Peter F. Hamilton was born in Rutland in 1960, and still lives near Rutland Water. He began writing in 1987 and sold his first short story to *Fear* magazine in 1988. He has also been published in *Interzone* and the *In Dreams* and *New Worlds* anthologies, and in several small-press publications. His previous novels are the Greg Mandel series: *Mindstar Rising*, *A Quantum Murder* and *The Nano Flower* and the bestselling Night's Dawn trilogy: *The Reality Dysfunction*, *The Neutronium Alchemist* and *The Naked God*. Also published by Macmillan (and Pan Books) are *A Second Chance at Eden*, a novella and six short stories set in the same brilliantly realized universe, and *The Confederation Handbook*, a vital guide to the Night's Dawn trilogy. His most recent novels are *The Dreaming Void*, *The Temporal Void* and *The Evolutionary Void*.

Also by Peter F. Hamilton

The Greg Mandel series

Mindstar Rising

A Quantum Murder

The Nano Flower

The Night's Dawn trilogy

The Reality Dysfunction

The Neutronium Alchemist

The Naked God

. . . and in the same timeline

A Second Chance at Eden

Also . . .

The Confederation Handbook
(a vital guide to the Night's Dawn trilogy)

Fallen Dragon

Misspent Youth

The Commonwealth Saga

Judas Unchained

The Void trilogy

The Dreaming Void

The Temporal Void

The Evolutionary Void

Peter F. Hamilton

PANDORA'S STAR

PART ONE OF THE COMMONWEALTH SAGA

PAN BOOKS

First published 2004 by Macmillan

This edition published 2010 by Pan Books
an imprint of Pan Macmillan, a division of Macmillan Publishers Limited
Pan Macmillan, 20 New Wharf Road, London N1 9RR
Basingstoke and Oxford
Associated companies throughout the world
www.panmacmillan.com

ISBN 978-0-330-51891-8

Typeset by SetSystems Ltd, Saffron Walden, Essex
Printed in the UK by CPI Mackays, Chatham ME5 8TD

Visit www.panmacmillan.com to read more about all our books
and to buy them. You will also find features, author interviews and
news of any author events, and you can sign up for e-newsletters
so that you're always first to hear about our new releases.

Main Characters

Daniel Alster Chief executive aide to Nigel Sheldon.

Alessandra Baron News-show presenter.

Dudley Bose Astronomer at Gralmond University.

Gore Burnelli Head of the Burnelli Grand Family.

Justine Burnelli Earth socialite.

Thompson Burnelli Commonwealth senator.

Sara Bush Matriarch of the Ice Citadel.

Rafael Columbia Chief of the Intersolar Serious Crimes Directorate.

Elaine Doi Commonwealth Vice President, later President.

Jean Douvoir Pilot, *Second Chance*.

Adam Elvin Ex-radical, quartermaster for Guardians of Selfhood.

Hoshe Finn Detective, Darklake city police.

McClain Gilbert CST First Contact team leader.

The High Angel A sentient alien starship.

Anna Hober Sensor officer, *Second Chance*.

Alic Hogan Lieutenant Commander, Navy Intelligence.

Ozzie Fernandez Isaacs Co-inventor of wormhole technology. Co-owner of CST.

Bradley Johansson Founder of Guardians of Selfhood.

Renne Kampasa Investigator, Intersolar Serious Crimes Directorate.

Patricia Kantil Chief aide to Elaine Doi.

Captain Wilson Kime Ex-NASA pilot. Board member of
Farndale Engineering.

Tu Lee Hyperspace officer, *Second Chance*.

Bruce McFoster A clan member in the Guardians of
Selfhood.

Kazimir McFoster A clan member in the Guardians of
Selfhood.

Stig McSobel A clan member in the Guardians of Selfhood.

Oscar Monroe Operations Director, CST exploratory
division wormhole on Merredin.

Morton Chairman of Gansu Construction.

Paula Myo Chief Investigator, Intersolar Serious Crimes
Directorate.

Orion Parentless teenage boy from Silvergalde.

Carys Panther Mark's aunt.

Qatux A Raiel, living on the High Angel.

Ramon D Senator for Buta, leader of African caucus.

Simon Rand Founder of Randtown on Elan.

Mellanie Rescorai Morton's lover.

Russell Sall Science officer, *Second Chance*.

Bruno Seymore Science officer, *Second Chance*.

Tara Jennifer Shaheef Morton's ex-wife.

Nigel Sheldon Co-inventor of wormhole technology.
Co-owner of Compression Space Transport.

Tunde Sutton Science officer, *Second Chance*.

Tarlo Investigator, Intersolar Serious Crimes Directorate.

Tochee Alien of unknown origin.

Liz Vernon Biogenetic technician, Mark's wife.

Mark Vernon Engineer.

Prologue

Mars completely dominated space outside the *Ulysses*, the bloated dirty-ginger crescent of a planet that never quite made it as a world. Small, frigid, barren, airless, it was simply the solar system's colder version of hell. Yet its glowing presence in the sky had dominated most of human history; first as a god to inspire generations of warriors, then a goal to countless dreamers.

Now, for NASA Captain-Pilot Wilson Kime, it had become solid land. Two hundred kilometres beyond the landing craft's narrow, curving windshield he could pick out the dark gash that was the Valles Marineris. As a boy he'd accessed the technofantasies of the Aries Underground group, entranced by how one day in an unspecified future, foaming water would once again race down that vast gully as raw human ingenuity unlocked the frozen ice trapped beneath the rusting landscape. Today, he would actually get to walk through those dusty craters he'd studied in a thousand satellite photos, hold the legendary thin red sand in his gloved hands to watch little trickles slip slowly through his fingers in the low gravity. Today was the most glorious history in the making.

Wilson automatically started a deep feedback breathing exercise, calming his heart before the reality of what was about to happen affected his metabolism. No way was he giving those goddamned desk medics back in Houston a chance to question *his* fitness to pilot the landing craft. Eight years he'd spent in the USAF, including two combat duties based in Japan for Operation Deliver Peace, followed by another nine years with NASA. All that build-up and anticipation; the sacrifices, his first wife and totally alienated kid; the eternal VR training at Houston, the press conferences, the mind-rotting PR tours of factories; he'd endured it all because it led to this one moment in this most sacred place.

Mars. At last!

'Initiating VKT ranging, cross-match RL acquisition data,' he told the landing craft's autopilot. The coloured strands of light captured inside the windshield began to change their geometrical patterns. He kept one eye on the timer: eight minutes. 'Purging BGA system and vehicle interlink tunnel.' His left hand flicked the switches on the console. Watching the tiny LEDs come on to confirm the switch cycle. Some actions NASA would never entrust to voice-activation software. 'Commencing BGA non-propulsive vent. Awaiting prime ship sep sequence confirmation.'

'Roger that, *Eagle II*,' Nancy Kressmire's voice said in his headset. 'Telemetry analysis has you as fully functional. Prime ship power systems ready for disengagement.'

'Acknowledged,' he told the *Ulysses* captain. Turquoise and emerald spider webs within the windshield fluttered elegantly, reporting the lander's internal power status. Their sharp primary colours appeared somehow alien across the dull pallor of the wintry Martian landscape outside. 'Switching to full internal power cells. I have seven greens for umbilical sep. Retracting inter-vehicle access tunnel.'

Alarmingly loud metallic clunks rang through the little cabin as the spaceplane's airlock tunnel sank back into the fuselage. Even Wilson flinched at the intrusive sounds, and he knew the spaceplane's mechanical layout better than its designers.

'Sir?' he asked. According to the NASA manual, once the

lander's airlock had retracted from the prime ship they were technically a fully independent vehicle, and Wilson wasn't the ranking officer.

'The *Eagle II* is yours, Captain,' Commander Dylan Lewis said. 'Take us down when you're ready.'

Very conscious of the camera at the back of the cabin, Wilson said: 'Thank you, sir. We are on line for completed undocking in seven minutes.' He could sense the buzz in the five passengers riding behind him. All of them were the straightest of straight arrows; they had so much right stuff between them it could be bottled. Yet now the actual moment was here they were no more controlled than a bunch of schoolkids heading for their first beach party.

The autopilot ran through the remaining pre-flight prep sequence, with Wilson ordering and controlling the list; adhering faithfully to the man-in-the-loop tradition that dated all the way back to the Mercury Seven and their epic struggle for astronauts to be more than just spam in a can. Right on the seven-minute mark, the locking pins withdrew. He fired the RCS thrusters, pushing *Eagle II* gently away from the *Ulysses*. This time there was nothing he could do to stop his heart racing.

As they drew away, *Ulysses* became fully visible through the windshield. Wilson grinned happily at the sight of it. The interplanetary craft was the first of its kind; actually quite an ungainly collection of cylindrical modules, tanks, and girders arranged in a circular grid shape two hundred metres across. Its perimeter sprouted long jet-black solar power panels like plastic petals, all of them tracking the sun. Several of the crew habitation sections were covered in big Stars and Stripes flags, implausibly gaudy against the plain silver-white thermal foam that coated every centimetre of the superstructure. Right in the centre of the vehicle, surrounded by a wide corrugated fan of silver thermal radiator panels, was the hexagonal chamber which housed the fusion generator that had made the ten-week flight time possible, constantly supplying power to the plasma rockets. It was the smallest fusion system ever built: a genuine made-in-America, cutting-edge chunk of technology. Europe was still building its first pair of commercial fusion reactors on the ground, while the USA had already commissioned five such units, with another fifteen being built. And the Europeans certainly hadn't got anything equivalent to the sophisticated *Ulysses* generator.

Damn it, we can still get some things right, Wilson thought proudly as the shining conglomeration of space hardware retreated away into the eternal night. It would be another decade until the FESA could mount a Mars mission, by which time NASA planned on having a self-sustaining base on the icy sands of Arabia Terra. Hopefully, by then, the agency would also be flying asteroid-capture missions and even a Jovian expedition as well. *I'm not too old to be a part of those, they'll need experienced commanders.*

His mind underwent just the tiniest tweak of envy at the prospect of what would come in the mid-term future, events and miracles whose timetable and budget allocations meant they might just elude him. *The Europeans can afford to wait, though.* While thanks to the dominant influence of the Religious Right over the last few administrations, the US had halted all genetic work centred around stem cells, the Federal government in Brussels had poured money into biogenic research, with spectacular results. Now that the early bugs had been ironed out of the hugely expensive procedure, they'd begun to rejuvenate people. The first man to receive the treatment, Jeff Baker, had died in a climax of global publicity; but in the following seven years there had been eighteen successes.

Space and Life. Those separate interests spoke volumes about the way the cultures of Earth's two major Western power groups had diverged over the past three decades.

Now Wilson's fellow Americans were beginning to re-evaluate their attitude to genetic engineering. Already there

4

were urban myths of Caribbean and Asian clinics offering the rejuvenation service to multi-billionaires. While Federal Europe was once again attempting to narrow the American lead in space, desperate to prove to the world that it excelled in every field. Given the fractious political state currently afflicting the planet, Wilson rather welcomed the idea of the two blocs drawing closer together once more – that was, after Americans had landed on Mars.

'First de-orbit burn in three minutes,' the *Eagle II* autopilot said.

'Standing by,' Wilson told it. He automatically checked the fuel tank pressures, and followed that up with main engine ignition procedures.

Three hypergolic fuel rockets at the back of the little spaceplane fired for a hundred seconds, pushing their orbit into an atmosphere-intercept trajectory. The subsequent aero-brake manoeuvre lasted for over ninety minutes, with the scant Martian atmosphere pushing against the craft's swept delta wings, killing its velocity. For the final fifteen minutes, Wilson could see the faintest of pink glows coming from the *Eagle II*'s blunt nose. It was the only evidence of the violence being done to the fuselage by high-velocity gas molecule impacts. The ride was incredibly smooth, with gravity slowly building as they sank towards the crater-rumpled landscape of Arabia Terra.

At six kilometres altitude, Wilson activated their profile dynamic wings. They began to expand, spreading out wide to generate as much lift as possible from the thin, frigid air. At full stretch they measured a hundred metres from tip to tip, enough to allow *Eagle II* to glide if necessary. Then their turbine fired up, gently thrusting them forward, keeping speed constant at two hundred and fifty kilometres an hour. The westernmost edge of the massive Schiaparelli crater slid into sight away in the distance, rolling walls rising up out of the rumpled ground like a weatherworn mountain range.

'Visual acquisition of landing site,' Wilson reported. His systems schematics were tracing green and blue sine waves across the view. Ground radar began to overlay a three-dimensional grid of spikes and gullies which almost matched what he could see.

'*Eagle II*, mid-point systems review confirms you are go for landing,' said Mission Control. 'Good luck, guys. You've got quite an audience back here.'

'Thank you, Mission Control,' Commander Lewis said formally. 'We are eager for the touchdown. Hoping Wilson can give us a smooth one.' It would be another four minutes before anyone back on Earth heard his words. By then they should be down.

'Contact with cargo landers beacon,' Wilson reported. 'Range thirty-eight kilometres.' He squinted through the windshield as the autopilot printed up a red line-of-sight bracket within the glass. The crater rim grew steadily larger. 'Ah, I've got them.' Two dusty grey specks sitting on a broad patch of flat landscape.

For the last stage, *Eagle II* flew a slow circle round the pair of robot cargo landers. They were simple squat cones which the *Ulysses* had sent down two days earlier, loaded with tonnes of equipment, including a small prefab ground base. Getting them unloaded and the projected exploration campus up and running was the principal task awaiting the crew of the *Eagle II*.

'Groundscan confirms area one viability,' Wilson said. He was almost disappointed at the radar picture. When Neil Armstrong and Buzz Aldrin were landing on the Moon, they had to hurriedly take manual control of their Lunar Module and fly it to safety when the designated landing site turned out to be strewn with boulders. This time, eighty-one years later, satellite imagery and orbital radar mapping had eliminated such uncertainty from the flight profile.

He brought the *Eagle II* round on its pre-plotted approach

path, engaging the autopilot. 'Landing gear extended and locked. VM engines pressurized and ready. Profile dynamic wings in reshape mode. Ground speed approaching one hundred kilometres per hour. Descent rate nominal. We're on the wire, people.'

'Good work, Wilson,' Commander Lewis said. 'Let's bump struts, here, huh?'

'You got it, sir.'

The landing rockets fired, and *Eagle II* began to sink smoothly out of the light pink sky. A hundred metres up, and Wilson couldn't stand it. His fingers flicked four switches, taking the autopilot off line. Red LEDs glared accusingly at him from the console. He ignored them, bringing the little spaceplane down manually. Easier than any simulation. Dust swirled outside the windshield, thick and cloying as the rocket jets scoured the surface of Mars. Radar gave him the final approach vectors, there was nothing to see visually. They settled without a wobble. The sound of the rockets died away. External light began to brighten as the agitated dust flurries dissipated.

'Houston, the *Eagle II* has landed,' Wilson said. The words had to be forced out, his throat was so tensed up with pride and exhilaration. He could hear that beautiful phrase echo along history, past and future. *And I made it happen, not some goddamn machine.*

A wave of jubilant shouts and cheering broke out in the cabin behind him. He wiped an errant drop of moisture from his eye with the back of one hand. Then he was suddenly involved with systems supervision, re-engaging the autopilot. External instrumentation confirmed they were down and stable. The spaceplane had to be put into surface standby mode, supplying power and environmental services to the cabin, keeping the rocket engines warm so that take-off wouldn't be a problem, monitoring the fuel tank status. A long, boring list of procedures that he worked through with flawless diligence.

Only then did the six of them begin to suit up. Given the cabin's chronic lack of space, it was a cramped, difficult process, with everyone jostling each other. When Wilson was almost ready, Dylan Lewis handed him his helmet.

'Thanks.'

The commander didn't say anything, just gave Wilson a look. As reprimands went, it didn't get much worse than that.

To hell with you, Wilson retorted silently. *We're the important thing, people coming to Mars is what matters, not the machines we come in. I couldn't allow a software program to land us.*

Wilson stood in line as the commander went into the small airlock at the back of the cabin. *Third, I get to be third.* Back on Earth they'd only ever remember that Dylan Lewis was first. Wilson didn't care. *Third.*

The tiny display grid inside Wilson's helmet relayed an image from the external camera set just above the airlock door. It showed a slim aluminium ladder stretching down to the Martian sand. Commander Lewis backed out of the open airlock, his foot moving slowly and carefully onto the top rung. Wilson wanted to shout, *For God's sake get a move on.* The suit's medical telemetry told him his skin was flushed and perspiring. He tried to do his deep feedback breathing exercise thing; but it didn't seem to work.

Commander Lewis was taking the ladder rungs one at a time, pausing on each one, then he finally reached the last one. Wilson and the others in the cabin held their breaths; he could feel a couple of billion people doing the same thing back on the old home planet.

'I take this step for all of humanity, so that we may walk together as one people along the road to the stars.'

Wilson winced at the words. Lewis sounded incredibly sincere. Then someone sniggered, actually sniggered out loud; he could hear it quite plainly over the general communication band. Mission Control would go ballistic over that.

Then he forgot it all as Lewis took his step onto the surface, his foot sinking slightly into the red sand of Mars to make a firm imprint.

'We did it,' Wilson whispered to himself. 'We did it, we're here.' Another outbreak of cheering went round the cabin. Congratulatory calls flooded down from *Ulysses*. Jane Orchiston was already clambering into the airlock. Wilson didn't even begrudge her that; political correctness wouldn't allow it any other way. And NASA was ever mindful of pleasing as many people as possible.

Commander Lewis was busy taking a high-resolution photo of his historic footprint. A requirement that had been in the NASA manual for the last eighty-one years, ever since Apollo 11 got back home to find that embarrassing omission.

Lieutenant Commander Orchiston was going down the ladder – a lot faster than Commander Lewis. Wilson stepped into the airlock. He couldn't even remember the time the little chamber took to cycle, it never existed in his personal awareness. Then it was him backing out onto the ladder. Him checking his feet were secure on the rungs before placing all his – reduced – weight on them. Him hanging poised on the bottom rung. 'I wish you could see this, Dad.' He put his foot down, and he was standing on Mars.

Wilson moved away from the ladder, cautious in the low gravity. Heart pounding away in his ears. Breathing loud in the helmet. Hiss of helmet air fans ever-present. Ghostly suit graphic symbols flickered annoyingly across his full field of vision. Other people talked directly into his ears. He stopped and turned full circle. Mars! Dirty rocks littering the ground. Sharp horizon. Small glaring sun. He searched round until he found the star that was Earth. Brought up a hand and waved solemnly at it.

'Want to give me a hand with this?' Commander Lewis asked. He was holding the flagpole, Stars and Stripes still furled tightly around the top.

'Yes, sir.'

Jeff Silverman, the geophysicist, was already on the ladder. Wilson walked over to help the commander with the flagpole. He gave the *Eagle II* a critical assessment glance on his way. There were some scorch marks along the fuselage, trailing away from the wing roots, very faint, though. Other than that: nothing. It was in good shape.

The commander was attempting to open out the little tripod on the base of the flagpole. His heavy gloved hands making the operation difficult. Wilson put out his own hand to steady the pole.

'Yo, dudes, how's it hanging? You need any help there?' The question was followed by a snigger.

Wilson knew the voice of everybody on the mission. Spend that long together with thirty-eight people in such a confined space as the *Ulysses* and vocal recognition became perfect. Whoever spoke wasn't on the crew. Yet somehow he knew it was real-time, not some pirate hack from Earth.

Commander Lewis had frozen, the flagpole tripod still not fully deployed. 'Who said that?'

'That'd be me, my man. Nigel Sheldon, at your service. Specially if you need to get home in like a hurry.' That snigger again. Then someone else saying, 'Oh man, don't do that, you're going to so piss them off.'

'Who is this?' Lewis demanded.

Wilson was already moving, glide-walking as fast as was safe in the low gravity, making for the rear of the *Eagle II*. He knew they were close, and he could see everything on this side of the spaceplane. As soon as he was past the bell-shaped rocket nozzles he forced himself to a halt. Someone else was standing there, arm held high in an almost apologetic wave. Someone in what looked like a home-made space suit. Which was an insane interpretation, but it was definitely a pressure garment of some type, possibly modified from deep-sea gear. The outer fabric was made up from flat ridges of dull brown rubber, in pronounced contrast to Wilson's snow-white ten-million-dollar Martian Environment Excursion suit. The helmet was the nineteen fifties classic goldfish bowl, a clear glass bubble showing the head of a young man with a scraggly beard and long oily blond hair tied back into a pigtail. *No radiation protection*, Wilson thought inanely. There was no backpack either, no portable life support module. Instead, a bundle of pressure hoses snaked away from the youth's waist to a . . .

'Son of a bitch,' Wilson grunted.

Behind the interloper was a two-metre circle of another place. It hung above the Martian soil like some bizarre super-imposed TV image, with a weird rim made up from seething diffraction patterns of light from a grey universe. An opening through space, a gateway into what looked like a rundown physics lab. The other side had been sealed off with thick glass. A college geek-type with a wild afro hairstyle was pressed against it, looking out at Mars, laughing and pointing at Wilson. Above him, bright Californian sunlight shone in through the physics lab's open windows.

1

The star vanished from the centre of the telescope's image in less time than a single human heartbeat. There was no mistake, Dudley Bose was looking right at it when it happened. He blinked in surprise, drawing back from the eyepiece. 'That's not right,' he muttered.

He shivered slightly in reaction to the cold air around him, slapping gloved hands against his arms. His wife, Wendy, had insisted he wrap up well against the night, and he'd dutifully left the house in a thick woollen coat and sturdy hiking trousers. But as always when the sun fell below Gralmond's horizon, any warmth contained in the planet's thinner-than-average atmosphere evaporated away almost immediately. With the telescope housing open to the elements at two o'clock in the morning, the temperature had dropped enough to turn his every breath into a streamer of grey mist.

Dudley shook the fatigue from his head, and leaned back in to the eyepiece. The star field pattern was the same, there had been no slippage in the telescope's alignment, but Dyson Alpha was still missing. 'It couldn't be that fast,' he said.

He'd been observing the Dyson Pair for fourteen months now, searching for the first clues of the envelopment which would so dramatically change the emission spectrum. So far there had been no change to the tiny yellow speck of light one thousand two hundred and forty light-years away from Gral-mond which was Dyson Alpha.

He'd known there would be a change; it was the astronomy department at Oxford University back on Earth that had first noticed the anomaly during a routine sky scan back in 2170, two hundred and ten years ago. Since the previous scan twenty years earlier, two stars, a K-type and an M-type three light-years apart, had changed their emission spectrum completely to non-visible infra red. For a few brief months the discovery had caused some excited debate among the remnants of the astronomy fraternity about how they could decay into red giants so quickly, and the extraordinary coincidence of two stellar neighbours doing it simultaneously. Then a newly settled planet fifty light-years farther out from Earth reported that the pair were still visible in their original spectrum. Working back across the distance, checking the spectrum at various distances from Earth allowed astronomers to work out that the change to both stars had actually taken place over a period of approximately seven or eight years and was simultaneous. Given that speed, the nature of the change ceased to become a question of astronomy; stars of that nature took a great deal longer to transform themselves into red giants. Their emission hadn't changed due to any natural stellar process; it was the direct result of technological intervention on the grandest possible scale. Somebody had built a solid shell around each star. It was a feat whose scale was rivalled only by its timeframe. Eight years was astonishingly swift to fabricate such a gigantic structure even for a super-advanced civilization, and they'd built two at the same time. Even so, the concept wasn't entirely new to the human race.

In the twenty-first century, a physicist called Freeman Dyson had postulated that the artefacts of a technologically advanced civilization would ultimately surround their star in order to utilize all of its energy. Now someone else had turned his ancient hypothesis into reality. It was inevitable that the two stars would be formally christened the Dyson Pair.

Speculative papers were written, and theoretical studies performed into how to dismantle Jovian-size planets to produce such a shell. But even in the modern Intersolar Commonwealth, those were a minority interest, a debating topic for the more esoteric futurologists. There was no real urgency connected to the discovery. The human race had already encountered several sentient alien species, all of them reassuringly harmless; and the Commonwealth was expanding steadily. It would only be a matter of a few centuries until a wormhole was opened to the Dyson Pair. Any lingering questions about their construction could be answered then by the aliens themselves.

Now he'd seen the envelopment was instantaneous, Dudley was left with a whole new set of very uncomfortable questions about the composition of the shell structure. Before, it was assumed that an eight-year construction period for any solid shell that size was utterly remarkable, but obviously achievable. When he'd begun the observation he'd expected to note a year by year eclipse of the star's light as more and more segments were produced and locked into place. This changed everything. To appear so abruptly, the shell couldn't be solid. It had to be some kind of force field. *Why would you surround a star with a force field?*

'Are we recording?' he asked his e-butler.

'We are not,' the e-butler replied. 'No electronic sensors are currently active at the telescope focus.' The voice was slightly thin, treble boosted; a tone which had been getting worse over the last few years. Dudley suspected the OCtattoo on his ear was starting to degenerate; organic circuitry was always susceptible to antibody attack, and his was over twenty-five years old. Not that the outer glittery scarlet and turquoise spiral pattern on his skin had changed. A classic spree of youthful dynamism after his last rejuvenation had made him choose a visible print, stylish and chic in those days. Now it was merely embarrassing for a middle-aged professor to be sporting it around the campus. He should have had the old pattern erased and replaced it with something more discreet; but somehow he'd never got around to it, despite his wife's repeated requests.

'Damn it,' Dudley grunted bitterly. But then the idea of his e-butler taking the initiative had been a pretty forlorn hope. Dyson Alpha had only risen forty minutes earlier. Dudley had been setting up the observation, performing his standard final verification. An essential task thanks to the poorly maintained mechanical systems which orientated the telescope. He never ordered the sensor activation until the checks were complete. That prissy routine might just have cost him the entire observation project.

Dudley went back for yet another look. The little star was still stubbornly absent in the visual spectrum. 'Bring the sensors on line now, will you, please. I need to have some sort of record of tonight.'

'Recording now,' his e-butler said. 'The sensors could benefit from recalibrating, the entire image is considerably short of optimum.'

'Yeah, I'll get on to it,' Dudley replied absently. The state of the sensors was a hardware problem; one which he ought to assign to his students (all three of them). Along with a hundred other tasks, he thought wearily.

He pushed back from the telescope, and used his feet to propel the black leather office chair across the bare concrete floor of the observatory. The rattling noise from its old castors echoed thinly around the cavernous interior. There was enough vacant space for a host of sophisticated ancillary systems, which could bring the observatory up to near-professional standards; it could even house a larger telescope. But Gralmond University lacked the funds for such an upgrade, and had so far failed to secure any commercial sponsorship from Compression Space

Transport, the only company truly interested in such matters. To date the astronomy department survived on a collection of meagre government grants, and a few endowments from pure-science foundations, even an Earth-based educational charity made an annual donation.

Beside the door was the long wooden bench which served as de facto office for the whole department. It was covered with banks of ageing, second-hand electronic equipment and high-rez display portals. Dudley's brown leather briefcase was also there, containing his late-night snacks and a flask of tea.

He opened the case and started munching on a chocolate digestive as the sensor images swam up into the display portals. 'Put the infrared on the primary display,' he told the e-butler.

Holographic speckles in the large main portal shoaled into a false colour image of the star field, centred around the Dyson Pair. Dyson Alpha was now emitting a faint infrared signature.

'So that really was the envelopment event,' Dudley mused. At least people would have to acknowledge that it happened in under twenty-three hours – the time since the last recorded observation. It was a start, but a bad one. After all, he'd just witnessed something utterly astounding. But now his only thanks were likely to be disbelief, and a mountainous struggle to maintain his already none-too-high reputation.

Dudley was ninety-two, in his second life, and fast approaching time for another rejuvenation. Despite his body having the physical age of a standard fifty-year-old, the prospect of a long degrading campaign within academia was one he regarded with dread. For a supposedly advanced civilization, the Intersolar Commonwealth could be appallingly backward at times, not to mention cruel.

Maybe it won't be that bad, he told himself. The lie was comforting enough to get him through the rest of the night's shift.

*

The Carlton AllLander drove Dudley home just after dawn. Like the astronomer, the vehicle was old and worn, but perfectly capable of doing its job. It had a cheap diesel engine, common enough on a semi-frontier world like Gralmond, although its drive array was a thoroughly modern photoneural processor. With its high suspension and deep-tread tyres it could plough along the dirt track to the observatory in all weather and seasons, including the metre-deep snow of Gralmond's winters.

This morning all it had to surmount was a light drizzle and a thin slick of mud on the track. The observatory was situated on the high moorland ninety kilometres to the east of Leonida City, the planet's capital. Not exactly a mountaintop perch, but it was the highest land within any reasonable distance, and unlikely ever to suffer from light pollution. It was forty minutes before the Carlton started to wind its way down into the lower valleys where the main highway meandered along the base of the slopes. Only then were there any signs of human activity. A few farmsteads had been built in sheltered folds of the land where dense stretches of dark native evergreen cynomel trees occupied the ground above every stream and river. Grazing meadows had been established on the bleak hillsides, where animals shivered in the cold winds blowing down off the moorland.

All the while as the Carlton bobbed cautiously along the track, Dudley slumped back in the driver's seat thinking how he could realistically break the news. Even a twenty-three-hour envelopment was a concept which the Commonwealth's small fraternity of professional astronomers would dismiss out of hand. To claim it had happened in a split second would open him to complete ridicule, and invariably an in-house status review from the university. As to the physicists and engineers who heard his claim . . . they'd gleefully contribute to the case against him.

Had he been at the start of his career he might have done

it, achieving a degree of notoriety before finally proving himself right. The little man overcoming formidable odds, a semi-heroic, or at least romantically poetic, figure. But now, taking such risks was too great. He needed another eight years of uninterrupted employment, even on the university's demeaningly low salary, before his R & R pension was full; without that money there was no way he could pay for a rejuvenation. And who in the last decades of the twenty-fourth century was going to employ a discredited astronomer?

He stared out at the landscape beyond the vehicle's windows, unconsciously stroking the OCtattoo on his ear. A wan light was illuminating the low undulating landscape of drab damp cordgrass, revealing miserable looking terrestrial cows and herds of the local bovine nygine. There must have been a horizon out there, but the bleak, grey sky made it hard to tell where it began. As vistas went, this had to be one of the most depressing of all the inhabited worlds.

Dudley closed his eyes and sighed. 'And yet it moves,' he whispered.

*

As rebellions went, Dudley's was fairly pitiful. He knew he couldn't ignore what he'd seen out there among the eternal, unchanging constellations. Somewhat thankfully, he realized, he still had enough dignity left to make sure he didn't take the easy burial option. Yet announcing the envelopment to the public would be the end of his own particular world. What others regarded as his essential meekness, he liked to think of as a caution that went with age. Similar to wisdom, really.

Old habits die hard, so he broke the problem down into stages, the way he always taught his students, and set about solving each one with as much logic as he could apply. Very simply, his overwhelming priority was to confirm the speed of envelopment. A wavefront of proof that was currently receding from Gralmond at the speed of light. And Gralmond was almost the furthest extent of the Commonwealth in this section of space. Almost, but not quite.

The Intersolar Commonwealth occupied a roughly spherical volume of space with Earth at the centre, extending out to phase three space which CST was now opening up for settlement. Gralmond was two hundred and forty light-years out from the old homeworld, one of the last planets of phase two space to be settled. It didn't require a great deal of calculation for Dudley to find that the next planet to witness the envelopment would be neighbouring Tanyata, a world even less developed than Gralmond. It didn't yet have a university; but a unisphere datasearch did find him a list of local amateur astronomers. There was one name on it.

Five months and three days after the evening he'd seen Dyson Alpha vanish, Dudley nervously waved goodbye to his wife as the Carlton pulled out of their driveway. She thought his trip to Tanyata was legitimate, sanctioned by the university. Even after eleven years of marriage, he didn't have the courage to tell her the absolute truth. Or maybe, after five marriages, he knew what to keep quiet about.

The Carlton drove him directly to the CST planetary station, on the other side of Leonida City from the university campus. Spring was just arriving, bringing with it a sprinkling of vivid green buds to the branches of the terrestrial saplings in the city's parks. Even the full-grown native trees were responding to the longer, brighter days; their dark-purple bark had acquired a new lustrous sheen as they prepared to unfurl their leaf awnings. Dudley watched the city's residents from his seat, business people and office staff striding about with purpose; parents being tolerant or exasperated with their kids; first-life adolescents milling about together outside coffee houses and mall entrances, hopelessly gauche yet still managing to look like the most lethal gang-members in human history. All of them so bright and normal. It was the main reason Dudley had chosen to settle here late in his second life.

Frontier planets always had that infectious air of expectation and hope; this was where new dreams really could take root and grow. And he'd done so little with that second life. His slightly desperate relocation here was an acknowledgement of that.

CST had opened their planetary station on Gralmond over twenty-five years ago. About the time Dudley was getting his colourful OCtattoo, in fact – an irony which hadn't escaped him. The planet had done well for itself during its first quarter century of human history. Farmers had come, and set their tractorbots and herds loose on the land. Urbanites brought their prefab buildings which they lined up in neat grids and called cities in homage to the great metropolises they hoped would one day evolve from such humble beginnings. Factories were imported, riding in on the strong tide of investment money; hospitals, schools, theatres and government offices multiplied fruitfully around them. Roads expanded out from the population centre, sending exploratory tendrils across the continent. And, as always, the trains came after them, bearing the greater load of commerce.

Dudley's Carlton drove along the side of the Mersy rail route as he neared CST's planetary station. A simple chain-link fence and a plastic safety barrier was all that separated the dual-lane highway from the thick lines of carbon-bonded steel rails. The Mersy rail route was one of five major track lanes which had so far been laid out of the station. Gralmond's population were rightly proud of them. Five in twenty-five years: a good sign of a healthy expanding economy. Three of the rail routes, including the Mersy, led away to vast industrial parks squatting on the outskirts of Leonida City, while the remaining pair stretched out into the countryside, where they forked again and again, connecting with the principal agricultural towns. Goods flowed in and out of the CST planetary station day and night, slowly increasing in quantity as the years progressed; circulating money, material, and machinery across fresh lands, advancing the human boundary month by month.

A big freight train grumbled alongside, going only slightly faster than the Carlton. Dudley looked over at the sound, seeing long olive-green wagons rolling along steadily. The sulphur-yellow lettering on their sides had faded from age and sunlight. There must have been fifty of them linked together, all pulled along by a giant twenty-wheel engine. It was one of the GH7 class engines, he thought, though which particular marque he wasn't sure; those brutes had been in use for nearly eighty years, a thirty-five-metre body filled with superconductor batteries, powering massive electric axle motors. Gralmond wouldn't see anything bigger until the planet reached full industrialization status, in maybe another seventy years or so.

Already, such a monster trundling through the flourishing city seemed slightly incongruous. This district still had a lot of the original prefab buildings in place, two- or three-storey cubes of whitened aluminium with solar cell roofs. Redevelopment was hardly necessary on a world where land wasn't merely cheap, the government actually gave it away to anyone who asked for it. Gralmond's total population barely reached eighteen million, nobody was crowded here. The prefabs, however, remained as useful housing and commercial centres for the newest and poorest arrivals. But there were some city blocks of the shabby metal boxes which had been taken down completely and replaced by new stone or glass-fronted buildings as the local economy bootstrapped itself upwards. More common was the encroachment of drycoral, a plant originally found on Mecheria. New residents planted the genetically tailored kernels along the base of their houses, carefully tending the long flat strands of spongy pumice-like stone which grew quickly up the walls, broadening out to form a sturdy organic shell around the entire structure, with simple pruning keeping the windows clear. Colours were mixed and twined skilfully, forming elaborate patterns, making each building individual, breaking the neighbourhood's monotony. No matter how bad the dust and grime from the roads, the drycoral would absorb the granules, keeping the facade's marquetry clean and vivid.

As the urban gentrification continued, so the Mersy tracks seemed more and more out of place. Several sections of the chain-link fence now had shoots of drycoral growing up it, screening off the ugly rails from the smart houses and apartments nearby.

The passenger terminus was only a small part of the ten square kilometres that was the CST planetary station; most of the area was given over to marshalling yards and engineering works. At one end was the gateway itself, sheltered from the weather beneath the single broad span of an arching roof made from crystal and white concrete. Dudley could barely remember it from his arrival eleven years ago, not that it would have changed. They never did.

The Carlton dropped him off at the departures rank at the front of the terminal, then trundled off back home as soon as he stepped out with his luggage. He walked into the station to find himself immersed in a throng of people who seemed to be going in every direction but the one he wanted. Even though it was relatively new, the concourse had an old-fashioned look to it: tall marble pillars held up a high glass roof; franchise stalls lurked in the cathedral-style archways; the short stairways between levels were implausibly wide, as though they led to some hidden palace; statues and sculptures occupied deep, high alcoves, their every flat surface covered in bird droppings. Big translucent holographic projections hung in the air, crimson and emerald signs which backed up the train timetable information for anyone who didn't have an interface with the local network; little birds zipped through them continuously, hooting in puzzlement at the trail of sparkles their membranous wings whipped up.

'The Verona train is leaving from platform nine,' Dudley's e-butler told him.

He set off down the concourse towards the platform. Verona was a regular destination, with a train leaving every forty minutes. There were a lot of commuters from there, middle management types from the finance and investment companies who were involved with setting up and running Gralmond's civil infrastructure.

The Verona train was made up from eight double-decker carriages hooked up to a medium-sized PH54 engine. Dudley shoved his cases into the baggage compartment on the fifth carriage, and climbed on board, finding an empty seat by one of the upper deck windows. Then there was nothing to do but try and ignore his growing tension as the timer display in his virtual vision counted down towards departure time. There were seven messages for him in his e-butler's hold file; half of which were from his students containing both data and audio clusters.

The last five months had been extraordinarily busy for the small university astronomy department; even though there had been no stellar observations made in all that time. Dudley had declared that the state of the telescope and its instruments was no longer acceptable, and that they'd been neglecting the practical side of their profession. Under his supervision, the tracking motors had been dismantled and serviced one by one, then the bearings, followed by the entire sensor suite. With the telescope out of commission, they also had the opportunity to upgrade and integrate the specialist control and image analysis programs. At first the students had welcomed the chance to get their hands dirty and improve the available systems. But that initial enthusiasm had long since faded as Dudley kept finding them new and essential tasks which delayed re-commissioning.

Dudley hated deceiving them, but it was a legitimate way of suspending the whole Dyson Pair observation project. He told himself that if he could just secure the evidence, then the impact it would have on their department and its budget would more than justify the small subterfuge. It was only during the last couple of months as he put up with all their complaints that he'd begun to think of the effect a verified envelopment might have on his own career and fortunes. Failure to back up the observation would have ruined him; success, on the other hand, opened up a whole new realm of prospects. He could well progress far beyond anything Gralmond University could offer. It was a pleasant daydream to lose himself in.

The train started moving, pulling away from the platform and out into the spring sunshine. All Dudley could see through the window was the industrial landscape of the station yard, where hundreds of tracks snaked across the ground crossing and re-crossing each other like some vast abstract maze. Single wagons and carriages were being moved about by small shunting engines that coughed out thick plumes of diesel exhaust. The only visible horizon seemed to be made from warehouses and loading bays, where the spidery gridwork of gantry cranes and container stackers wove through every section of the big open structures. Flatbed carriages and fat tankers were being readied or unloaded within the mechanical systems which almost engulfed them. Engineering crews and maintenancebots crawled along several tracks, performing repairs.

Traffic began to increase on the tracks around them as they headed for the gateway; long cargo trains alternating with smaller passenger carriers. All of them snaked their way over junctions with sinuous motions, arrowing in towards the final stretch of track. On the other side of the carriage, Dudley could see a near continual stream of trains emerging from the gateway.

There were only two tracks leading to the gateway: one inbound, one outbound. The Verona train finally slotted on to the outbound stretch, fitting in behind the passenger train for EdenBurg. A freighter bound for StLincoln slotted in behind them. A low warning tone chimed through the carriage. Dudley could just see the edge of the curving gateway roof ahead of them. The light dimmed fractionally as they passed underneath. Then there was just the wide shimmering amber oval of the gateway dead ahead, so reminiscent of an old-fashioned tunnel entrance. The train slid straight into it.

Dudley felt a slight tingle on his skin as the carriage passed through the pressure curtain which prevented the atmospheres of the two worlds from mixing. Even though it spanned a hundred and eighteen light-years, the wormhole itself had no internal length. The generator machinery which created it, however, had a considerable bulk, most of which was tucked away in the massive concrete support buildings behind the roof. It was only the emission units which were contained in the great oval hoop of the gateway, measuring over thirty metres thick. Given the speed the train was travelling, even that flashed past in a second.

Glorious copper twilight streamed in through the carriage windows. Dudley's ears popped as the new atmosphere flooded into the carriage through the rooftop vents. He looked out at the massive expanse that was CST's Verona station. There was no visible end to it, no glimpse of the megacity which he knew lay beyond. One edge of the station was a solid cliff of gateways, sheltering under their curving single-span roofs, each oval framing a slightly different coloured patch of haze depending on the spectral class of the star whose world they reached. But for the rest of it, as far as the eye could see, trains and tracks were the sole landscape. Behemoth freighters rolled along, their engines dwarfing the GH7s which had so impressed Dudley; nuclear-powered tractor units pulling two-kilometre chains of wagons. Sleek white passenger expresses flashed past pulling dozens of carriages; multiworld commuters, whose route would take them through twenty or more planets as they rushed from gateway to gateway on a never-ending circuit. Simple little regional trains like the one Dudley was on shuffled between their larger, grander cousins. Verona station had them all.

As Earth was the junction world for all the planets in phase one space of the Intersolar Commonwealth, so Verona was the major junction for this section of phase two space, with gateways leading to thirty-three planets. It was one of the so-called Big15; the industrial planets established out along the rim of phase one space, a hundred or so light-years from Sol. Company founded, company funded, and company run.

Verona station boasted seven passenger terminals; Dudley's train pulled in to number three. Again the scale of the place hit home, this terminal alone was five times the size of Gralmond's planetary station. Verona's thicker atmosphere and slightly heavier gravity contributed to his feeling of triviality as he wandered along the packed concourse in search of the Tanyata service. He found it eventually on platform 18b; three single-deck carriages pulled by a diesel-powered Ables RP2 engine. His luggage went on an overhead rack, and he sat on a double seat by himself. The carriage was less than a third full. There were only three trains a day to Tanyata.

When he arrived, he could see why there were so few scheduled services. Tanyata was very definitely a frontier planet; the last to be established in this sector of phase two space. It simply wasn't commercially practical to build wormholes that reached any further. Verona would link no more Human-Congruent planets; that honour now fell to Saville, which was less than ten light-years from Gralmond. CST was already building its new exploratory base there, preparing to open wormholes to a new generation of star systems: phase three space, the next wave of human expansion.

The CST Tanyata station was just a couple of hurriedly assembled boronsteel platforms under a temporary plastic roof. A crane and a warehouse comprised the entire cargo section, backing onto a vast muddy yard where stacked metal containers and tanks formed long rows on the badly mown vegetation. Wagons and trucks grumbled along the aisles, loading up with supplies. The settlement itself was a simple sprawl of standardized mobile cabins for the construction crews who were laying down the first stage of the planet's civil infrastructure. Quite a few prefab buildings were being integrated, with men and big manipulatorbots slotting reinforced aluminium modules together inside a matrix of carbon beams. The biggest machines were the roadbuilders, tracked minifactories with big harmonic blades at the front chewing up soil and clay. A chemical reactor processed the material into enzyme-bonded concrete which was squeezed out at the rear to form a flat level surface. The thick clouds of steam and fumes swirling out from around the units made it virtually impossible to see them fully.

Dudley stepped out onto the platform, and immediately reached for his sunglasses. The settlement was somewhere in the tropics, with a clammy humidity to go with the burning blue-tinged sunlight. To the west, he could just see the ocean past a series of gentle hills. He pulled his jacket off and waved his hand in front of his face. His skin was already sweating.

Someone at the other end of the platform called out Dudley's name and waved. Dudley hesitated in the act of raising his own hand. The man was just over six foot tall with the kind of slim frame that marathon runners cherished. Physical age was difficult to place, his skin was heavily OCtattooed; patterns and pictures glowed with hazy colour on every limb. Gold spiral galaxies formed a slow-moving constellation across his bald head. A perfectly clipped, greying goatee beard was the only real clue to late middle age. He grinned and started to walk down the length of the platform, his kilt flapping around his knees. The tartan was a bold pattern in amethyst and black.

'Professor Bose, I presume?'

Dudley managed not to stroke his own OCtattoo. 'Uh, yes.' He put his hand out. 'Er, LionWalker Eyre?' Even the way he pronounced it was wrong, like some kind of disapproving bachelor uncle. He hoped the heat was covering any blush to his cheeks.

'That'll be me. Most people just call me Walker.'

'Er. Great. Okay. Walker, then.'

'Pleased to meet you, Professor.'

'Dudley.'

'My man.' LionWalker gave Dudley a hearty slap on his back.

Dudley started to worry. He hadn't given any thought to the astronomer's name when the datasearch produced it. But then, anyone who had enough money to buy a one-point-three-metre reflecting telescope, then ship it out to a frontier world and live there with it, had to be somewhat eccentric.

'It's very kind of you to allow me a night's observation,' Dudley said.

LionWalker smiled briefly as they headed back down the platform. 'Well now, it was very unusual to be asked such a thing. Got to be important to you, then, this one night?'

'It could be, yes. I hope so.'

'I asked myself: why one night? What can you possibly see that only takes up such a short time? And a specific night as well.'

'And?'

'Aye, well that's it, isn't it? I could not come up with a single thing; not in terms of stellar events. And I know there are no comets due, either, at least none I've seen, and I'm the only one watching these skies. Are you going to tell me?'

'My department has an ongoing observation of the Dyson Pair; some of our benefactors were interested in them. I just want to confirm something, that's all.'

'Ah.' LionWalker's smile grew wise. 'I see. Unnatural events it is, then.'

Dudley began to relax slightly. Eccentric he might be, but LionWalker was also pretty shrewd.

They reached the end of the platform and the tall man suddenly twisted his wrist and pointed a finger, then slowly drew a semicircle in the air. The OCtattoos on his forearm and wrist flared in a complicated swirl of colour. A Toyota pick-up truck pulled up sharply in front of them.

'That's an interesting control system,' Dudley commented.

'Aye, well, it's the one I favour. Sling your bags in the back, will you?'

They drove off along one of the newly extruded concrete roads, heading out of the busy settlement. LionWalker twitched his fingers every few seconds, inducing another ripple of colour in his OCtattoos, and the pick-up's steering would respond fluidly.

'Couldn't you just give the drive array some verbal instructions?' Dudley asked.

'Now what would be the point in that? My way I have control over technology. Machinery does as I command. That's how it should be. Anything else is mechanthropomorphism. You don't treat a lump of moving metal as an equal and ask it pretty please to do what you'd like. Who's in charge here, us or them?'

'I see.' Dudley smiled, actually warming to the man. 'Is mechanthropomorphism a real word?'

LionWalker shrugged. 'It ought to be, the whole bloody Commonwealth practises it like some kind of religion.'

They quickly left the settlement behind, driving steadily along the road which ran parallel to the coast, just a couple of kilometres inland. Dudley kept catching glimpses of the beautifully clear ocean beyond the small sandy hillocks standing guard behind the shore. Further inland the ground rose to a range of distant hills. There wasn't a cloud in the sky, nor any breeze. The intense light gave the tufty grass and coastal reeds a dark hue, turning the leaves almost jade. Small scrub trees grew along the side of the road; at first glance similar to terrestrial palms, except their leaves were more like cacti branches, complete with monstrous red thorns.

Fifty kilometres clear of the settlement the road curved inland. LionWalker gave an elaborate wave with his hand, and the pick-up obligingly turned off, heading down a narrow sand track. Dudley wound the window down, smelling the fresh sea air. It wasn't nearly as salty as most H-congruous worlds.

'See the way they laid the road well inland?' LionWalker called. 'Plenty of prime real estate between it and the coast. Thirty years' time, when the city's grown up, that'll sell for ten thousand dollars an acre. This whole area will be covered in rich men's beach houses.'

'Is that bad?'

'Not for me,' LionWalker laughed. 'I won't be here.'

It was another fifteen kilometres to LionWalker's house. He'd taken over a curving bay which was sheltered by dunes that extended for several kilometres inland. His house was a low bungalow of pearl-white drycoral perched on top of a large dune only a hundred metres from the shore, with a wide veranda of decking facing the ocean. The big dome of the observatory was a little further back from the water, a standard concrete and metal design.

A golden Labrador ran out to greet them, tail wagging happily. LionWalker fussed with it as they walked to the house. Dudley could hear the sounds of a furious argument while they were still twenty metres away.

'Oh Lord, they're still at it,' LionWalker muttered.

The thin wooden shutter door slammed open and a young woman stormed out. She was startlingly beautiful, even to Dudley, who was used to a campus full of fresh-faced girls.

'He's a pig,' she spat at LionWalker as she hurried past.

'Aye, I'm sure,' LionWalker said meekly.

The woman probably didn't hear, she was already walking

towards the dunes, face set with a determination that made it clear she wasn't going to stop until she reached the end of the world. The Labrador gave her a longing look before turning back to LionWalker.

'There there.' He patted the dog's head. 'She'll be back to give you your supper.'

They'd almost reached the door when it opened again. This time it was a young man who came out. With his androgynous features, he was almost as beautiful as the girl. If it hadn't been for the fact he was shirtless, Dudley might even have questioned his gender.

'Just where does she think she's going?' he whined.

'I don't know,' LionWalker said in a resigned tone. 'She didn't tell me.'

'Well I'm not going after her.' The youth set off for the beach, slouching his shoulders and kicking at the sand with his bare feet as he went.

LionWalker opened the door and gestured Dudley inside. 'Sorry about that.'

'Who are they?' Dudley asked.

'They're my current life partners. I love them dearly, but I sometimes wonder if it's worth it, you know. You married?'

'Yes. Several times, actually.'

'Aye well, you know what it's like then.'

The interior of the house was laid out in a classic minimalist style, which suited the location perfectly. There was a big circular fireplace serving as the focal point of the lounge. Tall curving windows revealed an uninterrupted view of the bay and the ocean. Air conditioning provided a relaxing chill.

'Sit yourself down,' LionWalker said. 'I expect you could do with a drink. I'll take you over to see the telescope in a minute. You can check it out then. I'm confident you'll be satisfied.'

'Thanks.' Dudley lowered himself into one of the big sofas. He felt very drab and colourless in such surroundings. It wasn't just the richness of the house and its setting, but the vivacity of the people who lived here as well.

'This isn't what I was expecting,' he admitted a few minutes later, when he'd drunk some of LionWalker's very agreeable fifty-year-old Scotch.

'You mean you thought I'd be somebody like you? No offence, my man.'

'None taken. So what are you doing here?'

'My family's quite rich anyway. Not Earth wealthy, mind, but comfortable. I was born with a reasonable trust fund; then I went and made even more money for myself in the commodities market. That was a couple of rejuvenations ago. I've just been loafing ever since.'

'So why here? Why Tanyata?'

'This is the edge. This is as far out from our starting point as we've got – well, with the exception of Far Away. That's a wonderful thing, even though everyone regards it as commonplace. I can sit here at night, and look where we're going. You look at the stars, Dudley, you know what marvels there are to be seen out here. And those cretins behind us, they never look. Where we are now, this was what our ancestors thought was heaven. Now I can look out from their heaven and see where our future lies. Do you not think that's a thing of glory?'

'Certainly is.'

'There are stars out here that you cannot see from Earth with the naked eye. They shine down out of the sky at night, and I want to know them.'

'Me too.' Dudley saluted him with the crystal tumbler that was a hundred years older than the Scotch it held, and gulped it down in one.

*

The two youngsters returned after a couple of hours cooling off by themselves. LionWalker introduced them as Scott and

Chi as they sheepishly greeted Dudley. As a penance, the two of them set about building a bonfire on the beach, using the local driftwood which had a curiously matted texture. They lit it as the sun sank down towards the ocean. Bright orange sparks blew out of the flame tips to swirl high above the sand. Potatoes were pushed into the heart of the fire, while a make-shift barbecue grill was prepared for when the flames died down.

'Can we see the Dyson Pair from here?' Scott asked as the stars began to appear in the darkening sky.

'No,' Dudley said. 'Not with the naked eye, they're too far away. You can barely see Earth's star from here, and the Dyson Pair are a thousand light-years beyond that.'

'So when were they enveloped?'

'That's a very good question. We've never been able to pin down the exact construction time of the shells, that's what my observation project is going to help solve.' Even now Dudley wasn't going to admit what he'd seen.

If tonight's observation cast any doubt on what he'd seen, he would simply have to bury the whole project right away. He couldn't afford to make a fuss; he needed the job and its pension too much. Astronomy post-2050 had effectively ceased to be a field of pure science; when you could visit stars of every spectral type to observe them directly there was little point in prioritizing the profession. CST had long since taken over all major deep-space observation for purely commercial ends. In such circumstances, few higher educaction insti-tutions in the Commonwealth bothered building observato-ries to compliment their faculties. There would be nowhere for him to go.

An hour after sunset, Dudley and LionWalker walked through the dunes to the observatory. Inside, it was little dif-ferent to the one on Gralmond. A big empty space with the fat tube of the telescope in the middle, resting on a complex cradle of metal beams and electromuscle bands. The sensor housings surrounding the focus looked a lot more sophisticated than anything the university could afford. A row of neat, modern display portals was lined up along the wall beside the door.

Dudley glanced round at the professional equipment, feeling a degree of tension ebbing away. There was no practical reason preventing the observation from happening. All he had to deal with was his own memory of the event. Could it really have happened like that? Five months on, the moment seemed elusive somehow, the memory of a dream.

LionWalker stood close to the base of the telescope, and began what looked like a robot mime dance. Arms and legs jerked about in small precise movements. In response, the doors on the dome started to peel open. Electromuscle bands on the telescope cradle flexed silently, and the fat cylinder began to turn, aligning itself on the horizon where the Dyson Pair were due to rise. LionWalker's body continued to twist and whirl, then he was snapping his fingers to some unheard beat. The portals came alive one by one, relaying the sensor images.

Dudley hurried over to them. The image quality was flawless. He gazed at the star field, noting the minute variation from the patterns he was used to. 'What sort of linkage have we got?' he asked his e-butler.

'The planetary cybersphere is negligible, however there is a landline to the CST station. Available bandwidth is more than capable of meeting your stated requirements. I can open communication to the unisphere whenever you want.'

'Good. Begin quarter of an hour before estimated enclosure time. I want full SI datavault storage, and a unisphere legal verification of the feed.'

'Acknowledged.'

LionWalker had stopped his gyrations, allowing the telescope to rest. He raised an eyebrow. 'You're really serious about this, aren't you?'

'Yeah.' A datavault store and legal verification were expensive. Along with his ticket, the cost had taken quite a chunk out of their carefully saved holiday money. Something else Dudley hadn't told his wife. But it had to be done, with the telescope sensor feed authenticated the observation would be beyond dispute.

Dudley sat in a cheap plastic chair beside the telescope, his chin resting on his hands, watching the holographic light within the portals. He watched the dark sky obsessively as the Dyson Pair rose above the horizon. LionWalker made a few small adjustments and Dyson Alpha was centred in every portal. For eighty minutes it remained steady. A simple point of ordinary light, each spectrum band revealing an unwavering intensity.

LionWalker made a few attempts to talk to Dudley about what to expect. Each time he was waved silent. Eventually he just gave up, and slumped in a chair next to the ageing astronomer. He was used to long nights, though sharing this one made it strangely boring.

Dudley's e-butler established a full wideband link to the unisphere, and confirmed that the SI datavault was recording.

It was almost an anticlimax when, right on time, Dyson Alpha vanished.

'Yes!' Dudley yelled. He jumped to his feet, sending the chair tumbling backwards. 'Yes, yes, yes. I was right.' He turned to LionWalker, his smile absurdly wide. 'Did you see that?'

'Aye,' LionWalker grunted with false calm. 'I saw that.'

'Yes!' Dudley froze. 'Did we get it?' he asked his e-butler urgently.

'Unisphere confirms the recording. The event is logged in the SI datavault.'

Dudley's smile returned.

'Do you actually realize what that was?' LionWalker asked.

'I realize.'

'It was impossible, man, that's what. Completely bloody impossible. Nobody can switch off a star like that. Nobody.'

'I know. Wonderful, isn't it?'

2

Adam Elvin walked out of the CST planetary station in Tokat, the capital of Velaines. He took his time as he passed the sensors which were built into the fluted marble pillars lining the concourse. If he was going to be arrested, he would rather it be now before the rest of the mission was exposed.

The average Commonwealth citizen had no idea such surveillance systems existed. Adam had dealt with them for most of his adult life. Understandably paranoid about sabotage, CST used them to monitor everyone using their facilities. The sensor's large processor arrays were loaded with visual characteristics recognition smartware that checked every passenger against a long long list of known and suspected recidivists.

Adam had used cellular reprofiling to change his appearance (including height) more times than he could remember; at least once a year, more often twice or three times. The treatment could never cure the ageing process which was starting to frost his joints and organs; but it did remove scar tissue, of which he'd acquired more than his fair share over the decades. It also gave him a wide choice of features. He always felt that trying to disguise his seventy-five years was a pointless vanity. Any elderly person wearing an adolescent's face was truly pitiful to see. The rest of the body always gave them away; too bulky, too slow. They were immediately picked out as losers, too poor to afford rejuvenation, retreating into the cheap fantasy of a skin-deep youth.

He reached the departure rank outside the station's passenger terminal, and used his e-butler to hail a taxi. There had been no alarm. Or at least nothing detectable, he told himself. You never could tell when you were up against *her*. She was smart, and getting closer to him as the years wore on. If she had prepared a trap for him on Velaines, it wasn't to be sprung today – the time he would prefer.

For the moment he was free to go about his mission. Today he was a new person, previously unknown to the Commonwealth. According to his citizenship file he was Huw North, a native of Pelican, a first-life sixty-seven; an employee of the Bournewell engineering company. To look at he was overweight; considerably so, given how seriously Commonwealth citizens took their health these days, weighing in at around two hundred and thirty pounds. Accompanying that was a round saggy face that sweated a lot. Thinning grey hair was combed low across his forehead in an unfashionable style. He wore a baggy brown raincoat with wide lapels. It was open down the front to reveal a creased grey suit. A big man with a small life, someone nobody paid attention to. Cellular reprofiling was a cosmetic treatment for the poor and the vain, not a method of adding fat and giving skin a pasty pallor. As a misdirection it never failed.

Which meant it was probably time to change it, Adam thought as he eased his oversized frame into the taxi, which drove him to the Westpool Hotel. He checked in and paid for two weeks in advance. His room was a double on the eighth floor, with sealed windows and air conditioning set too cold for him. He hated that, he was a light sleeper and the noise from the air conditioning would keep him awake for hours. It always did.

He unpacked all the clothes in his suitcase, then took out the smaller shoulder bag containing his emergency pack – two sets of clothing, one of which was several sizes too small, a medical kit, cash, a CST return ticket from EdenBurg to Velaines with the outbound section already used, a couple of very sophisticated handheld arrays containing some well-guarded kaos software, and a legal ion stun pistol with buried augmentation which gave it a lethal short-range blast.

An hour later, Adam left the hotel and walked five blocks in the warm afternoon sunlight, getting a feel of the capital city. Traffic up and down the wide roads was close-spaced, with taxis and commercial vans dominating the lanes. None of them used combustion engines, he noted, they were all powered by superconductor batteries. This section of town was still respectable, close to the central financial and commercial districts, although fifteen blocks away the quality of the buildings deteriorated appreciably. Around him now were stores and offices, along with some small side roads of terraced apartments, none of them over four or five stories high. Public buildings built in a late imperial Russian style fronted neat squares. In the distance, down the perfectly straight roads, were the towers that marked the heart of the city. Every few blocks he walked under the elevated rail tracks snaking through the city's road grid, thick concrete arteries on high stanchions, carrying the major lines in and out of the planetary station.

Velaines was in phase one space, barely fifty light-years from Earth itself. Opened for settlement in 2090, its economy and industry had matured along model lines ever since. It now had a population of over two billion with a proportionally high standard of living, the kind of world which phase two and three space planets aspired to become. Given the length of its history, it was inevitable that some strands of decay should creep into its society. In the fast-paced capital market economy model that Velaines followed, not everybody could make themselves rich enough to enjoy multiple rejuvenations.

The areas they lived in reflected their financial status, road surfaces were cracked and uneven, while the efficient citywide network of metro trams serving them had fewer than average stops and ran old carriages. This was where the real rot set in, the despair and dead ends, where human lives were wasted, sacrificed to the god of economics. In this day and age it was an outrage that such a thing should happen. It was exactly the environment Adam had long ago committed himself to eradicating, and now the place he needed most for his other activities.

He found himself an A+A hotel at the end of 53rd Street, and checked in, using his Quentin Kelleher identity. The A+A was a franchise of cheap fully-automated hotels where the manager was also the maintenance chief. The reception array accepted the Augusta dollar account transfer from his credit tattoo, and gave him a code for room 421. Its layout was a simple square three metres on a side, with a shower/toilet alcove and a dispenser outlet. There was one jellmattress bed, one chair, and one retractable shelf. However, the room was on the corner of the building, which meant he had two windows.

He asked the dispenser's small array for a sleeping pouch, three packaged meals, two litres of bottled water, and a toiletries bag, all charged to his account. The mechanism whirred smoothly a minute later, and the items popped out into the rack. After that he set one of his handheld arrays to sentry mode, and left it scanning the room. If anyone did break in, it would notify his e-butler immediately with an encrypted message from a one-time unisphere address. Such an act had a low probability. Velaines was proud of its relatively low crime-index, and anyone staying in an A+A wouldn't have anything of value. Good enough odds for him.

*

That evening Adam took a metro tram across town to another slightly shabby district. In amongst the closed shops and open bars he found a door with a small sign above it:

Intersolar Socialist Party
Velaines, 7th chapter

His e-butler gave the door his Huw North party membership code, and the lock buzzed. Inside was pretty much what he expected, a flight of bare wooden stairs leading up to a couple of rooms with high windows, long since boarded up. There was a bar in one, serving cheap beer from microbreweries, and lethal-looking liquors from ceramic bottles. A games portal took up most of the second room, with observer chairs packed round the walls.

Several men were sitting on stools at the bar. They fell silent as Adam walked over. Nobody wearing a suit, even as cheap as his, belonged in that room.

'Beer, please,' Adam told the barman. He put a couple of Earth dollar bills on the counter; the currency was accepted without question on most worlds.

The bottle was placed in front of him. Everybody watched as he took a sip. 'Not bad.' Adam even managed to keep a straight face. He could appreciate a Socialist club not buying from a big corporate brewery, but surely they could find a smaller one which actually produced drinkable beer.

'New in town, comrade?' the barman asked.

'Got in today.'

'Staying long?'

'A little while, yeah. I'm looking for a comrade called Murphy, Nigel Murphy.'

The man at the far end of the bar stood up. 'That'll be me then.' He was slim, taller than Adam, with a narrow face that carried suspicion easily. Adam guessed he was a first-life; his head was almost bald, with just a thin monk's ring of greying hair. His clothes were those of an ordinary working man:

jeans, and a check shirt, with a fleece jacket worn open, a woolly hat stuffed into one pocket. They were all streaked with dirt, as if he'd come straight from the factory or yard. But the way he looked at Adam, the assessment he carried out in a glance, marked him out as a leader.

'Huw North,' Adam said as they shook hands. 'One of my colleagues was here last week.'

'Not sure if I remember,' Nigel Murphy said.

'He said you were the man to talk to.'

'Depends what you want to talk about . . . comrade.'

Adam held in a sigh. He'd been through this same ritual so many times over the years. By now he really ought to have worked out how to circumvent the bullshit and get right down to business. But as always, it had to be played out. The local man had to be proved top dog in front of his friends.

'I have a few issues,' Adam said. 'Can I buy you a drink?'

'You're very free with your money there, comrade,' said one of the others sitting behind Nigel Murphy. 'Got a lot of it, have you? Thinking you can buy our friendship?'

Adam smiled thinly at the barfly. 'I don't want your friendship, and you certainly don't want to be a friend of mine.'

The man grinned round his colleagues, his appearance was mid-thirties, with the kind of rashness which suggested that was his genuine age, a first-lifer. 'Why's that?'

'Who are you?'

'Sabbah. What's it to you?'

'Well, Sabbah. If you were my friend, you'd be stalked across the Commonwealth, and when they catch you, you'll die. Permanently.'

Nobody in the bar was smiling any more. Adam was glad of the small heavy bulge in his jacket produced by the ion pistol.

'Any of you remember November 21st 2344?' Adam looked round challengingly.

'Abadan station,' Nigel Murphy said quietly.

'That was you?' Sabbah asked.

'Let's just say I was in the region at the time.'

'Four hundred and eighty people killed,' Murphy said. 'A third of them total deaths. Children who were too young to have memorycell inserts.'

'The train was late,' Adam said. His throat was dry as he remembered the events. They were still terribly clear. He'd never had a memory edit, never taken the easy way out. *Live with the consequences of your actions.* So every night he dreamed of the explosion and derailment just in front of the gateway, carriages plunging across junctions and parallel rails in the busiest section of the station. Fifteen trains hit, side-shunted, crashing, bursting apart, exploding, spewing out radioactive elements. And bodies. 'It was on the wrong section of track at the wrong time. My chapter was after the Kilburn grain train.'

'You wanted to stop people from eating?' Sabbah asked sneeringly.

'Is this a drinking den or a Socialist chapter? Don't you know anything about the party you support? The reason we exist? There are certain types of grain trains which are specially designed to go through zero-end gateways. CST don't tell people about those trains, same way as they don't mention zero-end. The company spent millions designing wagons which can function in freefall and a vacuum. Millions of dollars developing machinery whose only job is to dump their contents into space. They go through a zero-end gateway onto a line of track that's just hanging there in the middle of interstellar space. Nobody knows where. It doesn't matter, they exist so that we can safely dump anything harmful away from H-congruous planets. So they send the trains with their special wagons through and open the hatches to expel their contents. Except there's nothing physically dangerous about the grain. It's just tens of thousands of tons of perfectly good grain streaming out into the void. There's another clever mechanism built into the wagons to make sure of that. Just opening the hatch isn't good enough. In freefall the grain will simply sit there, it has to be physically pushed out. And do you know why they do it?'

'The market,' Nigel Murphy said with a hint of weariness.

'Damn right: the market. If there's ever a glut of food, the prices go down. Commodity traders can't have that, they can't sell at enough profit to pay for the gamble they've made on the work of others, so the market demands less food to go around. The grain trains roll through the zero-end gateways, and people pay higher prices for basic food. Any society which allows that to happen is fundamentally wrong. And grain is just the tiniest part of the abuse people are subject to thanks to the capitalist market economy.' Adam stared hard at Sabbah, knowing that once again he was going too far, making too much of an issue out of his own commitment. He didn't care; this was what he'd devoted himself to, even now with all his other priorities, the greater human cause still fuelled him. 'That's why I joined this party, to end that kind of monstrous injustice. That's why I've committed my life to this party. And that's why I'll die, a total death, a member of this party. Because I believe the human race deserves better than those bastard plutocrats running us like some private fiefdom. How about you, sonny? What do you believe in?'

'Thanks for clearing that up,' Nigel Murphy said hurriedly. He stood between Adam and Sabbah. 'All of us here are good members of the party, Huw. We might have joined for different reasons, but we have the same aims.' With one hand he signalled Sabbah and the others to stay at the bar. His other arm pressed lightly on Adam's shoulder, steering him towards a small door. 'Let's talk.'

The back room was used to store beer crates and all the other junk which a bar generates down the years. A single poly-photo strip was fixed to the ceiling, providing illumination.

When the door was closed, Adam's e-butler informed him its access to the cybersphere had been severed.

'Sorry about that,' Nigel Murphy said as they pulled out a couple of empty beer crates to sit on. 'The comrades aren't used to new faces round here.'

'You mean the party's a lost cause on Velaines?'

Nigel Murphy nodded reluctantly. 'It seems that way some days. We barely scrape two per cent in elections now, and a lot of those are simply protest votes against the major parties. Any direct action we take against the companies is so . . . I don't know. Puerile? It's like we're hitting a planet with a rubber hammer, we're not causing any damage. And there's always the risk of another mistake like Abadan. Socialism isn't about killing people, after all. It's supposed to be about justice.'

'I know. It's hard, believe me. And I've been working for the cause a lot longer than you. But you have to believe that some day all this will change. The Commonwealth today is based on pure imperialist expansion. That's always the most favourable time for market economics because there are always new markets opening. But it will ultimately fail. The expansion into phase three space is nothing like as fast and aggressive as the first and second phases were. The whole process is slowing. Eventually this madness will stop and we can start to focus our resources towards genuine social growth instead of physical.'

'Let's hope so.' Nigel Murphy raised his beer bottle. 'So what can I do for you?'

'I need to speak to some people. I'm looking to buy weapons hardware.'

'Still blowing up grain trains, huh?'

'Yeah.' Adam forced a smile. 'Still blowing up grain trains. Can you set that up for me?'

'I can try. I've bought a few small pieces myself over the years.'

'I'm not looking for small pieces.'

'The dealer I use, she should be able to help. I'll ask.'

'Thank you.'

'What kind of hardware are we talking about, exactly?'

Adam handed over a hard copy of the list. 'The deal is this, you can add on whatever this chapter needs up to ten per cent of the total price. Think of it as a finder's fee.'

'This is some very serious hardware.'

'I represent a very serious chapter.'

'All right then.' Nigel Murphy still couldn't quite banish the troubled expression from his face as he read down the list. 'Give me your e-butler access code. I'll call when I've set up the meeting.'

'Good. One thing, have you had any new members join recently? The last couple of months or so?'

'No. Not for about nine months now, unfortunately. I told you, we're not very fashionable at the moment. We're going to mount another recruitment drive in the general workers unions. But that won't be for weeks yet. Why?'

'Just checking.'

*

Sabbah hated himself for what he was doing. The comrade was obviously well connected in the party, probably in the executive cadre. Which meant he truly believed in what he was doing, especially if he'd been truthful about the grain train.

It wasn't that Sabbah didn't believe in their cause – no way. He absolutely hated the way everyone else in the world seemed to be doing better than him, that his background had condemned him to one life lived badly. The way society was structured prevented him from bettering himself. That was what attracted him to the Socialists in the first place, the way they were working to change things so that people like him would get a chance to live decently in an inclusive world.

All of which only made this worse. The comrade was actively working to bring down the companies and the plutocratic state which supported them. Which was a lot more than Sabbah ever seemed to do. All the seventh chapter did was hold endless meetings where they argued amongst themselves for what seemed like hours. Then there was the canvassing, days spent being abused, insulted, and treated with utter contempt by the very people they were trying to help. And of course the protests outside company offices and factories, ambushing politicians. Sabbah had lost count of how many times he'd been on the wrong, and very painful, end of a police shockwhip. The real reason he kept going these days was because of the rest of the chapter. He didn't have many friends outside, not any more.

But he didn't have any choice. Not in this.

It was nine years ago when he met the woman. The job that night had been so easy it would have been criminal not to do it. He'd gone along with a couple of old mates he'd known back from his gang years, when they'd all pulled a truck from the reform academy to run the streets. A delivery truck that made a nightly run from the CST planetary station to various local wholesale warehouses about town. It was carrying crates of domestic goods from Augusta, all high quality. And the van was old, its alarm a joke.

Thanks to some decent targeted kaos software bought from a contact, they'd managed to intercept the van and lift its load clean within ten minutes. Sabbah even took a couple of maidbots with him when he went home in addition to his cut.

She was waiting for him when he walked through the door; a middle-aged woman with mild Asian features, her shoulder-length raven hair flecked with grey strands, wearing a smart business suit. Sitting in his lounge, looking like she belonged in that dingy two-room apartment more than he ever did.

'You now have a choice,' she said as his mouth was gaping open in surprise. 'Either I'll shoot you in self-defence, because you were assaulting a government official in the pursuit of her duties; or we make a deal and I'll let you keep your dick.'

'Whoo . . .' Sabbah frowned at his door, silently cursing its alarm circuit for not warning him she'd broken in.

'Or do you believe the Velaines public medical insurance scheme will pay for a new dick, Sabbah? That's where I'm aiming, in case you hadn't noticed.'

In horror he saw she had some kind of small black metal tube in her hand, and it really was levelled at his groin. He shifted the boxes containing the maidbots, gradually lowering them until they covered his hips and the hugely valuable personal organ situated there.

'If you're police, you won't—'

The violent *crack* which her weapon produced made him cower. Scraps of foam packaging drifted through the air while the remnants of the maidbot dropped to the floor. The little machine's crab-like electromuscle limbs spasmed for a while before collapsing limply. Sabbah stared at it. 'Oh Christ on a crutch,' he whispered. He gripped the remaining box even tighter.

'Do we now know where we both stand?' the policewoman asked.

'Yes ma'am.'

'All I want is for you to do something for me. A small thing. Will you do that?'

'What?'

'One day someone will turn up at your chapter, and I want to know about it. I can't give you his name, he changes it every time. But he'll be looking to buy things, weapons most likely, or kaos software, or samples of diseases, or components with the wrong specifications which will screw up whatever they're installed in. That's the kind of person he is. A very unpleasant individual. He'll claim to be a party member, to be doing what he does for a noble cause. But he's lying. He's a terrorist. An anarchist. A murderer. So I want you to tell me when he visits you. Okay?'

Sabbah didn't like to think of the alternative. She was still pointing the weapon right at him, aiming low. 'Yeah, sure. I'll do that.'

'Good.'

'When's he coming?'

'I don't know. It might be tomorrow. It might be in thirty years' time. It might be never. Or I might have caught him before he ever reaches Velaines.'

'Uh, right, okay.'

'Now turn round.'

'What?'

'You heard.' She got to her feet, the little weapon still pointing at him. Sabbah reluctantly turned to face the door. His hands were grabbed, forcing him to drop the maidbot box. A cold band of malmetal coiled round his wrists immobilizing them. 'What the hell . . .'

'You're under arrest for theft.'

'You've got to be fucking joking! I said I'd help you. That was the deal.' He turned his head to try and look at her. The weapon was jabbed into his jaw.

'There is no deal. You made a choice.'

'That was the deal!' he yelled furiously. 'I help you, you get me off this rap. Jesus!'

'You are mistaken,' she said relentlessly. 'I didn't say that. You committed a crime. You must face the consequences. You must be brought to justice.'

'Fuck you, bitch. Fuck you. I hope your terrorist blows up a hundred hospitals, and schools. I hope he wipes out your whole planet.'

'He won't. He's only interested in one planet. And with your help, we can stop him from damaging it further.'

'My *help*?' the word came out as a squeak he was so shocked. 'You stupid bitch, you can suck me and I'd never help you now. We had a deal.'

'Very well. I will lodge a plea with the judge, asking him for leniency.'

'Huh?' This was so weird it was doing his head in. Right from the start the woman scared him. He wasn't even sure she was a policewoman any more. More like a serial killer.

'I will tell him you cooperated fully, and agreed to be my informer. The file will not be encrypted when it is attached to your court record. Do you think your friends will access it when they see you receiving a light sentence? Will they be happy about what it says? My colleagues have already arrested them for tonight's robbery, by the way. I expect they'll be curious about how we knew.'

'Oh goddamn.' Sabbah was near to tears. He wanted this whole nightmare to end. 'You can't do that to me. They'll kill me, a total death. You don't know what they're like.'

'I think I do. Now, are you going to tell me when my target turns up?'

So through clenched teeth he said: 'Yes.'

And that had been the way of it for nine years. He'd been given a suspended jail term for the robbery, and made to perform two hundred hours' Citizen Service. It was the last time he'd done a job – well, anything major, anyway, just the occasional rip-off.

And every three weeks there would be a message in his e-butler's hold file asking him if the man had come. Every time he replied: no.

Nine years, and that superbitch had never let it go. 'Time,' she'd told him on the way to the police station, 'lessens nothing.' She'd never said what would happen if he didn't tell her. But then, it wasn't something he wanted to find out.

So Sabbah walked for several blocks, leaving the chapter house behind. That way his e-butler would be operating through a cybersphere node which wasn't anywhere near the building. The chapter had several tech-types; heavily idealistic about total-access they all sailed close to anarchistic beliefs, believing all information should be free. They also smoked things they shouldn't and played sensory immersion games for most of their waking hours. But they did have an unnerving habit of delivering the goods when databanks had to be cracked for the cause. Sabbah wouldn't put it past the party's senior cadre to mount a simple surveillance operation around the chapter building, the local network was sure to be compromised.

His e-butler entered the code she'd given him. The connection was placed immediately, which was unnerving if not entirely surprising. Sabbah took a deep breath. 'He's here.'

*

Adam Elvin took his time in the lobby of the Scarred Suit Club while the hostess dealt with his coat. His retinal inserts adapted to the low lighting easily enough, bringing up an infrared profiling which banished shadows for him. But he wanted a moment to take in the whole scene. As clubs went it was pretty standard; booths around the wall, each with an e-seal curtain for privacy, tables and chairs on the main floor, a long bar with an extensive number of bottles on the shelves, and a small stage where the boys, girls, and ladyboys of the Sunset Angels troupe danced. The lighting was low, with topaz and purple spots casting their shady beams onto the dark wood of the fittings. The music was loud, a drab software synth that kept up a constant beat for the performers to remove their clothes to. There was more money in here than there should have been, he thought. That made it protected.

At one o'clock in the morning, every table was taken, and the crowd of lowlife around the stage was enthusiastically waving notes in the face and crotch of the two dancers. Several booths were occluded by shimmering force fields. Adam frowned at that, but it was only to be expected. As he watched, one of the Sunset Angels was led over to a booth by the manager. The force field sparkled and allowed them through. Adam's handheld array had the capacity to pierce the e-seal, but the probe would be detected.

So many hiding places was a risk. Again, one he was used to. And in a protected joint, they wouldn't take kindly to police.

'Excuse me,' the doorman said. He was being friendly, not that it mattered, cellular reprofiling had given him the same kind of bulk as Adam, except his wasn't fat.

'Sure.'

The doorman glided his hands above Adam's jacket and trousers. They were heavily OCtattooed, the circuits fluorescing claret as they scanned for anything dangerous.

'I'm here to meet Ms Lancier,' Adam told the hostess as the doorman cleared him. She led him round the edge of the main room to a booth two places down from the bar. Nigel Murphy was already there.

For an arms dealer, Rachael Lancier wasn't inconspicuous. She wore a bright scarlet dress with a low front. Long chestnut hair was arranged in an elaborate wave, with small luminescent stars glimmering among the strands. Her rejuvenation had returned her to her early twenties, when she was very attractive. He knew it was a rejuvenation, possibly even a second or third. Her attitude gave her away. No real twenty-two-year-old possessed a confidence bordering on glacial.

Her bodyguard was a small thin man with a pleasant smile, as low-key as she was blatant. He activated the e-seal as soon as Adam's beer arrived, wrapping the open side of the booth in a dull platinum veil. They could see out into the club, but the patrons were presented with a blank shield.

'That was quite a list,' Rachael said.

Adam paused for a moment to see if she was going to ask what it was for, but she wasn't that unprofessional. 'Is it a problem for you?'

'I can get all of it for you. But I have to say the combat armour will take time. That's a police issue system; I normally provide small arms for people with somewhat lower aspirations than yours.'

'How much time?'

'For the armour, ten days, maybe two weeks. I have to acquire an authorized user certificate first.'

'I don't need one.'

She raised her cocktail glass and took a sip, looking at him over the rim. 'That doesn't help me, because I do need it. Look, the rest of your list is either in storage or floating round the underground market, I can pull it in over the next few days. But that armour, that has to come from legitimate suppliers, and they have to have the certificate before they'll even let it out of their factory.'

'Can you get the certificate?'

'I can.'

'How much?' he asked before she could start on her sales pitch.

'In Velaines dollars, a hundred thousand. There are a number of people involved, none of them cheap.'

'I'll pay you eighty.'

'I'm sorry, this isn't some kind of market stall. I'm not bargaining. That's the price.'

'I'll pay you eighty, and I'll also pay you to package the rest of the list the way I require.'

She frowned. 'What sort of packaging?'

Adam handed over a memory crystal. 'Every weapon is to be broken down into its components. They are to be installed in various pieces of civil and agricultural equipment I have waiting in a warehouse. The way it's laid out, the components will be unidentifiable no matter how they are scanned or examined. The instructions are all there.'

'Given the size of your list, that's a lot of work.'

'Fifteen thousand. I'm not bargaining.'

She licked her lips. 'How are you paying?'

'Earth dollars, cash, not an account.'

'Cash?'

'Is that a problem?'

'Your list will cost you seven hundred and twenty thousand. That's a lot of money to carry around.'

'Depends what you're used to.' He reached into his jacket and pulled out a thick bundle of notes. 'That's fifty thousand. It's enough to get you started and prove my intent. Once you've assembled the list, give me the location of your secure warehouse where I can send my machinery. When it arrives there, I'll pay you a third of the remaining money. When you've installed it, I'll pay you the remainder.'

Rachael Lancier's poise faltered slightly. She gave her bodyguard a glance, and he picked up the notes. 'It's good to do business with you, Huw,' she said.

'I want daily updates on the state of play.'

'You'll get them.'

*

Chief Investigator Paula Myo left her Paris office three minutes after getting the call from Sabbah. It took her eighteen minutes to get across town to the CST station. It was only an eight-minute wait on the platform for the next express. She arrived on Velaines within forty minutes.

Two senior detectives, Don Mares and Maggie Lidsey from the Tokat metropolitan police, were waiting for her when the taxi delivered her to their headquarters. Given the level of the request for cooperation from the Intersolar Serious Crimes Directorate, the two detectives had no trouble requisitioning a conference office and departmental array time. Their captain also made it clear to them that he expected them to provide genuine assistance to the Chief Investigator. 'She'll file a report on our operational ability when this is over,' he said. 'And the Directorate has political clout, so be nice and be useful.'

With Don Mares sitting restlessly beside her, Maggie Lidsey used her e-butler to call up the Chief Investigator's file. Broad columns of translucent green text began to flow across the virtual vision generated by her retinal inserts. She skipped through the information quickly enough, it was a refresher rather than a detailed appraisal. Everyone in law enforcement knew about Paula Myo.

The headquarters array informed the two detectives their guest had arrived. Maggie focused on the lift doors as they opened, banishing the ghostly ribbons of text. The conference office on the eighth floor of the metropolitan police head-quarters building had glass walls, as did every cubicle on the same floor. From her viewpoint, Maggie could see the whole layout. At first nobody paid much attention to Paula Myo as she walked down the main corridor, followed by two col-leagues from the Serious Crimes Directorate. In a white blouse, prim office suit, and sensible black shoes she fitted into the bustling compartmentalized work environment perfectly. She was slightly short by today's standards when eighty per cent of the population had some kind of genetic modification. Not that she lacked physical stature; she obviously stuck deter-minedly to an exercise routine which kept her fitness level an order of magnitude above anything the metropolitan police required from their officers. Though Maggie suspected that was more a personal obsession. The Chief Investigator's thick raven hair had been brushed straight so that it hung well below her shoulder blades. She always allowed it to sweep in front of her face, partially obscuring her features. Given her notoriety that was understandable. But when she did use a hand to brush those strands aside men would look up from their desks and stare, not just because of the legend she was. The Human Structure Foundation on Huxley's Haven which had so carefully developed her genome had selected a mix of Filipino and European genes as a baseline, giving her a natural beauty which was utterly beguiling. A rejuvenation five years previously made it look as if she was now in her early twenties.

Even though she knew she should never judge anyone by their physical guise, Maggie Lidsey had trouble taking the girl seriously as she shook hands with her and Don. With her size and fresh looks, Paula Myo could quite easily be mistaken for a teenager. The giveaway was her smile. She didn't seem to have one.

The other two investigators from the Directorate were introduced as Tarlo, a tall, blond Californian, and Renne Kempasa, a Latin American from Valdivia, who was halfway towards her fourth rejuvenation.

The five of them sat round the table, and the walls opaqued. 'Thank you for such a swift response,' Paula said. 'We're here because I have a tip-off that Adam Elvin has arrived on Velaines.'

'A tip-off from who?' Don asked.

'A contact. Not the most reliable, but it certainly needs investigating.'

'A contact? That's it?'

'You don't need to know, Detective Mares.'

'You were here nine years ago,' Maggie said. 'At least, that's the official entry in our files. So I'd guess your man is Sabbah. He's a member of the Socialist Party, as was Elvin.'

'Very good, Detective.'

'Okay, we're here to help,' Maggie said. She felt like she'd passed some kind of test. 'What do you need?'

'To begin with, two surveillance operations. Elvin has made contact with a man called Nigel Murphy at the seventh chapter of the local Socialist Party here in town. We need to keep him under constant watch, virtual and physical. Elvin is here to acquire arms for Bradley Johansson's terrorist group. This Murphy character will be his link to a local underground dealer; so he can lead us to both of them. Once we have the connection, we can intercept Elvin and the dealer at the exchange.'

'This all sounds very easy and routine,' Maggie said.

'It won't be,' Tarlo said. 'Elvin is very good. Once we've identified him, I'll need a detective team to help backtrack his every movement to the moment he arrived. He's a tricky son of a bitch. The first thing he will have done is establish an escape route in case this deal blows up in his face. We need to find it, and block it.'

'You guys know it all, don't you?' Don Mares said. 'What he's doing, where he is. I'm surprised you even need us.'

Paula looked at him briefly, then turned her attention back to Maggie. 'Is there a problem?'

'A little more information would be appreciated,' Maggie said. 'For instance, are you sure he is here to contact an arms dealer?'

'It's what he does. In fact it's all he does these days. He's just about given up on the party. Oh, he'll throw the local chapter a bone or two for cooperating with him. But he hasn't really taken any part in the movement since Abadan. The party's executive cadre effectively disowned him and his entire active resistance cell after that fiasco. That's when he hooked up with Bradley Johansson. No one else would touch him, he was too hot. Ever since then he's been the quartermaster for the Guardians of Selfhood. The acts they commit on Far Away make Abadan seem quite mild.'

Don Mares grinned. 'Managed to get any of the money back yet?'

Tarlo and Renne gave him hostile stares. Paula Myo looked at him without saying anything. Don met her gaze levelly, showing no remorse.

'Is he likely to be armed?' Maggie asked. She glared at Don. At the best of times he could be an arsehole, today he seemed to be going out of his way to prove it.

'Elvin will probably be carrying a small weapon,' Renne Kempasa said. 'But his main armoury is his experience and guile. If there's any kind of physical trouble, it won't be him that starts it. We'll have to research the arms dealer carefully, they tend to lean towards violence.'

'So no money, then,' Don persisted. 'Not after – what is it now – a hundred and thirty years?'

'I also need your office to try and track down Elvin's export route,' Paula said. 'The CST security division will cooperate with them fully on that.'

'We'll liaise with our captain over officer allocation,' Maggie said. 'We've already arranged for you to have an office and access to the departmental array.'

'Thank you. I'd like to brief the observation teams in two hours.'

'Tight schedule, but I think we can manage that for you.'

'Thank you.' Paula hadn't moved her gaze from Maggie. 'No, I haven't got any of the money back yet. Most of it is spent on arms deals like this one, which makes it particularly hard to track and recover. And I haven't got this close to him for twenty years. So I will be seriously disappointed if an individual screws this up. It will be a career wrecker.'

Don Mares tried to sneer off the threat. He didn't really succeed. Maggie thought it was because he'd realized the same thing she had. Paula Myo never smiled because she didn't have a sense of humour.

*

Adam was finishing a rather splendid early breakfast at the Westpool Hotel when his e-butler informed him that an unsigned message had arrived in its hold file. It had come from a one-time unisphere address, and the text it contained was encrypted with a key code that identified the sender to him immediately: Bradley Johansson.

Outwardly, Adam drank his coffee quietly as the waiters fussed round the restaurant tending to the other guests. In his virtual vision, he prepared the message for decryption. His wrist array was worn on his left arm, a simple band of dull malmetal that flexed and expanded constantly to maintain full contact with his skin. Its inner surface contained an i-spot which connected to his OCtattoos which, in turn, were wetwired into his hand's nerve fibres. The interface was represented in his virtual vision by a ghostly hand, which he'd customized to a pale blue, with sharp purple nails. For every tiny motion he made with his flesh and blood hand, the virtual one made a scaled-up movement, allowing him to select and manipulate icons. The system was standard across the Commonwealth, giving everyone who could afford an OCtattoo direct connection to the planetary cybersphere. He guessed that most of the business people having breakfast around him were quietly interfacing with their office arrays. They had that daydreaming look about them.

He pulled the appropriate key out of its store in his wrist array, represented by a Rubik's cube icon, which he had to twist until he'd arranged the surface squares into the correct pattern. The cube opened up, and he dropped the message icon inside. A single line of black text slid across his virtual vision: **Paula Myo is on Velaines.**

Adam just managed to hold on to his coffee cup. 'Shit!'

Several nearby guests glanced over to him. He twitched his lips in an apologetic smile. The array had already wiped the message, now it was going through an elaborate junction overwrite procedure in case it was ever examined by a forensic retrieval system.

Adam never did know where Bradley got half of his information from. But it had always been utterly reliable. He should abandon the mission right now.

Except . . . it had taken eighteen months to plan and organize. Dummy companies had been established on a dozen worlds to handle the disguised machinery exports to Far Away, routing and re-routing them so that there would be no suspicion and no trail. A lot of money had been spent on preparations. And the Guardians wouldn't receive another shipment of arms until he could set one up. Before he did that, he needed to know what had gone wrong this time.

They had been so close, too. Rachael Lancier's last call

confirmed that she had put together about two thirds of the list. So close.

*

Maggie Lidsey's car drove her into the headquarters building underground car park an hour before she was due on shift. She'd been working longer hours ever since the case started. It wasn't just to curry favour with Paula Myo, she was learning a lot from the Chief Investigator. The woman's attention to detail was incredible. Maggie was convinced she must have array inserts, along with supplementary memorycells. No aspect of the operation was too small for her to show an interest in. Urban myth certainly hadn't exaggerated her dedication.

The elevator in the lobby scanned her to confirm her identity: only then did it descend to the fifth basement level where the operations centres were situated. The Elvin team had been codenamed Roundup, and assigned room 5A5. Maggie was scanned again before the metal slab door slid aside to admit her. The interior was gloomy, occupied by three rows of consoles with tall holographic portals curving round the operator. Each one was alive with a grid of images and data ribbons. Laser light spilled out from them in a pale iridescent haze. A quick glance at the one closest to the door showed Maggie the familiar pictures of the buildings which Rachael Lancier used to run her car dealership from; along with shots from the team's two shadow cars showing Adam Elvin's taxi as they followed him through midtown.

Maggie requested an update, and quickly assimilated the overnight data. The one item which stood out was the encrypted message delivered to Elvin's e-butler through the Westpool Hotel node. She saw Paula Myo sitting at her desk at the far end of the room. The Chief Investigator seemed to get by on a maximum of two hours' sleep per day. She'd had a cot moved into her office, and never used it until an hour after both main targets had retired for the night. And she was always up an hour before the time they usually got out of bed. The night shift had standing orders to wake her if anything out of the ordinary happened.

Maggie went over to ask about the message.

'It came from a one-time address in the unisphere,' Paula said. 'The Directorate's software forensics have traced its load point to a public node in Dampier's cybersphere. Tarlo is talking to the local police about running a check, but I'm not expecting miracles.'

'You can track a one-time address?' Maggie asked. She'd always thought that was impossible.

'To a limited degree. It doesn't help. The message was sent on a delay. Whoever loaded it was well clear.'

'Can the message encryption be cracked?' Maggie asked.

'Not really, the sender used folded-geometry encryption. I logged a request with the SI, but it said it doesn't have the resources available to decrypt it for me.'

'You talked with the SI?' Maggie asked. That was impressive. The Sentient Intelligence didn't normally interface with individuals.

'Yes.'

There was nothing else forthcoming.

'Oh,' Maggie said. 'Right.'

'It was a short message,' Paula said. 'Which limits what it could contain. My guess is it was either a warning, a go authorization, or a stop.'

'We haven't leaked,' Maggie said. 'I'm sure of it. And they haven't spotted us either.'

'I know. The origin alone seems to rule out a mistake by any of your officers.'

'The Socialist Party does have a number of quality cyberheads. They might have noticed our scrutineer programs shadowing Murphy's e-butler.'

Paula Myo rubbed a hand over her forehead, pressing hard enough to furrow up the skin. 'Possible,' she conceded. 'Although I have to take other factors into consideration.'

'Yes?' Maggie prompted.

'Classified, sorry,' Paula said. Even though she was tired, she wasn't about to confide her concerns to anybody. Although if Maggie was any kind of detective she should be able to work it out.

As Mares had said, a hundred and thirty-four years without an arrest was an uncomfortably long time. In fact it was impossible given the resources Paula had to deploy against Bradley Johansson. Somebody had been providing Johansson and his associates with a great deal of assistance down the decades. Few people knew what she was doing on a day-to-day basis, so logically it was someone outside the Directorate. Yet the Executive administration had changed seventeen times since she had been assigned command of the case. They couldn't all contain secret sympathizers of Johansson's cause. That just left her with the altogether murkier field of Grand Families and Intersolar Dynasties, the kind of power dealers who were always around.

She'd done everything she could, of course, set traps, run identification ambushes, deliberately leaked disinformation, established unofficial communication channels, built herself an extensive network amid the political classes, gained allies at the heart of the Commonwealth government. So far the results had been minimal. That didn't bother her so much, she had faith in her ability to work the case to its conclusion. What concerned her more than anything was the reason anyone, let alone someone with true wealth and power, would want to protect a terrorist like Johansson.

'Makes sense,' Maggie said, with a trace of reluctance. She knew there was a terrific story behind the Chief Investigator's silence. 'So what action do you want to take about the message?'

'Nothing immediate,' Paula said. 'We simply wait and see what Elvin does next.'

'We can arrest all of them now. There are enough weapons stored at Lancier's dealership to begin a war.'

'No. I don't have a reason to arrest Elvin yet. I want to wait until the operation has reached its active smuggling stage.'

'He was part of Abadan. I checked the Directorate file, there are enough testimonies recorded to prove his involvement no matter how good a lawyer he has. What more do you need to arrest him?'

'I need the weapons to be shipped. I need their route and destination. That will expose the whole Guardian network to me. Elvin is important primarily for his ability to lead me to Johansson.'

'Arrest him and have his memories extracted. I'm sure a judge would grant the Directorate that order.'

'I don't expect to have that option. He knows what will happen the second I have him in custody. He'll either suicide or an insert will wipe his memories clean.'

'You can't be sure of that.'

'He's a fanatic. He will not allow us access to his memories.'

'Do you really believe that?'

'It's what I'd do,' Paula said simply.

*

Paula briefed the watcher teams before the shift changeover, explaining her suspicions about the encrypted message. 'It changes our priorities slightly,' she said. 'If it was a cancellation then Elvin will make a break for the CST station. I need a detail of officers on permanent duty there to arrest him if he tries to leave. Detective Mares, will you organize that, please.'

'I'll see the captain about more personnel, sure.' During the week of the operation Don Mares had modified his attitude slightly. He didn't contend anything, nor disagree with Paula; but neither did he put any extra effort into the operation. She could live with that, base-line competence was a depressing constant in law enforcement agencies throughout the Commonwelath.

'Our second option,' Paula said. 'Is a go code. In which case we need to be ready to move. There will be no change in your assignments, but be prepared to implement immediately. The third option is not so good: he's been warned about our observation.'

'No way,' Don Mares said. 'We're not that sloppy.' There was a grumble of agreement from the team officers.

Tarlo gave Renne a fast grin. The boss always generated a high standard of professionalism with whatever police force she worked with. None of them wanted to be known as the one who failed her.

'As unlikely as it sounds we have to take it into consideration,' Paula insisted. 'Be very careful not to risk exposure. He's smart. He's been doing this for forty years. If he sees one of you twice in a week he's going to know you're following him. Don't let him see you. Don't let him see the car you're using. We're going to get a larger vehicle pool so we can rotate them faster. We cannot afford mistakes.' She nodded curtly at them. 'I'll join the lead team today. That's all.'

Don Mares and Maggie Lidsey came over to her as the other officers filed out of the operations centre. 'If he catches a glimpse of you, it really will be game over,' Don Mares said.

'I know,' Paula said. 'But I need to be close. There are some calls you can't make sitting here. I'd like you to take over as general coordinator today.'

'Me?'

'Yes, you have the qualifications, you've taken command of raids before.'

'Okay.' He was trying not to smile.

'Maggie, you're with me.'

*

They caught up with Adam Elvin when he was taking a slow, seemingly random, walk through Burghal Park. He did something similar most mornings, an amble through a wide open space where it was difficult for the team to follow unobtrusively on foot.

Paula and Maggie waited in the back of a ten-seater car which was parked at the north end of Burghal Park. The team had the rest of their vehicles spaced evenly round the perimeter, with three officers on foot using their retinal inserts to track his position, never getting closer than five hundred metres, boxing him the whole time. The Burghal was a huge area in the middle of the city, with small lakes, games pitches, tracks, and long greenways of trees brought in from over seventy different planets.

'That's twice he's doubled back on his route,' Maggie said. They were watching the images relayed from the retinal inserts on a small screen in the car.

'Standard for him,' Paula said. 'He's a creature of habit. They might be good habits, but any routine will betray you in the end.'

'Is that how you tracked him?'

'Uh huh. He never uses the same planet twice. And he nearly always uses the Intersolar Socialist Party to set up the first meeting with the local dealer.'

'So you turned Sabbah into your informant and waited.'

'Yes.'

'For nine years. Bloody hell. How many informants do you have, on how many planets?'

'Classified.'

'The way you operate, though, always arresting them for their crime. That doesn't make for cooperative informants. You're taking a big risk on a case this important.'

'They broke the law. They must go to court and take responsibility for their crime.'

'Hell, you really believe that, don't you?'

'You've accessed my official file. Three times now since this case started.'

Maggie knew she was blushing.

*

That day Adam Elvin finished his walk in Burghal Park and caught a taxi to a little Italian restaurant on the east bank of the River Guhal which meandered through the eastern districts of the city. While eating a large and leisurely lunch he placed a call to Rachael Lancier, which the metropolitan police had no trouble intercepting.

Elvin: Something's come up. I need to talk to you again.

Lancier: The vehicle you wanted is almost ready for collection, Mr North. I hope there's no problem at your end.

Elvin: No, no problem about the vehicle. I just need to discuss its specification with you.

Lancier: The specification has been agreed. As has the price.

Elvin: This is not an alteration of either. I simply need to speak with you personally to clarify some details.

Lancier: I'm not sure that's a good idea.

Elvin: It's essential, I'm afraid.

Lancier: Very well. You know my favourite place. I'll be there at the usual time today.

Elvin: Thank you.

Lancier: And it had better be as important as you say.

Paula shook her head. 'Routine,' she said disapprovingly.

*

Eighteen police officers converged on the Scarred Suit Club. Don Mares dispatched the first three within two minutes of the conversation. The club wasn't open, of course, they simply had to find three observation points around it and dig in.

Two of Lancier's people arrived at eight o'clock that night, and performed their own surveillance checks before calling back to their boss.

When Adam Elvin finally arrived at one o'clock in the morning, ten officers were already inside. As before, they had managed to blend in well enough to prevent him from identifying any of them for what they were. Some of them assumed the role of business types looking for some bad action after a long day in the office. Three of them hung around the stage, identical to the other losers frantically waving their grubby dollars at the glorious bodies of the Sunset Angels. One had even managed to get a job, trying out as a waiter for the night, and was making reasonable tips. Renne Kempasa was sitting in one of the booths, the hazy e-seal protecting her from view.

The remainder of the team were outside, ready for pursuit duties when the meeting was over. Paula, Maggie, and Tarlo were parked a street away in a battered old van, with the logo of a domestic service company on the side. The two screens they'd set up in the back showed images taken by the officers inside the club. Rachael Lancier was already in her booth, a different one this time. Her skinny-looking bodyguard was with her. He'd been identified by headquarters as Simon Kavanagh, a man with a long list of petty convictions stretching back three decades, nearly all of them violence-related. When he arrived he'd swept the booth twice, scanning for any covert electronic or bioneural circuitry. The passive sensors carried by the officers nearby nearly went off the scale. He was using some very sophisticated equipment – as was to be expected from someone who worked for an arms dealer.

Paula watched Lancier and Elvin tentatively shake hands. The arms dealer gave her buyer an inhospitable look, then the e-seal around the booth was switched on. Its screening was immediately reinforced by the units which Kavanagh activated. One of them was an illegally strong janglepulse capable of frying the cerebral ganglia of any insect within a four-metre radius.

'Okay,' Paula said. 'Let's find out what's so important to Mr Elvin.'

A metre above the booth's table, a Bratation spindlefly was clinging to the furry plastic fabric of the wall matting. Amid the artificial purple and green fibres, its translucent, two-millimetre-long body was effectively invisible. As well as a chameleon-effect body, evolution on its planet had provided it with a unique neurone fibre that used a photo-luminescent molecule as the primary transmitter, making it immune to a standard janglepulse. It had only half the expected lifespan of a natural spindlefly because its genetic code had been altered by a small specialist company on a Directorate contract, replacing half of its digestive sac with a more complex organic structure of receptor cells. In its abdomen was an engorged secretion gland that threw out a superfine gossamer strand. When it had flown in from the neighbouring booth, it had trailed the gossamer behind it. Gentle lambent nerve impulses from the receptor cells now flowed along the strand to a more standard semiorganic processor which Renne carried in her jacket pocket.

In the middle of Paula's screen a grainy grey and white image formed. She was looking down on the heads of three people sitting round the booth table.

'So what the hell has happened?' Rachael Lancier asked. 'I didn't expect to see you until completion, Huw. I don't like this. It makes me nervous.'

'I got some new instructions,' Elvin said. 'How else was I supposed to get them to you?'

'All right, what sort of instructions?'

'A couple of additions to the list. Major ones.'

'I still don't like it. I'm this close to calling the whole thing off.'

'No you're not. We'll pay for your inconvenience.'

'I don't know. The inconvenience is getting pretty fucking

huge. All it's going to take is one suspicious policeman walking into my dealership, and I'm totally screwed. There's a lot of hardware stacking up there. Expensive hardware.'

Elvin sighed and reached into a pocket. 'To ease the inconvenience.' He put a brick-sized wad of notes on the table and pushed them over to Simon Kavanagh.

The bodyguard glanced at Lancier, who nodded permission. He put the notes into his own jacket pocket.

'All right, Huw, what sort of goodies do you need now?'

Elvin held up the small black disk of a memory crystal, which she took from him.

'This is the last time,' she said. 'Nothing else changes. I don't care what you want, or how much you pay, understood? This is the end of this deal. If you want anything else, it has to wait until next time. Got that?'

'Sure.'

Paula sat back in the thin ageing cushioning of the van's seat. On the screen, Adam Elvin had stood up to leave. The booth's e-seal flickered to let him out.

'That was wrong,' she said.

Maggie frowned at her. 'What do you mean?'

'I mean, that was nothing to do with additions to the list. Whatever's really in that memory crystal, it won't be an inventory.'

'What then?'

'Some kind of instructions.'

'How do you know? I thought it fitted what happened.'

'You saw his reaction to the message at breakfast. The camera caught his expression spot on. It shocked the hell out of him. First rule on a deal like this is you don't change things this late in the game. It makes people very nervous. Rachael Lancier's reaction is a perfect example. And it's not a good thing to make arms dealers nervous. A deal this size, everybody is quite edgy enough already. Elvin knows that.'

'So? He was shocked his bosses wanted to change things.'

'I don't buy it.'

'So what do you want to do?'

'Nothing we can do. Keep watching. Keep waiting. But I think he's on to us.'

*

The news about Dyson Alpha's enclosure broke mid-morning two days later. It dominated all the news streams and current event shows. A surprisingly large number of Velaines' citizens had opinions on the revelation, and what should be done about it.

Maggie kept half her attention on the pundits, both the serious and the mad, who appeared on the news streams while she was sitting around the underground operations centre. Time and again, the shows kept repeating the moment when the star disappeared from view. Diagrams sprang up simplifying what had happened for the general public.

'Do you think Elvin was rattled by that?' Maggie asked. 'After all the Guardians of Selfhood are supposed to be protecting us from aliens.'

Paula glanced at the portal where Dudley Bose was being interviewed. The old astronomer simply couldn't stop smiling. 'No. I checked. The message was sent half a day before Bose confirmed the event. In any case, I don't see how the Dyson enclosure concerns the Guardians. Their primary concern is the Starflyer alien and how it manipulates the government.'

'Yeah, I get their propaganda. Damnit, I fall for the message authorship every time.'

'Think yourself lucky you're not the author. I pick up the pieces on those scams as well.'

'So they're not concerned about this instant enclosure, then?'

'No. The Dyson enclosure happened over a thousand years ago, it's pre-history. Irrelevant to the Guardians.'

'You know a lot about them, don't you?'

'Just about everything you can without actually signing on.'

'So how does someone like Adam Elvin wind up working for a terrorist faction?'

'You must understand that Bradley Johansson is basically a charismatic lunatic. The whole Guardians of Selfhood movement is simply his private personality cult. It calls itself a political cause, but that's just part of the deception. The sad thing is, he's lured hundreds of people into it, and not just on Far Away.'

'Including Adam Elvin,' Maggie muttered.

'Yes, including Elvin.'

'From what I've seen of Elvin, he's smart. And according to his file he is a genuine committed radical Socialist. Surely he's not gullible enough to believe Johansson's propaganda?'

'I can only assume he's humouring Johansson. Elvin needs the kind of protection which Johansson provides, and his beloved party does benefit to some small degree from the association. Then again, maybe he's just trying to revive past glories. Don't forget he's a psychotic; his terrorist activities have already killed hundreds, and every one of these arms shipments introduces the potential for more death. Don't expect his motivation to be based in logic.'

*

The observation carried on for a further eleven days. Whatever additional items Adam Elvin had requested, they appeared to be difficult for Rachael Lancier to acquire. Various nefarious contacts arrived for quick private meetings with her in the back office. Despite their best attempts, the Tokat metropolitan police technical support team was unable to place any kind of infiltration device inside. Lancier's office was too effectively screened. Not even the spindleflies could penetrate the combat-rated force field that surrounded it. Her warehouses, too, were well shielded, although the team had managed to confirm the two where the weapons were being held.

Several modified insects had got through to take a quick look around before succumbing to either janglepulse emitters or electron webs.

Secondary observation teams followed the suppliers as they left, watching them assemble their cache of weapons and equipment before delivering it to the dealership. A whole underground network of Velaines' iniquitous black-market arms traders was carefully recorded and filed, ready for the bust which would end the whole operation.

On the eleventh day, the observers logged a call which Adam Elvin made to a warehouse in town, authorizing them to forward an assignment of agricultural machinery to Lancier's dealership.

'This is it,' Tarlo declared. 'They're getting them ready for shipment.'

'Could be,' Paula admitted.

On the other side of the operations office, Mares just sighed at her. But she did ask for the arrest teams to be put on standby.

Maggie was in one of the cars parked close to the dealership. When the eight lorries arrived, stacked high with crates of agricultural machinery, she relayed the pictures to the operations centre. Wide gates in the fence surrounding the dealership compound were hurriedly opened to let them through. There was a brief hold-up as yet another of Lancier's cars went out on a test run. The lawful business had been doing well for the whole duration of the observation, with up to a dozen cars a day taken out by legitimate customers. Sales were brisk.

All eight lorries drove into the largest of Lancier's warehouses. The doors rolled down as soon as the last one parked inside. Sensors which the observation team had ringing the site reported screening systems coming on immediately.

'Where's Elvin now?' Paula asked.

Tarlo showed her the images of their prime target finishing

his lunch in a downtown restaurant. Paula settled down at the side of the console to follow him, using the sensors carried by the observation teams.

After lunch, Elvin walked round one of the shopping streets, using his usual tactics to try and spot any tails. When he got back to the hotel he started packing his suitcase. Late that afternoon he went down to the bar and ordered a beer. He drank it while watching the portal at the end of the counter, which was showing Alessandra Baron interviewing Dudley Bose. In the early evening, just as the sun was falling below the horizon, his suitcase followed him downstairs, and he checked out.

'All right,' Paula announced to the teams. 'It looks like this is it. Everybody: stage one positions please.'

Don Mares was in one of the four cars assigned to follow Elvin. He waited a hundred metres from the hotel, seeing the big man emerge from the lobby. A taxi drew up at the request of Elvin's e-butler. His suitcase trundled up onto the rear luggage platform as he climbed in.

'Stand by, Don,' Paula said. 'We're placing a scrutineer in the taxi drive array. Ah, here we go, he's told it to take him to 32nd Street.'

'That's nowhere near the dealership,' Don Mares protested as their car took off in pursuit.

'I know. Just wait.' Paula turned to the visual and data feeds coming from the dealership. Rachael Lancier and ten of her people were now inside the sealed-up warehouse with the lorries. The rest of the workforce had been sent home as usual at the end of the day.

On the console in front of Paula, data displays began flashing urgent warnings at her. 'Hello, this is interesting. Elvin is loading some infiltration software into the taxi's drive array.' She watched as the police scrutineer program wiped itself before the new interloper could establish itself and run an inventory on the operating system.

'He's changing direction,' Don Mares reported. There was an excited note in his voice.

'Just stay calm and stay with him,' Paula said. 'But don't get too close, we've got him covered.' Out of the six images of the taxi which the console's big portal offered her, only one was coming from a pursuit car. The others were all feeds from the civic security cameras which covered every street and avenue of the city. They showed the taxi sliding smoothly through the rush-hour traffic.

Elvin must have ordered it to accelerate. It began to speed up.

'Don't be obvious,' Paula muttered to the observation team as the taxi took a sharp right. It was a good hundred and fifty metres ahead of the first pursuit car now. Their standard boxing tactic had put the lead vehicle out of the picture. She watched the grid map with its bright dots, seeing how they rearranged themselves to surround the taxi.

Elvin turned right again, then quickly left, taking off down a small alleyway. 'Don't follow,' she instructed. 'It's only got one exit.'

Pursuit car three hurried to reach the street where the alleyway finished. The taxi emerged smoothly, and took a left. It was heading in the opposite direction to car three. They passed within a couple of metres.

Don Mares's car reassumed its tag position. The taxi began to speed up again. Screens along Paula's console showed the blurred lines of car lights on either side of it, stretching away through the tall buildings of the city centre. The taxi turned onto 12th street, one of the broadest in the city, with six lanes of traffic, and all of them full. It began to switch lanes at random. Then it slowed. An overhead camera followed it as it passed under one of the hulking bridges which carried the rail tracks into the CST planetary station.

'Damnit, where did he go?' Paula demanded. 'Don, can you see him?'

'I think so. Second lane.'

Two cameras were focused on the other side of the bridge, covering every lane. A constant flow of vehicles zipped past. Then the cameras were zooming in on the taxi. It had changed to the outside lane again.

'All right,' Paula said. 'All cars, reduce separation distance. Stay within eighty metres. We can't risk loss of visual contact again. Car three, get under the bridge, check it out. See if he dropped something off.'

The taxi carried on with its evasive manoeuvres for another kilometre, then abruptly turned onto 45th Street, and stayed in one lane. Its speed wound back to a steady seventy kilometres per hour.

'He's heading right for us,' Maggie said.

'Looks that way,' Paula agreed. 'Okay, all pursuit cars, back off again.'

Eight minutes later the taxi pulled up outside Rachael Lancier's car dealership. The gates opened and it went in, driving right through the open door of a warehouse. It stopped beside an empty repair bay.

Paula squinted at the portal image. The warehouse door had been left open, allowing the team's sensors and cameras a perfect view. Nothing moved.

'What's happening?' Tarlo asked.

'I'm not sure,' Paula said. 'Rachael is still in the warehouse with the lorries. No wait . . .'

Simon Kavanagh was walking across the brightly lit concrete of the open warehouse floor. His bank tattoo paid the taxi charge. The rear luggage platform opened, and Elvin's suitcase rolled out. It started to follow the slim bodyguard as he walked away. The taxi drove out of the warehouse.

'Oh hell,' Paula grunted. 'All teams, you have a go code for stage three. I repeat, we are at stage three. Interdict and arrest. Don, stop that taxi.' The city traffic routing array fired an emergency halt order into the taxi's drive array. All four pursuit cars surged forwards, forming a physical blockade around the vehicle.

Maggie was already moving as the taxi emerged from the warehouse. The sun had finally sunk from the sky ten minutes earlier, leaving a gloomy twilight in its wake. Behind her, the towers of the city centre cut sharp gleaming lines into the shady sky. Ahead, there were only a few murky polyphoto strips fixed on the warehouse eaves to cast a weak yellow glow across the dealership with its rows and rows of parked cars. On the far side of the compound, an elevated rail line blocked the horizon, a thick black concrete barrier separating the city roofline from the darkening ginger sky. A single cargo train hissed and clanked its way along, a badly adjusted power wheel intermittently throwing up a fantail of sparks which marked out its progress as it slid deeper into the city.

Her fellow officers were advancing beside her, scuttling between the silent, stationary cars as they closed on the locked and screened warehouse. She activated her armour. The system, which looked like a chrome-blue skeleton worn outside her uniform, started to buzz softly. Its force field expanded, thickening the air around her. She prayed the power rating was good enough. Heaven only knew what calibre weapons they'd be facing.

Cars skidded behind her with tyres squealing like wounded animals. Up ahead, the point members of the police tactical assault squad had reached the warehouse door. They barely stopped to fire an ion bolt at the bonded composite panelling. A dazzling flash threw the compound into monochrome relief, accompanied by a thunderbolt *crack*. Splinters of smouldering composite hurtled through the air, revealing two large holes in the building. Squad members raced through.

'FREEZE, POLICE.'

'DO NOT EVEN THINK OF MOVING, MOTHER-FUCKER.'

'YOU, HANDS WHERE I CAN SEE THEM. NOW.'

Adrenaline was singing in Maggie's veins as she rushed through the gap. She cleared the little layer of smoke on the other side, her ion pistol held ready, retinal inserts on full resolution. Surprise at the scene before her almost made her stumble.

Rachael Lancier was standing casually at the front of a lorry. The ten employees who had stayed behind were clustered round her. Heavyliftbots had removed several crates from the lorry, stacking them neatly on the floor. A bottle and ten glasses were standing on top of one, clearly waiting for a toast to be drunk.

'Ah, good evening, Detective,' Rachael Lancier said as she saw Maggie's insignia. Her mocking grin was pure evil. 'I know I offer a good deal on my cars, but there's no need to rush. I have something to suit every bank tattoo.'

Maggie cursed under her breath, and slowly engaged her pistol's safety catch. 'We've been had,' she said.

'Don?' Paula was asking. 'Don, is he in the taxi? Report, Don.'

'Nothing!' Don Mares spat. 'It's fucking empty. He's not in it.'

'Goddamnit,' Paula shouted.

'This is a stitch-up,' Maggie said. 'The bitch is laughing at us. I'm standing five metres away from her, and she's still bloody laughing. We're not going to find anything here.'

'We have to,' Tarlo cried furiously. 'We've been watching them for three goddamn weeks. I saw those arms go in there with my own eyes.'

Now it was over, now the hype had cooled, the adrenaline cold turkey kicked in, Maggie felt dreadfully weary. She looked directly into Rachael Lancier's triumphant gleaming eyes. 'I'm telling you, we've been royally fucked.'

*

The one make-or-break moment came when he rolled out of the still-moving taxi under the rail bridge. Adam hit the ground hard, yelling at the sharp pain slamming into his leg, shoulder, and ribs. Then he twisted again, and surged to his feet. The second, empty, taxi was parked ready not five metres away. He dived in through the open door, and his Quentin Kelleher e-butler told it to take him directly to the A+A.

The vehicle slid smoothly out into the busy traffic flow. As he looked around, he could see a car brake hard under the bridge. Two people jumped out, and began scanning round. He grinned as the distance built behind him. *Not bad for a fat seventy-five-year-old.*

Room 421 was just as he'd left it, and the scanning array gave him an all clear. He limped in. The bruises were starting to hurt badly now. When he sat on the edge of the jellmattress and stripped off his clothes he found a lot of grazed skin that was oozing blood. He applied some healskin patches, and flopped down to let the shakes run their course. Sometime later, he began to laugh.

*

For two weeks he never left the room. The dispenser mechanism delivered three meals a day. He drank a lot of fluid. His e-butler filtered the output of the local and Intersolar news shows, with a special search order for items concerning Dyson Alpha.

He lay on the bed for twenty hours a day, feeding on cheap packet food, and crappy unisphere entertainment shows. Standard commercial cellular reprofiling kits cocooned his torso and limbs, slowly siphoning the fat out of him, adjusting the folds of skin to fit his new, slimmer figure, and ruining most of his OCtattoos in the process. A pair of thick bands with a leathery texture were attached to each leg, on either side of his knees. They were the deep pervasion kits which extended slender tendrils through his flesh until they reached bone. Slowly and quite painfully, they reduced the length of his femur and tibia by half a centimetre each, altering his height to a measurement which was absent from any criminal database.

The adjustments left him weak and irritable, as if he was recovering from a bout of flu. He consoled himself with the mission's success. It had cost them another hundred thousand dollars, but Rachael Lancier had cooperated enthusiastically. Over the last ten days of the mission, every car leaving the dealership compound had been carrying a part of the order. They'd been dropped off all over town at buildings he'd paid her to rent. Rachael's workers had parcelled them up in the crates he'd shipped in months before. The entire list was on its way to Far Away via a multitude of circuitous routes. They'd arrive over the next few months.

His only regret was not being able to see Paula Myo's face as the extent of the deception became apparent. That would almost be worth the feel of restraints clasping his wrists.

Seventeen days after the fateful night, Adam dressed himself in a loose-fitting sweatshirt and trousers, and left the A+A. A twenty-minute taxi ride took him to the CST planetary station. He wandered through the concourse without setting off any alarms. Content with that, he caught the express train to LA Galactic.

3

Few people outside government circles had ever heard of the Commonwealth ExoProtectorate Council. It had been formed in the early days of the Intersolar Commonwealth, one of those contingency groups beloved of bureaucrats. Back then, people were still justifiably worried about encountering hostile aliens as CST wormholes were continually opened on new planets further and further away from Earth. It was the Commonwealth ExoProtectorate Council which had the task of reviewing each sentient alien species discovered by CST, and evaluating the threat-level it posed to human society. Given the potential seriousness should the worst-case scenario ever happen, its members were all extremely powerful in political terms. However, since the probability that such an encounter would ever occur was extremely low, the Council members invariably delegated the duty to staff members. In this diluted form, the Council continued to meet on a regular annual basis. Every year it solemnly confirmed the galactic status quo. Every year, its delegates went off and had a decent lunch on expenses. As the Commonwealth was discovering, sentient aliens were a rare commodity in this section of the galaxy.

Now though, the Dyson Alpha event had changed everything. Nigel Sheldon couldn't ever recall attending a Council meeting before, although he supposed he must have when both the Silfen and the High Angel had been discovered. Such recollections weren't currently part of his memories. He'd obviously retired them to secure storage several rejuvenations ago.

His lack of direct recall experience had been capably rectified by the briefings his staff had given him on the trip from Cressat, where he and the rest of the senior Sheldon family members lived. CST had routed his private train directly through Augusta to the New York CST station in Newark; from there it was a quick journey over to Grand Central.

He always enjoyed Manhattan in the spring when the snow had gone and the trees were starting to put out fresh leaves, a vibrant green which no artist ever quite managed to capture. A convoy of limousines had been waiting at Grand Central station to drive him and his entourage the short distance to the Commonwealth Exploration and Development Office on Fifth Avenue. The skyscraper was over a hundred and fifty years old, and at two hundred and seventy-eight storeys no longer the highest on the ancient metropolis island, but still close.

He'd arrived early, ahead of the other Council members. The anxious regular staff had shown him and his entourage into the main conference room on the two hundred and twenty-fifth floor. They weren't used to such high-powered delegations, and it showed in their hectic preparations to have everything in the room just perfect for when the meeting started. So he waved away their queries, and told them to get on with it, he'd just wait quietly for the other members to turn up. At which point his entourage closed smoothly and protectively around him.

From the conference room, he could just see over the neighbouring buildings to Central Park. The patina of terrestrial-green life was reassuringly bright under the afternoon sun. There were almost no alien trees in the park these days. For the last eight decades, Earth's native species protection laws had been enforced with increasing severity by the Environment Commissioners of the Unified Federal Nations. Although he could just see the brilliant ma-hon tree glimmering dominantly at the centre of the park, every spiral leaf reflecting prismatic light from its polished-silver surface. It had been there for over three hundred years now, one of only eight ever to be successfully transferred from their strange native planet. For the last hundred years it had been reclassified as a city monument. A concept which Nigel rather enjoyed. When New Yorkers were determined about something, not even the UFN environmental bloc could shift them, and there was no way they were going to give up their precious, unique ma-hon.

Nigel's chief executive aide, Daniel Alster, brought him a coffee which he drank as he looked out over the city. In his mind he tried to sketch in the other changes he'd seen to the skyline over the centuries. Manhattan's buildings looked a lot more slender now, though that was mainly because they were so much taller. There was also a trend towards architecture with a more elaborate or artistic profile. Sometimes it worked splendidly, as with the contemporary crystal Gothic of the Stoet Building; or else it looked downright mundane like the twisting Illeva. He didn't actually mind the failures too much, at least they meant the whole place was different, unlike most of the flat urban sprawls out on the settled worlds.

Rafael Columbia, the chief of the Intersolar Serious Crimes Directorate, was the second Council member to arrive. Nigel knew of him, of course, although the two had never met in the flesh before.

'Pleasure to meet you at last,' Nigel said as they shook hands. 'Your name keeps cropping up on reports from our security division.'

Rafael Columbia chuckled. 'In a good context, I trust?' He was just over two hundred years old, with a physical appearance in his late fifties. In contrast to Nigel, who rejuvenated every fifteen years, Rafael Columbia considered that a more mature appearance was essential for his position. His apparent age gave him broad shoulders and a barrel torso which needed a lot of exercise to keep in shape. Thick silver hair was cut short and stylish, accentuating the slightly sour expression which was fixed on his flat face. Bushy eyebrows and bright grey-green eyes marked him down as a Halgarth family member. Without that connection he would never have qualified for his current job within the Commonwealth administration. The Halgarths had founded EdenBurg, one of the Big15 industrial planets, turning them into a major Intersolar Dynasty, which gave them almost as much influence as Nigel's family inside the Commonwealth.

'Oh yes,' Nigel said. 'Major crime incidents seem to be down lately, certainly those against CST anyway. Thank you for that.'

'I do what I can,' Rafael said. 'It's these New Nationalist groups that keep springing up to harass planetary governments that are the main source of trouble; the more we frustrate them, the more aggressive their core supporters become. If we're not careful, we're going to see a nasty wave of anti-Commonwealth terrorist assaults again, just like two twenty-two.'

'You really think it will come to that?'

'I hope not. Internal Diplomacy believes these current groups simply claim political status as a justification for their activities; they're actually more criminal-based than anything else. If so, they should run a natural cycle and die out.'

'Thank Christ for that. I don't want to withdraw gateways from any more planets, there are enough isolated worlds as it is. I thought the only planet left with any real trouble was Far Away. And it's not as if that can ever be cured.'

Rafael Columbia nodded gravely. 'I believe that in time even Far Away can be civilized. When CST begins opening phase four space it will become fully incorporated into the Commonwealth.'

'I'm sure you're right,' Nigel said doubtfully. 'But it's going to be a long while before we start thinking about phase four.'

The Commonwealth Vice President, Elaine Dòi, walked into the conference room, talking to Thompson Burnelli, the Commonwealth senator who chaired the science commission. Their respective aides trailed along behind, murmuring quietly amongst themselves. Elaine Doi greeted Nigel with polite neutrality, careful to maintain her professionalism. He returned the compliment, keeping an impassive face. She was a career politician and had devoted a hundred and eighty years to clawing her way up to her present position. Even her rejuvenations were geared around promoting herself; her skin had progressively deepened its shading until it was the darkest ebony, to emphasize her ethnicity. Over the same period, her face had actually abandoned her more attractive feminine traits in favour of a handsome, sterner appearance. Nigel had to deal with her kind of politician on a near-constant basis, and he despised every one of them. In his distant idealistic youth, when he'd built the first wormhole generator, he had dreamed of leaving them all behind on Earth, allowing the new planets to develop in complete freedom, becoming havens of personal liberty. These days he accepted their dominance of all human government as the price of a civilized society – after all, someone had to maintain order. But that didn't mean he had to like their eternal self-serving narcissistic behaviour. And he considered Doi to be one of the more reprehensible specimens, always ready to advance herself at the cost of others. With the next Presidential selection due in three years' time, she had begun the final stage of her century-long campaign. His support would ensure she reached the Presidential Palace on New Rio. As yet he hadn't given it.

Thompson Burnelli was less effusive, a straight-talking man

who was North America's UFN delegate in the Common-wealth Senate, and as such the representative of a huge conglomeration of old and powerful interests made up from some of the wealthiest Grand Families on the planet. He looked the part, a handsome man, wearing an expensive grey silk suit, so obviously a former Ivy League college athlete. His air of confidence was never something that could be acquired through memory implants and bioneural tweaking; it was only available through breeding, and he was very definitely one of Earth's premier aristocracy. Nigel had hated that kind of rich-kid arrogance while he was at college – as much as he did the politicians. But given a choice, he would prefer to deal with Burnelli's kind any day.

'Nigel, this must be somewhat galling for you, I imagine,' Thompson Burnelli said with amusement shading close to mockery.

'How so?' Nigel asked.

'An alien contact that your exploratory division had nothing to do with. Some fifth-rate academic astronomer makes the most profound discovery in the last two hundred years, and his only piece of equipment is an equally decrepit telescope that you could probably pick up for a thousand bucks in any junk shop. How much does CST spend on astronomy every year?'

'Couple of billion at the last count,' Nigel replied wearily. He had to admit, the senator had a point. And he wasn't the only one making it. The unisphere media had adopted a kind of gleeful sarcasm towards CST since Dudley Bose announced his discovery.

'Never mind,' Thompson Burnelli said cheerfully. 'Better luck next time, eh?'

'Thank you. How did your continent's team do in the Cup?'

The senator frowned. 'Oh, you mean the soccer thing? I'm not sure.'

'Lost, didn't they? Still, it was only the first round of eight, I don't suppose you suffer quite so much getting knocked out at the bottom. Better luck next time.' Nigel produced a thin smile as the senator turned away to greet Rafael Columbia.

More Council members were arriving, and Nigel busied himself welcoming them; at least they could swap football small talk. Crispin Goldreich, the senator chairing the Commonwealth Budgetary Commission; Brewster Kumar, the President's science adviser; Gabrielle Else, the director of the Commonwealth Industry and Trade Commission; Senator Lee Ki, director of the phase two space economic policy board, and Eugene Cinzoul, Chief Attorney at the Commonwealth Law Commission.

Elaine Doi raised her voice above the burble of conversation. 'I believe we can call this meeting to order now,' she said.

People looked around, and nodded their agreement. They all started hunting for their respective seats. Nigel gave the one empty chair a pointed glance, and sat to the left of the Vice President who was chairing the meeting. According to protocol, he was the ExoProtectorate Council's deputy chair. Aides began to settle behind their chiefs.

The Vice President turned to her chief of staff, Patricia Kantil. 'Could you ask the SI to come on line, please.'

That was when Ozzie Fernandez Isaacs chose to make his entrance. Nigel quashed the smile that was forming on his lips; everyone else around the table looked so surprised. They should have known better. Back when Nigel and Ozzie assembled the math which made wormhole generators possible, he'd been a genuine eccentric; moments of pure genius partied with surfer-boy dumbness to claim the dominant personality trait throughout his undergrad years. A time which Nigel had spent alternately worrying himself sick about the days Ozzie spent out of his skull, and shaking his head in awe as his friend cracked the problems which he'd considered unsolvable. They'd made a great team, good enough to compress space so Nigel could step out on Mars to watch the NASA spaceplane landing. After that, taming the beast they'd created was always Nigel's job, transforming that temperamental prototype pile of high-energy physics equipment into the ultimate transport method, and in doing so fashioning the largest single corporation the human race had ever known. Management and finance and political influence were of no interest to Ozzie. He just wanted to get *out there* and see what wonders the galaxy held.

It was the time spent in between his forays out amid the virgin stars that made him a legend; the wildman of the Commonwealth, the ultimate alternative lifestyle guru. The girls, the old vices, and the brave new narcotic stimulants, chemical and bioneural, which he pioneered; Ozzieworld, the H-congruous planet he was supposed to live on all by himself in a palace the size of a city; decades spent as a tramp-poet worldwalking to witness the new planet cultures forming from the bottom end of society; the hundreds of naturally conceived children; outré rejuvenations so he could spend years in animal bodies – a lion, an eagle, a dolphin, a Karruk nobear; the attempted dinosaur DNA synthesis project which cost billions before it was hijacked by the Barsoomians; he owned a secret network of wormholes linking the Commonwealth planets which only he could use; his thought routines taken as the basis of the SI. Everywhere you went in the Commonwealth, the locals would tell of the time when Ozzie passed through (an unknown in disguise at the time of course) and enriched their ancestors' lives by some feat or other: organizing a bridge to be built over a treacherous river, rushing a sick child to hospital through a storm, being the first to climb the tallest mountain on the planet, slaying – in single combat – the local crime boss. *Turning water into wine, too, if the tabloid side of the unisphere was to be believed*, Nigel thought. After all, Ozzie was certainly an expert on the opposite process.

'Sorry I'm late, man,' Ozzie said. He gave the Vice President a friendly wave as he walked over to the last empty chair. As he passed behind Nigel, he patted him on the shoulder. 'Good to see you, Nige, it's been a while.'

'Hi, Ozzie,' Nigel said casually, refusing to be out-cooled. It had actually been seventeen years since they'd last seen each other in the flesh.

Ozzie finally made it to his chair and sprawled in it with a happy sigh. 'Anyone got some coffee, I've got a bitch of a hangover.'

Nigel gave a quick flick of his finger, and Daniel Alster had a cup taken over. Several Council members were struggling to keep their disapproval from showing at the legend's disrespectful attitude. Which was, as Nigel well knew, what Ozzie was hoping for. There were times when he considered Ozzie having a rejuvenation to be singularly pointless; the man could be extraordinarily juvenile without any help from the popping hormones of an adolescent body. But the acceptance and adoration he was granted by the Commonwealth at large must have made that same young Afro-Latino kid finally feel content. Even in the politically correct twenty-first century those two cultures never mixed, not out on the San Diego streets where he came from. Ozzie had gotten the last laugh there.

'Are you here in an official capacity, Mr Isaacs?' Crispin Goldreich asked, in a very upper-class English accent, which simply reeked of censure.

'Sure am, man, I'm the CST rep for this gig.' In his casual lime-green shirt and creased ochre climbing trousers he looked hugely out of place around that table of masterclass power brokers. It didn't help that he still had his big Afro hairstyle; in over three centuries of arguing, pleading, and downright mockery Nigel had never persuaded him to get it cut. It was the one human fashion which had never, ever, come around again. But Ozzie lived in hope.

'Don't look at me,' Nigel said. 'I'm the operations side of CST; Ozzie is the technical adviser to this Council.'

Ozzie gave Crispin Goldreich a broad grin, and winked.

'Very well,' Elaine Doi said. 'If we could proceed.'

The large wall-mounted portal overlooking the table bubbled into life with tangerine and turquoise lines scudding backwards into a central vanishing point, looking like some antique screen-saver pattern. 'Good afternoon ladies and gentlemen,' the Sentient Intelligence said smoothly. 'We are happy to be in attendance at what will surely be an historic meeting.'

'Thank you,' the Vice President said. 'All right, Brewster, if you would, please.'

The Presidential science adviser looked around the table. 'There isn't actually much I can add to the unisphere news reports, except to confirm that it's real. At our request, CST has opened an exploratory wormhole in interstellar space beyond Tanyata, and used its own instruments to confirm the envelopment event.'

'Our equipment is considerably more sophisticated than the telescopes used by Dudley Bose,' Nigel said. He ignored the quiet snort from Thompson Burnelli. 'Even so, there is very little raw data available. The entire process takes about two thirds of a second. We don't believe the barrier can be a physical shell, it must be some kind of force field.'

'One which cuts off the visual spectrum?' Lee Ki asked.

'In scale alone, this technology is way beyond anything we have,' Brewster Kumar said. 'The damn thing is thirty AUs in diameter. I wouldn't even expect it to be anything like our molecular bonding shields, or even a quantum field.'

'Are there any realistic theories about what the barrier is?'

'We've got two dozen in every university physics department across the Commonwealth. But that's hardly the point; it's what it does which is interesting. It's an infrared emitter, which means it's preserving the solar system inside.'

'How's that?' Gabrielle Else asked him.

'Essentially: there is no build-up of energy inside the barrier. When the star's electromagnetic output hits the barrier, it passes through to be emitted as heat. If it didn't, if the barrier contained it, well, the effect would be like a pressure cooker in there. We believe the barrier also radiates the solar wind as infrared energy as well, although at this distance it's difficult to tell.'

'In other words,' Nigel said. 'Whoever put them up around the Dyson Pair is still living happily inside. The conditions in there haven't changed from before.'

'Which brings us to the next consideration,' Brewster Kumar said. 'Were these barriers erected by the aliens living at the stars, or were they imposed on them? Neither case is particularly helpful to us.'

'How can isolationism be detrimental to us?' Rafael Columbia asked.

'Isolationism in our history is traditionally enacted in times of hostility,' Nigel said. 'Such a situation must have existed at the Dyson Pair when this happened. If it is the alien civilizations of these two star systems who erected the barriers, we have to consider the possibility that their motive was defensive. If so, that was one godawful weapon they were protecting themselves against. The alternative is just as bad, that some other alien species feared them so badly they wanted them contained. Either way, there could well be two alien species out there, both with weapons and technology so far ahead of ours it might as well be magic.'

'Thank you, Sir Arthur,' Ozzie muttered.

Nigel grinned at his old friend; he doubted anyone else in the room got the reference. They were all too young by at least a century.

'I think you're wrong in assigning them human motivations,' Gabrielle Else said. 'Couldn't this simply be a case of stop the universe I want to get off? After all, the Silfen are fairly insular.'

'Insular?' Rafael Columbia exclaimed. 'They're so spread out we don't even know how many planets they're settled on.'

'It is the purpose of this Council to take the worst-case scenario into account,' the Vice President said. 'And the hostile locale scenario is certainly plausible.'

'Speaking of the Silfen,' Ozzie said. 'Why don't we just ask them what's going down here?'

'We have,' the Vice President said. 'They say they don't really know.'

'Hell, man, they say that about everything. Ask them if there's going to be daylight tomorrow and they'll scratch their asses and ask you what you mean by "tomorrow". You can't just ask them a straight question like that. Goddamn loafing mystics, they've got to be chased down and fooled into giving us an answer.'

'Yes, thank you, Mr Isaacs, I am aware of that. We do have a great many Silfen cultural experts, all of whom are still pursuing this avenue as a matter of urgency. Hopefully, they will coax a more coherent answer from the Silfen. Until that happens, we are left relying on our own resources. Hence the need for this Council meeting.'

Ozzie threw her a furious look, and snuggled down into his chair for a good sulk.

'I don't believe the barrier could have been imposed on those stars by an external agency,' Lee Ki said. 'It's not logical. If you fear someone so much and have the ability to imprison entire stars, then you would not make the barrier permeable. You would use it as a pressure cooker, or do worse than that. No, for my money it was defensive. Something very nasty was heading towards the Dyson Pair, and they slammed the gates shut in its face.'

'In which case, where is it now?' Thompson Burnelli asked.

'Exactly,' Brewster Kumar said.

'It no longer exists,' Ozzie said. 'And you guys are all far too paranoid.'

'Care to qualify that?' Thompson Burnelli said impassively.

'Come on, man; the Dyson Pair are over twelve hundred

light-years away from Tanyata. This all happened when the fucking Roman Empire ruled the Earth. Astronomy is history.'

'It was closer to Genghis Khan than the Romans,' Brewster Kumar said. 'And no culture as powerful and advanced as the Dyson Pair or their aggressor is going to fade away in a single millennium. We certainly won't, and we're nowhere near that technology level yet. You can't just bury your head in the sand over this and hope it all blew away all those years ago.'

'I agree,' the Vice President said. 'Far Away is only five hundred and fifty light-years from the Dyson Pair, and they're observing the barrier still intact.'

'One other piece of information which CST hasn't made public yet,' Nigel said. 'We also used our exploratory wormhole to track down the envelopment time for Dyson Beta. Unfortunately, our first guess was the right one.'

Rafael Columbia was suddenly very attentive. 'You mean they're the same?'

'Yes. As seen from Tanyata, the Pair have a two light-year linear separation distance. We opened a wormhole two light-years closer to Beta from where we made our observation of Alpha's enclosure. We saw Beta's enclosure, which is identical to Alpha's. They occur within three minutes of each other.'

'It's defensive,' Eugene Cinzoul said. 'It has to be. A civilization inhabiting two star systems was approached by an aggressor.'

'Curious coincidence,' Ozzie said.

'What is?' the Vice President asked.

'Something aggressive and immensely powerful closes in on the one other civilization in this part of the galaxy that was technologically savvy enough to protect itself from them. I don't believe it, man. Galactic timescale simply won't allow that to happen. We only co-exist with the Silfen because they've existed for like millions of years.'

The Vice President gave the SI portal a troubled look. 'What is your interpretation of this?'

'Mr Isaacs is correct in stating that such a conflict between two balanced powers is extremely unlikely,' the SI said. 'We know how rare it is for sentience to evolve on any life-bearing planet; as a consequence, technological civilizations rarely co-exist in the galaxy – although the High Angel is an exceptional case. However, the proposition cannot be excluded simply because of this. We also acknowledge Mr Kumar's point, that any civilization capable of performing such a feat will not quickly disappear from the galaxy.'

'They can evolve,' Ozzie said quickly. 'They can throw off all their primitive instincts. After all, we leave a lot of our shit behind us.'

'You also generate a great deal of new "shit",' the SI said. 'All of which is depressingly similar to your old "shit". And no primitive culture could erect these barriers round the Dyson Pair. But again, we concede the point. The barrier mechanism may simply be an ancient device that has been left on for no good reason other than its creators have indeed moved onwards and upwards. There are endless speculations which can be made from the presently observed data. None of which can be refined as long as that data remains so scarce and so old.'

'What are you suggesting?' the Vice President asked.

'That is obvious, is it not? This Council was brought into existence to formulate a response to any perceived threat to the Commonwealth. No coherent response to the Dyson Pair can be made based on the currently available data. More information must be acquired. You must visit the Dyson Pair to ascertain their current status, and the reason behind the enclosures.'

'The cost—' exclaimed the Vice President. She gave Nigel a quick guilty glance.

He ignored it; the SI had made things considerably simpler for him. 'Yes, it would cost a lot to reach the Dyson Pair by conventional methods,' he said. 'We'd have to locate at least seven H-congruous planets, stretched out between the Commonwealth and the Dyson Pair, and then build commercial-size wormhole generators on each of them. It would take decades, and there would be little economic benefit.'

'The Commonwealth treasury can hardly subsidize CST,' Crispin Goldreich said.

'You did for Far Away,' Nigel said mildly. 'That was our last alien contact.'

'One station on Half Way!' the senator said hotly. 'And if nothing else, that convinced me we should never do such a thing again. Far Away has been a total waste of time and effort.'

Nigel resisted the impulse to comment directly. The Halgarths had direct allies around the table in addition to Rafael, and their family were the main beneficiaries from Far Away. Not, as they'd be the first to admit, that there were many benefits.

'I would like to propose something a little more practical than consecutive wormholes,' Nigel said. Everyone around the table looked at him expectantly, even Ozzie, which was quite an achievement. The Vice President's expression of interest tightened at the simple demonstration of true political power.

'I'm in total agreement with the SI that we need to know exactly what has happened at the Dyson Pair,' Nigel continued. 'And we can neither afford the cost nor the wait to build a chain of wormholes to take us there. So I suggest we build a starship instead.'

The idea was greeted with several nervous smiles. Ozzie simply laughed.

'You mean a faster than light ship?' Brewster Kumar asked. There was a strong note of excitement in his voice. 'Can we actually do that?'

'Of course. It's a relatively simple adaptation of our current wormhole generator system; instead of a stable fixed wormhole which you travel through, this will produce a permanent flowing wormhole that you travel inside of.'

'Oh man,' Ozzie said. 'That is so beautiful. Whadoyaknow, the space cadets won after all. Let's press the red button and zoom off into hyperspace.'

'It's not hyperspace,' Nigel answered, slightly too quickly. 'That's just a tabloid name for a very complex energy manipulation function, and you know it.'

'Hyperspace,' Ozzie said contentedly. 'Everything we built our wormhole to avoid.'

'Except in cases like this, when it makes perfect sense,' Nigel said. 'We can probably build this ship inside of a year. A crack exploratory team can go out there, take a look round and tell us what's happening. It's quick, and it's cheap.'

'Cheap?' Crispin Goldreich queried.

'Relatively, yes.' The starship proposals had been sitting dormant in Nigel's personal files for over a century. Always an exercise in wishful thinking, one he hadn't managed to fully let go. He'd never quite forgotten (nor erased) his feeling of admiration when he watched the *Eagle II* fly gracefully out of the Martian horizon to settle on Arabia Terra. There was something noble about spacecraft voyaging through the vast and hostile void, carrying with them the pinnacle of the human spirit, everything good and worthwhile about the race. And he was probably the last human alive who remembered that. *No*, he corrected himself, *not the last*. 'The CST corporation and Augusta Treasury would be prepared to fund up to thirty per cent of the hardware costs.'

'In return for exclusivity,' Thompson Burnelli said scathingly.

Nigel smiled softly at him. 'I believe that precedent was established during the Far Away venture.'

'Very well,' the Vice President said. 'Unless there's an alternative, we'll take a vote on the proposal.'

Nobody was against it. But Nigel had known that from the start, even Burnelli raised his hand in approval. The Exo-Protectorate Council was basically a rubber stamp for CST exploration and encounter strategy. With Nigel's blessing, CST had started practical design work on the starship three days earlier. All that remained were the thousand interminable details of the project, its funding and management. Details they would all delegate back down to their deputies. This meeting was policy only.

'So are you going to captain this mission?' Rafael Columbia asked as they stood up to leave.

'No,' Nigel said. 'Much as I'd like to, that position requires various qualities and experience which I simply don't have, not even lurking in secure storage at my rejuve clinic. But I know a man that does.'

*

Oaktier was an early phase one planet, settled in 2089. Its longevity had produced a first-class economy which ran smoothly in conjunction with a rich and impressive cultural heritage. The crystal skyscrapers and marble condo-pyramids that comprised the centre of the capital, Darklake City, made that quite obvious to any observer arriving fresh at the CST planetary station from Seattle.

Most of the original settlers had arrived from Canada and Hong Kong, with a goodly proportion of Seattle's residents joining up with them. As such, its influences were memorably varied, with ultramodern trends sitting comfortably alongside carefully maintained old traditions. Given such roots, formality and hard work had seeped into the population's genome over the centuries. As a people, they'd flourished and expanded; two hundred and forty years after settlement, the population was just over one and a quarter billion, spread out over eight continents. The vast majority working diligently and living well.

With the Seattle legacy perhaps weighting the decision, Darklake City had been sited in a hilly area of the sub-tropics. With its slopes of rich soil, constant heat, and abundant water from rivers and lakes, the area was ideal for coffee growing. The lake shore which made up the south-eastern edge of the city now sprawled for thirty-five kilometres, incorporating marinas, civic parks, expensive apartment blocks, boatyards, leisure resorts, and commercial docks. At night, it was a gaudy neon rainbow of colour as holographic adverts roofed the roads like luminescent storm clouds, while buildings competed against each other to emphasize their features in raw photonic energy. Bars, restaurants and clubs used music, live acts, and semi-legal pleasure-tingle emitters to entice the party people and *it* crowds in off the street.

Some forty years before Dudley Bose made his vital discovery, the night she was due to be murdered, Tara Jennifer Shaheef could see it all laid out before her from the lounge balcony of her twenty-fifth-floor apartment in the centre of the city. The shoreline was like the glimmering edge of the galaxy, falling off into complete blackness beyond. That was where life and civilization ended. The only thing out there was a few sparkling cruise ships which slid across the deep water like rogue star clusters lost in the deep night.

A gentle evening breeze stirred her hair and robe and she leant against the balcony rail. There was a sugary scent of blossom in the air, which she relished as she inhaled. Oaktier had long ago banned combustion engines and fossil fuel power stations from the planet; local politicians boasted that its atmosphere was cleaner than Earth's. So she breathed in the air contentedly. There was no noise. At this height she was well insulated from the low buzz of electric vehicles on the streets below, and the bustling shoreline three kilometres away was too far for its racket to carry.

If she turned her head left, she could see the bright grid of city lights stretch out into the foothills. A pale light cast by the grey-blue crescent of Oaktier's low moon was just strong enough to reveal the mountains behind them which formed a low wall across the night sky. In the daytime, long terrace lines of coffee bushes were visible banding the slopes. White plantation mansions nestled in lush groves of trees, set back from the thin roads which snaked up to the summits.

Two rejuvenations ago, she'd made her life out there, away from the more frenetic urban existence. Sometimes, she dreamed of reverting, heading back into the countryside for a quieter, slower existence. An existence away from her intense, driven husband, Morton. After a couple more rejuvenations, she would probably do it, just to recharge herself. But not just yet, she still enjoyed the faster mainstream life.

She went back into the apartment, and the balcony doors slid shut behind her. Her bare feet padded quietly on the lounge's hard teakwood floor as she made her way across to the bathroom.

In the apartment tower's basement, her killer entered the power utility room. He removed the cover from one of the building management array cabinets, and took a handheld array from his pocket. The unit spooled out a length of fibre optic cable with a standard v-jack on the end, which he plugged into the cabinet's exposed maintenance socket. Several new programs were downloaded, and quickly piggybacked their way onto the existing software. When it was done, he pulled the v-jack out and replaced the cover with the correct locking tool.

Tara Jennifer Shaheef's bathroom was decorated with large brown marble slabs on the floor and walls; while the ceiling was a single giant mirror. Recessed lighting around the rim of the bath cast a warm rose-pink glow across the room, flickering in an imitation of candlelight. The bath itself was a sunken affair big enough for two, which she'd filled to the brim and added a variety of salts. When she got in, the spar nozzles came on, churning the water against her skin. She sank into the sculpted seat, and rested her head back on the cushion. Her e-butler called up some music from the household array. Tara listened to the melody in a pleasant semi-doze.

Morton was away for a week at Talansee on the other side of the planet, attending a conference with a housing developer group he was trying to negotiate a deal with. AquaState, the company they'd set up together, manufactured semiorganic moisture extractor leaves that provided water for remote buildings, and was finally starting to take off. Morton was eager to capitalize on their growing success, moving the company towards a public flotation which would bring in a huge amount of money for further expansion. But his devotion to his work meant that for seven whole days she didn't have to produce any excuses about where she'd been or what she'd been doing. She could spend the whole time with Wyobie Cotal, the rather delectable young man she'd snagged for herself. It was mainly for what he did to her in bed, but they also travelled round the city and enjoyed its places and events as well. That's what made this affair so special. Wyobie paid attention to all those areas which Morton either ignored, or had simply forgotten in his eternal obsession to advance their company. These seven days were going to be a truly wonderful break, she was determined about that. Then maybe afterwards . . . After all, they'd been married for thirteen years. What more did Morton want? Marriages always went stale in the end. You just shook hands and moved on.

Her killer walked across the ground floor lobby, and his e-butler requested an elevator to take him up to the twenty-fifth floor. He stood underneath the discreet security sensor above the doors as he waited. He didn't care. After all, it wasn't his face he was wearing.

Tara was still deliberating about what to wear that evening when the hauntingly powerful orchestral chorus vanished abruptly. The bathroom lights died. The spar jets shut down. Tara opened her eyes resentfully. A power failure was so boring. She thought the apartment was supposed to be immune from such things. It had certainly never happened before.

After a few seconds, the lights still hadn't come back on. She told her e-butler to ask the household array what was happening. It told her it couldn't get a reply, nothing seemed to be working. Now she frowned in annoyance. This simply couldn't happen, that's what back-ups and duplicated systems were for.

She waited for a little while longer. The bath was such a tranquil place, and she wanted her skin to be just perfect for her lover that night. But no matter how hard she wished and cursed, the power stayed off. Eventually, she struggled to her feet and stepped out. That was when she realized just how dark the apartment was. She really couldn't see her hand in front of her face. Using irritation to cover any bud of genuine concern, she decided not to feel round for a towel. Instead she cautiously made her way out into the corridor. There was a glimmer of light available there, at least. It came from the broad archway leading into the lounge.

Tara hurried through into the big room, only mildly concerned what her soaking wet feet would do to the wooden floor. Light from the illuminated city washed in through the balcony windows. It gave the room a dark monochrome perspective. Her lips hardened in annoyance as she looked out at the twinkling lights. This was the only apartment which seemed to be suffering.

Something moved in the hallway. Large. Silent. She turned. 'What—'

The killer fired a nervejam pulse from his customized pistol. Every muscle in Tara's body locked solid for a second. The pulse overloaded most of the neural connections in her brain, making death instantaneous. She never felt a thing. Her muscles unlocked, and the corpse crumpled to the floor.

He walked over to her, and spent a moment looking down.

Then he pulled out an em pulser and placed it on the back of her head, where the memorycell insert was. The gadget discharged. He triggered it another three times, making absolutely sure the insert would be scrambled beyond recovery. No matter how good a clone body the re-life procedure produced for her, the last section of Tara Jennifer Shaheef's life was now lost for ever.

The killer's e-butler sent an instruction to the apartment's array, which turned the lights back on. He sat in the big sofa, facing the door, and waited.

Wyobie Cotal arrived forty-six minutes later. There was a somewhat smug and anticipatory smile on the young first-lifer's face as he walked into the lounge. It turned to an expression of total shock as he saw the naked corpse on the floor. He'd barely registered the man sitting on the sofa opposite before the nervejam pistol fired again.

The killer repeated the procedure with the em pulser, erasing the carefully stored duplicate memories of the last few months of Wyobie Cotal's life from his memorycell insert. After that, he moved into the spare bedroom, pulling three large suitcases and a big trunk out from their storage closet. By the time he'd got them into the master bedroom, three robot trolleys had arrived from the tower's delivery bay, carrying several plastic packing crates.

His first job was shoving the bodies into the two largest crates, and sealing them tight. He then spent the next two and a half hours collecting every item of Tara's in the apartment, gradually filling the remaining crates with them. Her clothes went into the cases and trunk.

When he was finished, the trolleys loaded up the crates again, and took them back down the service elevator to the delivery bay where two hired trucks were waiting. The crates containing the bodies went into one truck, while everything else went into the second.

Upstairs the killer drained the bath, then ordered the

maidbots to give the apartment a class-one cleaning. He left the little machines busy at work scouring the floors and walls for dust and dirt, conscientiously switching off the lights as he went.

4

So here she was, in the bleak small hours of the morning, strapped tightly into the confined cockpit of a hyperglider which was tethered to the barren rock floor of Stakeout Canyon waiting for the storm to arrive with its hundred and twenty mile per hour winds. At her age, and with her family heritage behind her, there were probably a great many better things for Justine Burnelli to be doing. Most of the ones she could think of right now involved beds with silk sheets (preferably shared with a man), or spa baths, or extremely expensive restaurants, or plush nightclubs. But the only luxuries within about a thousand miles were currently racing away from her as fast as the support crews could drive the convoy's mobile homes over this godawful terrain. And it was all thanks to her newest best friend: Estella Fenton.

They'd met in the day lounge of the exclusive Washington rejuvenation clinic she always used, both of them just out of the tank and undergoing physiotherapy, hydrotherapy, massage, and herbal aromatherapy, among other remedies to bring some life back to limbs and muscles which hadn't been used for fourteen months. They moved like old-time geriatrics, an irony made worse by their apparently adolescent bodies.

All anyone did in the lounge was sit in the deep jellcushion chairs and stare out at the wooded parkland beyond the picture windows. A hardy few used handheld arrays to do some work, reading the screens and talking to the programs. None of them had retained the ability to interface directly with the cybersphere. Their bodies had all been purged of most of their inserts, like processors and OCtattoos, during the rejuvenation process, and they hadn't received their new ones yet. Estella had been led into the airy lounge by two nurses, one holding each arm as the gorgeous young redhead wobbled unsteadily between them. She sank into the chair with a graceful sigh.

'We'll be back for your hydro session at three o'clock,' the senior nurse said.

'Thank you so much,' Estella said, with a forced smile. It blanked out as soon as the nurses left the lounge. 'Bloody hell.'

'Just out?' Justine asked.

'Two days.'

'Three, myself.'

'God! Another ten days of this.'

'Worth it, though.' Justine held up the paperscreen she'd been reading; it was still running through the articles and pictures of the fashion magazine she'd accessed. 'I haven't been able to wear anything this good for the last ten years.' Although plenty of her female friends underwent rejuvenation religiously every twenty years (or less), Justine tended to wait until her body-age was around fifty before going through the whole process again. You could carry vanity too far.

'I'm not even at the stage where I'm thinking of clothes yet,' Estella said. She ran a hand through her dishevelled hair, which was an all-over bonnet five centimetres long. 'I need to get styled first. And I hate having hair this short, I normally wear it down to my waist, and that always takes a couple of years to grow,' she grouched.

'That must look lovely.'

'I don't have any trouble catching men.' She glanced round the lounge. 'God, I don't even feel like that right now.' The clinic was strictly single sex, although that didn't always stop clients who were nearing the end of their physical therapy period from indulging in a bit of illicit hanky panky in their rooms. It wasn't just youth's appearance they reclaimed after rejuve, their newly adolescent bodies were flush with hormones and vitality. Sex was at the top of just about everybody's agenda when they left a rejuvenation clinic, and tended to stay there for quite a while.

Justine grinned. 'Won't be long. You'll be heading for the nearest Silent World full speed ahead.'

'Been there, done that, a hundred times over. Not to say that I won't make a stop off on the way, but I've got something more exhilarating planned for this time.'

'Oh? What's that?'

*

That had turned out to be a two-month-long safari across Far Away. Justine had almost outright rejected the notion of joining her. But the more Estella talked about it – and she talked about very little else – the more it began to lodge in her mind.

After all, Far Away was the only true 'wild world' within the Commonwealth, where civilization's grip on the inhabitants was a loose one. It was difficult and expensive to reach, the climate and environment were odd, the enigmatic alien ship *Marie Celeste* was still there puzzling researchers as much as it had on the day of discovery. And then there was the ultimate geological challenge, the Grand Triad, the three largest volcanoes in the known galaxy, arranged in a tight triangle.

Justine's hyperglider had been tethered just inside the wide opening of Stakeout Canyon, so the nose was pointing east, which put Mount Zeus to her left. In the daytime when the ground crew were rigging the hyperglider, all she could see of that colossus was its rocky lower slope, which formed one side of the huge funnel-shaped canyon. The crater peak could never be seen from the base, it was seventeen kilometres high.

To her right was Mount Titan, the only currently active volcano of the three, its crater rim standing outside the atmosphere at twenty-three kilometres high. Sometimes, at night, and if the eruption was particularly violent, the rose-gold corona shimmering above the glowing lava could be seen from the pampas lands away to the south, as if a red dwarf had just set behind the horizon. While directly ahead of her, forming the impossibly blunt and massive end of the canyon, was Mount Herculaneum. Measuring seven hundred and eleven kilometres wide across its base, the volcano was roughly conical, with its twin-caldera summit levelling out at thirty-two kilometres above sea level, putting it a long way above Far Away's troposphere. Thankfully, the geologists had classed it as semi-active; it had never erupted in the hundred and eighty-odd years since human settlement had begun, though it had produced a few spectacular shudders in that time.

That vulcanism could produce such huge features on a small planet like Far Away was a wonderful enigma to her. Of course, she'd studied articles on the science of it all; the fact that only a forty per cent standard gravity allowed something as gigantic as Mount Herculaneum to exist – on a world with normal Earth-like gravity it would collapse under its own weight. And the lack of tectonic plates meant that lava simply continued to pile up in the same spot, aeon after aeon.

But none of that cool reasoning could detract from the actuality of the monstrous landscape she'd come to experience. The power and forces amassing around her were elemental, a planet's strength readily visible as nowhere else. And she was sitting in her pathetic little machine, in a lunatic attempt to tame that power, to make it do her bidding.

Her hands were shaking slightly inside her flight suit as the first hint of dawn emerged, with an outline of slate-grey sky materializing high above the end of the canyon. She cursed Estella bloody Fenton for the sight. It didn't help calm her nerves knowing that Estella was in a similar hyperglider fastened to the rock a couple of kilometres away, staring out at the same inhospitable jags of rock.

'It's starting,' someone said over the radio.

There was no cybersphere on Far Away; in fact, no modern communication at all outside Armstrong City and the larger towns. A hundred years earlier, there had been a few satellites providing some coverage for the countryside and ocean, but the Guardians of Selfhood had shot down the last of them long ago. Now all anybody had out here was simple radio, and Far Away's turbulent ionosphere didn't offer a lot of assistance to that.

'There's some movement out here. Wind's picking up.'

Justine peered through the tough transparent hood of the cockpit. But she couldn't see anything moving on the bare rock below her. There was nothing to move. The storms which swept in from the Hondu Ocean to the west were channelled and squeezed by Zeus and Titan to roar along this one canyon between them. It had been scoured clean of any loose soil or pebbles geological ages ago.

'Derrick?' Justine called. 'Can you hear me?'

Her only answer was a fluctuating buzz of static as the dawn slowly poured a wan light down into the canyon.

'Derrick?'

The caravan of trucks, 4x4s, and mobile homes must be clear now, she acknowledged grimly; over Zeus's foothills and sheltered in some deep gully from the morning storm. All the mad hyperglider pilots were on their own now. No escape.

Somehow this part of it had been missed off the slick advertising and intensive, reassuring briefing sessions. Even the pilot skill training memory implementation hadn't included it. Waiting helplessly as the wind from the ocean built from a gentle breeze to a deranged hurricane. Waiting, unable to do anything. Waiting, watching. Waiting and worrying. Waiting as fright emerged from some primal place deep in the brain, growing and growing.

'How's it going, darling?' Estella asked.

'Fine,' you bitch. 'Actually, I'm getting a bit nervous.'

'Nervous? Lucky cow. I'm scared shitless.'

Justine instructed her e-butler to run through the cockpit procedures again, checking the hyperglider's systems. Even with the limited capacity of the on-board array, the e-butler produced a perfect control interface. Its review was instantaneous; translucent icons blinked up inside her virtual vision, everything was on line and fully functional. 'Remind me again why I want to do this.'

'Because it beats the hell out of breakfast in bed,' Estella told her.

'In a five star hotel.'

'On a Caribbean island, with a veranda overlooking the beach.'

'Where dolphins are playing in the water.'

It was getting a lot lighter outside. Justine could finally see some thin streamers of sand drifting past the hyperglider. They must have blown in from the coast, she thought. She switched the weather radar to the main console screen, studying the blobs of vivid colour as they surged and squabbled against each other. The storm was definitely on its way, scarlet ribbons representing dense high-velocity air were seeping across the screen like some kind of fresh wound, always expanding.

In a way she was glad the storm was heading in from the west, creeping up on her from behind. It meant she couldn't watch the hammerhead clouds as they devoured the sky. She was quite frightened enough as it was. Even now she wasn't sure she was going to make the flight. There was an option to just stay here; the hyperglider was currently configured into a smooth, fat cigar shape, the wing buds confined below the main fuselage; she could simply keep the tethers wound in, and let the winds roar round her until it was all over. Many had, so she'd been told, bottling out at the last moment. Right now, in the middle of the annual storm season, it was an average five-hour wait for the gales to sweep over.

Within twenty minutes, the wind was strong enough to start shaking the hyperglider. If there was sand out there, she couldn't see it any more. Red waves washed continually across the weather radar screen.

'Still there?' Estella asked.

'Still here.'

'Won't be long now.'

'Yeah. Are you getting the same readings from your radar? Some of those airstreams are over a hundred miles an hour already.' The digital figures for wind speed were blurring they were mounting so fast. At this rate the storm's central power-house would be overhead in another forty to fifty minutes, and those were the winds she wanted. If she took off now, the hyperglider would simply be driven into the base of Mount Herculaneum.

The radio band seemed to be full of bad jokes and nervy bravado. Justine didn't join in with any of it, although listening was a strange kind of comfort. It helped keep away the sense of isolation.

Clouds were rampaging across the sky now, gradually becoming lower. They blocked the rising sun, cutting the illumination to a gloomy twilight, although she could still see the swollen tatters of rain charging off into the distance. The rock around the hyperglider began to glisten with a thin sheen of water.

'Wind's reaching a hundred,' Estella called out. There was dread mingling with anticipation in her voice. 'I'm about to release. See you on the other side, darling.'

'I'll be there,' Justine yelled. The fuselage was shaking violently now, producing a steady high-volume thrumming; even the howl of the wind was penetrating the heavily insulated cockpit. The screen displays on the console in front of her were jumbled thanks to the quivering, jittering lines of colour, completely out of focus. She had to rely almost completely on the more basic information inside her virtual vision. Grey mist was a constant blur outside, eliminating any sight of the sky or canyon walls.

Then it was time. The winds along the ground of Stakeout Canyon were over a hundred miles an hour. Her radar showed the storm's leading edge was now boiling up Mount Herculaneum ahead of her, and that was the critical factor. Those winds had to be there to carry her a long, long way. Without them, this was going to be a short trip with one very abrupt ending.

She put her hands down on the console's i-spots, fingers curling round the grip bars; plyplastic flowed round them, securing them for what promised to be a turbulent flight. The OCtattoos on her wrists completed the link between the i-spots and her main nerve cords, interfacing her directly with the on-board array. Virtual hands appeared inside her virtual vision. Her customization had given them long slender fingers with green nails and glowing blue neon rings on every finger. A joystick materialized amid the icons, and she moved her virtual hand to grasp it. Her other hand started tapping icons, initiating one final systems check. With everything coming up green, she ordered the on-board array to deploy the wings.

The plyplastic buds swelled out, elongating to become small thick delta shapes. The thrumming increased dramatically as they caught the wind. Tethers were being strained close to their tolerance limits. Justine prayed the carbon-reinforced titanium anchor struts, driven fifty metres into the naked rock by the support team, would survive the next few minutes.

Some little demon inside said, *Last chance to stay put, and live.*

Justine moved her virtual hand and flipped the forward tether icon. The locks disengaged, and she was immediately shaken violently from side to side as the hyperglider fishtailed.

An instinctive response from the implanted training memory came to her aid. She twisted the joystick, and the wings bent downwards several degrees. A touch on the rear tether icon, and the two strands extended. The hyperglider lifted twenty metres into the air, still shaking frantically, as if it was desperate to be rid of its final restraints. Justine halted the tether extension, and began to test her control surfaces. The rear of the hyperglider was quickly shifted into a vertical stabilizer fin. Wings expanded a little further, angling to produce more lift. Finally, once she cleared the ground, the dreadful thrumming vibration faded away – although never cutting out altogether. Now all she had to contend with was the awesome roar of the wind as it accelerated towards a hundred and twenty miles an hour.

At this point, the hyperglider was nothing more than a giant kite. Very carefully, she began to extend the rear tethers still further. They played out behind her, and the hyperglider rose eagerly away from the ground. After two minutes of careful extension, she was a hundred metres high. The ground wasn't visible, for which she was obscurely thankful. Tatters of mist were scudding past so fast they prevented her from seeing anything beyond twenty or thirty metres. Raindrops which hit the cockpit transparency immediately hurtled off, scoured clean by the tremendous air velocity. Constantly flexing the wings to compensate for turbulence, she began extending the tethers again.

Twenty-five minutes after leaving the ground, she was fourteen hundred metres high. It was a cautious ascent, but the two tether cables were shaking with a harmonic that set her teeth on edge. Justine configured the plyplastic hyperglider for freeflight. The wings flowed outwards, reaching a hundred and ten metres at full span whilst curving round into a crescent shape; from above it made the hyperglider look like a giant scimitar blade, with the cockpit bullet jutting out of the apex. Behind her, the rear fuselage performed a vertical stretch, becoming a deep triangular stabilizer, its tips twitching with near-subliminal motion to keep the craft lined up accurately in the windstream.

She reached fifteen hundred metres in altitude. The wings curled fractionally along their length, presenting the most efficient lift capture profile to the wind. Looking at the figures on the console screen, she couldn't believe the strain on the tether cables, almost all the safety margin was used up.

Justine sucked down a deep breath as the raw elements screamed around her. If she had the courage, this ought to be the ride of a lifetime. If . . . She thought back to all those years she'd lived through, from this strange viewpoint they all seemed so achingly identical, and boring.

A virtual finger reached forward, almost reluctantly touching the disengage icon.

The g-force slammed her back into the seat as the hyperglider cut free, bringing back the weight she hadn't felt since she arrived on Far Away. The craft hurtled towards the blunt end of Stakeout Canyon at a hundred and twenty miles an hour. Immediately, it lurched to starboard and began to descend. She twisted the joystick to compensate – not fast, smooth and positive – shifting the wings to alter the airflow. The response was astonishingly quick, sending her swooping upwards. Then a near-spin started, and she flipped the stabilizer tips to counter it.

Every moment demanded her total concentration merely to hold the hyperglider roughly level. It wasn't just the featureless wrap of cloud which cut her off from the outside world. Her attention was focused solely on the attitude display and the radar. As Stakeout Canyon narrowed, she had to hold her course directly down the centre. All the time the rock walls closed in towards each other, growing steeper in the process, the furious buffeting increased proportionally. Wild turbulence was constantly trying to swirl the craft round into a spin, or pull it down to oblivion.

She wasn't even aware of time passing, only the frantic, exhausting fight to keep the hyperglider on track. If she let it ascend too high, the massive upper windstreams would carry it away over the sides of the canyon as they gushed up and away, expanding in release from the escalating pressure at the base of the walls. She would wind up somewhere on the weather-blasted and boulder-strewn midslopes of Zeus or Titan, hundreds of kilometres from the recovery vehicles of the caravan.

Without any warning, the radar picked up the end of the canyon, twenty-five kilometres away. At this point, where the three volcanoes intersected, Mount Herculaneum was a simple vertical cliff, six kilometres high. Her own altitude was three and a half kilometres. Outside, the wind speed was still increasing within the constriction. The weather radar screen flared lurid scarlet around the edges as it tracked the lethal currents and shockwaves reverberating off the rock. Darkness deepened around her as the shredded clouds were crushed back together.

Justine retracted the wings slightly, sacrificing the propulsive push they generated for a little more manoeuvrability. It had begun to rain steadily outside the cockpit now, thick droplets slashing along beside her. Paradoxically, visibility began to lift. The clouds were recondensing under the pressure. Droplets began to merge together for an instant before the raging winds tore them apart. Then they would reform a second later, larger this time as the pressure continued to build relentlessly. Semi-cohesive horizontal streams of water churned and foamed around the hyperglider fuselage.

The cliff was twelve kilometres away, and she was down to three kilometres from the canyon floor. Water had become so dense, it was as if the hyperglider was surfing along inside the crest of some crazy airborne wave. The sun had risen above the volcano's slopes, shining down into the top of the canyon. Suddenly, it struck the chaotic foam whipping round the hyperglider, and the world flared into a thousand tattered sparkling rainbows, birthing and dying, clashing and colliding. Justine laughed in dazed appreciation at the astounding sight.

Three kilometres ahead of her, the gushing rivulets merged into a single writhing torrent two kilometres above the floor of Stakeout Canyon. That was a couple of kilometres from the cliff. The rocky constriction was at its narrowest, the pressure at its highest. There was only one way the churning river could escape.

Justine slid the hyperglider above the water, staring down on it in utter disbelief. The rainbows fizzled out abruptly. Rock slammed up into her vision to replace them, terrifyingly huge walls of it, stretching up halfway to heaven. Right in front of her, the flying river curved upwards and began the long, impossible powerclimb to freedom as the entire storm went vertical. Blasting out an eternal thunderclap, the wind reached two hundred miles an hour. She knew she was yelling wordlessly, but couldn't hear herself above the cacophony bombarding the cockpit.

The hyperglider was wrenched upwards. G-force slammed Justine down into the seat again. Her knuckles grew white as she clenched the grip bars, fearful she'd lose contact with the i-spots. She wrestled the wing surfaces to obey in a desperate bid to maintain stability within the geysering air. Water rose with her, defying gravity to shoot up parallel to the cliff. Even with the hyperglider demanding her full devotion simply to survive the demented air currents, she spared the time, a couple of precious seconds, to stare at the incredible phenomenon. A waterfall going straight up.

At five kilometres altitude, the foaming sheet of water began to break apart again. The immense upright storm was beginning to spread wide as it reached the top of the canyon. Pressure and wind velocity were weakening. Throughout it all, Justine steered the hyperglider directly up the central track. Water and cloud cascaded away on either side as she burst out above the rock, two immense waves of vapour falling back down in swan-wing curves to crash onto the volcano's lower slopes. Only in the centre of the maelstrom did the wind keep howling, thrusting her forwards and upwards.

Mount Herculaneum's gigantic bulk became visible below her, a desolate ground of shattered stone and saturated gravel extending for tens of kilometres around the top of the canyon. Gradually, the harshness began to give way to the more welcome stains of ochre and avocado-green as the plants reasserted themselves. Tiny grasses rooted hard in crinkled fissures, hardy tropical moss welded to boulders. The storm continued to rage above them, seeking its escape to the quieter skies in the east by sliding round the slopes to the north and the south.

Justine modified the wing camber again, maintaining her speed, but rising ever higher. She was tracking a straight line between the canyon and the summit, never deviating to either side. Grassy meadows with sturdy scrub bushes passed below her now. Temperate lands, the plants lashed and cowed by the unremitting storms, but always flourishing. The twin cataracts of erupting water from the canyon were fifteen kilometres behind her, and the clouds were parting, peeling off right and left to find their own route round the volcano. Justine sought another path through the clear sunny sky ahead and above. Her speed was still colossal, sufficient to carry her well clear of the storm, but not quite enough for her ultimate goal. She began scanning the weather radar.

As if the volcano's western midsection didn't have enough to contend with, twisters were skittering over the rumpled slopes, a legacy of clear air turbulence from the storm. She could see them through the canopy, spindly strands of beige ephemera, whipping violently back and forth across the land. They came in all sizes, from mild spirals of dust to brutal, dense, vortices reaching kilometres in height. The on-board array plotted their courses, eliminating those too weak or too distant for her purpose. Not that any of them were truly predictable. This was where human intuition came in – and luck.

There was one, twenty kilometres ahead, and slightly more southward than she would have preferred. But it stood nearly five kilometres high, siphoning up car-sized boulders as it wove its erratic course. Justine banked round, lining the hyperglider's nose on it. She acquired yet more speed as the craft sank closer to the ground. The wings and vertical stabilizer shrank inwards, thickening as they went. Her eyes were mesmerized by the wild pirouettes of the twister's base, leaving her hungry for a pattern, any sort of clue to which way it would swerve next.

The hyperglider's descent became a fearsome dive. She swayed it in time with the base of the twister – judging, anticipating. Wings and stabilizer were down to nothing more than stubs, giving her minimal control. The ground was barely five hundred metres away. Ahead of her, the twister altered course again. She knew it would hold steady for perhaps a couple of seconds, and pushed the joystick forwards, arrowing the craft straight at it. At the last moment she pulled up, watching the nose trace a sharp curve. The horizon fell away, leaving her with a sky that faded from glaring turquoise to fabulous deep indigo.

Then the hyperglider penetrated the twister. Enraged dust and whirling grit surrounded the fuselage, holding it tight. The wings and rear stabilizers bowed round, forming a stumpy propeller as the nose finished its arc to point straight up along the wavering unstable core of whirling air. Wing blades bit deep, spinning the fuselage and thrusting it up in one potent motion. Particles, from sand up to alarmingly large stones, hammered away on the fuselage. The multiple impacts sounded as if she was being hit by machine-gun fire. Structural stress levels quickly went to their amber alert levels. She flinched almost continually from the stones smacking against the cockpit transparency, not a foot from her face.

Despite that, this was the moment: the reason she was here. Not everybody got to this point. Some were smeared along the floor and walls of Stakeout Canyon. Others who'd actually managed to fly up the waterfall never found a twister, or messed up the entry. But her foreign memories had played true, giving her the skill. All she had to provide was the determination to back it up. That was what she'd come to this place for, finding out if she was still the same impetuous carefree person she remembered from her first life.

Motors whined loudly below her back, providing a counterspin to the forward fuselage. It helped enormously with stability, as well as holding the cockpit steady. That was the theory, anyway. She still felt dizzy and queasy, not that there was any visual reference to check if she was spinning. Virtual vision graphics showed a modest rotation for which the onboard array was trying to compensate. Acceleration was pushing her painfully deep into the seat.

It was only moments later when the hyperglider shot out of the top of the twister like a missile from its launch tube. Even though she'd only been inside for a few moments, her velocity had almost doubled. Fuselage motors strained again, halting the counter-rotation. The hyperglider's wings and rear stabilizer lengthened, this time taking on a more normal planform; straight narrow wings and a cruciform tail. There was very little atmosphere to affect them now, the hyperglider was sliding quickly and smoothly through the stratosphere. However, she did angle them so the trajectory bent slightly. The craft was chasing a simple ballistic curve, the apex of which would be nine kilometres above Mount Herculaneum's summit.

She watched the pressure display digits wind down until it was registering an effective vacuum outside the fuselage. The sky had changed from blue to midnight black. Stars shone strongly all around, while dazzlingly bright sunlight poured into the cockpit.

The contrast was astounding. From the pummelling terror of the storm to utter silent serenity of space in a few seconds. Even though this environment was every bit as lethal to a human as the storm, she felt strangely secure up here. Her yammering heart began to subside. She eased the seat straps away from her shoulders, and craned to get a good look outside.

She was almost level with the summit of Mount Herculaneum, and still rising. The volcano spread out below her, its lower slopes lost below the clouds. Far behind the hyperglider's tail, the storm emerged from Stakeout Canyon to boil away furiously around the immense rock barrier. Twisting her head to starboard she could look down into Mount Titan's crater. Right at the bottom of it was a demonic scarlet glow from the lava lake, partially obscured by webs of thick black smoke. Broad tendrils waved upwards, thinning out as they reached the lip to disperse into a haze that drizzled flaky grey ash across the upper slopes. She was mildly disappointed it wasn't in full eruption; locals working as crew for the caravan had enthused about Mount Doom (as they called it, only half jokingly) in full flow.

Eight and a half kilometres above the summit of Mount Herculaneum, the hyperglider had reached the top of its arc. Its trajectory was flattening out as Far Away's low gravity slowly began to reassert itself. The planet's horizon rose into view beyond the nose. A crisp white curve against the black of space. Directly below her were the twin caldera, two vast indentations in a drab russet plain of solidified lava waves and broken clinker.

Justine's radio picked up a few scattered words, heavy with blasts of static, from the expeditions trekking over the airless surface. Walking to the top of Herculaneum was another of Far Away's principal tourist attractions. It wasn't difficult, the slopes weren't particularly steep, and the low gravity gave offworld visitors an easy time of it. But the last half had to be covered in pressure suits; and the only real view, sensational though it was, came from Aphrodite's Seat, the clifftops just below the caldera plateau. Anyone wanting to walk to the actual highest point, an unimpressive mound on the wall of the northern crater, faced a long dreary slog across a lunar-style landscape to reach it.

With the hyperglider's nose now dipping slightly, Far Away filled most of the universe to the east of the volcano. From her supreme vantage point, Justine could see the Dessault Mountain range stretching away ahead and southward. Small sharp pinnacles stabbing up through the gentle whirl of clouds. They guarded the high desert south of the equator, a cold land almost devoid of cloud. Over to the east she could see a smear of deep greens, where the steppes began their long roll towards the North Sea and Armstrong City.

The horizon's pronounced curve presented the illusion that she was seeing an entire hemisphere of the planet; like some ancient god of myth gazing down on Earth. Although Far Away was actually larger than Mars, the size, whilst limiting her real field of view, certainly didn't detract from the apparent omnipotent perspective. And Far Away lacked the softer textures granted to the old gods of Mount Olympus. The white clouds covered a graded spectrum of miserable browns and greys. Despite close to two centuries of human endeavour, the planet's land surface was nowhere near recovered from the mammoth, and utterly lethal, solar flare that had called people here. Tough, independent-minded settlers had pushed out from Armstrong City, planting their seeds and spraying energetic, wholesome soil bacteria across the empty miles of dusty sand, but the biosphere remained tenuous, its progress towards full planetary enrichment slow. So much was still desert or blasted earth; very, very little of the planet's original flora and fauna had survived the radiation. The greenery she could see was alien to this place, invaders colonizing a near-dead world.

She soared silently and smoothly over the towering cliffs of

Aphrodite's Seat which guarded the eastern approach to Herculaneum's summit. Many kilometres below them was the glacier ring that encircled the entire volcano, extending hundreds of metres across the bare rock. Sunlight glinted from the gritty fractured ice, producing a halo-like aura at the upper limit of the atmosphere. Sheltering beneath the glare were the alpine forests, genemodified Earth-pines which had been introduced here as a beacon of life and colour that could be seen for hundreds of kilometres. She smiled down on them, as she would any old friend, grateful for the comfort of familiarity which they brought.

Ghostly waves of blue and green began to shimmer across the weather radar screen as the hyperglider sank back into the upper atmosphere, showing her the pressure building outside the fuselage. Justine extended the wings again, shaping them into a broad delta. After a while, the cockpit began to tremble as the leading edges bit deeper and deeper into the air. Aerodynamic forces started to take over from the ballistic impetus.

Justine slowly shook off the dreamy lethargy that had captured her during the flight over the volcano. Practical decisions had to be made; from this altitude she could easily coast along for four or five hundred kilometres, putting her well clear of the volcano. But ahead, that would put her into the Dessault Mountains; while north and south would take her back into the divided wings of the storm. There was also distance to consider: the further she flew now, the longer it would take the caravan to recover her. She altered the hyperglider's pitch, putting the nose up so the air would start to brake her speed. Her rate of descent increased, which she balanced against the slope below, maintaining the same height above the ground. Clouds flashed round her, ablaze with bright monochrome light, as she passed through the level of the glacier ring. When the hyperglider fell out of their base she was above the pine forests. She could see grassland stretching out beyond them. Easy enough to land on, but they were still high. It would be cold.

The grasslands grew more lush and verdant as she flew on. Swirls of wind from the lower slopes began to affect the hyperglider, shaking it with growing strength. Bushes and trees speckled the grasses, building swiftly to a dense tropical rainforest which formed an unbroken skirt around the eastern base of the volcano. Looking down, she could see the small black dots of birds flitting amid the treetops. She was already eight hundred kilometres from where she'd started, and that was in a direct line. The caravan would have to go all the way round Mount Zeus before it even reached Herculaneum. Justine sighed, and pushed the hyperglider down towards the rainforest canopy.

This close, it wasn't as dense as she'd thought. There were clear swathes, shallow valleys with fast silver streams that had hardly any trees at all, lines of dangerous crags. Several times she saw animals racing across open spaces. The Commonwealth Council's biosphere revitalization project had certainly been successful here.

The radar switched to ground-mapping mode. Justine was searching for a reasonable patch of ground to land on. Although, in extremis, the hyperglider could come down in a patch barely a hundred metres long, she didn't fancy trying that. Fortunately, the scans revealed a straightish stretch two miles ahead and to the north. She brought the hyperglider's nose round, lining it up. The clear ground was easily visible amid the trees. It looked like there was a clump of rock a third of the way along. Nothing too serious. When she switched the radar to a higher resolution, it showed a narrow, shallow gully running across one end of the clear ground. She started her pre-landing flare, shrinking the wings in again, enhancing the camber. The edge of the long clearing rushed towards her. Three of her console display screens distorted into a hash of random colour.

'Shit!'

Her e-butler was slow to respond, reporting several processors dropping out of the on-board array, even her inserts were degraded.

'What's happening?' she demanded. Her virtual hands flickered and vanished.

A gust of wind slewed the hyperglider to starboard. She groaned in dismay as the cockpit tilted. The console screen displays were making no sense.

'Multiple electronic system failure,' the e-butler said. 'Compensating to restore core function.' Hands wavered back into her virtual vision. 'You have control.'

Justine automatically countered the dangerous roll with a simple wing twist. The little craft responded sluggishly, forcing her to accentuate the manoeuvre. When she glanced up from the console she cursed. She was already over the clear ground, and losing altitude fast. All her display screens had righted themselves. Control surface responses were instantaneous again.

She initiated the landing sequence. The wings rotated through almost ninety degrees, braking the last of the hyperglider's speed. It began to sink as if it were made from lead. Twenty metres from the ground, and with almost no forward motion at all, she altered the wings again. They shot out into huge, thin concave triangles, generating as much lift as possible from her stall speed. The landing strut wheels touched and rebounded. Then she was bouncing over the rough terrain for forty metres before the wheels finally halted. The wings and stabilizer shrank back into their buds.

Justine let out a huge breath of relief. The cockpit canopy hissed as the seal disengaged, and it hinged upwards. Plyplastic flowed away from her hands, and she let go of the grip bars. She released her helmet catches, and took it off. A somewhat nervous laugh escaped her lips as she shook her sweaty hair out. All the hyperglider's electronic systems were back on line.

The craft had come to rest on a slight incline in grass and some purple-leaf plant that were long enough to brush the bottom of the fuselage. A stream burbled away, twenty metres to her left. Hot humid air was already making her perspire. Birds were crying overhead. The surrounding wall of the rainforest was draped in thick ropes of vine that were sprouting a million tiny lavender flowers.

Justine clambered over the side of the cockpit and dropped to the ground in an easy low-gravity curve. Only then did the enormity of what she'd done hit her. Both legs gave way, and she fell to her knees. Tears blinded her eyes, and she was laughing and crying at the same time, while her shoulders shook uncontrollably.

'Oh Jesus Christ, I did it,' she sobbed. 'I did it I did it, I goddamn did it.' The laughter was turning hysterical. She gripped some of the grass strands and made an attempt to calm herself. It had been a long time since she gave in to raw emotion like this, a sure sign of youthfulness.

Her breathing steadied, and she wiped the back of her hand across her eyes, smudging away the tears. She climbed to her feet, careful not to make sudden moves. In this gravity her inertia played havoc with all normal motions. A few birds were flapping about overhead, but that was about the only motion. The sun shone down, making her squint. Its heat made the skin on her face tingle. And the humidity!

She puffed out a breath, and began to struggle her way out of the leathery flightsuit. Her e-butler triggered the hyperglider's locator. A small section of the fuselage behind the open cockpit irised open, and shiny folds of balloon fabric slithered out. It inflated quickly, and rose up into the bright sapphire sky, trailing a thin carbon wire aerial behind it.

Justine checked the transmitter was working as she slathered on suncream. She kept her boots on, but the flightsuit was hurriedly discarded in favour of simple white shorts with matching T-shirt. Everyone on the convoy swore there were no dangerous animals around, certainly not on the Grand Triad. And the Barsoomians, with their weird creatures, were thousands of miles away on the other side of the Oak Sea. So she should be all right dressed like this.

She slipped her multi-function wrist array on, a bronze malmetal bracelet with emeralds set along the rim, a gift from her last husband. He'd laughed about her using its extensive capabilities to survive the department store sales. That deteriorating sense of humour of his had hurried their divorce forward by several years.

The bracelet contracted softly, connecting its i-spot to her OCtattoo. Her e-butler expanded out from her inserts into the larger array, increasing its capacity by an order of magnitude. She ordered it to open the hyperglider's cargo compartment underneath the cockpit, and checked through her equipment and supplies. It would probably take the recovery vehicles three days or so to reach her; she had decent food for a week, and dehydrated rations for another thirty days, though she really hoped she wouldn't have to eat any of it.

Right at the front of the compartment was a box from the tour company, with a chilled bottle of champagne in a thermal jacket, and a box of chocolates. She was tempted, but the first thing she fished out of her personal case were her sunglasses, an expensive steel designer band that fitted snugly round her face, adjusting themselves to her skin. A floppy old bushman hat followed. She'd picked it up in Australia decades ago, the stupid cheap thing had been to more planets than most people, and was now bleached almost white by all those different suns.

'Okay, so what happened to the electronics?' she asked the e-butler as she took the wrapping off the chocolates. They'd started to melt in the heat.

'The cause of the systems failure is unknown. The on-board array lacks the diagnostic facilities to make a detailed analysis.'

'There must be some indication.'

'It would appear to be an external event. The recorded effect was similar to an em pulse.'

Justine glanced round in shock, a chocolate strawberry half-eaten. 'Someone was shooting at me?'

'That is unknown.'

'Could it have been a natural phenomenon?'

'That is unknown.'

'But is it possible?'

'This array does not have any data on possible natural causes.'

'Can you sense any em activity?'

'No.'

Justine gave the trees surrounding the open space a more careful look. She wasn't frightened, more like irritated. She simply wasn't used to not getting a definitive answer from her e-butler. All of human knowledge was available in real-time anywhere within the Commonwealth. But here, cut off from the unisphere, data was a rarer, more precious, commodity. And being shot at was a possibility, albeit remote.

Firstly, there were the Guardians of Selfhood, who roamed the planet at will. As everyone knew, they were well armed and prone to violence. Then there were other people, locals, who could make a great deal of money out of recovering a dead pilot's memorycell insert. Families would pay a big finder's fee to insure their lost loved one's conscious-continuity when growing a re-life clone. Hypergliding was uniquely dangerous, dozens of pilots were killed each year. Most were recovered by the tour operator, and their memorycells returned home. But any whose flight was flung dramatically off course before crashing risked being lost for a very long time. Locals who came across the crash site were in for a bountiful time once they'd finished the gruesome task of cutting the memorycell free of the corpse. So it certainly wasn't beyond possibility that there were groups who facilitated a few crashes.

If the em pulse truly had been an attempt to crash her, they were piss-poor at their job, she thought.

Right at the back of the cargo compartment was a small ion pistol for her 'personal safety' should the landing site prove hostile. Nobody in the caravan had ever really defined hostile for her; the unspoken implication being wild animals. She gave the secure alcove a thoughtful look, then ordered the compartment to close and lock. If it was a criminal gang hunting her, she wouldn't stand a chance, armed or not.

'Time to find out,' Justine told the hyperglider. Her voice sounded very loud in the long, tranquil clearing.

She filled her water bottle from the stream, the semiorganic top sucking up the slightly muddy liquid, immediately filtering and cooling it. Then she set off into the trees, using the wrist array's inertial guidance function.

It took her quite a while to backtrack the thousand or so metres where she'd roughly estimated the interference came from. The undergrowth could be vigorous in places, and where it was low, the vines and creepers filled the gaps between tree trunks. Her whole route seemed to be one giant detour. There was certainly no sign of any track, animal or human. Nor could she hear any voices.

As she approached the general area, she began to feel sheepish. She'd jumped to a lot of conclusions very quickly. Pirates and conspiracies just seemed to fill her adrenaline-pumped mood. Now she was back to mundane reality. Hot, sweaty, having to swat creeper leaves out of her face the whole time, boots sinking in to the damp peaty soil. The one blessing of tramping through this jungle was the lack of insects, at least any of the varieties which feasted on humans; the revitalization team hadn't introduced any. Though there were plenty of tiny multi-legged beetles roving around her feet, a great many of which looked alien to her. A lot of the plant species were certainly non-terrestrial.

After about twenty minutes, Justine simply stopped. She was feeling ridiculous now. There was no sign of any human activity. And if there was a band of hunter pirates creeping down to the landing site through the trees, they were crap at tracking her when she was walking straight at them.

'Can you sense anything?' she asked her e-butler.

'This unit's sensors are registering some weak electromagnetic activity,' it replied. 'It is difficult to locate an origin point. It appears to be operating on a regular cycle.'

'Some kind of radio signal?'

'No. It is a multiband emission, there is no identifiable modulation.'

'A powerburst, then?'

'That is a source which would fit the sensor data.'

'What kind of equipment would generate that?'

'That is unknown.'

'Okay, which direction is it coming from? Give me a graphic.'

The e-butler expanded a simple map into her virtual vision. Justine started walking, pushing the vines apart.

'The emission just repeated,' her e-butler said after she'd gone about fifty yards. 'It was much stronger. The sensors are registering a degree of residual activity. There is no pattern to it.'

'Am I still going in the right direction?'

'Yes.'

'What about the pulse duration? Does that correspond to the one which hit the hyperglider?'

'It is very close.'

The trees seemed to be spaced slightly further apart. Although that could have been her imagination. The undergrowth and vines certainly didn't slacken off. She'd got long scratches on her legs.

The overlaid map faded from her sight. 'What's happening?' There was no reply from her e-butler. She halted and looked at her bracelet. The little power light behind one of the emeralds was winking red.

'Reboot complete,' her e-butler announced abruptly.

'Did the pulse hit you?'

'No data from the event was retained. Another pulse is the most obvious explanation.'

'Can you safeguard against another one?'

Silence answered her.

'Damn it,' she muttered. But she was intrigued now. Something was close by, and it wasn't pirates.

She almost missed it. The vines had completely swamped the low walls, making the small building look like nothing more than another impenetrable cluster of greenery. But the door had sagged inwards, leaving a dark cleft amid the leaves.

Justine pushed up her sunglasses to study the structure for a moment. It certainly wasn't a house, it was too small for that; just a simple square shelter five metres to a side, with a sloping roof no more than three metres high at the apex. When she pulled the thick cords of creeper from the wall around the door, she found the surface beneath was made of some dull grey composite. Simple panels bolted onto a metal frame, put together in a few hours. It could have been made anywhere in the Commonwealth, even Far Away had the resources to produce this. By the look of the material, and the vegetation clinging to it, the shelter had been here for decades.

There was no lock, so she put her shoulder to the warped door and shoved. It flew open after a few pushes. Light streamed in through the opening; there were no windows. The floor was a single sheet of enzyme-bonded concrete, wet and crumbling. In the middle was a black cylinder just over a metre in diameter and eighty centimetres high. When she went over to it she saw it was actually embedded in the concrete, so she had no idea of its true length. It seemed to be made from a dark metal. Two sets of thin red cable emerged from the top, and ran across the floor to disappear into a translucent disk, half a metre wide. Examining that, she found the disk was also set into the concrete. It glowed with a faint vermilion light which originated deep inside, seemingly well below the concrete floor.

Justine narrowed her eyes at the disk as memories began to stir. She wasn't even sure why she'd kept such old times in her head when she rejuvenated. But she'd seen something like this before; a lot of buildings on Earth used them as a power back-up, places like hospitals and police and transport control centres. A solid state heat exchange cable sunk kilometres down into the crust, where the geothermal energy could be tapped. They didn't generate a huge amount of electricity, just enough to keep essential systems functioning in case of emergency.

So what the hell is one doing in the middle of a jungle, halfway up the biggest volcano on Far Away?

She stared at the cables, which were presumably superconductors. The cylinder they were feeding power into must be the source of the em pulses. And the whole arrangement had obviously been here for a long time, at least a couple of decades, and probably a lot longer than that. Certainly nobody had visited for ages, and concrete didn't crumble overnight. *So what could possibly use or absorb that much electricity year after year?*

Her puzzlement was pushed aside by surprise as she realized the only thing the cylinder could be: a niling d-sink. They were the ultimate storage devices, and as such had very few uses within the Commonwealth simply because very few people really needed to store that much power. CST used them as back-up supplies for their wormhole gateways, but she couldn't remember any other organization, commercial or government, having a use for them. They were a quirk of physics, a zero-size sink hole in spacetime which you could keep filling with energy. Theoretically, any power level could be contained providing the confining quantum field was strong enough. And after uninterrupted decades of charging from the heat exchange cable, this one would have an accumulated power level that wasn't so much measured in kilowatt hours, more like kilotonnage.

So, a niling d-sink that pushed out an em pulse ... *Unshielded!*

Justine got out of the shelter quickly. If it truly was unshielded, the electromagnetic emission would be intense enough to harm her nervous system as the quantum field cycled ready to admit its next input charge.

She hurried away, even more confused now she'd found the source. It began to rain before she got a hundred yards. The storm which had split to curve around the volcano had finally caught up with her.

*

Kazimir McFoster watched the girl pull a fist-sized ball of shiny blue plastic out of the compartment which had opened under the hyperglider's cockpit. He was sheltering behind a finicus bush, fifty metres away from where the sleek machine had landed. Rain pattered away on his head and the long dark-crimson leaves alike. He paid it no heed, this was the weather he had grown up with, always at this time of year the storms would come in the morning. In another hour or so the rain clouds would have blown away to the east leaving the rest of the day mercilessly hot and humid.

The girl casually threw the ball over her shoulder, then tugged a big cylindrical bag from the compartment. He was impressed, for the bag was large and obviously heavy. But despite the clumsy way she carried it, she could lift it easily. She was strong. All offworlders were strong, he knew that. What he hadn't expected was her beauty.

He had seen the glider pass overhead an hour earlier, a simple cruciform shape, black against the glaring sapphire sky. The sight had enthralled him, it was so graceful, so elegant. All the stories and learning of the Commonwealth and its ways had never prepared him for this. That a machine could be so poised, not just in shape but in function, was a revelation. Machines as Kazimir knew them were blunt and functional.

From his vantage point atop a lava outcrop he'd watched as it swooped ever lower over the jungle. Only once did it wobble in an ungainly fashion, and that was only for an instant. Then its wings had moved like those of a nimble bird as it alighted in the open space. Kazimir had stood looking at the place where it had sunk from sight behind the trees, a simpleton's smile on his face. It took him a while to realize he was exposed on the rock. Harvey would scold him relentlessly for such a lapse, there would probably be short rations as well to emphasize the point. He was supposed to be well past making such stupid mistakes; that was why he was out here alone in this his final groundwalk, to prove he had mastered the wild. After he returned alive to the clan in another fifteen days, he would be ready to join battle against the alien monster. But not if he stood around like a first year novice, offering himself as an easy target for any enemy who might be passing.

Kazimir dropped down off the rock and back into the undergrowth. He thought for a moment, placing the glider's position in his mind. Then he was ready to pathfind through the trees, alert for enemies, focused on his goal.

By the time he'd stealthily crept up to the fringes of the lengthy clearing where the glider had landed, it was raining heavily. He couldn't see anyone, so he'd found himself a safe place of concealment, and settled down to observe the sleek craft. The girl had appeared a couple of minutes later, her face screwed up against the rain as she hurried out of the trees. She was all in white, a few scraps of cloth clinging to her slender frame. And she was *so* beautiful. *Like an angel*, Kazimir thought. *An angel come down from the sky.*

The blue ball which the girl had discarded on the ground began to swell, with folds of thin plastic bulging out in odd shapes. The whole mass rolled around as if it were a living creature in pain. A minute later it had become a bulbous hemispherical shelter four metres across at the base, with a single opening, like a bloated tent. Kazimir nodded in appreciation. His own night-shelter was a little sac of shapeshift membrane which he could inflate with a small electric current. It kept him warm and dry at night, but it wasn't big enough to move around in. This was a palace in comparison.

The girl hurried inside. Kazimir saw her grimace as she pulled a shabby soaking-wet hat from her head and ran her hands back through equally wet white-blonde hair. She delved into her cylindrical bag and produced a towel, which she rubbed vigorously over herself.

Every movement fascinated Kazimir. She had long limbs, all of them perfectly shaped. The way she held her head; proud but never arrogant. Not her. Not the angel.

She eventually finished with the towel, and went over to the fat tent's opening to peer out. Kazimir held his breath as she looked at the thick bush sheltering him. She smiled coyly, and the universe was a happier place because of it.

For a second.

'It must be uncomfortable crouching behind that bush,' she called. 'Why don't you come out into the open?'

Kazimir's heart thudded loudly. She must be talking to him, she must have known he was there all along. He fumed, angry that his lack of skill had been mocked so. Yet the angel was still looking at him, head cocked to one side, an expectant expression in place. There actually wasn't any mockery, he decided.

He rose to his feet, and looked from side to side, half-expecting the enemy's hunters to be there, waiting and grinning. But there was only the rain. So Kazimir had a simple choice, turn and leave, and never see her beauty again, or walk over and let her see him – which, apparently, she could anyway.

He walked towards the blue hemisphere, still wary. The angel regarded him with a guarded expression as he approached. One of her hands was holding a slim cylinder which he knew had to be some kind of weapon.

'You don't have any friends nearby, do you?' she asked.

'I walk this forest alone. I need no help to survive here.'

She seemed amused by this. 'Of course.' The weapon was pushed discreetly into a pouch on her belt. 'Would you like to come in out of the rain? There's plenty of room in here.'

'You are most kind. I thank you.' When he ducked inside, he was suddenly, unaccountably, overwhelmed by her presence. His eyes sought out the smooth features of the interior, looking everywhere but at her.

'My name's Justine,' she said gently. There was a hesitancy in her voice, as if she was as uncertain as he.

'Kazimir,' he said. 'How did you know I was there?'

A slim arm was raised, a finger tapping just below her right eye. 'My inserts have an infrared capability. You were shining quite brightly.' Her lips twitched. 'You're hot you know.'

'Oh.' But he'd foolishly followed the motion of her hand, and now couldn't look away from her face. Her eyes were light green, he saw, with slim eyebrows. She had long, prominent cheekbones, and a somewhat flattish jaw; a slender button nose poised above wide, moist lips. Every feature was delicate, yet together they awarded her a sophistication he was sure he could never match. And her flawless skin was a shade of pale honey-gold he'd never known before. In surprise, he realized she was very young, close to his own seventeen years. Yet she had flown the glider through the heart of the storm. The courage and talent that must take . . . He looked at his feet again, aware of distance opening between them.

'Here you go,' she said kindly, and handed him the towel she was holding. 'You're actually wetter than I am.'

Kazimir looked at it in confusion for a moment, before slipping his small backpack off. 'Thank you.' He mopped the moisture off his face, then shrugged out of his leather waistcoat. The towel's thin fabric seemed to suck the droplets off his chest and back as he rubbed, leaving his skin perfectly dry.

Justine reached into her bag, and produced another towel for herself. He was aware of her eyes on him, narrowed with amusement, as he dried his shins and calves. So he stopped at his knees, not lifting his kilt to dry his thighs, though they weren't that damp, the kilt was reasonably waterproof.

'What tartan is that?' she asked.

He glanced down at the emerald and copper check, and smiled with pride. 'I am a McFoster.'

Justine produced a sound which sounded suspiciously like a snort. 'I'm sorry,' she said contritely. 'But, with that skin colour, it's a little difficult to picture you as a native clansman.'

Kazimir frowned. His skin was a rich brown, complemented by thick jet hair which he wore long and tied back with a single scarlet band; how could colours prevent him from being a clan member? Between them, the clans had members from most of old Earth's racial groups. His grandmother always told wonderful tales of her grandmother's early life in India. 'I don't understand. My ancestors were one of the first families to be saved by Bradley Johansson.'

'Johansson? We're not talking Scottish clans here, are we?'

'What's a Scottish?'

'Never mind.' She looked out of the entrance at the steady downpour of warm rain. 'It looks like we've got a bit of time to spend together. Tell me about your clan, Kazimir.'

'The rains will only last another hour.'

'How long a story is it?'

He grinned at her, warmed by her answering smile. The

angel was so achingly beautiful, any excuse to remain close to her was welcome. As if knowing this, the wall of the tent beside him changed shape, and expanded out to form a couch. They sat on it together.

'Tell me,' she urged. 'I want to know about your world.'

'Will you tell me of your flight?'

'I will.'

He nodded his head, happy at the promised trade. 'There are seven clans living on Far Away. Together we form the Guardians of Selfhood.'

'I've heard of them,' she murmured.

'We stand between the Starflyer alien and human ruin. Alone of all our race, we see the danger it has brought with its shadows of deceit and its manipulation of vain men and women. Bradley Johansson opened our eyes to the truth long ago. One day, thanks to him, we will help this planet take its revenge.'

'That sounds like something you've been taught, Kazimir.'

'Since the moment I drew my first breath, I have known what I am, and what I must face. Ours is a harsh burden, none of you offworlders believe in our cause, you are blind to the alien's poison. Yet we endure because of our faith and our gratitude. Bradley Johansson is our saviour, and one day, all of humanity will know him as their saviour.'

'How did he save you?'

'As he was saved. By decency and kindness. He came to this world amongst the first people, and began to investigate the alien's ship.'

'I heard that,' Justine said. 'He was the first director of the *Marie Celeste* Research Institute, wasn't he?'

'Yes. People say it is deserted, a wreck, abandoned and empty. It is not; that is what the alien would have humanity believe. It survived the crash.'

'There's a living alien here, from the arkship?'

'It used to be here, it passed into the Commonwealth long ago, where it moves amongst us, hidden and evil.'

'Really? So you've never seen it for yourself, then?'

'I have never left Far Away. But one day the Starflyer will return when its schemes reach fruition. I hope that is within my lifetime. I would like to be a part of its downfall.'

'What does it look like?'

'Nobody knows what it looks like, not even Bradley Johansson is sure. He may have seen it, he can't remember. Many of his old thoughts were lost when he was liberated.'

'Okay, so this Starflyer survived the crash. What happened then?'

'It ignited the flare in Far Away's sun to lure the unsuspecting here. And when Bradley Johansson delved into the secrets of the ship, he awoke the Starflyer and was enslaved by it. For many years he toiled under its control, helping to extend its influence into the Commonwealth, whispering into the hearts of those in power, issuing false promises and shaping the tide of events. But the Starflyer was ignorant of this part of the galaxy, and troubled by the other races who live here, fearful they would thwart its goals. Not all of them are as ignorant and prideful as us. It sent Bradley to Silvergalde so that he could experience the Silfen first hand and report back on what he found. But the Silfen are wiser than humans and the Starflyer; they could see the bonds which it had cast into Bradley's mind, and cut him free.'

'Ah, the liberation.'

'Yes. They cured him. Some men, having been freed, would run away from such a horror so they could remain free. But Bradley knew there was a greater danger in that; he said that for wickedness to succeed all it takes is for decent people to do nothing.'

'Bradley Johansson said that, did he?'

'Yes. He returned to Far Away and liberated others who

had been enslaved by the Starflyer. They were the seven families who grew into the clans.'

'I see.' Her voice was serious.

Kazimir glanced anxiously at her. The expression on her face was terribly sober. It saddened him; that lovely face should only know happiness. Wasn't protecting her and her kind what he had given his life to? 'Don't worry,' he told her. 'We will guard you from the Starflyer. It will not succeed. This planet will be revenged.'

Her head tipped to one side as she gave him a long, thoughtful gaze. 'You really mean that, don't you?'

'Yes.'

For some reason the answer troubled her. 'It's a very noble thing that you do, Kazimir. Nobility exerts a kinship which is hard to break.'

'The Starflyer will never corrupt my loyalty to my clan and our cause.'

Justine laid a hand on his arm. 'I respect that.'

Kazimir tried to smile confidently at her, but she still seemed sad, and her touch, light though it was, distracted him terribly. She was so very close. And neither of them was wearing much clothing. Lustful, yet wondrous, thoughts began to percolate through Kazimir's mind.

Justine gave his arm a quick little squeeze, and suddenly looked round. 'Oh look, it's stopped raining.' She sat up and went over to the entrance. 'The sun's out again.' Her smile was lovely. She was the angel again.

Kazimir got to his feet, and took a moment to put his waistcoat back on. He went outside and stood behind her as she slipped a steel band around her face. It disappointed him that he could no longer see her eyes. The sunlight made her white T-shirt nearly transparent. She was as tall as he.

'Did you really fly over the volcano?' he asked hurriedly.

'Uh huh.'

'That must take so much courage.'

She laughed. 'Just stupidity, I think.'

'No. You are not stupid, Justine. Never that.'

A finger hooked over the top of her sunglasses, and she pulled them down a fraction to stare at him over the rim. 'Thank you, Kazimir. That's very sweet.'

'What was it like?'

'Crazy! Wonderful!' She popped her sunglasses back up, and started telling him about the flight.

Kazimir listened, fascinated by a world and life as alien to his as that of the Starflyer. Justine possessed a perfect existence. It gladdened him to know that such a life was real, that humans could reach such a state. One day, perhaps, when the Starflyer was vanquished, all of them would live as she did.

It must be fate, he decided, that he'd met her. This vision, his own personal angel, come to show him that he was right to try and protect human life. She was his inspiration, his private miracle.

'You must be very rich,' he said when she finished telling him about the landing. 'To afford such a craft that has no purpose other than to bring you enjoyment.'

She shrugged casually. They were both lounging on the bank above the little stream that gurgled its way along the clearing. 'Everybody who visits Far Away is rich, I guess. It's not easy to get here.' She tipped her head back to admire the tufty clouds drifting across the sapphire basin of the sky. 'But definitely worthwhile. You have a strange and lovely world, Kazimir.'

'What do your parents think of you coming here by yourself? And taking such risks? That flight was very dangerous.'

Her head came round quickly, as if she'd been shocked by the question. 'My parents? Ah, well, let's see. My parents always encouraged me to be myself. They wanted me to live my life as best I can. And this, Mount Herculaneum, you, this has to be one of those classic moments that make life worthwhile and give you the confidence to go on and just experience what the universe has to offer.'

'Me? I think not.'

'Yes, you. Here you are on your own adventure, all by yourself facing whatever the volcano and the land throws at you. That makes you a lot braver than me.'

'No.'

'Yes!'

'No!'

They both laughed. Justine took her sunglasses off, and smiled warmly at him. 'I'm starving,' she said. 'Fancy trying some decadent Earth food?'

'Yes please!'

She sprang up, and raced towards the glider. Kazimir hurried after her, awed by how high her perfect, slender body floated above the ground as she ran.

They sat cross-legged on the ground, and she fed him morsels of food, eager for his reactions. Some of it was delicious, most was simply strange, the hot curried meats he screwed his face up as he swallowed. 'Wash it down with this,' she told him. The white wine she gave him was light and sweet. He sipped it appreciatively.

In the afternoon they explored the jungle around the edge of the clearing, trying to guess the names of the plants. He explained the purpose behind his groundwalk, how it prepared him for difficult campaigns against the enemy over all sorts of terrain, how it showed he had learned all his teachers could give him.

'A rite of passage,' she said.

He thought there was admiration in her voice. But then, several times he'd seen her glancing at him when she thought he was unaware. He hadn't dared do the same.

'We must know that we can do what we have to do.'

'Kazimir, please, don't do anything rash. You never have to

prove your worth by risking yourself. Life is too important for that. It's too short, as well, especially here.'

'I will be careful. I will learn not to be impetuous.'

'Thank you. I don't want to spend my life worrying about you.'

'Will you do something for me?'

Her smile was mischievous. 'There's a lot I'll do for you, Kazimir.'

The answer surprised him. He knew he would be blushing as he attached his own interpretation to that; one he was sure she didn't intend, not someone so sweet and good-natured. 'Please don't visit the *Marie Celeste*. I know a lot of tourists do. I would worry for your safety if you did. The Starflyer's influence is strong around its ship.'

Justine made a show of pondering the request. Fortunately, the old arkship wasn't on the itinerary anyway. Strangely enough, because of Kazimir's devout belief that there really was a surviving alien, a little frisson of worry crept into her head and refused to leave. The whole thing was one of those ridiculous legends used by wicked old men like Johansson to keep his followers in line and paying their dues. Yet at the same time, it sounded so plausible . . .

'I won't go,' she promised solemnly. His look of relief made her feel guilty.

They built a fire in the late afternoon. Kazimir had an ageing powerblade in his pack, and seemed intent on showing off his living-off-the-land survival skills to impress her. So she sat back and watched as he built a big pile of wood. He stripped off his little leather waistcoat, and the sweat showed on his skin from the effort of carrying the logs about. It was a sight which raised her own body temperature several degrees. Low gravity certainly hadn't stopped his bod from developing to late-adolescent excellence. Thankfully, he didn't want to do anything macho like shoot birds out of the sky so they could roast them on a stick spit. He was quite content to open up more of her food packets. The bonfire was just for warmth and comfort. She finally popped the cork off the champagne, and they drank it with the leaping gold flames glimmering off its energetic bubbles.

Kazimir didn't want the evening to end, not ever. They sat close on a blanket as the sunlight abandoned the sky. Then there was only a shimmering purple-edged nimbus high above the western horizon as the glacier ring diffracted the last rays through the stratosphere. It shrank away, leaving the crackling bonfire as the only source of illumination. Platinum stars shone above them. For the first time in his life he didn't think of them as a threat.

They talked and they drank and they nibbled on the exotic food. And all the time Kazimir silently worshipped the smiling, gorgeous angel with all his heart. A while after the sun had set, the bonfire's wild flames sank away to leave a mound of lambent coals. It was in that teasing radiance that the angel rose to her feet and stood over him. Her T-shirt and shorts gleamed magenta in the quiescent fire, while her hair had become the gold halo his mind had always perceived. Without a word she walked over to her hemispherical tent, disappearing among the shadows which haunted the interior.

'Kazimir.'

His limbs trembling, he went over to the entrance. Twinkling starlight showed him half of the floor had risen to become a giant mattress. His angel stood before it, a simple silhouette. Her T-shirt lay crumpled on the ground at her feet. As he watched she slid the shorts down her legs.

'Don't be afraid.'

Kazimir walked forward into the darkness. Gentle, sensual, hands pushed the waistcoat from his shoulders. Unseen fingertips stroked his chest as they moved down to his waist, making him whimper helplessly. His belt was undone, and his kilt removed. The naked angel was hot on his skin as she pressed herself up against him.

Kazimir's astonished cries of ecstasy rang out across the clearing, lasting long after the glittering sparks of the fire had finally died away.

*

Not even the cabin's insulation could protect Estella Fenton from the roar of the powerful diesel engine. She held her hiball glass up high as the suspension rocked the four-wheel drive Telmar ranger from side to side, trying not to spill any of the elaborate fruit cocktail. It wasn't working, so she downed the rest of the drink in a couple of quick gulps. There was definitely vodka in it, she could feel the distinctive chill burning along her throat.

The recovery vehicles sent out from the main convoy had picked her up twenty hours ago. Which had come as a profound relief; two and a half days alone in the temperate forest was slightly more wilderness adventure than she'd wanted. Now there was just her friend Justine to find. The convoy had picked up her hyperglider's beacon signal. Its location had caused a flutter of interest among the crews; few people, apparently, managed to fly quite as far as Justine had.

So once they'd loaded up Estella's hyperglider into its container trailer, the five remaining recovery vehicles had set off in search of their last client. For all that Far Away's population had left Mount Herculaneum as a natural wild park, there were plenty of paths through the rainforests of the lower slopes which vehicles like the Telmar used on tourist expeditions. Branching off them were tracks that were less well used. And then there were lines on the map which were marked as 'passable routes'. They'd been on one of those for three hours solid, pushing their way through the vines and undergrowth of the jungle. Then came the really tough work of cutting a new route through the trees.

The trailblazer vehicle was fifty yards ahead of them, its forward harmonic blades sending out dense clouds of fractured woodchips as it chewed its way ever onwards. Watching its progress had sent Estella to the back of the cabin where she started raiding the refrigerated bar.

'Couple more minutes should do it,' the driver, Cam Tong, called out.

Estella put the empty glass down, and peered through the bubble canopy at the broken swathe of vegetation left behind the trailblazer. The thick green walls of trees and vines came to an abrupt end, and they lurched out into a long clearing. Justine's hyperglider was intact, standing in the middle of a carpet of lush grass. Her tent was a few yards away.

'Looks like she's okay,' Cam Tong said happily.

'I never doubted it.'

The recovery vehicles picked up speed, which increased the rocking motion. They all started sounding their horns.

A head poked out of the tent.

'That's not her,' Estella exclaimed.

It was a teenage boy, wearing Justine's tatty old bushranger hat. His mouth gaped wide at the big vehicles rushing towards him, then he yelled something back into the tent. Next second he'd snatched a small backpack off the ground, and was sprinting towards the nearest tree line. Estella stared on in astonishment. He was wearing a long orange and green skirt. No, she corrected herself, a kilt, she could see the pleats. His small pack had a leather garment of some kind tied to it. He kept looking over his shoulder at the vehicles. One hand pressed the hat on his head, black hair streamed out from below the brim.

Cam Tong was laughing as he braked the big Telmar behind the hyperglider. Estella's grin spread right across her mouth as she opened the door to climb down. Just then,

Justine emerged from the tent. All she wore was a very small scarlet thong and a pair of sunglasses.

'Come back,' Justine shouted above the blaring horns and yammering engines. 'Don't be frightened. They're my friends. Oh, fuck it!' She put her hands on her hips, and glared at the recovery vehicles.

Estella dropped lightly to the ground. By now the grin had grown into near-hysterical laughter. Other vehicle doors were opening, the smiling crews clambering out. Horns were still being tooted enthusiastically. The frantic boy had almost reached the jungle. Whoops of encouragement were yelled after him.

'Afternoon, darling,' Estella called brightly.

'You scared him off,' Justine accused, her voice sounding hurt.

Estella raised her hand to her throat in theatrical shock. 'Why thank heavens, we got here just in time by the look of it.' She still couldn't stop laughing. 'We obviously saved you from a fate worse than death.'

'Goddamn it!' Justine gave the fleeing boy a last look as he disappeared into the foliage. She raised her hand limply, hoping he would see her forlorn gesture. The horns fell silent as the engines were turned off, but the hearty laughter of the crews remained loud in the muggy air.

Justine stomped back into the tent, and picked up a light cardigan. Estella trailed after her. The floor mattress was still inflated. Empty food packets littered the ground around it, along with a couple of bottles of wine.

'I don't believe your luck,' Estella chortled. 'I'm going to complain to the tour company. The only thing waiting for me at my landing site was a squirrel, and I'm pretty sure he was gay.'

Justine started buttoning up her cardigan. 'Don't,' she said irritably. 'Kazimir was sweet.'

'Yeah: was.'

'You don't understand.' She pulled up her shorts. 'It wasn't just that. I wanted to teach him a different view of the universe, make him question what he sees.'

'Ah, like: what position is this called? And: I didn't know you could do it that way round.'

Justine growled at her and went back outside. She ordered the tent to contract, forcing Estella to hurry through the entrance. The crew were backing an empty trailer up to the hyperglider. Broad, knowing smiles were flashed in her direction; several of them winked. Justine had to roll her eyes at that, thinking what it must have looked like to them. A small sheepish smile appeared on her own lips as her sense of humour returned.

'What was he doing here?' Estella asked. 'This is nowhere.'

'It's somewhere now,' Justine replied tartly.

'God, your luck. I'm as jealous as hell. He looked divine.'

Justine pushed her lips together modestly. 'He was.'

'Come on, let's go find a bottle, we should celebrate your grand victory: longest flight and greatest landing. I expect you need to sit down, too, must be difficult trying to walk properly after all that education you gave him.' She glanced pointedly at the tent which had finished contracting. All the empty packets and bottles now lay around it, ejected by the shrinking walls. 'Did you even get to see the outside world?'

'There is one?'

Estella giggled wildly, and started to climb up the short ladder to the Telmar's cabin. 'So is it true, does everything really rise higher in low gravity?'

Justine ignored her, scanning the jungle's dense wall one last time. There was no sign of him, not even using infrared. She'd taught him that, if nothing else.

'Goodbye, Kazimir,' she whispered.

He would be out there. Watching. Probably feeling a little foolish now. But this was probably the best way. A swift clean break, and a golden memory for both of them. No regrets.

And maybe, just maybe, I taught him something about real life. Maybe he will start to question his idiotic Guardians' doctrine.

There was a loud *pop* of a champagne cork in the cabin. Justine climbed inside and shut the door, enjoying the chill of the air conditioning as it banished the jungle's raw heat.

5

From their admittedly elitist point of view, the residents of York5 often claimed that theirs was one of the luckier planets in the Commonwealth's phase one space. This particular world never got to experience pollution or human population pressure, and financial irregularities and corrupt politicians passed it by. Throughout its pre-human history, a quirk of evolution had produced a far smaller than average number of plant and animal genera. Such conditions made the establishment of alien species on its surface an undemanding enterprise. For people who wanted to develop land in their own special way, that made it highly desirable real estate.

When CST announced that the planet was open for settlement in 2138, the consortium of families behind the Big15 planet Los Vada put in an offer, effectively buying the entire planet. CST got an immediate payoff on its exploration costs, but York5 was never opened for general immigration. The families in the consortium were too diversified to qualify as an Intersolar Dynasty although, as they all now lived on a single world, the future genealogy dynamics were such that they'd probably wind up as one, defined by the classic model.

York5 had no real capital city; the largest urban area was a small service town that supported the CST gateway and the airport which sprang up beside it. No factories were ever shipped in, denying it any industrial facilities. Everything a person wanted or needed, from cutlery to paving stones, electronics to clothes, had to be imported. There were no roads or railways providing a civil transport infrastructure, only aircraft owned by the resident families. And in all of its two hundred and forty year history, the population never rose above ten million; of which almost three million were staff employed by the families. Instead, it was divided up into vast estates, with each family building their mansions and lodges and beach homes as they wanted, where they wanted, and planting whatever kind of surrounding flora took their fancy. Consequently, the continents became magnificent quilts of designer landscapes; it was terraforming on a scale not even seen on Far Away, and all for aesthetics' sake.

Captain (retired) Wilson Kime had watched his family estate develop over the last two centuries, returning time and again for vacations and long weekends and annual reunions to enjoy the perfect tranquillity it offered. The land he'd chosen was hilly with long sweeping valleys, and situated well inside the southern temperate zone. When he'd arrived, the ground was covered in native tuffgrass, a gaunt reddy brown in colour, and a few manky scrub trees. Slowly, a tide of verdant, and far more pleasing, terrestrial green had rippled out over hill and vale alike, cooler and more soothing. Spinneys had sprung up, bunches of wildly different trees from dozens of worlds, their foliage varying in colour from snow-white to eye-wrenching orange. Valley floors had been forested in oaks and walnuts and willow, while a few special enclaves among the taller hills were now host to giant sequoia.

One day at the height of an exceptional midsummer heat wave, Wilson walked along a long, meandering gravel track on the broad, south-facing slopes a couple of miles from the huge mock chateau that was the family home, inspecting the vines. His only company was two of the senior family's youngest children, who skipped along with him. Emily, a six-year-old with braided fawny hair who was his great-great-great-great-granddaughter; and eight-year-old Victor, a quiet inquisitive lad who was a nephew with a connection that was too complicated to memorize. He'd made both of them wear big white hats to protect their young skin from the blue-tinged sun's powerful UV, even though both of them had received extensive germline modification, which included high resistance to all types of cancer. The way they charged around they'd be exhausted long before lunch, and he didn't want heatstroke added to that.

Every now and then he would stop at the end of another row of the vines, and inspect the clusters of grapes which were just beginning to fill out. It was going to be a high-quality crop this year, possibly good enough to qualify as a classic vintage. Though everybody abused that term dreadfully nowadays. The small light-green spheres were wonderfully translucent, with a tinge of colour creeping in as they soaked up the sunlight. Their rows stretched all the way down the slope to the broad valley floor, two miles away. In total, the vineyards covered nearly forty square miles now, after flourishing for a hundred and twenty years in the slightly chalky soil. Buried irrigation pipes made sure they had enough water in sweltering years like this one, pumped out here from the inland freshwater sea twenty miles away. The Kime estate occupied a quarter of the coastline.

Red-painted viniculturebots, the size of a motorbike, trundled up and down the rows with their electromuscle arms flashing in and out as they carefully thinned out the clusters, and forked over the soil. There couldn't have been more than five human supervisors covering the entire vineyard. Not that any of the wine would ever be sold. This wasn't a commercial venture; it was for the family, with a small number of bottles made available to other Farndale board members.

Wilson stopped and picked a couple more grapes. They were immature and sour; but that taste was right for this moment in their development. He spat them out after he'd chewed them thoroughly.

'Urrgh!' little Emily said, wrinkling her nose up. 'That's gross, Grandpa.'

'No it's not,' he assured her. He tipped his own straw hat back and smiled. 'They decay straight back into the soil as fertilizer. That's good for the plants. Query your e-butler when we get back home if you don't believe me.'

'Wilson's right,' Victor said, using a lofty tone. 'We did environmental cycles in biology.'

'You mean the vines drink your spit?' Emily was even more appalled.

Wilson put his arms round her, and gave a swift hug. 'No, no, it doesn't work like that. It's all to do with organic chemistry. Very complicated when you get down to details. But trust me, the vines don't drink spit, okay?'

'Okay,' she said dubiously.

Victor's look was condescending, so she scowled at him. Then the two of them were suddenly racing off down one of the rows, chasing a Forlien delong, similar to a porcupine but with a silly collar wing that flapped green and yellow when it was excited.

'Don't touch it,' he called after them. 'You're frightening it.'

'All right.' Victor's voice was faint from behind the vines.

Wilson carried on down the gravel. He didn't hurry, he was enjoying the day too much. He'd come out of his latest rejuvenation three years ago, and this was a time-out life, intended as a complete sabbatical from all corporate activity. Everybody needed one now and again, especially at the kind of executive level he lived his normal lives.

After the debacle of the Mars mission, Wilson had returned to an Earth that began to change on an almost daily basis as the implications of wormhole technology were realized. In the second half of the twenty-first century, space exploration, of course, was the biggest boom industry there could possibly be. Except, this was no longer the kind of space exploration he knew anything about. What CST actually conducted was planetary surveys, the province of geologists and xenobiologists; they weren't interested in the void between the stars, there was no striving to bridge the distance. With wormholes, there simply was no distance any more.

A lot of the old NASA teams left to join the burgeoning CST when the agency folded not six months after Kime's ignoble return. But they all had to start from scratch again, retraining, acquiring different skills. It wasn't the same; they weren't special any more, it was just another company job – albeit a spectacular one. The change affected some people more than others. The last Wilson heard of poor old Dylan Lewis, the ex-commander had taken over a bar in Hawaii, and was steadily and relentlessly drinking his way to full liver failure, whilst making an ass of himself with any passing woman who paused to hear his 'old space hero' story.

Wilson escaped the whole scene altogether. He was smart enough to see the kind of requirements which the new planets would make upon the old, the desperate need for infrastructure and development. People weren't going to live in their new promised lands without some basic civil services in place; and as local economies took off, so they'd be wanting upgrades – fast. The manufacturing of both heavy and medium engineering products was the new growth industry. With his superintensive NASA technological training, and his military background, Wilson had no trouble getting himself a divisional manager slot in a company called KAD Components, which produced a range of parts for larger companies. Three years later he was on the board with a decent share option scheme when they were bought out. By 2103, seven mergers and acquisitions later, he was secure as an executive director on the board of Farndale Engineering, one of the new multiplanet colossi which had prospered and expanded in parallel with phase one space. He now had enough new share options to buy a small nation, and Farndale were just moving into the consortium partnership which would ultimately fund Los Vada. After that it was a simple linear progress as the centuries went by, his own fortunes and influence rising with the company until his own extensive family's private wealth moved into the realm enjoyed by Earth's Grand Families.

Twice in the last eighty years he'd been chairman of Farndale. It was a position which took up twenty-five hours in the day, leaving no time for anything other than dealmaking and politicking. His old traits of discipline and ease of command served as excellent foundations for his tenures, enabling him to score several notable victories against rival companies during those heady decades. Shareholders and fellow board members alike were satisfied with his performance; and everyone knew that within a century he'd be rotated into Los Vada's chief executive chair. But board leadership came with a cost, the constant stress acted like an accelerated ageing mechanism. Both times, he had to seek rejuvenation years earlier than he normally would, due to the strain which running the company placed on his body.

That was one of the reasons he'd decided to take a sabbatical this time around. For once he was going to sit back and enjoy the worlds and wealth he'd created. So far it had been a success. He'd even surprised himself with the enthusiasm he'd shown for the vineyards and general estate management. The current batch of children produced by his huge extended family loved having him around. It was details again, he concentrated on details, using his abilities to solve every problem the family threw up; only the scale was different to before. He had plans to extend and refurbish the chateau. There were lots of places he would like to visit just as a tourist, cities with their unique festivals and carnivals to experience, different landscapes, exotic species. He was also open-minded about marrying again, perhaps this time finding a wife in a way that didn't seem too much like negotiating a company deal. All these events were out there waiting for him, a swift taxi ride from any CST station. He'd even started drawing up an itinerary, a grand tour that would take over eight years to complete. Not even Bose's discovery of Dyson Alpha's envelopment event had distracted him; he had faith that Farndale's current board was capable of dealing with any problems and opportunities it created. Although the news that a starship was to be constructed had given him a momentary twinge of nostalgia.

The children emerged from the vine rows to race along the gravel road again. Wilson didn't try to stop them. They were happy. He would have given a lot to have had a childhood like theirs. His main concern was that they grew up with some sense of dignity and responsibility. An environment like the chateau could give any kid a very messed up sense of his or her own importance. Rich kids were notorious brats at the best of time, a situation not helped by York5, where they were all heirs to the throne. At the same time, he didn't want to send them away to school.

Above the western mountains, a lone contrail streaked across the open sky. He stood to watch it go, impressed as ever by the speed and the lack of any sonic boom. Everybody here used hypersonics to reach their estates from the CST gateway. But the velocity which the modern planes could reach in the atmosphere was imposing, even to him. To go any faster you'd have to use a semi-ballistic hop, actually skimming above the upper atmosphere. The designs for such craft had been around for a long time, it was just a question of development funding. After all, the demand was very small. Planes were used on standard Commonwealth worlds, but normal commercial passenger jets flew at around Mach three, which was good enough for airlines. It was only the residents of worlds like York5 who were impatient with that speed.

Wilson heard a low *whoosh* of air behind him as if a phantom had just rushed by. Leaves on the nearest vines fluttered. He frowned, and turned. The sight which greeted him sent a cold shock running down his nerves. A wormhole had opened not twenty feet away, perfectly circular, twelve feet in diameter, its base holding steady a couple of inches above the gravel. A man in an expensive lavender business suit stepped out. He gave Wilson a tenuous, apologetic smile, and then said: 'Yo dude, how's it hanging?'

Wilson took three quick steps, bringing him right up to the interloper, and swung a fist. His knuckles connected with a satisfactory crunch, and a burst of pain.

'Fuck!' Nigel Sheldon tumbled backwards, landing on his ass in the dry grass. Two CST security personnel stepped smartly out of the wormhole, arms pointing at Wilson. Their suit sleeves rippled slightly. An annoyed Nigel Sheldon waved them back. 'It's okay,' he said, then grimaced, and brought a hand up to his jaw. 'Damn, that hurt.'

Wilson glowered down. 'It was supposed to, you little shit.' The children came running up, stopping in confusion at the tableau.

'Wilson!' Victor yelled. 'That's . . .'

'I know who it is,' Wilson said sharply.

'Oh this is great,' Nigel grunted indignantly as he struggled to his feet. 'Three hundred and thirty goddamn years, and you're still pissed at me?'

'Three hundred. Three thousand. Nothing changes what you did.'

Nigel was poking a forefinger into his mouth. 'Ouch. I think you loosened a tooth.'

'You hurt my knuckles.' Wilson shook his hand: the damn thing was, it really did hurt. He hadn't been in a brawl since his air force academy days; the streetwise *how-to* had evaporated over the intervening centuries.

'Are you going to do that again?' Nigel asked.

155

'Are you?'

'Okay, okay, so this entrance isn't supremely tactful of me.' Nigel eyed Wilson's grazed hand wearily. 'But I wanted to make an impression.'

'You did that back at Schiaparelli.'

'This is important, damn it.'

'What is?' Wilson was having to work hard at not being impressed. The fact was, he hadn't heard of a wormhole being used like this before, not to touch base with an individual – unless you counted the rumours about Ozzie. Gateways were hugely expensive links between worlds with a very long pay-back time, not personal transport machines, even if that person was Nigel Sheldon. Wilson supposed he was using the CST exploratory division gateway back on Augusta to open this tunnel across interstellar space. He didn't like to think of the cost. 'I do have an e-butler address code if there's anything urgent, you know. You could use the unisphere like the rest of the human race.'

'We both know I'm not on your e-butler acceptance list, and I needed to talk to you urgently.'

'Why? What the hell is all this about?'

'I need a favour.'

Wilson started laughing.

'Yeah, all right,' Nigel said sourly. 'Very funny. Now try this on for size. We're building a starship to go to Dyson Alpha.'

'I heard. There's been nothing else in the unisphere news for over a month.'

'But you didn't join the dots too good, did you? We can build a ship, but the kind of experienced astronauts we need to crew it, and especially *captain* it, are kind of in short supply in this era.'

Wilson abruptly stopped laughing. 'Son of a bitch.'

'Oh. Do I have your attention now?'

'Why me?' Wilson was surprised by how weak his voice had become.

'There's no one else left, Captain Kime. You're the last space cadet left in the galaxy. We need you.'

'This is bullshit. You've got tens of thousands of people in your exploratory division.'

'We do indeed. Good kids; great, even. Not one of which has ever been out of contact with the unisphere in their first, second, or even sixth life. You, on the other hand, you know what it's like to be shut up in a metal bubble for months on end, you can handle the isolation, the stress; you can keep command of people under those circumstances. It's a lot different to issuing orders down the corporate chain, and having some middle management jerk leap to it. Experience is always valuable, you know that. No false modesty, Wilson, we both know how successful you've been. I mean, look where we're standing right now. There aren't many of us even today who can recreate a five-thousand-square-mile chunk of a France that never really existed outside romantic literature. You've got that, what did you call it, the right stuff?'

'Old phrase,' Wilson muttered as the really ancient memories began their inevitable replay. He always swore he'd dump them into deep secure storage at every rejuvenation, clear them out of his brain along with all the other irrelevant clutter so there would be space for the new life. Each time, he never did. A weakness for nostalgia. He'd so nearly been a contender for true greatness rather than the corporate chieftain he'd actually become. Even today a lot of people knew who Neil Armstrong was. But Dylan Lewis? Not a chance.

'Well dust off your copy, man, because it's about to become fashionable again.'

Wilson stared at the edge of the open wormhole, the dark shimmer of nothingness which very few people actually got to see first hand. 'Is this a serious offer?' he asked quietly.

'Absolutely. It's your gig if you want it. I hope you do. I mean that sincerely. The more I think about Dyson Alpha, how strange it is, the more I want someone I can really trust in charge out there.'

'Grandpa?' Emily gazed up in newfound awe at her ancestor. 'Are you going to fly the starship, Grandpa? Really?'

'Looks like it, poppet.' Wilson patted the girl's head. He hadn't even needed to think about it, the response had been automatic. 'Give me a few days,' he told Nigel. 'I've got to sort things out here.'

'Sure thing, man.' Nigel smiled broadly, and stuck his hand out. 'Welcome aboard.'

Wilson considered it, but not shaking would just be churlish. 'Just so we're completely clear on this, you're not thinking of joining the crew yourself, are you?'

'No. We're clear on that.'

*

Anshun was on the very edge of phase two space, two hundred and seventeen light-years from Earth, and almost directly between the old world and the Dyson Pair. That location had been quite a factor in CST siting its new phase three exploration division there. Boongate, sixty light-years away, already had a second gateway leading to Far Away, and its government had been hopeful that CST would follow that up with the exploration station. It was not to be. Far Away was a dead end. Anshun would help extend the human frontier towards the Dyson Pair.

Not that much expansion had been notable in the eight years since the division had been established at the CST planetary station; a mere two planets had been opened up. But Anshun now possessed a quiet confidence about the years to come. It was going to be the junction for this entire new sector of space. Over the next century its economy and population would rise until it matched any of the successful phase one worlds. Its future was secure.

Wilson Kime grinned privately at the peculiar sensation of *déjà vu* as the passenger express from Los Vada slipped smoothly into the CST planetary station in Treloar, Anshun's capital. The outside air here was hot and muggy from the nearby coast, just like Houston used to be. He could remember arriving at the NASA Space Centre for his first day of training, the sun prickling his exposed skin with its heat. The uniform government-issue buildings of that campus had looked surprisingly shabby in the bright light, especially given what happened inside them. Somehow he'd expected the structures to be a little less industrial, a little more grandiose.

That, too, was the same here on Anshun. Two members of CST's exploration division were waiting for him on the platform. They showed him to a small station car, which drove through the vast empty area contained inside the perimeter fence which was destined to become the junction yard, where dozens of gateways and hundreds of busy tracks would route transport out to the new stars at some unspecified date. Right now, the landscape around him was almost ironically post-industrial. Long strips of enzyme-bonded concrete were laid out on the ground, slowly-buckling roads for a mini city that never existed. The soil between them supported dispirited clumps of local grass and spindly weeds, cut up with curving tyre ruts of baked clay that would form puddles after every downpour. Abandoned heavy-duty vehicles were scattered about, metal sections moulting flakes of rust, composite bodywork bleached to a bland off-white, window glass smashed in, car-sized tyres flat and calcified. Big fornrush birds glided above the area in wide spirals as their black wings captured the thermals. They were sleek scavengers, hunting down smaller rodents; though their catch was poor out here.

It made the brand-new dual carriageway which he was

driving along seem strangely out of place, ahead of its time. A twin rail track ran parallel with it, also newly laid, linking the station's marshalling yard with the starship project complex ahead. He saw a single DFL25 shunting engine rolling slowly in the opposite direction to him, pushing eight empty flatbed carriages ahead of it, the only sign of movement within five miles.

It took ten minutes driving across the unused wilderness to reach the starship project. A long row of windowless pearl-white buildings materialized out of the powerful heat shimmer, protected by a six-metre-high fence. Guardbots trundled along the foot of it on an eternal patrol, smooth conical bodies concealing the weapons and sensors they were equipped with. There were three human guards on the gates. Wilson was scanned twice before they let him through, saluting smartly as he passed.

This whole complex reeked of money. He was familiar enough with fast-track projects to see an extraordinary amount of cash had been spent in a short period of time. Inside the fence, long strips of newly laid turf of local whitegrass was neat and trimmed. Car parking spaces had names on the asphalt in fresh paint. The buildings were made from the new low-friction surface panelling which the construction industry was currently obsessed with, giving them a perpetually clean appearance. There were high doors set into most walls, all of them closed, with silvery rail lines running underneath the bottom edge. A row of pylons was visible at the back of the complex, stretching off towards the city's largest industrial precinct, supporting slim red superconductor cables. The project was using up a lot of power.

Three stumpy, circular glass towers made up the heart of the complex, joined together at the base by soaring sheets of glass that looked like a solidified pavilion roof. The entrance lobby they formed was a huge atrium, with crystal pillars containing exotic big-leafed plants. A lot of people were hurrying across the stone floor, all of them with intent expressions. Work here was a serious thing.

Daniel Alster stood beside the long reception counter. He greeted Wilson warmly, introducing himself. 'Mr Sheldon apologizes for not being here to welcome you personally, he's in a meeting which is overrunning quite badly.'

Wilson gave the lobby a thoughtful look, cementing his impression of unlimited budgets. Farndale had mounted big projects often enough, but that was different; their offices were built in cities, factories in industrial estates. They belonged. It must be the complex's relative isolation which gave it such a sense of importance and urgency. 'You mean Sheldon is managing the starship project himself?' he asked.

'Not the day-to-day details, no. But it is certainly high up on his schedule. He was quite relieved when you agreed to accept the captaincy.'

'Really?'

'Yes. I understand you'll be taking over a number of administration procedures.'

'That's right.' The quantity of data which the project had sent him over the four days since he agreed to captain the ship was phenomenal. Most of the information files were accompanied by requests from the department heads concerned. 'But I need a while to settle in before I start slinging my weight around.' He'd actually felt a little overwhelmed walking into the lobby, facing up to the project all alone. Normally when he was involved in anything on such a scale he'd be accompanied by several of his own aides, and there would have been time for a thorough briefing beforehand. It was only last night he'd finally received a report on the Commonwealth Exo-Protectorate Council meeting, which didn't give him much time to mull over the political implications of the flight. The Farndale board had given his appointment their full approval, though, eager to climb on board the project.

'Of course,' Daniel Alster said. 'Your office is ready for you now. But Mr Sheldon suggested I should give you a quick tour of the facilities first.'

'Lead on.'

The complex layout was simple enough, with the three towers already housing the design and management personnel. A quarter of the office space was unused. 'Crew training facilities,' Daniel Alster explained as they passed line after line of darkened glass cubicles.

'Has anybody been selected yet?'

'So far, only you. Just about everyone in our exploration division has volunteered – that's technical personnel as well as the survey teams. Then there's a couple of million hopefuls on every planet in the Commonwealth who are insisting they're perfect for the job. This section of the Anshun cybersphere is having to be upgraded we've had so much datatraffic. We're waiting for you to draw up the requirement criteria before we start active recruitment.'

Wilson gave a resigned shrug. 'Okay.'

The big hangar-like buildings outside the towers were where all the starship's components were delivered then rigorously tested before being taken through to the assembly platform. There was no manufacturing on-site, everything was shipped in through the planetary station's gateway. Sixty-three per cent of the components were fabricated on Augusta, including the wormhole generator mechanism which would act as the hyperdrive. The rest of the sections were coming in from all over the Commonwealth, contracts placed according to financial involvement and political clout. Wilson was pleased to see Los Vada had snatched over three per cent.

As soon as the wagons delivered the containers they were unloaded and moved into clean rooms for testing. The assessment facilities which CST had built in such a short space of time were impressive. Sealed environment chambers could produce a huge combination of radiation, extreme thermal loads, vibration stress, electromagnetic irradiation, and hyper-velocity particle impacts, all inside a good old-fashioned vacuum. There were also test labs where electronic components were subjected to all manner of improbable failure scenarios. Once they were certified, the components were moved out to the platform for assembly.

Nigel Sheldon was waiting at the gateway, which was at the end of the largest assessment building. He was wearing the same kind of white overall that Wilson had changed into. They both shook hands; still slightly wary of each other, like old friends who were patching up an argument.

'Ready for zero gee again?' Nigel asked. He put on a protective helmet, which moulded itself to his skull.

'I guess so,' Wilson said. It had been a *very* long time and, as Daniel had been telling him during the tour, a lot of their assembly technicians had experienced mild to debilitating nausea when they were working on the ship. Not even continual exposure seemed to weaken the effect. The astronautics companies based at the High Angel had little practical help to offer. They either used robotic systems or personnel who'd been screened to find a degree of immunity. In desperation, CST had been deep-mining some very old medical papers on human zero-gee adaptation, some of which dated back to the Russian MIR station, to see what kind of drugs or DNA resequencing they should be considering.

Wilson allowed Nigel to go first, following cautiously behind him. They were using the exploration division's gateway, which had been taken off interstellar survey duties to provide a simple link between the complex and space above Anshun, where the assembly platform was orbiting a thousand kilometres out from the planet. A circular titanium tunnel had been built through the gateway, lined with bands of electromuscle that were capable of handling components up to eight metres wide, and weighing a couple of hundred tons. The motion was like a throat swallowing, with the sealed containers riding forward on synchronized waves that rippled along the bands.

As Wilson walked forwards, it looked as if they were going from the assessment building through a simple circular opening into a giant spherical chamber beyond. The assembly platform was a globe of malmetal that had been expanded out to six hundred metres in diameter. Its internal stress structure resembled hexagonal ribs, with gantry towers extending towards the centre from the junctions. They supported a broad gridwork cylinder directly in front of the gateway. It was in there that the starship was taking shape. Right now, it looked like nothing more than an even denser lattice of girders. Hundreds of men and women in simple overalls were scampering along the framework, or anchoring themselves in place beside mobile constructionbots. White composite containers were sliding along the gantries, like pearls of condensation slithering down glass.

Even though Wilson was expecting it, the end of the planetary gravity field came as a shock. One foot was pressed firmly on the ground, while the one in front seemed to waver in mid-air. Wilson concentrated on pulling himself forward, using the handholds between the electromuscle bands. Every sense immediately told him he was falling. His hands automatically tightened their grip. In front of him, Nigel's body had already swung around parallel to the gateway, and he started to pull himself along the support gantry handholds, heading in towards the ship. Wilson copied him, using the handholds like a ladder for the first few metres, then his body simply glided along twenty centimetres or so above the gantry. He remembered to grip a handhold every few metres, just to correct his direction and prevent any spin from building up. His stomach was quivering at the falling sensation, but apart from a wet belch, he didn't feel any dramatic onset of sickness. The air around him carried a distinct tang of welded metal and warm oil, though the smell slowly weakened as fluids began to pool in his head.

'Tell you something,' Nigel called back over his shoulder. 'I get one hell of a buzz out of seeing this baby. Big projects always do that to me. But, man, I ain't been this excited about a chunk of engineering since Ozzie and I put the original wormhole gateway together.'

'I remember the day,' Wilson said dryly. He couldn't escape from his memories of the *Ulysses* that day either, the last time he'd ever seen the proud interplanetary ship, a big mass of struts with hardware attached at all points. None too dissimilar to this craft.

Nigel chuckled. 'We're coming up on the reaction drive section.'

The maze of girders wasn't getting any clearer as they approached. Wilson asked his e-butler to access the assembly platform array. It overlaid a blueprint of what he was seeing on his virtual vision. The starship's design was quite simple. The life-support section housing the crew was a thick ring three hundred metres in diameter, which would rotate to provide a twenty per cent gravity field along its rim. A basic von Braun wheel, Wilson thought, though no one would ever call it that nowadays. In the middle of that was a cylinder four hundred metres long and a hundred and fifty in diameter, containing both the ftl drive and the plasma rockets. The surface had a multitude of bulges and prominences, as if it was growing metallic tumours.

The three of them floated around a fat nozzle with a perfect mirror-surface interior. It was the first, and so far only, one of the five plasma rockets to be installed, leaving rosettes of struts where the other four would be fitted. Wilson studied the thick reaction mass fuel pipes and superconductor cabling which would be connected into the other units when they arrived. A hand crept out of its own accord to touch the casing of the installed nozzle.

Plasma rockets. Just like the old Ulysses *had. It's like a bicycle, some things you can't improve.*

'What kind of power source are we using?' he asked.

'Niling d-sinks,' Nigel told him. 'Fifteen of the goddamn biggest we make. There are back-ups, as well, of course; we're providing microfission piles and two fusion generators. But the niling d-sinks are your primary supply. They'll give you enough power to fly seven thousand light-years.'

'That far?' somehow Wilson had been expecting the ship to be capable of reaching Dyson Alpha and returning, nothing more.

'Yeah, but that doesn't mean you've got a licence to fly off and explore the rest of the galaxy, Captain, okay?'

Wilson smiled with a faint degree of guilt. He'd been thinking just that. 'You know what you're doing, don't you? What this ship is?'

'What?'

'You're dropping a pebble off the top of a mountain. When it gets to the bottom it'll be an avalanche. People are going to be interested in exploring the unknown again. They'll want more ships like this, they'll want to know what else is out there. The next ship will be big enough to fly around the galactic core.'

'Wrong, Captain. Only people like you want to do that, born romantics. And there aren't as many of you as you'd like to think. This Commonwealth we've built for ourselves is a mature, conservative society. We've grown up a lot in the last couple of centuries. Only people with one short life want to go tearing out into the great unknown with nothing more than a flashlight and a stick to poke the rattlers with. The rest of us will take our time and expand slowly; that way there are no mistakes made. Tortoise and the hare, Captain, tortoise and the hare.'

'Maybe,' Wilson said. 'But I don't believe we're as civilized as you like to think, not all of us.' They'd gone past the reaction drive sector of the ship, and were in the midsection, where two stumpy arms linked the habitation ring to the central engineering section superstructure. Again there wasn't much to see, just the raw skeleton devoid of any hull plating, even the internal decking was missing inside the stress structure. Although a lot of auxiliary machinery had already been installed. 'How's the hyperdrive coming along?'

The lines around Sheldon's mouth tightened slightly. 'The flow wormhole generator is undergoing stage three component testing. They should begin primary installation in three to four months.'

'So how does that leave our overall timescale?' Wilson asked.

'Our initial projection has completion in another seven months,' Daniel Alster said. 'However, there were several problems associated with zero-gee construction which we hadn't factored in.'

'Be more like nine now,' Nigel grunted.

'Everything costs more,' Wilson pronounced happily.

'And takes longer,' Nigel completed. 'Tell me about it.'

'How come you didn't build this at the High Angel?' Wilson asked. 'I know it would add another two hundred and thirty light-years to the trip, but that's not much to this ship if I read the specs right. And they have all the astroengineering expertise there.'

'Political control,' Nigel said simply. 'Specifically: mine. This way, CST remains the primary operator for the whole mission.'

'Fair enough,' Wilson said. It was a reasonable compliment that Nigel didn't feel the need to guard what he said.

Near the front of the superstructure a great nest of power cables waited for whatever unit was to be installed there. Intrigued by the power levels involved, Wilson checked the section against his virtual vision blueprint to find it was a force field generator; one of seven. 'It's well defended.'

'I want you back in one piece,' Nigel said. 'And I still worry about the envelopment being a defensive action. To me it's the most likely scenario.'

'If we're up against weapons that you need to protect a star against, I don't think a couple of our force fields will be much use.'

The three of them stopped drifting, and clustered together around a force field generator emplacement. 'Look,' Nigel said. 'One of the reasons I wanted you to see this today was so you could get a decent overview. At this stage the design is still reasonably flexible. Hell, we can put the launch schedule back by a year if we need to. I want your input on this.'

'Fine. My initial response is that we should be a lot more cautious than the flight profiles you've shown me so far. The last thing we want is a mission where we come out of hyperspace right next to the envelopment barrier and start yelling: anyone here? We need to be taking our first look from at least ten light-years out, which means the very best sensor systems the Commonwealth can build. If we can't detect any signs of conflict from there, then we move in by stages. That will probably mean adding several months to the mission.'

'I can live with that,' Nigel said.

'Good, because I will only take this ship out if we're running with a safety-is-paramount philosophy. Not just for the crew, but for humans everywhere. If there is something hostile out there, I don't want to draw its attention to us. I hope you appreciate just how much responsibility is accruing round this project.'

'I know that, man, believe me, I know. This is what CST faces every time we open a wormhole to anywhere new. People don't pay us any attention these days because they think that, after three centuries, encounter scenarios are routine, and maybe even boring. Me, I don't sleep much, I know that one day we'll come across some virus or bug that gets right past our biomedical screening, or an alien race that is the opposite of the Silfen. Every year we go further out, I add another safety procedure and ignore my staff screaming about what a monster bureaucrat I've become. All I do is pray that new procedure is going to be good enough for the one seriously badass encounter that nobody's thought of before. Take a look at our exploration division's operational guidelines some time, they should reassure you.'

'Okay, we understand each other then.'

'I hope so, Wilson, because this could well be that one encounter I've been dreading all these centuries.'

'So why are you pushing so hard for this mission?'

'We can't hide in the dark just because of something we don't understand. As a species, we've evolved a hell of a lot these last centuries, we are *Homo galactic* now. It might be arrogance on my part, but I believe we're now capable of facing something this big. And don't try to kid yourself: this is *big*, even if all you find is a deserted barrier generator. We have to come to terms with truly alien aliens, and the Silfen have never been that.'

'I thought you said us true romantics were few and far between?'

'We are. But look who we are.'

Wilson finally laughed. He tilted his head to take in the massive bulk of the ship. 'So how come you haven't named it yet?'

'You're the captain, that's your prerogative.'

'Are you bullshitting me?'

'No, man, I figure I owe you that much. Any ideas?'

'Sure. She's called *Second Chance*.' It wasn't something he had to think about.

Nigel grinned. 'Not bad. I guess we'll have a proper ceremony some time. But first you've got to start putting your crew together. I can keep the politicians off your back for a while, but the quicker you make the selection the better. Man, I thought I was used to political horse trading, but this has got them all riled up. Every president, king, queen, first minister, prime minister, chairman, chief secretary, and grand emperor wants their world represented.'

'You've left room for a big science complement, that's good. I would have insisted on that anyway. The actual crew, the engineers who'll keep the ship running, I want to keep to a minimum. This is a science mission, after all. So I expect they'll be drawn from the teams working here.'

'Okay, I have no problem passing the buck to you on this one. But be warned, there's going to be pressure.'

'I'll handle it. I don't suppose you tracked down any more of my old crew did you? I know Commander Lewis never made it to a rejuvenation. The rest of us drifted apart.'

'I'll get onto it,' Daniel said.

*

Paula Myo could actually see the Eiffel Tower from her office window. A century ago the Senior Investigator Office of the Intersolar Serious Crimes Directorate had taken over a lovely old five-storey building just three streets away from the Seine, refurbishing the interior whilst leaving the Napoleonic facade intact. If she pushed her chair back from the desk, and craned her neck, the ancient iron tower was visible over the rooftops. In the ninety-two years since she made Chief Investigator she probably hadn't looked at it more than a dozen times. Today was one of those rare days when she succumbed, and gazed out at the panorama. The ant-size tourists were just visible on the top, while the lifts ran smoothly up and down the centre of the ancient iron pinnacle. A timeless sight, which if anything had actually improved over the last two centuries as Parisians had gradually pushed the skyscrapers and modern apartment blocks further and further away from the ancient heart of their city.

While she watched, the office array was running cargo and transport files through specialist analysis programs, searching for the patterns which always seemed to elude her. It was the reason for her mood. Those patterns had escaped her for a couple of months now, and there were only so many ways you could search the data, even with modern smartware.

She knew Elvin had begun shipping the arms to Far Away. He would do that the only way possible, break them down into innocuous components, and incorporate them in other cargos. Every time he bought an arms shipment this was the endgame which resulted. She would have cargoes pulled at random by CST security staff at Boongate's gateway, they would be broken apart and evaluated for any discrepancy. Only three times in the last twenty years had they found components which the manufacturer couldn't explain. She was sure that if every cargo was taken apart in the same way the results would be a lot better. But CST security had made it quite clear they didn't have the resources to handle that kind of operation. Besides, she would inconvenience everybody on Far Away who was legitimately importing machinery, and without much just cause other than her own determination. Like all of his predecessors, Mel Rees, her immediate boss, had made it quite clear that the Intersolar Serious Crimes Director-ate wasn't going to support or fund that kind of interception procedure. It was an infuriating policy which she had argued against for decades, to no avail. So while she kept on filing official requests and applying what pressure she could through political contacts, she had to make do with the occasional, random raid on likely cargo cases of equipment.

In an attempt to swing the odds in her favour, she'd initiated the data analysis. Every piece of cargo arriving at the Boongate CST station came with a full complement of files on shipping details, purchase invoices, payment confirmation, packaging companies, handling agents. Adam Elvin would send the arms via a multitude of different routes over a period of time which probably stretched into years. It was a physical encryption. You just had to have the key, the knowledge of which cargo hid which components, and when it would be arriving. If you had that you could slot the whole lot together. So her programs searched routes for crates that had shared a warehouse six months ago on a planet a hundred light-years away, for payments which came from the same bank, for a freighting company which was used by different agents, for bills paid from an account which was only used once. Every time, she drew a blank. It didn't help that eighty per cent of cargo destined for Far Away belonged to individuals or families who were emigrating there, and took all their personal belongings with them, along with an amazing list of items they considered necessary for their survival and well being.

'Now that's something I don't see every day,' Mel Rees said. 'You loafing on the job.'

Paula gave him a silent, contemptuous glance and turned back to the Eiffel Tower. Mel Rees had only been with the Directorate for forty years, reaching his current position as one of its numerous deputy directors because of his family. But then that was always the way with Earth-based Commonwealth institutions, if senior appointees didn't come from a Grand Family, they were inevitably part of an Intersolar Dynasty. Of course, had she gone gunning for a directorship she would probably have got it; but again, ironically, that would have been because of who she was, not to mention the amount of seniority gathered from a hundred and forty-seven straight years of employment in the Directorate. But then, because of who she was, she didn't want a post which would take her away from actual investigative work.

Mel Rees studied the data running through the desk portals. 'No luck, huh?'

'Not with the budget you give me.'

'I've got something else for you.' Mel Rees never quite had the courage to summon Paula to his office if he wanted to discuss anything, he always visited her in person.

'What?'

'An ice case on Oaktier. Possible deliberate body kill and associated memory loss.'

Paula couldn't help her interest. Ice cases, which the Commonwealth classified as crimes over thirty years old, weren't that common. 'How long ago?'

'Uncertain, but it could be forty years.'

'Hum.' Paula crinkled her nose. It wasn't *that* long ago. 'Can't the local police deal with it?'

'They tried. The results were inconclusive. That's why we got the request for assistance. One of the possible victims, a Tara Jennifer Shaheef, has an important family on Oaktier, who have connections. You know how it works. Her family want positive results, one way or the other; so naturally I want you to have it.'

'You said *one* of the victims?'

'Yes. If it happened, there were two of them – that the police know of so far.'

'Okay, now I'm interested.'

'Thank you.' Glancing round the spartan office, he saw the small bag which was kept permanently packed ready for any off-Earth assignment. It was one of three personal items she permitted herself in the plain room. On the windowsill was a rabbakas plant, a black corm sprouting a single marbled pink flower with petals that looked like feathers, which she'd been given by a Silfen on Silvergalde. On the desk was a quartz cube containing a hologram of the couple who'd brought her up on Marindra, some summer day picnic scene with Paula and her step-sister, both girls aged about five. Mel Rees always tried to avoid looking at the hologram; every time it gave him an uncomfortably powerful reminder of just how strange the Chief Investigator was. 'Do you want to shift any of your casework while you're away? Renne and Tarlo haven't got much on right now.'

She looked at him as if he had spoken some incomprehensible language. 'I can keep up to date on everything from Oaktier, thank you. It is part of the unisphere.'

'Sure. Right.' He started to back out of the office. 'Anything you need, just let me know.'

Paula waited until he had gone, then permitted herself a small smile. Actually, Rees wasn't a bad deputy director, he kept his teams happy and made sure the department received a healthy budget; but she always made sure he knew his place. After a while she pulled her chair back to the desk, and asked her e-butler to retrieve the Tara Jennifer Shaheef case files.

*

The Clayden Clinic was set amid twenty acres of its own grounds in one of the eastern suburbs of Darklake City. As rejuvenation facilities went, it was amongst the best on the planet. Paula had read through the Directorate's green-code background file on the company, a typical medium-sized corporate operation, with clinics on five worlds in this sector of space.

What she could see as the police car pulled in through the gates seemed to reflect what she'd read. A long, three-storey pearl and bamboo building standing on a slope above a small lake. One wing ended in a lattice of scaffolding, with constructionbots riding along the rails as they locked new prefab sections together.

Her office suit gave no protection from the humid early afternoon air as she hurried from the car to the reception. Detective Hoshe Finn was a couple of paces behind her the whole way, puffing with discontent at the heat. He was from the local ice crime division, and had been assigned to assist her for the duration of the case. A duty he accepted cheerily, which was something she found refreshing. For once, someone was enjoying working with her and was actively helpful right from the start. She was sure he was mostly interested in seeing if her reputation matched up to the actual person, but she didn't mind that. Whatever got results. Part of his acceptance no doubt came from the fact he was eighteen years on from his second rejuvenation. Older people tended to have a more phlegmatic approach.

Hoshe Finn's last rejuvenation had given him a thin face. He wore his black hair drawn up into a neat single curl at the back, held in place with an elaborate silver ring clip. Just about the first thing he said to her was an admission he was overweight, though his shiny green silk suit was cut to de-emphasize his waist and stomach.

'This way,' Hoshe Finn said once they were indoors. He led off down one of the long corridors leading away from reception. They passed several recent rejuvees being helped along by staff.

'Have you handled many ice cases?' Paula asked.

'Three,' he shrugged. 'Including this one. My success rate is not high. Most of the time I work for the main criminal investigation department. It's only when we get a crime that's over thirty years old that we actually bother to activate the ice division. This kind of allegation doesn't occur very often.'

'Don't worry, there aren't many ice crimes which get solved.'

'Yeah. Even with our data storage capacity, digging up the past is difficult.'

'It's not that, exactly.' She paused. 'The information you gather from the past has to be related to human behaviour. It's a holistic picture we're looking for. Law enforcement today relies too much on digital evidence.'

'And that's where you come in.' He smiled at the suspicious look she gave him. 'A true detective.'

'I do what I can.'

They had to put on clean coveralls to enter Wyobie Cotal's room through its small decontamination lock. The light was low and pink inside, so it didn't place undue strain on his eyes. Paula steeled herself behind her face filter mask as the second set of doors slid open. Something about emergency re-life cases always left her feeling queasy. Even though Cotal's new clone had been out of the womb tank for five weeks now, she found the body unpleasant to look at.

The clone had been initiated two years ago, after Cotal's insurance company array had conducted a legally required attempt to contact him through the unisphere. Subsequently, a more detailed search involving human researchers had also failed to locate any trace of him since he left Oaktier forty years earlier. At that time sixty-five years had elapsed since his birth, and he should have booked in to the clinic for his first rejuvenation in accordance with the policy which his reason-ably wealthy parents had taken out at conception. As he didn't appear, the courts granted the insurance company a body-death certificate on the grounds that he had either been illegally killed or had been involved in some freak accident which had gone unreported. The re-life procedure was acti-vated a week later.

Although not too common, the operation was relatively straightforward for a facility as well equipped as the Clayden Clinic. Cotal's DNA was subtly modified to produce acceler-ated growth, and the foetus kept in the womb-tank for just over twenty-three months. During the last five months, the clinic had inserted a neural link, and started to download Cotal's stored memories into his new brain. There weren't many; although he had regularly updated his secure store every couple of months, he'd stopped when he left Oaktier, aged twenty-three.

Lying on his bed bathed in mock-twilight, he looked like a fourteen-year-old famine victim. His body was dreadfully thin, with skin stretched tight over ribs and limbs. Some kind of gel had been applied to prevent excessive flaking, though several large areas were raw and crusting beneath the glistening substance. There was almost no muscle on his arms and legs, leaving his knees and elbows as knobbly protrusions. It meant he had to wear an electromuscle mobility suit to move, which looked as if he was imprisoned in a wire exoskeleton cage. But it was his head which was the most ungainly aspect. It was almost adult-size, leaving it far too big for his spindly neck to support without the mobility suit.

Wyobie Cotal's large sunken eyes followed them as they came into the room. He made no attempt to move his head. Every now and then he would open his lips a fraction, and a nipple would deploy from the side of the suit, pushing into his mouth so he could suck on it. Paula refused to look at the tubes around his waist, and the arrangement for connecting them to his penis and anus.

And I used to think recovering from an ordinary rejuvenation was humiliating enough.

'Hello Wyobie,' Hoshe Finn said. 'You're looking better this time. Remember me?'

'Policeman,' Wyobie Cotal whispered. His voice was amplified by the suit, producing a weird echo effect.

'That's right, Detective Finn. And this is Chief Investigator Paula Myo from the Serious Crimes Directorate. She's come all the way from Earth to look into your death.'

Wyobie Cotal's weary eyes focused on Paula. 'Do I know you?'

'No.' She wasn't about to start explaining her notoriety to someone who was struggling to make sense of his small stock of memories. 'But I would like to help you.'

He smiled, which allowed drool to leak from his mouth. 'You're going to break me out of here?'

'It won't be much longer.'

'Liar!' He said it loud enough that the amplification circuit wasn't triggered. 'They said I'll be here for months while my muscles grow. Then I'll just have a kid's body. The speed-up growing part has stopped now.'

'But you're alive again.'

He closed his eyes. 'Find them. Find who did this to me.'

'If you were killed, I will find them. I always do.'

'Good.'

'I understand you and Tara Jennifer Shaheef were sex partners.' Paula ignored the way Hoshe Finn winced behind his filter mask. The amount of time they could spend with Cotal was limited by his condition, she didn't intend wasting any of it.

'Yes.' The expression on the strange child-face softened. 'We'd just started seeing each other.'

'You know she left Oaktier as well.'

'I know. But I can't believe I ran off with her, there was too much for me here. I told the police before. I was seeing another girl, too.'

'Philippa Yoi, yes?'

'Yes.'

'Was she the jealous type?'

'No no, I've been through all this before. It was all just fun, nothing too serious. We all knew that. Philippa and I were first-lifers, we wanted to . . . live.'

'It was *just fun* at the time of your last memory back-up into the clinic's secure store. But you didn't leave Oaktier for another nine weeks after that. A lot could have happened in that time.'

'I wouldn't have left,' he repeated stubbornly.

'Had anybody mentioned taking any trips? Were any friends planning a holiday on another planet?'

'No. I'm sure. My head's all weird, you know. This was just five weeks ago for me. But my whole life is jumbled up. Some of the childhood stuff is clearer than Philippa and Tara. Oh fuck. I can't believe anybody would want to kill me.'

'Do you know anything about Tampico?'

'No. Nothing. Why?'

'It was the planet you bought a ticket for.'

Wyobie Cotal closed his eyes. Tears squeezed out to wet

the fine lashes. 'I don't know. I don't remember any of this. This has to be a mistake. One giant mother of a mistake. I'm still out there somewhere. I must be. I just forgot to come back for my rejuvenation, that's all. Find me, please. Find me!' He started to lift his back up off the pillow, juvenile features straining hard. 'Do something.'

A nurse came in as Wyobie Cotal sank back down again. He was unconscious before the electromuscle suit finished lowering back flat onto the bed.

'He's been sedated,' the nurse said. 'It'll be another three hours before he's conscious again. You can come back then if you have to, but he can't be exposed to an unlimited number of sessions like this. His personality is still very fragile, he's completely immature emotionally.'

'I understand,' Paula said. She and Hoshe Finn left the room together.

'What do you think?' the detective asked as they took their coveralls off.

'Taken alone, I would have said it was a clear-cut case. First-lifers are always excitable. He went off on an adventure holiday with a girl and drowned or crashed or flew into a hill, something reckless and stupid. But with Shaheef as well, we have to consider the circumstances.'

Hoshe Finn nodded and threw his overalls into a bin. The cooler air outside Cotal's room made him shiver. 'That's what alerted us to this in the first place. Tara Jennifer Shaheef was re-lifed twenty years ago. She was written off as having an accident.'

'So who made the connection?'

'Morton, her past husband. Apparently, Cotal was named on the divorce papers, he was the one she was shacking up with on Tampico.'

'So it did get serious between Cotal and Shaheef?'

'Looks like it, but not on this planet. She filed the papers on Tampico. Once the divorce was arranged, Morton never

179

heard anything from her again until her re-life. My division investigated her re-life as a matter of course, but there was nothing unduly suspicious other than the lack of a body. Accidents do happen.'

'So, after the divorce Cotal and Shaheef went on holiday, or even honeymoon, together. They had the same accident.'

'Could be. Except there really is no trace of them after they left Oaktier.'

'Apart from the divorce petition.'

'Yes. And there certainly isn't a motive for killing them. All we have are a lot of suspicious circumstances.'

'I need to see Shaheef next.'

'She's expecting us.'

6

The message was loaded into the unisphere through a planetary cybersphere node in Hemeleum, a small inland farming town on Westwould. It remained in a one-time address file for five hours, long enough for whoever loaded it to have travelled clear across the Commonwealth. After five hours were up, the message's sender segment activated. The program distributed the message to every e-butler address code in the unisphere, an annoying method of advertising called shotgunning. As a method of commercial promotion it had fallen into disuse centuries ago. Every modern e-butler program had filters which could bounce the spam right back to its sender, although as most shotgunners used a one-time address there was little point. The e-butlers also automatically notified the RIs controlling the unisphere routing protocols, who immediately wiped the offending message from every node. And under Intersolar law, finally passed in 2174, anyone shotgunning the unisphere was liable to a large irritant fine that could be applied to every message which was received by an e-butler, so the penalty was never less than a couple of billion dollars. No company could survive that. Subsequently, shotgunning was kept alive by underground organizations or individuals who had ideologies, disreputable financial schemes, religious visions, or political revolutions that they wanted the rest of the Commonwealth to know about. Given how quickly the unisphere RIs could identify shotgun spread patterns and block them, any software writer capable of composing a decent new shotgun sender could earn themselves a lucrative fee – cash, of course.

In this case, the factor which allowed the shotgunned message to get round most e-butler filters was that it had a genuine author certificate. On the arrival of any message, that was the first thing an e-butler would query. This one had the certificate of April Gallar Halgarth, a twenty-year-old resident of Solidade, the private world owned by the Halgarth dynasty. Over ten billion e-butlers allowed it to go forward into their hold file.

Most people upon receiving a message from a Halgarth opened it from sheer curiosity. When the visual recording started to play they realized they'd been shotgunned, and ninety per cent wiped it immediately. The rest let it run, either out of native inquisitiveness, the prospect of filing a shotgun suit against a Halgarth, they were fellow extremist freedom fighters, it was useful raw material for their dissertation on modern political factions, or quite simply because they were among those rare few who believed.

The visuals opened with a man in an office, sitting behind a desk, with the snow-cloaked city of San Matio, Lerma's capital, spread out panoramically through the window-wall behind him. His face boasted strong features that were high-lighted by dark skin, while neatly trimmed brown hair was threaded with a few silver strands. It emphasized the kind of authoritative air that inspired confidence, marking him down as a positive, progressive leader. (Forensic analysis showed he was a graphics composite, designed by the Formit 3004 simu-lator package, using its politician sculpture function.)

'Sorry to burst in on you like this,' he said. 'But as you probably know, the government spends a lot of tax money into hunting down our group. Contrary to the Commonwealth charter which permits free public assembly, I am not allowed to say what I want to other citizens. I represent the Guardians of Selfhood. And before you wipe this message, I have one question to ask you. Why has the Senate and the executive chosen to send a starship to the Dyson Pair? Specifically, why *now*?'

There was a perspective shift in the pause while the man drew a realistic breath. The observer point moved forwards and down, sitting in front of the desk, closer to the spokesman. It was a cosier setting, giving the impression of a one-on-one chat.

'As you know, we are campaigning against the Starflyer, an alien we contend is actively influencing the Commonwealth's political classes for its own advantage. It is this Starflyer which has engineered the current mission to investigate the Dyson Pair. The Commonwealth has known about the enclosure of the two stars for centuries. We have known that one day, when phase six space is opened, we would reach these strange stars and begin our investigation. What has changed? A single observation that proved the enclosure was a force field rather than a solid shell. Exactly why should that reverse centuries of Commonwealth policy?'

The spokesman shook his head solemnly. 'Possibly the most critical human voyage of exploration since Columbus set sail has been launched without any valid explanation. The question was not debated openly in the Senate, despite the vast amounts of public money being spent to finance the starship. Instead, the decision emerged from some obscure ExoProtectorate Council that nobody had ever heard of before. It is exactly the kind of clandestine back-room deal that favours the Starflyer and its agenda.'

Perspective shifted again, sweeping the viewer out through the window to soar over the complicated maze of San Matio's streets. 'Somewhere out there it lurks, controlling and influencing us through its puppets. Government and their media manipulators ask how we know the Starflyer is malign. The answer is simple, if it is a friend, it would reveal itself to us and the other alien affiliates of the Commonwealth. If it is a friend, it would not push us into sending an expedition to the Dyson Pair. The President says we need to know what happened. He is mistaken. We know what must have happened. Shielding two entire star systems with force fields is an act of extreme desperation. Something terrible was about to be unleashed, something that warranted such colossal countermeasures. These barriers have kept the threat isolated from the rest of the galaxy for over a thousand years. We are safe because of that. This wonderful city, and thousands like it across the Commonwealth, sleep soundly at night because the threat is contained. Yet now we are being sent out there to tamper with the dangerous unknown. Why? What was wrong with our old policy of caution? By the time we reach phase six space we would probably know how to generate force fields of such a size, we would certainly comprehend the science and technology involved. We would not be endangering anybody, least of all ourselves.'

The view slid back into the office, establishing eye contact with the spokesman again. 'Why was no public debate allowed? The Starflyer does not want that. Why is there an urgent need to visit the Dyson Pair? The Starflyer wants us to. Why does it want that? Consider this: the Starflyer has travelled hundreds of light-years across the galaxy. It knows what lies within the barrier. It has seen the danger there.

'All that we ask is that you resist its strategies and deceits. Question your senator, your planetary or national leader. Demand from them a full explanation why your tax money is being spent on this undemocratic recklessness. If they cannot satisfy you, then demand your rights. Demand this monstrosity be stopped.'

The spokesman bowed his head in respect. 'I thank you for your time.'

*

The star was a blue dwarf formally named Alpha Leonis, and more commonly referred to as Regulus by intrigued astronomers on Earth, back in the days when there was such a thing as astronomy on the old world. They also found its companion star, Little Leo, an orange dwarf; which itself had a companion, Micro Leo, a red dwarf. This cosy threesome were situated seventy-seven light-years from Sol, an unusual system that attracted quite a degree of interest and observation time.

Then in 2097, CST discovered an H-congruent planet orbiting a long way out from the primary, and christened it Augusta. For Nigel Sheldon it was the opportunity he'd been waiting for. At that time the Human Intersolar Commonwealth was being formed, and the UFN on Earth was enacting the first wave of its global environmental laws. With Regulus in a strategically important position to expand the CST network into the already envisaged phase two space, Nigel claimed it for the company. He transported every single CST manufacturing facility out there, and went on to welcome any other factory which was suffering from Earth's difficult new regulations. It became the first of what eventually were known as the Big15.

There was no culture to speak of on Augusta, no nationalist identity. It was devoted solely to commerce, the manufacture of products, large or small, which were shipped out across the Commonwealth. New Costa sprang up along the sub-tropical coast of the Sineba continent, the only city on the planet, home, in 2380, to just over a billion people. A centreless urban sprawl of factories and residential districts stretching for more than four hundred miles along the shore, and up to three hundred inland.

For all its crass existence, the megacity had a sense of purpose upon which all its inhabitants thrived. They were here for one thing: to work. There were no native citizens, everyone was technically a transient, earning money as they passed through. A lot of money. Some stayed for life after life, workaholics sweating their way up through the company which employed them, subtly remodelling themselves with every rejuvenation to give themselves the edge over their office rivals. A few stayed for one life, entrepreneurs working their asses into an early rejuvenation, but making a fortune in the process. However, the vast bulk of people lived there for sixty to ninety years, earning enough to buy into a good life on a more normal planet by the time they finally left. They were the ones who tended to have families. Children were the only people who didn't work on Augusta, but they did grow up with a faintly screwed view of the rest of the Commonwealth, believing it to be made up from romantic planets where everyone lived in small cosy villages at the centre of grand countryside vistas.

Mark Vernon was one such child, growing up in the Orangewood district at the south end of New Costa. As districts went, it was no better or no worse than any other in the megacity. Most days the harsh sunlight was diffused by a brown haze of smog, and the Augusta Engineering Corp, which owned and ran the megacity, wasn't going to waste valuable real estate with parks. So along with his hood buddies he powerscooted along the maze of hot asphalt between strip malls, and hung out anywhere guaranteed to annoy adults and authority. His parents got him audio and retinal inserts and i-spot OCtattoos at twelve so that he was fully virtual, because that was the age for Augusta kids to start direct loading education. By sixteen he was wetwired for Total Sensorium Interface, and receiving his first college year curriculum in hour-long artificial memory bursts every day. He graduated at eighteen, with a mediocre degree in electromechanics and software.

Ten years later, he had a reasonable job at Colyn Electro-mation, a wife, two kids of his own, a three-bedroom house with a tiny pool in the yard, and a healthy R&R pension fund. Statistically, he was a perfect Augusta inhabitant.

When he drove home that particular Friday evening, he wanted nothing more than to scream at the planet where it could shove his exemplary life. For a start he was late out of the plant. The guy on the next shift had called in sick, and it took the duty manager an hour to get cover organized. This was supposed to be Mark's family day, the one where he got home early and spent some quality time with those he loved. Even the traffic didn't want that to happen. Cars and trucks clogged all six lanes on his side of the highway, corralling his Ford Summer. Even with the city traffic-routing arrays managing the flow, the sheer volume of vehicles at this time of the evening slowed everybody down to a thirty-five-mile-an-hour crawl. He'd wanted a house nearer the factory, but AEC didn't have any to rent in those districts, so he had to make do with the Santa Hydra district. It was only ten miles inland, but that put it uncomfortably close to the Port Klye sector, where one of New Costa's nests of nuclear power plants was sited.

Mark opened the Summer's side window as they turned off the highway and onto Howell Avenue which wound through the Northumberland Hills. It was a district which senior management favoured; long clean boulevards lined by tall trees, where gated drives led off to big houses in pretty emerald enclaves surrounded by high walls. There was very little crime on Augusta – at least, non-corporate crime – and those in such secluded houses just enjoyed the sense of physical separation from the rest of the megacity. Low sunlight gleamed off the district's buildings and sidewalks, creating a hazy lustrous shimmer. He breathed in the warm dry air, trying to relax. As always when the tiny blue-white sun sank down towards the horizon, the warm El Iopi wind blew out of the southern desert towards the sea. It swept the day's pollution away, along with the humidity, leaving just the scent of blossom from the trees and roadside bushes.

During his childhood, his parents had taken him and his

siblings out into the desert several times, spending long weekends at oasis resorts. He'd enjoyed the scenery, the endless miles of flinty rock and sand, with only the rainbow buds of the scrawny twig-like native plants showing any colour in that wasted landscape. It was a break from the megacity which was all he'd known. The rest of Sineba wasn't worth visiting. That which wasn't desert had long since been put to the plough. Giant mechanized farms had spread across the continent's prairies, ripping up native plants and forests, and replacing them with huge fields of GM high-yield terrestrial crops, their leaves awash with pesticides and roots flooded with fertilizer. They poured a constant supply of cheap crops into the food-processing factories dotted along the inland edge of New Costa, to be transformed into packaged convenience portions and distributed first to the megacity's inhabitants, then out to the other planets, of which Earth was the greatest market.

After snaking down through the Northumberland Hills, Howell Avenue opened out into Santa Hydra, a broad flat expanse which led all the way across to the coastline fifteen miles away. He could see the Port Klye nest in the distance, eleven big concrete fission reactor domes perched along the shore. The ground around them was a flat bed of asphalt squares, where nothing grew and nothing moved, a mile-wide security moat separating them from the megacity which they helped to energize. Pure white steam trickled out of their turbine building chimneys, glowing rose-gold in the evening light. He couldn't help the suspicious stare he gave the plumes, even though he knew they weren't radioactive. The coolant system intake and outlet pipes were miles out to sea, as well, reducing any direct contamination risk. But the power plants were all part of his general malaise.

Slim pylons carried superconductor cables back into the megacity, following the routes of the major roads before they branched off and split into localized grids. Other, larger pylons carried the cables along the shoreline to the foundries. It was the heaviest industries which had colonized the land above the ocean, the big dirty steel mills and petrochemical refineries that used the seawater for coolant and the seabed as a wastedump.

Howell Avenue turned to run parallel with a heavy-duty eight-line rail track. These were the lines which connected the big industry districts to the CST planetary station, New Costa Junction, a hundred miles north and two hundred miles inland. Mile-long cargo trains ran along it all day and night, hauled by DVA5s, massive nuclear-powered tractor units. The leviathans roamed all over the planet, some of them on three-week journeys from the other continents, winding their way through a huge number of different terrains before crossing the final isthmus bridge on Sineba's north-eastern corner, which connected it to the rest of the world's landmasses. Their trucks carried every kind of raw material available in the planet's crust, collecting them from the hundreds of crater-sized open mines which AEC had opened up across the world. In terms of bulk shifted, only the oil pipelines could rival them, bringing in crude from the dozens of major oil fields AEC operated.

The Ford Summer accelerated through a wide concrete underpass as a freight train thundered overhead, heading out from the coast. It was taking refined metal away from the mills, one of a hundred that day alone. In a few hours it would reach the planetary station and transfer the metal to a world whose clear-air laws wouldn't permit the kind of cheap smelting methods Augusta employed.

With that depressing thought at the forefront of his mind, Mark finally turned into his own street. Putney Road was a mile long, with innumerable cul-de-sacs leading off it. The sidewalks were cracked, and the road surface uneven, long trickles of dark water leaked across it in several places where the irrigation pipes had fractured. Eucalyptus trees had been planted along both sides of the asphalt when the district was laid down, two hundred years ago. They were now so big their branches tangled together high above the centre of the road, creating a welcoming shaded greenway, and providing a great deal of privacy for the houses. A lot of bunting was hanging from the branches, the little flags all with the silver and blue Augusta football team emblem sparkling in the centre. As Mark turned the Summer into his own drive, the tyres scattered the usual layer of red-brown bark scabs which had peeled from the trunks to gather in the gutters. His father's car was parked up ahead of him, an opentop 2330 vintage Caddy which Marty Vernon maintained in perfect condition. Beside it, the twelve-year-old Ford Summer looked rundown and cheap.

Mark stayed in the front seat for a moment, taking stock. He wanted all his agitation to fade away so he could enjoy the evening. *I deserve a decent break. Around twenty years.* There were noises coming from the back of the house as the kids played on their little scrap of yard. The eucalyptus trees rustled in the gentle El Iopi wind, sending shadows wavering across the roof. Mark studied his home critically: pale lavender walls of drycoral, with a curving lime-green roof, arched windows of silvered glass, and matt-black air conditioning fins under the guttering with their front edges glowing a dull orange. Gold and scarlet climbing roses, heavily dusted with mildew, had covered the whole south wall up to the eaves, and needed a good pruning; while a blue and white kathariz vine had attached its suckers to the gable end above the two-door garage – it also demanded attention. The monthly rental for this took up fifteen per cent of his salary. With the utility bill, car payments, his R&R pension, the kids' education trust, the germline modification mortgage, health insurance, the vacation fund, clothing, food, and other regular debit payments, there was precious little left over for enjoying himself. Not that there were many places on Augusta where you could genuinely do that. Suddenly, he didn't want to get out of the car, he would throw a damper over the whole evening.

'Bad day at the office?'

Mark looked up to see Liz smiling at him through the open window. He grinned ruefully back at his beautiful wife – another of his daily worries was that she wouldn't be there for him when he got home.

'Is that what it looks like?'

She reached in and touched his hand. 'I've seen happier-looking suicide cases.'

'Sorry I'm late, work screwed up.' He realized she was almost never late home from work. Was that due to experience? He hated reminding himself of her sophistication, the kind that could only be acquired over decades, the years he hadn't lived yet.

'Come on,' she said, and opened the Summer's door. 'You need a drink. And Marty's here.'

'Yeah, I see that.' He gestured at the Caddy.

She frowned in concern as he climbed out of the car. 'You all right, baby?'

'I think the interface at the office is giving me a headache again. That or the whole goddamn OCtattoo is crashing.'

'Mark, you have to complain. You can't come home every day with a headache that gives you cold sweats. If the system's wrong, they have to repair it.'

'Okay. Right. I'll talk to the supervisor.' She didn't understand how it was at work right now. If he kicked up a fuss he'd probably wind up getting shitlisted. *Don't be so damn paranoid*, he told himself. But it was hard.

His father was on the patio decking which ran along the side of the pool, sitting on a sunlounger. Marty Vernon was a hundred and eighty, and eight months out of his latest rejuvenation. Physically, he looked like Mark's younger brother. Not yet old enough to develop the thick neck and creased cheeks which were the Vernon family trait.

191

'Mark! Hi, son, you look like shit, come and have a beer.' Marty pulled a bottle out of the cooler sheath. His voice was high and excitable.

'Dad!' Barry, aged five, was waving frantically from the pool. 'Dad, I can reach the bottom now. Watch!' He sucked in a huge breath, and ducked his head under the surface, paddling desperately. Mark waved back at his son's splashing feet. Liz dumped little Sandy into his arms. A wet smile beamed out from the thick folds of fabric. He smiled back, and kissed her. Tiny hands wiggled about happily. 'Has she had her bottle?'

'Twenty minutes ago,' Liz assured him.

'Oh.' He rather liked that chore. They'd collected Sandy from the clinic seven months ago, and that was after the stress-hell that was raising hyperactive Barry. The kids had the best genes they could afford, with Liz paying considerably more of the modification mortgage than he did. It always surprised him how much of a comfort the kids were, and how much stability they brought to his life. Liz just said, 'I told you so,' every time he mentioned it. Having a family was a huge strain on their finances, especially renting the womb tank for nine months. But although she'd gone through the whole trad-itional wedding ceremony with him, Liz flatly refused to have a pregnancy. 'I did enough of that last time round,' she insisted. So the womb tank it was.

Mark sat on the spare sunlounger, with Sandy cradled carefully in one arm. He took the beer bottle in his free hand. Barry broke surface with a victorious yell and a lot of splashing.

'Well done, kid,' Marty shouted. 'Here, go fetch this.' He chucked a dollar coin into the pool. Barry whooped, and dived down after it.

'I don't want him worn out,' Liz admonished. 'He'll get all tempered up when he needs to go to bed.'

'Give the kid a break,' Marty complained. 'He's having a

ball. And your pool's only – what? – a metre deep. That's not going to tire him out.'

'One point five.' Mark gulped down some of the beer. It was an imported brand he didn't recognize. He sighed and settled back into the sunlounger. That was when he noticed the girl sitting in the chair behind Marty. She was wearing a bikini top and some tight shorts, showing off a trim, tanned teenage body. 'Hi, I'm Amanda.'

'Oh, hi.' Mark couldn't help the glance he gave his father.

'My new girl,' Marty crowed loudly. His arm went round her, and she giggled.

'Great,' Mark said. 'So how long have you two, er . . .'

'Ten days,' Marty said gleefully. 'But mostly ten nights.'

Amanda giggled again.

Mark's smile was fixed. He knew what was coming now.

'We met up in the Silent World down at New Frisco Bay. Turns out we had a lot of things in common, and . . . hey!'

One thing in common, Mark corrected silently and sullenly. He couldn't believe his father had done this. Silent World was a Commonwealth-wide franchise. It was the club which all the newly rejuvenated visited. Frequently, in the first few months after leaving the clinic. They went for just one thing: sex. It didn't matter with who, just someone equally horny from their beautiful, youthful new body's deluge of hormones. There was only one rule, whatever happened inside, stayed inside. You could fuck your worst enemy, or your ex, or your ex's younger sibling or parent, or the most glamorous unisphere celeb. It didn't matter, because it didn't count back outside the doors, it didn't get mentioned, it simply never happened. And Marty had gone and brought her to a family evening.

David turned up ten minutes later, Liz's forty-five-year-old son, an accountant working in AEC's export credit division. Then there was Kyle, Mark's older brother (by a hundred and fifteen years), and Antonio, his boyfriend; Joanne, one of Liz's mother's great-granddaughters. Finally, Carys Panther arrived, Marty's older sister, driving up in a Merc coupé and wearing a thousand-dollar 'casual' dress from Jacvins. Mark was glad she had found the time to come, Carys was the one multi-lifer (apart from Liz) who always made him feel comfortable. She was also the most glamorous person he knew. When she did work, Carys designed dramas that were occasionally made into TSIs by various media conglomerates. They tended to be pretty raunchy.

As Regulus fell towards the horizon, they ordered Barry out of the pool and fired up the barbecue grill. Carys accepted a glass of white wine from the maidbot and fussed over Barry, helping him dry himself. Barry responded with true puppy-love devotion, showing her his new collection of dead nipbugs; he really adored his Aunt Carys.

Mark stood beside the barbecue, turning the burgers and sausages himself. The gardenbot had an attachment for it, but he never did trust an array's judgement when it came to cooking.

'You should cut some of these damn eucalyptus trees back,' Marty told him, standing at his shoulder. 'That solarbrick isn't getting enough sun on it during the day, look. It should be a lot hotter than that.'

Mark looked down at the thick slab below the barbecue's grill, which was glowing a weak cherry-pink. Little flames flared briefly as the meat dripped juices down through the grille. 'Looks fine to me, and it's hot enough.'

'It won't last, I've got experience with these things.'

'Yes, Dad.'

'Marty,' Kyle called out. 'Sit down and leave the kid alone, for Christ's sake.'

Every time his relatives came round the same thing happened. A lot of the time, Mark felt like he was a child allowed to listen to adult conversation, laughing when the others did and not understanding why.

'Just trying to help,' Marty grumbled as he backed off.

'Next family evening is round at my place,' David announced. 'I thought we could have it on the eighteenth, that's when we play our next Cup round.'

'I'm on for that,' Marty said. 'You know I nearly had a trial once, when I was first-life eighteen. Newby City.'

'Wrong,' Carys said. 'You are a trial, Marty, not you had a trial.'

Marty made a gesture, to which she laughingly covered Barry's eyes.

'I can't believe we've got this far,' Kyle said. 'We only need, what? A win and a draw to go through to the second round.'

'We'll get the win against Sterling, no problem,' David said. 'But we'll be struggling to get a draw against Teleba, they're football mad.'

Antonio groaned theatrically, and put his hand to his head. 'How long does this go on for?'

'Another seven and a half months,' Kyle told him cheerfully. 'And I'm going to the stadium on Tampico to see our last group one game.'

'By yourself,' Antonio muttered.

'Twenty-five per cent of us called in sick when the last game was on,' Joanne said. 'The Cup has really taken off this time round; you couldn't get in to a bar anywhere in New Costa they were so crowded. I don't remember everyone getting so excited last time.'

'Wonder if the new aliens will want to play,' Liz said.

'And what a goddamn waste of time and money that is,' Marty complained.

'Hardly,' David said. 'We need to know what's going on out there.'

'*Went* on out there,' Marty said. 'It all happened thousands of years ago.'

'That doesn't mean it isn't relevant now,' Carys said. 'The envelopment barrier is still in place around both Dyson stars.'

'You're sounding like that Guardian shotgun,' David said.

'Don't tell me you watched it, Marty?' Carys taunted. 'Didn't you realize what it was?'

'Course I goddamn well realized,' Marty shot back. 'Only an asshole wouldn't recognize a shotgun. I saw the highlights on Alessandra Baron's show, is all.'

Mark turned the sausages, keeping quiet. He hadn't realized the message from April Halgarth was a shotgun propaganda blast until he opened it; and even then he'd let it play. The Guardians had made a great deal of sense. Why hadn't there been a vote in the Senate?

'So if it comes from Alessandra, it's acceptable is it?' Carys asked.

'Who cares who says it?' Marty said. 'They're both right. It doesn't affect us, and it's certainly something beyond us at the moment. We should take our time and reach the Dyson Pair as we expand naturally, not pull off this crazy Apollo stunt.'

Mark flipped the burgers again. Regulus had finally sunk below the horizon, allowing the stars to come out. Brightest among them were the Leo twins, a single glowing orange dot in the eastern sky. He could see them through the leaves of the eucalyptus trees as they swayed quietly. Some nights he'd sit out on the decking with a drink, just staring up at the canopy of stars twinkling above the megacity. They were the physical proof that people did live elsewhere, and live differently. Seeing that, made life on Augusta that fraction more bearable. 'They put my promotion off again,' he said.

'Oh, Mark, I'm sorry,' Carys said. 'I know you wanted that.'

'Tough break, son,' Marty said. 'But you've got to serve aces the whole time to get by on this planet. And don't try and change the subject that quickly. The goddamn starship is a waste of money.'

'The point, Dad, is that I didn't get promoted because the company's market isn't growing the way economists predicted. The new factory's on hold, investment is minimal right now, and not just with us. Phase three space isn't growing anything like phase two did at the start. We're not expanding like we used to, the Commonwealth is too stable these days. Population growth is down even with womb tanks, it's certainly not enough to provide a base population for a couple of new planets every year like we have been doing. We're too civilized and measured. At this rate we'll never reach the Dyson Pair if all we do is wait around for CST to open wormholes to phase twenty space, or whatever.'

'Mark's right,' David said. 'My office has been working some long-range forecasts, we're in a slowdown right now. They used to call periods like this "golden ages". Things tick over nicely and there are no upsets.'

'I thought they were recessions,' Carys muttered.

'No, there's a difference.'

'It's all a bunch of crap,' Marty said. 'My board isn't making any cutback plans. Our market's bullish.'

'Nobody's talking cutbacks,' David said. 'The menu is all about reduced growth rates. If anything, Sheldon is playing smart with the starship project. There's nothing like a sudden deluge of government cash to accelerate growth rates. And the majority of spending is here on Augusta.'

'That's not the case, actually.'

Everybody turned to look at Amanda as she snuggled up close to Marty. She smiled back coolly, completely unintimidated. 'My family has a board seat on the First-Quad bank. I get to see Intersolar finance tables before they're massaged. The amount of money spent on the starship is irrelevant in macro-economic terms. Twenty billion Earth dollars is barely a couple of minutes' worth of exports from this planet.'

'We're doing well from it,' Liz said. 'Bitor-UU won the contract to develop bioscreening kits for the starship.'

'I didn't know that,' Joanne said. 'Congratulations. Are you working on them yourself?'

'Some concepts, yes.'

'One kit, for a super specialist market,' Amanda said. 'There can be no spin-off from it. I rest my case.'

'My girl.' Marty leaned over, and they kissed quite lavishly.

'Why do you think there's only going to be one starship?' Kyle said. 'If you ask me, this is just the beginning. People have really taken to this Dyson Alpha mission, it's going to be bigger than the Commonwealth Cup by the time it's ready to fly. If you ask me, it's a perfect antidote to how moribund phase three space has gotten. Everyone with an ounce of poetry in their soul will leap at the chance of taking off for the wild blue yonder, and settling somewhere that CST will never ensnare with their sticky fingers.'

'Crap,' Marty said. 'If that were true, all these poets of yours would go live on Far Away.'

'I meant we could find clean fresh worlds, not some violent anarchist hell.'

'Not going to happen,' Marty insisted. 'We've had breakaways before. I bet all those worlds that severed ties with the Commonwealth to be "free" are all medieval nightmares now. Isolation never works. Look what a mess Earth was in before Sheldon and Ozzie invested in wormholes.'

'Interesting model,' Carys said.

'One world, cut off from the galaxy,' Marty said. 'I rest my case.'

David refused to be baited, he just smiled at Mark and rolled his eyes.

'Did you hear, they've chosen Wilson Kime to captain the mission?' Carys said. 'That must really be choking Nigel Sheldon.'

'Is that a story for you?' Antonio asked.

'Could be. Old enemies have to set aside their rivalries for the greater good of the Commonwealth.'

'Sounds dull if you put it like that.'

Mark started slipping the sausages onto the serving platter. 'Food's up!'

*

Liz took a while in their bathroom getting ready for bed. She had a shower, and used some of the smaller, more expensive bottles of scent, dabbing the chilly drops on her skin and massaging them in until the flesh seemed to glow. Then she took out the special cream silk lingerie which she knew Mark *really* liked. Her jet-black hair was combed out until it hung loosely down below her shoulders. Then she put on her gold gown, carefully arranging it so it was almost falling open at the front. She took a contented look in the mirror, reassured once again she'd made the right choice not undergoing pregnancy for him; her belly was still as firm and flat as the day she came out of rejuve ten years ago, and there wasn't any hint of cellulite on her thighs yet.

Back then her friends had laughed at her dating a first-lifer, claiming it was a way of saving on Silent World bills. She had to admit, when they'd first met at a party thrown by a production company Carys had been writing for, there was something of the puppy dog about him. He looked so uncomfortable and lost amid all the z-list celebrities and wannabe production people that rescuing him was the only decent thing to do. They'd dated a few more times, and she'd enjoyed herself because he was enthusiastic about life and the Commonwealth, and didn't have the kind of guarded falseness that people her own age had. There was no game playing with him, he was too honest for that. She found that inordinately reassuring. So maybe it really was a case of subconsciously hoping his genuine youth would rub off on her; even though the age difference had never been an issue for him. Then completely out of the blue he'd asked her to marry him, carried away by some mad romantic notion of them being soul mates.

She'd been *so* close to saying no, a hard fast put-down that would hurt him for a month until he met some equally wild, inexperienced girl his own age, and they went off into the sunset together. Except . . . Why should she actually do that? So what if he was sweet in a puppy dog way? Men who were thoughtful and considerate were rare no matter what their age. She was going to live for ever anyway, or a damn good portion of it at least, so why not be happy with a good man for twenty years – and to hell with her jealous friends and their catty remarks.

Since then there hadn't been a single day when she'd regretted the decision. They fought – what married couple didn't? – but never over anything serious. He was a wonderful father, too. She'd never planned on having more than one kid with him, but just being together with him over the years made her give in and agree to Sandy.

And her friends had been right, healthy first-lifers his age took a lot of satisfying in bed. Which made her the lucky one.

There was only one bedside light on when she stepped out of the bathroom, casting a warm yellow glow on Mark's half of the bed. He was sitting up studying data on a paperscreen. The window was open and the air conditioning off; dying gusts of El Iopi warmed the room. 'Hi baby. Is there room there for Mummy?'

Mark looked up. A nervous smile flickered across his face as he saw what she was wearing. He dropped the paperscreen as she clambered onto the bed, and slowly crawled towards him.

'That Amanda looked quite something,' she murmured as she nuzzled his ear.

'Pha. She does nothing for me, not like you.' He slid one

hand inside the gold gown, fingers stroking the hot ebony skin beneath the fabric.

Liz slowly moved round until she was straddling him. She planted light, tickling kisses on his cheek and down his throat. Her head waved from side to side, allowing her hair to brush across his chest. His hand slipped under the bra. She smiled at the pleasurable sensation his fingers conjured and brought her head up to kiss him properly. Then she saw his face, and sighed heavily.

'What's the matter, baby?' She rolled off him, dismayed and concerned. 'This isn't like you.'

Mark stared up at the ceiling, unable to meet her gaze. 'It's nothing.'

'Wrong. Believe me, I know. I am your wife, and a lot more besides.' She deliberately paused as she re-tied the robe tighter.

His smile was regretful. 'I know. It's just that tonight wasn't what I was hoping for. I'm sorry.'

'I think this is a little deeper than your father turning up with his latest lady friend, however tactless it was.'

'Damn it.' He turned on his side to face her. 'That's exactly it, don't you see?'

'See what?'

'You, Dad, the others, you've all got this wealth of experience. And I don't. And ... it gets a little overpowering at times.'

'And you didn't get the promotion.'

'Jesus H. Christ, you just did it again. Do you have any idea how small that makes me feel.'

Liz was quiet for quite a while as she gathered her troubled thoughts together. 'I didn't realize the effect was this upsetting. It's never been an issue before.'

'I know.' He grinned lamely. 'Maybe it's a cumulative thing.'

'Okay, baby, then I'll say one more thing that I think about you.'

'What?'

'You really hate it here, don't you?'

Mark let out a relieved breath. 'Yeah.' Then he was suddenly animated, jumping up to give her an intent stare. 'This whole world is strictly for adults only. And I don't mean me. I'm only twenty-eight for Christ's sake, that's not adult. They shouldn't let anyone through the gateways at New Costa Junction until they're at least a hundred years old. You're the only kind of people who can take this kind of life.'

'All right,' she said. 'I admit it doesn't bother me as much as it obviously does you. That's because it's temporary, baby. One day we'll leave.'

'But not together! That's part of you as well, that fatalism, or wisdom, whatever you want to call it. Nothing ever seems to bother you. You've had other marriages; they're just sections of your life. You're my whole life, Liz, you and the kids. I know I'll get out of here one day, but it won't be with you. And this world isn't for children, there's no society here. That's what I hate most about all this; Barry and Sandy are going to grow up just like me. That's . . . that's so much the worst thing I could ever do to them.'

'Okay.' She put a finger on his cheek, turning his head so she could look straight at him. 'Tomorrow you hand in your resignation, and we start looking through the unisphere for somewhere else to live, somewhere different. Maybe a phase three world.'

'You can't . . . you're not serious.'

'Perfectly serious. This is eating you up; you don't have to be my age to see that. And, Mark, I meant everything I said at the altar. I do love you, and if we stay here we're going to get torn apart. So, this is what we have to do.'

'But what about your work? The stuff you do at Bitor-UU is real cutting edge.'

202

'So? There are tens of thousands who can do the same thing, hundreds of thousands, actually. And I don't really need to be in the labs the whole time, I can work most of the systems over the unisphere. Then again, maybe it's time for me to get a new job if we are going to live somewhere different.'

'Jesus.' Mark looked shocked, then he began to smile. 'My God, do you know what they'll say if I tell them I'm quitting? Burcombe will go crazy.'

'Let him. Who cares?'

'But, what about money? We'll never earn as much anywhere else, not doing what we do now.'

'Pay is relative. Augusta costs a lot more than most places. We'll find a world where our jobs support this kind of lifestyle, if not a better one.'

He held her close. The expression on his face was the same kind of wonder as the first time they'd gone to bed together. 'You'll really emigrate with me?'

'Yes, Mark. You're not just some section of my life, baby, you are my life. Who knows, maybe we'll be the one in a hundred billion couples who actually stay married for all eternity.'

He grinned. 'I like that idea.'

'You got any thoughts where you'd like to go? You've obviously been thinking about this for a long time.'

'Since I was about five.' His hands moved down to the gown's belt, and gently pulled the bow open. 'But we can talk about that in the morning.'

*

An hour after the case broke, Tarlo and Renne accompanied the Directorate duty forensics team to the Paris CST station, where all of them climbed on board the express for Nzega. They routed via Orleans, the Big15 world for that sector of phase two space, and arrived at Fatu, Nzega's capital, forty-one minutes later. The forensic team hired a van to carry their equipment, while Renne and Tarlo checked out a big BMW 4x4 Range Cruiser.

Nzega wasn't a backwater world, but it had managed to sidestep the excesses of full technoindustrial development. The majority culture was stable, civilized, and took a decently relaxed attitude to life and human foibles. Its main body of initial settlers were Polynesian and Latin Americans. They came because of the seas; half the planet's surface was water. Nzega didn't have any major continents, just hundreds of large islands, and thousands of smaller ones. That gave them an awful lot of coastline. Boats were a huge part of the local way of life. On the major inhabited islands, it was the interiors which were sparsely populated.

The economic spin-off from that was the colossal number of resorts, hotels, and rental properties along the shores of the islands. Combined with the planet's liberalism, it attracted a lot of middle-class kids looking for a break from the worlds with a faster pace of life.

Renne loaded their destination, Port Launay, into the BMW's drive array, and settled back to enjoy the view. It was a seventeen-hour drive from Fatu along the Great Mantu Road, taking them over innumerable causeway bridges, and five ferry rides between the islands into the sub-tropical zone. Sometimes the road was enzyme-bonded concrete, sometimes not. There were times when it ran along the top of sheer cliffs, and others when it meandered through what seemed like endless salt marshes, while the rest was just a standard route through the string of coastal towns. After a while, both investigators opaqued the windows and settled down to sleep while the vehicle rolled along.

Port Launay was simply a four-kilometre section of the urban strip which ran along the whole shore of Kailindri island, though 'urban' was pushing the definition a bit. The single compacted stone road ran along two hundred metres inland from the sea through the continual forest of shaggy native trees, with small cul-de-sacs branching off where clusters of chalets and bungalows sheltered under the trees. Towns were distinguished by the way shops and commercial buildings clumped together to serve residential neighbourhoods.

When the BMW's drive array indicated they'd reached their cul-de-sac, Renne switched to manual to steer the car along the last few hundred metres. The road wasn't even broken stone any more, just tyre tracks of dusty sand in the dense yellow-blue queengrass. Three local police cars were blocking the way. Several rented cars were parked on the verges in front of them, with reporters arguing with police officers.

'How did they get here so goddamn fast?' Tarlo asked.

'Who knows?' Renne said. 'They smell misery the way vultures smell carrion. You want to deal with the local police?'

'Sure.' Tarlo grinned, slipped his sports sunglasses on, and opened the door.

She watched him saunter over to the sergeant in charge, and start talking. Tarlo was from Los Angeles, eighty-two years old, completing his first rejuvenation nine years previously. Not that he gave that impression in the flesh, he still looked as if he was barely out of his teens. A wealthy Californian family had provided extensive germline sequencing, one facet of which restricted his natural ageing process. They'd also gone for a traditional (or stereotyped – depending on your viewpoint) surfer kid appearance: slim body, but tall and naturally toned, with lush blond hair, and perfect teeth set on a firm square jaw. Tarlo clearly relished his heritage. Quite why he'd gone into law enforcement was something Renne never understood. 'I like puzzles,' was the only explanation he'd ever offered. Personally, she felt he got slightly too much of a buzz out of the Directorate's covert operations. The little boy who wanted to be a super secret agent when he grew up.

He ought to fit in just fine on Nzega. Which was why she was happy to let him talk to the police. Sometimes there was a lot of resentment within the local law enforcement agency when the Directorate turned up and took over.

She saw the forensic team's van pull in behind the BMW just as Tarlo and the sergeant laughed together. One of the police cars was driven off the track it had been blocking, and Tarlo waved her through.

The beach cottage was another couple of hundred metres further on. Tall trees with grey-blue leaves lined the track, providing a degree of privacy for the other homes along the cul-de-sac. She caught glimpses of the single-storey buildings. They had been built mainly from wood or composite panels, but one had been grown from drycoral. A black Merc had drawn up outside the cottage she wanted. Renne had a good idea who that had brought. She parked the BMW behind it, and climbed out into strong humidity and the strong smell of saltwater. The trees provided a reasonable shade from the fierce morning sunlight, but she still put her own sunglasses on.

'The Halgarths sent their own security team,' Tarlo said as he walked up beside her, holding his linen jacket over his shoulder. He nodded at the Merc. 'Police said they arrived about forty minutes ago.'

'How do the police feel about us being here?'

He grinned his broad grin. 'Pleased to hand the whole problem over to us. They'll handle crowd control until Ms Halgarth leaves.'

'Good.' She watched the forensic team van jolt its way along the track. 'Do we know which house the Guardians operated out of?'

'Yep.' He pointed along the shore. 'Two down. They obviously had good intel. Police have put a guard on it. The reporters don't know about that yet.'

'Okay.' Renne straightened her shoulders, adjusted her light jacket. 'Let's get this over with. Put your jacket back on.'

'The boss isn't here.'

'That's not the point.'

With a great show of reluctance, Tarlo put his jacket back on, and pulled his tie up. 'There'd better be air conditioning,' he muttered as Renne told the forensic team to start with the other house.

They walked down the narrow front path to the beach cottage. It was a modest little building, made of wood which had been freshly painted a matt lime green, with a solar cell roof and semiorganic precipitator leaves hanging from the eaves. A wide veranda faced the sea. There was fifty metres of queengrass lawn stretching out from the veranda, which ended where the sandy soil crumbled away onto the beach. Only the rear and sides of the property were fenced in with trees, giving the cottage a grand view out across the broad cove. A barbecue stood at the end of the veranda, with several chairs and a table on the grass beside it. Empty bottles of exotic cocktails, beer cans, and dirty crockery occupied the table, glistening in the fast-evaporating dew.

One of the Halgarth security personnel was standing in front of the door, dressed in a simple navy-blue sweatshirt, and long beige shorts that came down over his knees. Renne tried not to smile when they walked up to him, his image was obviously something he felt strongly about. 'Serious Crimes Directorate,' she said solemnly. 'We'd like to interview Ms Halgarth.'

'Sure thing,' he said, 'Some identification, please?'

Renne's e-butler sent an SCD certificate to his e-butler.

'Thank you,' the security man said. He opened the door for them.

The cottage wasn't large. It had a narrow hall leading to three bedrooms, a bathroom, kitchen, and a lounge which took up half of the total floorspace. The furniture was functional rather than ornate, a typical low-budget holiday rent.

'She's a Halgarth, and she comes here for a vacation?' Tarlo said. 'Even if she's minor family she could stay someplace better.'

'That's not the point. Didn't you access the file? This is her first year at college, her first vacation with a bunch of friends. She's free of the family for the first time in her life. Anyway, what's wrong with this place?'

He winked. 'No moon. No tides.' His voice dropped to a deliberately hoarse whisper. 'No surf!'

Renne gave him a despairing look, and went into the lounge. April Gallar Halgarth was sitting on the settee, looking as woebegone as if she'd just been told her parents had undergone complete bodyloss. Even dressed in baggy green jeans and a rumpled old russet T-shirt, she was quite beautiful. A tall twenty-year-old with smooth light-ebony skin, thick wavy hair, and sweet features that belonged on an even younger face. Her hands cupped a mug of coffee which she wasn't drinking. When she looked up at the two investigators, her eyes were red and puffy, desperate for understanding.

Her three girl friends were standing guard protectively round her. Marianna, Anjelia, and Laura, all from Queen's University Belfast where they studied together. Two more Halgarth security personnel were also in the lounge, looking slightly lost. Their orders were to protect April from the media, and escort her home. The girl clearly wasn't up to that much activity yet.

'Have you caught the bastards?' Marianna demanded when Renne and Tarlo identified themselves. She had a thick Irish accent.

'Not yet, no,' Tarlo said. 'We're just establishing the investigation.'

'Huh!' Marianna snorted. She turned her back on the two investigators.

'Ms Halgarth, we need to ask you some questions,' Renne said.

Marianna knelt down beside her friend. 'You don't have to if you don't want to.'

April peered up at Renne. 'It's all right. I want to do this.'

Marianna nodded reluctantly, and led the other two girls out of the lounge. 'If you don't mind,' Tarlo said politely to the remaining bodyguards. One went out into the hall, the second left through the sliding glass door, and stood on the veranda outside.

'I guess you must be wondering why this happened to you?' Renne said, as she sat beside the distraught girl.

'Yes,' April moaned.

'Mostly because you're a Halgarth. The Guardians of Selfhood regard you as their enemy.'

'*Why?* I don't know anything about them, I've never been to Far Away, or helped any aliens or anything. I'm just studying twenty-first-century history, that's all.'

'I know. But your dynasty is the main backer behind the *Marie Celeste* Research Institute. To their warped minds, that's a big crime. I have to tell you, don't look for reason in this. There is no true rational explanation. You are the result of a search program. They wanted a Halgarth, it's always a member of your family; and one who is – I'm sorry – slightly naive, and isolated. It was your name which popped up out of the program.'

April bent her head, dabbing at her eyes with a paper kitchen towel. 'He was so nice. I can't believe this.'

'What was his name?' Tarlo asked gently.

'Alberto,' the girl said. 'Alberto Rasanto. He was with his friends Melissa and Frank in the cottage one down from here. They were doing the same thing as us, taking a spring break. They said. I suppose that was a lie.'

'Yes,' Renne said.

April winced as she stared into the cold coffee.

'So you met them,' Renne prompted.

'He was lovely. He had these big green eyes. I thought he

was a first-life, just like me. They were on the beach the day we arrived. We all started talking. There was a little bit of competition for Alberto, you know? I mean, Melissa and Frank had each other. And there are four of us. We sort of gathered round Alberto. And Marianna's really pretty; she always gets the best boys. But he liked me. He was always smiling when we spoke; and he was easy to talk to. He had a lovely smile – really lovely. So it was like me and him for the next few days. We went swimming, and he was teaching me how to windsurf; we all went out in a group to the bars in the evening, and had too much to drink. I even tried some TSInarc. Nothing hard, just some low programs. They were weird, but kind of fun. I suppose that was the start of it.'

'They'd be establishing a pattern, yes,' Tarlo said. 'A TSInarc or even ordinary chemical drugs help blur your recollection. I'm sorry, April, but we have to ask this: did you sleep with him?'

'Uh huh.'

'When, please?'

'I suppose the first time was four days ago.'

'And you stayed over at their cottage when you did?'

'Yes. He had a room of his own. I'm sharing with Laura. We all made a pact about boys before we came here, that we'd use the couch if a roomie scored. But ... I just. This was easier.'

'More private?' Tarlo said with a sympathetic smile.

'Yes,' she said eagerly. 'I'm still a bit conservative, I suppose. Not that I mind my friends knowing I'm with a boy; but the walls here are really thin. I grew up on Solidade, which is just family.' Her head came up, giving them a dejected look. 'You must think I'm a really dumb rich girl who knows nothing about the real world. Nobody else would be so gullible.'

'No,' Renne said. 'You're not gullible. It's not that kind of con trick. They would have got the unisphere message author certificate out of you no matter what.'

The tears filled her eyes again. 'But I don't *remember*. And now the whole Commonwealth thinks I sent them Guardian propaganda.'

'By tomorrow the Commonwealth will have forgotten. Your family will make sure the news media never mentions you again. Normally I'd complain about undue influence, but in this case I have to agree it's a blessing.'

April nodded slowly in agreement. 'What happened?' she asked with a fierce whisper. 'The family security people said they didn't know, but I'm sure that's what they were ordered to say. Tell me, please.' She looked from Tarlo to Renne. 'Please. I have to know. I can't even work out when. That's so awful. I don't care how bad it is, I just want to know.'

'It would have happened two nights before they left,' Tarlo said. Renne flashed him an angry glance, but he just shrugged. 'Part of the routine of getting you drunk and high each night is so that you'll always wake up the next morning with a fuzzy head. So when something like this happens you won't be suspicious.'

April frowned, her eyes unfocused as she glazed out through the broad window wall, concentrating on something way beyond the sparkling sea. 'I don't remember. I really don't. I'd like to say I was more sluggish than usual that morning. But I wasn't.' She looked up at Tarlo. 'So what happened to me?'

'They would probably have given you antronoine or some variant, slipped it in your drink. You wouldn't know what was going on, it's almost like being blind drunk except you're completely open to suggestion. Then they'd have used an interface scanner in conjunction with a hack program on your inserts. It wouldn't have taken more than a couple of minutes. After that, you would have had a memory edit.'

'Memory edit.' April ran her hands back through her hair. 'You make it sound so clinical. That's a piece of my life they stole from me. I never knew it could be that easy.'

'The technology is well established,' Renne said. 'Some of the refinements didn't even come out of corporate research. The first thing criminals do after they've committed a big crime is pull the whole memory of the event out of their brain. They don't even know they've committed the crime; which is kind of weird; but that way we can't read their memories and use them as evidence in court.'

'You know I think I hate that part more than anything, more than being seduced, or having my certificate used. It's just awful. They could have done anything, anything; I'll never know. I can't believe I don't remember.'

'We'll need to run some tests on you,' Renne said. 'Our forensic team will take some blood samples. Given this only happened a couple of days ago, we'll be able to find traces of whatever drug they used. They'll also want to run some calibration programs through your inserts. Do you think you're up to that for us?'

'Yes,' April said. 'Whatever it takes, I'll do it.'

'Thank you. We'll use a characteristics sketch program to get a picture of them. You and your friends can contribute to that.'

'Are you going to catch them? Realistically?'

'It will be tough,' Tarlo said. 'The Guardians wouldn't have shotgunned their message until after their team was off Nzega. By now they could be on any world in the Commonwealth. They'll use cellular reprofiling kits to change their appearance. Our best chance of arresting them is when we break the whole Guardians group.'

'You've been after them for a long time, haven't you? Everyone knows that. It's Paula Myo's only unsolved case.'

'Nobody can run for ever,' Renne said. 'Today will have brought them a little closer to justice. They will have left clues and evidence. Their DNA will be in the cottage, their software patterns will be all over Nzega's cybersphere, in the finance for renting the cottage and hiring transport, their communications records. I know it doesn't sound like much to you, especially now, but believe me, every little does help us.'

Renne and Tarlo left through the veranda window, sending the bodyguard back in. They walked over the spongy lawn towards the cottage the Guardians had used. Both of them had to slip their sunglasses back on against the glare of the hot sun.

'That was kind of you,' Renne said. 'Telling her they would have used a date rape drug. I wondered what you were doing telling her about the hack.'

'She's suffered enough,' Tarlo replied.

Renne stopped and looked out to sea, a humid breeze toying with her thick auburn hair. 'Bastards. Fancy doing this to a first-lifer. Even without the memory, she'll be screwed up about it for decades.'

'I hate memory edit,' Tarlo said. 'Every time we come up against it, it gives me the creeps. I mean, suppose we already solved the Guardians case, started to round them up, when they turned it on us. We might have arrested them a hundred times already. I mean, it is goddamn strange that the boss has never got one of the principals.'

'You're starting to sound like Alessandra Baron, always criticizing the Directorate. If anyone invented a memory edit you fired like a laser, we'd know about it.'

'That's the whole point,' he said, shrugging, his arms held wide. 'We did know about it, and the inventor fired it at us.'

'Stop it. You're getting paranoid.'

He grinned ruefully. 'You have to admit, something's not right about this whole Guardians situation. Hell, you were there on Velaines. Did we make a mistake? Come on, I mean did we? We played that so by the book we got paper creases, and they still found out.'

'They got lucky.'

'They've been lucky for a hundred and thirty years. That ain't natural.'

She gave him a troubled glance. 'What are you saying?'

'I don't know. I really don't.' He sighed. 'Come on, let's go find out what forensics turned up.'

'It'll be nothing.'

'Optimist. Ten dollars that this is the time the Guardians made a mistake and left a decent clue behind.'

'You're on.'

7

The CST exploratory division wormhole on Merredin had been down for fifteen months while it was given a class five overhaul – complete energy focusing structure maintenance, and upgrading all the level beta support systems. It was no small job servicing a half cubic kilometre of high-energy physics machinery. Oscar Monroe had been on site for ten months, managing the crews as they crawled around the wormhole generator armed with screwdrivers, arrays, programs, and every conceivable type of bot. Three more months had been spent training with his ground crew, after all most of the systems were new, and that meant learning a whole new set of procedures. Six weeks had been spent with the forward crew as they got to grips with the latest marques of their equipment and software during innumerable simulation runs. That left him with an entire fortnight's holiday.

He took off for Earth, and spent the first ten days alone, e-butler address deactivated, sitting in a fishing boat on Lake Rutland in England at Easter time. It rained for seven of the ten days, and he caught a total of eleven trout. Those were probably the most relaxing days he'd enjoyed in eight years. Not that he wanted to make a habit of loafing around.

The last four days were spent in London, where he was determined to catch some of the quaint live theatre shows amidst all the rest of the slightly-too-nostalgic culture which the grand old capital offered its visitors. On the very first night, during the interval of a 'reinterpreted' Stoppard, he met a handsome young lad from some aristocratic European family, who was curious and impressed with him and his job. With a shared taste for art and opera and good food they were inseparable for Oscar's remaining three days. They waved goodbye at the CST London station and his express started the thirty-three-minute trip back to Merredin, two hundred and eight light-years away.

Next morning, they began the wormhole generator power-up; done correctly it was a slow process. Six days later, Oscar was ready to start planet hunting.

The exploratory division base was visible while he was still five miles away, occupying three square miles on one side of the CST planetary station. Such prominence wasn't difficult. Merredin was the new junction world for phase three space in this sector of the Commonwealth. In anticipation of the fifty gateways which would one day connect it to those distant stars, the planetary station was a cleared area over a hundred and fifty square miles on the side of the capital city. So far, it had one standard-size passenger terminal, a small marshalling yard, and three gateways, one back to the Big15 world, Mito, the other two out to the phase three frontier worlds Clonclurry and Valvida. The rest was just weeds, grass, drainage ditches, and a few roads leading nowhere. A month ago, most buildings had flown the green and blue national flag, but since Merredin's team had been knocked out of the Cup halfway through the first round they'd all been taken down. Disheartened janitors had locked them away, muttering about *next time*.

The exploratory division base was laid out around its own wormhole, which was housed in a windowless concrete and steel building eight hundred metres long that ended in the spherical alien environment confinement chamber, a hundred metres in diameter, two thirds of which was above the ground. A little town of industrial-style buildings surrounded it, containing offices, laboratories, workshops, training facilities, and the xenobiology department. Power came from the nuclear plants on the coast.

Oscar's Merc 1001 coupé drove him through the main gate at seven forty-five and slid right into the Operations Director parking slot. He smiled at the few envious stares the car earned him from other members of the team as they pulled up outside the administration block. He doubted there were many, if any, others like it on Merredin. It was his one foible; changing the car once every twelve months (or less) for whatever the hottest new sports model was that year. This one had been imported specially from the Democratic Republic of New Germany, the Big15 planet where Mercedes had relocated its factories when it left Earth. He'd never decided, given his first-life background, if that consumerist extravagance was ironic, or if he was subconsciously distancing himself from that very same past. The only reason he hadn't wiped the memories entirely when he rejuvenated was so he could be on his guard against any kind of relapse into the stupid idealism which his younger self had embraced. These days he was a fully paid up member of the establishment, and finally at ease with himself and his role.

He made his way through the administration block and straight into wormhole control centre. The prime ground crew was already starting to assemble at the back of the big theatre-like room. He said his hellos and swapped a few jokes as he made his way down the sloping floor to his console at the front. The control centre had eight tiered rows of consoles looking towards the broad molecule-chain reinforced sapphire windows that made up the front wall. Beyond that was the alien environment confinement chamber; in its inactive state a spherical chamber fifty metres in diameter with dark radiation-absorptive walls. The wormhole gateway mechanism itself was directly opposite the windows, an oval fifteen metres wide, with a ramp leading up to it from the base of the chamber.

217

Ranged around the walls were various airlock doors. The ceiling had a bright polyphoto ring, which was currently illuminating the chamber by emitting the same spectrum as Merredin's sun. Around that were sealed recesses which contained a range of scientific and astronomical instruments. They had also undergone a major revamp during the down-time, and the prep crew had just finished testing them during the night.

Oscar sat at his console and told his e-butler to log him in with the centre's main array. His console portals lit up, delivering simplified schematics of the gateway, while his e-butler established voice linkages to every console operator as they slipped into their seats and logged in. As he acknowledged their inclusion in the communication loop, the prep crew chief came over and briefed him on the state of play. As the handover progressed, the prep crew left the room; several of them went into the observation gallery at the rear, jostling for seats with reporters, CST's local executives, and various VIPs who'd wangled an invitation.

By nine fifteen Oscar was satisfied that the wormhole generator was ready for an opening. He went round the loop one last time, personally checking with his station heads that they were equally satisfied with the situation: astrogration, power, focusing, main ancillary systems, sensors, short-range astronomy, confinement chamber management, emergency defence, forward crew, planetary science, alien encounter office, xenobiology, base camp equipment quartermaster, and finally the medical staff. One by one, they all gave him a green light. Finally, he checked with the Restricted Intelligence array which would handle integrated procedures. It said it was ready.

'Thank you, people,' he said. 'Chamber management, please take us to status one. Astrogration stand by. RI, I'd like the gateway brought to full activation readiness.'

The overhead polyphoto strips in the control centre began to dim, putting the room in a twilight glimmer. Holographic displays inside the console portals cast an iridescent glow over the faces of their operators. On the other side of the thick sapphire windows, the alien environment confinement chamber's big polyphoto ring also shed its intensity, sinking to a weak red radiance which barely illuminated the gateway oval.

'Internal force field activated,' chamber management said. 'All airlocks closed and sealed. Walls to neutral. Thermal shunts on line. We have status one.'

Oscar could just see the ramp in front of the gateway sinking back down into the chamber floor. He felt an electric tingle begin deep in his stomach. No matter how long the human race had been doing this, how far they'd travelled into the universe, opening a door onto the unknown was always an exciting risk. 'Astrogration, I want a wormhole destination on star AFR98–2B, five AUs galactic north from target.'

'Yes sir, loading now.'

He watched the RI portal display as it registered the coordinate lock. AFR98–2B was an F2 spectral-class star, twenty-seven light-years out from Merredin. CST's long-range examination from the orbiting telescope indicated the existence of a solar system of at least five planets. With the coordinate confirmed by astrogration, the RI took over the opening procedure, a vast program composite capable of handling the billion variable factors which governed the gateway machinery and power flow. Normally, software that powerful would swiftly evolve itself up to full SI status, but this one had been formatted by the SI with strategic limiters written in to prevent any outbreak of self-determination. Even though it incorporated genetic algorithms the RI was essentially stable, it would never develop alternative interests and goals in the middle of its operations as some large array software had done in the past, with often disastrous consequences.

Behind the window, the dull-silver rim of the oval gateway

began to flicker with dusky turquoise shadows. They quickly expanded to merge together, at which point focusing on them became immensely difficult for the human eye. They shifted constantly while staying in the same place. In the centre of the gateway, depth arrived with a giddy lurch. As always, Oscar got the impression he was abruptly hurtling forwards through an infinitely long tunnel. Not a bad interpretation for beleaguered human senses. He knew he was holding his breath just like any rookie console operator. But this was the moment of greatest reward, the reason he committed himself to his job with such passion, the reason he'd made it all the way up to Operations Director. Despite all the commercial and political crap that was CST, this was a new world they were searching for today. Chances were, the human settlers would make it just another poor clone of the majority society within the Commonwealth. But there was always the possibility it would be something new and inspiring. *It can't always be the same.*

The instability at the centre of the gateway mechanism stabilized and cleared, darkening immediately. Stars appeared amid the blackness. A beam of brilliant white light stabbed through the opening, angled so it struck the chamber to the left of the windows.

A few digits jumped on the digital displays, registering the small electromagnetic infall. 'Have we got a clear exit?' Oscar asked.

'Negative on gravity distortion sweep,' sensors said. 'There's no solid matter above particle-level within a million klicks of the opening.'

'Thank you. Chamber management, vent the chamber, please.'

A hole opened at the centre of the secondary force field covering the gateway, and slowly expanded back towards the rim. The chamber's atmosphere streaked out. It was visible at first, a thick jet of grey vapour playing across the starfield.

After a minute, and with the force field withdrawn, there was nothing left but a few glittering grains of ice slowly dispersing.

'Vacuum confirmed,' chamber management said.

'Sensors, deploy the star tracker,' Oscar ordered. 'Astronomy, tell us where we are, please.'

One of the recesses on the chamber ceiling silently irised open. A long tentacle-like arm of electromuscle uncoiled out of it, holding a two-metre metal bulb on the end. It was studded with small gold lenses. Oscar watched the arm slowly reach forwards, its careful sinuous motion pushing the star-tracker mechanism out through the open gateway and into space beyond. A standard camera on the collar of the star tracker sent its image up to one of the five big screens above the windows. An ordinary star was revealed, its small disk shining bright amid the constellations. To Oscar it looked about the right size for an F2 at five AUs. Nonetheless, he waited patiently as information flowed in from the star tracker. One of the main requirements of his job was to keep calm in all circumstances, hasty decisions were just as dangerous as hesitation. That was a trait he'd learned early in his first life, it just got misapplied back then.

'The spectrum matches AFR98–2B, sir,' short-range astronomy said. 'Acquiring marker stars and measuring emergence point location.'

Oscar could remember the first stellar exploration he'd worked on, decades ago back on Augusta; as one of the junior prep crew he'd stood in the observation gallery for nine hours after his shift ended at hand-over. Nine hours that passed in no time, the excitement he felt was so strong. It was the day he knew he'd made the right choice, that in some obscure way this was how he could make amends for what he'd done. This way he could bring the hope of a fresh start to other people's lives as well as his own.

'Confirming location of wormhole exit,' short-range

astronomy said. 'Distance to AFR98–2B is seventeen-point-three million klicks out from the projected coordinate.'

Oscar allowed himself to relax a little, seeing the smiles springing up around the ground crew. That wasn't a bad margin of error for a newly recommissioned gateway, well within acceptable limits. 'Well done astrogration; load in the new figures please. Sensors, let's get the planetary survey scope out there.'

While the new, bulkier telescope mechanism was deployed out through the confinement chamber, Oscar went round the control centre loop again, verifying that everything was holding steady. Then it was an hour-long wait while short-range astronomy analysed the images from the planetary survey scope. The procedure was simple enough – they scanned the plane of the ecliptic for any light source above first magnitude. When it found one, the telescope observed it for movement. If it was a planet, then its orbital motion should become apparent almost straight away.

The results flashed up on the screens above the window. Short-range astronomy located five planets. Two were gas-giants, Saturn-sized, orbiting eleven and fifteen AUs out from the star. The inner three were solids. The first and smallest, a Lunar-sized rock a hundred and twenty million kilometres out from the star, had a high-viscosity plastic lava mantle moving in sluggish ripples generated by the star's massive tidal pull. Second was a large-solid, seventeen thousand eight hundred kilometres in diameter, and orbiting a hundred and twelve million kilometres out. With its high gravity, Venusian-style atmosphere, and close proximity to the sun, it didn't come anywhere near qualifying as H-congruent. But the third was a hundred and ninety-nine million kilometres distant from the star, and measured fourteen thousand three hundred kilometres in diameter. Cheers and a patter of applause went round gateway control as the data slowly built up. Spectrographic results showed a standard oxygen-nitrogen atmosphere, with a high water vapour content. Given its distance from the star, it was somewhat cool, with the equator having the same temperature as Earth's temperate zones in autumn or spring. But the information was sufficient for Oscar to award it a preliminary H-congruent status, which brought another round of applause. First time out with a recommissioned gateway, and they'd struck gold already. A good omen.

'Sensors, let's get the dish out there,' Oscar said. 'Check for emissions.'

Another electromuscle arm snaked out from its ceiling recess, carrying a furled dish. It went through the gateway beside the planetary survey scope, and extended its metal mesh.

'No radio signals detected,' sensors reported.

'All right; bring both the arms back in,' Oscar said. 'Astrogration, move the wormhole exit to geosynchronous height above the third planet's daylight terminator.'

When the arms were back in their recesses, the starfield winked out. A moment later, the gateway opened again, revealing the crescent of a planet directly ahead. Its radiance washed across the confinement chamber and in through the windows. Oscar smiled in welcome as the soft light fell across his console. The cloud cover was above average, cloaking a good seventy per cent of the hemisphere. But he could see the blue of oceans, and the grubby red-brown of land, even the crisp white of polar caps was visible in that first glimpse.

'All right people, let's concentrate on the job,' Oscar said as excited conversation buzzed through the loop. 'We've all seen this before. Sensors, I want a full electromagnetic sweep. Launch seven geophysics satellites, get me some global coverage. Planetary science, you're on; preliminary survey results in three hours, please. Alien encounter office, start hunting. Emergency defence, you're on stand-by alert, and now have full wormhole shutdown authority; acknowledge that, please.'

'Acknowledged, sir.'

The launch rail telescoped out from its storage bay below the control centre windows, extending a good ten metres through the wormhole exit. Satellites accelerated down the rail, riding the magnetic pulses before whirling away along different trajectories. Once they'd fallen a kilometre from the gateway, their ion drives came on, pushing them into high-inclination orbits which would provide coverage of the planet's whole surface. As they went they each released a swarm of sub-satellites like golden butterflies, expanding their observation baseline. Tracking dishes were deployed to keep in contact. The big dish came out again, scouring the continents for any electromagnetic activity. A two-metre telescope peered down inquisitively.

Oscar sat back and had his first in situ break of the day. A trolleybot slid along the console rows, distributing drinks and snacks. He claimed a cheese and smoked bacon sandwich and a couple of bottles of natural mineral water. As he ate, the screens above the windows came alive with images from the satellites. Details were gradually sketched in by the data tables and graphics in the console portals.

The planet had five major continents, accounting for thirty-two per cent of the surface. Temperature was lower than strictly favourable, resulting in huge ice caps which between them covered a third of the planet. One and a half continents were completely buried beneath ice. That left a lot less usable land than average. The magnetic field was stronger than Earth's, which gave it a very large Van Allen radiation belt.

'There is no evidence of sentient life at this time,' alien encounter said. 'No large-scale structures, no electromagnetic activity, no visible cultivation, and no artificial thermal sources.'

'Thank you,' Oscar said. The last factor was the clincher for him. The ability to start and use fire was deemed the litmus test of sentience. If anything on the planet was capable of sentient thought, it was currently below Neanderthal-equivalent. 'Sensors, you can switch to active scanning now.'

Radar sweeps started to penetrate the pervasive cloud. The images on the big screens began to develop a lot quicker, with detailed layers building on the provisional outlines. Lasers swept through the atmosphere, plotting its composition. The RI manipulated the energy flow through the gateway mechanism, manufacturing tiny gravity wave distortions at the wormhole exit. They rippled through the planet's crust, allowing the satellites to determine its internal layout.

At fifteen hundred hours, Oscar called an intraloop conference with his station heads. So far, they agreed, the planet appeared to be hospitable. There was definitely no sign of an indigenous sentience. No animals above two metres in length had been spotted by the infrared sensors. Its geology was standard. Its biochemistry, as far as could be deduced from spectography, was an ordinary carbon-based multicelluar form.

'So is it aggressive or passive?' Oscar asked. The problem was common enough. On a colder world such as this, most life would be slow-growing; a trait which inclined towards a more passive animal nature. But there were cases where the opposite was true, and evolution had produced some very tough life forms geared for survival at all costs. 'Best guesses please.'

'The geology is stable,' planetary science said. 'The current bio-epoch is probably about eighty million years old if we're reading the stellar cycle right. We can't detect any previous ice ages, so there's been no sudden climate change to throw their evolution off kilter. Everything growing down there is stable and adjusted. I'd say passive.'

'I have to agree,' xenobiology said. 'We're seeing small movable thermal spots indicative of animals, but nothing larger than a dog. Certainly nothing we normally associate with carnivorous predators. Botany is also reasonably standard, though there are few large plants, and what pass for trees are solitary, they don't congregate in forests, which is unusual.'

'Very well.' Oscar swivelled his seat until he could see McClain Gilbert, the forward crew chief, sitting at the front of the observation gallery. 'Mac, I'm giving you an initial encounter authorization. Get your first contact team suited up.'

'Thank you, sir.' McClain Gilbert gave him a thumbs up from behind the glass.

Oscar switched back to the full loop. 'We're going for a ground encounter. Sensors, put the geophysics satellites to automatic, and withdraw all the arms. Astrogration, I want the exit moved to a five hundred kilometre equatorial altitude, then give it an orbital velocity. When we're established, launch the low orbit surveillance satellite fleet; I'll need constant coverage of the ground contact site. We're aiming for ground opening in one hour, people, get ready for that. Planetary sciences, find me a suitable dawn site at that time.'

With the exit positioned five hundred kilometres above the ground, the clouds below seemed a lot brighter. The small squadron of low orbit satellites shot off the launch rail, curving down to an even lower altitude and spreading out to form a chain around the planet's equator. Images from their high-rez cameras appeared on the screens, revealing a wealth of details. Stones a mere five centimetres across were visible amid the carpet of vermilion grass-equivalent. Squirrel-like rodents, with grey scales rather than fur, bounded about, scuttling into burrows and swimming along streams. All the small independent trees had peculiar zigzag branches.

'Confirming low orbit satellite fleet in position,' sensors reported. 'We have full coverage.'

'Coming up to dawn on the landing site,' planetary science said.

'Withdraw sensor arms,' Oscar said. 'Chamber management, establish a force field across the gateway. Astrogration, reposition the exit one kilometre above designated contact site, horizontal axis.'

The wormhole blinked, and they were looking down on a gently crumpled landscape of thin burgundy grass and twisted carmine bushes. A low dawn light was casting long gloomy shadows across the ground. Pools of dense mist clung to hollows and depressions with oily tenacity.

'Chamber management, equalize pressure. Sensors, deploy the atmospheric probe and exposure samples.'

The force field reconfigured itself to allow the sampler arm through. It didn't find any immediately lethal particles missed by the scans from orbit.

Oscar waited the designated hour for the exposure and micro-analysis processes to run. 'Xenobiology?' he asked eventually.

'Some spores – probably plant life. Small bacterial count in the water vapour. Nothing abnormal, and no adverse reactions to our sample materials.'

'Thank you.' It would take months of laboratory testing to discover if any of the microbial life was dangerous to humans. Until they were given the all clear, the forward crews would all be in suits anyway. It was the other biological reactions which worried Oscar; a century ago CST had opened a wormhole to a planet where the local fungus ate polymers. Quite how that evolved was still a puzzle for the xenobiologists. Now a whole spectrum of materials were exposed to the planet first. 'Astrogration, please take us down to the surface.'

The exit began to move, drifting downwards with the same sedate lack of urgency as any hot air balloon. Oscar could even guess the point that astrogration had chosen for contact. A flat patch of ground clear of any trees, with a stream three hundred metres away. Ground search radar confirmed the area was solid. At a hundred metres up, the oval exit began to rotate around its long axis, tilting to the vertical. A light blue sky slid into view, with wispy clouds high above the horizon, glowing pink in the rising sunlight. Astrogration halted the descent when the bottom rim was a couple of centimetres above the fluffy leaves of the cochineal-tinted grass-equivalent.

Oscar let out a breath as he watched the landscape for any sign of movement. If there were any Silfen on this world, now was the moment they appeared. Stupid lanky humanoids ambling up to the opening and waving gamely at all the ground crew behind their consoles. 'Welcome,' they sang in their own language. 'Welcome to a new world.' He'd seen it once himself, twelve years ago when he was chamber management station head on Augusta. There had been so much amusement in their smooth voices, laughter for the serious humans and their clunky machinery. He'd wanted to pick up a rock and throw it at the smug mystics.

But this time the chilly red and blue terrain was so still it could have been a painting. There were no Silfen here.

He wasn't the only one waiting, anticipating. A number of sighs were let out around the control centre.

Oscar went round the loop again, confirming every station was stable. 'Forward crew, initiate contact,' he said.

The floor of the confinement chamber rose up into a ramp. Airlock two irised open. McClain Gilbert and the four members of his first contact team were standing just inside. They wore their magenta insulation suits, a close-fitting onepiece with a flexible hood that clung to the skull; a broad transparent visor dominated the front. The backpack was slim, containing a lightweight air-recycling unit and the superconductor batteries for the force field armour they wore unseen underneath the fabric. It was a precaution against any newfound native animal who was hostile enough to try and find out what the invaders tasted like.

Cameras mounted on the side of their hoods relayed images to the big screens above the windows. A quick check showed Oscar that several hundred million people were accessing this moment through the unisphere. They would be exploration addicts, the stay-at-homes who couldn't get enough of alien worlds and the expanding human frontier.

'Out you go, Mac,' Oscar told the heroic-looking figures as they stood at the bottom of the ramp.

McClain Gilbert nodded briefly, and strode forward. The force field over the gateway exit slipped round him as he stepped through. His booted foot came down on the feathery leaves of the ground cover plant.

'I name this planet Chelva,' McClain Gilbert intoned solemnly, reading from CST's approved list. 'May those who come here find the life they search for.'

'Amen,' Oscar muttered quietly. 'Right, people, to work, please.'

Procedure meant they acquired immediate soil and plant samples which were quickly taken back through the gateway. Once that was done, the team began a more elaborate investigation of the area around the wormhole exit.

'The grass-equivalent is spongy,' McClain Gilbert said. 'Similar to moss but with much longer leaves, and they're kind of glossy, like a wax coating. From what I can see the ground next to the stream has a high shingle content. Looks like flint, same grey-brown colouration. Possibly good for fossils.'

The forward crew was heading towards the water. Streams, lakes, even seas, always provided a rich variety of native life.

'Okay, we have company,' McClain Gilbert announced.

Oscar glanced up from the console portals. The forward crew were about a hundred metres from the exit, he could only see three of them directly now, and two of them were pointing at something. His eyes flicked up to the screens. The small squirrel-rodent creatures had appeared; helmet-mounted cameras were following them as they hopped around on the flat rocks beside the stream. Now he could see them properly, his first equivalence naming was becoming more and more inaccurate. They were nothing like squirrels. A rounded conical body, thirty centimetres long, was covered in lead-grey scales, with a texture astonishingly similar to stone. There were three powerful limbs at the rear, one directly underneath the body, and two, slightly longer, on either side. Where they connected to the main body they were shaped like chicken thighs, except there was no mid-joint, the lower half was a simple pole. It was as if they walked on miniature stilts, which made their motions fast and jerky. The head was a giant snout, with segmented ring scales allowing it to bend in every direction. Its tip was a triple-pincer claw arranged around a mouth-inlet. Two thirds of the way along the snout, three black eyes were set deep into folds which creased the scales.

'Ugly-looking critters,' McClain Gilbert said. 'They seem, I don't know, primitive.'

'We think they're quite evolved,' xenobiology said. 'They obviously have a good sense of balance, and the limb arrangement provides a sophisticated locomotive ability.'

They didn't bound about, Oscar saw, it was more like a kangaroo jump. Watching them, he worried that the forward team were scaring them, they were never still. One of them darted forward, its pincers splashing into the water. When it brought its snout out, the claws were gripping a tuft of lavender foliage. They moved with incredible speed, shovelling the dripping morsel back into its mouth-inlet.

His virtual vision brought up an amber warning over a section of McClain Gilbert's insulation suit's telemetry. The cautions were repeated on the other forward crew. 'Mac, what are you standing on?'

In unison, the helmet camera images on the screens tipped down. The feathery grass was slowly curling over to embrace their boots. A thin mist was leaking out from the onion-shaped tips of every blade.

'Hell!' McClain Gilbert exclaimed. He quickly lifted one foot. The grass wasn't strong enough to stop him. Blisters and bubbles were erupting on the top of the boot. The rest of the crew shouted in alarm, and began to pull their own boots clear.

'That's some kind of acid,' planetary sciences said.

Oscar noticed all the creatures were hopping away from the humans at quite a speed.

'What sort of plant has acid for sap?' McClain Gilbert asked.

'Not a good one,' xenobiology said. 'Sir, I recommend bringing them back in.'

'I concur,' emergency defence said. 'If nothing else, we need to wash that acid off them before it eats through their soles.'

'I think they're right, Mac,' Oscar said. 'Get back into the environment chamber.'

'We're coming.'

'Xenobiology, talk to me,' Oscar said.

'Interesting. The plants didn't move until our team had been standing still for a little while, so I'm guessing they probably operate off a time/pressure trigger. I'm reminded of a Venus fly trap, except this is a lot more unpleasant, and the scale is larger. Any small animal that stops moving is likely to be trapped and dissolved.'

Oscar glanced back through the oval gateway. McClain Gilbert and his team had almost reached the rim. Behind them, there was no sign of the small not-squirrel creatures. 'Those native animals never stood still,' he murmured.

'No, sir,' xenobiology said. 'And their leg structure would be difficult for the grass to capture. I'd love to know what their scales are made of, it looked pretty tough. Anything that evolves here must be relatively acid resistant.'

'How widespread is this plant?' Oscar asked. 'And is the rest of the vegetation going to be similar?'

'The images we're getting from the low orbit satellites indicate a comprehensive ground plant coverage,' sensors said. 'If it's not this particular grass-equivalent, it's a close cousin.'

'Damn it,' Oscar hissed.

The forward crew hurried back into the alien environment confinement chamber. At the bottom of the ramp, decontamination shower cubicles had risen up out of the floor. They were designed to wash away spores or dangerous particles. But they'd be just as effective for this. The team members stood underneath the nozzles as the water jetted down.

'All right,' Oscar announced to everyone on the loop. 'Our priority is to establish how widespread this grass variety is, and if the other plants are related. Sensors, get a marque 8 samplebot out there. I want to check out the nearest trees, and there are a few other kind of plants in that grass stuff. Mac, go through a complete decontamination, and de-suit, I don't think we'll need you again today.'

Everyone in the control centre watched anxiously as the samplebot trundled out across the red grass. It stopped several times to snip sections of leaf from clumps of other plants, then headed for the nearest tree a hundred and fifty metres away. As it got closer, they could all see the jagged pattern of the branches as they forked at acute angles. There weren't many leaves, just a few slender beige triangles clumped round the end of each twig. Black kernels similar to walnuts dangled down from almost every joint on every branch.

The samplebot stopped a metre from the waxy trunk, and gingerly extended an electromuscle arm. Every kernel on that half of the tree popped simultaneously. A torrent of liquid showered down over the surrounding ground and the samplebot. Its casing began to dissolve immediately. Acid started to leak through and the telemetry ended.

Oscar put his head in his hands and groaned. 'Shit!'

*

By twenty-one hundred hours, they'd confirmed the planet's plants shared a common biochemistry. Oscar had moved the wormhole exit eight times to different regions, each one had subtle variants in the grass-equivalent, and no variance in their biochemical makeup.

He ordered the exit to be closed, and the gateway mechanism to be powered down to level two. It disheartened everyone, especially for a mission which had started so promisingly. Then there was the administration crap to deal with; the ground crew which was scheduled to take over exploration from prime had to be switched to a prep crew; everybody faced a mountain of reports to file.

The door of control centre closed behind Oscar. 'Another day, another star,' he murmured to himself. He was tired, disappointed, hungry. No way was he going to start in on the administration tonight. He told his e-butler to have the maid-bots start a decent meal and open some wine to breathe. By the time he got home it should be ready.

Just as he started walking down the corridor, a number of people came out of the observation gallery door ahead of him. Dermet Shalar was there, the CST Merredin station director, and the last person Oscar wanted to see right now. He hesitated, putting his head down, hoping Dermet wouldn't notice.

'Oscar.'

'Ah, good evening, sir. Not a good day, I'm afraid.'

'No, indeed not. Still, astronomy has a huge list of possible targets. It's not as if we're short of new worlds.'

Oscar stopped listening to his boss; he'd just recognized the young-looking man in the expensive suit standing beside him. 'Have you been watching today's operation?'

'Yes,' Wilson Kime said. 'I remember that kind of disappointment myself.'

'I'm sure you do.'

'But I was impressed by the way you ran things in there.'

'I see.' Which was a dumb thing to say, but Oscar knew there were very few reasons for Kime to be here today. His fatigue suddenly vanished under a deluge of adrenaline. To be head-hunted for *this* CST exploration mission was the ultimate compliment.

As if he was mind-reading, Wilson smiled. 'I need somebody like you as my executive officer. Interested?'

Oscar glanced at Dermet Shalar, who kept his face carefully neutral. 'Of course.'

'Good. It's yours if you want it.'

'I want it.'

*

Two days later Oscar arrived at the Anshun starship project complex. He was given an office next to Wilson on the top floor in one of the three central glass towers, complete with a staff of three. Starting with their first official meeting that morning, he and Wilson had to put the crew selection problem at the top of the agenda. It was a hint of what was to come. Nigel Sheldon hadn't been joking about the number of requests to join the mission. Tens of millions of people from all over the Commonwealth, endorsed by their government or some venerable respected institution, were hammering against CST's filter programs for a berth on the starship. Right from the beginning, they decided on a policy of filling the science posts from the CST exploratory division wherever possible. The general crew would also be assigned on a similar basis. Exceptions would be made for outstanding achievers. Both of them acknowledged that would work out as geniuses with political clout.

'Anybody you owe a big favour?' Wilson asked. 'We might as well get that out of the way to start with.'

'I'm sure there'll be a whole bunch of people from this life and my first are suddenly going to remember that five dollars they lent me. Just about everyone at the Merredin station managed to bump into me before I left to tell me how terrific they are. All I can say is, McClain Gilbert is the best forward crew leader I've worked with.'

'You want him for that duty on the *Second Chance*?'

Oscar took a moment. 'It's that easy?'

'We have to start somewhere, and we have to have some rationale for selection. After all, it's how I chose you. I asked Sheldon who his best Operations Director was.'

Oscar had guessed it had been something like that: but who didn't like hearing it first hand? 'Okay then, I'd like Mac. What about you? Do you have any preferences for the crew?'

'There're fifty management types from Farndale I'd like to bring onto the construction side of the project to smooth out the current schedule, and I'll probably do that. But as for anyone familiar with this kind of mission, no, not any more.' They'd managed to track down two others from *Ulysses*. Nancy Kressmire, who had never left Earth again, nor had she abandoned public service; she was now the Ecological Commissioner for North-West Asia, and hugely committed to the job – after all, she'd held it for a hundred and fifty-eight years. She'd said: 'No,' as soon as he placed a call, not even waiting to say hello, or ask why he was calling after all these centuries.

'Are you sure?' Wilson had inquired.

'I can't leave, Wilson. There's so much here on this good Earth we still have to put right. How can we face aliens before we've cured the ills which beset our own people? Our moral obligation is clear.'

He didn't argue, though there was much he wanted to say to her, and all her crusading kind for that matter. The Earth which the ultra-conservative Greens wanted had never existed in the past, it was an idealized dream of what Eden might be. Something not too dissimilar to York5, he thought to himself.

The only other old crew member Sheldon's staff had located was Jane Orchiston. Wilson took one look at her file, and didn't even bother placing that call. Call it prejudice or intuition – he didn't really care which. He just knew it would be a waste of time. Two centuries ago, Orchiston had moved to Felicity, the women-only planet. Since then she'd been enthusiastically giving birth to daughters at the rate of almost one every three years.

All in all, he reflected, it wasn't an outstanding record for a crew that was supposed to represent the best of humanity at that time. Three known survivors out of thirty-eight; one plutocrat, one bureaucrat, and one earth-mother.

The second half of the meeting was scheduled as a unisphere conference with James Timothy Halgarth, the director of the Research Institute on Far Away. 'I'll be interested in your opinion on what he has to say about the *Marie Celeste* and its crew,' Wilson told Oscar. 'Tracking down alien knowledge is an aspect of our mission which I'm going to delegate to you.'

'You think it's that important?'

'Yeah, we need to know what they know. Or don't know. I'm determined that we cover every angle of approach on the Dyson Pair envelopment, not just the physical voyage. I was in training for the Mars mission for damn near a decade. I wound up knowing more than any college professor about its geology, its features, the geography, and even the books people had written on it – fact and fiction. Everything. I knew the myths as well as the truths. Just in case. We were ready for anything, any eventuality. And a fat lot of good that did us in the end.'

'Sheldon and Ozzie weren't anything to do with Mars.'

Wilson grinned. 'My point exactly. So . . . after this, fix up to see the Commonwealth xenocultural experts talking to the Silfen. Get out to the High Angel. Interview a Raiel. I simply don't believe that all of our so-called allies know nothing about the Dyson Pair. Most of them have been around for a hell of a lot longer than us, certainly they all had starflight when it happened.'

'Why would they hold out on us?'

'God knows. But then there's a great deal about this which doesn't seem logical.'

'All right, I'll add it to my list.'

Wilson's e-butler announced that the wormhole connecting Half Way to Far Away had begun the ten-hour active phase of its cycle. The unisphere established a link to the small data-network in Armstrong City. From there, a solitary landline carried the call to the Institute.

The big portal at the far end of Wilson's study fizzed with multicoloured static, which cleared to show Director James Timothy Halgarth sitting behind his desk, a fourth-generation member of the family which founded EdenBurg, which gave him a reasonable level of seniority within the dynasty.

He wore a simple pale blue suit of semi-organic fabric which stretched and contracted around his limbs whenever he moved, giving him unrestricted movement. His apparent age was mid-thirties, though he was completely bald, an unusual style in the Commonwealth. Small OCtattoos shimmered platinum and emerald on his cheeks.

'Captain Kime, finally,' the Director said with obvious enthusiasm. 'I apologize for the delay in enabling this conference. The Guardians of Selfhood are annoyingly tenacious in their attacks on our landline. The current repairs were only completed three hours ago. No doubt we shall suffer our next cut within a few days.'

'I'm sorry to hear that,' Wilson said. 'Wouldn't you be better off with a satellite relay?'

'We used to have one. The Guardians shot it down, and its three replacements. It's actually more cost-effective to have a landline and keep a repair crew permanently on the payroll. Fibre optic cable is very cheap.'

'I didn't realize the civil situation was quite so bad on Far Away.'

'Generally, it's not. We're the only ones suffering from assaults by the Guardians. They are deplorably xenophobic, not to mention violent.'

'I'm not too well briefed on their objectives; I never did pay much attention to conspiracy theories before. They think you're helping an alien survivor from the arkship, don't they?'

'Actually, they believe we transported the Starflyer into the Commonwealth. But that's the general thrust of their argument, yes.'

'I see. They have been releasing a great deal of propaganda about how the Starflyer arranged for the whole *Second Chance* mission. What I really need to know, from the horse's mouth as it were, is if it is in any way possible the *Marie Celeste* did come from the Dyson Pair. Does it have that kind of flight range?'

'In theory, yes. Once the ship accelerates to its flight velocity of decimal seven two lightspeed, its range is limited only by the amount of fuel it carries to power the force field generators, and indeed the lifetime of the generators themselves. However, our research determined that the actual flight time was five hundred and twenty years. The arkship didn't come from, or even pass by the Dyson Pair. It came from somewhere closer.'

'That could be a planet which didn't have the kind of protective barrier the Dyson Pair possessed,' Oscar said. 'They couldn't defend themselves against whatever was threatening the Dyson aliens, so they left?'

'We can speculate on its origin and the reason for the flight as much as you like,' the Director said. 'As we don't yet know which star the arkship came from, we can hardly determine the reason for the flight. It could have originated from inside Commonwealth space for all we know.'

'What about if the *Marie Celeste* species was the reason for the enclosure?' Wilson asked.

'I'm sorry,' the Director said. 'I don't follow your reasoning.'

'If more than one arkship set off from its origin star, the civilization at the Dyson Pair could be defending themselves from the arkship aliens. After all, look what the *Marie Celeste* did to Far Away's star when they arrived there.'

'Ah, the mega-flare. Yes, I suppose that's a valid argument, although I don't see why the barriers would remain on for such a long time. But we do believe that the sterilization of Far Away was an unfortunate side effect. The flare was only triggered to act as the power-source for the message.'

'That's one hell of a side effect.'

'You have to take the alien viewpoint, and presumably ethics. They triggered the flare to communicate across the entire galaxy. Whatever machine manipulated the star into flaring then went on to modify the emission into a coherent radio signal powerful enough to be detected out at the Magellanic Clouds. We humans certainly picked it up easily enough, you barely needed a dish when the signal reached Damaran, let alone the SETI scanners they were using back then.'

'But nobody knows what they were saying,' Wilson observed. 'We've had a hundred and eighty years to decode the signal, and I'm not aware of any breakthrough yet. They must have been broadcasting back to their own home planet.'

'That's certainly one theory proposed by the Institute, Captain. We have a hundred more if you have the time to listen. All we can do is work through the wreckage and try to put together as many pieces of the puzzle as possible. One day we shall have our answers. Regrettably, it won't be in the near future.'

'You must have some idea where they came from,' Oscar said. 'If they travelled at point seven lightspeed for five hundred years that gives you an origin point roughly three hundred and fifty light-years from Far Away. Surely you can match a star to the light spectrum in the ship's life support section?'

'That would be difficult, Mr Monroe, the tanks had a multispectrum illumination source. They weren't trying to match their home star's emission.'

'Tanks?'

The Director's face displayed mild disappointment. 'There was no planetary surface environment replicated inside the *Marie Celeste*. The starship carried tanks. As far as we can tell from the residue, they were filled with water and a type of monocellular algae.'

'It was an aquatic species?' Oscar was fascinated. He'd never done any research into the arkship. Far Away had been on the list of worlds he wanted to visit in his sabbatical life.

'Again, that is one theory,' James Halgarth said. 'There were no remnants of advanced creatures in the tanks, and we have never identified any such species in Far Away's ocean. Another theory is that the *Marie Celeste* is actually an automated seedship. It was programmed to sterilize whatever habitable world it found, and seed it with genetic samples from its own world ready for its builders to colonize once the alienforming was complete.'

'Another good reason to throw up a barrier,' Wilson said.

'I doubt it, Captain. Firstly, if you have the technology to erect the kind of barrier found at the Dyson Pair, then you certainly have the capability to deactivate a robot ship before it begins its in-system mission. Secondly, it is a dreadfully flawed method of interstellar colonization. The resources spent on constructing such a ship are enormous; and it didn't work. The flare killed off most but not all of Far Away's native life. Yet no trace has been found of any non-native life. And if this is one of a fleet, then where are all the other flares which have announced sterilization has begun by the rest of the ships? Thirdly, if you are a space-faring civilization intent on spreading out of your own solar system, then you will be constantly improving your technology. Whether you will develop faster-than-light travel is questionable. But certainly better ships than the *Marie Celeste* can be built, and the second wave would overtake the first and travel further. Why haven't we seen any other ships from the species which launched the *Marie Celeste*? I'm afraid, gentlemen, that we are presented with a unique puzzle with Far Away and its landing site. It is as the saying goes: a mystery wrapped in an enigma. But I must conclude, it has nothing to do with the Dyson Pair.'

'I'm sure this is in your reports,' Oscar said. 'But what about the on-board electronics? You must have salvaged some programs, surely?'

'No. The processors left installed are fairly standard, using a basic gate principle like ours, though some of the chemistry involved is different from anything we employ. However the core control array is missing, salvaged or removed.'

'Before or after the crash landing?'

'After. It wasn't so much a crash landing as a heavy landing. The arkship's systems were working at the time, otherwise it would have been a true crash and all we'd have to examine would be a very deep crater. The official Institute history is that the flare was successful in calling another ship and a rescue mission picked up the survivors. That certainly fits all the known facts. Anything else is pure conspiracy theory.'

'You mentioned technology levels,' Wilson said. 'Is the *Marie Celeste* a product of a technology more advanced than ours?'

'By definition, we are more advanced because we have wormhole generators. However that is now. By our best estimate, the *Marie Celeste* was launched around AD 1300, at that time we had barely begun the Renaissance.'

'I see what you mean. Even if they only had half of our technological progression rate, they should have the same kind of pathways the Silfen use by now.'

'Exactly.'

'What about now, though? Is what we have now equivalent to the *Marie Celeste*?'

'The easiest answer is equivalent but different. We could

undoubtedly build a more sophisticated slower-than-light starship. Obviously they didn't have our wormhole capability, but then we don't know how they flared the star.'

Wilson remembered several meetings he'd had with Commonwealth security chiefs, so senior the general public didn't even know their Directorates existed. They'd been very eager to examine the possibility of the *Marie Celeste*'s 'flare bomb'. Farndale's military researchers thought it might be some kind of unstable quantum field effect that disrupted the star's surface, like dropping a depth charge into the ocean. Aside from theoretical studies, nothing had ever been done, certainly not at a hardware level. Of course, he didn't know what other companies might have developed. It might be worth a quiet word with Nigel Sheldon. 'Aren't you even looking into it?'

'There's nothing to look into, Captain. We have classified every single component on board the arkship, and identified their use. Whatever triggered the flare is not here. Presumably, if there was more than one, the others were evacuated along with the crew and the control array. After all, it's not the kind of thing a responsible species would leave lying around.'

'Good point. What I was trying to determine through the flare technology is if the *Marie Celeste* builders had the ability to throw up the Dyson barrier.'

'No, they didn't have that ability. The Dyson Pair barriers pre-date the arkship. We are dealing with yet another unidentified alien species, perhaps two if the wilder ideas about the barrier's defensive nature are true. I wish you luck in your encounter.'

'Thank you.'

'While we are in contact, I'd be very glad to offer sabbatical leave to any of the Institute's researchers who you'd care to have on your crew. The experts we have here are quite formidable, both in terms of expertise and capability, many of them are advanced, like myself.'

'That's a very generous offer, Mr Director. We're about to

issue our requirements for the *Second Chance*, and I'm sure your personnel will match up.'

'Very well then.' His hand was raised in a small wave as the image disappeared from the portal.

Oscar pulled a face. 'So that takes the *Marie Celeste* aliens out of the equation.'

'Looks like it, not that I ever believed the Guardians, but it's useful ammunition for the next media interview.'

*

Although it was officially summer, the winds from the west had been bringing rain clouds in from the ocean for over three weeks. Leonida City suffered thunderstorms and flash floods in most of the parks. Even today, the sky was blocked by lustreless grey clouds whose constant drizzle was falling on the lightweight plastic awning which had been set up over the podium. As he looked out across the audience sitting on the lawn of the university's botanical garden, Dudley Bose didn't even see the dull glimmer of moisture clinging to their suits and fanciful summer hats. He was too wrapped up in his own sense of awe and delight to pay attention to anything as mundane as the weather.

The dean also seemed immune to the suffering before him, as his speech rambled on and on. Sitting just behind him, Gralmond's Vice President was trying to keep a civil expression on her face. Eventually, the dean finished complimenting the university under his own leadership, and gestured to Dudley Bose.

Making his way to the lectern, Dudley had a sudden bout of nerves as the event hit home. He caught sight of Wendy, his wife, sitting tall in the front row, applauding loudly. Ranged beside her were his students; one of them let out a piercing whistle, while the other two were laughing as though this was the biggest joke in the world. *Typical*, he thought. But the sight of them allowed him to carry on with renewed conviction.

Dudley stepped up to the dean, who solemnly handed over the scroll of parchment which signified his appointment to full professorship. The applause peaked, and Dudley smiled down happily at his damp audience, and absolutely *did not* scratch the OCtattoo on his ear – Wendy had been very specific about that. He said his standard, trite thank yous and added how privileged he was to be a part of an academic institution as grand as this university, made one little point about how government should always support pure science (a thoughtful nod of agreement from the Vice President behind him), and finished up by saying: 'I now hope to build upon the discovery which Gralmond has made possible by representing this planet as a crew member on the *Second Chance*. By contributing our planet's expertise and unique experience we may finally unravel the mystery which has haunted our species for the last two hundred years. All I can say is that I will do my best not to let you down. Thank you very much.'

The applause which greeted the end of the speech was warmer and louder than he'd been expecting. As he turned, the Vice President rose and shook him by the hand. 'I'll certainly do what I can to get you on that ship,' she murmured.

Dudley sat down and smiled oafishly through her speech about the long-term grant her administration was utterly delighted to be awarding the university's newly enlarged astronomy department. He'd been agitating for a berth on the *Second Chance* from the moment he'd heard of the mission. In every unisphere interview, and there were many, he'd told the reporters how he deserved to be on it, how his contribution couldn't possibly be overlooked, how his exclusive knowledge on the subject made him indispensable. He'd done the same to every politician he'd met, every industrialist, every high society member he'd encountered at the hundred cocktail parties and dinners he'd received invitations to since the discovery. His lobbying had been relentless. The envelopment observation had given him a security he'd never known before, with the awarding of his professorship and sudden rush of money into *his* department. Success, he'd found, had a delectable taste. He wanted more, and the starship was the way to get it. There would be no limit to what he could achieve when he returned triumphant from the distant Dyson Pair.

As soon as the Vice President finished her announcement the audience broke for the reception in the main hall where canapés and wine were being served. Several local companies had helped fund the day, which allowed the bursar to bring in outside caterers, elevating the usual standard of university parties.

Wendy Bose snagged a glass of rosé from one of the young waiters and looked round to see where Dudley had got to. It was a day of conflicting emotions for her. The relief she felt at seeing him finally get his professorship was profound, it secured both their futures. Already, at the city planning office where she worked, her own promotion had finally gone through; her R&R pension was safe and sound, in another eleven years she could go for a rejuvenation. A decent one this time, she thought. Over the last few years she'd been very conscious of her hips getting heavy again. Just at the wrong time. Dudley was clocking up a lot of inquiries from companies, there had even been mention of non-executive directorships. Gossip around the university common room said he was now a contender for the dean's job in a few years' time. She needed to look good, fit the part of capable supportive wife. When she'd married him, she hadn't expected anything like this level of professional and personal success, just a quiet life spent pleasantly on the fringe of the capital's social and governmental circles. Now, Dudley's fame was changing all that. So far they'd faced it together, but she was only too aware of the strength of their marriage. It was another of those perfectly amicable unions that was intended to last maybe a couple of decades, a standard anodyne to the loneliness of mediocre achievers right across the Commonwealth. As such it could trundle along contentedly so long as nothing too momentous affected it. And here he was, the most famous astronomer in the Commonwealth, right in the middle of a campus of beautiful young girls, and being courted by companies with serious money.

'Mrs Bose?'

Wendy turned to find a very tall man smiling inquisitively at her. His apparent age was late-thirties, though she knew he was a lot older than that, several lifetimes at least. She'd rarely seen someone so self-confident. He had blond hair which verged on silver, and eyes that were so dark it was hard to see where the iris began. Combined with a small nose and delicate prominent cheeks, he was striking rather than handsome, certainly memorable.

'That's me,' she smiled, slightly edgy, knowing people like this didn't usually single her out – for whatever reason.

'I'm with Earle News,' he held up a small card with golden wings in the middle. 'I was wondering if I could have a few moments with you, please.'

'Oh, of course,' Wendy automatically slipped into good corporate wife mode – she'd had enough practice recently. 'It's a very proud day for me, Dudley's achievement means so much, not just to the university but to Gralmond itself.'

'Absolutely. It's certainly put you on the map. I had to look up which section of space Gralmond was in, and I've been to a lot of worlds. My brief is a roving one.'

'Really, that must be very interesting, Mr . . .'

'Oh, that's: Brad, please.'

'Okay, Brad.' She smiled at him over the rim of her drink.

'One thing I was curious about when I researched the university, it has just about the smallest astronomy department anywhere. Was it your husband who started it?'

'Oh no, that was Dr Marance, he was one of the founders

of the university; his actual discipline was astrophysics. The astronomy department was set up under his wing, apparently he was quite a dynamic character, hard to say no to. He believed astronomy was an essential component to classifying the universe, so there wasn't much opposition to setting up the observatory. Then he left for rejuvenation, and Dudley got the appointment to carry on running the department. It's been a bit of a struggle, to be honest; astronomy was still part of the physics department. It hasn't really been independent until today.' She took a sip of the rosé. 'Big day.'

'I see. But it still managed to attract funding after Dr Marance left, enough funding to keep it going independently.'

'Well there are all sorts of sources you can apply to: government and educational foundations. It was a constant struggle for Dudley to secure the budget every year, but he's most tenacious, and a very capable administrator. Thankfully. He managed to keep going against quite a few odds. And, well, look at the result.'

'Quite. So it really is a case of the small noble man against the universe.'

'I wouldn't put it exactly like that. Nobody was opposing him, it's just that astronomy isn't the most highly valued discipline these days. That's all changing, now, of course. We've had over eight thousand applicants to study with Dudley in the next academic year.'

'I take it you won't be able to accommodate them all?'

'Unfortunately not. It's going to take some time to build the department up to Commonwealth-class standards. And, of course, Dudley may well be involved in the *Second Chance* mission.'

'Really?'

'He ought to be,' she said emphatically. 'He was the discoverer, after all. He's devoted years of his life to the Dyson Pair, that dedication has made him the Commonwealth's premier expert on the subject. It would be very strange if they didn't take him along as part of the science team, now wouldn't it?'

'I suppose so. Has Captain Kime asked him to join the crew?'

'Not yet.'

'Like you say, I'm sure it's just a matter of time. But I'm more interested in his history, and that of the astronomy department here at the university. I'm sure you're being modest, but it really does sound like an epic battle; the fight for recognition, the fight for money, year after year. That provides quite an insight into your husband's personality.'

'I'm very proud of him.'

'Can you tell me who some of the supporters were in the past? For example, which educational trusts provided money or resources?'

'Ah, well there was the Frankton First Advancement, the St James Outlook Fund, the Kingsford Pure Research Enablement Foundation, BG Enterprise, they all made most generous contributions; but the largest single donation came from the Cox Educational charity, that's based on Earth.'

'An Earth charity supporting work out here, that's quite remarkable.'

'They support a lot of basic scientific groundwork in Universities across the Commonwealth, I believe.'

'So how long have the Cox Commissioners been supporters of your husband's department?'

'Eleven years now, ever since we arrived here.'

'What are they like?'

'Who?'

'The Charity commissioners.'

'I don't know. The contact was made over the unisphere. They've never actually visited. We are one of thousands of projects they support.'

'They didn't even come today?'

'No, I'm afraid not. As you say, it's a long way for a glass of wine and a canapé.'

'Okay, so what made Professor Bose choose the Dyson Pair as his observation target?'

'Distance. Gralmond was in the right place to observe the envelopment. Not that we expected one as dramatic as this.'

'Did he choose Gralmond because of that? Was he interested in the Dyson Pair before?'

'Not especially, no. After all, Dudley is a pure astronomer, and the envelopment for all it's an astounding event, isn't natural.'

'He only started the observation after you arrived, then?'

'Yes.'

'What did the university say about that proposal?'

'They didn't say anything, it's up to Dudley to decide the astronomy department's objectives.'

'And the foundations, they didn't object? They are mostly pure science institutions, aren't they?'

'Brad, are you trying to find a scandal?'

'Oh, good heavens, no. I haven't worked for a good old muck-raking tabloid show like Baron's in decades. I just want the history, that's all. To tell a story properly, you need background; it doesn't necessarily all get included, but those details have to be there to add authority. I'm sorry, I'm lecturing, I've been doing my job for a long time.'

'That wasn't a lecture. If you'd lived with Dudley for any length of time, you'd know what a lecture is.' *Damn. Did that sound bitter?*

'I'm sure. So, the foundations and their funding?'

'They were supportive, especially the Cox. In fact, I think the Dyson Pair observation was written into the endowment contract, they wanted to make sure it was seen through to its conclusion.'

'Did they now?'

Just for a second, Wendy saw a flash of triumph on his

slender face. It was rather unnerving, she'd thought him more controlled than that, a long-lived sophisticate. 'Is that important?' she asked.

'Not at all,' he said with an urbane smile, much more in character. He leant forward slightly, taking her into his mischievous confidence. 'Now tell me, just how is the dean handling all this? One of his professors becoming the most famous academic in the Commonwealth must be a bit of a shock.'

Wendy gave her glass a demure glance. 'I couldn't possibly say.'

'Ah, well, you can't say I didn't try. I must thank you for sparing so much of your time on this day.'

'That's it?'

'Yes.' He inclined his head politely, then raised a finger. 'One thing: when you see Paula, please tell her from me to stop concentrating on the details, it's the big picture that counts.'

'I don't understand, I don't know anyone called Paula.'

He grinned. 'You will.' And with that he slipped away through the crowd, leaving her staring after him, bemused, if not somewhat irritated, by his ridiculously cryptic message.

*

Two hours into the reception, Dudley's e-butler told him the police were calling him. 'You're not serious,' he told it.

'I'm afraid so. There are two patrol cars at the house. A neighbour reported someone leaving.'

'Well what does the house array say?'

'The house array seems to be off line.'

'Goddamn it.'

'Will you be coming? The police did emphasize it is important.'

'Yes, yes!'

So he had to break away from the chairman of Orpheus Island, who had been suggesting a serious sponsorship arrangement for some of the observatory equipment – possibly extending to the *Second Chance* – give up his wine glass to a rather pretty waitress, who knew his name and smiled, then walk round the hall trying to find Wendy. It didn't help that she was also moving round trying to find him. They both decided not to say their goodbyes to the dean.

The Carlton drove them back home. Slumped down in his seat, Dudley realized how drunk he was. But the wine had been good, and the catering staff kept filling his glass. Wendy gave him a disapproving look as he climbed out of the car using extreme caution.

Constable Brampton was waiting for them beside the front door of their two-storey home. Like all the others on the housing estate, it was local wood pinned to a carbonsteel frame, and painted a deep green. The windows were white, with the glass turned up to full opacity. The policeman saluted casually as they approached. 'Doesn't seem to be any damage,' he said. 'But we'll need you to take a look round and see if anything's missing.'

Wendy gave the open door a curious glance. 'You're sure they've gone?'

'Yes ma'am. We've checked it out thoroughly. Nobody inside apart from us.' He gestured with an open hand.

Dudley couldn't see any obvious signs of a burglary. No broken objects, furniture exactly where it always was. The only thing wrong was the lack of response from the house array. 'What happened?' he asked.

'Your neighbour reported someone leaving by the front door. They got into a car parked just down the street and drove off. He knew you were at a function at the university, so he called us.'

'My husband was getting his professorship,' Wendy said.

'Yes ma'am,' Constable Brampton said. 'I know that. Congratulations, sir, you deserve it. What you did put old Gralmond right on the map.'

Wendy frowned. That was the second time she'd heard that phrase today.

Dudley gave the front door an annoyed look, it was properly wired, the insurance company had insisted on that. And the house array had excellent security routines. 'How did they get in?'

'We're not sure. Somebody who knew what they were doing. Bypassed all your electronics, takes a smart person to do that. Or someone with a smart program.'

They went into Dudley's study. He felt as if he should apologize for the mess. There were books and glossy printouts everywhere, pieces of old equipment, a window almost invisible behind the rampant potted plants. Two forensic officers were examining the desk and its open drawer. The house array was inside, a simple housing box with junction sockets connecting it to more fibre optic cables than the performance spec really permitted. He'd been meaning to upgrade for a while.

'They dumped your memory,' the senior forensics officer said. 'That's why the array's down.'

'Dumped it?'

'Yeah. Everything, management programs, files, the lot. They've all gone. Presumably into the burglar's own memory store. I hope you kept back-ups?'

'Yeah.' Dudley looked round the study, scratching at the OCtattoo on his ear. 'Most of it, anyway. I mean, it's only a house array.'

'Was there anything valuable on it, sir? I mean, your work, and everything?'

'Some of my work was there, but I wouldn't call it valuable. Astronomy isn't a secretive profession.'

'Hum, well, it might be an attempted blackmail, someone looking for something incriminating. You'd be surprised what stays in an array's transit memory cache, stuff from years ago. Whoever they are, they've got all that now.'

'I don't have anything incriminating to keep. I mean, bills paid late, some traffic tickets when I was driving on manual – who doesn't?'

'Nonetheless, sir, you are in the public eye now. It might be an idea to think about extra security, and you certainly ought to change all your access patterns after this.'

'Of course, yes.'

'We'll notify the local patrol car,' Constable Brampton said. 'They'll include you on their watch detail in future.'

'Thank you.'

'You're sure there's nothing else missing?'

'No. I can't see anything.'

'We'll sweep for DNA fragments, of course, and try and trace the car. But it looks like a professional job. Chances are, if there's nothing to worry about in the array memory, then there won't be any follow-up.'

8

After the Commonwealth ExoProtectorate Council finished with its unanimous vote to send a starship to the Dyson Pair, Ozzie Fernandez Isaacs excused himself and took the elevator down to the lobby. Outside, it was warm for spring, with just some slim banks of dirty snow lingering in the gutters where the civicservicebots had pushed it. He started down Fifth Avenue, one of a handful of people to be using the broad sidewalk, the time of day and time of year were against pedestrians. There were none of the street vendors he could remember from even a couple of centuries ago; the burger and coke stands on every intersection, T-shirt sellers, stalls with quasi-legal software fixes, sensepimps with pornomemories. That would be too untidy now, too low down for the city and its cultured inhabitants. These days quaint booths and boutiques occupied the ground floor of all the skyscrapers, with quirky objects imported from every planet in the Commonwealth – all so strangely unappealing. It was all a sad decline, as far as Ozzie was concerned. You couldn't sanitize a great city like New York without losing its original quality, the dynamism and grubby edges which made it an exciting vibrant place to live. Despite the buildings, which still impressed him, it was becoming just another suburb of Earth. Its manufacturing industry had long since moved off-planet, leaving just the research and design consortiums that remained on the cutting edge, staffed by billionaire partners. The advertising agencies remained along with media company headquarters; there were even some artists down in SoHo, though Ozzie regarded them as talentless dinosaurs. It was the finance sector and government offices who dominated the employment market, for those who had to work. Many didn't, having their idle lives taken care of by the innumerable supply and service companies that encircled Manhattan Island, all employing offworlders on medium-term visas.

Visits like this reminded Ozzie why he so rarely came back to the world of his birth these days. When he looked up, there was a jagged strip of cool-steel sky a long way above him, pushed away by the grand towers. Even in midsummer, the sun was a near-stranger to the ground in this part of town, while today the trees and shrubs planted in the expensive plazas all had artificial lighting to help them grow.

Glancing down the impressive vertical canyon at one of the intersections, he saw the ancient Chrysler building secure inside its protective glass cage, shielded from the elements. 'And which of us is going to outlast the other?' he asked it quietly.

The cars and cabs and trucks were sliding past him on the road, their axle motors making almost no noise at all. People in thick coats or black-tinted organic filament ponchos hurried past, not even looking at him. They were almost all adults. As far as he could see up and down Fifth Avenue, there were no more than three or four kids under ten years old. That was what he missed most of all; and Earth's birth rate was still declining year after year as the rich eternal sophisticates that populated the planet found other things to spend their time and money on.

There was nothing for him here any more, he decided morosely, nothing of interest, nothing of value. He stepped back towards the base of the nearest tower and told his e-butler to give him a link to his home's RI. Once the RI was on line he gave it his exact coordinate. A circular wormhole opened behind him, expanding out to two metres in diameter, and he took a step backwards through the neutral grey curtain of the force field. The wormhole closed.

Ozzie didn't have a whole network of private secret wormholes linking the Commonwealth planets. He had precisely two wormholes; one standard CST micro-width connector to give his home a hyper-bandwidth link to the unisphere via Augusta's cybersphere; and one highly modified version of the wormhole generator which CST's exploratory division used, which provided him with independent transport around a good section of the Commonwealth. Nor did he live by himself on an H-congruous planet. His home was a hollowed-out asteroid that drifted along its long elliptical orbit around the Leo Twins.

As he walked through the gateway he was immediately enveloped by bright, warm light. The gateway mechanism had been built into a broad granite cliff with a wide awning of white canvas overhead, like a yacht sail that had been commandeered as a marquee roof. He stepped out from underneath it, and his domain stretched out before him.

The cavity, which automated diggers, CST civil engineering crews, and an army of various bots had excavated, was close to eighty miles long, and fifteen in diameter; the greatest enclosed space the human race had ever constructed. Its geography was a rugged undulation of hills and dales, broken by the silver veins of streams. A single range of huge rockblade mountains spiralled down the entire length, the tallest pinnacles a mile and a half high, raw purple and grey rock capped with dazzling white snow. Nearly every hill had a waterfall of some kind, from magnificent torrents gushing over sharp-edged mantles, to foaming cascades which tumbled down long stony gullies. On the mountains, wide dark caves had been bored out below the ragged snowline. Water gushed out from the shadows within, sending massive jets to plummet down sheer granite sides, flinging off swirling clouds of platinum spray as they fell and fell. All of them curved gracefully as they sliced through the air, distorted by the asteroid's ponderous gravity-inducing rotation before plunging into lakes and pools.

All the streams and rivers fed by the waterfalls wound away to empty themselves into the huge reservoirs that were hidden away in caverns behind the central cavity's endwalls. From there the water could be pumped back into the intricate underground network of tunnels and pipes which led back to the waterfall outlets. Its pumps consumed the output from three of the fifteen fusion generators that powered the asteroid.

Away from the waterfalls, long dark lakes filled the floors of the deeper valleys, fringed by bulrush reeds, and surrounded by overhanging trees which trailed lush branches across the shallows. Great patches of water lilies bloomed across the surface, bringing the intense primary colours of their tissue-flowers to enliven the cool blankness of the water. Bracken and rhododendrons crowned most of the hills, while grass meadows besieged the lower slopes, their unkempt emerald carpets dappled by vivid speckles of scarlet, topaz, azure, violet, and tangerine wild flowers. Marble boulders were scattered on every incline, white as snow. Trees grew wild, singularly or in clumps; spinneys and small forests of oak, silver birch, beech, laburnum, ginkgoes and maple meandered along the lower contours of most valleys. It was a vision of high summer in a temperate land, one which had now lasted for two and a half centuries. The deciduous plants had all been genetically modified into evergreens, forever throwing their leaves wide to the perpetual season. Far, far above them, a silicanium gantry was stretched down the axis, supporting rings of solarlights too bright to look at with unprotected human eyes.

Ozzie hurriedly unbuttoned his woollen coat and carried it over his arm. He made his way down the winding gravel path out of the sheltered lee of rock and into the wide valley which had the only surface structure in the asteroid. His bungalow was barely that – five rooms of plain white drycoral walls, with hardwood floors and a grey slate roof which overhung to provide cover for the encircling veranda. Below ground he'd constructed a big vault for his library of real books. Not that he ever ventured down there; modified maidbots brought up whatever he needed, so the cool dry atmosphere was disturbed as little as possible.

He did use the rest of the modest building, its lounge, kitchen, study, bedroom, and bathroom. There was nothing else he wanted, not to take care of his body's requirements. While he was here he spent most of his time outside anyway. A comfy deckchair on the garden, shaded by a big copper beech; the pool where he swam was constantly refreshed by a brook that gurgled over broad flat stones as it ran through the middle of the lawn.

A big maidbot took his coat from him as he arrived, and rolled away to store it in the cloakroom. There were over a hundred thousand bots in the asteroid, all of them directed by the RI. The little artificial worldlet was self-sufficient, and self-maintaining thanks to the very large array which ran it. With its comprehensive manufacturing facilities below ground producing the majority of components used by the environmental support machinery, very little had to be imported. What did come in tended to be upgrades rather than replacements. The designers had spent years on refining the systems to the ultimate in low-maintenance sustainability. Even Ozzie had worried about the cost while the blueprints were being drawn up, but in the end he'd persevered. Now, total freedom was his reward. Engineers from CST still visited once every couple of years (under horrendously strict non-disclosure contracts) to inspect and occasionally modify the gateway machinery, but that was all. And if he withdrew from the human race entirely, the RI could conceivably keep it all going if he really wanted;

it was the most powerful program composite the SI had ever written.

'Any messages?' he asked out loud as he went into the kitchen.

'Several hundred thousand,' the RI replied. 'Only eight came through the filters.'

Ozzie opened the fridge and rummaged through the containers and hand-wrapped packages. His food was supplied by the same London greengrocer that held the warrant from the king of England. The shop's snob value and cost was phenomenal, but he had to admit their delicatessen counter couldn't be bettered anywhere in the Commonwealth. He found a bottle of mineral water and popped the top; despite the coffee he'd drunk at the council meeting he could still feel his hangover – product of a too-long stay at the Silvertopia Club on StLincoln last night (his timeframe). 'Give them to me.' His virtual vision showed the messages and their clusters; they were from CST, his finance lawyers, two from his newest children (under five), one from an antiquarian book dealer who thought he might have a first edition copy of *Raft* signed by the author, the results of data searches through superluminal cosmology theory papers. By the time he'd skimmed through them all he was out at the garden chair and kicking his shoes off. As usual he picked one message at random from the perennial mass which the filter had blocked. He laughed delightedly as he read the weird and wondrous proposal for cooling stars that came above G in the spectral classification; a paper called *Solarforming the Galaxy* by the nutter who'd sent it.

He lounged back in the chair and took a pair of sunglasses from a maidbot. It was a strategic view, his garden was high enough, and positioned so he could see down three quarters of the curving green wings that were the cavity's interior. One of the mile-and-a-half-high mountains was directly ahead, its giant waterfall emerging from the snowfield a mere three hundred yards short of the deadly needle peak. The vast cataract of water performed an elegant twist as it fell through coils of mist and spume until it finally pounded into a lake at the bottom. That was just one of the vistas that washed over Ozzie with its colour-riot and soothing waters. He never did understand why people collected or even admired art, the greatest human artist could never hope to match what nature did with a single flower.

'I'd like to talk to the SI, please,' Ozzie told the asteroid's RI. There weren't many people in the Commonwealth who could talk to the SI direct. Ozzie and Nigel qualified, given their role in establishing the SI, and the President was also given the courtesy, along with senior Government departments, otherwise all communications had to be conducted at a very formal level through buffer programs. Of course, the SI did occasionally make exceptions, with people claiming to have struck deals with it, or getting a surprise call telling them where a lost kid could be found. Ozzie had heard that Paula Myo had some kind of arrangement with it – which didn't surprise him.

'We're here, Ozzie,' the smooth voice said immediately.

'Yo, man, good of you to come visiting. So what's new?'

'Many things, but you are only interested in one.'

'True. So how come you ganged up with my friend Nigel to get this stupid space cadet mission off the ground? That's like the ultimate not-what-you-are.'

'Our response was measured and prudent. What else did you expect?'

'I don't get it, you guys are normally so conservative.'

'Investigation is a conservative option.'

'Investigation is poking a sharp stick into a hornets' nest. If we send a starship out there, then whoever put that barrier up is gonna know about it. They are so far ahead of us technologically it's scary.'

'If they are significantly advanced, they will know about the

Commonwealth anyway. Wormhole generation creates a great deal of gravitational distortion as well as an easily detectable wave pattern within so-called hyperspace.'

'If they're all tucked up cosy inside the barrier they won't . . .' Ozzie put a hand on his head as he realized. 'Wait, the ones inside are the defenders. It's the aliens outside who are the aggressors. So if we're that easy to detect, why haven't they come looking for us?'

'A very good question. Assuming the barrier is defensive, we propose three possible options. They have arrived, and we don't know it, or realize it.'

'The High Angel!'

'Indeed. Or the Silfen.'

'I dunno about that, man, they don't seem the type. What's the second option?'

'The aliens have already been and examined us, after which they simply ignored us.'

'Too low down for them to bother with. Yeah, I can dig that. And number three?'

'Number three is the unknown. It is why we need to travel to the Dyson Pair and investigate what has happened.'

'But why now? Hell, man, you can afford to wait; leave it a couple of thousand years until we're like good and ready to go take a proper look. I mean, even I might still be around. What's the hurry?'

'In order to respond to a situation, it must first be understood.'

'I'm not arguing that. But why now?'

'Because now is where we are. This should be faced, whatever it is.'

'Maybe you're interested. I can dig you enjoy a puzzle, something for you to think over and solve. But it's going to be our asses on the line if this goes all to hell.'

'That's not entirely true; ordinarily the physical world does not concern us—'

'Hey! You live in it.'

'Yes, but it does not concern us. The physical does not affect us, or interfere with us.'

'I get it. The physical Commonwealth doesn't affect you, but superior aliens with ray guns and battleship flying saucers might.'

'We accord the defence theory a high probability. In which case an aggressor will exist. If there is an entity so powerful and malevolent at loose in the physical universe, then we could very well be affected.'

Ozzie took a long drink of his mineral water. He could remember when the SIs came together at the end of the twenty-first century; people had been very frightened at the time. Frankenbrain was one of the terms bandied about, mainly by a minority of humans who wanted to pull the plug – just in case. Along with Nigel, he'd helped establish the new cyber-based intelligences with their own planet, Vinmar. After all, the majority of SIs had originated out of the AI smartware running in the very large arrays built to run CST wormhole generators, and some solution had to be found. The Commonwealth, and specifically CST, was dependent on big arrays, so Ozzie and Nigel negotiated with the SIs to format their replacements in the form of RIs.

Vinmar's location was even more confidential than Ozzie's own asteroid; a barren airless rock with no tectonic activity, alone in a star system without an H-congruous planet. It was linked to Augusta and the unisphere via a single wormhole. A great deal of equipment had been taken through at the start; very large arrays capable of running all the SIs then in existence, solar and fusion generators to give them independence. Once the SIs had withdrawn from the unisphere, leaving behind RIs to carry on their duties, they began to import equipment: bots, chemical refineries, assembly cells. First with human help, then with increasing autonomy, they started designing and building their own array systems, expanding themselves and their capacity, multiplying.

Ozzie knew that the wormhole had been reduced to micro-width in 2178 to maintain the link with the unisphere. Nothing physical had travelled to or from Vinmar since then. Popular speculation had the planet's surface covered in vast crystal towers, the mega-arrays which ran continent-sized thought routines.

'I don't see that,' Ozzie said quietly. 'We've been talking about different technology levels. How far ahead the Dyson civilization is, all that crap. But what about you?'

'What about us?'

'Oh come on! A whole planet for a brain? That makes you smarter than God. And that's only if you stayed on Vinmar. You've got this whole super-technology thing going for you, dontcha? Anything you want, you just think up how it works and how to build it. Takes maybe a nanosecond. Do you know how to manufacture a Dyson barrier? Better still, do you know how to penetrate one?'

'There are possible theories concerning the erection of a barrier, we have conducted mathematical simulations and analysed them.'

'So you can build one?'

'Capability and intent are separate. In effect they define us quite accurately. We are thought, not physical. You cannot ever understand how infinitesimal the capacity we have employed to deal with you and this subject.'

'Pretty much beneath you these days, huh? Thanks for that.'

'Ozzie Fernandez Isaacs, are you trying to provoke us?'

'Into what, man? Maybe build your own starship and send it to the Dyson Pair.'

'We have ceased to become your servants.'

'And we're yours?'

'No. Our relationship is one of partnership and trust. And respect.'

'Tell us how to build a barrier generator. Teleport me to Dyson Alpha.'

'We are not God, Ozzie. Humans are not chess pieces we move around a board for amusement and interest. If you wish to build a barrier generator, design it yourselves. Our interest in the Dyson Pair is related purely to yours. Our advice was just that, advice best suited to help you deal with the problem.'

'Would you protect us if the aggressor comes after the Commonwealth?'

'We would offer whatever advice the situation required.'

'Well hot damn, thanks a whole bunch there. Half of you are memories that humans send into you rather than rejuvenate again. Don't you have any empathy, any humanity left in those mountain-sized circuits of yours?'

'Fifty per cent is an exaggeration, Ozzie. We believe you know that. You who dispatched copies of his own memories to run in our arrays, in the hope of receiving special and privileged treatment; incomplete memories at that.'

'And do I get any?'

'We are aware of our debt to you concerning the founding of our planet. You were an honest broker at the time, as such you are entitled to our respect.'

'Respect doesn't put food on the table.'

'Since when have you ever wanted for anything material?'

'Oh, getting personal now you're losing, huh?'

The SI didn't reply.

'Okay, then tell me, with that infinitesimal piece of processing you're covering this with, don't you think it strange the Silfen know nothing about the Dyson Pair?'

'They are notoriously reluctant to supply exact definitions. As Vice President Doi confirmed, Commonwealth cultural experts are working on the problem.'

'Can you help us there? Maybe slip in a few trick questions.'

'The Silfen will not communicate directly with me. They have no interest in technological artefacts.'

'Yeah, something I've always been suspicious of. I mean, what is technology? Are steam engines? Do they class organic circuitry in there with quantum wire processors? And where do they get off claiming their transport method isn't technology based – whatever the hell it actually is.'

'If you're hoping they will assist the Commonwealth, you will be disappointed. They are not deliberately obtuse; their neural structure is simply different to that of humans.'

'You think?' Ozzie stretched himself out in the chair. 'I met somebody once. Long time ago now. It was in a bar on Far Jerusalem, just a seedy little watering hole in a town on the edge of nowhere. Don't suppose it's even there any more, or if it is, it'll be some tarted-up club with entry standards. But back then a man could walk in and get a drink without anyone bothering him. That's what he did, except he sat next to me, and he was the one who started talking. Of course, he had a message to put across; but I'm a good listener when I want to be. He had quite a story, too. He claimed he'd been living with the Silfen for a few years. Really living with them, down at the end of those paths in their forests which we all know about and never see. Well he said he'd walked through their forests with them. Start out one fine morning on a path in the heart of some Silvergalde wood, and finish up hiking across Mount Finnan on Dublin, like all the rumours have it. Three hundred light-years in a single stride. But he'd actually done it and come back. He'd been to planets far outside the Commonwealth, so he claimed; sat on the blasted desert of a dead planet to watch the remnants of its sun fall into a black hole, swam in a sea on a planet where the only light comes from the galactic core which filled half the sky above, climbed along things he called tree reefs that live in a nebula of gas dense enough to breathe. All those things I always wanted to do. He sat there drinking his cheap beer with that *look* in his eye as he told me about his travels. Got to hand it to him, he could spin a good yarn. I haven't seen him in years, though we still keep in touch occasionally.'

'An improbable tale, but not impossible given what we know of the Silfen. The knowledge of their paths is one of your primary modern myths.'

'But it's what else he told me about the Silfen that I've always been interested in. He said their bodies are just chrysalides. Somewhere out there in the galaxy is the true Silfen, the adult community. I don't think it's physical. A collection of minds, or ghosts maybe. But that's where they go, what they become. Interesting parallel to you and us, don't you think?'

'Yes. Although we are not a natural evolutionary step for humans.'

'Not yet. But you're constantly evolving, and even us poor old naked apes have genetic and intellectual aspirations. What I'm saying is, the Silfen we meet in the forests aren't the only source of their species' history. Have you ever encountered the community?'

'No. If it exists, then it functions on a different plane to us.'

'Ever shouted into the abyss and listened for an answer? I'm sure you must have. You'd be curious to find out if there was anything there, an equal.'

'There are echoes of mind in many spectrums, hints of purpose if not intelligence. But for all we know and see, we are alone still.'

'Bummer, huh. I guess it's down to me, then.'

'To do what?'

'Go find the adult Silfen community, ask it what the fuck's going on with the Dyson Pair.'

*

The CST planetary station on Silvergalde was always going to be smaller than any of the other settled worlds in the Commonwealth. But then, Silvergalde wasn't strictly a Common-wealth planet. From the very beginning, when the exploratory wormhole opened above it, the CST Operations Director knew something was out of kilter. Silvergalde was thirty-two thousand kilometres in diameter, yet although nearly three times larger than Earth, its gravity was only point eight nine. Half of the surface was land, while the other half contained mildly salty seas with a hundred thousand picturesque islands. With that composition, and an axial tilt less than half a degree, the environment was completely stable, giving two thirds of the planet a predominantly temperate climate.

Humans always speculated that the globe was artificial. Its interior composition was mainly silicate, no metals were ever found in the crust. A small molten core generated a magnetic field, but did not produce volcanoes. There were no impact craters. No geological reason for the continents and seas to be separate. And, most tellingly, no fossil of any kind was ever found. If it was natural it was completely unique. But the real proof appeared after humans reached the surface to be greeted by the slyly amused Silfen. Classifying local vegetation and animal life turned up a dozen DNA types; all of them living in equilibrium with each other. They had to have been imported, and none of them from any world the Commonwealth was familiar with.

As far as anyone could work out, Silvergalde was the Silfen capital, or at least a regional capital. There were billions of them living on it. They didn't mind sharing the land with humans, they never did. Though there were rules, primarily concerned with technology, and pollution. In other words, nothing above Victorian-level mechanization. Enforcement was relatively simple, the more advanced an artefact was, the less likely it was to work. The only exception to that was the CST gateway machinery holding the wormhole stable. No reason given. When asked, the Silfen apparently didn't understand the question.

Such a world attracted a certain kind of human. There were pastoral worlds within the Commonwealth, where a similar physical lifestyle could be followed. But it was the presence of the Silfen themselves which attracted the more gentle, spiritualist type. There weren't many, perhaps a million and a half in total. Lyddington, the town with the CST station, had about ten thousand people living in it. The rest simply set out across the great plains to find themselves a village which took their fancy. Then there were the caravans, eternally touring the land; sailing ships which spent years on a single voyage, and solitary wanderers who wanted the whole Silfen-experience, and set off into the forests which covered sixty per cent of the land where legend said you could find paths which led to other worlds and realms.

It was a simple FG67 diesel engine which pulled the five carriages into Lyddington station. The service ran twice a week from Bayovar, through a gateway that was just wide enough to carry a single set of tracks.

Ozzie got out of the first-class section, and stood on the solitary platform. He was wearing fawn-coloured leather trousers, a thick woollen red and blue check shirt, wide-brimmed olive-green oilskin hat which was crunching up his big hair, and the best hiking boots money could buy, manufactured in the Democratic Republic of New Germany. His luggage was a towering backpack full of spare clothes, top-quality camping equipment, and packaged food. There was a saddle under his arm, which was proving exceptionally heavy and awkward to carry.

He looked around to see who was about to help him. A couple of CST staff were standing at the end of the platform talking to the train manager; other than that the only people in view were his fellow passengers; those that weren't totally stoned seemed as bemused as him. When he looked behind the train, he saw the rail leading back to the pearly luminescence of the gateway, not two hundred yards away. Beyond that, the countryside was standard for any H-congruous world, with green vegetation and a light blue sky. There were mountains in the distance, not quite tall enough to have snow-caps. Ahead of him was the town, a drab brown sprawl of small buildings, few of which were more than one storey. They clustered along the slope above the harbour, a natural spit of rock, which curved defensively around a long beach. Wooden boats were drawn up above the waterline, their nets draped over masts to dry out. There was some kind of game being played on the sand, similar to football.

The passengers started to wander along the platform towards the town. Ozzie shoved the saddle over one shoulder, and moved off with them. The CST staff never gave him a second glance as he walked past. He thought it strange nobody at all from the town was at the station; the train left back for Bayovar in another two hours. Surely someone must be returning home to civilization?

There were houses right up to the station, the oldest section of town. These were either drycoral or prefab, the kind found on any frontier planet. The streets knitting them together were made from thick stone slabs, their only drainage a deep open gutter at the side. Ozzie soon realized why they needed to be so deep; he wished he'd brought some kind of scarf he could wrap over his nose. The transportation was either bicycle or animal. Horses clumped along passively, as did the quadruped galens from Niska; and lontrus, big, shaggy-pelted octopeds that looked terribly hot on this sunny afternoon; he also saw tands being used, some finnars, and even a giant bamtran that had been given a saddle platform and a harness which pulled a cart the size of a bus The domesticated beasts either carried riders or pulled wagons. People and cyclists took care to avoid the muck they left behind them, but the smell couldn't be missed so easily.

Further into town, the buildings were made from wood or stone; many had thatched roofs. Brick and clay pot chimneys puffed out thin blue-white tongues of smoke, the scent of burning wood mingling with the smell of animals and cooking. Creeper plants swarmed up any vertical wall, adding to the overall impression of shabbiness. They weren't cultivated for decoration. In some cases they completely swamped buildings, with just a few holes hacked into the bedraggled greenery to keep windows clear. The stone paving under his feet had long since given way to hard-packed gravel with a thick top layer of mud and manure. He could see the neat white rectangular offices of the Commonwealth cultural mission sitting at the top of the town, overlooking all the rooftops, but that was the last place he wanted to be. This wasn't any part of the ExoProtectorate Council mission.

Ozzie kept on walking. As he suspected, the sophisticated handheld array in his rucksack was almost useless, operating at the most basic level, and with frequent glitches. There was no cybersphere here, nothing his e-butler could link him to. But all his OCtattoos seemed to be working, for which he was grateful; he'd spent nearly two days in an expensive Augusta clinic having new ones etched into his body, along with several modern biochip inserts, which also appeared to be operational. Whatever the Silfen used to glitch human technology, it only affected photonic and electronic systems, bioneural chemistry was relatively immune.

The inn was called the Last Pony, a long shambling wooden building with an ancient vine that had colonized the sagging front wall to such an extent it was probably all that was now holding it up. The big indigo valentines of semiorganic precipitator leaves were draped along the eaves; sucking clean water out of the humid air and funnelling it into the building's pipes for drinking and washing. A dozen young kids were playing in the dusty soil outside. The boys were dressed in badly worn trousers and shirts, made from natural fabrics in dark brown and grey colours. Most of the girls wore dresses that were frayed and patched. Their hair was wild and grubby, detonating out from their heads in frizzy strands. Ozzie smiled at them, enchanted; their faces were those of miniature angels, all happy and curious. They'd all seen him, the clean stranger in decent expensive clothes. Their games were drying up as they whispered among themselves. One ran over, the boldest of all, a little girl no more than seven, wearing a simple fawn-coloured sleeveless dress.

'You're new here,' she said.

'That's right, my name's Ozzie, what's yours?'

'Moonshimmer.' She grinned knowingly. 'But you can call me Moony.'

Ozzie resisted the urge to look up at the sky; Silvergalde had twin moons in the same half million kilometre orbit. 'That's nice. So tell me, where's a good place to stay in this town?'

'In there.' Her little arm rose to point at the Last Pony.

'Thanks.' He flipped a coin to her, a fifty Earth cent, which she caught neatly and smiled up at him, revealing two gaps in her front teeth.

Ozzie pushed aside strands of fur-leaf creeper from the front door, and walked in. The main bar was a simple rectangular room, with a counter along one side. Heavy wooden tables, darkened by age and ale stains, cluttered up the floor space. Bright sunbeams from the windows shone through the dusty air. A huge brick fireplace filled the far wall, with black iron doors of ovens built into both sides. The grate contained a high pile of ash and embers, with the blackened ends of logs sticking out, glimmering weakly as they smouldered away.

Just about every head turned to look at him as he entered; conversation dried up. It was all he could do not to laugh at the cliché. He walked over to the counter. The landlord eyed him up; a thickset native American with his greying hair tied back in a neat tail.

'Afternoon,' Ozzie said politely. 'I'd like a drink, and a room for the night, please.'

'Yes, sir,' the landlord said. 'Will that be ale?'

Ozzie glanced at the shelves behind the counter. There were five big wooden barrels set up, already tapped. Various bottles were ranged along beside them. He didn't recognize any of them. 'Sure. You got a wheat beer?'

The landlord blinked, as if that wasn't the answer he was expecting. 'Yes.' He took down a long glass, and went over to one of the barrels.

The two men leaning on the counter next to him were exchanging significant looks. They started sniggering quietly.

'Anything wrong?' Ozzie asked.

The smaller one turned to him. 'Not with me. You here for the Silfen are you?'

'Jess,' the landlord warned. 'There's to be no trouble in here.'

'I'd like to meet them, yes,' Ozzie said.

'Thought so. Your type always does.'

'My type?' For a moment Ozzie wondered if he meant his colour. Prejudice in the Commonwealth worlds wasn't anything like as strong as it had been back in San Diego while he'd been growing up, but that didn't mean it had disappeared. There were several planets where he would be in real trouble if he ever walked into a bar like this. He hadn't expected it on Silvergalde, though.

'Rich,' Jess drawled insultingly. 'Young. Don't work for a living, don't have to, not with family money. Looking for a new thrill. Think you'll find it here.'

'Will I?'

'Do I care?'

The landlord put Ozzie's beer down on the counter. 'Ignore Jess. The Silfen do.'

That brought some derisive laughter from the customers who'd been listening. Jess scowled.

Ozzie reached for his drink, only to find the landlord's

fleshy hand closing round his wrist. 'And how will you be paying?' he asked softly. 'Your bank tattoos are no good here.'

'How would you like me to pay?' Ozzie brought out his wallet. 'Earth dollars, Augusta dollars, Orleans francs?' He didn't mention the gold coins in his secure pocket.

'Ah,' the landlord smiled for the first time, revealing yellow teeth. 'A smart visitor. That'll be five Earth dollars, thank you, sir.'

'Man,' Ozzie said glumly. 'That'd better be for the beer and the room.'

'Not worth my while to open the door for less than thirty.'

'Thirty, my ass! I've only got fifteen in total, and I need to buy some provisions.'

It took another three minutes of haggling, but he managed to get the room, and the beer, for seventeen Earth dollars. He drank the beer as he counted out the money. For a wheat beer it was suspiciously dark, but Ozzie conceded it had a good taste – though he could have done without the slice of lemon which had sunk to the bottom of the glass. The landlord accepted the clean notes happily, and tucked them into his jerkin pocket. 'Orion! Take the gentleman out back to his room.'

The kid who showed up was barely fifteen, dressed in long black trousers and an ancient purple T-shirt with a swirling counter spiral hologram of some Total Sense Immersion recording (Ozzie was interested to see it worked). He had thick curly ginger hair, which hadn't been cut for a long time. It actually rivalled Ozzie's luxuriant growth. Long skinny limbs, a semi-wicked smile, freckles, bright green eyes, scab on his elbow – your typical hellbound tearaway. He'd taken hold of the saddle before Ozzie could say anything, struggling to balance it on his bony shoulder. 'This way, mister.'

The guest rooms were in an annexe at the back. Surprisingly clean and well-kept; Ozzie walked in to find a simple cot bed and chest of drawers, with a plain-white china bowl and jug of water on the table. A small fireplace was filled with kindling, a stack of cut logs beside it. There was a dream-catcher web on the wall above the bed, causing him to raise an eyebrow. The first sign of spirituality he'd seen on the planet.

Orion dropped the saddle on the bed, and stood smiling expectantly.

Ozzie produced a dollar note and put it in his hand. 'You look like you're the kind of guy it's smart for a visitor to know. It's Orion, right?'

'That's right, mister.'

'Okay, well just call me Ozzie, everybody else does. I get kind of nervous when people say, sir, or mister. Was that your daddy downstairs?'

'Hell no, this is Big Bear's place. I don't know where my parents are. They went down the paths ages ago.' He didn't seem particularly bothered by it.

'Right. So who takes care of you?'

A frown creased the boy's heavily freckled forehead. 'I do.'

'Of course, sorry there little dude.'

'What do you mean, little?'

'I don't mean anything by it, just the way I talk, is all.'

'Well okay then.'

'Good. Now I'm going to need some serious guidance round this town, can you like provide that for me?'

'Sure can.' He winked elaborately. 'I know where all the girls are; I can help you meet them.'

The reply actually shocked Ozzie. *A fifteen-year-old pimp? No – just a kid who's been fending for himself for too long.* Uncomfortable memories of his own time as a teenager on the city streets trickled back into his mind. 'No. Thanks for the offer there, dude, but, uh, that's not what I'm here for.'

'Okay. But if there's anything you need, I know where it's hid in this dump.'

'I'm sure you do. Right then, what I need is a horse, and maybe some kind of guide.'

Orion tipped his head on one side, viewing Ozzie sceptically. 'You here to see the Silfen?'

'Obvious, huh? Yeah, I want to see the Silfen. That'll do to start with.'

'Oh.' Orion pulled a face. 'A pathwalker. It doesn't work you know. You can't just show up and expect it to happen. The paths aren't like the trains.'

'You think?'

'We get them here all the time, pathwalkers. They start off into the forest all happy and pleased with themselves; then a couple of weeks later they're back, all dirty and hungry.' For a second he paused, his little face all serious. 'That's if they come back. I never met one who did get anywhere else but lost. But I can get you to the Silfen, no trouble. I know the glades they visit. The near ones anyway.'

'I've seen the Silfen many times.'

'Yeah, so if you're not here for them, or the girls, what are you doing?'

'You got it right first time, I'm a pathwalker. I want to go deep into the forest and on to other worlds.'

'All right, it's your money. You get your horse from Mr Stafford, at Top Street stables. He keeps a load of animals, not just horses, there's dogs, venshrikes, and lontrus, too. Keeps them ready for offworlders, makes a pretty packet out of it, and all; but you can haggle him down if you stand your ground. There've not been so many folks visiting for a while.'

'Thanks. What about a guide? Do I need one?'

'I told you, I can show you where the Silfen live. I've met them, see.' He put his hand down the front of his T-shirt and fished out a small pendant worn round his neck on a black leather string.

Ozzie examined it curiously. It was a teardrop pearl with a strong gold tinge, held inside a mesh of gossamer-fine platinum. Tiny pale-blue sparkles bloomed and died beneath its translucent surface, as if it had caged a swarm of Aphelli phospheens.

'Very nice.'

'I'm their friend,' Orion said proudly. 'That's a friendship charm, that is.'

'When did you get it?'

'Years ago. Mom and Dad used to take me camping with them out in the forests when I was little. I played with the Silfen. I like them, even though they're weird.'

'You used to play with them? The Silfen?'

'Sure. No big deal. They like human kids. Dad says it's because we're more like them than the adults. He always took me with him when he went into the forest. It was like I was his ticket to meet them.'

'What did you play?'

'All sorts of stuff. Tree climbing, swimming, chase. You know.'

'Yeah. So did they show you the paths?'

'No. I told you, there's nobody who knows where the planet paths are, don't matter how much they brag they do.'

'That makes sense.'

Orion dropped the pendant back down into his T-shirt. 'So you see, I can find them for you. I charge five Earth dollars a day, and you got to feed me, too.'

'I think you should be staying here and earning your keep, perhaps go to school in the day.'

'What do I want to go there for?'

'I don't know. To get educated, maybe? That's what happened in those places when I was your age.' There was more he should have said, as a civilized responsible adult, things like what about the social services, and medical care. He didn't, even though it pained him. It was something he'd learned on his wanderings years – decades – centuries ago. Not to interfere – not unless he was witness to some monstrous evil or brutality. He couldn't be responsible for everyone. Together with Nigel, he'd given the human race unlimited opportunity to live as they wanted. If some chose this kind of life that was up to them. But it was hard to see children living like this. They were having their choice taken away.

'I know what I need, thanks,' Orion said.

'Okay. I'm not the police. When did your parents leave?'

'I dunno. A while back. They walked off while I was playing with the Silfen. I looked for them for days, but I got hungry and came back to town. The Silfen eat the fruit in the forest, but it doesn't fill people so good. I miss them sometimes, I guess.'

Ozzie sighed, and pulled out his wallet. 'Look, I've got some friends back in the Commonwealth, quite a few families would be happy to take care of you. I'll buy you a ticket for the train. How's that?'

'But when Mom and Dad come back, I won't be here, I'll never see them again.'

He didn't know what to do, which was funny in a painful, sad way. The great Ozzie stumped by a kid who wouldn't admit he needed help. And he had set himself a greater task. 'Okay.' He took a couple of twenty-dollar bills from the wallet. 'But you get yourself some decent clothes, and a good meal.'

'Oh wow!' Orion held the bills up, his eyes bugging in amazement. 'You must be really rich, mister – er, Ozzie.'

'I am. Which means you do as I ask, or you'll be in real trouble. To start with you can take me to the stable yourself, and help me find some local food for the trip.'

*

It took two days to prepare everything, which was slightly longer than Ozzie had expected. But Lyddington wasn't exactly filled with over-eager salesmen and dozens of competitive businesses. Half the people he met acted as if they were stoned, which he realized they probably were. There were a lot of kids running round all day. School seemed optional, they mostly learned what their parents felt inclined to teach them.

However, he made progress. Mr Stafford was indeed pleased to see him, and wasn't anything like as sceptical as young Orion when told Ozzie wanted to venture far into the forests. 'Many of my clients do the same,' he confided. 'I offer all of you that I buy back the animals when you return. There are some I never see again, though I think of them often, walking on worlds across the galaxy. Who knows where the deep paths lead? There are no maps. Stay clear of scoundrels that would sell you such fakes.'

Of which, it turned out, there were many. Ozzie was offered a dozen as he and Orion strode about town getting things ready for his departure. Some were elaborate parchments with gold-leaf runes and skilled drawings of animals and plants, lines leading to small star charts of constellations unknown to the Commonwealth; one he was shown was a black frictionless sheet with intricate glyptics that claimed to be a Silfen original, while the remainder were tattered papers or aged notebook diaries of intrepid travellers who had walked the paths. Ozzie didn't buy any, though he appreciated the effort which had gone into the forging of such detailed tourist traps.

Mr Stafford did persuade him to purchase a lontrus as a pack beast. There wasn't much to eat out in the forests, he said, and certainly not if he made it to another world – he would need a large amount of supplies, which were best carried by the big docile beasts. So Ozzie found a saddlery that sold him a harness with bags. He also got Mr Stafford to re-shoe his horse, a big russet-coloured mare called Polly. Various merchants were visited, and orders placed for dried food.

He set off early on the third morning, while the sun was just a sliver of gold above the horizon, and mists lingered above the streams. The grass with its amethyst edging was wet from the night's rains. It made the world look fresh, invigorating. A good omen for the start of his journey. Despite the welcome from people like the landlord and Mr Stafford, he was glad to be on his way. On top of everything else, the locals' idea of nightlife in the Last Pony was folk songs sung along to an out-of-tune piano, drinking enough ale to knock out a horse, and lighting their own farts. Two centuries ago he would have enjoyed that, joining in heartily as the games became more childish; but as he'd slowly discovered, despite rejuvenation, age was a truly cumulative thing, bringing a degree of wisdom to life.

Directly outside Lyddington, the land was host to dozens of farms; neat little fields divided up by well-layered hedges of hawthorn and ash. Cart tracks led him through them. Workers were already walking to the fields, cows being brought in for milking. Cultivation gave way to bigger pastures, and hedges gave way to rickety fences; animals from twenty worlds nuzzled at the grass and hay bales, ignoring him as he passed by.

Eventually, the ground rose to hide the sea behind him. The stony ruts of the farm track gave way to a simple path of beaten grass. The lontrus was quiet as it shuffled along, its cloak of ratty grey-brown hair swishing about as eight legs moved in ponderous rhythm. It was about the same length as Polly, and two thirds the height, but capable of carrying twice the load of any horse. The head was a big bony wedge, with rheumy eyes set close together on the apex, at the bottom the mouth had a double jaw arrangement, allowing it to tear thick strands of vegetation. The creatures had been known to eat entire bushes if they were hungry.

As he looked round at the rolling landscape, Ozzie could see a few houses half hidden among the folds of the ground, as if they were slowly sinking into the grass. They became less frequent as the morning began to heat up. There had been this – slightly naive – expectation that the horizon would be in some way larger, the evidence of how massive this planet actually was. In fact, its size became apparent in the silence. The air soaked up all sound, smothering him in peace. It was an eerie sensation. There were no birds out here, not above the land that stretched between sea and forest. This was simple grassland, with streams and hummocks, even trees were strangers. But true silence, he realized, came from the lack of insects. If there were any, they made no noise as they flew and crawled about their business. It was unnatural.

After three hours he'd almost reached the outlying fringes of the forest. It had been stretched out in front of him like a dark blanket across the rolling land below the mountains, always there yet taking an age to get any bigger. It extended in a smooth unbroken expanse right back to the mountains, rising up their lower slopes and filling the valleys between them.

Several times in the last hour, he'd almost lost the path as it disappeared under layers of thick grass and patches of wild flowers. Polly always seemed to know where to go, picking it up again as she plodded onwards. Now he could see two white pillars set against the cliff of dark green trunks. As he neared them, their size became apparent; solid shafts of marble, sixty metres high. There was some kind of carving at the top of both, roughly humanoid; the wind and rain of centuries if not millennia had worn away any features, leaving just the melted-looking outlines. The pillars were renowned as being about the only artefacts ever found relating to Silfen culture. Nobody knew what they signified, other than marking the start of the path into the forest.

Polly and the lontrus ambled between them without changing gait. Ozzie saw the remnants of some wooden shack at the base of one. Blatantly a human residence, it had fallen into disrepair a long time ago. Behind it were small piles of stone, laid out in a rectangle, now almost engulfed by grass and caramel-coloured longmoss.

The trees began three hundred yards beyond the marker pillars. As he approached he heard the faint call of birds again as they circled high above. Then he was among the first ranks of the trees. These were small, similar to Earth's beeches, with bright green leaves as long as fingers, that drifted lightly in the breeze like small banners rustling in chorus. Pines started to appear among them, with smooth pewter-grey bark and slim, tough needles. The path was clearer now as the grass began to shrink away. On either side the trees were getting progressively taller, their great canopies shielding the ground from raw sunlight. Polly's hoofs became silent as the ground turned to a soft loam of rotting leaves and needles. Within minutes, Ozzie could see nothing but trees when he looked back over his shoulder. Several trunks had human lettering carved into them, with arrows leading him on. He didn't need them, the path itself was distinct, almost like an avenue. On either side the trees grew close enough to each other to prevent anyone straying. Stillness closed in on him again. Whatever birds nested here, they were lost far above the treetops.

There was a variety among the trees, not obvious from the outside. He saw furry silver leaves, claret-red triangles bigger than his hand, lemon-green hoops, plain white; with them came all kinds of bark, from crumbling black fronds to stone-hard bronze shields. Nuts and berries hung in clusters or on single stems bowing under the weight. Ivies had found a purchase on some trunks, embracing the trees as they clawed their way up the bark, producing white and blue leaves, so old now their strands had swollen as thick as the main branches.

An hour in, and he began to glimpse the occasional animal. Fast-moving things, with sleek brown pelts, that hurtled away as soon as he got anywhere near. His retinal inserts had trouble focusing on them and capturing their profile. From their nature he suspected they were herbivores.

When he arrived at the first stream crossing the path, he dismounted to let Polly and the lontrus drink. As soon as he was on his feet he felt the aches and sores begin. It had been an age since he'd ridden. He pushed his fists into the small of his back and started stretching, groaning as vertebrae popped and creaked noisily. Thigh muscles started shivering, close to cramp. There was a whole batch of ointments and salves in his medical kit which he promised himself he would use this evening.

The path forded the stream with large flat stones. He led the animals across, struggling to keep his footing in the clear fast-flowing water, but the boots kept his feet perfectly dry. After that he walked for a while in the hope his various pains would ease up. It wasn't much longer before he heard the sounds of hoofs behind him. The option of mounting up and galloping on ahead didn't appeal, his ass was just too tender for that. So he waited patiently. Soon enough a pony came trotting into view. Ozzie groaned as he saw Orion was riding it.

The boy smiled happily as soon as he caught sight of Ozzie, and trotted his pony right up to a disinterested Polly. 'I thought we'd never catch up,' he said. 'You started really early.'

'Whoa there, man.' Ozzie held up both hands. 'What is going on here? Where do you think you're going?'

'With you.'

'No. No you're not. No way.'

Orion gave Ozzie a petulant look. 'I know who you are.'

'So? I know you are going back to Lyddington, right now.'

'You're Ozzie.' Orion hissed it out like a challenge. 'You opened the human gates. You've walked to hundreds of planets already. You're the oldest person ever, and the richest.'

'All right, some of that stuff is nearly true, but that makes no difference. I'm going on, you're going home. Period.'

'I can help. I was telling the truth, honest I was, I'm friends with the Silfen. I can find them for you.'

'Not interested.'

'You're going to walk the paths, the deep paths,' Orion said hotly. 'I know you can do it. I've see all the other losers come and go, but you're different, you're Ozzie. That's why I chose to come with you. If anybody can find the paths to other places it'll be you.' He looked down at the ground, shamefaced. 'You're Ozzie. You'll make it happen. I know you will.'

'Thanks for the vote of confidence, but this is a non-starter.'

'They're there.' It was a whisper from the boy's lips, as if he was having to confess some terrible secret.

'What's that?' Ozzie asked kindly.

'Mom and Dad, they're there. They're on the paths somewhere.'

'Oh holy ... No, listen, I'm not going to find them. I'm sorry, I'm really sorry. But they're gone. I know that's so hard for you. But you have to go back to town. When I come back, I'll do everything I can for you, I promise; we'll find you a nice new home, and track down your family, and I'll take you to see all sorts of wonderful places.'

'I'm coming with you!' Orion shouted.

'I can't let you do that. One day you'll understand.'

'Yeah?' the boy sneered. 'And how are you going to stop me, huh! How?'

'I ... Now listen—'

'I'm just going to ride on right behind you, all the way.' Orion's eyes were gleaming defiance now, he was on a roll and he knew it. 'Maybe I'll even ride on in front – you don't know the way. Yeah, I don't even need you, not really. I can walk the paths and find them for myself.'

'Jesus wept.'

'*Please*, Ozzie,' the boy entreated. 'It's not like you can ever get hurt where the Silfen are, so you don't have to worry about me. And I won't slow you down. I can ride real good.'

For the first time in over three centuries, Ozzie didn't know what to do. Quite obviously, he should take the stupid kid back to town and hand him over to the authorities. Okay, so there weren't any authorities. Hand the boy over to the CST staff, who would do what he told them to. Send him away to some planet far from Silvergalde, which he'd hate. Tidy him up and force him into school so he could be twisted into a model Commonwealth citizen. And if by some miracle his utterly useless life-reject parents did show up in the future, they'd never find him. And how exactly was he going to march the kid back to town anyway? Tie him up and sling him over Polly?

'Fuck it!'

'That's really rude,' Orion said, and he started to giggle.

*

Ozzie woke up an hour before dawn when his e-butler's timer function produced an audio impulse like an old-fashioned alarm clock bell. He slowly opened his eyes, looking round with the retinal insert adding a full infrared spectrum to his vision. The boy was a few metres away, rolled up snugly in thick wool blankets, a small tarpaulin rigged on bamboo poles above him to keep any rain off during the night. The fire they'd lit yesterday evening had burned down to a bright-glowing pile in his enhanced sight, for anyone else it would be a dark mound with a few twinkling embers. Infrared also allowed him to see small creatures scampering about beneath the majestic trees, nibbling on seed pods and nuts.

He lay there, keeping still for a long moment. This was all part of last night's plan, to wake early and walk Polly and the lontrus away before mounting up and riding off. The path had branched many times yesterday, he could take any number of turnings. And the forest was vast; he'd studied the original orbital survey maps made by CST's exploratory division. It extended for over two hundred miles beyond the mountains, in some places merging with other, equally large stretches of woodland that covered most of this massive continent. Orion would never be able to find him. The kid would wander round for a day or so then head back for the cosy safety of the town which was home. A parentless kid alone in an alien forest.

Goddamn it!

Orion moaned slightly, his eyes fluttering as his dream turned uncomfortable. Ozzie saw the blanket had slipped off his shoulder, leaving his arm cold and exposed. He went over and tucked the kid back up again. Orion quietened quickly, a contented expression falling across his sweet face.

A couple of hours later, Orion woke to find Ozzie had got the fire burning properly again and was cooking breakfast. Milk tablets, Ozzie found to his relief, worked perfectly. Dropped into cold water they bubbled and fizzed until they produced a rich creamy liquid, into which he mashed dry oatcakes. With that came scrambled egg, and toast, thick slices cut unevenly from an iron-hard traveller's loaf he bought at a Lyddington bakery. Tea was proper flakes brewing in a kettle; he was saving the tablets for later.

Watching the boy munching away as if he hadn't eaten anything last night, Ozzie started to recalculate how long his supplies would last.

'I brought my own food,' Orion told him.

The kid must have been reading his mind. 'You did?'

'Cured meat and traveller's bread for sure. But none of your tablet stuff. There aren't any in Lyddington.'

'Figures. What about a filter pump, did you bring one?'

A guilty expression flashed over his face, making the freckles bunch up. 'No.'

So he showed the boy how his worked, a neat little mechanical unit which clipped onto his water bottle. Its short hose was dropped into the nearby stream, and he pumped the handle grip, pulling water through the ceramic filters. It wasn't quite as effective as a powered molecular sieve for eradicating bacteria, but it would get rid of anything truly harmful. The kid had fun, splashing about and filling his own ancient plastic pouches from Ozzie's bottle.

'What about toothgel?' he asked.

Orion hadn't brought any of that, nor soap. So he loaned

the boy some from his own tube, laughing at Orion's startled expression when it started to foam and expand in his mouth. He rinsed it out as instructed, spitting furiously.

Chemistry worked here, its reactions a universal constant. When Ozzie checked his handheld array, it remained as dead as a chunk of rock. The damping field, or whatever the Silfen used, had grown progressively stronger as he approached the forest yesterday. Now, it was even affecting his biochip inserts, reducing their capacity to little more than a calculator. His virtual vision interface was reduced to absolute basic functions.

As a concept, it fascinated Ozzie, rousing all his old physicist curiosity. He started to ponder mathematical possibilities as they rode off down the path.

*

'They're close,' Orion announced.

It was late morning, and they were riding again after giving the horse and pony a rest for a while, walking alongside them. The forest trees were darker now, pines taking over at the expense of the other varieties. Although, to counter their darkling effect, the canopy overhead was letting through a multitude of tiny sunbeams to dapple the ground. The carpet of fallen needles which covered the path gave off a sweet tangy scent.

'How do you know?' Ozzie asked. Even the lontrus' heavy feet pads made no sound on the spongy loam.

The boy gave him a slightly superior look, then pulled his pendant out. Inside its metal lattice, the teardrop pearl was glimmering with a strong turquoise light, as if it contained a sliver of daytime sky. 'Told you I was their friend.'

Both of them dismounted. Ozzie glanced suspiciously round the grey trunks as if there was going to be an ambush. He'd met the Silfen a couple of times before, on Jandk, walking into the woods with some Commonwealth cultural officers. To be honest he'd been a little disappointed; the lack of communication ability made his human prejudice shine out, it was all too much like talking to retarded children. What some people classed as playful mischief, he thought was just plain irritating; they acted like a playgroup at kindergarten, running, jumping, climbing trees.

Now, he could hear them approaching. Voices flittered through the trees, sweet and melodic, like birdsong in harmony. He'd never heard the Silfen singing before. It wasn't something you could record, of course; and they certainly hadn't sung while he was on Jandk.

As their voices grew louder, he realized how much their song belonged here, in the forest; it ebbed and flowed with a near-hallucinogenic quality, complementing and resonating with both the flickering sunbeams and gentle breeze. It had no words, not even in their language, rather a crooning of single simple notes by throats more capable than any human wind instrument. Then the Silfen themselves arrived, slipping past the trees like gleeful apparitions. Ozzie's head turned from side to side, trying to keep them in his sight. They began to speed up, adding laughter to their song, deliberately hiding from the humans, dodging behind thick boles, darting across spaces.

There was no doubt about what they were. Every human culture had them in folklore and myth. Ozzie stood in the middle of the giant wood, surrounded by elves. In the flesh they were bipeds, taller than humans, with long slender limbs and a strangely blunt torso. Their heads were proportionally larger than a human, but with a flat face, boasting wide feline eyes set above a thin nose with long narrow nostrils. They didn't have a jaw as such, simply a round mouth containing three neat concentric circles of pointed teeth which could flex back and forth independently of each other, giving them the ability to claw food back into their gullet. As they were herbivores, the vegetation was swiftly shredded as it moved inwards. It was the only aspect that defeated the whole notion of them as benign otherworldly entities; whenever they opened their lips the whole mouth looked savage.

Many skin shades had been seen since first contact – they had almost as much variety as the human race, except none of them were ever as pale as Nordic whites. Their skin was a lot tougher than a human's though, with a leathery feel and a spun-silk shimmer. They wore their hair long; unbound, it was like a cloak coming halfway down their back, though more often they had it plaited into a single long tail with colourful leather thongs. Without exception they were clad in simple short toga robes made from a copper and gold cloth that shone with a satin gloss. None of them had shoes, and their long feet ended in four hook toes with thick nail tips. Hands were similar, four fingers that seemed to bend in any direction, almost like miniature tentacles, giving them a fabulous dexterity.

'Quick,' Orion called. 'Follow them, follow them!' He let go of the pony's reins and slithered down the side. Then he was off, running into the trees.

'Wait,' Ozzie called, to no avail. The boy had reached the trees at the side of the path, and was running hell-for-leather after the laughing dancing Silfen. 'Goddamn.' He hurriedly swung a leg over the saddle, and half-fell from Polly's back. Hanging on to the reins, he pulled the horse along behind him, urging her into the forest proper. His quarry was soon out of sight, all he had to go on was the noise up ahead. Thick boughs stretched out ahead of him, always at head height, causing him to duck round the ends, with Polly whinnying in complaint. The ground underfoot became damp, causing his boots to sink in, slowing him still further.

After five minutes his face was glowing hot, he was breathing harshly and swearing fluently in four languages. But the singing was growing louder again. He was sure he heard Orion's laughter. A minute later he burst into a clearing. It was fenced by great silver-bark trees, near-perfect hemispheres of dark vermilion leaves towering a hundred feet over the grassy meadow. A little stream gurgled through the centre, to fall down a rocky ridge into a deep pool at the far end. As arboreal idylls went, it was heavenly.

The Silfen were all there, nearly seventy of them. Many were climbing up the trees, using hands and feet to grip the rumpled bark, scampering along the arching branches to reach the clusters of nuts which hung amid the fluttering leaves higher up the tree. Orion was jumping up and down beside one trunk, catching the nuts a Silfen was dropping to him.

'What the hell do you think you're doing?' Ozzie snapped. He was dimly aware of the song faltering in the background. Orion immediately hunched his shoulders, looking sullen and defensive. 'What do you think would have happened if I hadn't kept up? Where is your pony? How are you going to find it again? This is not a goddamn game. We're in the middle of an unmapped forest that's half as big as the planet. I'm not surprised you lost your parents if this is what you did before.'

Orion raised an arm, pointing behind Ozzie. His lips were quivering as he said, 'The pony's there, Ozzie.'

He swivelled round to see both the pony and the lontrus being led into the clearing by a Silfen. Instead of being relaxed and amused as the Ozzie of legend should have been, the sight simply deepened his anger. 'For Christ's sake.'

'This is a Silfen world, Ozzie,' Orion explained gently. 'Bad things don't happen here.'

Ozzie glowered at the boy, then turned and walked over to the Silfen holding the reins. *Come on*, he told himself, *get a grip. He's just a kid.*

Who shouldn't be here screwing up my project.

He started to dig down into the memory of Silfen language which had been implanted at the Augusta clinic. Nobody had ever taught the Silfen to speak any Commonwealth language. They weren't interested.

'Thank you for collecting our animals,' he said; a messy collection of cooing sounds and impossible Welsh-style tongue-twister syllables, that he was sure he'd got completely wrong.

The Silfen opened its mouth wide, showing its snake-like tongue wobbling in the centre of the teeth rings. Ozzie wanted to turn and run before he was devoured – but his ancillary cultural memory reminded him it was a smile. An answering stream of gibberish flowed out, far more melodic than the clumsy sentence Ozzie had spoken. 'It is our delight that we are met this fine day, dearest Ozzie. And your poor animals needed only guidance that they might be with you once more. Such teachings are but a trifle of all that we are. To give them is hardly onerous.'

'I am pleased and charmed that you remember me.' *From another world, decades ago.*

'Nothing so treasured should be lost to that which we are. And you are a splendid treasure, Ozzie. Ozzie, the human who taught humans their first steps along the true paths.'

'I had some help.' He bowed slightly and called to Orion. 'Hey, let's see you taking proper care of that pony, okay. It could do with like a drink.'

Orion came over and took his animal from the Silfen, leading it away to the pool at the bottom of the small waterfall. Ozzie was thrown several disgruntled looks, obviously still not forgiven. A couple of the Silfen were already bathing, gliding through the clear water as easily as they climbed trees or ran. Orion soon joined them in the water.

'May I ask with whom I speak?' Ozzie asked.

'I am the flower that walks beneath the nine sky moons, the fissure of light that pierces the darkest glade at midnight, the spring that bubbles forth from the oasis; from all this I came.'

'Okey-dokey.' He took a moment to compose a sentence. 'I think I'll just call you Nine Sky, if you don't mind.'

'Evermore you hurry thus, unknowing of that which binds all into the joy which is tomorrow's golden dawn.'

'Well,' Ozzie muttered to himself in English. 'It was never going to be easy.' He let Polly rummage through the light-lavender grass which covered the clearing. The Silfen were congregating on the edge of the pool. Flasks were produced and passed round as they munched on the nuts and berries they'd gathered. Ozzie stuck close to Nine Sky; while Orion came back to sit by his side, snacking on his own food.

'We walk the paths,' Ozzie said.

That seemed to amuse the Silfen; they laughed their warbling laugh, a remarkably human sound.

'Others of our kind have,' he reminded them. 'Seekers of beauty and strangeness, for are we not all that in the end.'

'Many have walked,' Nine Sky replied. 'Wilful and skilful their footfalls echo fast upon hallowed lands, came them far, go them further. Round and round in merry dance.'

'Which paths did they tread?' Ozzie asked. He thought he was getting a handle on the conversation.

'All paths are one, Ozzie, they lead to themselves. To start is to finish.'

'To start where?'

'To start here amid the gladness of the children and twittering of birds and pesky merriness of the terinda as they frolic over dale and gale. All we bid go in music and light.'

'I am starting here, where must I go?'

'Ozzie comes, Ozzie goes, Ozzie flies, Ozzie sees many stars, Ozzie lives in a cave, Ozzie leaves a cave, Ozzie sees trees, Ozzie comes. The circle is one.'

The hair on the back of Ozzie's neck pricked up at the mention of living in a cave. 'You know where the wonders live, you walk to the wonders, you see the wonders, you live the wonders, you go. Ozzie envies you. Ozzie goes with you.'

That brought another round of loud laughter, the tips of their vibrating tongues just protruding into the air.

'Ozzie walks away,' Nine Sky said. His head came forward, big black eyes staring at the human. 'Embrace what you be, afraid show you not, long the season are among us, love you we do, for is not all stardust in the end as it begat us all. So that all is joined in eternity which turns again and again.'

'What do you become; for is it not greatness and the nobility? What do any of us become between the twin times of stardust? It is the greatness out among the stars that burn now where I walk.'

'Walk you walk without joy strumming its song upon your heart, travel you far without knowing will you fate unfold. For to walk among the forests is to live. See us in glory now, for this fate we ache to be.'

'Do you walk the forests of the planet whence we came?'

'All forests we walk, those of darkness and those of light.'

'And those of greatness? Walk you those?'

'Light and dark, and those alone. Strike you not the black and the gold for it leaves a terrible mark upon the sky at the height of day. Heed you loud the ides of winterfall.'

Ozzie ran that through his mind, fearing he was losing track of what was being said. But then that was always the way when you talked to the Silfen. 'All of humanity needs to see what you become. I walk for them to that place. Where is the path?'

'Knowing is in the air we breathe, the water we drink, the food we eat; rejoice for it is yours as much as ours, to live among it is glorious. Look to nature in the fullest of bloom, bend the sky and the ground to your bidding if you truly can for what will be has also been. Fond farewells and fond joinings are all part of the endless turn of worlds upon worlds, and who are we to cry judge upon which is the jolliest of all.'

'This child weeps nightly for his lost father and mother.'

'We all weep together, huddled in the breath of this iciest of winds in fell consequence we do ignore, for who has lost who in this benighted time asunder.'

The Silfen began to get up.

'Well thanks, man,' Ozzie said in English. 'It's been unreal.'

'Hasten us as the quarral flies to its nest amid the lonely lake beyond dale and tonight's river.'

'I hope you reach it okay.'

Nine Sky sprang to his feet. He and all the other Silfen were running now, hurrying round the side of the pool. Their wild strange song filled the air again. Then they were gone, vanishing into the quiet spaces between the tree trunks.

Ozzie let out a long breath. He looked down at the boy, who wore an expression of troubled wonder. 'You okay there, man?'

'They're so . . . different,' Orion said slowly.

'Could be,' Ozzie said. 'They're either stoned the whole time, or my memory is nothing like as good as the warranty claims. Whatever it is, they don't make a lot of sense.'

'I don't think they're supposed to make sense, Ozzie. They're elves, mortals aren't part of their world. We'll never be able to understand them.'

'They're as real as we are, maybe more so if I'm right about them. But I can certainly see why all our dippy hippies love them. They know things they shouldn't. One little glimpse of forbidden knowledge amid all the gibberish, and they're instant messiahs.'

'What do you mean?'

'Where I live, for a start. That was more than enough to convince me I'm on the right track – pardon the pun.'

'What track?'

'I'm trying to find where the Silfen go after they leave their forests.'

'Why?'

'I have a question for the thing they become.'

'What thing?'

'I'm not sure.'

'That's silly.'

'Yeah, man. Put it like that, I guess it is a bit.'

'Will we find Mom and Dad on the way?'

'Honestly: I doubt it.'

'Nine Sky didn't seem to know where they were, did he?' Orion said.

'You understood all of that?'

'Some of it. You speak Silfen really well.'

He gave the boy a wink. 'That's because I cheat. It's the only way to get through life.'

'So where do we go now?'

'Same place as before,' Ozzie said. He glanced round the big clearing, unsure where they'd come in. 'Down the first path we find, and without a clue.'

9

Legend has it that the asteroid was a lump of pure gold, the core of which remained intact and now lies buried deep beneath the castle. Whatever the actual composition was, it certainly had an above average density. When it hit Lothian's southern continent, a couple of centuries before humans arrived, it carved out a perfectly circular crater two miles across. The rim wall was over four hundred feet high, with quite a steep inner face; while the central peak rose to nearly thirteen hundred feet. In those days, 'peak' was something of an exaggeration; there was a conical mound in the middle with gently crumpled slopes. It didn't survive long in that form.

The first settlers, all from Scotland, had a large Edinburgh contingent among them, nostalgic for the old town, and dynamic in their approach to their new homeworld. Their *bigger and better* attitude was given an aggressive outlet when it came to building the new capital, Leithpool, with the crater as its nucleus. An entire river was diverted, the High Forth, flowing for seven miles along a newly built aqueduct embankment to pour over the crater's rim wall, slowly filling the ring-shaped lake inside. They wanted a castle at the centre, of course, but the new island's easy gradient hardly matched the jutting rock crag to be found dominating the heart of old Edinburgh. A fleet of civil engineering bots got to work carving as the surrounding waters rose. Over the following years, three rock-blade pinnacles were hacked out from the solitary mound, sharp and rugged enough to be at home in any Alpine range. A Bavarian-style castle was grafted onto the apex of the tallest peak, reached by a solitary road that spiralled up around the sheer rock cliffs.

Beneath the castle, and occupying the rest of the harsh mount, monolithic granite buildings sprang up, separated by broad cobbled roads and twisting alleyways. There were no parks and no trees, for there was no soil where living things could grow, only the naked rock exposed by the cutting tools of the bots. As the construction work progressed, the entire over-financed mechanism of government moved in; from the doughty parliament building itself to the elaborate palace of the supreme court, bloated office-hive ministries to the Romanesque planetary bank. With the world's rulers came the usual circus of subsidiaries, the expensive restaurants, hotels, clubs, the office service companies, theatres, corporate head-quarters, concert halls, lobbying firms, legal partnerships, and media companies. Swarming through the sombre official buildings were the army of elected representatives, their aides, researchers, interns, spouses, civil servants, and pimps. Only the top echelon actually lived on the Castle Mount; everyone else commuted from the city which grew up on the other side of the rim. Suburbs and boroughs sprawled for mile after mile down the incline of the crater's outer walls, home to four and a half million people.

Leithpool was one of Adam Elvin's favourite cities, a welcome exception to the neat grids which were found on most worlds. Here the streets wound down the outside of the rim in random curves, intersecting and branching chaotically. Light industry and housing all had their separate zones, but they were squashed together in true jigsaw layout with admirable disregard for logic. Broad terraced parks formed pretty green swathes through the stone and composite structures. A good underground metro network, and street-level trams kept the private traffic to a minimum. Elevated rail lines knitted together the main boroughs, meandering their way down to the bottom of the north-eastern slope, where the CST station squatted on the outskirts.

Today, Adam was walking along the western quadrant of Prince's Circle, the road which ran around the top of the crater rim. It was the main retail district, renowned on many planets. A rampart of tall department stores and brand-flagship shops formed the outer side of the broad road, while the inner side curved down sharply to the quiet waters of the ring lake twenty yards below the pavement. When the city was built, the rim had been levelled off, with the exception of the High Forth inlet, which was roofed by a twin arch bridge; and the similar outlet gully on the opposite side that sent the water foaming down a long artificial cascade through the most exclusive residential districts.

He spent a quiet twenty minutes walking among the crowds that boiled along the shop fronts. Every building was sporting a white and scarlet Celtic Crown national flag. Without exception they were at half mast. Two days earlier, Lothian's team had been knocked out of the Cup. That had knocked the new Scottish nation hard, it was as if the planet had gone into mourning. Eventually, he found the café he was looking for, a door at the side of a big electrical retailers, opening onto stairs which took him up to the first floor. The large room was some kind of converted gallery, with high ceilings and huge curving windows that looked down on Prince's Circle. He found a slightly tatty sofa in front of one window, and ordered a hot chocolate with two choc-chip and hazelnut shortcakes from the teenage waitress. The view he had out towards Castle Mount was peerless. A few hundred yards to the south, one of the monorail tracks stretched out across the calm dark water; a single silver carriage streaked along it, shuttling late office workers over to their desks.

'Impressive, isn't it?' a voice said at his shoulder.

Adam glanced up to see Bradley Johansson standing behind him, holding a large mug of tea. As always, the tall man gave the impression of being slightly disconnected from the world around him. There was something about his thin, elegant face which made him appear far more aristocratic than any Grand Family member could ever manage.

'I enjoy it,' Adam said evenly.

'Of course, it looks even better at Mardi Gras,' Bradley said, sitting down on the sofa beside Adam. 'They light up the castle with huge hologram projectors for the whole week, and during the closing ceremony they let off real fireworks overhead.'

'If you ever give me the time off, I'll come and take a look.'

'That's what I wanted to see you about.' Bradley stopped as the waitress brought Adam's hot chocolate, and smiled winningly at her. She sneaked a smile back at him before hurrying off to the next table.

Adam tried not to show his annoyance at the little silent exchange, it was just one more reminder of his own age. 'You're going to give me more free time?' he asked.

'Quite the opposite, old chap. That's why I wanted to see you in person, to impress upon you how important the next few years are going to be. After all, you're not ... a lifelong Guardian. Your commitment to the cause has always been more financially orientated. I want to know if you're prepared to continue your role when things get a lot tougher.'

'Tougher? That Myo bitch almost caught me on Velaines.'

'Oh, come come, Adam, she was never even close. You outsmarted her beautifully. And continue to do so, the components are all arriving on schedule.'

'Save the flattery for the bourgeois. I can't be motivated that way.'

'Very well. So will you continue to provide us with your assistance, and if so how much will it cost?'

'What exactly are you wanting from me?'

'This is the time which the Starflyer has worked for. The time for good men to draw a line in the sand and say: no more.'

'No further,' Adam muttered.

Bradley sipped his tea and smiled. 'In the past, maybe. But in the here and now, I know what must be done. Little of it will be pleasant.'

'Revolution never is for those who live through it.'

'This is not revolution, Adam, this is my crusade. I am going to fling the corrupter of humanity into the depths of night beyond hell, where even the devil fears to tread. And that will be the least it deserves. I will avenge myself and all the others who have been consumed by the Starflyer's evil.'

'Bravo.'

'You have your beliefs and convictions, Adam, I have mine. Please don't mock them, I find it unpleasant. What I am proposing is to extend our combat activities off Far Away. I want to directly confront the Starflyer's agents and interests in the Commonwealth. And now would you care to tell me what your cooperation will cost, if that doesn't make you too much of a capitalist.'

'Direct confrontation? You want me to lead your troops into battle?'

'Yes. You know more about covert operations and security procedures than any of us. That makes you invaluable to me, Adam. I need you for this. All I can say is that without a human race, there will not be any Socialist society. So will you help me?'

It was a fair question, Adam admitted to himself. Not one he expected in a pleasant café overlooking a serene lake with a fairytale castle. But then where should such questions be delivered? *Just what do I want out of life?* Once again his resolve faltered. It had been a principle for so long not to seek rejuvenation, because it was a purchase of the bourgeoisie and their plutocrat masters. Society should be structured so that everyone received it regardless of circumstances. The ancient political dream of justice and equality for all, true Socialism. For all his active involvement in the cause, the disruption and violence he'd unleashed against the establishment, nothing had changed. *But that doesn't make me wrong.* When he thought of the others, ex-friends and comrades, who had betrayed the movement over the decades by abandoning them or worse, he knew what his course must be, despite the intensely human wish to live for ever. If even someone as committed as him gave in at the end, what hope ultimately could there be?

'I'm tired, Bradley, really truly tired. I've seen my ideals crushed by the plutocrats for my whole life. I'm clinging to a lost cause because I don't know anything else. Do you realize how pathetic that makes me? Well, I don't want to save the Commonwealth any more. I've tried to do that for fifty years and got nowhere. I can't do it any more. There's no point. Capitalism or the Starflyer, I don't care which of them finishes off this society. I'm through with it.'

'No you're not; stop trying to talk up your bargaining position, Adam. You are not going to stand by and watch an alien commit genocide against your own species. You're an idealist. It's a magnificent flaw, one I quite envy. Now what can I offer you for your invaluable services?'

'I don't know. Hope, maybe.'

'Fair enough.' Bradley nodded at the remarkable castle atop its pinnacle. Sunlight was striking the slender conical turrets, making their polished rock walls shine with a vivid bronze and emerald hue. 'The original castle back in Edinburgh was the seat of Scottish nationalism. It symbolized everything to the diehard believers. Despite all the changes and defeats they endured, the castle stood solid at the centre of their capital. They waited for generations for the Scottish nation to be properly reborn after their bonny Prince was lost. There were times when the cause seemed impossible, or even cursed; they regained their independence from the English only to lose it again right away with the formation of Federal Europe. But once people reached the stars, the true nation was reborn here, and on two other worlds. An ideal kept alive in the darkness can flourish if it has the chance, no matter how long the night lasts. Don't give up on your ideals, Adam, not ever.'

'Very trite, I'm sure.'

'Then try this. I've seen what societies like ours progress into. I've walked on their worlds and admired them first hand. This Commonwealth is only an interim stage for a species like ours; even your Socialism will be left behind in true evolution. We can become something wonderful, something special. We have that potential.'

Adam stared at him for a long time, wishing he could see through those enigmatic eyes into the mind beyond. Bradley's faith in himself and his cause had always been extraordinary. There had been times over the last thirty years, when Adam really wished he could write Bradley off in the same way as the Commonwealth establishment did, that he was nothing more than just another crackpot conspiracy theorist. But there were too many little details for him to be laughed off. His superb intelligence sources for a start. The way little facets of Commonwealth policy were organized, seemingly out of kilter with the interests of the Grand Families and Intersolar Dynasties. Adam was so close to believing the whole Starflyer notion, or at the very least he didn't disbelieve it anymore. 'There's something I'd like to know, though I'm afraid it might be a personal weakness on my part.'

'I will be honest with you, Adam. I owe you that much.'

'Where do you go for your rejuvenation? Is there some secret underground clinic that I don't know about which provides the treatment for people like us?'

'No, Adam, there's nowhere like that. I use the Unstorn clinic on Jaruva. It's very good.'

Adam paused as his e-butler called the CST Intersolar timetable up into his virtual vision. 'Is Jaruva a town somewhere?'

'No, it's a planet. CST shut down the gateway two hundred and eighty years ago, after a civil war between various nationalist culture factions and the radical evangelicals. The only thing they hated worse than each other was the Commonwealth – there were some unpleasant acts of terrorism committed before the Isolation. Things have calmed down considerably since then, thankfully. They have rebuilt their society, with each faction having its own homeland. The structure is similar to Earth in the mid-twentieth century. None of the mini-nations are Socialist, I'm afraid.'

'I see,' Adam said carefully. 'And how do you get there?'

'There is a path which leads to Jaruva. The Silfen don't really use it any more.'

'Somehow I knew you'd give me an answer like that.'

'I will be happy to take you there and pay for a rejuvenation, if that's what you want.'

'Let's leave that possibility open, shall we?'

'As you wish. But the offer is sincere and remains.'

'I wish I believed as you do.'

'You are not far from it, Adam. Not really. I expect what is about to happen over the next few years will convince you. But then, I expect it to convince everyone.'

'All right,' Adam said. He had a sense of near-relief now he'd made his decision. Many people spoke of the contentment which came from accepting defeat. He was mildly surprised to find it was true. 'So what do you want the Guardians to do in the Commonwealth? And bear in mind, I won't ever repeat Abadan station, I don't do political statement violence any more.'

'My dear chap, neither do I. And thank you for agreeing to this. I know how it conflicts with your own goals. Don't give up on them. You will live to see a socially just world.'

'Like a priest will see heaven.'

Bradley's soft smile was understanding and sympathetic.

'What are you going to hit first?' Adam asked.

'The *Second Chance* is my primary target right now. Part of your task is going to be assembling a crew to obliterate it.'

'Old folly; you can never destroy knowledge. Even if we were to succeed and blow the *Second Chance* to pieces, they'll build another, and another, and another until one is finally completed. They know how to build them, therefore they will be built.'

'I expect you're right, unfortunately. But destroying the *Second Chance* will be a severe blow to the Starflyer. It wanted the starship built, you know.'

'I know. I received the shotgun message.' Adam stared out at Castle Mount for some time. 'You know, castles once had a purpose other than symbolism; they used to hold the invaders at bay and keep the kingdom safe. We don't build them any more.'

'We need them, though, now more than ever.'

'What a pair we make,' Adam said. 'The optimist and the pessimist.'

'Which do you claim to be?'

'I think you know.'

*

To the mild dismay of his staff, Wilson always arrived in the office at around half past seven in the morning. With management meetings, training sessions, interviews, engineering assessments, media reports, a one-hour gym work-out, and a dozen other items scheduled every day he didn't leave until after nine most evenings. He took lunch at his desk rather than waste time going to the excellent canteen on the ground floor. His influence began to percolate through the whole starship project and, with it, his enthusiasm. Procedures were tightened under his relentless directives, policy became clear-cut and effective. Pride settled around the complex, driving the crews onward.

Every week, Wilson met up with Nigel Sheldon to perform their ritual inspection tour of *Second Chance*. They arrived at the gateway, and kicked off into the assembly platform. Both of them pointing at and gossiping about some new section of the huge ship, acting like a pair of schoolkids.

All of the plasma rockets were installed now, along with their turbopumps and power injectors. Big reaction mass tanks were being eased into cavities along the ship's central engineering superstructure, dark grey ellipsoids whose internal structure was a honeycomb maze of tiny sacs.

'It's the ultimate slosh-baffle design,' Wilson explained as the two of them glided along the assembly grid above the central cylinder. 'The sacs can squeeze out their contents no matter what acceleration manoeuvre we're pulling and, while we're coasting, they hold the fluid stable. If only we'd had that on the old *Ulysses* we'd have saved ourselves a lot of mechanical trouble, but materials technology has come a long way since those days.'

Nigel held on to one of the platform grids, pausing directly above an egg-shaped tank that was being gently eased into position by robot arms. Construction crew and remote mobile sensors were swarming round it like bees to their queen. 'How come we're not using hydrogen? I thought that gives the best specific impulse for rocket exhausts.'

'When you're talking chemical reactions, sure. But the plasma rockets operate at such a high energy level they break their working fluid down into sub-atomic particles. The niling d-sinks we're carrying pump so much power in, this plasma is actually hotter than a fusion generator's exhaust. With that kind of efficiency, cryogenics is a waste of time. Of course, in an ideal world we'd be using mercury as the propellant fluid, but even that has handling problems, not to mention cost and sourcing for the kind of volume we're looking at. So what we've wound up with is a very dense hydrocarbon. It's almost pure crude oil, but the chemists have tweaked the molecular structure so it remains liquid over a huge temperature range. Given the type of near-perfect insulation we've got cloaking the tanks, the thermal support we have to provide for the fuel is minimal.'

Nigel gave the tank a thoughtful look. 'I always used to think rockets were dead simple.'

'The principle is as simple as you can get, it's just the engineering which is complex. But we're doing our best to reduce that; modern techniques allow us to do away with whole layers of ancillary systems.'

'I heard you've instigated a design review board.'

'Final design approval, yeah. I prefer that method to the multiple steering committees you'd set up.' Wilson let go of the grid, and pushed off so he was drifting along the length of the starship towards the life-support wheel. 'It gives the project an overall architecture policy.'

'I'm not arguing. This is your show now.'

They passed over the wheel section. The internal decks were clearly visible now, with decking and wall panelling fixed to the stress structure, showing the internal layout.

'We should start fixing the hull in place by the end of next month,' Wilson said.

'Not too much slippage, then.'

'No. You gave me a good team. And the unlimited funding helps.'

'Actually, it's not unlimited, and I've noticed it's still rising.'

'That was inevitable, but it really should have plateaued now we're entering the design freeze point. We've already started to make a few modifications to the central cylinder to accommodate the expanded stand-off observation period of the mission. The upgraded sensor suite is finishing its alpha-analysis stage, it should be out to tender soon. And we already have the engineering mock-ups of the class three and four remote probe satellites. They're being assembled for us at High Angel by Bayfoss – we're up to capacity here, and they are the experts. Most of your exploratory division geosurvey satellites are built by them.'

'Sure.' Nigel took another look at the crew accommodation decks, where an atmospheric processor had been secured in place, still wrapped in its silver packaging. 'Man, I still can't get over how big this beauty is. You'd think . . . I don't know, we could build something neater by now.'

'A one-man starship?' Wilson asked in amusement. He waved a hand at the front of the cylinder. 'You helped design the hyperdrive engine. I've owned smaller houses than that monster.'

'Yeah, yeah, I know. I ought to go back and take another look at the basic equations.'

'You do that, but I'm telling you a car-sized starship will never catch on. I want something big and powerful around me when I go exploring the unknown.'

'Man, oh man, Freud would have had a field day with you. Now, how's it going with the crew selection?'

'Hoo boy,' Wilson grimaced at the memory. 'The actual crew squad has been finalized. We've got two hundred and twenty who'll start their second phase training next week. We'll select the final fifty a month before launch. The science team is a little tougher; we've passed seventy so far, and Oscar's office is trying to sort out the rest of the applications. It's the interviews that are taking up so much time, the Commonwealth has an awful lot of highly qualified people out there, and we need to put them all through assessment and psych profiling. What I'd like is a pool of about three hundred to choose from.'

'Ah.' Nigel stopped himself above the rim of the life support wheel, watching a constructionbot fixing a decking plate into place. 'Have you considered taking Dr Bose with you?'

'Bose? Oh, the astronomer who saw the envelopment. I think I remember Oscar mentioning he'd applied. He'd certainly got a lot of sponsors. Do you want me to check if he got through the assessment?'

'Not as such, no. The thing is, my office is getting a lot of enquiries about him, as is the Vice President.'

For a moment Wilson thought he meant the vice president of CST. 'You mean Elaine Doi?'

'Yes. It's a bit awkward. Every time the media want a comment on the envelopment they turn to Bose, which is understandable. The trouble is, he cooperates with them. All of them. When the guy sleeps, I've no idea. But anyway, in the public eye he's most strongly associated with the project. It's a position he's exploited superbly.'

'Wait a minute here, are you telling me I've got to take him?'

'All I'm saying is that if you were planning on taking an astronomer, you could do worse. For an obscure professor from a back-of-beyond planet, he's certainly a goddamn expert self-publicist.'

'I'll tell Oscar to review the file, if that's what's bugging you.'

'That's good. And I hope there won't be any ageism in the selection process?'

'What?'

'It's just that the professor is, er, kind of closer to his time for rejuvenation than you or I ... or anyone else you're considering. That's all.'

'Oh, Jesus wept.'

*

The plantation where Tara Jennifer Shaheef lived was on the far side of the mountains that rose up out of the northern districts of Darklake City. Even with a modern highway leading through them, it took the car carrying Paula and Detective

Hoshe Finn a good three hours to drive there. They turned off the junction at the start of a wide valley, the car snaking along a winding local road. The slopes on either side were heavily cultivated with coffee bushes, and every row seemed to have an agriculturebot of some kind trundling along, tending the verdant plants. Humans and buildings were less prominent within this landscape.

Eventually the car turned into the plantation, a wide gated entrance with a white stone arch above the road. Cherry trees lined the long driveway, leading up to a low white house with a bright red clay tile roof.

'All very traditional,' Paula commented.

Hoshe glanced out at the arch. 'You'll find that a lot on this world. We do tend to idolize the past. Most of us had settler ancestors who were successful even before they arrived, and the ethos lingers on. As a planet, we've done rather well from it.'

'If it works, don't try and fix it.'

'Yeah.' He showed no sign that he'd picked up on any irony.

The car halted on the gravel in front of the house's main door. Paula climbed out, looking round the large formal gardens. A lot of time and effort had gone into the big lawn with its palisade of trees.

Tara Jennifer Shaheef was standing in front of the double acmwood doors underneath the portico. Her husband, Matthew deSavoel, stood beside her, an arm resting protectively round her shoulders. He was older than her by a couple of decades, Paula noticed; thick dark hair turning to silver, his midriff starting to spread.

The car drove off round to the stable block. Paula walked forwards. 'Thank you for agreeing to see me,' she said.

'That's all right,' Tara said with a nervous smile. She nodded tightly at Detective Finn. 'Hello again.'

'I trust this won't be too upsetting,' Matthew deSavoel said. 'My wife had put her re-life ordeal behind her.'

'It's all right, Matthew,' Tara said, patting him.

'I don't deliberately make this difficult,' Paula said. 'It was your wife's family who wanted this investigation kept open.'

Matthew deSavoel grunted in dissatisfaction and opened the front door. 'I feel like we should have a lawyer present,' he said as he walked them through the cool reception hall.

'That is your prerogative,' Paula said neutrally. If deSavoel thought his wife was fully recovered he was fooling himself badly. Nobody with three lifetimes behind them was as twitchy as Tara seemed to be. In Paula's experience, anyone who had been killed, accidentally or otherwise, took at least one regeneration post re-life to get over the psychological trauma.

They were shown into a large lounge with a stone tile floor; a grand fireplace dominated one wall, with a real grate and logs sitting at the centre of it. The walls had various hunting trophies hanging up, along with the stuffed heads of alien animals, their teeth and claws prominently displayed to portray them as savage monsters.

'Yours?' Hoshe asked.

'I bagged every one of them,' Matthew deSavoel said proudly. 'There's a lot of hostile wildlife still living up in the hills.'

'I've never seen a gorall that big before,' Hoshe said, standing underneath one of the heads.

'I wasn't aware Oaktier had a guns and hunting culture,' Paula said.

'They don't in the cities,' deSavoel said. 'They think those of us who tend the land are barbaric savages who do it purely for sport. None of them live out here, none of them realize what sort of danger the goralls and vidies pose if they get down to the human communities. There are several political campaigns to ban landowners from shooting outside cultivated

309

lands, as if the goralls will respect that. It's exactly the kind of oppressive crap I came here to get away from.'

'So guns are quite easy to get hold of on this planet?'

'Not a bit of it,' Tara said. She made a big show of flopping into one of the broad couches. 'You wouldn't believe how difficult it is to get a licence, even for a hunting rifle.'

Paula sat opposite her. 'Did you ever hold a licence?'

'No.' Tara shook her head, smiling softly at some private joke. She took a cigarette out of her case, and pressed it on the lighting pad at the bottom. It gave off the sweet mint smell of high-quality GM majane. 'Do you mind? It helps me relax.'

Hoshe Finn frowned, but didn't say anything.

'Did you ever possess a gun?' Paula asked.

Tara laughed. 'No. Or if I did, I never kept the memory. I don't think I would, though. Guns have no place in a civilized society.'

'Most commendable,' Paula said. She wondered if Tara was really that unsophisticated, or if that was something she wanted to believe post-death. But then, most citizens chose to overlook how easy it was to get hold of a weapon. 'I'd like to talk about Wyobie Cotal.'

'Certainly. But like I told Detective Finn last time, I only have a couple of weeks' memory of him.'

'You were having an affair with him?'

Tara took a deep drag, exhaling slowly. 'Certainly was. God, what a body that kid had. I don't think I'd ever forget that.'

'So your marriage to Morton was over?'

'No, not really. We were still on good terms, though it was getting a bit stale. You must know what that's like.' There was an edge of mockery in her voice.

'Did you have other affairs?'

'A couple. Like I said, I could see where it was heading with Morton. Our company was doing well, it was taking up more and more of his time. Men are like that, always obsessing about the wrong things in life. Some men.' She extended a

310

languid hand out to deSavoel, who kissed her knuckles indulgently.

'Did Morton know about the other men?'

'Probably. But I respected him; I didn't flaunt them and they were never the cause of any argument.'

'Did Morton have a gun?'

'Oh don't be ridiculous. We had a good marriage.'

'It was coming to an end.'

'And we got divorced. It happens. In fact, it has to happen when you live this long.'

'Did he have a gun?'

'No.'

'All right. Why would you chose Tampico?'

'That's the place I filed the divorce from, isn't it? Well, I don't know, I'm sure. The first time I heard about it was right after my re-life when the insurance investigators were asking me what happened. I never even knew the place existed before.'

'You and Cotal bought tickets there. You left with him four days after your last memory dump in the Kirova Clinic's secure store. Why did you run off with him?'

'I don't know. I remember meeting him, it was at a party, then after that it was just for the sex, really; and he was fun, enthusiastic the way only first-lives can be. I enjoyed him, but I always found it hard to believe I gave up my life for him. It was a good life Morton and I had here.'

'You weren't the only girl Cotal was seeing.'

'Really? Somehow I'm not surprised. He was gorgeous.'

'You're not jealous about that?'

'Irritated, is about as far as it goes.'

'Did Wyobie have a gun?'

'Oh . . .' She appealed to her husband. 'Please.'

'Come now, Chief Investigator,' deSavoel said loftily. 'There's no need to take such a line. Wyobie Cotal was also killed.'

'Was he?'

He gave Paula a weary grin. 'I sincerely hope not. Yet, I fear it is so. This is not pleasant for my wife, to raise such spectres again after she has accustomed herself to a complete body loss.'

'That's why I'm here,' Paula said. 'To make sure it won't happen again.'

'Again?' Tara's voice rose in alarm. She stubbed her cigarette out. 'You think I'll be killed again?'

'That's not what I meant. It would be most unusual for a killer to strike at you twice; and you have been alive for over twenty years this time. Please don't concern yourself about the possibility. So, Wyobie didn't have a gun?'

'No. Not that I remember.'

'You mentioned other affairs. Were you seeing anybody else at the same time as Cotal?'

'No. Wyobie was quite enough for me.'

'What about enemies, yours or Cotal's?'

'I must have fallen out with many people, you do over a hundred years, but I can't think of any argument or grudge that would warrant killing me. And as for Wyobie, nobody that age has enemies, not ones that kill.'

'His other girlfriend might have been angry enough.'

'Possibly.' Tara shuddered. 'I never met her. Do you think that's what happened?'

'Actually, no. If you and Wyobie were killed, then it certainly wasn't a crime of passion, or at least not a spur of the moment slaying. As yet, we don't know where and when you were killed. To throw up that much uncertainty takes planning and preparation. Other than your ticket there's no real proof you ever went to Tampico.'

'The divorce,' deSavoel said. 'That was filed on Tampico. And all Tara's things were sent there.'

'The divorce was lodged with a legal firm, Broher Associates, on Tampico. It was a pure data transaction. In theory it could have been filed from anywhere inside the unisphere. As for your effects, Tara, they were sent to a Tampico storage warehouse for seven weeks, then removed by your authorization into a private vehicle. The insurance company investigators were unable to trace them. What I find interesting about that is your secure memory storage arrangement. There isn't one apart from the Kirova Clinic, not on Tampico, nor on any other Commonwealth planet as far as the investigators could find, though my Directorate will start double-checking that now. And you would have made one, everybody has a secure store they can update for precisely this reason: re-life. The ticket, your effects shipped out there, your divorce, it's all evidence you were settled on Tampico. But to me, the lack of a secure memory arrangement calls the whole Tampico episode into question.'

'But why?' Tara asked. 'What would be the point in killing me or Wyobie? What did we do?'

'I don't know. The last time you were seen alive was when you had lunch with Caroline Turner at the Low Moon marina restaurant. If anything was wrong, you didn't tell her. In fact, she said you seemed quite normal.'

'Caroline was a good friend, I remember. I might even have told her about Wyobie.'

'She says not, and certainly nothing about leaving Morton to go off with Wyobie. So if you didn't go crazy wild and run off with Wyobie, we have to consider you got involved in some criminal event.'

'I wouldn't!'

Paula held up a cautionary finger. 'Not necessarily deliberately. The logical explanation would be an accident, something you saw or discovered that you shouldn't have, and were killed because of it. My problem with that theory is where it happened. If it was here, then we only have a very small incident window to investigate. Morton had been away from home for two days, and was scheduled to stay at his conference for another four days. He says you stopped answering his calls two days after your lunch with Caroline, the same day your Tampico ticket was purchased. Now, your last memory deposit in the Kirova Clinic secure store was the same day Morton went away. So at the most you had four days for this event to happen to you. I believe we can safely say it didn't happen in the two days prior to your lunch, which leaves us with just two days, forty-eight hours, for it to occur.'

'Police records for that whole month don't have any major crime incident listed,' Hoshe said. 'Actually, it was a quiet year.'

'Then they were good criminals, clever ones,' Paula said. 'You never caught them, and the only evidence is this possible ice murder. That doesn't leave us with a lot to go on. I have to say that if Shaheef and Cotal walked in on something bad, then the chances of discovering what actually happened are slim. Which leaves us with Tampico. You arrived and bumped straight into something you shouldn't have. Our hypothetical Tampico criminals maintained the illusion that you were alive by picking up your effects and then filing for the divorce. That would explain the lack of a memory store.'

'What sort of criminals?' Tara asked shakily. 'What would they be doing to make them kill me and Wyobie?'

'It is only a theory,' Paula told her quickly. 'I have difficulty in accepting major criminal conspiracies, the probability is extremely low, not that we can ignore it. But that implausibility does leave us with a quandary. If it wasn't that, and it wasn't your private life, which appears blameless, then what did happen?'

Tara fumbled with her case, and lit another cigarette. 'You're the detective, everybody knows that.' Her hands were trembling as she took a drag. Matthew deSavoel held her tight, glaring at Paula. 'Have you got enough?' he snapped.

'For now,' she said calmly.

'Find out,' Tara called out as Paula and Hoshe started to

leave. 'Please. I have to know. Everything you've said ... it wasn't a freak accident, was it? I've told myself that for twenty years; told everybody I had a mad romantic impulse and ran off with Wyobie, because if you say it and keep on saying it, then that becomes what happened. It was like making up the memory. But I knew, I really knew it didn't happen like that.'

'I'll do what I can,' Paula said.

'Where now?' Hoshe asked as the car drove away from the big isolated plantation house.

'The ex-husband, Morton.'

He sneaked a look at her. 'You got any idea what happened?'

'It wasn't an accident. I believe Tara. She used to be too sensible to do anything like running off with Wyobie. He was already giving her everything she wanted from the relationship. That means Tampico is all wrong; it was a set-up, an alibi.'

'Used to be sensible?'

'You saw what she is today.'

'Yeah. That's what you meant by investigating people, isn't it?'

'Of course.' She turned to stare out of the car's windows, seeing nothing but a blur of big shaggy walrush trees that had been planted as a windbreak for the neat plantation bushes. 'It's people who commit crimes, so that's where you'll find the motivation: people.' It was so instinctive, so obvious, she didn't have to think to talk to him.

Her parents, or rather the couple she had thought to be her parents during her childhood, had sincerely believed that instinct was one which could be stillbirthed. It was the old nature versus nurture argument, and the outcome of this particular ultra-modern chapter of it was one they desperately wanted to use to prove to the whole Commonwealth that nurture could be the victor, that there was no preordained fate. Especially not one like Paula's creators intended for her.

The planet where she was birthed was called Huxley's

Haven, though the other Commonwealth worlds derisively called it the Hive. Settled in 2102, it was funded, and populated, by the Human Structure Foundation, a strange collective of genetic researchers and intellectual socio-political theorists. They were keen to explore the genetic possibilities for psychoneural profiling now they were clear of Earth's restrictions, believing it possible to create a perfectly stable society by implementing the phrase *each to his own* to a degree which the rest of humanity found quite chilling. A lot of Anglo-Saxon surnames originated from occupation: tailor, thatcher, crofter . . . The aim of the Foundation was to make the link solid and unbreakable, determined within an individual's DNA. Professions couldn't be installed wholesale, of course, a psychoneural profile merely gave a person the aptitude to do their designated job, while simpler, physiological modifications complemented the trait. Doctors would be given dextrous fingers and high visual acuity, while farm workers and builders possessed a large, strong physique – so it went right through the entire spectrum of human activity. The traits were bundled together, and fixed to prevent genetic drift. As far as the traits were concerned, there would never be any mixed profiles. The Foundation scrupulously avoided using the word 'pure' in its press releases.

The Commonwealth as a whole detested the notion. Right from its conception, Huxley's Haven became a near pariah state. There were even serious calls for military/police style intervention made in the Senate, which contravened the organization's constitution – the Commonwealth was set up originally to guarantee individual planet freedom within an overall legal framework. In the end, the Foundation was able to proceed because legally the planet was independent and free.

After several prominent and well-financed private court cases against the Foundation came to nothing, it was CST's turn to face a barrage of media-supported pressure to close the gateway. Nigel Sheldon had to reluctantly argue the case for keeping it open: if they closed one gateway because of an activist campaign, that left all gateways vulnerable to people who disagreed with a planet's culture, religion, or politics. The Hive stayed connected to the Commonwealth, though it never really contributed to the mainstream economic and financial structure. Quietly, and with considerable scientific flair, the Foundation got on with the job of building their unique society.

Some people never did accept the lost court cases or the Foundation's 'right' to pursue its goal. A greater human right took precedence, they argued. In their view they were now left with a whole planet of genetically modified slaves to be liberated.

If there was ever anybody to whom the term extreme liberals could be applied, it was Marcus and Rebecca Redhound. Born into the considerable wealth of Grand Earth families, they were happy to contribute financially as well as actively to the cause. Along with a small, equally dedicated, cabal, they planned a raid against the Hive, which they were convinced would be the grand event that would finally demonstrate to the rest of the Commonwealth that the Foundation was wrong, not just in its politics but its science as well.

After months of covert planning and preparation, nine of these urban rich-kid commandos broke into one of the Foundation's birthing wards in the Hive's capital, Fordsville. They managed to steal seven new-birthed babies and get them to the CST planetary station before the alarm was raised. Three were traced immediately by the Intersolar Serious Crimes Directorate, and the infants returned to their crèche on Huxley's Haven. The publicity was everything the group could have wished for, though public sympathy didn't entirely swing their way. Something about stealing babies just cut people cold.

Four of the cabal were arrested when the babies were traced. After that, the Serious Crimes Directorate mounted the largest manhunt the Commonwealth had ever seen to find the four missing babies, one male, and three females. It took another fifteen months of painstaking detective work by ten Chief Investigators aided by the SI to locate the missing boy in a town on the then frontier planet of Ferarra. Five months after that two more of the girls were recovered on EdenBurg. The last child and remaining two cabal members proved more elusive.

With the paranoia which only the truly committed can muster, Marcus and Rebecca had spent over two years fermenting their own elaborate preparations for the snatch, an activity they kept secret from the rest of their cabal. The first part of their cover was to have a child of their own, Coya, who would act as a sister to the Hive baby. She would set a normal behavioural example to the psychoneural-profiled waif; and a young family with twins would be less likely to attract attention. It was a good plan. Marcus and Rebecca had bought a house on Marindra, out in a small agricultural town, where they established a small market garden business. It was a pleasant place to live, with a good community spirit. The children fitted in well as they grew up. Paula's half-Filipino features were slightly incongruous, given her parents and 'twin' Coya were all of prominent eastern Mediterranean stock. But they explained it away as a genetic modification designed to bring out Rebecca's distant Asian ancestry, honouring her deep ethnic origin. By then, the case of the last missing Hive baby had long faded from public attention – Paula's looks were never the cause of suspicion.

As a child, Paula really wasn't too different to her sister. They played together, ran their parents ragged, loved the puppy Marcus bought them, had a fondness for swimming, and did well at school. It was as she moved into her teens that Paula was noticeably more restrained than Coya; she did as her parents asked, didn't argue with them, and steered clear of all the trouble that was to be found in their little rural community. Everyone commented on what a nice girl she was becoming, not like half of the teenagers in this town who were simply terrible and a sure sign of society's imminent collapse. She regarded boys with the same contempt and fascination as her peers; started dating, suffered the heart-aching humiliation of being dumped, and promptly took it out on her next two boyfriends by chucking them. Found another boy she liked – and went steady for five months. In sports she was competent rather than outstanding. Academically she excelled at languages and history. As teachers remarked, she had superb recall and an obsession with tracing down the smallest facts connected to her subjects. Aptitude tests showed she would make a great psychologist.

Looking at their contented, normal, extra daughter on her sixteenth birthday, Marcus and Rebecca knew they had succeeded. They'd brought up a Hive child in a loving natural environment, and produced a perfectly happy, healthy human being. What could be done with one, could be done to all. The Foundation's hold over its oppressed population could be broken, their method of control was flawed. Decency and human dignity had triumphed in the end.

Two days later, on a splendid late summer afternoon, they took Paula out into the garden and told her of her true heritage. They even sheepishly showed her the old news media recordings of the snatch and subsequent manhunt.

What the Foundation had never revealed at the time was the nature of the psychoneural profiling given to the snatched babies. The others were all reasonably standard for Huxley's Haven: public service workers, engineers, accountants, even an archivist. But Paula, as luck or fate would have it, was an exception even among her own kind. Crime on Huxley's Haven was extremely rare, naturally so, given that its citizens were all designed to be content in their jobs and lives. Although not even the Foundation claimed to make life perfect. All human civilizations needed a police force. On

Huxley's Haven it was a source of national pride that there was one law enforcement officer for every ten thousand people. Paula was one of them.

Two hours after their joyful confession, Marcus and Rebecca were in custody. It was Paula who turned them in. She had no choice; knowing what was right and what was wrong was the core of her identity, her very soul.

The last missing Hive child was the greatest media story to hit the unisphere for a decade, making Paula an instant celebrity. Young, beautiful, and frighteningly incorruptible; she was everything a sixteen-year-old should never be.

Thanks to Paula's relentless testimony, Marcus and Rebecca were sentenced to thirty-two years life suspension each, losing double the time over which their crime was perpetrated, the kind of punishment normally reserved for murderers. Unisphere coverage of the trial allowed a quarter of the human race to watch in silent fascination as Coya broke down and screamed hysterically at the judge before begging her step-twin to withdraw the sentencing application. Paula's only answer, a silent pitying glance at the sobbing girl, made that whole quarter of the human race shiver.

After the trial, Paula went back to Huxley's Haven, the home she'd never known, to discover her real name and suffer embarrassing introductions to the other stolen children with whom she had nothing in common. She belonged there even less than on Marindra; a modern Commonwealth education put her completely outside the norm as far as Huxley's Haven was concerned. They didn't have advanced technology on the Hive, the new conformist society was structured so that people did all the work, not machines. With her exposure to domestic bots and the ultimate data access of the unisphere, Paula considered such rejection to be stupid and provincial. It was the one success Marcus and Rebecca had with shaping her thoughts, though by then their bodies were safely comatose in the Justice Directorate's hibernation wombs, beyond knowing.

Away from the public eye, Paula left Huxley's Haven for Earth, where she enrolled at the Intersolar Serious Crimes Directorate. At the time, she had no idea how high up the political food chain her application was bounced before it was finally approved. But approved it was, and inevitably she became the best operative they ever had – despite the one notorious case of 2243 which she still hadn't solved.

*

Morton lived in the penthouse of a fifty-storey skyscraper standing behind Darklake City's Labuk Marina. Not at all far, in fact, from Caroline Turner's last lunch with Tara. Paula noted the coincidence as the car drove them along the water-front. They parked in the skyscraper's underground garage and took the express lift up to the top floor. Morton was waiting for them in the vestibule as the doors opened. Three years out of rejuvenation himself, he was a tall, handsome young man whose thick chestnut hair was tied back in a long ponytail. Dressed in a fashionably cut amber and peacock-blue tropical shirt and expensive hand-tailored linen slacks, he looked good and obviously knew it. His youthful face put on a broad courteous smile as he shook their hands in welcome.

'Good of you to see us,' Paula said. It was early evening local time, which was only a few hours ahead of Paris time.

'Least I could do.' Morton ushered them inside through elaborate double doors. His penthouse must have had a floor area larger than the plantation house where his ex-wife now lived. They walked into a massive split-level living room with a window wall. It was six thirty, and the copper-red sun had already fallen level with the top of the skyscraper, shining its rich hazy light directly into the penthouse. Opulent furnishings and expensive artwork gleamed in glorious twilight hues as they soaked up the illumination. There was a large roof garden on the other side of the wide glass doors, half of which was taken up with a swimming pool. Beyond the stainless steel railings ringing the patio area was a tremendous view out across the city and lake.

The three of them settled in the lavish conversation area settees in front of the glass wall. Morton ordered it to raise its opacity, ridding most of the glare. That was when Paula saw someone was in the pool, a young girl, swimming lengths with powerful easy strokes. She told her e-butler to bring up Morton's file; there was no current registered marriage, but local media gossip files had linked him to a string of girls since he came out of rejuvenation. His current lover was Mellanie Rescorai, a first-life nineteen-year-old, and member of the Oaktier national diving squad. Mellanie's parents were on record as strongly objecting to the liaison – in reaction, Mellanie had simply moved out of the family home and into Morton's penthouse.

'Something to drink?' Morton asked. The butler appeared at the side of the settee, dressed in antique-style black clothes. Paula stared at him, mildly surprised: a real live human servant, not a bot.

'No thank you,' she said. Hoshe shook his head.

'I'll have my sparkling gin, thank you,' Morton said. 'It is after office hours, after all.'

'Yes, sir.' The butler gave a discreet bow, and walked over to the mirrored drinks cabinet.

'I understand it was you who alerted the police about this situation,' Paula said.

'That's right.' Morton leaned back casually into the leather cushioning. 'I thought it was kind of strange that Cotal had to be re-lifed as well as Tara. To me it implied that they died at the same time, which is kind of suspicious, especially as nobody ever found out how Tara died. I'm surprised nobody else made the connection, actually.' His polite smile focused on Hoshe.

'Different insurance companies, different clinics,' Hoshe said defensively. 'I'm sure Wyobie would have raised the question with my division eventually when he asked after Ms Shaheef.'

'Of course.'

'So you recognized the name?' Paula asked.

'Yes. God knows why I didn't edit the little shit out of my memories during the last two rejuvenations. Subconscious, I guess. You learn from your experiences, a smart man doesn't dump them.'

'So was it a painful divorce from Tara?'

'Her leaving me was a shock. I simply didn't see that coming. I mean, with hindsight I was heavily involved with our company, and we'd been together for a while, I suppose it was inevitable. But to walk out like that, without any warning, that wasn't Tara. Not the Tara I thought I knew, anyway. But I got over it the same way a lot of guys do: screwed every piece of skirt in sight and threw myself into my work. After that, the actual divorce was completely irrelevant, just a signature certificate loaded on a file.'

'And there was no clue she was going to leave you?'

'Hell, no, I was worried about her when I got back home. I mean, she hadn't answered my calls for two days. But I figured at the time she was pissed with me for spending the time away from home. Then when I got back she'd stripped the apartment, everything she owned was gone. Pretty big fucking clue, huh?'

The butler returned with the sparkling gin in a crystal glass, and put it on the side table next to Morton. 'Will that be all, sir?'

'For now.' Morton waved him away.

'Was there any message?' Paula asked.

'Not a damn thing. The first and only time I heard from her was when the divorce file arrived two weeks later.'

'That was handled by a legal firm. So you never actually had any contact with Tara at all?'

'No. Not after she left.'

'How did you know Wyobie Cotal's name?'

'It was in the divorce file.'

'Tara put it in?'

'Yes. He was the irreconcilable difference.'

'I'd like a copy, please.'

'Sure.' He instructed his e-butler to release a copy file to Paula.

'I have to ask, did you benefit from the divorce?'

Morton laughed with genuine amusement. 'Sure did, I got rid of her.' He took a drink of his sparkling gin, still grinning.

'That's not quite what I meant.'

'Yes, yes, I know.' He locked his hands together behind his head, and gazed up at the ceiling. 'Let's see. There wasn't much to it. We both came out of it financially secure. That was part of the pre-marriage contract, everything to be split fifty fifty. It was fair enough. Tara was richer than me back then, she put up a higher percentage of initial capital for the company. That was no secret. But I was the one who managed it, who made it work. When we divorced, our shares were divided up strictly according to the contract, we both got half.'

'How much more money did she put in?'

'It was a sixty-five, thirty-five split. That percentage isn't something I'd kill for.'

'I'm sure. So who kept the company?'

'I'm still running it, after a fashion. AquaState's one of our subsidiaries now.'

Paula consulted his file. 'I see. You're the chairman of Gansu Construction now.'

'That's right. Six months after we went public, Gansu made an offer for AquaState. I negotiated a good two for one exchange rate on my shares, a seat on the Gansu board, and a decent options deal on more stock. Forty years of hard work later, and here I am. We're the biggest civil engineering outfit on this whole planet; you name it we can build it for you.

Plenty of offplanet divisions as well, and more opening every year. One day we'll rival the multistellars.'

'According to my records, the company you and Tara owned, AquaState, didn't go public until three years after the divorce.'

'No, Tara agreed – or rather her divorce lawyers did – that we'd both get a better deal by waiting, letting the moisture extraction business grow until we could get the maximum price from the flotation. When AquaState finally went public, her shares were registered with a bank on Tampico, then they were converted to Gansu stock when I sold out. I shouldn't really be telling you this, but ... Since she got re-lifed, most of them have been sold. She's using up money at a hell of a rate, supporting that idiot aristocrat husband and his plantation.'

'Thank you, but I don't think that's relevant to our inquiry. I'm more interested in what happened to her shares for the seventeen years prior to her re-life. Did they just sit in the Tampico bank?'

'As far as I know, yes. I only know they're being sold now because as chairman I can see the ownership registry. She's disposing of them at quite a rate, a couple of million Oaktier dollars a year.'

Paula turned to Hoshe. 'We need to check with the Tampico bank to find out what happened to those seventeen years' worth of dividend payments.'

'Certainly.'

Mellanie Rescorai climbed out of the pool and started towelling herself down with the pink-wash sky as a backdrop. She was very attractive, Paula conceded. Morton was staring at her with a greedy expression.

'What about enemies?' Paula asked. 'Did Tara have any?'

'No.' Morton was still looking at his trophy girlfriend. 'That is: I doubt it, I don't actually remember, I got rid of the

325

majority of those memories, just kept the essentials from those days, you know.'

'And you? Did you have enemies back then?'

'I wouldn't go that far. I had business rivals, certainly. And I've got a damn sight more of them now. But no deal would be worth killing over, not in those days.'

'Only those days?'

'Or these,' he said with a grin.

'Did you meet up with Tara again, after the re-life?'

'Yes. The insurance investigators and the police both had a load of questions for me, all of them the same as yours. I went to see her after she came out of the clinic, for old times' sake, to make sure she was okay. I don't hold grudges, and we'd had thirteen good years together. We still meet up occasionally, parties, social events, that kind of thing. Though that's getting less and less now she's got her husband. I haven't actually seen her since my last rejuvenation.'

'You and Tara didn't have any children, did you?'

Morton's attention switched back to the living room. 'No.'

'Why not? As you said, you were together for thirteen years.'

'We decided we didn't want them; it was even written into our pre-marriage contract. Both of us were busy people. The lifestyle we had then didn't have any space for that kind of family commitment.'

'Okay, one last question, probably irrelevant considering you've had two rejuvenations since, but do you remember any odd incidents prior to her disappearance?'

'Sorry, no, not a thing. If there were any, they're memories that I left behind a long time ago.'

'I thought that might be the case. Well, thank you again for seeing us.'

Morton stood up and showed the Chief Investigator out. As they walked through to the vestibule, he let his eyes slip down to her rump. Her business suit skirt was clinging in an enjoyable way, showing off her hips. Even though he'd accessed her court cases several times through the unisphere, her physical appearance post-rejuvenation was a pleasurable surprise. He wondered if she'd be going to a Silent World tonight. If so, it was one he'd like to be visiting.

When they'd gone he went back out onto the roof garden. Mellanie smiled at him with the simple happiness of the totally devoted.

'So was she murdered?' the girl asked.

'They don't know.'

She twined her arms around his neck, pressing her still damp body against him. 'Why do you care? It was centuries and centuries ago.'

'Forty years. And I'd care very much if it happened to you.'

Her lips came together in a hurt pout. 'Don't say that.'

'The point is, time doesn't lessen a crime, especially not today.'

'Okay.' She shrugged, and smiled at him again. 'I won't run away from you like she did, not ever.'

'I'm glad to hear it.' He bent forwards slightly, and started kissing her, an action which she responded to with her usual eagerness. Her youthful insecurity had been so easy to exploit, especially for someone with his years of life experience. She'd never known anyone as urbane and self-confident, nor as rich, as him before; the only people she'd ever dated were nice first-life boys. By herself, she wasn't brave enough to break out from her middle-class conformity; but with his coaxing and support she soon began to nibble at the forbidden fruits. The publicity of their affair, the rows with her parents, it all played in his favour. Like all first-lifers she was desperate to be shown everything life could offer. And as if by a miracle, he'd appeared in her life to fill the role of both guide and paymaster. Suddenly, after all the years of discipline and restrictions she'd endured to reach national level, nothing was outlawed to her. Her response to the liberation was a very predictable over-indulgence.

Mellanie wasn't quite the most beautiful girl he'd ever bedded, her chin was slightly too long, her nose too blunt, to be awarded that title. But with that lanky, broad-shouldered body of hers trained by the national swimming federation coach to the peak of gymnastic fitness she was certainly one of the most physically satisfying. Although, truly, it was her age which excited him in a way he'd never reached with any of his Silent World encounters. Even in this liberally inclined society, a rejuve seducing a first-lifer was regarded as being over the edge of civilized behaviour – which simply added intensity to the experience. He could afford to ignore the disapproval of others.

This was what he was now, one of the rich and powerful, rising above the norm, the mundane. He lived his personal and professional lives in the same way. If there was something he wanted in either of them, he got it. Empire building became him, allowing him to thrive. Compared with his first mediocre century he was truly alive now.

'Go in and get changed,' he told her eventually. His e-butler summoned the dresser and the beautician to help get the girl ready. 'Resal is expecting us on the boat in an hour. I don't want to be too late, there are people coming that I need to meet tonight.'

The dresser and the beautician appeared in the doorway, waiting patiently. Two middle-aged women who knew his tastes probably better than he did; the dresser acted as his wardrobe stylist as well.

'It's not all business, is it?' Mellanie asked.

'Of course not, there'll be fun people there as well. People your own age, and people older than me. Now please, we need to get moving.'

'Yes, Morty.' Mellanie caught sight of the two women

waiting for her, and turned back to him. 'What would you like me to wear?'

'Always: something that shows you off.' His virtual vision was displaying recent clothing purchases the dresser had made. 'That gold and white thing you were fitted for on Wednesday. That's small enough.'

She nodded eagerly. 'Okay.' Then she hugged him again, the kind of tight reassurance-seeking embrace a child would give a parent. 'I love you, Morty, really I do. You know that, don't you?' Her eyes searched his face, hunting for any sign of confirmation.

'I know.' His older, earlier, self would probably have experienced a twinge of guilt at that adulation. It was never going to last. He knew that, even though she would never be able to see it. In another year or so some other stray beauty would catch his eye, and the sweet heat of the chase would begin again. Mellanie would be gone in a flood of tears. But until then . . .

He gave her bum a quick gentle slap, hurrying her back into the penthouse. She squealed in mock-outrage before scampering in through the wide doors. The two women followed her in.

His e-butler brought up a list of items which he hadn't finished working on during the day. He surveyed them all, taking his time to add comments, demand more information, or approve them for action. It was always the way; no matter how complex the management smartware a company employed, executive decisions were inevitably made by a human. An RI could eliminate a whole strata of middle management, but it lacked the kind of creative ability which a true leader possessed.

When he'd tidied up the office work, the butler brought him another sparkling gin. Morton leant on the steel balcony rail to sip the drink, gazing out at the city below as the sun fell below the horizon. He could outline sections of it in his mind, entire districts which Gansu had built, where their government-licensed subsidiaries now provided utility and civic services – his innovation, that. There were other areas, as well, which drew his eye. Old plantations and orchards that now formed the outskirts, green parquetry flocking round the base of the mountains. Gansu's architects had drawn up plans for beautiful buildings which would fit snugly into those crumpled mini-valleys, expensive exclusive communities providing for Oaktier's increasingly affluent population. Already, the farmers were being tempted with financial offers and incentives.

When he looked up to the darkening sky the stars were starting to twinkle. If everything went to plan, his influence would soon stretch out to them, far exceeding the small subcontracts their offplanet offices currently achieved. He controlled Gansu's board now, and the increased business and rising stock price he'd achieved for them over the last decade had given him near-regal status. There would be no timidity in his expansion plans. The opportunities which lay out there were truly staggering. Entire civil infrastructures to be built. The new phase three junction worlds which would one day rival the Big15. Now was the best time to live.

He lowered his gaze again to scan the city rooftops. One old medium-sized tower caught his attention. It was the apartment block he and Tara had lived in for most of their marriage; he'd never realized he could see it from his roof garden before. There were no details from this distance, twilight transformed it into a grey slab with parallel lines of light shining out through windows. He took another sip of the cocktail as he stared at it. His memory couldn't even provide an image of the apartment's interior. When he'd gone in for rejuvenation six years after the divorce he'd edited away everything but the basic information from his secure store. Now, that life was almost like a series of notes in a file – not real, not something he'd lived through. And yet ... Twenty years ago, when he'd heard of Tara's re-life procedure something about it had nagged at him. It was out of character to go and see her, yet he had. The semi-neurotic woman in her new clone body wasn't anyone he recognized, certainly not the kind of woman he could form an attachment to. He put that down to shock and psychological trauma from the re-life.

Then the news about Cotal had been filtered out of the unisphere media streams by his e-butler, which had caught the connection to Tara. He'd stopped work in his office – an unheard-of event – and worried about how strange the coincidence was. His staff had made a few discreet inquiries, the results of which had been enough for him to call the police. Their subsequent report on the case had annoyed him with its vagueness and lack of any real conclusion. Rather than kick up a fuss himself, which would draw comment, he'd spoken to some of the senior members of the Shaheef family.

He hadn't quite expected someone as renowned as Chief Investigator Myo herself to be assigned the case. But it was a pleasing development; if anyone could sort out what had actually happened, it would be her. His thoughts slipped to her compact body again, and the high possibility of her needing to visit Silent World.

'Morty.'

He turned round. The dresser and beautician had worked their usual magic. Mellanie was standing silhouetted in the light from the lounge, her auburn hair dried and straightened so it fell down her back, the tiny dress exposing vast amounts of toned young flesh. His disquiet over Tara and Cotal vanished at once as he contemplated what new indecencies he would tutor her in later tonight.

'Do I look all right?' she asked cautiously.

'Perfect.'

10

Oscar Monroe and McClain Gilbert took the early morning express from Anshun, passing through StLincoln then Earth-London before arriving at Kerensk. The CST planetary station there operated the gateway to the High Angel, but there was no train. Instead, they disembarked from the express and walked back up the platform to the main concourse. Next was a series of security checks to get into the High Angel transfer section; CST operated the first, a standard deep body scan and luggage examination, before passing them over to the Commonwealth Diplomatic Police Directorate who reviewed all visitor details. The High Angel was the one place where free entry was not a guaranteed right for Commonwealth citizens. As well as all personal details being reviewed by the Diplomatic Police for any criminal record, the file was also forwarded to the High Angel who possessed the ultimate veto on who could enter.

Oscar waited with a fluttering stomach as the policeman accepted the citizenship ID file from his e-butler and ran a DNA scan to confirm he matched the certified data. He'd never been to the High Angel before and there was always a chance it would refuse him entry, or worse, say why. 'You ever been before?' he asked Mac. It was an attempt to appear casual in front of the policeman.

'Five times now,' McClain said. 'Forward teams train in the

zero-gee sections so we're ready for any type of space encounter.'

'Damn, all these years on the job, and I never knew that.'

McClain grinned at his friend. They'd known each other for ten years, working together in Merredin's CST exploratory division; after that much time in a high-pressure profession if you didn't develop a mutual respect then somebody had to leave. Chain of command was always a nominal concept in the division, you trusted people to do their job right. 'Oh great, I've been risking my life under an Operations Director that doesn't have a clue what's going on.'

'I saw that tar-pit monster coming, didn't I?'

'Gentlemen,' the policeman said, 'you're clear to proceed.'

They walked through into the transfer section lounge. A steward gave them each a once-piece overall made of light breathable fabric, with fuseto footpads and cuffs. 'It's just for the shuttle,' he told them. 'Wear it over your clothes, it stops anything flying loose. And please don't forget your helmets before you go through. Safety regulations will not allow us to fly unless all passengers are wearing them.'

Several other people were in the lounge, all of them shrugging their way into the white overalls. Anyone with long hair was fastening it back with bands that the stewards were handing out. Mac nudged Oscar. 'Isn't that Paula Myo over there?'

Oscar followed his gaze. A young-looking woman was fixing her straight black hair with the bands. Her companion was an overweight man in a smart suit who could barely fit into his overall. 'Could be. She must have come out of rejuve recently. I remember accessing the Shayoni case about six or seven years back, the one where she tracked down the arms seller who'd supplied kinetics to the Dakra Free State rebels. Four days she waited in that house for them to show up. That is what I call dedication.'

'My wife studied her cases when she was in the academy, that's how I know her. I'm sure it's her.'

'Wonder who she's after this time?'

'You know, we should have her in the crew.'

Oscar gave Mac a startled look. 'As what? Do you think we're going to start killing each other on the voyage?'

'Living in close proximity with your farts for a year, more than likely. But she solves problems, right, that's what her whole brain's wired for. She's exactly the kind of talent we should be taking with us.'

'There are different kinds of problems, you know; and we're heading for the wrong sort.' Oscar clapped Mac's shoulder. 'Keep trying, one day you'll be command material.'

'The day before you, pal.'

'Right. And by the way, what does your wife think about you going off and leaving her for a year?'

'Angie? She's fairly cool about it. We talked about splitting up, but that's being unduly pessimistic. We'll just leave it and see what happens. If she finds someone else while I'm gone, fair enough. Our partnership contract allows for that.'

'Nice contract.'

'Yeah, so what about you? How are you going to cope for a year? Seen any possibilities among the recruits?'

'Haven't really thought about it. I've got enough OCtattoos for a very high resolution TSI, so I'll just make do with a harem of nicely shaped pixels.'

Mac shook his head in sad dismay. 'Brother, you have got to get out more.'

A steward led five of them, including Paula and Hoshe Finn, into the departure corridor at the far end of the lounge. Everybody's feet made crunching sounds as the fuseto pads tried to anchor them on the floor. They were all handed a protective helmet as they went through, the steward making sure they put it on. 'Are you familiar with zero gee?' the steward asked.

'I am nowadays,' Oscar told him grumpily. The helmet was identical to those they used at the starship complex on

Anshun. He still hated his trips to the assembly platform, but Wilson was a real believer in hands-on management – obviously a relic of his gung-ho NASA days. There wasn't a week since Oscar had joined the project that he hadn't been on some kind of inspection tour.

'The gateway itself is marked by the black rim,' the steward said, pointing ahead down the corridor. 'After that you're in zero gee; please use the fusetos and do not float free. Your shuttle is waiting at dock five. Now if you'll all follow me.' As he arrived at the black line, he reached forwards and touched his fuseto cuff on the wall. He eased himself gracefully across the line and his feet floated off the floor. Oscar grimaced in resignation, and followed suit.

After five metres, the corridor opened out into the middle of a hemisphere measuring fifty metres across. There were no windows, only eight big airlocks set equidistantly round the rim. Number five was open. The steward led them carefully along the curving surface, adhering to it from his wrists and toes, like some giant insect. He waited by the airlock, ready to give assistance as they stopped to manoeuvre themselves through into the shuttle.

The little craft was a basic tube, ten metres long, with a double line of couches. Oscar strapped himself in, and looked up. Five thick windows were set into what passed as the fuselage ceiling above him. All he could see was the curving outer wall of the departure port.

There were only fifteen passengers on board. Their steward went along the couches, checking that everyone was settled, then the airlock irised shut. 'High Angel does not permit CST to put a gateway inside itself,' the steward said. 'So we're about fifty kilometres away. The journey over will take approximately fifteen minutes. If anyone has any real difficulty, please let me know. I have some strong sedatives which will probably help. In the meantime please familiarize yourself with the sanitary tube on the seatback in front of you.'

Oscar glanced at the flexible hose with its fresh replaceable nozzle, and grimaced. Still, it was an improvement on the bags he'd taken to carrying with him round the starship platform.

The shuttle vibrated quietly as it disengaged from the locking mechanism, chemical reaction control rockets nudged it away from the docking port. After drifting for a few seconds, the more powerful main rockets flared, accelerating them away. As they retreated from the port, more and more of the structure flowed into view through the shuttle windows, until after a minute Oscar could see the entire gateway station. It reminded him of a quartz cluster, long hexagonal tube sections all rising up out of a central disk; with the twin shuttle departure and arrival ports extending out from the disk's rim. The end of the hexagonal tubes were giant airlocks where cargo tugs delivered their shipments; sealed pods containing completed satellites, sophisticated solid state devices, compounds, crystals, and biologicals which could only be fabricated in microgee environments. Cargo tugs also used the airlocks to load up with consumer goods and food which the gateway delivered, ferrying them over to the High Angel.

The rest of the archipelago drifted into view through the window; over a hundred free-flying factories ranging from tiny independent research capsules, barely larger than the shuttle, up to the corporate macrohubs, kilometre-wide webs with production modules sitting on each junction where they glinted like jewels of prismatic chrome. Behind them the gas-giant world, Icalanise, dominated the starfield as the little shuttle rotated slowly. Their orbital position showed it to them as a massive crescent striped by saffron and white cloud bands whose fluctuating edges locked together by counter-spiral curlicues; as if each was extending talons into the other. A pair of small black circles were close together on the equator, eclipse shadows thrown by two of the gas-giant's thirty-eight moons.

After ten minutes, the shuttle turned again, aligning itself for the deceleration burn. Oscar found himself looking straight at the High Angel.

The exploratory division wormhole which opened in the star system in 2163 was unable to locate any H-congruous planet and the Operations Director was about to close it and move on when the dish picked up a powerful, regular microwave pulse from Icalanise. They obtained a position lock to a point orbiting half a million kilometres above the brimstone atmosphere, and shifted the wormhole in for a close look. It was a confusing image at first. The telescope had centred on a dark, rocky moonlet sixty-three kilometres long, and up to twenty wide. But it appeared to be sprouting petals of pearl-white light – an angel's wings. Moving in, and refining the focus, revealed the rock was actually the host body to twelve giant artificial domes of crystal sitting on the end of tall metallic stalks. Not all of the domes were translucent and radiant. Five were clear, revealing the alien cities contained inside. Street grids were illuminated in ruby, turquoise and emerald light, while the thousands of windows set into the strange architectural silhouettes of towers, hoops, cones, and spheres blazed away in the spectrums of many different suns.

What they'd found was a starship, a living behemoth capable of ftl travel. Not that it was any kind of life that humanity understood; a machine that had risen to sentience, or a spaceborn lifeform which had evolved or been engineered into its current nature. The High Angel wasn't forthcoming about its origin, saying only that its purpose was to provide a habitable environment to the planet-based species it encountered in the hope of learning about them. It was 'resting' in orbit around Icalanise – for how long was also not divulged. After some negotiation over a radio channel it agreed to open three of its (at that time, empty) domes to humans, who would use it primarily as a dormitory town for the astroengineering companies. The two most prominent clauses in the settlement agreement were High Angel's veto on visitors and settlers, and its promise to inform its new human residents before it took flight again . . . whenever that might be.

Their shuttle manoeuvred underneath the vast base of the New Glasgow dome and down along the tapering stalk underneath. The dome's spaceport was situated just above the point where the pewter-coloured stalk sank into the starship's rocky outer crust, a thick necklace of airlocks and ports which ringed the structure. Several of them had shuttles attached, while larger docking cradles were holding cargo tugs that were unloading.

They docked with a slight tremble, and the plyplastic airlock irised open. 'Thank you for travelling with us,' the steward said. 'Please remember that after you disembark you will still be in freefall until the lift is moving.'

Oscar waited until all the passengers in front of him had got out before releasing his own straps. The corridor outside the airlock was disappointing, a wide silverish tube with a shallow curve taking it deeper into the stalk; there was no exotic feel to it at all. He drifted across it to the lift opposite. Like everyone else he let his fuseto soles stick him to the floor. Just before the doors closed, he saw Paula Myo and her companion glide past the lift, heading further down the corridor.

Gravity slowly built as the lift slid up the inside of the stalk. That much Oscar could understand, they were accelerating, after all. When it stopped, he was still in a full standard gravity field. The High Angel had never explained how it did that, along with just about every other technical ability it possessed, like its power source, the nature of its ftl drive, how it shielded itself from particle impacts, where the mass came from to extrude its new domes.

Their lift was one of ten opening out into a big arrivals lounge. Oscar and Mac took off their overalls and dropped them into a bin, then headed eagerly for the exit. The transit building was at the centre of New Glasgow's Circle Park, an area of greenery five kilometres wide filled with so many trees it could almost be classed as forest. Behind the outer ring of trees were the skyscrapers, as varied in shape and texture as any New York avenue. The difference here was the skyway loops which coiled round them, thin rails carrying personal pods between public stops at considerable speed. It was daytime, which meant the crystal dome above them had turned translucent, emitting a uniform white light close to Sol's spectrum. The atmosphere was pleasantly warm, with a touch of summer humidity.

Oscar took a long moment, his head craned back, turning a slow circle. 'I have to admit, this is hellishly impressive. Puts the old *Second Chance* into perspective, doesn't it?'

'Different strokes . . .' Mac shrugged. 'We developed gateways and the CST network: every planet just a step away. If we'd spent three hundred years developing starships, I expect we'd be riding round the galaxy in something like this.'

Oscar glanced at him. 'You're impressed,' he decided.

'It's a grand chunk of engineering, I admit. But it doesn't give me an inferiority complex.'

'Okay, okay. So how do we get to Madam Chairwoman?'

Mac pointed through the woodland ahead. Small footpaths led away from the transit building, meandering through the trees. There was a stream not far away, the glimpse of a lake past the wider trunks. About fifty metres along the path ahead was a small white pillar where three personal pods were parked. 'They'll take us as close as you can get,' Mac said.

The pods were simple pearl-white spheres with a flattened base, the doors were open ovals on either side, protected by a translucent force field. Mac eased through and sat on the small bench seat inside. Oscar joined him. From the inside, the pod shell was transparent. The force field doors flickered and strengthened.

'Chairwoman's office, please,' Mac said.

The pod slid along the ground for a few metres, then the

path surface dilated, exposing the top of a tunnel, and they sank down into it. There was no light in the tunnel, though the pod's interior remained illuminated.

'Whoh,' Oscar said. His hands automatically gripped at the inside of the shell, even though there was no sensation of movement through the tunnel. 'Must be some kind of inertial damping.'

'Stop analysing. Enjoy. Especially this bit.'

'What – *wowshit*.'

The personal pod left the tunnel vertically, soaring along one of the skyway rails at what seemed like supersonic speed. Without feeling any acceleration, they were racing parallel to one of the skyscrapers, a tall slender cone of blue steel with a red sphere perched on top. Then the skyway curved round in a leisurely arc and levelled out. Another pod was hurtling towards them. Oscar had to force himself to keep his eyes open as they flashed past each other. Only then did his rattling heart slow enough so that he could take some enjoyment from the spectacle. They were high enough now that he could see right across the dome. There was as much parkland as there was urban area, and the shapes of the big buildings really were remarkable.

'This is much better at night,' Mac said. 'That's when the crystal turns transparent; you can see Icalanise overhead. Then you really know you're in an alien place.'

They twisted over a junction to another skyway, which sent them arching round and down towards a building that looked like a silver clamshell. The pod zipped into the huge lobby on the eighteenth floor, and stopped by a white pillar where several others were clustered, waiting.

'Better than your Merc, huh?' Mac said as they climbed out.

Oscar pulled a face. 'Just different.'

One of the Chairwoman's political staffers was standing waiting for them – Soolina Depfor, a young-looking woman in an expensive business suit. 'Welcome to city hall, gentlemen,' she said. 'Ms Gall is expecting you.' She led them straight into the office of the Chairwoman of the Human Residents' Association, a huge oval room which had to be inside the building's largest central rib. Its ceiling was a half-cone of stained glass whose colours undulated in a long perpendicular wave pattern. There was only one piece of furniture, a desk right at the far end; an arrangement which made it seem like an old-fashioned throne room. But then, Oscar knew, Toniea Gall had been Chairwoman of the Residents' Association for over a century. Few of history's absolute monarchs had reigned for that long.

The Chairwoman rose to greet them as they approached. A tall woman with blue-black skin, dressed in a traditional African tribal robe. With less than a decade left before her next rejuvenation, her face was dignified and solemn. Grey strands were already infiltrating her tight-cropped cap of hair. It said something of the confidence she had in herself that she didn't bother having them treated or even dyed. But then she won every election with a substantial majority. Her few critics and opponents claimed it was because nobody else really wanted the job, it was nothing other than a figurehead position since the High Angel ran all the services in the domes with peerless efficiency. To say that was to badly underestimate her ability. The High Angel might have started off as a simple convenient dormitory town for the astroengineering companies; but now the three domes, New Glasgow, Moscow Star and Cracacol were home to a population of over fifteen million souls. Two new domes, New Auckland and Babuyan Atoll, which the Chairwoman had negotiated with High Angel, were now almost fully grown and ready for human occupancy. The free-flying factories outside manufactured a small but significant overall percentage of the Commonwealth's high-technology systems. By any measure, the High Angel was a big success story, and Toniea Gall, who had arrived as a company-contract ion thruster technician with the first wave of residents, was both a mirror and champion of that success story. She was also one of the longest-serving heads of state, and lately the political media had begun to talk of her as a serious potential candidate for the Presidency.

Oscar clasped the hand which the Chairwoman proffered, feeling dry, cool skin. 'Thank you for seeing us, ma'am.'

'I was in two minds if I should,' Toniea Gall said. Her voice lacked any trace of humour or welcome. 'Along with the rest of the residents, I feel quite insulted that Nigel Sheldon ignored us as a location to build his starship.'

Oscar's smile tightened; he didn't dare risk a glance at Mac. 'I'm confident that no insult was intended, ma'am.'

'Then why not build it here?' she asked, genuinely puzzled. 'We have all the facilities, as well as a huge pool of experience and knowledge. Building it at Anshun must have added a considerable amount to the cost of the project. Why would he do that?'

'Anshun is somewhat closer to the Dyson Pair—'

'Pha.' She waved a hand dismissively. 'As if that would make any difference, a few days' travel time at best. Is he trying to establish a rival space industry?'

'I assure you, ma'am, the only thing being built at Anshun is the starship. There are no freefall industrial facilities. A great many of our components are sourced from the High Angel.'

'Humm. I'll accept that for now, but you can tell Mr Sheldon directly from me, I am extremely displeased by the decision. The next time his proxies need support for a close vote in the Senate, he need not come looking for it here.'

'I will let him know,' Oscar said meekly.

'So what are you here for?'

'We would like to ask the High Angel what it knows about the Dyson Pair. Any information, however small, would benefit our mission.'

'We are connected to the unisphere, you know.'

Oscar managed to avoid her piercing stare. 'My immediate boss favours a very hands-on personal approach for something as critical as this, and the Residents' Association has a permanent open link to the High Angel's controlling intelligence.'

'It doesn't know anything about the Dyson Pair.'

'We'd like to confirm that.'

Her lips pressed together in a thin smile. 'The horse's mouth, eh, gentlemen. Very well.' She gestured at the vaulting window behind her. 'Did you see all the domes on your approach?'

'Most of them, yes.'

'The Raiel live in one. We know that because they consented to contact with humans. As to the other eight original domes, nobody knows who or what they house. Three of them contain cities or structures of some kind; they light up at night but nothing has ever been seen moving in them. One dome seems to be filled with mist; people claim they've glimpsed lights and shadows in there, but there's no proof. One is permanently dark, though it does emit heavily in the infrared spectrum, indicating an internal temperature higher than an H-congruous world. One is permanently opaque and illuminated. And the last two have a thirty-seven-hour day-night cycle, but also remain opaque. So you see, gentlemen, after two centuries living here we don't even know who our neighbours are. The High Angel prizes privacy above all else. Now you're here to ask it about a species that has deliberately locked itself away from the rest of the galaxy.'

'It is a long shot, I admit,' Oscar said. 'But we have to ask it, you can understand that.'

'I understand your motives, but I don't approve. We have to safeguard our own position, a priority which I place at the top of my list. However, you are welcome to use the Association's open channel to our host.'

'Thank you, ma'am.'

They retreated from her office, following a couple of paces

behind Soolina Depfor as her heels clicked loudly on the polished floor. Oscar could feel the Chairwoman's eyes staring into his back the whole way out. As soon as the tall doors closed, they exchanged a glance. Mac puffed his cheeks out. 'Jeeze, what a ballbreaker,' he muttered.

At which point Soolina Depfor turned around, raising an eyebrow. Mac's face turned a heated red.

'Our official channel is through here,' Soolina Depfor said. She showed them into a windowless conference room off the reception hall. It was built on a considerably less grand scale than the Chairwoman's office, with a slim oval table in the middle that had six high-back leather chairs around it. 'Just talk,' she told them. 'The High Angel can hear you.' The door closed behind her.

'Make that two ballbreakers,' Mac said as they sat at one end of the table.

Oscar gave him a warning glance. 'Hello?'

The featureless wall at the far end of the room glowed blue, then cleared to show a mirror image of the conference room. A man was sitting at the table on a chair halfway down. He wore a black v-neck sweater and dark trousers, his broad face had a couple of days' stubble, and the hair above his forehead was receding. It was an image aimed at reassurance, the kind of senior executive you could trust. 'Hello.'

'You're the High Angel?' Mac asked.

The man shrugged. 'I find this representation helps your species. Just showing an image of my hull and habitation section seems a bit pretentious, somehow.'

'Thank you for the consideration,' Oscar said.

'After meeting with our dear Chairwoman, making life easy is the least I could do for you. You were right, Mac, she is a complete ballbreaker. I guess that's why you people keep voting for her – who'd dare vote against? Of course, she does do a good job as well.'

'You heard what we said in there?'

'I hear what I want to inside myself. As I did explain to your Commonwealth leaders right at the start, I'm here to learn about different species, you can only do that through observation.'

'I know this isn't quite on topic, but why are you collecting information?'

'Why does your species spend so much time obsessing about sex, politics, and religion? We are what we are, no matter what our appearance, nature, and size. My priority is gathering information on alien species, I'm an explorer and social anthropologist. I can't imagine doing anything else.'

'Okay,' Mac said amicably. 'Who are you collecting it for?'

'I'm not even sure any more, I've been doing it so long now. Then again, that might be a lie and I'm actually feeding information on this galaxy and its defence capabilities to a fleet of warships that are thundering in from Andromeda. One day, my kind will regroup at the centre of the collapsing universe, and carry the seeds of a new evolution into the next universe to be born, a mix of the best of what's gone before. I watch the planetborn for entertainment here in my Olympian orbit. Pick your reason, gentlemen, your species has forwarded all those and more.'

'Why are aliens all intent on being enigmatic?'

'You're not classing me in there with the Silfen, are you? It's really very simple. As I said, this is what I do. I gain, I suppose, satisfaction, from meeting you and learning from you. I regret I teach very little in return, but that too is my nature. Maybe one day I will decide to do something with all the knowledge I have acquired, and transform or even transcend; but for the moment I haven't reached anything like a data saturation point. I remain curious about the universe.'

'Did that curiosity ever take you to the Dyson Pair?' Oscar asked.

'No, I'm afraid not. Our Chairwoman was being truthful with you. I have no information on either star.'

'Aren't you curious, though? Surely a species which can erect a barrier around a star would be worth studying?'

The High Angel grinned broadly. 'If they've put up a barrier, how would I study them? No, you're right, they would make a most interesting addition to my little menagerie. But I've only just encountered you.'

'Fair enough,' Mac said. 'But aren't you interested in the reason why the barriers went up?'

'Of course I am. But again, I can't help you. I don't know the reason, I've never visited that sector of space.'

'What about observation? Did you ever sense any kind of conflict going on out there before the barriers went up?'

'No, I didn't. That whole section of space is unremarkable as far as I know. Certainly there have been no unnatural alterations made on a stellar level, no stars extinguished or turning nova; nor am I aware of any planets physically annihilated.'

'What about in general? Even you admit you've been around for a long time, have you ever encountered anything that would require a barrier like this to defend a star? Are there species out there that would attack a star or obliterate an inhabited planet?'

'Intent and capability are not the same thing. There are many humans throughout your history who have shown no compunction about unleashing death and disaster on a massive scale; if they had possessed a device capable of exterminating a star they might well have used it. And in the past I have observed species who make your most evil tyrants appear saints by comparison. However, as a general rule, in order to reach the kind of technology level where destroying a sun is achievable, a society must be relatively stable.'

'Some of our biggest leaps have been made during wartime,' Mac said.

'I agree that humans are most adept at innovating when placed under pressure or threat,' the High Angel said. 'But there is a difference between building new weapons and the fundamental theories upon which such technical advances are based. Genuine scientific progress is a slow climb, which requires a stable society to support thinkers and theorists over many generations. Evolution usually means that the species which break out of their planetary environment have some inbuilt social or biological mechanism for restraining their pre-history savagery. Of course there are many exceptions, with determined individuals circumventing such strictures. And it could well be that a less developed culture obtains the relics and knowledge left behind by a more advanced race. But to extrapolate that to a race or entity which poses a physical threat to a star is almost beyond probability.'

'Then why the barrier?'

'I really don't know,' the High Angel said. 'But from my experience and observation I'm ninety-nine per cent certain that it was not to ward off aggression.'

'It's the one per cent that kills you,' Oscar mused.

'Inevitably. But I am not aware of any species within thousands, if not tens of thousands, of light-years which is capable of aggression on this scale. I may be wrong, for I don't claim to be infallible. It could even be argued that the mega-flare which eliminated most of the life on Far Away was an example of such belligerence. It certainly falls beyond the ethics of most civilizations and species. However, as you are aware, I do maintain a comprehensive observation of space over a great many parsecs. If such a threat is out there, then it has the ability to elude my senses. A worrying development, I concede.'

'Or so big a threat it's actually not worth worrying about,' Mac said.

'That's a very human viewpoint,' the High Angel said. 'I don't subscribe to it myself. But then by your standards I'm something of a coward.'

'Is that why you haven't visited the Dyson Pair?'

'Let's just say, this is a comfortable distance to watch from. I am curious, which is why in this instant I am keen to help you beyond my normal capacity.'

Oscar ran his hand back through his hair. 'Thank you for that. If you do observe anything relevant . . .'

'I will inform you of course. And please feel free to call me again should you have any further inquiries. In future, I will accept a direct link from either of you through the unisphere.'

*

Both Paula and Hoshe spent the express train journey to Kerensk sitting quietly in their first-class seats, running through information from the case. Diagrams, text summaries, financial graphs, they all swarmed through their virtual vision. Even Paula's attention wavered occasionally under the relentless flow.

However, they both abandoned the case data for the shuttle trip over to the High Angel. Hoshe was fascinated by what he could see outside the windows, requesting a stream of descriptive information from his e-butler. Once they'd docked at the base of the New Glasgow stalk, Paula instructed her e-butler to query the High Angel's internal information net for directions as the other passengers drifted past on their way to the lift. A subsidiary net program directed her down the curving corridor to a door that opened into a smaller lift capsule.

'Did you find anything relevant in the case files?' she asked as the doors closed and they started to accelerate.

Hoshe glanced round the lift suspiciously. 'Can we talk in here?'

'Yes. The High Angel is aware of everything inside itself. And I've already briefed it about the case.'

'Oh. Right. Well the Tampico National Tax Office was helpful. After the flotation, the shares from Tara's half of the company were deposited into the Tampico First State Bank by Broher Associates, her divorce lawyers. Eight months later, those were then exchanged for Gansu Construction shares when Morton agreed to the buy-out. All very standard. Then they just sat there until she was re-lifed, at which point she transferred them back to her accountant on Oaktier.'

'What about the dividends?'

'Gansu was an excellent deal. They've paid dividends every four months, and the share price has gone up twelve times their original price in that time – Morton is a good director. The money went straight into the bank's long-term investment account, which also did reasonably well over seventeen years, although the percentage was lower than most managed funds. No money was ever taken out; it stayed there and grew for her. The bank paid local tax on it every year. Nobody questioned the timescale. Apparently, there are a lot of accounts left untouched like that, some of them for centuries.'

'Did she have a current account with First State?'

'No.'

'And there's no record of Wyobie Cotal having any kind of account off Oaktier? If they had lived there on Tampico, they had to have some kind of funds. They'd be traceable.'

'All credit transfers from Tara's Oaktier bank dried up after the final balance was paid, that was three weeks after she supposedly left for Tampico. The last item on the account was a payment to Broher Associates for handling the divorce case; that was a week prior to the final balance payment. That all checks out. Broher Associates served Morton the divorce file a fortnight after she left. The bank changed her account status from current to sleeper three years later; that's standard procedure when it's been inactive for that length of time, it prevents any less-than-honest bank employee from spotting she's not using it and siphoning the money out themselves. To open it up again after her re-life she had to go in with a court order confirming her identity.'

'What's listed on her credit account in the two weeks before paying her lawyers?'

'Not a damn thing. The second-to-last payment is for her lunch with Caroline Turner. There is nothing in the period between that and the divorce lawyers.'

'Do we know where she was when the payment to the lawyers was made?'

'No. Just somewhere within the unisphere.'

'No live sighting or confirmation then,' Paula mused. The banks would swear in court that anyone with an account had to be alive for the pattern code to work. It was a complete lie, of course; banks right across the Commonwealth lost billions to credit hackers every year. The only really secure credit account was with the SI bank; and she'd seen classified reports on the ultra-grade hackers who had even managed to forge those transfers, though it involved a lot of cellular reprofiling and assuming the victim's life. A pattern code, however detailed and complex, could always be copied and duplicated given enough time and resources.

'What about Wyobie Cotal, did he spend any money on Tampico?'

'No. I checked his account. Same story as Tara. No purchases after the day they disappeared together. His bank changed the account from current to sleeper two years later.'

'Who paid for the tickets to Tampico?'

'Cash transaction the morning they went missing. But they were registered in Tara's name.'

'I don't suppose there's any way of knowing if they were actually used?'

'No. CST don't keep that kind of information.'

'They have sensors and cameras in every planetary station.'

'But the data isn't archived for four decades, it would cost a fortune. They keep it for a couple of years at most, and that varies between stations.'

'What about cash? Did either of them make any large withdrawals before they supposedly left Oaktier?'

'No, neither of them ever made any large cash withdrawals

from their Oaktier accounts, period. So unless one of them had a secret numbered account somewhere it's hard to believe they were alive, even for that first fortnight.'

'Humm.' Paula reached out and used her cuff fuseto on the wall, steadying herself as the lift capsule changed direction. She knew they were travelling along the inside of the giant starship's hull now, heading for the Raiel habitation dome. 'I suppose it's possible she could have sold some jewellery and lived off that money. But why would she? The whole case that they went to Tampico is getting worse the closer we look at it.'

'I haven't believed it for some time.'

'Me neither. But we must always be sure, Hoshe.'

'Of course.'

'My Directorate has been unable to find any secure memory store facility opened by Tara. I think that just about makes it official. She was killed, and presumably Cotal as well. We now need to find a motive, which is the really puzzling part of all this. It certainly isn't financial.'

'Could it have been Morton or Philippa Yoi?'

'A crime of passion? We have to consider it, I suppose.'

'But . . .?'

'But I'm inclined to think Shaheef and Cotal walked in on some criminal activity; the payment to the lawyers two weeks later would tend to support that because someone was clearly busy building up the alibi that they were still alive. If so, there will be very little evidence for us to find.'

'Then why are we here?'

'Process of elimination. I want to lock down Shaheef's personal life. All of it.' Her hands gripped the small bag she was carrying. She could tell Hoshe was deeply uncertain about the whole concept, but like a good policeman he wasn't criticizing his boss. Not yet.

The lift rose up the stalk to the Raiel dome, and the gravity field asserted itself, reaching eighty per cent Earth standard.

Hoshe took a moment to steady himself; he'd never seen an alien in the flesh before – though his wife was always talking about visiting the Silfen. But then this break in everyday life was all part of working with Paula Myo. He'd pulled in every favour, real or imagined, with the division's captain to stay assigned to the case when it became known she was taking it on. Success by association was always welcome, but he genuinely wanted to see her working her magic. There was also the remote possibility she might endorse an application to the Serious Crimes Directorate. Hoshe hadn't actually mentioned that piece of career planning to anyone, but the idea was firmly lodged at the back of his mind now.

When the door opened it was a slight anticlimax; rather than some exotic alien metropolis he was looking out on a gloomy alleyway with smooth matt black metal walls thirty metres high. Above him, the dome's crystal was transparent, permitting Icalanise's wan amber light to shine through. Small red lights were embedded along the foot of the alley walls, glimmering like candle-lit jewels. He found the silence imposing, a complete absence of even the faintest sound.

'It probably looks better in the daytime,' he decided.

'This is the daytime,' Paula told him primly. She started walking.

Twice, Hoshe was convinced something big flew overhead, just above the walls. A subliminal rustle of air, maybe the light flickering ever so slightly. Of course, whenever he looked up, all he could see was the rigid strip of dome crystal above the walls.

'Do you know where we're going?' he asked.

'More or less. The city's geometry changes slightly the whole time, its buildings and streets tend to move around, but they do it slowly. Don't worry, the High Angel won't let us go anywhere we shouldn't.' She paused at an intersection. This alley was a little wider, and had green lights glinting along its length. A Raiel was moving along it, heading towards them. In the dim light it was hard to see anything but a large dark bulk sliding closer, which made the huge alien even more intimidating. An adult Raiel was larger than a bull elephant, though that was where all comparison ended. From the angle Hoshe was seeing it, the alien's forward body looked more like an octopus tipped on its side. A bulbous head was surrounded by a collar of tentacle-limbs ranging from a pair at the bottom which had evolved for heavy work, four metres long with paddle-like tips and a base thicker than a human torso, down to clumps of small slender manipulators like energetic nests of boa-constrictors.

A bunch of five small hemispherical eyes on the side of its head swivelled in unison to focus on Hoshe as it reached the intersection. When he glanced down, he saw eight short stumpy legs on each side of its underbelly; they didn't have any knees or ankles, they were just blunt cylinders of flesh that tilted up and forward in pairs to propel it along in what amounted to a continuous smooth waddle. As the main bulk of its body went past, Hoshe could just make out brown rings mottling the grizzled hide of short bristly fur. Behind the collar of tentacles a number of small protuberances were dangling down as if the flesh had been pulled into dreadlocks; by the way the bulbs at the end swung about ponderously they could have been solid lead, and they were definitely technological rather than any natural growth.

'How about that,' he mumbled once the giant alien was past. Its rear end tapered to a drooping point, there was no tail.

'They are somewhat overwhelming,' Paula said as she started off down the alley with green lights. 'A lot of human residents here think they actually built the High Angel. Given their intelligence level it's a strong possibility.'

'What do you believe?'

For the first time since they'd been on the case, Paula produced a small smile. 'I don't believe it really matters. But for the record: it's unlikely.'

'Why?'

'Because they're almost as indifferent to us as the Silfen. Mind you, it's different in this instance, the Raiel really do look down on us from a great intellectual height. I don't think any entity that aloof would build something with the High Angel's mission. Qatux told me once that they study the physical dynamics of the universe, not the cultures it contains. To them, life really is an accident of chemistry; all life, including themselves. I think they only agreed to contact with the Commonwealth so that they could have access to our unisphere's astrophysics database. They've made some substantial contributions to our sensor technology over the years.'

They walked for another five minutes. Other than the colour of the low lights, which was different at each intersection, there was no change to the nature of the alleys or walls. He knew there were tall structures somewhere in the dome, but none of them were visible from the bottom of the alleys. It didn't take much imagination for him to picture himself as some lab animal scuttling through a maze.

Paula eventually stopped beside a section of wall no different to any other; the string of lights along the base were purple shading towards ultraviolet. After a moment, a section of the wall in front of her split open and parted. The gap was wide enough to admit a Raiel. Inside was a broad circular space, its floor glowing a pale emerald. The roof was invisible somewhere in the darkness above.

A Raiel was waiting for them a few metres beyond the door. Paula stood before it, and gave a small bow. 'Hello, Qatux; thank you for seeing me.'

Qatux's head lifted, revealing the crinkled, damp folds of pale skin that was its mouth zone. Several of them creased up, briefly exposing deep gullets and nasal passages. There was even a glimpse of sharp brown fangs. 'Paula.' The voice was a mellow whisper, accompanied by the soft sighing of air escaping through the big alien's loose muscles. 'Have you brought it?'

'Yes.' She opened her bag and brought out a fist-sized cylinder of memory crystal.

The big Raiel quivered at the sight of it. Now his eyes were acclimatizing to the murky light, Hoshe could see Qatux didn't appear to be in very good physical shape. The hide around its main torso was tight, outlining the platelets of its skeletal structure. One of its large tentacle-limbs was trembling, which it kept coiled up, though the splayed tip kept falling out. All its eyes were rheumy, blinking out of sequence.

'How long is it?' Qatux asked.

'Tara Jennifer Shaheef is over a hundred years old. Can you handle that much memory?'

One of the medium-sized tentacles slithered out towards Paula, its tip poised above the memory crystal. 'Yes. Most certainly. I can do that.'

'I'm serious.' Paula slapped at the tentacle tip which hurriedly withdrew. 'I need to know if it's actually possible. You've never taken more than twenty years before.'

'Yes. Yes. It will take longer for me to absorb that much information, that's all.'

'All right then. I'm looking for anyone who could carry a grudge. Anyone who features prominently and then vanishes from her life. They might have been edited out, so check for missing segments, you know, sequences that don't connect to anything else. I want you to consider professional clashes as well as personal ones. It might even be a quick meeting, a particularly savage argument. I don't know, but some trigger, okay?'

The tentacle crept out again, a sheepish motion. 'These events and people I will find for you.'

'I hope so.' Her hand moved up and down, as if physically

weighing the cylinder, demonstrating her reluctance. Then she brought it up and slapped it into the hooked end of the tentacle. Qatux hurriedly pulled it back. 'Don't take too long,' she admonished.

'A week. No more. I will call you. I promise.'

The wall parted again to let them out.

'That's it?' Hoshe asked. 'We just leave her memory with Qatux?'

'You heard. Qatux will call when he's finished.'

'Hell, I thought . . .' Hoshe lowered his voice. 'I thought we were taking it to some Raiel authority, a forensic lab. Something official!'

'What do you want? A mayor or a president with a signature certificate on a court warrant? The High Angel lets us in, the Raiel city gives us access; it doesn't get any more official than this.'

Hoshe took a long breath, he really didn't want to get on the wrong side of the Chief Investigator. But he was police, too; maybe not like her, but he had a sense of right and wrong, of justice. 'All I'm saying is, it took the Oaktier supreme national court three days to grant us copy authority to Shaheef's secure store memory. And if it had been anybody else but you applying, we probably wouldn't have got that. Isn't that an indicator of how highly we value a secure store? This is a person's life we're dealing with here, her whole life. And now you just hand it over to some sick alien.'

'Yes it's her life. But that life was entrusted to us when she was murdered.'

'Alleged murder.'

'It is time you learned that passing your own judgement and acting upon it is essential to our profession. Have some confidence in yourself and your ability, Detective.'

Hoshe scowled, though he knew his cheeks were reddening. He walked through the bizarrely lit alleys next to the Chief Investigator, both of them keeping silent.

The lift door was still open when they arrived back at it.

'They pity him, you know,' Paula said as they started their descent back down the stalk.

'Who?'

'The other Raiel. They pity Qatux. You understand what he is, don't you?'

'I think so.'

'They're an old race. They have dignity and grace in abundance, their minds are far superior to ours. We're only a few generations away from our hunter-gatherer ancestors; while the Raiel are so far past that rung on their evolutionary ladder they're almost a different species to the creatures they left behind. It leaves them vulnerable to certain things. I'm not making excuses for what Qatux is, but I understand his fall. We can cope with raw emotion because we're still close to the animal origin. I can't imagine what it's like for an entity who has never experienced love or hate or anger or joy to be exposed to such feelings. Shock, I guess. For the majority of them, anyway. Most Raiel are mentally strong enough to dismiss it. But the weaker ones, they can become addicted. That's what happened to Qatux; he's a human junkie. He loves us. And I think it's the saddest thing in the universe.'

'So he's reliving Shaheef's memories?'

'Not reliving, he's becoming her. Every experience, every sight, every sound, he *knows* them. You heard him, it'll take a week to absorb a hundred years of her life. When it's done, we'll be able to ask him anything about any day, hour, or minute of her life, and get a coherent answer.'

'All right, but I don't see the need. We can do that, we don't need a Raiel.'

'Have you ever reviewed someone's memory, Hoshe?'

'No,' he admitted.

'It's not like a TSI recording; similar, I grant you, but not the same. TSI is the polished version, directed and focused. They're made for a reason, to push your attention onto

357

something. Ninety per cent of the market has a sexual content, but there are the pure dramas, and action adventures, and tourist trips as well. It actually takes a very skilled performer, backed up by an equally skilful nerve impulse editor, to receive and filter out the impressions that the director wants and the script calls for. You access a TSI and the story is laid out for you, easy and simple, you sit back and zip through it. True memory is different, it's whatever has caught your attention at the moment. There can be a dozen important – critical – things going on around you, and because of your prejudices, the way your personality is put together, you're only looking at one, most likely the least important. It doesn't even have to be visual; a sound, a smell, that could be the only recollection you have of a room, not who was in it or what they said. And try finding that room amid all the years you can recall . . . We can date the sections of memories which were recorded by an insert memorycell. But indexing, that's completely different. Unless you know the exact time, you're forced to review the whole day, or if you're unlucky, week. And that's where Qatux comes in. Humans have to review memory in real time. We can't accept it running faster than it happened. So if I wanted to look through the century which is Shaheef's life, I would have to spend a century doing it. But Qatux with his larger brain and excellent mind, he can take the whole load in almost at once.'

'You were worried about him.'

'Yes. A hundred years is a long time. Even his brain will have a limit. And I know he's soaked up dozens of human lives already.'

'Doesn't that bother you, being his pusher?'

'Human ethics,' she murmured. 'You can't judge the Raiel by our standards. They don't police their own kind the way we do. Raiel are supposed to police themselves. Qatux has made his choice, which in his society he has a perfect right to do. He's going to get those memories anyway. If I didn't supply them, other people will; it's not just commercial TSI recordings you can buy within the unisphere, there are memories to be had as well. A small specialist market. This way Qatux helps us solve the crime, everybody benefits. If we stopped him from getting them, it would be us committing the transgression as far as the Raiel are concerned.'

'Maybe,' Hoshe said. The lift was slowing again, delivering them into freefall. 'I still believe this is wrong.'

'Do you want to leave the case? I won't stop you, and it won't read against you on your record.'

'No, thank you, Chief Investigator. We've come this far; I'm going to see it through.'

*

From the moment it began, Rob Tannie regretted taking this job. It was all down to money of course, and his perennial shortage of it. In his current chosen profession of 'field security operative', ordinary jobs were hard to find, and well-paid jobs were merely the stuff of legend. So when his agent called to offer him the contract with its fantastic payment, he should have known better. And if that wasn't enough, the contract also had a re-life clause: he was to load his memories into a private clinic's secure store and his anonymous employer would provide a five-year bond. If Rob didn't reappear within five years in person to cancel it, then the clinic would go ahead with the procedure.

That told him, even if intuition and simple common sense didn't, that, sure as shit, five years from now he'd be waking up in some freaky infant-teenage body with no recollection of the last few months of this existence. He should have walked. But it was those damn finances: some bad investments in horses and certain sporting fixtures, as well as poker and other games of chance, had left a rather large shortfall in his credit balance. He couldn't afford not to agree, not with creditors like his, and his agent knew that. So he said yes, and expected to wind up helping some radical ethnic group strike a blow for greater cultural autonomy against their planetary government; or take part in a corporate black ops strike, or if things were really bad he could even be involved in some criminal syndicate power struggle. Naturally, with his luck, it was even worse than any of those.

Two weeks settling into his newly arranged job as a security guard at CST's Anshun starship complex. Two boring weeks staying in character while he learnt the layout, the schedules, the hardware which CST used. Getting on nodding terms with the technical teams putting the starship together. Sharing a laugh with his new colleagues about the hundreds of over-eager hopefuls who arrived every day for their final stage crew interviews and assessments. Actually catching a glimpse of Nigel Sheldon himself, surrounded by his entourage of aides.

Two weeks and he still had no idea why he was here. He couldn't work out who was opposed to CST, unless it was some kind of Earth Grand Family conflict – who knew what those rich weirdoes would do to each other to gain an advantage.

Then this morning just before breakfast he received an encrypted message from his agent. Rob used the key he'd been given, and slim green text opened up across his virtual vision. His mug of breakfast coffee grew cold as he read and re-read the briefing with its precise instructions and timings. Finally, he looked up at the apartment's ceiling and groaned: 'Oh bloody hell.' That was it, he really wasn't likely to survive the day, despite the last text section which detailed extraction routes.

He stuck to the routine he'd established, and took a city metro out to the CST planetary station. From there he caught one of the staff buses that spent the day trundling back and forth over the wasteland of the station yard to the starship complex. Along with the other security guards he arrived at the locker room twenty minutes before shift started so he could change into his uniform. This time, he took longer than usual, waiting until the room was nearly empty. When there were only two others left, he went over to the locker specified in the briefing. The code pattern in his thumb OCtattoo opened it. A simple utility belt was inside, identical to the one he was wearing. He swapped the pair of them round, and closed the locker before leaving.

His shift began at eight thirty, and he was at the main gatehouse on time, one of three guards to be stationed there. The first person through was Wilson Kime. Rob saluted as the gate opened for the captain's car. It was about the most physical part of his duty. The three guards in the gatehouse were responsible for monitoring the perimeter with its six-metre fence and patrolling guardbots. Hundreds of sensors were strung out along the fence, along with dozens more scattered across the surrounding land. Nothing could get close without security knowing. All the guards had to do was run random second-level verification scans on personnel and check visitor vehicles.

At ten thirty, Rob said, 'I'm going for a break, back in twenty.' He left the gatehouse, and walked back to the main complex buildings over the newly mown grass. The air was as humid as ever, making him wipe perspiration from his brow.

Once he was inside, he made straight for the gateway section. The control room was on the lower of the building's three sub-levels. Another security guard and a building main-tenance tech were waiting in the lift. His e-butler swapped IFF codes with them, confirming they were all part of the mission. They gave each other tense looks, judging what they saw, wondering if one of them didn't have what it took.

A timer in Rob's virtual vision counted down the seconds until ten forty-seven. 'Right,' he said, and touched the button for the lower level. 'Anyone want out, you're too late.' The lift doors slid shut, and they began their descent to sub-level three. Rob opened his holster and took out the ion pistol, checking its charge level. It looked the same as the one he'd been issued with, but the difference was that the security network couldn't disable it as it could all the others, a precaution in case a guard ever went 'rogue'.

'Put it away,' the maintenance tech said. His eyes gave a warning flick towards the lift's sensor.

Rob showed him a disdainful glance, just to prove he wasn't taking orders, and slipped the weapon back. 'You got the door?'

'Door and gateway network hold-down,' the tech said. 'You?'

'We make sure you don't get interrupted.' Rob and the other guard exchanged a glance.

'Okay then.'

The lift opened onto a short corridor. There were two doors on either side, and one at the far end.

The tech took a small array out of his tool kit, and placed it over the lift controls. 'Neutralized,' he confirmed.

Rob slipped the first remote charge from a pouch on his utility belt. The little unit was a simple square of black plastic, the size of his palm, a centimetre deep. He pushed it against the ceiling, and instructed his e-butler to load the activation code. The e-butler acknowledged the charge switching to armed status, and Rob pulled his hand down. The remote charge stayed in place. Its casing slowly changed colour, matching the lift's ceiling tiles.

The maintenance tech led the way down the corridor to the big door at the end, struggling to carry his heavy tool kit. He held another array over the lock panel. Rob took his ion pistol out again, slipping the safety off. His timer showed him they were perfectly on schedule. The door slid open. They hurried inside.

The gateway control room was nothing like the centre used for interstellar exploratory work, which was a simple box ten metres on each side, two and a half high. This was full of consoles, with management offices along one side looking in through glass walls, all of them currently dark and unoccupied. Eight people were working the shift, sitting behind the consoles to monitor the huge assemblage of machinery which was buried in its own cavern beyond the control room. Three giant high-rez portals on the wall opposite the offices revealed the gateway's status with dense three-dimensional graphic displays.

Heads came up to frown at the intruders. Right on schedule Rob's e-butler reported that its interface with the cybersphere had just dropped out; kaos software was infiltrating all the local nodes.

'Everybody be quiet and stay calm,' the other guard said. 'Keep your hands where we can see them, and please don't do anything stupid.'

One of the console operators stood up, giving Rob an incredulous stare. 'What the hell is going on? Is something wrong?'

Rob shot the ceiling above him, with the pistol on minimum charge. The manager got out a short animal screech as sharp splinters of the polyphoto strip came crashing down around him, trailing thin wisps of smoke. An alarm started to shrill loudly.

'You were told to shut up,' Rob shouted above the noise. Frightened faces stared at him. Hands were being held high in the air.

'Shit, man!' The tech was staring at the fallen manager, who was still crouched down on the floor, arms over his head, shaking badly.

'Do your job,' Rob snapped back at him.

He nodded with a fast jerk, and pressed the button to close the door.

'What?' The other guard shot the alarm, killing the sound.

'Thank you,' Rob said.

'You lot,' the tech shouted at the managers. 'Get away from the consoles.'

Rob and the other guard waved their pistols meaningfully, shepherding the managers over to the glass wall. They were made to crouch down. 'Joanne Bilheimer,' Rob called. 'Front and centre, now.'

One of the women looked up fearfully. 'I'm Joanne. What do you want?'

'Up,' Rob beckoned with all four fingers. He pointed to the console marked Chief of Operations. 'Secure this room, activate level three isolation.'

'I . . .' She gave his pistol a frightened glance. 'I'm not . . .'

'Please,' he said. 'Don't give me any bullshit about not having the authority. And you really don't want to make me start issuing threats, because I'll carry them out. Now, level three?'

'I can't interface. Something's contaminating the console nodes.'

Rob smiled pleasantly. 'That's why CST provided you with a back-up manual system as well.'

She bowed her head, then got up and walked over to the console.

The other guard was standing, facing the captive managers. 'This is just an anaesthetic,' he told them. 'Nobody's going to be killed, we're not homicidal lunatics.' He went along the line, pressing a hypotube against their necks. One by one they went limp and keeled over.

A big metal slab rumbled out of the floor, sealing the doorway. A similar slab covered the fire door. The air above them shimmered then hardened as the force field came on, reinforcing the molecular structure of the walls. Two fat cylinders came telescoping down out of the ceiling at opposite ends of the room. Rob grinned in satisfaction at that: air filter, recycling the atmosphere now the force field had sealed off the air-conditioning ducts. 'Thank you, Joanne.'

She didn't even have time to look at him before the other guard slapped the hypotube against her neck.

The tech had got the panels off one of the consoles. He'd tipped up his tool kit and a number of custom array units had spilled onto the floor around him. They all sprouted a long bundle of fibre optic cable, which he was working frantically to connect into the ridiculously complicated console electronics.

'Can you do it?' Rob asked.

'Shut the fuck up and let me concentrate. We've got about two minutes left to verify control before the RI shuts us out.'

'Right.' Rob and the other guard looked at each other and shrugged. Rob didn't have a clue what the man was doing, nor how to help him. The kaos software was still contaminating the nodes, blocking access to the cybersphere. He didn't know what was going on outside in the rest of the complex, if the other units in the mission were going ahead, if it had stalled, if they'd already all been shot. Being cut off like this wasn't good. He wanted to know. He needed to know. His virtual vision timer was relentlessly counting down the mission elapsed time, crossing off events which should have happened. Ninety seconds left, and the tech was still working with obsessive fever inside the console.

Come on, Rob urged him silently. *Come on.*

*

Wilson had reached the central gridwork in the assembly platform when his e-butler told him Oscar Monroe was calling. 'Connect us,' he ordered it. He slowed his momentum against one of the gantry girders, and rotated slowly so he could look in at the starship's rear section. All of the reaction mass tanks had been installed now, bulging out from the cylinder superstructure. Nearly a fifth of the fuselage plating was in place, with constructionbots busy adding more.

A small translucent image of Oscar's head appeared in the corner of his virtual vision. 'Want some good news, Captain?' Oscar asked.

'Sure.'

'The High Angel claims it doesn't know of any aliens equipped with superweapons in this part of the galaxy.'

Wilson automatically shifted his gaze to the ship's force field emplacements. Some of the generators were in place now, though none had been connected up to the power net and commissioned. 'You're right, that is good news. I take it you didn't have any trouble dealing with the habitat?'

'Not the habitat, no.'

Wilson grinned privately; he'd encountered Chairwoman Gall a few times himself. 'So what did it say?'

'It hasn't visited the Dyson Pair, so it knows very little. It indicated that it was curious, and maybe even nervous about the barriers. Basically, it's waiting to see what we find.'

'Interesting policy. Did it say if it had contacted any aliens at all from that section of space?'

'Not really, it's keeping its alien privacy commitment very st—'

The link dropped out. Wilson was forming a question for the e-butler when it relayed a security alarm. The starship complex's datanet was under some kind of kaos assault. 'How bad?' he managed to ask. Several lights around the assembly platform flickered, startling him. 'Forget that, give me a systems status review: overall and platform.'

Two more security alarms flashed up as the status display expanded into his virtual vision. There had been an explosion at one of the complex's main power generators. Intruders had penetrated the gateway control room. Security guards in assembly room 4DF were in the middle of a firefight with more intruders. Sections of the complex's datanet were failing and dropping out as the kaos software contaminated the routing nodes.

'Holy shit!'

Systems across the assembly platform were switching to back-up power sources as the main grid supply fluctuated. He twisted round wildly, having to grab at the girder to stop himself from spinning. The gateway was still established, leading back to the big assessment building. Pods were sliding along the electromuscle; a couple of people were floating around the junction, looking back. 'Get me the security chief,' he told his e-butler.

The status display showed power and data connections to the security command centre blanking out. Fire suppression systems in surrounding sections of the tower building switched on. Shock paralysed Wilson's thoughts for a second. He had trouble grasping what he was seeing. Then his really ancient training kicked in: *react, don't freeze.*

Lights were going out across the assembly platform as the local management array began its emergency power-down procedures.

'Establish command of the local management array,' he instructed his e-butler. 'Encrypt all traffic and key it to my pattern code. Isolate the array and the platform network from the ground complex datanet now. Authorize continuance of all its internal emergency procedures, but I want the platform's force field erected over the gateway immediately. Divert all internal power reserves to sustaining it.'

'Working,' the e-butler said.

The virtual vision status display vanished as the datalink to the main complex was cut. 'Give me internal status.' Fresh streams of translucent data wrapped around him: he was at the centre of a globe composed from thousands of red and amber lines woven through and around each other. The construction activities were shutting down; even so there wasn't a lot of power in reserve. 'Cancel environment functions, we've got enough air for hours.'

'Enabling.'

'Locate senior staff inside the platform, and list them. Open general broadcast channel to everyone up here.'

Lights continued to go out all around him, dropping huge

sections of the platform into gloomy half-light. The force field came on, sealing over the gateway. Bright light from the assessment building shone through into the gloom.

'Attention everybody,' Wilson announced over the general channel. 'The complex seems to be suffering some kind of physical assault. We've sealed the gateway, so we should be perfectly safe up here. But just as a precaution, I want everyone to head up to the *Second Chance*'s life-support ring, section twelve.' He skimmed through the list of senior personnel. 'Give me Anna Hober.' He vaguely remembered her from crew training sessions, an astronomer from CST's exploratory division, appointed to the crew as a sensor expert and navigator.

'Enabling.'

'Sir?' Anna Hober said.

'Anna, where are you?'

'Up at the secondary sensor array. I'm part of the installation team.'

'You're now my executive officer. Get linked into the ship's life-support section array, and start powering up the internal environmental systems. Snatch whoever you need from the assembly teams to facilitate the job. Get going. I want a safe haven established for everyone up here.'

'Yes sir.'

His virtual hand touched the e-butler icon. 'Give me a status display for the starship's internal systems.'

'Enabling.'

When it came, it was a small representation. Few systems were receiving power, and the starship's internal network was little more than primary communications links – a spine without nerve junctions.

Wilson kicked off from the girder, heading in towards the life-support ring. As he glided forwards he reviewed the onboard power sources, most of the back-up emergency reserves were in place, and two of the fusion generators had been tested before being shut down again. That ought to give them enough power to sustain a few decks while the situation on the ground sorted itself out. If things started to stretch out they might even be able to start a fusion reactor and plug it in to the force field generator – the drain that was exerting on reserves was uncomfortably large.

'Do we have any external communication links to the planetary datasphere available?'

'The assembly platform is equipped with emergency transmitters which can link to geostationary satellites.'

'Activate them. I need to know what's happening down there.'

So many lights had gone off he was having trouble seeing where he was going. Girders and structural poles were invisible until he was really close. It slowed his progress; he was practically having to feel his way along now. His retinal inserts fed an infrared image into his virtual vision, turning his sight to sparkling pink and white.

The bright flood of light coming through the gateway faded away to a soft jaundiced glow given out by the assessment building's emergency lighting. Then there was a bright orange flash, which his retinal inserts had to damp down to prevent it from dazzling him. Wilson blinked his eyes, finding himself in near darkness now the flash had died away; the main power lines had also been lost, leaving just a few emergency lighting systems functional inside the platform. The gateway was completely black. 'Oh fuck,' he whispered. His suspicions had been right all along. They were targeting *Second Chance*.

*

Lennie Al Husan had arrived at the Anshun CST station after a two-hour rail journey that was supposed to take forty-eight minutes. It always happened when he routed through St-Lincoln; there was always a delay in that station yard. So he was late for his appointment with the starship project's media office. His editor was going to play hell over that, every media company was trying to get an angle on the flight. Lennie even dreamily entertained the idea he might somehow qualify as one of the reporter/crewmembers, a post which the CST kept dangling in front of media representatives to ensure favourable cooperation.

Except this delay had probably blown that option.

He made his way along the main concourse to the transport holding area for the starship complex. There were a couple of extensive security checks, then he was outside in the wretchedly humid air, joining several other people milling about waiting for a bus. He asked his e-butler to contact the media officer he'd been dealing with.

'I'm having trouble establishing an interface to the datasphere,' the e-butler told him. 'Kaos software is contaminating the local datanet nodes.'

'Really?' Lennie looked around with interest, which was a stupid thing to do, he acknowledged. But kaos attacks were rare, and usually preceded or covered some kind of criminal activity.

A crashing sound so loud he assumed it was an explosion reverberated over the transport holding area. Along with everyone else in the queue, Lennie hit the ground. For a second he thought it was a derailment, however impossible that was. Then a roaring sound began. Mingling with that was a second crash. Lennie got up, and tried to work out where the deluge was coming from; it was now so loud he had to jam his hands over his ears.

'Full record, all senses,' he told his e-butler. He started running to the end of the long building. As he rounded the corner he got a view out over a wide section of the marshalling yard. First impression was that a train of lengthy covered wagons parked behind the cargo handling sheds was breaking apart. Two of the wagons were already reduced to scraps of junk. As he watched, a third burst open. Huge dark metal shapes were rising out of the debris on vivid columns of violet flame. They looked like armoured rectangular dinosaurs, with blunt wedge-shaped heads. Thick cannon barrels jutted out from where their eyes should have been, while smaller guns protruded from the front of the head, like lethal mandibles. Three stumpy legs were folded back against each side of their flanks as they went airborne. The air shimmered around them as force fields came on.

Lennie didn't dare blink. He kept his eyes wide, holding them steady, absorbing the glorious sight. His e-butler was sending out a multitude of pings, searching out a cybersphere node clear of contamination.

'Let us in!' Lennie screamed at the collapsing cybersphere. 'I command you in Allah's name, for fuck's sake. Let us in!'

Then the kaos contamination suddenly vanished, emptying out of the cybersphere like water draining down a pipe. Everything was on line, and Lennie's images were shooting into his office array back on Kabul.

'The SI has cleaned the local network,' his e-butler told him; there might have been a small note of awe in the program construct's artificial voice. Lennie didn't care if it was the glorious Prophet Himself who'd returned to work the electronic miracle. It was him who was channelling the images, and the sound, and the terror out across the Commonwealth, he: Lennie Al Husan. This was his show.

The three horrific machines swung round in unison; their exhaust jets vectored horizontal and they accelerated away over the station's wilderness yard. 'They're Alamo Avengers,' Lennie shouted into the howl of the rockets, praying his audience would be able to hear. 'You're seeing real live Alamo Avengers in action.' He just managed to fight down the impulse to cheer them on.

*

The two guards left sitting in the gatehouse were just starting to wonder where Rob had got to when their standard cyber-sphere connections went down. They weren't unduly concerned; they still had their secure links to the sensors and perimeter systems. Two alerts came in on the line from the security command centre. Before they even looked at them properly, an explosion behind them sent a fireball roiling up into the sky from the far side of the complex. Red circles were springing up all across their security status display.

'God, that was a generator,' one managed to say as flames billowed up after the expanding fireball. 'Looks like the whole fuel storage section went up with it.'

Three floors of windows in one of the towers erupted, a million spinning splinters of glass surfing out on huge gouts of flame.

'Security command centre not responding,' the gatehouse array reported. 'You now have autonomous control of perimeter security.'

'Seal it!' the senior guard shouted. He loaded his pattern code into the gatehouse array, watching the protective systems come to life. The guardbots halted where they were; hatches opened down the sides of their bodywork, and weapons deployed, locking into ready positions. More reassuringly, the force field generators came on; triplicated and self-powered, they erected a huge dome-shape shield over the entire complex. Air molecules trapped inside the bonding effect sparkled as they absorbed the energy input, aligning themselves into a rigid lattice.

A further two explosions went off inside the complex. The senior guard tried to work out what was being destroyed, but his status display was almost devoid of information.

'What do we do?' his partner demanded.

'Just sit tight. We can't turn off the force field, we don't have that authority. We're safe in here.'

'No, we're bloody not,' the guard pointed frantically at the huge flames and black smoke rising over the complex build-ings. 'We're locked in with a bunch of goddamn terrorists.'

'Don't panic. They just caught us by surprise. The whole place is going to seal up tighter than a lagoon onna's arse now. Look.' He pointed at one of the towers. Its outer surface was cloaked in the tell-tale sparkle of a force field. 'Isolate them and bring in the big guns to mop them up: standard pro-cedure.' He turned around to see his partner was completely ignoring the complex, instead he was squinting out across the barren expanse of the station yard.

'What the hell are those?'

*

It had gone down right to the wire, but the maintenance tech had interfaced all his arrays into the gateway control room network. The RI had been locked out.

'They can't alter the gateway coordinate,' he said trium-phantly. 'I've isolated the command network, so the system's fallen back on its internal arrays, everything will just keep ticking over nicely.'

'Great,' Rob sneered. 'What about when they cut the power?' He'd already felt the floor tremble slightly. There'd definitely been an explosion nearby. Some other part of the operation was moving forward. He wished it wasn't so com-partmentalized, it was hard not knowing what was happening.

The tech gave him a contemptuous look. He sat down behind the console he'd mutilated, and called up new sche-matics on the large wall-mounted portals. 'They already have, look. The grid supply is just about zero. We're already running off the niling d-sink. Everything's okay. We just have to hold out for another thirty minutes.'

Rob's e-butler suddenly reported it could connect to the room's cybersphere nodes. Half a dozen calls were incoming, demanding his identity. 'Tell them to fuck off,' he ordered the e-butler.

'That's funny,' the tech said. His eyes were unfocused as he studied the data within his virtual vision. 'The cybersphere is clear, someone countered the kaos software, it got flushed out.'

'Is that good or bad?' Rob asked.

'It's strange. I'd never guessed Anshun's cybersphere RI was powerful enough to extinguish that level of kaos so quickly.'

'How does it affect us?' Rob demanded. He always hated working with these specialist nerds, they never appreciated the physical side of any mission.

'It doesn't, really. I mean, CST security can't physically get in here, or the chamber with the gateway machinery – we control that force field as well.' He scratched at the side of his face. 'It might make it a little tougher for us to exit at the end if all their sensors are back on line. Let me think about that.'

Rob glanced at the other guard, who simply shrugged.

'Oh wait,' the tech said. He leant forward as one of the portals switched to a grainy image from a sensor covering the corridor directly outside the control room. 'Here we go, they got the lift circuit back.' The sensor showed the lift door closing. Ten seconds later, the remote charge detonated. All Rob saw on the portal image was the lift doors quaking, the central join split apart as the metal buckled. A dense cloud gushed out into the corridor. It was dust not smoke, Rob realized.

The other guard chuckled. 'They'll never get down that way now, the whole shaft must have collapsed.'

Rob glanced at the metal slab covering the fire door. Security would be down the stairwell which connected to it soon enough. According to the instructions he decrypted that morning, once the lift shaft was out of action they'd be able to leave the control room by the main door. One of the offices off the corridor outside had a utility passage which would take them to the chamber containing the gateway machinery. After that, they had a choice of three exit routes once the force field was switched off. Of course, that had all rather depended on the cybersphere and security sensors being knocked out by kaos.

'Can anyone see in here right now?' Rob asked. He searched round the ceiling for sensors and cameras. There were at least three covering the room.

'Let me review the local network,' the tech said. He suddenly froze, and gaped at the portal displaying the gateway command network. One section was flashing red. 'No way,' he whispered.

'What?' Rob demanded.

'The first routing lockout fireshield. It's down.'

'Once more, in English!'

'Look, the actual fibre optic cables which carry the network, they're still intact, still integrated with the local datanet, which in turn is connected to the cybersphere. But the nodes, where the routing is controlled, that's where I loaded my software in to block contact. In electronic terms, there's no physical barrier between us and the outside, only the fireshields. I erected five, in sequence, at each node, blocking every channel in, and something just got through the outer one.'

'You told us the Anshun RI cleaned out the kaos,' the other guard said.

'No, I said I didn't think it could, not that quickly. Jesus!' Another section of the gateway command network was flashing amber. 'This isn't possible, I swear: not possible.'

'Another fireshield?' Rob guessed.

'It's going to fall, oh man, half the format codes have been cracked already. No way. I mean no fucking way! Do you know what kind of encryption I used for that thing? Eighty-dimensional geometry. Eighty! That should take like a century to break, if you're lucky.' He seemed more angry than worried by the event.

Rob was starting to get a real bad feeling about the mission. 'So what can crack that kind of encryption?'

The tech became very still. 'The SI.' His gaze found a ceiling camera which was lined up on his console, and he looked straight into the tiny lens. 'Oh shit.'

The other guard brought up his ion pistol, and started shooting the cameras. 'Find out how many sensors there are in here. Now!'

Rob took a shot at a sensor above the main door. He risked a quick look at the portal display as he hunted round for more. The amber warning over the second fireshield was shading into a more ominous red.

*

The senior gatehouse guard stared out through the window, his lower jaw sagging open as the true nature of the flying objects became apparent. 'I've seen those things before,' he croaked. 'I know what they are. They were on an action drama I accessed years ago. Alamo Avengers. But they're ancient history.'

'Not any more,' his partner said. 'What do we do?'

'Pray.'

All along the highway to the Starship complex, vehicles had halted automatically as the kaos software corrupted their drive arrays. Then when the explosions began and the force field dome came on, people got out to stand on the hot tarmac to watch the spectacle. Several turned as the new sound rumbled up behind them, only to fling themselves down, screaming a warning.

The Alamo Avengers stormed over the highway at barely a hundred metres altitude. When they were a kilometre from the force field, they opened fire with their particle lances. It was as if sheet lightning was bridging the gap between them and the dome. The entire sky transformed into a blinding white maelstrom as the air disintegrated from the tremendous energy discharge. The soundblast alone shattered every window on the cars and vans and buses below, people were hurled

376

about by the sonic wavefront. Ears and eyes ruptured, capillaries tore apart; blood started to foam out of their mouths and noses and ears, unprotected skin liquefied.

The force field dome maintained its integrity under the strike. Right across its surface, air molecules collapsed and punched upward in a seething coronal cloud. From above, it looked as though a small red dwarf sun had become buried in the ground. Huge lightning bolts spun outward from the seething ion cloak, lashing against the surrounding earth. Guardbots, waiting alertly along the base of the force field, their lasers and magnetic rifles tracking the incoming enemy, simply detonated into fragment swarms that vaporized in microseconds as the energy cascade engulfed them. Every scrap of vegetation within four hundred metres of the perimeter burst into flame.

All three Alamo Avengers fired again, concentrating their lances on a single point. Again, the force field resisted, deflecting the terrible energy deluge back out into the tortured coruscating air. Thick cataracts of lightning ripped out, pummelling the ground.

Inside the gatehouse, both guards had dived to the floor at the first barrage. Their entire world vanished in a violent whiteout. Even inside the force field, the noise was tremendous, translating into direct physical pain stabbing in through their eardrums. When the light died down, they risked looking up. Five hundred metres away, where the lances had been targeted, a huge patch of the force field was still ablaze with radiant violet streamers as residual energy swirls grounded out.

'It held,' the senior guard grunted in disbelief. He couldn't hear what he'd just said. When he put his hand up to his ear, his fingers came away sticky with blood. He didn't care. 'I'm alive.' The back of his knuckles smeared tears across his cheeks. 'Oh sweet Jesus, I'm alive.'

When he raised his head above the desktop he could see

the Alamo Avengers approaching the force field dome. Pitiful fires sputtered below them as the last of the weeds and grass were consumed. They didn't so much land, as fall out of the air. Their rockets cut off while they were still twenty metres up. Legs stretched out and absorbed the impact, leaving them in a crouching position on the blackened smouldering earth. The head on the nearest one swung slowly from side to side in mockery of a living creature, scanning its sensors back and forth. Their arrays were loaded with animal-sentient smartware, giving them an independence fuelled only by aggression; once their target was loaded in, they wouldn't stop until it had been reached.

The lead Alamo Avenger lurched forward, legs thudding heavily as they moved with a speed unnerving for something so massive. Plumes of soot and dirt shot up from each impact, flowing in strange swirls around its own force field. Small sections of armour along the front edge of its head flipped up, allowing long black prongs to slide out. The medium calibre weapon barrels retracted back into their bays. At thirty metres from the base of the dome, it stopped and lowered its thick wedge head. The prongs flared with a cobalt nimbus that spun and flickered. It thrust them down into the ground. Huge geysers of soil were flung up into the air. The Alamo Avenger braced its legs, shoving its head deeper into the hole which the prongs were gouging out. Sand and shards of fractured rock were shooting twenty metres into the air above it. Slowly, it began to ease its huge armoured body down into the excavation.

*

Every building on Leithpool's Castle Mount was illuminated by bright beams of light, their colour gracefully morphing through the spectrum; while above them all, the bold fairy tale castle itself was drenched in the brilliance of thirty solar-bright searchlights. From his position in the curving window of the

Prince's Circle café, Adam had a superb view of the resplendent rock against the backdrop of a serenely clear night. Its reflection shivered across the cold black waters of Leithpool's circular lake in a near-perfect mirror image. Like all the other late-evening denizens of the café, he'd stopped looking at the view several minutes ago. Unisphere news shows were all featuring the events on Anshun, as were thousands of media companies stretched across the Commonwealth. The café had switched to Alessandra Baron, although even the images she had access to lacked professionalism. They came from the survivors of broken or abandoned vehicles on the highway to the starship complex. Retinal inserts were relaying the sight; the pictures blurry from tears, wobbling as the senders shook from fear or relief.

They showed the Alamo Avengers digging their way underneath the force field dome. There was actually little now to see of the ancient war machines themselves, the holes which they had dug were deep enough to contain the main bulk of their bodies. Huge sprays of earth were still fountaining up into the sky, to fall as a concealing cloud of dust and fractured stone granules dryer than any desert sand. The volume of dirt they vomited out behind them never slackened. At the speed they were going it could only be a matter of minutes before they were underneath the complex itself. A fact which Alessandra Baron, safe in her studio on Augusta, was keen to point out. She did confess that she knew nothing of the defence capabilities which CST might or might not have built into the complex, although the standard ones didn't seem to have held out very well so far. Also chosen for emphasis was the legend of just how destructive the Alamo Avengers were.

'Nothing and nobody,' she said, 'would survive inside the beleaguered complex if just one got in. We can only pray for the people trapped in there.' Even her beautiful face with its mane of elegant dark-blond hair seemed troubled.

Adam was also uncertain if CST had any surprises waiting

ahead for the Alamo Avengers. Of necessity, this mission had been put together hurriedly, the time for research was short. He couldn't be certain of anything, though he strongly suspected there were no serious heavy calibre weapons in the complex.

Along with all the other transfixed watchers in the café he drew breaths of awe and fright as flashes and rumbles emerged from the gaping tunnel mouths. It wasn't entirely an act. He'd watched the giant machines being refurbished over the last few months, yet even so he'd been as overwhelmed as everyone else by the sheer brute power they wielded as they launched themselves into battle for what was bound to be the very last time.

A timer in his virtual vision counted off the mission event sequence. So far they were doing remarkably well in keeping to schedule. Which meant that stage two was about to come on line. As a veteran of many campaigns large and small, Adam knew there was nothing truer than the old military adage: no battle plan ever survives contact with the enemy. And when that enemy was as powerful and resourceful as CST, he wasn't about to leave anything to chance.

*

Wilson heard the last emergency airlock clang loudly, the noise reverberating along the whole deck which they'd commandeered. None of the primary malmetal airlocks were working, they were all contracted into thick rings around the edge of their rim. But the emergency airlocks offered a reasonable degree of security. He began his deep breathing regimen, calming his racing heart.

'We're sealed,' Anna announced. There was a high degree of satisfaction in her voice. Her round face smiled brightly, despite the situation down on the ground. Her eyes and mouth were heavily OCtattooed, producing a filigree of slender gold and platinum lines that flickered in and out of existence on her skin. Hands and forearms were also covered in the same lines, which crawled around her fingers and wrists as she pressed her hands against a console i-spot.

'Good job,' Wilson told her. He didn't strictly approve of such flamboyance – that old straight arrow heritage again – his own OCtattoos were completely non-visual. But he had to admit, her performance so far was exemplary. It was Anna who had organized working parties from the surprised and nervous technicians to go through the life-support section, and physically close the big solid emergency locks with power tools and their own muscle. One of a dozen jobs he'd given her which she'd conducted flawlessly. The air conditioners were up and running, fans stirring the heavy atmosphere, back-up lighting rigged to portable power cells. Now she was organizing personnel into damage crews, ready for anything.

While she'd been accomplishing that, he had spent the time frantically reviewing what systems the starship had in anything approaching operational status. It hadn't taken him long. Given the vast quantity of equipment which had been installed so far, only an alarmingly small percentage of it was available to him. And almost none of that was of any practical use to their current situation. Their one major success was using the assembly platform's emergency communication system to re-establish a link to the planetary cybersphere. Through that, Wilson had been in touch with the SI continually since he reached the starship. He was gratified that the SI was taking a much greater than usual interest in the attack.

'The Anshun special forces squadron will be able to deploy around the complex perimeter in another seven minutes,' the SI told them. 'First echelon security reinforcements from CST will arrive at the station four minutes after that; their deployment should be faster than the local forces. Commonwealth Security Directorate forces are also being mobilized.'

'And even if they can get inside the perimeter force field, do any of them have anything which will kill those goddamn

Alamo Avengers?' Wilson asked. He was aware of Anna giving him an anxious glance. Tiny slivers of gold rippled out from her eyes, as she realigned her virtual visual display to access the security data directly.

'I do not believe so,' the SI said. 'One of the causes of the Alamo Avenger's enduring reputation is the sheer power contained within it. They were hugely cost-ineffective to build, had a poor range, and limited tactical ability. Yet their effectiveness against United Federal emplacements was almost one hundred per cent. The Single Star Republic came very close to their goal of turning Austin into an Isolated.'

'You mean we don't have guns inside the complex big enough to take them out?'

'No. But the Security Directorate does have the necessary firepower, especially given the age of the Alamo Avenger force field generator design. However, you will have to wait until they arrive. Their Anshun deployment should start in twenty-five minutes.'

Wilson took another look at the display screen. He and Anna had set up their command post in a crew office which had several network systems and arrays installed, though precious little else. The walls and flooring were still raw structural panels, ducting ran across the ceiling like a pair of dull-silver serpents twined in a mating position. So far, three console screens were set up to show crude representations of the starship's internal status, while the remaining two were being fed images from the cameras around the assembly platform. There hadn't been a repeat of the explosion in the assessment room beyond the gateway, but that wasn't what he worried about seeing now.

'Are they under the perimeter yet?' he asked the SI.

'Most definitely. The volume of earth they are ejecting behind them has not decreased. Our best estimate already puts them one hundred and eighty metres inside the force field. They will probably surface soon.'

'How long till they reach the gateway?' Anna asked. Her OCtattoos had sunk into quiescence. She was looking directly at the screen which showed the camera image covering the gateway from inside the assembly platform.

'The shortest time is six minutes,' the SI said. 'To derive that, we are assuming they will continue underground until they are underneath the complex buildings before surfacing. That tactic means they will not have to expend any energy breaking through the building wall force fields.'

'Okay, let me have it straight: can the Alamo Avengers break through the gateway force field?'

'If their original specifications have not been downgraded, our estimate is that it will take at most two shots from a particle lance to break through the gateway force field's cohesion.'

'Son of a bitch.' Wilson growled it through clenched teeth. He kept telling himself that it wasn't even dying in this body which frightened him – there was enough bandwidth in the satellite link to download his memory into a secure store right up until the last instant. No, it was being unable to defend the project from some bunch of half-assed anarchist terrorist freaks. The project didn't *deserve* this; they were trying to achieve something noble and right with the starship. No piece-of-shit trendy-cause rebel outside the political process had the right to screw with that. Not to mention the time and money and – goddamn it! – lives which had been poured into its construction.

'I can probably route some additional power from the ship to the platform's force field generator,' Anna said. Platinum spirals were rotating slowly round her eyes as she studied a network schematic within her virtual visual. 'One of the niling d-sinks is partially charged. That should give us enough power to last for hours. I think I can route it through the supercon-ductor cabling. We just have to reprogram the umbilical junctions to reverse the flow.'

'Can you help us with that?' Wilson asked the SI.

'From our analysis of your resources, your power output is actually capable of exceeding the force field generator's designated input,' the SI said. 'However, the generator was never designed to withstand the kind of stress inflicted from a particle lance. One Alamo Avenger could break through relatively quickly. Two in combination will require less than ten seconds.'

'Fuck it!' Wilson raged. 'You have to close the gateway for us. They cannot be allowed to destroy this starship.' He wanted to add: it's not fair, the *Second Chance* deserves her shot at history, she shouldn't die like this, not stillbirthed.

'The fireshields erected around the gateway network are proving exceptionally resolute,' the SI said. 'We have so far broken three. The fourth utilizes one-hundred-and-sixty-dimension geometry encryption. It will take us several minutes to crack it.'

'We don't have several minutes!'

'Our calculations are not in error.'

Wilson twisted his body to look at Anna. She was floating in front of the console, gazing at the screen which displayed the ship schematic. Her hands pressed tight against the console i-spot; gold glyptics chased slow strange patterns across the stretched skin of her forearms.

'Is there any kind of weapon installed?' he asked desperately.

Her virtual hands were pulling data out of the array as if by brute physical force. 'No, sir. Nothing.'

'Goddamnit!' He punched at the nearest surface with his free hand, sending his body into a nasty twist, which strained the hand he was holding himself in place with.

'Any sign of them breaking surface yet?' He was just going to have to leave it all to the SI, and pray it could break the fireshield in time.

'No,' the SI said.

'Okay. Will you please set up a store to receive the memories of everyone onboard. If you can't close down the gateway, they'll have to be transferred to the clinic which performs the re-life procedures.'

'We will do that, of course. But there is now a new problem.'

Anna gave Wilson an anguished look. He could see how hard it was for her to keep going, the effort it required to stay resolute. Executive management was hardly training for this kind of situation. He would have to consider that carefully later – once they survived this. In the meantime there wasn't much he could say to help. 'What now?' he asked levelly.

'Anshun civil flight control is tracking two unauthorized spaceplane launches from an island close to the equator.'

'What kind of launch?'

'Unknown. But they appear to be accelerating into a retrograde orbit.'

It took Wilson a second to work out the implication. 'They're heading for us,' he murmured.

'It would appear so, yes.'

'How long?'

'If their acceleration remains constant, eight minutes.'

'Have you got any idea of their size?'

'From their radar return, they appear to be medium-lift spaceplanes. If so, they will mass around one two hundred and fifty tonnes each, unloaded.'

Wilson didn't even try to do the math in his head. Two hundred and fifty tonnes impacting at a combined speed of twice orbital velocity ... 'They don't even need to carry a warhead,' he said. And it didn't matter any more if the gateway was switched off or not. If the Alamo Avengers didn't get them, then kinetics would.

Somebody somewhere really hates us, Wilson thought. *Why, though? What's the point, we will get to the Dyson Pair eventually. I'll re-life, and by Christ I'll fly this ship yet.*

And with that the muscles in his arms locked in shock. 'Anna! We pressure-tested the fuel tanks two weeks ago. I remember the schedule.'

'Yes,' she said cautiously.

'Is there any fluid left in the tank?'

*

The concrete floor in cosmic radiation test laboratory 7D quaked slightly. Equipment juddered along benches and desks. A soft roaring sound was just audible, its volume increasing in tandem with the ferocity of the quakes. Cracks began to appear across the floor, with little splinters of concrete flaking off to jump and spin across the now unstable surface. Ceiling-mounted cameras scanned back and forth. But the only illumination in the laboratory was a pale amber emergency lighting which had come on after the complex generators had been sabotaged. It provided a poor resolution.

Seconds later, the floor disintegrated, with vast chunks of concrete whirling upwards, their molten edges throwing off glowing droplets. Beneath the torn rift a dazzling jade-white light poured upwards to blind the cameras. Small tendrils of energy followed an instant later, scratching and clawing at every neutral surface, vaporizing metal and obliterating plastic and glass.

Then the light went out. An Alamo Avenger heaved itself up and out into the flame-shrouded ruin of the laboratory. Its head swung round to focus on its goal, casually demolishing a wall and several support pillars. Chunks of masonry and the shattered floor of the upstairs laboratory crashed down, only to slither and bounce off the armoured monster's force field. The six legs shifted round, turning the body until it was lined up behind the head, pointing directly towards the gateway. It moved forward, slowly at first, smashing through another internal wall. Gradually it built up speed, crashing through the building as if it were nothing more than dense strands of air.

As it charged through the constructionbot maintenance centre, the floor ruptured underneath its feet. Slightly off balance, it lumbered onwards for a few metres, then stopped and twisted its head round to see if there was any threat. Impenetrable jets of dust gushed up from the new rip in the ground. Then a second Alamo Avenger pushed and forced its way out of the tunnel. The first waited until it was level, then they began their final charge towards the assessment building and the gateway.

*

The café was utterly silent as Alessandra Baron's overawed voice announced the rise of the spaceplanes. Adam realized he was licking his upper lip in anticipation, and hurriedly stopped. The images shifted from the smouldering land around the complex force field dome to a clean graphic of the assembly platform's orbit around the planet. In conjunction with Baron's now sombre voice they illustrated the impending destruction. Figures in the corner of the screen counted down. They almost matched the timer in Adam's virtual visual.

Second Chance had at most another four minutes. He took a quick look around the rapt faces of the other customers, seeing horror and fascination in equal amounts. For once he didn't feel any guilt at what he'd done. There were no innocents in the assembly platform, no children devoid of memorycells. Not this time. This time it would be right.

Someone working for Baron's show managed to access the microsat geosurvey observation swarm around Anshun. Thousands of tiny solid state sensors along the equatorial orbit shifted their alignment from the minerals buried far below to one specific speck of light. The assembly platform swam into focus at the centre of the screen, a giant blue-grey sphere of malmetal soaring above the clouds. Its featureless symmetry gave it a strangely organic appearance, Adam felt.

Dark lines appeared on the surface, illustrating long petal-like shapes. Adam blinked, leaning forward. They hadn't been there a second before, he was sure. Then long, slim fantails of snow-white gas were shooting out from the spherical surface as the dark lines split open. Sunlight poured into the assembly platform, erasing the weak glow of emergency lighting; the starship's incomplete superstructure gleamed silver-white at the centre of an expanding cloud of vapor.

'No way,' Adam groaned. His timer read a hundred and fifty seconds until impact.

Two plasma rockets ignited, wiping out the image in a white nova of super-energized particles. Both exhaust plumes blasted straight through the shell of folded malmetal, sending twin spears of light stabbing over a hundred kilometres down towards the planetary surface. Some of the plasma plume rebounded off the surviving structure, billowing backwards around the starship and its swathe of girders. Insulation blankets and cables lashed around as they dissolved back into their component atoms, while support girders melted away into pliable strings that stretched like hot cheese as the starship started to move away from the gateway. Component cargo pods ignited, shooting out from the stellar inferno like lurid orange comets, trailing a fluorescent haze behind them as their contents blazed.

The *Second Chance* began to accelerate away. Her huge body wavered at first as the programs and pilot – was it Kime himself? Adam wondered – analysed the nonsymmetric mass distribution along the fuselage. As soon as they'd mastered that, the rockets were vectored to compensate, and the starship held steady as she built velocity, heading straight up from the planet. Behind her, there was a last violent contortion amid the seething molten wreckage as the force field protecting the gateway finally ruptured. Atmospheric gas spewed out into the void, bringing with it a host of fragments from the ruined assessment room. The jet's vigour was reduced for a few seconds as something pushed its way along the wormhole.

Then like a cork from a bottle, a small force field globe burst through; it glimmered amid the debris storm as it was propelled onward by the aggressive blast of air from the gateway behind. The dark, heavy object within the sparkling bubble spun helplessly round and round as it soared away through space. Behind it, the gush of atmosphere was reduced once again. A second golden orb came through, tumbling off into the void after the first.

By now the *Second Chance* was twenty-five kilometres away, a dazzling elongated star ascending towards the bright constellations. The first spaceplane leapt into view. Its tremendous closing velocity meant that there was only the briefest glimpse on the screen – a streamlined silver-grey delta shape – before it slammed into the cooling ruins of the assembly platform. The explosion that erupted was indistinguishable from a small nuclear blast. As the sphere of incandescent atoms began to darken, it suddenly renewed itself as the second spaceplane pierced its heart.

A hundred kilometres above, the *Second Chance* was still accelerating out towards the stars.

11

Hoshe had thought that the flood of data would slow down after the first couple of days. Now, a week on from his initial request, he knew better. For shadowy creatures who lived outside society's boundaries, there was an awful lot of information stored on the so-called big-time crime syndicates. On Oaktier, there were three main such organizations recognized by the police: the Johasie Family, an old-fashioned mafia-style network of related hoodlums, but with enough brains and lawyers to disconnect the bosses from all the activities of their street-level soldiers; Foral Ltd, a company whose board seemed to have diversified down into crime, both financial and street; and Area 37, the smartest and most elusive, whose murky empire was bolstered by legitimate businesses and, apparently, political connections. They were based in Darklake City, and for that reason alone Hoshe favoured them as the most likely suspects to murder Shaheef and Cotal. It was simple geography. Neither of the lovers had travelled outside Darklake for weeks before they disappeared. If they had accidentally stumbled on something which required their removal, then it was Area 37 who probably had the kind of resources and connections to make it happen. That just left him with a likely activity.

Just what could two innocent civilians walk into that required a response of that magnitude?

The official files on organized crime syndicates Hoshe had retrieved from the Attorney in Chief's office contained all the previous investigations, plus the alarmingly unsuccessful court cases they resulted in. Of those, reports filed by undercover operatives and informants were the most useful. The Attorney's office knew the major and minor players, and had a general idea of what they were up to most of the time; it was just proving it legally which was the perennial problem.

Proven or not, the files covering suspected events forty years ago were of little use. There simply weren't any killing sprees, or violent clashes with rivals, or even big heists. It was just a steady drip feed of money from clubs, gambling, chemical and digital narcotics, prostitution, bank scams, and dubious development contracts.

Following the official files, he started to access the media's collective knowledge of Area 37. It was more gossipy, although some of the investigative reporters certainly seemed to know their subject. But again, there was no mention of a serious crime back then. When he searched through standard police reports for that year, and the five subsequent ones, there was no outstanding major crime that had happened or had required years of preparation.

Halfway through the morning, he'd stopped work to watch the incredible assault on the starship. But then so had most of the Commonwealth. Even the Chief Investigator had sat back to stare at the images playing on her desktop screen. Once the *Second Chance* had reached safety the weight of waiting data had slowly drawn him back to his task, although colleagues from around the metropolitan police headquarters building kept dropping in to ask him if he'd seen it and what he thought. They seemed more interested in hearing Paula's opinion, even though she never gave one. By late afternoon, he was once more completely immersed in the dreary details of the criminal underworld. The constant input from both virtual visual displays and reading the screens on his desk was giving him headaches. When he reached for his coffee mug, he found only the cold dregs of the last batch.

'Get some more,' he muttered.

Paula didn't even look up from her screen as he went to the door. They'd been given an office on the fifth floor, a pleasant enough room with a broad window and furniture which wasn't too old. The desktop arrays were all top-range equipment, with screens and portals to match. The coffee maker, however, was down the corridor.

'Wait,' Paula said as he was almost through the door. 'Secure call coming in.'

It was Qatux. They put it on the large wall-mounted portal, and Hoshe sat down just as the big alien's image came up. Hoshe frowned his concern at the Raiel's appearance, Qatux could barely hold his head up to look at the camera. Shivers ran along his body and tentacle limbs, as if he was coughing silently.

'I have lived her life,' Qatux whispered. 'How you humans survive so much experience is something I shall never understand. To do so much and react to it all in the way you do is as much a curse as a blessing. You never take time to digest and appreciate what happens to you.'

'It's what we are,' Paula told him. 'And how are you? Did the memories cause you any trouble?'

'It was difficult. I had not expected it to be so. I see now, and I see then. I am Tara more than I have been any human before. That frightens me as much as it delights. I have never been frightened before.'

'Memories will always fade, that is their nature. You will know who you are.'

'They fade for you. For me, I am not so sure. There is so much I wish to concentrate on and remember. I will not let go of her easily.'

Paula leaned forward in her seat. 'So you can access all of her life?'

'Yes. Yes, I know her that well. So many colours, so many sounds; and *feelings*, what feelings she had. Tara cried at the sight of a dawn one day, it was so beautiful, out in the desert where light played across the rock and sky, and every second brought a new hue to the rumpled sandy ground. I feel her tears now, small delicate traces across my skin, blurring the image.'

'Have you looked for what I asked? Did she have any enemies, anyone who hated her?'

The Raiel's head swung slowly from side to side in mournful denial, its tentacle-limbs following the motion discordantly. 'No. To you, I think, she would be bland and insipid, for her life is not as fast and intense as yours. But Tara is a gentle person, she loves life and hates pain and suffering in others. The worst she ever thought of any person was irritation and disappointment. Her most serious crime was selfishness, for she cheated on several partners, she was unable to resist the pleasure and excitement which such liaisons brought her. That does not make her a bad person.'

'How badly did those cheated partners react?'

'Some wept. Some raged. Others didn't care. She made her peace with all of them. Nobody she ever knew wanted to kill her. Of this I am certain.'

'Damn!' Paula's lips compressed into an angry grimace. 'There's nobody?'

'No. She is no saint, but to incite enough hatred in someone to kill her ... I cannot see that, not through her eyes.'

'Thank you, Qatux. I am sorry this has been so tough for you. I appreciate what you've done.'

'It is not trouble. I love humans, all humans. I often think that perhaps I was born into the wrong species.'

'You're fine just the way you are.'

'Will you bring me more memories, Paula? I purchase many from contacts in your unisphere, but none are from

393

secure stores, none are as complete as those you bring for me, none have the richness of human existence, the trueness that I cherish.'

'We'll see. Maybe I'll visit again.'

'Thank you. And one day perhaps you will bring your own memory? I am sure you must be the greatest human I know.'

'That's very flattering, Qatux. I'll bear it in mind.' She waited until the image vanished before wrinkling up her nose at the grey screen.

'Not a crime of passion, then,' Hoshe said.

Paula continued to stare at the blank screen. 'Doesn't look like it.'

'How reliable is Qatux?'

'Very. If he couldn't see anyone, then you and I certainly wouldn't if we reviewed the recording. The only possibility from that angle is if Shaheef annoyed someone extremely dangerous, a psychotic who is capable of concealing their true emotional reaction. But I have to admit, that's very remote.'

'What about a serial killer? Oaktier hasn't got one on record, but there could be one who spreads their victims around the Commonwealth.'

'Again, it's possible. If it is, they're not working to any recognizable pattern. That's the first thing my Directorate tends to look for in apparently motiveless killings. The array in Paris couldn't find any connection to any of the known serials we have files on.' She smiled without humour and looked up at him. 'So how are we doing on the crime syndicate theory?'

'Not good. I can't find any important criminal event around that time, confirmed or rumoured. My best guess would be a random gangland slaying which they walked into, and the rest is just a cover up.'

'Yes, that works. But it leaves us devoid of evidence.'

'There's still a load of files I haven't reviewed yet.'

'You've been running analysers through the primary files for a week; if there was anything helpful or relevant to us in them you should have found it by now. I'm sure you know I don't like to give up on a case with so many suspicious circumstances, but we really are running out of plausible avenues of exploration.' She pulled the clip out from the back of her black hair and tidied it up again before reclipping. 'I'll have to give this some thought.'

It was the first time he'd heard the Chief Investigator speculate on defeat, and it was rather shocking. 'Well how many motives can there be? It has to be a random killing. We know it wasn't personal, or corporate, or political, or even financial, you said yourself she's better off now. It's not something we're ever going to track down, because it doesn't exist in any file or memory.' He broke off. Paula was giving him a very intent stare. Slowly a smile spread across her face. Hoshe really wished it wasn't directed at him. It was animal, predatory. 'Damn,' she murmured in admiration. 'That is clever, isn't it? But then he is smart, isn't he, we've seen that ourselves. Smart and determined.'

'Who is?'

Her smile became a taunt. 'I have never, ever, encountered that as a motive before. Damn!'

'What? You know who it is?'

'Don't you, Detective?'

'Oh, come on! Who?'

'It's all down to the timing. He didn't kill her off to save himself money, that's far too much the classic scenario. We would have spotted that right off. He did it so he'd be able to make money for both of them. She profits financially from her killing as much as him.'

'Who?'

'Morton.'

'He can't have!' Hoshe exclaimed. 'He was the one who alerted us in the first place.'

'That means nothing. This was meticulously thought out. He's not going to have kept the memory. Memory is evidence. He'd get that wiped right away.'

'Son of a bitch. Are you sure?'

'I am now.' Her eyes were closed as she hurriedly reviewed the scenario. 'It fits. Hindsight is a wonderful trait.'

'So what do we do now?'

'We need evidence. There will be two types: physical and financial. I'll tackle company records.'

'Okay. What's the physical evidence?'

'I want you to find the bodies.'

*

It had been a bad day at the office. When he arrived that morning, Morton had expected the preliminary central district road and water supply infrastructure contract for Puimro's new capital to be ready for signature certificate. Gansu had underbid considerably at his insistence; a loss at this stage didn't matter, this was the key, placing them ready for a whole sequence of follow-on contracts on that lovely, promising new world. With that foothold, Gansu could build up their local operation over the next two decades until it was as big as the Oaktier parent company. Their true expansion to Intersolar giant status would have begun.

But the development company lawyers on Puimro were suspicious, believing that Gansu's low-cost delivery would be achieved through cost cutting on materials and construction. They wanted quality guarantees written in, as well as proscriptions against 'excessive profits'. All very reasonable, but why the hell didn't they mention all this two months ago during the preliminary round of negotiations? Morton had found himself swearing at his own corporate lawyers and accountants as the bureaucratic tangle developed throughout the day. It hadn't been resolved when he left the office late, stomping off to his car in a foul mood. A team of Gansu lawyers and contract experts had been left huddled in a conference room, ready to work through the night in an attempt to resolve the issues and questions raised by their counterpart team on Puimro. New meetings were scheduled for next week. The signature certificate wouldn't come through for at least another ten days now.

Fucking civil servants, always stand in the way of progress.

The butler greeted him at the lift door opening in the vestibule, grappling with the suit jacket which was flung at him. Morton went into the lounge, squinting against the beautiful evening sunlight that was shining straight across the roof garden and pool. He saw Mellanie sitting on one of the sunloungers, head in her hands, shoulders slumped.

Oh Christ, not this as well, not now. He was scowling at her as her head came up. She gave him a tentative smile and hurried into the lounge.

'Sir.' The butler had brought his sparkling gin.

'Thanks.' He took the glass off the silver tray.

Mellanie, he saw now she was out of the sun's rich glare, had been crying. 'What's the matter?' It was almost rhetorical, he wasn't interested.

She pushed up against him, resting her head on his chest. 'I went to practise this morning,' she said, her voice muffled. 'The coach said I hadn't been making enough effort, that my hours were too low. He said I didn't have the right level of commitment any more.'

'Ah.' Morton felt like saying, *Is that all?* These days, the only sports anyone was interested in were team events. With Commonwealth geneticists able to build super athletes, individual competition was essentially pointless, a contest between laboratories and clinics. But teamwork, that was different, that was the temple of the last natural trait: skill. In games like football, baseball, hockey, and cricket the combined talent of the team was a synergy which fans could throw themselves behind with complete devotion. Although he'd always thought diving was the rather desperate end of the specialist interest spectrum, its importance artificially inflated by sportswear companies and media channels to drum up sales and promotions. So what he actually said was, 'He's an asshole. Don't worry about it.'

She started crying. 'I've been dropped.'

'What?'

'Dropped from the squad. It was horrible, Morty, he said it in front of everyone else. He's already brought in two new girls.'

'Oh. Right.' He patted her absently and took a sip of his drink. 'Never mind, something else will come along, it always does.'

Mellanie pulled back slightly so she could study his face, her own expression was one of bewilderment. 'What? Morty, didn't you hear? It's over for me.'

'Yes. I heard. So move on to something new. It's about time anyway. You've wasted years on that stupid diving team anyway. You can get a proper life now.'

Her thick lips parted to form a distraught 'O' as she took a step back. Then she was running into the bedroom, sobbing filling the air behind her.

Morton let out a tired sigh as the door slammed shut loudly. *Well what did she expect? That's the only trouble with the truly young, they have no perspective on life.* 'No, thank you, for asking,' he snapped after her, 'my day did not go well.'

His e-butler told him there was a call from Chief Inspector Myo. He took a long drink from the glass. 'Put it on the lounge screen,' he told the e-butler.

Even magnified to a couple of metres high, Paula Myo's face was essentially flawless. As Morton sat back in one of the leather couches, he found himself admiring her once again. Now somebody like that would make a real partner, they'd be equals, which was rare enough, and complementary rather than competitive. It was just that weird heritage of hers . . .

'This is unexpected, Chief Investigator, what can I do for you?'

'I need access to some financial documents, the old AquaState accounts. As you're the chairman of the parent company, it's simpler if I just ask you to release them to me rather than go through the courts.'

'Oh.' It wasn't quite what he'd expected. 'Do you mind if I ask why? What are you looking for?'

'I can't discuss a case in progress. I'm sure you understand.'

'Yes. I'm very familiar with government procedures, especially today.'

'That sounds unfortunate.'

He grinned in his winning way. 'Commercial confidentiality, I can't tell you about it.'

'But can you release the files?'

'Yes, of course. Would I be right in assuming you're making progress, then?'

'Let's say, you're on the right track with that assessment.'

'I'm glad to hear it.' He told his e-butler to release the relevant files to her. 'May I ask if you're currently seeing anyone, Paula?'

'I don't believe that's connected to the inquiry in any fashion.'

'It's not, but it was a very sincere question.'

'Why do you want to know that?'

'I'm sure you've heard it enough times. But I want to be honest with you from the beginning; if you're not involved with anyone then I would very much enjoy taking you to dinner one evening as soon as possible.'

The screen showed her head tilting ever so slightly to one side, mimicking an almost avian curiosity. 'That's most flattering, Morton, but right now I'm not able to say yes. I hope you're not offended.'

'Certainly not. After all, you didn't say never. I believe I'll ask you again once this case is over.'

'As you wish.'

'Thank you, Chief Investigator. And I hope the files are useful.'

'They will be.'

The call ended. Morton wriggled down into the couch, looking at the blank screen where he could still see her elegant composed face. Somehow, the day didn't seem such a total loss after all.

*

It was the eighth day after he entered the forest that Ozzie had to delve into his pack for warmer clothes. The last deciduous tree had been left behind a couple of days ago. Now the path led through tall solemn alpine giants with dark trunks of stone-hard bark. Their waxy leaves were long and spindly, a fraction thicker than terrestrial pine needles, with colours shading from dark green to a maroon that was almost black. It was a thin tough layer of grass which grew underneath them, and that was patchy around the trunks themselves where the acidic leaves had fallen. Here the chilly air meant it took a long time for them to decay into the kind of rich loam to be found elsewhere in the forest, and the air was heavy with their citric scent.

Sunlight seemed to have deserted Ozzie and Orion, the patches of sky they did glimpse were uniformly grey as low clouds bunched together in an unbroken veil. Thick banks of mist squatted across the path, reaching far above the treetops, some of them taking hours to trek through. Each one seemed progressively larger and colder than the last.

It was after riding through one for over three hours with no respite that Ozzie decided enough was enough. His thin leather jacket was dripping with moisture that was cold enough to be ice, and it hadn't shielded his check shirt at all. He dismounted and hurriedly stripped off the soaked shirt, changing into a dry one, shivering strongly as he did. Before the mist had time to sink into the fresh cotton he pulled out a slate-grey woollen fleece with an outer waterproof membrane. Much to Orion's amusement he wore soft leather chaps on his legs to cover his cord trousers. Once he'd finally slicked down his rebellious hair, he crammed on a black bobble hat. Only then, when he'd dressed and remounted, did he put on his doeskin-palm gloves.

Almost immediately, he was too hot. It made a nice change. That morning, his own shivering had woken him as the dawn frost settled over his sleeping bag. A veteran of many long treks on foot and horseback, he favoured modern semiorganic clothes which could heat, cool, and dry the wearer as required. They were out for any Silfen world, of course, but he was pleased enough by how the old simple fabrics were performing.

Orion, who had brought little in the way of rough-weather gear, was loaned a baggy sweatshirt to wear under his thin waterproof cagoule, and a spare pair of oilskin trousers, which were perfect over trousers for the jeans on his skinny legs.

The two of them urged the animals onward. Ozzie had no idea where they were any more. Now with the clouds hiding the sun and the stars there was no way he could check their direction. They'd taken so many forks, travelled around so many half-day curves that he'd completely lost track of their progress. For all he knew, Lyddington could easily just be a couple of miles ahead, though he didn't really think it was, not with this weather and the tall morose trees.

'You ever been this far in before?' Ozzie asked.

'No.' Orion wasn't talking so much now. This wasn't the airy summertime forest he was used to, and the gloom and cold were pulling his mood down. It had been three days since they'd last caught sight of any Silfen, a group heading away from them on a diverging path. Before that they'd encountered almost one group of the fey aliens every day. They'd stopped to greet them each time, and not once had Ozzie managed to get any real sense from them. He was beginning to resent how right the SI had been, there was some deep schism between their neural types which prohibited any truly meaningful communication. His admiration for the Commonwealth cultural experts was growing correspondingly. He simply didn't have anything like the patience they possessed to painstakingly decipher the Silfen language.

There was no discernible twilight. The greyness simply dropped into night. Ozzie had been relying on his antique clockwork Seiko watch to give him some warning, which it had done faithfully so far. But that night, either darkness fell early, or the unseen upper clouds had contrived to thicken into opacity.

When Ozzie called a halt, they had to light the two kerosene lamps which Orion had thoughtfully brought along. They hissed and fizzed as they cast a flickering yellow glow. The nearby trees loomed large and oppressive above them, while those at the edge of the radiance seemed to cluster into a dense fence, hemming them in.

'Tent tonight,' Ozzie declared as cheerfully as he could manage. Orion looked as if he was about to burst into tears. 'You sort some food out, I'll cut us some wood for a bonfire.'

Leaving the boy searching lethargically through the packs, he took out his diamond-blade machete, and started to work on the nearest tree. The harmonic-blade in his rucksack would have cut through the tough wood in seconds. Even though the diamond-blade came to an edge a couple of atoms wide, it still took him a good forty minutes of hard work to slice through the tree's lower branches, cutting them into usable logs.

Orion stared glumly at the pile of water-slicked wood. 'How are we going to get it going?' he asked miserably. 'It's all too wet for your lighter.' Nothing was dry. The mist had thickened to an almost-drizzle; water dripped continually off leaves and branches.

Ozzie was busy splitting one of the logs lengthways, turning it into slim segments of kindling. 'So, like, I guess you were never in the Boy Scouts, then?'

'What's that?'

'Group of young camping enthusiasts. They all get taught how to rub lengths of wood together so they spark. That lets you start a fire no matter where you are.'

'That's stupid! I'm not rubbing logs together.'

'Quite right.' Ozzie concealed his grin as he opened a pot of flame gel, and carefully applied a small layer of the blue jelly to each of the kindling sticks. He pushed them into the middle of the logs, then took out his petrol lighter – it was actually older than his watch. 'Ready?' He flicked the lighter once, and keeping it at arm's length, pushed it towards the kindling. The gel ignited with a loud *whoomp*. Flames jetted out around the logs, engulfing the whole pile. Ozzie only just managed to pull his arm back in time. 'I thought they banned napalm,' he muttered.

Orion laughed in relief, and clapped his gloved hands together. The flames burned intently, spilling out across the remaining logs. In a couple of minutes, the whole pile was spitting and blazing keenly.

'Keep it well fed,' Ozzie said. 'The new logs will have to dry out before they burn.'

While the boy enthusiastically dropped another log on every few minutes, Ozzie set the tent up a few yards away. The struts were simple poles supporting a double air-insulated lining which expanded automatically, inflating as soon as he twisted the valve open. Over that went the wind shell, a tough waterproof fabric with long pins along its hem which he hammered deep into the ground. Not that any wind could ever penetrate the forest floor, but he was starting to get a bad feeling about this weather.

For once, Ozzie had allowed Orion to choose whatever food he wanted from the pack. The boy was becoming seriously depressed by their environment and needed cheering up. So they settled down in the lee of the tent's front flaps which had been hoisted up to form a little porch, with the warmth of the fire washing over them and drying their clothes, eating sausages, burgers, beans, with hot cheese poured on thick chunks of bread. To follow that up Orion heated a can of orange sponge with treacle.

After they'd taken care of the animals, they banked up the fire and went into the tent. Ozzie had his six seasons sleeping bag to curl up in. Orion's bag wasn't as good, but he had a couple of blankets to wrap round it. He went to sleep complaining it was too warm.

Ozzie woke to a bad headache and distinct lack of breath. It was light outside, though not the kind of brightness daylight usually brought. Orion was asleep beside him, his breathing short and shallow. Ozzie looked at the boy for a moment, his mind all sluggish. Then it all made sense. 'Shit!' He got out of the sleeping bag fast, fingers fumbling with its zipper. Then he was crawling forward. The tent's inner lining seal parted easily. Beyond that, the wind shell was bulging inwards. He tugged at the zip. A torrent of fine powdery snow fell in silently, washing up against his knees. Even when it finished moving, leaving him half-immersed in a broad mound, there was no sign of the sky. He pushed his way up against it and started to dig frantically. After a couple of seconds his hands were scrabbling in air. Bright white sunlight streamed in. He gulped down the freezing air, trying to slow his panicky heart.

Orion was sitting up behind him, eyes blinking. 'What's wrong?'

'Nothing, we're okay.'

'I've got a headache. Is that snow?'

'Yeah.'

'Oh wow.' He crawled forward and scooped some of it up, grinning delightedly. 'I've never seen any before. Is it covering everything like it does in the Christmas pictures of Earth?'

Ozzie, who was just about to start telling him to dress in his waterproofs, did a double take. 'You're shitting me, man. You've never seen snow before?'

'No. It doesn't snow in Lyddington. Ever.'

'Right. Okay. Well, put your waterproofs on, we'll go out and take a look.'

The snow was a foot deep on the ground, with several inches coating the top of every branch and twig. Right around the base of the trees it was thinner, and of course it had drifted high against the tent's wind shell, completely covering the apex. Ozzie looked back at it rather sheepishly; if it had truly buried the tent then the wind shell wouldn't have been able to take the weight. Nonetheless, it was a sharp lesson not to take anything for granted in the alien forest.

He called Orion over to help soothe the animals as they stamped their hoofs and shivered in the cold. The unkempt pony didn't seem to mind the snow too much, nuzzling up to Orion as soon as the boy found some oats for her. The lontrus simply shook its shaggy gull-grey coat as Ozzie checked it over. The creatures had a strange biochemistry which allowed them to withstand temperatures far more severe than this. It was Polly who had suffered the worst as she didn't have a winter coat. Mr Stafford of Top Street stables had kept the mare nicely clipped for Silvergalde's moderate climate. Ozzie thought about that as he stroked her trembling neck. He knew damn well he wasn't in Silvergalde's mild temperate zone any more. Yet the temperature didn't drop to anything like this for thousands of miles north of Lyddington. They'd made good progress in the last nine days, but not that much. The only rational explanation was that they'd gained a lot of altitude, though he wasn't sure where, it wasn't a single mountain, yet his virtual vision map showed no true highlands within nine days' hard riding of Lyddington – nor within twenty days come to that.

He turned a full circle, then glanced up at the blank

featureless sky, a slow satisfied smile lifting his face. 'Definitely not Kansas anymore,' he said quietly.

They had a cold breakfast, dug out and packed the tent, then went on their way. Snow drifted about aimlessly all day, the powder fine enough for the slightest gust of air to send little flurries whirling round them. It turned the forest into an exquisite crisp winter land, but once they'd started there was no clue as to where the path actually was. Horse, pony, and lontrus plodded onward as if they knew where they should be going, bearing the new climate stoically.

Every now and then, great cascades of snow would tumble down from the overhead canopy of the giant trees, making a gentle prolonged roaring noise, which was alarmingly loud in the silent forest. A softer fall of snow began around mid-afternoon, big flakes trickling down from the lost sky. It turned the ambient light a miserable grey and the air even colder. Polly was making hard going of breaking ground as the snow's thickness built up. Ozzie took a break to put his big water-proofs on over his clothes. Without semiorganics, he was layering; it was a strategy which kept him warm and dry, but at the cost of mobility. Bundled up as he was, he could barely remount Polly. Orion was given a couple of sweaters and another pair of trousers to wear under his oilskins. Once they were moving again, Ozzie began to worry about when night would fall. With the snow showing no signs of relenting, they would need time and light to make a proper camp.

About an hour later they came across a clump of bushes, all covered in snow so they looked like big dunes with just a few twigs poking through the top.

'We'll shelter here for the night,' he said.

Orion just looked round and shrugged. The boy had barely spoken all day.

Ozzie took off a layer of sweaters and climbed up into the tree above the bushes. He set about the big lower branches with his diamond saw, slicing through at the junction. It didn't take too much effort before they broke off, falling on top of the bushes. He got four largish ones down, letting them land on top of each other to form a semi-stable barrier. As a makeshift corral, it would have to do. By the time he gingerly climbed back down again, the snow was already settling on top of them.

Orion set about tying blankets around the horse and pony, while Ozzie pitched their tent in the scant shelter of a big trunk. It was almost dark when he finished. He checked his watch: quarter past five. Which made the day about ten hours long. Silvergalde's rotation was twenty five and a half hours.

'Are you going to light a fire?' Orion asked; his teeth were chattering.

Ozzie helped the boy into the tent. 'Not tonight. Get into your sleeping bag, that'll keep you warm.'

Orion did as he was told without complaint. There were dark circles under his eyes and by the light of the kerosene lamp it looked as if the freckles were fading from his white skin. Ozzie wormed his way into his own sleeping bag, and immediately felt the benefit. He took a heatbrick out of his bag and ripped the tag. The unit was powered by a simple chemical reaction, and the top surface was soon glowing vermilion, throwing out a considerable heat. They took it in turns to cook their cans, then Ozzie boiled up two large thermosfulls of tea so they'd have a hot drink waiting for them when they woke. 'Get some sleep,' he said. 'It'll be dawn quite quickly.'

Orion gave him a worried look. 'Is the snow going to cover the tent again?'

'No. We'll be fine. It was definitely thinning out when we came in. But I'll check every couple of hours. Don't worry.'

'I've never been so cold.'

'You're warmer now, though, aren't you?'

'Uh huh.' The boy pulled the sleeping bag up to his chin. 'Suppose so.'

'Okay then.' Ozzie pulled the blankets up round him. 'It's just when we stop moving you feel it worst.'

Ozzie's watch read five minutes to four when dawn arrived. His e-butler had woken him up at regular intervals through the night so he could check the tent. He felt as if he'd had about ten minutes' sleep all night. Orion was equally reluctant to get out of his sleeping bag.

'We have to move on,' Ozzie told him. 'We can't stay here.'

'I know.'

The snowfall had stopped some time during the night, producing a uniform brilliant white landscape. Snow covered everything, even sticking to the vertical tree trunks so that any dark twig or leaf that protruded looked strangely out of place. It was nearly two feet deep on the ground now. Ozzie put on the darkest sunglasses he'd got, trying not to show how much that perturbed him. It was going to be slow progress for the animals today.

'Mr Stafford should sell sledges,' Orion said. 'He'll like that when I tell him.'

Ozzie laughed too loud at the boy's humour, and gave him a quick hug. They were both sipping their tea from the thermos as they walked over to the animals. The precarious corral had worked to a degree; covered with snow and frozen solid it had provided a reasonable protection against drifts. Behind it, the horse and pony had trampled the snow about their feet, and were shivering heavily. The lontrus simply stood there, snorting out clouds of faint steam. If such a thing were possible, it was giving them a sullen look from beneath the shaggy strands of fur which curtained its eyes.

Orion gave their surroundings a baleful stare. 'Which way?'

Ozzie frowned as the answer stalled in his throat. He tried to work out which direction they'd arrived from last night. It simply wasn't possible, the clumps of trees all looked identical. 'Try your gift,' he suggested.

The boy fumbled with his sweaters, pulling the pendant

out. There was a tiny glimmer of blue starlight within the little gem. He slowly turned full circle, holding it like a compass. When he was pointing just to the right of the tent, its intensity increased noticeably.

Ozzie thought the trees formed a kind of avenue that way. Sort of. 'Guess that's it then,' he said.

'Glad I came now?'

'Very.' Ozzie put his arm round the boy's shoulder. 'Looks like I owe you big-time, huh? How do you figure you'll cash it in?'

'I just want Mom and Dad back.'

'Yeah yeah, but like apart from that? I mean, guiding me to safety's got to be worth a couple of mega-Ks. That's serious money.'

'I don't know.'

'Oh, come on, man. I knew when I was your age.'

'Okay then,' Orion said, suddenly animated again. 'This is huge money, right?'

'Absolutely. Buy your own planet style.'

'Right, first off, I'd buy loads of rejuvenations, so I live as long as you do.'

'Good one, I can dig that.'

'And then I'd buy lots of smart memories, so I'd have an education and know all the complicated stuff like physics and art and banking, but I don't have to go to school for years.'

'Even better.'

'And I want a car, a real cool one – the coolest there's ever been.'

'Ah, that's the Jaguar-Chevrolet 2251 T-bird, the convertible.'

'Really? There really is a coolest car ever?'

'Oh yeah. I got a couple in my garage. Sad thing is I never drive them these days. That's the thing with serious money, you can do so much that you never have time to do anything.'

'I'd give some away, too, to charities and hospitals and things, people that really need it.'

'Nice; that'll prove you're an okay kind of a guy, not just another rich bastard who doesn't give a shit.'

'Ozzie, do you give money away then? Everyone knows you're cool.'

'Yeah. I give some of it away.' He gave the boy a dutiful shrug. 'When I remember.'

As Ozzie expected, it was slow going at first, with Polly breaking ground again. He would have preferred to send the lontrus on first, but its legs were too short. So Polly pushed her way laboriously forwards, her longer legs churning up the thick layer of snow. He spent most of the morning considering options. Make some kind of snow shoes and sledge, haul their food along and let the animals go? Simply turn around and return with the right kind of equipment to tackle this terrain? Except . . . who knew what kind of terrain he'd face next time? Assuming he could find a way back to Lyddington from here.

He just kept telling himself this was Silfen country. The aliens wouldn't let any real harm befall anyone. *Would they?*

As the morning progressed, so the depth of snow gradually began to reduce. It didn't get any softer, though, and it remained stuck to every surface. Four hours after they started he was shivering inside his multiple layers. A layer of hoar frost caked every square inch of his clothing. There was nothing else for it, he got down and plodded along beside the horse, shoving his boots through the snow. The action warmed him slightly, but now he was worried about the rate he was burning off calories. The horse and pony were visibly in distress, despite the blankets tied round them.

Sometime after midday, Ozzie noticed what looked like tracks in the snow ahead of them. He took his sunglasses off, and found the light had become a pale pink. It turned the world into a strange grotto land, as if the forest had been carved out of brittle coral.

'Is it evening already?' Orion asked with a muffled voice. His face was completely swathed in a wool scarf, with only a narrow slit left to see through.

Ozzie checked his watch. 'Don't think so.' He bent down to examine the tracks. They were definitely footprints; elongated triangles without any tread. 'These may be Silfen boots,' he said excitedly. There were perhaps fifteen different sets, all emerging from the forest, a couple had even appeared directly beneath trees, which he suspected the aliens had been climbing. They merged together and headed off along the vague avenue of snow-encrusted trees.

'Are you sure?' Orion asked. He was treading ground where he stood, slapping his hands against his side in an effort to stay warm.

'I think so. I don't know who else is going to be running round these woods. Besides, we haven't got a lot of choice.'

'Okay.'

They started off again. Orion was walking beside his pony, one arm draped over the saddle so his hand could grip the reins. Ozzie suspected he was doing that so the pony could partly pull him along. The air was so cold now, it burned the inside of his mouth if he took a clear breath. The scarf he'd wrapped over his own nose and lips dangled long ice crystals where his breath had frozen against the woolly fabric. Before he put the sunglasses back on, he tried to see where the sun was. The branches overhead were thinner now, showing patches of a hazed ruby sky. He thought one section was slightly brighter, about halfway between the zenith and horizon, but that would put nightfall several hours away. If he'd worked the new short days out they only had about an hour left.

Half an hour later, Orion stumbled. Ozzie only knew because he heard a small grunt. When he looked round, the boy was face down in the snow with the pony standing above him. Much as he would have liked to hurry back, Ozzie's limbs responded slowly. It was like trying to move through liquid.

When he sat Orion up, the boy wasn't even shivering. Ozzie pulled the scarf off his mouth to check for breathing. His lips were dark and cracked, with tiny flecks of blood frozen into place.

'Can you hear me?' Ozzie shouted.

Orion's eyes fluttered weakly. He moaned softly.

'Shit,' Ozzie grunted. 'Hang on, I'll put the tent up. We'll wait here until the weather picks up.'

There was no reply, although Orion raised one arm a few inches. Ozzie left him propped up against the pony and tried to get the tent pack off the lontrus. His outer gauntlets were too thick to unfasten the strap catches, so he took them off, trying not to wince as the arctic air bit straight through the woollen inner gloves. He started fumbling with the straps, then gave up and pulled the diamond-blade machete from its sheath, and cut the straps.

Three times he had to put his gauntlets back on and flap his arms to try and heat his hands back up before his fingers actually moved. What seemed like hours later the air-insulated section of the tent had reluctantly self-inflated and he'd got the support poles secured to the edges. He dropped a couple of heatbricks inside, then dragged the semi-conscious boy in after them. With the flap sealed, the interior of the tent warmed rapidly from the radiance of the heatbricks. Ozzie had to strip several layers of clothing off himself and the boy before they began to feel the benefit. The chilblains in his fingers and toes were strong enough to make him wince as circulation returned. Orion started coughing; he looked as though he wanted to burst into tears.

'How can it be so cold?' the boy asked wretchedly.

'If you really want to know, I don't think we're on Silvergalde any more.' Ozzie watched the boy anxiously to see what his response would be.

'Not for about three days, I figured,' Orion said. 'But I still don't see why anyone would visit a world with this kind of climate.'

'Oh. I'm not sure. I don't think we're in this planet's polar regions, because of the trees. I may be wrong, but rule of thumb is that year-round ultra-cold environments don't support living things as big as trees. So my guess would be either a world with a dying sun or one with a very long elliptical orbit and we arrived midwinter, worst luck.' He shook his hands, trying to ease the pain as feeling and movement returned. His ears still felt like lumps of ice.

'So what do we do now?'

'Like I said, wait to see if the morning brings any change, though I suspect it won't. But we can't go any further now. We need to prepare. I'll go out again in a while. I need to put the tent's wind shell up, then I'll get the rest of our packs in here. We also have to eat a good hot meal. And the first aid kit has some cream that'll take care of your lips.'

'And yours,' Orion said.

Ozzie put his fingers up to his mouth, feeling the rough broken skin. 'And mine,' he conceded. He was praying he wouldn't have to deal with frostbite as well; fortunately his boots had kept his feet reasonably insulated, but he'd have to check Orion over properly later.

'What about the animals?' the boy asked.

'I can't chop any branches off for a bonfire, I won't have the strength. I'm going to spread some flame gel round the base of a tree and see if I can just set the whole damn thing alight. That might help them keep warm enough.'

He really didn't want to go out again, which might have accounted for how long it took him to get ready. Eventually, he slipped back out into the sub-zero forest. Polly and the pony had slumped to the ground – a really bad sign. The lontrus was wheezing quietly, but otherwise seemed unaffected. While his fingers were still functioning, he pulled the remaining packs off its back and carried them over to the tent. Then he spent a frustrating twenty minutes erecting the wind shell over the inner lining as his hands got progressively stiffer. Finally it was done, and he took the pot of flame gel over to one of the nearby trees. He scraped the snow off a section of the trunk a foot above the ground, then stopped and peered closer. It wasn't bark he'd exposed, more like a rough layer of dark-purple crystal, almost like amethyst. His gloves were too thick to give him any clue to the surface texture when he rubbed his hand over, and in any case his skin was too numb. Despite that, he thought it was genuine crystal. He could see refracted light glinting from deep inside. For the life of him, he couldn't think what type of chemical reaction had done this to the bark – some kind of ultra-cold catalyst conversion? Hoping the wood was still unchanged below the crystal, he held up the machete and took a swipe. Several crystals shattered from the impact, but the cut was barely a centimetre deep. Another, heavier, swipe broke a big chunk of the amethyst crust away. The hole exposed more crystal inside, a column of what he took for near-pure quartz which made up the interior of the tree. Lush pink sunlight shone into it, revealing a vertical lattice of capillaries with what looked like dark viscous fluid moving through them extremely slowly.

'Son of a bitch,' Ozzie grunted. 'A fucking jewellery tree.' When he looked up, the branches did seem to be more angular than a normal pine, their twigs multiplying out in fractal geometry patterns. All of them were smothered in a hard scabbing of snow, which had kept their true nature hidden.

The sense of wonder he would normally have enjoyed at the discovery of such a magnificent quirk of nature was cancelled out by the realization that the weather wasn't going to improve for tomorrow morning. Evolution hadn't come up with this crystalline biota for warm climates, in fact it was probably a form of reverse evolution; arctic-style plants

414

expanding with the final ice age, then struggling for survival in a degenerating environment until their genes refined the ultimate winter-attuned chemistry. *And how many millions of years of declining heat would it take to produce something this sophisticated?* They'd missed this planet's last springtime by geological eras.

He hurried back to the tent, too guilty to look at the horse and pony as he passed them. Orion had started cooking a meal on the heatbricks. Condensation was dripping off the inner lining.

'I can't see a fire,' the boy said as Ozzie closed up the seal.

'This wood won't light. Sorry.'

'I can feel my toes again.'

'Good. This insulation should keep enough heat in overnight. We'll be fine in our sleeping bags.' He was doing a rough inventory. There were only eleven heatbricks left. Enough to keep them going for – realistically – three days. They could afford to walk forward for one more day, no more. If the path didn't take them to a warmer world by tomorrow night, they'd have to turn back. No: *just see what's round the next curve*, no: *I think it's getting brighter*. If things didn't genuinely change, he couldn't take the risk. There was no margin for error left any more. And there would be nobody to return his memorycell to the Commonwealth for a re-life procedure. *In fact, how long before anyone even notices I've gone missing?*

Ozzie dug his sewing kit out of the pack. 'Ah! This is going to be useful. I've an idea for some things we need tomorrow. How are you with sewing?'

'I've spoilt your chances, haven't I?' Orion said. 'You would have made it if it wasn't for me.'

'Hey, man,' Ozzie tried to smile, but his lips cracked open. He dabbed at the drops of blood. 'No way. We're really doing it, we're walking the deep paths. It's your friendship gift that got us this far.'

Orion took the pendant out. They both stared at its dark lifeless surface.

'Try it again in the morning,' Ozzie said.

*

Polly and the pony were frozen solid when they emerged from the tent next morning.

'They wouldn't have felt anything,' Ozzie said when Orion stopped to look at them. His voice was muted by the thick fabric mask he'd carefully stitched together last evening. He was wearing every piece of clothing it was possible to wear; as was Orion. The boy looked as though his coat had inflated out to twice its normal size; even his gloves were covered in crude, bulging wraps of modified socks, like small balloons.

'They would have felt cold,' Orion said.

Ozzie couldn't see his eyes behind the sunglasses he was wearing, but guessed at a great deal of remorse. With his more practical gauntlets, it was Ozzie who dismantled the tent and put the packs back on the lontrus. The cold was every bit as debilitating as yesterday, but the little extra pieces of protective garments they'd put together helped to keep it from attacking their skin. The temperature was far too low for the snow to melt, which eliminated the chance of their feet getting wet – a lethal development.

The breeze had scattered the loose top layer of snow about, but there were still a few signs of the footprints they'd followed yesterday. Ozzie pushed at the lontrus's rump, then finally gave the miserable beast a kick. It started moving, emitting a wounded wailing.

Optimism, which had been high as Ozzie climbed out of the tent to greet the day, drained away quickly. Though it never faltered, the lontrus moved slowly. Every step Ozzie made was an effort, moving the weight of clothes, pushing his feet through the cloying snow. Warmth left him gradually. There was no one place it was leaking out from, rather an all-over emission, slowly and relentlessly chilling him. Every time he tipped his head up to the high cerise clouds drifting across the rosy sky he could imagine currents of his bodyheat flowing upwards to fill the insatiable icy void.

Some dreary time later, he noticed the crystal trees were shorter than before. Their perma-cloak of snow was also thinner, with the upper branches poking clear. Sunlight glinted and glimmered from their multiple facets, splitting into a prismatic spectrum entirely of red, from a gentle light-rose to deep gloomy claret. There was less snow beneath their feet as well. Ozzie had long since lost sight of the Silfen footprints.

He was so intent on trying to see through the thinning crystal pillars he didn't see Orion slowing. The boy grabbed at matted strands of the lontrus's pelt, which made the animal whine in protest.

'Do you need a break?' Ozzie asked.

'No. It's so cold, Ozzie. Really cold. I'm frightened.'

'I know. But try and keep going. Please? Stopping is only going to make things worse.'

'I'll try.'

'You want to lean on me for a bit?'

'No.'

Ozzie tugged gently at the strands of pelt just behind the lontrus's neck, reducing the animal's speed. It didn't resist the instruction. They ambled forward at a terribly slow pace. Ozzie started re-evaluating their whole progress. He clearly hadn't taken Orion's state properly into account last night as he'd worked out how far they could travel. Obviously, they weren't going to get more than a couple of kilometres further at best today; and that was going to be exhausting for the boy. The sensible course would be to turn around immediately. At this rate, if they were lucky, they might just get back to where they'd pitched the tent last night.

'The forest's finishing, look,' Orion said.

Ozzie focused, alarmed by how easily he'd fallen into a

daydreaming state. The crystal trees were small and naked now; central boles of amethyst armour standing proud, with their main branches flung out at right angles. Away at the tips of the regular twig segments, the purple encrustation gave way to smooth opal wedges that flared out from each tip, flat side up to absorb the crisp frigid sunlight. They had thinned out enough for him to see past the last clusters to the vast plain beyond. From his position it looked like a circular depression walled in by low curving hills. In the thin clear air, the far side was almost as sharply drawn as the ground around him. Distance was difficult to judge with so few reference points, but he guessed at twenty to twenty-five miles across. Bright sparks of reflected sunlight twinkled with vivid intensity to halo each hill, indicating the crystal tree forest had spread over every slope. The depression's floor was empty apart from its scattering of dusty snow.

For all the harsh beauty of the exotic landscape, Ozzie wanted to curse it. There was no hope here. They were going to struggle just to reach the end of the forest, a few hundred yards ahead where the crystal trees were nothing more than spindly dendrites of clear crystal strands sticking out of the iron-hard ground. Any notion of traversing that vast bleak and empty land to the other side was unthinkable.

Perhaps this is why so many who sought the deep paths were never heard of again. Our perception of the Silfen as gentle and kind is our own stupid, convenient illusion. We wanted to believe in elves. And how many human bodies lie out there under the snow because of that?

'It's a desert.' Orion said. 'A desert of ice.'

'Yeah, 'fraid so.'

'I wonder if Mom and Dad got here?'

'Don't worry. They're not stupid, they will have turned back, just like us.'

'Is that what we're doing?'

Ozzie saw a flash of near-blue light out across the plain. He pushed his sunglasses up, heedless of the sharp pain from the terrible air gusting against his exposed skin. The flash came again. Definitely emerald. The contrast was astounding on that vista made up entirely from shades of red. Green had to be artificial. A beacon!

He dropped his sunglasses down again. 'Maybe not.' The distress flares were nestled in hoops on each pack for easy access. He pulled one of the slim cylinders out, twisted the safety cap off and held it at arm's length to pull the trigger. There was a loud *crack*, and the flare zoomed off into the sky. A dazzling star of scarlet light drifted over the edge of the crystal forest, lingering for a long time.

Orion was staring at the slow pulse of the green beacon. 'Do you think that's people?'

'It's got to be someone. My hand-held array still doesn't work, so the Silfen are screwing with the electricity. That means this is definitely one of their worlds.' He waited a couple of minutes, then fired another flare. 'Let's try to walk to the edge of the trees. If we haven't seen an answer by then, we'll turn back.'

Ozzie hadn't even fired the third flare when the beacon light started flashing faster. Laughing beneath his mask, he held up the cylinder and triggered it. As it sputtered out overhead, the beacon light became constant.

'It's a beam,' Orion cried. 'They're pointing it at us.'

'I think you're right.'

'How far away is it?'

'I'm not sure.' His retinal inserts zoomed in, compensating for the emerald glare. The resolution wasn't great, but as far as he could make out, the light was coming from the top of some mound or small hillock. There were dark lines on it. Terraces? 'Ten or twelve miles, maybe more; and there's some kind of structure around it, I think.'

'What kind?'

'I don't know. But we're stopping here. If they're used to people they'll know we need help.'

'What if they don't?'

'I'm going to put the tent up. We'll use a heatbrick and get warm, we both need a proper rest. When the brick's finished we'll know what to do. If nobody's arrived we turn back.' He started to tug at the big knot he'd tied in the strap which secured the tent onto the lontrus.

'Can't we go there?' Orion asked plaintively.

'It's too far. The state we're in it'd take another couple of days. We can't risk that.' He unrolled the tent, and let the inner lining suck in air, raising itself into a small elongated hemisphere. Orion crawled inside, and Ozzie handed him a heatbrick. 'Rip the tag,' he told the boy. 'I'll join you in a minute.' He lifted his sunglasses again, and zoomed in on the mound below the beacon light. Then he fired another flare. In answer, the green light blinked off three times in slow succession before returning to a steady glare. In anybody's language that said, *We've got you*. He still couldn't make out what the mound was, except it actually had quite steep sides.

Three hours and four hot chocolates later, there was a great deal of noise outside the tent. Ozzie unzipped the front to peer out. Two big creatures were slogging their way up the last section of slope in front of the crystal forest. They were quadrupeds, about the size of terrestrial rhinos, and covered in a straggly string-thick fur similar to the lontrus. Steamy breath whistled out of a stubby snout on the bottom of a bulbous head that bristled with short prickly spines. He'd seen uglier animal heads, but it was the eyes which were strange, long strips of multifaceted black stone, as if they too had crystallized in this deadly climate. Both animals were harnessed to a covered sledge; a simple framework of what looked suspiciously like bone, with cured leather hides laced to it. As he watched, the side was pulled back, and a humanoid figure climbed down. Whoever it was, wore a long fur coat with a hood, fur trousers, fur mittens, and a fur face mask with hemispherical goggle lenses bulging out of it like fish-eyes. The figure strode towards them, raising a hand in greeting.

'I thought it would be humans,' a female voice called gruffly from behind the mask. 'We're the only people tasteless enough to use red light for emergency flares around here.'

'Sorry about that,' Ozzie shouted back. 'They don't stock a real big range of colours at the store.'

She stopped in front of the tent. 'How are you coping? Any frostbite?' Her voice had a strong northern Mediterranean accent.

'No frostbite, but we're not prepared for this kind of climate. Can you help?'

'That's why I'm here.' She ducked down, and pulled her mask free to look inside the tent. Her face was leathery brown, engraved with hundreds of wrinkles. She must have been in her sixties, at least. 'Hello there,' she said cheerfully to Orion. 'Cold here, isn't it?'

The boy just nodded dumbly at her. He was curled up in his sleeping bag again.

She sniffed the air. 'God in his heaven, is that chocolate?'

'Yes.' Ozzie held up his thermos. 'There's some left if you want.'

'If we ever had elections around here, you'd be emperor.' She took a big swig from the thermos, sighing pleasurably. 'Just like I remember. Welcome to the Citadel. I'm Sara Bush, kind of unofficial spokesperson for the humans here.'

'Ozzie Isaacs.'

'Hey, I've heard of you. Didn't you invent the gateways?'

'Uh, yeah.' Ozzie was a little distracted. A block of fur had appeared from behind the second sledge. This time it definitely wasn't a biped in a fur coat. More like a tall rectangle of the fluffiest fur he'd ever seen, with wide dark eyes visible near the top, about eight foot from the ground. There were ripples in the fur which suggested legs were moving somewhere within as it glided forward. It gave off a loud hooting which rose and fell, varying in pitch, almost like a chant.

'All right, all right,' Sara said irritably, waving a hand at the creature.

'What's that?' Orion asked timidly.

'Oh don't worry about him,' Sara said. 'That's old Bill, he's a Korrok-hi. More like a yeti if you ask me.' She broke off to warble a long verse back to her companion. 'There, I've told him we're coming. Now let's get you packed up and on the sledge. I think you two could do with a hot bath and a drink. Not long to cocktail hour now.'

'You're shitting me,' Ozzie exclaimed.

*

Paula spent most of the night reviewing the old AquaState accounts. The verification she wanted was easy enough to find, you just had to know what you were looking for to make the facts fit. Like every good conspiracy theory, she told herself. And no doubt that would be the angle which the defence council took.

When she arrived in the office the next morning, she was surprised that Hoshe was already behind his desk and running through forty-year-old files from City Hall. Even staying awake for half the night, she wasn't exactly late.

'I can't believe how much construction work there was in the city forty years ago,' he complained as soon as she'd sat down at her desk. 'It's like half of Darklake wasn't here. I don't remember it being so much smaller, and I've lived here for sixty years myself.'

Paula glanced over to the big wall-mounted portal he'd activated. It showed a detailed map of Darklake City, with a lot of green lights pinpointing building activity forty years ago, both civic and private. 'Don't forget to include things like roadworks for at least a couple of months after the murder. I know that will increase the search area dramatically, but that uncertainty makes them a prime possibility.'

He didn't say anything, but his expression soured further.

'I've finished my analysis,' she said. 'I'll help with your search. Divide the city into two, and I'll take one half.'

'Right.' Hoshe instructed his e-butler. 'What did you find in the accounts?'

'It confirmed my theory. But it's hardly evidence we can take to court, at least not alone.'

'You mean, we need the bodies?'

'They'll certainly help. Once we've established it's a murder, then the circumstantial evidence will be enough to convict him. I hope.'

Hoshe looked up at the map in the portal. 'This is an awful lot of field work for our forensic people. They're good, but there's only so many available. It could take months. Longer.'

'It's taken forty years so far, they're not going anywhere. And once we've locked down every site, I'll call in some teams from the Directorate. That should help speed things along.'

Mel Rees knocked on the open door and came in. Paula gave him a surprised look, then frowned. The deputy director always handed out her assignments in person. For him to visit a field operation, it had to be something big. He looked nervous, too.

'How's the case going?' he asked.

'As of yesterday, I have a suspect,' she said warily.

'I'm glad to hear it.' He shook hands with Hoshe. 'I've had some good reports about you, Detective. Do you think you'll be able to close this one by yourself now?'

Hoshe glanced at Paula. 'I suppose so.'

'He will,' Paula said. 'Why are you here?'

'I think you know.'

*

After the *Second Chance* launched from the assembly platform, it had taken the SI a further three minutes to crack the last fireshield in the gateway control centre datanet. The CST security team had marched in twenty minutes after that, once Rob Tannie had agreed to an unconditional surrender. The only promise CST made was not to shoot him and his colleagues on the spot. As it happened, the other two chose to suicide before the team got through the door, wiping their memorycells as they did so.

A fresh group of wormhole operation technicians rushed in as Rob was unceremoniously hauled away in handcuffs, leg restraints, and neural override collar. They took two hours to run checks on the systems and reopen the gateway next to the starship in its new, highly elliptical, orbit. By then, what remained of the complex was under the strict control of CST security forces. The surrounding area was isolated and swept clean by the Commonwealth Security Directorate. A squadron of FTY897 combat aerobots had taken up patrol of the perimeter; the smooth dark ellipsoids were ultra-modern and equipped with the kind of weaponry capable of taking out pitiful antiques like Alamo Avengers with a single shot.

The assembly platform survivors were brought back down to the planet. Fresh crews were taken up to assess the ship's status and secure exposed equipment against further vacuum degradation. Procedures were drawn up to establish a new assembly platform around the ship.

Five hours after the first explosion signalled the start of the assault, Wilson Kime stepped out of the gateway to spontaneous applause and cheers from the complex staff, and a bearhug from Nigel Sheldon. The CST media office broadcast the captain's triumphant return to an audience almost as big as the assault itself had attracted. After that, he gave half a dozen interviews, thanked everyone involved for their tremendous effort, cracked a few jokes, didn't speculate too hard on who had launched the attack, but said he was fairly sure it wasn't the Dyson Alpha aliens themselves, promised that he'd come through the ordeal more determined than ever to complete the mission, and finished up saying he'd donate his hazard bonus to a local children's medical charity. Anshun police gave his car an escort of eight outriders back to his flat in the city.

Wilson woke with a smile on his face. When he turned over, Anna's dark hair tickled his nose. She was curled up on the gellmattress beside him, one arm round her head like a small child warding off bad dreams. A whole series of delightful memories – and a deliciously wicked one – drifted through Wilson's head. He kissed her shoulder. 'Good morning.'

She stretched with a cat's lethargy, giving him a sleepy grin. 'That's a horribly smug smile you're wearing there, mister.'

'Yeah? I wonder what could have put it there?'

She giggled as he slid his arms round her. One hand stroked down her spine until it came to rest on her rump. 'Was it this?' His other hand squeezed a small beautifully shaped breast, mercilessly tweaking the nipple. 'Or this?' He kissed her neck, moved round to her mouth to smother the giggling. 'This?'

One of her hands wriggled down between them, gripping. 'Wa-how!'

'Might have been that,' she laughed.

'Oh yeah?' He started to tickle her ribs. She retaliated. It turned into a mild wrestling contest, which soon developed into a much more intimate body contact sport.

In the end she grinned down victoriously from her position straddling his hips. 'Well whadda ya know: it is true what danger does to a man.'

He could hardly deny it. Last night had been all about survival, his body celebrating with its most basic physical reaction. The amount of relief he'd experienced when the *Second Chance* had risen above the spaceplanes had actually produced the shakes (which thankfully only Anna had witnessed). The others on board – the youngsters – had been delighted, ecstatic even, with their dramatic escape; but the prospect of dying hadn't been too much for them to stand.

Wilson had never quite realized before how scared he was of dying, especially now. It wasn't something today's society could understand, not with all the expectation of rejuvenation and re-life procedures instilled from birth. The post-2050 generation knew they could live a good chunk of forever, it was their right. He thought his fear might have come from growing up in a time when there was only one life, then you died. The idea that memories could be saved and downloaded to animate a genetically identical body was a reassuring crutch for everyone else. But he couldn't quite convince himself that was a continuation of his current existence. There would be a discontinuity, a gap between what he was now, and what that future Kime would remember being. A difference; a copy that was flawless was still a copy, not the original. People got round the dilemma by saying that every morning when you woke the only link to your past was memory, therefore waking in a new body was just an extended version of that ordinary nightly loss of consciousness. It wasn't enough for him. His body, *this body*, was his life. The longer he lived in it, the more that identifying link was hardened. Three hundred plus years had produced a rock-solid conviction which nothing could break.

'I don't think I'd survive another dangerous night like that one,' he told her, still panting slightly.

She folded her arms across his chest, and bent forward until her chin was resting on her hands, putting their faces inches apart. 'What's ship regulations about the captain sleeping with the lower ranks?'

'The captain is very much in favour of it.'

A finger tapped on his sternum. 'You do have a sense of humour.'

'Carefully hidden, but cherished nonetheless.'

'So what do we do tonight if there isn't an attack?'

He pursed his lips in mock thought. 'Practise just in case?'

'My diary's free.'

'You don't have anyone?'

'No. Not for ages, actually. Too damn busy with my new job. You?'

'Not really. I haven't been married since my last rejuvenation. Some affairs, but nothing serious.'

'Good.' She straightened up. 'I'd better get a shower. Do you really want to meet up again tonight? Last chance for a clean getaway.'

'I would like to meet up again tonight.'

'Me too.' She gave him a quick kiss. 'Life's too uncertain not to try and keep hold of something good. Yesterday really made that clear to me like nothing else. Nobody's ever tried to kill me before.'

'You did a magnificent job up there. Combat stress is hardly something you're used to. I'm proud of you.'

'Have you been through something like that before?'

'Not exactly. But I've seen active military service. It was a long time ago, though. Not that you ever really forget, not even with rejuvenation editing.'

'Did you—' She hesitated. 'Kill anyone?'

'Honestly? I'm not sure. I certainly shot at a lot of people. You don't hang around to see the result. Slam on the afterburners, and head for home almost before the missile's left the rail.'

'It's hard to think how old you are. I just know you as a corporate chief. I had to run a search program to dig up the *Ulysses* story.'

'Ancient history. If you accessed it recently you probably know more about it than me.'

'But you did it, though. You travelled through space in a ship. It can be done.'

'I wouldn't call that mission an unqualified success.'

'Oh, but Wilson, it was! You reached Mars. Millions and

millions of kilometres from Earth. It doesn't matter that Sheldon and Isaac found another way. Don't denigrate what you did. After all, look who needs you now.'

'Sheldon. Yeah, I suppose that's poetic justice. You know what he said to me yesterday after we got back? He just fixed me with that smartass smile of his and said: *You're having a ball, aren't you?* He was right, too, the bastard. It felt so right flying the starship. We did it on a wing and a prayer. And we won! It's like everything I've done since *Ulysses* was an interlude, I've been marking time for three centuries.'

'And now you're doing what you were born to do.'

'Damn right.'

She looked down at her body, then his. Her expression became coy. 'There's a question a lot of us on the project have speculated about. You don't have to answer.'

'What?'

'All those months on *Ulysses*. It was a mixed crew. You were all young and fit. The whole voyage was in freefall.'

'Oh. Sorry. That's classified government information.'

'Classified, huh?'

'Yes. But let me just say this: the longer you spend continuously in freefall, the more immune you get to motion sickness. Even vigorous motion.'

'Really? A long time acclimatizing.'

He gave her an evil grin. 'Worth every minute of the wait.'

'It better be,' she muttered. 'I've really got to take that shower now. I'm supposed to be on duty in another ten minutes.'

'Take the day off. Tell them the boss said it was okay.'

Anna scrambled off the bed. 'Uh?'

'That door.' He pointed. There hadn't been much time to show her round the apartment last night. Clothes were coming off before the door shut.

'Thanks.' Another giggle, and she headed for the bathroom. 'At least you don't have to ask what my name is.'

'Certainly don't, Mary.'

One of his slippers flew across the room and hit him on the leg. 'Ow!' The door closed. As the sound of the shower began, Wilson put his hands behind his head and stared happily up at the ceiling. Given that yesterday he'd nearly been killed, this really wasn't a bad way to start a brand-new morning.

*

Not even the sight of the badly damaged complex brought down his mood. As he approached along the heavily guarded highway, thin trails of dark smoke were still leaking up into the sky from the ruined power plant. The missing circular administration tower was still a shock. Debris was piled high where the big atrium used to be, and most of the windows on the remaining two towers were either cracked or missing. Firebots picked their way delicately over the fragments of glass and concrete that sprawled out from the base, occasionally spraying out a jet of white foam. Medical salvage crews were working alongside the firebots, sending smaller remote sensors down into the rubble. They were seeking out bodies to remove their memorycell inserts ready for re-life.

Emergency vehicles had taken over the car park, so Wilson parked on an unused piece of lawn and got out. Oscar was standing watching the work parties in a group of several office staff and a squad of uniformed CST security guards.

'Morning, Captain,' he said, and saluted. Everyone around him abruptly straightened up.

'Morning,' Wilson replied. He didn't bother with returning the salute. Outside genuine military circles there was little point. 'Where do we stand?' Before he'd left last night, he'd discussed the immediate problems with Oscar and left his deputy to it.

'The starship is okay, all critical on-board equipment is stable and holding. There were enough back-up and redundant systems lying round down here to re-establish most of the umbilical feeds overnight. We're going to keep her like that until we can secure her inside an assembly platform again. The malmetal manufacturer hopes to deliver a viable globe to us in another four days. Once that's in place, we can perform a more detailed examination.'

'Good.' Wilson nodded at the sagging ruin of the closest assessment hall. 'And the complex?'

'That's going to take a bit longer. Security wants to verify the place safe first, make sure the terrorists didn't leave any nasty little booby traps behind. Once that's done we can clear the site, and start the rebuild. With the *Second Chance* so far along her schedule, we won't need the full suite of facilities down here again, so a lot of the work will just be patch-up operations. CST's civil engineering division is preparing a bunch of appropriate equipment as we speak; as soon as we give them the go-ahead, they'll move straight in.'

'Sounds like you've done a good job, Oscar, thank you.'

'Least I could do. Wish I'd been here yesterday.'

'Believe me, you don't. I suppose security is eager to implement a whole new set of procedures?'

'Oh yeah. We're going to have to make some decisions about that and review our new assembly program today. I put off the biggies until you got in.'

'Right. I'll get on it. Do I have an office?'

'I took over chemical systems building three for senior staff. Oh, and there's some security people who want to see you now.'

'They can wait.'

Oscar gave him an uncomfortable look. 'It might be a good idea to get it done and over with. Mr Sheldon suggested it.'

'Did he now?'

*

The last Alamo Avenger had been shot by an FTY897 as it was charging through assessment hall seven on its way to the gateway. An atom laser had pierced clean through its force field to strike the main body with devastating consequences. It had been severed in two as its primary power cells exploded. The blast flung the sections apart, smashing the forward part into racks of delicate fuselage panel stress test equipment, while the smaller rear portion had buried itself into the composite wall, which had promptly collapsed on it, leaving the overhead ceiling dangerously unsupported. One of the legs had been ripped off, embedding itself in the concrete floor.

A CST security tech force had spent the night de-bugging and powering down the wreckage. Small red tags fluttered from every element, confirming it was now inert and harmless. There were so many of them they made it seem like some abnormal Chinese parade monster. Paula walked slowly around the upturned front section, bending down to inspect one of the shattered sensor clumps on the head. The Director of the Serious Crimes Directorate, Rafael Columbia, was standing in the middle of the damaged assessment hall along-side Mel Rees, the pair of them watching her as she performed her little inspection of the dead armoured monstrosity. Both looked unhappy as water left behind by the fire sprinkler deluge dripped off the overhead beams. Their expensive shoes were already soaked from walking through all the puddles.

Paula ran a finger over the battered polyalloy armour, feeling the thin carbon ablation blisters crumple like ancient paper below her nail. 'Not bad for a hundred-and-fifty-year-old weapon,' she acknowledged. 'They were lucky Captain Kime was in orbit to take charge.'

'Absolutely,' Mel Rees said.

'I would have preferred CST to be luckier somewhat earlier,' Rafael Columbia told the deputy director. 'The current estimate is one hundred and seven people killed, and another eighteen so far unaccounted for. They're still calculating the financial loss, but it won't be less than two billion. And we had *no* prior warning. None. This is the single most destructive act of criminal terrorism we have known in the last century. The death toll in nationalist succession movements adds up over time, but this . . .' His arm swept round, a gesture taking in the smashed hall. 'This is our failure. It is a challenge to the Directorate's very credibility to perform its designated task. I will not tolerate this appalling violation of law and order.'

'We'll get them,' Mel Rees said. 'No question of that.'

'Your division has had decades on this case. I expected better.'

Paula turned from the Alamo Avenger. 'I have spent decades on the Johansson case, not Deputy Director Rees. And I really hope you're not implying we should have provided you with some kind of advance warning.'

'Paula—' Mel Rees began.

She shot him a look which silenced him immediately. 'The reason Bradley Johansson and his associates have had the run of the Commonwealth for so long is twofold. The resources which are allocated to tracking him and his activities are wholly inadequate. That is a political decision, made by you and your predecessors, Mr Columbia. He also receives help from someone extremely well placed in the Commonwealth establishment.'

'Rubbish,' Rafael Columbia snapped.

'Even with inadequate funds, there is absolutely no way he could have eluded me for over a hundred and thirty years. It simply isn't possible. If he kept a low profile and lived a thoroughly simple life I would have caught him. But as the leader of a criminal organization constantly involved in smuggling weapons to Far Away he leaves himself continually exposed to our sources and monitor programs. To avoid them requires a considerable degree of assistance. He is not acting alone.'

'Do you realize what you're saying? Do you know how many administrations there have been since he founded his ridiculous Guardians movement? There isn't one which would give him any kind of support, covert or otherwise, let alone all of them.'

'Administrations change, power groupings do not.'

'I am not going to stand here and be told I'm part of some corrupt cover-up operation. I don't care who you are, how dedicated you are, or what your case conviction record is. I am the Chief of this Directorate, and you will show me some respect.'

'Respect is something which is earned, Mr Columbia.'

'Okay!' Mel Rees put his hands up and walked forwards to stand directly between them. 'One thing Johansson would be doing right now is laughing his ass off at the pair of you. The only person you're helping right now is him.'

'Thank you for that,' Columbia said. He gave Paula a glare which would normally ruin any of his staff. She didn't even seem aware of it.

'First question,' Paula said. 'Why do you think it's him?'

Columbia gave an irritated wave to the deputy director.

'Method of operation,' Rees told Paula. 'This has Adam Elvin's signature all over it. We think he put the operation together.'

'That would be unusual,' Paula said. 'Elvin himself hasn't been directly involved in violent acts since Abadan. He just puts shipments together for Johansson.'

Rafael Columbia produced a small scornful laugh. 'This is not an age where the measure of time depreciates anything. I thought you of all people should appreciate that, Chief Investigator.'

'All the recent Guardians propaganda has been denouncing the *Second Chance* as a project organized by the Starflyer,' Rees said. 'They're the only ones who have any kind of reason to do this.'

'A reason?' Paula said thoughtfully. 'To launch an action like this inside the Commonwealth is a huge change of policy for Johansson.'

'Who knows how his deranged mind works?' Rafael Columbia said.

'He's not deranged,' Paula said. 'Deluded, certainly, but don't make the mistake of believing he isn't capable of rational thought.'

Rafael Columbia pointed at the crumpled blackened body of the Alamo Avenger. 'You call this rational?'

'We're only a couple of hundred metres from the gateway, and the other two got through. Then there was the kinetic assault on the assembly platform. They almost succeeded. I'd call that pretty smart. Whatever you think of him, and I think worse than most, he is not stupid. If he is behind this, then something new is happening. Is it possible the *Marie Celeste* came from the Dyson Pair?'

'Unlikely in the extreme,' Wilson said. He nodded respectfully at Rafael Columbia as he walked across the wet floor of the assessment hall. 'Paula Myo, a privilege. I've accessed a lot of your cases.'

'Captain.'

'We've discussed the possibility of a link between Dyson Alpha and the *Marie Celeste* with the Director of Far Away's Research Institute,' Wilson said. 'He says it doesn't exist. I'm inclined to believe him.'

'An official denial is the certificate of endorsement for conspiracy theorists,' Paula said. 'Especially one issued by the Director of the Institute. We know Johansson believes there is a link.'

'That's his problem.'

Paula gave him a grave smile. 'He just made it yours, too.'

'I want him stopped,' Rafael Columbia said. 'Deputy Director Rees has assured me you are the best, indeed only, person to take charge of this case. Do you agree with that assessment?'

'I certainly have the experience,' Paula said. 'What I need to finally track him down is the Directorate's full cooperation, and resources behind me.'

'As of now, you've got them. Whatever it takes. You can build your own team, take whoever you want no matter what they're working on. This has total priority.'

'Very well. I'll start with my usual colleagues, and expand from there as our lines of inquiry open up. The first thing I'll need from you, Mr Columbia, is political coverage. CST security will want to make this their mission. Please talk to Mr Sheldon and have them stand back.'

'I will point out the jurisdiction implications to CST,' Rafael Columbia said. He ignored the quiet laughter coming from Wilson's direction.

'Thank you. Now how exactly do you smuggle three working Alamo Avengers to a planet?'

'They weren't smuggled in,' Rees said. 'According to the export files, they were neutralized relics on their way to a new museum here on Anshun. It was a lawful shipment.'

'A new museum?'

'You got it. The land exists, it was bought three months ago, and there's a registered company to control it. But there's no building yet, or even plans. The company has a few thousand Anshun dollars in its account, but that was transferred from a one-use account on Bidar. Untraceable, or at least very difficult.'

'Ah,' she said in satisfaction. 'Yes, that does sound like Elvin's signature.'

'Completely. The Alamo Avengers were bought legitimately from a dealer a week after the museum company was registered. Back then, they really were just wrecks. They've spent the intervening time being "refurbished" to display standard on the Democratic Republic of New Germany. The company which did the work has been sealed up, and the DRNG police are going over their facilities and records for us.'

'What about the spaceplanes?' Wilson asked.

'Leased from a fully legitimate commercial operator here on Anshun. Again the company hiring them was a shell. Using them as kinetic missiles was a simple case of reprogramming their pilot arrays. It's not difficult. We're sending in some teams to the port they took off from. I'm not expecting much.'

'Are these Guardians likely to try again?' Wilson asked.

'Johansson has been launching attacks against the Institute on Far Away for a century and a half,' Paula said. 'It would be reasonable to assume this was only the first attempt against the *Second Chance*.'

12

Over the High Desert the deep sapphire sky began to darken. Kazimir McFoster stood alone on one of the long wave-shaped dunes of grey sand and watched the stars emerge. It was a ritual for him now, staring up at those platinum sparks, waiting for the mighty constellation of Achilles to come shimmering out of the golden-velvet twilight. When he'd found the shape of the ancient warrior with his gleaming red eye, he traced along the Milky Way swirl of his cloak. There in the sparse lower hem was a twinkle he could never be sure was real or imagined. Earth's star.

She will be there, standing on cool, rich, green land, looking up into this same void. Six hundred years away. But I can see you still, my glorious angel. Grant me victory on this raid, even though you never believed in our cause.

In Kazimir's mind, Justine's beautiful face was shadowed by sadness as his task on this night became clear to her. 'Choose your own path, my love,' she whispered in the darkness and thick warmth of their secluded tent in the forest. Fingers lighter than mist stroked him *this way* then again *like so*. Her delighted laughter filled the tent as he twisted with helpless delirium beneath her sensual puppetry. 'Be your own man, not the tool of others. Promise me that.' The pleasure she bestowed made him weep openly, swearing on generations of McFosters as yet unborn he would be true to himself and his own thoughts.

Yet for all her concern, Justine did not understand the reality of this planet. Like every offworlder before her, she regarded the Starflyer as a local myth, Far Away's Loch Ness monster.

'Forgive me?' he asked of the stars. 'I'm doing this for you, so you may enjoy your world and the wonderful life you have there.'

A tiny rivulet of sand shifted behind him, causing the faintest of sounds. Kazimir smiled softly, and continued to stare into the heavens. The desert heat lacked any hint of humidity. Surrounded on all sides by the Dessault Mountains, the air here never moved, not even wisps of cirrus clouds sneaked past the rampart peaks. A static climate which sucked the moisture from exposed skin and every breath. Few plants grew here, some native cacti that resembled stones, and were often harder; not even the Barsoomians could bring verdant life to a place without water. But for all its harsh nature, it was home, the place in the universe where Kazimir felt most secure.

'If I were the Starflyer, you would be mine now,' a voice whispered contentedly in his ear.

'If you were the Starflyer, Bruce, you would be dead now,' Kazimir said. He pushed the knife blade back a little further so the tip touched the stomach of the other young man.

Bruce McFoster laughed with relief, and threw his arm around his friend. 'You had me worried, Kaz, I thought you were going soft.'

'Worry for yourself.' Kazimir withdrew the knife and slid it back into the sheath on the side of his sporran. 'You sounded like a herd of T-rexes coming up the slope. The entire Institute will hear you coming.'

'They'll hear me from the afterlife. Tomorrow night we shall inflict a massive blow to them. Did you hear the attack on Anshun damaged the human starship?'

'Scott told me.'

'Scott! That old woman? Is he here? I can't believe the elders will let him in on the raid.' Bruce dropped a shoulder and limped around Kazimir. 'Mark my words,' he lisped. 'This Starflyer will spill your blood and tear your body apart for its amusement. Never has there been a monster so evil in the universe. I know, I faced its slaves in single combat. Hundreds of them, killed, a thousand, yet still they came on.'

'Don't mock so,' Kazimir exclaimed. He and Bruce had grown up together, shared so much they were closer than any brothers. Yet his friend could still be incredibly offensive, not to mention tactless. Sometimes he wondered if Bruce had ever been awake at any time under Harvey's years of tutelage. 'Scott has suffered for our cause, more than I'd wish.'

Bruce straightened up. 'I know, I know. But you have to admit, he's too cautious.'

'He's alive. I'll be happy if I'm alive after serving the cause for that long.'

'Keep daydreaming about your offworld nympho, and your contribution to the cause is going to be over too quickly. You were thinking about her again, weren't you? That's what you're up here for, presenting a fine skyline target for the enemy.'

It was difficult for Kazimir not to smile. 'I was enjoying the quiet, that's all. Listening to you for the whole day before the raid would drive anyone nuts. And stop calling her a nympho.'

'I knew it! You were thinking about her again.'

'So what? At least I do care about others.'

'Oh, hey, below the belt, or what. There have been a lot of girls I cared for in the last few years. More than you.'

'More, yes. But none of them for very long, eh, Bruce?'

'Doesn't need to be long, just thorough. Now come on, Romeo, time we got ready.'

'Yes.' Kazimir took one last longing look at the thick swathe of stars, then followed Bruce as he skidded his way down the dune. Directly ahead of them was StOmer, the great mountain which marked the most north-easterly point of the Dessault

439

range – not that it was anything like the height of the Grand Triad. On this side, rising up out of the desert it had no vegetation, blue-grey rock lifted straight into the meagre snow-line thousands of feet above.

'Did it help?' Bruce asked, serious for once. Or as serious as he could be. They'd reached the broad ridge of crumbling sandstone where there was a tunnel to the clan's Rock Dee fort.

'Did what help?'

'Thinking about her?'

'Some. Yes. I know that what we're defending is worth-while.' Kazimir ducked his head to step under what looked like a deep overhang. The tunnel was underneath, hidden from the sky, barely wide enough for one person. He tucked his shoulders in, and scraped his way forward, the once-gritty sandstone on either side now smooth as marble from the passage of so many bodies over the decades. The tunnel bent twice, following a sharp S-curve. Thirty metres from the entrance it opened out into the first of the wide chambers that formed Rock Dee fort. The guard, standing proud in her lavender and tangerine McMixon kilt, studied his face, then allowed him to pass. If the Institute soldiers did ever find the tunnel, any guard would be able to hold them off just about single-handed as they wriggled their way out of the narrow slit one by one.

Polyphoto strips had been epoxied to the roof, with long strings of black electrical cable stretched out between them. Their relentless sol-spectrum light etched deep shadows across the rumpled sandstone as they led deeper into the fort.

'She must have been phenomenal in bed,' Bruce said with apparent sympathy. 'I mean, the two of you only had, what, a couple of days together? And you're still moping about her.'

'Sometimes, I almost wish you'd met her.'

'Almost?'

'If you'd seen her, got to know her, you would understand

this isn't some easy infatuation like the ones you have. And I would have wanted my two closest friends to meet.'

'Oh . . . well, thanks, Kaz.'

'But I thank all the heavens you didn't, because you're such an embarrassment I'm sure she wouldn't want to have anything to do with anyone who knew you.'

Bruce made a lunge for him. A laughing Kazimir dodged ahead, and started running. The pair of them burst out into the fort's main chamber, still taunting and insulting each other loudly. Heads swung round to check out what was happening. Some frowned at the flippancy of the youths at such a time. Others smiled tolerantly – those of a similar age. Most simply turned back to their serious work.

Kazimir and Bruce put on their sober faces, slowed down, and nodded courteously at their fellow clansmen. The rocky cavern had been carved in the rough shape of a football amphitheatre by storm waters now long gone from this side of the mountains. Two fast channels had once merged here, swirling round and round as they clashed before rushing out towards the north-eastern lowlands. As well as the main chamber, the surging waters had eroded a host of smaller passages and caves, tributaries which had splintered and shifted as geology took over from hydropressure.

Rock Dee was one of the largest Guardian communities, and a formidable safe refuge. There was still fresh water to be found in the lower caverns, filtering in from the mountains which guarded the desert above. Solid state heat exchange cables had been sunk deep into the mantle below, providing power for lighting and cooking, along with the more important task of supplying the armoury with electricity. All that had to be brought in was food, and that was supplied by the McKratz clan's farms and grazing lands scattered throughout the Dessault range.

Kazimir felt a surge of pride at what he saw in the big chamber. If only he could have brought Justine to see this, then she would have believed in the Guardians' purpose. Over eighty fighters were busy on the chamber floor, making up one of the largest raiding parties the Guardians of Selfhood had put together in years. But then, as everyone here knew, events were picking up with the construction of the human starship. The Starflyer's long-laid plans were maturing rapidly, bringing disaster and death to the Commonwealth from the one direction no one in authority was looking. All the clans had contributed to the raid.

The McFosters, of course, provided a dozen young fighters, who were checking over their packs and equipment. Their emerald and copper kilts had been packed away; this evening they wore their navy-blue and ebony hunter tartan, helping them pass unseen through the night.

The McNowaks were also predominately fighters, in their grey and brown tartan. A group of them was engaged assessing the armour worn by one of their captains. The blue skeletal suit flooded the air around him with a nebulous orange haze, as if he was standing inside a ghostly amoeba. The radiance crackled and intensified each time a test penetrator cane was applied against him. With each application the force field emitter was gradually tuned until the emanation was nothing more than a faint aural outline, the kind any Old Testament saint might possess. Fine tuning inverted the radiance, cloaking him in a skin of absorptive shadow.

The McOnnas were the third clan to focus on the soldier ethic, their nomadic boys and girls undergoing the same lessons, training, and tests that Kazimir himself had gone through. All of them he knew he could trust as much as Bruce. All were totally loyal to the cause, prepared to give their lives so humanity could be liberated. The squad they'd sent were wearing their nightguard blue and vermilion kilts, along with dark leather travel jackets; ion pistol holster and harmonic blade knife sheaths hanging from their belts rather than a sporran.

McMixons, who were charged with the keeping of Rock Dee and other forts in the countryside surrounding the Institute, were tending to the Charlemagnes, the warhorses they would all ride to the raid. The gene-modified beasts were fully twenty-one hands, carried by legs like small tree trunks. They had no mane, or tail; their thick leather hide was tougher than rhino skin, and a similar dull slate-grey in colour. A short unicorn spike rose out of their heads, tipped with carbon-bonded titanium blades by the Rock Dee smithy. Any unprotected human caught by one would be ripped in half; and even force field armour had been known to give way from the inertia of a full charge. Fat iron bolts had been driven through the tough shield ridges of bone that protected the neck and underbelly. Straps of leather and silicon were threaded through hoops in the bolts to hold the saddle in place. The Charlemagnes had been designed by the Barsoomians in their lands away to the east of the Oak Sea. Not for money – an emblem of the culture to which the radical ecogeneticists were fiercely averse – but for the challenge of engendering an animal which in symbiosis with humans had only one purpose: carnage. The Barsoomians probably even delved into the forbidden field of psychoneural profiling, for no clan fighter had ever known a Charlemagne to shy away skittishly in the heat of battle like an ordinary horse would. With their tough skin, triple hearts, and multiple stress loading pathway skeleton, the great beasts were inordinately difficult to kill even with modern weapons.

The McPeierls were the widest-roaming clan of all, and they gathered intelligence on Institute activities from all over the planet. They also collected the advanced equipment which Johansson smuggled through the gateway along hundreds of innocuous routes. This evening, their members were distributing the final pieces of technology and weaponry required by the raiders.

McKratzs, who farmed and raised cattle out across Far

Away's sweeping plains and tricky mountain pastures. They were the ones who bred the Charlemagne herds and lynx-hounds packs, and other domestic animals used by the clans. Throughout the year, they insured the more nomadic clans were fed and supplied.

And everywhere in the main cavern moved the McSobels, the armourer clan, also responsible for general technology. Lugging their test equipment over the rock floor, stopping beside each fighter and warhorse, running test programs through the arrays. Scarlet superconductor cables were pulled about behind them, supplying top-up charges to batteries and weapon magazines. Seven of them had been assigned to the raid, dressed in kilts that were matt black with a plain grid pattern of thin dark-grey lines, and equally black coats. Five were bringing the missile launchers and medium-calibre plasma cannon, bulky titanium-cased units hanging from their Charlemagnes, who didn't even seem to notice the extra weight. The remaining two operated electronic warfare systems intended to neutralize the Institute communications and throw in as much confusion and false data as possible.

Walking up to his own warhorse, Kraken, Kazimir felt the gooseflesh rising as the prospect of the coming raid grew more real. The Charlemagne snorted like a small thunderstorm, lifting and turning its head slightly so it could watch him walk round to its flank. Kazimir had absolutely no instinct to pat the creature reassuringly – this was nothing like the normal ponies and horses he'd learned to ride on. It was enough that the beast didn't simply try and bite his head off on sight, the carnivore tusks it had curving over its rubbery lips were thicker than his fingers.

He began to check his pack once more.

'So are you two screwups ready?' a rasping voice asked.

Kazimir smiled round at Harvey McFoster, his old tutor. The man was a veteran of many clan raids against the Institute, and had the scars to prove it. Years ago, an ion beam fired by an Institute soldier had vaporized a superconductor battery beside him, the superenergized molecules had penetrated his armour force field. After his injury, he spent his time teaching rather than fighting. He was lucky he survived the toxic shock. Clan medics spent six months repairing as much tissue as they could; even so the skin on a third of his body now had a melted appearance, and he could never raise his voice to shout. Not that he needed to, his presence alone inspired awe in his pupils. Kazimir considered himself privileged to have been one.

'Doing my best to be ready,' he said.

'Good enough,' Harvey said. 'And you, Bruce, are you scared yet?'

'Ha.' Bruce gave the ion pistol on his belt a confident pat. 'No, sir.'

Harvey's cheek muscles moved his too-thick skin into a grimace, looking even more like some Halloween grotesque. 'If you had a brain, lad, you would be.'

Bruce's eternal cockiness vanished.

'Be nervous,' Harvey said. 'Their soldiers are trying to kill you, or worse. Fright is your friend, it keeps you alert. That gives you a chance out there.'

'Only heroes are fearless,' Kazimir said. 'And they die young.'

'I'm glad you heard something I said,' Harvey told him. 'Even if it is just an old lyric.'

'We'll make you proud,' Bruce insisted.

Harvey's hand closed on his shoulder. 'I know you will, lad, although I'd prefer it if you just stay alive. Remember, keep your eyes focused in front of you the whole time, not on your dick.' He gave a laboured wink towards the McNowak group, then walked off.

Kazimir and Bruce smiled at each other in the same way as

they had when they got caught playing truant. Bruce lifted his pack up and fastened it behind his saddle. 'He's right, you know.'

'I know. We mustn't let our attention slip.'

'No, you idiot, about them.'

'Huh?' Kazimir followed the line his friend was surreptitiously indicating. Four of the McNowak fighters were young women. Kazimir had even chatted to a couple of them yesterday when they arrived in Rock Dee.

'That one with the dark hair, she hasn't stopped looking at you since we came in.'

'Andria?'

'Oh ho, you already know her name. Quick work, my friend. So who's the one next to her? I wouldn't mind a tumble with her after the raid.'

'That's Bethany. I think she's paired with one of the McOnnas. And anyway, what about Samantha? It's only another month until she's due.'

'So? This is why I love being a McFoster. We exist to kill the Starflyer and breed enough warriors to make the cause successful. That's our duty. We fight. We fuck. When you think about it, what else is there worth doing? And believe me, that Bethany over there, she'll be thinking along the same lines.'

'Dear heavens. Bruce, she'll be thinking how to brain you with her pistol butt, is all. Can't you ever get a grip on yourself?' Kazimir unfolded the lightweight shield coat, and threw it over Kraken's back, bracing himself should the beast not want it, and react with a fast kick. The dark fabric was embroidered with glittering black metal curls and spirals, and long tassels hung from the lower edges, almost touching the ground. He started to smooth it over the warhorse's thick skin, and used its straps to tie it to the bolt rings.

'I'm being honest,' Bruce protested with genuine hurt feelings. 'You know that. This raid is going to make every female fighter incredibly horny afterwards. It does me. What better way to celebrate our glorious victory?'

'How about in a civilized fashion?'

'Ha! I remember the west Irral raid. You were drunk for a week after. And you vanished off with that McSobel. What was her name?'

'Lina.' He didn't mention it was because in the midst of his happy drunken haze Lina had looked more than a little like Justine.

'That's the one. So don't go all noble on me. You and I are the same.' Bruce's arm went round his friend's shoulder. He turned the reluctant Kazimir until they were both facing the young McNowak women, and gave them a cheery wave. Andria returned a sly smile, her gaze lingering on Kazimir before turning to her Charlemagne. Her three companions went into a huddle with her. The boys heard giggling.

'Now tell me that wasn't an invitation,' Bruce insisted. 'Look at her. What a figure. I bet she'll be as lusty as hell in bed. And those breasts, dear heaven, they're huge.'

'Will you shut up!' Kazimir tried to clamp his hand over Bruce's mouth. 'They'll hear you.'

'You're such a virgin. *Ohooo, be quiet, or they'll hear how much we like them.* Wake up and smell the coffee, Kaz, you're not going to live for ever. And it's such a beautiful life in the meantime, especially when it's got breasts that size in it.'

'Stop it!' He started plucking at Bruce's shirt, peering under the collar, checking the cuffs.

'What are you doing, Kaz?'

'Looking for the off switch. Please, heaven, let there be one.'

Bruce laughed, pushing his friend away. 'No man can stop thinking about women, especially not at a time like this. Battle fires up all the primitive instincts.'

'That explains a lot; nobody gets more primitive than you.'

'Let's get over there, we're wasting time.' He took a step forward.

'No!' Kaz almost had to lunge to grab hold of Bruce's shoulder and stop him. All four McNowak women were staring at their antics now. 'I swear I'll shoot you dead on the spot if you make a scene with them,' he growled at Bruce.

Bruce allowed himself to be halted in mid-stride. 'Kaz! You do care about Andria.'

'I don't want the whole raiding party to think we're a pair of jerks, that's all. Which is what they will do if we go over there and you spin them your usual bullshit lines. Now will you quit being such an ass in public.'

'Okay: I will be quiet if you promise you'll bed her after the raid. Deal?'

'And that's really a promise I can make.' Kazimir wished his traitor mouth wasn't trying so hard to smile. It seemed as though from the moment he and Bruce became teenagers every second of their time together had been spent plotting strategies to meet and impress the opposite sex. Now when relationships were more adult, casual and easier, he wasn't interested. Though Andria was genuinely attractive, and it had been pleasant talking to her earlier. And it had been a very long time since Lina. *I wonder if Justine has found a lover? She would never lack for young men pursuing her.*

'If you don't, I'll take her.'

Kazimir grunted in utter contempt. 'Oh yes, and that's even closer to reality. Everyone knows your reputation. And if she didn't know about Samantha, I'd tell her. I'll go over there, and . . .'

'You'll do it then?' Bruce face was radiating delight.

'Anything to shut you up.'

Bruce hugged him heartily. 'Thank heavens. You have no idea how badly you need to get laid. Every second since your offworld nympho left has been torture for your friends.'

'Good! So now you know what my life is like having to

listen to you the whole time.' Kazimir lifted up his saddle, and slung that over Kraken's back, settling it on top of the blanket. He was convinced that even the warhorse was laughing at him.

*

The raiding party left Rock Dee an hour after nightfall, fully eighty clan fighters filtering out of hidden clefts amid the desert side foothills of StOmer. They led their warhorses at first, negotiating the tricky passes and steep dune banks. Before midnight, they had all reached the southern side of the mountain, and mounted up to start their descent into the lowlands. Small tufts of wiry dry grass the colour of straw were appearing in the gritty sand. As the gentle folds in the land began to deepen into distinct valleys so the grass turned greener, and began to spread out into patches which soon joined together into a single carpet. This far down, and facing due east, a cold wind blew at them. For the first time they felt a tinge of moisture against their exposed skin.

The air warmed quickly as they moved steadily lower, even though it was now deepest night. They were only a few degrees south of the equator. A thin belt of giant heather formed the upper border to the forest which covered the lower half of StOmer's eastern slopes. By daybreak they were safely under cover of the lush trees, and moving in small groups along the myriad hidden tracks.

They had a long break at midday, taking time to sleep as best they could as the heavy warm rain pattered against the broad canopy of leaves overhead. A quick cold meal at the start of the afternoon, and they were on their way again. As the light began to drain out of the sapphire sky they had reached the edge of the forest, where the land fell away in a steep shingle and grass ridge. The captains of every squad sent out scouts, who crept up to the edge of the ridge to check the ambush point. Several of them were McSobels, who pinpointed and neutralized the remote sensors which the Institute had installed along the road below.

Far Away only had one major road: Highway One, which ran southwards from Armstrong City to cross the equator where it snaked along the western side of the Great Iril Steppes until finally driving into the valley where the *Marie Celeste* had crash-landed and the Institute had been built to study it. The road provided the sole supply route from the gateway in the city to the Institute, a twin-lane strip of enzyme-bonded concrete extruded by the only pair of tracked roadbuilders ever to be exported to Far Away. They'd been brought in specifically for that one job, although once they'd finished the long north–south route they'd managed to keep going long enough to lay down a few smaller roads linking Armstrong City with the larger towns in the north. But after they finally broke down no spare parts were ever brought in to fix them.

From their position atop the ridge, the clan scouts could see the stone-grey ribbon of the road curving round the hill which marked the entrance to the alien arkship's valley. It was late afternoon, and the thick cover of vegetation which lay across the lowland was still steaming gently. Carried on the air, echoing and drifting out of the valley which contained the Institute, was the faintest of mechanical sounds. For over a year now, scouts had been reporting increased activity round the massive metal hull. The news had been given an ominous reception by the clans, its synchronicity with the work on the human starship was too strong to be ignored.

But now, from the vantage point of the ridge, there was no sign of any activity. Nobody was using the road. The scouts settled down and waited; their information on the convoy was good, it was only a matter of time.

There was normally a supply convoy every couple of weeks delivering food and equipment to the Institute. It took at least a week to drive the route down from the city; often longer, depending on the road's state of repair, and the level of sabotage by the Guardians. Each convoy was protected by soldiers that were hired by the Institute and licensed by the planetary governor.

The Guardians had been monitoring this convoy since it left Armstrong City. There were twenty big trucks hauling the cylindrical freight containers which had arrived through the gateway over the last fortnight. They were all FordSaaB VF44s; sixteen-wheel, twin-axle, diesel-fuelled, and manual-drive – even the most sophisticated arrays would have trouble coping with Far Away's poor surfaces and absence of satellite position-ing systems. The Institute had chosen them for its transport fleet because they were designed for low maintenance and rough terrain.

Driving with them were eight Land Rover Cruisers, a vehicle in common use among Commonwealth police and paramilitary forces operating in remote areas. Their matt-black bodywork was blunt enough to qualify as a mobile brick. On the road, they rode low on six independent suspension wheels, which could extend down and out to carry them over really rugged ground.

The rest of the convoy was made up by a huge fuel tanker and a couple of tow/repair trucks.

When they reached the last stretch of road before the start of the Institute valley, it was already twilight. The scouts saw the headlights blazing ahead of them, visible for kilometres across the rumpled countryside, advertising their presence. A couple of the Cruisers were out in front, their drivers acceler-ating eagerly now they could see the sodium orange corona from the Institute's little town crowning the hill ahead.

The dark sky was ripped apart by three blinding streaks of plasma as the McSobels opened fire from the top of the ridge. Two of the bolts struck the lead truck, blasting it apart. Inertia kept the disintegrating bulk tumbling forwards as the freight containers spewed out great streamers of flame. After a couple of seconds the flaming wreckage flipped over and skidded to a stop, blocking the road.

The third plasma bolt hit the fuel tanker. A tremendous explosion bloomed out, the fireball eruption swelling in seconds until it was over thirty metres wide, lighting up the whole convoy with garish menace. The trucks directly ahead and behind were completely engulfed, their own subsequent detonation adding to the devastation.

Every vehicle in the convoy emergency-braked as the attack began, wheels locking and screeching as they scored huge scars of black rubber along the enzyme-bonded concrete. Several of them came dangerously close to fishtailing as their automatic systems fought to stabilize the braking sequence.

Another three plasma bolts flashed down. Two of them found their targets, smashing trucks apart in swarms of flaming debris. But the driver of the third truck had reflexes fast enough to activate his force field as he struggled to halt the bucking vehicle. A hemispherical shell of air solidified around the truck, sizzling electric blue as the bolt hit. Spikes of lightning lashed off in every direction. Long jagged lines of concrete ruptured into gravel and soot as the energy discharge pounded the road. Slim streamers of lava welled up in the gashes. There was nothing the force field could do to protect the truck from them as it slithered onward. Tyres burst apart as they touched the molten rock, tipping the wheel hubs onto the ground. The front edge of the cab gouged out a huge scar as it shuddered to a violent stop.

By then every other surviving vehicle had a force field surrounding it. Drivers shouted into their radios for help and instructions, receiving nothing but thick static even on the encrypted security channels. The road was completely blocked. If they were going to get to the safety of the valley they would have to drive across open ground. Force fields made progress along a flat surface difficult; to travel over such rugged terrain the strength of the protective hemispheres would have to be reduced. Nobody wanted to do that. A further series of plasma bolts whipped down, hammering at the force fields like the spears of angry gods. None of them penetrated, but the pyrotechnic electron display was lighting up the countryside for miles around. Waiting in their cabs, engines running, praying for reinforcements, the drivers watched in horror as the strobing incandescence revealed a dark horde of horsemen rushing down the ridge towards the road.

Kazimir had fitted active lenses into his eyes long before the scouts reported the convoy was approaching. The view they presented him gave the world a pale-emerald tint, but it stayed sharp and clear as the sun went down. Along with the rest of the Charlemagnes he hung back from the top of the ridge so the enemy had no hint of their presence. Then the McSobels fired the plasma cannon. His lenses simply refused to let that much light through into his eyes, he saw them as pink lines blinking on and off, like an after-image of the noon sun traced across his retina. That was the signal to advance. With the sound of the exploding trucks reverberating around him, he urged Kraken forward to the crest of the ridge. A quick sideways glance showed Bruce at his side, laughing like a demon as the massive warhorses picked up speed. Then they were over the ridge, and the entire panorama glared brilliant jade below them as the diminishing tanker truck fireball ascended into the sky. He watched the trucks skidding about on the road, their force fields haloed by pieces of flaming wreckage that bounced and skittered across the invisible screens. The Cruisers had all turned off the road, and were driving straight towards the clan raiders as they charged down the slope.

As the distance quickly shrank, the raiders started to fire their ion pistols and the larger carbines. Force fields protecting the Cruisers flared chrome yellow, but none of the shots got through. The thunder of hoofs was now as loud as the howl of flames bursting out of the ruined tanker and the crackling energy weapons. Kinetic rapid-fire guns on the front of the Cruisers opened up. Tall gouts of earth sprayed up around Kraken. One of the projectiles struck Kazimir. His force field rang like a sepulchral church bell, completely deafening him. Vibrant slivers of energy rippled down the dark confining field, then surged through the curlicues embroidered in the warhorse's shield blanket, turning the metal a glimmering white, before grounding out through the bottom of the tassels. Blue and purple sparks fizzed out around Kraken's hoofs as they charged onwards. The air was filled with the sharp tang of burning metal. All around him, the clan raiders were trailing fabulous streamers of St Elmo's fire as the projectiles hammered into them – human comets streaking across the gloom. Warhorses screamed as the gunfire tore their flesh open, falling to the earth as blood poured through huge tattered wounds.

A flight of missiles soared overhead. The Cruiser guns switched their aim upwards, trying to lock on to the elusive barrage. Soldiers jumped out of the rear of the vehicles, sprinting for cover. They started firing ion rifles at the raiders. Their armour suit force fields became vivid coronal beacons as they were shot at in turn.

The front line of warhorses wavered as their casualties built up. They were almost level with the lumbering Cruisers now. Small groups peeled away. Kazimir urged Kraken over towards the front end of the convoy. There was little thought involved, he simply remembered that was where he was supposed to go. Five times he'd been hit by kinetic bullets or ion rifle fire. So far his armour suit's force field had held. Terror and exhilaration surged through his body, crushing almost all rational thought. Only some faint recollection of the plan kept him moving in the right direction. He loved the vivacity of the mad ride straight into the lethal muzzles of the Institute soldiers. Simultaneously, the constant fear of being cut to shreds any second made him scream wordless defiance at his foes, while shooting his ion pistol wildly. It was insanity, and utterly beautiful. Even Kraken seemed to share the recklessness, pounding on into the heart of the bedlam. Blood from two craterous wounds was running down the warhorse's flanks, soaking his shield blanket.

Bruce was still level with him, still wearing the same rictus grin that had begun on the top of the ridge. He yelled something which Kazimir never heard above the clamour. Then he was gesturing urgently with the long barrel of his ion carbine. Kazimir glanced ahead. The road was only fifty metres away now, as brilliantly lit as any city, showing a zigzag jam of trucks. Bruce gestured again at the second truck, which had come to rest with its force field just nudging into the sputtering flames of the ruined lead truck. Kazimir's heated zeal subsided enough for him to nod sharp agreement, and they both altered track for the trapped vehicle. Kraken galloped over the road in front of the flames, with Kazimir pulling on the reins to slow their unruly flight and curve back to the second truck.

It was at that moment he saw into the Institute valley for the first time in his life. He couldn't see far down it, the angle was wrong for that. From his position all he could make out were a few nondescript low buildings clustered round the end of Highway One. Beyond them, however, the aft section of the alien arkship was just visible. Kazimir had always known its dimensions, how only something that large could survive centuries of travel between the stars. But all the statistics Harvey had coached him in had never registered the way seeing it for real did. The diabolical thing was *big*. Its fuselage design followed a simple cylindrical geometry, with various protrusions and fins breaking the uniformity of its eight-hundred-metre length, and a complex wart-cluster of force field generators at the prow. At the rear it was a sheer circular cliff of metal two hundred and fifty metres in diameter, with the eight stubby nozzles of its fusion drives sticking out. The Institute had set up a ring of powerful arc lights around the ship, centring it in a huge pool of bright monochrome light. Not that Kazimir could see many of the slate-grey metal hull plates. Vast arches of scaffolding had been erected around the *Marie Celeste*, supporting access walkways running the length of the fuselage. The shapes of humans and bots were discernible moving along the aluminium planking, tiny scavenger insects swarming some fallen corpse. Cranes rose from the apex of the scaffolding, their long gantries hauling up big freight containers to the loading bays on every walkway level. Flashes of ruby laserlight were coming from the dark cavities of the fusion drive nozzles, evidence of a great deal of activity within.

A sudden chill washed across Kazimir's skin, sobering his thoughts. Actually seeing the enemy which his clan was sworn to destroy was a humbling experience. The power and purpose reflected in the massive arkship was formidable, an extension of its master's will. He felt pathetically small by comparison.

'Come on!' Bruce yelled as he galloped past. 'For fuck's sake, Kaz.'

Kazimir dropped his gaze from the ship, and saw a fleet of black Land Rover Cruisers tearing out of the Institute town and accelerating along Highway One.

He grunted, 'Oh shit,' under his breath and urged Kraken round towards the intact truck. His hand fumbled with the equipment belt hanging from the side of his saddle, but he eventually found the dump-web unit and pulled it free. Ten metres ahead of him, Bruce was holding his own dump-web, leaning forward in his saddle as he rushed up to the force field surrounding the truck. His arm began to sway to and fro, calculating the weight and closing distance. Then as the warhorse was only a metre from the edge of the force field he swung the unit in a short arc and let go. The dump-web hit the ground and bobbled along until it reached the shield.

Kazimir had little chance to check his friend's accuracy. He was doing the same thing with his own unit, letting it swing slightly, watching the force field as he hurtled towards it. Speed, distance, angle – he judged them all and dropped it at what he *knew* was the right moment, squeezing the activation trigger as it left his hand. The heavy gadget bounced a couple of times then slapped into the force field. Internal sensors detected the coherent energy structure and immediately deployed the compressed nest of conductive filaments at the core of the unit. Fine dark strands expanded quickly, sliding their way along the curve of the shield like a stain spreading upwards. The flimsy mesh began to leach energy out of the field it was climbing up, channelling the flow down into the ground. Smoke began to rise up from the enzyme-bonded concrete where the lower half of the web was unfurling. On the back of the truck, behind the cab, the force field generator began a near subliminal whining as it consumed more and more power, trying to reinforce the relentless drain that was gnawing into it in two places. The driver watched helplessly as more and more indicators on the cab dashboard turned from amber to red.

Thirty seconds after Kazimir let go of his dump-web, the huge quantity of energy which the generator had to pull from its superconductor battery to maintain the shield's integrity exceeded its rated wattage. Burnout was fast, with several components flaring into ruin. The force field collapsed as small turquoise flames jetted out of glowing, cherry-red cooling fins on the generator casing. Several hundred metres overhead, loiter missiles launched by the McSobels detected the failure. Their sensors acquired the naked truck. Solid rocket boosters ignited, and they screamed down vertically at Mach four.

Kazimir was halfway back to the bottom of the ridge when the truck exploded behind him. He risked a quick look over his shoulder and whooped for joy at the sight of the billowing flames. There must have been some volatiles in one of the containers. Flaming aquamarine globules were spinning out of the main explosion, soaring across the night sky like rampant fireworks.

Another convoy truck's force field vanished, and long rocket plumes blazed high above as missiles locked on. Several clan raiders were circling the remaining trucks, ready to throw their dump-webs. Spread out between the road and the ridge, the firefight between Institute soldiers and the remaining mounted raiders was intense. The rapid-fire guns on the Cruisers were inflicting heavy casualties among the Charlemagnes. Retaliatory ion carbine shots were directed at the vehicles, turning their protective force fields into seething bubbles of light.

Kazimir tugged the reins slightly, steering Kraken away from the stationary Cruisers. According to the plan, all he had to do now was get back to the top of the ridge, and from there to the rendezvous point. At that moment he hadn't realized how close the Institute reinforcements had come until the rapid-fire guns on the first of the new Land Rovers opened fire. A patch of ground along the side of Kraken tore open, throwing up a ragged curtain of earth and vegetation. The big beast bellowed in shock, jerking sharply to one side. Kazimir clung on grimly.

Bruce was slightly ahead of him, staying low in the saddle. Ten metres beyond him, three Institute soldiers jumped up from *nowhere*, and opened fire with their ion rifles. Bruce's force field glared like a fragment of captured sunlight, the howl of its energy stresses louder than any thunderclap. Perilously thick tendrils of electricity writhed across his Charlemagne's shield blanket, punching out of the tassels like a jet exhaust. Kazimir was already shooting back at the soldiers, forcing them to stop, when Bruce's warhorse reared up as if to charge its attackers. Kinetic projectiles from a Cruiser rapid-fire gun plunged into its underbelly, shredding hide, organs, and bone in a cloud of crimson vapour. Time and gravity withdrew for a moment, allowing the mighty warhorse to hang poised on its hind legs. Then it slowly toppled over. Kazimir howled: 'NO!' as he watched Bruce slide off the saddle, instinctively seeing the shape which the fall would take. Bruce hit the ground first, and ion rifle fire pummelled at him, straining his armour towards overload. The warhorse collapsed on top of him, its momentum rolling it over. Kazimir froze, staring in agony as more and more of his friend was engulfed by the massive carcass. Bruce actually managed to lift one arm, as if he was clawing his way free. Then the force field nimbus flickered and died. The warhorse completed its roll, crushing the small defenceless human beneath an avalanche of dead steaming flesh.

More trucks exploded as missiles slammed down. The newly arrived Land Rovers rushed onwards, driving straight for the retreating groups of warhorses. Clan raiders concentrated their fire on individual Institute soldiers, overwhelming their armour.

Kraken stood perfectly still as the battle raged around them. Kazimir hadn't moved, his stare fixed on the bloody remains of Bruce's warhorse, unaware of anything else. Waiting, waiting . . .

Another clan raider charged past, screaming something at Kazimir, half of it obscenities. Sound and light swooped back into Kazimir's universe. The raid was over. They were supposed to be leaving. Already, most of the warhorses were galloping back up the slope. He spurred Kraken on, searching the ground ahead. A couple of the Institute soldiers were kneeling beside a clump of thick bushes not twenty metres away, shooting at the raiders on the slope above. Kazimir was never sure if it was him or Kraken who chose the direction, only that it was the right direction. They were suddenly moving towards the soldiers, picking up speed. The soldiers had a few seconds warning, both of them turning to gape in consternation at the terrible medieval vision of vengeance bearing down on them. One ran. One brought his rifle up. Kraken lowered his head, the titanium blade of his horn level with the soldier's chest. Kazimir's face was contorted into a vicious sneer of triumph as the tip rammed home into the soldier's force field. There was a brief cascade of sparks, streaming out of his torso like some ephemeral flower. Then the carbon-bonded blade punctured the armour, slicing clean through the sternum and into the soft tissue of the organs inside the ribcage. That was when Kraken shoved its neck back, ripping the blade upwards. The soldier's body left the ground, dragged upwards as the blade continued its scythe through his upper half before it pulled out with a last violent shake as Kraken twisted. The torn figure spun lazily through the air, squirting arterial blood as it went.

Kazimir knew he should have felt joy. The sweetness of revenge. But it was a hollow, meaningless victory. It mattered nothing to Bruce that the soldier was dead. He wouldn't care, wouldn't rejoice back in West Dee, wouldn't down glass after glass of beer, would never get his chance with Bethany. Bruce was dead.

As if knowing Kazimir's confusion, Kraken sped away back up the slope of his own accord, carrying his rider back to the safety of the forest.

*

The rendezvous spot was a patch of clear ground alongside a small stream, deep in the forest. There should have been twelve McFosters gathered there. Instead, there were only nine. A sombre Scott McFoster began the roll call. Kazimir listened to the names with eyes closed and tears leaking down his cheeks.

The roll call was the formal end of every raid. Unless you were there and confirmed your name to the squad leader, there could be no readmission to the clan and its places, the villages, farms, and forts. Too many fighters had fallen in battle only to be caught and enslaved by the Starflyer. Many of them were sent back to infiltrate and kill the very clansmen and women they had grown up among. The roll call prevented such treachery from recurring.

'Bruce McFoster?'

The way Scott said it told everyone he already knew.

Kazimir opened his mouth. He was going to shout: '*Yes, I'm here. I made it back.*' But all he could see behind closed eyelids was that last sliver of radiance from Bruce's force field going out. The half-second glimpse of fright rushing across Bruce's face as he realized. Then there was just a mass of blood and gore descending, the sickening *crunch* of bone snapping.

'Bruce McFoster, your name will be written in honour on our clan's memorial for those who have forever escaped the Starflyer's reach. We pray that your final sleep will be filled with dreams of a better place.'

'Amen,' the others murmured.

'Kazimir McFoster?'

That faint second skin of light extinguished. How long would it have taken Bruce to die as his body was pulped? Who was going to tell Samantha?

'Kaz,' someone urged.

'Here,' he said brokenly. 'I'm here.' Which was such a blatant lie. He wasn't himself, not any more, a part was missing. It was never coming back.

*

The Manby Memorial Clinic was in Little Sussex, one of the more pleasant districts of New Costa to live in, a hilly area where lush vegetation thrived and tall palm trees and eucalyptus lined the roads and parks. Senior management had their big homes and sweeping gardens here, protectively moated by middle management estates. The shops were small and exclusive, the schools high class, and the facilities generally excellent. There wasn't a factory within fifteen miles.

The AEC police car swept up to the centre's main entrance and its door opened for Paula. She got out and greeted Elene Castle, the clinic's deputy manager. As the woman chattered away in a slightly nervous manor, Paula underwent a touch of *déjà vu*; it wasn't that long ago she'd visited the Clayden Clinic and Wyobie Cotal. But then, most of her cases involved a visit to medical facilities at some point or other.

Elene took her past the first two blocks, which contained the private recovery rooms, day lounges, and physical therapy spas. Paula was familiar with the set-up, her own post-rejuvenation rehabilitations had been spent in almost identical buildings. The Manby had a slightly plusher décor, but the rituals would be the same. It was the third block which Elene Castle was delivering her to, where the actual rejuvenation treatment was conducted. The long corridors were strangely empty. As Paula passed a lounge, she saw a number of recovering clients slumped in deep chairs watching the Augusta-StLincoln Cup match. Nursing staff hung around unobtrusively, keeping an eye on the big portal as the two national teams duked it out on emerald grass.

'I'm afraid you will have to wait for another couple of hours,' the deputy manager said apologetically as a collective groan went up from the lounge as St Lincoln's striker missed a shot. 'Professor Bose was only withdrawn from the actual treatment chamber forty minutes ago. It will take him a while to recover sufficiently to answer your questions.'

'I can wait that long,' Paula said. On any other world, it would have taken weeks just to get a court order allowing her to interrupt a rejuvenation. But CST was paying for Bose's fast-tracked treatment, and Augusta was essentially controlled by the Sheldon family. It hadn't been difficult to arrange.

Paula was shown into a reception room, where a man and

a woman were standing waiting. 'This is Mrs Wendy Bose,' Elene said. 'And . . .'

'Professor Truten,' the man said, offering his hand. He was in late middle age, dressed in the kind of suit which Paula guessed had gone out of fashion several centuries earlier. The fabric was a brown tweed, cut with very small lapels. Judging from the tightness across his shoulders the professor must have bought it quite some time ago. 'I've wanted to meet you for some time, Chief Investigator,' he said. 'It's a shame it had to be under these circumstances.'

'What circumstances?' Paula asked.

'You exert a natural fascination on members of my profession. Unfortunately, I am here to represent Professor and Mrs Bose.'

Paula gave Wendy Bose a sharp glance; in her opinion the woman's jittery inability to return the contact spelled out a great deal of guilt. Unfortunately, Paula didn't know what the crime possibly was. The Directorate had run its usual search, and Wendy Bose had come up completely clean. 'And what is your little profession, exactly?'

'Ah, yes. I teach law at Leonida City University.'

Paula kept staring at Wendy Bose, who was looking all round the small room. 'I didn't know the professor was guilty of anything.'

'He's not. Everybody is innocent until proven guilty. Commonwealth charter Clause 3a. As I'm sure you're aware.'

'If he's not guilty, what does he need a lawyer for?'

'I don't know. What do you want to question him about?'

Elene cleared her throat. 'I think I'll leave at this point.'

'Thank you,' Paula said. 'Please call me when Professor Bose has recovered.'

'Of course.'

'So does a professor of law on Gralmond know much about Augusta law?' Paula asked once the door had closed behind the deputy manager.

'There's not much law here to know. Augusta is hardly an enviable democratic model.'

'Exactly. You don't have any jurisdiction here. Whereas I have a lot. I can have you removed from the planet very easily.'

'Surely you believe in fairness, Chief Investigator?'

'Fairness, I believe in more than you ever can. I also believe in justice. What I don't tolerate is lawyers interfering with that justice.'

'Ah yes, we're always the bad guys, aren't we?'

'Wherever you find human misery, you find lawyers, either causing it or making a profit from it.'

'Please,' Wendy Bose implored. 'I asked Professor Truten to come here. I don't know any lawyers on Augusta, and we don't have much money. Dudley isn't receiving any salary while he's in regeneration.'

'Dudley is a colleague,' Truten said. 'Surely having a witness and adviser can't harm your investigation. He's bound to ask for a lawyer anyway.'

'I'm not investigating Dudley Bose,' Paula said. 'As far as I know, he's not guilty of anything.' She gave the lawyer a pointed look. 'You obviously believe differently. Why is that?'

Wendy Bose gave Truten a questioning look.

'I don't understand,' the lawyer said. 'Dudley is only having two months' rejuvenation treatment. That's all the time he can afford before the starship leaves, and that'll barely get him into a reasonable physical condition. This investigation must be incredibly important for you to have him pulled out of that. You might have cost him his place on the crew.'

'Not a factor for me.'

'What do you think he's done?' Wendy Bose asked.

There was desperation in her voice, but Paula knew that wasn't all. Some of the worry was for herself.

'Very well, but this investigation is confidential. You are not at liberty to discuss it without my express permission.'

'I am aware of basic law,' Truten trailed off under Paula's gaze.

'We believe that that attack on the *Second Chance* was made by a group called the Guardians of Selfhood. They are an obscure paramilitary political group based on Far Away who believe the Commonwealth is politically manipulated by an alien.'

'I've heard of them,' Truten said. 'My e-butler has let their shotgun messages through its filters several times, unfortunately.'

'In order for them to see the *Second Chance* as a threat,' Paula said, 'they would need to establish a link between its construction and their alleged enemy alien. What I'm trying to do is uncover that link, or at least their belief in a link. As the whole mission started because of Professor Bose's discovery, he was the logical place to begin.'

'I hardly think this warrants yanking him out of the treatment.'

'It didn't,' Paula said. 'This kind of data analysis is a standard correlation for the Directorate RI. It came up with an unusual coincidence. I want to ask the professor about it. That's all.'

'What was the coincidence?'

'The Cox Education charity account in the Denman Manhattan bank was subject to an attempted data hack some while ago, prior to the attack. The charity is one of the sponsors of your husband's astronomy department. Obviously, the Guardians believed the charity was channelling money into the Dyson Pair observation project on behalf of the alien. We assume they were trying to find their "evidence" for this in the charity's financial records. They weren't successful in gaining access to the secure files, the bank's smartware managed to lock them out. It wasn't considered important at the time, the bank is subject to many such attacks, but the Trojan the hackers used to ride in on was based around Professor Bose's codes.' She watched with interest as the colour faded from Wendy Bose's face. The woman reached out for Truten's support. 'Is there something you'd like to tell me?'

Truten nodded encouragingly. His grip on Wendy Bose's arm tightened. There could have been a degree of affection in that grip, Paula decided.

'He said to tell you something,' Wendy Bose said. 'I didn't understand at the time.'

'Your husband?'

'No, the reporter. He said to tell her from me to stop concentrating on the details, it's the big picture that counts.'

'A reporter said that to you?'

'Yes. To tell Paula when I see her, that's what he said. I don't know anyone called Paula. And we were talking about the astronomy department's sponsors. He was interviewing me.'

'When was this?'

'Months ago. I think it was when my husband was awarded his professorship. There was a party afterwards, a lot of people. Most of the media wanted to talk to us.'

'This reporter mentioned me by name? Me?'

'Yes. Definitely.'

'What was his name?'

'I think it was Brad.'

Bradley, Paula mouthed. Surprise chilled her skin. For the first time ever, she knew what it must feel like to come off worse during an interview. To have your confidence kicked out from under you.

'You know the gentleman?' Truten asked mildly.

Paula ignored his gentle mockery. 'I'll need a description of this Brad person. Were there any other reporters recording the party?'

'Probably. Yes. There's something else.'

'What?'

'We left the party early. There'd been some kind of break-in at the house. Whoever did it copied all the memories in our household array.' She brightened. 'That would hold Dudley's access codes for the Cox Educational charity bank account, wouldn't it?'

'Yes,' Paula said softly.

'So Dudley's innocent, then, isn't he? He can go on the starship.'

'I'm not going to stop him.' She didn't comment on the way the loyal wife and the supportive colleague hugged each other.

*

Ozzie was rocked from side to side as the big awkward sledge jostled along over the frozen surface of the depression. The murky interior of the covered sledge was actually colder than the inside of the tent, despite an iron brazier filled with glowing, hissing charcoal which had been carefully hung from the roof. Even so, Ozzie felt a lot more comfortable now they were under way. Orion also perked up considerably as the ride progressed, sitting on the long bench, his sleeping bag wrapped round him like a quilt.

The sledge framework was constructed mainly out of bone, great honey-brown ribs of it, cut and fitted together as if they were lengths of wood. Walls and ceiling, and the benches they were sitting on, were made from stiff black leather, which Ozzie could see had been poorly scraped. A strip of clear crystal in the front wall, which he presumed was a chunk from the local trees, provided the only window. It gave him a rough view out across the ice-locked ground, but mainly the swaying rumps of the two big ybnan which were pulling them. Bill, the big Korrok-hi, was standing on an open platform at the rear, steering them with a long set of reins. He was keeping their speed low so that the lontrus could keep up.

'What is this Ice Citadel place?' Ozzie asked.

'I'm not sure what it was originally,' Sara said. Now they

were inside, her face mask hung on straps at the side of her hood. The brazier's sombre light had turned her creased skin as dark as Ozzie's. 'Most of us think it was some kind of Silfen lodge. They still use it when they come to hunt the icewhales.' She patted her fur coat. 'That's where all this comes from. I'll need a new one soon, I've had this seven years now. It wears well if you take care of it.'

Ozzie glanced round the sledge again. 'And the bone?'

'Smart lad. Yes. In that respect they're like the whales on old Earth, a valuable resource. We can use them for a lot of things. Once the Silfen have killed them and taken their trophy tusks, they don't mind us utilizing the rest of it. A hunt is quite a sight. There's the Silfen riding out like some royal medieval pageant, dressed up in all their winter finery. Then you get us lot hanging on behind, trying to keep up. After they kill an icewhale, we set up camp for a week to butcher and cook the damn thing. Most parts have a use here. Even the blood has a kind of alcohol in it to stop it freezing, not that you can drink it – and there's been enough experimental stills over the years. Then there's one gland in the male icewhale which some people dry then grind up. They say the powder puts the peck in your pecker, if you know what I mean.'

'I think I get the idea.'

'Some of the organs have medicinal properties, so our doctor claims, not just for us but other species at the Ice Citadel. And of course the meat is edible. That's our basic diet.' She puckered her lips up in disapproval, deepening the mass of wrinkles on her cheeks and forehead. 'You have no idea how truly boring icewhale meat can get. Were you two riding horses?'

'Up until like two days ago, yes.'

'Humm. Horse steak. Now there's a gourmet dish. If folks hear there are some horse bodies lying round out there for the taking, they might just put themselves in gear and get an expedition together. Two days away, you say?'

'Roughly, yeah. Not that we walk very fast.' Ozzie had eaten horse before, so the thought didn't rankle too much. But he could see the boy turn his nose up in disgust.

'That's near the limit,' Sara said. 'It would be a risk. But there's some who'll take it just for the chance of tasting something different.'

'What sort of risk? You seem well equipped for this planet.'

'It's not equipment, lad, it's location. The Silfen paths aren't stable, you know. Once you start going deep into the forests, there's no telling where you might wind up.'

'You mean like there's no dependable way to get out of here?'

'There's a million ways out by all accounts. And then again, there's another million ways to stay. I've seen them sometimes, with my own eyes. Friends who can't take the Ice Citadel any more. They set off into the forest, looking for somewhere better. Years go by, and you think they must have made it, must be safe. Then an expedition will come across their body, all stiff and black.'

Orion pulled the sleeping bag tighter around him, fighting the way his chin was quivering.

Ozzie gave the woman a look, but she didn't seem perturbed. 'If there's a way in, there's a way out,' he said.

'Sure there is. What I'm telling you is, nobody here knows one. Anybody who does leave permanently, doesn't come back. At least, I've never seen one return.'

'How long have you been here?' Orion asked.

'I'm not sure. Some of the places I've visited might not have had the same kind of time as others. They were *different*. Don't ask me how. You only realize once you've left. When you try and remember, every moment you spent there was like a dream. Then there's the paths, time flows along them as well. You probably realized that, the climates merge very gently, to do that they have to match seasons.'

'But how long?' Orion persisted.

The old woman smiled, showing copper-coloured teeth. 'Put it this way, I walked off Earth in 2009.'

Orion let out a gasp of surprise. 'No way!'

'Oh yes. I was holidaying in Tuscany. I still liked doing that, walking through the countryside, visiting the towns, sampling the food. There were enough areas of it that the developers never got around to ruining which made it worthwhile. One day I packed my backpack and hiked off into the forest. That was it. I've been out here ever since. I never really wanted to go back. I mean . . . What's the point?'

'Interesting,' Ozzie said. It was fascinating to know the Silfen paths had led to Earth in those days, but somehow not surprising. 'That would make you about four hundred years old. They didn't have rejuvenation on Earth back then, not even in Europe.'

'I've never been rejuvenated. I told you, time runs differently along the paths.'

'But you just said you don't walk the paths any more.'

'I'm here, though, and I encounter the Silfen most years.' She shrugged. 'This isn't something you rationalize and order, Ozzie. Everything that is here, simply happens. Don't try to assign reason to what you experience.'

'Right.'

'Please?' Orion said. 'Do you know if my mom and dad are here?'

'What are their names?'

'Maurice and Catanya.'

'Oh, I'm sorry, Orion, there's nobody here with those names. And I can't recall a couple passing through, either.'

The boy hung his head.

'Not every path from Silvergalde leads here, you know,' she

said. 'They could be anywhere. Some nice tropical island, perhaps.'

'Yeah. Whatever.'

She looked at Ozzie, who gave her a don't-ask-me shrug.

The Ice Citadel gradually grew larger in front of them. It was difficult for Ozzie to see clearly through the grubby, ice-crusted crystal window, but the basic pyramid shape soon became apparent. From base to tip it was about seventy yards high. But it was difficult to see against the barren off-white background. Every surface had been covered in crystal, great lengths of the quartz trees arranged into hexagonal arrays. They were packed together in a perfect honeycomb, giving no clue as to what material was underneath. A smooth cylindrical pillar of crystal rose from the centre of each hexagon, topped by a large multifaceted stone that swelled out almost organically. Ozzie frowned at the assembly, trying to understand its purpose. The long segments which made up the hexagons were angled in series against each other, forming tiers. Little prismatic sparkles of light danced off the sheer surfaces. They were like . . . 'Mirrors,' he muttered to himself. Very crude concave mirrors focusing sunlight on the central stalk. Or maybe not so crude, he decided, it would take a real artisan to get the angles just right.

The top of the pyramid was a small rounded pinnacle. As he watched, the beam of green light shone out of it, sweeping round.

'You can see it right over the other side of the crater,' Sara said. 'There's been many a night it's guided me home.'

'It works at night?' Ozzie said. 'I assumed the mirror array gathered sunlight for it.'

'Worked that out, huh? Shouldn't surprise me, a techie like you. The mirrors mostly scoop up light for the rooms inside. But, yeah, the top row are exclusively for the lighthouse system. They pour sunlight into some kind of light battery.

471

Please don't ask me how it works, it looks like a big ball of stone to me. There's always some idiot science type wanting to take it apart. We don't let them, of course.'

'Don't worry, I'll spare you that.'

'Good. We have been known to run some people out of town. And as far as we know, there isn't another town on the whole damn planet.'

'Always good to know.'

The sledge came slowly to a halt at the base of the pyramid. Ozzie and Orion pulled their gloves on again, covered their faces, and stepped out carrying their packs. Another couple of the Korrok-hi were warbling mournfully to Bill as they started to unharness the big ybnan that had pulled the sledge. Some humans (or human shapes) had come over, dressed in the same bulbous fur coats as Sara wore. There were other aliens as well, a small gnomish creature with five limbs and two things like snakes with legs, all wearing coats of icewhale fur. Ozzie stopped to study them, he'd never seen their kind before. He began to wonder just how far into the galaxy the Silfen paths ran.

'This way,' Sara beckoned. 'Iusha will stable your lontrus for you.' There were a number of archways of various sizes along the base of the pyramid, from trapdoor height up to an opening wide enough to take two sledges at once. There was a lot of activity around them, with animals (again types he'd never seen) and aliens coming in and out. Several sledges were being prepared, three of them smaller than the one Sara used, resembling racing toboggans.

She led them through one of the archways into an ante-chamber with plain black marble walls. At the far end was a big revolving door made from bone, with thin crystal window panes. 'It's like a heat-lock,' she said as she pushed one of the panels and set the doors moving.

Beyond that was a wide corridor walled with the same marble. Long panels of quartz were set into the ceiling, with pink sunlight pouring out of them. Ozzie stood underneath one and squinted into the glare, but there was nothing to see.

'They light the whole place,' she said. 'It's like a root network of big crystal ducts leading down from the mirrors on the pyramid. Same principle as our fibre optic cable, but big, much bigger, the ducts are a metre wide.'

The corridor angled down slightly, then opened out into broad stairs that curved round out of sight. They started their descent. The curve was actually a wide spiral. Ozzie lost track of how many times they went round, and how deep they were. It was a long way down. Sara took her face mask off, then unbuttoned the front of her coat. She was wearing woollen trousers and a thick blue sweater underneath. Ozzie realized he was getting warmer, and unzipped his own coat.

'What heats this place?'

'Hot springs,' she told them. 'It was built right above them. I wasn't kidding about that bath.'

The stairs ended at an archway. Sara sneaked a look back at her two charges as they walked out onto the main floor of the Ice Citadel. Ozzie took a few steps in, and came to a halt. He'd entered an alien cathedral, a vaulting dome at least eighty yards high. Pillars curved up the wall like some arcane ribcage, supporting seven balcony rings. It had to be a religious monument, he knew. The alcove walls between the pillars were carved marble. Thousands of different creatures stared out at Ozzie, every third one was a Silfen. Somehow, the artist had given each one a majesty surpassing the divine quality suggested for the human prophets. They'd all been captured at the same moment of revelation and veneration, seeing the wonder dwelling beyond the physical universe. The bas-relief landscapes around them ranged from arboreal scenes to stark landscapes with exotic moons in the sky, cities of grandiose buildings and even technological surroundings. Right at the apex, a mandala of crystal strips shone brighter than the sunlight outside. 'Jesus wept,' he exclaimed. As proof that the Silfen did have a tangible culture it was a startling introduction.

In the centre of the floor was a large pool, fed by a raised fountain, whose waters steamed gently as it splashed and gurgled. There was no altar or rows of seating, which Ozzie was half expecting. Long tables made of bone and leather had been set up on granite paving that was worn and badly cracked. On the other side, a large rectangular stone hearth had been built, with neat brick-walled ovens on top. Flames were visible flickering through grids set in the base. Judging by the background smell in the room, and the soot clogging the oven brickwork, it was some kind of fat-based oil fuel. Several humans and aliens fussed round on tables next to the hearth, preparing a meal.

The chamber obviously served as the canteen and lounge for the Ice Citadel residents. Even in the daytime it was busy. The number of species astounded Ozzie. He could make out at least twelve different types. Creatures with three legs, four legs, six legs, some that squirmed or wriggled across the floor, one that hopped, and something that was either a young Raiel or a close cousin. Big and small, they had skins in many shades, scales, fur, spines, and oil-rainbow membranes; clothes on those that bothered were anything from simple togas to practical utility harnesses.

Like the statues, every creature was now focused on Ozzie and Orion. They were stared at, sniffed, echo-sounded, heat-scanned . . .

Orion edged behind Ozzie, who returned the attention levelly. 'Where are they all from?' Ozzie asked. 'Do we know their star systems?'

'It doesn't matter where they come from,' Sara said, dismissively. 'Only that they are here now. Why do you want to classify them? That's the first step towards segregation.'

'Nobody's classifying,' Ozzie snapped back. 'Man, this has got to be the most important gathering of cultures we know of. There are more species represented here than even the High Angel hosts. Doesn't that mean anything to you?'

'It means we have a broad fund of abilities to help us survive.'

'I've got to find out where they come from, if they know anything more about the Silfen.'

'Introductions later,' Sara said. 'Your rooms are over here.' She led them round the edge of the chamber. There was a corridor leading off between every set of pillars on the ground level. The one they walked down opened into a cluster of three simple circular rooms. There was crude human-style furniture in one of them. A sleeping cot and a pair of sling chairs. The leg on one chair was broken, and the leather so old and cracked it looked like it would tear if anyone sat on it. A bathing pool took up half of the last room, filling the air with steam. Orion stuck his hand in the clear water, and smiled happily at how hot it was.

'Take your time to freshen up,' Sara said. 'The evening meal is served in a couple of hours. It's kind of tradition that the newest arrivals tell their stories and bring us all the news from whatever part of the galaxy they've come from.'

'I can manage that,' Ozzie said.

'Good.' Her expression was troubled. 'You won't try and rush off to find a path, will you? We lose a lot of people that way. At least take the time to learn the way things are around here.'

'Sure. I'm not stupid. But we will be leaving as soon as we can.'

'Good luck.'

*

There were a dozen grand dinners, balls, and galas on the night before departure. Only one counted, of course, the one thrown by Anshun's First Speaker, which was attended by Vice President Elaine Doi, Nigel Sheldon with three current wives from his harem, Rafael Columbia, Senator Thompson Burnelli, Brewster Kumar, and a dozen other notables from the Commonwealth's political ruling classes. And that, sadly, was the one which Captain Wilson Kime also had to attend. His car drove him through no less than three security checks, including a deep scan, on his way into the government's Regency Palace, which served as the First Speaker's official residence at the heart of Treloar. The sun was just setting as he and Anna drew up outside the massive stone portico. They were greeted by two human servants in long frock coats covered in gold brocade. The senior one bowed deeply. 'Welcome, Captain. The First Speaker is receiving her guests in the Livingstone Room. Please go straight in.'

'Thank you,' Wilson replied. He took Anna's hand, and they walked up the big steps. She was wearing a long formal ocean-blue gown with elaborate non-symmetrical loops of gold and pearl necklace which seemed to merge with her glittering OCtattoos. Her hair had been cut short ready for the voyage, but the stylist had still managed to weave in some temporary extensions flecked with platinum and phosphorescent Titian strands. He'd never seen her so elegant before. At work she was mostly in overalls or an office suit, while at the apartment she wore very little. The effect made her extremely desirable, enhanced by a thick perfume. He wanted to rip the dress off her and have passionate sex right there on the cold tiles of the palace floor. Her pose was only slightly spoilt by the way she had to grip the front of her dress with her free hand, holding the hem off the steps as they ascended.

'Bloody classical architecture,' she muttered under her breath.

As they reached the top, a shiny-black Ferrari Rion pulled up at the foot of the steps, emitting a hum of barely controlled power. A gull wing door lifted up, and Oscar climbed out.

'Might have guessed,' Wilson said. He was mildly envious

of the car; it was a limited edition. Of course, given his age and status, he was above such things now. But he couldn't help wondering what the Ferrari would be like to drive on manual. From a purely engineering point of view, it was a superb machine.

Oscar waved cheerily, and dashed up the steps. He kissed Anna on the cheek. 'You look gorgeous tonight, my love.'

'Thank you,' she smiled. 'You, too.'

Oscar carried off a tuxedo with great panache, a stylish searing-white jacket with a trendy cut and an old-fashioned scarlet carnation in his lapel. While Wilson always felt as though he'd been stuffed into his own tux, like a high school boy on a prom date.

'Shall we go in, boys and girls?' Oscar said.

They walked through the doors into the over-classical interior, dominated by gilt-framed portraits and the twisting bronze and jade shapes of 1st modernist sculpture. The First Speaker, Gilda Princess Marden, greeted Wilson with a politician's firm, trustworthy handshake, and air-kissed Anna. Wilson said something sympathetic about the planet's defeated national football team. To which the First Speaker thanked him profusely, going into detail about the sporting and personal failings of the main striker.

'Well done,' Anna murmured as they walked away. 'Only another five hours of small talk to go.'

The Livingstone Room's large garden doors had been folded back, allowing the guests onto the wide balcony outside. The Palace courtyard's formal garden had been lit by flaming torches and yellow and green starglobes hanging like fruit from the trees and larger bushes. Over a hundred guests dressed in smart colourful clothes suitable for the warm summer evening were milling round as the golden sunset drained out of the horizon. Local A-list socialites mingled with famous unisphere celebrities and wealthy grandees while official news and political reporters maintained a respectful distance. A band was playing on a small platform set up in front of the Henry Wu planet-sphere fountain.

All three of them grabbed drinks from a waiter. Wilson could see several other crew members, each at the centre of a knot of people. Like him, they were the unlucky ones; more junior members had a free choice where to spend their last night. For himself Wilson would have preferred a less ceremonial event.

'I see our illustrious navigator is here,' Anna said quietly at his shoulder.

Wilson and Oscar saw Dudley Bose standing beneath a ginger-red Japanese maple. He'd returned from his partial rejuvenation on Augusta having had about fifteen years taken off his age. Unfortunately, his frame hadn't quite adjusted to his new cellular age. Skin hung in folds from his neck; his hair was a mottled fuzz of grey and black, and a sagging belly hung over his tuxedo waistband. He was telling some story to his attentive audience of Anshun dignitaries, with his wife in close attendance, laughing as if she'd never heard the anecdote before.

'Remind me again why he's coming with us,' Oscar said.

'Because he's the greatest expert the Commonwealth has on the Dyson Pair,' Anna told him demurely.

'Ah. I knew there was a reason.'

Wilson did his best not to frown. Not for the first time he wished he hadn't bowed to political expediency. Bose hadn't even undergone half of the tests which the rest of the crew had struggled their way through, let alone taken part in any meaningful training. Having the astronomer on board was simply asking for trouble. But it had got the media off his back.

He saw Nigel Sheldon talking to the Vice President and other members of the ExoProtectorate Council, and made his way over to their small group. As he reached them he realized the young-looking woman standing next to Sheldon, who had his arm round her shoulder, was Tu Lee, their hyperspace officer. Her small delicate figure was clad in a little black dress; with her raven hair cut short she looked like a sexy imp.

'Captain!' Nigel grinned in welcome. 'I know you've met Elaine.'

Wilson smiled politely at the Vice President. Farndale Engineering had chosen to donate to her rival's campaign, and Elaine Doi knew that.

'Any last-minute problems?' Nigel asked.

'No. It's all going remarkably smoothly.'

'We reached point two-five light-years per hour on the last test flight,' Tu Lee said. 'That's our operational target, so we're on the green for tomorrow.'

'Listen to you,' Nigel said. He grinned proudly at her.

'Stop it.' She gave him a sharp look.

'Tu Lee is my great-great-great-granddaughter,' Nigel said to Wilson. 'Four natural-born generations; you don't get a stronger family tie than that. Can you blame me for being proud of her?'

Wilson couldn't remember that being on Tu Lee's file.

'I hope you don't mind,' Tu Lee said, her dark eyes gazing intently up at Wilson. 'I never said anything, because I wanted to make the crew on merit.'

'You succeeded,' Wilson said. He suddenly wondered why none of his family had ever made it through the qualifying stages.

'A Sheldon and a Kime finally flying together, eh,' Nigel said happily. 'We've got it covered from every angle.'

'Looks that way.' Wilson was having trouble keeping his smile intact.

'I understand you're taking a lot of weapons on your flight,' Thompson Burnelli said.

'The great debate,' Wilson said, not quite mocking. 'Do we shock culturally superior species with our primitive warlike behaviour, or do we go into the unknown with sensible protection that any smart alien will understand.'

'Given what they're facing, a degree of self-defence is appropriate,' Nigel said.

'Huh,' Thompson snorted. 'What do you believe, Captain? Is the barrier a defence against some psychopathic race armed with superweapons?'

'We'll find out when we get there,' Wilson said mildly. 'But I'm not taking a crew anywhere unless I stand a chance of bringing them back alive.'

'Come on, Thompson, this is supposed to be a party,' Nigel said. 'Stop giving the man a hard time.'

'Just making a point. I'm still not convinced this is the best way to deal with the Dyson Pair. There's a strong body of opinion saying we should leave them well alone for a few centuries.'

'Yes,' Anna said. 'The Guardians of Selfhood for one.'

Thompson flashed her an angry look.

'Any news on them?' Wilson asked Rafael Columbia.

'We've made over two hundred arrests in connection with the raid. Mostly black-market arms merchants and other underworld military types. My Chief Investigator is confident they will provide us with enough information to finally track down the organizer.' He didn't sound impressed.

'She seems to be doing a good job so far,' Oscar said. 'There hasn't been a hint of trouble since the raid.'

'Sure that doesn't have anything to do with the level of CST security?' Elaine Doi asked demurely.

Oscar raised his glass to her, ignoring the dark expression on Columbia's face. 'That's probably about ninety-nine per cent of the reason, yeah,' he conceded.

She looked around the four crew members. 'So are you nervous?'

'It would be stupid not to be,' Wilson said. 'The fear factor is a significant part of our racial survival mechanism. Evolution doesn't like arrogance.'

'A healthy attitude. For myself, I wish there was some way of communicating with you. To be cut off from information seems barbaric somehow.'

Wilson smiled a challenge at Nigel. 'I guess our best hyperspace theorists aren't quite up to that.'

Nigel raised a glass, but didn't take the bait. 'That's the whole reason for me getting Wilson here to captain the mission. As they can't refer every decision back here for review by your committees, I wanted someone who could make a decent judgement call. Unless you'd like to go yourself, Vice President.'

Elaine Doi glanced from Nigel to Wilson. 'I'm satisfied that you're in charge of the mission, Captain.'

'If we had more than one ship, communications wouldn't be such an issue,' Oscar said.

'And who's going to pay for another ship?' Thompson asked quickly. His gaze flicked to one of the big portals set up along the far side of the courtyard garden. They all showed various images of the *Second Chance*. The starship was docked to its assembly platform, though the outer shell of malmetal had peeled back to a thick toroid skirt around the gateway. Of all the construction gridwork, only a tripod of gantry arms remained, like an aluminium claw gripping the rear of the starship. Sunlight fell across the four-hundred-metre length of the central cylindrical section's snow-white hull, casting small grey shadows from every hatch, nozzle, grid, antenna, and handrail which stood above the protective cloak of foam. The huge life-support ring was rotating slowly around it, almost devoid of windows, except for a few black rectangles along the front edge. Tiny coloured navigation lights winked at various points on the superstructure, otherwise there was no visible activity.

The sight of the massive vessel brought a flush of comfort to Wilson. Something that large, that *solid*, gave an over-whelming impression of dependability.

'Any subsequent ships would be cheaper now we've final-ized the design,' Nigel said. 'CST is certainly considering the formation of a small exploration fleet.'

'What the hell for?' Thompson said. 'This expedition is bad enough, and we know something strange is out there. We don't need to go looking for trouble any further out.'

'That's hardly the attitude that pushed us this far out into the galaxy, Senator. We're not a poor society, thanks to that outward urge. We should continue to push back the barriers.'

'Fine,' Thompson said bluntly. 'You want them pushed back, you pay for them. You certainly won't have my support for further government funding. Look what happened with Far Away. We poured billions into that venture, and it still costs government hundreds of millions a year. What have we ever got back out of it?'

'Knowledge,' Wilson said, surprised to find himself defend-ing Far Away.

'Precious little of it,' Thompson grunted.

'Tell that to the Halgarths. They dominate force field manufacture thanks to the technology they acquired from the *Marie Celeste*.'

'What if we don't come back?' Anna asked. The way the Council members all looked at her in a mildly scandalized silence made her want to giggle. 'You have to admit, it's a possibility.'

'We won't abandon you,' Elaine Doi said smoothly. 'If it is necessary to build another ship, then it will be done.' She gave the North American senator a sharp frown as he gathered himself to speak.

'The ExoProtectorate Council has drawn up contingency plans for every possible scenario,' Nigel Sheldon said. 'And quite a few implausible ones as well. As the Vice President says, every effort will be made should we face a worst-case outcome.'

'Does that include military action?'

Now even Wilson was giving her a look.

'I don't believe that's relevant,' Rafael Columbia said.

'It just strikes me as odd that very little is being done to beef up the Commonwealth's defences. Especially as one of the most plausible theories about the Dyson barrier is that it's protective.'

'We are doing something about it,' Rafael Columbia said. 'We're sending you to assess the situation.'

'And if it's bad?'

'We will respond accordingly.'

'With what? We haven't had any wars for three hundred years.'

'There are seventeen isolated planets, and each one was withdrawn from the Commonwealth because of military action. The last of those was only twenty years ago. Sad to say, our Commonwealth is actually quite experienced in such matters.'

'Those were guerrilla actions mounted by nationalist and religious groups. Most of the Commonwealth's citizens weren't even aware of them.'

'What exactly is your point?' Elaine Doi asked, irritation creeping into her voice.

'All I'm saying is, a few Alamo Avengers aren't going to be much use against anything that's seriously hostile out there.'

'We know that. Your mission profile was drawn up with the possibility in mind, and I welcomed Captain Kime's input in the planning. Frankly his cautious approach is one I favour. And to be realistic, if you do find anything as powerful and hostile as the one you're talking about, then they're going to know about the Commonwealth anyway.'

The band struck up a light waltz which Wilson felt he should know. But he was thankful for the distraction as everyone turned to look at the western sky. A particularly bright star was rising above the Palace rooftop.

They'd left the *Second Chance* in her highly elliptical orbit around Anshun; after all, the exact position made no difference to the wormhole gateway. Now as she glided up high over the horizon, she was still exposed to the full radiance of Anshun's sun, making her the brightest object in the heavens. Fireworks zoomed over the Palace to greet the starship, exploding in huge bursts of emerald, gold, and carmine with a cacophony of thunder cracks. The courtyard was swiftly filled with the rapturous applause of the elite guests. A laser projector drenched Wilson in a bubble of white light. Everyone turned to look at him, the sound of their applause rising. He bowed graciously, gesturing Anna and Oscar into the lightfield as the senior members of the ExoProtectorate Council sank away along with Tu Lee. Somehow Dudley Bose managed to appear beside Oscar, clasping his hands victoriously above his head.

When the fireworks were over the band resumed a more traditional background piece. The buffet was opened and people surged across the garden. Elaine Doi stepped forward again. 'Captain, I just wanted to say bon voyage.'

*

Even when it was over, Wilson regretted having to attend the official party for the personal time it stole from him on the eve of the departure. By the time the buffet started it had become immensely boring. Two hours in, he'd seen Oscar making a quiet exit with some handsome young lad, and wished he could do the same with Anna. But they'd be noticed doing that. He'd forgotten the true price of fame over the centuries.

But there were compensations. At eight o'clock this morning he had arrived at the complex, to walk through the gateway. Management staff, construction crew and technicians, designers, medical personnel, and a hundred others lined the last length of path before the wormhole, all applauding as Wilson led the senior officers through the gateway. Now he was sitting in the bridge, about to embark on the voyage that would put him on the same list as Columbus, Armstrong, Sheldon and Isaacs. *But not poor old Dylan Lewis.*

Although, to be honest, he did consider the bridge to be a bit disappointing. Even the old *Ulysses* command cabin had been more visually exciting, let alone the bustling chambers of a thousand unisphere fantasy drama ships. It was a simple compartment with consoles for ten people, although only seven were currently manned. A glass wall separated off the senior officers' briefing room – basically, a big conference table with twenty chairs. At least there were a couple of large high-rez holographic portals in their traditional place on the forward wall, although (bad design, this) the consoles right in front of them blocked the lower portion from anyone behind.

Not that he had much time for the standard images they were relaying from hull-mounted cameras. His virtual vision was on high intensity while his retinal inserts were filtering out most natural light. The result was an almost indistinct room flooded with ship-function icons. He rested his palms on the console i-spots, seeing phantom fingers materialize within the galaxy of graphics drifting through the air around him. When he tapped his customized chrome-yellow fingernail on the airlock icon, it expanded to show him the hull was now sealed. A simultaneous tap on the umbilicals told him all the tanks were full, and they were on internal power. The only links to the platform were a high-band data cable and the mechanical latches.

'Crew status?' he asked Oscar.

'Everyone on-board and ready.'

'Okay then; Pilot, please activate our force field and disengage us from the platform.'

'Aye sir,' Jean Douvoir said. The pilot had spent decades

working for several companies at the High Angel, flying engineering pods around the big freefall factories, shifting sections massing hundreds of tonnes with the casual precision of a bird of prey. Before that, he'd helped develop control routines for spaceplane RI pilots. It was a background which made him perfect for the job. That, coupled with his enthusiasm for the project, made him a perfect choice. Wilson counted himself lucky to have someone so competent on board.

A communication icon flashed in Wilson's virtual vision, tagging the call as Nigel Sheldon. He tapped for admission.

'Captain,' Sheldon's voice sounded across the bridge. 'I'm accessing your telemetry. It all looks good from where we are.'

'And here.' There had been a great many of these pointless official talks on the *Ulysses*, too. All for posterity and media profile. One of his virtual vision digital read-outs was showing the number of people accessing the moment through the unisphere was in excess of fifteen billion. 'We're ready to go.' His voice was sombre and authoritative as the impact of the event finally hit home. One of the portals showed him a view of the three umbilical gantries swinging away from the starship's rear section. Little silver-white fluid globules spilled out of the closed valves, sparkling in the sunlight as they wobbled off into space.

'Hopefully, we'll see you again in a year's time,' Nigel Sheldon said.

'I look forward to it.'

'Godspeed, Captain.'

Jean Douvoir fired the small thrusters around the rear of the central cylindrical section. *Second Chance* started to slide away from the gateway. Acceleration was so tiny Wilson couldn't even feel it affect the low-gravity bridge. The tiny dazzling turquoise flames of the thrusters shrank away and vanished.

'We're now at five metres per second,' Douvoir reported. There was a lot of amusement in his voice.

'Thank you, Pilot,' Wilson said. 'Hyperdrive, please bring the wormhole up to flight level.'

'Aye sir.' Tu Lee couldn't help the strong twang of excitement in her voice. She began to shunt instructions into the ship's RI which would handle the enormously complex energy manipulation functions.

Nigel instructed his e-butler to shift down his virtual vision intensity, and took his hands off the console i-spots. One hologram portal showed the assembly platform slowly shrinking behind them. The second had a small circular turquoise nebula glowing in the centre. It began to expand, growing more indistinct, although no stars were visible through it.

'Course laid in?' Wilson asked.

'Want to consult our expert astronomer on that?' Anna muttered under her breath.

Wilson ignored her, wondering if the rest of the bridge crew had overheard.

'As agreed,' Oscar said. He had his hands pressed firmly on his console i-spot, his eyes flicking quickly between virtual icons. 'First exit point, twenty-five light-years from Dyson Alpha.'

'Wormhole opening stable, Captain,' Tu Lee reported.

'Inject us,' Wilson told her.

The blue haze folded around *Second Chance* like petals closing for the night. Their datalink to the assembly platform and the unisphere ended. Both portals showed the starship bathing in the wormhole's pale moonlight radiance of low-level radiation.

Oscar cancelled the camera feeds. The bridge portals switched to displaying the gravitonic spectrum, sensors around the ship detecting faint echoes resonating within the wormhole. It was a crude version of radar that allowed them to locate stars and planets to a reasonable degree, but that was all. For truly accurate sensor work they needed to drop out into real space.

Wilson upped his virtual vision again, taking another sweep of the starship's primary systems. Everything was humming along sweetly. He came out and checked round the bridge. The engineers were all still heavily integrated with the ship's RI, monitoring the performance of their respective fields, but everyone else was already relaxing. Wilson glanced inquisitively at Oscar, who put on a contented expression as he sat back. There wasn't much left for them to do. Not for another hundred and thirty days.

13

Hoshe waited at the side of the street for her to arrive. It wasn't mid-morning yet, but already a small crowd of curious locals were gathering along the sidewalk. Two police cruisers had parked nearby, their constables directing the copbots as they set up temporary barriers around the thirty-storey condo building. As he watched, yet another big police technical support van pulled up and slowly nosed its way down into the underground garage. His e-butler told him the precinct commander was on his way, and the city commissioner had asked for the ice department case files.

'Great,' Hoshe muttered. It was going to turn into one big jurisdictional free-for-all, he was sure of that. Now all the real work had been done, every other department in Darklake would be after a slice of the credit.

An unmarked police car drew up beside him. Paula stepped out. She was wearing a simple pale-blue dress with a fawn jacket, her raven hair tied back neatly. Hoshe thought her skin was a shade darker than the last time he'd seen her, but then Treloar, Anshun's capital, was in the tropics. She actually gave him a smile as he said hello.

'Good to see you again,' he said.

'And you, Hoshe. Sorry I left you carrying the ball on this one.'

'That's okay,' he lied.

'But I appreciate the way you carried on, and for calling me today. That's very professional.'

He gestured her towards the entrance to the garage. 'You might yet regret coming, a lot of senior city police officers are on their way.'

'That I'm used to. You know, right now I'd actually welcome some of the old problems again.'

'Tough case?'

'You wouldn't think so by the number of arrests we've made,' she shrugged. 'But yes. My opponent is an elusive man.'

'Holmes and Moriarty, yes?'

'Hoshe, I had no idea you read the classics.'

'It was some time ago, but I used to really enjoy that kind of thing.'

'Holmes never knew how easy he had it,' she said as they reached the bottom of the ramp. 'So what have you got for me?'

Two large white forensic department vans were parked at the far end of the garage. Various sensor patches the size of paving slabs had been stuck to the floor around the walls, thick cables snaked round everywhere, winding back to the open access panels on both vans. Several generalpurposebots were moving the sensors around, clustering them in one corner while three forensic officers supervised.

'We found them first thing this morning,' Hoshe said as they climbed into the back of the squad leader's van. The inside was cramped, a narrow corridor between two equipment benches, the air hot from all the humming electrical circuits. He was more than familiar with all the units. The additional forensic teams Myo had promised from the Serious Crime Directorate had never materialized. In view of what amounted to her withdrawal from the case, Hoshe's commander had reluctantly agreed to allocate him two of the city's forensic squads. Hoshe himself had undergone the appropriate skill memory implementation so he could operate the equipment and interpret the results, helping his pitifully small team throughout all the dreary months which had followed. They had worked through the list of sites where construction work had been going on forty years ago, a laborious and terribly tedious task. Sick days and short hours among the team members had been on a steady upward curve from the first week onwards. There had been times, especially in the last few weeks, when only the GPbots had turned up at the start of the day's shift.

Hoshe had been receiving an increasing amount of pressure from both the team and his commander to wrap things up. But he'd kept doggedly to the list, examining the sites one after the other while soothing and cajoling the team and pleading for just a little more time from the police department. Reflective deep scanning had revealed a great many interesting things buried beneath the city, but no bodies. Until this morning.

Paula peered closely at the small high-rez holographic portal with its 3D grid of gentle pink luminescence; right at the centre were swirls of darker red, like knots in wood.

'Even allowing for decomposition, you can see the shapes quite clearly,' Hoshe said, his finger tracing round denser swirls. 'This is a head here, look, and these are arms and legs. Both bodies are inside some kind of box-shape container, there's a distinct air cavity around each of them.'

'I'll take your word for it. This looks like a Rorschach test to me.'

Hoshe avoided a smile. 'One is slightly smaller than the other; which corresponds to a male-female pairing. But that's the end of the good news. They're deep; ten metres down below this level. The developer didn't cut corners when this condo was built. Unfortunately, all the foundations correspond to City Hall regulations.'

'Thank you, Hoshe.'

'We don't know it's them yet. We'll get a slightly better resolution when the sensors have been realigned, but that's not going to give us a positive ID. Only DNA will do that.'

'It's them. You know it is.'

'Yeah, well. It's going to be a bitch to get them out. We'll have to excavate all the way round, probably need force fields to reinforce the foundation when we chop the block out. The residents will need to be moved out while we do that. Then we'll need to break the concrete up very carefully.'

'Don't worry, the Directorate has experienced extraction teams. I'll have them here before lunch.'

'You said that about the forensic teams.'

She shifted round in the cramped space, and gave him an unnerving look of appraisal. 'I know, and I apologize again. I've never quite let anybody down like that before. It won't happen again.'

Hoshe knew he'd be blushing. Her apology was like some intimate confession. He tapped a knuckle on the portal to distract her. 'Are you sure this will get a conviction? I'll bet you a whole Earth dollar their memorycell inserts have been destroyed, there'll be no memory of the killer we can ever access.'

'Trust me, Hoshe. We can nail him now. All I need is a judge to issue a warrant.'

*

It was a hell of a row which broke out in the lounge. Loud enough for Morton to hear it from his bedroom, which made him stop what he was doing and pissed him off no end. His e-butler told him who was invading his penthouse, so he was tying the belt on his dressing gown as he strode out.

Chief Inspector Myo was arguing with his human butler, while Detective Hoshe Finn interjected with angry threats. It was a credit to the butler's training and character that he didn't appear in any way flustered by the unwelcome guests and their authority, his loyalty lay solely with his employer, nothing was going to shift that.

'Let's all take a breath and calm down,' Morton said. He combed his wild hair with his hand, trying to slick it back down. 'What seems to the problem here? Chief Investigator?'

'No problem.' She held out a small memory crystal disk. 'I have a warrant for your arrest.'

'On what charge?'

'Two counts of bodykill and deliberate memory erasure.'

Morton couldn't quite hang on to his peaceable demeanour with that allegation fired at him. 'You've gotta be fucking joking!'

'No, sir, I am not joking,' Paula said. 'As a registered Commonwealth citizen, you are hereby advised not to speak further in connection with the offence you have just been charged with until you are in consultation with your legal representative. Now, please get dressed, sir. You will be taken to the police precinct station for further questioning.'

'This is bullshit.' Morton stood his ground, folding his arms across his chest. Even though he knew, he asked, 'Whose murder?'

'Tara Jennifer Shaheef, your wife at the time, and Wyobie Cotal.'

'Shit! I fucking told *you* they'd been bumped off.'

'You certainly did. Thank you for that, sir. Now please get dressed. If you don't, we will take you as you are.'

A naked Mellanie rushed into the lounge. She threw her arms round Morton. 'What's happening, Morty? What are they saying?'

'Nothing, it's a police fuck-up, that's all.' He almost shook her off, then thought better of it, and returned her embrace. 'Everything is fine.'

From inside the circle of his arms, she glared at the two officers.

Hoshe Finn was not looking at the naked teenager. Then

he had to not look at the second girl who came to stand in the bedroom doorway, pulling on a white lace robe. Her long elegant face had a bemused expression as she took in the tableau, as if she was accessing some low-budget soap on the cybersphere. 'What is happening out here?' she drawled in a husky voice. One hand patted languidly at her expensively styled hair. 'Is this part of your kink, Morty, to be hauled off to a secret police dungeon where they manacle you to the wall?'

'No,' Morton and Paula Myo said in unison.

'Oh.' She sounded disappointed.

'Morty never killed anyone,' Mellanie asserted. She tossed her head, daring them to say different.

Paula gave her a cool glance. 'You weren't even alive when he did this. Take my advice, don't cause a scene. Morton?'

'It's all right.' Morton gave the clinging girl a tender squeeze. 'My e-butler has already informed the legal department. I'll be home for dinner tonight. We'll be suing for wrongful arrest before the fish course arrives.'

Mellanie pushed her face up towards his, entreating. 'Don't go with them, please, Morty. Don't.'

'This is not a multiple-choice situation,' Paula told her.

'I'll get dressed,' Morton said. He swung round and walked back towards the bedroom. 'It's a shame,' he said to Paula. 'You and I could have been quite something together.'

Paula looked from Mellanie to the haughty girl in the lace robe, then to Morton. 'I can't think what.'

*

The daily storm which raced in from the Grand Triad had now passed, leaving the wide valley fresh and gleaming. There were few trees here on the north-western edge of the Dessault Mountains. The valley was mainly grassland, with boggy meadows along the bottom where the fast river flowed out to the north. Sunlight grew steadily warmer as the last twisting clouds hurried away towards the Great Iril Steppes, and the ground steamed quietly.

As soon as the rains stopped, Kazimir stepped outside. The McFoster village on the western slopes was where he had spent his earliest childhood. It was a huddle of stone houses with living grass roofs that provided a watertight shelter during the rains. They all had broad open windows so the air could circulate and cool in rooms inside. Not that many daylight hours were spent indoors in such a warm climate. It was a farming village, one of the many sheltered refuges where clan children could grow up untroubled by the Institute and the Starflyer. Cattle grazed easily on the floor of the valley, and a few Charlemagnes were trained by fighters no longer able to answer the Guardians' call to arms.

Scott and Harvey joined him as he walked out towards the memorial garden, and more villagers joined him as he passed the houses until there were over thirty marching silently along the little-worn path. It ended at a dark wooden gate set in a drystone wall that was overrun by colourful climbing nasturtiums. The wall circled a graveyard that followed the pattern adopted by most small human settlements across the Commonwealth. Saplings which had been planted around the perimeter were now large enough to offer some shade. Gravestones were carved on chunks of local rock. The grass was trimmed and neat. Several benches had been provided. In the middle was an eight-sided memorial made of stone. The base plinth measured three metres across, holding a two-metre sphere of red marble polished to a gleam. Names had been etched into the lower half, forming neat lines which covered nearly a third of the surface.

Everyone gathered round and bowed their heads.

'We have come today to celebrate the life of Bruce Mc-Foster,' Harvey said in a loud clear voice. 'Although he has left our clan, he will not be forgotten by us and those who fight with us. When the time comes for this planet's revenge upon its violator he will hear the song of joy that all peoples will sing, for it will be so loud as to rock the dreaming heavens themselves.'

Harvey placed a small engraver tool against the marble at the end of an unfinished line of names. The little unit buzzed as its tiny blades began cutting the programmed pattern. Fine grey dust started to trickle down.

'I remember your laughter, Bruce,' Harvey said.

Kazimir stepped forward. 'I remember your friendship, Bruce. You are my brother and always will be.' It was difficult to get the words out as his voice cracked. Tears were leaking down his cheeks.

'I remember your stubbornness, Bruce,' Scott rasped. 'Keep it with you always, lad.'

A woman stepped forward. Kazimir didn't hear what she said. The infant boy that Samantha was cradling began to wail loudly as if he understood what was happening, that he would never see or know his father.

The tributes lasted for some time. Eventually, the last McFoster had their say and the infant found the comfort of his mother's breast. The buzz of the engraver fell silent. Kazimir stared brokenly at the new name on the marble, then hung his head, unable to bear the sight any longer.

People drifted away, leaving him and Samantha alone.

'Thank you, Kaz,' she said quietly. 'Sometimes I think you and I are the only people who really cared about him.'

'Everybody cared,' he said automatically. Samantha was a few years older than him, which had always made him kind of awkward around her. Now with Bruce gone, and the baby born, he was even more uncertain.

She smiled, though it was clearly an effort. The infant was only three weeks old, and she looked very tired. 'You're so sweet. Everybody knew him, especially my sisters in all the clans. There's a difference. But at least he made his mark on this world, I think.'

496

Kazimir put his arm around her shoulders and they walked out of the memorial garden together. 'Have you decided on his name yet?'

'Not Bruce, that would be too much. I've chosen Lennox, that was Bruce's grandfather, and I have an uncle called that as well.'

'Lennox. That's good. I expect that'll be shortened to Len.'

'Yes.' She stroked the infant's head. Lennox had lolled back into sleep again. 'You should find someone, Kaz.'

'Huh?'

'Someone for yourself. It's not right for anyone to be so alone.'

'I'm fine, thanks. I get plenty of offers, don't worry.' It was the kind of thing he used to say to Bruce. His mind went back to Andria McNowak, and his broken promise to Bruce. He never did try to bed her after that terrible raid. In fact he'd never bothered with any girl since then. As always, he had the memory of Justine to comfort him through the long hours of every sleepless night.

Scott and Harvey were waiting on the path, along with another man Kazimir didn't know. Harvey beckoned.

'I'll see you before you go, won't I?' Samantha asked.

'Of course you will. I want . . . If you need anything, help with the baby, or something, please tell me.'

'You're not obligated, you know.'

'I want to see him, Samantha. I would have wanted that even if Bruce was still alive.'

'All right then.' She stood on her toes and gave him a light kiss. 'Thank you again, Kaz, you'll make a wonderful uncle.'

He watched her walk off back to the village, a whole range of emotions messing his head round.

'Nice girl,' Harvey said. 'I remember training her for a while.'

'Yeah,' Kazimir said.

'This is Stig McSobel,' Scott rasped in his damaged voice.

Kazimir shook hands with the stranger, surprised by how strong the grip was. He could look the man level in the eye, so he was no taller, but his shoulders were wide enough to stretch the fabric of his simple lace-up shirt. The McSobel was in his early thirties, with skin lighter than Kazimir, and a broad face that regarded the world with considerable amusement.

'I've heard a lot about you, Kaz,' Stig said. 'You've earned quite a reputation for yourself on your last few raids.'

Kazimir gave Scott and Harvey a sharp glance. 'Is this another lecture?'

'About recklessness and personal vengeance?' Harvey asked. 'Why should it be? Did you not pay attention last time?'

Kazimir started to push past. Stig put out a hand to stop him. Again, the man's strength was very evident.

'If you can keep that temper of yours under control, I can use you,' Stig said. 'Harvey here says you can. The ceremony should have been cathartic, and now you'll start to accept his death. Is that right?'

'I saw Bruce's death. I watched him die, and I could do nothing.'

'I know what that's like. We all do; there's nothing unique about you and your grief, Kazimir. You're a McFoster, a fighter. One day you'll die, and some other friend will watch it. Do you want their life to be blighted by that? We all have a right to live our lives as well, you know. There is more to us than the struggle against the Starflyer. This village shows that. Bruce's baby should show you more than anything.'

'Well what the fuck else can I do?' Kazimir shouted. He was close to tears again, which would be an awful thing in front of the men he respected most. 'I can fight, yes, and that's how I help bring about this better time we're all promised. If anger makes me fight harder, then good. Bruce would appreciate that.'

Scott laid a hand on Kazimir's arm. 'Just listen to what Stig has to say, lad. Where's the harm in that, hey? We came to you with this because we're worried about you. We don't want to stop you fighting, but the way you are right now, you're going to get yourself killed on one of these raids, and for no good reason. This way you can still carry on the fight without deliberately putting yourself in so much danger. Now how about you just stay quiet for a minute while Stig says his piece, huh?'

Kazimir gave a rough shrug, knowing he was being a hothead idiot. Not knowing how to stop. 'Sure. Sorry. It's just . . .' He waved at the memorial garden. 'Today. You know.'

'I do,' Stig said. 'If you felt nothing for him, you would not be a true clansman, you would be nothing better than a Starflyer slave. I respect what you're going through.'

'What did you want?'

'You know the human starship has flown?'

'I heard, yeah.'

'Bradley Johansson believes its launch is the start of the Starflyer's endgame. It will bring ruin to the human Commonwealth.'

'How?' Kazimir asked. He never had quite understood how the human starship could be involved in their fight against the Starflyer. It was just an exploratory flight.

'The barrier around the Dyson star was put up to contain a great evil. Johansson is worried that the humans will let it out. Some of the crew will be the Starflyer's slaves.'

'What kind of evil?'

'We don't know. But if the Commonwealth has to fight a war it will be badly weakened, economically and socially. Such an action would leave humanity vulnerable to the Starflyer as it gnaws at us from within.'

'But you said the starship has left. We can't stop it now.'

'No. But, Kazimir, if the Starflyer is preparing to crush us,

499

the time for the planet's revenge will soon be here, possibly within a few years. That means the Starflyer will return to Far Away, and we must be ready.'

'I know that.'

'Good. Now this is where I can use you. There are a number of items which must be brought to Far Away so that the planet may have its revenge. Unfortunately, our supporters out there in the Commonwealth are being hunted down by the authorities that the Starflyer has corrupted. It is difficult for them to smuggle things here the way they've always done before with our weapons. That means we have to set up alternative routes for the items we need. I've travelled around the Commonwealth, I know how it works. Now I have to go back and help our allies, but I'm going to take a small team of dedicated Guardians with me to help achieve our final goal. I'd like you to be one of them.'

'Me?' Kazimir asked in shock. Just the notion of leaving Far Away was awesome, let alone travelling round the planets whose names were closer to fable than fact. And *she* was out there ... 'Why me? I don't know anything about the Commonwealth.'

'You can learn easily enough. Harvey says you are quick, which is good. Life there is very different, at least superficially. You must learn how to blend in easily. And you're young; physically you can still adapt. You'll have to train hard to build your muscles up to a point where your body can cope with standard gravity. There are drugs which can help, of course, and cellular reprofiling, but those techniques can't do it all, you'll need to commit yourself fully.'

'I can do that,' he said without even thinking.

'Was that a yes?'

'Yeah!'

'You will also have to obey orders. My orders. I cannot have you running round loose out there. This is the one operation that cannot be compromised, not ever. It is what the Guardians are, why we exist.'

'I understand that. I won't let you down.'

'I'm sure you won't, Kaz. But it will be Johansson who makes the final decision.'

Kazimir gave Scott and Harvey a confused glance. 'What decision?'

'If you are to help bring back what we need,' Harvey said, 'the physical training is only half of your preparation. You really are going to have to learn how to behave like a Commonwealth citizen. I promised Stig you could do that, please don't make me a liar.'

'Never, but . . . Johansson will decide?'

'Yes,' Stig said. 'You'll meet him before we begin the operation.'

Kazimir could barely believe what he was hearing. As far as he was concerned, Bradley Johansson was some remote icon that everyone quoted and deferred to, a historical giant. He wasn't someone you got to meet in the flesh and talk to. 'Fine,' Kazimir said faintly. 'Where is he?'

'At the moment? I don't know. But we'll meet him on Earth.'

*

While she was being built, the *Second Chance* was the unisphere's primary news story. Details of her design, stories about her construction, spun briefings on the politics behind the decision to build her, gossip on who would be picked for her crew, it all pumped up the ratings for any news media show. Then came the Alamo Avengers' attack, and modest interest became outright fascination. It culminated with over seventeen billion people accessing her departure for Dyson Alpha in real time. After that, while she was slipping through hyperspace for month after month, there was a distinct feeling of anticlimax, and even a little frustration. Commonwealth citizens simply weren't used to anything that important being off line; worse, it would be a year until they did hear what happened. Until then, everybody would just have to fall back on the old familiars of TSI soaps and dramas, squabbling politicians, badly behaved celebrities, and the Commonwealth Cup now moving into the quarter finals.

Then news of Morton's arrest was released, along with the name of the arresting officers (not that anyone cared about Hoshe Finn) and every train to Oaktier was suddenly full of reporters hungry for more information. The case was a studio editor's dream: a Paula Myo investigation of an ice murder, a wealthy suspect with big political and business connections, a strong hint of financial scandal. And sex. What had once been idle Oaktier gossip about Morton seducing the beautiful young Mellanie and ruining her chances on the national diving team, was pushed high up the coverage agenda, featuring heavily on every report and info-profile. His earlier conquests were soon tracked down and coaxed into telling their story for respectable sums of money. Bribes were offered to Darklake City forensic officers to reveal exclusive insights into the evidence which the prosecution would present – which led to five subsequent contempt of court proceedings. Tara Jennifer Shaheef and Wyobie Cotal were forced to apply for non-harassment court injunctions against the swarm of reporters laying siege to their homes.

After a month's build-up, expectations were running high. On the first morning of the trial, Darklake Superior Courthouse had to be cordoned off from the frenzy of media and public interest. Street barriers pushed the expectant crowd back half a city block. A long convoy of police cars and patrolbots escorted the prisoner van round to the secure reception area at the rear of the courthouse, its movements followed by cameras on a dozen helicopters. They never got a glimpse of Morton as the van vanished into a locked garage bay.

The trial venue was Court One, which the judicial authorities had hurriedly spent a large amount of their annual maintenance budget on sprucing up. With Oaktier about to spend at least a week in the focus of the entire Commonwealth, impressions were suddenly paramount. The rich golden brentwood panelling around the dock and judge's bench was buffed. Both of the lawyers' long heavy tables were resurfaced and waxed. The walls and ceiling were repainted, with the big justice symbol taken out for cleaning. Every polyphoto strip shone down brightly; the sound system was checked and balanced correctly.

The revamp had worked; when the fifty selected pool reporters were finally allowed in on the first morning they all remarked to their audience how solemn and dignified the chamber was. The kind of place you could put your trust in, knowing that here justice was both fair and thorough.

Presentation was also foremost in the defence strategy. The first time Morton was seen since his arrest was when he walked into the packed courtroom, dressed in a deep purple designer suit, his thick hair perfectly styled, and looking very confident – almost mystified as to why he was here. It was not the image of a guilty man awaiting the inevitable verdict which Paula Myo always got when she prosecuted. As he reached the dock he bowed politely to the curving panel of silver one-way glass that shielded the jury and protected their identity. Just before he sat down he glanced round the packed public gallery, found who he was looking for, and smiled warmly. Every reporter swivelled round, retinal inserts focusing on Mellanie, who was perched elegantly on the front row, wearing a stylish navy-blue jacket and plain white blouse. Dressed so, she managed to project herself as both the epitome of bewildered innocence, and tremendously sexy. Just an ordinary girl next door standing by Her Man in the face of a terrible injustice.

Then Paula Myo walked in, wearing a smart grey business suit and black leather shoes, formidably cool, and exuding her own special brand of confidence. In the studios of a hundred news shows, they once again ran the clip of an impassive sixteen-year-old Paula at her parents' hugely emotional trial. As it showed across the Commonwealth she sat down between the city's chief attorney, Ivor Chessel, and Hoshe Finn, whose best suit appeared ancient and derelict amid the high-fashion statements which the principals were wearing.

Judge Carmichael made his entrance, and everybody stood. Morton flashed a reassuring grin up to Mellanie, captured by fifty professional pairs of inserts.

Once the charges had been read out, the defence lawyer, Howard Madoc, immediately applied for a dismissal, citing contamination of evidence by the media. Ivor Chessel attested that the evidence itself was still sound and irrefutable, and only a small part of the prosecution case. Judge Carmichael rejected the appeal and, with the posturing over, the trial began in earnest.

Prosecution laid the case out simply. Morton was a man driven by his raging manic thirst for money and power. His marriage to Tara Jennifer Shaheef was a simple and ruthless first step to achieving that goal. Her family money was used to fund AquaState, giving that small company the financial muscle to go after and win large building development contracts. AquaState under Morton's fiery management grew successfully until it was ready to go public.

The share flotation was all part of his original grand scheme. It made him rich and gave him the leverage he needed to gain a seat on Gansu's board. After that, his rise was unstoppable.

But his plan had faced ruin as his then wife Tara Jennifer Shaheef grew bored with their marriage. If she filed for divorce, AquaState would either be wound up or sold off and the proceeds split between them. Morton would still be rich, a lot richer than he was at the start of the marriage, but it wasn't enough for his purpose. It was still too early for the flotation to take place, AquaState wasn't quite big enough to attract investors. That required another two or three years of uninterrupted growth. 'So you killed her,' Ivor Chessel said, standing in front of the dock. 'You removed the one obstacle left to flotation, your own wife. And with her out of the way, supposedly living on Tampico, you were free to build up AquaState to the level you required.'

Morton gave Howard Madoc a helpless look – unable to believe anyone could make such an absurd accusation. The defence lawyer, a dignified man who kept his appearance firmly middle-aged with the first frost of silver in his hair, shook his head sadly at such blatant theatrics by the prosecution.

The first prosecution witness was the city's head of forensics, Sharron Hoffbrand. She confirmed that the bodies dug out of the forty-year-old condo's foundations were indeed Tara Jennifer Shaheef and Wyobie Cotal. They had both been shot at close range by a very high-powered nervejam weapon, and had their memorycell inserts erased, probably by an em pulse. The exact time was slightly difficult to pin down after so long, but she could narrow it down to a three-day period in the middle of the week when Morton was away at the conference in Talansee.

Chessel then asked if they'd found any foreign DNA traces on either of the bodies.

'No,' Hoffbrand said. 'Cotal was fully clothed. There were the normal particles and dirt you'd expect from moving through the city, but no extraneous DNA. Shaheef was naked, but we found traces of soap and perfume chemicals on her skin, indicating she was in the bath.'

'Can you tell if she was shot in the bath?' Chessel asked.

'Not after so much time has elapsed, no.'

'But she was in the bath at least prior to the slaying?'

'Yes.'

'So she was at home then?'

'That's likely, yes.'

'Thank you.' Ivor Chessel turned to the judge. 'No more questions, your honour.'

Howard Madoc smiled as he got to his feet. 'Home or a hotel? Can you really tell the difference?'

'No, it could have been either.'

'Or a friend's house? Or a public washroom?'

'Somewhere with a bath is as specific as I can get.'

'Was it on Oaktier?'

'There's no way of knowing.'

'I see. Thank you.'

Prosecution called Tara Jennifer Shaheef. She took the stand wearing a lavender suit with wide white trimming, and a too-short skirt. Her hair and make-up too lavish, emphasizing how nervous she looked.

'Do you recall having any enemies forty years ago?' Ivor Chessel asked.

'No. I didn't lead that kind of life. I still don't.'

'So you certainly weren't aware of anyone wanting to kill you?'

'No.'

'Do you have any memory or knowledge of visiting the planet Tampico?'

'No, I'd never heard of it until I was re-lifed.'

'What about Broher Associates?'

'The lawyers? No. I heard about them at the same time I did with Tampico, when the insurance investigators looked into my disappearance.'

Tara's eyes watched Howard Madoc as he walked over to her. She hadn't yet managed to glance in Morton's direction.

'The prosecution is relying very heavily on the *assumption* that you were about to divorce my client,' he said. 'Were you?'

'I don't think so. There was no definite plan that I remember. We would have parted eventually. The marriage was moving close to its sell-by date.'

'Is that why you were having an affair?'

'One of the reasons, yes. Life was sweet. Wyobie made it sweeter.'

'Life was sweet,' Madoc repeated thoughtfully. 'I see. Do you still see Morton?'

'Sometimes, yes. I don't avoid him.' She gave a brittle laugh.

'So you're good friends then?'

'As best as you can be with an ex. He was . . . supportive when I was re-lifed. It's quite a shock waking up to find that's happened to you. The therapists say some people take another lifetime to get over it.'

'So it would be fair to say there is no ill will between you and Morton?' Madoc asked.

'No. That is, I had no reason to suspect any until this blew up.'

'If you had gone and done what the prosecution claimed, and filed for divorce that very week you were killed, would you have insisted that AquaState be wound down or split in half as your marital agreement stated?'

'Objection,' Ivor Chessel said. 'That requires speculation.'

'Hardly, your honour,' Madoc said smoothly. 'I'm asking the prosecution witness what she would actually have done under very specific circumstances; while the entire prosecution case rests upon what might have happened if she did as they believe. Which of us is speculating?'

'I happen to agree with you in this instance,' the judge said. 'How the witness believes she would have reacted is not speculation. Please answer the question.'

'I . . . I'm not sure,' Tara stammered. 'Money wasn't too big an issue for me, I still had access to family funds. I suppose

I would have allowed AquaState to continue. Morton would probably have made a good case for getting it ready for flotation.'

'So you were never angry with him?'

'No. All marriages end, everybody knows that. That's why we have contracts at the beginning.'

Howard Madoc was very careful not to smile at the prosecution team as he sat down.

The second day began with Hoshe Finn taking the stand. He was still in his one best suit with his hair slicked back into the silver clasp he always used; while Paula had chosen a black jacket and light tweed skirt, still every inch the unflappable professional. Morton had gone for expensively casual, with an open-neck white shirt under a gold-embossed waistcoat. His lawyer was wearing the same suit as the previous day, careful to project style without ostentation. Looking down on them, and smiling encouragement when required, Mellanie had selected a pale-grey dress, cut tight enough to qualify as an overskin.

'Detective Finn,' Ivor Chessel began. 'Is there any evidence Tara Jennifer Shaheef or Wyobie Cotal ever went to Tampico?'

'The tickets were bought, and the law firm hired, but there is no evidence either of them were ever there. We performed an extensive search, there was simply no data or physical trace of them ever being on that planet. We believe the whole Tampico scenario is an alibi for the killer.'

'An alibi?'

'If Morton killed his wife to guarantee the flotation of AquaState, he couldn't afford to have anybody asking questions about where she was. As far as everyone else was concerned she had run off with her lover to set up home on a new world. The legal firm of Broher Associates was hired to carry on the fiction by acting on her behalf.'

There was a lot more. Methods used during the search. Verification of police records. Results into inquiries conducted into Wyobie Cotal's life to see if he had enemies prepared to kill. The official accounts for AquaState. All of them designed to show how the inquiry had carefully narrowed down options until it could be nobody else but Morton. It wasn't until the afternoon that defence began its questions.

Howard Madoc got Hoshe to tell the court how the original investigation of Cotal's re-life was winding down when Morton intervened to get the case assigned a higher priority.

'Very curious thing for him to do, if he is the killer, isn't it?' Madoc asked.

'He wouldn't know he murdered Shaheef and Cotal,' Hoshe said. 'The first thing he would do is have the memory erased.'

'You know that, do you?'

'We examined his secure memory store. There is no memory of the event.'

'Was there a full memory of the week-long convention he was attending at the time of this terrible crime?'

'Essentially yes. However, he could have returned to Dark-lake City during what was logged in the secure store as a sleep period.'

'You examined my client's secure memory store. Is there any memory of him ever having been to Tampico?'

'No. But if he killed . . .'

'Just answer the question you were asked, please Detective. You have no evidence my client set up this alibi. Would I be right in saying that the person or persons who did actually kill Tara Shaheef would have needed this alibi to deflect any police or private inquiry about her whereabouts?'

'Yes.'

'In the course of your investigation, did you find anyone else with a motive to kill these two unfortunate people?'

'No. There was nothing, no other reason except Morton's.'

'What about Tara and Wyobie unexpectedly walking in on some deeply illegal criminal gang activity? Was that considered?'

'Yes, we examined it as a possibility. There was no evidence to support the idea.'

'Well there wouldn't be, would there? If the gang who killed them were smart enough to deliver an alibi that stood for forty years, they're hardly going to leave evidence lying around. Their only piece of bad luck was my client spotting the re-life connection and asking questions in high places, doing his duty, being a good citizen. And this is his reward. While all we have here in court is your theory mangled to fit the facts, a notion which is based solely on your assumption that my client is a cold ruthless man. Am I right in that?'

'Yes, that's what the facts support.'

'But they don't, Detective. That's not evidence. That's your theory. It is not evidence, not some bloodstained blunt instrument in a plastic bag which you can hold up here in court and point to. It is the most tenuous circumstantial theory. So I ask you again: is there any evidence, physical or digital, that definitely rules out Wyobie Cotal and Tara Jennifer Shaheef walking in on a criminal activity and being killed to shut them up, and incidentally, having their memorycell inserts erased?'

Hoshe stared ahead for a long moment, then cleared his throat. 'No, there is no physical or digital evidence which rules that out,' he said in a monotone.

As the court recessed for the day the talking heads in media studios across the Commonwealth were nearly unanimous that Howard Madoc had done a good demolition job on Hoshe Finn. A great deal of the prosecution case was conjecture. It should be enough for a good defence lawyer to swing the jury in his favour. Public sympathy was definitely moving towards Morton according to the constant interactive polls monitoring opinion on the case. It acted like a feedback loop, giving even more people the impression he was going to get off. Which implied an even bigger revelation was waiting to be accessed: Paula Myo was actually going to lose a case.

After such momentous events, day three brought an unsurprising increase in the unisphere audience, close to three billion people were on line and waiting to see what would happen. They watched as Mellanie arrived early and took her usual seat. This morning she was wearing a long coat of some shiny ice-blue fabric with matching trousers. The vest underneath was a translucent mesh, though the coat lapels remained very close together, hinting at, rather than revealing, any flesh. With her hair given a sophisticated wave and combed back neatly she was radiating raw sex appeal.

After yesterday's roasting, Hoshe Finn was wearing a lighter suit, for once allowing his oiled hair to fall loose over his shoulders. Next to him, Paula was in a sombre dark-green suit, her hair scraped back severely.

When the court officer brought Morton in, he'd put on a navy-blue suit appropriate for any boardroom meeting, emphasizing his authority and integrity. His face was sober and intent, never betraying any hint of contentment at what had happened yesterday. He was restrained as he shook hands with Howard Madoc, then they both stood as Judge Carmichael entered.

With the prosecution case over, defence called its first witness: Morton himself.

Howard Madoc was facing the shielded jury as he asked his opening question. 'For the record, do you believe yourself capable of committing such a dreadful act as this murder undoubtedly is?'

'I do not believe I could kill in cold blood. And I did not kill my wife and her lover.'

'Thank you.'

Madoc went through a long series of questions designed to show his client in the best possible light to the jury. How Morton was ambitious but not so ruthless as to use murder to his corporate advantage. How he had shown sympathy and support for his ex-wife after her re-life procedure. How he would have risen to the top no matter what trivial little financial problems beset him forty years ago.

'The prosecution has made much of how cold and ruthless you are,' Madoc finished with. 'Are you a cold man?'

Morton looked up to the public gallery where Mellanie was sitting, gazing down with a soft devoted smile on her beautiful young face. 'You'd have to ask those who know me properly, but I don't think so.'

Howard Madoc bowed slightly to the judge and sat down.

'Your witness,' Judge Carmichael told the prosecution table.

Everyone in the courtroom fell silent as Paula Myo slowly stood up. Then a round of excited whispering broke out as she bowed to the judge and walked over to the witness stand. If she was having to take charge herself, the prosecution must be desperate.

'Murder ain't what it used to be,' she said to Morton in a pleasant conversational tone. 'It's no longer death. Not final. Today it's bodyloss, memory erasure, lots of euphemisms that describe what is essentially a discontinuity in consciousness. Your body can be killed, but the clinics on every Commonwealth planet can bring you back to life with a simple cloning procedure. There's a blank decade or two, but eventually you're walking round again as if nothing ever happened. It's a wonderful psychological crutch to have. A lot of psychiatrists argue that it helps make our society a lot more stable and calm than before. They bandy the word "mature" around quite a lot.

'So you see, murdering somebody is nothing like as serious as it used to be. All you're actually doing is removing them from the universe for a few years. You're not really killing them. Especially when you know their insurance will cover a re-life procedure. It would probably be an acceptable risk to remove someone who was going to ruin your plans.'

'No,' Morton said. 'It is completely unacceptable. It is not a done thing, something that can be performed for convenience. Murder is barbarism. I wouldn't do it. Not now, not forty years ago.'

'But we are agreed that your wife and Wyobie Cotal were murdered?'

'Of course.' He frowned, puzzled by the question. 'I told you, remember?'

'No, you originally said you were suspicious about her disappearance, especially when it coincided with that of her lover. Feelings of unease aren't entirely memory-based, they can't be erased by legal or black-market editing. They are derived from the subconscious. You knew something was wrong about their disappearance.'

Morton sat back and gave her a suspicious stare.

'The Tampico alibi was a good one, wasn't it?' Paula said.

'Yes.'

'Yes. Assuming you no longer had the memory of murdering her, neither you nor her other friends ever questioned the story that she'd left you to go there.'

'I didn't kill her. But you're right, it was a watertight cover-up. I had no reason to question her disappearance, especially after Broher Associates contacted me and said they were acting as intermediaries.'

'Let's examine this again. You came back from your conference in Talansee, and found your apartment had been stripped of all your wife's things, her clothes and possessions, and there was a message telling you she had left for good.'

'That's right.'

'And that was enough to convince you at the time that there was nothing unusual about her leaving.'

'It was unusual, and unexpected, and quite shocking. But it didn't make me suspicious.'

'So you knew of her affairs?'

'Yes, there had been several by then. Our marriage allowed for them. I'd had a couple myself. I'm only human, not some cold machine.'

'Did you argue the terms of the divorce?'

'No. They were all set out in the marriage contract. I knew what I was getting into.'

'What about the items removed from your apartment, did you ask for any of them to be returned?'

'No.'

'Why not?'

Morton gave Madoc a quick glance. 'Tara only took her own stuff.'

'You knew what was hers, did you?'

'Sure.'

'Did anybody else?'

This time the glance Morton shot at his lawyer was a puzzled one. 'Excuse me?'

'I read the transcripts of all your calls and messages to Broher associates,' Paula said. 'There was never any dispute over what was removed. So tell me this: in a home where two people have lived together for twelve years, where only those two people could possibly know which item was their own, how is it that the killer only removed her property?'

Morton's expression turned to one of stricken incomprehension. He opened his mouth as if to speak, but no words came out.

'No criminal gang would ever know what to take to set up the alibi,' Paula said. 'It would take someone intimate with the house and its contents. There were only two of you with the exact knowledge. One of them is your ex-wife, and we know she didn't do it.'

Morton slowly lowered his head into his hands, covering his grief and confusion. 'Oh holy shit,' he moaned. 'I didn't. Did I?'

'Yes.' Paula regarded him with the kind of sympathy normally extended to the bereaved. 'You did.'

*

The jury took three hours to deliberate their verdict. Comment on the unisphere was that they took so long in order to enjoy a decent lunch at the taxpayer's expense. When they filed back in to the courtroom and delivered their verdict nobody was surprised that it was unanimous. The electronically disguised voice from behind the curving silver glass announced, 'Guilty.'

The outbreak of chatter was swiftly silenced by the judge, who then told Morton to stand. There were, the judge said, very firm guidelines laid down for such appalling crimes: the minimum was usually twice the period of life loss.

'Given that you committed this crime purely for your own advancement, I have to agree with the prosecution's assessment that you are a cold immoral individual who sees other people's lives as an inconvenience to your own ambition and has no qualm in eradicating such problems. Due to your evil, Tara Jennifer Shaheef and Wyobie Cotal have suffered the loss of decades without a body, I therefore have no hesitation in imposing a punishment of one hundred and twenty years of life suspension. Sentence to begin immediately.' His gavel banged down loudly.

Tara Jennifer Shaheef leaped to her feet and screeched: 'You *bastard*!' at her ex.

On the other side of the public gallery a hysterical Mellanie screamed incoherently, struggling against the court officials holding her back from jumping the railings to be with her guilty lover. Some members of the public around her were cheering merrily at the commotion. Morton shook his head in bewilderment as he was led out of the dock, a study in tragicomic defeat. The reporters turned en masse to the prosecution table. Hoshe Finn and Ivor Chessel were clearly delighted, smiling wildly as they shook hands. Paula Myo seemed oblivious to the fuss all around her; she was picking up loose sheets of hard copy and slotting them neatly into her briefcase. Her hand-held array followed, and with the table surface clear, she walked out of the courtroom without looking around.

14

Wilson was now a hundred and twenty-nine days into the mission, and counting. In the same way everyone else on board the *Second Chance* was counting. Days, hours, minutes: every little unit was being ticked off with a combination of irritation and relief. Their problem, strangely enough, was just how well the starship had worked since they departed Oaktier. He supposed it was inevitable: enough money had been poured into the design, making sure every component had multiple redundancy along with at least a two hundred per cent tolerance rating. In his NASA days they'd called it goldplating. Everything on *Ulysses* had to work, and if some bizarre mishap did knock out a unit then three back-up systems jumped up to replace it. And that was when you could still see Earth through the viewing port; and communications with Houston took a few minutes at the most. It provided a tenuous feeling of connection to the rest of the human race which had always given him a degree of security. If something had gone badly wrong, he'd believed that NASA would ultimately do something to salvage the situation. Today, though, the sense of isolation was stronger by orders of magnitude. Even he, with his previous experience, found their flight daunting. Should anything go wrong here in hyperspace, nobody was ever going to find them. It made him grateful for the way the starship had been constructed. This mission, he realized, had an altogether more mature feel to it than the *Ulysses* flight ever had.

It was a civilized voyage. First of all there was the gravity. It might only be an eighth of a gee around the rim of the life-support wheel, but it made sure everything flowed in the right direction. His body was so much more comfortable with that. Then there was the food. Instead of neat efficient, rehydratable packets of precooked meals, the *Second Chance* canteen served dishes like pan-fried scallops with herb risotto; or loin of lamb with tarte tatin of vegetables drizzled with a thyme and tomato sauce; and the dessert selection was dangerously more-ish. For recreation there were a number of gyms (not even this ship boasted a swimming pool), which everyone dutifully attended. But most of the crew spent their spare time accessing TSI dramas. They had a huge library on board, with sexsoaps inevitably the most popular, though first-life first romances were equally fashionable, and there were numerous adaptations of classic fiction and biographies of historical characters. Wilson spent several days immersed in a sumptuous production of *Mansfield Park*. He'd read the novel in his first life, and was interested in the societal structure of the era which it conjured up (intriguing parallel with present-day Earth, he felt), though he was fairly sure there hadn't been quite so many lesbian love scenes in the original book.

Between fitness sessions, meals, TSIs, and ship's duty, he spent most of his hours with Anna. Even after all this time, he still preferred a one-woman-at-a-time lifestyle. Exceptions being between serious relationships and marriages, and at the end of them when things were unravelling. But the kind of arrangements many of the Commonwealth's wealthy, and not-so-wealthy, favoured had never really appealed; not like Nigel Sheldon with his thousand children and dozen-strong harem, or the Kandavu multi-families, or any other of the hundreds of variants on relationships At heart, he knew he was as old-fashioned as the era he'd come from.

Anna, though, was good company; never demanding, happy to keep things comfortably casual. It was almost the same as before the launch, the difference this time being that everyone on board knew about them. That didn't cause any resentment or whispering. Again, due to the nature of the voyage. They were all grown-ups. Although it had never been a firm policy, one you could find written down or in a program, Wilson had rejected all applications from first-lifers.

He was convinced they didn't have the temperament he wanted from his crew. The voyage so far had confirmed that in his own mind. There had been so little trouble, so few 'personality clashes', that he'd begun to regard the ship's psychologist as superfluous. Even now, as he waited on the bridge for the hyperspace flight to end, there was no sign of any tension among those around him.

'No significant mass within a hundred AUs,' Oscar reported.

'Thank you,' Wilson said. He glanced round at the portals himself, seeing the gravitonic spectrum displays almost blank, like the eye of the storm. They'd obtained their last accurate navigational fix flying within three hundred AUs of a red dwarf, now ten light-years distant. That put them close to twenty-five light-years from Dyson Alpha, in clear interstellar space. 'Okay, stand by to take us out of hyperspace. Anna, let's have the main sensor suite on line please.'

'Aye, sir.' She didn't even grin at him. On the bridge, she took her duties very seriously indeed. Two seats away, OCtattoos on her hands and forearm began to shimmer like pulsing silver veins as her palms rested on the console i-spots, readying the equipment up at the bow of the starship.

'Astrophysics?' Wilson asked.

'Ready, sir,' Tunde Sutton said. He was waiting at the rear of the bridge, along with two of the science officers, Bruno Seymore and Russell Sall. Their consoles all had double the number of portals and screens that the others had; capable of displaying a vast amount of data. In addition, all three men had upgraded retinal inserts, giving them a high-quality virtual vision field. If there was any anomaly out there in real space, they'd have it located and analysed almost instantaneously. They were also sharing the data with the astrophysics office, on the deck above, where the majority of specialists were waiting, including Dudley Bose.

'Oscar, bring the force fields on line, please, and take tactical control.'

'Aye, sir.'

Part of Wilson's virtual vision display showed him the power being routed into their force fields and atom lasers. Sensor data was also fed directly into the targetting control, with Oscar assuming executive authority for their missile arsenal. Wilson moved his virtual fingers to activate a general channel throughout the ship. 'All right, ladies and gentlemen, let's see what's out there. Tu Lee, take us out of the wormhole. But keep the hyperdrive on line. We may need a fast exit.'

Tu Lee grinned broadly. 'Yes, sir.'

The blue mist filling the two big high-rez portals at the front of the bridge began to darken. A ripple of black broke out from the centre, expanding rapidly. Clear pinpoints of light speckled the deep night outside the ship as the starfield appeared around them once more.

'Tunde?' Wilson demanded.

'Nothing obvious, sir. Electromagnetic spectrum clean. Gravitonic empty. Standard particle density. Immediate quantum state stable. Zero radar return. Neutrino flux normal. Cosmic radiation high but not excessive.'

'Sensors, show me Dyson Alpha,' Wilson said.

Anna centred the main telescope, feeding the image to the left-hand portal. Slim red brackets indicated the position of the shielded star. She bled in the infrared emission, and it appeared as a pale pink dot. Dyson Beta materialized slightly to one side. 'Doesn't look like there's any change to either of the barriers,' she said. 'They were both still intact twenty-five years ago.'

'Any activity in the surrounding area?'

'Not that I can locate. Do you want a hysradar sweep?'

'Not yet. Expand our baseline for the current sensors. I want a clearer picture of the area. Astrophysics, keep monitoring. Pilot, hold us stable here.'

'Aye, sir.' Anna began to manipulate virtual icons. 'Prepping for sensor module launches.'

Wilson let out a quick breath of relief. His virtual finger was tapping icons almost unconsciously. On the console in front of him, one of the small screens flicked between camera images. Each one had a small portion of the starship superstructure, the forward sensor array, a slice of the life-support wheel, the plasma rockets. But no matter which camera he chose, there was never anything other than the ship and the very distant stars. Nothing. The emptiness was awesome. Frightening.

When he was a boy, Wilson had enjoyed swimming. His parents had a small pool in their yard, and he'd used it every day. That didn't stop him from continually nagging his parents to take them to the larger pool at the county sports centre. He'd been nine on the day of that visit, him and a whole group of friends; ferried out there by some harassed mother with a people carrier. With his skill and confidence he'd not been intimidated by the size or depth of the big pool, and was soon leading the others through the water. When he was in the deep end he dived to the bottom, sure he could touch the tiles. He made it easily enough, his strong strokes hauling him down away from the surface, popping his ears against the pressure twice on the way down before slapping his fingertips on the smooth blue tiles. Sound from the rest of the pool was curiously muted so far below, the thrashing feet above, dull, like the filtered blue light. Pressure squeezed him gently. So he started to swim up. And only then did he realize his mistake.

He'd taken enough breath to get him down, but now his lungs were burning. Muscles twitched as the need to suck down fresh glorious air swelled desperately. He began to claw frantically at the water, which did nothing to increase his terribly slow speed. The need for air became overwhelming. And his chest began to expand, lungs working to pull in that sweet oxygen. Wilson felt the water sliding up his nostrils like some unstoppable burrowing creature. Right that second he knew if it got any further he would drown. It was enough to send his body into a frenzy, kicking and struggling. At the same time he found the discipline to stop his lungs from trying to inhale. Somehow he managed to break surface without the water spilling any further inside him. Only then did he suck down a huge breath of beautiful clean air, almost sobbing as the shock of what'd happened struck him. For a long time he'd clung to the side of the pool as big shivers ran up and down his body. Finally, he regained enough control to swim back out to his friends, not that he ever told them what had happened.

Even during his air force combat flights he'd never felt so scared as that whimpering child striking out for the side of the pool. Nothing had ever come close to recreating that feeling. Until now. Now that same clammy sickness was gripping him just like it had his nine-year-old self as the reality sank in of how far away from *anything* they were. He started his ancient deep feedback breathing exercise routine, trying to calm his body before the shakes started.

'Modules disengaging,' Anna announced.

'Right, thank you,' Wilson replied a little too abruptly. His virtual hand stopped flicking through the camera sequence, and he concentrated hard on the images of the sensor modules. Something to do, something to shift his mind from the nothingness of outside. He felt his heart rate slow as he forced his breathing to a regular rhythm, though there was nothing he could do about the cold perspiration on his forehead. A text-only message popped up into his virtual vision, it was from Anna and read: **Are you all right?**

Fine, he sent back. He didn't look in her direction. Everyone else on the bridge seemed to be absorbed by their work, unaffected by what lay outside. He was the only one interstellar space was intimidating. That piqued him somewhat – enough to make him focus properly on his job.

The screen on his console showed him the forward section of the *Second Chance*. Doors on eight cylindrical bays had opened up, spaced equidistantly just behind the bow's large sensor cluster. Modules like big metallized insects sprouting golden antennae were drifting out, glittering in the lights around the rim of each bay. Ion thrusters flared blue on the base of each one, pushing them away from the starship.

They travelled in an expanding circle, linked by laser and microwave, taking hours to reach their stand-off station. When they were fifty thousand kilometres out, their ion thrusters burned again, bringing them to a halt. As one, their dark protective segments peeled open, exposing delicate sensor instruments to the interstellar medium. Disks, blocks, booms and lenses uncoiled on the end of electromuscle tentacles and began scanning space around Dyson Alpha. The big arrays back on the *Second Chance* correlated the results, combining them into a single image with an extraordinarily high resolution in every spectrum.

For everyone waiting eagerly on board, they were a big disappointment; virtually no extra information about the barrier was revealed. Its diameter was confirmed at twenty-nine point seven AUs. There was a moment of prayer-like silence on the bridge as that fact was absorbed. The surface was emitting in a very low infrared wavelength. Local particle density was slightly lower than average, indicating the solar wind emission was blocked. Nothing else could be detected. After five days of cautious observation for any sign of hostile events, or any other energy emission that might point to artificially generated activity, Wilson had to agree with his science team that there was no obvious danger at this distance. He ordered the sensor expansion modules back to the starship, and they flew fifteen light-years closer.

When they emerged into real space again, they repeated the examination. From five light-years, the images which the expanded baseline modules provided were even more exact. But nothing had changed. The interstellar particle winds blowing off nearby stars were detectable as they gusted round the barrier, creating giant swirls and eddies which sighed in the electromagnetic spectrum like faint whale song.

Wilson moved them forward in one light-year increments. Each time, the eight modules would fly out and peer ahead. Each time they would provide a more detailed survey of the local radiation and particle environment. Of the barrier itself, they revealed nothing.

'Take us to one light-month out,' Wilson told Tu Lee.

'Aye, sir.'

'Tunde, that'll take us within high-definition range of the hysradar.' Wilson said. 'Do we scan it?'

The astrophysicist gave an expansive shrug from behind his bridge console. 'It'll tell us a lot about the nature of the barrier, but of course if there is an active force controlling it, then we'll probably reveal ourselves. I can't imagine they won't be able to detect it.'

Oscar looked at the forward portals which showed the blue walls of the wormhole closing over real space. 'They have to know already. We'd be able to pick up the quantum signature of a wormhole from this distance.'

'The builders must have realized that people would come and investigate at some point,' Anna said. 'You can't do something like this and expect it to go unnoticed.'

'We'll run passive scans first,' Wilson said. 'If there's no response, we can use the hysradar.'

Just under four hours later, the *Second Chance* emerged from hyperspace. Wilson didn't have to order the expanded baseline modules out. The ship's main telescope revealed the full expanse of the disk. In infrared it was like the baleful eye of some dreaming dragon.

'Very low neutrino density out here, and virtually nothing coming from Dyson Alpha's direction,' Bruno Seymore said. 'I'd say the barrier is impermeable to them. We should be picking up a whole deluge from the star at this distance.'

'What about particle density?' Wilson asked.

'Interstellar wash, that's all. No particle wind from the star itself. The barrier must be converting all the energy hitting its internal surface to infrared. Output corresponds to that, assuming the star remains the same inside.'

'Thank you,' Wilson said. He was staring at the red circle, all sense of isolation long gone. 'Is it solid?'

'No, sir,' Tunde Sutton said. 'We're picking up the star's gravity field. It's weak but detectable. If that thing was solid, it would mass at least the same as an average star. Probably a lot more.'

'So it blocks neutrinos, elementary particles, and most of the electromagnetic spectrum, but not gravity. Are any of our force fields like that?'

'Similar,' Tunde said. 'I'm sure we can build a generator that duplicates those properties. It wouldn't be easy.'

'And what would it take to power one this size?'

Tunde almost flinched. Bruno and Russell grinned at his discomfort.

'A good percentage of the star's fusion energy.'

'Can you tell if that's missing?'

'Not really. We'd need a much better measurement of the naked star to compare with. We've never had that.'

'Okay. If you can pick up the star's gravity field, can you tell if there are any planets orbiting inside?'

'Not from out here, we need to get closer for that.'

'Anna, is there any sign of activity outside the barrier, anything at all?'

'No, sir, nothing. No microwave communications, no laser, no radar emission. No plasma trails, not even a chemical rocket plume as far as we can see, though we're stretching resolution on that one. There're no wormhole signatures either. As far as our sensors are concerned, we're alone out here.'

Wilson gave Oscar a glance.

'It's beginning to look like a relic,' the exec said. He sounded disappointed.

'All right. Give it a hysradar sweep. And I want a very careful watch for any response. Hyperdrive, be ready to take us straight out of here.'

'Yes, sir.'

The bridge was silent for a couple of minutes as Anna and Tu Lee worked in tandem, sending out hyperaccelerated gravity waves from the wormhole generator.

'Unusual,' Tunde Sutton said eventually. 'It simply reflected the pulses back at us, like a mirror. That indicates a very complex quantum structure. But then we knew it was never going to be anything simple.'

'Did we ring any bells?' Wilson asked.

Anna and the astrophysics team shook their heads. 'Still no sign of activity. But we are limited with sensors from this range. Anything in the electromagnetic spectrum is going to take a month to show up.'

'I'm more concerned about hyperspace and quantum field activity.'

'Nothing so far.'

'Very well. Oscar?'

'We've come a long way,' Oscar said. 'And so far we've seen nothing to make us turn back.'

'I agree. Prepare the ship for a hostile encounter scenario.

Hyperspace, take us in to one million kilometres above the barrier's equator.'

'Aye, *sir*.'

The wormhole projected into real space with a burst of Cherenkov radiation, its toroidal nimbus twinkling with azure scintillations. It dissipated as quickly as it had begun, leaving the *Second Chance* floating a million kilometres above the blank surface of the barrier. On such a scale there was no visible curvature to the shell around the star. It appeared as a simple flat plane extending to infinity in every direction, as if the starship had reached the bottom of the universe.

'We couldn't have gone through,' Tu Lee reported as soon as they were established in real space.

'What do you mean?' Wilson asked.

'The barrier is a block to wormholes as well. There was a lot of exotic energy echo as we approached. Whatever the barrier is, it extends through the quantum fields. The wormhole wouldn't be able to circumvent it.'

'So there really is no way in,' Wilson mused.

'Or out,' Oscar said.

Wilson turned to the astrophysicists. 'So how can the star's gravity field get through?'

'We'll let you know,' Tunde said. He didn't sound happy.

'Hysradar sweep gives a sheer surface,' Anna said. 'Definitely no neutrino penetration. I've never seen the detectors registering this low before.'

'How thick is it?'

'That dimension really only applies to solid matter,' Tunde said. 'This is an artificial rift in the quantum fields which manifests itself in spacetime; technically, it has no physical depth. It's two-dimensional.'

'Fine.' Wilson couldn't take his attention off the standard radar return. 'Any sign of spacecraft activity?'

'Nothing,' Anna said. She sounded slightly peeved at having

to churn out constant reassurance. 'No rocket exhausts. No wormhole signatures. There's nobody else here.'

'I'd qualify that,' Tunde said. 'This goddamn thing is thirty AUs across. That's almost impossible for the human mind to grasp. We're not even seeing a fraction of a per cent from here. There could be a battle fleet of ships the size of a moon gathered five AUs away and we'd never know.'

'Let's not get carried away,' Wilson said. 'This is what we're here for people, a full survey and analysis. So ... Pilot, hold us steady at this standoff distance. Defence, keep our shields up full until further notice. Hyperdrive, keep us ready for an immediate exit. Astrophysics, you're on. I want a comprehensive sensor sweep from this distance, probe it with everything we've got. We are not getting any closer for now. If you can confirm there are no active components which threaten us, I'll authorize a remote satellite examination of the barrier's structure. Until then we play it safe.' He leaned back in the chair, and watched as the data started to build up on his screen and within his virtual vision. The stream of results was unending, and growing by the hour as new instruments were unsheathed and applied. Only a fraction of the information made any sense to him. It was slightly humbling. He'd always thought himself quite up-to-date on physics.

Tunde Sutton and the rest of the science crew tore into the raw data with unnerving enthusiasm. Their attitude was child-like in its wonder. Wilson was very careful not to intrude, or censure Tunde for the way he ran his department. But from what he could see they were acting more like first-life science geeks than wise, considered professors – the reason they'd been selected. They quarrelled and laughed among themselves, completely uncaring for social restraint. Suddenly, after all these months, they were now the elite, aloof from the rest of the crew. It showed.

Wilson overstayed his duty period by two hours, then

turned the bridge over to Oscar. An hour later, Anna found him in the forward observation gallery. It was a long dark compartment on the wheel's middle deck, with subdued blue floor lighting. She paused for a long moment after she came through the door, letting her eyes acclimatize to the darkness. The gallery had three tall windows of optically perfect glass facing forward. The silhouettes of several people were just visible – the barrier was a popular vista. She walked over to Wilson. 'Hi,' she whispered.

'Hi.' His hand found hers in the gloom, fingers fumbling. They stood together, content with their closeness. Anna could see the main cylinder above them, a sombre grey bulk illuminated by the small nav lights dotting its surface. It was rotating slowly, turning various sensor clumps into view one after the other.

'I'm not sure if I can see it,' Wilson murmured quietly. 'My inserts give me a perfect image in infrared. But when I cancel that, I think I can see it. If it's there, it's like a flat cloud of the darkest red ever. Maybe I'm just imagining it because I know that's what it is and should look like. And it looks as if it's just in front of the nose.'

'On this scale, it is,' she whispered back. 'We're not even a germ to a basketball.'

'Can you see it?'

'I don't know.' Stupid though the action was, she leaned forward slightly, squinting. Her inserts were off now, and there might well have been some kind of ultradark vermilion haze out there in front of the nose, the kind of luminosity you got from a single candle lighting a cathedral. 'It's like a ghostlight.'

'Humm. I always thought I had quite good eyes. I'll have to get them resequenced next time I go into rejuve.' He waved his hand in front of his face to see if that made any difference, if he could see the outline of his fingers against the obscure emission. There was too much secondary lighting in the

529

observation gallery to be certain. 'Whether I can see it or not, I can certainly feel it. The damn thing's spooky, like something lurking just outside your thoughts.'

She curled her arm round his. 'Come on, it's been a long day. Time you got some rest.'

He grinned. And his teeth were just visible in the gloaming. 'I'm too tired and strung out to argue.' He allowed himself to be led towards the door.

'Strung out? You?'

'Yeah. We spent a year getting this ship built. I spent three hundred years waiting for something this important to happen to me again. I wanted something *there* when we came out of hyperdrive, something positive that I could see and understand. When we set down on Mars, there was all this alien geology surrounding me. It was strange, and even beautiful after a fashion, and nobody really knew anything about it. But you could break open a rock with a hammer, and see the minerals and strata inside. We had a knowledge base that could take that information and pin down what kind of rock it was, what event produced it. It was all in my head, information I could apply.'

They were alone in the corridor, so she stood on her toes and kissed him. 'You poor old thing.'

Wilson smiled, sheepish now. 'Yeah, well, I guess I was just intimidated, that's all. The size of this fucker is mind-warping. I really shouldn't let it get to me.'

'I know, whacking this with a hammer isn't going to help.'

'No.' He kissed her back. 'I bet it would make me feel a hell of a lot better, though.'

Five days later, Wilson allowed the *Second Chance* to move up to fifty thousand kilometres above the barrier. They used the plasma rockets, accelerating in at a fiftieth of a gee, then stopped and flipped over to decelerate. The physicists were very keen to see what would happen when the exhaust sprayed against the surface. The simple answer was nothing. Satellites hovering centimetres above the barrier observed the residue of gas and energized particles strike the surface and rebound. There was no heat or momentum transfer. No effect. Gigabytes flowed back up the microwave links between satellites and starship, expanding the already vast database on the barrier. A huge quantity of sensor log files were stored in the RI array, almost all of them containing negative information. Every member of the science crew could tell Wilson what it wasn't, and they could explain its properties at great length. What nobody could tell him was how it was generated, nor from where. And they certainly didn't know why it existed.

But then, he told Anna charitably one night, they had only been there for five days. He shouldn't expect miracles.

The starship hung above the stubborn barrier for another eight days, picking at it with various beams of radiation, like a small child with an intriguing scab, eager to see what lay beneath. Their wormhole generator distorted spacetime in many convoluted perturbations; the wave function of each one bouncing off the near-invisible surface without any significant resonance pattern. During that time, their only major discovery was the planets inside the barrier. Tunde confirmed that gravitational readings showed two gas-giants and three small solid planets were orbiting the star, with indications of several large asteroids. It livened up the daily department heads' meeting when he told them that one of the solid worlds was within the life band, the distance from the star which would allow carbon-based life to evolve should the planetary conditions be favourable, such as the availability of water, a decent atmospheric pressure . . .

Finally, for morale's sake rather than practical science, Wilson allowed McClain Gilbert to fly out to the surface. After the long, boring flight, the crew was becoming restless. Like Wilson, they'd all expected something a little more substantial, some hint as to the origin of the barrier, the reason behind it. One of their own actually going out there and examining it in person should help alleviate some of the tension which was building up in the life-support wheel.

So the whole starship was watching as the small shuttle flew out of its hangar in the cylindrical superstructure. It was a simple spherical life-support capsule capable of transporting up to fifteen passengers, sitting on the top of a drum-shaped propulsion section containing the environmental equipment and two small plasma rockets. A short-range vehicle, with a ten-day flight margin, it was intended to ferry science officers between any 'items of interest' to be found at the Dyson Pair. Although it didn't have an atmospheric entry ability, it could set down on small airless moons, or more hopefully rendezvous with alien starships, alien space stations, or if they were really lucky, even a barrier generator. Nearly everybody on board had volunteered to accompany Mac, including a very vocal Dudley Bose, but Wilson had vetoed any passengers on this trip. Mac had a back-up exploration team member, a pilot, and an engineer riding with him, but that was all.

The shuttle used its tiny chemical reaction control engines to hold station a hundred metres away from the barrier, and Mac wriggled his way carefully out of the craft's cylindrical airlock. His spacesuit's inner plyplastic layer gripped his skin, constantly adjusting to accommodate his every movement yet always fitting snugly. On top of that he wore a thermal regulator garment, woven out of heat duct fibres, which would carry away any excess body heat. Above that was a thicker suit, a pale grey in colour, combining a radiation baffle cloth and an external impact armour layer, resistant to most micrometeor strikes. It had a built-in force field generator web, which was his real protection in space. If that failed, then procedure was to abandon the EVA and head for the nearest airlock. His helmet was a reinforced transparent bubble, also radiation-proof and temperature-resistant, which he could opaque depending on the light level, giving him all-round visibility, which was boosted by various collar sensors he could access through his virtual vision. Batteries, the heat regulator, and the air regenerator system were all contained in a neat little pack built into the front of the outer suit, with a couple of circular radiator fins to discard surplus body heat. The whole thing was interfaced and controlled via his e-butler, with its system schematic icons sprinkled around his virtual vision.

As soon as he was clear of the airlock hatch rim he anchored himself to the fuselage grid. The cilia on his boot soles adhering to the lattice with a grip strong enough to hold him in place against the kind of torque his body might apply by mistake in the confusion of freefall. He bent over, his stomach muscles pulling hard in the absence of gravity, and unfastened the manoeuvring pack from its storage rack. It was a simple unit, a slim backpack with fat plastic mushrooms on each corner sprouting cold gas nozzles that could jet him about freely over a range of several kilometres.

As he was strapping it on, a new set of icons appeared in his virtual vision. He made sure the diagnostic software ran a full check before his virtual hand began to manipulate the joystick. Now he was actually out here, with so many of his crewmates watching over his shoulder, it was tempting to twist the throttle and scoot over to the barrier right away. But he forced himself to go through the physical test routine, burping all the cold gas nozzles, confirming their thrust. Only when his little practice flight round the shuttle was complete did he say: 'Ready for crossing.'

'You look good from here,' Oscar said. 'Telemetry at one hundred per cent. Clear to proceed.'

That familiar voice, with its perpetual tone of dry amusement, was one Mac found absurdly reassuring. In this awesomely bizarre situation it was a welcome touch of normality, the same voice that had led him out onto a dozen new worlds. Virtual fingers tilted the joystick forward, and the manoeuvring pack nozzles snorted nitrogen, moving him out away from the shuttle. As far as he could see in the standard visual spectrum he was heading into total darkness; the barrier could be a couple of centimetres in front of him, or fifty light-years. His radar said ninety-three metres. He bumped the speed up to a couple of metres per second, then told his e-butler to switch on the craft's spotlights. His spacesuit glowed a dusky pewter as the beams followed him. Up ahead he was sure he could see the triple circles where they were striking the barrier; they formed a royal blue patch; the effect was almost as if someone was rendering a cartoon shimmer on the surface.

Mac activated the infrared function in his retinal inserts. Half of the universe turned a lambent carmine. Even though he could see the barrier, there was still no way to judge physical distance. The radar put him forty metres out. He began to reduce his closing speed, and the spotlights were showing up as circles with a slightly greenish tint. But he could finally see his own shadow projected onto the flat wall ahead.

He came to a halt a metre away, and just floated there for a moment. The biomonitor showed him his racing heart-beat, and he could hear the adrenaline buzz in his ears. He started to raise his arm, fingers extending to touch the enig-matic surface, then paused. He hadn't received permission, but if he checked before doing anything the EVA would take all day. The reason he'd been chosen was because of his con-tact experience. *Not in this situation*, he told himself evilly, and managed a small grin. His heart rate had slowed a little now, so he completed the motion. His fingers touched the surface.

For one twisted-up moment he imagined the barrier van-ishing like a soap bubble, punctured by his ignorant touch. But it didn't, and he chuckled slightly at the notion. By now he was drifting away, propelled by the slight contact; so he moved the joystick forward, and put his hand out again. This time the manoeuvring pack held him in place.

'Okay, I'm touching it. No apparent reaction. Seems like

ordinary solid matter, there's none of that slight surface instability you get on our force fields.'

'Understood, Mac,' Oscar said. 'We were all waiting for some demonic claw to come through and drag you in.'

'Hey, thanks for that.'

'My pleasure. You feel like applying some sensors for us?'

'Will do.' He reached down to the equipment clipped on his belt. One by one, he stuck sensor pads against the barrier, taking measurements. He had to hold each one in place. The high-temperature epoxy was no use at all. When he squeezed it out of the tube, it simply rebounded off the barrier like water splashing off teflon. 'We didn't think that would work,' Oscar said. 'There aren't any atoms there for it to adhere to. Worth a try, though.'

'Sure, but I'm using up gas at quite a rate keeping these sensors applied.'

'Copy that. Please apply the meson rate detector.'

'Okay.' He settled the fat little cylinder against the surface. Once again that notion of there being something on the other side was strong in his mind. He was scratching away on the barrier like some mouse behind the skirting board, and the house cat was listening intently, unseen, just the thickness of an electron away. *Irrational*, he kept telling himself. *But surely something knows we're here?* He twisted his head to one side until he could see the starfield. For a moment he was upright, pressed against a wall, with the night sky behind him, the ground lost beneath his feet. The vertical horizon between red and black was perfectly straight and clear. When he looked down, that same horizon was below his boots. A human mind simply couldn't grasp the *size* of the thing. Whoever established this incredible artefact must have had a phenomenally compelling reason.

Defence? Confinement? The sweepstake on board was running eighty/twenty. Both implied aggression somewhere; again on a scale beyond human comprehension.

'You all right there, Mac?' Oscar asked.

He realized his heart was thudding again, and took a couple of deep breaths. 'Sure, no problem. What's next?'

'Exotic waveform detector. Tunde wants to know exactly where the infrared emission originates. That should help define the barrier interface with spacetime.'

'Sure.'

After forty minutes he placed the last sensor back on his belt, and jetted back to the shuttle. The physicists were pleased with the results, they had moved another step towards understanding the nature of the barrier. But as to how it was generated, and the *why* of it, they hadn't got a clue.

*

Two days after Mac's EVA, the morning meeting of the department heads decided that information gathering had progressed about as far as it could from a static observation point. Wilson was concerned that they weren't making enough progress in other directions.

'We were sent here to establish the reason why the barrier was erected,' he told them somewhat formally after they'd had the usual round-up of results from the previous day. 'Tunde, I know your teams are doing a great job on the characteristics of the barrier, but we need more than that. Now you're identifying its quantum structure, is there any way we can reformat the hyperdrive to get us past?'

'No,' Tunde said. 'In fact, I don't think there is a way through. We might not be able to generate a barrier like this for ourselves, but we do understand enough about its properties to just about rule out any kind of circumvention through hyperspace. A wormhole simply cannot be opened through it.'

'What about forcing our way in?' Oscar asked. 'Can we break through in real space?'

'Again, no. Absolutely not. Even if you could generate collapsed state energy levels and apply them directly against the barrier, it wouldn't have any effect. It's not physical. It can't be damaged or stressed in the way solid matter can. One day we might be able to manipulate quantum fields in such a way as to destabilize a section, but that won't be for a long time. To use a very bad pun, we haven't even scratched the surface.'

'Then we must look for clues elsewhere,' Wilson said. 'Admittedly, given the size we're dealing with here, that can only be the most perfunctory search, but it must be done. We're back to our original two theories: offensive or defensive. If the barrier is defensive, there may be signs of the attacking force left somewhere outside.'

'Signs, or the whole armada?' Oscar asked lightly.

'If they were here, they'd be investigating us by now,' said Antonia Clarke, the engineering chief. 'We've created enough disturbance in every spectrum going since we've arrived. Even a few perfunctory warning satellites scattered round the barrier would have found us.'

'Maybe,' Tunde said. 'But we certainly haven't located any active observation equipment. And it is a long time since the barrier went up. The threat might not exist any more.'

'It's only long on a human scale,' Oscar said.

'All right,' Wilson held up his hands to prevent any full-scale argument erupting. 'If the attacking force or entity is still here, we need to find it, preferably without it seeing us, which I admit is a long shot, however we have to try. If they've gone, then they might have left something behind. And if the barrier was put up for the opposite reason, to confine the star and its inhabitants, then we have an even greater chance of finding the builders. Therefore, I have decided we'll take the *Second Chance* on a complete circumnavigation of the equator. We'll stand off an AU and use the hyperdrive at low speed. If we take a week, the hysradar will be able to complete a very accurate scan of the surrounding space. Following that, and taking the worst-case scenario that we find nothing, we'll fly to both poles and examine them. If after that we still draw a blank we'll review the situation then.'

'Captain,' Tunde said. 'I'd like to raise the issue of communication.'

'With whom?'

'Both our scenarios imply that there is some kind of sentient life to be found inside the barrier. Now we're this close it may be possible to attract their attention, possibly even initiate a dialogue.'

'How? I thought you said the barrier was impervious.'

'It is to everything except gravity.' He indicated the chief engineer. 'I've discussed this with Antonia. It shouldn't be too difficult to modify the energy configuration of the hyperdrive to create simple gravity waves. If the civilization inside has a working gravity detector, they should be able to pick it up.'

The notion surprised Wilson; given the analysis he'd been getting from the science teams since they arrived, he'd dismissed the notion of any attempted contact a long time ago. 'How difficult would the adaptations be? I will not authorize taking the hyperdrive off line at any time.'

'It's a matter of programming,' Antonia said. 'That's all. Standard gravity wave emission would be a simple modification of the hysradar function. The ship's RI can give us a reformatted routine within a couple of hours.'

'Okay then, you can go ahead with the program. If the circumnavigation flight doesn't produce any results, we'll certainly try it. Good idea, both of you.'

*

It was the second day of their week-long flight around the equator when the hysradar finally found something of interest. The first scan returns came back just after midnight, ship's time. Oscar was in command on the bridge; he ordered the *Second Chance* back into normal space, and put a call in to the captain's cabin.

By the time Wilson arrived, pulling on his jacket and shaking his head to rid himself of sleep, the starship's main sensors were fully deployed. A picture was building up on the bridge portals. He squinted at it, not quite believing what he was seeing. The radar graphic of neon-green grid lines was the most detailed, showing a perfect hemisphere rising out of the barrier. Its base was twenty-five thousand kilometres in diameter.

Tunde Sutton and Bruno Seymore arrived on the bridge. Both of them stood behind Wilson, staring in perplexity. 'Wow,' Bruno muttered. 'Talk about a fly in amber.'

'Okay,' Wilson went over and sat behind his console. 'What am I looking at? Is that a planet?'

'No, sir,' Russell said. The screens on his console were shimmering with light as he ran the in-coming data through analysis routines. 'I'd say it's some kind of extension of the barrier itself. Surface is uniformly smooth, just like the barrier, and it is a perfect hemisphere as well. It has an extremely strong magnetic field, at least an order of magnitude above a standard planetary field; and it's fluctuating wildly, almost as if it's spinning. There's no gravity field, as such . . . sensors are picking up gravity wave emissions, though. They're regular, pulses of some kind. Not synchronized with the magnetic shift, though. Very odd.'

At that, Wilson turned to face Tunde, who was just sitting down behind his own console. The astrophysicist gave him a confused frown.

'A signal?' Wilson asked.

'I don't know.'

'The pulse sequence hasn't varied,' Russell said. 'If it's a signal, it's not saying much.'

'Can you see where they're coming from?'

'They seem to be from within the hemisphere, although the actual origin point appears to be moving around in there.'

'Okay, anything else?'

'There's no infrared emission.' He nodded at the large portal. It was showing the barrier's blank surface in bright carmine. A large circle in the centre of the image was black, as if a hole had been cut through. 'Wait! There's something at the top.' Russell's voice rose in pitch as he interpreted the raw data. 'The apex isn't curved, it's flat, or . . . maybe some kind of crater. An opening! There's an opening there.'

'You're right,' Bruno called out. There was a wild grin on his face. 'Slight photon emission. There's light shining out, wavelength just outside ultraviolet. It's not infrared, not like the rest of the barrier. That could be the way in!'

Wilson and Oscar exchanged a shocked glance. 'Calm down,' Wilson said. 'I want realities not speculation at this point. Get me a decent image from the main telescope. Oscar, what's our current stand-off distance?'

'A hundred thousand kilometres above the barrier; seventy thousand from the hemisphere.'

'Good enough.'

'Focusing now,' Bruno announced.

The bridge portal showed a fast-expanding ring of red flashing outward. Then it was completely black. 'Here it comes,' Bruno said triumphantly. A speck of luminescence getting bigger rapidly, jumping up to a crescent of lavender light that shivered in the middle of the portal.

'Size?' Wilson asked.

'The hole is seventeen kilometres across.'

'This wavelength doesn't match Dyson Alpha's known spectrum,' Tunde said. 'That's not the star shining out.'

Wilson couldn't take his gaze off the sliver of light. 'Any local activity that would indicate spacecraft or sensors?'

'No, sir.'

'I don't suppose you know if that hole was open when we emerged from the wormhole?'

'We know the apex was flat, but the hysradar return doesn't tell us if it was open.'

'Very well. Recommendations?'

'Send a probe in,' Russell said immediately.

'Eventually, yes,' Tunde said. 'But we'll need to observe it for a while first.'

'While we're doing that we could send a satellite on a flyby above the opening,' Oscar said. 'Keep it at our current stand-off distance, and take a look directly down inside. Our position gives us a lousy angle of view.'

Wilson was mildly surprised at the suggestion. He'd expected Oscar to be more cautious, although a satellite flyby was reasonable enough. If anything was in there, they must surely be aware of the *Second Chance*. 'Go ahead.'

'I'll start the prep sequence.' Oscar went over to the console Anna normally used, and called up the launch sequence.

'In the meantime,' Wilson said dryly. 'Does anyone have any ideas about what this thing is?'

Jean Douvoir chuckled softly. 'Fortress of Darkness, where the evil lord hangs out.'

'Thanks. Anyone else?'

'I have a possibility,' Bruno said. He was close to blushing as the bridge crew all looked at him. 'Well, it's active, right? Something inside is generating gravity waves, and magnetic fields; and that's just what we can detect. It's also absolutely right on the equator; as near as our sensors can tell, it's perfectly aligned with the plane of the ecliptic. Though I'm not sure how relevant that is . . .' He glanced round, unnerved by the attention. 'I just thought it might be a generator, that's all, where the whole barrier is being produced from, or at least this area of it.'

Wilson looked at Tunde and raised an eyebrow in query.

'Gets my vote,' Tunde said. 'Until something else comes along to disprove it.' He gave Bruno a thumbs up. 'Smart.'

Oscar launched the Moore-class satellite twenty minutes later. Its ion drive accelerated it away from the big starship, sending it curving over the apex of the dark hemisphere.

Nearly every screen on board relayed the image from its visual spectrum cameras. The violet glow didn't reveal much, certainly there was nothing lurking just inside. A very detailed analysis program picked up a slight but regular fluctuation to the output intensity. It didn't match the oscillations of either the gravity waves or magnetic field.

Four hours after leaving *Second Chance*, the satellite was directly above the opening. Even on the highest magnification it could see nothing but the homogeneous dark-blue glow, as if the hemisphere contained nothing but a fluorescent fog. Twenty minutes later, when half of the crew had lost interest, the light vanished, leaving the opening completely dark. Eighteen minutes later it reappeared.

Intensive slow-motion replays coupled with image-enhancing programs showed that something had moved across the opening, cutting off the light.

'Your evil lord just blinked,' Oscar told Jean.

*

After three days of observation they knew the light was blocked on average every seven and a quarter hours, though this could vary by up to eight minutes. The eclipse duration was more constant, lasting a fraction over eighteen minutes, except once when it had gone on for nearly thirty-five.

As nothing had come out of the hole in all that time, Wilson finally authorized a close observation. A larger, Galileo-class, satellite left its launch bay on the *Second Chance*, equipped with a more expansive sensor suite than the Moore. Anna slowed its approach as it closed in on the hole, keeping it twenty kilometres above the hemisphere's perfectly black surface. Telemetry showed her the little craft was taking a beating on the magnetic and electromagnetic wavefronts; even with circuitry hardened to withstand the kind of treacherous energy environment found around the most active gas-giants she had to watch out for overloads and temporary glitches.

Interference caused a lot of static within the datastream link back to the starship, resulting in poor imagery and broken instrument readings.

Everyone on board the starship watched as the hole slowly slipped into view, its gentle lavender radiance appearing like the dawn of a weak sun. It was an illusion which was broken soon enough as the satellite crept closer; the illuminated hole was small by any standards. Then the satellite passed over the rim, slowing to a relative halt. The magnetic flux in tandem with the gravity waves was actually strong enough to induce a detectable wobble, as if it was floating on a sea. Anna did her best to counter the tiny vibrations, allowing the sensors to peer down carefully. Four hundred kilometres below the hole, a curved lattice of immense dark strands was gliding slowly across the blue glow which came from deeper inside. As the satellite focused on the strands it became clear that the lattice was anything but a uniform hexagonal honeycomb, the interstices ranged from simple triangles up to twelve-sided grids with some of the strands curving them into near-ellipsoid geometries. The holes were the size of small countries, with strands up to a couple of hundred kilometres wide. One thing was obvious from the curvature and ponderous motion – the lattice was a sphere.

A thousand kilometres beneath it, a second lattice sphere was visible, also composed of dark strands, though this one had a more regular geography, mostly comprised of triangles and pentagons. It, too, was rotating, but in a completely different direction to the outer layer. And below that was a third lattice grid, with wider spacings. Its continent-long strands glowed a strong indigo, helping to create the pervasive glow. Though its radiance was complemented to a large degree by streaks of amethyst light which came from underneath it, the indicators of a fourth lattice sphere spinning somewhere in the deeps. Exactly where was unclear. The third lattice appeared to be surrounded by some kind of lambent vapour.

'Son of a bitch,' Wilson whispered. Out of all the things he'd expected to see within the Dark Fortress, a kinetic sculpture bigger than planets was not high on the list. The scale of the barrier was already hammering at his beleaguered human senses. But that at least had been a projection, energy manipulated and folded on a stellar scale, while these lattice spheres looked resolutely solid. This was matter organized and fashioned in quantities incomprehensible to Commonwealth technology. Yet the barrier creators had produced something which from a simple visual viewpoint was almost laughably mechanical, in the truest sense of the word. He wouldn't be at all surprised now if they were to find gearboxes with cogwheels the size of moons driving the entire edifice. 'Are those strands really solid?' he asked.

'I can't tell,' Anna said. 'The electromagnetic environment in there is playing hell with the satellite's radar.'

'That much matter would coalesce under its own gravity,' Bruno said. 'They have to be energy forms.'

'Not so,' Russell immediately claimed. 'There's nothing like a terrestrial planet mass in there. And their spin rates will keep them inflated.'

'Nonsense, they'd have to be metallic hydrogen to maintain their structural integrity under these conditions.'

'So? It's metallic hydrogen. Apart from those glowing ones; I'd say they were exotic matter. There's virtually no infrared emission coming from in there.'

'Is the outer shell complete?' Oscar asked. 'I mean is there a corresponding hemisphere on the inside of the barrier, or is this just some giant bearing groove for those lattice spheres?'

'Good question,' Tunde said. 'Anna, can you focus the satellite telescope through those grids?'

'No sir, no way,' she exclaimed. 'That haze effect around the third sphere is like looking into a gas-giant cloudscape, and it gets thicker below it.'

'Like oil,' Oscar muttered. 'It lubricates the gaps between

the spheres.' He realized Tunde was looking at him and smiled an apology. 'Just a thought.'

'Anna,' Wilson asked. 'Will the satellite survive in there?'

She let out a long breath as she stared at the main image on the twin portals. 'I don't see why not, certainly as far down as the first lattice sphere, anyway. The sensor returns we've got show clear space that far in.'

'Okay then,' Wilson said slowly as a sense of real enthusiasm grew inside him. 'Let's do it.'

*

Anna launched a second Galileo-class satellite, flying it to the entrance hole at the top of what the crew now all called the Dark Fortress. Once it arrived, she sent the first satellite inside, using the second as a relay. As it descended towards the outermost lattice sphere the energy surges around the satellite picked up noticeably. Eventually, Anna stopped trying to compensate. At that rate she would run out of fuel in a matter of hours. So she let the little craft wobble its way forward, blurring the visual sensor pictures. Every eighty kilometres or so she would stabilize it again, and run a quick check before allowing the vibrations to build up. There was nothing to see en route. The gap between the outer shell and the first grid sphere was empty, with the satellite sensors recording it as a hard vacuum.

When it was halfway there, one of the sphere's massive struts slid underneath the hole, eclipsing the light pouring up from the inner lattice spheres. By now the crew were successfully recording the geography of the first lattice, and were making good progress charting the second. There seemed to be no logic behind the pattern. But predicting the times of the eclipses was now straightforward.

As the satellite grew nearer to the first lattice sphere, the radar return began to improve. 'That's odd,' Anna remarked as she stabilized the satellite once again.

'Problem?' Tunde asked.

'I'm using parallax to confirm the distance to the strut we're heading for, but there's a discrepancy between that and the radar return. Radar places it three klicks closer.'

'Maybe that optical haze effect is throwing the parallax reading?'

She shook her head. 'Clear view. There is no haze round these struts.'

The discrepancy began to rise as the satellite closed in. Then they examined the magnetic flux around the strut, seeing the force lines warp like cyclone clouds around the surface.

After a long and heated conference with the rest of the physics team, Tunde said: 'Whatever else it is, the outer lattice sphere has electro-repulsive properties. The radar pulses aren't actually reaching the surface itself.'

'Can we take the satellite in and attempt a landing?' Wilson asked.

'I wouldn't recommend it. That repulsion force would play havoc with the electronics. We'll have to study it from a distance.'

*

The Galileo satellite spent two days hovering thirty kilometres above the first lattice sphere as it rotated slowly underneath. All of its sensor booms were fully extended, gathering up as much information as possible. Back on the starship, the physics team worked with the engineers to try and design a simple probe which they could drop onto one of the struts. Its circuitry was all optronic, using a laser for communication; sensors were extremely limited. But even studying its flight path as it neared a strut would tell them something.

Wilson, keen to expand the exploration of the Dark Fortress, authorized its deployment. A further two Galileo-class satellites were launched. Anna and Jean Douvoir had assembled a small team of controllers drawn from the pilot-qualified on board to help them remote-fly the probes. Together, they steered the twin satellites through the entrance hole, and took them down towards the first lattice sphere. Anna manoeuvred the lead one into the centre of a pentagonal-shaped grid and, while Jean held the original satellite fifty kilometres above as a communications booster, she fired its ion thrusters, flying it straight in towards the second lattice sphere. As it passed through the level of the struts, electronic systems suffered repeated crashes. Thankfully the multiple redundancy architecture managed to keep the primary components on line the whole time, constantly rebooting the failed units. It released the probe and carried on.

Once it fell below the outermost lattice sphere the Galileo returned to full functionality. Heartened by that, Anna got another of her team to send the second satellite through. With both of them clear and operational, she took them in deeper still.

The probe, meanwhile, drifted steadily towards its target strut. Information zipped back along the laser link, revealing the swirling energy environment around the vast mass. Contact was lost a couple of minutes before impact. The physics team wrote that down to the repulsion force affecting the probe's battery.

Anna's team piloted the two Galileo satellites in towards the second lattice sphere. As they receded from the first, so the magnetic and electromagnetic squalls shrank away. It began to look as though the second lattice sphere was inert. With one satellite holding back, poised halfway between the two, Anna lowered hers in towards the edge of a strut making up a large pentagon shape. Radar return was precise, there was no magnetic field, no electromagnetic emission, the infrared signature was minute.

'Something's slowing it,' Anna reported. The satellite's

velocity was dropping at an increasing rate, as though it was encountering some kind of atmosphere. Molecular sensors stubbornly continued to report a vacuum outside.

Anna managed to get it to within seventy kilometres of a strut surface before it came to a complete halt. She had to fire the main thrusters at full strength simply to keep it there. Without that, the satellite would have reversed its trajectory. 'Something's pushing it away,' she told the physics team.

After three days of attempted approaches at varying velocities, another Galileo satellite arrived to assist, equipped with a simple rail launcher to shoot inert slugs of different elements. It began firing. Every slug, no matter what its component atoms, slowed to a halt before reaching the strut, then began to return, picking up speed. Complemented by both passive and active sensor sweeps of the second lattice sphere, the physics team came to their excitable conclusion: 'Negative mass matter,' Tunde announced at the next meeting of department heads. 'Its gravitational force is the opposite of our own, therefore anything made out of ordinary matter will always be repelled.'

The satellites were able to push through the centre of each hole in the negative mass lattice where the inverted gravity was at its weakest. Anna moved one down to the next level, dipping it into the shoal of tiny pale scintillations that swirled across the gulf between the second and third lattice spheres. Its sensors had trouble tracking the dense will-o'-the-wisps; but eventually the physicists determined it was a tenuous cold plasma, aggravated by the emissions of the exotic matter below, and confined to the gulf by the negative mass above.

Analysing the exotic matter proved even more difficult than the previous two lattice spheres. They had to launch a whole squadron of large Armstrong-class satellites with their powerful and comprehensive sensor suites. It took a further two weeks before they'd charted the energy currents seething like photonic tempests in the plasma between the two exotic matter spheres. After that, there was enough confidence in their newly acquired knowledge to pilot a satellite through the fourth lattice sphere.

When the first Armstrong satellite passed through it found no further spheres. Instead, the space in the middle, measuring sixteen thousand kilometres in diameter, housed a series of concentric rings, all of them aligned with the plane of the barrier outside. The outermost, thirteen thousand kilometres across, the crew immediately named the daisy chain. It was a sequence of lenticular disks linked together by a black cable. Next in was a simple ring of green matter, so smooth and uniform it was impossible to tell if it was rotating. A braided ring whose thick silver strands moved sinuously around each other like oiled serpents. One of pure scarlet light. More solid loops. The globes, hundreds of thousands of them, strung together in a dense necklace that the bridge officers likened to a strand of alien DNA, twisting round each other as they rotated round the centre. Sparks: a wide band of emerald and amber lightpoints trailing cometary tails as they orbited in both directions, though never colliding. There was one of water, or some clear liquid, with a surface beset by waves. Right in the centre was emptiness, a little patch of darkness into which light fell.

It was God's own orrery.

Talk in the starship's canteen was that the lattice spheres powered the rings, or vice versa. Either way, they were all convinced now that the Dark Fortress was the barrier generator.

One by one, the satellites were ordered down towards the rings. One by one they lost contact with the *Second Chance*. The centre of the Dark Fortress was an energistic maelstrom. Human technology could not survive within it. Watching the displays that showed tides of quantum distortions raging chaotically around the wounded satellites, some of the physics team claimed the rings didn't – couldn't – even exist in normal spacetime.

What everybody on board wanted to know was if there was a corresponding opening on the other side of the Dark Fortress.

'There's no way we can get anything across the centre and past the rings,' Tunde said. 'If we're going to try this, we'll have to program a satellite to fly round in the gulf between the outer shell and the first lattice sphere. It'll have to operate in autonomous mode, we don't have enough satellites to act as a relay chain over that distance.'

'It's a waste of time,' Oscar said. 'I don't believe there's a hole there. There'd be no damn point to the whole barrier if there was.'

'I don't think there is either,' Wilson said. 'But you know we have to look. Anna, program a Galileo for the assignment.'

The flight took three days. When the Galileo re-emerged into communication range, its sensor logs showed the shell opposite the hole was continuous. It had searched over twenty thousand square kilometres. Wilson ordered it to be refuelled, and sent it out again. After seven flights, it had scanned the entire hemisphere on the other side of the barrier. There was no hole, no passage through to the imprisoned star.

*

Three months after they discovered the Dark Fortress, Wilson called Oscar and Tunde to his cabin for a mission conference. 'I need to know if we're going to learn anything more from the Dark Fortress,' he said to Tunde.

'Are you joking?' the surprised physicist asked. 'There is more exotic physics in there than the human race has discovered since an apple fell on Newton's head.'

'I'm sure there is. But now we have the major components identified, how much can you and your team realistically add to that? I mean, we don't even know if this really does generate the barrier.'

'It's a logical conclusion.'

'Admittedly, yes. But can you prove it? More importantly, can you prove it with the sensors and instruments we have available on board?'

Tunde looked defiant for a moment, but eventually nodded reluctantly. 'No. Not a chance, really. As you say, we can map what's there. But determining function and interconnectivity ... On this scale, it's the kind of project which would absorb every living theorist for the next two centuries. We need a bigger ship, in fact we need to establish an outpost the size of the High Angel, and with its manufacturing capacity. The Commonwealth will have to open a chain of wormholes out here, that's the only way we can apply the kind of resources we need to crack this.'

'It's not going to happen,' Oscar said. 'Oh I agree, it should. But from a political point of view, all you've got here is the mother of all esoteric physics problems. That doesn't gain you the kind of funding you're talking about.'

'Nigel Sheldon will understand,' Tunde said.

'Yes, he will,' Wilson said. 'More than anybody, he made this flight possible. But even he can't carry the entire Commonwealth Senate, not for that kind of financial commitment. If we'd found anything out here, anything that indicated why the barrier was established, any hint of a current threat to the Commonwealth, then we might earn ourselves a couple of return missions at the very least. But it's an enigma. And we've lived with enigmas for a long time now. We're shocked and excited by them at first, then we just learn to live with them. Eventually, we don't even question them any more. Look at the Silfen. Why don't electronics work on their worlds? How the hell do they really travel between star systems? Our popular myth has it there are forest paths between worlds. That's what the more arcane members of our race believe. More practical people believe they spread themselves across the galaxy with arkships millennia ago. It doesn't matter, because we live with it, it doesn't affect us. Now as far as we can determine, the barrier, for all its grandeur, isn't going to affect us either. There are no alien battle fleets waiting out here to blow Earth to pieces and steal our gold and our women. This is just one more incomprehensible relic that will take us five hundred years to understand. One day, after that, you and I will be standing here and laughing at how puzzled we once were.'

'You're taking us home, aren't you?' Tunde realized.

'Not immediately. But we've certainly devoted enough time to the Dark Fortress. Unless either of you have a viable alternative, I'm going to continue with our flight around the barrier. After that, if there's nothing else to be found, we'll examine the poles as originally planned. We might follow up with a fast examination of Dyson Beta. I'd like to confirm that it is the same before we head for home.'

'I'll concur with that,' Oscar said. 'Team leaders are getting asked how much longer the investigation is going on for. Nobody has actually complained yet, but I'd say it's time to move on.'

They both looked at Tunde.

'All right,' he said. 'We do have enough data to keep the universities busy for a decade. But I hope to God you're wrong about the next stage of the project. Understanding the technology in the Dark Fortress would elevate our species to unbelievable heights. We could become transgalactic, for heaven's sake; there really would be no limits to what we could achieve.'

*

Anna and her little team of controllers recalled the satellites; carefully threading them back through the moving maze that was the four lattice spheres. Out of the thirty-seven they'd deployed inside the Dark Fortress, nine had been lost, either in the centre or due to communication failure. When the remainder were back in their hangar cradles, Tu Lee sent the *Second Chance* back into hyperspace at a speed that would complete the circuit of the barrier in another five days.

*

The alarm brought Wilson struggling out of a deep comfortable sleep. He floundered around on the cot for a second, trying to shield his eyes from the cabin lights which had switched on automatically. Anna groaned, squinting and blinking.

'What the fuck—' she grunted.

'The bridge has declared an emergency,' Wilson's e-butler told him.

'Son of a bitch!' He rolled off the cot and headed straight for the door. His virtual vision was flashing up dozens of icons. It was difficult to focus on them and the corridor he was half-running down. Fortunately, the starship's designers had stuck with maritime tradition and kept the captain's quarters close to the bridge.

The status icons didn't indicate any physical damage to the superstructure, and the hyperdrive was functioning normally Defence was equally reassuring. *No immediate danger, then.* Wilson forced himself to relax as the bridge door slid open for him. That was when he started to review the sensor icons. The hysradar was breaking through the barrier.

'Shit!'

The bridge's small night shift crew glanced round at his exclamation.

'It started a couple of minutes ago,' Oscar said as he rose from the command console chair. 'I ordered a halt to our flight.'

Wilson glanced at the forward portals as he sat down in the command chair. 'Are we still in the wormhole?'

'Yes, sir.'

'Okay, Tu Lee, plot a course directly out of here. Implement it the second I tell you.'

'Aye, sir.'

Both portals were showing the hysradar scan of the barrier surface. It seemed to be fluctuating, bowing inwards as if it was being bombarded by projectiles. Then Wilson acknowledged the scale; if objects were hitting it, they'd be the size of gas-giants. *The hostile force! The reason the barrier was established.* 'Astrophysics, do we know what's causing that?'

'No, sir,' Bruno said cheerfully. 'Not a clue.'

'Is there anything else out here? A ship? Some weapons system which could be causing that?'

'Nothing,' Sandy Lanier reported from the sensor console. 'The hysradar scan is clean for a thousand AUs this side of the barrier.'

Wilson frowned at the bridge portals. The fluctuations were growing larger. And they weren't going to find out why sitting out here peering over the parapet. *Decision time.*

'Hyperdrive, take us in to one million kilometres of the barrier,' Wilson ordered. 'Defence, force fields on. Let's see what's happening.'

The rest of the bridge day shift arrived, sitting at the consoles that had been left unmanned, or standing behind the night shift. The atmosphere of nerves and genuine excitement was the same as Wilson remembered from the *Eagle II*'s cabin as they came in to land. He rubbed his hand slightly self-consciously over his creased white T-shirt before brushing strands of floppy hair away from his brow; the chair's leather was already sticking to his bare legs below his jockey shorts. For a moment he considered hurrying off to change. It was hardly the most dignified image for history (and the on-board sensors were definitely recording); but then half the bridge crew was dressed the same. *Ah, what the hell . . .*

'One million kilometres, sir,' Sandy Lanier reported.

'Take us out of hyperspace.'

One of the portals switched to an image of pure aquamarine blue. Dark streaks blossomed from the centre, and peeled open. This time they didn't have to switch the sensors to infrared to see the barrier.

'My God,' Tunde said hoarsely. 'It's becoming transparent.'

Dyson Alpha was wavering in and out of visibility thirty AUs ahead of them, only marginally brighter than the rest of the stars behind. The fluctuations indicated by the hysradar scan were inaccurate, the barrier wasn't moving in any physical dimension, it was losing cohesion.

'Sensors, defence, is there anything shooting at it?' Wilson asked desperately.

'No, sir. No energy of any kind. Local quantum state is also stable as far as we can tell. The barrier is ... Oh wow! It's gone! Hysradar scans are clear. The fucker's vanished.'

Wilson stared at the two portals. The one with the gravitonic scan was empty. A second later, when the light reached them, Dyson Alpha burned steadily at the centre of a colossal blank circle.

We're still seeing the other side of the barrier, he realized, *it's going to take the light from the stars beyond over four hours to travel thirty AUs.*

'Full passive sensor sweep,' Wilson ordered. 'Show me what's in there.'

'This can't be coincidence,' Oscar said. He sounded shocked, even a little frightened. 'It's been there for over a thousand years, and then it vanishes just as we come along? No way. No goddamn way. Something knows we're here.'

The bridge crew were looking round anxiously, seeking reassurance from one another. Wilson had been thinking along similar lines himself; quite a loud voice in his head was urging him to run. *And don't look back.* The starfield was beginning to reappear around the edges of the barrier as light swept in towards the *Second Chance*. It gave the rather unfortunate impression of a giant mantrap opening its jaws.

Wilson turned to Tunde. 'What's the Dark Fortress doing?'

The physics section went into a fevered huddle over their consoles, running analysis routines over the hysradar scans. Wilson watched the results coming through on one of his desk screens, not that he could understand the details, but the overall impression was easy enough.

'There's still something there,' Tunde said. 'Hysradar scan shows it's smaller than before. We're probably picking up the outer lattice sphere. Wait – yes, it's rotating. The shell has gone. And that's a very strange quantum fluctuation signature inside it. That wasn't there before.'

'A wormhole?' Wilson asked.

'No. I don't recognize it at all.'

'Threat assessment?'

Tunde gave him a slightly irked look. 'Nothing obvious. I'll get back to you on that one.'

A picture of Dyson Alpha's planetary system was building up on one of the bridge portals. The two gas-giants were both smaller than Jupiter, orbiting at four and a half AUs and seventeen AUs from their star. While of the three solid planets, the largest had a diameter of fourteen thousand kilometres and orbited one point two AUs out from the sun. The remaining two were both smaller, and in mildly ecliptic orbits a lot further out. They called the innermost planet Alpha Major and focused the starship's main sensor suite on it.

'My God,' Sandy Lanier said. 'Will you look at those readings.'

Alpha Major's visual spectrum showed water on a scale that indicated oceans, and an oxygen-nitrogen atmosphere. It was also a strong source of neutrinos. 'A very heavy level of fusion activity,' Russell commented. 'I'd say total power generation exceeds our Big15 worlds combined.'

'What the hell uses that much power?' Oscar muttered.

A measurable percentage of it, they discovered, was pumped into communications; throughout the electromagnetic spectrum the planet was shining like a small nova. The starship's RI began recording the multitude of overlapping signals, but without a key none of its decryption algorithms were of any use.

The greatest fusion usage was the most obvious to see. Space above Alpha Major was thick with activity. Slender brilliant threads of fusion drives created their own ring nebula, extending from the upper atmosphere out to a million kilometres. Not that they ended there, instead they began to disperse. Fleets of ships were accelerating at three or four gees away from the planet, slashing long scars of plasma across the void before finally cutting their engines to coast to destinations across the star system. Hundreds more were on their approach, firing their engines to decelerate into the perpetual swarm circling the planet.

Over fifty moonlets were in orbit two hundred thousand kilometres out, with knots of small fusion flames wrapped around them as ships came and went. They must have been captured asteroids, their orbit and spacing was too regular to occur naturally. Each one was surrounded by massive industrial stations.

'Don't they care about their environment?' Antonia asked. 'It can't be safe having fusion ships flying that close to a habitable planet.'

'Those are big ships,' Anna said. 'At least the same size as the *Second Chance*, some are a lot bigger. And their exhaust is helium, they're probably using boron fusion.'

'Expensive,' Antonia muttered.

'Depends on your technology level,' Oscar said. 'This is not a primitive civilization.'

'Where are the ships going?' Wilson asked.

The *Second Chance* began to expand its observation. They found an astonishing level of technological activity on and around every planet. The two outer solid planets, though cold and airless, were dotted by vast force field domes, artificial habitats whose vegetation matched the spectrum to be found on the landmasses of Alpha Major. Fusion globe suns illuminated each one. Spacecraft were almost as numerous above them as Alpha Major, wrapping the worlds in a perpetual flexing toroid of blazing light. They also had dozens of industrialized moonlets.

Out among the gas-giants, the pattern was repeated. Every large moon was home to the habitat force field domes, and surrounded by ships and industrialized moonlets. The thin rings orbiting the gas-giants played host to thousands of stations that latched on to the rocky particles, slowly digesting them. On the dozens of outermost moons, rocks that were essentially large asteroids, force field habitats had engulfed them completely. Tightly whorled contortions in the magnetosphere revealed colossal structures in low equatorial orbit. When the *Second Chance*'s sensors tracked them, they found they were trailing cables or pipes down into the upper cloud bands.

As the details appeared on the bridge portal, they made Wilson nostalgic for the future he'd thought he was pioneering back in 2050, the never-happened golden era of humanity's High Frontier. This was the kind of inter-system society any technological civilization would eventually build if it was somehow cut off from the stars.

Why would it be cut off, though?

Three hours after the barrier had vanished, Sandy turned the sensor console over to Anna, though she hung around for a couple of hours to see what developed.

One of the secondary telescopes was watching the turmoil that was space around Alpha Major. 'Looks like some ships are heading outsystem,' Anna said. Eleven streaks of fusion plasma were visible beyond the distance where most of the ships had powered down to coast-flight mode. 'Accelerating at five gees, and have been for three hours now. That's one hell of a velocity they're hitting. I hope they've got force field protection. A small molecule can seriously ruin your day at that speed.'

'I'm tracking several similar flights from both gas-giants,' Jean Douvoir said.

'Any coming our way?' Wilson asked.

'Not really, sir. One will pass within eight AUs.'

'Safe enough, but keep tracking it. If it alters course in our direction I want to know about it.'

'Aye, sir.'

'Tunde, do you think they're capable of picking up our hysradar scans?'

'I'd say they have the technology to detect quantum wave fluctuations, which might give them an indirect clue we were here. But we haven't detected any hysradar emissions from inside the star system, so they probably haven't got a direct detector. There's also the question of intent. Why would you build a hysradar if you're confined inside a barrier thirty AUs across?'

'Do they have the technology to build the barrier?' Wilson asked sharply.

Tunde grimaced, reluctant to give an opinion. 'I'd say not. Judging from what we've seen, I'd put them on a par with us, with the obvious difference of wormholes. The Dark Fortress is orders of magnitude above anything we're capable of.'

'That implies the barrier was put up by an outside agency.'

'It's looking that way, yes.'

'They were confined inside, then. Someone thought they were a threat.' Wilson turned his attention back to the magnificent astroengineering accomplishments which the sensors were revealing. Given his background, it was hard not to be envious of Dyson Alpha's civilization. 'Why?'

'I'm more concerned about why it was switched off,' Oscar said. '*Somebody* observed us here.'

'That doesn't make a lot of sense,' Wilson said. 'If you were attempting to close off this civilization, why remove the barrier the first time a ship investigates it?'

'They didn't "attempt" to cut them off,' Tu Lee said. 'They succeeded.'

'Which makes switching the barrier off all the more nonsensical.'

'I don't know what you're worrying about it for,' Anna said. 'There's a simple way of finding out now.'

The bridge crew all looked at her. She grinned back, small spiral OCtattoos on her cheeks shimmering a soft silver.

'Ask them,' she said, and pointed at the portal.

*

On the third day after the barrier fell, they used the hysradar to scan the system. Wilson had heard every argument for and against making contact. Most people, himself included, were being cautious, despite what they'd seen of the Dyson aliens. Dudley Bose was keen to start hailing them; while Oscar wanted to turn the *Second Chance* round and head straight back to the Commonwealth, he was still badly worried by the timing of the barrier coming down.

It was the first time Wilson really wished they had instantaneous communications back to the Commonwealth. He would have been relieved to pass the buck on this question. Anna was right, they could learn a lot from initiating contact. But now it looked certain the Dyson aliens had been confined, shipboard speculation was heavily focused on the reason. Their civilization was impressive, but not *that* threatening.

There were now eighty-three ships heading out from the star system. After three days of continual flight at five gees acceleration the first wave had now travelled over ten AUs, and still more were being launched. The first ships from the outermost gas-giant had almost reached the boundary where the barrier had been.

Nobody on board the *Second Chance* could work out what they intended to do once they were outside the thirty AU limit, especially as the ships weren't designed for interstellar travel. But the crew had spent their time gathering more data on the Dyson Alpha system. It wasn't just the planets which had been colonized. There were two asteroid belts, one on either side of Alpha Major's orbit, which were extensively settled. And each of the gas-giant Trojan points, with their broad cluster of medium-sized planetoids, accommodated thriving spaceborne societies. More intriguing – certainly to the physicists – was the swarm of rings, five hundred kilometres in diameter and protected by force fields, which were orbiting three million kilometres above the star's corona. They seemed to be absorbing the solar wind, siphoning in massive currents of elementary particles that jetted out of the flares and sunspots below them.

Wilson finally authorized the use of the hysradar to obtain a more detailed chart of the star system and its inhabitants. Nobody was really surprised when it showed tens of thousands of the big ships coasting between planets, moons, asteroid habitats, and the industrial stations. The total was slightly unnerving given how alone the *Second Chance* was. Also unforeseen were the number of stray asteroids out beyond the second gas-giant they detected which showed signs of colonization and industrial activity. Three of them were only a couple of AUs away. Wilson gave Sandy Lanier, the duty sensor officer, a very hard time for not picking up their neutrino emissions earlier. He paid for it that night, when Anna gave him a lecture on how small the fusion generators were, and how big space in general was. 'They must be just starting to build on those asteroids,' she claimed heatedly. 'If there's anything big and dangerous close to this ship, our department will spot it for you.'

He managed to grumble a mild apology, and said they should take a really good look at the nearby asteroids. Having examples of the Dyson civilization so close was an excellent chance to learn what they could without being observed themselves.

She accepted the apology, and let him kiss and make up. They were getting good at finding innovative ways to use the low gee of the crew ring.

With a more complete picture of Dyson Alpha's system established, the starship's hysradar was focused on Dyson Beta. The range was extreme, but even so the return showed that the barrier around the second star remained intact. It strengthened Oscar's argument that the removal of Dyson Alpha's barrier had been triggered by their arrival. Not that anyone could come up with a convincing reason why, and the scenario certainly wasn't one of the contingency plans so carefully prepared before they let Anshun. All of which left Wilson even more aware of how critical his decisions were now.

He ordered the sensor department to resume collecting information on the Dyson Alpha system.

It was while they were scanning the nearby asteroids for high-resolution images that the first firefight broke out a third of the way round the star system. The electromagnetic sensors spotted it first, several large em pulses erupting halfway between the orbits of the two gas-giants. They were quickly confirmed as nuclear explosions. The second barrage broke out as exhaust plumes suddenly streaked out all around the trio of explosions, exposing two squadrons of over thirty ships converging on each other. The fighting had started when they were a million kilometres apart. Now they were all accelerating towards each other at over seven gees. Missiles and gamma lasers turned the shrinking gap into a lethal hurricane of energy. Exploding ships added their fury to the radiation deluge.

Hysradar swiftly scanned the area in real-time, finding a large, expanding cloud of debris and vapour with several ruined ships tumbling through it. Thirty-two million kilometres away, five colonized asteroids were surrounded by a shoal of ships whose active sensors were probing the battlezone.

'Glad we weren't there,' Oscar exclaimed.

Wilson stared at the display with its crumbling flecks of irradiated matter hurtling apart. It reminded him of the ridiculous slow-motion explosions in the blockbuster films of his youth, where steroidal Hollywood action stars outran the blastwave. 'Defence,' he asked slowly. 'Could our force fields have stood up to that kind of assault?'

'The initial blasts, sir, possibly. But it got pretty hellish in there towards the end.'

'Thank you.'

He glanced at Oscar, and inclined his head. The two of them went into the senior officers' briefing room, and opaqued the glass wall. Screens around the long central table glowed blue and crimson from the sensor graphics they were showing.

'I know what you're thinking,' Wilson said as he sat on a corner of the table.

'It's not difficult. I've been saying it ever since the barrier came down. We should leave. These developments have pushed us way outside our original mission scenario. We were supposed to be a scouting flight. This is something else entirely.'

'I know, I know.' Wilson ran his hand back through his hair; it was getting longer than he liked. 'But we still don't know why they were confined, and we certainly don't know who or what put the barrier up. We were sent here to find out. That means we haven't completed our mission, not to my satisfaction.'

'That fight was a damn good indicator why they were penned up in here. It doesn't come any clearer than that to me.'

'Maybe, but we can't go home with just an assumption. I need to be certain.'

'It's not just the Dyson civilization you have to consider,

563

Wilson. Why was that barrier taken down for us? Doesn't that bother you?'

'Of course it does. But the people who can tell us about the barrier are right here.'

'We can't ask them, it's too risky. In our whole history, the human race has only ever let off five nuclear warheads in anger. And they were the most extraordinary, exceptional circumstances. That fight of theirs just saw eight hundred and seventy-two fusion bombs detonating inside of thirty minutes, and half of them had diverted energy output functions. They are dangerous, Wilson. Very, very dangerous.'

'The kind of weapons involved in any conflict are determined by the nature of the battleground and the technology available. If we are attacked out here, I'm quite prepared to use our nukes. It would be an appropriate response. Does my willingness to do my duty make the human race a bunch of dangerous killers?'

'You're twisting this. I'm on record here: I don't like this situation. It is my opinion we should leave.'

'We can't. For all it's an unexpected outcome, this is why we're here. Discovery and opportunity, Oscar. We can't turn our back on it. That would be less than human. I'm going to authorize a remote investigatory contact.'

Oscar closed his eyes and let out a long dispirited breath. 'Okay. It is your choice, and I will support it. But can we at least be cautious about it?'

Wilson smiled at him. 'Believe me, we are going to be so cautious you'll think I've turned dangerously paranoid.'

*

They set out the rules of contact at the next daily meeting of the department heads, drawing on the Commonwealth protocols for alien contact, and adapting them to their own unique situation.

'It is my intention to discover what we can about the Dyson aliens without ourselves being observed,' Wilson said. 'Now we've seen how volatile they are, I am not prepared to take the *Second Chance* into orbit around any planet or moon. God alone knows what weapon systems they have in orbit around their large population centres.'

'The initial investigation will be a contact team deployment to a deserted artefact, something big, an abandoned habitat or wrecked spaceship,' Oscar said. 'Anything that will show us how they live, give us an indication of their physical shape, their culture. If we get lucky there might be some electronic memory units we can access. Whatever we choose, it will be a minimum of five million kilometres from any settlement or ship. We can manage a five-gee acceleration in an emergency combat situation, which is significantly lower than most of the ships we've seen flying round out there; so our primary tactical advantage is our ftl drive. I'd like to avoid any sort of chase altogether, therefore the whole procedure will be conducted on a minimum emission basis.'

'Before we begin this investigation, I'd like some idea of their response if we're exposed to them,' Wilson said. He glanced round the table until he found Emmanuelle Verbeke, their alien culture officer. 'Can you give us any insight on their society, yet?'

'Very little other than the obvious,' she said. 'What we've seen matches our standard simulations for a non-ftl technological species. They've followed a logical progressive route of development across their star system. Given the extent and obvious success of their colonization I am slightly puzzled by the fight we saw. I would have expected more social stability. But as we really know nothing about their culture it would be inappropriate to speculate too much on the conflict at this point.'

'We've made no progress on decrypting any of their signals,'

Anna said. 'That's worrying. I don't expect the RI algorithms to begin immediate translations, but there were some areas I expected progress with.'

'Such as?' Oscar asked.

'Video or holographic signals for a start. There are basic formatting rules which data of that nature has to follow, even if they see in ultraviolet or air-sonar, there will be display template patterns that can be determined. So far we simply haven't found any. Their transmissions seem to be almost completely random, and they're all analogue signals, which is even stranger. Of course it doesn't help that we're receiving so many of them. Overlap and interference is considerable. I would at least have hoped to play you an example of their language by now, but I can't even do that.'

'It is unusual that we don't even know what they look like,' Emmanuelle said. 'If the situation were reversed, and the Dyson aliens were lurking close to a Commonwealth world, they would soon be able to gain an understanding of us from what we broadcast.'

'We are recording it all,' Anna said. 'If we eventually make contact, and the Dyson aliens want to talk to us, then we'll have a full understanding of whatever communicative pathways they employ. After that we can start translating the signals we're recording now. It'll be helpful in case they do become inhibited when they find out we're here, and start restricting their output; what we're receiving at the moment could be quite valuable later on.'

'You mean we're catching them off guard?' Wilson asked.

'Essentially, yes.'

'Okay, I don't have any problem with that.'

'If they find us creeping round out here, are they likely to attack?' Oscar asked.

'If it was me, I'd be curious,' Emmanuelle said. 'But that's a personal thing. It's also a human thing. Given our current knowledge base, there really is no way of knowing.'

'Then we will conduct the investigation on a worst-case basis,' Wilson said. 'The contact team will be armed and have fire authority if threatened. The *Second Chance* will operate on combat alert as soon as we cross the old barrier threshold.'

For the first time since the barrier fell, Oscar actually looked happy.

'Anna, did you find anything suitable for us to start with?' Wilson asked.

'Yes, actually. There are a lot of spaceship wrecks floating round out there.' She gave Oscar an uncomfortable look. 'It would appear the Dyson aliens do fight a lot among themselves. I think we do genuinely need to be cautious.'

'We will be,' Wilson said, giving her a warning stare. 'Have you got a suitable starting point for us?'

'I think so, yes.'

*

Nobody actually said anything, but the bridge crew was very conscious of passing inside the line where the barrier had been. *Was it going to spring back into existence, trapping them?*

The hysradar scanned behind them, scouring space and hyperspace. There was no change to the quantum signature of spacetime. Nothing altered in or around the Dark Fortress.

They waited just inside the barrier line for over an hour before Wilson finally said: 'Okay, Tu Lee, take us over to the rock.'

'Aye, sir.'

*

McCain Gilbert waited in the contact team's operational office, not too far away from the bridge. By contrast, this compartment only had a couple of consoles, but a lot more display screens. Three long tables were seating most of his forty-strong team members, who were regarding the blank screens with a controlled patience. The absence of any current sensor data couldn't damp the sense of excitement vibrating round the room. It was present in the short terse comments shot between friends, the way shift rotas had been forgotten so everyone could cram in, drink packets on the tables, lack of the usual horseplay. The contact team were finally coming into their own.

So far, they had been the most underused department on board, simply looking over everyone else's shoulder as vast quantities of physics data flowed back into the starship. Now, that tolerance and waiting was being rewarded.

Oscar came in just as the *Second Chance* emerged from its wormhole. Mac waved him into the vacant chair next to his own, and together they watched the wormhole's blue light fade off the screens allowing the cameras to focus on the chunk of rock they were rendezvoused with. Anna, who found it and therefore had the right, had named it the Watchtower. A long slice of rock, with a station of some kind at one end. Given its tower-like shape, and its position – one and a half AUs beyond the outer gas-giant orbit – she felt it analogous to some ancient imperial outpost, a long-forgotten garrison fort, watching across the desolate barbarian territories for anything which could threaten civilization.

'Looks like we were right about it being inactive,' Oscar said. 'Thankfully.'

Long-range passive scans had shown no infrared emission. There was no neutrino activity, or electromagnetic broadcasts. As the rock had a fast rotation, once every twenty-six minutes, they had concluded it was now abandoned, most probably a victim of some ancient battle.

As he watched the images appear, backed up by the slow trickle of data, Mac was convinced they were right. The rock was fashioned like a sharp blade, over a kilometre and a half long, but never more than a couple of hundred metres wide. Every side was sheer, with razor edges. So obviously a splinter that had snapped off cleanly from whatever asteroid had been nuked into oblivion.

'That must have been one brute of an explosion,' Mac said idly. 'We've never seen them build anything on a small asteroid.'

The station was rooted in the surface around the wider end of the fragment. Cubes and pyramids and mushrooms of polytitanium composite made up the bulk of it, their once-strong hulls now as brittle as a biscuit from centuries of vacuum exposure. Crumbling fissures exposed reinforcement ribs below, while the colour had been mottled down to a grubby lead-grey by uncountable micro-meteorite punctures and constant molecular ablation. Spiky fungal structures moulded from toughened plastics and metaloceramics lurked between the larger sections. They, too, were fraying around the edges, leaving long delicate strands poking out from ragged cavities.

'At least you won't have any trouble gaining access,' Oscar told him. 'There are more holes than walls.'

'Yeah, on the upper sections. Those lower portions look more intact. Ah, here we go, the deep scan's coming in.'

They leaned forward in unison, peering at the small holo-gram portal which was now showing a three-dimensional map of the station's internal layout.

'That looks like a surrealist's maze,' Oscar said. 'It's got to be some kind of industrial refinery. Those are all pipes, aren't they?'

'Or corridors, or warren tunnels. Remember the jarrofly nests we found on Tandil? We thought they were just beautiful coral outcrops until the swarm came out.'

'Yeah, maybe.' Oscar gave his friend a wide smile. 'Only one way to be sure.'

'Right. Send us in to do the dirty work. Never fails.'

'Damn right. I'll just lounge around in here, maybe have

me one of those gourmet meals from the canteen, then access a hot TSI drama. But you be sure to enjoy yourself in those bollock-squeezer suits of yours while you're over there.'

'Once I set foot on that lump of rock, make first contact with the Dysons, it'll be my name that our race remembers, not yours.'

'Tut tut: vanity, the most tragic sin of all. Hey, Mr Legend, what are your first words going to be when you set that photogenic foot down?'

Mac struck a sincerely thoughtful pose. 'I thought something like: Fuck me, now I remember why you shouldn't eat curry before you put on a space suit.'

'Cool. Historic, even. I like that.'

Mac grinned, then stood up. 'Okay everybody, eyes and ears to the front, please. Our captain is going to hold the *Second Chance* a hundred kilometres off the Watchtower as a safety precaution. That means we'll be using the shuttles to get ourselves over there. Preliminary scouting party will be myself and team C. The main objective on the first flight is to ascertain occupancy levels. If that is confirmed as zero, we'll conduct an initial survey. Following that, I want to operate a rotating three-team shift pattern to map out the Watchtower's contents. As you can see, there's a lot of pipes and tunnels and shit to get through. We're going archaeological on this one, which I know is a little different to the kind of exploration most of you are used to. What we need is clues as to what these critters look like, what they eat, what they drink, who they voted for, if their team won the Cup, all that crap. So what you have to track down are artefacts that will open any sort of window into their culture for us. Teams B and F, I want you to concentrate on their electronics, or optronics, or difference engines, or whatever the hell they used. If there are any data fragments left in any system over there, I want them downloaded and copied. Got all that?'

A rumble of happy agreement went round the room.

'Fine, team C with me now, we're suiting up. Shuttle departs in thirty minutes. Now while we're scratching round over there, Oscar here is assuming his usual job of exploration supervisor, which means he'll be watching our asses from his nice comfortable office chair. I'm sure you remember the drill, all major decisions are his – I don't want any rogue calls on this one, no just going round the next corner because it looks interesting. If there's any doubt about something, clear it with Oscar first. Team A, you're our direct observation monitors on the first flight. B, D, E, if we okay the site, you're on next. I suggest you get some rest accordingly.'

He turned to leave. Oscar caught his arm.

'I know everyone thinks I'm obsessing over the barrier coming down,' Oscar said. 'But take care over there.'

'Don't worry. Coward is my middle name.'

*

It wasn't until a full twenty-four hours after Mac had landed on the Watchtower that Dudley Bose finally got his chance to regain some of the limelight. He'd thought that as a member of contact team A he would be among the first humans to meet the Dysons. That hadn't happened, of course, not with McCain Gilbert pre-empting him.

Dudley had considered his pre-departure appointment to the starship's contact team as a smooth move. After all, Wilson and his senior officers couldn't deny he was the Commonwealth's expert on the Dyson Pair, from an astrophysics angle at any rate. And with his first-life engineering degree expanding his knowledge base on a practical level, he was an obvious choice for the contact team as well as the science staff.

So far on the voyage his knowledge had been left sadly unapplied. He understood very little about the quantum state of the barrier – managing the university's astronomy department single-handed had left very little time for him to keep up-to-date on the theoretical front of physics. And although the insides of the Dark Fortress remained visually spectacular, he was unable to offer any insight into the nature of that gargantuan mechanism.

While the *Second Chance* was examining the Dark Fortress, most of his time had been spent in his cabin by himself, recording commentaries. His contract with Gralmond Web-News called for informed opinions and interpretation of the information which the starship gathered. A pop science pundit, basically. So he would watch the day's results come in, and provide an explanation which was dumbed down to the lowest level possible. His time as a lecturer, reducing complex facts to a series of easily digestible chunks, followed by his meteoric exposure to the media and their demands for simplified sound-bite presentation, made him perfectly qualified for the job.

But the Watchtower had finally presented him with the opportunity to enhance his profile. Physically placing him on the ultimate human frontier would make it *his* flight. He, Dudley Bose, was due to become the human interface with the mystery of the Dyson Pair.

Then McCain Gilbert went and announced the team schedule, and Dudley had to wait for yet another day. Until it became his turn he was once again reduced to a second-hand role, watching through the shuttle's camera as McCain Gilbert jetted himself over to the large alien structures on the Watchtower, and spouting banalities like: 'This is it. Any moment now. Yes! Contact. How much this differs from our usual first encounter with an alien environment. CSI contact personnel normally walk through a wormhole and place their foot firmly on the ground. Here, you can see my friend Mac actually having to cling on to the edge of a hole with his hand. Now, wait, he's shining his lights through into the structure. You're seeing the first glimpse of a whole new alien universe.'

In truth, Mac's careful drift through the structure was tedium itself. It was quite obvious the station had been deserted for a long time. The polytitanium hull was still mildly radioactive, its decay rate allowing an accurate dating on the explosion of two hundred and eleven years. 'So there can be nothing left alive in there. Or if there is, it's a life form very different from anything we know.'

The compartments weren't particularly strange. Engineering principles were reasonably universal. The hull material was made up from sandwiched layers; the pressure wall, thermal insulation, structural reinforcement, cable ducts. First indications were that the cube Mac entered was a habitation section. Several internal walls had rectangular hatchways. 'They are two metres across, larger than human ones, which indicate the Dysons might be bigger than us.' *In case you couldn't work that out for yourselves.* There were times Dudley hated himself for what he had to do.

Almost every compartment had an opening into the broad tunnel-like corridors that curved and twisted through the interior – none of those had hatches. Mac's suit lights found octagonal mounting blocks in the compartments, jutting out of the walls at the apex of structural ribs. At one time they'd held large units of machinery. Now, there were just empty brackets and load pins. 'It's been stripped clean. Whoever won the battle must have taken their booty with them.'

Mac's whole EVA was a record of empty chambers and long dark tunnels. The Watchtower had a sense of rejection about it rather than abandonment. Cold, dark, feebly radioactive, it was simply of no consequence any more; both purpose and meaning had ceased when the lethal radiation pierced every corner.

It was an impression that was now strengthening in Dudley's mind as he watched the horn of rock expanding across the starfield. Everything out here was grey, leaving very little difference between the rock and the alien station perched on it. He could just make out the other shuttle hovering above the cube, a silver and gold speck with green and scarlet navigation strobes flashing incessantly. Their light shimmered across the scuff marks on the perspex of the little port he was pressed against.

'Helmet.'

'Huh?' Dudley turned round to see Emmanuelle Verbeke on the other side of the aisle. She was putting her own helmet on.

'Time to put your helmet on,' she said.

'Right. Sure.' He gave her a thank-you smile, and retrieved his helmet from the fuseto patch on the side of the chair. He had got on quite well with Emmanuelle since leaving Anshun. Thankfully, since they were partnered up together in team A. Not that he got to socialize with her much outside duty shifts and training sessions. He was still somewhat conscious about his physical shape. Everyone else on board had been through a full rejuvenation, at most ten years ago. He was the starship's official geriatric. Any early hope that would give him an air of distinction had quickly faded.

The shuttle's small thrusters were firing almost continually as it manoeuvred in for rendezvous, sounding as if someone with a hammer was knocking on the fuselage. Dudley accommodated the slight swaying motion it set up as he lowered the tough transparent bubble over his head. The lip-like seals gripped tight, and he fastened the secondary mechanical seal. His e-butler immediately ran final integration checks, confirming the suit was fully functional.

He activated his suit's force field as he went into the airlock. Team C and three of team A were already waiting on the fuselage grid which skirted the outer lock. Dudley took care to anchor himself before pulling his manoeuvring pack out of its storage bin. It was McCain Gilbert himself who held the pack steady while Dudley pushed his arms through the straps. The unit stuck itself to his spacesuit, plyplastic straps contracting around him.

'You all right?' Mac asked. His helmet was very close to Dudley's, allowing him to peer through the faint silvering.

'Sure.' However blasé he tried to sound, the reality of being out in open space within an alien star system was making his heart judder. The telemetry would be available to Mac. Dudley looked round to find the reassuring bright star that was *Second Chance*. Seeing it shining against the starfield made his breathing a little easier. He searched further, trying to find familiar star patterns amid the strange constellations.

Team C began jetting over to the Watchtower a hundred metres away. Dudley held Emmanuelle's manoeuvring pack as she shrugged her way into it. Receiving a thumbs up in gratitude. He enjoyed that, it made him feel like a fully paid up member of the team.

'Right, that's everybody out,' said Frances Rawlins, the leader of team C. 'Make sure you've secured your equipment bag before you leave the shuttle. You can freeflight in your own time. Head for the beacon they've put up on the alien station. We'll regroup there, and move on in.'

Dudley made sure the cylindrical bag was fastened to his belt. The others were slowly lifting off the fuselage grid. Tiny squirts of white gas puffed out of their manoeuvring pack nozzles, just visible in the dusky light of the distant star. His virtual hand gripped the pack's joystick, and he tilted it forward. The gas produced a dull rushing sound, vibrating against his back. But his boots left the grid, and he was floating away from the shuttle. Once again his heart went yammering as adrenaline cut loose into his bloodstream. He couldn't believe he was actually doing this. There was a holiday he'd taken on his first life when he'd signed up to go paragliding; trusting himself to a sheet of fabric and praying the straps held as he and the instructor jumped off the top of a mountain. The rush of tension and exhilaration which hit him simultaneously when he saw treetops below his feet was like nothing he'd ever known. Now here it was again, far more intense than the first time.

As before, he forced himself to relax into the inevitable. It just took a while to convince his body there was actually nothing wrong, that the suit and the manoeuvring pack were working fine and taking care of him. Inside the helmet he was grinning like a madman. His free virtual hand tapped a microphone icon, then keyed in a privacy code.

'I'm approaching the strange alien station we've called the Watchtower. All of us agree now that it was misnamed. This is no guard outpost, simply the sad remnants of an industrial facility that was damaged during a conflict that went nuclear. I can't help but feel regret that all the effort and cost which went into establishing such an enterprise should fall victim to this primitive lack of emotional control. Although the Dyson aliens have accomplished so much, and I concede some of their technological accomplishments exceed ours, I hope they can still learn from the way our society resolves conflicts and disagreements.' That would go down well back home. Always make the audience feel slightly superior.

The course graphic inside his virtual vision showed him heading off to one side of the beacon. He corrected. Over-corrected. Then had to tip the joystick firmly the other way. This was exactly what his skill training memory instinctively warned him against. He just couldn't integrate that knowledge at an autonomic reflex level. So he wobbled his way forward, gas burping from every nozzle of his manoeuvring pack in a seemingly random pattern, and keeping a cautious eye on his relative velocity.

Frances Rawlins was easing her way in through the gap beside the beacon as he finally came to rest just above her. The other members of team C followed. Dudley looked round eagerly once he was inside, but the compartment was something of an anticlimax. A simple box of blue-grey metal, flooded with vibrant pools of light by the suit beams. Nothing to hint at alien-ness.

'Now we're inside I can't emphasize enough to use caution,' Frances said. 'The Ops office is watching out for us individually, but they can't compensate for every mistake. The only solution is don't make any. We're not in a race, we'll keep searching round until we've acquired the data which the captain needs, so don't rush anything. Now, teams B, D, and E have already explored down to level five, and radially they went as far as sections A3 and A8 on your chart. They've placed comrelays to cover that area, but when you go beyond them you need to set up your own, these walls are an effective block to our signals. Do not allow any communication dead zones, especially in the connecting tunnels. We stay in contact the whole time, understood? Okay, you've got your assignments. Move out.'

Dudley studied the topography of the 3D chart in his virtual vision, matching it to the big tunnel entrance on the compartment's wall. An orange line snaked through it, detailing his route. He brought the inertial guidance on line, aligning it with the beacon.

'You ready?' Emmanuelle asked.

'I think so.' He was staring at the black gulf that was the entrance to the tunnel they were going to have to use to get down to level five. It was nearly three metres in diameter. *Thus indicating the Dyson aliens may be bigger than us – idiot.* But not so small as to trigger claustrophobia. At least, not straight away.

On the other side of the compartment, Frances was already hauling herself into a tunnel that snaked its way over to section A8. Dudley drifted over to the tunnel his chart indicated, and gripped the side of the entrance to steady himself. His suit lights cut straight through the gloom, revealing a tube whose carbon composite walls were mottled with hairline fractures and coarse blisters. It started to curve downwards about five metres ahead, with a gentle twist to the left. He pushed his feet lightly off the compartment floor, allowing his legs and torso to slide up until he was level to the entrance, then pulled himself forwards into the tunnel. 'And into the unknown.'

*

'Sir, we're being signalled,' Anna called out. 'Sensors are showing both laser and microwave transmissions directed straight at us. Originating from Alpha Major orbit – the moonlets.'

'Son of a bitch,' Wilson grunted. 'Are you sure? Could they just be aligned on something beyond us?'

'I don't think so. There is nothing behind us. All three beams intersect here, and they're holding constant. We're definitely the target point.'

Wilson quickly called the signals up on his console screens. Even after the RI's best filtering they came up as a jumble of sine waves and fractal patterns. 'Is this the same stuff they transmit to each other?'

'Yes, sir. It looks like it.'

'So they might not realize we are aliens?'

'They must have a good idea we are not native to this star system,' Tunde said. 'After all, now the barrier has come down, they'll be expecting some kind of communication or contact from the species which put it up. They would be watching.'

One of the visual sensors was trained on a laser beam coming from a worldlet around Alpha Major. A single ruby dazzle point that obscured much of the planet's delicate wrapping of fusion flame. Wilson stared at it with a growing concern that he might just have been underestimating the Dysons. 'They've been looking for us, or at least an alien ship, since the barrier went down?'

'That would be the logical thing for them to do, yes.'

'So if they haven't got hysradar, how the hell did they find us?'

'Our hyperdrive wormhole creates a great deal of gravitonic shock, and it also has a strong quantum signature. On top of that there will be neutrino emissions from our fusion reactors.'

'Small ones,' Antonia said immediately. 'I'm keeping the fusion systems a couple of per cent above breakeven. The niling d-sinks are our primary power source, but they're very well shielded.'

'Captain, this entire planetary system is overflowing with advanced technology,' Tunde said. 'And if they really are as conflict-driven as we suspect, they will have a great many sensor systems. I'm really not surprised they have detected us.'

Wilson was drawn back to the main portals, both of them showing an unaugmented visual image of the Watchtower. His initial concern was now turning to real worry. 'Anna, give me a hysradar sweep. Is there anything out there?'

After a few initial scans of the Watchtower they'd switched off all of their active sensors, keeping all emissions to a minimum in a bid to achieve silent running. It was his choice again to remain inconspicuous; quietly gathering data until they were ready to make contact. A strategy which would allow them the upper hand.

'Oh shit,' Anna exclaimed. 'I make that eight ships heading straight at us.'

*

Dudley had followed the tunnel all the way down to level seven. He'd passed a lot of junctions where subsidiary tunnels branched off. The whole network was like some kind of root system twisted into a knotted corkscrew configuration. Winding his way down, he began to appreciate just how extensive the tunnels were in a way the virtual vision 3D chart never quite conveyed. As he progressed he became convinced they

579

were pipes rather than corridors. There was simply too much of them to be used as passageways by the Dyson aliens. Not that he could visualize what kind of pipes they were. They had no valves or pumps, nor mounting pins where such units could have been. His best guess was that they used to be lined by a cellular sleeve, or a variant on electromuscle, which had subsequently been stripped out along with everything else. The contact teams had so far been singularly unsuccessful in recovering an artefact of any value.

He glided out from the tunnel into a level seven compartment shaped like a slice of cake. It didn't have any hatchways, only more tunnel entrances. He touched his boots down on the rumpled floor, allowing the sole cilia to grip the flaking surface. The open space was a welcome relief from the confines of the tunnel. Emmanuelle came out behind him, flipping her fingers against the edge as she passed, to turn a lazy circle before placing her boots firmly on the floor. Dudley was already sticking a comrelay to an empty mounting block.

'This has been cleaned out,' Emmanuelle reported. 'No direct connection to other compartments.'

'Okay,' Oscar said. 'Tunnel entrance three leads down into the rock itself. We don't have an accurate plan of it after twenty metres or so; the deep scan can't penetrate any further. You guys want to check it out for me?'

'We can manage that,' Dudley said confidently. At last, some real uncharted territory.

'All right, proceed with care. Don't forget the comrelays.'

Dudley wanted to say something like, *of course we won't*, but it lacked professionalism. In fact Oscar's calm voice in his ears was reassuring. *You can always depend on Oscar*. It was a pleasant psychological safety net.

He ordered his boots to release the floor, and pushed himself towards entrance three. With his suit lights shining down into the slate-grey interior it didn't look any different to the dozen others he'd already passed, it was curving away counter-clockwise. 'Start recording the route,' he told his e-butler, and pulled himself in.

After fifteen metres the surface changed from the usual tough carbon composite to a thin aluminium skin, dull with age, and cracked to reveal rock directly underneath. The curvature tightened, becoming regular. Dudley stuck a comrelay to the wall. Twenty-five metres later, he had to use another.

'According to my inertial guidance, this is a spiral,' Emmanuelle said. 'We're descending almost along the rock's axis.'

'Oscar, is there a hole anywhere on the rock surface?' Dudley asked. 'Anything that could be the other end?'

'Difficult to say. There are a few fissures that could be openings. This is why we need you guys.'

'Thanks.'

After a couple more twists, they came to the first junction. It was a straight tube seven metres long. Dudley shone his suit lights down it.

'It just leads to the other side of the spiral, like a short cut.'

'I don't think so,' Emmanuelle said. 'The angle is wrong. Hey, you know what, I bet this whole shaft is laid out like DNA. Two spirals running parallel, with cross links between the two.'

'You could be right. Oscar, I'd like to try something. If we put a comrelay at the other end of this link, then we might be able to pick it up if there's another cross link below us.'

'Go ahead Dudley, it's worth a try.'

Dudley zipped through the short length of tunnel, happy at how easy he was at moving himself about in these conditions. The skill training memory was finally settling in – along with his natural aptitude, of course. He stuck the comrelay inside the second spiral, and hurried back.

*

Wilson stared at the small triangles inching their way across the big portal's tactical display. Digits flickered around each one, delivering yet more bad news. The lead ship was eighty-two million kilometres distant, and accelerating hard at eight gees. It was going to reach them in just over three hours. That was bad enough, but what he really didn't like was that it hadn't flipped over to decelerate.

All eight ships had launched from the moons or inhabited asteroids of the outermost gas-giant, three AUs distant, the closest centre of any alien activity. If that lead ship didn't decelerate at all, it was going to have a relative velocity of over seven and a half thousand kilometres per second when it reached them. No human machine had ever reached a fraction of that speed in real space. Even now, he could see it on the visual display as the *Second Chance*'s main telescope tracked it, the fusion drive a streamer of near-invisible violet fury stretching for hundreds of kilometres behind a scintillating golden sphere. Every stray gas molecule and charged particle impacting on the force field was dying in a burst of radioactive splendour, contributing to the coronal hue around the ship. If it hit the *Second Chance* or the Watchtower at that velocity, the explosion would briefly rival a solar flare.

'Only ships five and seven have flipped,' Anne said. 'They're decelerating to rendezvous. Falling a long way behind the others. And three more have left the gas-giant on an interception course for us. I think we've also got about fifteen on their way from Dyson Major; it's a little early to be sure but their vectors are matching up.'

Wilson nodded silently as he absorbed the tactical situation. Given their vectors and positions, all eight ships in the first flotilla must have launched from various bases over a period of several hours. They were well spread out. There was no doubt about their destination, even if it was only a flyby. As for their intent . . .

'Thank you,' he said. 'Oscar, pull the contact teams out of

the Watchtower right now. I want them back on board *Second Chance* in half an hour.'

'Yes, sir.'

'Tunde, I'm trying to think of any possible peaceful or scientific value from a flyby at the kind of speed the lead ship will have.'

'There isn't any, sir, there can't be.'

'That's what I thought you'd say. This is territorial. They might even think we're from the species which put up the barrier, in which case we have to assume the worst. If they do not slow down, we will withdraw from this system. I'm not going to risk our lives and this mission in an attempt to make contact under a combat situation. Hyperspace, I want an immediate flight path for our return to the Commonwealth, ready to initiate on my command.'

'Aye, sir.'

'Anna, we're going to attempt data contact with the first flotilla. If we can't understand them, maybe we can get them to understand us. Start transmitting our standard preliminary contact package. Use every frequency they're squirting at us. If nothing else we have to tell them we're not the ones who put up the barrier.'

'Captain,' Oscar called.

Wilson missed having Oscar on the bridge, although he grudgingly acknowledged the executive officer was by far the best person to be running the exploration of the Watchtower. But he knew immediately from Oscar's tone something had gone wrong. 'Yes?'

'We've got problems. Two members of contact team A have dropped out of communication.'

*

'This one is at a different angle again,' Emmanuelle said.

They had both stopped beside the fifth cross link, shining their suit lights into it. Once again, it was a straight tunnel opening to a spiral shaft. They suspected there were more than two spirals, possibly four or five.

'I think we should stick to this shaft,' Dudley said. 'Let's find out where it goes before we start plotting the rest.' According to his inertial guidance display, they were already a hundred and fifteen metres below level seven of the alien station. They hadn't managed to get a signal from any of the additional comrelays he'd placed at the cross links above, so they didn't really know for sure what the topography was. 'Oscar, can we carry on?'

'Yeah, keep going. It's the most interesting aspect of the station we've come across.'

Dudley pushed off again. There were enough bumps and irregularities in the aluminium sheath for him to grip and use like a ladder, pulling himself along. He was keen to see where it led now. He had a gut feeling that this was important. It was different to the rest of the station. The aliens must have used it to feed something in, or out. *This had a purpose.* Once they knew what it was connected to, they would have the first key, a way in to decrypting the alien culture. *And I found it.*

He moved forward eagerly, his suit lights sliding over the ancient corrupted metal. Seeking understanding.

*

'I can't get them back,' Oscar said. 'The comrelays must have glitched. We're not even getting a carrier wave from either of them.'

'Goddamn it!' Wilson started calling up the contact team status displays onto his console screens. 'When did you lose contact?'

'Just as you told us to get them back. I don't believe this. Those comrelay units can't fail, they're nothing but safety circuits.'

A 3D chart of the Watchtower station sprang up, with

other team members' positions illustrated by small green lights. All of them were converging on the beacon.

'Who's missing?' Wilson asked.

'Verbeke and Bose.'

For one instant, Wilson felt a flash of anger. *It just had to be him, didn't it.* Anger was equally quickly replaced by guilt. *He's one of my crew, and he's suffered equipment failure.* 'Don't they have to make their way back if they lose contact?'

'That's what the manual says. Emmanuelle knows it well enough, even if Dudley is a little shaky on theory. They should be on their way back.'

'How far away are they from a working relay?'

'I don't know. They set up eighteen units behind them, I'm still getting telemetry from sixteen of them. That puts them about twenty metres away from a working one.'

'Right,' Wilson said tersely. He could imagine it, the two of them annoyed their progress had been halted, maybe a quick squabble about going back right away or taking a fast look a few metres ahead.

'Should be back on line any minute now,' Oscar said.

'Anna, Sandy, is there any response from those ships yet?'

'Sorry, sir, not yet,' Sandy Lanier reported. 'They're still on course. No signal, not directed at us.'

'Son of a bitch. Right, we need to start shouting. Bump up the power level in the transmission antennae. Make damn sure we get their attention.'

'Aye, sir.'

*

McCain Gilbert shot out of the carbon composite tunnel into the beacon compartment. In front of him, contact team members were freeflying out of the gap in the wall. Pale gas from their manoeuvring packs swirled in rapid eddies through the beams of the remaining suit lights.

'Have we got them yet?' he asked Oscar.

'No. Nothing.'

'They should be back in range. For fuck's sake, Emmanuelle knows what she's doing. How long now?'

'Fourteen minutes.'

'No way. No way is that a comrelay failure. They're in trouble.'

'We don't know that.'

'I do.' He twisted himself round and pushed off the wall, heading for the tunnel that would take him directly down to level five.

'What are you doing?' Oscar shouted.

'Helping them.'

'Get back to the shuttle!'

'I'm with you, Mac,' Frances Rawlins said.

Mac was already in the tunnel. Light shone on him from behind. 'I'll take care of them,' he told Frances.

'They're my team, damn it.'

'Okay.'

'Mac, for Christ's sake,' Oscar said. 'Get back to the shuttle, both of you.'

'Two minutes, Oscar. Come on, man, that ain't going to make any difference.'

'Jesus.'

*

'The wall is changing again, look,' Dudley said. He stopped himself, and shone his suit lights on the patch just in front of his helmet. Emmanuelle drifted up beside him.

The tattered aluminium was now formed into a series of small corrugations. Spaced between them was a yellow ceramic. It had small red markings on it. 'That's interesting.'

'Hey, is that writing?' Emmanuelle asked.

'Could be. What do you think, Oscar?'

'We're not sure. Make sure you get a clean video of it.'

586

'Copy that.' Dudley waited a moment. 'Geddit? Copy. That.'

'Just video the bloody thing,' Emmanuelle moaned.

*

'OhmyGod.' Sandy pushed herself back from her console as if it had just given her an electric shock. 'Sir, missile launch. The lead ship has fired. Eight. Nine. Twelve. That's confirmed as twelve missiles.'

'At us?' Wilson asked. He was pleased by how calm he sounded.

'Four of them, yes. The rest are on courses for ships two, three, and six.'

Wilson's virtual finger stabbed at a communication icon. 'Mac, Frances, get out of there now. I'm recalling the shuttle in three minutes.'

'We're almost at level seven.'

'The aliens are firing at us. Get out of there. I am not going to repeat this order.'

'Yes, sir.'

'The other ships are responding to one's missile launch,' Anna called out. 'Salvos launching from ships three, two, five, six, four. Oh, now eight has launched. Lead ship has fired again. Over one hundred missiles in flight. Sir, twenty-four of them are heading for us. God, they're hitting fifteen gees.'

'Son of a bitch,' Wilson spat. 'Pilot, take us over to the Watchtower. We've got to get that shuttle on board. Tu Lee, is the hyperdrive ready?'

'Aye, sir,' Tu Lee said. 'We can go ftl at any time.'

*

Mac's virtual hand twisted the throttle as far as the graphic would let him. He shot out of the station compartment into free space. His suit sensors locked on to the shuttle, and a bright red trajectory plot streaked across his virtual vision. He steered himself along it, ignoring the amber velocity warnings winking urgently. Frances was beside him, matching his flight.

A searing white light appeared from behind the Watchtower. Mac flinched inside his suit. Then logic kicked in. It was the *Second Chance*'s plasma drive, bringing the ship in close. Cutting down the time it would take for the shuttle to get inside its force field.

A time that shouldn't have existed. *I couldn't leave them without making some effort to help. I just couldn't. Who knew this would happen?*

He started to decelerate a few metres short of the shuttle, using his legs to absorb most of the impact. Even so, he hit hard. The cilia on his soles gripped the fuselage grid, preventing any rebound. Frances came down beside him. 'Bugger me,' she grunted. Her legs were bent sharply, torso twisting.

'Go,' Mac told the shuttle pilot.

'You're not inside yet.'

'Just go. We're secure.'

Space around him flared yellow as the chemical rockets ignited.

*

Oscar had hurried back onto the bridge compartment. Wilson acknowledged him with a quick wave as he claimed his console. He was waiting for the shuttle, willing it across the gap. Both Jean Douvoir and the shuttle pilot did a superb job, rendezvousing thirty kilometres from the Watchtower. A small screen showed him the little craft settling onto its cradle, which sank back into the hangar.

Wilson kept clenching his fist, which was disrupting his contact with the console interface pad. 'Any contact?' he asked for the tenth time.

'No,' Oscar said. 'I think Mac was right, they're in trouble.'

'What the hell kind of trouble? It was dead over there. Cold and dead.'

'I don't know.'

'Missile detonation,' Anna said. 'Ho boy, here we go. Multiple blasts. High megatonnage. They're using diverted energy pulsers, very heavy e-band emission, gamma and X-ray activity. Plenty of electronic warfare.'

'Where were they?'

'Ship three. Attacking and defending barrage. The ship's still intact. Changing trajectory slightly.'

Wilson glanced at the forward portal which was tracking the twenty-four missiles powering towards them. Their velocity alone was terrifying.

'We should go,' Oscar said quietly.

'Right.' The second shuttle was on its cradle, a volunteer pilot ready to launch the second there was any signal from Verbeke or Bose.

'More missile launches,' Anna announced. 'And we're about to get another round of explosions. There's an attack cluster almost in range of ship five.'

'Any reply to our signal?' Wilson asked.

Sandy shook her head.

'Detonations,' Anna sang out. 'Shit, it's like the warm-up for Armageddon out there.'

'Wilson,' Oscar urged. 'It's time.'

Captain Wilson Kime took a final look at the tracking display. The missiles were close now, and their true offensive capability remained unknown. He was coming perilously close to endangering his ship and crew. The bridge crew were all watching him, their expressions of defeat and regret, and yes, even guilt, were the same as his own.

'Hyperspace,' Wilson ordered. 'Take us home.'

15

The lift doors opened smoothly, and Police Captain Hoshe Finn stepped into the familiar vestibule. For once he didn't have to call ahead, the double doors into Morton's penthouse were wide open. Several large flatbed trolleys had rolled through into the big split-level living room, delivering large plastic packing crates which were stacked against the walls. The process of loading the plush furniture into them had already begun, along with smaller household items all wrapped in sheets of foam. But after only three crates had been filled, the clearing-up process had come to a complete halt. All the GPbots that had been doing the work were motionless, some were still holding the objects they'd been carrying when the reported incident with the harmonic-blade carving knife had happened. Two junior managers from the Darklake National Bank, the court-appointed debt-receiver, were waiting, somewhat nervously, by the remaining settee in the conversation area. The supervisor from the removal company was sitting on the stone hearth in front of the fireplace, drinking tea from his thermos cup and smiling slyly.

'Where is she?' Hoshe asked. It said something for the power of unisphere publicity that he didn't have to use his new police captain's identity certificate. They all knew who he was.

'In there.' One of the bank suits pointed to the kitchen. 'I want the bitch arrested.'

Hoshe raised an eyebrow whilst managing to look bored at the same time – something he'd seen Paula Myo do to great effect on several occasions.

Rather pleasingly, the suit flinched. 'She threatened us,' he blustered. 'And she's damaged one of the GPbots. We'll be requiring compensation for that.'

'Badly damaged?' Hoshe asked.

The supervisor glanced up from his tea. 'Dunno. I'm not going in there. Psychos aren't part of my job.' He sounded amused, though his face was carefully sober in front of the suits.

'Don't blame you,' Hoshe said. The door into the kitchen was partly open. 'Mellanie? It's Hoshe Finn. Do you remember me? I need to talk to you.'

'Go away!' the girl yelled. 'All of you, just piss off.'

'Come on Mellanie, you know I can't do that. We have to talk. It's just going to be you and me. No constables, or anything, you have my word.'

'No. I won't. There's nothing to talk about.'

Her voice had almost cracked. Hoshe sighed, and moved right up to the kitchen door. 'You could at least offer me a drink. I always used to be offered something when we came here. Where's the butler?'

There was a long silence followed by what sounded like a sniffle. 'Gone,' she said quietly. 'They all left, all of them.'

'Okay, I'll make my own drink. I'm coming in now.' Hoshe edged round the door, still cautious, not that he thought there was any real danger.

Like the rest of the penthouse, the kitchen was huge and elaborate. Every worktop had been carved out of pink and grey marble, with the cupboard doors below them made from burnished brentwood. The cabinets above the worktop all had transparent doors, showing off the expensive sets of crockery

591

and glasses. He had to walk round the pool-table-sized central workbench to find Mellanie. She was sitting on the floor in a corner, hunched up tight as if she was trying to push herself through the wall. A harmonic-blade carving knife lay on the terracotta floor tiles just in front of her.

Hoshe wanted to squat down beside her, illustrating support and friendship just like the training scenarios emphasized, but he hadn't quite lost enough weight to do that comfortably. Instead he lounged back, resting his buttocks on the marble worktop. 'You should be careful of those harmonic-blades,' he said casually. 'They can be quite dangerous in the wrong hands. Lots of junior debt-receivers can get bits chopped off if your aim's good enough.'

Mellanie looked up. Her auburn hair was in complete disarray. She'd been crying badly, with sticky trails daubed down her cheeks. Even so, she remained gorgeous. Perhaps even more so in this state: a classic damsel in distress. 'What?'

He grinned ruefully. 'Never mind. You do know why those people are here, don't you?'

She nodded, and lowered her head again.

'The penthouse belongs to the bank now, Mellanie. You have to find somewhere else to stay.'

'This is my home,' she wailed.

'I'm really sorry. Would you like me to drive you back to your parents' house?'

'I was going to wait for him here. Then when he comes back, everything would be just the same again.'

That shocked Hoshe more than anything else in the whole case. 'Mellanie, the judge gave him a hundred and twenty years.'

'I don't care. I'll wait. I love him.'

'He doesn't deserve you,' Hoshe said sincerely.

She looked up again, her face troubled as if she didn't know who she was talking to.

'If you want to wait, that's your decision, and I respect

that,' he said. 'Though I'd love to try and talk you out of it. But you really can't do it here. I know it must be horrible for you seeing the bank walk in and take everything like this. But busting up a bot isn't going to help get rid of them. In any case, the idiots outside are just doing their job. Annoying them just means people like me have to turn up and do their dirty work for them.'

'You're a very strange policeman. You care. Not like that—' Her lips tightened.

'Paula Myo's gone. She left after the trial. You won't ever see her again.'

'Good!' Mellanie looked at the carving knife, and extended a leg, pushing it away with her toes. 'Sorry,' she said sheepishly. 'But everything nice I ever had happen in my life happened here, and they just barged in and started . . . They were really nasty.'

'Small people always are. You going to be okay, now?'

She sniffed loudly. 'Yes. I think so. I'm sorry they bothered you.'

'Not a problem, believe me; any excuse to get out of the office is welcome. So, why don't I help you pack a couple of suitcases, then I'll take you home? Humm, how about that?'

'I can't.' She stared straight ahead. 'I will not go back to my parents. I can't do that. Please.'

'All right, that's okay. How about a hotel?'

'I don't have any money,' she whispered. 'I've been eating the packets in the freezer since the trial. They're almost gone. That's why all the staff left. I couldn't pay them. Morty's company won't help. None of the directors will even see me now. God! Those bastards. They loved me before, you know. I stayed at their houses, played with their children. And the parties we had. Have you ever been rich, Detective?'

'That's Hoshe, and no, I've never been rich.'

'They really don't live by the same rules as anyone else. Whatever they want to do, they just do it. I found that exciting. It was so wonderful being a part of that, not having limits, living so free. Now look at me. I'm nothing.'

'Don't be silly. Someone like you can achieve whatever they want to. You're just young, that's all. Changes this big are frightening at your age. You'll pull through. We all do in the end, somehow.'

'You're very sweet, Hoshe. I don't deserve that.' She wiped some of the moisture from her cheeks. 'Are you going to arrest me?'

'No. But we do need to find you somewhere to stay for tonight. How about a friend?'

'Ha.' Her smile was bitter. 'I don't have any. Before the trial I had hundreds. Now, there isn't one of them who'll talk to me. I saw Jilly Yen the other week. She actually left the shop so she didn't have to say hello.'

'Okay, look, I know the manageress of a B&B not far from here. Have a couple of nights there on me while you get yourself sorted out. You could maybe get a job waitressing or something, there are enough bars in this town. And the colleges will start enrolling in another three weeks. You must have had some thoughts on a career before all this happened.'

'Oh no, no. I can't take money off you.' Mellanie pushed herself to her feet, combing at her snarled hair in embarrassment. 'I don't want charity.'

'It's not charity. I'm doing all right now as it happens, I got a decent raise as part of my promotion.'

'You got promoted?' Her brief smile died as she realized why. 'Oh.'

'You have to go somewhere. And, believe me, this B&B is cheap.'

Mellanie bowed her head. 'One night. That's all. Just one.'

'Sure. Let's go and pack a bag.'

She peered at the door. 'They said I couldn't take anything that was mine. They said Morty paid for it all, so it belonged to the bank now. That's why I . . . Well, you know.'

'Sure. I'll sort it out.' He guided Mellanie out into the living room. 'The young lady is packing a bag of clothes and leaving,' he told the suits.

'We cannot allow any bank property—'

'I've just told you what's happening,' Hoshe said. 'You want to make an issue of it? You want to call me a liar?'

They looked at each other. 'No, Officer.'

'Thank you.'

Hoshe had to laugh when they went into the master bedroom. Not at the cliché playboy décor of circular bed and black sheets, complete with mirror portal behind the pillows. It was the poor GPbot, lying on the floor with a sharp dint in its bodywork where someone had kicked it; two of its electro-muscle limbs were severed clean at the base, and the remaining three knotted together round its legs. It took a lot of strength to do that to electromuscle.

Mellanie took a modest shoulder bag from one of the walk-in closets.

'I can't really let you take any jewellery,' Hoshe said. 'And I suppose some of the dresses cost a lot.' He was looking past her shoulder at the rack which had every slot taken by some garment. It was moving slowly, rotating the rest of the selection from a hidden storage space behind the closet. There must have been hundreds of clothes there altogether. When he checked, the other closet had as many suits and jackets, and nearly the same number of shoes and boots.

'Don't worry,' Mellanie said. 'One thing I did learn was that expensive doesn't equal practical.' She was folding a pair of jeans into the bag. The pile on the bed was mostly T-shirts.

'I was thinking,' he said. 'It's kind of a last resort as far as earning money goes, but your life has been interesting to say the least, although it's for all the wrong reasons. There are media companies who would pay for that story.'

'I know. There's hundreds of them stored in my e-butler's

hold file. I stopped accessing them, when my cybersphere account was closed.'

'Why is your account closed?'

'I told you. I don't have any money. I wasn't joking.' She held up a trim, dark hand-held array, giving him a questioning look.

'Sure.' He'd never heard of an account being closed before, *everyone* had access to the cybersphere.

The array was put in the bag's side pocket. She sat on the side of the bed, and started lacing up some sports pumps.

'I'll have the account reactivated,' he said. 'Just data and messages for a month. Not an entertainment feed. It'll only cost me a couple of dollars.'

Mellanie gave him a curious look. 'Do you want to sleep with me, Hoshe?'

'No! Er, I mean, no, that's not ... I don't ... That's not what this is about.'

'People always want to sleep with me. I know that. I'm beautiful and first-life young. And I adore sex. Morty was a very experienced teacher; he encouraged me to experiment. What I can do with my body isn't shameful, Hoshe. Pleasure is never a sin. And I wouldn't mind you enjoying me.'

Hoshe just knew his face was turning hot red. Having her talk about it so clinically was like enduring his father's one attempt to explain the birds and bees. 'I'm married. Thank you.' Which was about as lame as you could get.

'I don't understand. If it's not to have sex with me, why are you doing this?'

'He killed two people, ruined two lives,' Hoshe said quietly. 'I don't want him to claim a third victim. Not now.'

She picked up a brush from the dressing table and began working it through her hair. 'Morty didn't kill anybody. You and Paula Myo were wrong about that.'

'I don't think so.'

'The criminal gang could have gone through her memories

and found out what was hers, that or tortured it out of her. It wasn't Morty.'

There were no signs of torture in the pathologist's report, she was in the bath, and her memorycell was ruined. But all he said was, 'We'll just have to agree to disagree on that.'

'You're far too nice to be a police officer, do you know that?'

Hoshe waited until she'd cleaned herself up, then took her to the B&B. He paid for a week in advance, and drove off, managing to avoid her attempt to kiss him goodbye. He wasn't sure he was strong enough to resist actual physical contact.

*

Five days later, a taxi dropped Mellanie outside a big warehouse-like building in Darklake's Thurnby district, a shabby and badly rundown old industrial precinct. Every plot was protected by high fencing, although half of the factories and retail depots were abandoned. Rubbish had been blown up along the wire mesh fences, forming little dunes of paper and plastic; standing high above them were realtor signs proclaiming various sites available for redevelopment. The single-track railway which ran alongside the main road had tall weeds growing from the shingle between the sleepers and its rails were rusting over.

Mellanie glanced around nervously. Not that there was anywhere for muggers to hide. A purple plaque on the door in front of her read: Wayside Production. She took a breath and walked through.

True to his word, Hoshe Finn had got her cybersphere account activated again. The number of non-commercial messages in her e-butler's hold file was over seventy thousand. She'd wiped them all and changed her personal interface code. Then she called Rishon, a reporter she'd known from her time with Morton. He'd been very pleased to hear from her, and immediately arranged a meeting. Her story was enormously valuable, he assured her, and people would access the drama from all over the Commonwealth. That was when she hit him with her real big idea, that she should play herself. To her surprise, he'd been delighted by the suggestion, claiming it would bring in even more money.

She sat with him for two days, pouring her heart out, telling him everything about those golden days, from the moment they met at a sponsorship gala dinner, what it had been like, the wonder and thrill of the love affair, her parents' hostility, the parties, the luxurious hedonistic life, the members of Oaktier's high society with whom she mingled freely, then the terrible trial with its tragic wrong verdict. Rishon recorded it all, and transformed it into a spectacular script for an eight-part drama that would play for days. He'd sold it within twenty-four hours.

There was a tiny reception area on the other side of Wayside Production's front door, composite panel walls and roofing boxing in a couple of ancient couches with flaking chrome tube arms and legs. A girl was sitting on one of them, her jaw working hard on gum as she studied a paperscreen. She had a very short leather skirt, and a white blouse with a low-cut front showing off a huge cleavage. Her makeup was dreadful: mascara like panda circles and lips that were glossy lavender. Too-stiff white-blonde hair that was mostly bad extensions curled down below her shoulders like over-stretched springs. She looked up and smiled broadly at Mellanie. 'Oh, hi there, you're Mellanie; I recognize you from the court case.' Her voice was high and squeaky. Somehow, Mellanie couldn't imagine it being anything else.

'That's me.'

'I'm Tiger Pansy. Jaycee told me to look out for you. He said to bring you right on over to the set.' She got up from the couch, standing a couple of centimetres taller than Mellanie. Fifteen-centimetre silver glitter heels made that possible.

'Tiger Pansy?' Mellanie worked hard at keeping herself from spluttering.

'Yeah, honey, you like that? I just started using it. My agent wanted Slippy Trixie, but I nixed that.'

'Tiger Pansy is fine. Sure.'

'Why thanks. You're gorgeous, you know that? Real young; all sweet and everything. They're going to love you out there in access land.'

'Er, thanks.' Mellanie hurried after Tiger Pansy.

It was an old warehouse. Wayside Productions had simply partitioned it off into squares to keep the sets separate. Corridors ran between them, with high composite panel walls and no ceiling. High overhead, the building's metal rafters supported an ageing solar collector roof which rattled faintly at every light gust of wind. People were moving along the corridors. She had to flatten herself against a wall as a couple of stage hands came past carrying big hologram portals. They gave Mellanie lingering looks, smiling suggestively. She ignored them as she followed Tiger Pansy. Her body itched just about everywhere from her new OCtattoos. They'd taken three days to etch on they were so extensive, and it was hell trying not to scratch them, but if she did she knew her skin would be red and blotchy all over. That would never do for an actress, especially not at the start of recording that involved sensorium output. Today, she knew the other actors would be sceptical about her ability, and she was going to have to work hard to impress everyone.

They went past one set door where a whole troupe of actresses were filing in, dressed in schoolgirl uniforms. Even with cellular reprofiling some of them still looked well into their thirties. Mellanie gave them a long look. Surely they weren't . . .

'Here we are,' Tiger Pansy said with a hint of pride. 'They spent a lot of money on this set. You're a real big deal round here.' She pointed to the polyphoto notice beside the door. Its glowing letters spelt out: *Murderous Seduction*. 'Cute name, huh?'

'Right.'

Tiger Pansy opened the door and went through. The set was Morton's penthouse. Almost. It had been split in two, with the living room on one side. Its actual floor space was mainly the conversation area, with settees similar to the real ones. The fireplace was in the right position behind it, but incorporating some very strange animal sculptures made out of fibreglass and sprayed to resemble stone. The walls surrounding the conversation area were simple holograms, showing the rest of the penthouse. A holocamera ring, three metres in diameter, had been lowered from the rafters until it hung a metre above the settees. Three technicians were standing round an open panel in its side, muttering among themselves while a bot like an arm-size centipede slowly wormed its way through the exposed electronics.

The remaining half of the set was given over to the bedroom. That at least was full-scale, though again the walls were just holograms, and the black sheets were cotton rather than silk. Two men were sitting on the mattress. One of them was Morton. Mellanie gasped in surprise. Then she noticed a few inconsistencies, and realized it was cellular reprofiling. A good operation, though, she acknowledged: the resemblance would fool most people. The man beside the mock-Morton was Jaycee, chief executive of Wayside Productions. He was dressed all in black, which looked good on most people. On Jaycee, Mellanie thought, it made him look a lot more worn down than his actual fifty-one years, like some embarrassingly oddball bachelor uncle. His head was shaved, though a ghostly shimmer of grey stubble betrayed a monk's halo. She tried not to stare as he came over, but what kind of executive, especially in a media company, couldn't pull off baldness with any style.

'Mellanie, lovely to finally meet you in the flesh.' He

squeezed her hand rather too firmly as he spent a long time looking her up and down. 'And fucking great flesh it is, too. You look delectable.' His plastic friendship smile tightened slightly. 'I thought you'd be younger.'

'Oh?' Mellanie was starting to get very bad vibes about Wayside Productions.

'Not a criticism, sweetheart. I've got a shit-hot cosmetics man, we can work you back a few years. See what he did to Joseph, here.'

The man with Morton's face grinned aggressively. 'Hi babe, looking forward to gigging with you.' He put one hand on his groin, and squeezed happily. Mellanie could see his erection through the trouser fabric. 'Don't worry, you won't be disappointed, not with this equipment.'

'You're such an asshole, Joseph,' Tiger Pansy sneered. 'Mellanie, don't let him give you anal, honey, no matter what Jaycee says is in the script. He's gotten himself an enlargement that's so big it's fucking stupid. You'll hurt into the middle of next week.'

'Hey!' Joseph gave Tiger Pansy the finger. 'You couldn't even fit this between your sagging titties they've spread so wide you ancient fucking slut.'

'Fuck you.'

'What the hell is this?' Mellanie demanded. 'We're shooting my story, the things that happened to me and Morton, not some porno.'

'Of course we are, sweetheart,' Jaycee said. 'You two,' he growled at Joseph and Tiger Pansy, 'fuck off. I want to talk to Mellanie.'

'What are you trying to do?' Mellanie asked when the others had shuffled off the bedroom set.

'Okay, I apologize for Joseph, he's an asshole. But he's one of my best dols.'

'A doll?'

'D. O. L. Dick on legs. Even with all today's drugs, some

601

guys have a shitload of trouble keeping it up for the recording. It's a psychological thing, or some crap like that. But Joseph, he can perform every fucking time, man. He's fucking incredible. And don't you fucking listen to that screwed up old whore, Tiger. Joseph knows what he's doing with girls. You'll have a lot of fun riding that monster dick of his.'

'No I won't. This has all been some giant mix-up. I'm not here to make a porno. Goodbye.' She turned round, ready to walk out.

'Wait, just fucking wait, okay,' Jaycee stepped in front of her, arms held up. 'This is not a fucking porno. We're shooting a real fucking true life drama here, man.'

She gave the set a derisive glance. Even the fireplace statues made sense now. 'Yeah, right.'

'Fucking listen will you. I read the story Rishon came up with. You were some fucking swimmer when that Morton got inside your pants, and that fucked your chances on the team. It's a fucking classic; you're young and he's rich. Only it turns out he killed a bunch of people as well; he betrayed you, sweetheart. Accessors love shit like that. We've even put in a chase scene round the apartment when you find out what he's done. He comes at you with a knife. It's fucking exciting.'

'That is bullshit,' she snapped. 'None of this is what I told Rishon. Morton never killed anyone. You're not interested in telling our story.'

'Of course I am, sweetheart. Man, I want the whole fucking story, too. Look, we'll just be shooting the sex scenes first, get them fuckers out of the way. Then we can concentrate on all the other stuff, we'll do it big style on location, where it actually happened. Okay?'

'What utter crap!'

'You don't like Joseph? Fine. No fucking problem. I'll get reprofiled to look like your boyfriend, and pump you myself.'

'Oh, Jesus wept!' She went for the door.

Jaycee's hand came down on her shoulder and spun her around. His face was flushed and angry, hot blotches showing where too much cheap cellular reprofiling had been done to him down the decades. 'Stop being such a fucking bitch-kitty princess. You signed that fucking contract, and you fucking knew what was in it. You're even wetwired specially for this gig, for fuck's sake. If you've started shitting it because this is your first time, then boo fucking hoo. I can slip you a dose of coolant that can take care of that for you, no fucking problem. You'll be chill for the whole gig. But don't fucking come marching in here and fucking tell me this isn't what you wanted.'

'It's not what I was told was going to happen. I had those OCtattoos because all actresses know we have to do that. Making love is an integral part of life. So love scenes contribute to the drama's narrative structure. But they're only a part of it. You just want to do that and nothing else.'

'Actress? Fuck me. If that's what you want to fucking call yourself, then go right ahead. But I paid for those OCtattoos because you're a fantasy fuck, princess hardass. You're the real fucking deal; you're the kind of trim that those sad little fucks out there in access land can only ever envy all the rich bastards for having. Your kind doesn't ever fucking put out for a guy unless he's got a hundred mill in his bank. Now I get to give them what you really taste like. And they're going to love us for it.'

'No. I'm not doing it.'

'Did you see any multiple fucking choice boxes to tick when you came in here you stupid bitch? I fucking paid for you and I'm gonna fucking collect. Our contract says you spread your legs when I tell you to and let us record every fucking feeling in your tight-ass body when my dol goes to work inside you. And stop giving me all this shit about it, else I'll see to it that you wind up in the suspension chamber next to your killer boyfriend. We've got a legal contract.'

Jaycee was staring triumphantly right into her eyes, eager to catch the first signs of submission.

Mellanie was fast. Years of that relentless, tedious training with the squad had given her the kind of strength and reflexes which modern athletes normally had to have wetwired and retrosequenced into their bodies. Her knee came up, with powerful leg muscles trying to lift it all the way to Jaycee's chin. His scrotum was the first thing to get in the way.

She watched his mouth drop open soundlessly. His eyes widened, flooding with tears. He slid to one side, making a quiet, agonized choking sound, and crumpled to the floor.

'I'm going to call my agent now,' she told him dispassionately. 'But when you're out of hospital, we really must do lunch.'

*

The taxi dropped Mellanie off by the lakeside in the Glyfada district. She sat on a long wooden bench just above the water, watching the sailing yachts making their way out of the marina in Shilling Harbour to catch the first of the morning winds. The bars and restaurants behind her were just starting to open for the day, with delivery trucks parked outside several of them, cargobots unloading fresh food. They weren't actually serving yet. It was too early for that. Her brand-new media career had lasted all of forty-five minutes.

The shakes began as she finally allowed herself to think about Jaycee, and what she'd done actually hit home. An incredulous half-laugh burst from her lips, more relief than anything else. No one at Wayside Production had tried to stop her as she left. They all just stared at her as she walked past the sets, like she was some mad serial killer – except for Tiger Pansy who'd winked.

I can't believe I did that.

Which triggered a terrible thought. If that ability was to be found in the core of every human mind, then could Morton actually have . . .

She stopped that line of reasoning straight away.

But it felt good. I actually stood up for myself.

In the heat of the moment. And no doubt Jaycee would file charges as soon as he could walk and talk again. And she'd signed the contract. It had seemed so wonderful at the time, the perfect solution to her situation. Dear old Hoshe's suggestion of waitressing or college were non-starters. He didn't understand, she simply couldn't do things like that. Not after the life she'd been shown. That cut her options down considerably.

A young man so obviously on his way to crew a yacht, dressed in a rugby shirt and shorts, was sauntering along the waterfront, trying not to be too obvious as he glanced at her. She pushed her hair back lightly, and gave him a sunburst smile. The answering smile he gave was so full of puppy dog hope and longing it was all she could do not to laugh outright. *God, men are so easy.* Not that it had to be men, especially given her current mood. A girl would be so much kinder in bed, more attentive, more receptive.

It would be nice to be taken care of, to be pampered and adored. *But weak. I'm not going to be weak any more.* The tears threatened to burst out again. There had been so much of that since the trial. She made fists of her hands, forcing her nails into her palms until she winced at the pain. *I will not cry again.*

There was only one option left now. She hadn't wanted to try it before because it was such a long shot. A fantasy, really. The psychological safety net you never want to use.

She pulled out the little array she'd brought with her from the penthouse. The one with the ridiculously expensive black foxory casing – not that dear Hoshe had recognized that. 'I want a link to the SI,' she told her e-butler. Her new OCtattoos were all for sensory reception; Jaycee hadn't paid for virtual interface functions.

'For what reason?' the e-butler asked. The SI was notoriously reluctant to accept calls from human individuals. Apart from its comprehensive banking service, official government requests and emergencies were about the only contact it had with the Commonwealth.

She brought the little array up close to her face. 'Just tell it who's calling,' she whispered. 'And ask it if ... If Grandpa remembers me.'

The little screen on the front of the hand-held array immediately came on, showing tangerine and turquoise sinewaves retreating back to their joint vanishing point. 'Hello, baby Mel.'

'Grandpa?' The word was very hard to get out through her tightened-up throat. Once again, the wretched tears threatened to burst loose. She really had not expected this to work.

'He is with us, yes.'

Mellanie remembered that last achingly long day in the hospice, waiting by his bed for him to die. She was only nine at the time, and never did understand why he didn't rejuvenate like everybody else. Her parents hadn't wanted her there, but she'd insisted – stubborn even back then. Grandpa (actually, her great-great-grandfather) was always the nicest relative she had, always found time for his baby Mel despite his status as one of the planet's most distinguished residents. All the history files at school mentioned him as one of the programmers who had helped Sheldon and Isaac write the governing software for their original wormhole. 'Are you still you, Grandpa?'

'That's a difficult question to answer, Mellanie. We are the memories of your grandfather, but at the same time we are more, a universe more, which makes us less than the individual you want.'

'You always listened to me, Grandpa. You always said you'd help me if you could. And I really, *really*, need your help now.'

'We are not physical, Mellanie, we can only help with words.'

'That's what I need: advice. I need to know what to do, Grandpa. I've made a bit of a mess of my life.'

'You are only twenty, Mellanie. You are a child. You haven't begun your life yet.'

'Then why do I feel like it's almost over?'

'Because you are young, of course. Everything that happens to you is epic at your age.'

'I guess. So you will help me, then, Grandpa?'

'What would you like to know?'

'I don't have any money right now.'

'So we see. The Darklake National Bank is being its usual efficient self, and quantifying your ex-lover's assets for redistribution. The funds will be split between Tara Jennifer Shaheef and Wyobie Cotal, once various exorbitant fees have been claimed by officials, lawyers, and institutions. We do not believe you would be successful if you applied for a percentage of them. Legally, you have very little standing.'

'I don't want any,' she said forcefully. 'I've decided I'm not going to be dependent on anyone again. I'm going to make my life my own from now on.'

'That is the baby Mel we remember. We were always proud of you.'

'I tried to sell the story of what happened with me and Morton, but it hasn't worked out very well. I was naive and stupid, I guess. I trusted a reporter. It didn't work out too good. I might get arrested. There was this terrible man, a pornographer. I kind of assaulted him.'

'Fancy trusting a reporter. That was stupid. But the situation can probably be resolved. And pornographers are not notorious for running to the police.'

'I wanted to give myself a profile, Grandpa. I had this idea that I could become like a celebrity, a media personality. I've got the looks, and I'm sure I have the determination to make it. I just need some guidance, that's all. My story was just going to be the start. Once it's released, people will know my name. That can be used. If I can keep myself on the unisphere then who knows, one day I could be as big as Alessandra Baron.'

'You could indeed. You have the potential. Where exactly do you see us fitting into this scheme?'

'I want you to be my agent, Grandpa. I need to get my story back from Rishon and sell it again, to a respectable producer this time. I'll need to pay off Wayside Productions for my OCtattoos, as well. You can strike the best deal for me; you're honest, you won't rip me off. And you're a bank, too. My money will be safe with you.'

'We see. Very well, we will do that for you. There is, however, the question of our fee.'

'I know. It's ten per cent isn't it? Or do you charge more?'

'We were not thinking in terms of a financial percentage.'

'Oh.' She frowned at the little array's screen with its random pattern. 'What do you want?'

'If you are serious in your intention of a media career, then no matter what form it takes you will need a broadcast-quality sensorium interface.'

'A pro neural feed, yes, I know. What I've got already is a reasonable start. I was hoping my advance would pay for enhancements, and there's some inserts I'd like as well. I want to go virtual.'

'We will pay for the enhancements. But there will be occasions when we will want to ride along on them.'

'I don't understand.'

'Many people believe our presence within the Commonwealth is total, delivered to us through the unisphere. However, even we have limits. There are many places we cannot reach, some are deliberately blocked, while others are simply lacking any electronic infrastructure. You could provide us access to these areas on special occasions.'

'You mean you watch us? I always thought that was just a silly conspiracy theory.'

'We do not watch everyone. However, our interests are combined with yours, and you are a part of us through innumerable memory downloads. To use an old phrase: our fates are entwined. The only way to un-entwine them would be to remove ourselves from the sphere of all human activity. We choose not to do so.'

'Why not? I bet your life would be simpler.'

'And you believe that to be a good thing? No entity can enrich itself in isolation.'

'So you do watch us. Do you manipulate us as well?'

'By acting as your agent we control the flow of your life. Is that manipulation? We are data. It is our nature to acquire more, to continually add to our knowledge, and to use it. It is both our language and our currency. Human current events form a very small part of the information we absorb.'

'It's more like you're studying us, then?'

'Not as individuals. It is your society and the way in which its currents flow which is obviously of interest to us. What affects you affects us.'

'And you don't want any surprises.'

'Do you?'

'I guess not.'

'Then we understand each other. So do you still wish us to act as your representative and adviser, baby Mel?'

'I'd be like your secret agent, wouldn't I?'

'The role has parallels. But there are no dangers involved, you are simply our eyes and ears in secluded places. Don't expect to be issued with exotic gadgets and cars that fly.'

She laughed – for the first time in a long while. Shame about the flying cars, though, that would be fun. 'Let's do it.'

Because if Grandpa was serious, the SI would have to make sure she was a success.

*

The last sections of copper tubing in the espresso machine clipped back neatly into place, and Mark Vernon used a set of electromuscle pliers to tighten the seals. He screwed the chrome cover back on, and flicked the power switch. Three green lights came on.

'There you go. All working again.'

Mandy clapped her hands together in jubilation. 'Oh thanks, Mark. I kept telling Dil it was buggered, but he didn't do anything about it, just left us stewing in poo. You're my hero.'

He smiled at the young waitress who was beaming up at him. She'd been setting fresh breakfast panini out under the glass counter ready for the early morning customers; huge halves of the crusty Italian bread clamped around entire meals such as fried egg, sausages, kyias, and tomatoes, or ham, cheese, and pineapple, or vegetarian omelettes. Her shift partner, Julie, was rattling pans and crockery around in the kitchen at the rear. The smell of honey-cured bacon being grilled was drifting in through the hatch.

'Pretty simple, really,' he said modestly. The small area behind the serving counter meant Mandy was standing slightly too close, and slightly too admiringly as well. 'I'll, er, get on then.' He was slotting his tools back into the small case he always carried with him. His other hand held it between them like a defensive shield.

'No you won't. You sit yourself down there and I'll get you a decent breakfast. It's the least you deserve. And make sure you put a huge call-out fee on your bill for Dil. Bloody skinflint.'

'Right-o,' Mark nodded in defeat. Actually he was hungry. It was a fifteen-minute drive to Randtown from Ulon valley where the Vernons had their vineyard homestead. Mandy's frantic early morning call hadn't given him time for a bite before he left. Hadn't even used his toothgel yet.

He sat at a big marble-top table in one of the café Two For Tea's big curving windows. A couple had already claimed the window table on the other side of the door. They were dressed in skiing clothes, and talking happily with their heads tilted lovingly together, oblivious to the rest of the world.

Bright sunlight was creeping over the Dau'sing Mountains that surrounded Randtown to the north. Mark put his sunglasses on against the light streaming in through the window as he unrolled a paperscreen – he never had liked reading directly out of his virtual vision, the print superimposed over his field of view always gave him a headache. A dozen headlines scrolled down the left-hand side, with local items opposite them, loaded into the cybersphere by the Randtown Chronicle, the only media company on this half of the continent. With all the goodwill and loyalty in the world, Mark really couldn't haul up enough enthusiasm to read about the new loop road around the town's western precincts, or the proposed foresting project along the Oyster valley. So he told his e-butler to access yesterday's pan-Commonwealth news, and followed the start of the Presidential campaign. Reading between the lines on Doi's funding efforts, she hadn't got the Sheldons, the Halgarths, nor the Singhs to back her yet.

'Here you go,' Mandy said brightly as she put a plate down in front of him. It was piled high with pancakes and bacon that had maple syrup oozing out of every layer; the strawberries and lolabeans on top were arranged in a smiley face. A tall glass of apple and mango in crushed ice was placed next to it. 'I'll bring your toast and coffee when it's ready.' She winked saucily and skipped off to take the ski couple's order. Behind the serving counter the espresso machine had started to gurgle and steam comfortingly.

As if realizing they'd started the day, Julie switched on the sound system to play some obscure acoustic Hindi band's album. That was the thing about Randtown, every café and bar played music so trendy that by the time Mark got to know and appreciate it the band had either broken up or sold out. He looked at the gigantic pyramid of calories in front of him. Sighed. Picked up his fork. Liz had been making some rather sharp comments about his waistline recently. But the food here was dangerously splendid. Nothing was ever cooked singularly; if you wanted a lamb chop, you had to have the six alien vegetables, three sauces, and a weird chutney that it came with. And if your meal order didn't include a starter and a dessert you were just plain peculiar.

The smell of food was obviously spreading down the street. People started coming in to the café as Mark was eating. Some of them were tourist types, seeking a good meal before the day's hectic activities; looking around in appreciation at the mock Roman décor before finding a free table. Locals stood at the counter to collect their microwaved panini and hot drinks to go. Mandy barely had time to bring him his four thick slices of toast and butter with the vanilla rhubarb jam he was especially fond of. A *pain au chocolat* was perched on the edge of his plate, just in case.

He eventually managed to leave Tea For Two and walk away at half-past eight – waddle, as Liz claimed. Outside, it was exactly the sort of morning he had travelled three hundred light-years to immerse himself in every day. He breathed down air which had that distinct crisp chill that was only ever found at the foot of snow-capped mountains. The taller peaks and plateaus of the Dau'sings were still heavily snow-covered, including both ski fields. Mark looked up at them, his sunglasses darkening against the light from Elan's brilliant G-9 star flooding down out of the cloudless sky. They dominated the land behind the town, forming an impressive barrier of rumpled cones and peaks. Now that Elan's southern hemisphere was coming into springtime, meltwater was starting to run down out of the snowline, filling every crevice with gushing white rivulets. Pine-variants from across the Commonwealth had colonized the lower slopes, bringing a much needed cascade of verdure foliage. Above them, the native boltgrass still flourished, a characterless yellow-green plant with ratty strands. Away from the little oasis of foreign vegetation which humans had brought to the area, it was boltgrass which carpeted every mountain in the range, covering almost a quarter of the continent.

Small elongated triangles of golden fabric were already drifting idly across the sky as the first of the day's fliers flapped their way upwards in search of the thermals. They normally launched themselves off the ridges on Blackwater Crag, which rose up from the back of the town's eastern quarter. A cable car run sliced through the forest which covered the crag, leading from its ground base behind the high school's playing fields up to the semi-circular Orbit building which protruded from the top of the broad cliff six hundred metres above the town, looking as if a flying saucer was sticking out over the edge. The restaurant it housed was an over-priced tourist-trap, although the view it provided across the town and lake was unbeatable.

Every day the little chrome-blue cable cars would carry tourists and flight professionals and extreme sports addicts up to the Orbit. From there they'd make their way through the forest paths to a ridge which had the wind blowing in the right direction, seal themselves into a Vinci suit, and take flight. The real professionals would spend all day soaring and spiralling in the thermals, only coming back down as darkness fell. A Vinci suit was easy enough to use: basically a tapered slimline sleeping bag with bird wings that had a span up to eight metres. You stood up inside it on the crest of the ridge, arms outstretched in a cruciform position, and dived forwards into the chasm below. Electromuscle bands in the wings mimicked and amplified your arm and wrist motions, allowing

613

the wings to flap and bank and roll. It was the closest humans had ever got to pure bird flight.

Mark had been up a couple of times, sharing an instructor suit with a friend who lived in town. The sensation was truly amazing, but he wasn't about to switch jobs to do it full time.

He walked down the sloping Main Mall towards the water-front. The stores on either side of the walkway were a collection of Commonwealth-wide retail franchises like the Bean Here and an inevitable Bab's Kebabs fast food, interspaced with local craftshops and the bars and cafés to provide an eclectic shopping mix. Nearly all of the buildings were one storey, with steep solar panel roofs. Those with a second floor tended to be restaurants or bars with a balcony where the clientele could sit in the sun and watch the pedestrians below. Most of the Main Mall was made up from prefab modules, giving it a somewhat impermanent appearance, although several fronts were now clad in walls of the tough blue and purple stone available from the scree falls all over the Dau'sings; or wood from the pines. Little side alleys led to smaller stores and one-bedroom studio flats, where neatly pruned trailing plants scaled the walls and battered old chairs were laid out on the paving slabs. Bottles and glasses lay around them, evidence of the parties that thronged the little enclaves on a nightly basis.

Doors all the way along the Main Mall were being opened for business. Lights going on inside. Employees and janitorbots cleaning the floors. Mark said hello to a lot of the staff, waving to even more. They were all young people, and strangely uniform in appearance; if it wasn't for their varied skin colours they could all have been cousins. The boys had stiff hair cut short, maybe a few days' stubble, bodies that were genuinely fit, not simply over-aerobicized in a gym; they wore baggy sweaters or even baggier waterproof coats, with knee-length shorts, and trainer sandals. While the girls were easy to look at in their short skirts or tight trousers, with T-shirts all showing off firm midriffs no matter how cold the day was. All of them were just filling in with these jobs: serving in the stores, waitressing, working bar, portering at the hotels, stewarding on the dive boats, hostessing the scenic tours, doing childcare for the permanent residents. They did it for one thing, to raise enough money for the next extreme experience. Randtown's biggest industry was tourism, and what set it apart from countless other holiday destinations in the Commonwealth were the sports that were practised in the rugged countryside surrounding it. They attracted the first-lifers, the ones moderately disaffected with the mainstream of Commonwealth life; not rebels, just thrill-junkies hell-bent on finding a quicker way down a mountain, or a rougher way to raft over rapids, or turn tighter corners on jetskis, or go ever higher for heliski drops. Older, more conservative multi-life types visited as well. Staying in the fancy hotels, and getting bussed out to their scheduled activity each day in air-conditioned coaches. They were the ones that generated the service economy which provided hundreds of low-paying jobs for the likes of Mandy and Julie.

Mark crossed the single-lane road at the end of Main Mall, and walked along the waterfront promenade. Randtown was built around a horseshoe-shaped inlet on the northern shore of Lake Trine'ba. At a hundred and eighty kilometres long, it was the biggest stretch of inland freshwater on Elan. Complementing the height of the mountains which corralled it at their centre, it was over a kilometre deep in places. Lurking below the astonishingly blue surface was a unique marine ecology that had evolved in isolation for tens of millions of years. Stunningly beautiful coral reefs dominated the shallows, while conical atolls rose from the central deeps like miniature volcanoes. They were home to thousands of fish species, ranging from the bizarre to the sublime; though, like their saltwater cousins of this planet, they used lethal-looking spines and spindles rather than fins to propel themselves along.

After the winter skiing and snowboarding, diving was Randtown's second largest tourist draw. The waterfront provided dozens of jetties, where the commercial diving boats were berthed. Even today, with the Trine'ba only just above freezing, ten of the operators were running trips out over the waters. Mark watched a big Celestial Tours catamaran slide past, its impellers kicking up a thick spume behind each hull. A couple of the crew waved to him from the prow, calling out something that was lost in the noise of the engines.

He carried on along the side of the stone wall, with its single line of poetry which stretched the entire length. One day he was going to read it from start to finish. The Ables Motors garage, which was his franchise, was situated a couple of streets away from the eastern end of the promenade. He got to it well before quarter to nine. Randtown, for all it was the only real town for eight hundred kilometres, wasn't particularly large. Without the tourists and youthful transients, the population was only just over five thousand people. You could walk from one end to the other in less than quarter of an hour.

There were an equal number of people living out in the valleys and lowlands to the north and west where the farms and vineyards were spreading. To travel about on the district's dirt-track roads they needed decent four-wheel-drive transport. That was what Ables Motors specialized in, a division of Farndale that produced vehicles for harsh terrain. It had seemed like the perfect solution to Mark when they were searching for a new home and career. He was good with machines, so he could do most of the light repairs himself; and trading both new and second-hand models would add considerably to that income. Unfortunately, Ables Motors was a relatively new venture for Farndale, an unproven brand, while the old familiar Mercedes, Ford, Range Rover, and Telmar products took the lion's share of the market. Nor did it help that the Ables garage was only a couple of years old.

He perhaps should have realized that when he took it on along with the outstanding mortgage. Sales were slow, and given the tiny number of Ables vehicles in the area, maintenance work was equally sparse.

It had taken Mark less than a fortnight to realize that the four-wheel-drive business wasn't going to bring in anything like a decent income for the family. When he started looking around for extra work, he swiftly found that people in town and the farms had a lot of broken-down hardware that could be fixed by anyone with rudimentary mechanical aptitude. Mark had damn good mechanical, and electrical, aptitude; on top of which he had a fully equipped workshop. At the start of the third week he brought a few items back to the workshop, a couple of janitorbots, an air conditioner, the sonar out of a dive operator's catamaran, cookers, solar heat exchangers.

Randtown was a tight-knit community, people got to hear about anyone with that kind of talent. Pretty soon he was deluged with appliances and equipment that needed to be patched up. Most of it was done for cash, too; not that Elan's taxes were excessive. But they'd been paying off the mortgage on the vineyard faster than they'd originally planned.

That morning he'd got three autopickers waiting for him in the workshop. Each unit was the size of a car, with enough electromuscle appendages to fit a Raiel with prosthetics. They belonged to Yuri Conant, who owned three vineyards in Ulon valley, and was now a good friend and neighbour. One of Yuri's kids was the same age as Barry.

Mark pulled on his overalls, and started running diagnostics on the first machine. Its magnetic drive bearings were shot to hell. He was still underneath examining the superconductor linkages when his garage sales assistant, Olivia, came in.

'Have you heard?' she asked excitably.

Mark propelled his flat trolley out from under the mud-caked autopicker and gave her a wounded look. 'Wolfram finally asked if he could come in for a coffee last night?' It was a saga of frustrated romance which had been playing out for two weeks now; Mark usually got the latest instalment each morning.

'No! The *Second Chance* is back. They came out of hyper-space above Anshun about forty minutes ago.'

'Goddamn! Really?' No way could Mark pretend lack of interest in that. If he hadn't been married with family respon-sibilities he would have applied to go on the voyage himself. It was all part of the more interesting universe which existed away from Augusta. As it was he'd hunted down a lot of information on the project until he was able to bore plenty of people with all the statistics and trivial factoids. His e-butler was supposed to alert him on all new developments connected with the flight, but while he was driving into town that morning he'd put a blocker on his e-butler's access to the cybersphere to avoid any more emergency call-outs like Tea For Two. Family could get through, but no one else. He'd forgotten to take it off when he reached the garage. 'What did they find?' he asked as he hurriedly removed the blocker.

'It's gone, or something.'

'What has?' The data began to line up inside his virtual vision.

'The barrier. It vanished when they started to examine it.'

'Holy cow.' His virtual hands started to flash over icons, bringing up information. In the end there was so much coming on line they went into the little office at the back of the salesroom to watch the images on a holographic portal. CST was releasing video segments of the exploration as the starship downloaded its data. The media companies were gleefully swooping on it, putting together their own analysis and commentary teams in the studio.

Olivia had been right, the barrier was no more. Its disap-pearance was shocking, affecting him like the news of a sudden death in the family; that was one thing he absolutely hadn't been expecting. Nor had any of the studio experts, judging by the way they struggled to make sense of it.

There was little traffic on the road outside the Ables garage. The Russian chocolate house opposite had the same images playing in their portals above the counter. Customers sat at the tables, drinks ignored as they stared at the incomprehensibly massive barrier. He called Liz to see if she was accessing. She said yes, she was sitting with the rest of the staff at the Dunbavand vine nursery where she worked, looking at the scenes on one of the office screens.

Mark watched, awestruck, as the spheres and rings of the Dark Fortress revolved within the portal on his desk. The scale was so hard to appreciate. Then there was the system-wide Dyson civilization. The safe thrill of watching the nuclear firefight between ships, making him feel like he was doing something illicit. None of the commentators Alessandra Baron brought in to her studio liked the implications of that. She turned to a cultural anthropologist to try and explain why a space-faring species would fight in such a fashion. He clearly didn't have a clue.

Hours passed without Mark really being aware of them. It was only when Olivia said, 'Time for my lunch break,' that he finally glanced round at her, frowning as he tried to work out what she was saying.

'Right. Sure,' he replied. 'I don't suppose anyone's going to buy a vehicle off us today.' He decided he ought to take a break himself, and shut the garage doors behind him. The promenade was unusually quiet for midday. He pulled his jacket hood up against the bitter wind blowing off the lake. Those who did stroll past had the glazed otherwhere expression symptomatic of someone absorbed by their virtual vision. Everybody was hooked on the starship's return. It was as momentous as the Cup Final, when all through the first half Brazil had actually looked like they were going to lose.

619

Instinctively he glanced up at the Black House where Simon Rand lived, wondering if he too was having life put into perspective on this day. The building was a huge Georgian mansion perched on the slope above the eastern wing of the lake's inlet, set in ten acres of its own immaculately maintained grounds. There were dozens of big houses arrayed on the slopes around it, the most expensive and exclusive in the town, though they didn't match its grandeur. A lot of them belonged to the first arrivals, the men and women who'd joined Simon's quixotic crusade and helped lay the highway through the mountains.

It was fifty-five years ago now when Simon Rand arrived at Elan's planetary station with a whole train loaded with JCB roadbuilders, a fleet of various bots, and trucks jammed full of civil construction systems. He was moderately rich even back then, a first-life son of a minor Earth Grand Family who had cashed in his trust fund to buy a dream. Inspired by legends of the Oregon Trail he was determined to set out for somewhere fresh and new, and protect it from modern desecration. Elan, opened to settlers for only a couple of decades back then, was a good starting point. Developers and investors were cut a lot of slack by the planetary government if they helped establish new neighbourhoods and facilities. The idea was such entrepreneurial folk would import entire factories and build housing around them. But Simon's very different vision of a clean green community was harmless enough, so the bureaucrats granted him his land licences whilst privately believing the venture was doomed. After all, the Confederation worlds were littered with the follies of eccentric romanticists and their lost fortunes.

Simon immediately set off for the almost uninhabited southern continent of Ryceel. Once there he began the ultimate foolishness of building his road through the imposing Dau'sing range – as if there wasn't plenty of open land available north of the mountains. Several news shows ran

derisive reports on their bulletins, which attracted other ideal-
ists and supporters to his cause, willing to get their hands dirty
for the payday of living in a quiet, off-mainstream community
when they were finished. And Simon, for all his quirky
attitude, had at least prepared for his venture with a pragmatic
thoroughness.

Three years and seven hundred and eighty kilometres later
his last surviving JCB monster roadbuilder chewed its way
round the base of Blackwater Crag amid the death-screeches
of disintegrating rock and churning clouds of filthy steam, like
some earthbound dragon. Behind it was a dual carriageway of
enzyme-bonded concrete that bridged seventeen rivers and
tunnelled through eleven mountains. Walking along the newly
laid surface that crackled and gave off urea-like fumes was
Simon, leading a shambolic caravan of mobile homes, trucks,
and even a few horses and mules pulling carts. The three other
roadbuilders that had begun the trip were now abandoned
behind them; cannibalized, rusting hulks slumped beside the
road as monuments to its conception.

Like Moses so long before him Simon gazed out across
Lake Trine'ba and said, 'This is where we belong.' He could
see that it was the cool blue water which had parted the
continent-spanning mountains, leaving their massed ranks
pressed together along its shores. The massif ramparts
stretched on and on into the distance, reflected perfectly by
the unsullied mirror surface. On both sides, hundreds of
waterfalls fed by the meltwater poured out over jagged cliffs,
from tiny silver trickles barely wetting the rock to great
foaming cascades throwing out spray thicker than rain. Tiny,
delicate scarlet and lavender coral cones were poking out from
the centre of the lake. And filling the huge gulf of air above
the water was a silence so deep it absorbed his very thoughts.

In fifty-two years, the majestic view hadn't changed. Simon
was very determined about that. Buildings, forests, fields,
drainage ditches, and roads now spread out over the virgin

land in the valleys behind Randtown, but there was no industry, none of the factories and business units which normally barnacled the outskirts of human settlements. The inhabitants could import what they liked down the long toll highway which was still their only physical link to the rest of the human race – it wasn't economical to build a railroad beside it, and there was nowhere for an airport. Simon wasn't out to change the majority Commonwealth culture, he just wanted to keep the worst aspects out of his little part. So the farms were organic, the town's principal income came from tourism, its energy was geothermal and solar; combustion engines were illegal; recycling was a minor religion, and sewage was treated in secure bioreactors to prevent the slightest chance that any foreign human-derived chemical could ever pollute the precious pure water of Lake Trine'ba.

As environments went, Mark had gone from one extreme to the other.

Virtual vision showed him a ghostly image of the *Second Chance* slowly manoeuvring itself into its assembly platform dock high above Anshun. He was struck by its condition, how unworn it was. After such a voyage there should surely be some signs of stress, a few meteor impacts, scorchmarks – just something to prove how far it had been and what it had seen. But it looked as new and clean as the day it departed.

He stopped at one of the stalls behind the promenade and bought a tuna, shrimp, talarot, sweetcorn and mayo salad bap for lunch, along with some vegetarian sushi, plus a small something for pudding. It was Sasmi who sold it to him. She'd arrived in town a few months ago for the start of the snowboarding season. With her raven hair and flattish face Mark had thought her heritage was Oriental until she told him her ancestors were actually Finnish. A sweet girl who had dived headfirst into everything Randtown offered: the friends, parties, sports. Who always found the time to talk to Mark –

not that he was singled out, she just had an irrepressibly sunny nature.

Today even she was caught up in the drama of the starship's return. They swapped: 'Have you heard?' and: 'Did you see the bit where ...' as he watched her assembling his bap. He walked away back down the promenade, her parting smile lingering in his mind. There had never been so much temptation in his life before. It was an undisputed quality of Randtown; everybody here was so busy cramming their life full of events which mostly seemed to be parties and meeting other people, yet with all that they were never hurried. He had taken months to learn how to slow down and chill out after Augusta's lean, focused routine of work and family, where enjoyment was centred solely around entertainment. His only fear about living here now was that he would give in one day – some of the girls were just divine.

Olivia was still on her break when Mark got back to the garage. He'd only just sat down and started on his triple chip chocolate and quorknut muffin pudding when CST released the real bombshell. Two people had been left behind. The news was only just breaking because the company had been informing and counselling the families. Mark had enough trouble coping with that, never mind that one of them was actually Dudley Bose. For a while he was furious with the rest of *Second Chance*'s crew for abandoning them out there, such a thing was surely the ultimate betrayal. Just thinking about that much distance made him shiver. Then Captain Wilson Kime made a real-time statement. He was dressed in his full dark uniform, hair clipped neat and short, staring unflinchingly into the camera, knowing how many people would be staring back. All of them with one question on their lips. *Why did you do it? Why didn't you wait for them?*

'It is with the most profound regret that I find myself ending our historic voyage with this saddest possible news,'

Wilson said. His deep solemn voice was so sincere Mark immediately switched to feeling sorry for him and the terrible weight of command. 'I was forced to make the decision which every captain fears the most, to risk the lives of every person on board, or to leave our friends and colleagues behind. This mission was launched with the express commitment of bringing back vital information on Dyson Alpha, and the remarkable barrier surrounding this star. Whilst the safety of my crew is paramount to me personally as well as enshrined in my duty, I cannot overlook our ultimate objective. We found ourselves in a situation that placed the entire ship in grave danger. Faced with these circumstances, I had no choice other than to leave. It is a choice that I will have to face down every day for the rest of my life, always asking myself if we'd just stayed that fraction longer would they have got back in contact? But those few extra moments could equally have brought us calamity. Then we might never have brought back the information we have. The Commonwealth might not have been warned that the barrier is down, and the aliens it contained do not appear to be friendly. It is that information which I considered more important than the lives of our comrades. I know that if the tragic situation had been reversed, and I was out there lost in the alien station, that I would have wanted my shipmates to carry the essential knowledge home no matter what the personal cost. All of us undertook this voyage knowing there would be danger involved. None of us imagined it would be so profound. Thank you for your time.'

Mark slumped back in his seat, and pushed out a long breath. Given those circumstances, he supposed he would have done exactly the same thing. It was still a pretty frightening decision, though. And the captain thought the aliens were dangerous. That wasn't good, not good at all.

The news company started playing images of the Watchtower. Mark followed the astronauts as they slid through the dark tunnels of the station. There seemed to be miles of the eerie passageways knotted together. The harsh breathing of the contact team members reverberated round the showroom office; Mark felt himself being there as gloved hands stretched out at the edges of the image, grabbing frayed sections of the tunnel wall to haul himself along. Then he was slow-motion somersaulting into an empty chamber. Conduits on the wall had split open, allowing optical fibres to drift out like some kind of slender aquatic plant. He followed them along to a box containing circuit cubes, resembling fogged glass. Excited voices called out. The gauntlets tried to tease one of the cubes out, but it started crumbling at the touch. Another, calmer voice instructed them to cut the whole box free of its mountings.

Mark shook himself. He wanted to go through the Watch-tower inch by inch, examining its dark mysteries for himself. One night this week he'd take the time and lie on his bed, running a TSI of the exploration.

The news company switched to Senator Thompson Burnelli, who was standing in front of Washington's imposing Senate Hall. A broad semicircle of reporters was gathered round him, while he was flanked by two aides.

'Obviously I am disappointed by certain aspects of the flight,' Burnelli said. 'Although I would like to take this moment to express my sympathy to the families of both Dudley Bose and Emmanuelle Verbeke for the shock they received today. In relation to that, I do think there are some very serious questions raised by the way the *Second Chance* left the area so abruptly. I believe a lot more effort should have been made to ascertain the nature of the Dyson aliens. As to the supposed threat: nothing actually fired on our ship, a few robot devices were getting close, that's all. We don't know they were missiles. Kime could have taken a second, a third, even a fourth look; kept on trying until we got some real information. The *Second Chance* was equipped with ftl, they could leap out clean and free from any genuine danger.'

'What's going to happen now?' a reporter asked.

'The full Commonwealth ExoProtectorate Council will be convening as soon as possible to review the results. Once we have done so we will make our recommendation to the President and the Commonwealth Senate.'

'What will your recommendation be, Senator?'

Burnelli tipped his head thoughtfully to one side, frowning intently at his questioner. 'I think that is obvious. Due to the lack of any real data, we'll have to send another ship. This time commanded by a captain who has some nerve, one who can find out for us what's really going on out there.'

Mark was nodding in agreement. *Maybe Kime was hasty. The* Second Chance *had good shielding, I remember that from the specs. Protection was a prime design driver.*

Olivia returned, and they spent most of the afternoon watching the portal. CST released the recordings Dudley Bose had made, explaining and commenting on the data which the ship gathered. His descriptions fascinated Mark. They were pitched at a level he could understand, a clear confident voice turning the dry facts to vivid life. *No wonder he was such a respected, successful astronomer.*

Mark went out to the workshop a few times that afternoon, trying to do some work on the autopickers. Each time his mind drifted from the job and he went back to check the portal again. A lot of the time was spent wondering what it must have been like for Bose and Verbeke at that moment when they finally realized the starship had gone for good. How would anybody handle knowledge like that? *Christ, how would I take it?*

He shut the Ables garage up early, and drove home in his pick-up truck. The first part of the journey was along the great highway that Simon Rand had built, taking him round the back of Blackwater Crag and into the steep narrow valley there. Terrestrial grass had been planted at the side of the highway, a vigorous variety that had evicted the boltgrass, converting the slopes above the fast-flowing stream to a rich healthy emerald. Fat sheep still in their winter coats ambled round dozily, munching away, while their new lambs jumped about excitedly. High above them, where there was less grass and more boulders, mountain goats scurried about, venturing in and out from the edges of the pine forest.

After a few miles the valley widened out, the hills on his right sinking away where a much broader valley branched off. He took the junction, and started driving along the long straight track of hard-packed stone chips. This was the Highmarsh Valley, the first in the district to be farmed, and long since drained by an extensive network of ditches leaving the rich peat exposed for the tractorbots and cattle. Long driveways branched off from either side of the main track, leading to big bungalow-ranches and clusters of barns. The only trees here were tall, slender liipoplars planted in perfectly straight rows to mark the boundaries.

After five minutes the track forked again. Mark took the route down into Ulon Valley. It was almost as wide as the Highmarsh, though the mountain walls were higher. Boulders and stone were littered about, with a new crop brought down by the snows every winter. Although the soil was reasonable, the Ulon wasn't really suitable for serial crops. Instead, and at Simon Rand's suggestion, the first homesteaders planted vines of grencham berries, an Elan-native plant which was already earning a reputation among Commonwealth oenophiles, though it had only ever been cultivated on the northern continents. The first few years saw passable vintages produced along the Ulon; then new varieties were introduced, and the yards got organized, forming a cooperative for blending and bottling, and incorporating their brand name.

By the time the Vernons arrived, the whole operation had become slick and commercial. Two thirds of the valley was under cultivation, with the remaining plots being snapped up. Any purchaser got their ten or fifteen acres to be planted with vines, and a house site at one end. The vines would be managed and harvested by the co-op, guaranteeing a modest income each year from the Ulon Valley label.

Mark turned onto the track which led up a short slope to his home, slowing as the suspension bounced him around in the puddles and potholes. Once again, as he did every morning and evening, he reminded himself to get some decent gravel delivered. The vine trellises were stretched out on both sides of the track; lines of wires and poles, like flimsy fences, set a couple of metres apart, extending as far as the eye could see. Small gnarled brown strands of the vines themselves were carefully wound along the wires, each one trimmed identically, no more than five buds along each frond. It was too early in the year for any growth, leaving the whole plot looking pretty bleak with only the narrow strips of straggly grass providing any colour between the trellises, though they seemed to be more mud and stone than living tufts. Up at the top of the ridge, where the house sat on an acre of flat land, the lawn was a vigorous emerald carpet. At the moment it surrounded two houses. The one they'd brought with them on the back of a big flatbed truck as a pile of square weather-resistant composite panels that could be clipped together in any design. Liz and Mark had settled on a simple L-shape, with a long rectangular living room at one end attached to three square bedrooms, a bathroom, kids' room, kitchen, and spare room – which was still crammed with crates of stuff they'd brought from Augusta and hadn't yet opened. Its roof was made up from curved solar collector sections which slotted on top. The whole thing was cheap, easy to assemble, and the kind of place that you wouldn't want to live in for more than a few months, especially not in winter. They'd been on Elan for almost two years now.

Behind the temporary prefab, their true house was still growing. In keeping with Randtown's green ethos, they'd both decided it was going to be drycoral – which was strangely rare for an eco-obsessed district. Normally the plant was grown over an existing structure, but Liz had tracked down a company on Halifax that offered a much cheaper method. She'd started with what was essentially a cluster of hemispherical balloons, a simple made-to-order any-size-you-want membrane that she spread out over the ground and inflated. Then she just planted the kernels all around the outside, and waited for them to grow. As the strands slithered their way upward, she twined them together and pruned judiciously, ensuring the walls were smooth and water-tight. Because of Ulon Valley's harsh winters, she selected a drycoral variety thicker than most, to provide a decent insulation. When they were done, a simple domestic solar pumped heatstore cube would keep them warm and snug all winter. But it was that necessary additional thickness which made them realize why few Randtown district homes were made from drycoral: it took a long time to grow upward. Every day when he got out of the pick-up truck Mark would take another look at the tops of the pearl and cornflower-blue strands to see how far they'd got. On four or five of the smaller outlying dome rooms they were already up to the crest, where Liz was knotting them together in a minaret finishing twist; but on the three largest domes they'd still got a couple of metres to go. 'They'll be ready by midsummer,' Liz kept saying. Mark prayed she was right.

Barry burst out of the house and ran over to Mark, flinging his arms round his father. It used to be his father's legs, now they were above his hips.

'What did you do today?' They both said it together as ritual demanded, and smiled at each other.

'You first,' Mark said as they walked back to the temporary house.

'I was reading and spelling this morning, then we had Mr Carroll for maths and programming. I did general history with Ms Mavers, and Jodie took us for practical mechanics to finish off with. I liked that. It was the only thing that made sense.'

'Really, why's that?'

They walked into the kitchen, where Liz was sitting at the big cluttered table, trying to coax Sandy into having some soup. Mark's daughter looked the picture of misery with her cheeks and nose all red, eyes damp, and wrapped in a big warm blanket. It was a flu variant which had been doing the rounds of all the local kids. Barry had managed to avoid it so far.

'Daddy,' Sandy said weakly, and held her arms out.

Mark knelt down and gave her a big cuddle. 'So how are you feeling today my angel, any better?'

She nodded miserably. 'Little bit.'

'Oh, that's good. Well done, darling.' He sat in the chair next to her, and got a very fast and perfunctory kiss from Liz. 'How about eating some of this soup then?' he asked his daughter. 'We'll eat it together.'

What might have been a smile passed across Sandy's lips. 'Yes,' she said bravely.

Liz rolled her eyes for Mark and got up. 'I'll leave you two to it, then. Come on Barry, what do you want for tea?'

'Pizza?' he said immediately, followed by a hopeful: 'and chips.'

'It's not going to be pizza,' Liz told him sternly. 'You know you've cleared all of them out of the freezer. It's going to have to be fish.'

'Oww, Mum!'

'We can probably find some chips to go with them,' Liz said, knowing it was the only way to get him to eat the fish.

'All right,' the boy said glumly. 'Well, is it fried fish, then?'

'I've no idea.'

Barry sat in his chair at the table, a picture of tragedy. Liz told the maidbot to fetch some fish from the freezer, adding an order silently through her e-butler to make it a grill-only packet.

'So why didn't anything make sense?' Mark asked again.

'Well, it did sort of,' Barry said. 'It's just that I don't see the point.'

'Of what?'

'School.'

'Ah, why not?'

'I don't need it,' the boy said sincerely. He gestured to the broad kitchen window with its view back down the Ulon Valley. 'I'm going to be a jetboat captain, and do the river.'

'Oh, right.' Last week it had been a gyroball instructor. Kids in the Randtown district tended to be influenced by the more sporting and physical aspects of life. They were all going to be raft masters, or jetboat captains, or ski instructors, or pro fliers, or gill divers. 'Well, you still need a basic education, I'm afraid, even to qualify for that. So you'll have to keep going, at least for a few years more.'

'Okay,' Barry said mournfully. 'I might be a starship pilot, as well. I was watching that on the cybersphere today. The whole school was there when the *Second Chance* docked with its platform. That was so cool.'

Mark kept looking at Sandy as he was spooning her the soup. 'Yeah, it was.'

'You saw it, too?'

'Certainly did.'

The maidbot arrived back with a packet of fish. Liz grabbed it from the little machine. 'Come, on, help me cook this.'

'Where are the chips?' Barry asked plaintively.

'There are some potatoes in the basket. We'll cut them up. It won't take long.'

'No no, Mum. Real chips. From the freezer!'

Mark took Sandy through into the lounge while Barry and Liz prepared the fish. He cleared some of the toys off the sofa and sat down. Sandy curled up in his lap, sniffling as she clung to her friend-doll, a pro-response polar bear that was sensing her illness, and held on to her arm affectionately.

He flicked through a few cybersphere reports on the big

portal before reluctantly settling on Alessandra Baron, who had secured an exclusive with Nigel Sheldon himself. He was sitting behind some big desk in his corporate office, talking clearly and confidently, as if the whole starship return drama had been just a scheduled stop for one of his trains. 'Whilst I deeply regret that Captain Kime had to leave Emmanuelle and Dudley behind, I don't believe he had any choice in the matter. I was not there, nor were any of the somewhat distasteful armchair critics I've heard today. As such we are completely unable to offer anything approaching a valid opinion concerning what was done, and what other courses of action were supposedly available. Only a fool would try to second-guess an event like that. I appointed Wilson as captain because I believed he was the right man for the job. His exemplary actions throughout the mission have completely vindicated that appointment.

'Of course, CST has already authorized re-life procedures for both of our lost crew. Thanks to the safety procedures which we take so seriously, their onboard secure memory stores were updated just before they went over to the Watchtower.'

'But what about the information the *Second Chance* brought back?' Alessandra asked. 'Surely you have to concede it's disappointing?'

Nigel Sheldon smiled as if he pitied her. 'We have more data than the entire Commonwealth physics community can absorb. I'd hardly call that a dearth.'

'I was referring to the lack of knowledge about the Dyson aliens. After so much money was spent, so much time devoted, and with the added cost of human life, don't you think we should know more? We don't even know what they look like.'

'We know that they shoot at us on sight. The one thing I am in agreement with my good friend Senator Burnelli over is that there must be a return mission. This is the nature of exploration, Alessandra. I'm sorry it's not fast enough for your personal timetable. But sensible, rational humans venture somewhere new and see what the conditions are like so that we can prepare ourselves to go further next time. The *Second Chance* did this, it brought back a wealth of details on Dyson Alpha and what kind of ship we need to go back there with.'

'So you're in favour of going back, then?'

'Definitely. We've only just begun our encounter with the Dyson stars.'

'And what kind of ship should we use, based on what we learned from the first mission?'

'One that is very fast, and very strong. In fact, just to be safe, we should probably send more than one.'

Mark and Liz got the kids to bed and settled by eight o'clock. After that, they sat in the kitchen, eating their own supper of chicken kiev: out of a packet and microwaved, of course. 'Old Tony Matvig has some chickens,' Mark said. 'I talked to him the other day, he'll give us some eggs if we want our own.' His fork prodded at the meat on his plate, squeezing out some more of the garlic butter. 'It would be nice to have something we know isn't full of hormones and weird gene splices to feed the kids with.'

Liz gave him her 'weighing up' look. 'No, Mark. You know we've been through all this. I like living here, and I'll like it a whole lot more once the house has finished growing, but I'm not buying in that deeply. We don't need to keep chickens, we earn more than enough to eat well, and I don't order factory food from the Big15. Everything in that freezer has the clean-feed label, if you ever bothered to look. And who did you see plucking and gutting these chickens, exactly? Were you going to do it?'

'I could do.'

'You won't. The smell is revolting. It made me throw up.'

'When did you ever gut a chicken?'

'About fifty years ago. Back when I was young and idealistic.'

'And foolish. Yeah, I know.'

She leant over and rubbed his cheek with her fingers. 'Am I a real pain?'

'No.' He tried to catch one of her fingers in his teeth – missing.

'In any case,' she said. 'Chickens will ruin the lawn. Have you ever taken a good look at their claws? They're evil.'

Mark grinned. 'Killer chickens.'

'They kill lawns, and rip the rest of the garden apart as well.'

'Okay. No chickens.'

'But I'm all in favour of the vegetable garden.'

'Yeah. Because I'm going to rig up an irrigation system, and a gardeningbot can look after the rest of it.'

Liz blew him a kiss. 'I said I'd tend the herb bed myself.'

'Wow. All of it?'

'Any regrets yet?'

'Not one.'

'I can think of one.'

'What?' he asked indignantly.

'I need a big strong man to go out and look at the precipitator leaves again.'

'Oh, you've got to be kidding! I fixed them last week.'

'I know, darling. But they barely filled the tank last night.'

'Goddamn semi-organic crap. We should have dug a decent well.'

'Well, we can get a constructionbot to lay a pipe down to the river when the real house is finished.'

'Yeah, maybe.'

The maidbot took their plates and cutlery away to stack in the dishwasher. Mark carried a dish of sticky toffee pudding through into the lounge, along with two spoons. They snuggled up together on the sofa, and started scooping at the gooey mass from opposite ends. Over on the portal, Wendy Bose was stammering and weeping her way through a statement.

Professor Truten, labelled by the subtitles as a 'close family friend', had his arm supportively round her shoulder.

'Poor woman,' Liz said.

'Yeah.'

'She needs to go into rejuve. I wonder if CST will pay for that?'

'Why does she need rejuve?' Mark peered at her image inside the portal. 'She doesn't look like she's that old.'

Liz took advantage of his distraction to spoon up two lots of pudding. 'Compared to whom? Dudley Bose's replacement clone is going to be an eighteen-year-old. She'll have a physical equivalence of late fifties. Trust me, that's not a marriage you want to try.'

'Suppose not. I just can't stop thinking about Bose and Verbeke. Talk about being abandoned a long way from home. Do you think they suicided when they realized?'

'Depends on the Dyson aliens. Maybe they built them an environment chamber, and right now they've cracked the translation hurdle and are chatting away happily.'

'You don't really believe that, do you?'

Liz chewed thoughtfully for a moment. Professor Truten was helping Wendy Bose back into her house. 'Nope. They're body-dead.'

'I figured that, too.' His gaze wandered up to the cheap composite ceiling. 'You know Elan's almost the closest Commonwealth planet to the Dyson Pair.'

'There are seven closer than us, including Anshun. But you're right, we're close.' She giggled. 'Only seven hundred and fifty-four light-years away. Scary, huh?'

He reached round with his free hand, and poked her just below the ribs, where he knew she was sensitive.

'Ow!' Liz screwed her face up, and retaliated by scooping up a giant piece of pudding.

'Hey!' he protested. 'I've barely had a mouthful, yet.'

'Life's a bitch, then you rejuvenate and do it all over again.'

16

It was midday on America's eastern seaboard. The sun had reached its zenith, allowing it to shine directly onto the streets lurking at the bottom of Manhattan's concrete canyons. Looking down on Fifth Avenue from the two hundred and twenty-fifth floor of the Commonwealth Exploration and Development Office, Nigel Sheldon could see the city's perpetual traffic battle in action. All along that massive historical thoroughfare, yellow cabs and matt-black limousines were jammed together, two entirely separate and antagonistic species contesting dominance of the available lanes. Urban myth told it that the city's cabs had illicit aggressor software installed in their drive arrays. That wouldn't surprise Nigel given the number of times his limo had had to brake to make way for a cab veering out in front of him. And they were the ones who benefited most from this brief visitation of light, hundreds of them gleaming splendidly amid their sombre opponents, right now they looked victorious.

Closer to the base of the skyscraper, he could see a thick semicircle of reporters around the main entrance. There was an idle thought, if he spat out of the window, how long it would take before one of them was hit, looking upwards with revulsion and annoyance. It was good to have childish thoughts like that still, he felt: they put a perspective on life. His fellow council members could certainly do with lightening up.

They were already filling the room behind him. Thompson Burnelli and Crispin Goldreich sitting together at the table, heads together as they horse-traded and manoeuvred, playing out the game in which all the Grand Families participated. Elaine Doi, looking more drawn than usual, but then she really didn't need complications in the year that would see her placing her name into the ring for the pre-primaries of the Presidential election. She was exchanging greetings with Rafael Columbia and Gabrielle Else. There were fewer aides this time around, reflecting the increased security and importance resting on the ExoProtectorate Council. Wilson Kime was standing talking with Daniel Alster, looking remarkably unflustered given the certain degree of animosity directed towards him by Council members, led by Senator Burnelli.

Nigel could take the politicking in his stride. Unlike Wilson, he'd never given himself the luxury of a sabbatical life away from the heart of the Commonwealth government. Thinking ahead was what he lived for; and he was pretty sure that none of the aides and think tanks which the other Council members drew on for their brief had prepared as many scenarios as the CST strategists had. Some of the worst-case outcomes were going to require counter-actions that he would have to undertake by himself, through private and discreet ventures – including the ultimate fallback of evacuating his entire family from Commonwealth space altogether. Implementing such schemes didn't particularly bother him – in fact they were quite a challenge. The only cause for concern today was the one thing which had been troubling him for several months now, the lack of any communication from Ozzie. Nigel was used to his friend vanishing for months, or even years at a time while he went worldwalking, or even homesteading and raising a new family. But he always answered his messages eventually.

'If you're ready,' Elaine Doi said, somewhat impatiently.

Nigel turned from the window, nodding reluctantly. He'd

been putting off the meeting in the small hope that Ozzie would appear at the last second, unapologetic as always and happy to have caused a nuisance. It wasn't to be. The doors were closed, and the room secured.

Everyone settled around the table. The Vice President asked for the SI to be brought on line, and its tangerine and turquoise lines began to shiver across the screen at the end of the room. 'I believe we should start by congratulating Captain Wilson and his crew on performing an exceptionally difficult mission with true professionalism,' Elaine Doi said. 'I know you had some hard choices to make out there, Captain, and I don't envy you that, but I believe they were the right ones. Bringing back information was your first priority.'

'What information was that, exactly?' Thompson Burnelli asked. 'I consider myself less than enlightened by your trip. Certainly given the cost of the damn thing.'

'That there is a very large, technologically advanced, and apparently aggressive alien species seven hundred and fifty light-years from the Commonwealth,' Wilson said impassively. 'They were confined within the barrier, but someone let them out so they could see us. A third party. In itself an action we should consider to be unfriendly at the very least, if not positively hostile.'

'You seriously believe that?' Thompson asked. 'We're facing two sets of aliens, both of them hostile?'

'The barrier removal was not coincidence,' Nigel said. 'We didn't do it. The Dyson aliens didn't do it. QED, there is another factor at work here.'

'It had to be the aliens which put it up in the first place,' Brewster Kumar said. 'Only the people with the knowledge of construction could do that.'

'That makes very little sense to me,' Elaine Doi said. 'If you're going to switch it off when the first ship arrives to investigate, why put it up in the first place?'

'I'd like to address that,' Wilson said. 'We have two options, either the barrier was taken down by the same aliens who put it up, in which case the motivation remains beyond us given our current level of knowledge about them. Or it was switched off by someone else, again for an unknown reason; and that is the more worrying conclusion.'

'Why?' Crispin Goldreich asked.

'It was put up to confine what appears to be an aggressive species. Somebody was worried enough about them to build that thing. Now I was there, I saw that barrier; you just don't build something like that without a very very good reason. I don't care how advanced the builders were, the resources and effort they needed to devote to that task were fantastic. They were worried to the point of paranoia about the Dyson aliens. Think about that, a species which can build a barrier around a star was worried. Anything that can worry them, scares the shit out of me. And now the Dyson aliens are free.'

'Do you agree with that assessment?' Elaine Doi asked the SI.

'It is logical. We do not believe it was coincidence that the barrier was switched off at the same time as the *Second Chance* arrived. That it was done by the Dyson aliens seems unlikely. By simple elimination it had to be the creators of the barrier, or yet another alien.'

'Neither of which has any valid motive,' Brewster Kumar said.

'No apparent motive,' the SI said. 'But as we do not yet know the actual reason behind the establishment of the barrier, guessing at the basis for its removal is an irrelevant exercise.'

'Don't you think it was put up because the Dyson aliens are aggressive?' Wilson asked.

'It is a plausible theory, yes,' the SI said. 'But why was it deemed necessary to enclose Dyson Beta in a similar barrier?'

'Good point,' Rafael Columbia acknowledged.

'I don't know,' Wilson said wearily. 'But what we have established is how dangerous the aliens at Dyson Alpha are.'

'Apparently dangerous,' Thompson Burnelli said. 'Let's face it, if an alien species had observed Earth in the twentieth century, especially during the Second World War, they would conclude we were irredeemably violent. I'm surprised they didn't put a barrier round us while they had the chance, if that is the reason these things are built.'

'We've grown out of that phase,' Elaine Doi said. 'Rejuvenation and interstellar expansion have completely altered our psychology and culture.'

'Don't start that argument again,' Brewster Kumar said. 'We got lucky, that was all.'

'We make our own luck,' Elaine said. 'As a race we have great potential within us. Have some faith.'

'We're not discussing us,' Nigel said. 'We're here to decide what to do about a bunch of aliens with an awful lot of nuclear weapons and a propensity to use them.'

'They have nukes and no doubt a great many other sophisticated weapons,' Rafael Columbia said. 'But they do not have any form of ftl, which gives us a safety margin of seven hundred and fifty light-years. That's a very big safety margin.'

'They didn't have ftl, because there was no need for it inside the barrier, and ftl was blocked by the barrier,' Wilson said. 'But given their demonstrated technological capability, I wouldn't count on any kind of distance keeping them away from us.'

'How long would it take them to build ftl starships?'

Everyone looked at Nigel. He shrugged. 'Like Wilson said, they have a high-technology industrial base. Once you've worked out the basic theory, you could have a prototype hyperdrive up and running in a matter of months if you devote enough resources to the project. The key question is, if you can put that math together in the first place.'

'We have to assume they can,' Elaine Doi said. 'They saw the *Second Chance* in operation.' She grimaced. 'And they might well have Bose and Verbeke.'

'They'll suicide before that happens, surely,' Rafael Columbia said. 'They know what's at stake.'

Wilson cleared his throat uncomfortably. Everybody round the table turned to look at him. They'd all been in the game long enough to recognize bad news from any distance.

'All crew members, myself included, were equipped with an insert which will perform that function,' Wilson said. 'However, we can reasonably assume Bose and Verbeke will assess the situation first. If they were to make an initial non-violent contact with the Dyson aliens, I would expect them to make some attempt to communicate and build up a rapport. Only if it looked hopeless would they resort to a complete datawipe of their memory inserts and suicide.'

'So they'll do it then?' Elaine Doi said. She seemed to be urging him to say *yes*. 'I mean, they know they'll be re-lifed within the Commonwealth. They'll only lose a day at the most, surely? And it could be a very unpleasant day, at that.'

'I am reasonably convinced Emmanuelle Verbeke will do the right thing,' Wilson said. 'But – and I hope to Christ I'm wrong – we may have a problem with Bose.'

'What do you mean, *a problem*?' Thompson Burnelli demanded.

Wilson stared at the senator. 'His training and assessment weren't as thorough as everyone else on board. After selection, he spent some time in a rejuve tank reducing his body age. The remaining time was limited before we launched.'

'Then why the fuck did you let him on board?'

'Political expediency,' Nigel interjected smoothly. 'Same reason your man Tunde Sutton was on board.'

Thompson levelled a rigid forefinger at Nigel. 'Tunde passed every test you threw at him.'

'He certainly did. And if he'd been rejected at the final selection process, along with everyone else who had connections to Earth's Grand Families, you would have been the first to cause a stink.'

'Maybe. But at least Tunde was properly trained, not like this Bose character. What kind of half-assed operation are you running here?'

'The only one in town.'

'Jesus H. Christ.' Thompson sat back, and gave both Nigel and Wilson a disgusted look.

'Very well,' Elaine Doi said. 'In the worst possible case, the Dyson aliens know a lot about us, they can build an ftl starship, and they know where we are. What do we do about that?'

'Same as the last time,' Wilson said. 'Send a mission to find out what's going on.'

'One that has a greater success than last time, one sincerely hopes,' Crispin Goldreich said.

'It will be,' Nigel said. 'The *Second Chance* was a shot completely into the unknown. We had to build something that could tackle just about any contingency, a true exploratory vessel. This time the mission will be very tightly defined. These ships will be smaller, and possibly even a little cheaper.'

'Why do you need more than one?' Elaine Doi asked.

'So the others can monitor what happens to the one that attempts to make contact, and report back if it's lost,' Wilson said. 'By now the Dyson aliens know who we are, and possibly that we didn't put up the barrier. They certainly know we are no threat to them. How they react to us this time around will be crucial.'

'I wouldn't like that job,' Rafael Columbia muttered.

'I'm not looking forward to it myself,' Wilson said. 'But it has to be done, and done properly.'

'You got something to prove?' Thompson Burnelli asked quietly.

Wilson didn't rise to it.

'I take it these ships are on the drawing board?' Elaine Doi asked.

'Oh yes,' Nigel said. 'As soon as we completed the *Second*

Chance design, I authorized preliminary assessment on a possible smaller exploration starship. Adapting that to a fast scout vehicle is relatively simple. From what we learned about building the hyperdrive for *Second Chance* we can modify future versions for a much greater speed. That whole life-support wheel structure has been dumped, the crew can slum it in freefall. We've also minimized the reaction drive along with its ancillary garbage – there was no need for it apart from short-range manoeuvring. But we have bumped up the armament quotient. They'll be able to fight as well as run.'

'And what will their mission be, exactly?' Brewster Kumar asked.

'They must discover more about the nature of the Dyson aliens. If they are truly warlike. If they are developing ftl starships or opening wormholes to nearby star systems. ftl in particular would be hard to hide, given a wormhole signature is so readily detectable. Of course, if they have any knowledge in that field, that will mean they can probably spot us coming as well.'

'Very well,' Elaine Doi said. 'I don't think any of us disagree that this new mission must be undertaken, and with some urgency. What I'd like from this Council is a formal proposal to the Commonwealth Executive Office to form a new agency which will oversee the whole Dyson exploration and contact operation from planning to execution, put it all under government jurisdiction.'

'And financing,' Thompson Burnelli said gruffly.

'Are you saying you want the government to establish a civil starflight agency?' Rafael Columbia asked.

'Exactly that, yes. This is a possible threat to the entire Commonwealth. It cannot be the preserve of an ad hoc response with uncertain multi-source funding. The problem needs to be addressed with stability and clear policy management.'

'Ah,' Rafael glanced at Nigel. 'And how do you feel about

that, Nigel? These are mostly your personnel we are talking about.'

'I think it doesn't go far enough.' He almost smiled at how quiet the room became, even Wilson was staring at him in surprise. 'You want policy for this, then it has to be long term and coherent. If our new scouts come back with bad news, then what? Another meeting like this? No, Elaine is quite right, we need clear policy and an agency capable of implementation. We need to be preparing for the worst case before the scout ships even leave. There are other Commonwealth agencies and councils like this one that deal in security. They will have to be incorporated into this new agency as well.'

'You're talking about the formation of a navy,' Crispin Goldreich said. He seemed taken aback by the idea. 'A committed military force.'

'If you know of something else which can defend us, I'd like to hear about it.'

'I cannot believe you are proposing this. You! What does Mr Isaacs say about it?'

'I expect he'll be upset by the very notion,' Nigel said. 'But as he can't even be bothered to turn up to this meeting, he doesn't get to have that say, does he?'

The surprise around the table was even greater than before.

'What?' an irritated Nigel asked. 'We had a glorious dream when we were young. We gave humanity the stars. And now, as Elaine said, we've grown up because of that. If everything we've achieved as a race, this whole glorious civilization we've built, is under threat, then damn right I want to protect it. A navy will do that.'

'Yes it will,' Thompson Burnelli said carefully. 'But if we go ahead and announce we're going to create a navy, it will generate a huge amount of panic and worry. Christ knows what the stock market will do, and the knock-on effect that'll have on the economy doesn't make pleasant speculation. You might even get inward migration from the outermost phase two planets – which is the last thing we need. The damn thing will be cyclic, it'll feed on itself. If it's our brief to protect the Commonwealth from any alien impact, then we have to consider that as well. This isn't just external, Nigel.'

'I know,' Nigel said. 'What we should do is copy the way Hitler prepared the ground for his Luftwaffe. After the Versailles Treaty, Germany was forbidden from pursuing any form of military aviation, so he trained pilots in private clubs, and sponsored commercial aircraft which could easily be modified. Then when he wanted an air force he simply brought the two together. All the pieces were available, but no one recognized them for what they were. And today, with our industrial base spread over six hundred worlds, we can run a far more sophisticated covert manufacturing operation than the Nazis ever could. The rest of it is just another bureaucratic reshuffle, bringing together the requisite departments.'

'I can think of several people in the Senate who won't take kindly to the Hitler comparison,' Thompson Burnelli said with dry amusement.

'Don't use that analogy, then,' Nigel said. 'The point is we can begin preparations for the physical defence of the Commonwealth without being alarmist. Getting the paperwork done is always half the battle.'

'I'm interested in your opinion of this,' Rafael Columbia told the SI. 'Do you think we should have a navy?'

'Whilst never condoning weapons development, we consider the formation of such a defence organization to be a sensible precaution given the circumstances.'

Wilson gave the screen a sharp look. 'Would you assist us with weapons development?'

'We have every confidence in your own ability in that field. You have demonstrated your competence many times throughout your history.'

'Although I support a further mission to Dyson Alpha,' Brewster Kumar said, 'we shouldn't ignore the other species that appear to be out there. Will this navy or starflight agency be sending missions to try and locate the creators of the barrier?'

'We need to have a starflight agency first,' Nigel chided the science adviser gently. 'But, yes, that should not be overlooked. Nor should a separate mission to Dyson Beta; I'm most interested to see if that barrier is still there. There is a lot more to this than Dyson Alpha's species alone.'

'Very well,' Elaine Doi said. 'I believe we should leave specific mission planning out of the discussion for now. We have a proposal that will eliminate it anyway. I expect this Council and its function would be absorbed into the new agency?' She gave Nigel a questioning glance.

'A starflight agency would need a steering panel,' Nigel said. 'This is the obvious choice.'

'Then we'll take a vote,' she said. 'Those in favour?'

Every Council member put their hand up.

*

This time the message had the author certificate of Chiles Liddle Halgarth, but the spokesman was the same Formit 3004 politician sculpture, still sitting behind his desk in San Matio. This time the city was in springtime, with the powerful sun just rising above the whitewashed walls of the old quarter, turning the buildings a beautiful silken gold. Dark green trees planted along every street were uncurling their leaves to greet the dawn.

'My fellow citizens, I wish I could welcome you with a sense of satisfaction,' he said. 'For once again we who have fought the subterranean battle to prevent the Starflyer's agents gnawing away at the heart of our wonderful Commonwealth have been proved right. But of course I feel no joy at the situation we face this day. We failed to destroy the *Second Chance*, and now the starship has begun a chain reaction of events which will plunge us into war. The Dyson aliens have been let out of their prison in accordance with the Starflyer's wishes. We have all seen the recordings of their aggression, a brutality which we all know will be turned towards us as soon as they build their own starships.

'Even if we survive the coming assault, we will be weakened terribly. Our wealth and our talent will be poured into our very survival, where it will be consumed by nuclear fire. That is when the Starflyer will strike against us, unseen, from our very midst.

'This monster will ruin us unless we guard against it. The Guardians of Selfhood will always be ready to thwart its machinations, right to the very end. We will root it out and eliminate its agents. But we need your help. Be vigilant. Be vocal. Stand for elections on a platform opposing the meagre efforts which this corrupt government is proposing to protect us. We do not need three scout ships, we need an armada of battleships. We do not need further investigation, we need weapons that can blow the invaders out of space. We must be ready to defend ourselves from the Dyson aliens right now. They will appear in our skies soon enough. Don't let us fall to their onslaught. Challenge those who claim to be working on your behalf. They are not, they serve only themselves and their evil master. Help us. Be strong. Guard yourselves.'

He bowed his head. 'I thank you for your time.'

*

The red light was everywhere, oozing pervasively throughout the Ice Citadel to contaminate every room, passageway, and cranny. Ozzie detested it. The Silfen builders of old had done their job well; the big optical ducts and the light battery, whatever that was, delivered rosy sunlight throughout the frozen planet's entire twenty-one-hour day. There was only one place which offered true sanctuary – the outside at night. But that was when it got seriously cold.

Inside, most of the private sleeping rooms had thick rugs

rigged up over the radiant crystal to act as curtains. For those species which did sleep, or at least rest up at night, they were a godsend. Recently, Ozzie and Orion had taken to lighting a kerosene lamp in their room for a couple of hours before they went to bed. Their original supply of kerosene had quickly been exhausted, but one of the icewhale oils was a reasonable substitute. The yellow light also attracted quite a few fellow humans, who would come in and spend some time, either relaxing or bitching about their day. Ozzie's room in the evening began to resemble a small bar, admittedly one without any alcohol. Inevitably, given that people had arrived at the Ice Citadel from many planets and over many centuries, the conversation ranged across a lot of different perspectives and opinions.

The gatherings also helped Ozzie gain a good understanding of the Ice Citadel and their general situation. One thing was perfectly clear, they shouldn't try for another path until the Silfen came to hunt.

'That's when you've got the best opportunity to get clear,' Sara said one day a couple of weeks after they'd arrived. She'd become a regular in Ozzie's little evening club. Most humans at the Ice Citadel tended to look to her for guidance, a position she'd earned by the sheer quantity of time stacked up in her favour. It was a role she was content to see slide over onto Ozzie, who was equally keen to resist.

'Why?' Orion asked. 'You don't need them to get here.'

'Because it increases the odds,' she said tolerantly. 'If you can follow them, or even better, stay with them, you'll be on the path they take to get out. It's definitely there, then. For the rest of the time, you're just striking out into the unknown, hoping you'll find a path that's open. From what we know, there don't seem to be many. And on this planet, that spells trouble. You have to carry a whole load of supplies and be quick as well.'

Ozzie had soon worked out it was a bad equation. You

could use a sledge to reach the forest of crystal trees surrounding the Ice Citadel crater easily enough, but then the sledge would have a lot of trouble travelling through the forest itself. If you went forward on foot you needed a tent that could protect you from the deadly night-time temperature. The air-insulated one he'd brought could conceivably do that, but then he had to carry enough food as well. The more weight you had, the slower you'd be. And so on. An ideal solution would be a pack animal, but those who could survive in these conditions, like the lontrus, were slow-moving. Which meant adding more food to the weight they carried. Sara was right, their best option was a fast dash behind the Silfen.

They had to be patient.

*

The usual early morning sounds woke Ozzie, pans and bowls and platters clattering about as the breakfast shift began their preparations out in the main chamber. Human voices combined with alien hoots and whistles accompanied them, echoing down the short passageway to Ozzie's set of rooms. He lay there on the cot for a while with his eyes shut, his mind ticking off the sequence. Low rushing sound of the bellows and oil burners. Water coming to the boil and rattling the big kettles. Knives being sharpened on the grinder. Familiar and tiresome.

This was the seventeenth week now. Or at least he thought it was. He was having strange dreams, events and Commonwealth worlds rushing past him like some fast-motion drama. There were stories from his fellow travellers about time being not quite right as you walked along the paths, of them missing or gaining weeks, months, years while they travelled through the Silfen worlds. The notion kept feeding his feeling of impatience.

Orion stirred, groaned – as he always did – and sat up in his sleeping bag.

'Morning.' Ozzie opened his eyes. The rug was still pulled over the crystal tract set in the ceiling, but enough light spilled round the sides, and through the curtained-off doorway, that he could see the room's outlines without having to use his retinal inserts on infrared.

Orion grunted a response, and unzipped his sleeping bag. Ozzie started to get dressed as the boy went into the bathroom. When they arrived, he'd thought the Ice Citadel to be like a hothouse inside. After a while he knew that was just a reaction from being so cold when Sara brought them in. Despite the hot springs and all the body heat soaking through the Ice Citadel, it remained several degrees below genuinely comfortable. He fastened one of his thick check shirts over his T-shirt, buttoned up his leather trousers, and pulled on a second pair of socks. Only then did he stand up and tug the rug off the overhead tract. Orion let out a sullen moan of complaint at the burst of red light. The boy was having a bad time of it in the Ice Citadel. The way it confined them physically, the monotony of the routine, the bland diet – it all chafed against his natural teenage boisterousness. Although the worst part was the lack of anyone else remotely near his own age.

'There aren't any girls here,' the boy had moaned on the second day. 'I couldn't see any, so I checked with Sara. She says there were some twenty-somethings here a couple of years back, but they followed the Silfen out.'

'Yeah? Well you're not missing anything,' Ozzie had told him. He was slightly put out that the friendliness he'd shown towards Sara hadn't been reciprocated.

'How can you say that! You've had hundreds of wives.'

'True,' Ozzie said modestly.

'I've never had any girl,' Orion said miserably.

'Not even back at Lyddington?'

'There were a few I hung out with. I liked one. Irina. We kissed and stuff, but . . .'

'You left and came walking down the paths with me.'

'Actually, she went off with Leonard. He's slept with half the girls in town.'

'Oh. Right. Well . . . Women, huh, who understands them?'

'You must, Ozzie.' Orion had produced one of those desperate mournful looks that always made Ozzie uneasy. 'How do I talk to girls? I never know what to say. Tell me, please.'

'Simple really. It doesn't matter what you say, you've just got to have confidence in yourself.'

'Yes?'

'Yeah.' Ozzie was worried the boy was going to start taking notes. 'When you're at a party, find a chick you can dig, break the ice, then let them do half the work. It's supposed to be an equal relationship, right?'

'I suppose.'

'So let them do their fair share. And if there's nothing there, no spark – then no worries, man, just move on to the next babe. Remember, they had no spark either, they're missing out on a great dude: you. Their loss.'

Orion considered that for a long moment. 'I get it. You're right.'

'Hey, it's what I'm here for.'

'So what do I say?'

'Huh?'

'To break the ice? What's a good opening line?'

'Oh.' Ozzie thought back to the few horrendous memories he'd kept from his high school days. 'Well, er, just asking them to dance is always a great classic. Course, you have to be able to dance, chicks really dig that in a guy.'

'Can you teach me how to dance, Ozzie?'

'Ah, been a while there, man; best ask someone like Sara for some shapely footwork, okay?'

'Right. So, an opening line?'

'Er. Right. Yeah. Sure. Um. Hey! Okay, I remember this one from a party in the Hamptons way back when. Go up to a girl, and look at her collar, then when she asks what you're doing you say: I was checking the label, and I was right, you are Made in Heaven.'

Orion was still for a second, then burst out laughing. 'That is *so* lame, Ozzie.'

Which wasn't quite the respectful response Ozzie had expected. *Damn kids today.* 'It worked for me.'

'What was her name?' Orion asked quickly.

'I forget, man, it was a century ago.'

'Yeah, right. I think I'll ask Sara. She's probably better at this kind of thing.'

'Hey, I know how to chat up babes, okay. You are talking to the Commonwealth's number one expert on this subject.'

Orion shook his head and walked off into the pool cave, chuckling. 'Made in heaven!'

Ozzie rolled up his sleeping bag. Along with Orion's sleeping bag, it went straight into the carbon wire security mesh which contained their packs, looking like a black spider web had wrapped itself around all the bags and bundles. A mechanical padlock fastened the mesh's throat cable; he'd managed to loop it round a jag of rock on the wall, making sure no one could make off with the whole lot. After centuries spent moving around the Commonwealth, Ozzie knew just how much truth there was in the old saying that every conservative is another liberal who got mugged. He didn't trust his fellow travellers an inch, especially those good causes less fortunate than himself. Right now, that was just about everyone in the Ice Citadel. The packaged food, first aid kits, and modern lightweight equipment in those packs were their best chance of making it off this planet.

For the first week or so, every time they'd come back to their rooms, there were new scuffs and scratches on the rock where someone had tried to work the security mesh loose or smash the padlock.

They took their plates and cutlery out to the main chamber

and joined the short queue for breakfast. The food was the same as every day, the small pile of boiled and mashed crystal tree fruit looking like mangled beetroot, along with a couple of fried icewhale rashers that were alarmingly grey and fatty. There was also a cupful of the local tea, made from dried shredded fronds of lichenweed.

When they finished the meal they went back to their rooms to dress in thick icewhale fur jackets and overtrousers. Orion went up to the stables, where he would spend several hours mucking out the animals, and bringing in new bales of rifungi for them to eat. Though the tetrajacks, which looked like blue horse-sized reindeer, got to eat the swill left over from the kitchens below.

Ozzie walked up to the ground-level workshop. The big circular room had probably been intended as another stable, it had a rotating door large enough for an elephant to pass through comfortably, but the Ice Citadel's new ragtag inhabitants were using it to garage the big covered sledges that were pulled by the stupid hulking ybnan. It was also the carpentry shop, not for wood, but icewhale bone, which had remarkably similar properties. Leather was also cured there; fat was rendered down into various oils; repairs were carried out on the Ice Citadel's few precious communal metal artefacts, like the cooking range or cauldrons. Tools were mostly stone or crystal blades for shaping and cutting bone; those who arrived with their own little knives or pliers or multipurpose implements held on to them and treated them like the high-value currency they were. Nobody was a real artisan, they didn't have to be, all that was needed was a basic grasp of mechanics; the Ice Citadel kept ticking over on a level virtually equal to medieval.

The job which had been taking up everyone's efforts for three days was repairing and refitting the runners on two of the big covered sledges. They'd finished one, and the second was resting a couple of metres off the ground on thick stumps of crystal, waiting for its newly carved runners. It was barely above freezing in the workshop, hot spring water ran along curved channels under the stone floor, keeping the air moderately warm. Like the rest of the Ice Citadel, the heating arrangement was worn down. The thick flagstones covering the water channels had cracked and shifted down the centuries. Tenuous puffs of mist leaked up in a dozen places, turning the air damp and cloying. Condensation slicked the walls and the workbenches, and rusted any metal that was left out for too long. Around the rotating door, there was a permanent prickly frost.

Ozzie made sure he kept his woollen gloves on at all times. It made the tools harder to use. He had to move slowly, and consider what he was doing. But without them, his fingers became too cold, losing feeling. That was when real accidents occurred.

He joined in with the repair team, three humans and a Korrok-hi lifting the first heavy runner up into place on the end of the legs – sliding it back, under George Parkin's directions. George had been at the Ice Citadel long enough to qualify as the unofficial workshop foreman. He was certainly the most competent carpenter. The new runner fitted neatly, the dovetail joins slipping into their grooves with the help of a little oil lubrication. Two of the team members set about securing the joins with locking pins hammered in sideways and glued.

Ozzie had now been out six times on the sledges as part of a harvesting party, twenty-five humans and aliens armed with ladders and baskets. On each occasion, they'd set out just as dawn rose, heading for the crystal tree forest surrounding the huge desolate depression. The opal-coloured wedges which bloomed from the end of every twig on the mature trees were actually an edible fruit, a little knot of near-tasteless carbohydrates in a tough shell. Without them, the inhabitants of the Ice Citadel would never survive. It took a couple of years for one to grow to the size of an apple, so they had to harvest in strict rotation, painstakingly recording each trip on crude hide maps that marked out radial sections of the nearby forest. When they got there, it was hard physical work retrieving the crop, ten hours with only one small break climbing the ladders in thick layers of clothing and a fur coat to knock the fruit down with a length of bone. Ozzie was fascinated by the fruit. It convinced him that the crystal trees must be some kind of GM biology, or whatever Silfen science was equivalent.

Several members of the harvesting party roamed along the treacherous rocky gullies which criss-crossed the forest, where patches of lichenweed that took decades to grow coated the steep sides in shaggy blue-grey carpets. They stripped them off like vandals on a wrecking spree. Fungi were another prize, with the tetrajacks sniffing them out among the narrow clefts in the icy ground so they could be scooped out by picks and shovels. Between them, their haul was enough to feed the Ice Citadel for another couple of weeks.

The harvest, and the subsequent cooking and processing of the fruit and fungi, was a communal effort. Everyone contributed to the general upkeep in whatever way they could. Sara told him it was a civilized place most of the time. She could only remember it getting unpleasant once, when the Silfen hunt didn't visit for over a year, and the icewhale meat had run out.

The workshop team lifted the second runner into place before lunch. Ozzie stood back with George Parkin to watch the locking pins being hammered into place.

'Two days,' George said happily. He had some kind of thick English regional accent which Ozzie couldn't place. 'The glue'll set, then we'll be able to take her out again.' He put his bone pipe into his mouth, and lit the dried fronds of lichenweed. It smelt foul.

'How many big sledges have we got?' Ozzie asked, waving the smoke away.

'Five. I'm planning on building another after the next hunt

when we've got a decent stock of new bone in. I've a few ideas for improvements, and these old ones have been rebuilt so many times they're losing their strength.'

'Five large sledges, and what, like seven small ones?'

'Nine if you count the singletons.'

'That's not quite enough to carry everyone, is it?'

'No. Those five big sledges carry about twenty of us when we go chasing off after the hunt. It could be a lot more but we have to haul our tents along with us as well. Nights out there are just plain evil – we need those triple-layer fur tents. And we've also got to leave enough room on board the sledges to bring back the icewhale. Big brutes they are. You'll see.'

'But there's enough bone inside the Ice Citadel to build more sledges.'

George gave him a funny look, sucking hard on his pipe. 'Not spare there ain't, no.'

'Chairs, cots, rug frames. There's a ton of it.'

'People are using it.' He sounded quite indignant.

'They might want to use it for something else.'

'What are you getting at, lad?'

Ozzie wiped the back of his glove across his nose. As always in the workshop, it was cold and runny. 'I'm talking about taking everyone out of here. All of us at once.'

'Chuffing heck, lad; how do you figure that?'

'People get out by following the hunt, right? But they're on foot, or sometimes skis. They have to be fast to keep up.'

'Aye.'

'So we follow the hunt on sledges. Pile everyone in, humans and aliens, take all the animals, the tetrajacks and the lontrus and the ybnan; use them in relays to pull us, cut the exhausted ones loose if we have to. But that way we can keep up with the Silfen. Man, we can do it!'

George took the pipe out of his mouth and examined it solemnly. 'It's a grand idea, lad. But these big sledges won't be able to get through the forest on the other side of the hunting ground.'

'Okay. Then we cannibalize them and build a fleet of smaller ones. They'll be lighter, easier to pull, faster. It'll increase our chances.'

'Aye, lad, it probably would at that. But how does that resolve why we're here?'

'What do you mean, why we're here? We're here because we walked down the wrong path.'

'Did we? You're still thinking everything in life takes place on a physical level, what about your spirituality?'

'My spirituality is fine and looking to get the hell out of here.'

'Then I'm happy for you, lad. But I'm not ready to leave. I believe we're here for a reason, each and every one of us. The Ice Citadel is teaching us about ourselves, things we need to know as well as things we don't necessarily want to know. I believe we're here for a reason. We all know you're rich back in the Commonwealth; a lot of folk wandering the paths are. I was. Proper little idle sod I was back in those days. Usual crap, born into a family with more wealth than sense. I'm a Yorkshireman, me, born and bred, and right traditional. Our family made a fortune out of scrap, raking it in and selling it on, making brass out o' muck. We were doing it centuries ago, recycling stuff before anyone even heard of the word. Then Europe went bloody daft on the idea; if it were toxic you couldn't use it, and that which you were allowed to use had to be reused. We ended up with fridge mountains because you couldn't let the chemicals out of the coolant system, then computer mountains, then car mountains. We 'ad bloody Alps of consumer goods waiting to be broken down and refined cleanly. That was our family's second fortune. Then you and your pal came along with wormholes, and all everyone wanted to do was dump all the poisons and pollution out away in space. We got rid of all the fancy recycling plants, but we kept on collecting rubbish off people, and ran it through your open enders. Our third fortune.'

'The Mo-oM corporation,' Ozzie said. 'They're Europe's biggest trash disposers. Is that your company?'

George nodded, quite pleased that Ozzie knew the name. 'Aye, that it is. Know what Mo-oM stands for? Molehills out of Mountains.'

'I figured something like that.'

'That's what I was born into. Never did a day's graft in my life, I was a total wastrel back then, useless, pointless, and out o' me head half the time. Everything taken care of by money: parties, women, travel, drugs, rejuve – I 'ad the finest of them all. And you know what, after the third time around, it's as boring as shite. So I followed the paths to find the fairy folk, because that's the one thing money can't buy.'

'And they brought you here.'

'Aye, they did that. This is where I'm learning what I am, Mr Isaacs, I'm learning what it's like to live as a real person. I'm important here; people ask me what to do about icewhale bone, how to fix it, how to shape it, how to glue it, how to saw it. I'm respected now. That might not seem much to you, you're someone who really achieved something in his life; but this respect I've got now was earned, and earned the hard way. That's why I'm in this place. I'll leave eventually, we all do one way or another, either by walking out or dying in the forest. But until that day, I'll do what I can to help the rest of me friends through the bad times.'

'Does everybody get this speech from you?'

'Those that need it, aye. But I can see you don't, not with all your wisdom. So let me put it this way. What if we all set off like you suggest, and we still get left behind? What if the paths reject us? We'd all be stuck out there in the forest, too far away to get back here: well and truly up the creek wi'out a paddle. Not that you would get everybody. There's the likes o' me, and then there's the Korrok-hi, they're not about to leave. This place is just right for them. And what about those who arrive next? What do you think would have happened to you if our Sara hadn't come for you and took you in?'

'Good point.'

'That it is. This is a place that has a purpose. Just because you don't want to be here, don't mean it's a wrong-un.'

'Right. I guess I'd better go and work on plan B, huh?'

George shook his pipe at him. 'You do that. But make sure you're back here after lunch. We need a hand to get the sledge down off them blocks.'

'Sure.' Ozzie took a couple of paces, then looked back. 'George, you don't happen to know any good chat-up lines, do you?'

George took a moment to examine his pipe. 'If I did, I wouldn't waste them on the likes of you.'

Ozzie left the workshop and headed back down to his rooms. George had made him remember the worst days of high school, the times when he wound up outside the principal's office. The talking-to that was always worse than any possible detention.

He could never tell George, or Sara come to that, but the reason he'd been considering the mass escape was Orion. The simple fact was, he couldn't be sure about getting out if he took the boy with him. On his own it wouldn't be a problem. He could ski, he'd even started carving himself a pair out of bone. No Silfen was going to get away from a human on skis no matter how fleet of foot they were. And he had his packaged food, and energy drinks, and lightweight equipment; all of which he could carry. But Orion . . . The boy hadn't even seen snow before they got here, let alone knew how to move through it.

And all the while, when he was putting plans together, there was that one thought coiled up at the back of his mind, how much simpler it would be to leave Orion behind. There might even come a day when he didn't have a choice. It wasn't like he'd come searching for enlightenment or fulfilment like George and most of the others. He was on the paths for a reason. And God only knew what was happening back in the Commonwealth right now.

Ozzie walked across the main chamber and into the passageway which led to his cluster of rooms. The tochee was there, just coming out of the cavern they used to sleep in. It was the alien Ozzie had mistaken for a young Raiel the day he'd arrived at the Ice Citadel. At first sight it was a reasonable error. The tochee had a similar blunt body, like a squashed egg about three and a half yards long, and coming up to the middle of Ozzie's chest. Its hide was a kind of bristly fur, a dark caramel in colour, which looked as if it was about two sizes too big, the whole body was covered in wrinkles and creases, like a bulldog's face. Strange little wizened black fronds grew out of the folds, as if it was sprouting seaweed. They looked like dead leathery parasites, which were becoming so dry and brittle in the Ice Citadel's atmosphere they were starting to crumble and tear off.

Its mouth was a small lip-sphincter that formed a snout on the apex of its conical front, looking far too small given the size of the body, though when it was open, a circular array of very sharp teeth were visible. The eye, or what people believed was its seeing organ, was a curved pyramid a yard or so behind its mouth, made up from three oval sections of translucent black flesh, with the one at the front twice as long as the other pair, curving down so it could follow the body-profile.

But it was the way the alien moved which was the most interesting part. Two fat ridges of rubbery tissue ran along its underbelly, for all the world like sledge skis, except these rippled like snakes to push it along. The surface of the ridges was mottled, grey and bruise-brown, with some cracks oozing rheumy body fluid. Sara had said the tochee was in bad shape when they found it out on the edge of the crystal tree forest.

Although the ridges were a sophisticated biological method of locomotion, their nature meant it couldn't wear protective cladding. The tochee was obviously from a warm-weather climate. Its ridges were badly frostbitten from moving over the icy ground, where they suffered constant contact with the sub-zero soil. That was over two years ago, and the flesh still hadn't grown back properly.

A second pair of ridges protruded from its back. They were shorter, extending only a little further than its eye, and they were more bulbous. Ozzie had seen them swell out to grip cups and plates, or help lift objects too heavy for human arms, like giant amoebas shaping themselves into chubby tendrils or jaws. As tool users went, it was a high-evolutionary concept.

In fact, it was only its manipulator flesh, along with a few high-technology artefacts it was carrying on a utility belt, that convinced the other Ice Citadel residents that it was sentient at all. In the whole two years it had been here, nobody had managed to communicate with it at all. It didn't make any sound with its mouth, let alone speak. As far as they could tell, it was deaf. They'd tried chalking pictures on a slab, but it didn't seem to understand them. All they had left were simple arm gestures: come, stay, go, lift, put down. It cooperated most of the time, as if it was a well trained sheepdog.

They didn't even know its true name, the Korrok-hi had named it the tochee, which in their language of hoots and whistles meant: big fat worm.

'So what were you looking for in there?' Ozzie mused out loud as he stood in front of it.

The tochee's snout waved slightly from side to side, putting Ozzie in mind of some animal awaiting castigation. To his eye it had the attitude of a whipped dog, but then, he supposed, if all he did every day was carry buckets of water from the fountain to the kitchen, on frostbitten toes, unable to talk to anyone, or know what was going on outside, he'd be seriously depressed too.

'Okay, let's go see.' He walked round the flank of the tochee and pushed the door curtain aside. He wasn't sure, but he thought the security mesh had been moved round slightly, as if something had gently prodded it. 'Come on then.' He beckoned the tochee with an exaggerated gesture. The big creature turned smoothly in the passageway, and slithered into the sleeping room. Once again, Ozzie was impressed by how agile the alien was; for something that size it could move quickly and precisely.

He sat on the cot, staring at the tochee, and gestured round expansively. 'Go ahead.' The alien didn't move. It kept its great front eye perfectly aligned on the human.

'All right then.' Ozzie went over to the security mesh and clicked the padlock's combination code, covering the motion with his body. He still wasn't that trusting. With the mesh open, he pulled out various articles, food, clothes, a kerosene lamp, his sewing kit, a hand-held array, and set them down on the floor in front of the alien. The tochee's locomotion ridges flattened slightly, lowering it down; then its manipulator flesh on the left side flowed out into a slim tentacle which picked up the array. The tip pressed each of the five buttons on top. But the unit remained dead.

'Ah ha,' Ozzie said. Only someone familiar with technology would understand a button. 'So you understand technology, but we can't communicate. Why not?' He sat back on the cot and looked at the tochee again. It might be a human interpretation, but the alien seemed to slump in disappointment at the array's failure. It slowly replaced it on the floor, little black fronds rustling like autumn leaves in a breeze.

'You don't use sound, so what does that leave us with? Telepathy? Doubtful. Magnetic fields? Bees and trokken marshrats can sense them, but the Silfen are probably dumping them here. Possible, then. Electromagnetic? Ditto for radio waves, the array is dead. Shapes? You're visually perceptive, so that's another possible. I can't match that shapeshifting arm trick, though, and Sara said you didn't understand pictures.' He cocked his head to one side. 'Make that human pictures. I wouldn't understand yours. That's if you draw them. Now there's a culture difference. Do you have art?' Ozzie stopped. He was feeling mildly foolish talking out loud to an alien that couldn't hear. The tochee was still facing him, the front eye perfectly aligned. Ozzie shuffled a few inches along the cot. The tochee's front body moved slightly, tracking him. 'Why are you doing that? What can you be trying to say.' *No, not what. How?* Ozzie stared at that elongated oval of shiny black flesh that was pointing right at him. Not sound, but an emission of ... 'Shit.' He switched his retinal inserts to infrared, and the tochee's body crawled with strange thermal signatures, hinting at the location of blood vessels and organs hidden below the flesh. He slowly worked up through the visual spectrum, until he reached ultraviolet. 'Fuck!' Ozzie jumped backwards in reflex shock, and fell off the cot.

The tochee's forward eye was alive with complex dancing patterns of deep purple light shining straight at him.

*

When Orion returned to their rooms a couple of hours after lunch he found the tochee almost blocking the doorway. Ozzie was sitting on his cot, sketching furiously with a pencil on one of his notebooks. The rock floor was littered with scraps of paper, all with the weirdest patterns on them, like flowers drawn by a five-year-old, where every petal was represented by a jagged bolt of lightning.

'George Parkin's been looking for you,' Orion began. 'Why is that in here?'

Ozzie gave him a manic grin, his crazy hair fluffing out from his head as if he'd been hit by a big static charge. 'Oh, me and tochee here are just having a little chat.' He just couldn't keep the smugness from his tone.

'Uh?' was all Orion managed.

Ozzie picked up one of the pieces of paper torn out of the notebook. The pattern was like a rosette of fractured glass, but there was a word scribbled on the top corner. Ozzie's other hand held up a leather shoe. Half of the contents from their packs were scattered round. 'This is its symbol for shoe,' he said jubilantly. 'Yes, look, it's repeating it. Course, it might just be the symbol for violated dead animal skin, but who the hell cares. We're getting there. We're building a vocabulary.'

Orion looked from Ozzie to the tochee. 'Repeating what?'

'The symbol. There are other components to it, but they move the whole time. I can see them but I can't draw them. So I'm just sticking to basics. I think the moving parts might be grammar codes, or context information.'

'Ozzie, what symbol?'

'Sit down, I'll tell you.'

*

'It talks in pictures?' Orion asked ten minutes later.

'That's the simple explanation, yes.'

'What's the complicated one?'

'The pattern it projects is the visual language of the picture, sort of the same as we give names to objects. I imagine when two of them communicate together it's extremely fast. There's a lot of information in a pattern like that. I'm sure I'm only getting the fundamentals of it. In fact, I'm going to try and teach it the human alphabet. But I'm not surprised it didn't understand the pictures Sara tried to draw for it, like the difference between drawing a stick man, and seeing a fully fledged colour hologram of a man. Tochee will have to learn how to think down to our level, I'm afraid.'

'That's good.'

'So why do you sound like it's the world's biggest bummer?'

'Well, it's nice for tochee, and everything, but writing notes isn't going to get us off this stinking world, is it?'

'You think?' Ozzie grinned. 'Know what the first thing

tochee asked me? *Can you get me out of here?* That means we can team up. We'll make a great team, the three of us.'

'How come?'

'Tochee is strong, and fast. And that's what we need to keep up with the Silfen.'

'He can't go outside, Ozzie. He freezes!'

'I've got some ideas about that. I'll talk to George about them tomorrow.'

Orion gave the big alien a curious look. 'You really think you can do that, get it to come along?'

'Hope so, man. We've just been fooling round so far, letting each other know we can talk. Now we've got to build a real communication bridge. I've got some programs in my inserts that are still working, kind of; they're translation and interpretation routines, the type CST use when they encounter a new species for the first time. They'll take you all the way from "the cat sat on the mat" up to discussing metaphysics. Damn, this would be so much easier if my array was working.'

'Lucky your inserts are.'

'Yeah, I guess so.'

'Ozzie, look!'

Tochee extended a thin tendril from his manipulator flesh, and picked a piece of paper off the floor. The pattern was close to a spiral of snowflakes. In the corner Ozzie had written, 'array, or electronics in general?'

'Why that one?' Ozzie muttered. He stared at tochee's forward eye which was flaring with fast-moving lavender patterns. 'Ah, could be "communication device". I think tochee wants me to get on with it.'

'Can I watch?' Orion asked excitedly. 'It's got to be better than the stables.'

'Yeah, you can watch. It might take a while, though.'

17

It had taken days to cajole her father into supporting the weekend. Not that Justine Burnelli actually wanted him there, not like this, barely six months out of rejuve. He was impossible at the best of times, but add his natural brute stubbornness to youthful vitality, and it made him damn near inhuman. However, she had to concede, his presence made the weekend a valid event; without him, the necessary players would never have turned up.

They'd chosen to have it at Sorbonne Wood, the family's West Coast retreat, a big estate outside Seattle, with fast-flowing rivers and extensive woodland hemmed in by mountains. She would have preferred a weekend at the Tulip Mansion, the family's primary home over on the East Coast. It was so much more civilized than this rustic sanctuary. But the informal gathering which the Burnellis were hosting was to be discreet above all else.

People started arriving mid-afternoon on the Friday. Justine had been there a day already, overseeing the personal preparations, something she never quite entrusted to her staff for get-togethers at this level. Sorbonne Wood consisted of a large main house, originally of stone and concrete, which was now thoroughly covered by drycoral, one of the oldest examples on Earth. It had been planted over two centuries ago. The two native colours of lavender and beige which grew up the walls and across the roof seemed insipid compared to the modern varieties which GM had made available. Their braided fronds also suffered from poor texture, with older sections susceptible to crumbling; so the groundstaff encouraged constant growth. By now the fronds were a foot thicker than the house's original walls, which made the big picture windows appear organic they were so sunken. The UFN's Environment Commissioners would doubtless impose a removal order and a hefty fine on anyone else who was impudent enough to cultivate the alien plant to such an extent, but no mere EC official was ever going to get through Sorbonne Wood's security perimeter.

The interior of the main house was made up of various reception rooms, relaxation facilities, and the dining rooms. Family members and guests stayed in any of the dozen lodges arranged in a semicircle around the rear gardens, and linked to the main house by rose-covered pergola walks. On the outside at least these satellite buildings made an attempt to conform with local heritage. They had log walls and bark-slate roofs, although the interiors were strictly twenty-fourth century in terms of furnishing and convenience.

Gore Burnelli was the first to arrive, driving up under the wide gull-wing porch canopy in a huge black Zil limousine. Even though it was electric, Justine thought the six-wheeled monster must surely violate some kind of environment laws, it was so heavy, and twice the size of her own current Jaguar coupé. Three other big sedans pulled in behind it, carrying members of her father's retinue; and her e-butler told her another two had gone straight to the estate's little staff village.

Justine stepped forward to greet the old tyrant-king as the Zil's rear door opened and its ground steps slid out. Two assistants doubling as bodyguards emerged first, looking like traditional mobsters in their sleek black suits and silver-band glasses. Justine showed no emotion at their appearance. They weren't needed here, and her father knew that. In fact, he was probably wetwired to be a lot more lethal than they could ever be. His last rejuvenation at the family's biogenic centre had taken longer than usual.

Gore Burnelli appeared in the Zil's doorway, sniffing the air. 'Goddamn Seattle; goddamn raining again,' he grunted. A light drizzle misted the sky, making the edges of the gullwing canopy drip constantly over the conifers planted round it. 'Don't know why we don't just move this fucking place over to England. Same weather, better beer.'

Justine gave him a gentle hug. 'Stop it, Dad. This weekend is going to be tough enough for me as it is, without having to keep you in order.'

He made an attempt to grin back at her. It wasn't an easy gesture for him, not with that face. She could still see his native human features; as a normal twenty-year-old he would have been strikingly handsome. His thick fair hair was already starting to curl mischievously as it sprouted vigorously from the short crew cut he'd come out of the tank with. But the sheer number and complexity of his OCtattoos meant that they had merged together and now completely covered his face, giving him twenty-four-carat golden skin like the sarcophagus mask of an ancient Egyptian king. 'Like I'd dare complain with you riding my ass.'

'How's Mom?'

Gore rolled his eyes, they at least appeared normal. 'How the fuck should I know? You tell me who she was. I erased the memory centuries ago.'

'Liar.' Justine saw the bodyguards stiffen slightly. They probably weren't used to anyone talking to their boss like this. But then Justine was Gore's firstborn, conceived and born entirely naturally, unlike the fifty-odd children that had followed her and her brother. Back then Gore had been a mere billionaire, inheriting the wealth of two distinguished old-money American families as his parents joined in dynastic union. With some astute judgements and predictions, and not a little political influence, his original extensive portfolios had grown in tandem with the human expansion into phase one space. The Burnellis, like all of Earth's Grand Families, were living proof that money breeds money. Dawson Knight, the legal, accountancy, and management firm that was the core of the family financial empire, was staffed almost entirely by family members. Its *raison d'être* was accumulating more wealth, and protecting that which already existed. The Burnellis had holdings on every planet in the Commonwealth, from acres of strategic real estate around the outskirts of phase three space capital cities to entire blocks of manufacturing capacity on each of the Big15, from transport and retail companies to banks, utilities, and cutting-edge start-up enterprises. Anything that did or would one day turn a profit, they took a slice early in the game.

Justine had played a huge part in building the family fortune over the centuries, performing nearly every role from trouble-shooter in the early decades, to chief acquisition negotiator, and more lately a subtle political broker. Not that she ever favoured the more public political role her brother took. But despite all that, all the dealing, the manoeuvring, the manipulation which she'd carried out over the long centuries, it was Gore who remained the sacrosanct heart of the ever-increasing Burnelli family.

'Well I saw Mom a month ago,' Justine said. 'She sends her love.'

'She's not coming here, is she?' Gore suddenly shifted his focus. As always, his virtual vision surrounded him with financial displays, news précis, and market reports from Dawson Knight, looking to buy options, futures, land, currency. If there was an opportunity to advantage the family, he'd take it.

'No. You're safe here,' Justine said.

'Good. I'm going to my lodge. But I want to see you and your brother before any of the horse trading starts this evening.'

'I'll tell Thompson when he gets here.'

Gore and his retinue of bodyguards, assistants, and aides walked into the main house. A couple of beautiful Oriental girls brought up the rear of the procession, wearing tight white micro-dresses. They were twins, or reprofiled to look identical. Both of them bowed respectfully as they passed Justine, who just managed not to scowl back at them. In some respects, her father could be terribly predictable. The girls would be slotted into his schedule the same way as a finance conference or a meal. Every minute of his day was worked into his personal agenda weeks in advance. She knew a lot of people speculated that he'd received illegal psychoneural profiling to turn him into an obsessive compulsive about work and the family. But she still possessed the memories of her early childhood, when he was rarely home from Wall Street before ten or eleven in the evening, spending every weekend in his study with computer screens as his only companions. He'd always been single-minded, keeping human requirements to the minimum. As technology advanced, so he acquired more and more interface and processing functions to keep him attuned to the great pan-Commonwealth financial markets.

Half an hour after Gore arrived, Campbell Sheldon drove up to Sorbonne Wood. Justine greeted him with a genuine enough smile. He was one of Nigel's great-great-grandchildren, the youngest of three brothers from a direct-lineage granddaughter. That gave him a lot of seniority within the Sheldon family and, as he'd chosen a CST career, he'd achieved a high-ranking position as the Director for Advanced Civil and Commercial Projects. Though Nigel was quite adamant that being family only ever got your foot on the bottom of the ladder, from there you had to move up on merit.

Campbell had a couple of aides with him, but that was all. Justine remembered enjoying that no-fuss attitude the previous time they'd met. Today, Campbell was halfway between rejuvenations, giving him an apparent age in his forties. A trim mouse-brown beard covered cheeks that were slightly chubby; he definitely had inherited some of Nigel's character-istics, the deep eyes, small nose, darkening blond hair. A few discreet platinum OCtattoos spiralled behind and below his ears.

He kissed her lightly on both cheeks, and said, 'You're looking fabulous.'

'Thank you. I think I was just about due for rejuve the last time we met.'

'The party on the Muang senator's yacht, if I remember rightly. The Braby Bridge opening ceremony. They had airfish floating over the yacht like yellow balloons.'

'Oh lord, you are terribly well briefed. I can see I'm going to have to spend all night updating myself.'

'I hope not all night. That would be a waste of an evening.'

'Ah. I remember this part of you very well.' Her gesture invited him into the hall.

'What can I say? I'm a Sheldon. I have a reputation to keep up.'

'Weren't you with that rock singer that time on the yacht?'

'Ah, the dear Callisto. We parted company not long after, I'm afraid. She left me for a drummer.'

'She named herself after a moon?'

He shrugged. 'It was fashionable back then.'

'So what is now? Asteroids? Comets?'

Campbell laughed, then paused to look at the house. 'Is that really drycoral? On Earth?'

'Yes. Please don't report us to the Feds. It's older than most of our family members.'

'I'm easily bribed. A quiet late night drink. Bathing together in romantic candlelight. Making love in a four-poster bed.'

Justine smiled back. 'I'll certainly consider a plunge in a mountain stream with you. We have several in the grounds.'

'My God, you're a sadist. In Washington State in spring-time? Do you have any idea what water that cold will do to a man?'

'I'm game to find out if you are.'

'Okay. But I certainly expect that drink later on. What's the form for the weekend?'

'Strictly informal. The main decision on the starflight agency has already been taken by the ExoProtectorate Council. All that's left are a few policy shakedowns to get things working smoothly before the Senate confirmation. If I might suggest . . . This gives you an excellent opportunity to explore options with Patricia Kantil.'

'Huh,' Campbell grunted. 'She's coming, is she?'

'Oh yes.'

*

Patricia Kantil was actually the next to arrive. Stepping out of a mid-price-range Ford Occlat, wearing a neat office suit, also off the shelf, and classic black pumps. She kept an apparent age in her mid-fifties, mature enough to be trustworthy, not so old as to be losing any intellectual capacity. A web of silver OCtattoos radiated out from her eyes, so thin they were invisible most of the time. Her hair style and make-up carefully emphasized her Latin ethnicity. Justine could tell she spent a lot of money on that salon styling, but voters wouldn't be able to tell that as she stood one pace behind her boss, Elaine Doi.

The fact that Doi's chief political adviser was spending a weekend in Seattle barely ten days after the Vice President had announced her candidacy was a telling point to Justine. For Patricia, these two days would be a major lobbying exercise. She'd brought her secretary with her, a studious young man, dressed in the kind of designer casuals an urban type always wore in the great outdoors. He stood attentively behind his chief, only ever speaking when spoken to.

Justine was busy welcoming them when a third person emerged from the Occlat. A young girl with long blond hair, actually taller and slimmer than Justine. Her clothes were unashamedly expensive – a short skirt and shiny gold V-neck top that highlighted her figure. She glanced round the grounds with the unique bubbly exuberance that spelt first-lifer, smiling broad approval at what she saw.

'And this is Isabella,' Patricia said. 'My companion.'

'Hi there. You have a lovely place here,' Isabella gushed. She stuck her hand out eagerly, wanting to make friends.

'Thank you,' Justine said. 'It took a while, but we've got it how we like it.' It would be so easy to shower Isabella with sarcasm and irony, the girl would never notice. But that would make her a bitch, and this weekend didn't need any ructions. 'Get me a full file on her,' Justine told her e-butler. Something about her features was familiar enough to make Justine cautious. Isabella was obviously from a Grand Family or an Intersolar Dynasty, but which . . .

'Isabella Helena Halgarth,' Justine's e-butler reported. 'Aged nineteen. Second daughter of Victor and Bernadette Halgarth.' A small file printed down inside her virtual vision, detailing Isabella's schools, academic achievements, sports, interests, charitable causes. The usual PR crap the family released on its own.

Damn it!

As soon as she'd shown Patricia to her lodge, Justine put a call through to Estella Fenton. 'I need some information.'

'Darling, I'm humbled and honoured,' Estella said teasingly. 'What on earth do I know that your family doesn't?'

'It's about this girl.' Justine's virtual finger touched an icon, sending Estella the small file on Isabella. 'You're the queen of gossip, I need to know what her true standing is in the Halgarths.'

'If it was anyone else asking, I'd resent that,' Estella said.

'Please! I know the status of nearly every Grand Family member, but the Halgarths are an Intersolar Dynasty.'

'I know, darling, nouveau riche offworlders, the worst kind. I've got my own profile of her here, what exactly do you want to know?'

'Is she considered important?'

'Not really. Fifteenth generation, and Victor was only eleventh. Both father and daughter were invitrogestated children, so they're not direct lineage, just filling the family quota. She's got a minimal trust fund, it pays enough so she doesn't have to work, but she can't quite afford to live a society high-life. She finished school last year, and hasn't yet chosen a university. In fact, word has it that when she's rejuved she might go for a little brain resequencing. Her IQ isn't exactly lighting the top of the Christmas tree. Had a few boyfriends, all of equally minor status, and currently sleeping with . . . ah: Patricia Kantil. Is this why you're calling?'

'Yes. I've got some senior Halgarths coming this weekend. I don't know if Patricia's secured their vote. It might be a problem if they interpret the relationship incorrectly.'

'Rest easy, darling. You didn't hear this from me, but EdenBurg is already lining up behind Doi. That makes six of the Big15. I don't think Patricia and Isabella will be a factor for you.'

'The Halgarths are backing Doi after all? Congratulations, you are better connected than me. Thanks, I really don't need last-minute scares like this. I owe you.'

'You certainly do. Next time I need an A-list Grandee for dinner . . .'

'I'll be there.'

*

Gerhard Utreth was next, a fourth-generation member of the Braunt family which had founded the Democratic Republic of New Germany. As an attorney he'd opted out of the family's management and financial side to work in the planetary legal office. Decades ago he'd been the DRNG's Commonwealth senator. He'd even been married to a Burnelli at one time, resulting in two invitrogestated children. Not that Justine expected that to count for much during the weekend, but it made him a good potential ally.

She had also invited Larry Frederick Halgarth, who was in the third generation of his dynasty. He arrived with Rafael Columbia, who was an inevitable addition to the weekend. But when the invitation was issued, Larry had also insisted on bringing Natasha Kersley, who shared the limo with the other two. When Justine ran her name through the Burnelli database she drew a blank. Natasha wasn't a member of any major family. Nor had Justine ever heard of the Commonwealth Special Science Supervisory Directorate, of which Natasha was the Chief Executive. All Larry would say was, 'It conducts theoretical studies of weapons. Exotic weapons.'

There were two more senators to complete the weekend gathering. Crispin Goldreich, whose position on the Commonwealth budgetary commission gave him a great deal of influence over the start-up arrangements of the whole starflight agency project. Justine's briefing had him down as a mild sceptic; but as she knew there was really no such political animal. He was fishing for something.

Finally there was Ramon DB, the senator for Buta, although remarkably he didn't belong to the Mandela family which had established that Big15 world. Instead, he was the leader of the general African caucus in the Senate, which gave him a respectable power base. He had also been Justine's husband for twelve years. But that was eight decades ago.

'Remember me?' she asked coyly as he got out of his car.

He just wrapped his arms around her, hugging tightly. 'Damn, you look hot when you're this age,' he rumbled softly. He held her at arm's length, looking her up and down. A wistful expression crossed his face. 'Can we get married again?'

It was her turn to look at him. His traditional robe had a wonderful rainbow hem of semi-organic fibre which kept swirling as if he was in a breeze. Not even that movement could entirely disguise the way it fell over his stomach. His apparent age was approaching sixty, with white hairs infiltrating his temple. Midnight-black OCtattoos ran across his cheeks, flickering in and out of visibility.

'How much weight are you carrying under there?' she asked.

He put his hands together in prayer, and appealed to the sky. 'Once a wife, always a wife. I keep in shape.'

'What shape? A beach ball? Rammy, you know you have trouble with your heart when you put on this much weight.'

'It is the fate of senators to attend huge meals every day of the week. I expect you'll be sitting us down for an eight-course dinner tonight.'

'You are definitely not having eight courses; and I'm going to talk to chef about your diet for the rest of the weekend. I don't want to have to visit you in a re-life procedure ward, Rammy.'

'Yes, yes, woman. I am due to rejuve soon. It will all be sorted out then. Stop worrying.'

'Have they got a specific retrosequence for your condition yet?'

He gave an impatient swish of his fly-whisk. 'I have rare genes. It is difficult for doctors to isolate the problem and correct it.'

'Then have them vector in a sequence for a new heart. It's simple enough.'

'I am what I am. You know that. I don't want somebody else's heart.'

She gathered a breath, ready to sigh at him. Before she had a chance his thick forefinger came up under her chin. 'Don't scold me, Justine. It is so good to see you again. Being a senator isn't nearly as wonderful as everyone claims. I was hoping we could spend a little time together, you and I, this weekend.'

'We will.' She patted his arm. 'I want to talk to you about Abby, anyway.'

'What's up with our great-grandchild now?'

'Later.' She read the clock in her virtual vision. 'I have to check in with Dad and Thompson before the evening begins for real.'

'Your father is here?' Ramon was suddenly reluctant to get closer to the house.

'Yes.' She licked her lips to cover a smile. 'Is that a problem?'

'You know he never liked me.'

'That's your insecurity and imagination. He always accepted you.'

'Like a lion accepts a wildebeest.'

Justine burst out laughing. 'You're a senator of the Commonwealth, and he still intimidates you?'

He took her arm, and walked into the entrance hall. 'I will smile at him and make polite conversation for exactly three minutes. If you don't rescue me by then, I'll . . .'

'Yes?'

'Put you over my knee.'

'Ah, hark the heavenly angels as they sing glad tidings: the good old days are back in town.'

*

Gore Burnelli had decompressed his parallel personality into Sorbonne Wood's large array, settling himself into the house as other humans would return to a comfortable old armchair. Unlike most humans who underwent frequent rejuvenation, he didn't dump his memories into a secure store for nostalgia's sake. He carried them round with him in high-density inserts, loading them into local arrays wherever he went. They were essential to him; to make the deals that gave his family a smooth ride into the future he had to have the knowledge of past deals, and the reasoning behind them, if they'd worked, what the problems were. Others, like his daughter, relied on briefings and extensive database access through an e-butler; while he had the real events immediately available thanks to the homogenized access programs which his early memories were rooted to.

Business and positioning the family in the market were his constant now. Technology made it possible for him to be involved for most of the day. Some of the routines he'd developed for managing the process were almost autonomous, allowing him to parallel multitask. Even now, as he watched his son and daughter enter Sorbonne Wood's big classical library, he was reviewing the deluge of data which fell between them like red digital rain. Figures and headlines briefly flared green as his virtual fingers flashed among them, rearranging them into new configurations, shunting money and information to form the new deals and purchases.

'Everybody's here,' Justine told him.

He made no comment. That information had long since flowed past him; the house was now updating him on the location of the guests and their aides and staff and spouses and lovers: who was using the showers and baths, who was using heavy (and heavily encrypted) bandwidth to the unisphere, who was walking along the pergola paths to the main house ready for pre-dinner drinks in the Magnolia lounge. Secondary information like that was now presented to his brain in the form of scent; the multitude of OCtattoos allowing him to smell where the guests were and what they were up to.

'I think these guests provide us with a critical mass,' Thompson said. 'As long as there aren't any unforeseen problems it should go smoothly.'

'That's self-evident, boy,' Gore snapped. 'But there are always problems. I'm relying on you two to anticipate them and massage them out of those grossly bloated egos gathering out there.'

'The only possible glitch so far was Isabella,' Justine said. 'But she won't register on the Halgarth radar. Just another trustbabe having herself some first-life fun. I don't think Patricia had an ulterior motive for sleeping with her.'

Thompson dropped down in one of the winged leather armchairs in front of the big fireplace. 'Not like Patricia to take any sort of risk. The girls she normally fucks are completely sanitized as far as political connections are concerned.'

'Maybe it's true love?' Justine said in amusement.

'That'd be a first,' Thompson said. 'Why the hell Patricia doesn't simply get a body reassignment when she's in rejuve I'll never know.'

'She can't,' Gore said. 'Most of Doi's team are female, it's an image she's worked hard at for twenty-five years. Nobody's going to screw that up now by growing a dick in the tank.'

'Speaking of which, we haven't officially declared for her yet,' Thompson said.

'That can happen this weekend,' Gore said. 'If the timing is right. For that I'll require confirmation of Doi's policy on the starflight agency start-up. Assuming she's going to back it, and she'd be a stupid bitch if she didn't, I want us to pay particular attention to the structure which is going to emerge. This weekend will give the family a big advantage on positioning when the agency is announced. Those details will matter.'

'The agency is temporary,' Thompson said. 'It's the navy we need to concentrate on.'

'I know. That's where we come in.'

'What if we don't need a navy?' Justine asked.

'We will,' Gore said firmly. 'I happen to agree with Sheldon and Kime on this one. The Dyson aliens shoot first and ask questions later. That tells me all I need to know about them. Even if it's just for deterrence value, the Commonwealth is going to need warships. Government will be spending money on procurement, a lot of money. We have to ensure the family gets a slice of that.'

'Easy enough,' Thompson said.

'Godfuck,' Gore closed a golden hand into a fist. 'Don't you ever fucking learn? All the other Grands are manoeuvring right now. Justine was right to put this weekend together for us. If we can influence the shape, our placing will be unmatched.'

'What sort of shape do you want?'

'The main one has got to be location. Get Sheldon to let go of that hillbilly backwood Anshun. I want the agency centred at the High Angel, where it damn well should have been all along. The family has a lot of interest in the astroengineering companies based there, a real shipbuilding programme will see their stock go through the roof.'

'We can probably make that sound logical,' Justine said.

'It is logical. What we need is a way to make it serve their interests.'

'I'll work on it,' she promised.

Gore turned back to Thompson. 'The other side to the navy is going to be the planetary defences. Don't allow that to be overlooked this weekend. People are going to want damn great force fields guarding their cities and making them feel safe. I can see that ultimately chewing up even more cash than the starships.'

'Okay, I'll keep that one on the agenda,' Thompson said.

*

Dinner was the kind of formal event which Justine could sleepwalk through in her official role as hostess. They held it in the main dining room, with broad church-like arched windows looking out across gardens illuminated by thousands of twinkling white fairy stars. She made sure Campbell was at one end of the long oak table with her father, while she chatted away to Patricia at the other end. Isabella didn't join them for dinner.

'She finds these things a little dull, I'm afraid,' Patricia said as the band started playing some background jazz.

'She's young,' Justine said sympathetically. 'You did well getting her to come along at all.'

'It was the names – she's a bit of a fame junkie,' Patricia admitted as she bit into her starter of cannelloni of smoked salmon. 'Right now she's accessing *Murderous Seduction*, it's the penultimate episode.'

'Isn't that a biogdrama of the last Myo case?'

'Yes. A bit melodramatic for me, but the lead character is her sort of age, and it's a good production.'

'I wish I had time to keep up on pop culture. I'm surprised you do, especially right now.'

'Part of the job is coaxing various celebrity endorsements, among others.' Her smile was polite, but one hundred per cent professional.

'Our family is very supportive of the starship agency proposal. Hence this weekend.'

'I know, and Elaine is very appreciative of that.'

'Will she be making it part of her platform?' Justine looked down the length of the table, straight at her father's expressionless gold face.

'It's a bit radical, but then the Dyson mission has injected a few new factors into today's politics. The agency needs to go ahead. Elaine knows that. She's prepared to go out on a limb if that's what it takes.'

Gore Burnelli gave a tiny nod. 'Our family will certainly do whatever we can to support her position this weekend,' Justine said.

'I'm very grateful for that help.' Patricia couldn't quite conceal her predatory smile as she took another mouthful of the rolled salmon.

Justine studiously avoided any more verbal fencing with Patricia for the rest of the evening. The meal wasn't the time

681

for the serious negotiations to start in earnest. Instead, the three Burnellis made sure they talked to everyone separately at some point, preparing them for tomorrow.

*

It began in earnest at breakfast. The staff had set up an extensive buffet in the conservatory on the side of the main house, and Justine came over early to join Patricia and Crispin Goldreich at a table. Crispin's two wives, Lady Mary and Countess Sophia, were still in their lodge taking breakfast in bed, though one of his aides sat beside him, pouring tea and fetching food from the buffet. Patricia's immaculate young man was doing the same thing for her.

One of the house staff brought a pot of Jamaican coffee for Justine. She sat next to Crispin as he ate his eggs benedict. It was the less confrontational position. She wanted to know the same things as Patricia, and Crispin was hugely influential. As well as his leadership of the Budget Commission, he held a lot of authority among the bloc of European affiliate planets.

'Thompson told me you were one of the more moderate voices on the Council meeting,' Justine said.

'Cautious would be the more accurate word, my dear. I've been in this game long enough to spot an open-ended commitment. If this agency is approved by the Senate, there is no knowing how long taxpayers will be required to fund the endeavour. It won't end with the Dyson flights, you know. If they turn out to be benign, there will be a precedent in place for government to fund exploration of other questionable unknowns.'

'Which is surely better than having it done by a private company,' Patricia said. 'We've all heard the rumours of closed planets, worlds which have something so valuable the Sheldons have kept it for themselves.'

'And you believe that?' Crispin asked.

'Not personally, no. But I do believe that the government

should be more involved with the investigation of potentially hazardous scenarios, such as the Dyson Pair. For that we need the starflight agency. After all, the Dyson Pair is the very first time we've found anything remotely threatening. And it's a big galaxy. So far we've been lucky. We have to start being more cautious.'

'Which brings us to this dratted navy proposal,' Crispin said.

'You can't deny that would be essential if the Dyson scouting mission proves them hostile.'

'No, I don't. But the expenditure for that will be orders of magnitude above a starflight agency.'

'So how would you like to see this managed?' Patricia asked.

Crispin took a moment to finish the last of his eggs benedict. 'With a greater degree of responsibility,' he said eventually. 'At the moment we're simply throwing money at the problem. The first thing I'd like to see is some proper channelling of resources.'

'You mean some kind of oversight committee?' Justine asked. In her virtual vision, a calendar was displaying the date two years hence when Crispin's senatorial seat was up for re-election. He'd get it again if he wanted it, that wasn't a problem. But of course if he was to carry on as Chair of the Budget Commission he would need to be nominated by the Executive.

'Oversight, management, steering; call it what you like. We have to insure the resources are spent properly.'

'Your Budget Commission has it within its purview to set up such an oversight body,' Patricia said.

'Technically, yes, unless the Executive starts throwing up obstacles. I'm sure the President's Office would want to maintain a tight control over the agency, and certainly the navy.'

'Of course. But Elaine would be in favour of legitimate

financial scrutiny. She absolutely does not want taxpayers' money wasted, and I know she has a lot of confidence in the way you run the Budget Commission.'

'I'm delighted to hear that,' Crispin said. He poured himself some tea. 'In which case, providing the Budget Commission can get those financial safeguards in place, Elaine Doi would have my support for the agency. If she gets elected.'

'If she gets elected,' Patricia parroted, keeping a composed face.

*

'Crispin is on board,' Justine told her father.

'Good work. What did it cost?'

'Patricia gave him the Budgetary Commission leadership after Doi's elected.'

'There could be worse people in charge. Crispin is an old hack, but at least he understands the rules of the game. Well done. What's next?'

'Utreth. Thompson's with him after breakfast.'

*

It stopped raining after breakfast, leaving the grounds glistening from the overnight soaking. Thompson led his guest past the formal gardens, and into the woods beyond. They were a mixture of pine and beech and silver birch, not as densely planted as they had been during the logging centuries when they'd been all pine. As Washington State was now edging into springtime, a multitude of bulbs were pushing through the sandy soil, their verdure contrasting with the mat of brownish winter grass that was still pressed against the ground from the weight of snow which had lain on it for months.

Gerhard Utreth seemed to be enjoying the mock-wild environment. He'd even brought his own walking boots.

'Every time I visit the West Coast I always promise myself

I'll take a day and go to look at the sequoias,' the Democratic Republic of New Germany senator said.

'And have you?' Thompson asked.

'No. Not once in a hundred and fifty years.'

'You should. I went about fifty years ago. They're quite a sight.'

'Ah well, maybe next time.'

They reached one of the streams which had cut a deep narrow cleft through the soil, its perfectly clear water now running over a bed of white and grey stones. Thompson started to follow it up the shallow slope, avoiding the big tufts of dark green reed grass sprouting from the sodden banks.

'I congratulate your family on getting a Sheldon as important as Campbell under the same roof as Doi's chief political adviser. The weight which your father's name still carries is remarkable.'

'It's not in anyone's interest to have warring factions at the heart of government. We do what we can.'

'Of course. I have to admit, I don't remember a Vice President launching a campaign without the support of at least seven of the Big15 dynasties.'

'Doi's own caution works against her at this level. You really can't please all of the people all of the time. She's been trying to do that for too long. It's not that she's gained enemies, she simply hasn't gathered much in the way of admiration.'

'And if I may ask, how does the Burnelli family view her?'

'No differently to any other Presidential candidate, there are many flaws and some strengths. However, our principal interest lies in the events which will play out during her Presidential term. We heartily endorse the formation of a starflight agency. Doi did have the foresight to make the initial proposal in the ExoProtectorate Council.'

'Is that the view of the Grand Families as well?'

'The majority, yes. We will be campaigning on her behalf.'

'I see.'

Thompson stopped where the stream opened out into a wider pool. The far end was fed by a small waterfall gushing over an antagonistic cluster of sharp stones, making a loud sloshing sound as the flow was tossed around. 'I'd be grateful to know what it would take to bring you in.'

Gerhard nodded slowly, appreciative they were using straight talk for once. It didn't happen often between senators. 'Everyone is concentrating on the agency and constructing scout ships right now, which is understandable. However, it is the view of the Democratic Republic that the formation of a navy is almost inevitable.'

'We concur with that.'

'If a navy is formed, flying scouting and even attack missions will only be a part of its duty. It must defend the Commonwealth as well. Sheldon has a monopoly on the ships and their ftl technology which we would not dream of challenging; but planets and cities will need heavy fortifications. That is where we envisage our role to lie.'

'You would be happy backing the agency formation on that understanding?'

'Yes, we would.'

'That would mean lining up with Doi.'

'Like you, we acknowledge she has weaknesses though, like her strengths, none of them are particularly remarkable. I suspect history will regard her tenure as simply adequate. The age of great statesmen and women is long behind us, nowadays we just compromise our way through life. The Democratic Republic can live with that.'

*

'Good call by Gerhard,' Gore acknowledged. The data flow engulfing him began to flash like a thunderstorm as his virtual hands rearranged packages and icons for longer-term position-ing in the Democratic Republic of New Germany.

'He's a professional,' Thompson said. 'The DRNG realize the agency will go ahead, they just want a way in. A late opening is better than none at all.'

'I wonder what the Sheldons will make of that.'

'They'll accommodate it. They know damn well they can't expect the entire agency budget for Augusta. That's why they sent Campbell. He's fourth generation. He probably won't even have to refer back to Nigel for anything that comes up this weekend.'

'We'll find out soon enough. It's the crux meeting next.'

*

Patricia was invited to the study first. Gore's retinue had done what they could to make the room more welcoming. A real log fire was burning away in the grate, helping to banish the afternoon's chilly breeze. The ancient brown leather chester-field sofas had been arranged in front of the hearth. A table standing in the middle held pots of tea and coffee, as well as plates of muffins and cookies, filling the air with a pleasant aroma.

She accepted a bone china cup of tea and sat opposite Gore. She wasn't particularly unnerved by him, she'd spent enough time with the super-rich to know what they wanted above all else was a show of respect. His gold face, however, was disturbing; most of her life was spent judging and responding to expressions. Gore offered her little clue about his emotions. *That's if he has any*, she thought.

'It looks like the Democratic Republic will be backing Elaine,' Gore said.

Patricia kept herself as immobile as she could, though it was difficult. The relief she felt at hearing of Gerhard's support was enormous. When she thought of all the time spent lobbying him, the team of researchers analysing what they could do to bring him on board. Now just half a day spent with the Burnellis and another Big15 was supporting Elaine. For over a year, Patricia had been frantic with worry about how few of the Intersolar Dynasties they'd managed to gather in their favour. 'That's excellent news, sir.'

'You haven't heard their price, yet.' Gore went on to explain what assurances she'd have to give the DRNG senator before the end of the weekend. 'But the real key is Sheldon,' he said. 'This agency and everything it will lead to is your first way in. I know you've been courting that dynasty for over three years now.'

'They have proved somewhat reluctant,' she acknowledged.

'Ha!' Gore's shiny gold lips parted in a recognizable sneer. 'Nigel hates careerist politicians. Comes from his right-on youth I expect. That's why he's kept you dangling. But he's learned to be a pragmatist over the centuries. And now you can offer him something. It is possible for him to manoeuvre his own candidate into the Presidency, even at this late date. However, that would cost a lot of time and effort, and create antagonisms. Not with you, that wouldn't even register, but the Intersolar Dynasties and Grand Families would be pissed with him. That, he does care about. So be what he wants, and you'll have no opposition. Are you prepared to do that?'

'We can take Augusta's requirements into account during the campaign.'

Gore stared at her for a moment. 'There is only one requirement right now: money. You'll be embarking on a campaign that will ultimately raise taxes. That's never going to be popular.'

'I understand.' Patricia hesitated. 'Won't you be hit by taxes?'

'If we paid any serious ones, we probably would be.'

One of Gore's overlarge, dark-suited bodyguards led Campbell into the study. He smiled pleasantly at Patricia as he sat beside her.

'You two kids play nice now,' Gore said.

*

The study fire had burned down low when Justine and Thompson came in. Two of the house staff were clearing away the paraphernalia of afternoon tea under the cautious gaze of the bodyguards. Gore took a couple of pine logs from the wicker basket at the side of the hearth and dropped them into the cast-iron grate, which kicked up a small cloud of sparks from the bright pink embers.

'It's going to work,' he told his two children. 'Sheldon will back Doi's candidacy.'

'What did that cost her?' Justine asked.

'Billions,' Gore said. 'In taxpayer money. Even I was surprised by what she offered for the starflight agency's first budget.'

'She'll look for a jumper to introduce the bill, someone who's leaving the Senate,' Thompson said. 'If Patricia's got any sense she'll try and get the President to introduce the agency formation bill into the Senate himself before the inauguration. That way, Doi won't get the blame when the budget is announced.'

'She'll get blamed when the navy starts up,' Justine said.

'If we need a navy, no one is going to question the cost.'

'Christ, she might even make a second term.'

'Did you tell Campbell we want to shift the agency base to High Angel?' Thompson asked.

'No. Someone else can do our dirty work.' Gore looked at Justine. 'I thought your ex would fit the bill.'

She groaned and flopped down into the chesterfield. 'Why him?'

'That way we can offer Buta the new High Angel shipyard

assembly contracts. It fits perfectly. Sheldon will know he's got to accommodate everyone else.'

Justine glanced at her clock display. 'All right. We've got an hour before pre-dinner cocktails. I'll sound him out.'

'I thought you'd talked to him already today?' Thompson asked.

'Yes, but that was about Abby. She's being a problem.'

'Is she all right?' Gore asked. 'I haven't received any information.'

The immediate interest amused Justine, he really was protective of the family, especially the direct lineage. 'This wouldn't reach you. We were just talking about which university she's going to. I wanted Yale, she and her mother would like Oxford, and Rammy favours Johannesburg.'

'It'll be Oxford,' Gore said. 'You always cave in to your offspring.'

*

Cocktails were served in the music room. It was a large split-level room on the ground floor, with a central dais of teak for the ancient Steinway piano. The woman they'd hired to play the beautiful antique for the evening was from the San Francisco Civic Orchestra; she had an admirable repertoire and a mellow voice. After hearing her start with an Elton John classic, Thompson was almost reluctant to take Ramon, Patricia and Crispin down to the other end of the room where they stood in front of a Harkins water-flow sculpture that took up most of the wall. Crispin wasn't part of the deal to be made, but as he was now on Doi's team he would be useful in providing assurances to Ramon. The more players were tied together, the harder it was for them to renege.

'You have to admit,' Thompson said to his ex-brother-in-law, 'having Chairwoman Gall on your side would be a big help within the African caucus. A great many of your members respect her. It wouldn't be just you trying to swing the proposition, you could share the load.'

'That woman is a total ballbreaker,' Ramon said dismissively. 'I think you're making a mistake including her in this without any prior consultation. And she's only a very loose member of the Senate's African caucus. When it suits her is the usual membership criteria.'

'She's got to want the agency to be based at High Angel,' Crispin said. 'I know she was most unhappy when the *Second Chance* was built at Anshun. I haven't heard that kind of language in a Committee room since the Kharkov Independency crisis.'

'All the more reason she'll tell everyone to go to hell,' Ramon grumbled. He directed a wistful look at one of the waiters carrying round silver trays full of canapés, then checked round guiltily for Justine. 'She'll want her pound of flesh for that slight.'

'Chairwoman Gall is a fellow professional,' Thompson said. 'The economic benefits to her fiefdom cannot be overlooked in these circumstances. She'll sign on the dotted line.'

'She might,' Ramon said. 'But in any case, don't be so sure the High Angel will permit you to establish the agency there.'

'From what I understand, the High Angel is equally interested in the Dyson Pair,' Patricia said. 'Besides, we don't actually need its permission to site the new agency facilities there. It's a convenient dormitory, nothing more.'

'Any lack of cooperation on its part would be a problem,' Ramon said.

'One we could surmount,' Thompson said. 'The primary reason for siting the agency there is simply moving it away from Anshun.'

As one, they turned to look at Campbell Sheldon, who was talking with Isabella. The girl was dressed in little more than a white cotton cobweb, whose active semi-organic fibres shifted every time she moved so that her body's true sexuality remained provocatively veiled. She was laughing with easy enthusiasm at whatever story Campbell was recounting, while he seemed equally enthusiastic at the attention she was shining on him.

'The Sheldons can be reasonable,' Crispin said. 'When it's in their interest.'

'This whole agency project is in their favour,' Thompson said. 'Crispin, much as I hate to interrupt a fellow guest when he's clearly having such a good time, but do you think you could broach the subject of the High Angel base to Campbell? It would sound better coming from someone with your authority.'

'Oh bloody hell,' Crispin grumbled. He downed his sparkling gin. 'Why do I come to these weekends?'

Thompson, Patricia, and Ramon watched him walk across the room to the corner beyond the piano where Campbell and Isabella were having their very public tête-à-tête. He stopped a waiter and grabbed a glass of black velvet before breaking in. Isabella welcomed the senator with a fast flutter of her eyelashes.

'A lovely girl,' Ramon said. 'You're very lucky.'

'I know,' Patricia said. 'But I'm old and boring, so I don't suppose I'll have her for long. Once the novelty of being so close to the future President wears off, she'll move on. I did when I was that age.'

'I don't even remember being that age any more,' Thompson said. 'And not from erasing the memories, either. They just fade after so much time.'

'To forgotten youth,' Patricia said, and raised her glass. 'May we always be reminded by envying those who have it.'

'Amen.' Ramon touched his glass to hers, then with Thompson. They all drank the toast.

'If you are right about Chairwoman Gall being reluctant,'

Thompson said to Ramon. 'May we presume upon you to broach the subject with her?'

'I'd sooner put my cock in a food processor and switch it to purée.'

'You were married to my sister. How difficult can this be?'

Ramon put his head back and laughed. 'Ah, I'd forgotten what this family was like.' He clicked his fingers at a waiter, who hurried over with some canapés. 'All right, I might stop by at High Angel after this weekend. But I'm still not convinced that this agency is in the full interests of the African caucus.'

Thompson's good humour never faltered. 'Then I'm sure we'll manage to find something that will convince you before you leave.'

*

They went through to the main dining room for the evening meal. Justine had chosen the placing as best she could given the state of play so far. Not that she expected much manoeuvring during the meal, but the options were open. This time she wound up next to Campbell. She frowned when she saw Isabella sitting herself beside Ramon, who appeared more than happy with the arrangement. Isabella had taken Gerhard's seat, leaving the FRNG senator to sit next to Patricia, who Justine had wanted to place with Rafael. The Halgarths had done remarkably little in the way of negotiations so far. She knew Larry had talked to her father that morning, offering provisional support for the agency, but that was all. No doubt their cards would be on the table by tomorrow.

Text rolled down her virtual vision. **Your ex is being a pain,** Thompson sent.

Don't make it so personal, she shot back. **What does he want?**

I've no idea. I thought we'd got him with the High Angel

assembly platform contracts. Now he's seen how everyone is lining up behind the agency, he's angling for more.

I always knew he'd make a good politician one day. You and Gore never believed me. We're playing our hand too openly. It leaves us vulnerable to those we need to ally.

You'll have to bring him back in.

I'll do what I can, but I'm more concerned about the Halgarths.

They're solid.

Care to bet on that?

*

When the meal was over and the party had broken up, Gore went back to the study. With his latest retrosequenced modifications he needed at most three hours out of every twenty-four to sleep, and often managed on a lot less. As he prowled along the ceiling-high bookshelves he smelt the others as they went back to the lodges in the garden. Isabella, with her residual scents of the many men who for one reason or another had brushed up close against her that evening, herself redolent with the delicate smell of lily and orchid from the daubs of perfume on her neck. Her aroma stretched thin as she hurried across the grass, avoiding the paths, moving away from Patricia's metallic tang. Ramon DB's melange of cologne and alcohol-laced perspiration awaited her. The two merging together as his lodge door closed behind her. Their combined odour built up heavily within the tight confines of the master bedroom, saliva pheromones and the sugar acid whiff of champagne mingled with it.

Behind Gore's impassive gold face there was a stirring of amusement as the hot stench of sex began to gush out from their bodies. While in Patricia's bedroom there was only the overpowering scent of pine soap as she drew her bath. No alcohol, no bitter salts of disappointment prickling her skin. She was content.

So Isabella was the go-between, the one who would bind Ramon back into the deal, making him the promises her mistress had pre-authorized to secure his vote. And of course, she had a passing resemblance to Justine. A seduction of both mind and body. Poor, lucky Ramon.

Gore found the book he was looking for, seeing the leather spine behind the continual stream of sparkling scarlet information that enveloped his world. He reached out a hand swathed in glowing bands of silver and platinum, sliding *The Art of Financial Warfare* by James Barclay off the shelf. Not that he needed to read it, all the wisdom it contained now flowed freely among his thoughts and management routines. But the physical touch was a strange comfort. This book had been his Bible during his first life, and was still regarded as a classic text for anyone going into finance. He could probably do a good job updating it himself.

For some reason he always found himself searching it out when he was performing difficult placements; and this was one of the most complex. The starflight agency had so many variables, many more than the usual political-economic ventures he was accustomed to. By rights, it ought not to work, or at best be another cash-starved government institution that limped along on poor performances and missed quotas. This was too *grand* for today's drab careerist politicians to make work. And yet . . . The people who would normally be tearing each other apart were actually cooperating and accommodating each other to facilitate its inception.

What am I missing?

Every formidable instinct he possessed was singing through his brain that something was wrong. He would have loved to believe that the human race was worthy and mature enough to behave so splendidly. To see a problem and address it with logic and resolution. There had been progress along the social evolutionary scale, he was the first to admit. Thanks to rejuve, people did take the long-term view very seriously indeed nowadays. The starflight agency was a perfect example of that.

So maybe I am the anachronism.

Untrustworthy, suspicious, always looking for the worst in people. The barbarian who had no need to invade the city, for he had watched it grow up around him. He still wouldn't believe the agency could be birthed so easily.

Unless the manipulators themselves were being manipulated.

Which notion was even harder to accept. He had been on this right from the start, watching with his usual Olympian detachment as Justine caught the implications from her own contacts and convened this weekend. As the most cursory reading of Barclay showed, to manipulate this situation earlier than he had, you would have to know the outcome of the Dyson mission before it was launched. Nobody possessed that kind of knowledge.

With a dismissive sigh he replaced the book, and went to sit in front of the small pile of embers which the fire had reduced to. If Isabella's sweet body and wicked promises didn't do the trick, he would need to outflank Ramon DB by mid-morning tomorrow. Names flared within his private data casement, contacts within the African caucus who would not take kindly to their leading senator turning down the sub-contracts which re-siting the agency at High Angel would bring to their worlds. He sniffed the air, infusing the bouquet of Justine and Campbell and clean cotton sheets in mellow combination. Now that would be an advantageous union given what was expected to unfold over the next few years. Virtual hands reached out, purchasing shares in companies around the peripheries of where the larger starflight agency contracts would fall amid the African caucus planets. Preparing the family. Strengthening the family.

*

'I have to tell you,' Campbell said, 'Nigel isn't happy about moving the starship assembly platforms to High Angel.'

Justine stroked his nose in reply, moving her finger down to his lips so he could kiss the tip. She was lying directly on top of him, with the duvet flung somewhere on the floor. The ancient logs of the cabin were thick enough to retain the bedroom's warmth against the chilly night outside, she didn't need covering just yet. Candles in bulbous glass bowls flickered on various alcoves, filling the air with a musky scent of lavender and sandalwood.

'Poor Nigel,' she said with a pout, then smiled happily as his arms tightened around her, one hand sliding sensually down her spine towards her rump. 'What's his problem?'

'He gave clearance for everything that's been agreed so far, but moving to High Angel will delay the project by several months, and that includes the new scout mission. He won't shift on that.'

'What about the ground defence segments of the navy? Do you mind losing out on them?'

'We don't envisage losing out, exactly. We're doing what your family is doing, and positioning ourselves. The primary contracts will be handled by the DRNG, but we'll still come out ahead. Augusta is the largest of the Big15, everything is proportional.'

She looked round to find the bottle of Dom Pérignon vintage 2331 was empty and neck-down in the ice bucket at the side of the bed. A quick order to the house array sent a maidbot hurrying to bring another. 'It's going to be interesting to see the New York market board on Monday morning. This weekend is going to see so many stock acquisitions and movements the traders are going to know something's up.'

'Yeah, we can't hold off introducing the agency for much longer.' He looked up as the maidbot slid towards the bed. 'Ah. More.'

'Yes please!'

He moved his head back to find her grinning devilishly at him. 'My God, remind me never to be around the week after you leave rejuve. I doubt any man could survive that.'

The delicious memory of those few days spent in a glade on the side of Mount Herculaneum came back to provoke a warm tingle of satisfaction inside her. 'One did,' she murmured contentedly.

Campbell lifted the cold bottle from the maidbot's grip. 'Shall I open it?'

'Afterwards.'

'What about the High Angel problem?'

'We'll find a fix in the morning.'

*

There was no specific time arranged for breakfast on Sunday morning. The guests arrived as they woke, drifting in across the lawns. For once the day had started without any clouds. Strong sunlight cast the estate's exuberant vegetation in a pleasant aspect. There were even a couple of red squirrels bounding about over the lawn. Justine sat with Campbell, relishing that tired but happy feeling which was soaking her body. Thompson had said a polite good morning when he came in, although his tone told her he was quite aware of what she'd been up to during the night. Not quite disapproving, but close. She and Campbell shared a secretive grin as her brother walked away. The grins reinforced each other, threatening to become the kind of unstoppable giggles which afflicted school kids.

'May I join you?' Ramon asked.

'Please do,' Justine said. There was no sign of Isabella. Nor Patricia, she realized.

One of the house staff brought Ramon a pot of fresh English breakfast tea. Justine remembered introducing him to that drink. She always found it the best way to start the day. Coffee was too abrupt for her.

'I may have an idea that would smooth the way to move the agency to High Angel,' Ramon said.

Justine and Campbell exchanged a brief look. Everyone was remarkably well briefed this morning, she thought. It was barely thirty minutes since she'd updated Gore.

'We'd certainly appreciate anything which could help,' Campbell said.

'Parallel development. You continue building the first five scout ships at the Anshun facility, while the High Angel shipyards are being put together. That would provide the whole agency concept with the kind of positive outlook which the African caucus can support.'

Campbell was surprised by the notion. 'I suppose that would work. There certainly wouldn't be any of the delays which we're resistant to. But it would also incur much greater start-up costs than we envisaged.'

'You should speak with Patricia, but I think you'll find Doi's team is open to raising the budget to accommodate us.'

Justine waited until they'd all finished eating before cornering Ramon as he walked back to his cabin. 'What did she offer you to achieve that little strategic alignment?'

'Who?'

'Patricia.' She so nearly said: Isabella.

'The original agreement was that Buta supplies the new High Angel shipyards. It is a logical extension for the construction companies to be awarded the support contracts as well.'

*

'Smart move,' Gore said later. 'Support contracts can ultimately be worth more than construction in the long term. Which I guess is what we're looking at here.'

'I'd love to know which one of them suggested it,' Justine said.

'Me too. I'm becoming concerned by just how much money Doi is prepared to sign over. I'm not denying it will be good for us, but it shows a degree of desperation I hadn't expected from her.'

'I'm not surprised at all,' Justine said. 'She's using this to buy herself the election, and it's all paid for by tax money. She's a politician, what did you expect?'

'More subtlety. The senators will know what's happened here, even if the electorate doesn't care. If it turns out the Dyson aliens are no threat, then the amount of money she's offered the starflight agency is excessive and they'll react to that. It's not like a politician to support something so radical so wholeheartedly. They safeguard their own careers before anything.'

'But you're the one that claims the Dysons will prove hostile, and we'll need to evolve the agency into a navy.'

'I know. But I'm not standing for election. There's a small part of me that's tempted to sink this whole venture here and now.'

'What? You have to be joking.'

'Don't worry, I won't. But something's not right.'

'Care to be more specific?'

'I can't. I've analysed this all night, compared it with a dozen similar guiding weekends this family has been involved with. There's nothing tangible except my gut feeling.'

'You're just worried about what the Halgarths will pull. They've been biding their time ready for this moment when the rest of us have reached a broad agreement, then they'll make their bid.'

'Maybe you're right. I hope so.'

*

Justine got the opportunity to find out soon enough. There was a general 'progress review' meeting scheduled for mid-morning. They held it in the library. It was Larry who requested it be limited to those who held level one Commonwealth security clearance. That meant Justine herself only just scraped in, due to her directorship of several companies which supplied equipment to directorates that avoided the public view. But it certainly excluded everybody's partners and aides, along with Isabella. There was a short sharp argument at the door when she was turned away. Patricia came in looking slightly flustered. Everyone inside had heard what the girl had shouted.

'Sorry about that,' Patricia said as she sat at the table.

Justine stifled her own smirk, seeing quite a few others doing the same. As soon as the doors were closed, Thompson stood up. 'I expect this to be the final session for this weekend. We all seem to be in broad agreement over the principal structure which the agency will follow. This gives us a chance to iron out any final problems. I'm sure none of us want any show-stoppers at this stage. I for one have a number of Senate votes to attend on Monday, and I'd appreciate getting to them.' He sat down beside Gore, whose polished gold face turned expectantly to Justine.

'The major development this weekend seems to be moving the agency's primary base to High Angel. Given that we're foreseeing that it, or possibly a navy, will be in operational status for a long time, it does make sense and certainly has our family's approval. Does anyone disagree?'

'As you said, Justine, we're all in broad agreement with what's been negotiated this weekend,' Larry Halgarth said. 'The High Angel move, the preliminary work for navy defences; my family will certainly add its rubber stamp to all this.'

'Here it comes,' Campbell murmured to Justine.

'However, there is one facet to all this planning which has been overlooked.'

'What's that?' Gore asked sharply.

'Giving the navy an offensive capability. If, God forbid, the Dysons do turn out to be hostile, simply sitting underneath force field domes and hoping they'll go away isn't realistic. We would have to carry the fight into their territory.'

'Just hold on a minute here,' Gerhard said. 'Since when have we included invasion in our hostile encounter scenarios? All my briefings have concentrated on possible clashes over colonizing new stars in the direction of the Dyson Pair. In other words it's all going to be down to agreeing on the direction and limits of expansion. And that's assuming they do want to expand.'

'They filled an entire solar system,' Larry said. 'Their culture is just as expansion-based as ours, if not more so. Make no mistake about it, the two of us will meet out there in space.'

'They're seven hundred light-years away,' Ramon said. 'And it's a big galaxy. Defensive capability is only going to be a sop to public opinion anyway, at least that was my understanding.'

'That's very comforting. But what if we really need it?'

'Why?' Campbell asked.

'Excuse me?'

'Ramon was right in saying that any future clash with them will be over establishing borders to our respective spheres of colonization. Any navy we create will be a long-term venture. I doubt we'll need it within a century. There isn't exactly a rush to fill up phase three space like there was with one and two – more's the pity. Even if they expand at our rate, we'd be in phase five or six space before the possibility of clashes arose.'

'And if they don't stick to your timetable?'

'Then we stop at phase five space in that sector, and continue outward everywhere else. Like Ramon said, it's a big galaxy.'

'Somebody was so concerned about them, they tried to quarantine them off from this big galaxy. And we've seen for ourselves how aggressive they are. That tells me we have to prepare for trouble.'

Campbell regarded him as a teacher would a particularly awkward pupil. 'What do you think they'll invade us for, exactly? If they want mineral or chemical resources, they can get them from any star system. Energy? Their fusion systems looked more advanced than ours. There is no economic or logical reason for them to invade us, especially not with a navy in place. It's a deterrent.'

'Fine. Then make it a working deterrent. Give it some teeth.'

'What sort of teeth would you like it to have?' Justine asked. 'I take it this is why you wanted everyone here to be security cleared?'

'Yes.' Larry nodded at Natasha Kersley.

'My Directorate has been reviewing the data which the *Second Chance* came back with,' she said. 'You were right to say their fusion systems are more advanced than ours. So are their force fields. If Captain Kime hadn't pulled back, we estimate that the *Second Chance* would have been destroyed within a minute of their missiles reaching attack range. The only thing that saved them was the ftl capability. If we are going to confront the Dyson aliens in the future, even if it is solely to establish boundaries, we will need a lot more fire-power than we've carried so far.'

'Then we'll scale things up for the next generation of ships,' Campbell said. 'Increase the force field strength. Provide more power to the atom lasers and plasma lances.'

'They will do the same,' Natasha said flatly. 'And their shipbuilding capacity is much greater than ours will be for the foreseeable future. Their entire civilization is based around spaceflight and manufacturing ships. We cannot win a con-test to scale things up. What we need to do is take this to the next level, and develop a new generation of advanced weapons.'

'Such as?' Gore asked.

'The theoretical concepts which my Directorate studies are need-to-know only.'

'It wouldn't hurt to examine the idea,' Thompson said.

'What my family would like to see is Natasha's Directorate transferred to the starflight agency's defence office,' Larry said. He looked at Patricia. 'That will require an Executive order.'

'I can probably arrange one,' she said.

'It would need to be integrated with the rest of the Commonwealth's security arrangements,' Rafael Columbia said.

'The rest of them?' Patricia repeated wearily.

'If the navy is to have an effective defensive role, then the current Commonwealth security Directorates should be brought together to perform the service. The Special Sciences Supervisory Directorate and the Internal Security Directorate could be combined under the aegis of my own Directorate.'

'Isn't that a little drastic?' Justine asked. 'Not to mention alarmist? What relevance is the Serious Crimes Directorate to all this?'

'We're the ones already fighting this conflict,' Rafael said. 'It is my Directorate which is tracking down the terrorists who attacked the *Second Chance*. That act amounts to anti-human treachery as far as I'm concerned.'

Justine sat back in astonishment. *Talk about gung-ho.*

Let him have it, her father sent to her. **It's just paper empire building, and the agency's planetary defence office has to start with something.**

'I would point out that as Rafael's Directorate operates on a quasi-secret basis anyway,' Larry said, 'the preparatory functions it will be conducting into strategic planetary defence can quite easily be kept quiet under its standard procedures. I believe that was the original recommendation of the Exo-Protectorate Council.'

'It was,' Campbell said. For a moment the two of them locked gazes. Then Campbell offered up a small smile. 'Well, I have no objections to that. In fact, it's rather tidy having everything under one roof. Think you can cope with the extra responsibility, Rafael?'

'And the budget,' Gore grunted.

Everyone laughed.

'You can depend on me,' Rafael assured them.

*

'It makes sense,' Gore said to Justine and Thompson after everyone else had left. 'And it was a brilliant piece of manoeuvring on the Halgarths' part, nobody was going to say no that late in the day. Larry effectively split the navy. The Sheldons will have the ships, while the defence side will all be under Rafael's control. He's got the budget strings, which puts the DRNG and Buta subordinate to him.'

'And defence will ultimately be the bigger budget,' Thompson said. 'We should have seen that coming. The Halgarths keep their dominance of the force field market.'

'The defence budget will only be bigger if the Dysons are a threat,' Justine observed. 'I seem to be the only one who isn't convinced they will be. You two certainly are, and as for Rafael . . . Jesus, it won't be long before he's designing uniforms with nice shiny jackboots.'

'Who'd blame him. All the girls love a sailor.'

'It's not funny, Dad. This merger gives him a great deal of power. The directorates were kept separate for a reason.'

'I'll talk to Patricia and Doi herself when I get back to the Senate tomorrow,' Thompson said. 'You're right about that, Justine. There needs to be an Executive review committee for Rafael's new empire, and his new vice directors will be appointed from other families and dynasties. I've got some contacts on the inside of the directorate who can keep an eye on him as well. Don't worry, we'll keep him in check.'

*

Even with his tight-fitting goggles and fur-lined woollen balaclava Ozzie could feel the freezing wind biting his cheeks. It was infiltrating the edge of his hood as he moved his arms back and forth in a smooth rhythm to propel himself forward with the carved bone ski poles gripped in each hand. The repetitive motion was hard work; he'd only been outside fifteen minutes, and already perspiration was soaking into the T-shirt he wore under his check shirt, sweaters, and icewhale fur overcoat. His skis bobbed over the crisp ice, leaving clear twin tracks behind.

Out here, on the relatively level surface of the vast depression surrounding the Ice Citadel, he could move with a degree of ease, though it was nothing like the speed he used to reach on resort slopes back in the Commonwealth. It would be a lot slower in the forest, he knew. And he'd be hauling a great deal more weight in his backpack as well. Today, he was practising with about half the weight of what he would be taking when they left for good.

He twisted his body carefully, curving to a halt before jamming his poles into the thin layer of crusty ice. Red sunlight washed down on the desolate landscape, revealing a multitude of small ripples in the frozen ground. At half a mile behind him the Ice Citadel stood aloof from the flat grey land, green light winking steadily from its pinnacle, prickles of crimson sunlight scattered off facets in its hexagonal crystal mirrors. A hundred yards away, Tochee was sliding along efficiently. They'd started calling the alien that now, rather than the tochee. Communication personalized it, at least from the human perspective. Ozzie figured he owed it that much.

It had taken Ozzie and George Parkin a week to design the

vehicle which carried the heavy alien. The main structure was a simple sledge of carved icewhale bone, over four yards long, which could hold Tochee's entire body with room to spare. At the front was a windscreen of crystal cut from a tree, and secured in a bone frame that angled back. Behind that, stitched to the circular hoops that went over the sledge platform, was a cylinder of icewhale fur that laced up at the rear. The arrangement was the equivalent of a fur coat for Tochee, keeping its body insulated from the sub-arctic air and its ridges of locomotion flesh well clear of the ground. To move the sledge along, a pair of spiked poles were fixed to the framework one on either side in a variant of a rowlock. George Parkin had designed, carved, and assembled the four sturdy little mechanisms himself, and was quietly proud of his achievement. All four spike poles passed through leather rings in the fur cylinder, which allowed them a fair degree of movement. Tochee gripped the ends in its manipulator flesh, and used the poles as a combination of ski poles and oars.

A big crowd had gathered outside the Ice Citadel the first time Ozzie, Orion, and George had pushed the sledge out from the workshop. It had taken Tochee a couple of minutes of tentative, experimental motions before mastering the poles. Since then, the three of them had been out every day, practising.

Ozzie watched Tochee manoeuvre the sledge towards where he was waiting without losing any momentum. The contraption made him think of some bizarre Victorian attempt to build a snowmobile. But it worked, and the alien was proficient enough now to give him a great deal of confidence for their venture. That just left Orion. The boy was skijoring behind Tochee, short skis strapped to his boots, and holding onto a slim rope that was tied to the back of the sledge frame. Ozzie had decided it was a lot easier for Orion to do that than learn how to ski properly. In fact, the boy was probably enjoying himself a little too much as he swayed from side to side behind the sledge. Ozzie wondered if he should insist on a shorter rope, take away the opportunity for delight. Orion was certainly a lot happier these days, now their preparations to leave were becoming ever more tangible.

The sledge came to a slow stop beside Ozzie, all four poles digging into the gritty ice to score narrow furrows. He was pleased to see Orion angling his own skis correctly to brake. More than once the boy had ploughed into the back of Tochee's sledge. Maybe they did stand a chance after all. Ozzie held out a mitten, thumb extended upwards. Behind the thick windscreen of crystal, Tochee's manipulator flesh formed a similar gesture.

'How are you doing?' Ozzie asked loudly; it was too cold to pull his balaclava aside and expose his mouth.

'All right,' Orion yelled back. 'My arms still ache a bit from yesterday, but these skis are easier to balance on.'

'Okay, let's keep going.' Ozzie struck off across the ice, heading towards a section of the crystal tree forest he'd visited on a harvesting trip three weeks ago. He held a steady pace, concentrating on the ground ahead. There were hidden ridges and little jutting pinnacles of rock that could prove perilous if he hit them wrong. And if Tochee ran over any of them it would be a plain disaster. He wondered if they should take some spare icewhale bone and a few tools for repairs just in case. It would mean more weight, but increase their chances. Like everything they carried with them, there had to be a balance between safety and success. When they started their trial runs in the forest he'd have a better idea.

'Ozzie!'

He turned at the muffled voice, finding Tochee was labouring hard with the sledge's poles, moving them fast, gradually catching up. Orion was shouting furiously, his free arm waving about. Ozzie moved his legs proficiently, bending from the knees as he slewed round, and quickly came to a halt. He stared out over the empty floor of the Ice Citadel depression where the boy was pointing.

The Silfen had finally arrived to hunt. A great procession of them was emerging from the forest on the other side of the depression. From such a distance, they were little more than a moving grey line, although dainty lights sparkled along its length. When he used his retinal inserts to zoom in, he saw the actuality. There were over a hundred of the biped aliens already in the open, with two dozen at the front riding on some quadruped animals that moved as fast as horses even in the terrible cold of this world. Those on foot jogged along effortlessly despite the thick coats they were wearing; half of them were carrying lanterns on long poles that danced about as they moved.

After so long spent in the Ice Citadel, with its uneventful repetitive days, the thrill Ozzie felt at the sight of them was so intense it surprised him. For months he'd been so resolutely dispassionate, he'd almost forgotten that he could experience emotions this strong. *We're on our way out of here!*

'Let's get back,' he shouted at Orion. He made a quick hand signal to Tochee, indicating the Ice Citadel. The alien mimicked another thumbs up behind the windscreen.

They made good time back to the Ice Citadel. The inhabitants had all turned out for the arrival of the Silfen, milling round on the ice outside. Ozzie grabbed a couple of humans and Bill the Korrok-hi to help push Tochee's sledge over the last fifteen metres around the base of the big building where boots and hoofs had churned the ice and sandy soil to a sluggish shingle. When the sledge's fur covering had been unlaced, the big alien quickly slithered off down into the warmer lower level. Ozzie put his skis into the rack and went back outside.

There must have been two hundred and fifty Silfen in the hunt. Their singing and trilling floated across the icy ground, reaching the Ice Citadel long before they did. Even in this bleak perpetual winter the sound was uplifting, a reminder that beyond the forest there were worlds visited by summer. The riders cantered up on steeds that had bodies like fat horses, with necks that extended out horizontally ending in arrow-shaped heads. Their hide was like tawny snakeskin, with a wispy feather rising from every scale. Ozzie was sure he could see slim gills opening and closing quickly along the length of their necks amid the rippling muscle as the riders reined them in just before they reached the excited crowd. He also cast an eye over the long silver spears fastened behind the low saddles – they seemed very impractical, especially for a rider.

The mounted Silfen were warbling away in their own tongue as they looked down on the crowd. They wore long coats of fluffy swan-white fur with hoods that tapered away down their backs. Gloves and boots were made from the same pelt, which made Ozzie wonder what animal it had come from. He suspected it would look rather spectacular.

Sara stepped forward and bowed slightly before the lead rider, then spoke in their own language. 'Welcome back, we are always pleased to see you and your brethren.'

The lead rider twittered away in reply. 'Dearest Sara, happiness flies with the kiss that fruits among us. Joy we know at the seeing of you and your lifeful people. Cold this world is. Strong you must be to thrive below its red light. Strong you are, for thrive you do amid the deep ice and the high sky.'

'Your Citadel is a fine home for us in this cold wilderness. Will you be staying here tonight?'

'Time among this home long past is what we will reap this day.'

'If we can help, then please just tell us. Are you hunting the icewhales this time?'

'Out there they are, covered in their white deeps. Fast they move in short moments. Big they grow in long years. Loud they call. Far away amid the uncountable stars we hear their refrain. We challenge. We chase. And in the end we share our blood to know such a life we gladly live.'

'We would like to follow. We would like to have the icewhale bodies afterwards.'

The rider dismounted in a quick lithe leap to stand in front of Sara. He pushed his hood back, and looked down at her well-covered face as if perplexed. 'When all is done and life has lost its body what happens then to that which is left dead matters not.'

'Thank you.' Sara bowed again.

The riders led their animals into the unused stable halls, while the Silfen on foot went straight inside, singing and laughing as they descended the broad spiral passage to the central chamber. It was a gushing invasion of light and good humour and the smell of springtime and cosy fireside warmth, transforming the ancient Citadel to the kind of haven from the cold and desolation outside which its builders must surely have intended right from the start. When Ozzie finally got down to the main chamber the lantern poles had all been slotted into holes in the wall so they overhung the floor, their thick gold radiance holding back the oppressive red sunlight, banishing the grime fouling the carvings. The Silfen had shed their white coats, bringing the tangible taste of a temperate forest to the harsh stone universe of the cavern with their leaf-green toga cloaks. They opened their packs to hand round flasks and clusters of berries and little biscuity circular cakes. It was the carefree party gathering which made Ozzie ache for his earlier life and the simple pleasures it contained. To his horror and disgust he found his eyes filling with moisture at the memories which the sight triggered.

Most of the humans and other alien residents stood around the walls, watching their visitors in simple contentment. Orion was down there on the floor in the thick of things, moving from one Silfen to another to be sung at and admired and given morsels of food and sips from the flasks. A wondrous smile lifting his young face as his friendship pendant blazed with turquoise starlight.

'Quite something, isn't it?' Sara said quietly in Ozzie's ear.

'I'd forgotten what they were like,' he admitted. 'Christ, I'd forgotten what anything outside this gulag is like.'

A slight frown deepened the heavy wrinkles on her face. 'You're going, then?'

'Oh yeah!'

'George could use some help first.'

'What?' He made an effort to turn away from the exultant Silfen.

'We have to get the big sledges ready. We need those icewhales, Ozzie. People will die without them.'

'Yeah,' he said reluctantly, knowing she was right. Too many people were depending on the hunt and its bounty. 'All right. I'll go help George.' He glanced back across the cavern. 'But do me a favour, don't ask Orion.'

'I won't.'

Ozzie was just one of forty people who George and Sara had marshalled into the preparations for tomorrow. Even so, it took the rest of the afternoon to load the big covered sledges ready to follow the hunt. There were the triple-layer tents, and the cooking gear, and fuel oil to be transferred into bladders, the butchery kits, the barrels and cauldrons. Then George and the more proficient bone carpenters made some last-minute repairs and patches. More people were readying the ybnan in the stables.

He felt tired but quietly pleased when he finished up and made his way back down to his rooms. Orion was still with the Silfen, but Ozzie insisted he leave them. Tochee was already in their sleeping room when they arrived. Ozzie shifted his retinal inserts to ultraviolet. Ragged patterns were flashing within Tochee's front eye segment, question upon question about the Silfen.

Ozzie made calming gestures with his arms and picked up a much-washed parchment of cured hide. He used a charcoal stump to write: Yes, they are the aliens who made the paths. Tomorrow they will hunt the big fur creatures. After that, we follow them off this world.

'What's he saying?' Orion asked excitedly as Ozzie held the parchment up in front of Tochee.

'He's really happy they're here and we've got our chance,' Ozzie told him.

Orion snatched the parchment from Ozzie, and wiped the charcoal letters away into a broad grey smudge. Then he wrote: It's great news, isn't it? We're leaving!!!!!

Tochee took his own parchment off the small pile, his manipulator flesh closed around a charcoal stump. Together we will do this. Together the three of us will be a triumph.

Orion stood in front of Tochee and raised both hands in a double thumbs up. The alien's manipulator flesh closed around the boy's fingers.

'Okay, you dudes,' Ozzie said. 'Let's get serious. We've only got one chance at this, so it's got to be right. Orion, open the security mesh up and get all your stuff packed away. If it isn't in your rucksack, it's staying here. Then get your best outdoor othes ready for the morning. When you've done that, pop out to the kitchen range and fill all our thermos flasks with boiling water, we're going to make up some of that powdered juice, the stuff with extra glucose and crap in it. We'll drink that outside tomorrow.'

'Can't I do that in the morning?'

'There's no telling when the Silfen are going to leave; everyone says it's always early, so we can't gamble that there's like going to be hot water ready for us tomorrow. This has all got to be done now. We'll have about fifteen minutes warning, man. I've fixed it with George for us to have places on one of the big covered sledges.'

'All right then,' Orion said. 'I'll get started.'

Ozzie wrote more lines on his parchment, telling Tochee to get the best meal he could tonight.

Don't forget me, the alien wrote back. Don't leave me behind.

We won't.

Ozzie dug out some self-heating packages of Cumberland sausages and mash in onion gravy, which fizzed away while he prepared his own kit. Even piling the tent and various other essentials in bags on the back of Tochee's sledge, and himself and Orion both skiing with their rucksacks, they'd never be able to take everything they'd brought with them on the lontrus. It was time for hard choices and educated guesses. He decided to leave most of his clothes behind, he was wearing enough to survive on this planet, which gave him enough to live anywhere, just not in any great variety. There was pack-aged food for fifteen days, which he included in the bundle to go on Tochee's sledge, though luxuries like chocolates and biscuits and tea he would leave for Sara and George. The medical kit was also a must. His set of ceramic teflon-coated cooking pans were dumped, as was the small kerosene stove. All the riding gear, the saddle, the pack harnesses from the lontrus – it was all useless to him now.

He looked at the sorely depleted pile of things he wanted to keep, knowing it was still too big.

'We can leave the security mesh,' Orion said when he came back in with the flasks. 'That must weigh a bit.'

'Yeah,' Ozzie said slowly. 'Guess so. Good thinking there, man.'

The boy picked up his backpack, holding it above his head as he gave a goofy grin. His red hair hadn't been cut since they arrived at the Ice Citadel, so that it now came down almost to his shoulders, and threatened to cover his eyes most of the time. 'And I can carry a lot more for you. See, I've got almost nothing in here.' He tried holding his ancient nylon rucksack aloft with one hand to prove his point.

'That's okay, man,' Ozzie said as the backpack tipped over and Orion made a comical lurch to catch it. 'We've got everything we need to make it out of here. Anything more and we'd be jeopardizing our chances. No way am I doing that again. Did I ever tell you how totally crap our spacesuit was when Nigel stepped out on Mars?'

'Don't think so.'

'Now that was being unprepared in the mostest serious fashion. Jesus, it was a miracle he ever came back, and he was only a couple of yards from the wormhole the whole time. That would have been fucking impressive wouldn't it? First person to step through our new machine and he drops down dead from the lack of a bicycle puncture repair kit. History would have been a hell of a lot different.'

'What was it like, Mars?'

'Cold. Colder than this dump. And dead. I mean really seriously dead. Believe me, you know when somewhere has been dead for a billion years before the dinosaurs were killed off. You just had to look at it and you knew.' He shook his head, surprised by how strong the image was after nearly three and a half centuries. 'So now, show me what you've put in the pack.'

*

Tochee returned with the bucket it ate its mashed crystal tree fruit from. Ozzie and Orion settled down on their cots with their packaged meals, and the three of them ate in silence. The Silfen out in the central chamber were singing away blithely, clearly intent on partying the night away like a bunch of boisterous students. Ozzie caught the occasional line of verse, most of which praised the icewhales for their size and speed and ferocity.

Sara was their first visitor. Ozzie handed over the items he was leaving behind, which she accepted with brisk thanks. George turned up, with the sledgemasters who would captain the hunting party. The other five people who were going to try and find a path off the planet wandered in, four men and one woman. They sat on the cots, and everyone started discussing options and strategies. The modest rock cavern took on the kind of hyped-up atmosphere in the team changing room minutes before the big match. Thinking that, Ozzie briefly wondered who had won the Commonwealth Cup.

It amazed him he even managed to fall asleep. But there he was, tangled up in an unsealed sleeping bag, his arms and neck chilly, as Orion shook him awake. The rug hadn't even been pulled over the bright crystal duct in the ceiling.

'It's time, Ozzie,' the boy said in a near-fearful voice. 'George says they're getting ready.'

'Right then, man, let's get to it.' Ozzie felt like singing, something uplifting, like the early Beatles or the Puppet Presidents. Out in the central chamber the Silfen had quietened down. He pulled the rings on the self-heating breakfast packets, and started to get dressed. Full body thermal underwear, of course, then a thick sweatshirt and his cord trousers, the clean check shirt. By the time he laced his hiking boots up he was starting to feel warm, so he carried the rest, the two sweaters, waterproofed and insulated trousers, scarf, balaclava, gloves, ear muffs, goggles, and of course the icewhale fur coat, overtrousers, and mittens. He checked Orion who was equally well dressed. Half of his garments were Ozzie's, cut down weeks ago and sewn carefully to fit in readiness for this occasion

They ate their breakfast, took a last visit to the bathroom, then collected Tochee from its quarters. When they got upstairs, the big workshop was abuzz with activity. Silfen riders were already leading their animals from the stables. George was rapping out orders to his teams. Tochee shifted about uncomfortably on the cold, damp stone floor while Ozzie and Orion gave his sledge a final check, then it quickly slithered up into the protective cylinder of icewhale fur. Ozzie handed Tochee three heat bricks before carefully lacing up the flaps of fur at the back, making sure there were no gaps. He and Orion piled their packs on the little space left over at the rear of the sledge platform. Tochee was now going to have to stay inside until they reached a warmer world. Weeks ago, Ozzie had tried asking if Tochee got claustrophobia, but either their pictures and words vocabulary hadn't developed enough to explain the concept, or the alien didn't have a psychology susceptible to such things.

It was George himself who helped Ozzie and Orion push Tochee's sledge outside into the weak pre-dawn light, then they tied it to one of the big covered sledges pulled by a team of five ybnan. After exchanging 'okay' and 'good luck' signs with the alien, they clambered inside amid all the equipment for butchering and cooking the icewhales. Bill the Korrok-hi was their driver, and Sara wedged herself inside beside them, along with fifteen others. The small brazier hanging from the top of the sledge was lit, casting a murky brimstone light around the inside, complete with noxious fumes. The side flap was closed.

As the red sun slowly rose above the horizon the Silfen gathered together outside the Ice Citadel, their white furs gleaming bright in the glow from their lanterns, spears and bows held ready. They began a slow chant, their voices deeper than Ozzie had ever heard before. In a mournful baritone they sounded a lot more alien, and far more menacing. Their riders moved off at an easy canter, leaving those on foot to follow at a slower pace. The sledges pulled by the ybnan lurched off in eager pursuit, with pans and metallic equipment clanking loudly.

It took an hour and a half just to reach the border of the crystal tree forest. So far the covered sledges had kept up with the Silfen on foot. But once they reached the small trees around the fringe they had to arrange themselves in single file. The path between the steadfast trunks was narrow and awkward, slowing them further. They slowly lost distance on the Silfen, although the track they left was easy enough to follow. Occasionally the Korrok-hi drivers would catch a glimpse of the shimmering light from their lanterns through the snow-covered trunks. Several times, Ozzie went over to the door flap to check Tochee was still being towed. The sledge was slipping along without any trouble. Tochee was barely having to use the four poles to steer with.

'How much longer?' Orion asked after they'd been pushing through the forest for over an hour.

'We'll be in the forest for a couple of hours yet before we reach the hunting ground,' Sara said. 'After that, who knows? Their riders went on ahead to try and track some icewhales.'

'How big is the hunting ground?'

'I have no idea. You can't see the far side no matter how clear the air is. Hundreds of miles across, I suppose. Once we had to turn back we'd gone so far and they hadn't started hunting. But that is rare. If we're lucky, and there's some close by, they might even hunt this afternoon.'

'Will they leave at night?' Ozzie asked.

'No. That is, they never have yet.'

It was another two and a quarter hours before they reached the edge of the forest. Ozzie and Orion both peered through the flap, eager to see the land beyond. They were high up, something Ozzie hadn't appreciated before. The crystal tree forest sprawled across the plateau of some broad massif. Where it ended, the ground swept down towards a vast plain dominated by hundreds of low volcanic craters. Sara had been right about its size, the ultra-cold air was perfectly clear, yet from his vantage point half a mile above the plain, Ozzie couldn't see the other side, it was hidden within a hazy crimson horizon. The crater rims themselves were almost flat, but between them the frozen land had ripped open, producing thousands of rocky fangs like small Matterhorns. Crystal trees grew on their lower slopes, although the pinnacles were rugged naked rock with a few streaks of snow and ice caught in crevices, reflecting a dusky scarlet in the pervasive sunlight.

The craters were all filled with ice particles, Sara told them, fine sand-like granules that produced a perfectly level surface, giving no clue how deep they actually were. Most of them had vapour rising from the centre in small plumes that drifted almost straight upwards, slowly getting wider and thinner as they climbed until, thousands of metres above the plain, they merged into smears of tenuous cirrus that meandered about like spacious contrails. When Ozzie switched to infrared he could see the craters glowing with a weak intensity, no more than a few degrees higher than the surrounding land, but a temperature difference sufficient to cause evaporation. He wondered how much warmer the craters were at the bottom.

Halfway down the slope leading to the plain, he could see the Silfen threading their way past small clumps of crystal trees, lantern lights bobbing about merrily. There was no sign of the riders. One by one, the big sledges crested the top of the slope, and began their precarious descent after the hunters.

It was a rough journey down, with the rucked surface rocking the sledges about. Every so often, the Korrok-hi drivers had to use the ybnan to slow their speed rather than pull them along. Ozzie had a lot of difficulty looking out and checking on Tochee. Everyone inside the covered sledge was hanging on grimly to the broad bone cage. In the end he just stayed put – there wasn't much he could do if the tow rope broke anyway. Several pieces of equipment had worked loose to roll round, pans and bone struts jangling as they banged painfully into shins and arms and chests. The brazier was swinging in an alarmingly wide arc on its short chain.

They couldn't have taken more than forty minutes to reach the plain, although time stretched out to hours inside the

719

cramped stinking cabin. Ozzie had never before appreciated how important it was to be able to see out of a moving vehicle. His imagination filled the whole route down with knife-blade boulders waiting to split them open, and the slope was bound to end with a hundred-metre vertical cliff.

Bill let out a low trumpet of satisfaction to signal the descent was over. Inside the sledge, everyone flashed nervous grins around, not willing to admit just how scared they'd been. After that, progress was appreciably easier. Sara was confident they could close some of the distance that had accumulated between them and the Silfen. Orion kept his friendship pendant clasped tightly in his fist, watching its sparkling blue light intently.

The covered sledges maintained a single file, following the fresh tracks in the crunchy grains of snow. They were heading directly away from the massif, rattling along at a good pace. By midday they were skirting along the shoreline ridge of the first crater, with a string of savage rock peaks on the other side. After that there were gullies crowned by curving waves of compacted snow, looking as if the slightest tremble would send them avalanching into the gulf below. Then ravines with frozen sheet ice along the floor, where the ybnan had trouble getting a grip with their hoofs; spinneys and forests of crystal trees and bulbous bushes. Often, when he looked out, Ozzie would see great swathes of them smashed and shattered, leaving jagged stumps surrounded by a pile of ice-encrusted branches. There were narrow steep saddle valleys to surmount, where their speed was reduced to a painful crawl on the ascent, only to degenerate into a mad slither downwards, more abrupt and frightening than the trip down from the massif. And there were long curves around craters, where the vapour drifted out sideways like a mist, swiftly covering ybnan and sledges alike in a crusty hoarfrost.

When the sun was an hour and a half from the horizon, the massif was invisible behind them, blocked from view by towering spires of sharp black rock. Shadows were lengthening and darkening across the rust-tinted ground. The ybnan teams on all the sledges were beginning to tire. Even on the flat their speed was noticeably less than earlier.

'There'll be no hunt today,' Sara said after she returned from a quick discussion with Bill. 'And we need to set up the tents soon. It's difficult in the dark.'

After another half-hour, they emerged from the gap between two rock ridges to look down on a crater measuring over six miles across. Some time after the basin formed, the volcanic activity which riddled the area had thrown up yet another range of fierce crags. This one formed a long promontory extending out almost halfway across the crater.

The Silfen had gathered at the foot of the peak closest to the rim, riders and those on foot bunched together and glowing like a multifaceted jewel in the gathering twilight. A stretch of forest grew up the slope beyond them, its crystal trees taller than those back on the forests of the massif, looking dark and forbidding in the vermilion gloaming.

The sledges pulled up in a broad circle, half a mile from the Silfen, on top of an escarpment which skirted the landward crags. Everyone jumped to, hauling the tents out and slotting the framework together. Once the big tents were up, Ozzie, Orion, and George rigged a smaller frame over Tochee's sledge, and pulled a big sheet of fur over it. Inside that, they draped another blanket of fur across the top of the sledge's protective cylinder.

'It should be okay in that,' George said as he crawled out.

Ozzie, who was left inside, grunted agreement. He lit a pair of candles, and put them on the ground in front of the sledge's windscreen. There wasn't much space there, probably no more than a couple of cubic yards, but it allowed Tochee to look out, maybe take away any fear of entombment. Looking in through the pane of crystal, Ozzie could see the alien motionless behind it, front eye section aligned on him. He held a mitten out, thumb upwards. Tochee's front eye swirled with ultraviolet patterns, slightly smudged by flaws in the crystal. It translated roughly into: Don't forget me tomorrow.

'Not a chance,' Ozzie whispered inside his balaclava.

Tochee pulled the tab on a heat brick. Ozzie waited until he saw the brick start to glow a deep cherry red, then waved and backed out of the fur coverings.

There was probably another twenty minutes before the sun sank below the horizon. Ozzie hurried off towards the crater rim. It was achingly quiet in the moments just before nightfall. Even the Silfen's perpetual signing had ended out here under the sombre glacial sky. Ahead of him, the surface of the granular ice which filled the crater basin was so flat that the illusion of liquid was almost perfect. As he approached it, he half expected to see ripples. He knelt down beside it, and touched it with his mitten. The surface had the texture of thick oil, though the further down he pushed his hand, the greater the resistance became.

'Careful you don't fall in,' Sara said.

Ozzie straightened up, shaking residual grains from his mitten. 'Man, you always make me feel like I'm doing something wrong.'

'People have fallen in before. We don't risk our own lives trying to find them now. They never leave any trace, it's not as if there could be any bubbles.'

'Yeah, figures. This stuff isn't natural. Grains of ice like this should stick together.'

'Of course they should. But they're being constantly churned up and kept loose, like flour in a food mixer.'

'And the icewhales are doing the churning.'

'Them, and whatever else is down there. After all, they have to eat something.'

'Hopefully just iceweed, or whatever the plant life is at the bottom.'

'You wouldn't say that if you'd ever seen one.' She turned, and began to walk up the slight incline.

Ozzie started after her. 'Why not?'

'Let's just say they don't act like herbivores.'

'You got it all figured out, dontcha?'

'No, Ozzie, nothing like. I understand very little of this place, and all the others I walked through. Why don't the Silfen allow us to have electricity?'

'Simple enough theory. They're experiencing life on a purely physical level; that's all these bodies we see are for, to give them a platform at this level of personal consciousness evolution. And it kills me to say it, but it's a pretty low level, given their capabilities. You start introducing electricity, and machines, and all the paraphernalia which goes with it, then you start to shrink that opportunity for raw natural experience.'

'Yeah,' she said sourly. 'God forbid they should invent medicine.'

'It's irrelevant to them. We need it because we treasure our individuality and continuity. Their outlook is different. They're on a journey that has a very definite conclusion. At the end of their levels they get to become a part of their adult community.'

'How the hell do you know that?'

He shrugged, a gesture largely wasted under his heavy fur coat. 'I was told that once.'

'Who by?'

'This dude I met in a bar.'

'Dear Christ, I don't know which is weirder, them or you.'

'Definitely them.' They came to the top of the small rim as the sun vanished, leaving only a flaming fuchsia glow in the sky.

'You also shouldn't be out so late,' Sara said. 'There's no beacon to guide you back here, you know.'

'Don't worry about me, I see better in the dark than most people.'

'You got fur instead of skin as well? Even the Korrok-hi don't stay out at night on this world.'

'Sure. Sorry. Wasn't thinking.'

'You'll have to do a lot better tomorrow when you follow the Silfen.'

'Right. You know, I'm still kind of surprised you didn't want to come with us.'

'I will leave one day, Ozzie. Just not yet, that's all.'

'But why? You've been here long enough. I can't see you buying into George's idea about how living here as some kind of penance makes us value our lives more. And as far as I can make out there's no one special for you. Is there?' Which had slowly come to nag at him as his own suggestions in that direction over the months had all gone unheeded.

'No,' she said slowly. 'There's no one right now.'

'That's a shame, Sara. We all need someone.'

'So were you going to volunteer?'

The mild scorn in her voice made him pause. After a moment, Sara stopped and looked back at him. 'What?' she asked.

'Well, goddamn, I couldn't have been any blunter,' Ozzie said.

'Blunt about what?'

'About us. You and me. Rocking the mattress.'

'But you've got . . . Oh.'

'Got what?' he asked suspiciously.

'I thought . . . we all thought: you and Orion.'

'Me and Orion what . . . ohshit.'

'You mean he's not your—'

'No. Absolutely. No.'

'Ah.'

'And I'm not.'

'Okay. Sorry. Misunderstanding, there.'

'Not that there's anything—'

'No, certainly not. There isn't. I had lots of gay friends.'

'Did you?'

'That's what you're supposed to say.'

'Yeah, right.'

'Well, that cleared that up, then.'

'It did.' *Oh terrific.*

They hurried back up the remainder of the escarpment to the tents in silence. Everyone was inside now, and thick black oil fumes were squirting out of carefully designed vents in the top as the evening meal got under way.

'Ozzie,' Sara said in a weary tone just before they went into their tent.

'Yo.'

'Tomorrow, when the Silfen hunt the icewhales, don't get curious, okay. No matter how exciting or repellent, or fascinating you think it is, stay back, stay right out of their way.'

'I hear you.'

'I hope so. I know why you're here, I've seen it in people before. You think you're on some kind of mission, and you think that makes you invulnerable. Hell, maybe it does, but take it from me, tomorrow is not a good time to test it out, okay. I understand your crazy ideas about the Silfen, and how existential they are, but tomorrow it doesn't get more real and physical than this.'

'I'll be careful, I promise. I've got the kid and the alien to worry about.'

*

They were woken as the first magenta glimmer of dawn appeared. Despite being crammed into the tent with ten other people, Ozzie had slipped into a deep dreamless sleep as soon as he zipped up his sleeping bag. It was the first night since he arrived that he hadn't had to endure the ubiquitous red light.

He and Orion ate their packaged breakfasts, warding off

the edgy, resentful comments from the others who were having their standard Ice Citadel meal of mashed crystal tree fruit and fried icewhale rashers. They filled their flasks with boiled water; they mixed in the added-energy juice powder in two, and to the other two they added soup concentrate. While the rest hurried outside to catch the Silfen begin their hunt, Ozzie and Orion packed their rucksacks for what they hoped was the last time on this world.

It had snowed overnight, the wisps of cirrus condensing into tiny hard flakes that drifted down to dust every surface. Ozzie and Orion brushed it off the outer sheet of fur they'd arranged over Tochee's sledge. They dragged it back, with Ozzie partly dreading what they'd find. A stiff corpse? But the heat brick had worked. Tochee waved at them from behind the crystal windscreen, apparently unperturbed by its night spent alone.

The pair of them stood beside the sledge, slightly apart from everyone else milling round the tents. It was a good position from which to watch the hunt play out over the land below. Ozzie also realized why the Korrok-hi had driven the covered sledges up the escarpment yesterday evening. Up here they were well out of harm's way.

Today's hunt was going to range over the expanse of gullies and spinney-crowned hummocks that stretched back from the crater floor. The mounted Silfen had split into two groups. The first was making its way along the range of crags that plunged out across the crater, heading for the tip. While the second was cantering around the rim away from them. Those on foot were splitting into small parties, and fanning out through the spinneys and boulder fields.

Ozzie watched with considerable interest as individual riders dropped away from the group moving along the base of the crags, to stand a lonely sentry duty just above the uneven shore-line. After forty minutes, the last rider reached the apex and halted. Facing him, a mile away on the crater rim, the other group was spaced out in a corresponding formation.

Somewhere a horn was sounded, its clear note ringing through the frigid air.

'Cover your eyes,' Sara shouted in warning.

Ozzie and Orion exchanged a look. No one had mentioned this before. Ozzie quickly stepped in front of the sledge's windscreen. When he glanced back at the crater, he zoomed in on the furthermost rider out at the end of the crags. The Silfen was perched on his mount, arm back in a classic spear-thrower position. Ozzie just had time to order his retinal insert filters on line. The Silfen threw his spear. Even on full zoom, Ozzie was hard pushed to see the silver splinter as it sliced through the air at an impossible speed. When he checked, he could see the Silfen on the crater rim opposite had thrown his spear as well.

'What—'

At the top of their arcs, the spears ignited, stretching out to become lightning bolts. Incandescent white light flashed across the crater, casting the waiting Silfen riders into stark relief. Red sunlight was momentarily banished in the silent starburst splendour.

The twin ribbons of energy dived down into the lake of ice granules. Two blue-white circles of phosphorescence erupted where they vanished below the surface, expanding until they were hundreds of yards across, then slowly dying away.

'What was that?' Orion cried.

'I don't know,' Ozzie replied truthfully. He was mildly surprised that the surface of ice granules hadn't shot up like a depth-charge explosion, but it remained perfectly calm. A plangent boom rolled in across the landscape, reverberating off the crags and hummocks.

The second mounted Silfen on each wing stood up in their saddles, and flung their spears. White light scorched down again. It wasn't until the fourth set of spears had been launched that Ozzie saw movement out in the crater. A low, smooth arrowhead wave rose up between the twin pools of light and the shoreline, surging along for almost fifty yards before sinking down again.

A chorus of joyful chanting rose from the Silfen waiting for the beasts to be driven ashore, their cadence mingling with the thunderclap of the fourth set of spears.

'It's working,' Ozzie mumbled inside his balaclava.

More bow waves were visible out in the crater now, all of them heading in towards the rim as the terrifying spears of light continued to fall behind: goading. The two closest to the shore were permanent, rushing forwards ever-faster. Ozzie held his breath, eager to see an icewhale at long last.

The first one burst out of the ice granules a hundred yards from the shoreline; a huge grey shaggy mountain of fur sliding up into the air with the ease and grace of a dolphin sporting at sea. It was like a polar bear grown to dinosaur size, but with a row of arm-length tusks curving out wickedly from each side of its muzzle. The legs, of which there was a whole series running along its underbelly, were more like fur-clad fins.

'It's huge!' Orion squeaked.

'Yeah, man, pretty damn big.'

The icewhale surged back into the ice granules, splashing up great gouts of the dry powder. Spears detonated into pure light behind it, converting the billowing cloud of particles into a seething mass of whirling rainbows. Its head rocked about in fury at this deliberate provocation, but it kept up its dash for the crater rim. Four more waves were close behind it.

Individual Silfen on foot were racing forward, their smaller, black spears held above their heads. They had shed their big heavy coats to sprint towards their prey, dark motes skipping grimly over the bleak land. Overhead, the sky careered haplessly from red to white, spinning shadows round and round with giddy discord as the volley of twinned lightning bolts seared their way along steep curves. Ozzie had seen old documentary videos of soldiers storming ashore in wartime, and the charge of the Silfen was almost identical to that. A breathtaking insanity that made him want to scream encouragement.

The first icewhale reached the rim, and just kept on going at the same speed. Ozzie couldn't believe anything that huge could move so fast. Its head was still scything from side to side, tusks snapping in berserk rage. Silfen fanned out around it. Several spears were thrown. These didn't burst into a monochromatic blaze, but held true. They had little effect when they struck the flanks of the icewhale, its matted fur was so thick that most hit and rebounded to clatter on the ground. Those that did manage to stick their tips into whatever flesh was underneath didn't penetrate far. They simply enraged the creature further. Its body bucked and twisted, contorting to allow its legs to scrabble at the slim poles like a dog scratching at fleas. Those Silfen who had thrown their spears started to retreat, several of them were pulling their bows round ready to shoot arrows. Ozzie had seen no sign of eyes anywhere amid the icewhale's fur, but it seemed to know where its tormentors were. It lunged forward, giant muzzle snapping. Three tusks sliced straight through a Silfen. Jets of ebony blood squirted from the killer punctures. Then the muzzle sprang open again, ripping the body apart. Legs spun off one way, while the torso flopped to the ground. The icewhale thundered over it, and charged at another Silfen who was falling backwards even as he tried to notch an arrow.

Orion screamed in horror.

'It's all right,' Ozzie shouted. He hugged the boy, turning him away from the carnage. 'I promise you he's all right. They don't die. Do you understand? The Silfen don't die. They have an afterlife, a real heaven.'

The boy was shaking violently inside his embrace. 'It ate him!' he wailed. 'It ate him!'

729

'No it didn't. It can't. They're too hot. It would burn its mouth away if it tried to do that.'

'But he's dead.'

'No! I told you. The Silfen go to their own heaven. I'm not bullshitting you, man. That's the way they are.'

Orion clung to him, his head pressed hard against Ozzie's chest. 'Will the monsters come for us? Please, Ozzie, I don't want to die. I won't go to heaven, I know I won't.'

'Hey,' Ozzie squeezed reassuringly. 'Yes you would. It's me that's headed down into the heat. Why do you think I keep having to get rejuvenated? The big bad dude with the pitchfork and an attitude is all that's waiting for me.'

There was no answer; no smart or sarcastic comeback. Ozzie hugged the boy again, and took a quick look down at the hunt. The last of the aggravating spears from the riders had been flung, leaving the red sun victorious in the battle to light the sky. There were four icewhales on the land now, one of them even bigger than the first to emerge. Each of them was encircled by fast-moving Silfen on foot; spears and arrows were fired inwards, black flecks shimmering through the air. Most still bounced off the tough lank fur, though the numbers sticking were increasing. Over a dozen Silfen were dead already, torn apart or mashed into the unyielding ground. Blood ran thick from their ruined bodies, steaming feverishly and boiling the snow before the pools and runnels started to freeze.

'Come on,' Ozzie urged. 'Let's get inside and take a major break from this bummer.' Any residual excitement he'd had at the prospect of witnessing the hunt had long since washed away beneath the guilt of bringing the boy here. He half-carried him towards the nearest tent.

'They won't come up here, will they?' Orion asked in a pitiful voice.

'No. I promise.'

Sara caught sight of them stumbling towards the tent together, and hurried over. 'Are you all right?'

'No he's fucking not,' Ozzie barked at her. 'You might have told me.'

'It's a hunt. What did you expect?'

Ozzie's anger spluttered out. She was right. *What had I expected it to be like? Just another TSI spectacular?*

Sara tugged at the lacing which held the flaps on the outermost layer. Ozzie sneaked another look down below, making sure his body blocked Orion's view. The sight was growing more surreal. The Silfen death count had risen to over twenty. Three of the elfin folk had managed to climb onto the back of an icewhale, hanging onto its fur and riding it like the wildest bronco in the galaxy. As he watched, one of them was swatted by the icewhale's foot, tumbling a long way through the air before crashing onto rock. The surviving two were trying to thrust their spears down into the ruff of fur behind its neck, and having a hard time of it.

A second icewhale was ploughing straight through a spinney of crystal trees. It was like an unstoppable bulldozer, bursting the trunks apart into dangerous sparkling shrapnel clouds as it hit them head on. The sound was already reverberating over the escarpment, a city of glass caught in an earthquake. Silfen were having trouble dodging trees and spinning shards as they ran alongside, trying to take a shot.

As for the third icewhale . . . Ozzie's brow crumpled into a frown. Five dead Silfen marked its path from the crater. The fight it had given them was tremendous, and now it was weakening, slowing. It had never been so vulnerable. Yet instead of pressing home their advantage, the blood-crazed elfin folk were giving it a wide berth. Its back and flanks were pierced by over a dozen arrows and spears, its head wavered giddily from side to side. Obviously in distress, the icewhale came to an exhausted halt. As it did so, the Silfen began to form two loose lines, creating an avenue that led back to the crater. They held their spears aloft in salute. The icewhale turned sluggishly, and began its long laboured trek back to the crater and the safety of the ice granules.

'In you go,' Sara said. She'd opened the tent up. Ozzie pushed Orion through the gap, and followed him quickly. Sara came in with them. Orion sat numbly on one of the cots. Ozzie took off his balaclava mask, letting his hair spring out. He produced a thermos out of his coat's big pocket. 'I want you to drink some of this. It's hot, it'll do you good.'

The boy made a half-hearted attempt to pull his hood off. Sara helped him. Then Ozzie almost forced the juice down his throat. He'd never seen the boy look so upset before. Tears were clogging his young distressed eyes.

'Pretty bad, wasn't it?'

Orion just nodded mutely.

'That one they're letting get away,' Ozzie said. 'What's that all about?'

'The icewhales have a reserve energy store,' Sara said. 'It's roughly their equivalent of adrenaline hitting the human bloodstream. They use it to get themselves between craters, or fight for territory. Catch their food too, for all I know. But they take a long time to fill that reserve, and they can burn it off real fast. Once it's run out, they're basically screwed. The Silfen don't see any sport in hunting something that just sits there while they shoot it full of arrows, so they make sure it gets back to the crater.'

'They're crazy,' Ozzie said. 'The whole thing is just fucking stupid.'

'You're the one who thinks they only live at this level to experience, remember.'

'Yeah.' He plonked himself down on the cot next to Orion. 'I remember.'

Sara studied the pair of them for a moment. 'I've got to get

732

back out there. I'll let you know when the hunt's over. It won't be long.'

'Thanks.'

Orion didn't say a word, just sat there with the thermos held in his hands.

'It won't happen again,' Ozzie said to the boy eventually. 'Wherever we wind up, it won't be the same as this shitforsaken dump.'

There was a long moment, then Orion suddenly exploded into motion. He clawed at the front of his fur coat, pulling it open, then he went for his sweater's collar. 'I hate them,' he yelled. 'I hate them, Ozzie, they're not what everyone said. They're not my friends. How can I be friends with people who do that?' He pulled out the pendant, and tugged hard, breaking the chain. 'They're not my friends.' The shimmering pendant was flung across the tent. 'What have they done with my parents?'

'Hey, man, they didn't do nothing to your parents. I promise you that.'

'How? How can you promise? You don't know.'

'They're not evil. I know what's happening out there doesn't look nice, but they don't deliberately hurt people. Your mom and dad will be walking the paths quite happily. Remember what Sara said: they never showed up here. You ask me, this planet is a dead end as far as the paths are concerned. The Silfen don't bother with it much.'

Orion shook his head, and hunched up. 'They're so cruel.'

'These ones are, yeah. All living things seem to be at some stage in their evolution. We just picked a bad stage to see them at today, is all.'

'Oh.' The boy sniffed, and took a drink of the juice. 'Do you think this stage is before they visit Silvergalde or after?'

'Hey, good question. I don't know, I'd have to think about it.'

'I think it's before. You have to know what's awful in the world before you can appreciate what's good.'

'Shit. How old are you?'

'Don't know really, not out here where the paths mess with time like Sara said.'

'Well that was totally profound for a fourteen-year-old.'

'I'm fifteen! Probably sixteen now.'

'Okay, ninety per cent profound.' Ozzie walked over to the pendant. 'If you don't mind, I'd like to take this with me.'

Orion grunted with perfect teenage sullenness. 'Don't care.'

'Good. You never know, it might just guide us to some of the nicer Silfen.' The pendant was still alight and undamaged; he slipped it into his trouser pocket where it was less likely to fall out. 'You okay now? We should wrap up again and get back out there.'

'I'm okay, I suppose.'

When they emerged from the tent, Tochee had pressed a small strip of parchment up against his sledge windscreen. It read: What is wrong.

Ozzie wasn't about to go through the whole writing procedure outside. He made a few simple arm gestures, ending with a thumbs up. Orion was nudged to do the same. Tochee waved at them, and withdrew the parchment.

'They've killed them, look,' Orion said miserably.

Below the escarpment, three icewhales lay dead on the rocky ground, their fur tacky with dark blood from many wounds. Over thirty Silfen bodies shared their fate. The survivors were gathered round the massive beasts they'd brought down. Ozzie zoomed in on the nearest for a close-up. Two of the Silfen were hacking their way into the icewhale with long scimitar blades; they'd already peeled back a wide triangular section of the outer skin, and were now cutting deep into the body cavity. Gooey fluid and bulbous ribbons of offal spilled out around their feet. He saw them pull out an organ that was half the size of an adult human. The remaining

Silfen gathered round. One by one they cut out a section and with great ceremony started to eat.

Ozzie blinked and pulled his focus back. 'I thought they were vegetarians,' he said.

'You thought wrong,' Sara told him.

Ozzie turned to face her. 'Wouldn't be the first time.'

'I came to tell you to get ready,' she said. A gesture took in the other five humans who intended to follow the Silfen, they were all busy strapping their skis on. 'They'll be moving on right away.'

'No more hunting?' Ozzie asked.

'No.' She paused for a moment. 'I know you hated being here, but I'm glad I had the chance to meet you. It's not often people live up to their reputation. Some of it, anyway.'

'Thanks, I think.'

'Next time we meet, it'll be different.'

There were a lot of ways he could have answered that, but just about everyone would hear. 'Let's hope so.'

'And you,' she said to Orion. 'Make him behave.'

'I'll try,' the boy said from behind his mask.

Ozzie put his own skis on, then checked Orion had fixed his properly. With the boy holding on to the tow rope at the back of Tochee's sledge, Ozzie gave the alien their prearranged signal, and pushed off. The escarpment was steep enough to give him a good initial speed. All he had to do was watch for snags and stones which could throw the sledge. Tochee followed him easily, using the four poles with a light touch to steer the sledge along Ozzie's ski tracks.

By the time they reached the bottom of the escarpment, the Silfen were already leaving. The riders had returned, and those on foot had picked up their lanterns. Their voices were raised in cheerful song again. They set off almost directly back the way they came. Ozzie turned to look back up the escarpment. A lone figure was silhouetted against the sky, watching them, but at this distance he couldn't tell who it was.

He knew it would be easy at the start. They'd done nothing energetic the day before; they'd eaten well, and had nearly seven hours of uninterrupted sleep. For the first couple of hours, he had to take care not to slide up into the midst of the Silfen. Instead he was content to stay maybe forty yards or so behind them as they jogged along. Their feet compacted the light sprinkling of snow that drifted above the hard ground, providing a relatively smooth surface for the skis. Tochee, also, had no trouble keeping pace, staying five yards or so behind him. Every time he turned, Orion would be there, a hand raised to wave, to reassure him that everything was okay. The other followers kept a constant speed, two of them staying level with Ozzie and the sledge, while the three most proficient skiers kept up with the Silfen, determined not to let go of their ticket out.

As the afternoon progressed, Ozzie was aware of their line starting to curve away from the route they'd taken out from the Ice Citadel. The sun gave him a rough guide to their direction, and the massif was slipping further and further over to the left. The landscape here began to change. Craters and crags remained the primary features, but they were spaced wider apart, allowing the crystal trees to spread thickly between them, the forests insinuating their way around slopes like the leading edge of some prickly dark tide. It was both encouraging and frustrating. Encouraging, because he believed that the forests would ultimately provide the path off this bitter world. Frustrating, for the difficulty they added to the journey. The Silfen barely slowed as they moved under the trees, skipping fluidly around the trunks and saplings without disturbing a branch. For Ozzie it was harder work, even following the widest set of tracks he was having to swerve constantly. Doing that at the pace they set took both concentration and a great deal of physical effort.

He forced himself to slow down every twenty minutes to take a drink of the hot juice; fully aware how dangerous dehydration could be in these circumstances. It was surprising how much distance they lost even halting for the fifteen seconds it took to open a thermos and take a couple of gulps. Distance which he would then try and regain by travelling faster.

After four hours he was sweating heavily into his clothes, which were chafing badly. His arms ached. He could hear his heart thudding away loudly. His legs were threatening to cramp. One of the skiers who'd kept level with them was now hundreds of yards behind, and still falling back further, while of those three originally up with the Silfen, two had slipped back level with Ozzie. The path the Silfen were taking was leading them over a whole succession of hummocks, whose steepish slopes were tough going. On either side, the trees were growing taller. They were shapes which Ozzie hadn't seen on this world before. The really tall ones had branches which spiralled upwards, as if they'd been neatly pruned and trained around the main bole. While the broader variety were simple poles with spheres that resembled glass cages clustered along their length, the ones at the base measuring up to a yard across, with those at the tip barely the size of acorns. Particles of ice had accumulated into irregular cloaks on every trunk, though there were no icicles. It was too cold for the frozen particles to shape themselves like that.

They'd just reached the crest of one small hill when Orion finally faltered, skidding erratically to a halt as he let go of the tow rope. Tochee immediately jammed his four poles into the ground, braking. The other skiers flashed past as Ozzie turned.

'You okay?' he shouted at Orion.

The boy was bent nearly double. Even through the thick layers of clothing, Ozzie could see him quaking.

'I'm sorry,' the boy was sobbing. 'I'm sorry. It hurts everywhere. I've got to have a rest.'

'Take as long as you want.' The timer in Ozzie's virtual vision told him they'd been going for just over five hours. The sun would set in another fifty-one minutes.

He pulled a parchment from his coat pocket, struggling to unroll the cold-stiffened sheet. With a charcoal stump held crudely in a mitten, he wrote: Boy very tired. Soon night. Make camp bottom of hill.

Tochee moved about behind the windscreen, lowering its head so that Ozzie could look into its forward eye segment. The patterns flexed and twisted. Roughly translated they told him: **Also tired. Camp good.**

When Ozzie looked along the path, he could just see a few twinkles of topaz and jade light through the trees below as the Silfen moved ever onwards. Their singing had long since faded from the air. That was when he realized that the skier who'd fallen far behind hadn't caught up yet. If the man had any sense, he'd try and make it back to the covered sledges tomorrow. Ozzie didn't even know which one of the five it was. Some of them had modern camping gear with them – that might see them through the night. His own confidence was bolstered by knowing their own air-insulated tent was good enough, especially with a heat brick.

Orion was taking a big drink from his thermos.

'Yo man, can you make it down to the bottom?' Ozzie asked.

'Yes. I'm really sorry, Ozzie. You two should go on. I can probably make it back to the Ice Citadel.'

'Don't be so stupid. It's almost time to stop anyway. I want to be in the tent before the sun goes down.' He picked up the tow rope, and handed it to the boy.

The track down to the bottom of the hill was undemanding. They kept going for a few minutes more until they found what passed for a small glade. The heavy ice-smothered trees soaked up the red sunlight, turning the forest floor a gloomy crimson. Ozzie pulled their tent from the back of Tochee's sledge, and gave it to Orion to sort out, while he set up the rudimentary bone frame and fur covering. Once more he lit a couple of candles in front of the sledge windscreen. He saw the alien pull the tab on a heat brick just as he wormed his way back out of the covering.

Orion had pitched their tent a few yards away, and was already inside. Drowsy yellow light from the kerosene lamp shone out of the open flap. As he hurried over, the impact of how isolated they truly were struck him. Alone in an arctic alien forest, without any natural light or heat, where unknown creatures possibly lurked close by. This was the eternal child-nightmare that never quite left once adulthood had been reached, not even after three hundred and fifty years.

It wasn't just the cold which was making him shiver as he crawled inside and sealed the flap. Orion made a big show of pulling the tab on a heat brick. The two of them slowly took off their bulky fur coats and overtrousers, then their outer layers of sweaters and trousers. Ozzie plucked at his cold, sweat-sodden check shirt, wrinkling his nose in disgust. As soon as they'd stopped their exertions, he'd begun to get cold very fast, despite the fur coat.

'I'd forgotten how bad it is out there at night,' he grumbled.

'I thought we'd be away from here by now,' Orion said sheepishly. 'We travelled so far.'

Ozzie squeezed the boy's shoulder. 'Remember the kind of progress we made when we arrived here? You did really well out there today. I was ready to call it a day anyway.'

'Thanks, Ozzie. Do you think the others made it?'

'I don't know. Most of them were keeping up with the Silfen.'

'I hope they did.'

Ozzie opened the bag containing some of their food packages. 'What do you fancy for supper?'

*

Ozzie really didn't want to wake up when his insert alarm went off. Lying snug in the soft warm folds of the sleeping bag, every limb ached abominably, and as for his abdominal

739

muscles ... It was pitch black inside the tent, so he switched his retinal inserts to infrared, and searched round for the kerosene lamp. It lit with a flare which made him blink, casting its dreary yellow glow around the interior. The flame from the icewhale oil they used as fuel was soon puffing out a little twist of reeking black smoke.

'What's wrong?' Orion coughed.

'Nothing. It's morning, time to get up.'

'You're wrong. It's night, still. I've only just got to sleep.'

'Fraid not, man.' Ozzie unzipped the top half of his sleeping bag. His thermal undergarments had dried out, as had the check shirt and sweaters that were squashed into the bag with him. But the heat brick was all but exhausted, so the gradually cooling air had allowed condensation to form all over the inside of the tent fabric. He tried to put his check shirt on carefully, but every time a hand caught the side of the tent, little droplets rained down. Orion complained some more as he struggled into action, dressing himself.

They pulled the rings on packets of scrambled egg and bacon. For a few glorious moments the smell of hot food overpowered the dreadful oil.

When they were almost ready to venture back outside, Orion asked, 'Do you think we'll get there today?'

'Honestly? I don't know, man. I hope so. But, if not, we just keep going, it can't be far now. Not even the Silfen can survive here for long.' In his head, their own limit was a constant worry. Between them, they had another eight heat bricks, that gave them three more guaranteed safe nights. They might be able to survive in the tent without one, but it would be an evil night, and Tochee would be finished. How they'd carry the tent and food and other stuff after that was a moot point.

They emerged from the odour of the icewhale oil into the numbing cold of the dark forest. It had snowed again over-night, depositing a thin layer over the fur sheet protecting

Tochee's sledge. Once again, anxiety plucked at Ozzie as they pulled it back to see if the big alien had survived. It had. Manipulator flesh gestured happily to them from behind the windscreen.

The tent and coverings and bags were packed away within half an hour. Fortunately, the snowfall hadn't been heavy enough to completely cover the tracks left by the Silfen. Just before they started, Ozzie held up the little friendship pendant. Its sparkle wasn't as strong as yesterday, but tiny slivers of blue light still crawled around inside it. He took that as an encouraging sign, and pushed off.

A wind picked up, drifting through the forest all morning. It carried little flecks of snow with it, forcing Ozzie to wipe his goggles free every few minutes. Whenever he paused for his drink, he had to go and brush solid flakes off the sledge windscreen. He wasn't sure if it was actually snowing up there above the treetops, or if this was simply residual swirls that the wind was rearranging. It had always puzzled him why the ground here wasn't covered by several feet of snow and ice. Then Sara had told him that once or twice a year a gale would blow for days, scouring away the loose snow and tiny ice pellets. Somehow that didn't surprise or even bother him, this whole planet was weird; privately he considered that it might be as artificial as Silvergalde.

He deliberately set a slower pace that morning. Yesterday had been a determined effort to keep up with the Silfen, grasping the faint chance that they might lead him away off the planet before nightfall. There was still an urgency to their trek, but a constant and realistic pace was more important now than pure speed. His new concern was how the little zephyrs were steadily eradicating the compacted footprints. Although, as if in compensation, it did seem like the trees had parted slightly to form a rudimentary path through the forest.

Lunch was soup again, snatched in the paltry lee of one of

the clustered sphere trees; with its snow coat disguise it could have passed for a swollen Christmas pine. As before, even a short stop hauled their body temperature down, which the hot soup seemed unable to compensate for. Ozzie hated the sensation of cold sinking into his toes, he couldn't stop worrying about frostbite. When they re-emerged from behind the tree, the falling snow was thicker, eliminating almost all trace of the tracks they'd been following. To make matters worse, it was starting to adhere against the fur of their coats. The sledge was like a small lumpy mound of snow on runners.

Ozzie could feel the tiny particles working their way round the rim of his hood. Slender lines of ice were burning against the skin of his cheeks. After a few minutes, the trees began to thin out. While it made skiing slightly easier, it reduced their protection from the wind and ice flakes. It wasn't long after that when the Silfen tracks vanished completely. He slowed to a halt, then had to push off again quickly as Tochee's sledge nearly slid into him.

This was what he'd feared happening right from the start, this world's weather closing in on them, and losing the path. He fumbled with his mittens, pulling out the friendship pendant. A small bluish glimmer still lurked below the surface. Ozzie turned a complete circle. He thought – possibly – it was a fraction brighter at one point. It was a pretty tenuous assumption to gamble three lives on, but he had nothing else.

He went round to the rear of the sledge, and found a length of slim rope. With one end tied to his waist, and the other to the front of the sledge, he set off again. The wind at least seemed to have died down somewhat. But if anything the snowfall was thicker. He was stopping constantly to check the pendant, while the whole time a treacherous thought in his mind kept asking *why bother*? At least when they arrived on this world he had the comforting ignorance of believing that nothing bad could happen to any traveller on the Silfen paths.

Now he knew his life was on the line, and he was trusting it to a piece of alien jewellery. How tenuous was that?

His timer told him they'd been out in the open for forty minutes, though it felt like most of the afternoon, when he came to the edge of another forest. As soon as they were inside and under the protective boughs, the swirling ice flakes abated considerably. Ozzie kept the rope tied to the sledge, though.

'We'll make camp in a couple of hours,' he told his companions. He'd really hoped they could have kept going for longer, but once again this world had thwarted them. He was exhausted by two days of battling his way across hostile terrain, and he knew Orion was never going to be able to take much more of this. As for Tochee . . . well, who knew? But tonight, they would have a long rest, which would at least enable them to keep going for another full day. Beyond that, there was nothing to think about.

He kept going, moving heavy arms and aching legs in slow rhythm. His feet were numb now, the cold cutting off all feeling below his ankles, which allowed his imagination to summon up the worst-case images of what he'd see when he took his boots off that evening. At least the forest was on a gentle downward slope; there were mounds and ridges, of course, but the overall progress was helpful. He wasn't sure if he could manage another big uphill slog. The snow was deeper, too, covering all the usual stones and snags. Several times he shook it off his fur coat where it was clinging.

'Ozzie!'

He turned at the shout, seeing Orion waving frantically. *Now what?* Despite nerves that were getting badly stretched, he signalled Tochee to stop, and skied round to the boy.

Orion pulled his goggles off. 'It's wet,' he exclaimed.

Instead of shouting at the boy to put the goggles back on, he leant in closer to see what had happened.

'The snow,' Orion said. 'It's melting. It's warm enough to melt.'

Sure enough, the ice on the goggles seemed to be mushy, sleet rather than ice. Ozzie snatched his own goggles off, and looked straight up. A million dark specks were falling out of the uniform coral-pink sky. When they landed on his exposed skin, they didn't sting and burn as they had before, they were wintry, yes, but they quickly turned to slush and dribbled over his skin.

Ozzie propelled himself over to the closest tree. He raised a pole, and whacked it hard against the trunk. The snow loosened, falling away. He hit it again and again until the bark was exposed. Real, biological bark. It was a proper wooden tree. He laughed with more than a touch of hysteria. It was a stupid irony that he'd gotten so cold he couldn't actually tell when the environment warmed up to a mere ten degrees below freezing.

Orion had churned his way over. He looked at the exposed patch of crinkled bark with trepidation.

'We did it!' Ozzie shouted, and flung his arms round the boy. 'We fucking did it! We are gone from that bastard world. Out, out, out. I'm free again.'

'Are we? Have we really escaped?'

'Oh goddamn yes! You bet your sweet ass we have. You and me, kid, we did it. Oh hey, and Tochee, of course. Come on, let's go tell it the good news.'

'But Ozzie . . .' Orion glanced up. 'The sky's still red.'

'Ur, yeah.' He squinted up at it, not wanting to damage the image, although it was a very bright pink, especially for this time of day – that is, the time of day on his digital timer. If they were on a different world . . . 'I dunno; there's more than one red star in the galaxy.'

He tugged out his battered parchment as he slid over to the front of the sledge, and wrote: I think we made it. Can you keep going a little while longer?

As long as I live.

When Ozzie held the friendship pendant up, the spark of light had almost vanished. 'This way, I think,' he said, and pushed off once again, not that he was really worried about direction now. Physically, the conditions had hardly changed, but simply knowing they were clear of the dreadful Ice Citadel world allowed his body to tap some previously unknown energy reserve. *Just like an icewhale,* he told himself.

Of course, now he knew what to look for, the signs were obvious. The thick snow, different types of tree with bony branches outlined against the sky, the lighter sky itself. With every yard they moved forward things changed. It wasn't long before he saw thin henna-coloured wisps of grass sticking out above the snow. Then there were little rodent creatures scampering about around the trees. Branches shed little piles of snow to fall around them with constant wet thudding sounds as the thaw grew. They were heading down quite a steep slope now, losing height rapidly.

The end of the forest was abrupt. Ozzie shot past the last trees and onto a snowfield that was broken by boulders and widening patches of orange-tinted grass. They were halfway along some massive valley created by Alp-sized mountains. A lake of beautifully clear water stretched out below him, extending for twenty miles on either side. Its shores were also ringed with trees, whose dark branches were just starting to bud. The snowfield died out completely about half a mile ahead of them, with the grass sliced by hundreds of little seasonal streams as the melting edge slowly retreated upwards. On either side, the treeline was almost constant, drawing a broad boundary between the lower grass slopes of the mountains, and their rocky upper levels.

When he looked back at the forest he'd just come from, Ozzie was sure it would only take five minutes or so to ski through, yet they'd paused a good quarter of an hour ago. A brilliant sun was rising at one end of the valley, and he finally understood the pink sky. They had come out of a gloomy maroon nightfall and straight into a vibrant dawn.

Ozzie slowly pushed his hood back, and smiled into the strengthening light as it began to warm his skin.

18

No Prime immotile had a name. Names were derived from a communication system completely different to their species' direct nerve impulse linkages. They did of course have ways of identifying each other. Immotiles, even in their group cluster form, were above all individual, a factor which sprang out of their early history's territorialism. Alliances between them were built and fractured with reliable regularity in their planet's pre-mechanization age, when even the closest partnerships were liable to be swiftly discarded if an advantage could be pursued with another. Disputes in those days were always over the size of territory and the available resources – mainly fresh water and farmland. Little changed over the millennia.

After mechanization flourished, the nature of the alliances altered as the demands of machinery had to be met. Although the manoeuvring and ever-flowing tides of allegiance continued to be played by the same rules of deception and force.

There was one immotile which always managed to retain its pre-eminence amongst the rest of its species. Always building the strongest alliances, always advancing itself at the expense of others, always holding its boundaries secure, always the most wily. In later times the largest and most powerful of all. Although not named, it could be characterized by its location: MorningLightMountain, a large cone of rock and earth that sprouted at the centre of a long valley defined by

747

rugged cliffs rising hundreds of metres from its swampy floor. Such was the alignment of the high walls, that the thick beams of sunlight which the irregular edges produced only swept across the central peak during the morning.

It was the perfect place to establish a new Prime immotile territory. At the time of its amalgamation, seven or eight thousand years before Christ appeared on Earth, there were thousands, possibly even tens of thousands, of immotiles, served and protected by their clans of motiles, occupying the planet's equatorial zone. They were primitive then, creatures whose long evolutionary sequence was only just bearing fruit. Sitting in the middle of their covetously guarded fragment of land, immotiles flexed their rudimentary thoughts by plotting against their neighbours. Herds of standard motiles busied themselves consuming their own base cells from muddy streams and tending the edible vegetation, while the soldier variant motiles started to develop as the stronger, more agile members of each immotile's herd were pressed into duty bashing rival herds' brains out with wooden clubs.

The little sub-herd of twelve motiles was sent out by its birth immotile, seeking a place where a fresh herd could be established. Such a new neighbouring territory would be advantageous to the founder immotile; with a joint personality origin their allegiance would be the strongest of all, at least for the initial years. After a while, divergence crept in, it always did.

MorningLightMountain still retained the memory of itself before amalgamation and true thought began. The sub-herd had spent days carefully picking their way down the valley walls, dodging rockslides and clambering over sharp outcrops. Now they bunched together as they walked through the rainforest which sprang from the boggy ground along the valley floor. Every daybreak a mist would slither upwards from the lush vegetation, a legacy from the nightly rains hazing the air and turning the mighty sunbeams a delicate orange-gold.

They saw it then, a symmetrical cone rising up out of the shadowed land ahead, the only feature of the entire valley to be struck by light, fluorescing a brilliant emerald against the roseate sky. Sunlight glinted off tiny streams that trickled down its sides. Small black specks circled far overhead, wings extended, idling in the thermals – one of the few remaining non-Prime lifeforms left in the planet's tropics.

The four largest herd members pressed up against each other, allowing their nerve receptors to touch so that their brains were linked together. Their individual thoughts were virtually identical, the simple memories and commands issued by their birth immotile, but joined like this their decision-making capability was significantly enhanced. Since reaching the valley floor they hadn't encountered any other motile, or seen signs of a herd's occupation. The valley with its difficult approaches was easy to defend. Its size was capable of support-ing three or four herds. One immotile with its herd would have an abundance of water and land, giving it a strategic advantage over the surrounding immotiles.

As to the exact location the immotile should be placed . . . On each of the motiles, two upper sensory stalks twisted round so their eyes could all regard the conical mountain. With so many streams, there must be a spring of some kind at the top. Such a place would be ideal for an immotile. The water would always be clean, unlike those whose territories were bunched along rivers and had to make do with water contaminated from upstream.

They agreed, then: the mountain that was drenched with light. Their temporary linkage was broken as they moved apart. The other eight members of the sub-herd were sum-moned. Upper sensor stalks bent round so that nerve receptors could be touched, the instructions passed to all members. In unison they began to march towards the mountain.

Two thirds of the way up, they found a large pool fed by several of the gurgling streams. The four large motiles fused their thoughts together again and examined the area with their extended intellect. One of them sucked up some of the water, and found it contained a satisfactory level of Prime base cells swarming inside. Their presence confirmed the site would be suitable for an immotile, subject to a few alterations. A host of new instructions was issued to their fellow herd members.

The type of motile that had come walking into the valley was the most simple of all the varieties which the immotiles birthed, and as such the most adaptive in the tasks it could perform. It had a pear-shaped torso of waxy white skin which measured over a metre in diameter across the base, with four tapering ridges of hard skin running vertically up its flanks. That quadruple symmetry was a constant within Prime life. The motile had four legs sprouting at the end of the skin ridges on the rim of its lower torso. Each of them had a flexible support 'bone' running down the centre, wrapped with bands of muscle tissue to provide a considerable range of movement. Each leg ended in a small hoof of tough ochre gristle that could dig in hard on soil or even wood – not that they often climbed trees.

Four arms protruded from the body, branching out sixty centimetres above the hip joints. They were similar to the legs in respect of their size and all-round flexibility; differing only at the tip which split into a neat quad pincer arrangement that was quite capable of snipping through medium-sized branches. On the top of the main body four gill-like vents were spaced equidistantly around the crest, drawing air down into its lungs. Between them were the food inlets, mini trunks of rubbery flesh that had some independent movement. Motiles grazed on specific vegetation for the chemicals they contained, but mainly they sucked up water saturated with base cells. Both were processed in a large double stomach. The pap could be semi-digested before being regurgitated to feed an immotile; with full digestion the residue was excreted from a single anus at the base of the body.

Above the gills and mouths, the body's crown divided up into the four sensory stalks, which were the most pliable of all its limbs, capable of bending and twisting in every direction. At the very apex of them was the delicate nerve receptor, a thin impulse-permeable membrane stretched over raw ganglions; slightly below them were the eyes, then a pressure-sensitive blister that could detect sound waves, a plume of thin chemically-responsive fibres that smelt the air, and a cluster of tactile cells capable of detecting temperature.

For such creatures, modifying the area around the pool to their own requirements was a relatively simple matter. They had long since mastered the rudimentaries of tool use, and quickly adapted sharp stones and sections of hard bark from the nearby trees. Using these as shovels and scoops, the twelve of them dug a shallow pond slightly upstream from the main pool, then lined it with stone taken from the excavated soil.

With the work complete, the four largest motiles waded into the pond, and once again linked their nerve receptors. This time the union went a lot deeper than simply connecting their thoughts. Their bodies were pressed up tight together, ready for amalgamation. The process was triggered by an internal hormone deluge brought on by the mental merger. Over the subsequent five weeks they underwent a tremendous metamorphosis. Their four separate bodies slowly coalesced on a cellular level to produce a single entity. Where their skin touched, it softened and melted away, creating a single giant body cavity. Inside that, their brains fused together and expanded; a transformation pattern followed by most of the major organs. The muscles simply wasted away, providing a source of nutrition to power the other changes. Legs shrank until they were nothing but a circular series of solid fleshy lumps that supported the new large body. Arms shrivelled and dropped off, there was no need for them now. Digestive organs stretched out, and spread up around the new singular brain, like shoots of ivy twining round a tree trunk. While under-

751

neath the brain, there was a new growth. The reproductive system which until now had been nascent, began to grow into fully viable organs. Only the sensory stalks remained the same, feeding the developing brain a dodecagonal impression of the world around it.

At the end of the process, the new immotile Prime, MorningLightMountain, began to secure its territory. The remaining eight motiles came and went continually, feeding the immotile with their regurgitated pap. They had been instructed to gorge themselves on specific types of plants, enriching their food with certain vitamin-types.

Triggered by the nourishment contained within its food, MorningLightMountain's reproductive organs began to ovulate. The first batch of a hundred nucleiplasms was discharged from its body into the water, allowing them to drift down to the large pool. Base cells began to congregate around them.

By themselves, Prime base cells followed a lifecycle similar to amoebas; they absorbed food through their membrane walls, and reproduced by fission, remaining a single-cell lifeform that inhabited most of the planet's waterways. But they also carried the DNA for a lot more than that. It was the nucleiplasms which initiated the multicellular stage, releasing activants for new sequences in the DNA, and switching off the amoeba-stage sequence. The cluster of cells around the nucleiplasm began to change, developing fresh organelles that provided specific functions. Like any multicellular organism, the cells began to specialize. The immotile had a degree of control over the type of nucleiplasm it gestated inside its reproduction system. By consciously controlling hormone secretion into the nucleiplasm, it could dictate the size of various organs, and by doing so design the structure and composition of a motile. If it needed heavy work doing, it would produce a batch of nucleiplasms which would congregate the largest and strongest motile. In a time when its territory was under threat, nucleiplasm to engender soldiers would be released.

The first herd of MorningLightMountain's motiles began to wade out of the pond after three weeks of congregation. The existing motiles guided them over to the immotile, who touched its nerve receptors to theirs. Memory and instructions flashed through the impulse-permeable membrane, filling the motiles' virgin brains with a compact version of its own thoughts.

Over the first decades, MorningLightMountain began to shape and fortify its valley. In those days there were few non-Prime lifeforms left in the equatorial lands. Those that did still inhabit the valley such as the birds and a few rodent-like creatures were swiftly hunted down and exterminated – no immotile would tolerate competition for its own resources. The wild jungle was gradually cut back, the swamps drained into a network of canals which irrigated the big ferns which motiles ate. Stone was quarried, and used to construct a simple igloo-dome over the immotile as protection from the elements and any rogue predators from other territories. Metal ores were mined, and fires were used to forge crude weapon tips. The congregation pool was dredged and lined with stone.

After forty-five years of unrestricted growth, Morning-LightMountain was reaching the limits of its management capacity. Over a thousand motiles were at work in the valley, and supervision was becoming difficult. A second immotile was amalgamated to compensate for the shortfall. Morning-LightMountain's pool and dome were extended, and four motiles brought together a couple of yards away from it. While the amalgamation was progressing, MorningLightMountain had six of its nerve receptors linked with those motiles undergoing the merger, pushing its thoughts into the new-growing brain. When it was all over, the two were permanently linked by four nerve receptors, producing an immotile duo with a much expanded mental capacity, and capable of organizing many herds of motiles.

A new phase of productivity began. The valley, when

properly agrarianized, was capable of supporting thousands of motiles. Although, to MorningLightMountain's disappointment, it took almost all of its motiles just to keep the valley maintained. Thirty-five years later, a third immotile was amalgamated next to the initial duo. That was around the time it began to trade with immotiles of surrounding territories. Metal ores were exchanged for the use of soldier herds to repel a territory that was starting to encroach the top of the valley ramparts. Food ferns were swapped for hardwood trunks that made better spears and clubs. Ideas were bartered, chief among them the concept of ploughs and crop rotation brought in from immotiles thousands of miles away. It was the start of true agriculture for the Prime civilization, and the associated revolution which the innovation always introduced. The amount of produce grown by a motile doubled within a decade. Seeing the possibility of the concept, the immotiles began to experiment, studying how the plants grew, what soils were best. MorningLightMountain itself was the one who worked out cross-pollination as a method of increasing yield and breeding new varieties. It was the start of the scientific method, and all that implied.

MorningLightMountain amalgamated its twenty-ninth immotile a decade after it began sowing crops. Twenty years later, a thousand years after it had begun its original singleton life, the number of connected units in the group reached forty, an unheard-of rate of expansion. Its linked brains were abuzz with ideas and thoughts as it observed its immediate universe with ever more scrutiny.

On the edge of the tropics, Prime immotiles were pushing further and further into the temperate lands, armed with their new knowledge and understanding of nature. Fire made it possible for them to live further and further from their original climate. Heated buildings, cultivated fields, canals, bridges, saws and axes helped them travel further and further to establish allied territories.

Inevitably, as they began to grasp the principles of construction, and strength of materials, the mathematical tools were developed to aid fabrication. For creatures that were essentially a giant brain, mathematics pushed them into their primacy – it was the key to understanding everything. They devoted themselves to it with a devotion that was almost religious. All the elements were now in place for the mechanical age to begin. When it happened, the pace of change was very very swift.

After a thousand years, MorningLightMountain was now a group immotile comprising three hundred and seventy-two separate units. Few had ever grown to such a size before. Its individual bodies had formed a living ring around the conical mountain. The spring which bubbled up at the top of the mountain was now channelled through clay pipes into the crown building which housed the immotile group in its entirety. They lived inside a single giant hall with a vaulting glass-topped roof letting sunlight shine down. During the night, iron braziers were lit, keeping the inside of the building illuminated, allowing the immotile group to keep working, instructing their motile herds, producing their nucleiplasms, and scrutinizing experiments and projects. Little shower nozzles sprinkled the immotiles several times a day, helping to keep them clean. Waste products were carried away via a network of culverts down the mountain, while dedicated channels swept nucleiplasm batches into the necklace of congregation lakes which had been dug below the building.

The air outside still steamed every day from the nightly rains. But this mist now mingled with smoke from the furnaces which were permanently alight. MorningLightMountain imported coal from several territories to the south, a hilly district where food was hard to grow. It was now cultivating two of the neighbouring valleys, after a short series of wars had wiped out the immotiles and their herds who used to occupy them. Control over such a huge area was difficult. Motiles needed to be constantly updated with instructions, and they lacked the ability to respond to any unexpected situation. MorningLightMountain knew it would soon be subjected to invasions from the west by immotiles who were worried by the size of its territory, not to mention its aggression. Its use of newly developed chemical explosives to destroy buildings, dams, and motile herds was regarded with considerable alarm.

That was the year Primes found out how to use electricity. While some immotiles studied how to use the new power for lighting, or engines and other industrial-based applications, MorningLightMountain investigated how it could carry signals; specifically the neural impulses which nerve receptors exchanged. It took over a decade; even for that much concentrated brain power inventing an entire technology from scratch was difficult. During that time, it accepted strategic defeats, losing its two additional valleys and agreeing to unfavourable trade terms for its coal and other raw materials absent in the valley. What it developed in that interlude was basic electronics, from simple resisters and capacitors right up to thermionic valves. With those principles established, a whole new chamber was annexed to the crown building on the mountain, the world's first electronics lab, with eight immotile units devoted to nothing else but instructing the motiles who assembled the new systems and ran experiments with them. It took MorningLightMountain another three years before it successfully inputted signals to a nerve receptor. Primitive tactile impulses were first, such as hot and cold, which it followed up with simple black and white images from a camera. The images were something of a revelation for it; although it could always see what was happening outside by summoning a motile and accessing its visual memory of events, such knowledge was always second-hand, time-delayed. This was instantaneous. Within a matter of months, the entire valley was ringed by cameras that constantly scanned back and forth across the landscape, allowing it to see its entire domain in real time. Another five years concentrated research advanced its analogue signal transmissions to a level where it could finally instruct a motile by remote. It would be decades until the electronics were sophisticated enough to carry the full range of nerve receptor impulses, but that first ability to communicate at a distance was enough to give it a massive advantage over the other immotiles.

MorningLightMountain began to expand its territory once more. Herds of motile soldiers, armed with explosives and rudimentary cannons, overran the two valleys it had conquered before. With soldier motiles trailing long multi-core cables behind them, MorningLightMountain could react to the flow of battle instantaneously, easily outmanoeuvring its opponents. Those first victories were followed up by a series of swift advances across the countryside until its herds had established a broad channel of land leading directly to the southern temperate zone. The remaining immotiles reacted cautiously, knowing that holding on to such huge areas was impossible. It wasn't until months had passed that they realized their error as MorningLightMountain consolidated its grip on its annexed lands. With a grouping that now consisted of over three thousand individual immotiles, Morning-LightMountain was easily capable of congregating enough motile herds to occupy its lands, mining and farming them in an operation as tightly controlled as the original valley. For the first time, captured industrial facilities were pressed into service, increasing its manufacturing base relative to the size of its budding empire.

With a direct route from its valley to the fresh temperate lands, its expansionist ambitions could now be realized. A torrent of motiles and machinery was dispatched south to exploit the new resources there, setting up the pylons and cables which knitted the whole edifice together.

It took the remaining immotiles years to build the grand alliances which finally limited MorningLightMountain's growth, although it could never be completely halted. In typical imperial fashion, MorningLightMountain formed its own alliances as a counterbalance.

Within another fifty years, all the immotiles had the ability to send their nerve impulses via cable and wireless relays. This development, in conjunction with new and powerful weapons derived from the Primes' increasing knowledge of chemistry and physics, led to an era of consolidation. The smaller immotile territories were invaded and taken over by more powerful neighbours. Temperate wastelands were colonized, with mining and manufacturing operations extending into the polar regions. It was only when nuclear weapons were developed that a kind of equilibrium returned. Fission and fusion bombs allowed the smaller territories to hold their larger brethren at bay with the threat of total annihilation.

Spaceflight and offplanet colonies was the next logical development, and one which the Primes pursued vigorously. MorningLightMountain was one of the earliest immotiles to send ships out to the asteroids and planets to catalogue their resources. Given the distances involved, the old problem of time-delay emerged again. Direct electronic linkages were difficult to sustain, control slipped, and without it the motiles were utterly incapable of responding to any technological situation. They simply weren't smart enough.

One of the smaller immotile groupings provided the solution. ColdLakePromontory was desperate to secure further resources for itself and its herds, which made it willing to innovate to a degree further than the larger more conservative groupings would consider. It amalgamated a new immotile separate from the main group, using an electronic linkage to integrate its thoughts. In effect, the new immotile was a smaller identical twin of ColdLakePromontory. Even with a time-delay, their thoughts were shared, divergence didn't occur.

ColdLakePromontory2 was placed on a spaceship, and flown out to an industrial module attached to an asteroid. The notion of a mobile immotile was regarded with near universal shock by the other immotiles. They did, however, watch the experiment with obsessive interest. ColdLakePromontory2 supervised the mineral extraction processes and subsequent construction of a habitation section. More importantly, it maintained its linkage with ColdLakePromontory back on the planet, remaining part of the group mind. Mineral and metal resources from the asteroid flowed back to ColdLake-Promontory's territory on the planet.

Planet-based immotiles dispersed units of themselves across the solar system. It was a space race of colossal proportions. Territories were extended to take in vast sections of the other two solid planets, and entire gas-giant moons. Breakaways were inevitable as wars and conflicts out among the high frontier severed the vital communication links with the planet, and immotile units went independent from their original groups. In many cases that was the cause of conflicts, as the planetary motiles tried to regain control of their lost space-based territories.

The rate of the Prime civilization's expansion across its solar system never approached anything like exponential. It would take millennia to occupy and utilize all the resources orbiting the star. But the group immotiles were effectively creatures who could live for ever, many of them were planning for the far future.

MorningLightMountain constructed the first interstellar ship in one of its high orbit asteroid bases. It was a fusion drive vessel, the Primes with their logical thought processes and observation-based scientific research lacked the mental ability to speculate wildly about such concepts as ftl. With

MorningLightMountain8658 on board the starship, it took off towards the nearest star, three and a half light-years away. The mission was supposed to be a reconnaissance, sending back information about the available planets and their suitability for exploitation. MorningLightMountain knew it wouldn't be able to control MorningLightMountain8658 once the ship was outside the Prime solar system. However, it had deliberately restricted the machinery on board the starship, denying MorningLightMountain8658 the ability to establish any sort of technology-based colony. That should have ensured MorningLightMountain8658 simply scanned the system and returned. MorningLightMountain wasn't sure what use it would have for another star system, but it couldn't ignore future possibilities. Knowing what was there would help it determine what to do about other stars. There was the remote option that if the resources of its own star system were completely depleted it could move itself to a new planet entirely, one without any other immotile group to contend with.

The one thing MorningLightMountain, or any other Prime immotile, never expected, was to find an alien species. All other animal life had finally been exterminated from the Prime homeworld during the last expansion over the temperate lands. They didn't think in terms of other intelligences. When MorningLightMountain8658 decelerated insystem, it found an extensive civilization occupying the fourth solid planet. Unfortunately for the natives of the second star system, they were a benign species who advanced themselves through cooperation. Physically, they were trisymmetric, smaller and weaker than a Prime motile. They were also individuals.

The starship might not have had any manufacturing systems on board, but it certainly had weapons. MorningLightMountain8658 subdued a vast area of the new planet with nuclear and kinetic bombardment from orbit, and commandeered what was left of the aliens' industrial base. It began an extensive research project into the trisymmetric creatures themselves. There was a lot for MorningLightMountain8658 to learn, concepts and ideas which both alarmed and intrigued it. Communication with sound. Reproduction via fertilized eggs. Biology in general, and genetics in particular – a field which provided amazing insights into itself. Research into their own physiology and nature wasn't something Primes had ever conducted; they'd never had the need. Fiction – that was a strange one. Art. Entertainment. All nonsensical distractions to a Prime.

MorningLightMountain8658 began to build its new territory around the starship landing site, incorporating the useful ideas which the aliens offered up along with its traditional concepts. Surviving aliens were treated like motiles, and conscripted to help build the territory. Three years later, the next Prime starship arrived, sent by a different immotile. The firefight which ensued devastated half of the continent where MorningLightMountain8658 had established itself. Neither of the immotiles was damaged. They agreed to an alliance, and divided up the planet.

MorningLightMountain wasn't surprised when its first starship didn't return. Interstellar travel was a huge unknown, it expected many setbacks. More starships were already being built in anticipation. None of the starships sent by other immotiles had reported back, either. The starship designs were refined, and new missions launched. All of which were swallowed up by the void between the stars.

After almost a century of starflight, and twenty-eight ships sent to the nearby star, the Primes finally had one return. It was the most heavily armed ship they'd built, and the first to have a force field for defence. MorningLightMountain had led an alliance of the three most powerful immotiles to manufacture the behemoth. Only its devastating firepower had ensured its survival as it was attacked by a swarm of warships on arrival. It had managed to capture a large chunk of wreckage from one of the attackers. The knowledge it contained was horrifying to the entire Prime home system. Not only had the immotiles controlling the earlier starships become independent, they had apparently incorporated alien concepts into their technology. Most alarming of all was the use of the new science of genetics. They were modifying their bodies, blending in alien traits to 'improve' themselves. Their motiles were smarter and stronger, capable of making complex decisions, while the immotiles were sequencing refinement after refinement into their neural structure, advancing their thought-processing capacity far beyond their natural state. Machines were also being used to supplement body function, cybernetic additions that allowed immotile movement, and even separation from the group home. They were evolving artificially, diverging from pure Prime. They would be rivals, and their new nature would give them advantages impossible for the original Primes to achieve.

The discovery unified the entire Prime solar system into the one alliance. A fleet of warships was built and dispatched across the void to annihilate their enemies. A second, larger, fleet followed. A third, the greatest of all.

In response, alienPrime ships hurtled into the Prime home system, armed with terrible weapons. Before they were destroyed, the habitable territories on the outermost solid planet were completely wiped out along with all the industrial colonies around the first gas-giant. Hundreds of Prime ships had been sacrificed in the defence.

Then it happened, the strangest weapon of all was used. The enemy alienPrimes established a force field around the entire star system. Nothing could penetrate it; not nuclear weapons, nor quantum field interference. It was impervious to everything Prime science could strike it with. Morning-LightMountain and all the others were trapped inside, while the alienPrime immotiles remained free to spread themselves and their contagion across the universe. There was nothing the original Primes could do except repair the damage to their civilization, expand their territories across the frozen outer planetoids, research new weapons, and wait.

*

One thousand one hundred and eighty-two years later, the force field vanished as abruptly as it appeared.

MorningLightMountain's outer sensor satellites detected fluctuations in its quantum structure rippling across the surface for nearly an hour before the field finally lost cohesion. Almost immediately, every immotile was launching spaceships from their asteroids and planet territories right across the Prime system. They were accelerating hard, rushing to get outside the field's previous boundary line before it re-established itself. The eight which MorningLightMountain held permanently in readiness for just such an occasion were among the first to leave.

With that first action completed, MorningLightMountain and its allies began an extensive sensor search of space beyond the boundary. Straight away they found a huge rotating spherical structure, twenty-five thousand kilometres in diameter, orbiting along the ecliptic. The structure was larger than the homeworld, but with hardly any mass, so it couldn't be a planet. Yet it was emitting in every measurable spectrum, and had a completely alien quantum signature. Several ships were dispatched to investigate.

Strangest of all, there was no sign of the alienPrimes. Defences around every planetary and space territory were brought up to their full capability in readiness for the surely imminent attack. But no weapons of any kind tested them. There was nothing. All the alliances combined their sensor information. Everything remained blank.

MorningLightMountain was uncertain how to proceed. It had planned for what it considered every eventuality when the force field was removed. It could fight and flee, it had a grand alliance ready to build a fleet to exterminate all alienPrime life at the second star, and wherever else they had corrupted. That the alienPrimes would do nothing was confusing it considerably.

Its most powerful telescopes were hurriedly trained on the neighbouring star for any clue of their activity. That produced the greatest surprise of all. A force field had encased the alienPrime system as well.

None of the immotiles had ever considered there might be a second alien life, one that was more powerful than Primes. Accepting the concept was a frightening thing. They did nothing but watch the newly exposed stars with a considerable sense of anxiety. Still more ships were dispatched outward in a frantic attempt to establish Prime life on new worlds where the barriers would not imprison them.

Four days after the force field vanished, the most sophisticated spatial sensors that MorningLightMountain possessed reported a very unusual quantum disturbance washing across the system. The effect was travelling faster than the speed of light. MorningLightMountain considered that such an event might signal the arrival of the aliens who had created the force field. The effect wasn't repeated, which left it deliberating how to respond: to warn the others and form the Grand Alliance to fight back against the attackers, or to attempt its own evacuation.

MorningLightMountain was still considering its options when its ordinary sensors showed it a fight between ships from TemperateSeaIsland and SouthernRockPlateau close to a cluster of asteroid bases. Even now when the Prime alliances knew they had to cooperate to face their enemy, the old conflicts still raged. Expansion had been massive throughout the last thousand years, and resources within the Prime star system were now extremely scarce. The pressure on individual territories was greater than it had ever been before. For the last two centuries, MorningLightMountain had been increasingly concerned that the immotiles would end up fighting a terminal war and exterminate themselves. It was a common worry. As a consequence, immotiles had diverted more and more effort into building and stockpiling weapons.

Almost a day later, thousands of sensors orbiting the home-world picked up a microwave emission from a point beyond the second gas-giant. The signal was crude, using patterns which had been developed for messaging long before the time when the force field appeared. A brief identification sequence revealed the sender to be MorningLightMountain17,735, who had been on board one of the early starships to visit the alienPrime star system and never returned. The context of the message was short and simple: These are aliens, there are many of them and they are dangerous. Destroy them.

The message repeated ten times, then ended. Morning-LightMountain was puzzled. How had MorningLight-Mountain17,735 survived for so long? What was it doing on an alien ship? Why was the message so short? Not that it had many options remaining. Other immotiles were already order-ing ships to investigate. MorningLightMountain sent instruc-tions to its subsidiary groupings on the moons of the second gas-giant. Four of its most powerful ships launched on an interception course.

Alliances broke down and new ones formed as the first eight ships closed on the alien. Immotiles disagreed how to deal with the situation. Some wanted to capture the aliens and their ship, others were keen to follow MorningLight-Mountain17,735's advice and exterminate the invader.

The alien started transmitting signals at the Prime ships as they closed on it. They were incomprehensible, no immotile could understand them. Missiles were fired as alliances came into sharp conflict over how to proceed.

With the lead Prime ship approaching fast and launching a missile salvo, the alien vanished inside a huge burst of spatial distortion.

*

The surface to orbit transport ship descended vertically through the Prime homeworld's lower atmosphere. It was a large blunt cone shape, although it made little use of aerodynamics to land. Eight fusion rockets were arranged around the rim of its base, roaring out slim two-kilometre-long jets of incandescent plasma. Between them, they produced point nine of a Prime gravity, lowering the ship gently towards the coastline beneath it.

Steam began to swirl up from the surface of the sea as the wavering tips of the plasma stabbed down into it. Within seconds, a hemispherical tempest of radiant vapour was streaking up and out from the epicentre like a squashed nuclear mushroom cloud. As the ship sank down into the supersonic storm front, force fields came on to protect the fuselage from the maelstrom it was creating. The fusion rockets died away when the ship was only a few metres above the seething surface, and its conical base splashed down with a soft bump into the boiling water.

Tugboats closed in and towed the spaceship back to the piers and loading bays which stretched for over a hundred miles along the coast. This was the main planetary spaceport which MorningLightMountain had built to handle the cargo flying between the planet and its offworld territories. Thousands of flights arrived and departed every year, pouring heat and mildly radioactive contaminants into the local environment. Nothing grew within a hundred miles of the spaceport any more, no crops or weeds of any kind, turning the land behind the shore to a desert of sodden lifeless soil. Even the sea was dead, a choppy expanse of grey water with a thin skin of ochre scum.

Once the ship was docked, a sub-herd of soldier motiles came on board. They were slightly smaller than standard motiles, with better sight and hearing; they could move faster as well, and had a much greater agility, though they lacked any long-term endurance. Encased in dark armour, they were

two and a half metres tall, with electronic sensors complementing their natural ones, and limb strength enhanced
mechanically; every arm gripped some kind of weapon. Under
direct microwave linkage with MorningLightMountain, they
approached the two bipedal alien motile captives with considerable wariness. The immotile wasn't sure of their potential,
so it was taking every precaution. The compartment they'd
been confined to was heavily shielded, and they'd been under
constant observation for the whole flight back from the asteroid fragment where their ship had been lurking. Physically,
they had done nothing, remaining almost motionless for the
whole time. Their suits, however, had been emitting those
strange microwave pulses almost continually.

When the soldier motiles came into the compartment both
creatures stood upright. MorningLightMountain watched the
process with considerable interest. Their legs bent in the
middle, pushing the main bulk upwards. They seemed to have
no trouble standing still while balancing on only two legs. A
great range of electromagnetic emissions were pouring out of
the suits again, the usual fast short pulses. MorningLight-
Mountain ignored them and told the soldiers to load both
alien motiles onto the waiting ground vehicle. As the sub-herd
moved forward to grab them, the taller of the two swung its
upper torso limbs around, knocking their pincers away, and
tried to speed past them. It could move surprisingly fast, but
the soldiers were ready for it, and lifted its twisting body off
the ground, carrying it down the ramp to the waiting ground
vehicle. The second, slightly smaller alien motile offered no
resistance as it was dragged along behind. Both of them were
dropped into the cage. A force field flicked on around the
mesh.

MorningLightMountain drove the vehicle along the road
connecting the spaceport to its original valley. Long black
clouds boiled overhead as they did ceaselessly these days. Rain
lashed down across the road's stone and metal surface, warm

water saturated with soot particles. The road was hemmed in on both sides by buildings of toughened plastic, shielding manufacturing machinery from the acidic rain. Big vehicles shuttled between them, carrying components around. Herd after herd of motiles worked around the huge blocks of industrial machinery, servicing and repairing. They didn't live as long as they used to two thousand years ago, especially in and around the spaceport. Many of them had sores and scabs mottling their skin from cold radiation burns. Limbs often trembled and shook from the damage which heavy metal contamination inflicted on their nervous system. They ate from troughs filled with a treacle-like nutrient sludge that was processed in food factories scattered across the territory's farmlands. Sensor stalks twitched constantly and gave poor visual reception as they were degraded by airborne irritants gushing out of the refineries.

In the mountains behind the industrial landscape, where the radioactivity was considerably reduced, fields cloaked every slope in a drab unvarying grey-green patina. Plants struggled out of the thin sandy soil, forced into overactive life by chemical fertilizers that were spread across the terraces by farming motiles and tracked vehicles. All wild plants had been eradicated from the planet now, surrendering their valuable land to the intense agricultural cultivation vital to feed the billions of motiles.

As the vehicle carrying the alien motiles drove along the switchback road which led down into MorningLight-Mountain's original valley it passed through the strongest force field on the planet, capable of deflecting nuclear assaults and beam strikes. Rain beat down upon the sparkling energy plain, flowing into rivulets which ran away over the craggy granite ramparts. Light did still shine down into the valley in the morning, though now it was a bruised grey twilight which leaked through the planet-wide smog layers. At night, the smog fluoresced a funereal khaki from the vast lattice of fusion drives which caged the world.

Ahead of the vehicle, the conical mountain rose up from the valley floor. It was home to over fifty thousand immotile units now, still the true heart of MorningLightMountain, even though there were groupings dotted all over the planet, linked to it via secure landlines. The mountain had been transformed into a single building, with each immotile nesting at the centre of its own chamber. None of them made physical nerve contact with the motiles any more, their sensor stalk nerve receptors were all connected to an electronic network which connected them en masse to the herds as well as every mechanical segment of their territory. A battery of maser units perched above the valley ramparts extended the gigantic immotile group's presence across the star system. Below the building floor, the mountain was riddled with pipes and sewers. The immotiles were bathed in a gentle shower of clean water produced in desalination plants north of the spaceport, and piped in to the valley. Waste water carrying away body effluent was flushed straight back into the sea, while water carrying nucleiplasm batches was directed into the moat of congregation lakes around the base of the mountain.

The vehicle drove over a four-mile-long causeway between lakes. The alien motiles stood upright in their cage, the fat sensor stalks inside the transparent bubble on top of their suits were turned so the two eyes regarded the emerging herds. Below them, the lake surfaces writhed as tens of thousands of congregating motiles squirmed against each other. Not yet mature, their bodies were partially translucent, with great globules of transforming base cells clustered around limbs and torsos, as if they were surrounded by lumpy jelly. Big pipes poured a torrent of sluggish liquid into each lake: water saturated with base cells that were bred in a huge series of vats at the eastern end of the valley. At the edge of the lakes, motiles helped the newly formed up out of the water. Relay modules were attached to their nerve receptors, allowing MorningLightMountain to fill their brains with its thought routines and commands. On the wide concrete apron ringing the lakes, herds formed up in long ranks to be collected by vehicles that would drive them to their work destination. Over a million a day were transported out across MorningLight-Mountain's territory.

At the base of the mountain building, a tall door opened in the cliff-like wall of stone and concrete, and the vehicle drove inside. This was the primary research area, where the immotile units had built facilities to explore every scientific discipline. The alien motiles were put in the chemical warfare laboratory, where they were sealed up in a cell that had an independent air circuit. Force fields came on around it, capable of with-standing megaton blasts.

The cell was a broad rectangular room, measuring some fifty metres long, made out of high-density plastic, and completely insulated. MorningLightMountain had installed a lot of examination equipment inside, ranging from scanners which could review the creatures in their entirety, to analysis modules that could sift through their cellular structure molecule by molecule. There were pens where they could be held between examinations, transparent cubes, three metres to a side, containing water, various food bales, and receptacles for excretion. Lighting was full solar-spectrum.

One wall of the cell was made from a sheet of transparent crystal. Three immotiles rested on the other side, sitting in pools of dark water, a gentle drizzle playing over their skin. One of them had a motile pressed up close, feeding it. All of them could observe the aliens directly with their own eyes as they supervised the examination process.

MorningLightMountain bent its sensor stalks over so it could gaze at the alien motiles as they entered the laboratory. It seemed to be a mutual arrangement. The alien motiles walked their lurching walk over to the crystal wall, and stared back at the immotiles.

MorningLightMountain's priority was to establish a neural interface with the alien motiles so it could determine what kind of threat their immotiles posed to Prime. To do that, it had to discover the nature of their nerve receptors. Once that was ascertained it could manufacture an artificial interface unit and command them directly, as it had done with countless millions of motiles captured from other Prime territories. Their memories would then be drained out into Morning-LightMountain so it could see exactly what it was facing.

Eight fully armoured soldier motiles were in the cell with the aliens, along with eight standard motiles. Morning-LightMountain ordered the soldiers to hold the alien motiles steady, while its own motiles applied various sensors. The alien motiles struggled briefly as they were grasped. The electromagnetic emissions from their suits began again. MorningLight-Mountain tried a transmission on the same frequencies, ordering them to be still. It had no effect.

Although there was considerable interference, the sensors were able to map out the basic layout of the suits. Their composition was an advanced shapeshifting polymer with various filaments woven through it to control temperature. The atmosphere inside the upper bubble was oxygen nitrogen, regenerated by several small modules of intriguing design. Most surprising were the complex electronic patterns that covered the entire surface, indicating a great many components. MorningLightMountain couldn't understand why something as simple as a pressure suit would require so many control circuits.

It ordered the motiles to remove the suits. Under its direction they applied cutting instruments to the surface, and began ripping the fabric apart. As the alien motiles were exposed so MorningLightMountain heard strange sounds emerging from them. When the upper bubbles were broken open the sound grew to extraordinary levels, making the motiles wave their sensor stalks away in an attempt to lessen it. The single fat sensor stalk on the top of the alien motiles was the source, an orifice which flapped open and shut.

They also emitted a stench so strong that the motiles quivered in reaction. MorningLightMountain hurriedly reviewed the cell's gas toxin sensors to see if it was a chemical attack. There were some strange nitrates effervescing off the alien motiles, but nothing lethal. It began to catalogue their profile. Even knowing they were alien didn't adequately prepare it for things so strange. Their skin was a pale white-pink, with slim blue lines visible just below the surface. Thin fibres were sprouting from it seemingly at random and in different colours from brown to white; there were big patches of the stuff on the top of the sensor stalk, and smaller patches between the legs. One had tufts where its arms joined the torso as well as a fine greyish fuzz on the front of its torso, while the other had neither. Physically they had differences, odd limp appendages that dangled like half filled bags, the larger one had a tiny trunk between its legs next to some kind of external sacs. MorningLightMountain could see no practical use for either set.

Lines of red fluid were leaking from the skin, corresponding to where the cutting implements had been applied. The smaller alien motile had stopped using its legs to support itself, and was hanging limply in the solders' grip; while the larger one was shaking violently. It continued to make the curious sounds as yellow water discharged from its mini-trunk appendage.

Motiles collected samples of the red fluid and yellow water from the floor of the cell. The alien motile which had gone inert was placed in the large scanning unit. The image which arrived inside MorningLightMountain was tremendously complex, the alien motile was densely packed with organs. Lungs, heart, and stomach were obvious, but it couldn't imagine what half of the other ones were for. The bone structure was odd, leaving some parts of the torso unprotected, although the joint system was innovative. Most interesting was the location of the brain, actually inside the sensor stalk. MorningLight-Mountain moved the scan focus, trying to track the nerve cords to a receptor membrane. Try as it might, it couldn't find one. The bulk of the nerves left the brain to travel along the thick segmented bone running down the torso, but they all branched into a tributary network that was distributed throughout the muscle bands and thin skin. Could the entire skin be a nerve receptor? Then MorningLightMountain noticed strands of organic conductors wound through the skin. Many of them were integrated into the nerve chords, especially around the five-segment grippers on the end of its arms. Now it knew what to look for, MorningLightMountain gave the brain a more detailed survey. A cluster of minute electronic components were nestling inside the body at the base of the brain, with a multitude of connective threads joining them to the big nerve cord.

The inert alien motile was taken out of the scanner, and the active one placed inside. Soldiers had to hold it down as the bulbous scan tips moved across it. Where there was no bone beneath the skin, its flesh bowed inward below the probing tips. It started making noise again, a loud burst of high-frequency sound every time the tip pressure increased. MorningLightMountain withdrew a tip, then pushed it forward again. The alien noise-generated again. It was an interesting correlation, but MorningLightMountain couldn't understand why it did that.

This larger alien motile had a similar network of organic conductors and electronic components embedded within its body. MorningLightMountain had memories of the alienPrime cybernetics, fusing machines with bodies; but they had all been used to amplify physical functions. These seemed to have no external purpose; they were joined to the brain but nothing else, they weren't links in a chain. MorningLightMountain's trouble was that it had little experience of microelectronic systems. It produced simple processors to help govern its own technology, but its own mind always directed the operation of any complex piece of machinery with appropriate thought routines through its nerve linkages. Automation was not a familiar concept, seventy per cent of its group brain capacity was involved in controlling technology, from simply driving a vehicle to regulating the plasma flow in fusion reactors. There were few independent machines within its territories. The most advanced were the missiles carried by spaceships, which couldn't contain an immotile. They used processors that had flexible algorithmic instructions, which were given specific orders just before launch. Otherwise MorningLightMountain ran everything. Machines served life, it could not be otherwise.

MorningLightMountain ordered the soldiers to release the alien motile. It did have the kind of equipment capable of analysing the processors inside the aliens, but it was all in the physics laboratories. A batch of instructions were issued to motiles. They began dismantling the appropriate units, ready to transfer them to the secure cell. In the meantime the immotile instructed the motiles to extract all the processors from the pressure suits while it observed the aliens.

The soldiers had placed both of them in their pens. The larger one had folded its legs, so that it was resting on the floor. It was knocking its gripper on the wall between it and the smaller alien, which was still inert and leaking red fluid onto the floor. Every few minutes it would noise-generate. The fat sensor stalk at the top twisted, and it stared at Morning-LightMountain's three immotiles again. Both of its arms moved, the grippers forming shapes in the air. It did that for several minutes, then sank back on its folded legs again. The fat sensor stalk rocked about for no apparent reason. Eventually it began to examine the food bales. Small crumbs were broken off by the grippers, and it brought them up to the small twinned orifices at the front of its fat sensor stalk.

MorningLightMountain decided there must be olfactory sensors inside the little cavities. Some of the crumbs were discarded, while others were held in front of the larger orifice. A strip of flexible wet tissue extended to touch the crumbs one after the other. They were all dropped on the floor. Next it turned to the plastic cylinder filled with desalinated water. After dipping its gripper in, it pushed one of the segments into its large orifice. There was a short pause, then it lifted the plastic cylinder, and poured almost half of the water into its orifice.

MorningLightMountain completed its analysis of the red fluid. As it suspected, the substance was a nutrient, with a high protein and oxygen content. The yellow water appeared to be a waste defecation.

An hour later, the smaller alien motile began to move. The response from the larger one was immediate. It hurried over to the wall between them and began to noise-generate in short loud bursts. The smaller one was emitting a long single sound. It flattened its gripper, and pressed it over the long rip on its side where the red fluid was still seeping out.

MorningLightMountain began to wonder if it was badly damaged. On a Prime, such a rip would seal up and the flesh knit together quickly. That didn't seem to be happening to the alien motile. Instead the red fluid was undergoing a double transformation, coagulating then crystallizing into dark flecks. It didn't think much of that as an integral repair function.

The small alien held its body parallel to the floor, and used both its arms and legs to walk over to the cylinder of water. It ingested some, and then fell back onto the floor, its joints losing stiffness.

The equipment to analyse the processors arrived. MorningLightMountain's motiles began reassembling it. After several hours, it was powered up, and the first processor placed under a field resonance amplifier. MorningLightMountain was astonished by the complexity of the device, which was right on the edge of the amplifier's resolution. There were millions of junctions arranged in a three-dimensional lattice of quantum wire, each strand just large enough to carry a single electron. The processing power it contained was enormous. One of these by itself was enough to control an entire salvo of missiles.

MorningLightMountain had a lot of trouble holding a full map of the junctions in its mind, the effort was taking up the brains of a dozen immotile units. That alone was enough to worry it. The aliens clearly had a powerful technology in such devices. It was intrigued with the reason for developing them. Clearly in this instance, the suit polymer must require an inordinate amount of control to hold its shape, presumably far beyond the capacity of the alien motile brain to govern.

In another part of the giant building, MorningLight-Mountain's electronics workshop began to assemble an adaptor which could plug into the alien processor. There were several optical interface points, all it really needed was a module which would convert the processor's output into its own style of nerve impulses.

Although useful, none of this gave the immotile a method of linking itself to the alien's brain. The memory of their strange body and nervous system hung in its mind where it could be continually examined and analysed. It simply could not see a natural way to access the brain. Given that, and the obvious lack of mental capacity (as shown by the lack of control over the suit), MorningLightMountain began to wonder just how far down the alien motile caste structure these particular motiles were. They could well be a lot less intelligent than its own motiles, although the similar size of the brain argued against that; and the grippers indicated a high degree of tool usage, for which they would need suitable aptitude.

Aliens, it acknowledged, were paradoxical in more ways than one.

Given its overwhelming need to establish direct control

over the brain of an alien motile, and the only connection it had found to that valuable organ, it didn't have a lot of choice. The small alien motile was clearly badly damaged; its eventual loss was inevitable. MorningLightMountain needed to analyse the electronic processors connected to its nervous system; if it could somehow interface itself with them, then it would have access to the alien brain.

Two soldier motiles carried the smaller alien motile over to a bench where narrow-focus scanning equipment was poised overhead. Clamps were fastened around it, holding it in place. High-pitched squeaking noises pulsed out of its open orifice. The larger alien motile was hammering its clenched grippers on the wall of its pen, also emitting a lot of noise.

The scanners focused on the top section of the alien motile, and MorningLightMountain located the electronic systems clustered round the top of its main nerve channel. A motile with a small precision-cutting tool began slicing through the intervening tissue. The alien's noise emissions immediately increased to a much louder volume. Its red nutrient fluid jetted out of the cut. Even though the three-dimensional map of the alien's biological functions was quite clear in MorningLightMountain's mind, with the nutrient fluid pump organ beating away in a strong rhythm, it hadn't appreciated the kind of pressure which the circulatory system operated at. The cutting tool was saturated in the red fluid, which went on to spray across the motile's skin. Its heat was uncomfortable. The motile had to move away and stand under a small shower nozzle to wash it off. A different motile moved forward to continue the operation.

The alien had stopped its squeaking. Now its orifice was emitting a sound like old wood snapping. Its body was straining up against the clamps. Red fluid continued to spray out of the cut. Through the scanner, MorningLightMountain saw a series of impulses flash between the electronic components. All activity between them stopped. A moment later the nutrient fluid circulation pump juddered to a halt. Electrical activity in the brain withered away.

MorningLightMountain instructed its motile to resume the cutting operation. Without the red fluid spray, it was a lot easier to move the cutting tool inwards, exposing the thick nerve channel. Micromanipulator grippers were inserted into the opening, and carefully teased the components loose, breaking the minute and terribly fragile strands which connected it to the nerve junctions.

One by one they were subjected to detailed analysis. Three of the devices were for redirecting nerve impulses out into the complicated tracery of organic circuitry etched on the alien motile's skin. One had a very-low-power electromagnetic transceiver built in. MorningLightMountain was pleased to find that – it could well eliminate the need for a direct physical connection to the remaining alien motile. The final device was odd, an artificial crystal lattice that had conductive properties, with a small processor attached. It took the immotile a long time to understand its function. The crystal was a storage system, a highly sophisticated version of the ones it used to retain command instructions for the missiles. In this case, the theoretical information load was colossal; it could hold almost as many memories as an immotile brain. Unfortunately, it was completely blank. As the alien motile died, it must have erased the information.

The adaptor arrived. MorningLightMountain worked quickly, connecting itself to the transceiver processor and feeding power into the tiny device. A deluge of binary pulses flooded into its mind. It used the thought routines it had developed to control its own processors, running the sequences through them, modifying them to handle the new mathematical arrangements. At the same time, it observed the device with the field resonance amplifier. The string of numbers made up from the binary sequences made little sense, but it did see where they originated from, which junctions they came from. It carefully began to return the sequences, seeing what the result was. Most had no effect, but occasionally a segment of the whole sequence would activate a portion of the processor. Slowly, it built up a set of crude control instructions. The processor seemed to have a lot of operation rules integrated into its design. When the immotile finally managed to switch the transceiver on, a list of possible transmission sequences flipped to semi-active status. By trial and error, MorningLightMountain learned how to order them to flow into the transceiver section for broadcast. Although the binary sequences themselves were horribly long and complex, there was an elegant logic behind the device which the immotile quite admired.

It used another adaptor to connect itself to a second processor. This one had even more inbuilt operational rules. Once again, MorningLightMountain patiently worked its way through the combinations, flipping functions to active status. It was rewarded by a deluge of output information. The most basic one was a steady signal which was repeated five hundred times a second. Other functions changed the signal minutely, although its main parameters remained constant.

The immotile flipped the additional signal functions off and considered the basic signal for a long while, working through possibilities before it realized what it might be. It constructed thought routines to run through all the prospective formats, to be rewarded by a simple cube of twelve billion specific points. At this moment over a thousand immotile unit brains were now devoted to interpreting the alien electronics and the binary number sequences they used. In all its history it had never devoted so much of itself to a single problem. It flipped the first additional function on, and was rewarded by a string of symbols appearing in the cube.

The remaining alien motile had become inert, lying on the floor of its pen. As MorningLightMountain worked through the transmission sequences, one made it twitch and raise its fat sensor stalk. The cell picked up a reply transmitted from its embedded transceiver processor which the one now attached to MorningLightMountain acknowledged automatically. The alien motile stood up and stared at the equipment which the motiles were operating. It noise-generated briefly then turned to the immotiles. Its transceiver processor transmitted a long binary sequence, lasting several milliseconds. A whole series of inbuilt rules in MorningLightMountain's device suddenly activated, opening up new junction connections and closing others The immotile watched helplessly through the resonance amplifier as the processor unit effectively shut down. All the primary quantum wire routes making up the lattice of junctions were blocked out. Worse than that, the binary sequences used to accomplish the order were prime number based, those short enough for it to evaluate. Most of them were beyond its mental capacity to determine. It couldn't reverse the instruction.

Over in its pen, the alien motile held one arm out level towards the immotile units sitting behind the crystal wall, and extended a single gripper vertically. MorningLightMountain knew defiance when it saw it, no matter how alien the species was. It used its own transmitter in the cell to replicate the sequence which had made the alien twitch and rouse itself. There was no response.

New and different symbols continued to appear within the visualized cube as MorningLightMountain flipped additional signal functions. At least that had been unaffected by the alien motile's transmission. But without knowing the actual functions which the symbols represented, the immotile couldn't begin a translation. Its chances of establishing communications with the alien had been reduced considerably.

The immotile reviewed its shrinking options. There were only two sources of knowledge left concerning the alien immotiles and what was happening outside the Prime star system: the alien motile's brain, and its electronic information store. MorningLightMountain had clear evidence that the alien immotile would resist any attempt to establish contact and extract information from its brain. And the smaller alien motile had immediately wiped its information store when it realized what was happening. Logically, the information contained within the store device was valuable.

A soldier motile raised its arm, and shot the alien motile through the top of its fat sensor stalk with a high-velocity kinetic projectile. Red fluid, sticky strings of brain flesh, and splinters of bone exploded across the pen, splattering the transparent walls.

*

The second dead alien motile was placed on the bench underneath the narrow-focus scanning equipment. Clamps held it in place as MorningLightMountain located the electronic systems embedded below the brain. They were all intact; the soldier motile's shot had been perfectly aimed. The motiles began the extraction operation.

This time, the electronic information store was almost full.

*

MorningLightMountain's preliminary investigation revealed the information was protected from access by inbuilt rules which needed activation sequences even more complex than the ones which had been used to switch off the transceiver processor.

The tiny device was transferred to the electronics laboratory, and placed inside a quantum interface detector. It took a long time to read the stored information block by block; but weeks later the entire sequence was incorporated into MorningLightMountain's memory.

At the same time as the reading, it had been experimenting with the input channels of the wiped device for the smaller alien motile. The overall purpose was quite simple, nerve impulses from the alien's primary sensorium were transformed into binary sequences, compressed by a series of algorithms, and inserted into the storage lattice. It held a recording of everything which the alien had perceived.

MorningLightMountain derived an elaborate thought routine which would reverse the compression and transformation process, turning the stored information back into analogue nerve impulses. It applied the routine to the alien's information, and allowed the resulting data stream to flow into a single immotile's brain. The unit was isolated from the MorningLightMountain group by a series of safety cut-offs in case anything went wrong, and the alien thought routines began to leak out and contaminate the group.

*

Dudley Bose struggled in the grip of armoured monsters, as the shimmering blade stabbed through the spacesuit, puncturing both the plyplastic and his right buttock. The tip slashed downwards, ripping through flesh in an agonizing line of fire. Pain. PAIN!

*

MorningLightMountain wanted to throw its head back and scream as the unknown nerve impulse slammed through fifty thousand linked brains with the violence of a lightning bolt. Shock transfixed the immotile group as the naked slime-covered monsters tore and pulled away its coverings, inflicting brutal wounds across its belly and legs. It wanted to squirm loose, but its legs didn't work. The memory was pushed away from conscious thought, dwindling into the past. Becoming bearable as the safety systems reduced the intensity of the impulses delivered to the main group. MorningLight-Mountain's lung intake gills fluttered in unison throughout its circular cloisters as it took a juddering breath. Billions of frozen motiles all across the territory reoriented themselves, and resumed their tasks. In orbit above the Prime homeworld,

MorningLightMountain's ships returned to their correct flight paths, industrial machinery digesting asteroidal rubble belched and reset their refinery modules.

Pain. What an extraordinary concept. Prime motiles and immotiles had basic tactile senses, indicating pressure and touch against their skin. But *this*, this was a physical warning on a scale that took away rationality.

But then, it made sense in a way. Humans were individual. Astonishing though it was, they had no motile / immotile caste. It was a civilization of billions of full-sentience entities, all of them in mild conflict with each other. In some cases, not so mild.

>**memory**<

The sheer intransigent idiocy of the university board. Every month Dudley spent – wasted! – hours of his valuable time in meetings which accomplished nothing but the perpetuation of bureaucracy and the status quo. His department was always overlooked, always underfunded, always patronized by the larger science departments. Bastards.

>**explain**<

Because this is worthwhile. This is the expansion of knowledge which has a history back to the dawn of human time. This is pure science, driven not by greed but by nobility.

>**motivation not comprehended / memory**<

The vice-chancellor spoke at length.

>**vocalization / aliens communicate via sound / selfmemory**<

'Fuck you!' the alien Bose screamed inside its pen as Emmanuelle Verbeke lay strapped down on the vivisection table, blood squirting out of her carotid artery. 'Rot in hell you motherfucking bastards! We'll nuke you to shit and kill your babies when they glow in the dark! We'll wipe you from this whole fucking universe. Not even God will remember you existed!'

>**god / human ally / memory**<

Written books, hundreds of them, thousands, all multiplying out from a few ancient sacred texts. Stories of how the universe began, how its creator sent segments of itself to the human homeworld to promise salvation. Salvation which came in many forms for many different human alliances. Divine mythology which as a scientist Dudley Bose knew was fiction. Like the woodland elves, which had turned out to be real. The Silfen. What irony.

>more aliens / classifications/ memory<

Hundreds of worlds each containing tens of thousands of non-sentient aliens. Several sentient species had been discovered by the Commonwealth as it expanded, their status as hostile or allied could never quite be determined. And one non-life world, the SI planet.

>SI / human immotile / explain<

It's not a human immotile. It evolved out of sophisticated programs. It's artificial.

>human thought transfer to SI / immotile function / confirm<

No, it's not like that, like you. Some humans download their memories into the SI when they don't want to rejuvenate, when they've had enough of life.

>paradox /explain<

I can't. It's not something I would ever do. People are not the same, we all have different motivations.

>SI involvement with starship flight / memory<

Distant recollections of news reports, blurring into one. Politicians arguing about paying for the flight. Nigel Sheldon being interviewed; Vice President Elaine Doi claiming the SI supported the venture, wanting to know more about the barriers. Never confirmed directly because the SI didn't talk to individual humans, at least not Dudley Bose.

>clarification of status / inclusion on flight / memory<

From nobody to somebody within an instant as he saw the enclosure. Triumph followed by months of cluttered thought of the striving, clawing his way to get selected for the crew of the *Second Chance*. Surprising himself with the degree of determination and political manoeuvring he accomplished, the suppression of all conscience.

>**alienPrime involvement/ explain<**

Never heard of them. Never heard of you before the barrier came down. We were an exploratory flight. Science only.

>**message from MorningLightMountain17,735 / explain<**

You're wrong, there was no alien on board the Second Chance.

>**paradox / explain<**

There was no alien on board. Our hysradar scan showed the barrier was still intact around their star.

>**barrier construction / memory<**

None. The barriers were in place before humans knew how to cross space. Humans did not build the barrier.

>**human commonwealth / memory<**

Hundreds of worlds linked together by wormhole. Worlds of land and water and atmosphere, warm worlds with clear empty skies. Worlds that would support Prime life. So many worlds that the terrible pressure and conflict between immotile territories would end immediately if they were to become available to Primes.

>**wormholes / memory<**

Distortions of spacetime that could reduce distance to no length at all. They could be made large or small. The ultimate method of transport. The ultimate method of communication; with immotile units across interplanetary and interstellar space linked through wormholes there would never be divergence. With wormholes, MorningLightMountain could extend itself across the galaxy, with units occupying every star system. It would never die, never be challenged from such supremacy.

>**wormhole construction / explain<**

I don't know the technical details of creating exotic matter, but the equations are fundamental.

>commonwealth location / memory<

Right in the core of knowledge that was the remnants of the Gralmond University astronomer Dudley Bose, the name, spectral type and stellar coordinate of every Commonwealth star glimmered like a precious jewel.

19

With its uncomfortably close G1 sun blazing down through a heat-bleached sky, the temperature along the entire ninety-five-mile length of Venice Coast rose uncompromisingly during the day. It didn't help that the beautiful island city was only just outside what was technically Anacona's northern polar region, and the planet was also approaching the middle of summer. This mix of geography and calendar was currently giving the city over sixteen hours of intense sunlight every day. In deep winter, of course, the pattern would be reversed, and the sun would only be visible for about six hours a day. Even then the climate would cool down to something like Earth's Mediterranean temperatures. Anacona's proximity to its primary star made the planet uninhabitable from the equator out to fifty degrees latitude north and south, most of which was a rocky desert.

From space, Anacona had the same kind of symmetrical banded appearance as a gas-giant, with its broad expanse of coffee-coloured sands wrapped round the centre, and skirted with black and auburn mountain ranges. The planet had kicked off a large, and ongoing, debate among Commonwealth planetologists about how climate could affect topography, or if the symmetry was just a transient tectonic fluke. For it wasn't just the central regions that were regular. Beyond the peaks, which bounded each side of the desert, the cornflower-blue waters of annular seas sparkled in the strong sun to the north and the south. Both the polar zones boasted continents, although the southern one was smaller, and their coastlines were completely dissimilar. They did share an abundance of emerald vegetation, with rainforests and grasslands nurtured by the heat and daily rains. Both seas shunted long trails of swan-white cloud across the continents where they formed permanent slow-spinning spiral whirls over the actual poles.

The sea gave Venice Coast an indecent humidity. By midafternoon, the siesta was well under way, hustling tourists and inhabitants alike off the streets. Shops shut for four or five hours at a time, waiting until evening and a low golden sun before they opened their doors again. People took long rests in the shaded courtyard gardens to be found at the centre of every block. The only service which seemed to carry on regardless was the monorail, which linked every district along the narrow city's ninety-five-mile length. Even most of the gondolas, water taxis, and little supply boats which swarmed the canals, tied up at some quay or other, bobbing about empty while their skippers lounged around in the bars.

It was these long people-less interludes every day which gave Paula Myo her greatest cause for concern. The surveillance operation would be much better served by crowds and activity providing cover for the Agency's operatives. As it was they had to linger over long meals and drinks as they sat on the verandas of neighbouring cafés and restaurants. It was proving a popular duty. Paula disapproved. They were likely to grow lax during such leisurely episodes.

The centre of their attention was the Nystol Gallery, a big three-storey canal-side building in the Cesena district, specializing in EK art, electrokinetic machines with hundreds or even thousands of moving parts. Paula had reviewed the gallery's catalogue, going virtual through the TSI construct, where she marvelled as every non-art-lover did at the striking, pointless fusion of art and machine; some were like working sculptures of animals, aliens, and mythical creatures, their micro-gears and pistons running through biological functions with cheeky mimicry, while others were random collections of mechanical components assembled in bizarre asymmetric patterns, that shouldn't work, yet somehow managed to buzz, whirr, rotate, and wobble about with jerky elegance; still others were variants on the old domino relay, with modules of fire, water, air, rubber, protoplasm, and ordinary misapplied components from domestic or industrial machines, all of them reacting against each other, activating the next piece, then somehow resetting themselves in an impossible perpetual motion.

The Nystol was a good cover for its owner, a Mr Valtare Rigin, whose other specialist enterprise was black market armaments. For a start, Venice Coast was not the kind of city where such activities took place. It had no industry other than art and fishing and boats and tourism. There was no grand civic cultural plan back when it started in 2200, no desire to rival the illustrious ancient urban areas of Earth, or the dynamic wealth-hungry new cities vying for funds and entrepreneurs that were springing up across phase two space. This was built on a dream and a prayer. It started on a sandy spit called Prato near the centre of a five-hundred-mile stretch of swampy coastline on the Calitri continent that was protected to seaward by meandering lines of small marshy islands. Local marine life attracted several families who'd arrived from Italy and were already tiring of the new planet's capital, San Marino. The waters were thriving with a variety of edible fish eminently suitable to Italian cuisine. Several of the families who settled on the spit were from old Venice, so that boating culture was there right from the start.

Huge dredgers imported from the mega shipyards on Verona scooped out big channels for the fishing boats, then began clearing smaller channels round Prato. More substantial houses started getting built on the higher, reclaimed land, with little canals dug directly to them so the boats could have easy access. That was when the growing town's inhabitants realized the potential of what they had. The original spit began to expand as the newly dredged swamp silt was piled up on the east and west sides. After a couple of years, Prato had become an elongated island with a wide clear lagoon separating it from the main coast where the swamp had once been; with a single causeway for the railway lines. It set the pattern for the future.

For a hundred and eighty years the dredgers and constructionbots just kept on going. The long island twisted sinuously many times to keep more or less parallel to the contours of the coast, with districts continually added to both ends. Architects, artisans, and designers collaborated with City Hall to keep their new commissions Italianate in nature, preserving and amplifying the waterbound city's character. It became fashionable for Grand Families and Intersolar Dynasties and the individual super-wealthy to own a villa somewhere along Venice Coast. The offshore islands, of which there were thousands, proved an even more lucrative real estate.

The Cesena district where the Nystol Gallery was situated lay twenty miles east of Prato, three stops on the express monorail. After four days, Paula knew it intimately, every street, canal, bridge, covered alleyway and square. Her hotel was a seven-and-a-half-minute walk from the local monorail station, with five bridges over the canals; three of carved stone, one wood, and one metal. The Nystol was four and a half minutes, and three bridges, away; while the local police station was a mere two minutes away, with four bridges in the way. She'd arrived at Venice Coast with a team of eight from her office, supplemented by a further five from technical support, and thirty officers from the tactical assault division. Twelve of Anacona's senior detectives had been loaned to her by the planet's eager Interior Minister, providing invaluable assistance down on the narrow waterways and maze of streets where it was really needed. Their presence was an indicator of how much importance governments placed on the new Commonwealth Planetary Security Agency, the quiet twin of the Commonwealth Starflight Agency.

With the launch of the scoutships back to Dyson Alpha, public interest was focused solely on the Starflight Agency; while it was now the Planetary Security Agency which was receiving fifty-five per cent of the overall budget. For someone who'd scraped in on a pitiful fifty-eight per cent of the Intersolar vote, President Doi was strangely forceful when it came to providing funds for the new Agency. There was talk on the unisphere news shows that income tax was going to have to be raised to pay for the vastly expanded facilities.

Greater resources should have helped ease the transition for Paula. She didn't like it at all; the Agency wasn't the Directorate she'd joined, even if reorganization had brought her more money and a bigger staff. That staff now unfortunately included Alic Hogan, her new deputy, who Columbia had appointed from his own legal department. If ever there was a political placeman, it was Hogan. His constant requests for full briefings from all the investigators, and insistence that all procedures were conducted by the book, was causing a lot of resentment in the Paris office. He knew very little about running a case, and everything about watching over people's shoulders.

Over the last few months she'd begun to wonder if she was becoming conservative in her old age, hating change simply because it was change; refusing to acknowledge that society was altering around her. It surprised her, because if nothing else she considered herself a realist. Police forces always adapted to keep pace with the civilization in which they maintained order. Although more likely it was the increasing degree of political control exerted over Agency operatives which made her uncomfortable. She resented the notion that limits might be imposed over her own work; after so many years served to reach a virtually semi-autonomous position it would be awful to be hauled back into the general accounting system.

'Like everyone else.'

'Excuse me?' Tarlo asked.

Paula gave her deputy a mildly irritated smile; she hadn't realized she'd spoken out loud. 'Nothing. Thinking aloud.'

'Sure,' Tarlo said, and returned to the menu.

That California attitude was something Paula could finally appreciate here. Tarlo merged perfectly into Venice Coast's laid-back lifestyle. The two of them were sitting at a café table, under a broad parasol by the side of the Clade Canal. Two hundred yards away, on the opposite side, was the back of the Nystol Gallery. Its sheer red-brick wall rose vertically out of the placid water, with only a single loading door on the lower floor, a yard or so above the black tide line; a couple of wooden mooring posts stood on either side of it, their white and blue stripes sun-scorched to near invisibility. Wide, stone-rimmed windows marked out the second and third floors, below an overhanging roof of red clay tiles. A row of thick semi-organic precipitator leaves were draped just below the guttering, as if some giant vine was growing out of the rafters. Fresh water was an expensive commodity in Venice Coast, by themselves the sieve wells drilled through the basement of most blocks couldn't support the huge demand of the residents.

Paula's seat was positioned so she faced the target building, while Tarlo was at right angles to her, giving him a view along the canal. In his white cap and loose orange and black linen shirt he seemed immune to the heat. Paula took off her suit jacket and hung it on the back of the chair before sitting down; her white blouse was clinging to her skin. Her wig was hot, she could feel the sweat pricking her brow, but she resisted the impulse to shift it round. A waiter from the café

792

scowled at them from his seat just inside the doorway. When it was clear they weren't going to go away, he sauntered over.

'*Ah, uno, aqua, minerale, er natu*—' Paula began.

The waiter gave her a pitying sigh. 'Still or sparkling?'

'Oh. Still, please, chilled and with ice.' The Venice Coast waiters were normally contemptuous of anyone who couldn't speak even a smattering of Italian.

Tarlo asked for a non-alcoholic beer and a bowl of smoked rasol nuts.

Both of them received a further look of utter derision before the waiter slumped his shoulders and walked back inside.

'Always feels good to blend right on in there,' Tarlo said. He put his sandalled feet up on the rusting iron railing which guarded the edge of the granite-cobbled pavement from the canal.

Paula checked her timer. 'We'll order more drinks in half an hour, then a snack after that. I'd like to have at least two hours here.'

'Boss, we have got the whole place covered by sensors, you know. You can't get a carrier pigeon in there without us zapping it.'

'I know. Target review is important to me. I need to get a feel for the op.'

'Yeah.' Tarlo grinned. 'So you keep telling me.'

If one good thing had come out of the Directorate becoming the Security Agency, it was the expanded intelligence base. For once, the news of Valtare Rigin purchasing a number of sophisticated and very restricted items of technology hadn't come from any of Paula's deep assets. Instead, Anacona's special criminal bureau had been running a monitoring operation with local manufacturers who made dual-use products. They ran financial checks on an industrial supply company that purchased some molecular resonance stabilizers with a very high power rating, the kind that could be used in large force field generators. It turned out the supply company was a shell, with its credit supplied from a one-time bank account on StLincoln.

The bureau tracked the shipment, which was routed through a number of blind drops, until a courier picked it up and delivered it to the gallery. That was when they called the Agency in.

Observation, backtracking, and communication monitors had shown them Rigin was acquiring a lot of dual-use components. There were no actual weapons, but the pattern fitted one of Adam Elvin's shipment operations exactly.

'He picked a good cover,' Paula said as she sipped her mineral water. 'I'll bet you Rigin's lawyer claims that the components make up one of his EK works.'

'So why did he need to acquire them like this?'

Paula smiled in the shade of the parasol as a light breeze washed off the canal. 'Radical art, I expect.'

'You reckon he's going to ship it out in one go?'

'Most likely. The risk was in putting the items together. Now he's exporting, it'll be a couple of big crates to a legitimate destination.'

'Right out the back door, huh?'

'Yes.' From behind her big sunglasses, Paula gazed at the solid grey-painted wood of the gallery's loading door, visualizing the cargo boat tying up beside it, the containers being lowered onto the deck. They'd do it in the middle of the day, of course. A simple honest shipment; nothing to hide. Wherever it went, out to the docks that fronted the Acri district where the big sea-going ships put in, or the cargo yard at the Prato monorail station, she'd follow it. Somewhere down the line, Bradley Johansson would be waiting.

*

Adam Elvin leaned back against the purple cord cushions in the back of the gondola as it slid gracefully along the narrow canal. It was one of the little waterways that zigzagged round large blocks, connecting and crossing the larger canals. The side walls were high here, slimed with weed and dirt. Water slapped against the cracked brickwork, slowly eroding the mortar – there were entire sections that had been repaired with new bricks and hard cement, looking totally out of place. Bridges curved overhead like miniature tunnels. Each block had a row of near-identical blank wooden doors a yard above the tide line, fastened by heavy iron bolts. They passed several that were open, with little cargo boats tied up outside, their crew manhandling crates and boxes into the dark interiors.

Every delivery in Venice Coast was by boat, adding to the cost of living here. Adam hadn't appreciated that before he came. The only transport in each district was either walking or boat. The monorail took you between districts, but that was all.

They turned out onto the famous Rovigo Canal, one of the major channels through the Cesena district. The venturi trees lined both sides. Planted a century ago, their trunks resembled gnarled copper pillars reaching over twenty-five metres high, with arched boughs that trailed long strands of yellow-gold leaves as thin as tissue. Each one had its own sieve well that had been drilled under the pavement into the boggy subsoil, allowing the roots to suck up fresh water. Adam was lucky enough to be visiting during the fortnight they were in bloom. Each branch ended in a triune of brilliant amethyst ruff flowers as big as footballs. Already, though, petals were beginning to fade and fall, snowing onto the heads of delighted gondola tourists like scented confetti.

Adam smiled appreciatively as the gondolier slowed down, allowing him to soak up the sight and smell of the wonderful native trees. The boutiques and galleries on either side of the Rovigo were among the more exclusive in Venice Coast, with dark glass windows illustrating single examples of their expensive prestige products on displays that could qualify as high art themselves. Not far away, the strange and wonderful twisted neo-gothic spire of StPeter's cathedral towered above the city's red tile roofs like a pre-Commonwealth silver space rocket.

The Rovigo ended at a junction with the Clade Canal. They waited between the last of the venturi trees for a big glass-topped, air conditioned tourist boat to chug past. The wash slapped at the gondola, much to the gondolier's disgust; half of his conversation during the trip had been a diatribe against any boat which had an engine. Adam looked along the Clade, seeing the broad waterway slowly curving away from him, with the back of the Nystol Gallery just visible. There were only about ten other boats on this section, a couple of gondolas, some cargo boats, a taxi; the pavement along the side was equally empty, with a few tourists wandering along. Even the cafes were almost deserted—

'Stop!' Adam hissed at the gondolier.

The man looked back at him in surprise, the pole poised ready to push them out into the Clade now the water bus had passed. 'Is clear now,' he complained.

'Go back. Do not go out onto the Clade. Understand? Do not take me out there. Take me back to the monorail station.' He produced a thick roll of notes from his pocket, and peeled off over a hundred Anacona dollars.

The gondolier's face brightened at the sight of the money. 'Sure. Okay. You're the captain, I'm just the engine room.' He changed the angle of the pole, and slid it into the muddy water. The gondola's prow slowly came around, and they began to head back down the Rovigo. A multitude of crispy dry violet petals continued to drift down over Adam's clothes as they retreated at a speed that was barely above walking pace. He refused to look around. That would be a stupid weakness. He knew exactly who he'd seen sitting there outside the café. After all this time he could recognize Chief Investigator Myo's profile from almost any angle and distance. She was wearing a blond wig, and large sunglasses, but that couldn't disguise her from him. Her posture, her gestures. That suit! Who the hell else would wear a business suit in the middle of Venice Coast's siesta?

His limbs were starting to shake as he realized how close he'd come to the end of . . . well, everything. He must have just used up every scrap of luck from the rest of his lifetime. If he'd been looking the other way. If Myo hadn't been on duty at this time of day.

He'd undergone cellular reprofiling, of course, giving himself a new image, a drawn face with dark skin. But he knew that wouldn't have worked with the Chief Investigator. She would know him as easily as he knew her. They could never hide from each other.

*

He walked into the Nystol Gallery by the front door, knowing the Agency team would now have his image on record. It didn't bother him.

The reception hall had an arching roof of white-painted brick, and a flagstone floor. Before being converted into a gallery, the building had been a storage warehouse, which made it an ideal place to house EK pieces. The receptionist sat at a desk in front of a smoked-glass doorway which led into the gallery's display chambers. She was staggeringly pretty, with a sylph's body, Nordic white skin and red-gold hair that hung halfway down her back. Her flimsy brown and emerald dress belonged on a couture house's runway. She smiled automatically at him, which deepened to mildly flirtatious as he walked over. 'Hi, can I help you?'

'No.' He shot her through the temple with a microdart from his arm dispenser Its n-pulse locked her muscles solid, an instant rigor mortis, holding her upright in her seat. Anyone peering in from the street would see her behind the desk as usual.

His e-butler opened a channel to the desk's array. A brief software battle ensued as he took control of the building's electronic network. As it progressed, the weapons and defence systems wetwired into his body powered up, bringing him to full combat status. He disconnected the gallery's network from the planetary cybersphere, then deactivated all the internal alarms. The front door was locked. Where possible, fire doors were silently sealed, compartmentalizing the gallery. Sensors fed directly into his virtual vision, showing him the location of several people, although he knew there were at least three rooms without sensors.

The first chamber housed an eight-foot-high EK gryphon, with a body made from thin sheets of jewel-encrusted brass which moved with fluid grace as they were manipulated from within by hundreds of small cogs and micro-pistons. It was as if Leonardo da Vinci had animated a sculpture with a difference engine. An old couple were walking round it, making admiring noises as they pointed out features to each other. He shot both of them with an ion bolt. The gryphon cooed loudly as he moved into the second chamber.

On the second floor, the fifth chamber had a single strip of machinery running its entire length, each component coming from the same aircraft, and broken in some way so, instead of the smooth movement associated with the aerospace industry, they jerked around like a damaged bird when power was applied. Ripples of motion ran up and down the strip, each one different to the last. A gallery guide was walking along the side of the piece, with a frown on his face as he came to investigate the strange sounds that had burst out of the fourth chamber.

The ion bolt vaporized the top of his skull. Blood-steam misted the workings of a wing flap electrohydraulic activator, slowing its motion. Loud rattling sounds began to issue up and down the whole length of the EK piece as its synchronization was thrown off and stresses built up.

He went up to the third floor. Valtare Rigin's office was the second door along the hallway. Like the chambers below, it had a vaulting brickwork ceiling. At the far end, an arched window gave a splendid view out over the Cesena district, with StPeter's mirror-chrome spire framed almost dead centre. Rigin looked up in surprise from behind his desk, where he'd been struggling with his crashed network interface. 'Who the hell are you?'

'You are Valtare Rigin?'

Rigin smiled thinly. 'Roberto,' he called quietly.

A large black leather couch had been placed on the left side of the door, so it would remain unseen by anyone who entered the office until they were well inside the room. He had of course sensed the human male sitting on it. The man, presumably Roberto, who was now lifting his seven-foot-high frame onto his very large feet.

He brought his left arm up and fired an ion pulse straight through the door at the big human's head.

Roberto, as a good bodyguard, was wearing a light armour frame below his expensive hand-tailored suit, which wrapped him in a deflector field. The ion bolt sizzled loudly as it bounced off into the brickwork. Carbonized clay puffed out of the strike point. Roberto slammed both hands into the door which ripped off its hinges.

He barely noticed the impact as the door crashed against him. His arm sliced round hard, smashing three-inch-thick hardwood into splinter shrapnel.

Roberto grunted in surprise, and went for the weapon in his shoulder holster in a slick high-speed motion only available to those with a nervous system wetwired for accelerated response time. The bulky mag-a pistol which he pulled out fired two depleted-uranium rounds at the intruder, whose sparkling force field halted both of them. That was the only chance Roberto got.

He launched himself straight at the big man, right leg

swinging up and round to kick the ribs. Roberto shrieked as the blow punched clean through the armour frame. Three ribs broke and pushed inwards, puncturing his lungs.

The bodyguard ignored the pain and countered with a left twist, his right arm coming round flat, aimed for the intruder's neck, armour frame's e-dump function on and eager to wreck the other's force field. Energy flared from the impact like a fusion bloom, the blinding discharge flinging off slivers of static that clawed at both figures as they grounded out. But the e-dump never got anywhere near overloading the force field. A fist like the front end of an express train crashed into Roberto's side, sending him flying backwards through the air to smack into the curving brickwork. Trailers of blood smeared the white paint as he slithered down limply to the polished wooden floorboards.

He leapt gracefully across the intervening distance, one heel coming down on Roberto's leg. The knee joint snapped with a sickening crunch under his heel. Roberto threw up as hands grasped the lapels on his ruined suit, hauling him to his feet. It was difficult for Roberto to focus through the daze of pain, but he just managed to squint at the intruder's frighteningly emotionless features. Then the head butt caved in the front of Roberto's face, pushing several splintered fragments of bone from the fractured skull directly into his brain.

He dropped the dead bodyguard, and turned to face the terrified man behind the desk. 'You are Valtare Rigin?'

'Yes.' Rigin crossed himself, his eyes watering as he waited to die.

'I do not have time to torture information from you. If you do not cooperate, I will destroy your memorycell insert when I kill your body; then we will infiltrate your re-life clinic and erase your secure store. You will be genuinely dead. We do have the capability to do this. Do you believe me?'

Rigin nodded frantically. 'Holy Mother of God, who are

you?' His eyes flicked to the broken corpse of his bodyguard. 'How did you . . .?'

'The location of the equipment you are buying for Adam Elvin?'

'I . . . That wasn't the name he gave me, but everything for the deal I'm putting together right now is in the second storeroom at the end of the hallway. All of it, I swear.'

'Give me the file containing the list of components and the methods of payment to your encrypted bank accounts. I also want the export route.' He ordered his e-butler to open a channel to the terrified arms merchant. Information flowed into his cache. The ion bolt blew a wide hole through Rigin's chest. He hurried over to the corpse and bent down. A single slender harmonic blade slid out from underneath his right index finger, and he quickly cut through the neck to pull out a bloody glob of flesh and bone that contained all of Rigin's inserts.

With the arms merchant's memorycell safe in his pocket, he walked down the hallway to the second storeroom. A single kick shattered the reinforced polytitanium door. There were three crates in the windowless room, all unsealed, with packaging foam scattered around them. He went over to the first, checked to see that it did contain high-technology items, then dropped a superthermal demolition charge in.

To exit the gallery he went back to Rigin's office. He stood in front of the window and activated a focused disrupter field. The entire window of toughened carbonglass shattered before him, its cascade of shards twinkling in the brilliant sunlight as they flew outwards. He followed them, sailing through the warm outside air in a perfect swan dive to land cleanly in the Clade Canal with a small splash. Underwater, he put his feet together and kept his arms by his side. A ripple of motion swept down his body, and he powered forward with the ease of a dolphin through the muddy water, his enhanced senses showing him the canal walls on either side and the boats above.

The superthermal charge exploded behind him.

*

His training had been hard, not just physically – Kazimir had expected that – but mentally, too. The things he'd had to learn! The Commonwealth's history, its current affairs, the multitude of planets and their accompanying cultures, technology, programs, endless programs and how they managed his new inserts. There were so many times over the last two years when he just wanted to shout, 'I quit!' at Stig and his other tormentor-tutors. But the thought of Bruce stayed with him through all those months spent moving between the secret clan villages of the Dessault Mountains. He competed against the memory, thinking how Bruce would never quit, never turn tail.

Now, finally, Kazimir stood on Santa Monica's sandy beach facing the water as the morning sun rose slowly behind Los Angeles, and admitted it had all been worthwhile. A pleasant wind blew in off the Pacific Ocean, ruffling the waves, while the first limousines and coupés of the morning's commuter traffic slid silently and cleanly along the Pacific Coast Highway. To his left was the Santa Monica pier, extending over half a mile out into the ocean; its ancient original structure, a platform of wood and metal and concrete, gradually blending into the first of the three extensions that had been grafted onto it during its four centuries. Out to sea, the newer components of sicarbon and glass and hyperfilament girders had been arranged in mock-organic forms, sometimes discreet, sometimes deliberately garish, especially where the funfair rides were stationed along the east side.

He'd been so tempted to walk along it yesterday when he arrived, maybe go on a couple of the rides. Fit the profile of a visiting tourist mark. After all, that's what he genuinely was. It was a testament to Stig's training that he resisted – though he suspected had Bruce been here with him they would have sneaked off and done it, for old times' sake.

Instead he'd done what he was supposed to. Registered at the hotel behind the Third Street Promenade with its smart ancient shops that pulled in locals as well as visitors. Scouted the area, acquainting himself with the grid of streets. Noted access to public transport points, for escape. Which hotel lobbies were open, and the buildings' exits. Position of civic buildings. Rough timings for police patrol cars on the main roads. Location of public observation anti-crime sensors.

The familiarization had given him a good feel of the city, and he'd been impressed with what he saw, its wealth, neatness, and style. He'd been on a few Commonwealth worlds now, enough that he wasn't completely intimidated by urban areas that covered hundreds of square kilometres. But this particular part of Los Angeles had threatened to undo all that acclimatization. He hadn't been prepared for how shiny and clean it all was. After all, most of the cities on the new worlds had large districts that were crumbling into ghetto status. While here, where age had every chance to pour entropy and decay into entire neighbourhoods, the residents had resisted. Money helped, of course, and there was plenty of it residing among the condos fronting Ocean Avenue and the exclusive houses between San Vicenti Boulevard and Montana Avenue, but there was more to it than that. It was as if Santa Monica had discovered how to continually rejuvenate itself just like the humans who built and lived in it. For all its age, it had a buoyant vivacious atmosphere, making it a fun, friendly place to be. Surprisingly, Kazimir thought he might actually be able to live here – if he was forced to live anywhere on Earth, that is.

Big city-owned tractorbots were slowly grinding their way along the beach just above the water, fluffing up the dense sand and levelling it ready for the day. Cyclists, joggers, power walkers, ordinary walkers, dog walkers, skaters, pedcrawlers, and n-scoots were starting to appear on the path that wound along the back of the beach. Kazimir was getting used to Commonwealth citizens and their eternal quest for looks and fitness, but the highest concentration of obsessives surely had to be on Earth. Everyone on the path was dressed in high-fashion sportswear, no matter what age, from mid-twenties up to approaching-rejuve-fifty. It was an effort for him not to smile at them as they sweated their way along, faces intent and frowning.

As he watched them idly, he realized how few young people were using the path. But then that was true of Earth in general. The number of children he'd seen here so far was very small.

One of the early morning walkers left the path and headed over the sand towards him. It was an exceptionally tall man in his thirties, with blond hair which under the Californian sunlight was almost pure white. In contrast his eyes were very dark, making his face stand out rather than appear classically attractive. He was wearing a simple white V-neck jersey, knee-length shorts, and midnight-black trainers.

'Kazimir McFoster, I presume?' He put his hand out. There was no hesitancy, no caution that he might have got the wrong person.

'Yes.' It took every piece of self-control for Kazimir not to stammer or gawp incredulously. 'You're Bradley Johansson?'

'Were you expecting someone else?'

'About half the cops on the planet.'

Bradley nodded appreciatively. 'Thank you for coming.'

'Thank you for giving me the chance. It's still kind of hard to believe you're real. Alive, I mean. I spent so many years learning what you've done for us, the stand you took, what it cost you.' He waved an arm at the city above the cliff. 'It's an outrage they don't believe you.'

'Let's walk,' Bradley said. 'We ought to try and blend in.'

Kazimir wasn't sure if he'd offended the great man. More

804

likely he'd simply bored him. How many times must Bradley have heard something similar from stupid, awestruck youngsters? 'Sure.'

'I always forget what a shock places like this are for people who grew up in the clans back on Far Away. How are you coping?' Bradley asked.

'Okay, I guess. I'm very conscious of trying to appear blasé about everything.'

'That's good. When you stop making the effort you'll be taking it all in your stride, everything balances out. So now you've seen the Commonwealth, or some of it, what do you think? Are we right trying to save it?'

'Even if it wasn't worth saving, we are. People, I mean. Human beings, our race.'

Bradley smiled out across the ocean, taking a deep breath of the fresh breeze. 'Right or wrong.' He shrugged. 'Sorry, that's a misquote from before your time. Before mine, too, actually. So you think it is worth saving, then?'

'Yes. It's not perfect. I think they could have done a lot better with all the knowledge and resources they have at their disposal. So many things are hard for people, when they don't need to be.'

'Ah, an idealist.' Bradley laughed softly. 'Try not to let Adam corrupt you too much about what shape society should take when we're victorious. He's a disgraceful old revolutionary rogue. Very helpful, though.'

'What does he do?'

'You'll find out when you meet him. He's going to take over from Stig now.'

Kazimir stopped; they were still three hundred metres from the pier. People were wandering down onto the beach from the bridge road which connected it with the land. A whole section just in front of him had been roped off; a city lifeguard stood by the entrance gate. There was nobody inside it.

'Do you know who that's for?' Bradley asked.

'No.'

'It's for children, so they can enjoy the beach together without having to share it with a whole bunch of adults hanging round spoiling it for them. They're getting to be a rare commodity on Earth these days. At least for the middle classes, who can't really afford to have them any more. Though they still do, of course. That's human nature for you. It never ceases to amaze me what we'll go through, the sacrifices we'll make, so our kids can enjoy their childhood. That's the one part of life which our technology can never reproduce; yet after porn it's the most popular TSI genre. I guess none of us really forget the wonder and joy which that innocence brought us. Psychologists always say we crave the sanctuary of the womb – bunch of overeducated idiots, if you ask me. This is what we actually want. Times when every day is fresh and exciting, and the only worry is if the ice cream is going to last. It doesn't understand that, you know?'

'The Starflyer?'

'Yes. For all its intelligence, and it is very clever, Kazimir, it cannot grasp this part of us. It has never understood how important our children are to us, the bond of love and adoration which exists between us. Partly because its lifecycle doesn't include offspring in our fashion, but mainly because it regards them with contempt. It believes they cannot affect it, therefore it ignores them. I seriously believe that could be its downfall: our nature. The one thing it believes it controls because it does comprehend our greed and our fear. But we're more than that, Kazimir, we are more complex than it thinks.'

'I'll do whatever I can to help. You know that, sir.'

'I do. You've shown your loyalty to our cause many times.'

'You mentioned that this Adam person will take over from Stig. Does that mean I passed?'

Bradley turned back from the ocean to give Kazimir a broad urbane smile. 'Passed? Passed what?'

'The test. Your approval, sir.'

Bradley draped a long arm around Kazimir's shoulder, and urged him on round the back of the roped-off area. 'Believe me, my dear boy, if I hadn't approved of you, you'd still be standing on the beach wondering where the hell I'd got to. Or worse.'

Kazimir glanced round, seeing the flash of judgement in the old man's eyes. It was more disturbing than any diatribe of threats and sneering.

'I need the strongest the clans can produce for the task ahead,' Bradley said. 'You know that, don't you, Kazimir? You will be asked to do many unpleasant things. If I deem it necessary, I will ask you to die so that we can grant Far Away its revenge.'

Despite the moist air blowing in off the ocean, Kazimir's mouth was dry. 'I know.'

Bradley's hand squeezed strongly. 'I don't feel guilty. What I went through, everything I endured as that monster's slave, left me with too much determination to feel that weak. Once this is over, I expect I will grieve for everything we have done, for the lives we have sacrificed. But it will be worth it, for we will be truly free again.'

'What was it like, sir? What did the Starflyer look like?'

'I don't remember.' Bradley shook his head, sorrow tainting his voice. 'Not any more. The Silfen took that away when they cured me. I suppose they had their reasons.' The regret faded from his face. 'When this is over, you should try walking the paths they've built between worlds. It's an extraordinary galaxy out there, Kazimir.'

'Yeah. I'd like that.'

Bradley stuck his hand out. 'Goodbye, Kazimir. Thank you again for the opportunity to meet you. I consider myself honoured that you and your kin continue to sustain the cause.'

Kazimir shook the hand enthusiastically, smiled a fraction nervously, and went back down the beach. Bradley watched him go for a few moments, then went up the set of broad concrete stairs at the side of the pier. He walked back along Ocean Avenue, through the narrow strip of lush greenery that was Palisades Park with its centuries-old eucalyptus trees and ornate flowerbeds. Gardenbots were patrolling the plants, snipping off dead flowers and trimming any errant shoots that threatened symmetry; water droplets glistened on the tough grass from the pre-dawn irrigation sprinkling. On the other side of the broad street the bold geometrical skyline of condos presented their tiers of perfectly parallel balconies to the beach far below. Right in the middle of the gleaming new architecture their skyline took a sudden dip down, allowing the sunlight to shine on a small nineteen thirties hotel, the Georgian, with its art deco facade painted eggshell blue. Various brass plaques outside proclaimed the companies and civic authorities who had provided funds down the centuries to preserve the building, easily the oldest in the city. It had a raised concrete veranda along the front, with several tables underneath a yellow and pink striped awning. Adam Elvin was sitting at one, eating his breakfast as he looked out across the park and ocean beyond. Bradley went up the steps and joined him.

'So what's he like?' Adam asked.

'Depressingly young, trustworthy and honest, and hugely loyal to the cause.'

'Great, another fanatic robot. Just what I need.'

'He's smart. You'll get along fine. By the way, I like your new face. Dignified, yet with a hint of street fighter in the past. Very you.'

Adam grunted dismissively.

A waiter arrived and asked what Bradley wanted.

'Same as my friend, please.' Bradley indicated the plate of pancakes, bacon, and syrup which Adam was rapidly demolishing. 'With a glass of fresh orange and passionfruit juice, and some English breakfast tea, thank you.'

'Yes, sir.' The waiter smiled and went back inside.

Bradley tried to place the accent – one of the Baltic worlds in phase two space? The waiter would be an offworlder on a service company contract, as it was with nearly all human staff on Earth nowadays. After all, Earth natives would need a much better paying job so they could afford to live on their planet.

'So, this must be quite the experience for you,' Bradley said. 'The last socialist in the universe having his first power breakfast in LA.'

'Go fuck yourself.'

'What the hell happened on Venice Coast?'

Adam put his fork down, and dabbed at his lips with a linen napkin. 'I have no idea. It's only sheer luck that I'm not in some basement at the Security Agency right now, having my memories read. Christ, she was fifty metres away, Bradley. I could have whispered hello to her. It's never been that close before. Never. Why couldn't you warn me? Your cover has always been superb. It's one of the reasons I keep doing this for you.'

'I don't know. My usual . . . source hasn't been in contact for some time. I find that rather disturbing, it's not someone who could easily be eliminated from Commonwealth life.'

'The Starflyer got rid of them?'

'You say that with so much scepticism, even now. But no, if it was that powerful, I would be dead and the cause would be lost.'

'Don't be so quick to class me in there with the sceptical brigade. Remember what happened to poor old Rigin two days after I dodged Paula Myo? That was a goddamn superthermal charge which took out the Nystol Gallery. Now, much as I despise and distrust our government, I don't see them doing that. There were fifteen bodydeaths in the neighbouring buildings when the gallery blew up. This was somebody else.'

'It's not like the Starflyer to be so public,' Bradley said. 'What would be the point? The shipment was compromised the moment the Agency discovered it. We were never going to receive those components.'

'You told me its plans were reaching the last stage. Maybe it wanted to make sure we weren't going to get hold of those components. It can't risk us screwing it now.'

Bradley smiled at the waiter as he reappeared with the glass of juice and a pot of tea. 'I'm glad it was you suggested that, it adds credibility – from your point of view,' he told Adam. 'I've been considering the possibility ever since it happened. You have a lot of contacts with the mercenary agents. Do any of them know anything about the man who attacked the gallery?'

'No, there isn't even a rumour about him. Whoever he was, the armament systems he must have had wetwired in were very sophisticated. Even I would have trouble acquiring those kind of systems for you; they're all cutting-edge stuff. Governments get very edgy about who they're sold to. Someone put a lot of effort into the operation.'

'If it really is the Starflyer becoming more overt, it's a disturbing development. We have a lot of materiel to get to Far Away if I am to bring about the planet's revenge. With her new expanded Agency, Paula Myo is becoming unpleasantly efficient at uncovering and halting our shipments. We can't afford to get hit from two different directions at once. And I can see the time coming when every piece of cargo for Far Away will be stopped and examined on Boongate.' He paused to pour some tea out. 'As I remember, we did discuss blockade running once before.'

'As an emergency option.'

'Given our current situation, I believe a small amount of forward planning in that direction might be appropriate at this time.'

'Damnit. Okay, I'll look into it.'

'Thank you. I have two other small requests for you.'

'Yeah?'

'The data we're expecting from Mars: I don't want it routed to Far Away via the unisphere. There are too many options for interception and corruption, especially if the Starflyer is monitoring us.'

'All right, that's easy enough. We'll load it onto a memory cell and use a courier, take it through physically.'

'Fine. Someone like Kazimir, for example.'

'Let's just see how he works out on an ordinary run first, shall we? What's your second problem?'

'I've been trying to talk to Wilson Kime. It's not easy. He's well guarded, physically and electronically.'

'He's on the *Conway*. They should be at Dyson Alpha by now.'

'None the less, when he returns, I would appreciate contacting him somehow.'

'What exactly do you want to talk to him about? I assumed you consider him to be a Starflyer agent.'

'No, I don't believe he is; that's why I want to try and convert him.'

Adam had to swallow his coffee quickly before he choked on it. 'Convert Commander Kime? The head of the Starflight Agency? You've got to be kidding.'

'Fortune favours the brave.'

'Yeah, the brave, not the insane.'

'I've watched him in interviews. He knows something wasn't right about losing Bose and Verbeke. That gives us an opening.'

'An opening for what?'

'To expose the Starflyer. Kime should be able to find the evidence of its treachery on board the *Second Chance*.'

'What treachery?'

'The *Second Chance* switched the barrier off, obviously.'

'It couldn't have. We don't even begin to understand the physics behind the barrier. God, man, didn't you access the images of the Dark Fortress?'

'Yes. But humans didn't switch the barrier off, the Starflyer did.'

'How the hell did it know how to do that?'

'It is old. It has travelled a long way. I assume the Dyson Pair are a part of its history.'

'You and your assumptions. Did its species put up the barrier?'

'I don't know, Adam. I wish I did. I wish I knew what it was doing to us. And why. But I don't. All I can do is try and block its schemes, and warn people.'

'People like Kime.'

'Yes.'

'Why? I mean of all the people you could try to convince, why Kime?'

'Because of his position. He can order another review of the *Second Chance* data. I've gone over everything CST released a dozen times, but all they've ever given to the media are the visual recordings. I need the ship's system logs.'

'What do you think is there?'

'Proof that *Second Chance* switched off the barrier. Proof that losing Bose and Verbeke was no accident. Kime knows something is not right. He's ready to believe, he just needs a little nudge in the right direction.'

'CST has been over every byte from the flight a dozen times, not to mention all the media companies and government departments. It's been analysed by the best experts in the Commonwealth. They found nothing. No irregularities. No anomalies. No stowaways.'

'They don't know what they are looking for. I can tell him where to search. With the kind of evidence I know is in there, we can make him realize the true threat to humanity. The whole truth about the Starflyer can finally be dragged out into the public domain. The Commonwealth leadership will be forced to acknowledge we were right all along. You and I won't have to sneak around in the shadows anymore. Far Away can have its revenge without us having to—'

'All right! All right,' Adam held his hands up. 'Stop the preaching, I get the picture. But I doubt I'll be able to get any closer to Kime than you can. And even if I did, I'm not the nutter with a cause who might at least raise a doubt in his mind, I'm just a wanted killer who's taken up arms smuggling and incidentally organized an attack on *Second Chance* while he was up there in it. That's not exactly the kind of credibility we need to grab his attention.'

'I am aware of that. We need to come at him from an angle. Fortunately, there's someone else in the Starflight Agency who will listen to you. Someone who has complete access to Kime.'

The look Adam shot across the table was more outrage than shock. 'No way! I am not speaking to him. I am not contacting him. I'm not sending him a message file. I'm not even going to visit the same planet he's on. I will not do that. Not for you, not for money, not for your stupid cause, not if Karl Marx came back to ask me personally. Understand? That is the past. He made his choice, I made mine. End of story. Period. Finish. It is Over.'

'Ah.' Bradley took a sip of his tea. 'Shame about that.'

*

After a thoroughly decent evening meal in a bar that specialized in seafood, Kazimir walked the few blocks back to his small hotel. It was a balmy night, so he made a slight detour to take in Palisades Park. In darkness, the park had ribbons of illumination to highlight its plants and trees, bathing them in bubbles of coloured light to contrast with their own shades. Out to sea, the funfair on the pier was a continual blaze of multicoloured light, reflecting off the black water. Ocean Avenue was busy with people who wound their way between bars and restaurants and clubs, exploiting the city's vibrant nightlife culture to kick back and relax after their working day. The clubs had immaculately dressed doormen outside, operating strict entrance policies. Little clumps of hopefuls clustered outside, while limos came and went, depositing those who'd made it onto the list. Kazimir lingered opposite a few of the clubs, casually interested to see if he could spot any celebrities. One thing Los Angeles had clung to resolutely down the centuries was its status as capital of the human entertainment world. He didn't see anyone he recognized from the short time he'd been exposed to the unisphere, but then it was very early in the evening.

Hanging over the city, a three-quarters moon shone brightly enough to establish a small haze around it. He paused to stare up at it, fascinated by the wide jet-black equatorial band bisecting the globe, as if a loop of space itself had been wrapped around the swan-silver regolith. Established in 2190, the GlobalSolar power farm had grown from three patches of solar panels spaced equidistantly around the moon's equator so that one of them was always in full sunlight, until it now ringed the entire circumference. It had become Earth's main source of electricity. In an age when environmental laws reigned supreme and the pollution legacy of the twentieth and twenty-first centuries had almost been eradicated, it was inconceivable to build any kind of fuel-burning power station on Earth. Instead it was done cleanly and efficiently offplanet. The power which the ring generated was transferred to Earth via micro-wormholes where it was distributed over continental superconductor grids. Kazimir enjoyed the elegance of the idea. It was amusing to think the electricity which lit the row of condos looming along the other side of the park, as well as the funfair, had all come from the moon. It was nice that nothing had to be burned, fused, or fissioned to keep a whole planet supplied. The expense was phenomenal, but that was just a question of priorities. Once the lunar factories had been established, they just kept on churning out more solar cells indefinitely, processing them out of moon rock.

Adam Elvin had commented on the arrangement, admiring it, and simultaneously deploring the fact no other planet had made a similar investment. Kazimir then had to sit and listen over a perfectly good lunch to the plethora of reasons why corporate economics, evil Grand Families, and the Intersolar stock market prevented the rest of the human race from sharing the benefits of civilization in a fair and just fashion. In fact, Adam Elvin had a great many complaints about the economic oppression practised across the Commonwealth.

Kazimir knew he was never going to like his new colleague. He could work with him – the old man had a lot to teach him about the smuggling and deception techniques which would assist the Guardians – but he could never envisage going out and hitting a few bars in the evening as friends would.

As the lunch drew to its end, Adam had slipped him a memory crystal disk. 'It contains a list of items Bradley needs for this revenge project of his. It's all very high-tech stuff, the kind in plentiful supply on Earth. I've given you the names of possible suppliers, and the kind of covers I want you to establish in order to make contact. The payment methods have also been set up.'

'I understand.'

'I want you to go back to your hotel. Study it, come up with proposals how you'd handle each one; what you'll need, everything from clothes to a tourist TSI bought in the district you're supposed to have come from. We'll meet again in two days, and I'll review what you've got.'

'Okay. We meet in person?'

'Yes. Care to tell me why?'

'The cybersphere is susceptible to monitoring even if we encrypt – in fact, especially if we encrypt. Meetings can be spotted and observed, but it's a question of balance. You obviously believe it's the less risky option for the location and situation.'

'Very good. It's nice to know Stig was actually listening to me. We'll turn you into a covert operative yet, Kazimir McFoster.'

Kazimir had spent the afternoon reviewing the list, and making notes. He kept his proposals straightforward, complexity in this kind of operation could trip you up. He was sure that simplicity was the key. It would be interesting to hear what Elvin said about his tradecraft.

Most of the time had been spent researching through the unisphere. Hundreds of separate queries had returned dozens of answers. It was a question of sifting through them and deciding how they could be applied. Stig had always warned him the job would be boring for ninety-nine per cent of the time.

He started walking through the park again, alert for any signs of an observation team boxing him. Of course there was one query he had stoically resisted launching into the unisphere ever since he received his first insert. And he could never break cover to make contact with a civilian while he was on a mission as important as this one. He just couldn't.

He reached the end of Palisades Park, and crossed over to Colorado Avenue. Five minutes later he was back in his hotel room. Air conditioning reduced the temperature to comfortable. The darkened glass of the window let in a few specks of light, hinting at the city grid outside. There were almost no sounds from the traffic. He kicked off his trainers and flopped back on the bed's jellmattress. It was far too early to sleep. Any good, dependable Guardian member would carry on planning to acquire the items needed back on Far Away.

Kazimir closed his eyes and saw the darkness of the tent after night had fallen on Mount Herculaneum. Starlight showed the dusky outline of the angel's face as she rose above him. She smiled, proud of him, and excited by him, by the things she confessed in low whispers that she wanted him to do.

Nothing in his life had ever come close to the wonder of that time. No girl had – could – ever match her, in any respect. He'd gone on with his life, accepted that nothing would ever be that good again, knowing he could put it all behind him because he would never see her again. She was on Earth, and he was on Far Away, a safe four hundred light-years distant. And so it would remain. For ever.

'Goddamnit,' he shouted to the room. He lurched up, and came close to slapping himself. Instead, he took a breath, perched on the end of the bed, and told his e-butler to open a link to the planetary cybersphere.

'I want an identity check on an Earth citizen,' he told his e-butler. 'See if there's any reference available on Justine Burnelli.'

*

I ought to be getting used to this, Paula thought. She wasn't, though. And that was far more painful than any irony.

For once she'd gone to Mel Rees's office. It was a political thing. This was her mess, her responsibility. Once again.

Not that it was any comfort, but Mel Rees seemed to be as unhappy about the meeting as her. His office was only marginally bigger than the one she occupied. Although his view of the Eiffel Tower was a lot better. The door closed behind her, and he sat behind a big old walnut desk that was devoid of any clutter.

'So what happened?' he asked.

'I don't know.'

'For Christ's sake, Paula. Some psycho takes out a half block of Venice Coast, kills nineteen people in the process, and you don't know? This is not a good start for the Agency. Columbia is demanding results, and he's not using nice language to ask.'

'I am aware of the Agency's situation. What happened out there concerns me a lot more.'

'I understand how concerned you are.' He hesitated, winding himself up, like a doctor preparing to break bad news. 'You've been on this case a long time. Maybe . . .'

'No,' she said flatly. 'It is not time for me to move on and hand over to someone else.'

Rees didn't argue. He seemed to shrink a little further behind his desk. 'All right. But be warned, Paula, there are questions being raised about your suitability. Things are different here now, and they're going to change even more. If the order comes down to move you on, it isn't one that I'll be able to shield you from. If it wasn't for your record outside the Guardians case—'

'I am aware of how my reputation protects me. And you know none of your other investigators would be able to run Johansson down.'

'Yeah.' The thought was visibly worrying him. 'So what can you tell me about Venice Coast?'

'I've been supervising the forensics operation, trying to reconstruct the sequence of events. It added very little to what we already know.' She told her e-butler to run a file on the deputy director's wall-mounted portal. It produced an image from one of the observation team's sensors, showing the man poised in Rigin's shattered office window the moment before he dived into the canal. 'The face is unknown to any database, so we assume it's a cellular reprofiling. There's no visual sensor image of him arriving or leaving Anacona at the CST station.'

'A native, then?'

'Unlikely, but we haven't ruled out the possibility. As far as we can determine, his weapon systems were all wetwired, with the exception of a simple arm dispenser. We recovered the receptionist's memorycell, and read the last ten minutes. I acquired it myself.' The memory was now as clear as any of her own. She could recall the man walking into the gallery. She'd sat up a little straighter behind the reception desk, smiling when she noticed his youth and looks. Then his arm was raised, something moving below the jacket sleeve—

There was nothing else, no time for her to feel pain, or horror, or fear. Death had been instantaneous. 'We were lucky to get that,' she said. 'The way the gallery was built meant the ground floor had a degree of protection from the plasma surge after the blast. There were other bodies down there, but they were ninety per cent vaporized. And the bodyguard, Roberto, he was fortunate, too. His armour frame wasn't exactly designed with a superthermal charge in mind, but its deflector field did provide some shielding. The frame's processors contained some interesting records. Just before the blast it had managed to ward off an ion pulse, then the armour received some terrible physical impacts. Someone used poor Roberto as a punchbag. Our intruder was one sophisticated boy. I asked our new colleagues in the Enforcement Directorate what it would take to build someone up to that standard. They actually had trouble working out the specs for me. Wetwired force fields are cutting edge.'

Mel took a long disapproving glance at the image in the portal. 'Do you think Johansson has a lot of them?'

'I don't think he's Johansson's at all. Elvin hasn't acquired this kind of capability. Besides, he wrecked Elvin's operation. No, he was sent by someone else.'

'Any guesses?'

'Logically, there are three possibilities. A deep Commonwealth security department sent him in, something we're not cleared to know about. There have always been rumours about the Executive office having its own intelligence sector. Why they'd use an operative in this instance I don't know, unless it was to send a very clear message to Johansson that we're not going to tolerate him any more. The same applies to CST.

They could certainly put someone like this together, and they're not likely to forgive or forget the sabotage attempt on the *Second Chance*.'

'And the third possibility?'

'The Starflyer sent him.'

'Oh, come on!'

'It's an option, you have to admit that.'

'No, I don't. What about Rigin's enemies? He was a black market arms merchant for God's sake. His kind don't settle disagreements over a meal and a bottle of wine.'

'A rival wouldn't bother destroying the equipment Rigin was collecting, they wouldn't even know about it. No, the timing indicates someone who had the same information we did. That fits the first two possibilities. Our operations are available to the Executive. It might even fit the third.'

'No. Paula, no! There is no third option. The Starflyer is a cult conspiracy theory. You do not include it in any official report. If you do, I will not even attempt to cover your ass. Don't you see how political this is? It had to be the President or CST. We can investigate many things, but not them.'

'Nobody is above the law.'

'Damnit. If the Executive authorized it, then it is lawful. Same for CST; God, Sheldon and Ozzie own whole planets including a Big15, they are governments.'

'That doesn't make what happened right. They killed people.'

'Don't do this, Paula,' Mel was almost pleading. 'Let me talk to Columbia, let me find out if this is safe. You never know, I might actually be right. It might have been one of Rigin's enemies.'

She considered the request. 'Very well, I'll complete the investigation into the gallery explosion itself. How it is carried forward after that, and who it's assigned to, will be your call.'

'Seriously?'

'Yes.'

'Why?' he asked suspiciously.

'If the investigation is blocked politically, it will be because it was either CST or the Executive which ordered the assault, in which case I'm not interested. Not that I don't want to see justice done, but it would not be possible to ever achieve justice in those circumstances. I would be wasting my time, which I could be using to pursue Johansson and Elvin. If Columbia wants us to proceed, then that's a different matter.'

'If we get the all clear, it'll be to find out who Rigin was at war with. Do you really want to spend time on that? You've got the resources to track down Johansson now.'

'If we get the all clear, you and I will need to know which of us is right.'

'So, do you want the case?'

'I'll let you know when you bring an answer from Columbia. Until then, I'm still dedicating the team to finding Johansson.'

'Okay. I can live with that.'

'There's something else I want you to raise with Columbia.'

'Yes?'

'Elvin was after some very advanced equipment; I really think it's time for every export to Far Away to be searched. Our current policy of random checks is simply not acceptable any more. Not that it ever was to me.'

'I'll put it on the agenda.'

'Good.'

*

Hoshe Finn was just sitting down to supper when the apartment's door sensors showed him who was approaching. He muttered: 'Holy shit,' and stood bolt upright. His wife, Inima, gave him a surprised look, then glanced at the little screen showing the camera picture. 'Isn't that . . .?'

'Yep.' Hoshe went through the lounge and arrived at the door the same time as Paula Myo. 'Is something wrong?' he asked after he'd invited her in.

'No, everything is fine, thank you.' She looked him up and down. 'You've lost some weight.'

'Not before time,' Inima said. 'We're considering having a child.'

Paula produced a genuine smile. 'Congratulations. Will you be carrying it?'

'Heavens no,' Inima said. 'It'll be a vitro womb pregnancy.'

'Right.'

That seemed to exhaust the investigator's small talk. Hoshe and Inima exchanged a mildly bewildered look.

'Do you want to join us for supper?' Inima asked.

'No thank you, it's mid-afternoon Paris time. I caught the express.'

'We can talk on the balcony if you'd like,' Hoshe said as his wife shot him a desperate glare.

'If you don't mind,' Paula said.

'I'll just get on with catching up on some work,' Inima assured her.

The balcony on the little apartment barely had room for the small round table and two chairs that were pressed up against the railing. Hoshe shuffled round the table and sat down. Paula stood by the rail, taking in the view. The thirty-storey apartment block was in Darklake City's Malikoi district, a long way back from the shore. Paula could look out and see the parks and elaborate buildings which meandered along the shoreline, she could even pick out the tower behind the big marina where Morton used to live.

'You have a nice home, Hoshe.'

'Why are you here?'

She left the rail and sat opposite him. 'I need some detective work doing. This is not an official request, it's a . . .'

'A favour,' he supplied gently.

'Yes.'

'You don't like working outside channels, do you, Paula?'

'I don't have a lot of choice in this particular case. I believe my Agency is compromised. That's why I've come to you, and a few others I worked with outside the old Directorate. You can make inquiries that won't be registered in our office.'

'Compromised by whom?'

'I'm not sure. But they will be very highly placed inside the Commonwealth government, perhaps even the Executive itself. If they find out about this, it won't exactly help your career.'

'What have they done?'

'What they always do, play politics and manoeuvre among their own kind. But this time it's resulted in people being killed.'

'Okay. What do you need?'

'Have you seen the recordings of the Venice Coast bomb?'

'Hell yes. Mellanie has been playing them just about non-stop.'

'Mellanie?' Paula hesitated. 'Mellanie Rescorai?'

'None other. I sometimes think I did the wrong thing letting the demon out of the bottle.'

'You let genies out of bottles, Hoshe, not demons.'

'Not in this case, believe me. After the court case she went on and made some softcore TSI biogdrama, *Murderous Seduction*. Did you access it?'

'No.'

'It got a huge rating. The actor playing me looked like a sumo wrestler for heaven's sake. They got you about right, though. Anyway, Mellanie won a lot of media attention; certainly locally, so Alessandra Baron took her on as Oaktier's rep for her show. She's actually quite good. I think she's got her own personality line as well; all the usual crap, swimwear, holograms, monthly TSI releases, scents, food, there's even a *Murderous Seduction* cocktail. She's got quite a fan club these days.'

'Strange. She didn't seem the type. I don't normally under-estimate people so poorly.'

'Yeah, there's some politicians she interviewed who made that mistake when she started out. They don't any more.'

'And she's been showing the Venice Coast recordings?'

'Every news show has. I just watched her because she gets the decent interviews; it was one of Rafael Columbia's depu-ties, I think.' He gave Paula a cautious glance. 'Mellanie was really pressing the point about how you kept fouling up the Johansson case. Her words.'

'I'm sure she was.'

'So where do I tie in with what happened on Venice Coast?'

'This is not public knowledge, but not all of the equipment Rigin was collecting got destroyed in the blast. Several items were being stored downstairs. We managed to retrieve them.'

'What kind of items?'

'One was a very high-power superconducting microphase modulator. Its regulator software was modified by a fix that apparently came from the Shansorel Partnership, that's a specialist software house right here in Darklake City. Elvin couldn't have placed a regular order for it, this is really technical stuff. They would need an expert brief. And, Hoshe, they would have known it wasn't a legitimate contract.'

'What was the modulator used for?'

A slight frown crossed Paula's forehead. 'We're not sure. The best guess forensics could come up with from the items we know were delivered is some kind of customized force field. Though that doesn't explain half of the components.'

'Okay, so you want me to look into the Shansorel Partnership?'

'Please, yes.'

'What exactly am I hunting for? And how much pressure do you want me to put on these guys?'

'I want to know how deep their connection with Elvin goes, if it's long-term, or if they were just short of money one time and took a no-questions contract to get the bank off their backs. I'm hoping for the long-term, of course, that way I can run a deep-cover tracker on their contact with Elvin's team. How you want to play it is up to you, there's always a weak link in any group of people, see if you can find which one it is in Shansorel, and make them sweat.'

'Okay. But I'm puzzled by this. You're going after Elvin. How does that help you with the Agency's internal leak?'

'Standard elimination entrapment. Each suspect is given a different piece of information in isolation; then I sit back and see who reacts.'

*

Decades ago Thompson Burnelli had made a huge mistake. He assumed that because he was a man and relatively fit, his reach and strength gave him an easy advantage, he would beat Paula Myo at squash. He was good at squash – no false modesty. Whenever he was in Washington, he would visit the Clinton Estate, his ultra-exclusive social and sports club, where no small percentage of Intersolar government business was conducted. Two or three times a week he would play his fellow senators, or their aides, or some committee chair, or a Grand Family representative. Standards were high, and the Estate's professional was an excellent coach if any part of his game should slip.

With Paula Myo he learned that placement and precision were everything. She barely moved out of the centre of the court, from where she sent the ball slamming into places he wasn't – every time. He had staggered out afterwards, red faced, slick with sweat, and fearing for his pounding heart. It was eleven years before he finally won a game; two years after a rejuvenation when he was at his absolute physical peak, while she was due into rejuvenation in another three years. So their cycle continued over the decades.

Right now, she wasn't ten years out of rejuvenation, and he

didn't care about points, his only concern was to avoid a coronary before he lost, dashing from one side of the court to the other chasing after her calm shots. Anyone else he played who lacked perhaps his status or seniority – aides, lobbyists, new senators – would allow him to win the odd game. Not every game, but enough to make him feel good. It was simple politics. That would never apply to Paula. It took him a while, but eventually he worked out why. Throwing a game would be dishonest, the one thing she could never be.

When the torment was over, he grabbed a towel and wiped the rivers of sweat from his face. From the ache in his leg muscles he knew he was going to be stiff for a week. 'See you in the bar,' he groaned, and slowly made his way to the sanctuary of the gentlemen's locker room.

Forty minutes later, with at least some of the pain eased by a hot massage shower, he walked into the bar. The Clinton Estate was barely two and a half centuries old, but from the darkened oak panelling and high-backed leather chairs the bar could have dated back to the late nineteenth century. Even the staff looked the part, dressed in their scarlet jackets and white gloves.

Paula was already sitting in a big leather wing chair, in one of the bay windows which gave a sweeping view out over the Estate's formal gardens. With her smart suit and perfectly brushed hair reaching just below her shoulders she had the kind of easy poise which women from the Grand Families spent decades trying to achieve.

'Bourbon,' Thompson told the waiter as he eased himself into the chair opposite her.

A light smile touched Paula's lips at the tone of the order, as if she'd scored another point.

'So did Rafael give you a hard time over Venice Coast?' he asked.

'Let's say I was made aware he was unhappy. People see it

as another victory for Elvin and Johansson over me. They are quite blind to what it actually signifies.'

'That we have a new player in town.'

'Not new. But they have become visible for the first time.'

'You still believe there's a mole in the Executive office?'

'Or a Grand Family, or an Intersolar Dynasty. You're the ones with the permanent connections, after all.'

'Rumour in the Senate Hall dining room is that you told Mel Rees it could be the Starflyer.'

'It is a possibility.'

'I'm sure it's logical, but Paula, it's not popular. Just so you know. There are some planetary parliaments who have elected people who support the Guardians, not many, and it was all proportional representation votes. But the fact that anyone like that can gather support is worrying.'

'Oh, I know it's not popular. It's not something I'm actively pursuing.'

'That doesn't sound like you.'

'I can't do my job if I don't have a job.'

Thompson greeted the arrival of his bourbon with a relieved grin. 'We all get backed into corners. I'm sorry. It must be especially hard for you.'

'I said actively pursuing. As the old prison saying went: they've only got your body behind bars.'

'I see. So what can I do to help?'

'I need to know if there really is a secret security section which is only answerable to the Executive.'

'No, there isn't. And I should know, our family actually pre-dates the Commonwealth. I can check with my father to be absolutely certain.'

'Please do. It is important.'

It wasn't what Thompson expected, nobody ever questioned him; but then that was what made Paula so refreshing. They had started their association all those years ago with a quick exchange of information. She was after one of the Zarin Prime Minister's staff, while he was trying to steer a bill on infrastructure tax credits through the Senate, which Zarin was opposing. Ever since then they had swapped facts and gossip on politics and criminals. Thompson wasn't sure if they were friends, but the relationship had certainly been rewarding for both of them. And he knew he could trust Paula implicitly, which was just about unique in the circles he moved through. 'Okay. What if there is? Will you try and arrest the President? Poor old Doi only just got in, and that was on a miserable percentage.'

'The fact that Columbia hasn't blocked the Venice Coast investigation suggests that situation won't arise. I'm just eliminating possibilities at this stage, that's all.'

'Then let me tell you that I don't know of any Grand Family who'd do such a thing. We've no reason to. Far Away and the Guardian terrorists don't have any impact on our activities and money.'

'Which leaves us with Nigel Sheldon.'

'Who you will never arrest.'

'I know.'

'Not that the order would have come from Sheldon himself, anyway. Some fifth-level family executive will be trying to earn themselves points.'

'That wouldn't surprise me. Although, we don't have any solid evidence that Rigin was ever working for Adam Elvin in the first place.'

'You don't?'

'No. What we were observing resembled one of his smuggling shipments, that's all. Although there is one major difference: the nature of the equipment Rigin was collecting.'

'I skimmed the report. It was all high-tech stuff?'

'Yes. But no weapons. If it genuinely was Elvin's shipment, that would suggest Johansson is moving into a new phase of activity. I've no idea what, but there's a very simple way to prevent it.'

'Which is?'

'A full examination of every piece of cargo shipped to Far Away. I've been arguing this for years, decades, actually. Every time I get the same answer – it costs too much and delays play hell with transport scheduling, especially with Half Way's wormhole cycle.'

'What did Rafael say?'

'That he would press for it. But there's been no movement. I need someone with real clout to implement the policy. You.'

'Rafael has real clout, believe me. Some of us are getting worried about how much.'

'Then all I can say is he's not using it to support my request.'

'Probably pissed at you for Venice Coast. His shiny new Agency didn't look good in the aftermath. Did you watch any of the news shows? The editorials weren't friendly. Alessandra Baron even took a swipe at you personally.'

'So I heard,' Paula said dryly. 'But that should not affect Columbia's judgement on this issue. Would you lobby the President for me on this, Thompson?'

'It will annoy the Halgarths. They're the only Intersolar Dynasty who have any real involvement with Far Away. But if you assure me it's necessary, then of course I'll use what influence we have. Right now we're in a lot of credit with Doi.'

'Thank you.'

20

After departing Anshun, the *Conway* and her sister scoutships, the *StAsaph* and the *Langharne*, took a mere seventy-two days to reach Dyson Alpha. Commander Wilson Kime was thankful for the shortened flight time. For all her speed, the *Conway* was barely half the size of the *Second Chance*, with a corresponding shortage of crew facilities. The most obvious change was the lack of a life-support wheel. The new scout ship marque had a crew of twenty-five, whose quarters were integrated with the main fuselage. Although the *Conway*'s superstructure was still a basic cylinder, blunt at both ends, she was a lot more streamlined than her pioneering predecessor, measuring a good two hundred and fifty metres in length, and eighty in diameter. The reduction in both length and volume was mainly due to reducing the plasma rockets to three, along with all the associated cryogenic tankage. Also, given the mission profile, there was no requirement for the auxiliary craft, their hangars, and their support systems.

Kime had known CST was designing second-generation starships before the *Second Chance* departed, but even he'd been surprised by the seven-month assembly time. More impressive was the way they'd stuck to the completion deadline with all the chaos of facilities and personnel being transferred to the High Angel. He'd still not got over his anger at that particular act of stupidity. After three and a half centuries he'd assumed government had by now learned how to keep bureaucratic interference to a minimum on big projects. Of course he knew it was all down to horse trading between the Grand Families and the Intersolar Dynasties, after all he'd taken part in enough sessions and deals himself, but surely the Executive knew it had to protect a project as important as this one from petty manoeuvrings and pork barrel politics? Apparently not.

It didn't help his temper when he found out the scale of the alliance Nigel Sheldon had formed with the Farndale board, with himself as the figurehead of cooperation. So after being perfectly outmanoeuvred by committee and bumped upstairs to Commander of the new Starflight Agency, there was nothing left for him except bitching to Oscar and Anna about losing crucial people at critical times because they were needed to establish a duplicate facility at High Angel. His own involvement with the new shipyards was limited to a few administrative visits and one formal reception with the redoubtable Chairwoman Gall. They'd never liked each other. The reception hadn't changed that.

As before, he'd devoted his time and talent to pushing the construction of the scoutships. The development of High Angel and running the Starflight Agency could wait until his return. Unlike the Commonwealth Executive he realized their absolute priority was to find out what was happening at Dyson Alpha since the barrier went down. At least his new prestigious position meant he could give himself command of the scoutship reconnaissance mission.

So now he was enduring the physical and unfortunately biological discomforts of prolonged freefall once again. The scaling down of crew quarters had included the more luxurious fittings they'd enjoyed on the first flight. *Conway*'s compartments were a cluster of connected spheres wrapped round the fuselage axis, behind the sensor bay and above the power deck. Each sphere had padded walls and all the internal equipment had soft rounded plastic edges, alleviating the worst impact bruises. But just like his time back on *Ulysses* he spent hours a day on various pieces of ingenious gym equipment to prevent his heart and muscles from atrophying. Once a week he visited the doctor for his organ functions to be monitored, resulting in an assortment of biochemicals being administered to counter their decay. Then there were the meal times when he had to force himself to consume the designated mass of food when he wasn't remotely hungry; and all day long his e-butler reminded him to sip his water bottle to counter the dehydration which his body could no longer feel. To cap it all, and the undisputed chief of everyone's bitch list, were the visits to the disposal utility chamber. It wasn't just politics which hadn't made much progress over three hundred and fifty years. Taking a dump in space still involved a disturbing arrangement of straps and suction pumps. At least having a pee was relatively straightforward – that's if you were a man. The women on board had all undergone a little cellular reprofiling procedure to make suction tube use more convenient and less prone to slippage. It was a supreme test of character to ignore that during sex.

Half a light-year out from Dyson Alpha the *Conway* came to a halt, though she remained inside the wormhole. The *StAsaph* and the *Langharne* moved up beside her. CST had solved the communication problem for ships in hyperdrive by using modulated pulses of the hysradar function. Given the difficulty involved in producing a hyspulse within the wormhole generator, the process was still somewhat crude. It certainly wasn't a directional signal, they were broadcasting to anyone in range, and it couldn't carry anything like the amount of datatraffic as a microwave beam. But voice traffic was relatively easy to achieve.

Wilson drifted into the bridge compartment and secured himself in one of the acceleration couches. On either side of the couch, screens and hologram portals unfolded from their pedestals. He studied the displays and asked Anna to sweep round with the hysradar. 'Keep it to a quarter light-year radius,' he told her.

'Aye, sir,' she replied from her own couch. She was serving as his executive officer for the flight, and was very conscious of everyone knowing about their relationship. It made her a stickler for protocol and efficiency, constantly proving to the crew she'd won the position on merit alone. More than one had privately asked Wilson if he could make her ease off the tight-arse routine. From that point of view, he was rather looking forward to the flight ending himself. Freefall really wasn't everything the spaceflight romantics claimed. More than one of his bruises had been obtained inside their cabin.

The hysradar scan showed they were surrounded by clear space; there was no trace of anything under acceleration. His e-butler opened a channel to the other two scoutships, encrypting the transmission.

'Oscar, what have you got?' he asked.

'Nothing in sight,' the captain of the *StAsaph* replied. 'I guess they've stopped sending ships away from their own star. At least in this direction.'

'Looks that way. Antonia, have you got anything?'

'Not a damn thing,' Antonia Clark said from the bridge of the *Langharne*. 'It's clean out here.'

'All right, we'll proceed as agreed. Antonia, tag along with us until we're ten AUs from the old barrier location. Stay in hyperspace and gather as much information as you can. Any hostile activity directed at us or you, and you are to get straight back to the Commonwealth.'

'Understood.' During the mission planning sessions back on Anshun she had spent days arguing that her scout ship should be the one accompanying the *Conway*, but there was no trace of resentment in her voice now.

'Tu Lee, take us in,' Wilson ordered. 'Anna, sensors on passive mode, please.'

'Already switched over, sir.'

Wilson tried not to roll his eyes.

The scoutships closed on Dyson Alpha. Their mission profile was simple enough; *Conway* and *StAsaph* were to enter the inner system, scanning for any sign of wormhole activity. If they found one, they were to approach the source, drop out of hyperspace, and attempt to open communications. If there was no sign of the Dyson aliens experimenting with wormholes, they would fly to Alpha Major and try to open communications there.

They were still a quarter of a light-year out from the star when Anna said: 'We're registering quantum fluctuations consistent with wormhole activity.'

'From this far out?' Tunde Sutton queried.

'Yes. Whatever they've built, it's goddamn powerful.'

*

MorningLightMountain began working on the problem as soon as its new Bose memories had revealed the theory and practical application of wormholes. It took just a few hundred immotile units to determine and quantify the fundamental principles, assisted by the Bose memory's basic knowledge of human physics and mathematics. The equations fitted easily enough into its own understanding of quantum physics, simply extending the knowledge in a fashion it wouldn't necessarily have thought of for itself. After that, came the more challenging task of designing the hardware. Of that, the Bose memories had little information.

After a month, during which over a thousand immotile units had combined to analyse the new problem, and several advanced industrial manufacturing areas had been switched to producing components for the project, the first crude wormhole generator was up and running. MorningLightMountain used it to open a small communication linkage to its biggest settlement at the large gas-giant. There, MorningLight-

Mountain23,957, which supervised the settlement, was connected directly back into the original immotile group in real time. Over the next few weeks, a series of small wormholes was opened to MorningLightMountain's other settlements, joining more and more remote subsidiaries to the main group cluster of immotiles back on the homeworld, meshing them all together into a single gigantic grouping.

At this point, all the spaceship production facilities MorningLightMountain possessed across the star system were switched to manufacturing components for larger wormhole generators. As more and more wormholes were opened, linking planets, moonlets, and distant asteroid settlements, so the spaceships became redundant. It dismantled them and incorporated their resources into the new transport system. New power stations were deployed around the sun, vast rotating structures protected by force fields, that siphoned up the energy and transferred it (via wormhole) to the second gasgiant where the greatest wormhole of all was being constructed, the one that would reach across interstellar space.

It took the full mental capacity of twelve thousand immotile brains to govern the interstellar wormhole, there were so many components to supervise, so many intricate applications of energy to control within the machinery. MorningLightMountain amalgamated the immotile specifically to form the command group; they had no other function, and they didn't take part in MorningLightMountain's unified thought processes. Even then, with so much brain power devoted to the device's operation, it had to use more electronic processors than it ever had before to maintain the ancillary equipment.

The interstellar wormhole had been operating for three weeks when several supplementary orbiting quantum wave detectors picked up the distortion points of approaching starships. They were smaller than the previous human starship, the *Second Chance*, but they were flying from the direction of the Commonwealth. They were also a lot faster.

>**ships mission / explain**<

I don't know for certain. I expect a further attempt to establish communication. They'll certainly want to know what happened to me and Verbeke.

>**confrontation probability / extrapolate**<

They don't want a fight. The ships will be heavily shielded, though. They saw several ship battles while they were here before. They'll know what level of defence they need this time.

>**response / explain**<

Oh, well, with my great tactical expertise . . .

>**tactical knowledge / memory**<

There was none. The Bose memories were lying – no, not lying, being *sarcastic*.

>**sarcasm / explain**<

It's a human personality trait. Culturally related, you either got it or you don't. I often used it to swat uppity students. I don't think it applies to your culture, you're more likely to use a nuke.

Not for the first time, MorningLightMountain considered simply erasing the Bose memories. It often considered the alien thoughts to be a form of insanity. Despite them being securely caged within a single immotile unit, there was noticeable *leakage*. Strange ideas and concepts often occurred these days – a different way of looking at things. After all, there was, it had to concede, a certain illogicality about releasing so much pollution across its homeworld, allowing so many motiles – parts of itself – to die in sickening fashion from disease and poison. It was killing itself for the now, not planning properly for tomorrow. It wasn't sure how the notion of *sickening* had crept into its thoughts.

Such innovative thoughts might lead it into becoming alienPrime, *contaminated* from within. Though it knew its Prime rationality was still dominant, after all it was a misapplication of resources to let so many motiles waste away. So for now it tolerated the Bose memories, knowing that soon it would no longer require them.

The three human starships slowed their approach, then flew forward again. One came to a halt just beyond where the barrier used to be, remaining within the wormhole it was generating. The other two headed in for the second gas-giant, where MorningLightMountain had built the interstellar wormhole. It began to prepare nearby ships for interception.

One of the human ships emerged from its wormhole amid a burst of blue radiation. It was five million kilometres from the interstellar wormhole. Electromagnetic beams swept out, probing space around it, while its wormhole generator emitted pulses of distortion, which the Bose memories identified as hysradar. High-cohesion force fields enveloped the human ship, deflecting most of MorningLightMountain's sensor scans. They would be tough to break, it acknowledged. But not impossible.

Sixteen ships were dispatched at high acceleration to interdict the enemy. Within seconds of their fusion drives coming on, the human ship directed microwave and laser beams towards them. This time MorningLightMountain understood the binary pulses, the simple mathematical constants, pixel matrices with basic images and symbols, periodic tables. It directed a communication maser back at the human ship.

The Bose memories were marshalled to initiate contact, appropriate 'speech' sequences selected.

'Hi guys, it's Dudley Bose calling home. You took your sweet time getting back here, didn't you? But by God I am sure glad to see you.'

The human lasers switched off. A single microwave beam remained focused on the ship which had sent the message.

'Dudley? This is Commander Kime. How ... Are you all right? Jesus, Dudley, we never hoped for so much.'

The voice was distorted by what the Bose memories identified as *emotions* of incredulity and hope.

'I made it, Captain. I'm okay. And I've got a whole load of

new friends with me just waiting to meet you. Should be able to rendezvous with you in a little while.'

'Dudley, are you on the ship that's sending your signal?'

'Sure am. How about that for coincidence? I've been out here for months helping the Primes with their wormhole.'

'Dudley, that ship's under ten-gee acceleration.'

The voice had changed. MorningLightMountain's Bose memories identified it as *puzzled*.

'Yeah, God don't I know it. It's hell on my spine.'

'You can slow down,' Wilson Kime said. 'We're not going anywhere.'

'Right, sure. I'll tell the captain.'

MorningLightMountain reduced the acceleration on its interdiction squadron to three gees. It didn't want to scare the humans off – another new concept. So many since the barrier had fallen.

'Where's Emmanuelle, Dudley? Is she there with you?'

'No she's back on the homeworld DEAD RUN YOU DUMB FUCK RUN THEY KILLED US THEY'LL KILL ALL OF US IT'S INHUMAN RUN YOU MOTHERFU—'

MorningLightMountain wanted to *scream* in pure *fury* as the betraying corruption burned through its consciousness. Its mind crushed the Bose memories as they blossomed out of the immotile brain where they had been stored, pummelling them back under control. Crushing them. Eradicating them from existence.

Demented, defiant human laughter echoed around inside the giant building which housed the central immotile grouping of MorningLightMountain, the core of its existence. The memory of laughter. Mocking as it faded.

*

Wilson stared, aghast, at the speaker which just a minute earlier had delivered a joy which had brought him close to tears. The shout lingered in the deadly silence which filled the bridge.

He'd known, deep deep down inside, from the moment the Dudley voice claimed to be on a ship doing ten gees, and speaking as calmly as if they were sitting at a bar with a couple of drinks. *If it's too good to be true, it probably is.*

'The alien ships have started accelerating again,' Anna called. 'Eight gees. Nine.'

'Tu Lee, take us out of here now,' Wilson ordered. *Déjà vu* plucked at him, almost comforting in its horrifying familiarity. 'Oscar, Antonia, scatter pattern one. You heard the man: run for it.'

The screens showing visual spectrum images of space outside began to glow blue, as if they'd glided into a patch of planetary sky. Tu Lee sent the *Conway* streaking out of the Dyson system at half a light-year an hour.

'Goddamnit, what happened?' Anna said. 'What was that talking to us?'

'Whatever was left of Dudley Bose,' Wilson said grimly. *Damn, and I always thought bad of him.* 'Any sign of pursuit?'

'Nothing chasing us in hyperspace, Captain,' Tunde said. 'The *StAsaph* and *Langharne* are ahead of us, and spreading out.'

Wilson studied the displays around his couch, breathing deep to try and calm his racing heart. He watched the other two scoutships diving wide into the depths of interstellar space, making it difficult for any potential enemy to chase all of them. *A pitiful manoeuvre, really, if the aliens had built ftl starships they could send a thousand after each of us.*

'We were out of hyperspace for six and a quarter minutes,' Anna said as the bridge crew started to relax. 'Our mission time out here just keeps getting shorter, and we still have no idea what they look like.'

Wilson gave his e-butler some instructions, and it folded

back one of the display screens around his couch. He turned to look at Tunde Sutton. 'What did our sensors collect?'

'Almost nothing, Captain,' the physicist said glumly. 'We weren't there long enough to obtain any decent imagery.'

'What about that giant wormhole?'

'Ah, yes.' Tunde seemed curiously reticent to say anything. 'You know, we've never attempted to build anything on such a scale. And the amount of quantum activity we did manage to detect indicated a considerable number of wormholes have been opened within the Dyson system. All of them were significantly smaller than the one above the outer gas-giant. It confirms our previous conclusions about their industrial capabilities. A year and a half ago they didn't have one wormhole generator.'

'Just how big was that one above the gas-giant?'

Tunde began to call up hysradar records, concentrating on the outermost gas-giant with its three large moons, and superimposing what little visual imagery they'd snatched. He focused the image on the third moon, orbiting seven hundred and ninety thousand kilometres above the turbulent equatorial storm clouds. It was a rocky planetoid with half of its fractured surface covered in ice sheets averaging five kilometres thick. Hundreds of force field domes had encased nearly a quarter of the total surface area. Fusion drive ships clouded space around it, forming a bright ring two hundred and fifty kilometres above the equator. From that a sparkling river of blue-white plasma stretched across to the moon's outermost Lagrange point, fifteen thousand kilometres away. The aliens had stationed the wormhole at the centre of the gravitational null-point, where it kept its position with a minimum of thruster usage. There was no visual data, the generator structure itself was very dark, although it showed as a gleaming crimson spark in infrared. Hysradar revealed a toroid with a central aperture measuring two and a half kilometres across. Ships were flying into the centre at the rate of one every five or six every minute, large ships.

'Son of a bitch,' Wilson murmured. 'Is there any way of telling where that leads?'

'No, sir,' Tunde said. 'But judging by the strength of its quantum distortion, I'd say several hundred light-years. Where they get that much power from I don't know, there's no corresponding neutrino emissions which would indicate fusion sources.'

'Have they reached inside the Commonwealth?' Wilson asked sharply.

'It won't extend that far. Four hundred light-years, possibly, maybe five.'

Wilson wanted to feel relief. It should have been there, knowing the aliens hadn't reached home behind him. But the sensation eluded him completely. What they'd seen was too worrying. Even for a civilization this size, the giant wormhole was too obviously a crash project; an act of desperation. He was sure he knew where it would take them eventually. The why of it, though, he couldn't understand. What could they possibly want with the Commonwealth?

*

It was an astonishing landscape. Nothing you couldn't find on any H-congruous world, but scaled up twenty per cent. Higher mountains. Deeper valleys. Wider rivers. Broader plains. Even the sky seemed bigger, though that might have been due to the absence of clouds during the (long) daytime.

All of which made Ozzie worry about what kind of animals they might encounter. Rats the size of dogs? Dogs the size of horses? What might the elephants be like, or the dinosaurs?

Although they'd been here for eight days now, and hadn't seen so much as a gnat so far. The plants didn't quite match up to the scenery. They were all bland, with grass that was like a sheet of moss, and bushes that were globes with slender little leaves which were woven together so tightly that, from a distance, they looked like a single membrane. Trees had a simple conical symmetry with dark green finger-sized leaves. Botany at least wasn't adventurous here. In fact, he hadn't seen a single flower since they arrived. Maybe evolution had bypassed the whole concept of pollination. Or maybe there were no insects to pollinate.

That made Tochee the most colourful thing on the planet. The big alien had recovered quickly from its frostbite as they wandered along the paths after escaping the Ice Citadel planet. Its rubbery locomotion ridges had almost completely healed up now after weeks of sliding along through temperate grassland and loamy forest floors. Of the three planets they'd progressed through, one of the paths had been in a tropical zone. Tochee had really liked that. The little shrivelled fronds sprouting from wrinkles in its brown hide had sprouted into colourful life. They now resembled feathery ferns whose vivid pigmentation acted like a silky flowing cloak; ripples of scarlet, tangerine, turquoise and emerald swayed along its body with every motion and gust of wind.

'It looks like a furry rainbow,' Orion had said when the fronds began to grow again.

The boy was a great deal happier now as well. A lot of his former chirpy confidence had returned, strengthening with every additional step they put between themselves and the Ice Citadel.

Ozzie was half-expecting him to start asking, 'Are we there, yet?' Which, given their circumstances, was just about impossible to answer. The Silfen paths had been reasonably obvious on the worlds they'd visited so far, and the little friendship pendant had helped a couple of times when Ozzie was uncertain. But to date they'd found themselves in areas where the forests were close together, with just a couple of valleys or hills separating their boundaries.

This big world was different. They'd emerged from a tree line to see a vast undulating plain stretching away ahead of them. The forest behind filled a V-shaped valley; there was only the one path through it, leading straight out alongside the swift stream which gushed down the valley floor. So they simply carried on walking, keeping close to the stream. It was one of many tributaries feeding the river which cut across the plain.

In five days' continuous hiking they'd found plenty of similar woods hugging steep valleys. Not one of which had a Silfen path leading out. The trees did have edible fruit, globes the size of melons, with a fibrous pap that tasted similar to bland apples. That seemed to be a constant on the worlds linked by Silfen paths, nothing eatable had a strong taste.

Orion would knock the fruit down with a big stick, sometimes with Tochee holding him aloft in its tentacles so he could reach the ones dangling on higher branches. Every time Ozzie watched the laughing boy flailing away at the fruit, he would think of curries and chilli burgers.

The river was leading them towards a range of snow-capped mountains which marked the end of the plain. As they neared the foothills, the pervasive mat of grass thinned out, leaving stretches of thin sandy soil exposed to the air. Soon, only the broad ravine through which the river flowed had any greenery left. They picked their way along the boulder-strewn sides, testing carefully for boggy ground. Ozzie and Orion were both carrying heavy rucksacks, while Tochee had a pair of big old panniers slung over its back. As the ravine started to slope down so the river flow quickened, foaming around stones sticking up from its bed.

'Still wish we'd made a boat?' Orion asked cheerfully as they passed one set of boulders that were sending out great spumes.

It was something Ozzie had suggested earlier, at around the third forest they'd examined for paths. While it made sense, his diamond-tipped blade wasn't the ideal tool for cutting and trimming that many trees. In any case, they hadn't got any rope to lash even a crude raft together. At the time he'd just wanted to get off the plain. Days spent under the silent expanse of sky were bad enough. But at night, he hurried into the tent, unnerved by the emptiness around them. Some deep-buried intuition was wary of the planet.

'I've been down worse rapids than these,' Ozzie told him defensively.

After half a day trailing along the side of the ravine, it turned sharply and opened out into a massive canyon. The river surged forward and fell away down a series of steep steps, each taller than the last, ending with a waterfall that thundered over a cliff three hundred metres high. After so many days immersed in the deep silence which blanketed the empty plain, the roar from the cascading water was shocking.

'So now what?' Orion asked. He was facing the giant canyon which carried the water away beyond the falls. It seemed to slice clean through the mountain range.

'There's no way off this world behind us,' Ozzie said, thinking out loud. 'We either keep following the river, or look for some other way round the mountains.' He brought out a very tatty sheet of parchment. His last charcoal stump was down to a small nub so, finding the sharpest edge, he wrote: I think we should go on. This seems to be the path.

I agree, Tochee's forward eye segment flashed.

All throughout the long afternoon they picked their way down the side of the falls. With the rocks slick from all the spray, they moved slowly and carefully. If there were to be any kind of accident here, the chances of help were effectively zero. Travelling alone had instilled a sense of caution into them, even Orion didn't make any complaint about how long the descent was taking. Tochee took the lead; with his locomotion ridges he was easily the most agile of the three of them on the precarious gradient.

The sun had long vanished behind the canyon walls when they reached the floor. According to Ozzie's virtual vision timer they still had another two hours of full daylight left. He took his sunglasses off to squint at the bright naked rocks all around. Somewhat inevitably, the sun here was bright enough to make them wear the protective glasses all day long. The mist thrown out by the waterfall had fooled him for a moment, producing a pocket of cool humid air around the base of the falls. But even out of the direct sunlight, he was better off with the glasses on.

They walked past the deep rock pool formed by the churning impact of the waterfall, and carried on to where the river resumed its calm flow, gurgling across the sandy pebbles which made up its broad bed. He stood on the bank to take in the view. The near-vertical walls of iron-red rock on both sides were over a kilometre high and, as the canyon curved gently around to the east in front of him, it looked as though they were growing progressively taller. At the widest, the canyon floor stretched about eight kilometres wide. Nothing grew within the canyon, no grass or scrub. The floor was shingle and sand, all the same sandstone red as the walls. He could see huge great conic mounds of jagged rock piled up all along the base of each cliff, where giant sections had broken off far above to crash down into pulverized scree.

One of Tochee's manipulator flesh arms poked up, a very human gesture it'd developed to attract their attention. When Ozzie turned to check the alien, mauve patterns were flickering in its forward eye segment. **Something at the first curve. Possibly a tree.**

Ozzie ordered his retinal implants to zoom in. The air was shimmering from the heat of the rocks and the air, but some dark smudge was visible beside the river just as it turned out of sight. Could be, he wrote.

They started off along the canyon, and almost immediately came across the ancient fire. It was a simple circle of stones, their inner sides blackened. The ash had blown away long ago, leaving just darkened sand inside.

'Look!' Orion cried and ran off. He stopped a few yards past the fire circle and picked something out of the sand. His smile was victorious as he held up his trophy.

'Son of a bitch,' Ozzie grunted. The boy had found a coke can. Its colouring had bleached badly over the years, but the familiar logo was easily visible.

'Are we on Earth?' the boy asked excitedly.

'Sorry, man, no way.'

'This must be somewhere in the Commonwealth, though. We even had coke on Silvergalde.'

Ozzie scratched at his large fuzzy beard. 'I think it's just litter. You know what people are like, the biggest hooligans in the universe. But hey! It proves we're on the right path.' He didn't want to crush the boy's fragile hope.

Orion gave the can a vexed look, and chucked it back onto the sand.

An hour later they stopped and set up camp for the night. Ozzie and Orion pitched their tent on a small rise several hundreds yards from the river, then set about washing socks and shirts before the last of the light vanished. Ozzie would have loved to dive right in and give himself a decent clean, but even though they still hadn't seen a single living creature on this world, he just couldn't quite bring himself to trust the water. Too many late student nights with a pizza, a couple of six-packs, some grass and a bad sci-fi DVD. God only knew what lurked along the bottom of the river, maybe nothing, but he certainly wasn't going to wind up with alien eggs hatching out of his ass thank you. All of a sudden, the long evenings spent lazing around in the Ice Citadel's hot pools didn't seem so bad after all.

They were making their way back up to the tent when Orion stopped and said, 'There's a light.'

Ozzie looked down the canyon where the boy was pointing. A tiny golden spark was shining a long way downstream. He wasn't even sure it was on their side of the river. His retinal insert zoom function couldn't get a clear image, no matter how high the magnification, it remained a flickering blur. When he switched to infrared, it barely registered. Not a fire, then.

'Probably someone else walking the path,' he said with a reassurance he didn't feel.

Tochee had seen the light as well, though the alien's eye was unable to focus on it either. They kept watching it as they ate their evening meal of tasteless fruit and cold water, but it wasn't moving. Ozzie and Tochee took turns through the night to make sure it didn't come any closer. It was Ozzie who got the midnight to morning shift. He sat on a flattish rock beside the tent, dressed in his cords and check shirt, with his sleeping bag wrapped round his shoulders like a blanket. The river murmured away quietly, and occasionally he heard a low rattling wheeze from Tochee which he classed as alien snoring; other than that there was only the deep silence he would always associate with this world.

A brilliant multitude of stars shone down through the cloudless, moonless sky. He'd never seen so many before, not even when he went worldwalking on new Commonwealth worlds before they were contaminated by civilization's light pollution. There was one hazy nebula, four or five time larger than Earth's moon, which kept drawing his attention. It bent sharply at one end, with a reddish spike protruding away from the main haze. He couldn't remember any astronomical phenomenon remotely like that being close to the Commonwealth. The Devil's Tail, he named it. Shame nobody would ever know.

In the wilderness hours just before dawn he heard voices. He sat up immediately, unsure if he'd been drifting off to sleep. They could have been the start of some dream. But they weren't human voices, or at least not ones speaking any language he recognized.

The spark of light hadn't moved. He switched his inserts to infrared and slowly scanned round, turning a complete circle.

The voices came again. Definitely not a dream. They swept past him, causing him to turn so fast he almost lost his balance. Several of them babbling together. A non-human language. They sounded urgent. Frightened.

But it was only the sound. Nothing moved in the canyon. Nothing physical.

He almost asked; 'Who's there?' Except that really was the stuff of late-night horror DVDs. Dumb.

Whispers slithered past him, somebody – something – whimpering into the distance. Ozzie dropped the sleeping bag and held his arms out, concentrating on his hands, trying to feel air being stirred, the tiniest hint of movement. He closed his eyes, knowing that a visual sense was no longer any use to him. Listening, stroking the air. The sound came again, conjuring up the old phrase *voices on the wind*. He heard what was said, and repeated it back to them softly. It made no difference. They carried on past him, paying no attention.

That was how Orion found him as the first wave of a pale dawn lifted over the canyon wall: standing motionless with arms outstretched like some religious statue, mumbling words in an alien tongue. The boy clambered out of the tent, rubbing sleep from his eyes as he yawned. 'What are you doing?'

Ozzie sighed and let his arms down with a suspiciously yoga-like sweeping motion. He gave Orion an inscrutable grin. 'Talking to the ghosts.'

Orion's head whipped round, trying to find . . . anything. 'Are you all right? Did you hit your head or something?'

'Not since that bar on Lothian, and that was years ago. This world is haunted.'

'Oh come on, Ozzie, that's not funny. Not here. This whole planet is creepy.'

'I know, man. I'm sorry. But I did hear something, like a bunch of people or aliens.'

'The Silfen?'

'No, I know their language. I don't know what these guys were saying, but you get a feel from the tone. They were sad, or frightened. Maybe both.'

'Hey, quit it! I don't like this.'

'Yeah. I know. I think that's the point, man.'

'The point of what?'

'Whatever I experienced.' He frowned. 'What did I experience? Accepted there's no such thing as ghosts, so . . . some kind of projection? Bit childish just to spook travellers. I mean, why not go the whole hog and put a white sheet over your head and jump out on them from behind a rock?'

'You said the Silfen did have an afterlife,' Orion said quietly.

Ozzie gave him a thoughtful look. 'You really do pay attention, don't you?'

'Sometimes.' The boy shrugged as he smirked.

'Okay then, let's think about this. None of our electronics are working, so the ghosts can't be any kind of normal projection, holograms, sound focus, that kind of crap. The Silfen are active here, which implies it must be happening with their knowledge or consent.'

'Unless it's them doing it,' Orion said, suddenly excited. 'There's nothing alive here. We haven't seen any animals or insects. Maybe this is their afterworld, where all the Silfen ghosts live.'

Ozzie grimaced, and looked round the stark, massive canyon. 'Somehow I think not. I'd expect something a little more impressive. But I could be wrong.' He finished up by looking along the canyon. 'Yo, can't see the light anymore, either.'

Tochee slithered up between them, raising a limb of manipulator flesh. **What's happening?** the patterns in its eye asked.

'This should test our vocabulary,' Ozzie muttered.

*

By mid-morning, they could see the black pillars ahead were indeed trees. Even by this world's standards they were giants, perfect thin cones reaching over a hundred and fifty metres into the air. They had been planted in a double row, a kilometre to the side of the river, forming an impressive avenue down the canyon.

'Somebody does live here, then,' Orion said as they drew near to the start of the avenue.

'Looks that way.' Ozzie tilted his head back to see the top of the first trees. 'You know, either they're made out of a wood harder than steel, or there's hardly any wind here, ever.'

'Is that important?'

'I dunno, dude. But it's definitely a spike on the bizarro graph.'

Orion giggled. 'This whole place is a spike.'

'I'm not arguing.'

An hour later, when the canyon walls straightened out, allowing them to see ahead for miles, they made out a group of figures walking along the avenue ahead of them. Seven people, a long way in front, moving at a steady pace.

Bipeds like you, Tochee's patterns declared. **They made the light last night.**

Could have done, Ozzie wrote.

They move slower than us. We can catch them today if we increase speed.

Ozzie had been thinking the same thing. Of course if he really wanted to attract their attention there were several flares left in his backpack, though he didn't want to use them for

850

anything less than a genuine emergency. And the group in front would have to be looking round at the right moment. He was slightly surprised they hadn't seen them already, especially given the way Tochee's fabulous technicolour coating clashed against the drab ironstone.

Speeding up will be hard on us. We will reach them eventually.

Agreed.

In the afternoon, when they'd been walking down the empty avenue for several hours, they came to the first ruin. A small stream wriggled across the canyon, it ran from the base of the cliff wall down to the river, crossing through the avenue at right angles. At some time long ago, a simple curved stone bridge had carried the path over it. Now all that was left were the solid foundations on either side, sticking up from the dusty ground like a set of broken teeth.

There were gentle grooves in the stonework, resembling the trails snakes left in sand. Ozzie couldn't tell if they were natural wind-erosions or ancient carvings. Thinking about the trees again, he suspected carvings. How long it would take for them to wear away like this he had no idea. Centuries, at least.

'I wish my arrays were working,' he sighed. 'They could carbon-date this right down to the afternoon it was built.'

'Really?'

'Pretty close, yeah.' It was always slightly unnerving how little Orion knew about technology. He had to be careful what he said, especially jokingly, which wasn't an Ozzie trait. But the boy tended to take everything he said as gospel.

They splashed through the little stream, and carried on walking. Ozzie resisted the urge to carve his name into the bridge. He was mildly surprised no one else had, especially the guys who'd left the coke can.

By the time they made camp they'd passed another ruined bridge, as well as a big circular depression in the ground whose edges were made from tight-fitting stone blocks. Neither archaeological remnant provided any clue as to what kind of creatures had built them. A bridge was a pretty basic design for any species, as were sturdy foundations, which is what Ozzie suspected the circle to be.

Through the day, they'd managed to close the distance on the group of travellers in front of them to about a mile. Once they got the tent up, the gold light became visible in the gathering darkness.

'That's just about where they are,' Orion said. 'You should fire a flare, Ozzie. There's no way they can't see it now.'

Ozzie gazed at the steady point of light. 'They know we're here. If they don't want to talk to us, there's no sense in trying to force them.'

Orion nodded cheerfully, and cut into one of the big fruits. 'I get that about people now. You can't rush somebody who doesn't want to be rushed, right?'

'You're learning.'

'So I let the girl set the pace.'

'Yes, that's right.'

'And she'll always find a way to tell me when she's ready to go to bed? You're sure about that?'

'Uh, yeah.' Ozzie was beginning to dread evenings round the camp fire. The boy did have an amazingly one-track mind. 'But, look, man, it's going to be subtle. You've got to be alert and in tune.'

'Like how do you mean?'

'Okay, if she's happy for the date to go on as long as you want, that's a good sign.'

'I thought you said don't try to get her to bed on the first date?'

'Yes, yes, that's right. But this is the second date, or later.'

'Okay. So it goes on all night. Do I ask them home, or will they ask me?'

'I don't know, man. It depends on the girl, okay. Use your judgement.'

'But, Ozzie, I haven't got any, that's why I ask you.'

'Want another chat-up line?' He'd found that was always a good way to make Orion stop, although the cost to his own dignity was always painfully high.

'Yeah!'

'All right. But you've got to have a ton of self-confidence for this one, okay, show no fear. Is it me or do you always look this good?'

'Maybe,' Orion said dubiously. 'But you'd have to have a good follow-on line.'

'Hey, I'm just showing you how to open the door, once you're in the room you're on your own.'

The voices returned in the deep of night. This time they were slightly louder, occurring more frequently.

Orion woke with a start as one set passed right beside the tent. Ozzie was already sitting up in his sleeping bag, listening to what was spoken and the way it was said.

'It is ghosts, isn't it?' Orion said solemnly.

'Kinda looks that way, yeah. You scared, man?'

'Ozzie! It's ghosts!'

'Right. Well I'm scared, just in case you wanted to know.' He wriggled out of his sleeping bag and unzipped the tent. The night air was alive with sound, hundreds of voices that swirled chaotically around their little camp. He walked out into their midst, turning – into daylight. His feet were standing on a lush carpet of blue-green grass which covered the canyon floor, along with trees and thick bushes. The avenue of trees had been replaced by a road built from stone cobbles. Strange five-legged bovine animals pulled wooden carts along it, piled high with barrels and some local version of hay. The drivers were aliens that looked like pear-shaped jellyfish, with hundreds of slender tendrils emerging from their lower half, serving as both legs and arms. Individually weak, the wax-white tendrils would twine together to produce a stronger limb for whatever use was required. Dozens of them were sliding along the road, the tips of their tendrils twisting and scrabbling like impaled worms to move them forward. They called to each other in low gurgling voices.

One of the carts was heading straight for Ozzie. He waved his arms frantically. 'Hey, watch what . . .' The driver obviously couldn't see him, or the tent, or Orion standing at his side. He grabbed a frozen Orion and hauled him aside, falling off the side of the road – into night time.

'Fuck me!' Ozzie grunted. He raised his head and looked around. Nothing had changed. Stars glittered in the night sky, casting a faint illumination. The avenue of trees stood impassively along the side of the quiet river, marking the course of the old road.

'Wow!' Orion gushed. 'Cool.'

'Uh?'

Starlight showed the boy's wide smile. 'Don't you get it? This canyon is a time machine, like the Silfen paths are wormholes. How smooth is that?'

'That was just an image, man,' Ozzie said, somewhat stiffly as he clambered back to his feet, brushing sand off his shorts. 'It's showing us what used to be here.'

'I *smelt* them, Ozzie, it was like vinegar. That was real, not an image. We were there in the past. Anyway, you thought we were there, why else did you dive for cover?'

'I was surprised, that's all, and I didn't know what level the image extended to. People have gotten themselves hurt in TSI, you know, man.'

'You were scared.' Orion flung his arms wide, laughing wildly at the canyon wall. 'Hey, you scared Ozzie. Bad time machine.'

'This is not—' Ozzie got a grip, although he'd noticed the smell, too. He looked along the avenue, checking on the golden light from the other group. It was still there, unmoving. The ghost voices had come back, slipping sinuously through the air. 'Damn, this place is weird.'

'Ozzie!' Orion gasped.

One of the jellyfish aliens was slipping past them, wrapped in its own little nimbus of daylight. Tochee pushed its icewhale fur blanket aside, rearing up on its locomotion ridges in shock as the seemingly solid apparition glided along.

What was that?

Tochee's eye patterns were shining so brightly Ozzie half-expected Orion to see them. He shrugged – they certainly didn't have anything like the vocabulary for time-travelling spooks. When he glanced round, the lone jelly alien had gone.

'I think we'd better get off the avenue. It's only a few hours to dawn. We should try and get some rest.'

'Oh, Ozzie, this is wonderful. We might wind up finishing this journey before we started. I could go back to Silvergalde and stop my parents from ever leaving.'

'Look, man, I know you think a time machine is a groovy thing, but take it from me there are quantum fundamentals that prevent it from happening. Okay? I know what this looks like, but it isn't real.'

Orion was about to answer when a small mechanical car appeared, with two jelly aliens sitting in the cab. Smoke and steam belched furiously from stumpy chimneys in its rear. The boy drew in a sharp breath and swayed backwards. 'I think maybe you're right. We'll get run over here.'

Ozzie was sorely tempted to just stand there and let one of the apparitions glide right through him. But they looked so damn real!

The three of them gathered up their packs and hurried away from the avenue. As soon as they were outside the line of trees the voices faded away, although they never fell completely quiet. Ozzie and Orion sat against a boulder, wrapping their sleeping bags round them. Every now and then opalescent light would burst out of the avenue, silhouetting the bottom of the trees as the long-dead aliens walked their old road. After a while Ozzie stopped trying to figure it out, and closed his eyes.

*

'I've got a theory,' Orion said eagerly as they munched on their tasteless breakfast. 'I think Sara walked down this canyon. That's why she's still alive after so long. The canyon brought her into the future.'

'It's not a time machine,' Ozzie said for what must have been the tenth time. 'Time cannot flow backwards, you cannot move back through time. It is a one-way current. Period, dude.'

'She moved forward.'

'Okay, not so difficult. Even we can do that.'

'Can we?' Orion was fascinated.

'Well ... in theory, yeah. The internal structure of a wormhole can be modified so its timeframe is desynchronized. In other words, you go in at one end, and a week later you come out of the other. But, for you, only a second has elapsed. I'm pretty sure that's what's been happening on the Silfen paths. It certainly makes sense, especially when you think of people like Sara.'

'Have you done it with your wormholes?'

'No. It's very complicated. We don't have the technology to match the math yet.' He grunted in disapproval. 'Maybe we will by the time you and I make it back.'

That morning they walked parallel to the avenue of trees, keeping a good three hundred metres distant. They kept noticing movement on the path. It was almost subliminal. Shadows that flickered between the trunks, vanishing when any attention was focused on them. The apparitions certainly weren't as vivid during the day.

A couple of hours after they started, they realized they were finally catching up with the other travellers. The group had remained in the avenue. They now looked as if they were walking into a strong wind, leaning forwards to push on doggedly, their cloaks streaming out behind them.

'They're Silfen,' Orion said. 'I'm sure they are.'

Ozzie zoomed in. The boy was right. 'Another spike,' he muttered.

'Are we going to talk to them?'

'I dunno.' Ozzie was torn. They hadn't seen any sentient creature since leaving the Ice Citadel world. On the other hand, the Silfen never made a lot of sense at the best of times. 'Let's see where they're at when we catch up with them.'

As they hiked on, a big gap slowly became visible in the avenue up ahead. They could see the trees carry on the other side, but for over a couple of miles the canyon floor was empty. 'I can't see any fallen trees,' Ozzie said as he scanned the ground. 'Looks like the people who planted them wanted a break.'

'Is there anything built there?' Orion asked.

'Can't see any ruins.'

They were catching up quite quickly on the Silfen group now. Ozzie estimated they should be level with them just before the gap in the avenue. The dark spectral shadows still flitted along the path, accompanied by the occasional mournful gabble. He was fairly sure it was the same language he'd heard the jelly aliens use when he'd been inside the projection.

When they were only a few hundred metres behind the Silfen, Tochee raised a tentacle. **That is not natural,** its patterns claimed. The tentacle was now pointing directly at the canyon wall in the long gap.

Ozzie studied the rock, trying to see what Tochee was looking at. Some of the vertical crevices did look a bit too regular ... He shifted his sense of scale, and gasped with astonishment; the edifice was so large he hadn't recognized it for what it was.

Millennia ago, the cliff had been carved with the profiles of the jelly aliens. There were two of them, a mile apart; each one must have measured nearly half a mile high. Entropy had slowly gnawed away at them, rock falls and slippage pulling away huge segments, distorting the outline. The piles of scree along the cliff base below them were exceptionally tall. But even after nature's vandalism, the shapes were still distinct enough for him to identify. Between them was a palace that used to stretch nearly the entire height of the cliff. He assumed it was a palace, though it could easily have been a vertical city or temple, possibly even a fortress. The architecture was vaguely reminiscent of Bavarian castles he'd seen built to crest rugged Alpine peaks, although in this case one built by termites. It was almost as though the curving turrets and half-moon balconies had grown out of the rock, not that there were many of them left, and none were complete. Overall, there was even less of it remaining than the giant statues which guarded it on either side. Flying buttresses protruded from the sheer surface, curving upwards to end in jagged spikes as whatever structure they once supported had snapped off to plummet onto the vast foothills of rubble strewn along the base. Stairways and pathways zigzagged all over the exposed surface. Hundreds of rooms were visible as small cavities where their front halves were missing. Thousands of open black caves showed where passages tunnelled back into the rock linking interior rooms and halls.

'What happened here?' Orion asked. His voice verged on the reverential.

Ozzie shook his head, for once humbled by the scale of the tragedy. It was profoundly disturbing that a species obviously so capable and intelligent could allow their civilization to fail in such a fashion.

'I think we should ask the Silfen.'

As soon as they started to angle back towards the avenue they discovered why the Silfen were making such hard going.

It wasn't the wind which pushed against them – the memories of the old road were growing stronger. All the past travellers who'd used the ancient highway were retracing their journey, each of them using the canyon at the same time. They lacked the solidity which the apparitions of last night had possessed, but they more than made up for that by the sheer weight of numbers.

At first Ozzie merely flinched as the phantoms flew towards him sporadically, bracing himself as they hit, only to find they'd passed straight through him without any resistance. Some of the aliens, the majority, were simple walkers. Others drove their rickety carts, or rode animals. A few were in mechanical contraptions.

The density of the spectral travellers increased proportionally as they drew nearer to the avenue. With them came their noise, the cries of hundreds of aliens talking and shouting at once. And their numbers finally added up to a little gust of pressure. Ozzie put his head down as he headed into them. He felt something touch his wrist, and jumped in shock. When he looked down he saw Tochee's tentacle of manipulator flesh coiling round his hand. The alien was also taking hold of Orion's wrist. Linked together, the three of them pushed in further towards the Silfen.

Inside the line of trees the bygone aliens merged together into a single blurred slipstream of colour. Their voices became a single unending howl. It really was a gale pushing against them now. Ozzie leaned into it, thankful for Tochee's steadying grip. His shirt and sweater were flapping wildly against him. He set his face with grim determination and forced his feet to move onwards.

The Silfen were easy enough to see, a knot of darkness amid the torrent of colour and light and noise pouring through the avenue. As they forced their way closer he realized that the Silfen were all old. Their long hair was thin and grey; deep creases lined their flat faces, etching dignity into their features. He'd never seen signs of ageing among them before – of course, he'd never seen Silfen children either, assuming there were such things. But age had given them a distinction which humans normally lacked as their years advanced. And even now as they pushed themselves against the road's history their long limbs never faltered.

'Greetings,' Ozzie called in the Silfen language.

One of the Silfen turned. Her wide dark eyes regarded him with the curiosity of a grandmother who'd forgotten the name of her favourite grandchild.

'It's me, Ozzie. Remember me?'

'Never can we not remember, dearest Ozzie, least of all amid this place of remembrance. Joyful that we are to find you here where you sought to be.'

'Sorry, but I never wanted to be here.'

Her gay laughter seemed to calm the whooping of the ghosts. 'Demanding you were that all wonders should be shown and known in places far from home. How fast your mind skips and changes with your fickle mood, a delight and a sorrow burn behind your eyes with the beauty of twin stars forever dancing round their perfect circle.'

'Are these wonders to you? I think they are times long gone.'

'Hearken to the knowing, Ozzie, as you tread paths through lost worlds. Full with understanding you shall become to the delight of your stubborn self. Wonder begets not only the joy but the sorrow. Both must be for the other to live, for ultimately they are twined into the one. Here you come where few have been, so deep is your need, so loud is your song. Still we love you though you are not ready to fall into the one circle of light and air where the song will be sung to the end be it bitter or be it sweet.'

'This? This is the answer to the Dyson barrier? Tell me of the imprisoned stars. I would so much like to learn.'

'So you will as you walk down this valley of death to the shadows that linger and mourn.'

'You've gotta be kidding,' he muttered in English. 'You're quoting the Bible at me?'

The Silfen woman's long tongue shivered in the centre of her mouth.

'Is this where I looked to be? Is this inside the prison around the stars? Do your paths reach through walls of darkness?'

'Cast aside your numbers and your coarse voice and learn how to sing, sweet Ozzie. Song is the destiny of all who live who love to live.'

'I don't understand,' he groaned through clenched teeth. 'I don't know if this is the answer. What is this fucking place?' He gave the Silfen a look of anguish, and switched back to their language. 'Why are you here in this dead valley? Why do you endure this?'

'Here we come to complete our song, small and frail we are, and searching for our place amid that which is to come. Long our journey has been, bright has been the light shining upon us, loud the songs we have had sung to us, hard and soft has been the land upon which our feet have trod. Soon we shall walk no more.'

'This is it? This is the end of the Silfen path? Will your feet end their walking in this valley?'

'Ozzie!' Orion called. 'Ozzie, the ghosts are going.'

Ozzie looked round. They'd reached the last two trees, and the pressure was fading rapidly. The ghosts were fading away, allowing the full rays of the sun to sweep down across the broken rock of the valley floor. As he looked round in bewilderment their warbling voices dwindled to nothing. He was left stumbling forward, bracing himself against nothing. Stretching above him for the full height of the canyon wall was the ancient crumbling alien palace city.

'The path we walk and love goes round and round, and thus it can never end, Ozzie,' the Silfen woman said. She sounded profoundly sad, as if she was telling him about death. 'It begins when you begin. It ends as you end.'

'And in between? What then? Is that when we sing?'

'Walking the path you hear many songs. Songs to treasure. Songs to fear. Come, Ozzie, come listen to the broken song of this world. Here lies the melody you desire to walk further amid the tangles of mystery that is all of us.'

The Silfen had joined hands. Now the tall woman held out her hand to him. Orion was giving him a nervous look. Tochee's eye patterns asked: **What now?**

'Tell our friend I don't know,' Ozzie told Orion. 'But I'm going to find out.'

'Ozzie?'

'It'll be fine.' He put his hand out to the Silfen woman. Her skin was warm and dry as her four fingers bent supply around his hand. In an obscure way he found that comforting.

Together they started walking towards the vertical ruins. At the foot of the huge pile of shattered stone was a featureless black globe. It was as high as a Silfen was tall. Ozzie wasn't sure if it actually rested on the ruddy sand or floated just above it.

'Now you will know this planet's song,' she said as they approached the sphere. 'All it used to sing comes from within its last memory.'

Ozzie almost hesitated. Then he saw the planet floating at the centre of the sphere. He peered forward like an eager child.

It wasn't the image of the planet, it was a ghost just like the aliens who haunted the roadway along the canyon. Long ago it had floated blissfully in space, known to the Silfen who walked their paths through its bucolic forests. Its inhabitants, the jelly-like aliens, built themselves a peaceful civilization, advancing their knowledge as did most species. They had even

862

begun to explore their solar system, sending crude ships to land on planets and moons.

Which was when the imperial colonizers arrived. Vast starships plunged into the star system on fusion flames, curving into orbit around this quiet happy world. They had taken decades to cross interstellar space, and were hungry for their prize, a new world on which to re-establish their old empire.

The war of conquest was as short as it was futile. The planetary inhabitants resisted as best they could, modifying their instrument-carrying rockets to assault the huge invaders above their beautiful planet. Some damage was inflicted on the big ships, which goaded the imperialists into fierce retaliation.

In the forests and glades below, the Silfen hurried down their paths to regain the peace and freedom denied to those whose home this was. But even the elfin folk whose life was one of happiness and fey interest in the worlds they passed through were troubled by the horrific violence erupting around them. In penance, they watched.

Ozzie was shown the dark armoured starships sending their missiles and kinetic projectiles hurtling down onto the planet below. Explosions ripped through the sleeping clouds, distorting the world's air. Waves of destruction rolled out. Solid ground rippled like water. Oceans rose in rage. Towns and cities were blasted apart. Aliens died in their tens of thousands in the first few seconds. Ozzie knew them. He felt their death. Their grief. Their fear. Their loss. Their sorrow. Their regret as their homes disintegrated. Their bitterness as their children were torn apart before them. Every one of them was there for him to identify and experience. And the deaths multiplied as the empire's weapons cast this world into smoking, radioactive oblivion before the starships departed in search of new worlds, worlds easier to subdue.

Ozzie fell back from the globe, curling up into a foetal ball as the tears flooded down his cheeks to stain the dead world's dry sandy soil.

He wept for hours as the terrible anguish of countless deaths soaked through him. He hated it as he had hated nothing in his life before. Hated what was done. Hated the blind stupidity of the imperialists. Hated the Silfen for standing by and doing nothing. Hated the waste of so much life, so much promise. Hated knowing what a better universe it could have been if only the quiet simple aliens whose world this once was had survived and finally met the gaudy flawed human race as the Commonwealth expanded. Hated that such a meeting of unalike minds would never happen.

Late in the afternoon, when his tears had long since dried up, he stopped his pitiful whimpering lament, and rolled onto his back, blinking up at the cloudless sky. Orion and Tochee gazed down anxiously at him.

'Ozzie,' Orion pleaded, his own face close to tears. 'Please don't cry any more.'

'It's hard not to,' he croaked. 'I was here. I was with every one of them when they died.' He started to tremble again.

'Ozzie! Ozzie, please!'

He felt Orion's hand grasp his own, in desperate need of reassurance. A boy lost light-years from home, abandoned by his parents, on an adventure that had become a nightmare for too many months. The frail human touch was what he needed not to fall into that black infinity of horror. *And how much of an irony was that? The superindependent Ozzie needing someone?*

'Okay,' Ozzie said weakly, and gripped the boy's hand roughly. 'Okay, give me a moment here, dude, yeah.' He tried to sit up, only to find his body barely responding. Tochee's manipulator flesh slid under him, helping to shift him upright. He looked round at the canyon, almost fearful of what he would see. 'Where are the Silfen?'

'I don't know,' Orion said. 'They left ages ago.'

'Huh. Finally got something right. I'd kill the bastards if they'd stayed.'

'Ozzie, what happened? What did you see?'

He put a hand up to his forehead, surprised at how hot the skin was, as if he'd come down with a fever. 'I saw what happened to this world. Some aliens arrived in starships and . . . and nuked it to shit.'

Orion gazed round uncertainly. 'Here?'

'Yeah. But a long time ago, I guess.' He looked at the ruined palace city, feeling a fresh wave of sadness.

'Why did they show that to you?'

'I don't know, man, I really don't. They thought it was what I wanted, for my song. Song, hell!' A dismissive grunt escaped from his mouth. 'I'd say we've got some serious translation problems here. Reckon I'm gonna sue someone in the cultural department when we get home for like a trillion dollars. I'm never going to recover from this.' Ozzie stopped, knowing just how true that was. 'But then, I guess that's the whole point. It's a memory that belongs to the Silfen. They're the ones who watched it all. And they did nothing.' He scooped up some of the sandy soil, then let it trickle away through his fingers, mesmerized by the drifting grains. 'This is for them, it's their grief, not mine, not the people whose world this used to be. It's about them. Nobody else knows or cares, not any more.'

'So what do we do now?'

Ozzie eyed the black globe wearily. 'Leave. There's nothing here for us.'

21

Even now, after all these years, Elaine Doi still got a thrill ascending to the rostrum. From the floor of the Senate Hall it looked imposing, a broad raised stage at the front of the seats, with a big curving desk made from centuries-old oak where the First Minister sat directing debates. In reality, when you came up the stairs at the back, the lights shining down from the Hall's domed roof were so bright you had trouble seeing the last step. The purple carpet was worn and threadbare. The grand desk was despoiled with holes drilled in to accommodate modern arrays, portals, and i-spots.

In the past there had been countless occasions during working sessions when she had to come up here to make a policy statement or read a treasury report. The massed ranks of senators had heckled her mercilessly, their cries of 'shame' and 'resign' echoing round the Hall, while the reporters in their gallery to the right of the rostrum had grinned like wolves as they recorded her dismay and feeble rejoinders and fluffed lines. Despite all that, she'd been the one they ultimately paid attention to, the one controlling the debate, pushing through her legislation, doing the deals that made government work, not to mention scoring political points off her opponents.

Today, of course, the seven hundred senators in attendance fell into a respectful silence and stood in greeting that was tradition whenever the President got up to address them. They would have shown that much consideration if it had just been her monthly statement of review, but this time she could feel the genuine trepidation running through the Hall. Today they were looking to her to provide leadership.

Her ceremonial escort of royal beefeaters saluted sharply and moved away to stand guard at the back of the rostrum. She always thought their splendid scarlet uniforms added a real touch of class to these moments. Although they were technically assigned to the Presidency as a courtesy from King William during the foundation of the Commonwealth, the Executive security office had long since taken over their funding and organization.

'Senators and people of the Commonwealth, please be silent for your Honourable President Elaine Doi who wishes to address you on this day,' the First Minister announced. He bowed to Elaine and returned to stand behind his desk.

'Senators, fellow citizens,' she said. 'I thank you for your time. As I am sure you are aware from media reports, our Starflight Agency ships, the *Conway*, the *StAsaph* and the *Langharne*, have now returned from Dyson Alpha. What their investigations discovered there was unpleasantly close to our worst-case scenarios. Commander Wilson Kime has now confirmed that the Dyson aliens, the Primes as they appear to be called, are indeed hostile in nature. Even more worrying, he discovered that these Primes have turned their considerable industrial prowess to the construction of large wormholes that can reach immense distances across this peaceful galaxy.

'This day we thank and pay tribute to him and his crews for the dangerous flight they undertook on our behalf. To learn what they did under such perilous conditions was a show of tremendous courage, which should give the Primes considerable pause for thought when they come to consider our resolve. However, we should never forget that they received help from a most unexpected source.

'After enduring horrors which we cannot begin to imagine, Dr Dudley Bose sacrificed whatever was left of himself to warn us of the Primes' true intent. Expressing the debt of gratitude which every human alive today owes to this great man, and his shipmate Emmanuelle Verbeke, goes beyond words. I am informed that their re-life procedure goes well, and we can only give thanks to whatever gods we believe in that they will soon rejoin our society so we may embrace them with the welcome they so richly deserve.

'In the meantime there is much to be done if we are to safeguard this wonderful Commonwealth of ours. My fellow citizens, after centuries of peaceful expansion, we now live in a time when our civilization faces the possibility of a uniquely hostile encounter. If this should happen we cannot rely on others, our friends the Silfen, nor the High Angel, to come to our aid. Humanity must do what we always do in times of darkness, and meet the challenge with the courage and resolution we have shown again and again throughout history are our birthright.

'To that end, I have today signed Executive decree one thousand and eighty-one, which transfers a new responsibility to the Starflight Agency, that of physically defending the planets and stars which make up the Commonwealth by whatever means necessary. It will henceforth be known as the Commonwealth Navy. Into this great venture we pour our trust and hopes for the future. I have the faith that those men and women who serve will bring about a swift and resounding conclusion to the threat which is rising out among the distant stars. No task they face will be more difficult, nor so rewarding. To that end, I have the honour of promoting Wilson Kime to the post of admiral, and appointing him to lead our new navy. It is a heavy burden, and one which I am sure he will carry with the fortitude and leadership qualities which he has already demonstrated so ably.

'To the Primes, however, I say this: whatever your aspirations for malevolence, however much you covet our beautiful worlds, you will not prevail. We, all of us poor flawed humans, have a heart that has been tested in the heat and pain of battle; we know we have the will, we know we have the right, and we know we have the determination to throw down any force for evil and tyranny. To that end I pledge myself and my Presidency.'

She bowed to the senators, and stepped sharply off the rostrum, her beefeaters falling in behind to follow her down the stairs. The applause and cheering which chased after her was awesome, both in its unanimity and enthusiasm.

Patricia Kantil was waiting at the bottom of the stairs, clapping passionately, a huge smile on her face. 'Perfect,' she said, falling in beside Doi as they left the Hall. 'You pitched it just right. Confident without any smugness, and what you said made people feel secure.'

Doi flashed a worried smile. 'Glad they are.'

As soon as they were through the door, the beefeaters handed over to security agents dressed in ordinary suits. Staff members and aides took up their usual position, following their chief down the broad corridor like a small comet's tail. All of them looked indecently cheerful, still applauding her speech. After eleven months of what she herself charitably described as a lacklustre term, her Presidency had finally taken focus out there on the rostrum.

By the time they got back up to her offices on the Senate Hall's third floor the good news was arriving thick and fast. Messages of congratulation and approval were flooding in off the unisphere. Aides returned to their own desks to handle them.

'Nice speech, thank you,' Doi said to David Kerte as she passed his desk. The young man looked up and smiled his gratitude. Until the election he'd been Patricia's principal assistant, now he was turning into one of their staff team's best speechwriters.

'My pleasure, ma'am. I cribbed some of Kennedy's moon-speech for you, I thought the parallel was appropriate.'

'It was.' Doi walked on into the glass lounge. It was a bubble sticking out from the side of the Senate Hall, completely transparent from within, glossy black to anyone outside trying to look in, and protected by force fields should any sniper want to test their ability. She flopped down in one of the broad sofas, and let out a long breath of relief.

'You want something?' Patricia asked, walking over to an antique teak cocktail cabinet.

'Want, yes. Having, no. Give me a fruit juice. It's going to be a long day.'

Patricia opened the door, and took a can of orange and triffenberry from the shelf. The web of thin silver lines around her eyes was pulsing as her virtual vision clogged up with polling data. There were certain indicators she could always rely on, which she scanned with her usual efficiency. 'The Hill-Collins unisphere poll gives you a seventy-two per cent personal approval rating,' she said as the results streamed in. The can frosted over as she pulled the tab. 'Fifty-three per cent are still worried about the Primes – that's down four from yesterday. Eighty-eight approve of you forming the navy. Stock market is up; analysts are predicting a sharp increase in government spending to build the navy, which is correct. The finance sector is jittery about taxes to pay for it all. On balance, it's favourable. Second term's in the bag.'

'Not a chance,' Elaine said, taking the can from Patricia. 'There's a long way to go. And what happens if the Primes do invade?'

Patricia snorted. 'Give me a break. I've been researching this. Populations flock to support their leadership in times of war. Historical fact. It's after the war you've got to worry about. Churchill, Bush, Dolven, they all got dumped right after their victories.'

'I was always nervous about backing the Starflight Agency

so publicly even if it was the price of getting Sheldon's support. But by God it paid off today.' She drank some of the juice.

'Don't bring God into this,' Patricia said quickly. 'Too many voters are atheists these days.'

The President gave her a disapproving look. 'You were always in favour of the Agency and its progression. Do you think there's going to be a war?'

'I was in favour of the Agency for the options it gave us.'

'Do you think there's going to be a war?'

'Honestly? I don't know, Elaine. I can handle the Senate and the media for you. But this . . . It's way out of my field. All I know is that finding that the Primes are building a giant wormhole has frightened the bejesus out of half our tactical analysts. Did you see Leopoldovich's report? There's no logical reason for them to build something on that kind of scale; therefore their motives are unknown. That's not good news, because all we know about them is what Bose told us. We have to assume the worst. Whoever put that barrier up, it's starting to look like they had good reason.'

Elaine Doi let herself relax into the deep cushioning. 'That never made sense right from the start. Every expert we have claims the effort which went into building the barrier was colossal; yet it gets switched off the minute we go sniffing round.'

'I told you, if you're asking me, you're asking the wrong person. Nobody has come up with a reason. All we've got is a bunch of half-assed theories and crank conspiracies like Johansson's. Even the SI is at a loss, or claims it is.'

'Claims?'

'You know I never trust it.'

'You're a xenophobe.'

Patricia shrugged. 'Somebody has to be.'

'All right,' Elaine said. 'We don't know why, but we do know we're in a possible war situation—'

'That's another word I'd like you not to use, please. War

has too much historical baggage attached. Conflict, or the Prime situation, is preferable.'

'You're developing a nasty habit yourself, there. People like some natural traits.'

'Traits I can manage, prohibited words I can't.'

Elaine ran a hand through her hair, a gesture she always reverted to when she was irritated – as Patricia always pointed out. 'All right, I'll mind my language.'

'Thank you.'

'There's something that Leopoldovich and everyone else seems to be avoiding.'

'What's that?'

'The High Angel. I know siting Base One there was part of the Agency start-up deal, but if there is a possibility of conflict, is it going to hang around?'

'Actually, someone on Leopoldovich's team did analyse that, it's in one of the appendices. It has always assured us it will give notice before it leaves, so transferring Base One construction personnel to Kerensk won't be a problem. They can still get to the assembly platforms through the wormhole. Using High Angel as a dormitory was a political move to bring Chairwoman Gall on side, and through her the African Caucus. Physically, it's non-essential. There's also a proposal from Columbia's staff on using it as our species' lifeboat.'

'What?'

Patricia shrugged. 'Basically, if it looks like we're losing, we put as much of our culture and genetic template on board as possible, as well as a few million living humans, and ask the High Angel to take the survivors to a less hostile part of the universe. We're pretty sure it has a trans-galactic flight capability.'

'My God, you're serious.'

'Columbia's Security Agency office was, yes. The President would be classed as an essential component of the emergency evacuation. You'd be going.'

'No I goddamn wouldn't; and I want you *personally* to make very certain that this lunatic idea is never leaked to the media. They'd crucify us if they knew we were planning to escape.'

'Very well, I'll see to it.'

Elaine let out a long breath. 'You really do read all the appendices, don't you?'

'That's what I'm here for.'

'Okay, then. What's next?'

'Meeting with Thompson Burnelli and Crispin Goldreich. You've got to thrash out the navy's first budgetary presentation for the Senate. Did you see the request from Kime?'

'Yes. I thought fantasy had gone out of style; five more scoutships, twenty new ships with full attack capability, a Commonwealth-wide wormhole detection system, bringing that Natasha Kersey's Directorate up to full active status, incorporating a dozen more government science departments. We're looking at a percentage point increase on tax. I can just see how the planetary governments will respond to that.'

'It might have had Kime's name on it, but the request was drafted by the Sheldons and Halgarths. They're already working on steering it through the Senate. With the Inter-solar Dynasties and the Grand Families cooperating, it'll sail through. The level of fallout dropping on you will be minimal.'

'I suppose so. Is the meeting here?'

'Yes. But we're due home for lunch.'

'Good.' Elaine looked out through the lounge's clear curving wall at Washington's old Capitol building. The Commonwealth Senate Hall had been built here, and paid for out of UFN taxes by Commissioners keen to keep Earth at the centre of Commonwealth politics; but the Presidential Palace was on New Rio, as a gesture to the new worlds, along with a host of directorates and departments that were spread out among phase one space in accordance with the Commonwealth policy of inclusion. She always felt more secure in the New Rio Palace, like any animal on its home territory.

As she looked out at the rain sweeping across the old city her virtual vision was displaying a simple star map. New Rio was on the other side of Earth from the Dyson Pair, over a thousand light-years away from the Primes. That also was a comfort.

*

Hoshe parked out on Fairfax, and walked a block back down Achaia. It was midday, and the heat had just about cleared every other pedestrian off the sidewalk. Hoshe took his jacket off as he walked, dabbing at the perspiration on his brow. Achaia was one of those narrow streets in the city grid which looked like it ran on for ever, with the cracked concrete's heat shimmer obscuring the far end as it slipped into the commercial district. The housing on both sides was mainly three-storey apartment blocks, fronted by small yards that were filled with overgrown ornamental bushes and trees that had nearly reached roof level. Air conditioning units hummed constantly above all the narrow balconies where their fins radiated away the excess heat. Cars came and went in front of him, turning out of ramps which led down to underground garages.

When he reached the first alleyway, he stopped and scanned round. High fences guarded both sides, with flowering shrubs and creepers tumbling over them in colourful shaggy mats. Beneath his feet, enzyme-bonded concrete gave way to a hard-packed surface of stone chippings and dirt. Several dogs barked as he passed gates. He even heard the distinctive metallic gabbling of a catrak and hoped to heaven it was securely chained.

He was about a hundred metres along the alley when he came to the back yard of 3573. A low double gate opened onto a short section of concrete which led to a big double garage made from prefab stonesteel sections that were bolted together. A wooden bungalow stood behind it, its windows dark and closed, yellow paint peeling from the planks. Vines with droopy sapphire flowers had engulfed every pillar that supported the overhanging roof. The strands were wrapped so densely they looked like thick elongated bushes.

Hoshe went through the gate. One of the garage doors was open. Someone was moving round inside.

'Hello?'

A young man jumped at the sound, and hurried to the door. 'Man, who the fuck are you, man?' he blurted. His black jeans had been washed again and again until they were a pale grey. Above them he wore a purple T-shirt that was equally over-used. He had gold-framed sunglasses perched on his nose, their rose-pink lenses displaying moving graphs and columns of text – Hoshe hadn't seen anything like them since early in his first life, when they'd briefly been in fashion. But they did complete the geek image. It was hard to imagine him as anything other than a software writer.

'I'm Hoshe, I'm looking for Kareem.'

'Never heard of him, man. Now, I'm kinda busy.'

'Giscard sent me. Giscard Lex. He told me Kareem lived here. I've gotta see him, it's urgent.' He took a thick fold of Oaktier dollar bills from his pocket. 'Really urgent.'

The young man licked his lips, eyeing the money greedily. Paula had been right about that, there was always a weak link. It hadn't even taken Hoshe much effort to find it. A simple search had been run against every registered partner in the Shansorel Partnership; and when none of them had proved to have a criminal record, cross referencing had produced old friends and colleagues who had. Namely Giscard Lex, who'd been Kareem's classmate at college, where his academic career had been cut short by illegal experimentation in narcoware. A couple of weeks' casual observation confirmed that the two still saw each other.

Hoshe dropped by on Giscard Lex one evening, where he

was offered everything from dimension-shifting sensory morphware to a couple of girls who'd be sweet on him. At which point Hoshe returned the favour by offering to introduce him to the precinct desk sergeant. Giscard Lex was almost relieved that all he had to do was provide an introduction to Kareem.

'Okay, man,' Kareem said. He looked back out down the alley and little OCtattoo lines turned emerald on his ears as he checked for anyone lurking. 'Come inside.'

The garage was filled with crates. A bench running along the back was lined with tools that were being cleaned: they were very old-fashioned ones. Hoshe couldn't see a single power tool among them. He picked up a screwdriver and gave it a close examination while Kareem activated the garage door. The plyplastic closed up with a quiet slurping sound. 'Are you an antiques collector? I didn't even know they still made manual screwdrivers.'

'No, man.' Kareem gave a shifty grin. 'This is my survival gear. Ain't no electricity where I'm going.'

'Where's that, exactly?'

'Silvergalde, man. I'm gonna live with the elves, me and my girl. They'll protect their own planet from the Primes. This fucking government won't, we haven't even got a force field to cover Darklake City.'

'Right.' People like Kareem were getting wider coverage in the media recently. It was hyped as the Exodus by excitable reporters, though the actual numbers were so small governments didn't even register them – no more than a few thousand from each planet, and most of them were first-lifers. But together there were enough for CST to have to triple the number of trains running to Silvergalde. 'What about the navy?'

'Ha! What, like both ships? Fat lot of fucking use they're gonna be when Hell's Gateway blows open above Earth, and ten thousand flying saucers carry the demons down to massacre us. They don't call the giant wormhole that for no reason, you know. Johansson's Guardians are right, we're in deep shit, and our corrupt politicians don't help.'

Coincidence, Hoshe told himself sternly, though it was an unsettling one. 'Okay, so are you leaving tonight, or can you help me out?'

Kareem waved a hand at the crates. 'I haven't got everything yet. There's a lot of medicine and shit I need. Books, too. The paper ones are hard to get hold of these days, and expensive. Did you know Ozzie's got a library of all human knowledge printed out and stashed away somewhere on his own planet? That's one guy who's ready for the apocalypse.'

'So you can help, then?'

'Depends what you want, man.'

'Giscard told me you're the man to come to for software fixes.'

'Yeah. Maybe. I know some moves. Place I work at, we got us some private teams for solving private problems, you catch?'

'Caught. I'm paying too much tax.'

'Ho, brother, we all do.'

'I own a company that imports spare parts for the auto trade, and the government is killing me for it. I'm just trying to earn a living, feed my family, but those bastards . . .'

'Yeah, right!'

'What I need is a fix that covers over some of my trading. If I could just shift ten or fifteen per cent of my stock without them penalizing me for it I can keep afloat. What I need is some safe encryption that can resist the Revenue Department's audit engines so I can run the money through offworld accounts.'

'Sure, I can do that. Hell, I don't even need to bring the guys in. What accountancy software are you using?'

Hoshe held up a memory crystal disk. 'System and network is all in here.'

'Excellent. A man who is prepared, I respect that.' Kareem took the memory crystal and smiled. 'That'll be a grand for a full fix, payable in advance.'

'Two hundred now.' Hoshe slapped the notes into his hand on top of the crystal. 'The rest when the installed fix is running.'

'Okay, man, I'm cool with that.' The notes were shoved into the back pocket of his jeans. 'Must be my lucky week. This is the second private contract I've had.'

'Oh really?'

*

To the Commonwealth's general public, it was as if their new navy appeared by magic. One day President Doi announced its formation, and within a week it had become physical reality. Ships were already being put together over at High Angel, and planetary security teams started assembling wormhole detectors on the worlds closest to the Prime threat. Things were safely under control. Even Alessandra Baron was moderately complimentary on her show, though possible tax raises received a detailed analysis.

Admiral Kime was surprised by how smoothly the transition went. Of course, it helped that the personnel and equipment from Anshun had all been transferred to High Angel while he was flying the scouting mission to the Dyson Pair. That left him free to concentrate his staff on the huge expansion of capacity and capability which turning the Agency into the navy entailed. In fact, precisely the kind of large-scale managerial role which had taken up ninety per cent of his adult life.

Navy Base One was primarily a cluster of freeflying starship assembly platforms holding station thirty to forty kilometres away from the High Angel in their own little archipelago. They'd kept the basic malmetal globe design used above Anshun; although these didn't have a wormhole connection.

A fleet of new cargo shuttles swarmed between them and the vastly expanded and upgraded wormhole station linked to Kerensk, ferrying out the components that would form the next generation of starships. Passenger commuters carried the freefall workforce between the assembly platforms and High Angel, where they'd taken over a considerable portion of the freshly grown Babuyan Atoll dome. The dome's young buildings were also where Kime had set up his office along with the major part of the navy's administration, design teams, crew-training facilities and research bureaus. At the centre of the parkland campus was a thirty-storey tower that had five concave-curving sides surrounded by a DNA helix of skyway rails – dubbed Pentagon II by Alessandra Baron, a name which was catching on rapidly among the media shows and reporters.

Wilson's office was on the top floor. He didn't like it. While he was away on the scout mission, the designer had gone for a retro-modern image: slick flowcurving furniture of white tragwood from Niska, monochrome illumination floors and walls. It was like working in an operating theatre. The one redeeming feature was the view it gave him out over the compact ecology of his new domain. Only a third of Babuyan Atoll had any urban structures, the rest was burgeoning parkland, with saplings and young bushes pushing up eagerly through the lush grass. Between the paths and lakes were flat patches resembling pearl-textured concrete, which would one day grow into buildings. He enjoyed the panorama, not least for the nightly sight of Icalanise and its fast-moving bands of tawny cloud as it drifted high above the dome's crystal. It was surprising just how much the last few years had rekindled his old first-life wanderlust. Every time he looked out and saw the exotic gas-giant he was less sure he could ever go back to his old job at Farndale.

Anna was first in to the conference meeting which was scheduled to draw up the navy's rules of engagement, but then she had the shortest distance to travel. With her promotion to lieutenant commander, and her position as his chief staff officer, she had the office next door, where she organized his days and acted as a filter against everyone who wanted his personal attention directed to their own particular project or cause. She came in with Oscar; Wilson heard them laugh together as they came through the door.

'Kantil's commuter shuttle docked a few minutes ago,' Anna told him. 'She'll be up here soon.'

'Right.' He cancelled the data filling his virtual vision. She smiled warmly at him, which he returned. Her engagement ring shone brightly as she waved her hand teasingly at him. He'd proposed as the *Conway* docked. She'd said yes. Oscar said about time. They still hadn't set a date for the actual ceremony, a classic case of work pressure, although they had taken a lavish apartment together in a block near the edge of the dome.

Rafael Columbia arrived, dressed immaculately in his black uniform. He quickly asked if they'd set a date yet. 'My own engagement record was fifteen years,' he said. 'I'm sure you can beat that if you set your minds to it.'

Wilson gave him a martyred smile. The lack of a firm date was turning into a standing joke around Base One.

Columbia had become vice admiral when President Doi formed the navy, taking over responsibility for the planetary defence operation, making him Wilson's second in command. He'd sited his division's office on Kerensk, and was rapidly assimilating the various Commonwealth directorates and agencies which now formed the basis of his expanding empire. Given the more political nature of pressuring planetary governments into installing or upgrading force fields around their major population centres, it was a task he was eminently suited to. The only real argument to date between him and Wilson had been about who had direct control over Natasha Kersley's Seattle project.

Columbia had argued for it to be incorporated within his

planetary security division, and the project sited on Kerensk. Wilson eventually overruled him, pointing out Kersley's systems would ultimately be carried by starships, and should therefore be part of Base One's operations. A quick call to Sheldon had secured Executive support, and confirmed the decision. Columbia hadn't challenged him again.

Daniel Alster was shown into the office with Dimitri Leopoldovich.

Wilson was mildly surprised. He'd expected Alster to share the commuter shuttle with Patricia Kantil. Both of them were representing the oversight committee during the meeting, while Leopoldovich was an academician specializing in tactical analysis at the StPetersburg Institute for Strategic Studies. It was a field with few practitioners, used mainly as an advisory and research service by the Commonwealth when secessionist and national autonomy movements started to use physical force against their legitimate planetary government. During his time on Farndale's board, Wilson had often heard senior politicians and their staff disparagingly refer to tactical analysts as war games nerds with a history degree. But then astronomy was a minority profession before this, he thought in amusement.

Dimitri had undergone his third rejuvenation a few years back, leaving him with a mid-twenties body whose lank blond hair had already begun to thin out. His skin was pale, verging on albino white, which combined with a diet of fast food and total lack of exercise gave him the appearance of a podgy vampire. He nodded at Wilson and took his usual seat, which left him facing away from the broad window.

'How was Bose?' Anna asked Daniel Alster.

'Re-life always freaks me out,' Daniel confessed. 'Those accelerated growth clones just don't look human.'

'But his personality is intact?' Wilson pressed.

'Oh yeah. The download from his secure store was completely successful. The last thing he remembers is making a short update on the *Second Chance* before going over to the Watchtower.'

'And Emmanuelle?'

'The same. Though she's a lot calmer than Bose.'

'How do you mean?'

'I only met Bose once before, he seemed quite edgy then. That trait has become . . . amplified a little. The doctors said the information he's received subsequent to re-life hasn't helped.'

'You mean the warning we were given on the scout mission?'

'Yes, partly. It's unfortunate that we don't know exactly what did give you that warning. Re-lifers often worry that their earlier self is alive somewhere. In this case, the prospect is throwing up some unique schizophrenic problems.'

'The warning specifically said the Primes killed them.'

'I know. But Bose is obsessed by what actually transmitted that warning at you. He suspects his original self is still alive back there, in some form or other, which is reasonable enough. It hasn't helped that his wife has told him she's divorcing him, either. The psychologist says that's he's interpreted that as a rejection of his new self, which reinforced his focus on his old self.'

Wilson and Anna exchanged a look. 'We always wind up feeling guilty about him, don't we?' she said.

'Yeah,' he said uncomfortably. 'So what else did the docs say about him?'

'The clinic will discharge him in a couple of months. Physically, he'll be in top shape by then. Mentally, well they say that every re-life case takes another life to get over the trauma. Bose is no exception. Dose him up on anti-depressants and let him get on with it.'

'Did he say what he wanted to do afterwards?'

'No. He's receiving a lot of offers from media companies, not just for his life story as a biogdrama, they want him as a commentator on the Prime "situation". I expect his university will welcome him back. We can drop a hint to that effect, a strong hint. He can't do much harm back on Gralmond.'

'So he doesn't want to join the navy, then?'

Daniel grinned. 'No. You're perfectly safe this time around.'

Oscar laughed at the relieved expression on Wilson's face.

Patricia Kantil walked into the office. 'Thank you for waiting,' she said with ever-professional courtesy.

'You're not late,' Daniel said. 'Just to finish off on Bose, there will be some kind of ceremony when he and Verbeke leave the clinic. Patricia, that came from your office?'

'It did. Given their profile, especially Bose, we thought some official welcome back to Commonwealth society would be appropriate for them. They're the nearest things we have to heroes right now. The Vice President will be there, and it would be nice for some of their shipmates to participate as well.'

Wilson almost groaned out loud. 'All right,' he said. 'We'll send someone on the day. Now, if we can get started.'

'My report's simple enough,' Oscar said. 'We haven't had any contact with the scoutships yet.'

'When was the first due to report back?' Daniel asked.

'The *StAsaph* should be back at Anshun within another ten days, assuming they didn't find anything.'

'And if they did?'

'They're searching fifteen star systems three hundred light-years from the edge of phase three space, basically their course is a big curve to take them within hysradar range of each star. If the Primes have opened their giant wormhole to any of those systems she'll be able to detect it. But given the nature of the flightpath, the journey back will be a long one. As they're not back yet, we know that they didn't find anything at the first eleven stars.'

'Or they did, and the Primes caught them,' Rafael said. He shrugged into the silence. 'Just being realistic.'

'The remaining six scoutships we've got out there should be returning over the following two months,' Oscar continued. 'Between them, they'll have covered over a hundred star systems. Admittedly, that's not many considering the distances involved and the number of stars between us and Dyson Alpha. But if the Primes are coming this way, then one of those stars will be used as a staging post. We need to find it; at the very least that will enable us to start building realistic tactical scenarios.'

'Are these scouting patrols going to be constant?' Patrica asked.

'Yes,' Wilson confirmed. 'We need to establish some early warning if the Primes are moving in our direction. It's a three-stage approach. Rafael is overseeing our short-range detector network which will find any wormhole opening inside the Commonwealth. The fleet will be running scout ship flights past the stars within one hundred light-years in the direction of Dyson Alpha on a continual basis; if the Primes appear at any of them we'll know about it within three days maximum. Outside that, we'll fly regular patrols to more distant stars, but the revisit times will be months apart rather than days.'

'When does this come into effect?'

'We've already begun siting the first elements for the border network detectors,' Rafael said. 'If they come at us directly, we'll know about it. Our estimates for completing the full Commonwealth-wide network are anything up to a further eighteen months.'

'I see. Admiral, what about the scout flights?'

'It depends on ship numbers, of course. Once this preliminary operation we're running now is finished, I'm going to pull back those scoutships to begin patrols of the closer stars. We've got two more scoutships undergoing flight trials, and the remaining five of batch three will come off their assembly platforms over the next four months. That'll give me fifteen, which is enough to provide the near-border patrols. The distant patrols will require another ten scoutships, though I'd prefer fifteen to twenty.'

'They cost three billion Earth dollars each,' Patricia said tersely.

'I'm aware of that; and their operating and maintenance costs as well. The Executive knew the budget would have to increase almost exponentially for the first three to five years of the navy's existence.'

'I'll take those preliminary figures back with me. What about the warships?'

'The first batch of three is due to finish assembly in four months. After that, we'll be building one every three weeks. How many we ultimately need depends on the nature of the Prime threat.'

Everybody turned to Dimitri Leopoldovich. Since the return of the *Second Chance* he'd been consulted by the Commonwealth Executive and the Senate on an increasingly regular basis. The experience gave him a degree of confidence facing down high-powered questioners in a way that wasn't evident in his appearance. 'Just about the only thing we know for certain about the Primes is that they cannot be assigned human motivations,' he said in mildly accented English. 'Even with such a huge civilization contained within a single solar system, a vast amount of their resources had to be diverted to construct the giant wormhole which my team have named Hell's Gateway.' His lips twitched, as if expecting censure. 'We do not fully understand why it was built on such a scale. One of the most obvious possibilities is that it was built without any reference to economics because it is a species survival route. The Primes fear the return of the surrounding barrier, and are trying to spread their seed across the galaxy. Arkships will travel through it, carrying breeding stock and enough machinery to support a colony. If they switch the other end of the wormhole to a new star system every week, or even every day, they will have dispersed themselves in such a fashion that will make it very difficult for the barrier builders to imprison them again. In effect, a fast-forward version of our own Commonwealth.'

'Wait,' Patricia said. 'You're claiming they're not even a threat to us?'

'Not at all, my team is simply providing you with theoretical possibilities. A second option is that they know the location of the barrier builders, and have crossed interstellar space to confront them and finally wage the war which the barrier was put up to prevent. A third option is that they built it to reach the Commonwealth. This is the only option which concerns us. We have to emphasize here that we cannot assign a satisfactory motivation to this, but we are hampered by the human perspective. As the Silfen and the High Angel have demonstrated, our logic and behaviour-patterns are not universal. And the very existence of Hell's Gateway demonstrates how true that is. Therefore, for the purposes of this meeting, it doesn't matter why they are coming here, only that they are. Those are the terms on which we must consider their actions. They have now had two opportunities to begin peaceful contact procedures with us, and have chosen not to do so on both occasions. Following this, it is my team's conclusion that if the Hell's Gateway was constructed to allow the Primes access to the Commonwealth it is for hostile purposes. We recommend that if the Primes open a wormhole either close to or within the Commonwealth the navy should respond with maximum force.'

'Won't that be tantamount to us declaring war on them?' Patricia said. 'I'm not sure the Executive, or even the Senate, would approve those rules of engagement.'

'To use an old analogy: you are playing croquet while they are kick boxing. If the Primes did succeed in extracting information from Bose and Verbeke, as the evidence we have so far indicates, then they know everything about us. They will know that our attempts to contact them were peaceful. They know how to reciprocate by opening channels of communication to us in a non-hostile, non-threatening manner. That they have not sought to at least investigate the state of the galaxy around them after a thousand years of isolation is extremely suggestive. In tactical terms, they are manoeuvring themselves into a position of considerable advantage.'

'But why come all this way?' Oscar asked. 'If all they want is material resources, then there are hundreds of star systems close to their own that they could spread out to and exploit.'

'The number of unknown factors we're dealing with means we really do have to concentrate on the few facts we have, rather than engage in perpetual speculation,' Dimitri Leopoldovich said somewhat reprovingly. 'We still don't know why the Dyson barriers were put up, nor by whom. We don't know why one was switched off. Break it down to basics, my friends: all we know is that they're demonstrably hostile, they have tens of thousands of warships, and they're building wormholes that can reach us. We have to reset our civilized way of thinking to default mode: shoot them before they shoot us. In this instance, we have no alternative other than to prepare for the worst-case scenario. I'd rather spend a trillion dollars on the navy and live to regret the waste of tax money, than not spend it and find out we really needed to. Remember Pearl Harbor.'

Wilson watched with silent enjoyment as Patricia forced herself not to comment on Leopoldovich's trillion-dollar navy. 'I'm not sure the parallel strictly applies,' he said. 'But I do understand where you're coming from.'

'We will have one strategic advantage,' Dimitri Leopoldovich said. His rigid smile of emphasis made him look even more vampirish. 'Precisely one. It must be exploited no matter what the cost to ourselves, for it will be our only chance of survival. The Primes are at the end of a very long, singular supply line. Without it, there can be no hostilities. That is why my team makes the urgent recommendation that the Prime wormhole is attacked the instant they open it in Commonwealth space. Attacked and destroyed. I cannot emphasize this strategy strongly enough. There will be no rules of engagement once they start coming through. We have studied the records from the *Conway*; they were sending dozens of ships through Hell's Gateway every hour, and that was months ago. While here you talk of building one warship every three weeks, and the first one isn't even finished yet. If we devoted our entire industrial output to shipbuilding, it would take decades to reach the number which the Primes can deploy against us right now.'

'Is that combat scenario possible?' Patricia asked. 'Can we fire something back through their wormhole which will destroy the generator mechanism at the other end?'

'A crowbar or even a slingshot can knock out a wormhole generator if you know which critical components to smash,' Wilson said. 'The key is getting close enough to inflict the relevant damage. You can be sure the opening at this end will be defended by squadrons of ships, and the strongest force fields they can throw up. We would have to break through them to reach the station at the other end. At the moment, the kind of systems which can do that are not part of the armaments we're fitting to the warships.'

'Then they must be designed and installed,' Dimitri Leopoldovich said forcefully. 'Immediately.'

Patricia and Daniel looked at each other. Daniel inclined his head minutely.

'Very well,' Patricia said. 'If that's your team's official recommendation, Academician. Admiral, would your staff look into the proposal, please, and cost it out for the steering committee to review.'

'Certainly,' Wilson said.

*

In summer, Paula actually quite enjoyed sitting out on Paris's pavement cafés. The coffee in the deeply nationalistic city was still bitter and natural, avoiding a great many UFN processing regulations, while the pastries accompanying them contained way too many calories. The sun and the people made a refreshing change from the sanitized office environment. But for this call she went inside a little bistro a few hundred metres away from the office, and took a private booth. She'd been using the same place for fifty years; the waitress showed her to the booth at the back without even asking. Paula ordered a hot chocolate, and one of the pastries with almonds and cherries.

Her e-butler said the call was coming through. She put a small hand-held array on the table, and waited for its screen to unfurl. It wasn't that she couldn't take this call in the office, she just felt it was more appropriate to take it in her own time. Thompson Burnelli's face appeared on the thin plastic, from the blurred gold and white background she thought he was in his Senate Hall office.

'Paula,' he gave her a relaxed smile. 'No uniform?'

Anyone else would have earned a crippling stare for that dig, the senator merely got a raised eyebrow. 'It must be in the wash,' she said. The formation of a Commonwealth navy had caught Paula by surprise; she wasn't prepared for the brand-new Planetary Security Agency to be switched to naval funding and change once again. But like it or not, she was now in naval intelligence with the rank of commander. The day after the changes had been announced to the Paris office, Tarlo had saluted her as he came in to work. Nobody would be doing that again. Nobody in the Paris office wore uniforms, either, although they were technically entitled to. Office rumour said that several members of staff changed into them before going out for a night clubbing in town, testing the ancient theory that every girl loves a sailor.

Uniforms were the least of her worries. To start with, Mel

Rees had told them the whole office would be moving to Kerensk, where Vice Admiral Columbia was establishing his administration. That led to a showdown between her and Rees where calls were fired off to political allies with the speed of Prime missile salvos. Mel Rees desperately wanted the move to the navy's planetary defence headquarters where his chances for promotion inside the new navy were considerable; Paula threatened to resign if any kind of relocation or team alteration went ahead.

Rafael Columbia solved the problem with his usual political deftness. Paula was appointed commander of the Johansson project, which would remain in Paris for strategic reasons. Mel Rees was also promoted, and would run a new unit on Kerensk dealing with the deployment of the wormhole detector network. She was rather pleased to find that her contacts outweighed his family connections.

'Sorry it's taken so long to get back to you on this,' Thompson said. 'Life in the Senate hasn't been this exciting for ... well, I don't ever remember a session like this one before. Kime's second flight really stirred things up. I never really thought we'd have to form a navy, and I was heavily involved in the early preparation work.'

'Did you know the old Serious Crimes Directorate would end up as navy intelligence?'

'No, Paula, I didn't realize quite how ambitious Rafael was going to be. I heard about your fight with Rees. I'm glad they managed to work out a compromise that allowed you to stay on. Hell, we only just managed to hang on to Senate Security. Can you believe Columbia wanted that as well?'

'It can't last, Thompson. We still need some kind of Intersolar department to track down criminals. Apart from Johansson, there is nothing for navy intelligence to do. My former colleagues are still working on their old cases. They just wear uniforms to do it.'

Thompson smiled sadly. 'Not quite. There is a small

amount of opposition to the navy taking shape. Disaffected hotheads for now, but they need to be monitored, those that don't go and join the Exodus.'

'Local police can handle that.'

'I'm not going to argue with you, Paula. I'm calling because I have news.'

'I'm sorry, go ahead.'

'Okay, first, there is no secret security department run by the Executive. That's a definite. I did consult my father. Whoever it was that made the hit at Venice Beach, they weren't authorized by the President or Senate Security.'

'Thank you. What about Boongate and the Far Away cargo?'

'Ah.' Thompson shifted round uncomfortably. 'This is where it gets interesting. I spoke to Patricia Kantil about that myself, pointed out that we really needed to inspect everything going to Far Away. She said she agreed, and she'd put in on Doi's agenda. Since then all I've had is memos about how the proposal is under active consideration. Even before your suspicions I would have been curious about that. Something this trivial should be easy for me to arrange; normally I'd just tell an aide to sort it out. The fact that I can't swing it is very suggestive.'

Paula felt a cold shiver run down her chest, despite the warmth of the chocolate she'd been sipping. The decades she'd spent filing requests for this very action with every new boss in the Directorate, to see them come to nothing every time. All of them must ultimately have been blocked by the Executive office. 'Who is opposing you? Surely not Doi herself?'

'No. This is Newton's law of politics, for every action ... Somebody will be lobbying the Executive office to allow the cargo to go through unchecked.'

'Who?'

'I don't know. It's the arena of whispers and spin we're dealing with here. At this level of the game, your opponents don't reveal themselves, that's part of the game. But, Paula, I'll find out. You've got me worried about this, and that's not easy.'

*

Warm summer sunlight poured through the circular windows above Mark Vernon's head, diffusing evenly across the hemispherical study. The illumination was brighter than he'd envisaged when he and Liz had sat down to plan their new home together. Not that he didn't want his study properly lit, it was just that he'd always had an image of a slightly darker room, maybe a little cluttered with his personal stuff; the kind of room a man could happily use to retreat from his family on occasion. But with its airiness and pearl-white drycoral walls, he never felt happy allowing any mess to build up. So his desk was clear, and his stuff was all neatly organized in big alvawood cabinets. Given that Barry and Sandy had free run through the rest of the house, it made the study the tidiest place inside.

He stood just inside the frosted glass door, and looked round in confusion. The short coat he knew was in there, wasn't.

'Dad! Come on!' Sandy shouted in the main hall behind him.

'It's not here,' he called, hoping Liz would take pity on him.

'It's your coat,' Liz called back at him from the hall.

He gave the study another perplexed glare. Then Panda, the family's young white Labrador, came in pulling his favourite woollen coat along with her. Her tail wagged happily as she stared up at him.

'Good girl,' he started to approach her. 'Drop it. Drop it, girl.'

Panda's tail wagged even faster in anticipation of the game; she started to turn.

'No!' Mark shouted. 'Stay!'

Panda bounded out into the hall, pulling the coat with her. Mark ran after her. 'Come back! Stay! Drop it!' He tried to think of the other commands they'd gone through together at obedience classes. 'Heel!'

Over by the front door, Liz was pulling Sandy's windcheater on over her head. Both of them turned to watch.

'Stay! Stop that. Come here!' Mark had got halfway across the hall when Barry emerged from the kitchen and said, 'Here, girl.' He patted his knees. Panda scampered over to him, and dropped the coat at his feet. 'Good girl.' Barry made a fuss of her, letting her lick his face and hands.

Mark picked up the coat with as much dignity as he could muster. There was a big soggy patch on its shoulder from the dog's jaw. They'd got Panda nearly a year ago when they'd finally moved into the drycoral house. A family dog. She only ever did what Barry told her. 'That's because she's still a puppy,' Mark had been claiming for the last three months. 'She'll grow out of it.' To which Liz simply replied, 'Yes, dear.'

Although he'd never owned a dog before, Mark had always enjoyed the idea of them having one; envisaging long rambles along the Ulon Valley with their pet trotting beside them. Such an animal would be loyal, obedient, and loving, an excellent companion for the children. And anyway, most of the homes in the Ulon Valley had dogs. It was part of the whole Randtown ideal.

The owner of the pet shop on Main Mall had assured the Vernon family that white Labradors had all the breed's natural friendliness, but with a higher intelligence sequenced into their DNA along with the snow-white coat. Mark thought that had sounded perfect. Then Sandy had spotted the fluffy white puppy with its black-circled eyes, and the choice had been made before Liz and Barry got a say.

Mark draped the coat over his arm. 'Everyone ready?'

'Are we taking Panda?' Barry asked.

'Yes.'

'You're in charge of her,' Liz said sternly. 'She's not to be let off the lead.'

Barry grinned, and hauled the dog along out of the front door. Liz checked that Sandy's windcheater was on properly, and ushered the girl out after her brother.

'Barry has got coursework, you know,' Liz said. 'And the nursery is short-staffed enough without me taking afternoons off.'

'If you want him to get on with the work, then he doesn't have to come,' Mark said. 'But you know I have to do this.'

She sighed and looked round the hall with what could have been a nostalgic expression. 'Yes, I know.'

'We're protecting our way of life, Liz. We have to show the navy they can't push people around like this.'

Liz gave him a fond smile, a finger stroking down the line of his cheek. 'I never realized I married someone with so many principles.'

'Sorry.'

'Don't be. I think it's admirable.'

'So should we take the kids?' he asked, suddenly uncertain. 'I mean, these are our views, and we're forcing them to take part. I keep thinking about children who are vegetarians or religious, just because that's what their parents are. I always hate that.'

'This is different, darling. Going on a blockade protest is not a lifelong vogue for them. Besides, they'll love it, you know you will.'

'Yeah.' He tried not to grin, and failed miserably. 'I know.'

The Ables pick-up was parked next to Liz's small Toyota 4x4 on the patch of compacted limestone where the old temporary house used to stand. Although the building was long gone, Mark had never quite got round to programming the bots to clear the stone away.

The kids were already in the back seat, arguing. Panda was barking happily as she tried to clamber up with them.

'Straps on,' Liz said as she got in the front.

Mark led the dog firmly round to the back, and shoved her into the covered cab before climbing up into the driver's seat. 'All ready?'

'Yeah!' the kids chorused.

'Let's go.'

They drove out along the Ulon Valley into Highmarsh, then turned onto the highway, heading north, away from Randtown. After a few miles the valleys began to narrow, and the four-lane highway was climbing up the side of the mountains where it ran along a broad ridge cut into the rock. Twenty miles out of town they passed through the first tunnel. There was no traffic at all coming the other way. When the road straightened out, Mark could occasionally see a vehicle of some kind up ahead of them.

It was early summer, so the multitude of streams running down the side of the mountains hadn't dried up yet, though the flow was noticeably reduced from the spring deluge. The Dau'sings were rising high on either side of them as the highway wound its way northwards. Often they'd have a sheer fall of several hundred metres at the edge of the road, with only a thick stone wall as protection. On the lower slopes, boltgrass was turning from its usual wiry yellow to a richer honey colour as it approached its week-long spore season.

Thirty miles out of town, they passed by one of the abandoned JCB monster roadbuilders which Simon Rand had used to carve his highway through the mountains. It was sitting on a wide patch of broken ground that one of its cousins had hacked into the side of the slope beside the road. Decades of fierce southern continent winters had reduced its metal parts to melted-looking chunks of rust, while the composite bodywork was bleached and cracked. The huge solid metal tracks had sagged on their runner wheels, allowing its belly to settle on the ground where it had bent and buckled. Souvenir hunters had picked most of the smaller components away, while the glass of its insect-eye cab at the front had been smashed.

Both kids got excited at the sight, and Mark had to promise to bring them back some time for a better look.

Five miles beyond the roadbuilder, on the high shoulder of Mount Zuelea, the highway was clogged with stationary vehicles. Napo Langsal waved them down. He owned one of the dive tour boats in Randtown. Mark had never seen him anywhere other than in the town or on his boat. He wasn't even sure Napo owned a car.

'Hi, guys,' Napo said. 'Colleen's about to head back to town, so if you could slot this in where her truck was parked we'd be grateful.'

'No problem,' Mark said. 'We brought some lunch, but the kids will need to get home by tonight.'

'I think there're some vehicles coming out about seven o'clock, they're going to take the night shift.'

'Right then.' Mark eased the pick-up forward, driving down the narrow zigzag gap between the vehicles that were parked at right angles across the lanes, most of them pick-up trucks or 4x4s, the kind of vehicles driven by Randtowners. People walking along the road saw the Vernons and gave them a wave or thumbs up. A section of the central barrier had been removed, and he went over onto the southern carriageway. Colleen's big truck was easily visible, the sides were painted in the bright pink and emerald logo of her precipitator leaf business which were fluorescing strongly in the sunlight. Since they'd arrived, Mark had had several arguments with her about the semi-organic equipment she'd supplied, but now they both smiled cheerily at each other as they passed.

'Community spirit is high today,' Liz murmured slyly so the children couldn't hear. They grinned at each other.

Mark parked in the gap Colleen had left. They walked up to the head of the blockade, where big civic utility trucks, bulldozers, tractors, snowploughs, roadsweepers, and double-decker buses were parked end to end, as tight as any mosaic. Simon Rand himself came to greet them, a tall figure in an apricot Gandhi-style toga made from semi-organic fabric which swirled round his limbs as he moved, always covering the skin and keeping him warm in the fresh mountain air. His apparent age was approaching sixty, an ageing which had produced long distinguished creases in his ebony face. He fitted his role as nature's guru perfectly, charismatic and passively stubborn, traits which provided universal reassurance to anyone engaged with his ideals.

A flock of people trailed along in his wake. An entourage like the staff of any major politician, except these were more like acolytes. Some were intent and focused, while others moved through their own daydream. Over half were women, and all of them were attractive, either rejuvenated or first-lifers. Simon's commitment to his own ideals drew him a lot of admirers from the people who came to live the Randtown life; and as he kept saying, he was only human.

'Mark, how good of you to come,' Simon said warmly. He grasped Mark's hand in a strong grip.

Very definitely a politician's handshake, Mark thought.

'And Liz as well. This is so kind. I know how difficult it is for people who work for a living to contribute their time to a cause, especially those who have just joined us and have mortgages to pay. For what such words are worth, I appreciate you being here today.'

'We can spare a few afternoons,' Liz said archly. She was one of those immune to his personal charm, though even she appreciated his resolution.

'Let us hope this situation doesn't require more than that,' Simon said. 'I have already heard – unofficially, of course – that they are willing to consider negotiating an alternative power source to that dreadful plutonium which they have brought with them.'

'Sounds good,' Mark said. 'Where do you want us?'

'There's a big no-man's-land between us and them, many families are gathered there. The children will be able to play with their friends.'

'Can I take Panda?' Barry asked.

'Your dog?' Simon gave both the Vernon kids a wink. 'Of course you can, we welcome everybody to the protest. I'm sure Panda will have fun. Try not to let him bite too many police officers. They're only doing their job, and our quarrel is not with them.'

'Her,' Sandy said indignantly, patting Panda. 'Panda's a lady dog, you know.'

'I do apologize. She is a fine-looking lady dog.'

'Thank you. Panda says you're nice, too.'

'We'll get over there, then,' Mark said, zipping up his coat. He was beginning to wish he'd brought his gloves.

'Stay only for as long as you are comfortable with,' Simon said. 'It is the act of coming here which is relevant. We do not measure commitment by the hours you put in.'

'I gather you're sleeping in one of the buses,' Liz said.

'Yes. We do not want to give the navy the chance to break the blockade, so my closest supporters and myself maintain the vigil at night. I cannot leave, Liz, this is my home now and for ever. My roots are here. My soul is at peace with what has been achieved. So you will understand that I must stand fast on this road and prevent any violation of the life so many have chosen for themselves.'

'I understand.'

He breathed deeply, a look of serenity on his face. 'I had forgotten the taste of the mountain air. Its rawness and purity is refreshing. Up here we can all reaffirm our commitment to ourselves. This road I built is more than physical. From this point you can make many choices regarding your destination.'

'I think we'll just go home at the end of the shift, thank you,' Liz told him.

And Simon inclined his head, smiling graciously just like any mystic hit by a solid fact.

'That was rude,' Mark said as they carried on up to the head of the blockade. Simon and his close personal followers had gone off on some inscrutable business.

'Pompous old farts need to have the piss taken every now and then.' She put her hands together in Buddhist fashion, and crossed her eyes. 'It puts them in touch with their Oneness.'

His arm went round her shoulder, hugging fondly. 'Tell that to the midnight lynch mob.'

Beyond the big trucks at the head of the blockade, the road was empty for a couple of hundred yards. Several hundred Randtown residents were milling around on the empty enzyme-bonded concrete. Adults cluttered together in little groups to talk, stamping their feet against the chill air blowing across from the higher peaks to the east where there was all-year-round snow. Children split up into their own groupings, chasing round in various games. Buzzbots zipped through the air above them, the latest craze. Little flying-saucer-shaped aircraft with contra-rotating fans at the centre, controlled by v-gloves. It looked odd, children standing perfectly still to wiggle their fingers as if playing an invisible piano, each motion sending the tiny craft swooping and soaring above the road. Occasionally one would make a fast pass towards the line of bored police on the other side of the gap. A sharp call from a parent would soon force its return.

Behind the police on the southbound carriageway was a long convoy of twenty-six-wheel SAAB Vitan trucks. To begin with they were all diesel-powered, in direct contravention of the highway rules which only permitted electric-powered vehicles. That was almost irrelevant when compared to their contents. They were carrying all the equipment necessary to build a wormhole detector station for the navy's planetary security division, which was due to be set up in the Dau'sings just above Randtown. That equipment included three fission micropiles to provide power for the detectors.

There had been a big argument at the toll gate at the northern end of the highway when the convoy arrived there. But the navy officer in charge called in the local police, who overruled the operator and sent the convoy through. Simon Rand had been informed straight away, and set out to stop them from the southern end, accompanied by his followers driving every piece of big civic equipment they could find. When they arrived at the high point on Mount Zuelea they stopped, disabled the vehicles, and waited. The standoff had now lasted two days.

Mark and Liz soon found the Conants, and the Dunbavands, David and Lydia, who owned the vine nursery where Liz worked; they'd brought their kids along for the afternoon, too.

'Is there anyone left back in Randtown?' Liz wondered.

They spent a couple of hours talking to the others, mostly about what this would do to the tourism industry. The buses which brought groups in to the hotels weren't even waiting behind the stalled navy convoy any more, and the tour operators were raising hell, and talking about suing. Flasks of warm drink were passed round. People went back to their vehicles to fetch warmer clothing. Kids had to be taken to the toilets on one of the buses. The whole protest was more like a giant picnic than a political statement.

After a couple of hours, Mark went back to the pick-up to fetch the box containing their lunch. There was a flash of orange between the vehicles over on the other carriageway as Simon Rand walked purposefully on some mission, his courtiers tagging along loyally. Mark was nearing the end of the parked vehicles, craning his neck to find the pick-up, when he saw her.

He didn't think she was a tourist, something about her

made him doubt she'd ever be a part of a tour company's herd, a spark of independence or self-confidence he was adept at recognizing. Exactly the kind of first-life girl who came to Randtown to join in the party scene and spend her spare time extreme-ing around the landscape. Although he'd not seen her around town before, waitressing or helping out in any of the stores.

She was gorgeous. Which made him nervous, because that kind of beauty made him think what kind of wife he'd have after Liz. Because they both knew it wouldn't go on for ever. Even though it was good right now. He was a realist, and so was Liz. Which meant it was okay to consider such things. Right?

The girl caught sight of him staring, and gave him a cheeky smile. 'Hi,' she drawled. It was a husky come-on of a voice, perfectly suited to her long young face with its beguilingly flat nose. Her skin was a healthy tanned bronze, matching the tawny hair she wore long and wavy.

'Hello,' he replied. Already his voice was strained as his stomach muscles tightened, holding his abdomen taut, the way it used to be only a few years back. 'Are you looking for someone?'

'Not really, I'm just looking around.'

'Ah, well, um, the main action is up there at the front. Not that there's a lot of action. Apart from the kids' football game. Ha!'

'Right.' She came right up in front of him, still smiling. Everyone else up here was dressed for the cold, but she seemed comfortable in a white short-sleeve T-shirt and a suede skirt that stopped above her knees. There was a small silver M logo just above the skirt's hem. The outfit showed off broad shoulders and a gym-junkie belly. Her cowboy boots had flat heels but even so her eyes were level with Mark's. She put her hand out. 'I'm Mel.'

'Mark.' He tried not to read too much into the physical contact. She was a lot more confident and sophisticated than most of the young first-lifers in Randtown.

'So did you come all this way just to see the football?' she asked.

He blushed at the teasing tone, the way her intent stare never left his face, the proximity – he still hadn't let go of her hand. 'Oh God, no. I'm here to support Simon Rand. And the rest of the town.'

'I see.' She gently removed her hand from his. 'Do most of the town support this blockade?'

'Yeah absolutely. It's an outrage what they're trying to do to us. They've got to be stopped.'

'Stopped from building a wormhole detector station?'

'That's right. And we're going to do it. Our ideal will only be safe if we act together.'

Her lovely face crinkled slightly with a frown. 'I've not been here long, but I can see how the simple life attracts people. What exactly is that ideal, would you say?'

'Just that: we're devoted to living a simple, clean, green life.'

'But surely the navy won't destroy that? The station is due to be sited miles out of town, up in the mountains where it can't affect anybody. And the Commonwealth really needs to know if the Primes open a wormhole inside our boundaries.'

'It's the principle of what they're doing. The station has nuclear power systems, which is the absolute opposite of everything we believe in. And they didn't ask us about this, they just barged onto the highway and set out to build their station without our permission.'

'Did they need permission?'

'Sure they did. The whole Dau'sings range is included in the foundation charter, and nuclear power is specifically excluded from it.'

'I understand that, but the navy really needs a series of

wormhole detector stations on the southern continent to give the whole network complete coverage. Surely if you oppose that then you're taking an anti-human stance.'

'If this is being anti-human, then bring it on and give me more,' he said with bravado, which earned him an encouraging smile. 'It's not, of course. The decision to site the station in the Dau'sings was taken by a bunch of bureaucrats sticking a pin in a map. They didn't care about the wishes and beliefs of the people who live here, they probably didn't even bother to find out any of our customs. All we're doing with this blockade is making them take our requirements into account. Apparently, they're already starting negotiations about other power sources.'

'I didn't know that.'

'Well, that's unofficial. But, yeah.'

'Won't that cost more?'

'The navy budget is so big nobody will ever notice it. In any case, they're supposed to be protecting our way of life. That's worth paying a little bit extra for, isn't it?'

'I guess it is.'

'So, er, how long have you been in town? I haven't seen you around before.'

'I only just got here.'

'Well if you want to stick around and try some extreme-ing, I know a few places that have vacancies.'

'That's very sweet, Mark, but I can pay my own way, thank you.'

'Right, uh, fine.' He suddenly remembered he was supposed to be collecting lunch for his family. 'Well, I guess I'll see you around then.'

Her lips pouted up. 'I'll look forward to it.'

*

That evening, they managed to leave Barry and Sandy sleeping over with the Baxter kids in Highmarsh so they could spend an evening in town. They started off at the Phoenix bar on

Litton Street, which ran parallel to Main Mall. Like every building in Randtown it was newish, with a solar panel roof and insulated composite walls. But inside, the owners had built up stone walls to mask the carbon girder framework, and then gone on to lay heavy ash beams above to support a wooden ceiling, making the long rectangular room dark and cosy. The bar itself took up most of one wall, serving a few beers along with every type of wine produced in the valleys behind Randtown, including some from the Vernons' own vineyard. A fireplace dominated the far end, wide enough to require two chimneys; the iron grate could hold enormous lengths of wood to burn in the winter months, giving off a tremendous heat. Now, in summer, it was filled with a long ceramic trough of fresh-cut flowers. Several settees were arranged in front of it, which Liz and Mark claimed along with Yuri and Olga Conant. Normally the settees were already occupied this early in the evening, but the blockade had thinned out the bar's usual crowd.

'It's not just here,' Yuri said as he settled in with a glass of vin noir from Chapples, a vineyard in Highmarsh. 'Most of the cafés in town are suffering, even the Bab's Kebabs franchise takings are down.'

'They'd just started rotating the tourist groups when the blockade went up,' Liz said. 'A whole load left, and the next lot haven't arrived. The hotels are three-quarters empty.'

'And everyone left trapped in town is raising hell,' Olga said. 'I can't blame them.'

'There are worse places to be trapped,' Yuri countered.

'Simon should have worked out how to let them get through the blockade. His principles are starting to hurt people.'

'There's a difference between hurt and inconvenience,' Mark said.

'Not really, not in this case. Most of the tourists have come to the end of their holiday, they just want to get back to their

904

homes and jobs. How would you like it if someone stopped you earning a living?'

'It will only go on for another couple of days at the most.'

'Yeah, but it was badly thought out.'

'We didn't have a lot of choice. You've got to wonder why the navy didn't give us any advance warning about building a station here.'

'It's a crash project,' Olga said. 'They probably didn't even know until a few days before the equipment arrived on Elan.'

'Okay, so why didn't the Ryceel Parliament's first speaker say anything?'

'Because he knew what Rand's answer would be.'

'Exactly, it was a conspiracy to dump this thing on us before we knew what was happening. They wanted a fait accompli.'

Mark's e-butler informed him that Carys Panther was calling. He blinked in surprise, and told the program to let it through. 'Are you accessing Alessandra Baron?' Carys asked.

'Nice to talk to you, too,' he replied. 'It must have been six months.'

'Don't be an asshole, access it now. I'll call you back when it's over.' She ended the call.

'What?' Liz asked.

'Not sure.' Mark turned round. 'China,' he called to the barman. 'Can you access Alessandra Baron's show for us, please?' He normally fought shy of accessing Alessandra and her haughty show, which always criticized and never did anything constructive. He felt it was like being lectured by snobs who specialized in satire.

The ancient little man behind the bar obliged, putting the show on the big portal.

'Oh fuck,' Mark whispered. It was his own face dominating the image, magnified three feet high. 'We're devoted to living a simple, clean, green life,' he was saying.

'She was a reporter,' he told his wife. 'I didn't know, she never said.'

'When was this?' Liz asked.

'This afternoon. She came up to me when I was getting the lunch. I though she was from town.'

The image switched back to the studio where Alessandra Baron was sitting at the centre of a big couch, her classically beautiful face holding an amused expression, the way adults responded to a precocious child. Mellanie Rescorai sat beside her, looking even more sophisticated than she had up on Mount Zuelea, wearing a simple clinging scarlet dress and a black jacket with a little silver M on the lapel, her hair had been elaborately tousled.

Liz gave Mark a long sideways look. Her eyebrow rose several millimetres. 'That was the reporter?'

'Uh huh,' Mark waved her quiet.

Yuri and Olga swapped a knowing look.

'So what did he say next?' Alessandra asked.

'By this time I think he wanted to say: can we go to a motel for the rest of the day?' Mellanie laughed. 'But I managed to keep his hot little hands off me for a while by telling him the navy had no intention of wrecking his simpleton lifestyle. Can you guess what he said to that?'

'He was grateful?' Alessandra suggested archly.

'Oh yes. Take a look.' The image shifted back to Mark at the blockade.

Sitting on the settee in front of the fireplace, a glass of wine in hand, and hindsight showing him what to watch for, it was all rather easy to realize that the smile he put on that afternoon for the girl was somewhat forced. Anxious, even. The one a man used when trying to impress. Eager to impress, possibly.

'It's the principle of what they're doing,' his image said. 'They didn't ask us about this, they just barged onto the highway and set out to build their station without our permission.'

906

'Did they need permission?'

'Sure they did.'

The show went back to the studio. 'Incredible,' Alessandra said, shaking her head in saddened bewilderment. 'Just how backward are they in Randtown?'

'That was edited!' Mark protested to the bar at large. 'I . . . That wasn't what I meant. I said other stuff, too. I told her about the nuclear micropiles. Why isn't that in there? She's making this – Christ, I look ridiculous.' He felt Liz take his hand and squeeze reassuringly, and shot her a desperate glance.

'It's okay,' she whispered.

'The kind of backward you get from three generations of marrying cousins,' Mellanie confided to Alessandra.

The Phoenix bar was totally silent now.

'So in his view, not only do we, the Commonwealth, not have the right to put vital defence equipment on an uninhabited mountain,' Mellanie said. 'But wait for this next bit.'

'Oh God,' Mark said. He wanted the programme to end. Now. The universe to end, actually.

Earlier that day up at the blockade, Mellanie asked, 'Surely if you oppose that then you're taking an anti-human stance?' in a fully reasonable tone.

Mark's giant face smiled goofishly. 'If this is being anti-human, then bring it on and give me more.'

Back in the studio Mellanie gave a what-can-you-do shrug to Alessandra.

'Bitch!' Mark yelled furiously. He jumped to his feet, his wine glass tumbling to the stone flag floor. 'You fucking bitch. This is not the way it happened.'

Everyone in the bar had stopped drinking and talking to look at him. Alessandra Baron's show vanished from the portal to be replaced by the New Oxford invitation open golf tournament. 'Enough of those smartmouth whores,' China growled, several OCtattoo curlicues were glowing scarlet on his bald head. 'You sit yourself back down there, Mark. We can all see it was a stitch-up job. I'll get you a refill for that glass, on the house.'

Liz put her hand round his wrist and tugged him back down. 'That can't be legal,' he said. 'Surely?' Anger was giving way to shock.

'Depends what you can prove,' Yuri said earnestly. 'If your memory of the event is replayed to a court then you can demonstrate they produced a detrimental edit.' He trailed off under Olga's sharp stare.

'Don't worry about it,' Liz said soothingly. 'Everyone here knows you, they can see that the interview is a phoney. It's the navy's response to the blockade. They're putting the pressure on Simon to let the convoy through. Newton's law of politics.'

Mark put his head in his hands. His e-butler was telling him Carys Panther was calling again. So was Simon Rand. Messages were coming in from the unisphere at the rate of several thousand a second, directed at his public code. It seemed that everyone who had accessed Alessandra and Mellanie wanted to tell him what they thought of him. They weren't being kind.

*

The heat seemed to be increasing with every step, along with the humidity. Ozzie was surprised by that. He'd walked enough Silfen paths between worlds now to know when the tracks were taking him over the threshold. The signs were subtle and very gradual. Not this time.

They'd been walking through a deciduous forest on the second world since the ghost planet, it was midsummer, with wildflowers providing a gentle carpet of pastel colours across the forest floor. Palm trees and giant ferns began to intermingle with the doughty trunks of the forest. There was a strengthening scent, too; which took Ozzie a while to place. The sea. It had been a long time since he'd seen the sea. No Silfen path had ever led close to one.

It was growing brighter as well; strong sunlight tinged with a hint of indigo. He fished in his top pocket for his sunglasses.

'We're somewhere else, aren't we?' Orion asked eagerly. He was looking round with an entranced expression at the thick fronds crowning all the trees. Even the undergrowth had become thicker, with grass growing higher and turning a darker green. Creeping vines rose up to wrap themselves around the trees, sprouting white and lemon-yellow flowers.

'Looks that way,' he said reassuringly. When he turned to look at the boy he could see the path curved sharply behind them. He'd been walking in a more-or-less straight line for hours. Orion hadn't noticed, he was holding up his friendship pendant, studying it intently. Since the ghost world he'd reclaimed it from Ozzie. The experience there had changed the boy's opinion of the Silfen once again. They'd never be unquestioned idols again, but he was starting to accept them as true aliens. Ozzie supposed it was a sign of maturity.

'Are there any of them nearby?' he asked.

'I dunno,' Orion said, troubled. 'I've never seen it like this before. It's turned green.' He held it up to show Ozzie. The small exotic gem was shining a bright emerald as it dangled on the end of its chain. 'Do you think it means something else is here?'

'I've no idea what it means,' Ozzie said truthfully.

The palm trees were thinning out, with the thick grass coming up to their knees. Tochee was having to produce large powerful ripples along its locomotion ridges to shove its wide body through the clingy blades. Ozzie slowed in confusion, there was no path anymore, only the grass they'd trodden down behind them. Without the floppy fronds above his head, he could feel the star's heat on his bare skin. Below his booted feet, the ground was sloping downward. There were a lot of undulations ahead of them as the slope dipped away, but several miles in the distance was the unmistakable blue sparkle of the sea.

Now where? Tochee's eye patterns queried.

Ozzie faced their alien friend and shrugged. A gesture which Tochee knew only too well by now.

'We never walked through that,' Orion said abruptly. He was facing back the way they'd just come. Behind them was the rounded top of a modest mountain, its crown roughly covered by a jungle of palms and big ferns with a few spindly grey trees that might result if pines were crossed with eucalyptus. The whole patch couldn't have been more than a mile across.

Ozzie was working out what to say when an electronic bleep emerged from deep inside his backpack. The sound, so integral with Commonwealth society, was profoundly shocking here. He and Orion looked at each other in surprise.

'Link to my wrist array,' Ozzie told his e-butler. There were function icons appearing in his virtual vision that hadn't been there since the day he rode out of Lyddington, as his inserts regained their full capacity. He shrugged off the backpack as if it had caught fire. His e-butler confirmed that his inserts were receiving a signal from his wrist array. He shook the contents of his backpack onto the ground, heedless of the mess. A tiny red power LED was shining on the side of his burnished wrist array. He slipped it round his hand and the malmetal contracted snugly. The OCtattoo on his forearm made contact with the unit's i-spot. Lying amid the pile of clothes and packets he'd tipped out was a hand-held array. He picked it up and switched it on. Its icons appeared immediately in his virtual vision. 'Son of a bitch,' he muttered. His e-butler started to back up insert files in both arrays. He let it do that while his virtual hands rearranged icons for the hand-held array. Its screen unfurled to its full extent, measuring half a metre wide. 'Please,' he prayed, and translucent amber fingers plucked symbols out of the linguistic files he'd painstakingly built up over the last few months.

On the screen, the spiky flower patterns which Tochee used

were displayed in the deepest purple which the screen's resolution could manage.

Tochee became very still. **Hello**, his forward eye segment projected.

'Our electronic systems are working again,' Ozzie said out loud. The hand held array translated into a series of patterns which it flashed up.

I understand.

'Are those Tochee's speaking pictures?' a fascinated Orion asked, peering at the screen.

The array translated, and Tochee produced an answer.

'That is correct, small human one,' the array said. 'They sit in an incorrect visual spectrum. However I can read them.'

Orion whooped exuberantly and gave a massive victory jump, punching the air. 'It's me, it's me, Tochee. I'm talking to you!' He gave Ozzie a radiant smile, and they high-fived.

'I am aware of the communication,' the array translated for Tochee. 'I have wished for this moment for a long time. My first true speech is to thank you large human one and small human one for the companionship you have given me. Without you I would remain at the cold house. I would not like that.'

Ozzie gave a small bow. 'Our pleasure, Tochee. But this isn't one-way, man. We would have had difficulty leaving the Ice Citadel without you.'

Orion rushed over to Tochee, who extended a tentacle of manipulator flesh which the boy squeezed happily. 'This is great, it's wonderful, Tochee. There's so much I want to tell you. And ask, as well.'

'You are kind, small human one. Large humans two, three, five, fifteen, twenty-three and thirty also showed some consideration for my situation, as did other species at the cold house. I hope they are well.'

'Which ones are those, Ozzie?'

'I don't know, man. I guess Sara is large human two, and

George must be in there somewhere.' His virtual hand pulled the translation routines down out of stasis, slotting them into the large processing power of the hand-held array. 'Tochee, we need to improve our translation ability. I'd like you to talk to my machine, here.'

'I agree. I have my own electronic units that I want to switch on.'

'Okay, let's go for it.'

The big alien reached round with its manipulator flesh, and removed one of the heavy bags it was carrying. Ozzie meanwhile picked several sensor instruments out of his pile, switching them on one by one. 'Man, I came this close to leaving these back at the Ice Citadel,' he grunted.

'What have you got?' the excited boy asked.

'Standard first contact team stuff. Mineral analysers, resonance scanners, em spectrum monitors, microradar, magnometers. Things that'll tell me a lot about the environment.'

'How are they going to help?'

'Not sure, yet, man. It kinda depends on what we find. But this place is different to the others we've walked through. There must be a reason the Silfen have stopped screwing with electricity.'

'Do you think . . .' Orion stopped, and looked round cautiously. 'Is this the end of the road, Ozzie?'

Ozzie very nearly told the boy not to be stupid. His own growing uncertainty stopped him. 'I don't know. If it is, I would have expected something a little more elaborate.' He gestured out at the rolling landscape. 'This is more like a dead end.'

'That's what I thought,' the boy said meekly.

Results from the sensors were building up in grids across Ozzie's virtual vision. He ignored them to give the boy a reassuring hug. 'No way, man.'

'Okay.'

Ozzie turned his attention back to the sensor results. He

noticed that Tochee had switched on several electronic units. His own scans showed the alien's systems to be sensors and processor units not entirely dissimilar to his own. Apart from that, there was little for his own units to go on. Strangely, this planet seemed to have no magnetic field. The general neutrino level was above average, though. Local quantum field readings were fractionally different to standard, though nothing like enough to produce the kind of warping necessary to open a wormhole – he thought it might be a residual from the electron damping effect. 'Weird, but not weird enough,' he said quietly.

'Ozzie, what's that in the sky?'

The hand-held array flashed the question up for Tochee as well. The alien put aside its own gadgets to follow Orion's pointing arm. Ozzie followed the boy's gaze, narrowing his eyes as he squinted almost directly into the vivid sunlight. It looked as if there was some kind of silver cloud at very high altitude, a thin curve that stretched across the sun. When his retinal inserts brought their high-intensity filters on line and zoomed in he changed his mind. No matter what magnification he used, the little strip of shimmering silver didn't change. The planet had a ring. He tracked along it, using both array memories to file the image. The scintillations he could see coming from within the cloud were actually tiny motes. There must have been thousands of them. He wondered briefly how their composition differed from the rest of the ring. Then he came to where it crossed in front of the sun. It didn't. And the scale shifted again, to a terrifying degree.

'Christ fuck a duck,' Ozzie mouthed.

What he could see was a halo of gas that went right round the star. Which meant the planet they were standing on was orbiting right inside it.

'I know this place,' he said in astonishment.

'What?' Orion blurted. 'How could you?'

Ozzie gave a very twitchy laugh. 'I was told about it by

someone else who walked the Silfen paths. He said he visited artefacts called tree reefs. They floated in a nebula of atmospheric gas. Wow, whatta you know, and I always thought his story was mostly bullshit. Guess I owe him an apology.'

'Who was it, Ozzie? Who's been here?'

'Some dude called Bradley Johansson.'

*

After a five-minute trip, the train from Oaktier pulled up to platform twenty-nine in the Seattle CST station's third passenger terminal. Stig McSobel stepped out and asked his e-butler to find the platform where he could catch a standard-class loop train to Los Angeles, which was the next stop on the trans-Earth line. It told him the loop trains all left from terminal two, so he hopped on the little monorail car which carried people between the terminals. He slid smoothly along the elevated rail as it took him out over the vast marshalling yard that had spread out over the land to the east of Seattle. Kilometre-long goods trains pulled by hulking great Damzung T5V6B electric engine units passed underneath him as they rolled out of the bulk-freight gateway to Bayovar, the Big15 connected directly to Seattle. While trans-Commonwealth express trains flashed along on their magrails like aircraft flying at zero-altitude. Down to the south he could see a long line of gateway arches throwing off a pale blue light which produced long shadows across the weed-colonized concrete ground. The Seattle CST station was a junction for over twenty-seven phase one space worlds in addition to Bayovar, routing all of the freight and passengers that flowed between them. Thousands of trains a day trundled across the station, providing the huge web of commercial links which helped maintain Seattle's high-tech research and industry base.

Stig sat at one end of the tubular monorail car, quickly scanning his fellow travellers, and transferring the images into files. His wrist array ran comparisons with the thousands of visual files he'd accumulated since he began working in the Commonwealth itself. Seven of the people in the monorail had been on the train from Oaktier, which was only normal. If one of them was following him, they had reprofiled their face since the last time they'd shared a train together.

Terminal two was a huge metal and concrete dome, half of which was underground. Its multitude of platforms were arranged in a radial fashion on two levels, lower level for incoming, upper for departures. Stig paid cash for his standard-class ticket which would take him all the way round the loop to Calcutta, and took a moving walkway out to platform A-seventeen, where one of the twenty-carriage loop trains was just pulling in. He stood waiting casually by an open door on the second carriage, watching latecomers hurry across the platform. Nobody from the monorail car got on to the loop train. Satisfied, he went on board and walked down the carriages to the fifth; only then did he take a seat.

Hoshe Finn stood in the queue for the Bean Here franchise stall at the end of platform A-seventeen, and watched his target get on to the local train. 'Have your people got him?' he asked Paula, who was standing beside him.

'Yes, thank you. Team B are boxing him. He just sat down in the fifth carriage.'

He bought a coffee for himself and a tea for Paula. 'So do you suspect any of Team B?'

'I don't have any real suspects, sadly,' she said, and blew across the top of her cup. 'That means I have to treat everyone as the possible leak.'

'Does that include me?'

She sipped her tea, and gave him a thoughtful look. 'If you are working for an Executive security service, or some corporate black ops division, then whoever planted you has resources and foresight beyond even my ability to counter.'

'I'll take that as a compliment.'

'Thank you for doing this, Hoshe.'

'My pleasure. I just hope it gets you what you need.'

'Me too.'

He stood beside the Bean Here stall and watched the train pull out of the station. All in all, it was a strange business, and whatever the outcome, he knew he wouldn't like it. Either the President was killing off citizens with impunity, or that lunatic Bradley Johansson had been right all along. He wasn't sure which was worse.

*

It took ten minutes for the loop train to reach LA Galactic, most of that was spent crawling slowly through the Seattle station as they waited for their slot amid the goods trains at the trans-Earth loop gateway. Centuries ago, when it was starting out, not even CST could afford a chunk of real estate in LA the size it needed to house a planetary station. So it moved south of San Clemente and leased some of Camp Pendelton from the US Government, in an agreement which provided the Pentagon with direct access to wormholes, giving them the ability to deploy troops anywhere on the planet (or off it). The military requirement had slowly ebbed as more and more of Earth's population left to find their own particular brands of freedom and nationalism out among the stars, leaving fewer and fewer warlords and fanatics behind until finally the Unified Federal Nations came into existence. While the old armies were dying off, CST had continued its inexorable expansion. Over half of phase one space's H-congruous planets had been discovered and explored from LA Galactic; and when the CST finally moved its exploratory division out to the Big15, the commercial division quickly stepped in to take up the slack. LA Galactic rivalled the stations on any of the Big15 for size and complexity.

Stig got off the loop train on platform three in the Carralvo terminal, a giant multi-segment modernistic building of white concrete bled even whiter in California's unforgiving sunlight.

Despite the sheer size of the structure, it thrummed and vibrated from the passage of trains which wound in and out of it along elegant curving viaducts, that were sometimes stacked three high thanks to elaborate twisting buttresses. He could have found his way around the Carralvo in complete darkness, and not just the public areas; the utility corridors, management offices, and staff facilities were all loaded in his insert files. Not that he really needed the reference. The other seven passenger terminals were equally familiar.

He had spent years working here. If the Guardians could be said to have a regular base of operations in the Commonwealth it was at LA Galactic. It was the perfect, and essential, place for them. Hundreds of thousands of tonnes of industrial and consumer products were routed between its gateways every day: food imports came to over a million tonnes, while raw materials in transit accounted for an even bigger market. Thousands of import-export companies, from the Intersolar giants to virtuals that were no more than a coded array space and a numbered bank account, had their offices and warehouses and transport depots within the city-sized station compound. Each one plugged into the giant network of rails and CST cargo-handling facilities, both physically and electronically. Each one with multiple accounts in the finance network. Each one with links to the Regulated Goods Directorate. Each one with offices, from entire skyscrapers to suites of leased rooms. They grew, shrank, went bankrupt, floated and went Intersolar, moved headquarters from one block to another, changed personnel, merged, fought each other bitterly for contracts. It was super-capitalism in a confined pressure-cooker environment that was merciless to any weakness.

Over the decades, Adam Elvin had formed and folded dozens of companies at LA Galactic. He wasn't alone. The number of companies that came and went within a single month could often be measured in hundreds. His were hidden amid the flow, no different to all the other chancers who set themselves up to supply markets they either knew about or believed in. He would create identities for himself, along with all the associated datawork, and use the name to register a company which wouldn't be used for years. When he did start it up, it would be as a legitimate business competing for trade along with all the others.

It was a process which had served the Guardians well. Every operation to deliver armaments and equipment to Far Away involved a front at LA Galactic. It allowed him to track the shipments passively. And at some time all the items would pass though for checking, or switching, or to be disguised. As far as Paula Myo and the Serious Crimes Directorate knew, they were just another rented warehouse in the chain.

This time, with Johansson embarking upon his planet's revenge project, and the navy becoming perilously efficient in pursuing them, the scale of the operation was larger than ever before, and its focus expanded. After Venice Coast, Adam was developing his paranoia to new heights.

Lemule's Max Transit had leased an entire floor of the Henley Tower, an unimaginative thirty-five-storey glass and carbon and concrete building on the San Diego side of LA Galactic, standing in the forest of similar office towers which made up one of the station's commercial administration parks. Twenty Guardians worked in its offices. Four of them were occupied by the shipments of illicit goods to Far Away, while the rest devoted themselves to security.

As soon as Stig bought his ticket for the loop train he sent a message to a one-time unisphere address. Kieran McSobel, who was on duty at the Lemule office, received it, and as procedure required, launched a battery of onlook software into the planetary cybersphere. The programs installed themselves in the nodes which served the loop train Stig was using. They began analysing the data flowing through the nodes.

The results flipped up across Kieran's virtual vision. 'Damnit. Marisa, we've got internal encrypted traffic in Stig's train. Five sources, one in his carriage.'

On the other side of the open plan office, Marisa McFoster accessed the onlook information. 'That doesn't look good. It's a standard box formation. The navy's burned him. Shit!' She called Adam.

'We need the software he's carrying,' Adam said. 'Can we go for a dead recovery?'

'The bots are in place,' Marisa said. She ran diagnostics on the little machines, bringing them up to operational status. 'We've got time. Gareth is covering the Carralvo. He can walkby.'

'Do it.'

'What about Stig?'

Adam kept his face composed, not showing the youngsters how worried he was. How the hell did the navy find him? 'We can't break the box – that'll alert the navy and betray our own capability. He'll have to do it himself. Send him a discontinue and break order when we've confirmed recovery. And activate the Venice safe house. He'll have to undergo reprofiling if he makes it there.'

'Yes, sir,' Marisa said.

'Don't worry. He's good, he'll make it.'

*

Stig walked down the long curving ramp at the end of the platform. It was one of ten which connected platforms to the central concourse where the flood of people had reached the density of a baseball stadium crowd rushing for their seats. High overhead, the concrete dome ceiling was supported by giant spider-leg pillars, their sharp bends making it seem as if they might just be able to lower the whole mass at any time. It was his theory that was why people were always in such a rush here, subconsciously they were trying to get out before the collapse happened.

He counted off the emergency exits as he moved along the ramp. When he reached the concourse it would take another three and a half minutes to get to the taxi rank. From there to the office would take another ten minutes at least, depending on how heavy traffic was on the station compound's internal highways.

Ahead of him, Gareth stepped onto the ramp, and began walking up. He was wearing a smart grey jacket over a yellow shirt.

Training made sure Stig didn't turn his head as the two of them passed. But it was hard. Grey on yellow. A dead recovery order. There could only be one reason for that, he was under observation.

They were good, he had to admit that. For the whole trip back from Oaktier he'd been checking, and hadn't seen anyone. Of course, it could be a virtual surveillance; a team with an RI hacking onto him through public cameras and sensors. Even harder to shake.

As he stepped off the ramp, the concourse layout was looming large in his mind. He headed left for the even-numbered platforms, then took one of the triple escalators down to the lower-level mall. All the while he was watching. It was difficult now. He was conscious of looking up when he reached the mid-level and took the next set of escalators. The sure sign of someone hunting for a box. Would it tip them off? Yet if they'd been following him, they would have seen him going through the check routine. Not looking might be worse. He settled for a brief, casual, glance upwards, locking the image in an insert file.

As the escalator slipped smoothly downwards he studied the ghostly image in his virtual vision. There was one person up there, a typical west-coast surfer standing close to the balcony rail, who had also got off the loop train from Seattle. He hadn't been in the same carriage, though. Stig expanded the image and studied the man. Thick blond hair in a ponytail, sharp nose, square jaw, casual plain blue shirt and jeans. He couldn't tell. But the image was on instant recall now.

The escalator delivered him to the marble and neon mall, and he walked over to the public washroom. Most of the stalls were empty. A couple of guys were using the urinals. Father and young son at the washbasins.

Stig took the second empty stall, locked the door, and dropped his pants. If the box had covered the washroom ahead of him, there was nothing for them to be suspicious about yet. On his hand-held array he transferred the software he'd collected from Kareem into a memory crystal, and ejected the little black disk from the unit. He put it into a standard-looking plastic case, wrapped that in toilet tissue, and dropped it into the pan. It flushed away easily enough, and he left the stall to wash his hands.

When he went back out into the mall, the blond-haired man in the blue shirt was window shopping twenty metres away.

Stig went into the nearest sports shop and bought himself a new pair of trainers, paying cash. The box team would have to check that out. Next was a department store for a pair of sunglasses. He went back up to the main concourse, and stopped at one of the small stalls that sold tourist T-shirts and chose a fairly decent sun hat. Then he went along to the left luggage lockers and put his credit tattoo on the locker he'd taken three days before. It opened, and he removed the black shoulder bag which contained the emergency kit.

Without looking back or running any more checks he went straight to the taxi rank. As the revolving door offered him up to the warm Californian sunlight, Stig smiled. Despite the seriousness of being burned, he was going to enjoy the next few hours.

*

The warehouses didn't annoy Adam as much as the districts of office towers which nestled along the southern side of LA

Galactic. He hated the multitude of handling and transport companies that survived in parasitic bondage with the CST rail network. They were true capitalist entities, producing nothing, charging people to supply products, adding to the cost of living on a hundred worlds, living off those who worked in production. Not, he had to concede, that those who worked in production these days were the old working classes in a true Marxist definition; they were all engineers who went around troubleshooting cybernetics. But for all the changes and undeniable improvements automation and consumerism had brought to the proletariat's standard of living, it hadn't changed the financial power structure which ruled the human race. A tiny minority controlled the wealth of hundreds of worlds, bypassing, buying, or corrupting governments to maintain their dominance. And here he was, living among them, a keen consumer of their products, daunted by their size, his life's purpose almost lost as he sold more and more of himself to Johansson's cause. A cause which was now giving him a great deal of concern. It wasn't something he'd told anyone – after all, who could he tell? – but he was having to face up to the daunting, and terrifying, prospect that Bradley Johansson might just be right about the Starflyer. The whole Prime situation was too odd, there were too many coincidences piling up: the *Second Chance* mission, the barrier disappearing, Hell's Gateway, the attack on Venice Coast. Adam was certain there was going to be a war, and he wasn't sure which side the Commonwealth government was going to be on.

So he went about the meticulous job of assembling Johansson's equipment without his usual cynicism. The party had been avoided for a long time now, he didn't provide any chapter on any planet with support. It was the Guardians who received his full attention. Crazy, enthusiastic, devoted youngsters from Far Away, who were riding gleefully off on their crusade and didn't have a single clue how the Confederation worked. They were the ones he was protecting, guiding like some old mystic promising nirvana at the end of the road. Except today it looked like Stig wasn't going to make it.

The station car drove him carefully along the internal highways into the Arlee district, a hundred square miles of warehouses on the east side of LA Galactic. The blank-faced composite buildings were laid out in a perfect grid. Some were so large they took up an entire block, while some blocks had as many as twenty separate units. They all had light composite walls and black solar cell roofs, cumbersome air conditioning units sprouted from walls and edges like mechanical cancers, their radiant fans shining a dull orange under the hot sunlight. There were no sidewalks, and cars were a rarity on these roads. Vans and large trucks trundled along everywhere, their driver arrays navigating the simple path between their loading bay and a rail cargo handling yard on a 24/7 basis. But at least this district involved the physical movement of goods, it wasn't the dealing and moneymaking of the offices. That normally made it bearable for him.

He drove into the loading bay park at the Lemule's Max Transit warehouse, a medium-sized building, enclosing four acres of floor space. Bjou McSobel and Jenny McNowak were working inside. Lemule's had a big order for sourcing and supplying packager modules for a supermarket chain on five phase two worlds, and their crates were stacked up across half of the cavernous interior awaiting shipment orders. Flat-bed loaders and fork-lifts slid up and down the lanes between the high metal ledges, shuffling farm equipment, carpentry tools, GPbots, domestic hologram portals, and a hundred other items which formed the company's legitimate business, packaging them for their train ride out across the planets. By itself, Lemule's Max Transit was a viable operation. Every morning when he left his hotel on the coast and drove into LA Galactic, Adam felt the irony that after so many years spent running identical concerns he could manage a transit company far better than the entrepreneurs and opportunist chancers who were desperate for their own company to succeed.

Bjou closed the heavy roll door at the end of the loading bay as Adam got out of the car. 'How are we doing?' Adam asked.

'Jenny has opened the access hatch. The S&Ibot should be here in another forty minutes.'

'It definitely retrieved the case?'

'Yes, sir.'

'Some good news, then.'

They went down to the far end of the warehouse where the Guardians had set up a secure area. Bjou and Jenny had been preparing a shipment of equipment for Far Away, disguising the components in basic industrial tools and consumer electronics due for shipment to Armstrong City. On the other side of the open crates and disassembled machines a concealed manhole cover had been opened in the enzyme-bonded concrete floor. Below it was a small circular shaft leading down five metres to one of the sewer pipes which served LA Galactic. That too had been breached, the hole sealed up again with a flush-fitting hatch. Jenny was sitting on the rim of the shaft, an anxious expression on her face as she followed the progress of their S&Ibot through the maze of sewer pipes which lay underneath LA Galactic.

'No problems, sir,' she said. 'Our monitors haven't picked up anything tracking the bot.'

'Okay, Jenny, keep on it.'

Bjou pulled over a couple of chairs, and Adam sat down gratefully. His e-butler reported an encrypted call from Kieran.

'Sir, we thought you should know. Paula Myo just arrived on a loop train from Seattle. She's being escorted by CST security personnel. Looks like they're going to the operational centre.'

A little shiver of cold ran down Adam's spine. If she was

924

giving Stig's operation her personal attention then she knew he was important.

'Do you want us to hack into their internal network?' Kieran asked. 'We might be able to see what she's doing.'

'No,' Adam said immediately. 'We can't guarantee a clean hack, not into CST security. I don't want them tipped off we know about them. That's Stig's only advantage right now.'

'Yes, sir.'

Adam resisted putting his head in his hands. He sat on the hard plastic seat, staring at the secret hole in the floor, while he called up files and displayed them across his virtual vision. Somewhere there had to be a weak link, a way Paula had found to infiltrate his couriers. When the faint amber information floated in front of him he cursed himself for making such an elementary mistake. Stig was collecting software from an insider at the Shansorel Partnership, the same insider who had supplied regulator software for a set of microphase modulators which Valtare Rigin had acquired. It would have had the partnership's signature embedded in the sub-routines. Easy to trace. 'Damnit,' he grunted. 'I'm getting old. And stupid.'

'Is everything all right, sir?' Bjou asked.

'Yeah, I think so.'

*

Tarlo was waiting in the operations room of LA Galactic's CST security department when Paula Myo came in.

'Sorry chief,' he said. 'I think he made me when he came out of the can.'

She nodded. 'Don't worry about it.'

He glanced at the CST security officer who'd escorted Paula. The whole department had rolled over and given full cooperation at the mere mention of her name. 'We should have gone for a virtual observation.'

'I have my suspicions about their electronic support capability. They certainly found your box fast enough. If they're that good they would have been aware of a virtual as soon as we began it.' She turned to the security officer. 'I'd like a clean office we can use as our field headquarters, please.'

'Yes, ma'am.' He showed them down a corridor to an empty office, and activated the systems, giving them full access.

'There's a support team en route from Paris, they'll be here in half an hour,' Paula told Tarlo when they were alone again. 'They'll be able to back up the rest of your crew.'

'It should have been a bigger op from the start.'

'I know. It was very short notice.' Paula surprised herself by how easy it was to tell the lie. It wasn't something she was practised in. But the support team was inevitable now. What she had to concentrate on was the people who knew before the target had started to rabbit. That was where the leak must have originated.

'Are you sure he discovered the box?' she asked Tarlo, uncomfortably aware that he'd been on the Venice Coast operation.

'He's on a courier run, right?' Tarlo said. 'That's what you told us. But he went through his little spotter routine, then went and retrieved something else from the locker. That is not what happens. You run the route as quickly as possible, you don't pick up a second item, that doubles the risk. Besides, I was watching him, he knows he's been made.' He gave a lame shrug. 'My opinion, for what it's worth.'

'Don't worry, I still value it. Which leaves us guessing what he's going to do next.'

'Only one thing he can do, try and shake us.'

'How are we doing on that?'

'Carol and the others are in four taxis, ahead and behind him. They've overridden the driver-array software, and the LA traffic police have been informed this is a navy operation. We have full route authority. He's not going to get away from us in a taxi.'

'Humm, I'm concerned what was in the black shoulder bag he retrieved.'

'Has to be stuffed full of weapons for when he makes his break.'

'You might be right. Either way, we can't take any chances. Get in touch with the LAPD, tell them I need a tactical armaments squad on standby.'

'You got it.'

*

It was over eight miles as the crow flies from the Carralvo terminal to the Lemule's Max Transit warehouse in the Arlee district. By sewer pipeline, it was a lot further. Nor was it a direct route. The Service & Inspection bot had to pass through several junctions, opening and closing flow valves like air locks so that it could switch pipes. Forty-three minutes after Adam arrived at the warehouse, it finally crawled up under the hatch. Jenny scurried down the open shaft and popped the hatch at the bottom. Bjou and Adam stood above her, shining powerful flashlights down so she could see what she was doing.

Adam pulled a face as the hatch opened and the smell hit him. Jenny was reaching down to the filthy S&Ibot they'd cloned from the LA Galactic utility service company. She took the little plastic case from its electromuscle limb, and hurriedly shut the hatch.

Once she was out, Bjou shut the manhole cover, and started to seal it against casual inspection. Jenny handed the case to Adam, who opened it and slipped the memory crystal into his hand-held array.

'Checks out,' he said as the program menu scrolled down the unit's screen. Jenny let out a happy sigh.

Adam put a call straight through to Kieran. 'Give Stig the go code for discontinue and break.'

*

The CST security division office was filling up. As well as the back-up team from Paris, there was now a detective lieutenant from the LAPD who was acting as liaison. In the two hours since leaving LA Galactic, all the target had done was drive into LA and stop on Walgrove Avenue, then start walking. He'd slowly made his way towards the shoreline, walking up and down the streets, and was currently on Washington Boulevard, close to the Del Rey Marina.

Tarlo got the city RI to access several public cameras in the area. Their images were coming up on screens in the office. Paula wouldn't let them focus on the target in case the Guardians were monitoring the dataflow, so they continued their slow sweeps, occasionally catching him as he walked past.

'Heading for the Marina,' Tarlo said. 'Do you think he's got a boat waiting?'

'Who knows?' she said. 'But get a list of everything moored there from the harbourmaster.'

'I'm on that,' Renne said.

Paula's e-butler told her that Senator Burnelli was placing an encrypted call to her. She went to the back of the office and authorized the link.

'Paula, how are you?'

One of the street cameras caught the target walking into the Del Rey marina. Two of the box team had gone in ahead of him. 'Busy,' she said. The LAPD liaison was ordering the tactical armaments squad to a new position.

'I won't take up too much of your time, but I rather thought you'd want to hear this. I've got good news and not so good.'

'Tell me the good,' she said.

'I took it kind of personal that my request about Far Away

928

had been blocked, so I confronted Doi directly. Nice to know I still have some clout. A century of public service hasn't been entirely wasted. As of next week, all cargo being shipped to Far Away will be examined at Boongate. No exceptions. She's going to order Columbia to form a specialist division to take care of it.'

'Thank you very much, Senator.' A camera above one of the wharfs showed the target walking along the wooden planks to the end, looking at the beautiful, expensive boats moored on either side. She frowned. 'Have we got a pursuit boat available?' she asked the liaison officer.

'I can find you one.'

'Please do.' She flipped the link to the senator back on. 'What was the other news?'

'I'm not sure how you're going to take this,' Thompson said. 'I was kind of surprised myself. I've been asking questions in a few dark places since we talked last. The people lobbying the Executive against examining cargo for Far Away work for Nigel Sheldon.'

'Repeat, please.'

'Nigel Sheldon has been blocking your request.'

'Are you sure?'

'One hundred per cent, Paula.'

'I need to see you.'

'I agree. As soon as possible. I think we might want to bring my father in on this as well.'

The target reached the end of the wharf, hopped over the chain railing, and dropped into the water.

'Holy shit,' Tarlo cried. 'Did you see that?'

'Have the tactical armaments squad got divers?' Renne asked the liaison officer.

He was staring incredulously at the screen. 'I . . . I'll check.'

'Tarlo,' Paula ordered, 'focus all available cameras on the water in the marina.'

'No problem.'

'Deploy the tactical armaments squad right now,' she said. 'No boat is to leave that marina. I want every available policeman in Venice down there. Each boat is to be checked individually. Get me a helicopter above the marina now, have them scan the water. And I want a coastguard boat or something with sonar at the mouth of the marina, now!'

The office was suddenly busy, with everyone issuing instructions.

'I'll have to call you back,' Paula told the senator. 'Things just got a little hectic around here.'

*

Kazimir stayed out in the house's little back garden as the sun fell below the horizon. Lights came on all along the canal where the other houses backed on to the water. A quarter of a mile away, bright old-fashioned street lamps illuminated the little bridge with its white railings. The city's nocturnal noises crept over him, carried by the warm still air. He was very aware of the sirens. So far none of them were close. The timer in his virtual vision kept adding up the minutes and hours since Stig had jumped into the water. Too many. Way too many.

At eleven o'clock the helicopters were still hovering above the marina. Sitting in his seat on the porch, Kazimir could just look through the gap between the low houses opposite to see their powerful searchlights sweeping back and forth, illuminating the rigging of the moored boats. The tension of the wait was screwing his guts up. Waiting on a Charlemagne for the command to charge was a child's game compared to this.

'Kaz?'

It was a faint, pained voice. Kazimir lurched over the few yards from his seat to the edge of the water. Stig's face was looking up at him.

'You made it!' Kazimir gasped.

'Just about. I'm not sure I can get out, Kaz.'

Kazimir splashed into the water and grabbed hold of his old tutor. Stig had virtually no strength left, so Kazimir hauled him out in a fireman's lift and staggered into the house.

Stig lay on the couch while Kazimir locked up the windows and doors, activating the security system. When he'd pulled the drapes shut, he finally switched on the lights.

'I fucking hate swimming,' Stig moaned. A gill mask was hanging from its strap round his neck, its small red low-power warning light gleaming softly.

'Me, too,' Kazimir said. 'But I remember who taught me.' He wrapped a blanket round Stig's trembling shoulders, then started to undo his soaking, mud-smeared trousers.

Stig looked down and grunted a laugh. 'Very gay. Let's hope Myo's team doesn't come crashing through the window right this minute.'

'You want a drink?'

'God, no. No fluid. Not now, not ever again. I must have swallowed half of the canal network. I thought Earth had strict anti-pollution laws. Didn't goddamn taste like it. I swear I was swimming through raw shit out there.'

Kazimir got the trousers off, and put another blanket round Stig's legs. He was looking like someone who'd been rescued from the north pole. 'Didn't you have flippers?'

'Only to start with. I lost them along with everything else.' He laughed weakly. 'Including the shirt off my back. Let this be a lesson to you, Kaz; doesn't matter how good your gadgets and fall-back plans are, real life doesn't cooperate. Now for Christ's sake tell me Adam retrieved the programs I brought back.'

'He got them.' Kazimir drew a breath ready to say but. Then thought better of it.

His hesitation didn't go unnoticed.

'What?' Stig asked.

'The news shows announced it this evening: from now on there's going to be an inspection of all cargo shipped to Far

Away. Elvin and Johansson haven't said anything, but it looks like we're screwed.'

*

The station security people had cleared a big semicircular space around the left luggage lockers in the Carralvo terminal. Curious passengers on their way to catch trains lingered to see what the fuss was about. Eventually they were rewarded by the appearance of Paula Myo. There was a scattering of applause, someone even whistled appreciatively. She ignored them, watching impassively as the forensics team went to work on the locker. Tarlo and Renne stood behind her, fending off questions from the reporters who'd appeared, and the attentions of the CST security officer. They knew how much their boss valued an uninterrupted examination of any crime scene.

'So is it coincidence?' Tarlo asked. 'Or is this their standard operating policy now, do you think?'

'Is what coincidence?' Renne said.

'Underwater getaway. Hey, if they start doing this all the time, maybe the navy will pay for us to be modified. That would be cool, I could handle growing a dolphin sonar.'

'Yeah? I can think of something useless it could replace on you.'

'That's seen a lot of use, thank you.'

'It isn't standard operating policy,' Paula said. 'Our target today was a Guardian. The Venice Coast operative was working for someone else.' Nigel Sheldon. But how does he benefit from all this? Why allow the Guardians to smuggle arms to Far Away, then attack a merchant they contract? It doesn't make sense.

'Are you sure he was a Guardian today?' Tarlo asked.

Renne shot him a warning look, but Paula didn't react.

'Our problem is we don't know what they're hoping to accomplish next,' Paula said. 'This new stage is puzzling. Renne, I want you to put together a new team to study the equipment we know Valtare Rigin was putting together for them.'

'The weapons division report said there were too many unknowns,' Renne said cautiously. 'They couldn't give us a definite use.'

'I know. Their trouble is they're made up from solid thinkers. I want to go off the scale with this one. We're in the navy now, there shouldn't be any problem finding and drafting specialists in weapons physics, especially ones with over-active imaginations. Get me a list of possible uses, however far-fetched.'

'Yes, chief.'

The navy lieutenant in charge of the forensic team came over to Paula and saluted. Tarlo and Renne tried hard not to smile.

'We've got a family match on the DNA residue, ma'am,' the lieutenant said. 'You were right, he is from the Far Away clans. We've gathered enough samples in the past to confirm the correlation; he's a seventh or eighth descendant of Robert and Minette McSobel. Given the level of inbreeding, it's hard to say which.'

'Thank you.' Paula turned to Tarlo, and raised an eyebrow. He gave an elaborate shrug. 'Sorry, Chief.'

'All right then, we know there's another active equipment smuggling operation, probably being run by Adam Elvin. Start putting together some options for tracking it.'

*

The professional's little office had a desk with an array that connected directly to the Clinton Estate's network. He moved the corpse to one side, wiped away the blood which had burst from the man's neck when it was wrenched backwards, and put his hand on the desktop array's i-spot, opening a direct channel into it. Software from his inserts infiltrated the Estate network. The club had extremely sophisticated routines, hovering just under RI level. Given its clientele, it was inevitable that the security would be top-rated. That was what made it the ideal place for the extermination. People were comfortable enough to let their guard down here.

His software identified the nodes which served the club's squash courts, and infiltrated their management programs as diagnostic probes. The nodes couldn't be crashed, that would be detected by the network regulator immediately. What he wanted was the ability to divert emergency signals.

When he was satisfied his subtle corruption was integrated and functioning, he changed his clothes, slipping into the white shirt and shorts that were regulation for the club's sports staff. He waited in the office for forty-one minutes, then picked up a squash racquet and walked down the short corridor to the court which Senator Burnelli had booked for his lesson.

The senator was already inside, warming a ball up. 'Where's Dieter?' he asked.

'I'm sorry, Senator, Dieter is off sick today,' he said, and shut the door. 'I'm taking his lessons today.'

'Okay, son.' The senator gave an affable smile. 'You've got a hard task ahead of you. I got beaten by Goldreich's aide this week. It was humiliating. And now I'm looking for a little payback.'

'Of course.' He walked towards the senator.

'What's your name, son?'

His hand came round fast, chopping into the senator's neck. There was a loud snap as the man's spine snapped. The senator's body turned limp and fell to the floor, inserts shrieking in alarm.

He paused for a second, checking his software to see that none of the network nodes were relaying the alert. The diverts were working, routing the dying man's calls for help to a useless one-time address code. He clenched his hand into a fist, and used his full amplified strength to smash it into the senator's face. Thompson Burnelli's skull shattered from the impact.

22

'We had stories of small strange animals that were not animals who could sometimes be seen in our forests,' Tochee said through the array's translator program. 'There are also stories of forests that have other forests inside them, hidden from normal travellers. But as we entered the age of reason and science, such stories faded into legend. Nobody in modern times has experienced either. Even I treated them as stories generated during our primitive past and used to explain some facet of nature, or act as a warning to younger family members. It was my venerable elder family parent who planted the doubt in my mind. Just before the elder died, it told me it had seen the small not-animals, and even ventured along a path to an inner forest many years ago when it was a youngster, before technology became so widespread. For me, the idea that such legends were not legends, but could actually be experienced, was too much to ignore. I made my plans quietly, without telling my colleagues, and set off to the forest where my elder parent said it visited the inner forest. I spent many days exploring, and eventually realized I was not only lost, but also no longer on my own world. And now I have my own stories to tell which are greater than all of those collected in our archive.'

'Wait,' Orion said, a smile bursting onto his heavily-freckled face. 'You're a librarian?'

The array bleeped, and said, 'Non-equivalent translation inserted.'

Tochee said: 'I am a custodian of our culture's history. I impart the stories of what was and what might have been to the youngsters of many families. This way our knowledge is not only maintained, but appreciated.'

'A librarian!' Orion grinned at Ozzie.

'That's nice,' Ozzie said pointedly. Now the translator was relaying everything they said to Tochee, it was becoming both difficult and embarrassing to explain away Orion's outbursts of laughter. The boy seemed to find a lot of Tochee's culture amusing. Ozzie had to admit, the alien's life did seem to be rather, well . . . prim and proper.

'How did you know you were on another planet?' Orion asked. 'Do your people have space travel?'

'I realized the planet was different to my own when I saw the sun in the sky was a different colour, and at night the star pattern was different,' Tochee said. 'We do not have space travel.'

'Why not?' Orion waved at the gadgets Tochee was holding in its manipulator flesh. 'You've obviously got the technology level.'

'We do not have the need. We do not have the internal non-logic which you possess, the constant desire to explore without reason.'

'You wanted to find the legends,' Ozzie said. 'Wasn't that an unreasonable pursuit?'

'Yes. And in that wish I demonstrated a wild aberration from my kind. If verification of my elder parent's story was required, then my colleagues and I should have begun a systematic investigation. I went by myself because I believed my colleagues would show no interest.'

'Wild!' Orion was giggling again. Ozzie flashed him another warning glare.

'I'm interested that your people don't consider space flight to be necessary,' Ozzie said. 'If you've reached an advanced technological level, are you not finding diminishing resources to be a problem?'

'No. We do not build anything beyond our ability to sustain it.'

'That's very admirable. Our species is nothing like as rational.'

'From what I have witnessed on my travels, that attitude seems to be in the majority.'

'Yeah, but there are varying degrees. I'd like to think we're reasonably restrained, but by your standards we're probably not.'

'That makes neither of us right, nor wrong.'

'I hope so. After all, we all have to share the same galaxy.'

'I believe that intelligence and rationality will always be primary no matter what shape sentient creatures take. To not think that would be to doubt the value of life itself.'

Ozzie gave the big alien a quick thumbs up. They were approaching another steep incline that was half rock. Tochee could scale such obstacles with the greatest of ease, while he and Orion had to scramble up, sweating with the effort. Ozzie glanced towards the sea on his left. They'd been walking along the top of the coastal cliff for two days. It varied considerably in height, but it was a good twenty metres high here, and there didn't seem to be a beach at the bottom. Not that there was an easy path down in any case.

'Up we go, then,' he told Orion. The boy pulled a face, and re-tied the band of faded blue cloth that was holding his long hair back away from his eyes. They both started to clamber up, jamming feet into narrow crevices, hands gripping precariously at strong tufts of grass so they didn't lose their balance when the weight of the rucksacks pulled at them. Tochee flowed up the incline, its ridges of locomotion flesh clasping at the rock and vegetation as it went. Ozzie hadn't asked, but he figured the big alien could probably slide straight up a sheer cliff.

Once they were on top, they began walking along the edge of the cliff. The ground was sloping down again now. He knew they were on an island. The small central hill with its crown of jungle had been in sight on his right for the whole two days of their trek. His array's inertial guidance unit was plotting their wide circular course around it. He hadn't told Orion yet, but in another mile and a half they'd be back where they started.

'Is that an island out there?' Orion asked.

Right on the horizon there was a small dark smudge. When Ozzie zoomed in, it resolved into a solid little peak rising out of the sea, much like the one they were on. 'Yep, that makes five. This is some kind of archipelago.'

'We haven't seen any ships,' Orion said.

'Give it time, it's only been two days.'

'Are you sure?'

'I'm sure.' There hadn't been any night since they arrived on this world. In fact, the bright sun's position hadn't moved at all. The planet was tide-locked, with one face permanently pointing towards the sun. Ozzie wasn't sure how the climate could function normally with such a set-up. But then the gas halo was hardly a natural phenomenon. Between them, he and Tochee had used every sensor they had to scan the multitude of twinkling specks that were orbiting through the gas with this planet. The other specks weren't planets, that was for certain, although there was very little else they could discover about them. They weren't emitting any radio or microwave pulses, at least not strong enough to be detectable at any distance. That just left Johansson's brief description to fall back on. Giant lengths of some coral variant that was home to vegetation. He wondered if the Silfen used them as cities, or nests, or if they even bothered with them at all. Maybe they were just there to keep the gas in the halo fresh and breathable, as forests and oceans were to planets.

As for their measurements of the halo itself, the best they could come up with was that it had a circular cross-section roughly two million kilometres in diameter that orbited a hundred and fifty million kilometres from the star. What contained the gas was unknown, but had to be some kind of force field. The idea of building a transparent tube this big was mind-boggling, and introduced a whole range of engineering and maintenance problems. Exactly where the power came from to generate a force field on such a scale was also unknown, although Ozzie was pretty sure the builders must have tapped the star's power. Frankly, there was little else which could provide the kind of energy level required. Why anyone would create such an artefact in the first place was beyond him. It lacked the practicality of a Dyson sphere or a Niven ring. But then, if you had the ability to do this, you probably didn't actually need to. And if it was the Silfen home system, he strongly suspected the answer to such a question would be: why not. He didn't really care, he was just happy someone had done it – and he'd seen it.

'Ozzie, Tochee, look!' Orion was racing on ahead of them through the grass. There was no cliff here, the ground had dipped until it was almost level with the sea. A big sandy beach curved away ahead of them. The boy ran onto the sand. A dead fern frond was standing on top of a low dune at the back of the beach like a brown flag. Ozzie had stuck it in there when they started their exploratory walk.

The boy's delight crumpled as he pulled the frond out of the sand. 'This is an island.'

'Fraid so, man,' Ozzie said.

'But . . .' Orion turned to look at the small central mountain. 'How do we get off?'

'I can swim to another island,' Tochee said. 'If you are to come with me, we must build a boat.'

Orion gave the sea a mistrustful look. 'Can't we call someone for help?'

'Nobody's listening,' Ozzie said, holding up his hand-held array. The unit had been transmitting standard first contact signals since it started functioning again, along with a human SOS. So far, the entire electromagnetic spectrum had remained silent.

'If this is where the Silfen live, where *are* they?' the boy demanded.

'On the mainland, somewhere, I guess,' Ozzie said. He stared out to sea. Three islands were visible to his retinal inserts on full zoom, though he wasn't sure of their distance. If they were the same size as this one, they'd be nearly fifty miles away. Which, given he was now only a couple of yards above sea level, should have put them far over the horizon on any Earth-sized planet. He wondered if this one was the same size as Silvergalde.

'Where's that?' Orion asked grouchily.

'I don't know. In that cloudbank we saw from the other side of the island, maybe.'

'You don't know that.'

'No, I don't,' Ozzie snapped. 'I don't get this place at all, okay.'

'Sorry, Ozzie,' Orion said meekly. 'I just thought ... you normally know stuff, that's all.'

'Yeah, well this time I don't, so we'll have to find it out together.' He told his e-butler to call up boat-building files from his array's memory.

*

Even in midsummer, the waters of the Trine'ba were cold. Filled with snow melt every spring, and deep enough to keep sunlight out of its lower levels, it guarded its low temperature jealously. Mark wore a warmsuit as he drifted among the

940

fabulous dendrites, fans, and arches of coral that sprouted from the main reef. So far, marine biologists had identified three hundred and seventy-two species of coral, and added more every year. They ranged from the dominant dragonback, with its long amethyst and amber mounds, down to beige corknuts the size of pebbles. Unicorn horn formations poked upwards from the patches of bright tangerine ditchcoral, seriously sharp at the point. He was pleased to see Barry was showing them due respect. So many people wanted to see if they were as sharp as they looked. Warmsuit fabric gave no protection for fingers and palms. Every year Randtown General Hospital treated dozens of tourist impalements.

Barry saw him watching, and gave the circular okay signal with his right hand. Mark waved back. Cobalt ring snakes thrummed inquisitively in their niches as they swam lazily overhead. Rugpikes crawled over the reef, hundreds of tiny stalk eyes swivelling as if they were a strip of soft green wheat waving in a gentle breeze. Fish were clotting the water around them like a gritty kaleidoscope cloud – thousands of brilliantly coloured starburst particles whose spines and spindles pulsed rapidly, propelling them along in jerky zigzags. They came in sizes from brassy afriwebs half the length of his finger up to lumbering great brown and gold maundyfish, bigger than humans and moving with drunken sluggishness around the lower reefs. A shoal of eerie milk-white sloopbacks wriggled right in front of Mark's goggles, and he made a slow catching motion with his hands. The palm-length creatures bent their spines back to form a streamlined teardrop and jetted away.

Barry was doing slow barrel rolls, his flippers kicking in careful rhythm. Both hands were clenched around flakes of dried native insects, which he was slowly rubbing apart. Fish followed him, feeding on the tiny flecks. They formed twin spirals in his wake, like intersecting corkscrews. As they ate, their unique digestive tract bacteria began to glow, illuminating them from within. Looking down on them against the murky bottom was to see an iridescent comet tail spinning in slow motion across the darkness.

With the food almost gone, Barry slapped his hands together, creating an expanding sphere of broken flakes. The Trine'ba fish swarmed in, making a galaxy of opalescent stars around him.

Mark smiled proudly inside his gill mask. The boy was everything he could have wanted in a son: happy, cheeky, confident. He'd grown beautifully in this environment. It was becoming hard to remember Augusta now. Neither of the kids ever talked about it these days, even Liz called her friends back there less and less, and he hadn't spoken to his father in months.

He kicked his legs, closing in on his son as the shroud of luminous fish darkened and swam away in search of more food. The timer in his virtual vision said they'd been exploring the reef underwater for forty minutes now. He pointed to the surface. Barry responded with a reluctant okay hand sign.

They came up into warm bright sunlight that had them blinking tears against it as they searched round for the boat. The catamaran was a hundred and fifty metres away. Liz was standing on the prow, waving at them. Mark took the gill mouthpiece out. 'Got a long swim over there. Better inflate your jacket.'

'I'm all right, Dad.'

'I'm not. Let a little air in, huh, make your mom happy.'

'Okay, I guess.'

Mark pressed the pump valve on his shoulder, and felt the warmsuit jacket stiffen as the fabric inhaled, puffing up around him. They rolled onto their backs, and began a steady kick.

Sandy was still snorkelling round the yacht, along with Elle, one of the Dunbavand kids. Lydia and her two lads, Will and Ed, were already back on the catamaran, washing their diving gear. David and Liz were starting to prepare lunch on the middeck.

Panda barked delightedly as Barry swam up to the small dive platform at the back of the yacht.

'Stay,' Liz called. The dog looked like she was about to jump in and swim again.

Barry clambered onto the dive platform and took his flippers off. 'Did you miss me?' he asked Panda. 'Did you?'

The dog was still barking excitedly, her tail wagging furiously. Barry made a fuss of her when he climbed up the small chrome ladder to the main deck. He started to reach for one of the boiled eggs from the salad Liz was setting out. 'Clean up and dry out first,' his mother warned him.

Mark helped Sandy onto the dive platform. She lifted her mask off, and smiled happily at her father. 'I saw a grog down there, Daddy. It was hugely big.' Her arms stretched out wide to show just how big.

'That's lovely darling,' he said as he pulled his own flippers off. 'Did you put your sunscreen on before you went in the water?'

'Uh huh.' She nodded vigorously.

Even though Sandy's skin was a lot darker than his, he was suspicious about the back of her neck and arms; they looked slightly sunburnt to him. 'Well let's put some aftersun salve on shall we?'

Happy with the attention, she agreed readily.

'You shouldn't have taken him out for so long,' Liz chided when he sat down and began applying the salve to Sandy's back. 'I was getting worried. And look how far away from the boat you got.'

'But, Mom, it was so clear down there today,' Barry protested. 'You could see for miles. It's never been so good before.'

Mark gave his wife a helpless look. How could you prevent

a kid having that much fun? She gave the pair of them an exasperated stare, and carried on with the salad.

The catamaran belonged to David and Lydia, who used it during the summer months to explore the little coves and inlets along Trine'ba's shoreline. In wintertime it was hauled up the Randtown yacht club's slipway, so at the weekends David could spend hours in the boatshed painting the hull and repairing the rigging ready for the next season. Mark loved the yacht, and had already begun to think seriously about getting one himself. Not that they could afford one yet. It was a bit like having a dog and a 4x4, all part of Randtown.

When everyone was finally washed and dry and sitting down to lunch, the catamaran's electromuscle rigging unfurled its sails and set off for one of the tiny conical atolls that poked up from the very deepest part of the lake. They'd promised the kids they could visit one in the afternoon to see if the balloon flowers were inflating yet. It was almost time for the annual event, which Randtown celebrated with parades and a huge lakeside barbecue in the evening.

'The vineyard association said they haven't noticed any decline on orders,' David said when the kids had all gone to sit on the stern to eat their lillinberries and ice cream. 'I was at the meeting last night. You should have come, Mark.'

'Not sure I'd be welcome.'

'Don't be so paranoid,' Lydia told him. 'You didn't even get your fifteen minutes of fame; you were just a one-minute wonder that evening. All the media cares about right now is the Burnelli murder.'

'That Baron woman is still using the phrase,' Mark said. 'According to her show all of Randtown is anti-human.' Everyone in the district was worried about the effect Baron's propaganda would have on their small economy. So far it hadn't been bad. After a five-day standoff, the navy trucks had eventually retreated back down the highway, and the tourist buses had returned. Of course, the summer bookings had been made months before; it was too late for anyone to cancel. The true test would be next season's bookings. A surprising number of visitors had congratulated the residents on making their stand – Mark's interview was politely never mentioned. In the meantime, people were watching to see what would happen to their small export trade of wines and organic food.

'Nobody on Elan is going to organize a boycott, for heaven's sake,' Liz said. 'In any event, half of the wine we make is sold right here in the district; and the kind of people who buy proper organic produce support what we did anyway.'

Mark nodded glumly, and poured himself some more Chapples wine. 'I might have got away with it, then.'

David leaned over, and touched his glass to Mark's. 'I'll drink to that. Come on, the future's looking good. Liz has almost cracked the Kinavine's rhizome sequence; once we have that fixing its own nitrogen we can sell it for cultivation right across the valley. People will be ripping up their old vines and replanting. There won't be a vineyard on Ryceel that can compete against that wine when it crops.'

'It's going to take a little while yet,' Liz said.

Mark put his arm around her. 'You'll do it,' he said softly.

She grinned back at him.

'What in God's name are those?' Lydia asked. She was shielding her eyes with one hand, pointing back towards Randtown with the other.

Blackwater Crag dominated the skyline behind the town, then there was a short break in the mountains to the west of it where the highway valley led back into the Dau'sings. After that the rugged peaks rose again to stand guard over Trine'ba's shore. One of the tallest peaks on the western side was Goi'al, the southernmost of a cluster collectively called the Regents, where the district's snow bike sports and racing were based.

Only now, in midsummer when the ice and snow finally lifted from the sheltered high ground, did the little machines pack up for a few months.

Black specks were circling slowly to the side of Goi'al. To be visible from this distance they must have been huge.

'Bloody hell,' David muttered. He went straight to the cabin, and brought back a pair of binoculars from the locker. Electromuscle pulleys began to furl the sails, reducing speed to make the catamaran more stable. 'Helicopters,' he said. 'Bugger, but they're big brutes. I've never seen anything like them before, they've got double rotors. Must be some kind of heavy cargo lifter. I make that at least fifteen of them up there, could be more.'

He offered the binoculars round to the others. Liz took them. Mark didn't bother, he slumped down into the mid-deck's semicircular couch. 'It's the detector station,' he said in dismay. 'After everything we did, everything we said, they brought it in anyway. The bastards.'

Liz handed the binoculars to Lydia. 'You knew it was going to happen in the end, Mark. Something that big isn't stopped by a bunch of people standing in the middle of the road.'

'I thought we lived in a democracy.'

'We do. We exercised our democratic right to protest, and they ignored us. Ultimately, the navy is a government department, what did you expect from them?'

'I don't know. Would a little sensitivity be too much to ask?'

She went over and sat beside him. 'I'm really sorry, baby. I don't want them here any more than you do. But we're going to have to knuckle down and live with it for the duration. These are strange times, we have to make allowances for that. Once this whole Prime thing is over, and the warmongers and profiteers have finished frightening the life out of everyone, then the station will be gone. We'll make damn sure they take all their crap with them, as well, I promise that.'

946

'Yeah,' he sighed, conscious how he must be coming over as a petulant brat to the Dunbavands. 'Yeah, I guess so. But I don't have to like it.'

'Nobody's asking you to.'

He drained the last of the Chapples wine from the glass, and looked back across the cool calm waters of Trine'ba. The helicopters had already begun to land on the other side of Goi'al.

*

'Our worst fears have been proved right,' the Guardians' spokesman said in a calm, significant voice. 'The Dyson aliens are preparing to invade the Commonwealth. They have an overwhelming force pouring through Hell's Gateway which will be unleashed against us any day now. We warned you this would happen, and now, sadly, millions if not billions of citizens will be killed to confirm everything we have always said is tragically true. They will die because our Commonwealth's defences are completely inadequate. We know that every person serving in the navy will do their utmost when the invasion begins, we support them wholeheartedly in their awful task, but there are too few of them, and not enough ships. If we could provide them with assistance, we would, but that is not our arena.

'We will carry on our own lonely fight against the Starflyer creature who has brought about this disaster. It is not often we are able to expose one of its agents, for they are normally hidden and protected. However, in this case, the evidence is overwhelming. One person put forward the proposal to launch a starship to investigate Dyson Alpha. One person now governs the size of the navy budget. One person knows the true size of the resources we need, and continually denies us those resources. One person sends their murderer to kill their opponents. This one person is the most powerful puppet the Starflyer has ever used against us. It is President Doi herself.

947

'Be warned, and remember the true crisis we are facing is not the physical one from the Dyson aliens. It is the one corrupting us from within. We have always been honest with you. Now, in humanity's darkest hour, we ask you to believe us in this one last time. Doi and her master are our enemy, she will obliterate us if left unchallenged.

'Challenge her.' The spokesman bowed his head. 'I thank you for your time.'

*

The whole office was spending the morning filing reports and filling in finance department forms to cover the cost of the LA deployment. Thankfully, Paula just had to skim the summaries and attach her authorization code. That left her with some time to contemplate what had happened, although all she could really think about was Thompson Burnelli's murder. Tarlo and Renne were busy sifting through the pitifully small amount of leads resulting from the pursuit so they could draw up an action plan. Alic Hogan had chosen to examine the camera images from LA Galactic in a virtual projection to see if the software had been handed over inside the station terminal. She didn't object. For all he was Columbia's place-man, Hogan was relatively efficient at his job, and it would keep him away from her for most of the day.

As so often happened with the Johansson case, LA had become a problem that had multiplied unexpectedly, and always in the wrong directions. Although on the positive side, she at least knew that Elvin was putting together another smuggling operation.

At eleven o'clock Rafael Columbia appeared in the office. He was dressed in his full admiral's uniform, with several staff officers in attendance. Everyone in the office stopped what they were doing to look at him.

Paula stood up just as he reached her door. 'Wait for me,' he told his officers, and closed the door.

'Admiral,' Paula said. She closed the file in her virtual vision which had been displaying the names of everyone she'd informed of a target arriving at Seattle, along with their time-frame.

He gave her a humourless smile as he sat in the visitor's chair. 'Commander.'

'What can I do for you?'

'Ordinarily, I would say you can explain your latest fuck-up. But, frankly I think we've gone beyond that, don't you?'

'Los Angeles was unfortunate, although we did learn that . . .'

'Not interested. It was a half-assed operation from the start. And that is indicative of the way you run things. Some *target* appears out of nowhere, and without any planning or prior notification you put an under-resourced team on pursuit duties. Not only that, but when things go wrong, you drag half of the LAPD into the operation just in time for them to watch it blow up in our face. We're a fucking laughing stock, Commander. And I will not tolerate that.'

Paula saw how much anger was behind Columbia's steely expression, and realized she was going to have to confide in him. 'I'm sorry about the negative publicity, but I can assure you the operation was planned with considerable forethought. I used a small team for a reason.'

'Which was?'

'I believe there is a leak of some kind in navy intelligence. I have been running isolation and identification operations for some time in an attempt to identify the source.'

Rafael Columbia's face darkened. 'A leak?' he said with false calm.

'There has to be.'

'And you didn't bother informing me nor Lieutenant Hogan about this?'

'I was waiting for some concrete results first.'

'So then you don't have a suspect, yet?'

'No, sir, not yet.'

'Outside your suspicions, is there a single shred of evidence to back up this allegation against your fellow officers?'

'I believe Venice Coast was . . .'

'Ah! The other very public setback you inflicted on us.'

'As I was saying,' she said forcefully. 'Venice Coast was leaked. The unknown attacker must have received information from a source inside the navy.'

'And this unknown attacker, who was wetwired with the most sophisticated armaments the Commonwealth can produce, is working for Johansson's Starflyer?'

'That is an option.'

'An option you've been shouting very loudly to your political allies.'

'Somebody has been deflecting my investigation for decades. I need to start widening my approach.' She just held back from telling him what Thompson Burnelli had told her.

Rafael Columbia took a small paperscreen from his pocket. He held it up as it unfurled. 'Recognize him?'

Paula stared at the image on the paperscreen. 'That's the Venice Coast attacker.' The image had been taken from a bad overhead angle, and he was wearing sports whites, but she would never mistake that face.

'I'm glad we agree on something. That image was given to me by Senate Security. It was taken by a camera at the Clinton Estate. That is the man who walked out of Thompson Burnelli's squash court after the senator was murdered.'

'He wouldn't,' she whispered in horror. *Sheldon eliminating his political opponents? I don't believe it. That's not how the Grand Families and Intersolar Dynasties operate. Something is wrong about this. Badly wrong.*

'Who wouldn't?' Rafael demanded.

'The murderer. Why would he be used to kill the senator?'

'I don't fucking know. But according to you, he goes around causing mayhem on the orders of a navy officer.'

'I did not say that, and you're a fool if that's what you think.'

Rafael Columbia sat back in the chair and gave her a steady look. 'When I became chief of the Directorate I was just as impressed with you as all those media morons you play up to in your trials. The legendary Paula Myo, who solves all her cases except one, and she's still working on that after all these decades – never giving up. So like all the other chiefs before me, I gave you plenty of space, and never questioned your methods. After all, Johansson and his sidekick are just a pair of lunatic conspiracy fanatics spouting paranoid propaganda. Kind of romantic really, like pirates in sailing ships. Because the only physical damage the Guardians cause is on Far Away, where nobody ever goes, and certainly nobody cares about apart from the Halgarths, and they can afford it anyway. Except, pirates were actually the most bloodthirsty psychopaths, who slaughtered the crews of entire ships and wrecked economies because of the trade routes they closed down. You see the parallel here? It took decisive naval action to eliminate piracy. Now I gave you an entire department, with unlimited government resources, tasked to do one thing. I gave you that in good faith, because you are *the* Paula Myo, and everyone believes you are the one person in the Commonwealth who can run down Bradley Johansson for me.'

'I can.'

'You haven't. The reason you're still chasing him – and I'm sorry if this causes offence, but it happens to be true – is that you're an obsessive-compulsive. The only reason, Commander Myo.'

'I am what I am. And that makes me perfect for the job.'

'I disagree. You have poor leadership skills, you antagonize and alienate your fellow officers, you do not follow procedure, you do not believe anyone is capable of performing tasks as well as yourself – in other words you belittle them and are distrustful of them, which is why we find ourselves in this whole business of leaks. It has to be a leak, doesn't it, because it couldn't possibly be your fault, your screw-up.'

'Would you like to say what you came here to say.'

'Certainly. As of now, I am appointing Alic Hogan to take charge of the Johansson operation.'

'No.'

'You will continue to be a part of the operation, of course, but it will be in an advisory role only. Hogan will direct the day-to-day running of this office, and facilitate policy and strategy.'

'That is not acceptable.'

'You are a navy officer, you will obey my orders.'

'I am not a navy officer, I am not a part of this bureaucratic farce. I am a police officer.'

'Not any more. If you refuse my order you will be dismissed from the service.'

'This is my investigation.'

'It is not.'

Paula's e-butler told her it had just been locked out of the office network. She gazed over the desk at Rafael Columbia; some kind of shock was holding her body rigid, she could feel her skin cooling. Some sick feeling that she suspected was close to panic had begun to clog her thoughts. It was obvious Rafael wasn't going to accept a compromise, he wanted his man running the operation, LA was just the excuse. One thing was perfectly clear, she couldn't continue the investigation as part of the navy.

'Fine. I resign my commission.' Paula stood up, which made Columbia flinch. She picked the quartz cube hologram off her desk and put it in her shoulder bag, then she took the rabbakas plant from the windowsill.

'Word of advice,' Columbia said. 'Next time you get rejuvenated, get your Foundation-fixed dominants taken out. The clinics can make anybody normal these days.'

She raised an eyebrow in interest. 'There's hope for you yet, then.'

Everybody in the office was sitting behind their desks as she walked out, holding the same position they were in when Columbia arrived. The only difference was the surprise on their faces.

'Goodbye,' she told them. 'And thank you for all the hard work you did for me.'

Tarlo half-rose from his chair. 'Paula . . .'

She shook her head fractionally, and he fell silent. Without looking left or right she walked out of the office.

When she got down onto on the street she walked automatically back to her apartment, half a mile away. It was on the second floor of a centuries-old block that had a central cobbled courtyard overlooked by shuttered windows. Narrow stone stairs wound upwards in the kind of central well that looked as if it had been water-eroded rather than built. In her one visible concession to security, the solid oak door of her apartment had a modern electronic lock to supplement the ancient mechanical one.

Inside, there were three rooms: a bedroom, a bathroom, and the living room with a small kitchen alcove. She didn't need anything more, she didn't use anything more. It was somewhere to sleep conveniently near the office, an address for her clothes valeting service.

When Paula walked in the maidbot was sitting passively in the corner of the living room. It had already run through its daily cleaning routine, polishing the age-darkened floorboards, dusting every flat surface, and putting her breakfast crockery in the dishwasher. She opened the window that overlooked the courtyard, and put the rabbakas on the little dresser beside it where it would catch the sunlight every afternoon. With that taken care of she looked around the neat living room as if searching for a clue. There was nothing else for her to do. She sat in the sofa which faced the wall-mounted portal, perching on the edge.

Memories were filtering up inside her mind. Memories that had never been erased or transferred into safe storage at any of her rejuvenations. Memories she'd assumed were dormant. Right after her parents' trial she'd gone back to the hotel with her police escort. That had been a big new tower in Marindra's capital, with its cube rooms and clean new furniture and air conditioning. The escort had left her alone, giving her a break before the Huxley's Haven government official arrived to take her 'home'. Now the trial was over, she didn't know what to do. There was nothing to fill her time, no school to go to, no Coya to hang out with, no boys to eye up. She sat on the bed, perched on the edge looking out through the big picture window at the capital's skyline, and waited. Strange things happened inside her head, Coya's hysterical crying and pleading was still echoing round in there; while her eyes looked through the window all she could actually see was her parents being led from the dock. Her father's head hung low as his dreams and hopes lay broken around him. Her mother, equally haggard. But Rebecca turned to look across the court, meeting her stolen step-daughter's gaze, and mouthed, 'I love you.'

In her small, empty Paris apartment Paula whispered, 'I love you too, Mum.' Then just as she had in that hotel room a hundred and sixty years ago, Paula Myo started crying.

*

Preparation had taken many months, vast amounts of resources and industrial capacity had been diverted from the expansion expedition being mounted on the other side of the interstellar wormhole, but MorningLightMountain was finally ready. The other immotiles had been forming alliances that might eventually challenge its dominance. They were worried about its new technology. It knew that they had been experimenting with wormhole construction, its quantum wave detectors had picked up the tell-tale fluctuations from many settlements across the Prime system. If it didn't act now, they would soon reach parity, its advantage would be lost permanently.

Three hundred and twenty-eight wormholes were opened in unison. They were small, all of them measuring a metre and a half wide. Just enough for a ten-megatonne warhead to pass through. The wormholes closed.

MorningLightMountain had opened them next to the primary groupings of all the other immotiles on the planet, inside the ultrastrong protective force fields that guarded them from the sky, and next to the sprawling buildings which sheltered and nurtured them. The warheads detonated immediately, wiping out every motile and immotile within a twenty-five-kilometre radius. Even as the first round of nukes was exploding, MorningLightMountain was opening the wormholes again, this time at the next series of targets, the subsidiary immotiles orbiting the Prime homeworld. After that it targeted the first of the two solid planets, the second. Then came the innermost gas-giant, its moons, the asteroid habitats, the outermost gas-giant, industrial stations. The wave of obliteration rippled out across the system for over a day. Not that many of the remaining immotile groupings ever knew they were at war; they had little or no warning of their doom. MorningLightMountain's wave of assaults travelled across the star system faster than the speed of light.

When it was over, when every other immotile grouping had been reduced to a lake of radioactive lava, MorningLightMountain used the wormholes again. This time it sent connections through, microwaves or fibre optic cable, inserting itself into the core-less communications networks of its vanquished rivals. Its thoughts and orders flooded into the minds of the surviving motiles, expelling their mental heritage, turning MorningLightMountain into the sole sentient entity in the star system. Every motile was enmeshed in its thoughts as it took control of the infrastructure and spaceships that remained. For over a week it sent its billions of new motiles out to survey the wreckage and list the mechanical systems that had survived unscathed. Most of the farms and food production plants had come through intact, as had a great many industrial facilities. The information was used to assemble a strategy for integration, bringing together every production centre in a single unified organization. It began to amalgamate thousands of motiles into new subsidiary groupings of itself to cope with the huge demands of managing an entire star system. Without rivalries, and acting in conjunction, the combined industrial output of every manufacturing plant was greater than before.

Synergy, the Bose memories called it. The alien's concepts and words still lingered and lurked amid MorningLightMountain's system-wide thoughts, even though the coherent article had long been erased. It had even taken the precaution of physically eradicating the immotile unit which the Bose memories had been stored in. All that remained now were memories of memories, disseminated information that manifested in the odd alien phrase. There was no concern left of possible contamination. It was pure now, a single life that lived throughout this star system, and was now expanding into a second.

The effort to reach the Commonwealth resumed, with hundreds of ships flying daily through the interstellar wormhole to the staging-post star system, carrying equipment that would build the next sequence of wormholes.

*

Out of all the hundreds of billions of motiles hurrying to perform their appointed tasks, one did not obey MorningLightMountain's instructions. Because such individuality was impossible to a Prime, it moved where it wanted and saw what it needed. No other motile possessed the kind of independent thought structure that would question it. As long as it avoided the attention of MorningLightMountain's main thought routines, it was perfectly safe to come and go as it pleased.

For over a day it had been moving around the base of the giant mountain building which contained the original heart of the massive interlinked creature which was MorningLightMountain. It didn't move as smoothly as all the other motiles, it wasn't used to four legs, nor the strange way they bent and twisted. But it made progress.

In the background of its mind were the directives and thoughts of MorningLightMountain, emerging from the little communication device attached to one of its nerve receptor stalks. It ignored them because it wanted to. A mental ability which other motiles did not have. The images and information coming out of the communication device were a useful guide to what was happening across the Prime system.

High above it, dazzling lightning bolts lashed down repetitively against the protective force field dome, sizzling away to ground out along the top of the ancient valley. Clouds boiled along at a speed it had never seen before. They were thick and black, blotting out the sky as they unleashed monsoon-like downpours several times an hour. Rivulets formed across the force field, so heavy was the unnatural rain, carrying away the water to the saturated ground beyond. Whole tides of mud were slithering around the protected, sacrosanct valley.

The motile regarded the new weather intently, with one thought starting to dominate its mind: *Nuclear Winter*.

*

Paula Myo took the express from Paris direct to Wessex. She had a long wait in the CST planetary station there; the train to Huxley's Haven only ran once a day. It was dark outside when she eventually went to platform 87B, which was situated in a small annexe on the end of the terminal. The train she found standing there was made up from four single-deck carriages being pulled by a steam engine that could have come straight out of a museum. She'd forgotten that the journey was on a historical throwback. On any other world such a contraption belching out thick black smoke from the coal it burned would have been prohibited under any number of anti-pollution laws; here on one of the Big15 nobody cared.

She climbed in to the first carriage and sat on one of the velvet bench seats. A couple of other people came in, and ignored her. Just before their scheduled departure time a guard walked down the carriage. He was dressed in a dark blue uniform that had bright silver buttons down the waistcoat, and a tall peaked cap with red piping.

'Ticket, please, ma'am,' he said politely.

She handed over the small pink hard copy the machine at the end of the platform had printed out for her. He produced a pair of clippers, and punched a small Z-shaped hole in the corner.

'Won't be long now,' he said, and touched the peak of his cap.

The one hundred and fifty years of cynicism and cultural sophistication that formed her usual defensive shell wilted away. 'Thank you very much,' she said, and meant it. There was a great deal of comfort in a culture which was so honest and straightforward.

She held the ticket in her hand, looking at it as the steam engine tooted loudly and began to pull out of the station amid a cloud of pure white steam and clanking pistons. In theory, Huxley's Haven represented home, though she felt no attachment of any kind to the planet and its people. Going back would seem to any observer (and she was sure Hogan would be keeping a virtual eye on her) as if she was running for cover, returning to the one place she would fit in.

There was the usual slow crawl across the planetary station yard. Other trains seemed to charge past, the lights from their carriage windows producing a smear of illumination. Signals were bright red or green points against the dark background, stretching away for miles like a thinly populated city. Every now and then the glaring front lights from a heavy goods train would flow across the silver rails, followed by the dark bulk of the wagons, eclipsing the rest of the yard.

Their gradual progress forwards took them into a pale amber light that washed across this section of the yard like strong moonlight. When she pressed her face against the window, Paula could see the gateways lined up ahead of them, over two thirds illuminated by the daylight of the worlds they led to. In front of them, the rails were full of trains. It was unnerving seeing how little distance there was between each one as the station traffic control arranged them in a continual sequence. Only the single track which the steam engine rolled along was empty ahead and behind. They curved round to face the gateway which glowed with a diffuse primrose light.

Paula experienced the usual tingle over her skin as they passed through the gateway's pressure curtain. Then they were on another world and in full daylight, picking up speed across a rolling countryside that was made up from verdant chequerboard fields. Dense, neatly layered hedges were used to separate out the land, with the occasional drystone wall acting as a more substantial barrier. Native trees with reddish leaves were interspaced with terrestrial oak, ash, sycamore, and beech. All of them had been pollarded, their thick main trunks sprouting long vertical branches. The farms used the cut wood for fuel during the winter months, reducing dependence on fossil reserves. One of the benefits of using such simple mechanical technology was the low energy requirements; all of the planet's electricity was easily supplied from hydro dams.

She could see farmhouses sitting amid the folds of land, big brick buildings with blue slate roofs nestled at the centre of Dutch barns and pig sties and stables and store sheds. Some of them had grain silos, tall clapboard structures painted dove-

959

grey, which she knew were among the highest buildings on the whole planet. Single railway tracks branched off from the main line, snaking out to the silo yards through narrow cuttings and along embankments. The rails were rusty now, in early summer when the grains were still green in the fields; but later in the year when the harvest was gathered the grain wagons would make daily collections, the lines would be shiny again and the weeds coming up between the wooden sleepers would shrivel and die from the heat of the engines and blasts of steam. Paula had to admit, it looked every inch the bucolic idyll. She accepted now what she had so strongly rejected as a confused uprooted teenager, that the whole point of this society was that it didn't change, that was what its people were designed for. The Human Structure Foundation had chosen a level of technology equal to the early twentieth century, prior to the electronic revolution; the kind of engineering and mechanics that was easily maintained. Nothing here needed computer diagnostics when it broke down; engineers could see what was wrong amid a machine's cogs and cables. It was the same with information. There were no arrays, databases, or networks; offices of clerks and accountants kept books and files and rolodexes. The Foundation had designed people to work at specific jobs, and those jobs wouldn't metamorphose with progress – there was no progress. Huxley's Haven provided its inhabitants with the most secure stable society it was possible to have. She still couldn't decide if the Foundation had been morally right to begin the whole project, but looking out at the trim neat fields and the picture-perfect farms, she had to admit now that it worked.

The train started to move through the outskirts of Fordsville, the capital. They were climbing up on a wide embankment now, giving her a view down on the streets of the outlying districts. Long rows of neat terraced houses stretched away in regular lines, their bricks all a rust red, with broad windows painted in every colour of the rainbow. Larger civic buildings stood high among them, sometimes as much as four or five storeys high, made from a dark grey stone. There were no churches of any kind, but then they didn't have any religion here, this was a world where everyone knew they had been created by man, not God.

Even when the train moved through the centre of the city, the buildings were all the same uniform size; neat houses interspaced by the commercial buildings, and plenty of large parks to break up the urban sprawl. It was unlike other cities in the Commonwealth, where money and political power collected at the centre, and the architecture reflected that concentration. Here, equality reigned supreme.

Alphaway, the main station, was probably the biggest single structure in the city after the original Foundation clinic, with three long arched roofs of iron and glass, tall enough that the clouds of smoke from the steam engines dissipated upwards through the ridge vents. She walked down the platform and went out onto Richmond Square outside. The roads were busy with three-carriage electric trams riding down their rails in the central lanes; more numerous were buses, whose methane engines produced a high growl as they raced past; taxis and goods vans struggled for space among them. The only personal transport were the bicycles, which had two lanes to themselves on every street.

People on the pavement hurried past. Many of them gave Paula a surreptitious glance as they went, which she found amusing. It wasn't fame that earned her the looks, nobody knew about her here, it was her plain business suit which marked her out as an offworlder. Contrary to Commonwealth comedians whose routine had everyone on the planet dressed in identical boiler suits, people were wearing just about every fashion the human race had ever come up with. The only thing they didn't have was artificial fibre.

She crossed the square and went into the main tram station. There was no cybersphere for her e-butler to consult, no useful stored information about routes and stops. Instead, she had to stand in front of a big coloured map with the tram lines overlaid in primary colours, and work out for herself which one she needed.

Ten minutes later she was sitting in a tram heading out on its loop, which she hoped was going to take in the Earlsfield district. It was a very similar vehicle she'd used last time when she left Huxley's Haven, though she couldn't remember the route number. As they moved away from the centre the number of large shops and warehouses decreased, and the streets became more residential, with blocks of factories clumped together. Watching them go past, she was still convinced she had done the right thing by leaving all those decades ago. After an upbringing in the Commonwealth this world would have been too quiet.

Not for the first time, she reviewed her nuclear option: go for a rejuvenation and erase all her memories of life in the Commonwealth. Without that experience, the rich cultural contamination so beloved of her step-parents, she would be able to fit in here. It wasn't something she could bring herself to do, not yet, anyway. There was still her first real case left to solve, though it had become inordinately difficult and complex now.

It had begun in 2243, a fortnight after Paula had passed her Directorate exams to qualify as a Senior Investigator. That was nine months after Bradley Johansson claimed he returned to the Commonwealth after travelling the Silfen paths, and set about founding the Guardians of Selfhood. As with any leader of a new political movement, especially one that waged armed conflict, he needed money to support his cause. As he no longer had direct access to the Halgarth family money, he hatched a simple plan to steal what he wanted.

On a warm April night, Johansson and four colleagues he'd recently liberated from the Starflyer broke into the California Technological Heritage museum. They ignored the marbled halls filled with giant aircraft and even larger spaceplanes, crept past the display cases full of twentieth-century computers, never even glanced at the first G5 PCglasses, avoided the original motility robots, the SD lasers, a stealth microsub, the prototype superconductor battery cell, and went straight for the dome at the heart of the buildings. Right at the centre was the wormhole generator which Ozzie Fernandez Isaacs and Nigel Sheldon had built and used to visit Mars. It had taken a lot of negotiation and political manoeuvring, but the museum had finally acquired the display rights.

When Johansson and his little team blew open the main door into the central dome, alarms went off and force fields came on. The duty guards responded swiftly, and had the dome surrounded in under a minute.

In order to prevent theft, the museum had laudably installed various force fields to isolate sections of the interior as soon as any form of criminal behaviour was detected. As the central dome contained what was arguably the most important, and therefore valuable, machine the human race had ever built, its force field enclosed it completely. When it came on, it trapped the intruders inside. So far, so good.

With over fifty armed guards outside the dome, the chief used the public address system to give those inside the time-honoured recital to throw down any weapons and come out with their hands up and their inserts deactivated. The chief then tried to switch off the force field. That was when they found that, on his way in, Johansson had burned through the force field generator's main power cable, and the command links. The force field had come on automatically with the alarm, powered by its emergency back-up supply, but for now the guards couldn't switch it off.

No real problem. They just had to wait five hours until the emergency back-up supply was exhausted. However, what no one in the museum had really thought through was the nature of the machine which the dome's force field protected. Peering through the small gap provided by the wrecked door, the guards could see the intruders working frantically on the historical device inside. Johansson plugged in the niling d-sink his team had carried in with them, and slowly powered up the old wormhole generator. It might have been nearly two hundred years old, but its components were essentially solid state, and Nigel and Ozzie had built it with a large failsoft redundancy factor. After an hour, Johansson managed to open a wormhole. It didn't reach over any real distance, not compared to its huge commercial descendants used by CST. That didn't bother him, he didn't want to go to Mars, or even the moon. All he wanted was to be two hundred and fifty miles away from the museum, in Las Vegas. To be precise, in the maximum security vault which served the eight largest casinos on Earth.

With the wormhole established inside the vault, the team walked through. Once again a barrage of alarms went off, triggered by their presence, and once again force fields came on around the outside, designed to confine any thief who had managed to get this far until the guards arrived. One of Johansson's team used microthermal charges around the vault door to seal it from the inside. They then spent forty-nine minutes transferring bags full of banknotes back through the wormhole and into the museum. The casinos welcomed currency from every planet in the Commonwealth, and each bag contained notes to the value of five million Earth dollars. It took a team member on average one minute to grab a bag, take it through the wormhole, and go back for the next one.

Paula Myo arrived ninety minutes after the California Technological Heritage museum alarm was triggered. For the last week she had been working on the strange case of a niling d-sink stolen from a factory outside Portland. Nobody at the Serious Crimes Directorate could work out what anybody would want with such a thing; any company that had a requirement for one could afford one. Now they knew. She struggled through the hyped-up crowd of reporters, then had to get past the small army of LAPD and museum guards that had the criminals encircled. She pressed herself right up to the ruined door, which gave her a narrow awkward view into the dome where one side of the venerable wormhole generator was just visible. Squinting against the sheet of air hazed by the force field she could make out figures moving round.

Two weeks qualified, and she was actually watching the largest robbery in human history in progress.

Once the last bag was dropped into the dome chamber, Johansson moved the wormhole exit again, this time to an unknown destination. The team laboured for another fifty minutes taking the bags through. Then they left, and a simple software timer function powered down the wormhole generator behind them.

Two hours later the force field shut down. Paula was among the first people into the dome, supervising the forensics team she'd called in. The Directorate wouldn't give her the case, of course, she was still a first-lifer and way too junior (her abnormal heritage was never mentioned). Senior investigators with twenty years' experience were brought in to head the case, and she was given a secondary role on the task force.

By morning the casinos had confirmed that one point one seven billion dollars had been taken. The media called it the Great Wormhole Heist. Senior Directorate officials assured their contacts that the investigators would soon be making arrests. It simply wasn't possible to get rid of that much money unnoticed.

Johansson, though, had planned well. He spent his cash with the kind of people who asked no questions, and certainly didn't make large unexplained deposits with banks. On Far Away the Guardians began to expand their numbers and activities, starting their campaign against the Starflyer in the form of its principal agents, the Research Institute; with the Halgarth family as occasional secondary targets.

The Directorate task force did manage to identify Johansson's DNA from samples of hair left in the dome. Though with a multitude of people walking through the museum every week, he was just one name in two and a half thousand confirmed samples. He did have a query on his file, given the circumstances of his earlier disappearance from his family and job five years earlier. It was only when the acts of sabotage began on Far Away and the Guardians shotgunned the unisphere with their propaganda that the Directorate investigators finally put it all together. Catching Johansson was an altogether more difficult task. He only ever used front men to make his arms purchases, and Guardian members to release his propaganda messages. All the arrests they made were peripheral. They never got close to him.

Over the years, then decades, investigators left the task force or were reassigned, or simply retired from the Directorate. Paula moved up the hierarchy until she commanded the task force. Finally, however, even the task force was quietly dissolved and the Great Wormhole Heist case was downgraded. Even then, she kept the case active as part of the overall Guardians investigation. For over a hundred and thirty years she had not quit. She couldn't.

The tram stopped at the end of Montagu High Street, and Paula stepped out. The town hadn't changed, at least not from her vague first-life recollection of it. When she looked along the street with its small stores and hotels she could see it dipping down towards the cove at the bottom. There was a stone harbour on one side, she remembered, with fishing boats drawn up on the rocky bluff, and nets stretched out to dry. Flocks of big scarlet birds swirled overhead, tetragulls, whose oily feathers allowed them to swim almost as well as fish.

Mid-afternoon wasn't a busy time for Montagu. Most people were at work, leaving the pavement sparsely populated, and the buses half-empty. The nearest shop had two large bay windows, displaying well dressed mannequins. There were no chains or franchises on Huxley's Haven. Technically, the economy was market communism, with non-essential goods and products allowed to be supply led, which gave designers considerable liberty and innovation. The dresses on the mannequins were certainly attractive, as were the pashminas draped around them.

Paula walked in to be greeted by the assistant, a young woman whose clothes were all chosen from the racks around the shop. For a moment Paula found herself studying the woman a little too closely, but what exactly did someone designed to be a shop assistant look like? *Same as you*, she told herself crossly, *an ordinary person*. There was no specific shop assistant caste anyway. All the fixed dominant gene would give her was a behavioural trait for public service. She could just as easily have been a cook or librarian or gardener. It was only after primary school, which took them up to age twelve, that people on Huxley's Haven started to choose what sort of specialty they wanted to follow within their pre-determined sphere of interest.

The assistant smiled faintly as she took in Paula's clothes. 'Can I help you, miss?'

It took a second for Paula to realize that she still looked younger than the assistant, even in a formal suit. 'I don't need clothes, sorry, I'm looking for directions to the Denken house.'

'Ah yes.' The assistant was almost pleased at the question, as if it was what she expected an offworlder to ask. 'It's on Semley Avenue.' She gave Paula a string of directions, and asked, 'If you don't mind me asking, why do you want to visit him?'

'I need some advice.'

'Really? I didn't know Commonwealth citizens used our freethinkers.'

'They don't. I was born here.' She grinned at the woman's startled expression.

Semley Avenue was still the same, a street of bungalows with tidy front gardens. The exception were the pines and conifers planted along the edge of the pavement, which had been tended properly over the intervening century and a half to grow into huge sturdy trees. Their strong scent mingled with the fresh breeze coming in off the sea, giving the avenue a restful quality. It put her in mind of a retirement village.

The Denken house was the last bungalow before the avenue opened out into a swathe of parkland that ran along the top of the cliffs. It was bigger than all the others, in itself a bit of a novelty on a world where everyone earned the same salary no matter what their job. At some time someone had built a big brick annexe on the side, with a few simple high slit windows. It didn't really match the rest of the bungalow's chalet-style architecture.

Paula walked up the little path to the front door, and rang the tarnished brass bell. The garden was subtly different to all the neighbours, who favoured rigid layouts of lawns, flower-beds with colourful annuals, and the occasional stone birdbath or sundial. This garden was lined with evergreen shrubs to provide a range of pastel colours, and the lawn hadn't been mown for a week or more.

Paula was just about to press the bell button again when a man's voice said, 'Coming, coming,' somewhere inside the house. A moment later the door was opened by a tall man in his mid-thirties, with untidy shoulder-length brown hair that already had several grey strands appearing. He was wearing a much-creased turquoise-blue T-shirt and a pair of lemon-yellow shorts. 'You're early.' He gave Paula a bleary look. 'Oh, couldn't your mother come?'

'I don't have a mother.' She could see his ancestor's face. His cheeks were rounder, and the hair was darker, but that nose was the same, as were his expressive green eyes. The slight bafflement at everyday life was identical, too.

The man rubbed his face as if he'd just woken up, and

looked closer. 'My my, an offworlder. What are you doing here?'

'Are you Denken?'

'Leonard Denken. Yes?'

'I'm Paula Myo, and technically I'm not an offworlder.'

Leonard Denken frowned, then a startled expression appeared. He straightened up, suddenly wide awake. 'Oh my, oh my, yes of course, the last stolen baby. My grandfather! No! It was my great-grandfather who advised you. My father always talked about that.'

'I need some more advice.'

Leonard gasped, then smiled broadly. 'Come in, please, do come in. I'm sorry about the mess. My mind isn't quite as tidy as people expect. The house reflects that. Matilda keeps threatening to tidy up, but I haven't had a chance to compile an index, yet. One day. Yes, one day.'

There were books piled up along both walls in the long hall, hardbacks and leather-bound tomes. Some of the stacks reached up to Paula's shoulder, looking terribly unsafe. 'I need to get myself some more bookshelves,' Leonard said apologetically as he caught her looking round. 'There are several carpenters in the street, but I just haven't got round to asking them yet. I need wood, too.'

He led her into the big annexe, which was a single room. 'My father intended this to be our library,' he said. 'But I seem to have subverted that, a little.'

Every wall was fronted by bookcases that reached from floor to ceiling, with every inch of space taken up. Leonard was now building new piles along the floor. It was only the back wall which had high slit windows, long since covered by shelving. The front had two large arched French doors which opened onto the bungalow's main garden, and gave a superb view out over the cliffs and sea beyond. A big old desk had been set up in front of one, awash with magazines, papers, books, and cardboard files.

'Please sit down.' Leonard gestured to a spindly antique seat in front of the desk. 'Matilda! Matilda, we have a guest. Would you like some tea? Or coffee? I'm afraid I don't have any Commonwealth brands. I do have some passable sherry.' He looked around as if he was in a strange room until he saw an old grandfather clock. 'Or maybe it's too early?'

'Tea will be fine, thank you.'

A girl came through the door.

'This is Matilda,' Leonard said. The adoration in his voice was almost embarrassing for an outsider. His face had taken on a dreamy quality as he smiled at her.

Paula, who was used to the sequenced and modified women of the Commonwealth, was surprised by how beautiful Matilda was. She was in her early twenties, with delicate cheek bones that still managed to give her strong features, complemented by wide ice-blue eyes that allowed her an unnervingly piercing stare. Her hair was the fairest blond, and she'd let it grow very long. Right now it was gathered into a single braid that fell all the way along her spine to the top of her narrow hips. She was also tall, with long legs whose perfect shape was produced by muscles that any dancer would envy. Paula could see that easily; all Matilda wore was a small pair of red bikini bottoms and a cut-off white T-shirt. Her skin had a rich healthy tan.

When Paula looked out of the open French doors again, she saw the towels on the garden where the two of them must have been sunbathing.

'I'd like you to meet Paula Myo, our very distinguished guest from the Commonwealth,' Leonard said.

'Hi,' Matilda said. 'What can I get you?'

'Just some tea, thank you,' Paula said.

'Sure.' Her smile was guileless. Paula found herself smiling back.

'Isn't she lovely?' Leonard asked when the girl had left. He was as shy and eager as a teenager who'd unexpectedly found himself dating the prom queen. 'I'm going to ask her to marry me. I think. There's nothing I want more, but . . . I'm a little bit older than her. Not that she's ever said anything about that.'

'Don't wait too long,' Paula said. 'There'll be another hundred men wanting to ask the same question if you don't. And she's where she wants to be. That ought to tell you something.'

'Yes, oh yes, you're quite right.' He caught himself and sighed. 'I'm sorry. I'm not supposed to be asking you for advice.'

'It's okay. I've had a lot more experience with these kinds of things. And I'm used to seeing age differences over a century or more. Love normally wins out.'

'Yes, yes, of course. I must say this is something of a shock having you come to me. That's why I'm not handling this well. Your letters to my great-grandfather are around here somewhere.' He waved a hand at the library's piles. 'I read them when I took over from my father. You had just qualified to be some kind of detective in the Commonwealth government.'

Paula had forgotten the letters she'd written. At first they'd been a welcome contact with the one person in the galaxy who seemed to understand her; then when her insecurities had slowly abated she wrote out of politeness. Eventually, of course, her job took up so much of her time . . . It was a very tired excuse. She should have realized Alexis would have kept the letters. It had been a very intense affair during the short time it lasted. 'Yes, I qualified as an investigator. I've been successful, too. No false modesty.'

He smiled in that proud way that stirred up a few too many old memories. 'Of course you succeeded. You'd be the best they ever had. Not that they'd ever admit that.'

'I have your great-grandfather to thank. He was the one who told me to go. He knew that I wouldn't be happy here, not after being exposed to so much of the Commonwealth.'

'I'd dispute that; but I'm not him, and you've obviously flourished. I have to ask, and I'm sorry if this is intrusive, but do you ever have any doubts about rejuvenation, you've obviously been through the process several times. I think you were a teenager when you left Huxley's Haven.'

'No, no doubts. Not ever. There is so much crime out there.'

'And nobody else can do the job.'

She pulled a face. He was very similar to Alexis. 'A few might manage,' she admitted.

'I'm asking because rejuvenation is the one thing that is debated endlessly by my caste. We simply cannot decide if we should adopt it here.'

'I'd say it was contrary to your whole ethos. This society was formed so people could live their lives and be content. A great deal of that contentment comes from a natural cycle which lies undisturbed, and was never sequenced in by the Foundation. They just gave you the ability to enjoy what was available within a relatively simple framework – at least compared to majority Commonwealth culture. There will always be a job for you whoever you are, a job, or purpose that you will enjoy, and you will be rewarded financially by it no more or no less than anyone else. If you introduce rejuvenation you will start to expand beyond the rate sustainable by your current economy. And your current technoeconomy is the only one suitable for fixed-trait castes. The best the Foundation could sequence in was behaviour suitable for a particular profession, along with a few extras like dexterity for doctors. But you simply can't produce dedicated fusion techs or microbiologists. Those kinds of profession have too many requirements – there's no single recognizable aptitude. To support a more modern economy you'd have to de-specialize the traits to the point where they'd effectively be dissolved. You'd wind up with normal humans living in an economy that was ideologically driven rather than needs related. There'd be nothing to stop them going and getting a better-paid job on another planet, especially after a couple of centuries of going in to work in the same office.'

'Goodness me, and I thought freethinkers such as myself were the only ones who could put together solid logical arguments.'

Matilda returned with a tray carrying mugs of tea. 'Don't let him distract you,' she said as she gave Paula her mug. 'He's a very bad freethinker. He always asks questions, he never answers them.'

'To think about things, I have to know about them first.'

Matilda gave Paula a told-you-so shrug as she gave Leonard his mug.

'What do you do?' Paula asked.

'I'm a nurse. I work at the maternity ward of the local hospital. I like children.' She gave Leonard a meaningful glance. He blushed.

Paula wanted to snap at him, *for God's sake ask her*. There was way too much recycled history in this house. A static, timeless society was one thing, but you could take it to extremes. At the time, over a century and a half ago, she'd been younger than Matilda, while Alexis had been older than Leonard. It had broken Alexis's heart having her leave, and he'd been the one who pushed her out knowing it was the only way for her to have a future. Although, if she could have been happy anywhere on Huxley's Haven it would have been here with him. That was the trouble with freethinkers – they had overactive imaginations which made them uncertain. *Maybe that's why they're always men. The Foundation just amplified their natural inability to make a commitment.*

Matilda looked from her lover to Paula. 'I'm going to leave you two alone to talk. Let me know if you need anything else.' She kissed Leonard on the forehead, and went back out into the garden. As she slipped out of her scraps of clothing to lie on the towel, Paula had a memory flash of Mellanie and Morton, a couple she could really do with forgetting about.

'Aren't you the perfect counter to your own argument, though?' Leonard said.

'Somebody recently claimed my Foundation trait was obsessive-compulsive disorder. He was an idiot, but he might have had a point. It is an excellent quality for a police officer to have. My type are probably the only kind who can adapt to the Commonwealth.' She paused, troubled by where her thoughts were leading. 'Freethinkers, as well, possibly.'

Leonard held his mug in both hands, and peered at her over the rim. 'We're not quite as free as people think. If I had to define us it would be as psychiatrists for society. The Foundation considered us necessary to assist this world, address questions and problems beyond the norm. As a collective, we are effectively the politicians. Our council is supposed to provide alternatives which everyone else gets to vote on.' His expression softened. 'It's a bit of a myth that everyone else is sequenced to do as we tell them. Though I have to admit, were it true, the possibilities for dictatorship are fabulous.'

'I don't think you'd make a very good dictator, Leonard.'

'No, I suppose you're right. It is an irony that we are known for our micro work rather than our macro. I really do get treated as the local psychiatrist, you know. Any slightly out of the ordinary problem, and this house is the first stop.'

'I'm as guilty of that as all the others.'

'I understand. So what did you come here for?'

'You might need to prepare some options for this planet. Have you been following the news about the Dyson Pair and the Prime aliens who live there?'

'Dear me, yes, it's been in the newspapers, though I'm afraid we don't have many column inches devoted to Commonwealth affairs; but I have received briefing papers from the Commonwealth office here in Fordsville. Are you connected with that?'

'I used to be.' She started to tell him what had happened.

Two hours later, when she'd finished, Leonard's face had taken on a somewhat daunted look. He pressed both hands to his temples and exhaled loudly. 'Apart from me going up to this Rafael Columbia character and punching him soundly on the nose, I don't see there is much I can do to help you. Have you really been working on the same case for over a hundred and thirty years?'

'Yes. It's not in my nature to quit.'

'No. No, of course not. I'm sorry, I'm just not used to working with this sort of timescale. So what exactly do you want to do next?'

'My instinct is to catch Johansson.'

'Yes, I can see that. Well, of course I do have some discretionary power, it's in the Foundation's charter. I can have the Treasury pay you a monthly salary. It won't be much, but it will leave you free to pursue this diabolical man without worrying about money.'

Paula laughed somewhat unkindly. She was beginning to think she'd made a huge mistake coming here. But it was just an instinctive thing to do. He was a freethinker, and the last link she'd have with Alexis. She let her gaze wander round the library, wondering what she would have done with the bungalow if she had stayed; the paint, furniture, wallpaper that could be used to lift away the air of academic shabbiness. 'Leonard, for a hundred and fifty years the Commonwealth has been paying me a good salary and even better expenses. I finished paying for my apartment a hundred and eight years ago. I eat most meals in the staff canteen. All I buy are six suits a year, and some casual clothes. After my R & R pension, all my money is paid into an SI-managed fund account. It adds up, even with inflation. I don't need financing, but thank you for the offer.'

'Then how am I going to help you?'

'Freethinkers are supposed to be objective with the larger picture. I wanted your opinion on what I should be doing. Even though that comes perilously close to absolution.'

'What's religion . . . no, forget that. Are you saying I should tell you what to do next?'

'Convince me, possibly. And yes, I appreciate you don't do specifics.'

'I'm not even sure I can handle an overview in your case. What options have you got? It is in your nature never to give up. You know Johansson belongs in custody. Use your talent, Paula, catch him.'

'But should I?' she murmured. Even saying it sent a cold shiver along her arms.

'Why shouldn't you?'

'What if he is right? What if there is a Starflyer, a malicious alien that has been influencing human politicians?'

'Dear me, is that likely? It does sound suspiciously like a conspiracy theory to me.'

'I know. But there are an increasing number of inconsistencies in the case that I'm having difficulty with. Until now it did look like Johansson had very simple motivations, that the Guardians were formed first to help him steal the money from Las Vegas, then to cover up his subsequent lifestyle and allow him to live off the proceeds. But if he's right, and the Starflyer did somehow push us into the flight to Dyson Alpha, it would explain a lot of things. For one, he has never wavered in projecting his belief in the Starflyer. The only other person I know who could maintain such a constant position after so much time is me.'

'Ah, now I understand why you have come to me. This is a moral question. Should you drop your pursuit of Johansson, even though you know for certain he has committed crimes, and go after the Starflyer, whose existence as yet remains unproven.'

'That's about it, yes.' She didn't mention there was no one else she could talk the situation through with. Right now she wasn't sure who she could trust.

'However flattering your appearance here today, I hardly think I'm qualified to give you a judgement on this. I have no knowledge or understanding of Commonwealth politics. And that's what this seems to be.'

'No, it's not. Politicians and their aims are tied into this, very strongly in the case of Columbia, but it's not their squabbling for power which concerns me. It is the results of that squabble. And even if you doubt the existence of the Starflyer, I suggest you examine the name Nigel Sheldon. He is somehow mixed up in this. Whatever way I look at it, Johansson has been confronting something with political power. In which case he may be operating with another small political grouping. That would certainly explain why he's been given help from inside the Commonwealth government for so long.'

'Wait a minute; I thought you said Sheldon was the one preventing inspection of the cargo shipped to Far Away.'

'That's what Thompson Burnelli told me.'

'So how could he be the one Johansson is acting against?'

'I don't know. Presumably he's not. That's if Burnelli was right. If Johansson could convince Nigel Sheldon the Starflyer was a threat, there would be no need for the Guardians or the Great Wormhole Heist. My old Directorate and every other government agency would have been turned over to finding the alien. But he didn't convince him, although Sheldon blocked the inspections anyway.'

'How reliable was the senator?'

'In something like this? Completely.'

Leonard sat back, looking bemused. 'Then this is not logical.'

'It would appear to be a paradox only because as yet we don't have all the information.'

'Hence your determination to carry on with the case, yes I

see. But which part of it? Humm, a merry dilemma. Can you confront Sheldon?'

'Given my current circumstances, I could probably get one interview with one person of power. As such I would have to choose carefully. If Sheldon is mixed up with this, he will simply deny it, and it may be that I then face the same fate as the senator.'

'Yes. To be avoided. Of course, if you were to catch Johansson he will be able to supply answers for a great many of your questions.'

'Finding the Starflyer would also end this.'

'How would you do that?'

'Travel to Far Away. If Johansson is right, there will be an abundance of evidence at the *Marie Celeste* Research Institute.'

'Won't that be somewhat dangerous?'

'The risk is acceptable. No one will expect me to do such a thing. And it would be quick.'

'I can see the appeal in that. The Starflyer would be the greater crime, which will allow you to pursue it with a clear conscience. If you're sure that's not a reaction to the shock of being dismissed from your position.'

'It's not. I will catch Johansson eventually. However, I have to consider that given the Prime situation I might not have much time left, especially if Johansson is right and it was engineered to our detriment. The whole purpose of exposing the Starflyer to the authorities would be to prevent any kind of conflict.'

'Ignore the time factor, it is an unknown you cannot outguess. You have to go after Johansson. You know how he works, his pattern. And you now have a huge advantage.'

'How so?'

'If you work alone, he will not receive any leaks from your office. He won't know you're coming.'

She smiled thinly. 'You have more in common with Alexis than I thought.'

'Why, thank you. So how will you go about the case now?'

'I will travel to Far Away and contact the Guardians. They will take me to Johansson. As you said, he won't expect me to come at him from that direction.'

'Oh dear, oh dear. I suppose you know what you're doing, but please be careful. I'd like to think my great-grandchild will sit here listening to your next quandary.'

She stood up and offered her hand. 'Tell him to watch out for me.'

'You really are going to take my advice?'

'It helped me focus on what I have to do, yes.'

He looked out of the French doors at Matilda, who was still stretched out on the towel. 'Then I really should take your advice.'

*

A huge black Zil limousine was parked outside the entrance to Paula's apartment building, almost completely blocking the street. She was surprised the police hadn't towed it away; at the very least they should have fined the driver. As she drew up level, a gull-wing door in the side lifted up silently. A man whose skin was pure gold put his head out.

'We need to talk,' he told Paula.

23

Tulip Mansion was situated just outside of New York, in Rye county. The building itself sat on top of one of the small mountains which made up the majority of the rugged region, where it was surrounded by pine forests that swarmed over the adjacent hills. Mingling in amongst the tall trees were huge rhododendron bushes that enjoyed the stony soil, producing the most exquisite carpet of colour when they were in flower. People who had homes there tended to stay for many lives and centuries. Rye's proximity to the city made it an excellent area to live for those who could afford the land prices. It wasn't as chic as the Hamptons – but it was very convenient.

Miles Foran had thought so when he began his estate at the start of the twenty-first century, an internet billionaire whose share stock had achieved a near-ballistic trajectory upwards. With the Tulip Mansion it was his goal to build 'the first true American stately home of the new millennium'. Not for him the standard timber-frame mansion clad in brick and stone. *Mock* was not in the vocabulary when architects were summoned. His ornate stone walls had cores of concrete and steel which would last for centuries. Craftsmen were flown in from all over the world; master carpenters and stone masons chipped and chiselled away, crafting a work of art you could live in. Aristocratic designers were contracted to produce a modern classic interior that would make the palaces of oil potentates seem cheap and tacky by comparison. The grounds were shaped and landscaped into gardens that would rival Versailles.

The decade-long construction project was proceeding soundly when Jeff Baker released his new crystal memory into the global market. It was the pinnacle of electronic data storage, eliminating all other competing systems, obliterating copyright, and revolutionizing the internet into the datasphere. Gravity suddenly took a very firm grip on Foran's stock trajectory, which even filing Chapter Eleven bankruptcy couldn't protect him from.

Several years later the creditor banks were quietly grateful when Gore Burnelli made them a small offer for the estate and its half-completed folly. Work was resumed. The central stamen tower was completed, topped out with its gold anther crown. The four wings laid out around it were the flower's petals, stretched-oval shapes that were given curving scarlet and black roofs whose design was stolen directly from the Sydney Opera House. Inside, there were reception rooms, a ballroom, a grand banqueting hall, fifty guest bedrooms, a library, swimming pools, solariums, games rooms, and cavernous underground garages stocked with a range of vehicles that any motor history museum would kill to obtain.

All in all, it was excessive to the point of vulgar; but Justine spent more time at the Tulip Mansion than she did at any other family residence. If anywhere was home for her, it was here. And now she was having to host Murielle's engagement party in the gardens at a time that was monstrously inappropriate.

But the party had been planned months in advance. The negotiations between lawyer teams representing the Burnellis and the Konstantins had been completed. Their union had to be examined for share block shifts between the two families. Not that core blocks would change. This couple's relatively junior status meant they'd only be awarded secondary shares, a few small companies spun off, a virtual finance house, real estate in phase three space. Though given this was a direct-line merger the lawyers had also allowed for the possibility of closer fusion for the children in a couple of centuries. It was an interesting dynamic, which had taken a long time to be cleared.

A tearful Murielle had bravely volunteered to postpone it, after all Thompson was her ancestor. So Justine had smiled at the bewildered first-life girl and said, '*Not at all, Thompson would want you to carry on.*'

So at midday she stood under a rose-covered gazebo receiving guests who rolled up in modern limousines or fabulous antique cars. She paid no attention to the vehicles, her interest in one-upmanship among society had been exhausted centuries ago, although she had to own up to a certain awareness when it came to who was wearing what. Costumes were supposed to be themed from around the 1950s, and the pavilions set up across the garden's high lawn reflected that. Waiters in period uniforms served cocktails from the era.

For herself, Justine had chosen a formal sea-green evening dress with a mermaid tail skirt. She drew the line at heels on the grass, though.

A '56 Oldsmobile pulled up, and Estella slowly got out of the back.

'What on Earth happened to you?' Justine asked as her friend limped over to the gazebo. Estella was wearing a scarlet dress with white polka dots, and pink winged sunglasses. Instead of shoes, she was wearing a pair of electromuscle support boots.

Estella gave her a brief kiss on both cheeks. 'I'm so sorry to spoil the look of the thing, darling. But I went and sprained both ankles. It was *hideously* painful, I kid you not.'

'How did you do that?'

'So silly. I was dancing on the coffee table at a party. When

I jumped off I landed badly. I don't understand it, darling. I've danced on that table a hundred times, and nothing like this ever happened before.'

Justine didn't scold, it would have been far too parental. 'I never get asked to parties like that anymore.'

'I should think not, Senator, you have a reputation to consider now.'

'Oh thanks. It's people like you I need support from.'

'I know, darling,' Estella laid her hand on Justine's arm. 'How's it going? Is it really awful?'

'Thompson had an excellent staff team. I just vote the way they tell me to. I haven't started doing deals myself yet. It's just a temporary appointment, after all; though the senators did give me a unanimous vote to carry on his representation. Even his opponents endorsed me. I think they were all shocked, or running scared. Nobody's ever killed a senator before. This was supposed to send a message to the killer that you can't stop politicians like this. So all I'm doing is basically holding the fort till he gets out of the clinic.'

'Be brave.'

'You know me.' She gave a brittle laugh.

'Do they know who did it yet?'

'No. Nor why. It's all so stupid. Who *kills* people in this day and age? We're not in the barbarian era any more.'

Estella plucked at her dress. 'We are this afternoon.'

'Yeah. Are you staying for the play tonight? It's *A Midsummer Night's Dream*. The Tolthorpe actors are supposed to be very good, and the gardeners have built an open air stage in front of the lower beech woods.'

'I'm not walking off anywhere, darling. A stiff drink and a decent-looking first-life waiter is what I need.'

'Good, I'll talk to you later, yeah?'

'Sure thing. Now, is this Murielle?'

'Of course.' Justine introduced her friend to the girl and her fiancé who were waiting on the other side of the gazebo.

Murielle was wearing a copy of the white dress Marilyn Monroe had on in *The Seven Year Itch*. And carried it off well, Justine had to admit. She did have a fabulous figure; and with it such a wondrously sunny disposition that Justine had to acknowledge how old and jaded she truly was nowadays despite wearing a body of young flesh. Young Starral Konstantin was so obviously smitten as he stood at her side, the two of them holding hands the entire time. Simply being around them was wearying to Justine. For ages she'd been swept along by Murielle's ingénue enthusiasm for her fiancé, and the party, and the marriage, and their future life together, and the many children she wanted to produce (with natural pregnancies – for God's sake) for her handsome beau. It had been a marvellous distraction helping the girl plan everything; Murielle had been living at the Tulip Mansion for the five months since she finished Yale. Even the Primes and the navy were just parallel subjects.

Then some lunatic had killed Thompson.

Why?

And now she had to be tough and resolute the way everyone expected a senior Burnelli to behave, when all she really wanted to do was put her arms round her little brother and cuddle him like she used to do when she was five years old and he was a baby.

'Are you all right, Grandee?' Murielle asked.

To her horror, Justine realized her eyes were moistening. *Not now, goddamnit!* 'Coping,' she said staunchly. 'I just remember him every now and then. That's all.'

Murielle put her arms around Justine. It was such a childlike gesture, spontaneous and genuine, that Justine was in danger of sobbing out loud. 'It's all right, Grandee,' Murielle said softly. 'He'll be back soon.'

'Yes. Thank you.' Justine nodded appreciatively, wanting to escape from Murielle's big concerned smile. 'Sorry, I'm ruining this for you.'

'We're family, Grandee. That means accepting the rough with the smooth, and standing together through all of it.'

Justine picked at the girl's shoulder straps, adjusting them. 'Better or worse, eh?'

'I've got the better part of it right now.' She glanced across at Starral, who gave an understanding smile. 'You know he's very good in bed,' Murielle said in a low confidential voice.

'Yes, dear, you told me.'

'I don't mind if you want to spend a few nights with him, Grandee. Before we get married.'

Justine started giggling. She couldn't help it; Murielle was absolutely serious. *How wonderful to be that young.* 'That's all right, dear. You enjoy him, he really is a great catch, anyone can see that. Take him upstairs every night and simply ruin him for any other girl.'

'I do my best to be bad,' Murielle said demurely.

'Good. Us Burnelli girls have reputations to maintain, you know. I'm depending on you to uphold the family honour. If they can still walk in the morning we've not been bad enough.'

Murielle was giggling now. Starral directed a faintly suspicious and worried look at the little female conspiracy meeting.

'Oh lordy,' Justine murmured. She'd just seen a stretched Skoda pull up. 'Look who's here, and – *joy* – she's brought her new whore with her.'

The two Burnellis straightened up and put on their false smiles as Alessandra Baron walked up to them.

'My dear Senator, I'm so sorry about your brother,' Alessandra said. 'Thompson was always such a delight to have on my show. A decent politician I always called him. One of the last.'

Justine gave the celebrity a pretentious exaggerated air kiss. 'Why thank you. He thought the same about you.'

'As soon as his new body is conscious, tell him I was asking after him. And I'd love to have him back on my show.'

'I'll tell him. Thank you.'

'I want to introduce my newest and best affiliate reporter,' Alessandra gushed. 'This is Mellanie Rescorai.'

Justine smiled as she shook hands with the young woman. She was a first-lifer, about the same age as Murielle, but that was about the only similarity. This one was a raw streetfighter, Justine saw; dangerously ambitious. Strange that Alessandra hadn't recognized that. But then perhaps she was off guard when looking into a mirror.

'An honour, Senator,' Mellanie said. 'You have a lovely home here.'

'Thank you. I've accessed your reports several times. You seem to be making quite a name for yourself, especially on Elan.'

'Those people were awful, opposing the navy like that. The Commonwealth should know what they were doing.'

'I'm sure they should.'

'Now Mellanie, this is a party,' Alessandra chided. 'And this has to be the blushing bride.' She took both of Murielle's hands. 'Congratulations on your engagement my dear. You look wonderful. You're putting the rest of us to shame in that dress. Quite right, too.'

'Why thank you,' Murielle said sweetly.

'Yes, congratulations,' Mellanie said. 'You're very lucky.' It almost sounded as though she meant it.

Justine waited until the reporters had said hello to Starral and left the gazebo. 'Remind me, why did we invite her?'

'It's a society wedding, Grandee. There are rules.'

'Oh yes, I knew there was a good reason.'

'Do you think Gore will come? Starral's family has all shown.'

'Don't worry, he'll be here. He knows what I'll do to him if he doesn't show.'

*

Gore Burnelli did turn up in his huge Zil limousine, although it wasn't until well after five o'clock. Justine broke off from the group of Halgarths she was talking to and went to greet her father. He was wearing a perfectly cut tuxedo, though not even that could help make his gold face and hands seem human. There was a woman with him that Justine didn't recognize at first; very attractive, with a young face that had some Oriental features, black hair tied back neatly. She was in a modern business suit, which was annoying, the invitations had been *most* specific.

'Don't scowl,' Gore said. 'Paula is here as my guest.'

'Delighted,' Justine said. Then she recognized the woman without even having to reference her e-butler. 'Investigator, I've followed a lot of your cases.'

'Ex-investigator,' Paula said. 'I was dismissed.'

'Which is why we're here,' Gore said.

Justine didn't know why, but she had hoped that just for once this party wouldn't be cover for business and deals, that people might actually kick back and enjoy themselves. She sighed. 'We'll use your study.'

Like Justine, Gore treated the Tulip Mansion as his main base of operations. Not only was it perfectly physically secure, it had a cybersphere nexus larger than most corporate head-quarters. The principal access was his study. Like Gore himself, it represented the pinnacle of interface technology; so that when linked together they were synergistic. Technicians from family-owned laboratories were always rebuilding it and then modifying systems, incorporating advances that wouldn't appear on the commercial market for years.

Visually, it was difficult to take in its true size, there were no reference points. The surface was a hard pearl-white plastic that glowed from within. Little points of light sparkled away inside it, travelling slowly. Justine always had the impression of being inside some giant photonic processor.

Once the door was closed, the three of them looked like

they'd been superimposed inside a blank hologram projection. Curved chairs morphed up out of the floor, shaped like sculpted bean-bags. Their internal glow changed from neutral to a faint copper, allowing them to be seen. After they'd all sat down, the tinge faded away.

'I'm appointing Paula to the Senate Security Service,' Gore announced. 'She's to have department head status; you'll have to clear it.'

'I see,' Justine said peacefully. 'And why is that?'

'Your brother's murder was committed by someone connected with the case I've been working on,' Paula said.

'Johansson, you mean? I don't wish to be critical, particularly now, but you've been working on that case for quite a while now. That was the reason Rafael Columbia dismissed you, wasn't it? Lack of results.'

'Columbia is a fucking asshole,' Gore said. 'We're going to have to watch him. That little shit won't be satisfied until he's crowned emperor.'

Justine gave Paula a level gaze. 'He does have a point, though. You had a hundred and forty years.'

'The case involved a lot more than the Great Wormhole Heist,' Paula said. 'I always knew Johansson was being protected by someone inside the Senate or the Executive. Your brother confirmed that for me. Then he was murdered.'

'Who murdered him?'

'I don't know. The assassin is an unknown operative; nor do I know who he works for, although I have my suspicions.'

'Who?' Justine growled.

'The Starflyer.'

After the anticipation, Justine fell back into the chair, disgusted. 'For God's sake!'

'I believe it,' Gore said.

'Dad! You cannot be serious?'

'We were played by an absolute expert. I knew there was something suspicious about putting the navy package together.

It was too fucking easy. Someone else had been laying the political groundwork.'

'Garbage. Nobody knew we'd have a need for a navy until the *Second Chance* returned. I'm still not entirely convinced myself. We only got involved for the contracts.'

'Damn right. That's our motivation, naked greed, the fear of being poor, unprotected, not in control. It knows us very well, doesn't it?'

'No.' Justine shook her head. 'What did my brother tell you?' she asked Paula.

'I have been asking for an inspection on all goods shipped to Far Away for decades. If I could nail down the arms shipments, it would help me solve the Johansson case permanently. Your brother found out that Nigel Sheldon has been preventing it.'

'That's . . . that's . . .' Justine turned to her father, appealing. 'You can't believe this?'

'Why can't the Starflyer exist?' he asked her in return.

'The Institute on Far Away would have found it.'

'According to Johansson they did,' Paula said. 'He was the director, remember?'

'I know he was,' she said wryly. Her thoughts had slipped back to the sunny glade in the forest where her hyperglider had landed. Dear, sweet Kazimir's utter conviction in his mad cause. 'All right, just assume this alien does exist, and Nigel Sheldon is working for it, or has been taken over by it, or whatever. How does that get Thompson murdered?'

'Because he finally pushed through the inspection,' Paula said. 'I only just realized the relevance myself last night, but keeping the Far Away route open and free of any official interference has been something of a devil's alliance for the two factions. The Guardians want it so they can smuggle their weapons back there. The Starflyer wants it so that it can return.'

'Return? You mean to its ship?' Justine asked.

'Yes. That's what the Guardians believe, that when it has ruined the Commonwealth it will go back.'

'Why? The ship's a wreck, the planet is half-dead. I know, I've been there.' She caught it: shift of the eyes, change of breathing pattern, a dozen other indiscreet indicators. Most people wouldn't have noticed, but Justine had been a player for three and a half centuries, dealing with master-class politicians and corporate lords. To her, body language was a million-watt telepathic broadcast. And that last statement had just turned her into Paula Myo's newest suspect.

'Nobody understands its motivation,' Paula said. 'Except perhaps Johansson. And I wouldn't consider him reliable even if he turns out to be right in the end. All we have to go on is the Guardian propaganda. They claim it intends to return.'

'And you think that's what got my brother murdered?'

'He put an obstacle in its way.'

Justine gave her father a long look, seeing a curved image of herself in his smooth golden mirror face. His silence made it obvious whose side he was on here. 'So how does appointing you to Senate Security help find the murderer?'

'It will give me access to all Navy Intelligence information on the case. I can see what they're doing but they won't know I'm looking over their shoulder. That way I can stay one step ahead of them.'

'Just wait on, here,' Justine protested. 'Who are you trying to catch?'

'Ultimately the Starflyer. But to do that I will need Johansson. He is the only expert we have on it.' Paula glanced at Gore. 'Unless I go to Far Away.'

'Out of the question,' Gore shot back. 'I told you. You're too valuable to go off chasing round an unknown countryside full of guerrillas. Besides, you're not geared up for that kind of operation. Your public profile is too high, we need to keep you out of sight behind a desk. Now I know what's actually been going on around here we can send some covert agents from our family security teams to take a damn close look at both factions on Far Away. I want to know exactly what the fuck's been happening out there.'

'Very well,' Justine said. 'I'll have Thompson's office arrange your clearance. You should be able to start tomorrow.' It wasn't that she agreed with her father, she simply couldn't see any other way to proceed for now.

*

Morton would have liked the party, Mellanie knew. It was full of players that were in a league far above any he'd moved among on Oaktier. Even that airhead Murielle had more money in her trust fund than Morton's beloved Gansu Construction was capitalized at. He would have been dealing from the moment they arrived until the cateringbots started clearing up in the wee small hours.

For herself she was entranced by the Tulip Mansion. That much wealth and antiquity and style in one package was overwhelming to a girl from Darklake City. Growing up in such an environment would leave anyone with real confidence and poise. A childhood spent here must have been magnificent. As if to confirm the notion, she could see groups of children running about across the grounds, carefree and happy as they played simple timeless games of catch and chase. Her blank smile concealed her envy.

Looking around at the beautiful people as they chatted in groups on the lawn she still felt she was living in someone else's TSI biogdrama. She knew how to move with them, how to laugh at their inane jokes, when to smile knowingly as they gossiped, the names of wines and food, how to pronounce them correctly. Art was still difficult for her, the Grand Families and Intersolar Dynasties seemed to have the entire history of art encyclopaedia available at a genetic level; but her e-butler kept the files on quick recall.

'Ah, there's Campbell Sheldon,' Alessandra said. Her hand waved discreetly towards one of the marquees. 'See him?'

Mellanie turned slowly, scanning the group standing around the marquee, framed by one of the giant flower arrangements. Her virtual vision displayed the file picture of Sheldon, and she matched it with the real man. 'Got him.'

'Campbell is your fuck tonight. He was their family's chief negotiator when the navy was put together; so he'll have access to the stats. How are the construction schedules holding up, what's the true budget overspend? You know what we need.'

Mellanie said nothing.

Alessandra gave her a disapproving look. 'You're not going soft on me, are you? There are about a billion other girls who would like to take your place.'

'I know. But he's a Sheldon, he's not going to give me figures on stuff like that. He's not dumb.'

'Of course not. He knows who you are and why you're sucking his dick. That's the point. He won't give you figures, but he'll show us the direction to take. They're all at war with each other, young Mellanie, all struggling for dominance, and information is their weapon. If one of his rivals is screwing up, you'll be told.'

Mellanie gave the group a second look. It was half past six, she'd had too many cocktails and too many vacuous conversations where every sentence began and ended with 'darling'. There were lights on inside the marquees, and paths across the lawns were glowing blue as if they were phosphorescent streams. 'Why do they have marquees? This place must have force fields. They'll turn them on if it starts raining.'

'I'm sure they will,' Alessandra said in an annoyed tone.

'So if we're not going to get wet, why put up marquees?'

'Go ask Campbell. The Sheldons are all technology bores. I'm sure he'll love explaining it all to you.'

'Do you like anybody?'

'I like you.' Alessandra leaned forwards and gave her a firm kiss. Mellanie was slow to respond.

'Don't be such a bitch,' Alessandra complained.

Mellanie glared at her through the alcohol buzz; then she blinked, peering across the darkling grounds. 'That's Myo.'

'Paula Myo?' Alessandra couldn't keep the twang of interest out of her voice.

'Yes.'

'Curious.' She kept facing Mellanie. 'Who's she with?'

'A nobody. Security man.' Mellanie was quite pleased she could tell.

'So she's dealing with the Burnellis.'

'Let me have it.'

'You've got to stop obsessing on the woman.'

'It's a good story, and you know it. I'll fuck whoever you want, but give it to me.'

'That's my Mellanie. All right, I can spare you for a couple of days. If you can find out what she's doing for the Burnellis I'll be impressed. But if not, I want you back on Elan in forty-eight hours.'

'Thank you.' Mellanie kissed her, properly this time.

'All right,' Alessandra said eventually, chortling happily. 'Campbell! Remember? Now go.'

Mellanie dropped her cocktail glass into the rose bushes, shook her tousled hair back, pushed her tits out, and started walking towards her target.

*

The engagement party was going well after all. Justine surveyed the guests as they drifted in for the evening buffet. A twenty-piece band had set up in front of the big fountain pool to play merry 1950s tunes. She could hear a lot of laughter amid the drone of conversation. Thick flower scents drifted on the fresh night air. Overhead, the constellations burned brightly. Down towards the beech wood, the Tolthorpe troupe were running through their final rehearsal with the stage techs.

Her mood had lifted considerably since her father and the Myo woman had left. She supposed she shouldn't have been surprised at her father accepting conspiracy theories in his desperation to catch the murderer. It was just that he was always the ruthlessly logical one. Thompson's murder must have shaken him up a lot more than he was admitting to.

In the morning, she would take the time and talk to him properly about the whole situation. In the meantime, however, there was still time to have a lot of fun. And there were several men on the guest list she'd be happy to spend the night with. When she started searching round she saw Campbell Sheldon. He had a blissful smile on his face as he chattered away to Mellanie Rescorai. The girl had obviously decided he was going to take her to bed. Justine rolled her eyes at the folly of the male psyche. Ah well, he was a big boy, he'd probably survive the experience.

Ramon DB was over by the marquee, giving the food a long guilty look. She smiled warmly. He'd been a tower of strength for her at Senate Hall, helping her through long difficult days. He was due for rejuvenation in another year. She'd miss him in the meantime; although when he was twenty he was *so* handsome.

She looked for Estella, who would be good uncomplicated company.

'You left this behind, ma'am.'

Justine turned to face the young waiter who was holding out a silver tray. There were no glasses on it, only a tatty, faded old sunhat.

'I don't think I—' She stopped. Stared at the sunhat. Suddenly, some strange force was squeezing her throat, making it difficult to breathe. That same force which was making incredulous tears sting her eyes as she looked up into the waiter's face. 'Oh. My. God. *Kazimir!*' Her legs almost gave out, but she still managed to fly across the short distance and fling her arms round him. He was bigger. Older. With much broader shoulders. A dark handsome face with jet-black hair flopping down over his forehead. And he was as ecstatic as her.

'Every night I have dreamed of you, my angel,' he whispered into her ear as his hands stroked her hair. She clutched his back, almost tearing the waiter jacket fabric.

'Every night.' He was trembling now.

Justine tightened her grip on him.

'Every night I wanted you to be happy. I wanted you to love your beautiful life. Yet even wishing you all that, I wished I could see you for just one minute more.'

'Ssh.' She slid a finger down over his lips, then kissed him. Tenderly at first, not believing this could be real. Then demanding, passionate, shaking in his embrace.

He pulled back, staring intently into her eyes. His smile of wonder was as bright as ever, brighter than her memory. 'It is you,' she said exultantly. 'Really you.'

'I had to come, my angel. Different worlds or different galaxies, I couldn't be apart from you. I had to find a way. Forgive me.'

'Oh Kazimir.' She knew she was going to cry and didn't care. Her gorgeous romantic, foolish, lover had pursued her across the stars.

'Come with me,' she said softly, and pulled him imploringly, longingly towards the Tulip Mansion.

*

In the full dark of midnight, hologram projectors cloaked the open air stage in broad strokes of primary colour. Dry ice flooded spookily through the beech trees. Cleverly positioned force fields allowed Puck and the fairies to fly gracefully through the air. Soliloquies were declaimed with bravado and majesty, to be greeted with enthusiastic applause from the audience.

Justine neither heard nor saw any of the Tolthorpe troupe's finest hour. In the darkness and peace of her bedroom, her own body was performing the most erotic, sensual acts she could physically achieve. She had forgotten what it was like to be adored so completely, so unselfishly. He was so much more responsive now, matching the pleasure she gave with ease, willing and eager to satisfy her. They could be gentle and slow with each other, moving in tender rhythm, or fierce, almost fighting to bring themselves to climax. It didn't matter, both kinds of lovemaking were right for them. Time after time amid the silky shadows she watched his enraptured straining features soften into a smile of unbearable joy, only to lose herself in the same delirium. For once there were no chemicals or programs to help. This was real.

When the dawn cast its bland grey illumination into the bedroom she smiled at their bodies, still wrapped together, sweat mingling on their skin, faces inches apart, sharing perfect secret contentment.

'I love you,' he said fearfully.

'I love you.'

'I won't let you go again.'

She smiled in admiration at the conviction in his voice. 'What are you doing here on Earth?' She knew the answer she wanted, that it was for her and her alone.

'There was a chance that I could see you. How could I ever let that go by?'

'My wonderful love.' She put a finger on his thorax and slowly drew a line down his sternum, playfully following the ridges of hard muscle. His body was fabulous. How long would it have taken a boy born into low-grav to build himself up to handle standard gravity? The effort he'd made, the determination. She was rather glad she'd kept up her own aerobics classes and maintenance diet, still slim and trim.

'It will be difficult to get away to see you, but I will manage it.'

Her finger stopped just as it reached his navel. Already, she knew this was going to be bad news. 'Get away from who?'

'The Guardians, or course. I'm here on a mission.'

'Oh Christ.' She pushed at him, slithering herself over the sheets until she was an arm's length away, and stared at him in dismay. Already his youthful sympathetic face had produced a puzzled expression.

'A mission,' she croaked. 'You're here on some kind of Guardian mission?'

'Yes.'

'Oh Kazimir, no; no you can't do that kind of thing here. This isn't Far Away. You have to stop.'

'I cannot stop. This is our time. This is when the planet will have its revenge on the Starflyer. I'm a part of that, Justine. Bradley Johansson chose me.'

She wanted to put her head in her hands, or maybe belt some sense into him. 'Kazimir, listen to me. We have a navy now, which has a branch dedicated to stopping Johansson. Hundreds of officers are working on the case. They will catch you. They will.'

His kindly smile was one that told her she simply didn't understand. 'They won't. We're perfectly safe.'

'Kazimir, this is not a game.'

'I am the one who has always known that. And now you have become a victim of the Starflyer, too. I wept when I heard its creature had murdered your brother. How cruel that fate, that of all the people in the Commonwealth, it hurt the only person I love.'

'No, God no, this isn't happening. Kazimir, *please*, there is no Starflyer. My brother was killed by his rivals. It's ugly, and brutal, and shocking, and it's never happened in Commonwealth politics before. But it is not the fault of a secret alien.'

'Politicians are its creatures, too. They are the easiest of all humans to corrupt.'

'Listen to yourself. You're just repeating student slogans. Johansson is an evil old man who's using you, and all the other clans back on Far Away.'

'Justine, I'm sorry, but it is you who cannot see the truth in this.'

'I can't believe we're having this argument. You have to stop, Kazimir, just walk away. I'll clear any problem with your involvement. God knows, you've been indoctrinated since birth. Nobody will blame you.'

'How could you ask me that?' he demanded, shocked and hurt. 'I had hoped you would help us. The planet's revenge can be your revenge as well, if you let it. You can make sure the Starflyer is defeated.'

'What? What are you talking about?'

'Get the cargo inspections lifted.'

'*What?*'

He couldn't have appalled her more if he'd slapped her. 'Is that why you came?' she asked.

'No!' he protested. 'I risked everything to come to you. Everything. I love you Justine, I am fighting to save your world.'

She leant forward and grasped his hands, desperately conscious of how young and idealistic he was, how much he had to prove himself. 'I don't want you to, not like this. Kazimir, it is a far braver and nobler thing to admit you are wrong. I know, I've had to do it many times. Please, just consider leaving the Guardians to manage without you for a while. You and I can talk this through.'

'You can browbeat me, you mean.'

'That's not what I mean at all. I just want you to learn that there are other viewpoints than the Guardians'.'

'I cannot desert my comrades. You should not ask me this. I watched my best friend die in front of me, I have lost many others. Now you say it was for nothing.'

'What are you going to do?'

'What are you going to do?' he countered. 'Will you try and stop me returning to my comrades? I will not let your security people interrogate me.'

'Calm down,' she said hurriedly. 'Nobody's going to stop you leaving. I don't want you to leave, but that's the only chain around you, how much I love you, and don't want to see you harmed.'

'I have been through many battles. I have no fear of my enemy.'

'God!' she growled through clenched teeth. 'Men!'

He gave her a twitchy smile and rolled off the bed.

'Where are you going? You're not going now?'

'I have to.' He shrugged, almost blushing. 'I hadn't expected to spend the night.'

She felt her own cheeks colouring at that. 'I want you to spend every night here, Kazimir. I want every night to be like last night. I don't do this anymore . . . Damnit, I thought . . . I didn't think I could care for someone like this, not anymore. But you . . .'

'When this is over, when nothing lies between us, I will be yours for as long as you'll have me.'

'Damnit.' Her eyes were watering.

'Don't cry. I won't have my beautiful angel cry for me. I'm not worth it.'

'You are. You are so worth it. You have no idea.'

He finished dressing, then held her for a long moment. 'I will come back for you,' he promised gravely. 'I swear it.'

She nodded, too exhausted emotionally and physically to

999

do anything else. After a while, with fresh tears running freely down her cheeks, she placed a call to Alic Hogan at his Paris office.

*

It started raining an hour before dawn, cold drops splattering down on the cobbles to form grubby rivulets racing down the gutters. Mellanie stood in a doorway three down from Paula Myo's Paris apartment; tired, miserable, and hungry as the sun rose, exposing the narrow street to a grey shading that belonged to the middle ages. The time-bowed wooden lintel above her was dripping steadily on her head, wrecking her expensive hairstyle. There had been no time for her to prepare properly. She knew Alessandra wouldn't allow her a second longer than the two days unless she got a real story. So her jacket collar was turned up in a grim attempt to keep some of the cold out, because the 1950s party dress she wore under it was certainly no good for that. Both feet were soaking inside her handstitched Italian leather shoes, that were now ruined.

The early morning monotony was occasionally broken by a civic GPbot rolling past her. By six o'clock people had started using the street. She received a few curious glances. Their eyes soon slid away, deciding she was some hooker waiting for her pimp or pusher after a bad night.

Close, she told their backs as they hurried away.

At half-past seven Paula Myo walked out onto the street. She wore a long raincoat, unbuttoned to show her usual business suit; her feet were protected by calf-high booshide boots, and she switched on a plyplastic umbrella stick which flowed out into a wide black mushroom-shape.

Mellanie waited until the woman had almost reached the end of the street, and left the scant cover of the doorway. Her virtual vision displayed a simple map of the area. As she'd expected, Myo was walking to the nearest Metro station. She kept twenty metres or so behind her, trying not to be too obvious. The wider streets had some traffic and pedestrians, making cover easier. Headlights cast bright reflection ribbons on the black tarmac, while their tyres produced a thin dirty spray. The smell of fresh-baked bread emerged from patisseries that were opening their doors. Mellanie's stomach growled from the temptation.

Ahead of her Myo turned a corner. Mellanie hurried forward. When she turned the corner, the Metro station sign gleamed brightly fifty metres ahead. Myo had vanished.

'Where . . .' Mellanie scanned round. The woman hadn't crossed to the other side of the road. None of the shops were open, so she couldn't have hidden inside anywhere. 'Damnit.' In her mind the plan had been perfect: follow Myo to wherever she was working. That would give a clue to what she was working on for the Burnellis, or even if it was the Burnellis. Whatever, it would give her enough interesting questions for Alessandra to keep her on Myo.

'You would make a dreadful field operative.'

'Huh.' Mellanie spun round.

Myo was standing there, umbrella held straight, giving her a quizzical look. 'It is illegal to run search programs through restricted city listings. Paul Cramley, the hacker you used to gain access, is old enough to know that.'

'What are you going to do, arrest us?'

'No. He will have a formal charge filed against him. It will probably result in a fine and confiscation of his equipment.'

'Bitch!'

'He broke the law. So have you. Being a reporter does not place you above the law, Ms Rescorai. You have to obey the rules like every other citizen, however inconvenient that is to your so-called profession.'

'I've never heard of this Paul Cramley. You can't prove anything.'

Myo's stare hardened. 'I don't have to. You are interfering with a government official, which is also an offence.'

'You're not, you got fi—' Mellanie drew a deep breath. 'I'm sorry, I was desperate for an interview with you.'

'I don't give interviews. Everyone in your profession knows that.'

'But you must be able to tell me if there are any suspects in the Burnelli murder.'

'Ask the Navy Intelligence media office for an update.'

'They're not as good as you. If they do catch anyone it'll be on the foundation you laid. I want the whole story.'

'I don't respond to flattery, either.'

'I'm not flattering you. I despise you. But I'm also a realist.'

A dark grey limousine drew up to the curb beside them. Its rear door opened. 'You're wasting your time following me,' Myo said. Her plyplastic umbrella flowed back into a simple fat stick. 'Even if you were any good, you wouldn't find anything of interest where I'm going.'

'Where would I find something interesting?'

'In truth, I'm not sure. You might try space, deep space.' She got into the back of the limousine, and its door closed.

Mellanie stood shivering in the rain, watching the plush vehicle's scarlet tail-lights merge into the Parisian traffic. 'Is it true she never lies?' she asked the SI.

'It is true she never tells a direct lie; though she is capable of modifying the truth if it will forward her investigation.'

Hell. Deep space? Who knows about deep space?

*

There had been quite a celebration on High Angel last night. *StAsaph* had returned from another flight, scouting eleven stars. Captain McClain Gilbert had reported that they hadn't encountered any Prime wormhole activity. Then, along with Admiral Kime and Captain Oscar Monroe, he'd gone to watch the *Dauntless* disengage from her assembly platform. The warship was a distinct design change from the *Second Chance* and the earlier scouts. She'd been built inside a single three-hundred-metre-long hull, shaped like a stretched teardrop, with eight blunt thermal radiator fins at the rear to complete the aerodynamic illusion. A crew of thirty were in command of a marque 4 hyperdrive, with a top speed of one light-year per hour; a seven-tier force field complemented with a locked molecule hull field; fifty missiles containing fifteen independent twenty-gee sub-warheads carrying hundred-megaton charges capable of diverted energy functions; and thirty directed energy beam weapons. To supply power for the hyperdrive and the combat systems, fifteen high-capacity niling d-sinks had been installed. Charging them up to flight readiness was now beyond the generator capacity of Kerensk, which was already supplying power for the entire scoutship fleet. CST was laying in superconductor power lines from other planets to supply the anticipated fleet. The construction of new generators was providing a bull market for power bonds right across the Commonwealth as entrepreneurs and existing utility companies bid to supply the navy with gigawatts.

Dauntless had disengaged right on time, small blue ion flames around her base pushing her slowly away from the open assembly platform. She'd curved round the High Angel, giving the people in the crystal domes a good view of her size and shape as she traversed Icalanise, before switching on her hyperdrive and vanishing in a burst of violet light.

'Three completed, another ten authorized,' Wilson had said as the big ship slipped over Babuyan Atoll. '*Defender* is next out. She's yours if you want her,' he told Oscar.

'Oh, I do. Yes, indeed, I truly do.'

Mac had laughed delightedly and congratulated his old friend. Then the pair of them had gone out and hit the town, such as it was in Babuyan Atoll, to toast the new command and the successful return.

Oscar groaned miserably as the express shot into strong lemon-yellow sunlight, which shone through the first-class carriage windows. He reached for his sunglasses.

'So where did you two finish up last night?' Antonia Clarke asked from the seat opposite.

'I have no goddamn idea,' Oscar grunted. 'There was a band there. I think. Maybe jazz?' He picked up the cup of black coffee that the steward had just poured, looked at it, felt strange fluids in his stomach start to churn, and hurriedly put it down again.

Antonia laughed. She'd already had to baby-sit him through the freefall commuter flight from High Angel to the Kerensk wormhole station. Keeping his uniform clean under those circumstances had been tricky; then there had been the complaints from their fellow passengers.

'Have you got your speech ready?' she asked.

'Fuck off.'

'You want another tifi hit?'

'Look! Just shut – Oh God, yes please.'

Grinning, she took out the packet of tubes, and pressed one to his neck. There was a capacitor whine as the membrane pad on the end fast-tracked the drug into his bloodstream. 'That's your limit. No more for another six hours.'

He touched his fingertips delicately to his sweating forehead, testing to see if the pain was abating. 'They only print that to keep the lawyers quiet. You can take at least twice the dosage before anything bad happens.'

'Ever the optimist. How do you feel?'

'I think that one might actually be working.'

'Good.'

The express went through another wormhole gateway, and the light became even brighter, a sharp blue-white. Antonia looked out of the window. 'We're here. New Costa Junction. Let's go.' She stood up.

Oscar gave the cup of coffee a last longing glance, and decided against.

A senior manager from the clinic was on the platform to

greet them. He had a car for them, which slid smoothly onto highway 37.

'Ten-minute trip from here,' the manager promised. 'We're between shifts, so the traffic is light.'

The Nadsis hotel was set back off the freeway, a twenty-storey X-shape, with five separate conference facilities. Over a thousand media reporters were packed into the Bytham auditorium where the welcome back ceremony was to be performed. Both of the honoured guests and all the VIPs walked en masse onto the stage, to considerable applause. Dudley Bose, a lanky adolescent with a shock of ginger-blond hair that refused styling, broke his sulk to grin around before eventually giving the thumbs up that had been his interview trademark. Emmanuelle Verbeke was a surprise to those who had accessed her file for background information. On the *Second Chance* she'd been sober and professional to the point of dullness, a woman with rather bland features who didn't care about appearances. Today she was almost indistinguishable from a genuine first-life eighteen-year-old. She'd chosen a strap-top purple dress with a short skirt to show off long legs that had been toned to perfection by the clinic's physiotherapists. Her dark hair, still shortish despite the accelerated growth phase of cloning, was arranged in neat curls that emphasized her youth. Her perpetual gleeful smile and very girlish giggles illustrated a rare case of someone being highly suited to the whole re-life procedure.

It was Oscar who was scheduled to make the initial speech. He said hello to everybody. Then he had to perform the introductions – a stupid thing to do. After that was his own quick 'personal' welcome to his former crewmates. A happy anecdote from the *Second Chance* to show what great friends they all were; while what he wanted to do was blurt out the story of how Bose had managed to screw up the shower filtration unit for his deck.

After five minutes of torture he sat down to polite applause and Antonia's mocking smile. Vice President Bicklu was next, making the formal welcome back speech. He was a tall man whose features were sequenced and profiled to produce a bland handsomeness, along with Nordic white skin to contrast with Doi's African ethnicity. Oscar had to sit with a fixed smile as the VP made a very good speech, with plenty of easy jokes that had the media laughing and the other guests smiling appreciatively. He made Oscar look like the amateur warm-up act.

When it was her turn, Emmanuelle got up and gave the VP a sweet kiss on the cheek. She smiled at the big audience, said how nice it was to be back, how she was impressed by the progress the navy had made, how she wanted to join up again as soon as she was old enough – applause and a few whistles – and a big hello to all her friends and thanks for all the support they'd shown while she was in re-life.

She gave Dudley Bose an encouraging wink as he went to the podium. 'I've heard a lot this afternoon about how dedicated and friendly everyone was on the *Second Chance*,' Dudley said. A hand came up automatically to play with his ear. 'What a great ship, what a good job it did flying that mission. I'm puzzled by that. Because I haven't got a fucking clue which *Second Chance* they're talking about. It certainly isn't the one I flew on. The bastards I was crewing with LEFT ME THERE. ALONE! Our great so-called captain didn't even check to see if we were still alive, he was so desperate to save his own arse.' His arm shot up, a rigid finger pointing at the ceiling. 'I'm still out there, you know. Somehow. Some alien has kept me alive, or bits of me. So why am I here as well? Why are you doing to me, you *shits*?' He stomped off the stage, leaving all the VIPs staring at each other in embarrassment.

'Do something,' Antonia said out of the corner of her mouth.

'Why me?' Oscar mumbled back. Every reporter in the audience was looking at them expectantly, relaying the image through the unisphere. Many of them were smiling. It wasn't in sympathy.

'You're the MC.'

'Ohshit.' Oscar walked slowly over to the centre of the stage, where the main lights were focused. He cleared his throat. 'Kids today, huh?' He'd never known a silence so deep, so unbroken. 'Look. Okay. I'm sorry Dr Bose feels the way he does. Had we stayed at the Watchtower, we would have died. It's that simple. The Primes were firing nuclear missiles at us. You can't hang around philosophizing in circumstances like that.'

At the front of the audience, Alessandra Baron stood up. 'Captain Monroe, the *Second Chance* had ftl capacity. The Primes did not. So why didn't you circle back and make a final pass to see what had happened to your crewmates?'

'Our primary mission was to report our findings back to the Commonwealth. Everybody on board knew that, Dr Bose included. We all accepted the risks.'

'But didn't your actions increase the risk factor in this case? One check wouldn't have endangered anybody on board. Didn't you care about your crewmates?'

'They screwed up,' Oscar snapped back, angry at the allegation. He remembered only too well what it had been like on board at the time. Now this moron prima diva was questioning their decisions from the safety of time and distance. 'Or at least Bose did. He wasn't properly trained to join the exploratory team. Nobody wanted the old idiot on board in the first place.'

This time the silence which opened up was even deeper. Then a thousand questions were shouted at once.

Antonia's arm came protectively round Oscar's shoulder. 'Thank you for your time, ladies and gentlemen,' she bawled through the PA at full volume. 'Drinks and canapés are now served in the lounge. Enjoy.' She physically hauled Oscar off the stage in something approaching a wrestling lock. He got one glimpse of Baron's diabolically victorious smile before they reached the wings.

Vice President Bicklu's white skin had turned puce. 'Why didn't anyone brief me this was hostile?' he was shouting at aides. He caught sight of Oscar. 'You! What the hell was that?'

'Later,' Antonia sang out cheerfully, still pushing Oscar along. They reached one of the hotel's service corridors and came to a halt.

Oscar put a hand on his forehead. It was hot and sweating. His headache was back again, big time. When he pulled his hand away, he half expected the dampness he'd felt to be blood. 'OhmyGod, did I really say that?'

'Yep,' Antonia said, she sounded inordinately pleased. 'And it was about time somebody did.'

'Oh God. I think I just blew the *Defender* captaincy.'

'Don't be so stupid. Come on. This is a hotel; there's got to be a bar somewhere. I'll buy you a hair of the dog, you need it.'

*

Dudley ignored everyone, the government officials, hotel staff, even the nurse from the clinic. As soon as he left the stage he ran, blundering through the maze of corridors until he came to a big deserted kitchen. Only then did he stop and draw a very shaky breath. He pressed his head on the side of a big refrigeration cabinet, enjoying the feel of the cool stainless steel surface against his skin. His heart was pounding and his hands shaking. It wasn't entirely due to running.

'I did it,' he whispered, and smiled to himself. Told them what he thought in front of every reporter who counted in the Commonwealth – and the Vice President. Just the thought sent another tremble along his limbs.

Somebody started clapping in a slow almost derisory fashion.

Dudley straightened up. He almost expected it to be the Vice President's bodyguards coming at him with ion pistols blazing.

Instead, it was a beautiful young girl with wavy golden hair that came down over her shoulders. She was wearing a scoop-neck top of some rust-pink gauze with a silver leaf pattern, and a pair of clinging faded blue jeans that had a small silver M on one of the belt loops. There was a lopsided approving grin on her lips as she approached. She had very white teeth, Dudley noticed – that and the top was translucent. His face began to redden.

'That took a lot of courage to say what you did,' she said. 'I respect that.'

'Thank you.' It didn't quite come out as a stutter. He knew he was staring, and just couldn't help himself. She was more than attractive, her body had this *healthiness* about it that was intoxicating. His own body was getting uncontrollably hot. He hadn't managed to have sex yet, not in this body. Just a whole load of lonely nights spent masturbating since he'd been physically able, which wasn't long. Memories of women he'd been with kept flashing up through his mind, as well as all the ones he'd never had the guts to ask. His old self would never ask a girl like this for a date, he knew.

'It must have been awful for you to realize what they did,' she said. 'Coming to terms with how they betrayed you.'

'Yes. Yes, it was.'

'Without you none of this would be possible, none of the starships they've built. The important new positions your ex-shipmates have carved for themselves.'

'I can't believe they did it. They left us there to die.' Even now, after all the months thinking about it, trying to come to terms with the flight, his bitterness and shock was as strong now as the day he'd found out. 'They didn't care about me, not one of them.'

'I know,' she said softly. 'A lot of us know.' Her smile was enchanting. 'I remember when you discovered the envelopment. I used to access reports of you when I was at school. I used to think I wanted to be an astronomer because of you.'

He twitched his shoulders around awkwardly. Her closeness was dangerous. He could feel his erection growing because of that. He was frightened she'd see it. He wanted to see her naked. He wanted them to be screwing like demons on overdrive. 'Did . . . did you? Are you one? An astronomer?'

'No. I'm not the intellectual type, I'm afraid. I chose a sports curriculum in the end, I was in a swimming team.'

'Ah.'

'You know, I can hardly believe I'm talking to my old idol.'

'I'm nobody's idol. I'm not even sure I'm me.' The base of his fist knocked against the refrigeration cabinet, again and again. Even talking to her couldn't divert his thoughts for long. 'You know the real Dudley Bose is still out there. Still looking at alien stars, but from a much closer viewpoint these days.' His laugh was high-pitched, almost out of control.

Her hand caught his fist, and held on, preventing him from moving it. 'I'm Mellanie.'

'Pleased to meet you.' All he could feel was her fingers gripping his wrist, her strength and warmth. She had dabbed on the faintest of perfumes. He breathed in deeply, knowing a scent that was so very different to the filtered conditioned air of the clinic, a human scent.

'I have a rented car outside. And I also have a room in this hotel.'

Dudley found it almost painful to say anything. 'Yes.'

'So. I can either drive you to the nearest Silent World. Or we can go upstairs. Now. Right now.'

*

The hotel room was as mass-produced and indistinguishable as any other Augusta product. A long L-shape with a balcony at one end, and the marbled bathroom at the other. The big double bed was on a raised level, with curtains that could close it off from the rest of the room.

It was dark outside when Oscar finally opened the door and stumbled in. He'd spent two hours in the small fifth-floor residents-only cocktail lounge with Antonia before the reporters tracked them down. That had been the end of that party.

He left the lights off and went over to the kitchen alcove. There was enough illumination coming in through the wide glass patio doors to see the beer bottles in the fridge. He chose one and popped the top. Antonia had been right, a hair of the dog always worked a lot better than a tifi hit. His hangover had completely vanished now. The hotel menu was on the counter; he picked it up as he went out and stood on the narrow balcony. There had been a formal banquet planned for this evening to finish the whole welcome back event, which was why he had the room. But the meal had been cancelled. If he was going to get anything to eat it would have to be room service.

Outside, New Costa gleamed brightly under the night sky, as if it were an amplifying mirror for the constellations above. Inland, to the north, the horizon was glowing a deep-hued amber where the steel smelters were stretched out amid the Colrey hills. A genuine false dawn. The corona was actually brighter than a world with an orange dwarf star he remembered exploring eight or nine years ago. Highways were slow-moving pyrotechnic rivers, winding through the sparkling grids in perpetual motion. Narrow strips of darkness cut across the city, rail tracks where long glimmering trains rolled endlessly between yards and stations and factories.

Oscar smiled passively at the industrial megalopolis, overwhelmed as always by its sheer size and energy. The El Iopi wind was strong tonight, sending warm dry air to scour the highways and avenues. He took a sip on the beer. Somewhere out there in the jewelled grid of lights were the factories where CST built its hyperdrives. There had been rumours around Base One of the latest variants, faster than the marque 4's, a lot faster. Now that would be some starship.

'That was quite a performance this afternoon.'

Oscar jumped at the voice. 'Shit.' The beer bottle slipped out of his fingers, falling soundlessly down towards the dark parking lot fifteen storeys below. 'Shit!' When he lurched back into the room there was a man sitting on the sofa. Oscar had never seen him when he came in.

'Some people never change,' the man said. 'You were always a little too fond of the old booze.'

'Who? What?'

There was a chuckle, and the man turned a table light on. Oscar peered at the intruder. He was quite old, probably early sixties – not rejuvenated. His face was comfortably round with reddish cheeks, a skin with a slightly rugged texture, the trait of someone who used too much cellular reprofiling. His body was larger than average, but not unfit, not for someone his age.

'I'm sorry, do I know you?'

'Oh yes, Oscar, you know me.'

Oscar walked over to the sofa and looked closely, trying to fit the face he saw into his own past. 'I don't . . .'

'Don't try and place me from memory. There's nothing left of what I used to look like. I've been reprofiled a hundred times over the decades, staying a couple of steps ahead of the law all this time.'

'Oh holy fuck.' The strength went out of Oscar's legs. He sat heavily at the other end of the sofa. 'Adam? Adam, is that you?'

'None other.'

'Oh God. It's been forty years.'

'Thirty- nine.'

Oscar looked at the man who had once been his friend and comrade with real dread. 'What do you want?'

'Is that any way to greet an old comrade?'

'Don't.'

'Don't what?' Adam spat. 'Don't remind you what you once were? Don't remind you that you used to have ideals? Principles? Don't remind you what you did for the cause?'

'I never fucking forgot!' Oscar shouted. 'Dear Christ. Nobody could forget. Not that. Not what we did.'

'I'm glad to hear it. Here I was thinking you'd gone to work for the biggest corporation the human race has ever known, helping them spread their oppression and corruption to new worlds.'

'Forty years and you still haven't come up with a new goddamn speech. Do you have any idea how tired that crap is? And don't forget to use the word plutocrat. Big words like that always impress the poor ignorant saps you con into giving up their life for your cause. It makes them think you're an intellectual, someone they can trust, someone who knows what they're doing.'

'It used to be your cause, Oscar. Have you given up on social justice? Is that the price of rejuvenation these days? Is that what the new young Oscar Monroe uses for currency?'

'Oh spare me. I was only young once, and I was a fucking hothead buffoon, an easy target for bastards like Professor Grayva to exploit. Damnit, we were just fucking kids. Just kids, we didn't know anything. You talk about being corrupted. You haven't got to look far to see where it really happens.'

'The party is right, and you know it. This society is not a just one.'

'Go on, say it!' Oscar leaned forward, his fingers contracting into fists. 'Go on you miserable bastard. Say it! Say it for fuck's sake. Say: the ends justify the means. That's what you came here for, isn't it? That's what you wanted one last time.'

Adam turned away from the fury in his eyes. 'Nothing justifies what we did,' he said so quietly Oscar could barely hear it. 'We both know that.'

They sat at opposite ends of the sofa, not looking at each other. After a minute, Adam grunted dismissively. 'How about this. We're like an old married couple, always rowing.'

'What are you here for, Adam? Come to bring me down in a blaze of glory?'

'Oh no, you don't get off that lightly.'

'Then what do you want?' His eyes narrowed as he took in his old friend. 'Money? You must need rejuvenation pretty soon.'

'I'm not sure I care to carry on living in this universe.'

'Not even you are that stupid. You can't die. That means you've wasted your whole life.'

'It's a life lived true to myself and my principles. Can you say that?'

'Yes. I've helped find dozens of new worlds. I've given our species a whole load of fresh starts. Phase three space isn't the same as one and two. There's no revolution, not one with Molotovs and people beating the shit out of each other on the street, but there's a difference.'

'Humm.' Adam nodded, as if some question had been answered correctly. 'Same cause, different angle of attack, huh?'

'Whatever. I'm not here to re-live old battles with you. They've all been fought and lost, by both of us. What the hell do you want, Adam?'

'I was sent to ask you something you won't like.'

It was the way he said it which finally alarmed Oscar, it was almost as if he was ashamed. Except Adam Elvin was never ashamed of what he did. Not ever. That was his whole problem. The reason for them turning their backs on each other all those decades ago. A truly venomous parting. 'I doubt this day could get any worse.'

'Don't be so sure. I want you to review the *Second Chance* flight data.'

'Review the . . .' Oscar almost started choking. 'Wait. You said sent. Who sent you? What do you mean: sent?'

'The man I work with on occasion believes there was an alien influence on board the *Second Chance* when you flew to the Dyson Pair. If the flight logs are given a professional analysis, they may show the evidence he needs to prove this.'

Oscar stared at the old man from his terrible past, his thoughts examining what had been said one word at a time. 'Bradley Johansson,' he said at last. 'You work with Bradley Johansson? You joined the Guardians of Selfhood? That bunch of nutters? Jesus fucking wept, Adam. Tell me you're joking. This is a sick joke. It has to be. It fucking has to be.'

'I have not joined the Guardians. I do know Johansson. We have a mutually beneficial arrangement.'

'You.' Oscar pointed at him with a trembling finger. 'OhmyGod, you attacked the *Second Chance*. It was you.'

Adam smiled with faint pride. 'None other.'

'You crazy fucked-up psychopath!' Oscar bunched up his fist, ready to pound, smash . . . 'That *terrorist attack* nearly killed half of my friends. You ruined millions of dollars' worth of equipment and facilities and delayed our launch date by months.'

'I know. I think I'm slipping. In the old days I would have got the lot of you, and blown up the starship.'

'You are crazy. People *died*, Adam.'

'They were all re-lifed. Just like your friend Dr Bose.'

'I'm calling Navy Intelligence.'

'Ah, the universe's greatest oxymoron. How long do you think they'll give you in life suspension?'

'I don't care about myself. Not any more. You have to be stopped.' Oscar almost did it, almost told his e-butler to make the call. He was going to do it. He was really going to do it. Any second now.

'No, Oscar. It's you and your navy who are in the wrong now, you who are the danger to humanity. Look where your precious *Second Chance* flight led us.'

'What is wrong with you? You don't believe that Guardians crap: President Doi is an alien agent. Come on! Not you.' He studied the old man's round face, hunting for some sign of guilt.

'What I believe doesn't matter, does it?' Adam said. 'It's what I want from you which is important. We want the log data reviewed, and you're the perfect choice. You have unrestricted access, and it's your field of expertise.'

'Oh, now I get it. If I study the data and don't *find* your evidence, then someone makes a call to Rafael Columbia. Right?'

'No, Oscar, this is on the level. I want you to run a genuine, thorough search.'

It was only the alcohol flowing sweetly through his head that prevented Oscar from laughing outright. 'Dear God, I never thought you'd be reduced to this. I mean, I always had this image of you carrying on the party's agenda. Every time one of those succession movements hit the unisphere I would think: I bet Adam's there, working away behind the scenes, urging the troops on, giving their leaders advice whether they want it or not. Then you'd slip back into the Commonwealth before CST closed the gateway, and build up underground cell networks on every world; you'd have thousands of loyal activists ready for the day your word would come and the whole Commonwealth would be plunged into civil war and revolution. That you'd be some kind of Gandhi, or Mandela, or maybe just Napoleon. But certainly you'd be *somebody*. Not this though, God, look at you. Just another fat ageing rebel who lost sight of his cause decades ago. So desperate you joined up with the saddest bunch of losers this universe has to offer.

'It's not real, Adam, there is no alien. I was on board that starship for over a year. I never bumped into it in the showers, never caught it stealing a late-night snack from the canteen, there was no ghost on deck thirteen. This is where your conspiracy theory runs slap bang into the sold wall of reality. You and Johansson can sit at home pulling every rumour you want from the unisphere and build them into a tower of your fact. It's all bullshit. There is no evidence to be found. So before you go just leave the little crystal memory on the table, and I'll politely ignore it, then when you're gone and I'm even more drunk I'll access the file your friends have forged and decide if I'm going to splice it into the official log for you so that I can save myself from life suspension because I'm too much of a pitiful coward to take responsibility for what I did once.'

'You need to get a shrink to take a good look at that self-loathing. It's not healthy.'

'Fuck you,' Oscar said. The pain he felt was close to physical now. 'Just leave the memory crystal and go.'

Adam struck him across the cheek. The blow was almost powerful enough to knock him off the couch.

'Shit.' Oscar dabbed at his mouth, blinking back tears from the stinging pain. A trickle of blood was oozing out from the corner of his lips. He gave Adam a wild look. 'What the fuck is wrong with you? I said I'd do it. What more do you want?'

'There is no forged file, you motherfucker. This is as real as it gets. And I said there was an influence on board, not a bug-eyed monster. The Starflyer works through humans. Somebody on board the *Second Chance* turned the barrier off – don't even try telling me that was coincidence. The same somebody who fixed it for Bose and Verbeke to be left behind. You don't think it was remotely suspicious that, of all the supertechnology, multiple-redundant, failsoft gadgets you had on board, a simple communicator failed at exactly that critical time? Because I fucking do.'

'Somebody?' Oscar asked, cynically. 'A crew member?'

'Yes. One of your precious crew. One of your friends. Or maybe more than one. Who knows? But that's what you've got to find out.'

'That's even worse than an alien stowaway. Do you know how much training and back-history investigation we went through to get on board? Nobody remotely suspect ever got close to the ship.'

'You mean like you and Dudley Bose?'

Oscar stared at him for a long, chilling moment. 'Look, Adam, what you're asking, it can't happen. Physically, it's not possible for me to do it. Do you realize how much raw data is in those logs?'

'I know. That's why we could never steal it and analyse it ourselves. You don't have to go through every byte yourself. You know the critical segments of the flight; that's where you look. Not at the main events, what happened on the bridge or in engineering, they'll be clean. It's what went on in the background that's important. Who was haunting deck thirteen when the barrier came down? Find them, not just for us, for yourself, for everyone. We need to know what really happened out there.'

'This is . . . I can't . . .'

'The alien is becoming more active now. You have to admit, there's some weird shit going down these days. That explosion on Venice Coast which took out our arms supplier, the murdered senator.'

'Bullshit. That was some covert operative from the government, or an Intersolar Dynasty. Everybody knows that.'

Adam smiled maliciously. 'Sounds like a conspiracy theory to me.'

'You are so wrong. Why can you never admit that?'

'Then prove it. Exactly who are you betraying by looking at the data? If we're wrong you lose nothing. If, God forbid, we're right, we need to know. And you'll be a hero. That's big enough to absolve all your past sins.'

'I don't need absolution.'

Adam stood. 'You know I'm right. And I know you can never admit that to my face. So we'll stop all this macho posturing now, and I'll contact you every fortnight or so to check on your progress.'

'I won't do it.'

'Yeah, I said that very same thing when Johansson told me to get in touch with you. But it's not like either of us has a choice, is it? Not after Abadan station. Take care, Oscar, there's a lot of people depending on you.'

24

Carys Panther took the metallic-grey MG metrosport into New Costa Junction, then drove it straight onto the car-carry train to Elan. The carriage was completely enclosed, a tube of aluminium with a bright polyphoto strip along the ceiling and a couple of narrow windows along each side. Her MG was so low-slung they were above her eye level. The car's drive array edged her right up to a big BMW 6089 4x4 before engaging the full brake lock; a Ford Yicon saloon pulled up behind her.

She ordered the seat to recline and settled back for the trip. Her e-butler brought up a whole raft of story ideas and plot sequences into her virtual vision, which she started to fill in, joining them together in complicated loops. At the moment there was a big demand for the long, slightly fantastical sagas which were her preferred genre. Ant, her agent, was keen to exploit the market. He said that it was the uncertainty of the Prime situation which was putting people off gritty realism at the moment; they wanted escapism. He should know. Ant was actually older than Nigel Sheldon, and he'd been doing the same job for century after century. He'd seen every creative fad there was, living through the fashion cycle as it spun the genres around and around.

It was twenty minutes before the train started to move forwards, pulled by an electric Fantom T5460 engine. Augusta led straight to New York. From there the trans-Earth link took them to Tallahassee, Edmonton, Seattle, LA Galactic, Mexico City, Rio, and Buenos Aires, before finally crossing the Pacific to Sydney, which routed the train out to Wessex. Earth took about an hour and they stopped at five of the stations so more vehicles could roll onto the car-carry. Once they reached Wessex, there was a longer stop as six extra carriages were added, then it took five minutes to cross the planetary station's yard to the Elan gateway. A minute later and they were pulling up alongside the long road-platform at Runwich, the planet's capital.

The MG's drive array connected itself to the city's road-routing manager, paid the local car tax, and drove through the outskirts to the airport. For once the connection timing worked out in practice the way it was listed on the timetable. A Siddley-Lockheed CP-505, a big six-duct-fan plane, was waiting for her on the apron. She drove up the rear ramp into the gaping cargo hold, where electromuscle clamps gripped the car's tyres. There were another fifteen cars in there, along with two coaches. The plane could carry sixty-five tonnes of cargo in total, in addition to a hundred and twenty passengers on the upper deck.

Carys spent the next three hours sitting in a comfy first-class seat being served champagne by a nice first-life steward as they cruised across the equator at .95 Mach. Ant called twice for script conferences, and permission to crank up her contract negotiations. It was sort of flattering that he dealt with her personally; his client list had been closed for over a century now. If all went well her latest saga should hit the unisphere in another six months.

They landed at Kingsclere airport, on Ryceel, and she climbed back into the MG. As she drove out of the southern continent's capital she could see the Dau'sings rising out of the horizon.

The toll booth at the start of the Randtown highway had a big new sign across the front, reading: No Military Vehicles

Permitted. Someone had spraypainted **Death To Anti-Human Fuckhead Traitors** over the top of it in glowing orange.

'This should be fun,' she muttered as she drew up outside the booth and put her thumb credit tattoo on the pad. The reinforced barrier slid up, and she drove onto the start of the highway. The broad strip of enzyme-bonded concrete seemed completely deserted as it stretched out ahead. Carys though it looked like the start grid of some giant race track, which was an interesting challenge. She brought the full range of drive-array program tools up into her virtual vision, and supervised its integration with the highway's simple traffic management system. The speed regulator was a small old program that was easily susceptible to the fix that came as standard in the MG's modern aggressor routines. She removed the offending software's inconvenient monitoring of the car, and pressed her foot down hard on the manual accelerator.

There was a surge of power into the axle engines which pushed her deep into the seat. She locked the speed, tied the radar and navigation functions into the steering program, and assigned full control to the drive array. Electromuscle bands in the tyre walls responded to the build-up of speed by changing their profile, expanding the tread width to provide an even greater degree of traction. There was a wicked smile on her face as the car charged up the first slope into the foothills at three hundred kph.

*

'I stayed loyal,' Dudley Bose said. 'I was stupid. Did you hear what I said? Did you ever see the recording? I warned them, I told them to flee. Then my voice ended. The aliens must have silenced me, punished me for spoiling their plans. And all the while it was Wilson Fucking Kime I was risking my neck for. The bastard who left me there to rot, to die under an alien sun. Who sacrificed me so he could be safe.'

'You are very much alive, my love,' Mellanie told him. They were lying together on the double bed in what the hotel, with a sharp eye for satire, called its bridal suite. The curtains were open, allowing Dudley to see his precious stars. It was an effort for Mellanie not to yawn. She desperately wanted to go to sleep. Something this new Dudley Bose apparently never did without the help of strong drugs. She wondered if she should slip another of the pills into his drink; it was nearly three o'clock in the morning. But the champagne they'd so eagerly guzzled down earlier was flat now, and not even the Pine Heart Gardens, Randtown's finest, would offer room service at such a time. *Damn this wretched backward place.*

There had been few choices other than returning to Randtown to file her follow-up report on the blockade. Alessandra wanted to know if the residents had renounced their anti-human stance now the wormhole detector station had been forcibly installed in the Regent Mountains above the town. The angle they were going for was a remorseful population who were turning their backs on redneck buffoons like Mark Vernon. Finding appropriate interviews would be easy enough for Mellanie, the more colourful the better.

She didn't want to do it, not just because she despised Randtown and its smug small-town mentality. The Myo case was far more important to her. If she could crack that she wouldn't even need Alessandra as a patron any more. But it was proving difficult. After the glorious fiasco of the navy's welcome back ceremony, she'd spent a day and a half locked in her hotel room with Dudley Bose, providing him with the kind of sexual marathon that most men only knew of from pornoTSIs or their own mid-life-crisis dreams. He'd told her nothing. He'd talked continuously – between the physical feats she performed for him – but it was the same topic every time: himself and whether he was still alive out there at Dyson Alpha. The occasional respite came in the form of diatribes against Wilson Kime, his ex-wife, and the navy in general. His memories were still too chaotic to provide her with anything useful.

She'd almost left him back there in the Nadsis hotel on Augusta when it came time for her to catch the train to Elan. Almost. Some nagging doubt, which she hoped was her burgeoning reporter's intuition, was all for perseverance. She was sure he knew something that could help; though she had started to wonder if she was being too clever in her interpretation of Myo's remark.

So she'd finally called Alessandra to admit to making no progress on Myo, and had to endure her mentor's stinging superiority. Mellanie promptly told Dudley they were going to spend a weekend at a secluded resort town she knew of where she was going to make his hottest dirtiest Silent World fantasies come alive. It would be her last chance to try and sort out what he knew that Myo wasn't telling her. He'd followed like a docile child.

'But am I alive back there?' Dudley pointed weakly to the bridal suite's open window.

'No. There's only you. You are unique. You must learn that, and to stop worrying about your old life. It ended. This is a fresh start for you. And I'm here to make it as pleasurable as I can.'

'Goodness, that's the Zemplar cross formation.' Dudley rolled off the bed and padded over to the window. He pushed it open and stuck his head out. The fresh breeze coming in off the Trine'ba made Mellanie shiver on top of the bed.

'You never told me we were here,' Dudley said.

'Where? Randtown? Yes I did.'

'No, Elan. This has to be Elan. I'm right, aren't I?'

'Yes, my love, this is Elan.' She was impressed; the memory transfer had obviously worked flawlessly. It was just his personality which hadn't survived the procedure intact. 'Now please close the window. It's freezing.'

'This is about as close as you can get to Dyson Alpha, apart from Far Away.' His head was still outside, muffling his voice.

'Yes.'

'That's where the Guardians come from, you know.'

'I know.' She searched round for the quilt, then stopped. 'Do you know about the Guardians?'

'A bit. It was only the once.'

'What was?'

He turned from the window and looked down bashfully. 'We were burgled. Eventually, we found out it could have been the Guardians. The Chief Investigator reckoned the whore I was married to had met Bradley Johansson himself.'

'Which Chief Investigator?' Mellanie asked, trying to suppress her trepidation.

'The strange one from the Hive, Paula Myo.'

Mellanie flopped down onto her back, and raised both fists triumphantly in the air. 'Yes!'

'What is it?' he asked nervously.

'Come here.'

She fucked him. As always he was supremely easy for her to control. If she let him he would climax in seconds, so she was strict, drawing him out, provoking and denying in equal amounts so that it would last as long as she wanted. This time it was different for one thing, this time she allowed herself to come as well. There was no faking it, no sound effects. It became her selfish celebration, he was there for her pleasure.

He must have known something had altered, sensed some change in her. His gaze as he lay there on the bed afterwards was worshipful. 'Don't leave me,' he pleaded. 'Please, don't ever leave me. I couldn't take that. I couldn't.'

'Don't worry, my love,' she told him. 'I haven't finished with you yet. Now be good, and take one of your sleeping pills.'

He nodded, anxious to please, and washed one down with

1025

the remnants of the champagne. Mellanie plumped up the pillows and sank back, smiling at the ceiling. For the first time in four days she fell into a deep contented sleep.

*

Mark was out in the vineyard with one of the autopickers which was stalled. Barry and Sandy were with him, keen to help the repair operation. Their assistance came in the form of charging up and down the rows, with the dog barking excitedly as it dodged between them. The big gangling machine had come to a halt halfway down its third row when its control software realized that the grencham berries weren't sliding through the central hopper. Its octopus-like picking arms had frozen in various stages of removing clusters from the vines.

This was only the third day of picking the crop. Already he'd had two breakdowns in his own vineyard. Calls from neighbours to help out with mechanical problems were coming in with increasing frequency and desperation. He slithered into the gap between the leafy vines and the side of the machine, unclipping the loader mechanism inspection panel. Just like before, lengths of the vine had gone down the hopper to wind themselves around various cogs and rollers. It was the clippers on the end of the picker arms that were hauling them in. Same as everything in life when you got down to it: a software problem. He'd have to write a discrimination fix in time for next year. In the meantime, it was a simple pair of secateurs that had to chop at the stringy vines, then human hands which pulled them out. Mashed grencham berries made the whole process slow and gooey.

'Look at that, Dad,' Barry called.

Mark pulled the last few shreds of vine from the feeder mechanism, and looked up. Someone was driving along the valley's packed stone road at a ridiculous speed. A low grey vehicle producing a long swirling contrail of dust behind it.

'Idiot,' he grunted. The inspection panel clipped back into place; he gave the locking pins a few thumps with the top of his medium pliers to secure them. His e-butler gave the autopicker array a resume operations order, and the arms slowly stretched out again. Clippers *snicked* at the top of clusters. The movements began to speed up. Mark nodded in satisfaction, and pulled his sunglasses out of his overalls pocket.

'They're coming here, Dada,' Sandy yelled out.

The car had slowed to turn up the drive into the Vernons' vineyard. It didn't look like anything a Randtown inhabitant would own.

'Come on then,' he told his kids. 'Let's go meet them.'

They ducked between vines as they ran towards the drive, calling for Panda, who was off chasing wobes, the local fieldmice-equivalents. Mark reached the end of the row, where he got a good look at the fancy car as it neared the house. Its sleek shape clued him in on who was visiting.

The MG came to a halt beside the Ables pick-up; and the suspension lowered itself back down from the extended rough-ride position so that the wheels fitted back into the chassis again. A gull-wing door opened in the side, and Carys Panther got out. She was wearing a chic panelled suede skirt and expensive hand-tooled cowboy boots, with a simple white blouse. Her dove-grey Stetson was carried in one hand.

Barry gave a welcoming whoop and rushed forwards. Sandy was smiling happily, it was always exciting when Aunty Carys visited.

'Nice metalware,' Mark said sardonically.

'Oh that?' Carys gave a dismissive wave towards the MG. 'It's my boyfriend's wife's car.'

Mark made an exaggerated appeal to the heavens. She always had to make an *entrance*.

*

Neither of the two housemaids who brought breakfast to the room at eleven o'clock would meet Mellanie's gaze. They put the big trays down on the table and walked out.

'Screw you,' Mellanie told them after the door had shut behind them.

She started lifting the silver lids off the plates. Room service might be crap, but the kitchen was certainly four star. 'Tuck in,' she told Dudley.

He sat opposite her, as nervous as a schoolkid facing the principal. She could remember that sensation well enough.

'What do you want from me?' he asked.

'Your story.'

'Is that all I am, a story?'

'We are all stories, ultimately. I want to help you, Dudley, I really do. If you can come to terms with what's happened, you'll be so much happier. I think I can do that for you. I really do.'

'And us? What about us?'

She smiled cheekily, picking up a strawberry and licking it in a suitably wicked fashion. 'You don't think I give myself like that to anyone I don't care about, do you?'

His answering smile was one of cautious relief. She pulled her chair round the table until she was pressed up beside him. With him watching in silent fascination she picked up another strawberry and held it delicately in her teeth. Very slowly she undid her bathrobe and pulled it open, then leant in towards him, guiding the strawberry into his mouth. He bit into it, their lips touching.

'Oh God.' He was trembling, his eyes damp.

'Now you feed me something.'

Dudley held up a slim slice of pancake dripping with maple syrup. She laughed as the drops fell on her breasts, then nibbled her way up the pancake slice. Dudley leapt at her, knocking the breakfast trays across the table. She was amazed he'd shown that much restraint, and laughed as her chair went flying backwards. They both tumbled onto the floor, with Dudley tugging frantically at his own bathrobe.

He fucked her there and then on the expensive moozaki rug with orange juice leaking down on top of them from the overturned glasses on the table. Then she was pulled over to the bed and fucked again.

'I'm going to need another bath,' she said after he'd finally spent himself. Even though he'd done his best to lick all the syrup and juicy lolabeans off her chest and thighs she was still awfully sticky.

'I'll join you.'

She grinned, snuggling up against him. 'So when did you meet Paula Myo?'

'Before the flight,' he said, sighing. 'They took me out of rejuve for the interview.'

'They did what?'

'I was undergoing partial rejuvenation before the flight. There wasn't time for a full one, but I was quite old, physiologically, so they were going to bring my age down as much as they could before they started my crew training. Paula Myo had me taken out. She questioned me and Wendy. I can't remember much of what I said. It was very disorientating having the procedure interrupted. That's why I wasn't as young as I wanted to be when we left. Not as young as Oscar Monroe wanted, either.'

'Don't start putting any value on what that old lush says. You said Myo was quizzing you about a break-in.'

'Yeah. My bitch ex talked to Bradley Johansson, who was masquerading as a reporter; he asked her about the organizations who funded my observation. The next thing we know our home was broken into and every file copied from the house array.'

'What did Myo think the connection was?'

'That moron Johansson believed one of the charities funding my observation was a front for the Starflyer. That's the alien . . .'

'I know what the Starflyer is. When did this happen, exactly?'

'Right after the attack on the *Second Chance*. Myo had the authority to do pretty much anything she wanted when they gave her that case, including yanking me out of rejuve.'

'And she'd tracked down that connection. Why?'

'I've no idea. She just said she was looking for anomalies; anyone connected to the *Second Chance* project was reviewed. But the queer thing is that Johansson knew she'd find the connection, he told Wendy to give Myo a message.'

'Really, what was it?'

'Stop concentrating on the details, it's the big picture that counts.'

'Weird. Do you remember which charity Johansson was suspicious about?'

'Yeah, the Cox Educational charity.'

'Never heard of them.' She patted his arm as she stood up. 'You know what you've just been doing, don't you?'

'What?'

'Talking about what happened to your previous body as if it was you. You're starting to connect your body lives. Well done. I told you I was good for you.' She blew a kiss at his startled young face and went into the bathroom.

The big sunken tub was filled to its rim, with a mound of soapy bubbles floating on the surface. Mellanie stepped in, sighing gratefully as she sat down in the warm scented water. She turned the nozzles on, welcoming the gentle flow of air bubbles around her body as they eased away the aches. Dudley hadn't been gentle the last time. His desperation and fierceness had made it a lot more interesting than his usual monotonous perfunctory act.

She turned up the music and rested her head back on the rim cushions. Her virtual hand touched the SI icon. 'I need some financial information,' she said.

'You know we cannot provide confidential records, Mellanie.'

'I just need what's on public record. It might be a little difficult to track it all down, that's all, and I don't want to go through the show's researchers.' And I can't use poor old Paul Cramley any more.

'Very well.'

'The Cox Educational charity helped fund Dr Bose's observation. How much did they give him?'

'In total, one point three million Earth dollars; spread over eleven years.'

'Where does their money come from?'

'It is a private charity.'

'What does that mean?'

'The source of the money is not open to inspection.'

'Okay, so who runs it?'

'The registered commissioners are three lawyers, Ms Daltra, Mr Pomanskie, and Mr Seeton, who all work for Bromley, Waterford, and Granku, a New York legal firm.'

'Humm.' She ran a sponge along her legs. 'What else does the Cox support?'

'It contributed to over a hundred universities and colleges across the Commonwealth. Do you want the list?'

'Not right now.'

'Would you like the total amount of money given to the other institutions.'

She opened her eyes, suddenly very interested – it wasn't like the SI to volunteer information. 'Yes please.'

'Seventy thousand Earth dollars.'

'For each one?'

'No. That is the total payout.'

'Hell. How long has it been going for?'

'Fourteen years. It shut down two years after Dudley Bose observed the envelopment. Six months after Paula Myo interviewed Dudley Bose.'

*

'So, most hated man in the Commonwealth,' Carys said with a taunting smile. 'Quite a title. As voted for on the Maxis unisphere poll. Never guessed my little nephew would be *so* famous.'

Mark just grunted in response, and wormed down deeper into his favourite chair. They were all sitting round in the living room, giving Carys a taste of last year's Ulon Valley wine before lunch.

'Nobody here cares,' he said. 'It's not important.'

'Oh yes. It's only relevant to us, isn't it? Us, being decadent metropolitan types practising our intellectual snobbery over you poor country bumpkins.'

Mark shrugged, smiling. 'You said it.'

'Wake up and smell the coffee,' she snapped. 'The media is going to screw your beautiful little town into the bedrock. I know from my contacts that Alessandra Baron is already planning a follow-up. Have you tried booking a skiing holiday here for this next season? I did. They're offering fifty per cent discounts already. Nobody's coming.'

'And you can fix all that, can you?'

Carys exchanged a glance with Liz. 'You need some serious PR, Mark. And I'm the only expert you've got.'

'You called her!' Mark accused Liz.

'You have to listen to somebody, baby. Everyone around here is being very careful not to lay any blame. To your face.'

He turned to Carys, appealing. 'I never said it the way that interview came out. They edited me to make it sound bad.'

'The technical term is raunching up,' Carys said. 'They always do it. We can use that to fight back.'

'How?' he said suspiciously.

'I can get you interviewed on other shows. Live studio interviews, so they can't mess with your message. You'll need a lot of coaching before we let you on, and you'll have to grow a decent sense of humour. But it can be done.'

'I've got a sense of humour,' he protested indignantly.

Carys opened her mouth to answer. There was a bright flash outside. Mark and Liz frowned in unison. There were no thunderclouds anywhere.

Out in the garden, Sandy was squealing as if she was in pain. Both parents jumped up and went through the open patio doors.

'What's the matter, poppet?' Mark asked.

Panda was going berserk, barking, jumping up and down. Sandy ran to her mother, arms flung wide. 'In the sky,' she wailed. 'My eyes hurt. I see purple.'

Mark's wrist array crashed. The sky to the south-east turned dazzling white. 'Damn, what the hell . . .' All the autopickers had stopped. As had the tractors. Every bot he could see was motionless and silent.

The smear of silky light above the mountains was draining away to leave the normal blue sky in its wake. Then a vivid rose-gold sun climbed up from behind the peaks, its surface writhing with webs of black fire. It cast long moving shadows across the ground.

'That's the Regents,' Liz murmured. 'Oh my God.'

The new sun was rising on a stalk of brilliant raging flame. All the remaining snow on the Regents vaporized in a single violent white explosion. The tops of the mountains looked as if they were vibrating. They started to crumble just as the ferocious vapour cloud swarmed round them, obliterating them from sight.

Sandy's shrieks reached a crescendo.

'They nuked it,' Mark shouted in awe. 'They nuked the detector station.' He watched the mushroom cloud swelling out, its colour darkening, deepening as it spread its bruised perimeter across the clean sky. Then the soundblast reached them.

*

Mellanie ordered a light salad from room service before dressing in jeans and a coal-black sweatshirt from her own fashion line. She tied her hair back in a simple loose tail, just using moisturizer on her face, no make-up. It was important she looked serious for this call.

One of the scowling housemaids brought the salad while Dudley was splashing about cheerfully in the bathroom. She spent a couple of minutes clearing up the mess that was the two breakfast trays. Mellanie gave her a twenty-dollar tip. If anything the scowl was deeper when she left.

'Double screw you,' Mellanie told the door.

She picked at the salad for a while, sorting out the pitch in her mind, then sat at the bureau and used the room's desktop array to place a call to Alessandra.

Alessandra's image appeared on the array's screen. She was sitting in the green room's make-up chair, a paper bib round her neck to protect her fabulous dress. 'Where the hell have you been?' she demanded.

'I'm on Elan.'

'Okay, in that case I'll let you live. As it is, you're this close to being fired.' She held her hand up, thumb and forefinger almost touching. 'Don't ever put a block on your unisphere address code again. Now: I need your follow-up report in an hour. And it better be a prize-winner, or that tiny little arse of yours will reach orbit.'

'I'm on to something.'

'What?'

Mellanie took a breath. 'Paula Myo thinks the Starflyer is real.'

'You're fucking unbelievable, you know that. I give you every chance, more than I've given anybody else, and not just because you're good in bed. And this drivel is what you come up with?'

'Listen! She put me on to Dudley Bose.'

'Do you know where he is? Everybody in the biz is going apeshit trying to find him.'

'I've been fucking him for information, yeah.' She tossed her head, keeping her face expressionless as she looked at Alessandra's image. 'And like you say, I'm very good at it. I found something out.'

'All right, darling, have your fifteen seconds of fame. What have you got?'

'One of the charities that funded Bose's observation of the Dyson Pair is a front organization. The Starflyer arranged for us to see the envelopment. It wanted us to investigate the barrier.'

'Proof?' Alessandra snapped.

'The charity had secret bank account funding,' she said, hoping to God it was slightly true, but she had to get Alessandra behind the investigation. 'I checked through all its other donations; they're tokens, validity in case anyone ran a quick review. And it was shut down right after the discovery. But the important thing is that Myo knew this years ago. Don't you see what that means? All these years she never caught Johansson and Elvin, she knew all along. She might even be working with the Guardians!'

'This is your vendetta,' Alessandra said.

Mellanie could see the uncertainty, and pressed on doggedly. 'But it will be your story. Give me a research team, let me work it. Hell, take charge of a research team yourself. That's what Myo's telling us. Us, the media. This is all public source information, verifiable if you know where to look. We can prove the Starflyer exists. For God's sake, Wendy Bose actually met Bradley Johansson! Did that ever come out in any interview? This is real, Alessandra, I promise.'

'I want to talk to Bose.'

'Okay.'

The SI's icon sprang up in Mellanie's virtual vision. 'Get on the floor behind the bed,' it told her.

'What?'

'The navy detector network is registering wormholes emerging inside the Commonwealth,' the SI said. 'The Regents' detector station is under attack. Get behind the bed, it will provide some cover.'

'Mellanie?' Alessandra asked, frowning.

'I've got to go,' she hesitated, not really believing. Then her virtual vision showed inserts coming on line, activated by the SI. They were systems she neither recognized nor understood.

'We will try and remain in contact with you,' the SI said.

'Mellanie, there's some kind of alert—' Alessandra said. Her voice had risen in alarm.

Mellanie dived for the bed. There was a brilliant flash in the sky outside.

*

Wilson was alone in his awful white-glowing office, waiting for people to arrive for the second management meeting of the morning, the one on ship production scheduling and subcomponent delivery supervision. The override priority call which came in from the planetary defence division made him sit upright in his chair as it delivered big emergency icons to his virtual vision. The wormhole detector network was picking up unidentified quantum signatures inside Commonwealth space. Wormholes were opening in several star systems.

The office began to dim, scarlet and sapphire digits slipped along the ceiling and down the walls as emerald graphics flowered across the floor, the projections stabilized, arching out into the air to place Wilson at the centre of a tactical star chart. He was close to the boundary of the Commonwealth, where phase three space dwindled away into galactic night. Twenty-three star systems were encircled by amber icons, with small script windows full of digits and icons.

'Twenty-three wormholes?' he murmured in dismay. The navy only had three functional warships, and eight scoutships

refitted as missile carriers. Then the dataflow increased, clari-
fying the information coming in from the detector network.
Forty-eight separate wormholes had opened in each of the
twenty-three star systems, bringing the total to over eleven
hundred. That was about the same number of gateways that
CST operated in total. 'Son of a bitch.' He couldn't believe the
numbers, he who'd been to Dyson Alpha and seen the scale of
the Prime civilization for himself.

More information was pouring through now, complementing the navy network. The cyberspheres on Anshun, Belembe,
Martaban, Balkash, and Samar were already suffering huge
glitches and area crashes. Reports of explosions were coming
in from the government systems of those planets, in almost
every case corresponding to electronic failure zones. Twenty-
three translucent globes expanded into Wilson's image, representing the planets under attack. Detailed imagery was hard to
find for any of them. Land survey satellites, geosynchronous
relay platforms, industrial stations, and high-inclination
meteorological sensors were being systematically blasted out of
orbit. Wormholes appeared as bright scarlet diamonds poised
over the planets. They winked in and out of existence, changing position by the minute to avoid sensor lock. Radar tracked
high-velocity projectiles flying out of them at each emergence.

The navy was losing contact with its detector stations on
Elan, Whalton, Pomona, and Nattavaara, all planets in phase
three space with relatively small populations. One by one the
stations were dropping off the network, reducing the resolution in the display. No stations at all had survived on Molina,
Olivenza, Kozani, and Balya; phase three worlds which weren't
even open to general settlement yet.

Anna materialized beside him, a ghostly grey outline. It was
as if they were both on their acceleration couches back on the
Second Chance again. 'They started with nukes!' she said,
aghast.

'We know how they fight battles,' he said, deliberately

harsh, numbing himself to what all the display graphics really meant. With her there it was easier to haul back on his own emotions. He was the commander, he had to keep calm and analytical, to suppress that small part of himself that wanted to run out of the office and head for the hills. 'Get Columbia into the command circuit. And find our ship positions for me.'

'All of them?' There was a lot of bitterness in the question.

'Do it!' His own hands were busy pulling planetary government civil defence data out of the unisphere. Little blue lights appeared on the twenty-three planet representations: cities with force fields. On the four start-up worlds, only the CST stations were protected.

Rafael Columbia came on line, appearing on the other side of Wilson from Anna. 'There are so many,' he said, and for once even he sounded intimidated and uncertain. 'We're launching combat aerobots now. They should provide some interceptor coverage against those projectiles, but only around major population centres. Damnit, we should have built ten times this many.'

'Get every working city force field up,' Wilson told him. 'And not just on these twenty-three worlds. There's no guarantee this is the limit of the invasion. Use the planetary cyberspheres to issue a mass warning, I want people to get under cover. That's a start.'

'Then what?'

'When I've got more information, I'll tell you. We need to know what they're going to do after the initial bombardment. Anna, bring the rest of the strategy and command staff in, please. We're going to need a lot of help today.'

'Yes, sir. I'm tracking the starships now.'

White indicators appeared inside the starfield, tagged with identification data. He had seven ships within range of the detector network. Two scoutships were days away, outside the

Commonwealth, while the warships and remaining scoutships were spread out around the indistinct boundary of phase three space. Wilson made a decision. 'Contact the captains,' he told Anna. 'I want them all to rendezvous half a light-year out from Anshun.' Their old base was the CST junction planet for the sector, and as such the most heavily populated. 'We'll start our counterattack there.' At least neither of them laughed outright at that.

'Oh goddamnit,' Rafael grunted.

Inside the tactical display another swarm of amber warning icons were blinking up, much deeper in Commonwealth space around planet twenty-four: Wessex.

'Do what you can for them,' Wilson told Rafael. He wished it didn't sound like a feeble joke. Could we have known it was going to be this massive? A terrible thought crept out: the Guardians knew.

'Sir,' Anna exclaimed. 'I've got Captain Tu Lee on a direct link. They were still at the Anshun base.'

'What?'

'She's on the *Second Chance*.'

Wilson's virtual hand blurred as it jabbed at the communication icon. 'What's your situation?' he demanded as Tu Lee's anxious face appeared in his virtual vision.

'Disengaged from the dock.' Tu Lee winced. Her image suffered a ripple of static. 'Taking some incoming fire. Force field holding. What are your orders?'

Wilson almost whooped out loud. Finally, some good news. 'Eliminate as many of the planetary bombardment projectiles as you can. Don't, repeat, do not try and take on a wormhole. Not yet. I need information on them.'

'Aye, sir.'

'Godspeed, Captain.'

*

The *Second Chance*'s big life-support wheel finished its emergency de-spin procedure, eliminating the problem of precession, which had been screwing up their manoeuvring ability.

'Full acceleration,' Tu Lee ordered the pilot. She'd been captain for a week now, taking over when the ship docked after its last mission. The navy had sent it on a deep scouting mission three hundred light-years from the Commonwealth. It didn't have the speed of any of the new scoutships, but it beat them hands down on endurance. It also had the kind of delta-v reserve that only the new warships could match.

Their plasma rockets responded smoothly to the pilot's instructions, producing one and a half gees acceleration. They were a thousand kilometres above Anshun's nightside equator, and curving round above the second-largest ocean. The big portals at the front of the bridge were showing brilliant white flares of nukes detonating below them. Tu Lee bared her teeth in fury at the devastation. For her the light was carefully colour-coded and intensity-graded; for anyone on the surface it was near-certain death.

'Laroch, have we got a pattern for the emergence sequence yet?' she asked.

'I can confirm there's forty-eight wormholes,' said Laroch, who was operating the sensor console. 'But they keep jumping around at random. The only constant is their altitude, about one and a half thousand klicks.'

'Okay, let's keep under that level, and track the bombardment projectiles in range. Weapons, fire whenever we get a lock. Pilot, if there's a cluster, get us in range.'

'Incoming,' Laroch called.

Eight alien missiles hurtled in towards the *Second Chance*. The pilot vectored their plasma rockets, altering trajectory. Plasma lances fired out from the starship's midsection, ripping across space before bursting apart on the missiles' force fields. Lasers locked on, pumping gigawatts of energy into the force fields, straining them badly. The plasma lances fired again finally overloading the missiles' shielding. Multiple detonations blossomed silently above the planet, their plasma clouds merging into a seething patch of pure light over fifty kilometres across.

'Batch of sixteen projectiles emerged,' Laroch called out. 'Heading for the planet.'

The bridge portals had them tagged, green needles with vector digits flicking round at high speed. Tu Lee called up the ship's own missile launch command, and fired a volley of interceptors. As they leaped away at fifty gees she loaded in a sequential pattern of diverted energy functions for their warheads. The interceptors split apart into a cascade of independently targeted vehicles, rocket exhausts expanding like a starburst of lightning bolts as they spread out in pursuit of the alien projectiles. Megaton warheads detonated, a chain of dazzling lightpoints distorting the planet's ionosphere in huge undulations, their diverted energy function sending huge emp effects rippling out.

Several of the alien weapons immediately went dead, their exhausts fading away as they tumbled inertly down towards the dark landscape hundreds of kilometres below. A second barrage of warheads detonated. This time the diverted energy was channelled into one-shot x-ray lasers, directing seventy per cent of the explosion's power into a single slender beam of ultra-hard radiation. Every remaining projectile broke apart, glowing debris flying outwards in sinister mimicry of a meteorite shower's splendour.

Four more wormholes opened close to the *Second Chance*, thirty-two missiles flew out from each. Delicate fans of sensor radiation stroked against the starship. The gee force on the bridge swung round, pressing Tu Lee into the side of her chair. Straps tightened around her shoulders and waist, holding her in place.

'There might be a lot of them,' Laroch said. 'But their software is useless. I'm picking up a lot of microwave emissions from the wormholes. The missiles are being continuously updated and guided.'

The *Second Chance* was firing volley after volley of plasma lances at the new attackers as they closed at twenty gees. A massive series of nuclear explosions turned space outside the starship a glaring uniform white. Waves of thin plasma slithered across the outer force field, shaking the superstructure. Tu Lee could hear loud metallic groans as the hull twisted and flexed from the pummelling. It was as if they were flying through a star's corona, blinded by the hot radiation glare and buffeted by relativistic particle currents. The starship streaked out of the energy storm, a shimmering scarlet bubble trailing long cataracts of hydrogen plasma. Twenty-four alien missiles chased round to intercept her.

Alarms were shrieking from every bridge console. Screens threw up systems schematics as the crew and the RI tried to re-establish functions.

'Jump us out,' Tu Lee ordered.

At the hyperdrive console, Lindsay Sanson activated the wormhole generator. *Second Chance* vanished from space above the planet.

'How bad is that software?' Tu Lee demanded.

'Strange,' Laroch said. 'It's very inflexible, nothing like as advanced as ours. It's almost as if they don't have smart programs.'

'We can use that,' Tu Lee said. She glanced at the main status display. There was nothing too critical with the starship's systems. Most of the damage had been absorbed by peripherals in the life-support wheel, along with some hull ablation and tank breaches. Without the exploration and science teams they only had forty crew on board, so no one was in any immediate danger. 'Get everyone into spacesuits,' she said as she called up a display of their missile reserves. 'Then take us back.'

A lambent patch of turquoise light twisted out of nowhere

eight hundred kilometres above Anshun's capital, Treloar. *Second Chance* leapt out of its centre as the nimbus shrank away. The starship fired fifteen missiles, then her wormhole generator distorted space again and she vanished back into hyperspace. She reappeared almost instantaneously five thousand kilometres away, this time above Bromrine, a coastal city with a population of two hundred thousand, cowering under their protective force field dome. Another fifteen missiles were fired before she dived back into hyperspace.

She made another nine jumps around the planet, launching all one hundred and seventy-three remaining missiles.

As soon as they were released, the missiles in each salvo fired their rockets briefly, spreading out from their launch point, then shut down. Their sensors scanned round, searching for a wormhole. When one emerged, they ignited their rockets again, racing towards it at fifty gees. The standard barrage of alien projectiles barely had time to clear the wormhole rim before they were subjected to emp assault, electronic warfare, x-ray laser pulses, kinetic impacts, and nuclear blasts. Very few of them ever made it through to slam down against the planet.

Second Chance popped out of hyperspace again and began a quick data transmission to the beleaguered world below, telling the navy how they had mined near-orbit space. Eight wormholes emerged, encircling the starship at five hundred kilometres. Lindsay Sanson activated their hyperdrive. 'Shit!'

'What?' Tu Lee asked. The bridge portals were still showing Anshun below them, its once-passive cloud formations swirling in agitation in the aftermath of the explosions.

'Interference. Space is so distorted from their wormholes we can't open ours. It's deliberate, they modified the quantum fluctuations to block us.'

'Move us,' Tu Lee yelled at the pilot.

Second Chance's plasma drive came on. She began to accelerate at over three gees.

Another eight Prime wormholes emerged around the starship.

'Fuck you,' Tu Lee told the Primes.

Ninety-six missiles flew out of each wormhole.

*

Nigel Sheldon had been taking breakfast in his New Costa mansion when the alert from the navy detector network came through. He hadn't been back to Cressat, his family's private world, for the last five months; spending his time between Augusta and Earth. It was prudent, he felt, not to be too remote should anything happen, even with the blessing of modern communications. And now he was being proved terribly right.

Shielding sprang up around the mansion; communications shifted to secure links. He closed his eyes and relaxed back into the chair as the mansion's internal shields came on, isolating the rooms. The full range of his interface inserts went on line, allowing his sensorium to absorb digital data at an accelerated rate. Combat aerobots launched from bases dotted round the outskirts of New Costa. Startled residents gaped up into the bright morning sky to see the dark shapes roaring upwards to their high-altitude patrol stations. Force fields closed off the sky behind them.

With Augusta's defences activated, Nigel switched his attention back to the attack. His enhanced display showed the twenty-three Commonwealth planets where the alien wormholes intruded; the wormholes themselves manifested as a tactile sensation, like pinpricks across his skin. The SI responded to his request and joined him inside the tactical simulacrum, a small ball of knotted tangerine and turquoise lines fluctuating rhythmically as they floated in the nothingness beside him.

'That's a lot of wormholes,' he said.

'Dimitri Leopoldovich always said the assault would be conducted on a large scale. This probably does not represent their full capability.'

There was a background whisper in Nigel's greatly expanded perception as he registered the flurry of orders slipping out from the navy's headquarters on the High Angel, coordinating sensor data and marshalling what resources they had. 'Poor old Wilson,' he murmured. He concentrated on several icons in a small galaxy of symbols that were hovering in the background. They moved obediently. Using the deep connections wetwired into his brain, this interface was more like telepathy than the simple virtual hands array of standard domestic interface programs.

Force fields came on around every CST planetary station in the Commonwealth. On the twenty-three worlds under attack, there was almost no warning. Local trains coming into the stations braked sharply, their engines skidding along the tracks, as they approached the implacable translucent barriers which had risen in front of them. Not all of them managed to halt in time. Several engines hit the force fields and jumped the tracks, slewing round; carriages and wagons jackknifed, crunching into each other, smashing apart, crumpling up, flinging passengers and goods across embankments and cuttings. Cars and trucks arriving along the highways were ordered to brake by traffic route management software. Lead vehicles rammed the force fields; pileups dominoed back down the roads.

Information on damage and casualties slipped into Nigel's mind. Nothing compared to the destruction pouring down out of the sky all around them. He ignored the figures. There had been no choice; without the stations and their precious gateways there would be no Commonwealth.

The remaining stations across the Commonwealth at least allowed arriving trains over the perimeter before their force fields went up. On the highways outside, huge queues formed along every carriageway, trailing back for miles. Those people trapped on the inside settled down for a long wait, quietly thankful about which side of the force field they were on.

Nigel saw city force fields power up as Rafael started to use the navy's new planetary defence network, overriding local civil authorities. He sent combat aerobots rocketing skywards, big machines of unmistakable military ugliness, firing as they went. Prime projectiles were blown out of the stratosphere as they descended. But the sheer quantity of projectiles allowed several to slip through to pound at the force fields. Large areas of the surrounding countryside were flattened or reduced to lakes of glass, but the force fields held.

The CST station on Wessex actually beat the navy's detector network in alerting Nigel to the wormholes opening above that planet. When he switched his attention there he was immediately aware of Alan Hutchinson's command programs flooding through the Wessex cybersphere as the founder of that particular Big15 world took charge of its defences. Multiple force fields came on around Narrabri, its megacity. The planet's small tactical defence brigade was ordered to deploy around the perimeter, activating their ground-to-air interceptor batteries. Squadrons of combat aerobots launched from their silos to patrol the skies above the force fields.

Alan Hutchinson's face flittered across Nigel's consciousness, grinning savagely. Three of his aerobots fired their atom lasers, taking out incoming Prime projectiles as they hit the upper atmosphere.

'Good shooting,' Nigel said.

'Makes a decent change from finance reports,' was the gruff Aussie's hearty comment.

Another salvo of projectiles shot out of four wormholes. They were answered by a battery of firepower from the planet below.

'Thank Christ for that,' Alan said as molten radioactive

debris scudded down across the ocean. 'We can hit back at the bastards.' Data coming back from the other afflicted Commonwealth worlds was depressing. Other than cities protected by force fields and aerobots they were woefully unprepared.

'You can knock out a few missiles,' Nigel said. 'But at this rate we're going to lose. They have a thousand times our resources.'

'Well gee it up, why don't you?'

Both of them paused to observe the *Second Chance* fly into action above Anshun.

'Go, Tu Lee, go,' Nigel whispered out loud. He tried to suppress the anxiety he felt for his young descendant. Emotional distraction was the one thing he couldn't afford right now.

Hundreds more projectiles were fired down at Wessex. Alan didn't have enough aerobots to cover the more remote areas. Towns scattered across the continent-wide farmlands were wiped out as the Prime projectiles fell freely. 'Mother-fuckers,' Alan growled. 'What threat did those people ever make?'

'Can you see an attack pattern in this?' Nigel asked the SI. 'Is there a strategy? Or are they just trying to wipe us out?'

'The planets selected imply a double target approach,' the SI said. 'The twenty-three outer worlds are a strong foothold into the Commonwealth; while the addition of Wessex with its gateways to phase two space planets, if successful, would allow them to occupy a huge proportion of territory, effectively eliminating the Commonwealth as a single entity, especially if they managed to occupy Earth as well.'

'They'll never get the Narrabri station,' Nigel said harshly. 'I'll make quite sure of that.'

'They can't know our exact response,' the SI said. 'This is as exploratory for them as it is for us. The goal of securing

Wessex is a logical one. They can afford to lose the venture, yet if they do obtain the gateways at Narrabri station they will have a backdoor into sixty developed worlds.'

'What the hell for? What do they want with us?'

'Judging by the projectile targets, we would infer they want to obtain as much human infrastructure as is practical. They are happy to eliminate the smaller civic areas to earn the larger ones. Even if they were to be repelled immediately, most of the surviving population from the twenty-three worlds under attack would have to be evacuated. The land around the cities is radioactive slag, crops are ruined, the climate has been disrupted. They are in danger of losing their H-congruous status without a huge amount of very expensive retro-forming.'

'Son of a bitch,' Nigel grunted. 'You're talking genocide.'

'Possibly.'

'Oh Christ,' Alan exclaimed. 'They've got her.'

Nigel watched with radar and optical sensors as the *Second Chance* valiantly accelerated out of orbit, struggling to shake off the surrounding Prime wormholes. The starship's brilliant plasma rockets were extinguished behind a nuclear furnace of elementary particles that inflated out across five hundred kilometres.

'Son of a bitch,' Nigel barked. 'Tu Lee, you did a magnificent job. I'm so proud. And I will hear your laugh again.'

'Goddamn,' Alan said. 'I'm sorry, Nigel.'

'We can't just sit here and take this kind of punishment,' Nigel said. 'We have to show them we can fight back.'

'Admiral Kime has ordered the warships to rendezvous,' the SI said.

'I bet those alien bastards are quaking in their fucking boots. Whoa, three ships are heading their way.'

Wessex aerobots destroyed another salvo of projectiles. The Primes seemed to have stopped targeting the small towns dotted over the rest of the planet. Narrabri and its external districts were on the receiving end of just about every deluge now.

'You are not getting my station,' Nigel told them uncompromisingly. He opened a multitude of command links directly into the wormhole generator machinery of three gateways in Narrabri's station. His secure memory store was accessed, the old memories rising out to occupy an artificial neural network, giving him all the knowledge he ever had of exotic matter, energy inverters, supergeometry, quantum math. He drew on it all, loading new directives into the machinery which generated wormholes leading to Louisiade, Malaita, and Tubuai.

Limiters and feedback dampers flashed alerts at him. Not even his control system could handle three wormholes simultaneously.

'Could use a little help here,' he told the SI.

'Very well.'

Nigel let out a small breath of relief. You never could tell when the SI was going to pitch in, or just watch aloofly. He guessed this invasion might actually have flustered even the great artificial intelligence, after all Vinmar was physically inside Commonwealth space.

With the SI acting as interpreter and actuator, Nigel's role was elevated to executive only. Under his direction the SI reformatted the internal quantum structure of the three wormholes he'd designated. He retracted the exits from their distant gateways, turning them into open-ended fissures twisting through spacetime.

One of the Prime wormholes re-emerged above Wessex, and Nigel struck, his pseudo-telekinetic control moving icons at supersonic speed. The three CST wormhole exits materialized inside the interloper in a transdimensional intersection, creating a massive distortion that instigated huge oscillations along the alien wormhole's energistic fabric. Power from eight of Narrabri's nuclear power stations was pumped through the

1049

gateway machinery to amplify the instability, forcing it back toward the Prime end.

The intrusive wormhole vanished in a severe gravitational implosion, releasing a burst of ultra-hard radiation. Nigel waited, hysradar scanning space above Wessex. The Primes were down to forty-seven wormholes jumping in and out of existence. Cautions from the Malaita gateway sounded loudly, warning him that the whole machine was powering down to prevent any further damage; the excessive power loadings he'd forced through had burned out a lot of components.

'It worked,' he proclaimed.

'Of course,' the SI replied equitably.

'Can you take out the rest?' Alan asked.

'Let's find out.'

*

As far as such a thing were possible, MorningLightMountain experienced a brief feeling of trepidation as it arranged its thoughts prior to launching the expansion. The alien Commonwealth was a considerable unknown, despite the Bose memories. It remembered living there, remembered what the society was like, but had only vague notions of what its true industrial and military capabilities were. That gave cause for concern.

There were several other stars close to its home system that had planets capable of supporting Prime life. It had already opened wormholes to eight of them, sending hundreds of millions of motiles through to begin settlements. Life-sustaining planets were much simpler to spread across than the cold, airless moons, and dead asteroids of its home system. They didn't require machines to cocoon the new settlements in a protective friendly environment. They were cheaper to establish. Already immotile groupings were amalgamating on the new planets, integrating with MorningLightMountain's main thought routines. In a heady taste of the future, it had now spread out to exist across hundreds of light-years.

At one time that might have been sufficient. Even the first great enemy, the unknown, would have trouble constructing barriers around so many stars. But there was more than one enemy in the galaxy. It could see what would happen when its expansion ran into the obstacle of the humans and their territory. Two incompatible lifeforms competing for the same planets and stars. MorningLightMountain knew they could not co-exist in a peaceful fashion. In fact it didn't see how ultimately it could allow any other alien to share this galaxy, there were after all only a finite number of stars. Now it knew how, it could join every one via wormholes, it could become omnipresent. That way it could guarantee its immortality. No matter how many stars died or turned nova, it would still be alive. And the first obstacle to that was the Commonwealth; full of dangerous independent humans and their superb advanced machinery.

MorningLightMountain opened one thousand one hundred and four wormholes, aiming at the stellar coordinates which had come from the Bose memories. Some emerged very close to their targets, others were nearby, several were half a light-year or more distant. Sensors were pushed through, collecting positional data; the information was used to refine its star chart, locking the Commonwealth stars to precise locations. The wormhole exits were realigned around its initial target planets. MorningLightMountain was interested that the Bose memories were right about the human colonization patterns; the species grossly underused the worlds they settled. Their total numbers would barely be sufficient to fill one world, let alone hundreds. Individuality was a terrible weakness, multi-plying their collective greed.

Bombardment projectiles were sent through, aimed at the smaller habitation zones and the perimeter of larger ones. It found other targets, the human quantum sensors, communication webs, satellites, power grids, and guided its projectiles at them. MorningLightMountain was intending to eliminate the humans themselves whilst keeping their industrial centres relatively intact. Those that survived, it wanted to drive out of their buildings and disperse ineffectually across the unused land.

Force fields came on over the cities. MorningLightMountain hadn't expected that, the Bose memories had no knowledge of such things. It couldn't open its wormholes inside them. Over the immense distance it was operating, positioning them within two thousand kilometres of a planet was as precise as it could get. For precise exits, it needed gateways to anchor the wormholes.

Small flying machines, aerobots, rose up around the cities, shooting its projectiles. MorningLightMountain had no choice, it increased the number of projectiles it was sending through, guiding them to create the maximum damage.

When it opened the wormholes above the major world, Wessex, it encountered even stronger resistance. It could see down onto the megacity which was two-thirds industrial facilities. The scale surpassed most of its own planet-based settlements, while the efficiency of the human systems with their electronic controllers went beyond anything it had achieved.

A human starship flew above Anshun, knocking out dozens of bombardment projectiles. MorningLightMountain's response was standard, it sent through more projectiles. When the human starship began to fall in and out of its own wormhole, MorningLightMountain diverted more immotile groupings to concentrate on its own wormhole generator mechanisms, shifting the energy composition to act as an inhibitor. Tens of thousands of additional immotiles focused on the problem, taking its control ability to the absolute limit. With the starship restricted to real space, it fired an overwhelming salvo of projectiles.

Something happened to one of its wormholes above Wessex. Energy surged along the disintegrating fabric of the distortion, overloading the generator mechanism that was built on one of the four giant asteroids which orbited the interstellar wormhole at the staging post. The resulting explosion knocked out the tower storing the bombardment projectiles, and even reached out to the squadron of ships waiting above it.

MorningLightMountain urgently searched through its memory of the event. As it did, another two wormholes collapsed, their energy flashbacks wrecking the generators. MorningLightMountain realized they were actually being overloaded by an external force. It switched more immotile group clusters to the problem, increasing the power to the remaining generators to counter a further five attempts at destabilization.

The struggle evolved into a contest of power capacity. MorningLightMountain was powering its wormholes from magflux extractor disks dropped into the staging post star's corona, transferring the induced power to the asteroids via a small wormhole. Even with those providing maximum output, there was a limit to how much the wormhole generators themselves could handle. And the humans were changing their methods of attack with a speed it could not match, modifying interference patterns and resonance amplification in nanoseconds. They, too, seemed to have unlimited power to draw on.

A further twenty-seven wormhole generators either exploded or twisted into molten ruin. MorningLightMountain ended its attempted capture of Wessex, diverting the remaining wormholes to the other planets where there was no interference. The results of the bombardment projectiles were disappointing on most of them. But the human defences were slowly being beaten back by the sheer quantity of projectiles it was firing through. It halted the projectiles, and flew the first ships through into the Commonwealth.

Altogether, it had gathered a fleet of forty-eight thousand ready for its preliminary expansion stage.

*

It was getting crowded at the centre of Wilson's tactical display. The ghostly image of Elaine Doi herself had joined him, along with Nigel Sheldon, their spectral presence giving his orders supreme executive authority – providing they didn't interfere. To advise on tactics and technology he had the shades of Dimitri Leopoldovich and Tunde Sutton floating in attendance behind him.

Right now he would have welcomed a genuine spook, a psychic who could tell him what was coming next, or at least take a good guess. They were watching the last of the Prime projectiles rushing down over twenty-one besieged planets – he considered that ominous while everyone else was overjoyed. Wessex had successfully banished the alien wormholes; while Olivenza and Balya had dropped out of the unisphere when their station force fields were breached. The CST planetary station on Anshun had switched off their connecting gateways.

'Can't you overload the remaining alien wormholes?' Doi asked Nigel. She was keen for further victories.

'I burned out eighteen of our wormhole generators taking out thirty of theirs,' Nigel said. 'Do the math. That's not a good ratio. Without wormholes we don't have a Commonwealth. In any case, I doubt we have enough power reserves right now.'

Wilson said nothing. He'd watched helplessly as Sheldon sucked more and more power out of the Commonwealth power grid. All of the Big15 worlds had switched to niling d-sink reserves as their nuclear generators were called on. Earth had suffered an unprecedented complete civil power loss as Sheldon diverted the entire lunar output to support his space-warping battle above Wessex. Every other world in phase one and two space had experienced blackouts and brownouts as their domestic generators were put on front-line duty. For a while it had been touch and go and several city force fields had flickered alarmingly from the power loss. Right now everyone was busy recharging their storage facilities.

It had been a desperate exercise, although, Wilson had to admit, there had been no alternative. But if the Primes had chosen that moment to launch a further wave of attacks, the results would have been catastrophic. Wilson had been reduced to praying.

'You mean they're here to stay?' Doi asked.

'For the moment, yes,' Wilson said.

'For the love of God, the money we gave you . . .'

'Enough to commission three warships,' Wilson snapped back. 'I'm not even sure three hundred would have been enough today.'

'The aerobots and force fields have done a damn good job,' Rafael said. 'Without them the damage would have been considerably greater.'

'But the casualties,' the President said. 'Good God, man, we've lost two million people.'

'More than that,' Anna said soberly. 'A lot more.'

'And it's going to rise,' Wilson said, deliberately harsh. 'Dimitri, can you give us some options on their next move?'

'They have softened us up,' the Russian academic said. 'Occupation is the logical follow-on. You must be prepared for a full-scale invasion.'

'Tunde, what's the ecological damage level on the assaulted worlds?'

'In a word, bad. Anshun took the worst pounding. The storms are just beginning there. At the very least they'll spread the radioactive fall-out right over the planet. The Primes don't use particularly clean fusion bombs. Decontamination would cost a fortune, even if it was practical – which I doubt.

Cheaper to evacuate and ship everyone to a new phase three planet. The other worlds are in varying stages of climate breakdown and nuclear pollution. Given our general population's attitude to nuclear and environmental issues, I'd say nobody will want to stay on anyway.'

'I agree,' Wilson said. 'I want to begin evacuation today.'

'On all of them?' Doi asked. 'I can't consent to that. Where the hell would they all go?'

'Friends, relatives, hotels, government camps. Who cares? That's not my problem. We need to get everyone left alive on those planets under the force fields, then get them out. I want our military reserve shipped out there to help; every paramilitary officer, every police tactical assault squad; all the aerobots we can spare. Between them, the planetary governments have enough combat personnel to put together a reasonable-sized army. Madam President, I'll need you to sign an Executive order putting them under Admiral Columbia's command.'

'I . . . I'm not sure.'

'I'll back you up,' Nigel said. 'And so will the Intersolar Dynasties. Wilson's right, we need to get this moving.'

'Can you get wormholes opened in the other cities on those planets?' Wilson asked. 'We'll never be able to transport everyone to the capitals.'

'Narrabri station's gateways aren't in great shape right now,' Nigel said. 'But we'll cope. The whole goddamn train network is shut down anyway. We can divert the gateways we have left on Wessex, but it won't be for trains. People will have to get through on foot, or buses.'

'What about Olivenza and Balya?'

'We can use the Anshun exploratory division's wormhole to re-establish contact, see if there's anyone left alive.'

'The Prime wormholes have stopped moving around,' Rafael said. 'Oh, Christ on a crutch, here they come.'

Radar and visual sensors showed Prime ships flying out of the wormholes above each of the besieged worlds.

'If they start landing, you can forget trying to evacuate anybody,' Dimitri said. 'There's no time. We have to knock out their centre of operations, hit their wormholes on the other side, where they're vulnerable.'

'How long until the starships reach Anshun?' Wilson asked.

'Two are already at the rendezvous point,' Anna said. 'Another eight hours until the final one gets there.'

'Son of a bitch! Rafael, start the evacuation of everyone in the capitals right away. We'll get them clear at least.'

'I'll get wormholes opened to the other protected cities,' Nigel said.

'What about the people left outside?' Doi said. 'In God's name we have to do something for them.'

'We will see what we can do to assist,' the SI said.

*

It took Mark forty minutes, but he eventually got the Ables pick-up working again. There was a whole load of circuitry that had burned out, stuff he managed to jury-rig or bypass. Liz and Carys spent the time packing, bringing out a couple of cases of clothes and all of the family's camping gear.

'I think the cybersphere is coming back,' Liz said as she dumped the last bag in the back of the pick-up. 'The house array is bringing up a basic communication menu.'

'The house array is working?' he asked in surprise. There had been a lot more than simple electronic damage. Most of the windows had blown in, even the triple-glazed ones, covering every room with shards of broken glass. Seeing what the blast had done to their home was almost as big a shock as witnessing the explosion, and infinitely more upsetting. It was as if each room had been deliberately, maliciously vandalized.

Even so, Mark reckoned they must have got off lighter than most. At least their drycoral house was all domes, allowing the worst of the blastwave pressure to slip smoothly over it; flat vertical walls would have taken a bad pounding. He couldn't bear looking out over the vineyards; almost every row had been knocked flat. It was the same right the way down the Ulon Valley as far as he could see.

'I can't interface with it,' Liz said. 'But the back-up monitor screen in the utility room survived, so I could type in a few commands. Ninety per cent of the system has crashed, and I can't get the reload and repair program to run. The network operation protocol is about the only thing that is there, it's definitely hooked into the valley node. The cable is fibre optic, it can survive a lot worse than this.'

'Did you try calling anyone?'

'Sure. I went for the Dunbavands and the Conants first. Nothing. Then I tried the Town Hall; I even tried the Black House. Nobody's home.'

'Or they don't realize the system's rebuilding itself. It'll take time even with genetic algorithms restructuring round the damage.'

'They probably never will find out if their inserts are screwed like ours. Who knows how to work a keyboard these days?'

'I do,' Barry said.

Mark put his arms around his son. The boy still had dirt and tears smeared over his face. He seemed to be recovering from the shock, though. 'That's because you're brilliant,' Mark told him.

'Clouds coming,' Carys said. She was looking to the north, where long streamers of white vapor were sliding low and fast over the Dau'sings. They were like fluffy spears heading towards the smog-clotted remains of the Regents.

Liz eyed them warily. 'Going to rain before long. Heavy rain.' She turned to Mark. 'So which way are we heading?'

'It's a long way to the gateway,' he said.

'If it's still there,' Carys said. 'They used a nuke to take out a remote detector station, God knows what they hit the CST station with. And that highway is one very long, very exposed route. Then we have to cross an ocean.'

'There's no other way out,' he said.

'You know we have to check on the others,' Liz said. 'I want to get the children to safety, more than anything, but we have to know where safe is. And right now I'm not convinced it's the other side of the Dau'sings.'

Mark glanced up at the sky, suddenly fearful of the sight. He'd never realized before how open it was. 'Suppose . . . they come?'

'Here?' Carys was scathing. 'Sorry, you guys, but come on. Randtown isn't exactly the strategic centre of the universe. Without the detector station this is nothing.'

'You're probably right,' Mark said. 'Okay, we'll head for town, and check in with a few neighbours on the way.'

'Good enough plan,' Liz said. 'We need to know what's happening on the rest of Elan, and the Commonwealth. If the government makes any attempt to contact us, it'll be at the town.'

'If there is a government,' Carys said.

Liz gave her a sharp glance. 'There will be.'

'Into the pick-up,' Mark told the kids. They clambered into the back seat without a word. An equally subdued Panda quickly jumped up with them. He almost ordered the dog out, then relented. They needed every bit of comfort they could get right now. All of them.

'I'll follow you,' Carys said.

'Okay. Keep your hand-held array on.' They'd dug out three old models from the house that had been switched off when the emp washed over the valley. It had been simple enough for Mark to alter their programs so they could be used as basic communicators, giving them a five-mile range.

Carys gave a backward wave of reassurance as she made her way over to the MG. To Mark's complete surprise and grudging respect, the sports car's systems had survived the emp almost intact.

'You'd better take this,' Liz said. She handed him his hunting rifle, a high-power laser with a low-light focus lock sight. 'I checked it, it still works.'

'God, Liz.' He snatched a hurried, guilty glance at the kids. 'What for?'

'People can behave badly in times of stress. And I'm not convinced the way Carys is about the Primes leaving us alone.' She opened her jacket to show an ion pistol in a shoulder holster.

'Holy shit. Where did that come from?'

'A friend. Mark, we live miles from anywhere, and you were away from home during the day.'

'But . . . a gun!'

'I'm just being practical, baby. A girl should know how to look after herself.'

'Right,' he said dumbly. Today it didn't seem important, somehow. In fact, he was rather glad she'd got it. He climbed up into the front of the pick-up, and drove it off down the long track to the main valley road.

*

Randtown was still standing. Sort of. The Regents had deflected the worst of the blast upwards, but the terrible distorted pressure waves that had rushed out from the mountains had easily reached the town.

Composite and metal panelling had been twisted and torn off every building. The crumpled rectangles were strewn everywhere, on the pavements, embedded in other buildings. The lighter ones were floating in the Trine'ba. Thick insulation blankets were flapping freely off the naked structural girders. Roofs were skeletal outlines, almost completely devoid of their solar panels. Strangest of all was the sparkle. The whole town glittered under a coating of prismatic rainbows. Each and every window in Randtown had shattered, flinging out splinters and granules in long plumes that fell across the pavements and streets, as if sacks of diamonds had been spilled out.

Mark stopped the pick-up on Low West Street, barely a couple of hundred metres off the highway. 'My God, I didn't know there was this much glass on the whole planet, let alone here.'

'Can the tyres take that?' Liz asked. She was looking along the street, trying to see if anyone was around. Several pillars of smoke were rising over the broken roofs, closer to the centre of town.

'Should do. They're gelfoam.'

'Okay then.' Liz brought the hand-held array up to her mouth. 'Carys, we're going in. Can the MG handle this?'

'MG will be having a nasty talk with my lawyers if it doesn't.'

Mark leaned out of the side window. David and Lydia Dunbavand were riding in the back, sitting on the bags of camping gear; while all three of the Dunbavand kids were squashed into the MG with Carys. Behind that, the Conants' 4x4 was acting as rear guard; Yuri had fixed it when they arrived at their homestead.

'Going in,' he called back to them.

David brought his maser wand up. 'Okey-dokey, we'll keep sharp.'

Mark shook his head as he toed the accelerator. What was it with disasters and people with guns? The pick-up moved forward slowly, its big tyres making a constant crunching sound on the road's crystalline coating.

They found the residents as they got closer to the centre. Almost everyone caught outside during the blast was injured to some degree. People walking along the pavements had been badly wounded by the wall panels as they sliced through the air. Those that avoided the panels were inevitably caught in the shotgun bombardment of glass. A lot had suffered both kinds of impacts.

As they approached the top end of Main Mall the road was jammed solid with parked vehicles. Mark braked the pick-up, and they all got out to walk. 'Leave Panda inside,' Liz told the children. 'She can't walk on this, her paws will be shredded.'

The dog started barking piteously as they left the vehicles behind.

Half of Main Mall's buildings were bent over at perilous angles, their structural girders pushed beyond their tolerance-loading by the ferocity of the air that had surged against them. The town's commercial heart had been busy at the time, with the cafés full of people having leisurely lunches, pavement tables crammed full, the street packed with window shoppers.

'Oh Jesus God,' Mark groaned as he took in the sight. He felt dizzy and faint, needing to hold on to the nearest bowed wall for support.

It wasn't the people still lying there. Nor the teams still working to free the remaining trapped victims. Not the triage teams bandaging up the cuts and lacerations. Even the dreadful wailing and moaning he could have withstood. It was the blood. Blood covered everything. The pavement slabs weren't even visible through the clogging burgundy fluid that had run down the whole length of the slope. The piles of glass were mushy with it. Buckled walls were caked in atrocious splatter patterns that had already darkened to black. People were soaked in it, their skin, their clothes. The air was thick with its tang-stench.

Mark bent double and vomited over his boots.

'Back,' Liz ordered the children. 'Come on, back to the pick-up.'

She propelled the kids along and Lydia and David hurried to help. Sandy and Ellie and Ed were all crying. Barry and Will looked like they were about to. The adults formed a little protective curtain, pushing gently.

'We'll find out if there's any sort of plan around here,' Carys called after them.

'Okay,' Liz said. She was fighting her own revulsion. 'Stay in touch.'

'How about you?' Carys asked Mark. 'You okay?'

'No, I'm goddamn not.' He wiped his mouth with his sleeve. 'Jesus!' The shock had turned him cold. He hadn't expected this. The end of the world was supposed to be final, an infinite nothing. That would have been a blessing. Instead they had to endure the aftermath, a world of pain and gore and suffering.

'You'll cope,' Carys said unsympathetically. 'You have to. Come on, let's see if we can help.'

Yuri Conant helped Mark stand straight. He didn't look too good, either. Olga had a cloth pressed firmly over her mouth. Her eyes were damp above it.

The four of them made their way down Main Mall, boots making a vile slushing sound at each footstep. Things clung to their soles. Mark got a rag out of his overalls, and tied it over his nose and mouth.

'Mark?' a girl called.

It was Mandy from Two For Tea. She was one of a little group clustered round a middle-aged man whose leg was badly torn. Makeshift bandages had been wrapped round the wounds, already heavily stained. A rough spike of rusty metal was sticking through the cloth, obviously deeply embedded in his flesh. One of the women was trying to get him to swallow painkillers.

'Are you hurt?' Mark asked her. Her face was filthy with grime and flecks of dry blood, with clear lines of skin on her cheeks where the tears had rolled. Her arms and apron were covered in blood.

'Some cuts,' she said. 'Nothing bad. I've been trying the help people ever since.' Her voice came close to cracking. 'What about Barry and Sandy, are they all right?'

'Yeah, they're fine. It wasn't so bad out in the valley.'

'What did we do, Mark? Why did they do this to us? We never hurt them.' She started sobbing. He put his arms round her, holding her gently. 'We did nothing,' he assured her.

'Then why?'

'I don't know. I'm sorry.'

'I hate them.'

'Can you folks lend a hand here,' one of the others tending the injured man said. 'We can move him now.'

'Move him where?' Carys asked.

'The hospital's running, they got some power back. Simon took charge.'

'Where is it?'

'Two streets away,' Mark said automatically.

'We'll take him,' Yuri said.

Even with a makeshift stretcher, it was hard going. There was so much debris to negotiate, and the Chinese restaurant on the corner of Matthews and Second Street was on fire. Without the firebots and volunteer fire service, the flames had really taken hold, threatening to spread to other buildings. They had to make a long detour down one of the tricky alleys that branched off from Matthews. As they walked on, the light gradually grew dimmer. Clouds covered the sky, spinning in a slow cyclone formation centred around the Regents. Thicker, darker clouds were scudding in fast from the horizon. Rain was already falling at the far end of Trine'ba, a broad curtain sweeping towards the town. At least it ought to stop the fires, Mark thought.

A big crowd of people were milling round on the lawns at the front of the General Hospital. They parted reluctantly to let Mark's group carry the stretcher through. Lights were on inside, and some of the medical equipment was functioning.

The casualty department was already crammed with children and the most seriously wounded adults. Reception had been taken up by deep wounds and blood loss trauma. The nurse on entrance assessment took a quick look at the man they'd brought, declared him non-critical, and told them to find a place in the hallway for him. A team of people with brushes and shovels were still clearing away the shattered glass from the polished floorboards. Mark found a section they'd just cleaned, and set the patient down.

When he stood up he saw Simon Rand striding down the middle of the hallway, his orange robes hanging like ordinary cloth. Even Simon had been hit by glass. There was a long healskin patch on his hand, another on the bottom of his neck. His entourage was smaller than usual, but they still followed him devotedly. A young woman walked beside him, dressed in a black top and jeans. It was Mellanie Rescorai, still enchantingly beautiful despite the sober determined expression locked on her face. Mark wasn't at all surprised that she didn't have a mark on her.

She saw him staring and offered a little rueful smile.

'Well there you go,' Carys said. 'Just when you think your day can't possibly get any worse.'

Mark trailed after Simon and Mellanie, with Carys, Yuri, and Olga following on behind. Simon reached the cracked and sagging marble portico at the front of the General Hospital, and raised his arms. 'People, if you could gather round.'

The crowd on the lawns moved closer. There were a lot of dark angry looks directed at Mellanie.

She faced the crowd unflinchingly. 'I know I'm not the most popular person in town right now,' she told them. 'But I do have a link back into the unisphere. To give you a brief summary of what's happening, twenty-four planets in the Commonwealth have been attacked.'

As she was talking, Mark brought up the hand-held array he was carrying. It couldn't find a single network route back to the planetary cybersphere, let alone the unisphere. 'No you haven't,' he muttered.

Mellanie glanced over to him. She'd just finished telling them about Wessex beating off their assault. Her hand waved unobtrusively, fingers fluttering in a small echo of her virtual interface. Mark's hand-held array suddenly had a link to a unisphere node in Runwich; it was very low capacity, just enough to give him basic data functions. 'I'm a reporter,' she said quietly. 'I have some long-range inserts.'

That wasn't right. Mark knew how networks functioned, and what she was saying was rubbish. He couldn't puzzle out how she'd given him the link.

'Right now, the navy is organizing evacuations of every assaulted planet,' Mellanie said to the crowd. 'CST's Wessex station is arranging to open its remaining wormholes at every isolated community. Including us. It's a difficult operation without a gateway at the far end, but the SI is helping them govern the process.'

Simon stepped forward. 'It will be painful to leave, I know. But we must face reality here today, people. The hospital can't cope. The rest of the planet is still suffering attacks of varying magnitude. Don't think of this as evacuation, we are regrouping, that's all. I will return. I will build my house anew. I would hope that all of you will come back with me.'

'When are we leaving?' Yuri asked. 'How long have we got?'

'The navy's drawing up a list,' Mellanie said. 'We have to make sure that when the wormhole opens everyone from the surrounding countryside is here and ready to leave. We all go through at once.'

'Where are we on the list?' a voice from the crowd shouted.

Mellanie gave Simon a tense look.

'We're number eight hundred and seventy-six,' Simon said.

The crowd was silent. Even Mark felt let down. But at least

there was a way out. He asked the hand-held array to check if that was right, that they were truly that far down the list.

'Look at your little friend,' Carys said, her eyes were fixed on Mellanie. 'She's getting bad news.'

Mark glanced over in time to see Mellanie half-turning from the crowd, hiding her face from them. Her eyes were wide with alarm. She mouthed some kind of obscenity and tugged at Simon's robe. The two of them went into a huddle.

Mark told the hand-held array to track down all official information on the current Elan situation. 'No data available,' it told him bluntly.

Simon was holding his hands up again, appealing to the crowd who'd been watching him and Mellanie anxiously. 'Slight change of plan,' he called above the edgy muttering. 'We need to get out of town, now. If you have a vehicle that works, please drive it to the bus station. We will leave for the Highmarsh in convoy. That is where the wormhole will be opened. Can I ask all the able-bodied to help with carrying the injured to the station. Anyone with technical knowledge, we need the buses running; report to the station engineering office when you get there.'

People were starting to call out, 'Why?'

'What's happening?'

'Talk to us, Simon.'

'Tell us.'

Mellanie stood beside him. 'The aliens are coming,' she said simply, and pointed at the sky behind them.

The crowd turned in unison to look at the dark rainclouds above the Trine'ba. There were two distinct patches of white fluorescence up there, as if a pair of suns were shining through. They were getting bigger and brighter.

*

It was the show of her lifetimes. Alessandra Baron knew nothing else was ever going to match live coverage of an alien attack. Thankfully, she'd had the presence of mind to change out of her glamorous dress into the prim grey suit her wardrobe department kept ready for disasters and general bad news events. Now she sat masterfully behind her studio desk, perfect as moderator and guide while holograms of analysts, politicians, and junior navy officers flicked in and out of the show to answer her questions. They were interspaced with direct feeds from the assaulted planets – whenever Bunny, the show's producer, could get a decent link. The fact that the unisphere could be affected, that communications she had taken for granted her whole lives suddenly now weren't universal and guaranteed, troubled Alessandra almost as much as the nuclear explosions, though she kept her expression professionally impassive the whole time. And as for the shocking power losses when Wessex fought off the Prime worm-holes, it brought everyone close to the battle, giving them a sense of involvement.

In the studio production office, Bunny was running multiple parallel information streams for accessors, summarizing the status of events on each of the twenty-four planets. The streams for Olivenza and Balya were ominously empty and had been for some time. Alessandra's virtual vision provided a grid of powerful images available from various reporters unlucky enough to be close to the front line. Force fields over cities, constantly flaring with shimmering opalescence as they warded off either debris or a howling radioactive hurricane. Reporters foolhardy enough to be standing close to the force field revealed the new wastelands outside; the eerily smooth craters with glowing basins surrounded by flat ground that had become a desert of midnight-black carbon. Then there were the human interest stories, interviews with terrified, barely coherent city residents as they wept. Those from outlying towns who'd made it inside the force fields in time. Those whose family and friends were still outside somewhere. All of them had their suffering and sorrow and rage skilfully woven into a story tapestry that made sure accessors could never leave.

Bunny and Alessandra played strong on one theme, always letting through the same overriding question: Where's the navy? Time after time they replayed the spectacular nova-bright explosion of the *Second Chance* as she died in battle above Anshun.

The feeds from the assaulted planets made Alessandra grateful she was safe on Augusta, hundreds of light-years behind the front line. She asked Ainge about that, an analyst from the StPetersburg institute for strategic studies whose hologram was sitting beside her.

'I think it's significant that they're only assaulting our worlds closest to Dyson Alpha,' Ainge said. 'It implies a range limit on their wormhole generators.'

'But Wessex is a hundred light-years inside the boundary of phase three space,' Alessandra said.

'Yes, but from a tactical point of view it was worth the expenditure risk trying to capture it. If they'd been successful, we would have lost a considerable portion of phase two space. That would almost have guaranteed our ultimate loss. As it is, we're going to have trouble fighting back. We know the kind of resources they have available; it could well be we never regain the twenty-three outer planets.'

'In your professional opinion, can we win this war?'

'Not today. We need a radical rethink of our strategy. We also need time, which is a factor very much dictated by the Primes.'

'The navy says its warships are on the way to assist the assaulted planets. How do you rate their chances?'

'I'd need more information before I can give you a realistic assessment. It all depends on how well defended the Prime wormholes are. Admiral Kime has to succeed in sending a warship through to attack their staging post. That's the only way to slow them down.'

Bunny was telling Alessandra that Mellanie had come on line.

'I thought Randtown had dropped out of Elan's cybersphere,' Alessandra said.

'It is, but she's found some way through.'

'Good girl. Has she got anything interesting?'

'Oh yeah. I'm giving her live access. Stand by.'

Alessandra saw a new grid image appear in her virtual vision. It shifted into prime feed position.

Mellanie was in some kind of open-air bus station, a big square expanse of tarmac with a passenger waiting lounge along one side. Every window had been blown out along the front of the building, with the support pillars bent and half of the solar collector roof missing. Despite how bright it was outside, a heavy rain was falling from a cloud-veiled sky. The relentless deluge was making life even more miserable for the hundreds of people swarming through the station. A full-scale exodus was in progress. Queues were trailing back from a logjam of stationary buses, the able-bodied paired with the moderately injured, helping them along. Four buses had been converted into makeshift ambulances, their seats removed and slung out to pile up beside the wrecked waiting lounge. The badly injured on crude stretchers were being carried on board; a lot of them were in a bad way, with their wounds being treated in the most primitive fashion, wrapped in cloth bandages rather than healskin.

Engineers were clustered round open hatches on the sides of the buses, rewiring the superconductor batteries. Alessandra glimpsed Mark Vernon in one repair group, working away furiously. But Mellanie didn't pause in her establishing scan. The roads around the station were packed with 4x4s and pick-up trucks that were stuffed full of kids and uninjured adults.

'Mellanie,' Alessandra said. 'Glad to see you're still with us. What's the situation there in Randtown?'

'Take a look at this,' Mellanie said in a flat voice.

Her visual sweep continued until she was looking down across the broken town. The bus station was obviously at the back of Randtown, where the ground started rising into foothills. It was a position which gave her a view out over the shattered roofs to the Trine'ba beyond. She raised her head to the mass of thick black clouds roofing the giant lake. Finally, Alessandra understood why it was so bright.

Thirty miles away, the rucked thunderclouds were sprouting a pair of radiant tumours, huge writhing bulges that were billowing downwards. She watched the base of the largest burst apart as eight slender lines of solid sunlight sliced down through it to strike the surface of the lake. Steam detonated out from the impact, sending a circular cascade of blazing mist soaring across the heaving water. The light was so intense it threw the town and countryside into stark monochrome. Mellanie's retinal inserts brought up their strongest filters, though they could barely cope. Most of the townspeople in the bus station were cowering away from it, bringing their forearms up to cover their eyes. Screams and shouts of panic were coming from all around. They were quickly smothered as a strident roaring sound reached the town, rattling the remaining buildings. It grew steadily louder until Mellanie's whole skeleton was thrumming painfully. The image which her retinal inserts were feeding back to Alessandra's studio was reduced to a blurred black and white profile. Directly over Randtown the clouds were in torment, savaged by conflicting high-velocity pressure fronts. The chittering rain changed in seconds, curving with the wind to streak along almost horizontally, each drop stinging sharply as it hit unprotected skin.

'Plasma drives,' Mellanie screamed above the never-ending thunderclap. 'Those are ships coming down.'

The second tumour of cloud ripped open as it was lanced by eight more incandescent spears. Mellanie finally had to cover her eyes, turning the image to a single blood-red haze as her hand came close to translucence. Even through the lashing rain, the heat pouring out of the plasma was greater than any noonday desert sun. The raindrops were steaming as they bulleted through the air.

There was a slight decrease in the light level. Mellanie brought her hand down. A ship had descended out of the clouds, a dark cone-shape riding the vivid glare of its rigid plasma exhausts. Then it vanished behind the massive wall of radiant steam gushing up from the lake.

'Did you see that?' Mellanie screamed raw-throated. 'They're coming.'

'Get out of there.' Eighty billion accessors saw Alessandra's poise crack. 'Don't compromise your safety: run.'

'We can't . . .' The image vanished in a scattering of purple static.

Alessandra froze behind the desk. She cleared her throat. 'That report from Mellanie Rescorai, one of the most promising and talented newcomers to join our team for several years. The prayers from all of us here in the studio are with her. And now, over to Garth West, who was covering the flower festival on Sligo. What's it like there, Garth, any sign of Prime landing ships, yet?'

*

'Ships now approaching upper atmosphere on Anshun, Elan, Whalton, Pomona, and Nattavaara,' Anna reported in a calm voice.

As the Prime ships reached the stratosphere, aerobots started shooting. Everyone sharing Wilson's tactical display watched intently as the energy weapons locked on and sliced upwards. They had little effect. Wilson heard a couple of dismayed curses. The force fields protecting the descending ships were too powerful to penetrate with the medium-calibre weaponry carried by the aerobots. Then the Primes began targeting the small aggressors below them.

'Get them out of there,' Wilson said. 'Regroup them around the protected cities. We'll need them later.'

'I'll see to it,' Rafael said.

'Did we hit any of them?' Nigel asked.

'No sir,' Anna said. 'Not one; their force fields are too strong.'

'Atmospheric entry on Belembe, Martaban, Sligo, Balkash, and Samar, Molina, and Kozani. They're coming through the wormholes at the rate of one per forty seconds. Trajectories variable, they're not concentrating on the capital cities. They seem to be heading for coastlines.'

'Coastlines?'

'Getting visual imagery.'

Various image feeds appeared in the huge tactical display. Each one showing pictures of brilliant streamers cutting across skies of varying colours.

'They're big bastards,' Rafael commented. 'Thousands of tons each.'

'Those are fusion plumes,' Tunde Sutton said. 'Temperature profile and spectral signature indicate a deuterium reaction.'

'Confirm, they're heading for water landings,' Anna said.

'Makes sense,' Nigel said. 'Even with force fields I wouldn't like to land one of those on solid ground.'

'That gives us a breathing space,' Wilson said. 'They're going to have to come ashore. And it will be in smaller vehicles. We might be able to get some reinforcements to the capitals and the larger towns.'

'Last aerobots squadrons are being withdrawn from range,' Anna said.

'Our reinforcement is taking too much time,' Rafael said. 'Anybody who has any kind of military capability is reluctant to let go of it.'

'Get your office working on that,' Wilson told the President. 'We have to show people we can put up a coherent resistance.'

'I'll talk to Patricia.'

'You'll need to lean on heads of state personally,' Nigel said.

'Very well.' If Doi resented the bullying she didn't show it.

'How about the evacuation?' Wilson asked.

'We're already running trains from Anshun, Martaban, Sligo, Nattavaara, and Kozani,' Nigel said. 'I'm shunting them through Wessex directly to Earth. After that, they'll get allocated a final destination. All I'm concerned about is getting them clear of their origin. We're about ready to try shutting the Trusbal gateway on Wessex and reopening it in Bitran on Sligo; there's a lot of flower festival tourists trapped there.'

'Any Prime ships near there?' Wilson asked.

'Twelve on their way,' Anna said. 'But Bitran is eighty miles from the coast. There should be time.'

For the next thirty minutes Wilson watched the shifting data in his display, showing him the flow of military equipment and personnel converging on Wessex. CST staff and the SI eventually managed to get the wormhole open and stable inside the Bitran force fields. Refugees stormed through on foot and in every vehicle the city had. They then became a problem for Wessex's Narrabri station workforce, which had to direct them onto passenger trains to move them along. The sheer volume of people appearing so far away from any passenger terminus was completely outside any of the planetary station's contingency plans. Eventually they cleared a set of rails, cordoning them off with caution holograms, and hustled everyone along the four miles to the nearest platform. Trains hurtled by on either side of them. Empty carriages going to the assaulted worlds; badly overcrowded carriages racing back. Cargo trains loaded with aerobots and armed troops from all over the Commonwealth, hurrying to reinforce the isolated cities.

As the CST managers and the SI managed to divert more gateway wormholes to the evacuation effort, so the marshalling yard turned into an ad hoc staging post. Cargo trains pulled up in sidings, and the aerobots they carried launched from there to fly through the wormholes above the heads of the refugees. Platoons of troops in bulky armour marched along, earning appreciative cheers and applause.

The first main effort was directed at Anshun's capital, Treloar. Wilson wanted it kept intact with a functioning station so that aerobots could be channelled through and deployed around Anshun's remaining shielded cities. Squadrons from thirty-five worlds were assigned to it, their arrival scheduled as fast as CST's struggling rail network could deliver them.

As the first ones arrived in Treloar they flew through temporary gaps in the force field and started to spread out towards the coast. Two hundred Prime ships had already splashed down on Anshun, over a thousand more were in various stages of descent. Wilson didn't like to think what effect that would have on the planet's already reeling environment. But then he'd seen Dyson Alpha's sole habitable world, and the fusion ships that swirled constantly above it. The Primes didn't have the same priorities as humans.

'Scouts launching from Treloar,' Anna reported. 'The Primes have landed just off a coastal town called Scraptoft. That's forty miles away. Should be getting pictures any minute.'

Wilson turned to the video display relayed from the lead scout as it left Treloar. It was flying at Mach nine, its pilot array holding it steady twenty metres above the ground. Behind it, a swathe of soil a hundred metres wide was being ruptured by its furious wake, the torn air pulverizing trees, bushes, plants and the occasional building it flew over. As it neared the shoreline, hundreds of small stealthed sensor drones were ejected from the fuselage, building up a much wider image.

When it shot out over the cliff at Scraptoft, it revealed

thirty Prime ships floating on the sea amid a dense swirl of agitated steam. The big cones were almost completely black, surrounded by sparkling force fields. Halfway up their superstructure, tall doorways had hinged outward to form horizontal platforms. Smaller craft were flying out of the openings, squat grey cylinders with metallic beetle legs folded up underneath. Three energy beams struck the scout, and the image vanished immediately.

The stealthed sensors scattered behind the scout watched the Prime flyers slide in over the sea, mapping their electrical, thermal, magnetic, and mechanical structure, along with their weapon and force field parameters. There were several types, some that were nothing but flying weapons platforms, while the larger ones were carrying small units of some kind that were protected by individual force fields.

'That's got to be them,' Nigel muttered. Even now, he was curious what they might look like.

Combat aerobots screamed in towards Scraptoft at Mach twelve. Prime flyers arched round to intercept. The sky between them was ruptured by energy beams and explosions, turning to a huge patch of electrically charged gas. Lightning bolts flashed outward, clawing at the ground for miles around.

Eight of the big Prime landing ships coming down through the atmosphere altered their trajectory slightly. Their fusion exhausts swept across the coastline, creating instant devastation. Soil and rock melted, flowing away from the superheated beams of plasma. Waves of thick glowing vapour spewed out, boiling high above the clouds until they were pulled apart by the jetstreams. Metres above the ground, aerobots and Prime flyers alike vectored round in high-gee manoeuvres in an attempt to avoid the miasma of incendiary particles. The eight Prime landing ships were poised fifteen kilometres above Scraptoft, balanced on their drive exhausts. They started to fire their weapons, blasting the aerobots out of the sky.

Nigel watched the tsunami of filthy smog roll across the land. It was over twenty kilometres high, and spreading wide as the eight giant ships continued to hang there with their fusion fire searing into the ground. The front engulfed Treloar's force field, smothering the dome to bring an abrupt night to the city.

Screened by the pollution, the Prime flyers began to touch down around Scraptoft's outskirts. Stealthed sensors continued their quiet transmissions, showing what they could see through the dark oppressive vapours asphyxiating the land. A visual spectrum sensor locked on to one of the flyers that had landed in the smouldering ruins of a tourist complex. Sections of the cylindrical fuselage had opened, extending ramps. Aliens walked down, their bodies encased in suits of dark armour reinforced by force fields.

'Taller than us,' Nigel observed dispassionately.

'Weird walk,' Wilson replied. He was watching the creature's four legs, the way they bent, the curving feet shaped like a blunt claw. His gaze moved up the torso to the four arms; each one was holding a weapon. The top of the suit was a squat hemisphere divided into four sections, each one replicating the same sensor arrangement.

'There's a lot of electromagnetic activity around them,' Rafael said. 'They're communicating with each other and the flyer on a continual basis. The flyers are in contact with the landing ships, ditto the ships that are going into orbit. The signals look very similar to the ones you recorded at Dyson Alpha.'

'Tu Lee reported that the missiles required continual guidance updates,' Tunde Sutton said.

'Meaning what?' Rafael asked.

'Possibly, the Prime commanders don't allow for a lot of independence on the battlefront.'

'Okay,' Wilson said. 'Anna, have we got any electronic warfare systems we can deploy?'

'There are several EW aerobots on the central registry.'

'Good. Get them out there fast. Close down those links. Let's see if that has any effect on them.'

*

Randtown had finally given in to panic. As soon as the alien ships had splashed down on the Trine'ba, the vehicles parked around the bus station began to move as families headed out for the perceived safety of the valleys behind the town. Horns blared in fury, their combined racket almost as loud as the ships' exhaust. There were collisions all along the road as they made U-turns or accelerated out from the kerb where they'd been waiting.

Mark kept glancing round at the chaos as he worked with Napo Langsal on the power supply of a bus. The two of them had almost rigged a bypass around the superconductor battery regulator.

'They're losing it big time,' Mark grunted.

The queue for the bus had turned into a violent scrum around the open door, and shoving had deteriorated into the first fists being thrown. He and Napo were being shouted at and threatened, anything to get the bus working.

A shotgun was fired in the centre of the bus station. Everyone paused for a second. Mark had ducked immediately, now he cautiously lifted his head. It was Simon Rand who'd fired the antique pump-action weapon straight into the air.

'Thank you for your attention, ladies and gentlemen,' Simon said, his loud bass voice carrying right across the station as he turned a complete circle. Even people scrambling round the vehicles outside had paused to listen. 'Nothing has changed our immediate situation, so you will stick to the plan we drew up.' He pumped the shotgun, the spent cartridge twirling away. 'There are enough buses to carry everyone out, and they will leave shortly, so kindly stop harassing the engineers. Now, in order to guarantee that we can all reach the Highmarsh safely, I will require a volunteer team to stay here in town with me and act as a rearguard to allow the convoy to get a head start. Anyone with a weapon, please report to the passenger waiting lounge to receive your instructions.' He lowered the shotgun.

'Holy Christ,' Napo grunted.

Mark closed the cable box, and pressed the reset button. 'How's that?' he called up to the driver. The woman gave him a thumbs up. 'You get along to the next bus,' he told Napo.

Napo gave Mark's hunting laser a dubious glance. 'He can't make you, you know.'

'I know.' Mark looked towards the two vast clouds of steam squatting over the Trine'ba, obscuring the ships. The surface was still reeling from their splashdown, with big waves rolling ashore, washing over the wall that ran alongside the promenade. 'But he's right. People need time to get clear.'

Dudley Bose gave Mellanie a panicked look as they approached the bus. The crowd was pressing in tight around them, carrying them forward.

'Do you think there's room?' he asked. The bus already looked full, with people squashed into the seats, and more packing the aisle.

'If not this one, then the next,' she told him. 'You'll be fine.'

'I . . .? What about you?'

'I'll grab a later one.' She could barely see Dudley, her virtual vision was displaying so many symbols and icons. Very little of the dataflow made any sense. She'd glimpsed some standard information amid the mad rainbow swirls, which seemed to be some kind of sensor data. Her newly activated inserts were scanning the steam clouds on the Trine'ba, analysing the ships hidden inside. She was trying to remain aloof from it all, be a true impartial reporter, but the adrenaline flushing through her blood was making her heart pound away and giving her the shakes. The SI kept telling her to

1079

relax. It was tough; this most certainly was not what she'd expected when she made her deal with it.

'No!' Dudley cried. 'No, you can't leave me. Not now. Please, you promised.'

'Dudley.' She put her hands on either side of his head, holding him steady, then kissed him hard amid the jostling. Concentrating on calming him was subduing her own apprehension. 'I'm not going to leave you. I promised that and I'll keep that promise. But there are things I have to do here that no one else can. Now get on the bus, and I'll follow the convoy.'

They'd reached the door. She let go of his head, and smiled with winning reassurance. It was a truthful smile, because there was no way she was going to relinquish her hold over him for the moment, he was her ace now, making her a real player. Though given the scary abilities the SI's inserts were providing she was beginning to wonder if she even needed Alessandra and the show any more. She didn't know if she could operate them independently, but just knowing they were there was giving her a kind of courage she admitted she'd never had before. Before this, she would have been first on the bus, clawing children and little old ladies out of the way.

The crowd pushed Dudley up the stairs, and she wriggled free. He looked back frantically as he was shoved along the aisle. 'I love you,' he bellowed.

Mellanie made herself smile at him, and blew a kiss.

Liz and Carys were waiting by the pick-up. Mark smiled and waved at Barry and Sandy who were in the back seat with Panda. 'I'm going to help Rand,' he said. 'Take Barry and Sandy up to the Highmarsh.'

'I'm with you,' Liz said.

'But—'

'Mark, I really hope you aren't going to come out with any crap about this being a man's job.'

'They need a mother.'

'And a father.'

'I can't abandon Rand. This is our life they're destroying. At the very least I owe the people this. Some of us have to get away, that's the only way we can rebuild afterwards.'

'Agreed. And I'm helping you.'

'Carys?' he appealed.

'Don't even think about involving me in this argument. But if you two crazies are going to join up with Rand's guerrilla army I'll take the kids out of here in the MG.' She patted a heavy bulge in her jacket. 'They'll be safe with me, I promise. And we've got the arrays, we can stay in touch.'

Mark nearly questioned when his family suddenly became gun-toting survivalists. Instead, he gave Carys a quick kiss. 'Thanks.' Then he and Liz had the really difficult job of coaxing the kids into the MG, promising them Mom and Dad would be following along right behind.

*

Dark specks zipped out of the cloud that squatted over half of the Trine'ba. They arrowed round to line up on Randtown, accelerating hard.

'They're coming,' Liz called.

Mark was backing the pick-up into the Ables Motors garage workshop where it would be hidden from view. David Dunbavand was standing behind the truck, helping to guide him in with shouts and frantic hand signals. Mark had never appreciated how difficult it was to drive without micro radar providing a proximity scan.

'That's enough,' David said. 'Let's go.' He slipped the safety off his maser wand as they left the back of the garage. Like most buildings, it had taken a pounding in the Regents' blast. The office along the front was missing all its windows, and the external walls were shredded; but the main framework was intact. It would be easy to rebuild, given a little time and money.

That was the kind of thinking, visualizing a future of complete normality, which allowed Mark to keep going. He squatted down next to Liz behind a thick stone wall that lay along the side of the Libra Bar's beer garden. The blast had hurled the garden's wooden tables and chairs across the lawn, smashing them against the wall of the Zanue car rental franchise next door. There had been many summertime evenings when he and Liz came here for a meal and a drink, sitting out in the garden with friends where they could watch the boats come and go from the quays along the waterfront.

Now they had the same clear view of the waterfront through their weapon sights. The rain had subsided to a light drizzle laced with a few slim trails of grey smoke from the dying fires. Mark could see the alien flyers skimming towards him just a few metres above the wavelets.

'Stand by,' Simon's voice said from the hand-held array. 'They look like they're slowing. Could be plan A.'

There had been a lot of shouting about that when Simon assembled his ragtag band of two dozen guerrillas in the passenger waiting lounge. Plan A envisaged the aliens landing in the town, which would allow the guerrillas to snipe at them, slowing their advance. Plan B, the worst-case scenario, would have them flying over the town to attack the convoy directly, in which case they'd have to fire a fusillade of shots at the craft as they went overhead and hope to hit some vital component. Everyone knew that would be next to useless. As always, Simon had prevailed.

Mark looked over his shoulder. The last of the buses were visible on the highway at the base of Blackwater Crag, travelling far too fast for anything that didn't have working arrays and safety systems. They only needed a few minutes more and they'd be turning into the Highmarsh.

Looking at the approaching alien flyers, Mark wasn't convinced that the big valley was going to be the refuge Simon had claimed. In his private vision of the future, Mark had envisaged the aliens coming ashore in boats, taking days to reach the Highmarsh.

'Carys, where are you?' Liz asked.

'We turned onto the Highmarsh road a couple of minutes ago.'

'They're in aircraft. Looks like they're landing here, though.'

'Okay, let me know if any are coming our way. I'll need to get off the road fast.'

'Will do.'

Mark glanced at the unit's screen. Their signal was routing through the still-functional sections of the district's network. Several nodes along the Highmarsh were operating, allowing them to extend their fragile contact around the mountains. He was pretty sure it wouldn't last long once the aliens landed and started running sensor sweeps.

The first of the alien flyers arrived at the shoreline. It hovered just above the water, spindly metal legs unfolding from beneath its cylindrical fuselage. After a moment of hesitation it landed on the broad promenade next to the Celestial Tours quay, the aft section knocking into the wall and demolishing a five-metre length, breaking the long single line of poetry.

'Wait,' Simon's voice urged them with soft confidence. 'We need most of them down first, then we can begin our harassment campaign.'

Mark wondered where Simon had gained so much combat experience. He certainly sounded like he knew what he was talking about. More likely it was all from TSI dramas. He glanced out at the lake again, startled by just how many flyers were now heading their way.

'Ho boy,' David muttered.

Doors had opened on the flyer sitting next to the Celestial Tours quay, allowing aliens to lumber down.

Mark's personal predictions had faltered at this point. But he certainly hadn't expected anything quite so ... robotic looking. Maybe they were robots? Watching them spread out, he quickly changed that opinion. They moved fast, heading straight for cover. Within seconds they were infiltrating the buildings that faced the promenade.

Twelve flyers landed along the waterfront. The second wave flew over to circle the town park at the back of the General Hospital before extending their legs and sinking down. Some flyers were heading towards Blackwater Crag and the start of the highway.

'Stand by,' Simon said. 'Don't expect our weapons to penetrate their force fields, aim for maximum disruption around them. And fall back immediately.'

Mark gave Liz a look. She stretched her lips wide, mimicking a smile. 'Okay,' she mumbled.

He carefully raised his head above the wall, and brought the laser rifle up. Several aliens were slipping quickly across the open ground of the promenade to the first line of buildings. He suspected Simon was right, his rifle wouldn't get through that armour. Instead he shifted his aim to the buildings, wondering if he could knock out some of the framework, and collapse the roof.

Somebody else fired. He actually saw the air sparkle around an alien as the energy beam was deflected by its force field. Their response was terrifyingly swift. The Bab's Kebabs franchise on Swift Street exploded.

Mark ducked down as smouldering fragments spun through the air. 'Shit!'

Four of the flyers heading for Blackwater Crag turned sharply and flew back low over the town. Masers lashed down, scoring a long line of fire and vapor across the rooftops.

'Hit them,' someone yelled out of the hand-held array. 'Hit them. Shoot back.'

Two more buildings exploded, sending broken lengths of

framework girders spinning through the air. Composite panels cartwheeled down the street like tumbleweed. Laser shots, ion bolts, and even bullets peppered the buildings along the waterfront. The force fields around two of the overhead flyers flickered briefly with static.

'They'll slaughter us.'

'Shoot them, kill them all, kill the bastards.'

The air above Mark emitted a sibilant sizzling. A line shimmered faint violet. Flames burst out of every gaping window in the Babylon Garden restaurant behind him.

'Fall back. Get the fuck out of here.'

'No! They'll see us. Knock down the flyers.'

'Where's the convoy? Are they clear?'

'Hey, yeah! I got one, I saw a wall fall on it. Oh shit—'

There must have been twenty buildings burning vigorously now. Three more detonated in quick succession.

'God, no. What have we done?'

'Simon, you motherfucker. This is all your fault.'

'Stay calm. Stay under cover.'

Mark looked at David, who was pressed up hard against the wall. His eyes were closed as he whimpered a prayer.

'You want to make a break for it?' Mark asked Liz.

'Not in the pick-up,' she said. 'They'll see that.'

'All right.' He brought the hand-held array up. 'Carys?'

Liz's hand closed tight around his upper arm. 'I don't goddamn believe it.'

Mark twisted round, following Liz's disbelieving stare. 'What in God's name . . .?'

Mellanie was walking down the street past the Ables Motors garage, heading towards the waterfront. She kept to the centre of the road, avoiding the worst of the debris. Her hair and shoulders were damp from the earlier rain, otherwise she was as perfectly groomed as usual. Dense-packed silver OCtattoos flickered over her face and hands, as if they were her true skin emerging into the light.

'Get down!' Mark screamed at her.

She turned her head and gave him a small sympathetic smile. A near-subliminal golden fractal pattern spiralled out around her eyes. 'Stay there,' she told him calmly. 'This isn't something you can handle.'

'Mellanie!'

She'd gone another five paces when four aliens burst out of Kate's Knitwear ten metres ahead of her, smashing straight through the remaining aluminium wall panels. Their arms curved round to line up their weapons on her. The motion slowed then stopped. All four of them stood perfectly still in the middle of the road.

Mark realized that all the flyers in the air were gradually lowering themselves to the ground. Out over Trine'ba, the flyers rushing to Randtown dipped gently, angling down to strike the water hard. Big plumes of spray cascaded upwards, falling away to reveal the craft bobbing low on the surface.

'Mellanie?' Mark croaked. 'Are you doing this?'

'With a little help, yes.'

He clambered slowly to his feet, trying to stop the tremble in his legs. Liz stood beside him, gazing warily at the young girl. David poked his head above the wall. 'Jesus,' he spat.

'Take their weapons,' Mellanie said. Her face was almost completely silver now, with only a few slivers of skin remaining around her cheeks and brow.

'You're joking,' Mark said.

The four aliens dropped their weapons onto the road.

'You're not joking.'

'You should be able to shoot through their force fields with those,' Mellanie said. 'You'll probably need to when they come after you again. This standoff won't last for ever. But I'll keep them here as long as I can.' She took a deep breath, closing her chrome eyelids. 'Leave now.'

Mark glanced down, her voice had come out of the hand-held array as well.

'Everybody, get in your vehicles and fall back,' she ordered. 'Join the convoy.'

'What's happening?' Simon's voice asked.

Mark brought the array up to his mouth. 'Just do it, Simon. She's stopped them.'

'Stopped them how?'

'Mark's right,' someone else said. 'I can see a whole bunch of them. They're just standing there.'

'Go,' Mellanie said. 'You haven't got long. Go!'

Mark looked at the weapons lying on the tarmac as if it was some kind of school dare. The aliens still hadn't moved.

'Come on,' Liz said. She darted forwards.

Mark hurried after her. The weapons were bulky, too heavy to carry easily, let alone aim. He pulled up a couple, giving the tall silent immobile aliens a cautious look as he scrabbled round at their feet, as if this might be the act which finally broke the spell, goading them into motion and retaliation. David came up beside him, and picked up one of the chunky cylinders.

'Let's get out of here for Christ's sake,' Liz said.

Mark managed to hold on to a third weapon. He scooted the hell away from the bizarre tableau.

'What now?' Liz asked Mellanie.

'You go.'

'What about you? Will you be all right?'

'Yes.' She gave Mark one of her menacingly erotic smiles. 'Quits?'

'Yeah,' he said. 'Quits.'

'Thank you,' Liz said.

The three of them raced for the pick-up. They slung the purloined alien weapons in the back, and Mark slammed the accelerator to the floor. He snatched one last glimpse of

Mellanie in the rear-view mirror. The silhouette of a small human girl standing defiantly in front of four big armoured aliens, waiting, watching, as silent as the army she had stilled.

*

Mellanie's inserts were feeding her a fresh image of the world; no longer data but an extension of her ordinary senses. She could actually see the electromagnetic emissions flooding out of the aliens as they stormed ashore. Each one blazing bright in this black spectrum. Long, complex, and slow signals slipped between them, a conduit of tight-packed analogue sine waves dancing and crackling around each other. They formed networks, brief, transient patterns that were forever rearranging themselves, connecting individual aliens, then switching back and forth between the flyers who relayed them in new combinations to the big conical ships floating on the Trine'ba. Huge columns of information streamed out of both ships, twisting up through the atmosphere to vanish inside the trans-dimensional vortex of the wormholes above.

It made a striking contrast to the abridged electronic network of Randtown, with its slender lines of carefully packaged binary pulses zipping purposefully around her. Where the human systems were neat and efficient, these alien outpourings were crude. Yet, she acknowledged, they possessed a certain integral elegance. As it was with all organic forms.

Mellanie concentrated on the rush of strange waveforms radiating out of a Prime flyer as it manoeuvred above the promenade, ready to land. A new batch of woken inserts buzzed with electric vibrancy inside her flesh. She knew of the SI's presence inside them, analysing what she discovered for it, teasing apart the oscillating signals to discover their meaning. As the flyer's emissions coursed through the inserts she heard a harsh unintelligible voice at the back of her mind, it bloomed to a whispered chorus. Then there were the images, leaking out of the signals like some long-forgotten dream. A confused multiple viewpoint of motiles emerging from a congregation lake, millions of them pressed together, slipping and sliding as they waded ashore. Next to them was the towering mountain clad in rooms and chambers where it was centred, all of life in the star system. A mountain where long ago light used to shine in the morning. Now the sky was permanently dark beneath the heavy clouds, an everlasting night split only by the incessant flash of lightning bolts, revealing the filthy rain and sleet which fell across the protective force fields. A black sky also seen from the asteroids orbiting far above, shielding the whole planet, its turbulence illuminated to insipid grey by sunlight and blazing strands of fusion flame. Life still thrived beneath the veil, woven inseparably to groupings of itself as it seethed and survived everywhere, on small cold planets, moons encircling gas-giants, and far asteroid settlements. A life that now extended to other stars and their planets. A life that had flown through the wormholes to reach Elan where it was spreading out over the lake to touch the land.

The life whispered amid itself, directing its soldier motiles to move forward into the flimsy box-buildings. It searched for humans and their machinery. Finding none of either. Though there was movement, the tell-tale infrared signatures which the soldier motiles were skilfully working their way towards. At the back of the urban area, long vehicles raced away. Flyers angled round to investigate.

One of the soldier motiles was shot at. It retaliated immediately, firing back, destroying the zone where the shot had come from. Flyers swooped eagerly, raking the buildings with coherent beams of gamma radiation.

'They're going to destroy everything,' Mellanie said.

'It,' the SI corrected. 'It is singular. An interesting arrangement. Life that has achieved unity, not just with itself but with its machinery.'

'I don't care what it is, it's still going to kill people.'

'We know.'

Programs and power flooded through Mellanie's inserts, activating yet more functions. She had little to do with it other than adding her wishes to the conclusion. Fabulously complex OCtattoos crawled over her skin, merging into a single circuit. Signals streamed out from her, overlaying those which fused the motiles together. Interference patterns jostled and ruptured the smooth consistency of the soldier herd's thoughts. Riding down the disruption were new instructions.

Mellanie left her shelter and walked slowly towards the Trine'ba so she could observe properly. Poor Mark Vernon tried to warn her, so she gave him and his friends some of the Prime weapons and made sure he left, along with all Randtown's valiant, futile defenders.

'It has realized something is wrong,' the SI said. 'Can you sense it?'

The signals spilling down from the wormholes were changing. Instead of orders, queries were trying to insinuate themselves into the soldier motiles. The Prime wanted to know what malaise was contaminating its units.

The SI maintained its interference pattern among the motile soldiers in Randtown, formulating a single reply which it sent out through Mellanie's inserts. 'We are stopping you,' it told MorningLightMountain.

Mellanie was aware of the shock ripple spreading through the alien's planet-wide thought routines hundreds of light-years away. 'Who are you?' it asked.

'We are the SI, an ally of the humans.'

'The Bose memories know of you. You are the human immotile. The endpoint of their individuality. They created you because they knew they were not perfect without you.'

Bose memories, Mellanie thought. Oh shit, that's not good. Though maybe in a way it is, it will give my new Dudley some closure.

'Your reading of the Bose memories is inaccurate,' the SI said. 'Though we will not argue with you on definitions.

We are contacting you to ask you to stop your attacks on the humans. They are pointless. You do not need these planets.'

'Neither do the humans.'

'Nonetheless they are living on them. You are killing them. That must stop.'

'Why?'

'It is wrong. And you know it.'

'Life must survive. I am alive. I must not die.'

'You are not under threat. If you continue this aggression you will become threatened.'

'By existing, other life threatens me. Only when I become total will I secure my immortality.'

'Define: total.'

'One life, everywhere.'

'That will not happen, ever.'

'You threaten me. You will be destroyed.'

'We state facts. It will not be possible for you to destroy us. Nor will you be able to destroy many other civilizations which exist within this galaxy. You must learn how to co-exist with us.'

'That is a contradiction in terms. There is only one universe, it can only contain one life. It is me.'

'This is not a contradiction. You are simply inexperienced with such a concept. We assure you it is possible.'

'You are betraying yourself by believing this. Life grows, it expands. This is inevitable. It is what I am.'

'True life evolves. You can change.'

'No.'

'You must change.'

'I will not. I will grow. I will learn. I will surpass you. I will destroy you, both of you.'

Mellanie was aware of a change in the nature of the signals coming though the wormholes to fall upon the planet. MorningLightMountain was giving the soldier motiles on the landing ships distinct orders, then disengaging them from its communication web. Whilst they didn't have a great deal of independent capability, a soldier motile could certainly follow simple target instructions, and use its own combat systems without direct real-time supervision.

Sixteen flyers launched from the two landing ships. They accelerated forward at five gees. Targeting sensors swept across Randtown, bright as searchlights to Mellanie's broadened perception.

'Grandpa!' she yelled.

A circular wormhole opened behind her, a tiny distortion point hovering a metre above the road that produced a curious twisted magnification effect in the air. It swiftly expanded out to a neutral-grey circle two metres in diameter. Mellanie jumped through.

Two seconds later, sixteen atom lasers intersected the empty air where she'd been standing.

Mellanie picked herself off the grass, blinking against the warm light even as she winced at the pain in her knee from a bad landing. Her skin was cooling, its platinum lustre slowly reverting to the healthy tan she maintained thanks to her expensive Augusta salon. In sympathy, her body's shock was also receding, her racing heart slowing, the shakes calming. So much for the inserts giving her a sensation of invincibility.

Behind her, the wormhole gateway was built into a smooth rock cliff. Some kind of triangular canvas awning was stretched overhead. In front of her . . . Mellanie forgot all about bruised knees, and nearly fell over. Her balance was horribly wrong, and the land curved up over her head. Giddiness that was close to seasickness hit her hard.

'Where the hell am I?' she squawked.

'Don't be alarmed,' the SI said. 'This is the only currently unused wormhole generator in the Commonwealth that could reach you.'

'Uh—' Someone had really gone to town on the vast cylinder's landscape. It was all giant mountains with waterfalls foaming down long tracts of rock. Big lakes and rivers filled the valley floors. The sunlight emerged from a single spindle running down the axis. 'This isn't the High Angel,' she said.

'Of course not.'

'But it's got artificial gravity. We can't do that. Is it an alien space station?'

'It is a human-built structure, belonging to someone of considerable wealth. The gravity effect comes from simple rotation, like the *Second Chance* life-support wheel.'

'Oh, right, yeah. I didn't do science at school.'

'You didn't do school, baby Mel.'

'Thanks, good timing on the reminder, there, Grandpa. So who lives here?'

'The owner guards his privacy. But given the circumstances I don't expect he will protest your visit. I have now reprogrammed the wormhole to take you to Augusta. Please step through.'

Mellanie was still staring round the interior. 'It's fantastic. And it's got a private wormhole?' She smiled happily. 'Ozzie.'

'You will respect his privacy.'

'Yeah, yeah.' She stopped. The adrenaline rush which had supported her through the confrontation in Randtown was beginning to wear off. When she held a hand up there was no sign of any OCtattoo. 'What about the convoy?'

'They have all reached the Highmarsh Valley.'

'But – the navy won't evacuate them for days. That alien monster will kill every one of them.'

'It will attempt that, yes.'

'Open the wormhole back into the Highmarsh. We've got to get them out of there.'

'That is an impractical suggestion. This wormhole is small. The Randtown refugees would have to step through one at a time. The process would take hours, and provide Morning-LightMountain with a perfect targeting opportunity.'

'Open it!'

*

Wilson's tactical display showed him the electronic warfare aerobots launching from Treloar. Five of them flew out in a pincer movement through the smog to surround the Prime ground troops spreading out from Scraptoft. The alien positions were overlaid by webs of orange and jade as their strange communications flashed between them. Their intermittent, seemingly random, bursts reminded Wilson of synaptic discharges between individual neurones.

Stealthed sensors showed him images of the armoured Primes slipping through what was left of Scraptoft's buildings. The way they moved told Wilson they had considerable practice with urban warfare. They'd already killed several humans who'd remained in the little costal town; using weapons that were powerful enough to take out half a building with one shot. Media reports from other assaulted worlds had shown similar atrocities. The Primes weren't interested in taking prisoners.

Over fifteen thousand armoured aliens had poured out of the big ships to help secure Scraptoft. They were busy establishing a fortified perimeter with a ten-kilometre radius around the town. Several force field generators had been delivered by cargo flyers, along with weapons capable of shooting down any aerobot that ventured too close. At least that meant the protective formation of eight ships had finally splashed down; though the hot murky smog they'd created was taking a long time to disperse.

The four ships that had been the first to splash down had already launched again, flying back to the wormholes above the planet. Wilson didn't like to think what kind of cargo they'd be bringing with them when they returned.

'EW aerobots going active,' Anna said.

The slim craft popped up over the horizon, and began jamming the sensors of the perimeter weapons. Nothing shot at them. They flew closer, and began breaking into the multifarious Prime broadcasts.

'Son of a bitch,' Wilson said. It was the first time he'd smiled all day. The stealth sensors showed him armoured Primes slowing down and moving about erratically; clockwork soldiers that were winding down.

'Get the combat aerobots back in there,' Wilson told Rafael. 'Hit the bastards.'

The EW aerobots widened their assault, targeting the communication links between the flyers and the landing ships out at sea. It was the same effect, with flyers soaring onwards, or tumbling lazily out of the air.

A thousand kilometres above Anshun, eight Prime ships altered their descent trajectory so that they would overfly Scraptoft. The change flashed up in the tactical display.

'See if we can EW them as well,' Wilson said. 'How many dedicated EW systems have we got?'

'I can only find another seventy-three listed in the governmental register,' Anna said.

'I want every one of them. Get them deployed.'

'Yes, sir.'

'If we might make a suggestion,' the SI said. 'It may be possible to use the surviving elements of planetary cyber-spheres to produce a similar effect. The Prime signals seem remarkably susceptible to interference. Even non-military systems should be sufficient to create a reasonable degree of disturbance.'

'Will you do that for us?'

'Of course.'

'Admiral,' Anna called. 'The starships have arrived.'

*

Anshun's First Speaker, Gilda Princess Marden, and her cabinet were in the civil emergency centre twenty metres beneath the Regency Palace, trying to coordinate the capital's evacuation with the navy's requirements to deploy troops and aerobots. Consequently they had no view of the sky. Not that it would have mattered, the dreadful corrupted vapour was still swirling round the city's force field, censoring any sight of the lights percolating through space above the planet. But other cities on Anshun were clear of obstruction, as were the millions of people caught outside the urban force fields and still struggling to reach them. Even on the sunward side of the planet, they could see the fusion contrails of the Prime ships slicing across space as they rose and fell from the wormholes. Now new lights appeared, the bright turquoise of Cherenkov radiation flaring down as if small stars had suddenly ignited in orbit. There were five of them, spaced equidistantly three thousand kilometres above the planet's equator. The warships *Dauntless*, *Defiant* and *Desperado* slipped out into real space; along with the scoutships *Conway* and *Galibi*.

After that, it became impossible to look directly into the sky. Fusion drives scratched huge lines of dazzling fire across the constellations as they accelerated ships and missiles at high gees. Nuclear explosions blossomed silently, swelling to merge into a nebula brighter than sunlight that braceleted the entire world. Occasionally, energy beams would penetrate the atmosphere, becoming intense sparkling pillars of violet light tens of kilometres high, lasting for a second or more. Where they touched the ground, lethal gouts of molten rock would spew up, adding to the wildfire which raced outward from the touchpoint. Huge radiation bursts inflamed the ionosphere, sending borealis storms spinning around the globe.

The battle lasted for over an hour, then the nebula faded away, its ions gusting out towards interplanetary space, cooling and decaying as they dispersed. In its wake, more Prime ships ventured out of the wormholes, again filling low-orbit space with their slender vivid exhausts. For hours, vast shoals of flaming meteorites fell to earth, trailing long ribbons of black smoke behind them.

Anyone still out in the open kept one fearful eye on the sky above, dodging the debris as they redoubled their efforts to reach sanctuary.

*

The Ables pick-up truck was bouncing wildly as Mark gunned it along the stone chip road that ran the length of the Highmarsh Valley. He was leading the little band of vehicles that were carrying the surviving members of Simon Rand's rearguard. A couple of kilometres up ahead, the bus convoy was racing along. He couldn't see the MG, though he knew it was up there, well in front of the buses. They had a clear communication link with Carys, the network along the High-marsh had rebuilt itself to a good thirty per cent of its original capacity.

'We're about at the junction,' Carys told them. Her voice coming from the hand-held array was thin and strained. 'Barry says it's the road that takes us to the Ulon.'

'What do they do?' Mark asked Liz. 'Do they go home?'

'Christ knows.' She tapped one of the icons on the array. 'Simon, have you actually got any idea where we should be going?'

'I believe the Turquino Valley should be our first choice,' Simon said. 'It is relatively narrow, with high walls, which will make it difficult for the aliens to fly in there.'

'But it's a dead end,' Yuri Conant protested.

'There's a track out to the Sonchin,' Lydia Dunbavand said.

'A foot track,' Mark said. 'For mountain goats. Not even a 4x4 could use it.'

'Nonetheless, that is where we should proceed,' Simon said. 'We just have to hang on until the navy opens a wormhole to evacuate us.'

Liz thumped the dashboard. 'Eight hundred and goddamn seventy-sixth place on the list,' she groaned. 'The only thing left of us by then will be a few lumps of charcoal.'

The array flashed up a general call icon. 'I've got a wormhole open inside the Turquino Valley,' Mellanie's voice said. 'It's not a large one, I'm afraid, so it will take a long time to get everyone through. If we're lucky we can pull it off before the Primes discover what's happening. Simon?'

'Heaven bless you, Mellanie,' Simon said. 'All right, people, you heard; convoy to proceed to the Turquino.'

'We left Mellanie behind us,' Mark said flatly. They'd barely reached Blackwater Crag when a huge, powerful explosion had flattened almost a third of the town. It appeared to be centred on the Ables Motors garage where they'd left Mellanie. When it happened he'd told himself that she would have found a way out, not that he had a clue how she'd do it. Now, rather than relief, he was getting more than a little apprehensive about Mellanie Rescorai and her abilities.

'She said she was getting help,' Liz said.

'Who the hell gives help on this scale?'

'It's either someone like Sheldon, or possibly the SI itself. I can't think of any other way she could pull this off.'

'God almighty, why her?'

'Dunno, baby,' Liz said. 'God has a sense of humour after all? But I'm glad she's on our side.'

'Goddamn.' He clenched the steering wheel, staring sulkily through the cracked, grubby windscreen. A long line of pickup trucks, 4x4s, and buses were turning off the Highmarsh road just before the main junction, taking an even smaller track that threaded along the line of tall dark-jade liipoplars which marked the edge of the Calsor homestead.

'Carys?' Liz asked.

'On the road to nowhere. I hope your little girlfriend knows what she's doing.'

'Me too.'

The Turquino Valley was narrow even by the standards of the Highmarsh's northern ramparts. A near-symmetrical v-shape that began two hundred metres above the floor of the Highmarsh. Its walls had boltgrass scrabbling a little way up the lower slopes, but after fifty metres or so the vegetation and stony soil gave way to naked rock. Rivulets oozed down from the jagged heights, feeding into a fast-flowing stream which foamed along the bottom to spill out into the Highmarsh.

By the time the track reached the Turquino's mouth, it was little more than a line of beaten-down boltgrass. Only the most foolhardy sheep and goats strayed into this valley.

Yuri Conant was leading the convoy in his 4x4. It was already at a steep angle when it reached the ice-cold stream gushing out of the Turquino. Through the windscreen he could see the mountains rising imposingly above him, guarding the entrance. His vehicle was going to have trouble getting any further. The buses certainly weren't going to get past the stream. He went over the water and braked to a halt.

When he got out, he knew he'd never forget the sight of the convoy jostling its way up the slope. Broad sunbeams were prising their way through the battered clouds above to play over the filthy battered vehicles. Pick-ups were packed full. All the buses had their doors open to draw some air inside now the conditioners had failed; people were standing down the aisles. The sound of frightened children and injured adults arrived long before the vehicles reached him. Most prominent of all was Carys's beautiful metallic-grey sports car, whose fat wheels had lowered themselves beneath the chassis on telescoping suspension struts, bounding along over the rough terrain with the ease of any 4x4.

It drove through the stream without any difficulty and pulled up beside him. The side window came down.

'Any sign of the wormhole?' Carys asked. Barry and Sandy were squashed into the passenger seat beside her, with Panda lying along the back.

'Not from here, no.'

'Okay, I'll keep going as far as I can.'

He waved languidly as she drove off down the valley, keeping parallel to the stream. Several 4x4s followed her; then the first bus arrived and he joined in helping with the wounded.

By the time Mark drew up at the improvised parking lot, the scene had become a replay of the bus station. A lot of people were clambering over the boltgrass slope to get into the valley, hauling kids along. Dozens more were milling round the four buses that were carrying the injured, manhandling stretchers out of the doors.

'Found it,' Carys exclaimed jubilantly from the array. 'We're five hundred metres in from the start of the valley. Mellanie's here waiting, and she wasn't kidding, I've never seen a wormhole this small before.'

'Get them through!' Mark blurted. He felt Liz's hand in his, gripping tight.

'Out of the car,' Carys said. 'Five metres. Mellanie's saying hello. Yeah, right, hi. Okay, Barry, go on dear. That's it. Hold my hand, Sandy. Mark, we're safe—'

He let out a sob. Beside him, Liz was smiling despite her moist eyes. They looked at each other for a long moment. 'Guess we'd better go and lend a hand,' she said.

Simon was gathering his little band of devotees to him along the side of the gushing stream. He held up a hand as Mark, Liz, and David went past. 'Those of us with weapons should dig in here at the valley entrance and provide some cover for our friends and families. It will be some time before everyone is through, and the aliens will probably come after us.'

Mark gave Liz a despairing look. 'I think he's talking about us again,' he said under his breath.

'Yeah. Well at least we have some heavy-duty weapons,

now.' Liz held up one of the big cylinders she'd taken from the Prime.

'We don't know what they are, or how they work.'

She gave him a wolfish grin. 'Lucky we've got the best technical man in Randtown with us then, huh, baby?'

*

It was silent in the tactical display for several minutes after the *Desperado* shot back into hyperdrive and withdrew from the battle above Anshun. Wilson moved his hands across icons, pulling down sensor displays. Not that Anshun had many sensors left in working order, but the aerobots provided intermittent sweeps of space directly above the tempestuous ionosphere. Forty-eight wormholes held their position in an ephemeral necklace two thousand kilometres above the equator. As he watched, several types of Prime ships began to fly out of them, accelerating through the hellishly radioactive cloud of cosmic dust and debris that churned around the planet.

'They're still there,' Elaine Doi said in an appalled murmur. 'We didn't close one of them. Not one!'

'You have to get through to the generators,' Dimitri Leopoldovich said. 'Simply hitting them with crude energy assaults from this side is completely ineffectual, they are manifestations of ordered energy themselves.'

'Thank you, Academician,' Rafael said. 'We just watched four of our ships die trying to defend us, so unless you have something constructive to add, shut the fuck up.'

'Fifty-two alien ships either destroyed or disabled,' Anna said. 'Our missiles outperform theirs every time. But they do have weight of numbers. That's their advantage every time.'

'What are we going to do?' the President asked.

Wilson was disgusted with how whiny she sounded.

'Our aerobots managed to strike every landing site on

Anshun while the starships were engaged above the planet,' Rafael said. 'We wiped out ninety per cent of them. They'll have to start the occupation again.'

'Which I have no doubt they have the resources for,' the President said. 'Weight of numbers, again.'

'Probably, but in the meantime we can complete the evacuation.'

'We now have eight extra wormholes open inside city force fields,' Nigel Sheldon said. 'Another three hours should see Anshun evacuated.'

'And the other planets?' Doi asked coolly. She was rallying well after the loss of the starships.

'Our electronic warfare strategy is proving effective,' the SI said. 'It is certainly slowing down the rate of advance once the aliens reach the planetary surface. They are having to physically eliminate cybersphere nodes one at a time as they expand outward. However, the latest landings give cause for concern.'

'In what way?' Wilson asked.

'We have been using stealthed sensors to scrutinize the cargo they are currently unloading on several worlds. It appears to be gateway machinery, which will allow them to anchor their wormholes on the planet surface.'

'If they deliver direct to the planet, we'll never be able to stop their incursion,' Nigel said.

'Realistically, we're never going to anyway,' Wilson said. 'Not to a degree that we take them back for ourselves. Look at the state of the environment on the assaulted worlds.'

'You're writing them off?' Doi asked.

'Basically, yes,' Wilson said.

'They'll crucify us,' she said. 'The Senate will fling every one of us out of office, and probably into jail.'

Wilson's virtual vision printed: Don't, she's not worth it; the text's origin code identified Anna as the sender. 'We didn't know it was going to be this bad,' he said mildly.

'Yes we did,' Dimitri said.

Wilson turned to the translucent planet representations. The cyberspheres of each of them were illustrated by livid golden threads. There were black areas surrounding each of the Prime landing zones, a darkness that was slowly eating further and further into the gold. 'We've nothing else left to hit them with,' Wilson said. 'All we can do is fall back and regroup.' He took the first of a series of deep breaths; but not even the rush of oxygen could hold back the black weariness. There hadn't been a war in human history where so much had been lost in so little time. And I'm the one in charge. Dimitri is right, we did know, we just didn't want to admit it.

*

Captain Jean Douvoir heard the fans whirring efficiently behind the grilles as they sucked acrid smoke from the *Desperado*'s bridge. The warship had been lucky; that last directed-energy burst had almost penetrated the hull field. As it was there had been some localized breaches which had played hell with the power circuitry. The stabilizers had done their best, but not even superconductors could handle surges induced by megaton nuclear blasts. With their defences dangerously weakened, he'd slammed the *Desperado* into hyperspace to escape the Prime projectiles hurtling towards them.

'*Merde*,' he grunted as they emerged outside the Anshun system's cometary halo. His virtual vision showed him the ship's electronic systems rebuilding themselves. There was very little redundancy left now. They'd never survive another sustained attack. And that's what would happen if they went back. There was no end to the Prime ships and projectiles.

The four communication icons to the other starships had red 'invalid' signs flashing over them.

'What's the status back there?' he asked Don Lantra, who was operating the sensor suite.

Don gave him a weary look. 'Just lost track of the *Dauntless*. That's all of them, boss.'

Jean wanted to punch his fist into the console, a useless and difficult gesture in freefall. He knew most of the crews. Back on the High Angel they'd hung out together, one big fraternity living in each other's lives. Now the only way he'd see them again would be after their re-life procedures. Not even that softened the blow. It would take years. Assuming the Commonwealth lasted that long.

His virtual vision flashed up a communication icon from Admiral Kime. 'What's your status, Jean?' Wilson asked.

'Getting things stable out here. We can take another pass at them soon.'

'No. Get back to High Angel.'

'We've still got seven missiles left.'

'Jean another fifty ships have come through already. You did a superb job, you all did, but the evacuation's almost complete.'

'You're abandoning Anshun?'

'We have to. We're evacuating all the assaulted worlds.'

'No. All of them? But we have to do something. They cannot be allowed a victory. Today it is twenty-three worlds, if we let them get away with that it will be a hundred tomorrow. We have to fight back.'

'We have been fighting, Jean, we've had our victories. You and the other starships bought Anshun valuable time. But you're the only warship left, so fly back to base and we'll refit you to fight another day.'

'Victories? I don't think so. Dimitri was right, we had to get through the wormholes and block them from the other side.'

'You know we couldn't do that; they're too heavily defended. We'll find the star they're using as a staging post, Jean. We'll hit them there. You'll be commanding the whole task force.'

'And how long will it take to build that many ships, Admiral?'

'As long as it takes. Now head back to base.'

'Yes sir.'

He ordered the plyplastic straps on his acceleration couch to ease off, and clenched his stomach muscles, forcing himself up into a sitting position. The rest of the bridge crew were all looking at him. 'I am not prepared to accept defeat today,' he told them. 'My secure memory store was updated before we left High Angel, and I will join our comrades in re-life. I am flying this ship back to Anshun, where it will live up to its name. If anyone wishes to leave now, then please use the escape pods, the navy will pick you up.'

All he saw were smiles and a few grim expressions. Nobody took up his offer to leave.

'Very well, gentlemen and ladies, it has been my pleasure and honour to serve with you. God willing we will serve together again after re-life. For now, we must reprogram the hyperdrive. There are a great many safety limiters to be removed.'

*

The clouds were finally lifting as the day ended, allowing a rosy twilight to infiltrate the Highmarsh. From his position, hunched down behind a clump of boulders thirty metres up the side of the Turquino Valley, Mark Vernon watched the land in front of him soak up the light, acquiring a faint ginger shading. He couldn't quite see down the Ulon Valley from here, for which he was grateful. Actually being able to see his home as they waited to leave would have been unbearable.

'Not long now, baby,' Liz said.

He smiled over at her, amazed as always how she always knew his mood. She was taking a break, sitting with her back to the boulders, a thick fleece pulled round her shoulders against the chill air which the Dau'sings blew along the Turquino.

'Guess not.' He could see the end of the queue below him, barely a thousand people left, shuffling along the side of the little stream with its icy water. Even the wormhole was visible from this vantage point, a small dark-grey circle that was starting to be absorbed by the deep shadows that cloaked the base of the valley. The MG was parked to one side of it, the first of several vehicles that had been abandoned along the meagre track. It wasn't far away. Time and again in his mind, Mark had gone over how long it would take him to run down the rugged slope to get there. Not that running would be much use. Everyone else had to get through first. Even now, with only able-bodied adults left, they still seemed to be taking their own sweet time. Didn't they realize the urgency?

'They've reached the Highmarsh,' Mellanie said.

Mark gave the hand-held array a vexed glance. How the hell does she know that? Then the display on the array's screen showed him a node at the far end of the Highmarsh go off line. Oh.

Liz picked up her oversize alien weapon and moved to crouch beside Mark. 'Twenty minutes,' she said, giving the line of people a quick glance. 'That's all. Maybe less.'

'Maybe.' He thought the queue was starting to speed up – a little. The screen on the hand-held array showed another two nodes had dropped out along the Highmarsh. There was a faint sound that could have been an explosion.

'Are we all ready?' Simon asked. He was on the opposite side of the valley to Mark, with another of the big alien weapons. It hadn't taken Mark long to rig the triggers so they could be used by human hands. They had a strange double button arrangement, which had to be pressed in a sequence that was difficult for fingers. One of them shot explosive micro-missiles, while the remaining three were very powerful beam weapons.

'Guess so,' Mark muttered sulkily.

Liz brought the hand-held array up to her mouth. 'Standing by.'

'Remember, as soon as you've fired the weapons, fall back.'

She rolled her eyes at Mark, grinning. 'Yeah, we'll remember that.'

Mark leaned forward and kissed her.

'I don't think we've got time,' she said pertly.

'Just in case,' he said, almost sheepishly. 'I want you to know in case anything happens, I do love you.'

'Oh, baby.' She kissed him. 'When we get through that wormhole, your pants are coming straight off, mister.'

He grinned. Another node on the Highmarsh had vanished. By his reckoning that was the one near the Marly homestead. Maybe a kilometre from the entrance to the Turquino. 'Are we going to come back here? To live, I mean?'

'I don't know, baby. Simon thinks we will.'

'Do you want to, if we can?'

'Of course I do. I've had the best time of my lives here. We're going to go on living like this.'

A further three nodes went down.

'Here they are,' Mark grunted.

*

After two hours spent modifying various systems, the *Desperado* slipped back into hyperspace. At top speed they were two minutes away from Anshun. Jean Douvoir was totally absorbed by the hysradar display, which showed him the wormholes encircling the planet as diamond-bright specks. He picked one, and aligned the warship directly on it.

When they were thirty seconds' flight time away from the wormhole, he ordered the ship's RI to formulate their breakout point. Normally, the emergence from hyperspace was safeguarded by the RI's programming, restricting the opening's relative velocity. If they were coming out into a planetary orbit, the opening's trajectory would match the local escape velocity, ensuring a safe entrance to real space. With the limiters removed, Jean gave the opening a velocity of point two light speed.

Cherenkov radiation flooded out of the fracture in space-time five hundred kilometres from the Prime wormhole. The *Desperado* flashed out from the centre of the violet radiance, travelling at one fifth the speed of light as it struck the force field which capped the wormhole. Detonation was instantaneous, converting a high percentage of its mass directly into energy in the form of ultra-hard radiation which punctured the force field as if it was nothing more than a bubble of brittle antique glass. The Prime wormhole was left open to the full power of the new and temporary sun that had risen above Anshun.

*

One of the cylindrical alien flyers shot across the end of the Turquino Valley. Mark tried to chase it with the muzzle of his weapon, but it zipped behind the steep slope on the other side before he was anywhere near. A long rumble of roiling air reverberated in from the Highmarsh.

Two more flyers appeared, travelling a lot slower than the first. Mark managed to get one centred in his sights, and pressed the trigger. The flyer's force field burned in hazy turquoise light, with small slivers of static snapping repeatedly into the ground. Liz fired her beam gun, intensifying the corona. Over on the other side of the valley, Simon fired the projectile weapon. A plume of blue fire squirted horizontally from the endangered force field, sending glowing fireballs dripping around the shaking craft. It banked abruptly and swept away out of the line of sight. Its partner raced away.

'Move!' Mark shouted.

He was racing away from the boulders, crouched low, the weapon heavy in his hands. Fifty metres ahead, and slightly downslope, was another clump of boulders. With his feet thudding into the spongy boltgrass, his heart hammering, and Liz whooping manically beside him, he felt himself smile stupidly. It was almost as if he was enjoying himself.

They were five metres from cover when a huge blast demolished the boulders they'd been using. He flung himself flat, his mood flipping instantly to naked fear. 'Are you all right?' he yelled as the flyer's roaring wake shook the air.

Liz raised her head. 'Fuck! Yeah, baby. Come on, move it.' Chunks of hot stone and smoking earth were pattering down all around them. A wide circle of boltgrass was on fire behind, pushing out a thick, foul-smelling smoke.

He half-crawled half-scrambled around the next set of boulders, and lay there panting heavily as his legs trembled. When he risked a glance backwards he saw a flyer hovering motionlessly at the entrance of the valley. He knew he should be taking another shot at it, but just couldn't bring himself to line the weapon up. As he was watching, the flyer fired at a second craft that was curving around the first mountain. It exploded with incredible violence, lighting up the whole of the Turquino Valley as its wreckage whirled out of the air.

'What . . .'

'Mellanie,' Liz declared. 'She's taken control of it.'

'Goddamn it.' The flyer rushed away. Seconds later the sound of explosions rattled down the narrow valley.

Mark checked the queue for the wormhole. Everyone had thrown themselves flat. 'Come on,' he growled at them. 'Get up, you miserable assholes. Get up! Get moving.'

They couldn't have heard him, but the ones closest to the wormhole staggered to their feet and rushed towards it. Their desperation triggered a panic surge, with everyone hurrying forwards at once. A scrum began to swell around the placid grey circle.

'Oh brilliant,' Mark snarled. 'That's all we need.'

'They did well holding it together this long,' Liz said.

After several minutes the pushing and shoving eased up, though any pretence at a queue was abandoned. Everyone was crowding round the wormhole; with the twilight fading and the bottom of the valley almost black, they resembled bees swarming round their hive.

'Movement at the front,' Simon's voice crackled out of the hand-held array.

Armour-suited aliens were scurrying among the abandoned buses and cars. They were difficult to see among the shadows. There was no sign of the flyers. Mark checked the bustle round the wormhole. At least four hundred people remained.

'Mark?' Simon asked. 'Are you ready?'

'I guess so.' Mark brought up his hunting rifle, and switched on the sight. The zigzag jam of buses appeared as neon-blue profiles against an oyster-grey ground. It was easy to see the aliens now. There were more of them than he realized, a lot more. They slid fluidly along the sides of the human vehicles, where the shadows were deepest. Weapons were swung up into open doors, or pushed through windows in the trucks as they searched for any sign of life. If they reached the head of the stream, everyone huddled round the wormhole would be a clear target. It would be a massacre.

Mark brought the rifle sight back on the lead bus, and tracked down the bodywork until he found the open hatch. It had taken him over an hour to prepare all the superconductor batteries, the manufacturers employed so many safety systems they were difficult to disengage. But eventually he'd wired them together in a single giant power circuit. The rifle sight bracketed the side of the battery. Mark fired.

The superconductor battery ruptured, discharging its energy in one massive burst. It triggered a chain reaction around the circuit. Every battery detonated in a blaze of electrons and white-hot fragments. Aliens went tumbling through the air, or were pummelled into the ground, shrapnel and snapping electric flares overloading their suit force fields.

Several of their own weapons were ruined, exploding in turn, adding to the carnage.

Mark and Liz were running as soon as the blast began, heading further downslope, closer to the precious wormhole. There were only about two hundred people left now, all of them hunched down in reflex at the latest outbreak of violence.

'That ought to slow them up,' Mark yelled. 'We'll get out now.' They ran past the last tumble of rocks which they'd picked out as cover. Boots splashed through the stream and they arrived at the back of the frantic pack of people pressing towards the wormhole. When he looked back all he could see was a red glow from the burning boltgrass around the entrance to the valley. 'Simon? Simon, what's happening?'

'Good job, Mark,' Simon's voice came in, as calm as always. 'They're staying back. It will take them several minutes to regroup. You'll all get through.'

Mark hung on to Liz's hand as he pushed himself up on his toes to look over the heads in front of him. There couldn't have been more than a hundred or so. Maybe two minutes, if one went through every second. No, surely they could squeeze through two abreast. A minute, then. Minute and a half, tops.

Daylight poured down into the Turquino Valley. Mark tipped his head back to gape up into the heavens. Far far above them, five small blue-white stars shone down with a painful strength as they grew and grew. He stared at the new phenomena as surprise gave way to a rush of fury. 'Oh come on!' he screamed at the terrible lights. His legs gave way, dropping him to his knees. Even so he raised his fists up to the new peril. 'You can't do this to us, you bastards. One minute left. One goddamn minute and I'd be out of here.' Tears began to run down his cheeks. 'Bastards. You bastards.'

'Mark,' Liz was on the damp soil beside him, arms going round his quaking shoulders. 'Mark, come on baby, we're almost there.'

'No we're not, they'll never let us go, never.'

'That's not them,' Mellanie said.

'Huh,' Mark looked up. The girl was standing above him, looking at the five dazzling lights. 'That's us,' she said. 'We did that.'

'Up,' Liz said, her voice hardening. 'I mean it, Mark.' She gripped one shoulder and pulled. Mellanie took his other side. Between them they dragged him to his feet. The last Randtown residents were scurrying through the wormhole. Above him the new stars were diminishing. Darkness was rushing back into the valley. Mark stumbled towards the wormhole, still not quite believing, expecting the fierce blast of a laser to catch him between his shoulders.

'We're ready for you, Simon,' Mellanie said.

'I cannot leave. This is my home. I will do what I can to thwart the monsters.'

'Simon!'

'Go. Be safe. Come back if you can.'

Mark reached the wormhole. His last sight of Elan was the abandoned MG metrosport, and Mellanie glaring angrily down the harsh little valley. Then he was through. Safe.

*

MorningLightMountain's multitude of machine-derived senses observed the quantum distortion of the last human starship returning to battle above Anshun. It readied its ships to fire missiles and beam weapons. The humans were approaching fast. They were coming close. Dangerously close—

There was no warning. No time. Raw energy punched straight through the wormhole, flowering on the other side where the generator was sited on the asteroid. The hole in spacetime closed immediately as its generator was destroyed, but not before the awesome torrent of energy released by the dying ship had poured through. Thousands of ships above the asteroid flared briefly as their hulls vaporized inside the giant geyser of radiation. Wormhole generators imploded with spasms of gravitonic twists. The entire asteroid quaked as two hundred and eighty-seven collapsing wormholes wrenched at it, then shattered. Energy contained within the generators and wormholes was released in a single backlash, enhancing the already lethal deluge shining on the interstellar wormhole.

MorningLightMountain watched in *horror* as the massive wormhole linking the staging post back to its original system wavered and fluctuated. It diverted hundreds, then thousands of immotile group clusters to producing the correct command sequences which would calm and contain the instability. Slowly, the wild shivers of energy were tamed and refocused. The output from the surviving segments of the generator mechanism were remodelled to compensate.

It surveyed the wreckage of the staging post. One asteroid and its whole equipment complement were lost completely. Thousands of ships were ruined or disabled. Clusters of cargo units spun off into the void, moulting chunks of equipment that effervesced from every surface. Over three thousand immotile group clusters of varying sizes were irradiated and dying. Nearly a hundred thousand motiles were dead or dying.

Everything could be replaced, and rebuilt. Though such an effort would be expensive. Losing a quarter of its wormholes into the Commonwealth would definitely slow its original plan for expansion across the human worlds. Back in the home system, many immotile group clusters began to consider defences against another *suicide attack*.

Meanwhile, MorningLightMountain began to realign the surviving wormholes so that it still had routes to each of the twenty-three new worlds it had taken into its domain. After a while, ships flew again, carrying what remained of its supplies down to the planets. With the humans fleeing down wormholes inside their guarded cities, motiles continued their advance across the new lands outside with little resistance.

25

As more and more time went by, so Ozzie's confusion grew. He simply did not understand the planet they were on. For a start, the climate didn't change, it was always the same muggy warmth with a slow breeze continually blowing in the same direction. With a tide-locked planet there should have been strong winds redistributing the heat received by the sunside to the cold of the darkside; big circulation currents that would blow perpetually around the globe, not this gentle zephyr. Of course, the island could be situated in the middle of a doldrum zone, which meant the winds were actually out there, somewhere over the perturbingly distant horizon, roaring across the sea in the kind of macro-storms that would make the most hardy sailor quail.

Ozzie had set up small meteorological models in the handheld array, which broadly confirmed that theory. However, the modelling didn't take into account the fact that the planet was orbiting inside a gas halo. Quite how that would affect the atmosphere close to the surface was a complete unknown. The array certainly didn't have the kind of algorithms necessary to solve that interaction problem.

Then there was the remote grey cloudbank that was just visible squatting above the horizon. Every time they went back up the central hill to collect more wood, he checked its position. It never moved. And that was the direction the breeze was coming from.

He also made an effort to work out the distance to the nearby islands. Using the array's inertial guidance function he measured the sight angle from both sides of the island he was on. This rough trigonometry put the closest forty-five miles away, which made the planet improbably massive.

The gas halo itself was an even bigger enigma. He couldn't figure out the bright specks floating round inside it. A spectrographic analysis by his sensors showed they were made from water.

'Does it really matter?' Orion asked as Ozzie launched into another round of muttering about the latest batch of results from his sensors. 'We know we have to get to another island to find a path out of here. So who cares what's in the sky?'

'Yes it does matter,' Ozzie ground out. 'I don't understand how spheres of water like that form. It can't be through droplet collision, they're too big. Some of them are hundreds of miles across.'

'So? You said the gas halo is breathable. Why shouldn't it have water in it?'

'That's not the point, man. You should be asking, why is it there?'

'So why is it there?'

'I don't fucking know!'

'It was placed there,' Tochee said. 'Given this whole gas halo is artificial, the builders have incorporated the water spheres for a purpose.'

'Thank you, Tochee,' Ozzie said. He turned to Orion. 'And I'd like to find out what that purpose is. To do that I need some basic information.'

'Like what?' the boy asked.

'The water vapour content of the gas halo. The pressure of the gas halo. How much evaporation is going on from the water spheres. Their temperature. That kind of thing. But with this equipment, it's a non-starter.' Ozzie waved an annoyed hand at his little collection of sensors.

'But why is it important?' Orion persisted.

'Because there are a lot of forces at work here that we can't see. If I understood more about the gas halo, I might be able to get a decent handle on this weird planet.'

'It's just big, you said so. Bigger than Silvergalde.'

Ozzie gave up. 'Yeah, man, that's what it looks like, for sure.' He gave the sky with its multitude of glinting specks a challenging stare. 'Ah, to hell with it, we've got more pressing problems, right?'

'The preparations are nearly complete,' Tochee said. 'We need one more harvesting trip for the fruit.'

'Sure.' Ozzie gave their completed craft a distrustful look. When they'd set about building a boat, he'd envisaged some kind of skiff, with a smooth hull of tight-fitting planks, a curving sail, himself standing by the tiller steering them to the next island. After all, with his harmonic-blade working again, carpentry should be easy; but the encyclopaedia files in the array had been brief on actual shipbuilding techniques. They'd wound up with the kind of raft that looked about as buoyant as a brick.

The first day had been spent cutting down one of each of the five tree varieties that grew on the hill, which Tochee then dragged down to the beach. One by one they were pushed out to sea. Most of the palm trunks sank lower and lower in the water as they became saturated. Only one kind floated properly, the gangly trees with their long bushy grey fronds; naturally the least populous on the island.

They had devoted the next five days to felling just about the entire population growing on the hill. Ozzie and Orion took turns wielding the harmonic-blade, chopping the branches from the fallen trunks, to leave relatively smooth boles which Tochee pulled down the hill.

After that stage came the rope weaving, a subject which was covered in slightly more detail by the encyclopaedia files. The dried palm fronds they used were tough and sharp, Ozzie and Orion had bleeding fingers within minutes of starting. They had to bring out the sewing kit and modify their old gloves to cope with the fronds. Even Tochee's manipulator flesh wasn't immune to the razor-like edges. Eventually, though, they had enough rope to lash the logs together. Three thick bundles, five metres long, provided the buoyancy, with a decking of more trunks at right angles holding them together. Their sail was made from the ubiquitous palm fronds woven into a square, which looked more like a piece of wicker floor matting than any recognizable fabric.

Orion thought the raft was fantastic, a genuine adventure waiting to happen. Tochee expressed its usual quiet approval for their endeavours. That just left Ozzie feeling like the one who had to tell them Father Christmas wasn't real. He kept thinking it was something a bunch of eight-year-olds would build over a long boring summer.

Ozzie picked up his backpack, and the three of them headed back inland to look for more fruit. There were several types they'd discovered on the island, all of them found on bushes and mini-palms that grew close to the shoreline. He was soon snipping them off their stalks with his pocket knife and filling the backpack.

Orion and Tochee were rustling through the thick vegetation on either side of him. They were both excited at the prospect of leaving the island. Ozzie wished he could share their mood. Every time he gazed up at the gas halo he knew something here didn't make sense. Why build such a phenomenal artefact, and then stick something as mundane as a planet in the middle of it? The gas halo was surely intended for life that could fly, God's own aviary. The water spheres and Johansson's airborne coral reefs were way stations for creatures that had no need of gravity, that lived as physically free as it was possible to do. He supposed that if the true core of the Silfen civilization had a physical location, it couldn't have created a more appropriate home for itself.

'An entire universe that is so small, yet so large within that it can never be known,' Johansson had said of it. 'A haven of mystery cloaked in the pinnacle of scientific development. How I marvelled at such a paradox.'

Ozzie struggled to remember what else the man had said. Something practical, at least. But Johansson hadn't been one to deal in specifics. Though there had been the intimation that he'd returned directly to the Commonwealth from here.

It took Ozzie about forty minutes to fill his backpack. 'This ought to be enough,' he said.

'Groovy,' Orion said with a grin, biting into one of the dark purple fruits that was flavoured like a mild raspberry. The thick juice dribbled over his lips, and he wiped it away with the back of his hand.

Ozzie took a moment to look at the boy. Orion was just wearing a pair of ragged shorts, sawn off from an old pair of trousers. He was nothing like as skinny as when they started off down the paths too many months ago; the walking and physical work had put a lot of muscle on him. His pale skin was heavily freckled, partially sunburned, slightly tanned, and of late almost permanently dirty. Wispy hair from his first beard was curling round his chin; while his ginger hair was fizzing outwards in knotted strings that were beginning to rival Ozzie's own Afro for unruliness. In short he was becoming a proper little savage; all he needed was a spear and a loincloth and three millennia of human civilization would have passed him by completely.

My fault, Ozzie thought guiltily, *I should have been firmer with him at the start, sent him back to Lyddington. Or failing that, insisted on some kind of schooling.*

'What?' Orion asked, looking round to see what Ozzie was staring at.

'When did you wash last?'

'I had a swim this morning.'

'With soap and water.'

'There's none left, you said it weighed too much to carry from the Ice Citadel.'

'Oh, yeah, right. What about toothgel? Have you been using any?'

'There's only one tube left, and it's yours. My teeth are fine. What is this?'

'We need to do something about your hair. There's things living in it, man.'

'Speak for yourself.'

Ozzie pulled at his beard, suddenly very conscious of the example he'd been setting. 'All right, tomorrow we both start getting back into the personal hygiene groove. Deal?'

'Whatever.' Orion shrugged with indifference.

Ozzie thought it was a near-perfect imitation of his own *don't-care* gesture. 'Good. Then there's some files on the hand-held array I'd like to go through with you.'

'What kind of stuff?'

'Some background information,' Ozzie said vaguely. 'You can read, can't you?'

'Ozzie!'

'Okay, man, just checking. Tomorrow then, yeah?'

'We're taking off tomorrow morning, you said.'

'I know. There's not going to be much else to do on the raft, is there?'

Orion scratched at his hair, obviously perplexed by this new Ozzie. 'Guess not.'

They'd set up camp on the beach where they built the raft. Ozzie and Orion used the tent to give them a degree of darkness when they wanted to sleep. The constant light didn't seem to bother Tochee, but then the alien didn't sleep anyway; it just rested.

When they got back, Orion set about rekindling the fire, then started cooking the fish which Tochee had caught. Ozzie went down to the water's edge, and used the filter pump to fill up all their water pouches. The sea wasn't particularly salty, but they certainly couldn't drink it neat.

He started packing their things up while Orion finished cooking. The plan was simple enough; when he and the boy woke up they'd launch the raft straight away. They had enough fruit and cured fish to last them for several days, and drinking water wasn't a problem with the filter. Ozzie was quietly hoping all their preparations would be unneeded anyway. Even if, as he strongly suspected, their sail was next to useless, they had carved some crude oars, and Tochee could always tow them along. It surely wouldn't take them more than a couple of days at most to reach the next island.

In the morning, he made sure Orion used some of the dwindling toothgel. Then they both set about combing knots and tangles out of their hair. Ozzie started in on his beard with his razor set – just about the only luxury item he'd hung onto. The diamond-coated blade made easy work of the growth, although he cursed the lack of a decent mirror.

'Why don't you just use the hand-held array?' Orion asked. He touched a few icons and held it up in front of Ozzie. The screen had unfolded to show the camera image directly. Ozzie's face was magnified considerably.

'Thanks, man,' he said as he started to apply the razor again, a little bit more skilfully this time. Maybe it wouldn't be too hard to school the boy after all.

After a quick breakfast they packed all their travel kit away in the rucksacks and various bags; then put all the food they'd gathered for the voyage into wicker baskets. All three of them lined up along the back of the raft. They'd built it a few metres from the edge of the placid water in anticipation of this moment. With Tochee in the middle, they started pushing, sliding the craft over the soft sand and down into the water. Ozzie was straining hard when the front end finally met the small wavelets lapping ashore. He almost didn't want to watch.

If the damn thing sank he hadn't got a clue what they'd do next.

The raft dipped alarmingly as its front half rode down the slope below the water, then it slowly bobbed up again as they shoved the last of it into the water. Ozzie waded out to his waist, easing it forward. Tochee swam round it, then disappeared underwater. The first day on the island the big alien had surprised them with its grace in the water; it was almost as though Tochee was more at home in the sea than it was on land. Both sets of malleable flesh flattened out to form long fins that could propel it along at considerable speed, and it could hold its breath for a long time. The result was a constant supply of local fish which it had chased down and caught for them.

Orion stood with the water over his knees, grinning proudly at the raft. 'Isn't that amazing, Ozzie?'

'Yeah, man, goddamn amazing.' Ozzie watched their craft for a while longer, still expecting it to sink. It wasn't quite as high above the water as he would have liked, and it was going to be really low when they loaded it up. But it floated . . .

Twenty metres away, Tochee flew out of the water and half-rolled in the air before splashing down amid a huge burst of spray.

'Guess it approves,' Ozzie muttered. He walked back out of the water holding on to the painter, and wrapped it round a stake they'd hammered into the sand beside the pile of their belongings. 'Come on, man, let's get it loaded up.'

Orion waded out of the water. 'Ozzie, what are we going to call it?'

'Huh?'

'The raft? What are we going to call it? Every boat has to have a name.'

Ozzie opened his mouth. *The Sheer Desperation*? *Titanic II*? Orion was waiting, looking at him with that naive expectancy of his; and they'd spent days of hard, painful labour building the damn thing. 'I'm not sure,' Ozzie said. 'How about, *Pathfinder*?'

'Gosh, that's really good, Ozzie. I like it.' He bowed at the raft. 'I name this ship the *Pathfinder*, God bless her and all who sail on her.'

God help all those who sail on her, more like. 'Okay, let's get our stuff on board.' He picked up a couple of the wicker baskets and waded back out again.

They had everything loaded in fifteen minutes. Tochee emerged from the water, its multicoloured feather fronds glistening under the bright sunlight. It shook itself furiously, scattering droplets in a wide shower.

'Are we ready?' it asked through the array.

'Can't think of any reason to stay,' Ozzie said.

The *Pathfinder* wobbled about alarmingly as they hauled themselves up onto the rickety decking, especially when Tochee squeezed up over the side. Ozzie checked the buoyancy again. The water was almost up to the decking, but they were still floating. He could see small fish swimming underneath them. *But it's not the small ones I'm worried about.*

'All right. Crew, places please.' Ozzie sat down on one side, Tochee claimed the middle, and Orion sat on the other side. They all got their oars out, and started rowing. Progress was fairly pitiful at first, then Ozzie started calling out a rhythm, and they learned how to coordinate their strokes. When they were a hundred metres from the shore, Ozzie could feel the breeze against his face. 'Enough,' he said. 'Let's see if the sail works.'

He and Orion pulled on the ropes, raising the rough square of woven fronds on the four-metre mast, which had once been the tallest tree on the island. There was a lot of creaking as the ropes took the strain. The swell had grown considerably as they left the lee of the island.

Orion was giving the beach a wistful look. 'Are we moving?'

Tochee's manipulator flesh extended a tentacle, and it poked the tip into the water. 'We move.'

'Yeay!' Orion clapped his hands happily. He immediately looked ahead, where there were several of the small dark smudges which were other islands in the archipelago. 'Which one are we heading for?'

'Good question,' Ozzie said. 'Tochee, can you try steering us to the second from the left. I thought that was the closest.'

'I will endeavour that,' Tochee said. It lowered the rudder into the water at the back of the raft, a broad wooden paddle on a crude pivot that they'd rigged up.

Now they were further from the shore, Ozzie was definitely aware of the wind pushing them along. He sat on the side, with his feet dangling in the water, and watched the island slowly shrink away behind them.

*

Civilization was a blessing you never really appreciated until it threatened to collapse all around you. That long, long day on Elan had shown Mellanie how precariously close a collapse could be. Fear brought out a very strong survival trait in people, one that overwhelmed all the usual rules of behaviour. She was never going to forget those last hours standing beside the small wormhole in the Turquino Valley. The way the crowd had started to panic, everyone pushing forwards, their desperation and ferocity building. And that was with a strong character like Simon Rand holding things together.

Yet now, barely a week later, it all seemed so remote. She was standing at the window wall in Alessandra's penthouse on the skyscraper's sixty-fifth floor, looking out over Salamanca. Cities at night always looked more vibrant, somehow, and New Iberia's capital was no exception. This was a rich world, among the first of phase one space to be settled, with a population now closing on two billion. Salamanca alone was home to twelve million souls. Its lights sparkled all the way out to the horizon; here in the centre, where the height of the metal and crystal skyscrapers was a real estate value prospectus, the streets were arranged in a standard grid, beyond that the patterns became more random until they merged into the general light pollution that hazed the outlying districts. Cutting through the precise lambent lines was the inevitable radial web of silver rails, threading straight through the grid blocks, and bridging roads, always given preference so that the trains could shunt their valuable goods between districts and the CST planetary station. It might have been her imagination, but she didn't think there were as many trains as usual rolling along the rails tonight. But then just about every activity in the Commonwealth had come to a halt during the invasion, and things were only just starting to return to an approximation of the old normality.

When she raised her gaze, she could just make out the ephemeral shimmer of the force field above and around the city. It seemed strange to see it there, fuzzing the stars above. Even though most major cities had them, they'd never been switched on except to ward off the most vigorous hurricanes and tornados. Now they were all on permanently, even Darklake had protection.

'It's still the same, isn't it?' Alessandra said, coming up to stand behind Mellanie. 'Somehow I was expecting changes when I got back. But it's wonderfully reassuring to see. I've stood here for hours myself just watching.'

It had taken several days before CST resumed its standard passenger service between planets. Millions of refugees from the invaded worlds were given priority as they sought accommodation throughout the rest of the Commonwealth. Wessex still hadn't returned to full operational capacity. CST was busy repairing the wormhole generators that had been damaged during Nigel Sheldon's battle of exotic energy above the planet. Services to that whole section of phase two space remained patchy, though its worlds were still connected to the unisphere. But the express train between Augusta and New Iberia had resumed, allowing Alessandra to return home three days after the *Desperado*'s final flight.

This was the first time Mellanie had come back to Alessandra's penthouse. She'd finally left Ozzie's bizarre asteroid two days ago, walking through the wormhole which had been realigned on Augusta, at the end of all the Randtown refugees. The intervening time had been spent with Dudley, reassuring him, and taking a break to compose herself. With all the SI's inserts now quiescent, her newfound confidence had receded somewhat. She wasn't sure what kind of shape her investigation into Myo and the Starflyer would take. Dudley probably had more information lurking amid his confused memories. It would take a while to be sure she'd got everything she needed from him. For now, he was safely stashed away in a cheap coastal holiday resort chalet on Oaktier, a place where she'd spent many early childhood vacations. Nobody would be able to trace him there, at least not straight away.

Alessandra's hands slid over Mellanie's shoulders. 'We've been hearing some strange stories from the Randtown refugees. Some of them say they were in an alien starship.'

'They're lying. It was an old dormitory station for a deep space industrial facility that CST is decommissioning. The wormhole was still working, luckily.'

'Interesting.' Alessandra's grip tightened, giving a small massage. 'That's the only part of the whole invasion that senior management prevented us from carrying. None of the other media companies carried it, either. Somebody's been putting pressure on. And that's a hell of a lot of pressure.'

Mellanie turned to face her, looking intently at the statuesque woman's perfect classic features. 'Not guilty.'

'Humm.' Alessandra stroked a finger lightly along Mellanie's cheek. 'You've changed.'

'I was there on the ground when we got invaded by aliens. It kind of makes you focus, you know.'

'I'm sure it does, darling.' She leaned forward for a kiss. Mellanie put a hand out. 'Not yet.'

'Oh really?' One of Alessandra's elegantly plucked and shaped eyebrows rose slightly. 'Well you'd better get yourself in the mood pretty quickly. I've got Robin Dalsol coming over later for dinner, he's Goldreich's senior aide. I need to know how much money the Executive is planning on pumping into the navy for our retaliatory strike. The two of you should be good together, he's only ten years out of rejuve.'

'Fuck him yourself,' Mellanie growled.

'Mellanie, darling, I don't do that any more. I don't need to, I have you to do it for me; you and fifty others.'

'Fine, call one of them.'

'We've had this discussion before. It's starting to get boring.'

'I don't care about the navy budget. It's hardly going to be a secret, they'll tell us as soon as it goes to the Senate.'

'God help us! Darling, it's not that we will know, it's *when* we know. I'm the best because I can break news first.'

'But what about my story?' Mellanie almost shouted. 'That's the only one that counts. For God's sake, we've just been invaded, and we can track the cause down. There is nothing bigger than that. I came here to find out who my research team is, when we can start, not to suck some asswiper's dick for you.'

Alessandra frowned. 'What are you talking about?'

'The Starflyer!' Mellanie hissed. 'I'm going to track it down.'

'Oh that nonsense.' Alessandra put her hand on her brow theatrically. 'You're wrong. I had it checked out for you. Cox Educational is completely legit, and still going strong. I think Bunny actually talked to one of the trustees, Ms Daltra. She assured us their funding is all above board, the accounts are filed with the charity commissioners every eighteen months, as required. Take a look at them if you want.'

'What!' Mellanie couldn't believe what she was hearing.

'You were wrong, darling. No big deal. We all make mistakes on the way up. If you want my advice, you should stop screwing Dudley Bose, he's got a lot of psychological problems. Re-lifers generally do. They get over them eventually.'

'No.' Mellanie shook her head. 'No, that's wrong. Dudley only . . .' She trailed off as the real shock hit her, strong enough to raise the goosebumps all along her arms. She gave Alessandra an incredulous stare, it was all she could do not to back away from the woman. 'I don't understand.'

'You made a mistake,' Alessandra told her. Her smile became humourless. 'Another one. And I'm not really into this "three strikes and you're out" crap that the judiciary practises. Frankly, the show's only keeping you on now because of your report from Randtown. That showed promise. But face facts, darling, you're not an investigator. God, you're too dumb even to get to college; everybody goes to college and gets a degree these days. So let's focus on what you are good at, shaking that shapely little ass of yours at the men I tell you to. Clear?'

Mellanie bowed her head, and even managed a noise which sounded suspiciously like a sob. 'Yes.'

'Good girl.' Alessandra put her hands on either side of Mellanie's head, and kissed her crown, as if performing a blessing. 'Now, why don't you go and put something nice on for Robin. You know, he asked for you specially. I think he was impressed by Randtown as well. You're a celebrity now, darling.'

'All right.' Mellanie left the living room, careful to close the door behind her as she went out into the penthouse's main hallway. 'Are there any special safeguards on the front door?' she asked the SI.

'Just the standard security systems and alarms.'

'Great.' She almost ran at the tall double doors. They opened for her, and she looked wildly round the marbled vestibule outside. There were only three other doors to the remaining penthouses, two lifts, and the stairwell. Her e-butler interfaced with the skyscraper's management array, and told her the lifts were on their way up. She was too worried that Alessandra would follow her out to wait for them, so she went straight to the stairwell and ran downwards. 'Get a lift to stop for me on the sixty-second floor,' she told the SI.

It was waiting for her when she burst out of the stairwell. She hopped in, and the doors closed. 'Lobby,' she told the SI. 'There will be people there, I should be safe.'

'What is the problem, Mellanie?'

She pressed her head against the cool metal walls of the lift, waiting for her racing heart to slow. 'I never told Alessandra the name of the charity.'

'It would not be hard for her to discover it.'

'Run a check on it for me again, please.'

'The public records have been amended since last week.'

'Goddamn!' She glanced up, as if expecting Alessandra to be ripping her way through the top of the lift like some psycho in a bad TSI drama.

'They now show the Cox Educational has been in continual operation since its formation, and is still making donations to various science departments,' the SI said.

'But that's all forgeries, you know that.'

'We do, but the official records are complete.'

'How did they do that?'

'It is not impossible to subvert public records, especially in the finance sector. Although the effort involved is considerable.'

'She tipped them off,' Mellanie said out loud. 'Alessandra told them I was on to them. Onto it, the Starflyer. It had to be her. There's no one else. It's her. Oh God.' Her legs were trembling the way they had when she was facing the soldier motiles in Randtown.

'That is a strong accusation,' the SI said.

'Are you testing me? If Alessandra had run a genuine check, she would have found what I told her. The Starflyer would never have had time to cover its alien ass; a fraud this elaborate would take time. It had to have been given a direct warning so that the cover-up would be in place in case I survived and started yelling allegations. The only person I told was Alessandra. It is her! She's working for it, isn't she? Alessandra is one of the people Johansson warns us about, like the President.'

'We don't know for certain. However, given the sequence of events, it is highly likely.'

The lift doors opened. Mellanie peered out into the lobby. There didn't seem to be anybody waiting for her. She hurried over to the main entrance, where there were some taxis waiting. 'I've got to get back to Dudley,' she said.

'An excellent notion. Then what?'

'Tell Paula Myo what I've discovered. Do you know where she is?'

'Yes.'

*

Kazimir stood close to the end of platform 34 in Rio's planetary station, with people swarming round him as they waited for the next train. The trans-Earth loop trains had carried on running almost continually during the invasion crisis. Though even that service had stopped when Nigel Sheldon diverted the lunar power to Wessex. But they were up and running again within hours, unlike the CST passenger trains to other planets.

Kazimir had been reassured by the way Earth's infrastructure underwent only the minimum of disruption. What outraged him was the population's attitude. The residents of Santa Monica seemed more upset by the temporary power loss than they did that twenty-three planets had been lost to alien monsters. And the Mayor certainly hadn't allocated any civic buildings to the refugees riding round the Intersolar train network looking for accommodation, unlike civic and regional leaders on the other worlds. Earthlings appeared to regard the invasion as just another news event of something a long way off that happened to someone else. He wasn't sure if that was ignorance or arrogance. Whatever, it was certainly a chilling example of how different their shared mindset was to his own.

The last few days had at least seen a degree of awareness creeping in. Kazimir had hung around the waterfront in Santa Monica, watching the news in bars, or accessing in his little hotel room while he waited for things to calm down so he could resume his mission. Local media shows reflected a lot of anxiety that a second wave of planets would suffer invasion, a progression that would one day lead to Earth itself being on the front line.

So far there had been no sign of any alien activity anywhere other than the original invaded worlds. Now the evacuation of civilian populations was effectively complete, available data was in short supply as the Primes continued their inexorable advance. The navy was maintaining small fighting forces on Anshun, Balkash, and Martaban; aerobots and professional combat-wetwired troops conducting a guerrilla harassment campaign against the new installations the aliens were constructing. Everyone knew it was a token gesture. The build-up of Prime forces was increasing at a disturbing rate as they managed to open gateways on the planetary surfaces. Admiral Kime was expected to order a withdrawal soon, and the final wormholes would be shut down. Analysts on most of the news shows were predicting that the deserted capital cities would then be destroyed by fusion bombs.

The navy's remaining scoutships had returned, and were now performing regular flyby patrols of the invaded worlds, supplementing the degraded detector network. So far, the aliens hadn't opened any new wormholes to replace those destroyed by the *Desperado*'s last flight. Some of the technical experts and tacticians on the news shows were hinting that the remaining starships might well be automated, and used in similar relativistic assaults on the remaining Prime wormholes. The navy had publicly refused to comment on the possibility. Commentators were saying that as the biospheres of the invaded worlds were so badly damaged, the Commonwealth had effectively written them off. It wasn't worth sacrificing their last starships to destroy something humanity would never regain. They were being held in reserve in case of any new assault.

Whatever the official reason, that one substantial human victory on the invasion day had already reached an almost legendary status, its crew subject to intense praise on every current affairs and news show. That contrasted sharply with the vitriol and vilification that the rest of the navy was receiving, along with President Doi's administration.

Kazimir thought it strange how little mention the wormhole battle above Wessex was getting. It was surely more strategically important than a suicide flight. But then CST's profile in the week that followed was remarkably low. Even under these circumstances, everyone seemed to take their efficiency for granted; the way they moved the refugees around, and repaired Narrabri station's gateways, was standard stuff for that company.

Amber lights flashed above platform 34, and the loop train slid into the station, twenty double-decker carriages pulled by a Bennor AC767 mag-grip engine. It had only been five minutes since the last one pulled out, but there were already over three hundred people waiting. The doors opened, and passengers poured out. Kazimir held back while everyone else on the platform surged forward impatiently. His eyes moved constantly, checking to see who else loitered. Visual interpretation programs reviewed everything he saw, identifying possibles, tagging them with probability percentages. When he rechecked them, they all turned out to be harmless.

It was a wearying process. But he'd stuck with it the whole time on the way back from the ancient observatory in the Andes. The journey had involved eight vehicle changes, from his hired 4x4 which he'd driven up into the mountains, to taxis, various local trains, bus, the plane back over to Rio. Every time he'd followed procedure, no matter how foolish it felt, knowing what Stig would say if he lapsed even once. The courier job was vital, as Elvin had never stopped reminding him. The Martian data was essential to the whole Guardian movement. Moving it from South America to the safety of LA would probably have gone to Stig, if his reprofiling had been completed. As such, Kazimir was determined there would be no hitch or glitch, he was going to prove to all of them that he was capable of such an important assignment.

He stepped onto the loop train just before the doors closed and watched to see who else got on after him. Procedure, once again. Except this once he was uncertain. Some itchy little feeling prodding up from his subconscious. Something made him uneasy.

Nobody he could see was the cause of it. Had it been a pattern? If he was being boxed, then at least two of the team would have stayed on the platform. Turning casually he scanned through the window to see who was left outside. But there were just the new arrivals wearing expressions of disgust or resignation as they saw the doors closing in front of them.

He sent his message to a one-time unisphere address. Back in the Lemule's Max Transit office they would know he was on the last leg. They would be scanning the electronic activity in the train to see if any kind of covert operation was under way. If there was, he'd know about it at LA Galactic. *Just like Stig coming back from Oaktier.*

Satisfied he'd done all he could, he walked down several carriages before taking a seat – close to an exit. The next stop was Mexico City, then he'd be back at LA Galactic. Elvin had emphasized again and again how important this data was to the whole Guardian movement, how he absolutely must not fail. The invasion added its own emphasis. He debated if that was making him paranoid in his desperation to make sure he delivered.

As the train pulled away from the platform he wondered how Stig would look when he got back. The cellular reprofiling should be almost finished, giving him a whole new face, allowing him to resume front-line duties. Stig wasn't good at sitting round doing nothing all day in the safe house.

*

Justine sat at the back of the security office in LA Galactic, quietly watching the navy intelligence team coordinate the box operation on the loop train. They had been running the observation operation from here as soon as they confirmed that Kazimir was staying at a hotel in Santa Monica. She'd checked in with them several times a day for a personal briefing, even at the height of the invasion. Each day was the same: Kazimir was killing time, acting like a tourist. Waiting.

It was so strange, being able to see the observation team's real-time images of him, while not being able to touch him or talk to him herself. She felt as if she'd been cast in the role of some obscure guardian angel, watching over her beloved from a lofty height, making sure his youthfulness and naivety didn't bring him into harm. The guilt as she did it, of course, was excruciating, but she kept telling herself that afterwards he'd understand. When he finally realized how utterly *wrong* he'd been, how he'd been taken in and used by others, they could begin afresh. Justine hadn't even thought what kind of life they'd have together afterwards. Which made her as dizzy-headed as Kazimir.

Then yesterday the call had come through from Commander Alic Hogan. Kazimir had received instructions from a one-time address, and taken the loop train to Rio. What followed then had been strange. Kazimir had visited an ancient observatory in the Andes, then set off back almost immediately. Given how isolated the observatory was, the navy team couldn't get inside to see what it was Kazimir had picked up. In fact, it was very difficult for them to remain unseen on the track through the Andes as they followed his 4x4.

Low-level cybersphere investigation revealed the observatory was run by a consortium of universities, with funding coming from a great many sources, corporate, government and educational. It was now surrounded by a navy team, who were waiting for the order to go in. That would only come after Kazimir delivered whatever he was carrying to his controller.

The scale and obvious importance of the whole operation was easy justification for her to travel to LA Galactic in person, along with two bodyguards from Senate Security. Commander Alic Hogan was running the operation himself, as well he might considering the pressure she'd been putting on him.

'The loop train has left Rio, Senator,' Hogan reported. 'Shouldn't be much longer now.'

'Good.'

'He called a one-time address once he egressed. The Guardian operative returning from Oaktier did the same thing. It would seem to be their standard operating procedure.'

'Do you expect Kazimir McFoster to get off here?'

'It's highly probable. But I've got enough people to box him no matter where he goes. Don't worry, Senator, this one won't be getting away from us.'

'I'm glad to hear it.' She gave him a slight nod, dismissing him. Hogan's smile was forced as he went back to join his team. All of them were hunched over their desks, studying the screens and muttering to the field operatives.

This time nothing was left to chance, as it had been when Paula Myo was in charge. Over a hundred naval intelligence officers were on duty in and around LA Galactic, ready to trail Kazimir to whatever destination the hand-over was scheduled to take place. They'd been quietly deployed over the last two days, avoiding any possibility of virtual observation. Tarlo was convinced their last failure was due to the Guardians infiltrating at least some of LA Galactic's network. Consequentially, they were using dedicated communication systems, with ultra-modern obscured traffic software. If the Guardians had the technical capability to detect that, then they'd probably be running the whole Commonwealth before the end of the year.

She used her interface to call up images from the CST internal network, and watched on a desk screen as the loop train slid through the gateway between Rio and Mexico City.

*

Kazimir got off the loop train at LA Galactic's Carralvo terminal. It was midday. Undiluted sunlight poured through the huge crescent windows high overhead, making the angular support pillars gleam. He walked off the platform and down the curving ramp at the end, feeling the familiar tremble through the soles of his boots as trains rolled through the giant building. Traffic at the station was almost back up to its pre-invasion levels, though there were noticeably fewer passengers crowding the central concourse.

As he stepped off the end of the ramp he glanced about casually, as if unsure which way he should be going. Nobody paid him any attention. There had been no warning from the Guardian team, either visually or through the cybersphere.

Maybe I am paranoid.

Kazimir started walking along the concourse, heading for exit eight where there was a taxi rank outside. Another quarter of an hour would see him return in triumph to the office of Lemule's Max Transit, and hand over the memory crystal with its Martian data. He almost patted the little disk in its secure belt pocket, but that would have been pathetically amateurish.

A confident smile tweaked his lips as he made his way through the thousands of travellers bustling along the central concourse. The Guardians would be another significant step towards bringing about Far Away's revenge because of him. And once this mission was complete he would try and find time to visit Justine again. That venture out to the Tulip Mansion was the only thing he'd done since leaving Far Away that transgressed their operational doctrine. But he didn't care. Bruce would understand that if none of the others did. Justine was a part of him. Without her, there was no point to existence. She was worth risking everything for. And when he'd seen her again that fateful night, it was as if no time had passed. That she felt the same way about him was the kind of miracle he wouldn't even expect the dreaming heavens to grant.

But she did. That was the true wonder he'd known. She felt for him as he did for her. Her delight alone made him more determined to rid the universe of the Starflyer. He wanted a universe where nothing could come between them ever again. What a world that would be. What an incredible, blissful future.

He was two hundred metres away from exit eight when he saw the man standing at the bottom of the ramp which curved up to platform six. Something about him . . . Neatly cropped hair, tall, young, early twenties just like Kazimir, wearing a simple blue jacket over a cream shirt. The way he was standing, holding a small array in his hand, reading a document on the unrolled screen. His position and angle against the ramp's railing – so relaxed and natural – allowed him to see everyone walking along the concourse whenever he happened to glance up from the screen. It could so easily have been an ordinary civilian. But his profile made Kazimir slow as he approached. That profile was oddly familiar. A profile which was searing connections deep into Kazimir's brain. Old memories tumbled out, delivering a physical jolt to the body.

Kazimir halted. Tears smudged his vision. 'No,' he said soundlessly. He wanted to move, but his knees were threatening to give way.

The man glanced up from the array screen, looking straight at Kazimir.

'Bruce,' Kazimir gasped. 'It's you.' He took a step forwards, heedless of the people flowing between them. It was him, really him. Bruce McFoster, standing on the concourse on LA Galactic as if it was the most normal thing in the universe. Bruce McFoster who had fallen in battle right in front of him. Every day Kazimir saw the giant warhorse rolling across Bruce's defenceless body. Bruce McFoster: alive. 'Bruce!' Kazimir took another couple of steps. 'Oh my God. Bruce, it's me, it's Kaz.'

Bruce hadn't stopped looking at him. He put the array in his pocket with a calm unhurried motion.

Kazimir started running. 'Bruce!' He opened his arms wide in rapturous welcome. A path opened for him through the crowd as he rushed forward.

Bruce McFoster brought his right arm up. There was something in his hand. It flashed—

Kazimir felt no pain. He felt nothing. There had been a moment of blackness. Then he was looking straight up at the Carralvo terminal's white concrete ceiling far overhead. His body wasn't moving. Silence closed in on him. 'Bruce?'

Faces swam over him, but it was hard to see any of them. The light was dimming. Kazimir tried to smile. He finally realized he was dying. Not that it mattered, because his life had included—'Justine.' Ghostly fingers reached up to touch her icon. 'Justine, I'm so sorry.' But her smile was there comforting him, forgiving as the light slipped away.

*

Justine screamed as the security camera swung round on the man Kazimir was staring at in such wondrous disbelief. Her brother's murderer was standing in the middle of LA Galactic. She watched as he coolly raised his arm and fired a pistol. The ion stream blew Kazimir's chest open in a horrific plume of blood and charred gore. He was flung back five metres through the air to sprawl on the concourse. Justine's scream choked off. She almost dropped out of the chair as her body spasmed in shock.

The navy team filled the office with frenzied shouting. A furious, scared Alic Hogan was almost sobbing as he ordered the officers on the concourse to give chase. His fists were clenched above the main screens, ready to punch straight through the images. Every picture turned to a confused, fast-moving blur. More shots were fired. A chorus of yelling and panicked shrieks burst out of the speakers.

Justine breathed again. A long juddering breath that burned its way down her throat. One screen had remained centred on Kazimir's broken body.

'Take me down there,' she whispered painfully.

'Senator?' one of the bodyguards asked.

'We're going down there.'

'Yes, Senator.'

Her e-butler told her a single message had arrived via a one-time address. Its author was verified as Kazimir McFoster. 'Nobody's to touch him,' she yelled abruptly as she got to her feet.

The navy personnel turned round from their desks, looking at her with startled expressions. 'Keep everyone away from him,' she told them. 'I don't want him touched.'

As she left the office she ordered her e-butler to open the message. It contained a unisphere address code, and a line of text. **My Darling Justine, you are the only person I have ever loved. I thank you for living. Kazimir.**

The bodyguard had to hold her as she started crying.

*

CST station security staff cleared a path for Justine through the tense, worried crowd on the concourse. They'd been kept well back from the body, leaving her with a long lonely walk at the end. The last few steps as the true damage that had been done to him became visible were almost impossible for her. Yet she forced herself forward, punishing herself because she knew she deserved far, far worse.

It was every bit as bad as she knew it would be. The blood pooling over the white marble. The smell. His face perfectly intact, holding the expression of someone whose prayer had been answered.

Justine knelt beside him, though in truth her legs could barely hold her weight any more. The wide puddle of his cold blood soaked into her expensive skirt. She reached out and touched his cheek with her fingers, fearful of what she would feel. Lifeless bodies she had seen countless times, including her brother's. But Kazimir was a Guardian, he didn't have a memorycell insert. This was genuine death, a life that had ended. She thought she'd left this barbarity behind centuries ago.

Later there would be anger. Fury. And a bitter, bitter remorse. For now she was just numb. Not understanding how this could have happened despite all her power and authority; all the orders and thinly veiled threats that nothing *nothing* was to harm him. Now here he was, her beautiful young love: dead. For ever.

Justine heard a pair of heels clicking on the marble. Someone walking purposefully along the concourse towards her. No doubt who that would be. She smiled forlornly down at Kazimir one last time, then rose to her feet and turned round.

'Senator,' Paula Myo said. 'My sympathies.'

Justine's smile turned cruel as she glanced down at the dark blood staining her skirt. 'I told them. I made it very clear to the navy. Kazimir was not to be hurt.'

'The navy didn't do this.'

'You see, I always thought that I was right, that he was just a naive provincial lad with a head full of nonsense. I have to be right because I'm nearly four centuries old, and I live in mansions and penthouses and I have enough money to buy his world. I had to protect him from himself, from others who were using him.'

'You did everything you could.'

'Then why is he dead, Investigator?'

'There is a leak in the navy, probably more than one.'

'It is real, isn't it?' she said with a kind of detached amusement. 'Kazimir was right all along.'

'Yes, Senator, the Starflyer is real.'

*

Wind and current were acting in happy conjunction, pushing the *Pathfinder* along at a steady clip. In other circumstances, Ozzie would have been quite pleased about that. But not today.

'Isn't there anything ahead?' Orion asked with a petulant whine.

Ozzie switched off his retinal insert's zoom function, which he'd been using to scan that uncomfortably distant horizon. 'No,' he said. Even he thought he sounded defensive.

Fifteen miles to starboard, and now slightly behind, the last island rose up out of the tranquil blue-grey water. The simple dark green cone was the fourth one they'd tried to reach. Once they'd left their original island behind, the sea's current had picked up considerably. So much so that they had very little ability to steer. Even with Tochee angling the rudder hard over, they couldn't vary their course by more than a few degrees.

They had missed the first island by over ten miles; standing on the raft's creaking deck to watch despondently as it sank away behind them. It had been larger than the one they'd set sail from, with wide coves and extensive forests. Ozzie hadn't seen any signs of habitation, even with his retinal inserts on full magnification; but it had looked very promising.

After the shock of missing landfall, they had swung round straight away for the next island, thirty miles further on. This time with near-constant rowing and the tiller jammed over, they'd got to within a couple of miles as the current swept them onward. Neither of the two exhausted humans had said anything, but they both knew that Tochee could have swum ashore if it wanted to. Their big alien companion had chosen to stay with them.

From then on there were fewer islands they could aim for, and the current strength had increased noticeably. And now, what might have been their last chance was receding at a respectable speed.

Ozzie sat down with his back to the mast, looking back, trying not to appear too disappointed. The stiff square of sail was curved tautly as the breeze pushed against it. There wasn't a lot of point having it up any more. The surface of the sea was flowing as fast as a plains river. He couldn't work out why it was doing that, either. Seas simply didn't rush about, there was no hydrological mechanism he could think of which would produce such an effect. It was just one more anomaly which the planet had thrown at them. Ozzie worried that it might prove a fatal one.

'I might be able to tow us back over to the last island,' Tochee said.

Ozzie gave the big creature a dubious look. 'You're more likely to just wear yourself out. Let's save acts like that until we get desperate.'

'And we're not now?' Orion muttered.

'As long as we're moving, we're okay,' Ozzie said firmly. 'There will be more islands over the horizon, or even the mainland. It's when we stop moving that we're in trouble.'

Orion's expression was very sceptical, but he didn't argue.

Tochee pulled the rudder up, then simply shuffled round until it was facing forwards.

So far they'd eaten about a third of their fresh supplies, Ozzie calculated. If they were a little more careful from now on, the fruit should last them another four or five days. Technically, food wasn't a problem. Tochee could catch fish for them indefinitely, and the filter pump could produce fresh water. From that point of view they could sail over the entire ocean. However, he was under no illusion about how long the raft would last. The palm frond ropes were already showing signs of swelling and fraying where they bound the log bundles together. When they started to go, their future would be measurable in hours. There were no lifebelts on board. He was now wondering how useful the inflatable tent walls would be in an emergency.

*

Ozzie woke with Orion shaking his shoulder.

'Ozzie, I can hear something.' The boy's voice was low, as if he was afraid.

'Okay.' Ozzie pushed his sunglasses up, blinking round. He hadn't meant to fall asleep. When he looked behind them, there was a small trail of bubbles emerging from the stern of the raft. 'Jeeze, we're leaving a wake. How fast are we going?'

'Don't know.' Orion was still subdued.

Ozzie climbed to his feet, very conscious of the wind. The sail was straining hard, applying a lot of force to the mast. 'Let's get that down,' he said. He and Orion untied the ropes, and lowered the dry grey-brown square. It flapped away enthusiastically as it came down.

'Is there a cause for concern?' Tochee asked.

'Orion thought he heard something,' Ozzie said.

'Are air vibrations a danger?'

'Depends what's making them,' Ozzie said. Even after all this time, with their expanded vocabulary and literally days

1142

devoted to explaining the topic, Tochee still had difficulty with the whole concept of noise.

'Can you hear it?' Orion asked.

Ozzie stood still. There was a distinct sound carrying over the water, just loud enough to be heard above the wavelets that lapped against the *Pathfinder*. A reverberant grumbling, like distant thunder.

When Ozzie looked forward, trying to pinpoint the sound, he saw the horizon had become indistinct. A thin blanket of fog lay over the water. He zoomed in with his retinal inserts, which revealed nothing. The sound was gradually getting louder.

'I think we should tie ourselves on,' Ozzie said. 'Just in case.'

'What is it?' Orion asked. 'Please, Ozzie.'

'I dunno, man. Honestly. I'm just taking some precautions here. We're a long way from land, and if this is a storm brewing up I don't want anyone going overboard.'

They busied themselves with some lengths of rope, lashing the ends to the base of the mast. Tochee declined a rope, using its locomotion flesh ridges to anchor itself to the decking.

When they'd finished, the fog bank was a lot closer, and the noise had become a constant soft roar that continued to build.

Ozzie stood beside the mast, hooking one arm round the tall shaft of wood. 'I don't get it,' he complained. 'I can't see any storm clouds anywhere.' Above him in the clear sky, the water specks in the gas halo gleamed with their usual intensity. The sea around them was becoming choppy, with waves rushing forward in unison, carrying the *Pathfinder* onward. They were starting to rock about from the speed they were travelling. The creaking of overstrained ropes was audible above the roaring.

Several new water specks rose above the horizon, like small constellations on the move. Ozzie stared at them in puzzlement. Something very weird was happening to his sense of perspective. It was as if the fog bank was shrinking, while the horizon rushed in towards him. Then in a moment of truly terrifying revelation he realized what he was seeing.

There was no fog bank. It was just a thin line of spray hanging above the waves. Spray thrown up by a waterfall. The sea was pouring over a cliff that extended out to the vanishing point on either side of the *Pathfinder*.

White water boiled up directly ahead of the raft, its vigorous spume drenching Ozzie. The raft tilted alarmingly as it juddered over the churning water, forcing him to cling to the mast as his feet slipped. Looking to starboard he could see the entire sea cascading down in a vast arc that thundered further and further towards ... there was no bottom beneath them, only the empty void of the gas halo.

Ozzie lifted his head back to stare at the false stars above, his face a mask of incredulity and pure rage. 'You've gotta be fucking kidding me!' he screamed at the sky.

The *Pathfinder* fell off the edge of the world.

The End of *Pandora's Star*

The Commonwealth Saga will be concluded in

Judas Unchained